KAREN MILLER

KINGMAKER, KINGBREAKER

THE OMNIBUS EDITION

INCLUDES *THE INNOCENT MAGE* AND *THE AWAKENED MAGE*

**Without thinking, Asher jumped into the path
of the frightened horse.**

A lifetime of sailing boats in untamed weather had honed his reflexes and made him indifferent to danger. Catching those flapping reins was just like laying hold of a loose halyard in high winds; battling the best to a standstill not much harder than wrestling with a net-load of fish reluctant to die.

And besides, it seemed a shame for a fine animal like that to break a slender leg just 'cause some royal folderol couldn't keep his arse in the saddle.

"It'd be fine, I reckon," he said, determined that this elegantly clad prince was a man, like him, who pissed and farted same as all men did, and had nothing more special to recommend him than an expensive tailor. "Don't seem like the beast's taken any harm, barrin' a fright."

The prince glanced up at him. A flicker of recognition lit his eyes and he nodded. Standing straight, he looped the reins over one arm and then dusted his hands on his breeches. "So it would appear, Barl be praised." He kissed the solid gold holyring on his left forefinger. "He was a gift from His Majesty."

"A grand gift," said Asher. "Glad I could save 'im for you. I be fine too, by the way. You know. 'Case you were wonderin'."

Praise for

The KINGMAKER, KINGBREAKER Series

"Miller's debut is a blockbuster story crafted with a strong sense of wonder."
                                                             —*Nexus*

"Miller's prose is earnest and engaging, and h[er] complex story accelerates nicely toward a brutal cliffhanger finale."
                                                             —*Publishers Weekly*

"Intriguing characters and a finely tuned sense of drama..."
                                                             —*Library Journal Review*

KINGMAKER, KINGBREAKER

BOOKS BY KAREN MILLER

Kingmaker, Kingbreaker
The Innocent Mage
The Awakened Mage

The Godspeaker Trilogy
Empress
The Riven Kingdom
Hammer of God

The Fisherman's Children
The Prodigal Mage
The Reluctant Mage

Kingmaker, Kingbreaker *(omnibus edition)*

The Godspeaker Trilogy *(omnibus edition)*

Writing as K.E. Mills

The Rogue Agent Series
The Accidental Sorcerer
Witches Incorporated
Wizard Squared
Wizard Undercover

KINGMAKER, KINGBREAKER

Book 1: The Innocent Mage
Book 2: The Awakened Mage

KAREN MILLER

www.orbitbooks.net

Orbit
Hachette Book Group
237 Park Avenue, New York, NY 10017
www.HachetteBookGroup.com

First compilation edition: August 2012

Orbit is an imprint of Hachette Book Group, Inc.
The Orbit name and logo are trademarks of Little, Brown Book Group Limited.

The Hachette Speakers Bureau provides a wide range of authors for speaking events.
To find out more, go to www.hachettespeakersbureau.com or call (866) 376-6591.

The publisher is not responsible for websites (or their content)
that are not owned by the publisher.

The characters and events in this book are fictitious. Any similarity to real persons,
living or dead, is coincidental and not intended by the author.

Library of Congress Control Number: 2012933764

ISBN: 978-0-316-20127-8

10 9 8 7 6 5 4 3 2 1

RRD-C

Printed in the United States of America

KINGMAKER, KINGBREAKER

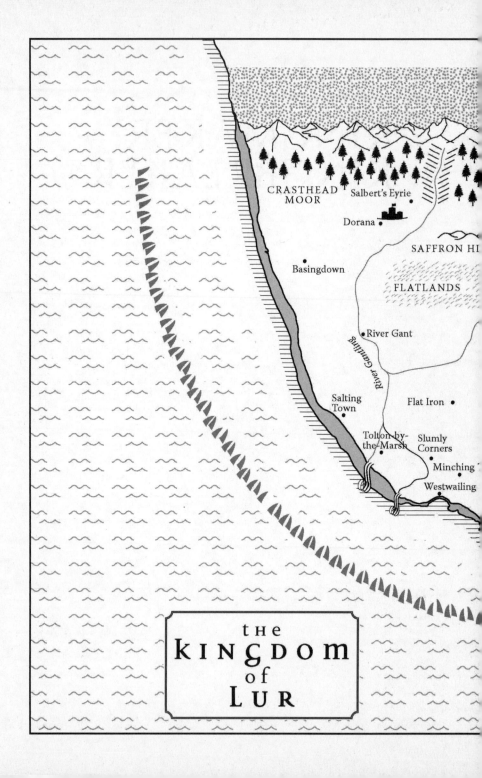

CRASTHEAD
MOOR

Salbert's Eyrie

Dorana

SAFFRON HI

Basingdown

FLATLANDS

River Gant

River Gamwling

Salting
Town

Flat Iron

Tolton-by-
the-Marsh

Slumly
Corners

Minching

Westwailing

THE
KINGDOM
OF
LUR

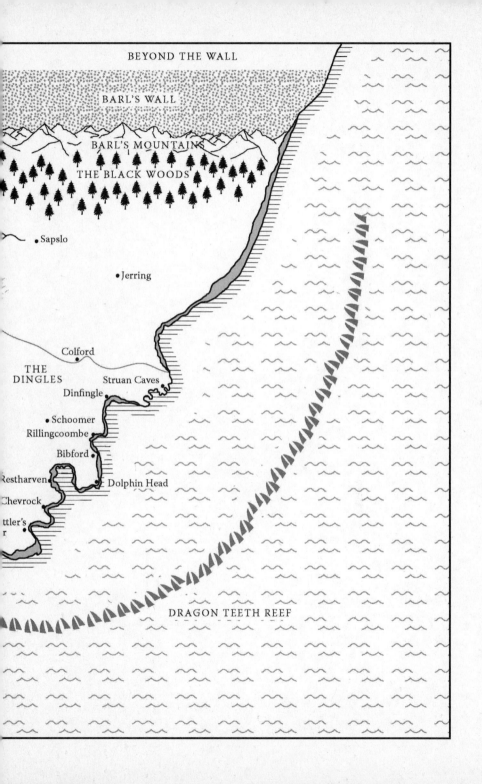

CONTENTS

BOOK 1

THE INNOCENT MAGE

To my parents, for their blind, unbending and oftentimes bemused faith. Couldn't have done it without you, guys.

PROLOGUE

Nine hundred and ninety-seven...nine hundred and ninety-eight...nine hundred and ninety-nine...one thousand!

Asher opened his eyes. At *last*.

Time to go.

Holding his breath, he slid out of his old, creaking bed and put his bare feet on the floor as lightly as the rising sun kissed the mouth of Restharven Harbour.

In the other bed his brother Bede, mired in sleep, stirred and grunted beneath his blankets. Asher waited, suspended between heartbeats. Bede grunted again, then started snoring, and Asher sighed his silent relief. Thank Barl they didn't still share this room with Niko. Bloody Niko woke cursing if a fly farted. There'd be no chance of creeping safely out of the house if Niko still slept here.

But after Wishus finally got hisself married to that shrew Pippa and moved out of his solitary chamber to his own stone cottage along Fishhook Lane, Niko had taken belligerent possession of the empty room. Claimed it as his own by right of being the oldest brother still living at home—and with his fists if nobody liked that reason.

As the youngest, Asher didn't rate a room of his own. As the youngest he didn't rate a lot of things. Even though he was twenty years old, and a man, and could be married his own damn self if he'd wanted to be. If there was a woman in Restharven or anywhere else on the coast who could make his heart beat fast for longer than a kiss and a fumble on the cliffs overlooking the ocean.

Pausing to scoop up his boots, left conveniently at the end of the bed, Asher tiptoed into the corridor and past Niko's closed door. At Da's room he hesitated. Looked in.

Da wasn't there. Shafting moonlight revealed the sagging double bed, empty. The blankets undisturbed. The single pillow undented. The room smelled musty. Abandoned, even though somebody still lived there. If he closed his eyes, he could almost catch the sweet sug-gestion of Ma's perfume.

But only almost, and only if he imagined it. Ma was long since dead and buried, and all that remained of her perfume was a single cracked and used-up bottle Da kept on the dusty windowsill.

Asher moved on, a ghost in his own house.

He found his father in the living room, sprawled snoring in his armchair. An empty ale jug sat on the table by his right hand; his tan-kard was tumbled on the carpet at his slippered feet. Asher wrinkled his nose at the sourness of spilled beer and soaked wool.

The living room curtains were still open. Moonlight painted the floor, the armchair. Da. Asher stared down at him and felt a pang of conscience. He looked so *tired*. But then he had a right to. Sailing towards sixty, Da was. When you saw him on the ocean, bellowing orders and hauling nets over the side of whichever family smack he'd chosen to captain that day, or watched him gutting fish and bargain-ing the prices afterwards, it was hard to believe he had seven sons grown and was a grandpa eleven times over. There wasn't a man in all the Kingdom of Lur, Olken or Doranen, who could beat back the waves like Da. Who could catch a leaping sawfish with just a hook and a rod, or snatch a bright-scaled volly from right over the side of the boat and kill it with his bare hands alone.

Looking at him now, though, all black and silver in the moonlight, his uncapped head sparse with greying hair, his weathered face sag-ging in sorrowed sleep, belief was all too easy.

Da was old. Old and wearing out fast, from work and worry.

Still holding his boots, Asher crouched beside the armchair. Gazed into his father's slumbering features and felt a great wave of love crash over him. He was going to miss this face, with its crooked nose, broke in a drunken brawl over Ma when they were courting, and its scarred chin, split by slipping on a storm-heaved deck five seasons gone.

"Past time somebody did the worryin' for you, Da," he whispered. "Past time y'had things soft, 'stead of hard. I said I'd do this for you, one day, and I reckon that day's come."

Trouble was, it was easier said than done. To make good on his promise he needed more than dreams, though he had plenty of those. He needed money. Lots and lots of money. But he wasn't going to find it in Restharven. Not just because it was Restharven, but because of his brothers. In a family business, money made was money shared... and the youngest got the smallest slice of the pie.

Well, sink that for a load of mackerel.

He was off to find his own pie, and he wasn't going to share it with anybody. Not till the pie was big enough to buy him a boat of his own, so he and Da could leave Zeth and the rest of them to their own devices, sink or swim, who cared? He and Da wouldn't. He and Da would have their own damn boat, and with all the money they'd make fishing it, just the two of them, they'd live as grand as the king hisself.

For two years now, he'd been scrimping and saving and going without, just so he'd have enough to get by. Enough to get him all the way to the grand City of Dorana. He had it all worked out.

"It's just for a year, Da," he whispered. "I'll only be gone a year. It ain't that long a time, really. And I'll be back afore y'know it. You'll see."

The clock on the wall struck half past ten, loud chiming in the silence. The Rusty Anchor would be closing soon, and Jed was waiting with his knapsack and purse. He had to go. Asher leaned over the armchair, pressed a kiss to his father's weathered cheek and slipped out of the small stone cottage he and all his brothers had lived in from birth.

When he was sure it was safe to make a noise he stamped into his boots then hurried from shadow to shadow until he reached the Rusty Anchor. The pub was full, as usual. Asher pressed his nose to the bobbled windowpane, trying not to be seen, and searched for Jed. Spying his friend at last amongst the crush of carousing fishermen, he tapped and waved and hoped Jed would notice him. Just as he was despairing, Jed leapt away from an enthusiastically swung arm, stumbled, turned, and saw him.

"I were about to give up on you!" his friend grumbled as he came outside, a fresh tankard of ale in his hand. "You said ten o'clock, or soon after. It be nigh on closin' time now!"

"Don't look like y'missed me over much." Asher swiped the tankard from Jed's clutches and took a deep swallow of cold, bitter ale. "Did y'bring 'em?"

Jed snatched the tankard back. "Course I brung 'em," he said, rolling his eyes. "I'm your friend, ain't I?"

"A friend would let me drink that tankard dry," said Asher, grinning. "It's a long ways between me and the next pub, and from the looks of you, one tankard more'll be one tankard too many."

"Ain't no such thing," said Jed. Then he relented. "Here." He shoved the tankard at him. "Bloody bully. Now come on. I've stashed your things round the corner. If you stop fritterin' my time and get along I'll manage a last mouthful meself afore the Anchor closes."

Asher took the tankard. Good ole Jed. There wasn't another soul he'd have trusted his precious purseful of trins and cuicks to, or his goatskin of water and knapsack stuffed with cheese and apples and bread and clothes. Nor his dreams, neither. They'd been friends their whole lives, him and Jed. He'd even offered to take Jed to the City with him, but there'd been no need. Jed wasn't plagued with a school of brothers. He was all set to inherit his da's fishing boat in a few more years.

Lucky bastard.

"You take care now," Jed said sternly as Asher guzzled the rest of his ale. "Dorana City's a long ways from here, and it be a powerful dry place. Not to mention swarmin' with Doranen. So just you watch your step, Meister Asher. You ain't the most respectful man I ever had the pleasure of knowin'. Fact is, I ain't sure those magic folk up yonder be ready for the likes of you."

Asher laughed and tossed him the empty tankard. "Reckon those magic folk up yonder can take care of 'emselves, Jed. Just like me. Now you won't forget to see my da first thing tomorrow and let him know I be fine and I'll be back a year from today, will you?"

"Course I won't. But I still reckon you ought to let me tell him where you'll be. He's bound to ask, y'know."

"Aye, I know, but it ain't to be helped," said Asher. "You got to keep that flappin' tongue of yours behind your teeth, Jed, 'cause two seconds after you tell him he'll tell Zeth and the rest of 'em and that'll be the end of that. They'll find me and drag me back here and I won't ever get enough money saved to set Da and me up all grand and comfy. Just 'cause we're related and I be the youngest they think they own me. But they don't. So it'll be safest all round if you just act like you ain't got the foggiest notion where I am."

"Lie, you mean?"

Asher pulled a face. "For 'is own good, Jed. And mine."

"All right," said Jed, belching. "If you say so."

Asher tied the water-filled goatskin to his belt and hitched his knapsack over his shoulders. "I say so."

Jed sighed mournfully. "You'll miss the festival."

"This year. We can drink twice as much next year to make up for it. My shout. Now get yourself into the Anchor, would you, afore somebody wonders where you've got to and comes lookin'."

"Aye, sir," said Jed, and bruised Asher's ribs with a clumsy hug. "Have a grand time, eh? Bring yourself home safe and sound."

"I aim to." Asher stepped back. "Safe and mighty plump in the pocket to boot. And mayhap I'll bring a tidy armful of City Olken lass home with me and my money!"

Jed snorted. "Mayhap you will at that. Provided she's half blind and all foolish. Now for the love of Barl, it be ten minutes till closing time. If you don't get out of here now you'll be leavin' with an audience."

Which was the last thing he needed. With a smile and a wave Asher turned and hurried up the street, away from his friend and the pub and the only life he'd ever known. If he walked all night, fast, he'd reach the village of Schoomer in time to hitch a ride on one of the potato wagons heading for Colford. From Colford he could hitch to Jerring, from Jerring to Sapslo, and in Sapslo he could buy a seat on one of the wagons travelling to Dorana.

No way would his sinkin' brothers ever work out *that* plan.

As he strode up the hill towards the Coast Road he looked out to the left, where Restharven Harbour shone like a newly minted trin beneath the full-bellied moon. The warm night was full of salt and sound. A rising breeze blew spray in his face and his ears echoed with the pounding boom of waves crashing against the cliffs on either side of the keyhole harbour.

He felt his heart knock against his ribs. A year in dry Dorana. A year without the ocean. No screaming gulls, no skin-scouring surf. No pitching deck beneath his feet, no snapping sails above his head. No racing the tide and his brothers back to port, or diving off Dolphin Head into surging blue water, or scoffing grease and vinegar fresh-fried fish for dinner with Jed and the other lads.

Could he stand it?

Ha. "Could" didn't come into it. He had to. There were dreams to fulfil and a promise to keep, and he couldn't do either without leaving his heart and soul behind him. Without leaving home.

Head up, whistling and unafraid, Asher hurried towards his future.

PART ONE

CHAPTER ONE

*H*e's here."

Caught unawares, Matt straightened sharply and stared at the woman framed in the stable doorway. Her thin fingers clung tight to the top of the bolted half-door and her angular face was taut with suppressed excitement. The startled horse he was saddling tossed its head and snorted.

"Easy, Ballodair, you fool," he said, one hand on the dancing brown hindquarters. "Sneak up on a body why don't you, Dathne?"

"Sorry." As usual, she didn't sound particularly repentant. "Did you hear what I said?"

Matt ducked under the stallion's neck and checked the girth buckles on the other side. "Not really."

Dathne glanced over her shoulder, unbolted the stable door and slipped inside. From the yard behind her, the sounds of voices raised in bantering laughter and the clip-clopping scrunch of iron-shod hooves on raked gravel as two of the stable lads led horses to pasture. "I *said*," she repeated, lowering her voice, "he's here."

The gold buckles on the horse's bridle weren't quite even. Tugging them straight, frowning, Matt glanced at her. "Who? His Highness?" He clicked his tongue. "Early again, drat him. Nine o'clock he asks me to have Ballodair ready, some meetin' or other somewhere, but it ain't even—"

Dathne made an impatient hissing sound. "Not Prince Gar, you clot-head! *Him*."

At first he couldn't make head or tail of what she meant. Then he looked, really looked, into her face, her eyes. His heart leapt, and he had to steady himself against Ballodair's warm, muscled neck.

"Are you sure? How do you know?" His voice sounded strange: cracked and dry and frightened. He was frightened. If Dathne was right...if the one so long awaited was here at last...then this life, which he loved despite its dangerous secrets, was ended. And this day, so bright and blue and warmly scented with jasmine and roses and fine-boned horseflesh, marked the beginning of the end of all things known and cherished.

The end of everything, should he and Dathne fail.

Dathne was staring at him, surprise and annoyance in her narrow, uncompromising face. "How do I know? You of all people ask me that?" she demanded. "I *know*. He woke me out of sleep with his coming, late last night. My skin crawls with him." Then she shrugged, an impatient twitch of her bony shoulders. "And anyway, I've seen him."

"Seen him?" said Matt, startled. "In the flesh, you mean? Not vision? When? Where?"

Pulling her light shawl tight about her, she took a straw-rustling step closer and dropped her voice to a near whisper. "Earlier. I followed my nose till I found him coming out of Verry's Hostelry." She sniffed. "Can't say I think much of his taste."

"Dathne, that was foolish." He wiped his sweaty palms down his breeches. "What if he'd seen you?"

Another shrug. "What if he had? He doesn't know me or what I'm about. Besides, he didn't. The City's thronging with folk for market day. I blended with the crowd well enough."

"You don't reckon..." Matt hesitated. "D'you think he *knows*?"

Dathne scowled and scuffed her toe in the yellow straw, thinking. "He might," she said at last. "I suppose." Then she shook her head. "But I think not. If he did, why would there be need of us? We've a part to play in all this that hasn't begun yet." Her dark eyes took on a daunting, familiar glow. "I wonder where it will lead us. Don't you?"

Matt shivered. That was the kind of question he'd rather wasn't asked, or answered. "So long as it's not to an early grave, I don't much care. Have you told Veira?"

"Not yet," Dathne replied after a heartbeat's hesitation. "She's got Circle business, trouble in Basingdown, and beyond him being here I've nothing to tell. Not yet."

"You sound so calm. So sure!" He knew he sounded accusing. Couldn't help it. There she stood, strong and certain and self-contained as always, while his guts were writhing into knots and fresh sweat damped his shirt. Sensing his distress, Ballodair blew a warning through blood-red nostrils and pinned back his sharply curved ears. Matt took a strangled breath and stroked the horse's glossy cheek, seeking comfort. "How is it you're so sure?" His voice was a plaintive whisper.

Dathne smiled. "Because I dreamed him and he came."

And that was that. Stupid of him to expect more. To expect comfort.

Dathne was Dathne: acerbic, cryptic, unflustered and alone. After six years of knowing her, arguing with her, deferring to her, a drab and fluttering moth to her flame, he knew it was pointless to protest. She would be as she was and there was an end to it. As well to complain that a horse had four legs and a tail.

A grin, fleeting and impish, lit her plain face. She could read him as easily as any of the books she sold in her shop, drat her. "I should go. The prince will be here for his horse any moment, and I have things to do."

Something in her gleaming eyes unsettled his innards all over again. "What things?"

"Meet me in the Goose tonight for a pint," she invited, fingers lightly resting on the stable door. "Could be I'll have a tale to tell."

"Dathne—!"

But she was out of the stable, bolting the door, *snick*, behind her, and the sun was bright on the raven-black hair bound in a knot close to her long straight neck. "No later than seven, mind!" she called over her shoulder, stepping neatly aside from young Bellybone with his buckets of water dangling left and right. "I need my beauty sleep... for all the good it's done me so far!"

Then she was gone, slipping like a shadow through the stable yard's arched main entrance, and coming through the door in the wall leading to the prince's Tower residence was the prince himself, ready for riding and for business, bright yellow hair like molten gold and the easy smile on his face that hid so much, so much.

With a sigh and a last frowning stare after the woman he was soul-sworn bound to serve and to follow, Matt thrust aside his worries and went forth to greet his sovereign's son.

In the great Central Square of Dorana, capital city of the Kingdom of Lur, market day was in full, uproarious swing. First Barl's Day of every month it was held, regular as rainfall, and even though the sun had barely cleared the tallest turret on the distant royal palace the square was crammed full of buyers and sellers and sightseers, flapping and jostling like fish in a net.

Asher stood in the midst of the madness and stared like a lackwit, his senses reeling. A rabble of noise dinned his ears and his nose was overwhelmed by so many different smells, sweat and smoke and cow dung and incense, flowers and sweetmeats and roasting fowl and fresh-baked bread and more, that his empty stomach churned.

Most of the stallholders were his own people, Olken, dark-haired and industrious, selling their wares with cheerful ferocity. Fresh fruit, vegetables, butchered meat, live chickens, cured fish, candles, books, jewellery, saddlery, furniture, paintings, haircuts, bread, clocks, sweet-meats, pastries, wool, work clothes, fancy clothes...it seemed there was nothing a man couldn't buy if he had a yearning, and the money.

"Ribbons! Buy yer pretty ribbons here, six cuicks a dozen!"

"Teshoes! Ripe teshoes!"

"Oy! Mind how ye go there, lad! Mind how ye go!"

Asher spun on his heel and stumbled clear just as a bull handler, chocolate-brown beast in tow, ambled past on his way to the Live-stock Quarter. The bull's polished nose ring flashed in the sunshine, and its splayed hooves clacked on the cobblestones.

"'Ere, you great lump, git out of me way!" grumbled the fruit seller, a fat Olken woman with her dark hair straggled back in a bun, her bright green dress swathed in a juice-stained apron and a brace of plump pink teshoes in one capable hand. "You be trippin' up me customers!"

Because he'd sworn a private promise to ask whoever he could, he said to her, "Would you be needin' a body to hire?"

The fruit seller winked at the crowd gathered about her barrows and cackled. "Thanks, sonny, but I already got me a man wot'd make two of you, I reckon, so just be on yer way if you ain't buyin' none of me wares!" A roll of her meaty shoulders heaved her abundant bosom, and her lips pursed in a mockery of invitation.

Around him, laughter. Hot-faced, Asher waited till the ole besom's back was turned, nicked a teshoe from the pile at the front of the stall and jumped into the swift-flowing stream of passers-by.

He finished the fruit in three gulps and licked the tart juice off his stubbly chin. It was all the breakfast he'd get. Lunch, too, and maybe even dinner if he didn't find work today. The purse tucked into his belt was ominously flat; it had taken nearly all his meagre savings just to get here, and then last night's board had gobbled up most of the rest. He had enough for one more night's lodging, a bowl of soup and a heel of bread. After that, he was looking at a spot of bother. But even as doubt set its gnawing rat teeth in his guts, he felt a wild grin escape him.

He was in Dorana. *Dorana*. The great walled City itself. If only Da could see him now. If his *brothers* could see...they'd puke their miserable guts out, right enough.

Ha.

Long before devising the plan that had brought him here, he'd dreamed of seeing this place. Had grown up feeding that dream on the stories Ole Hemp used to tell the eager crowd of boys who gathered round his feet of an afternoon, once the boats were in and the catch was cleaned and gutted and the gulls were squabbling their fill on the pier.

Ole Hemp was the only man in Restharven who'd ever seen the City. Sprawled on his favourite bench down by the harbour, puffing on his gnarly pipe, he used to tell tales that set all their hearts to thumping and nigh started their eyes right out of their heads.

"Dorana City," Ole Hemp would say, "be so big you could fit Restharven in it twenty times over, at least. Its houses and hostelries be tall, like inland trees, and painted every colour under the sky. And its ale houses, well, they never run dry, do they. And the smells! Enough to spill the juices from yer mouth in a river, for in their kitchens they roast pigs and lambs and fat juicy bullocks over fire pits so big and deep they'd hold a whole Restharven fambly, near enough."

And the listening boys would sigh, imagining, and rub their fish-full bellies.

But there was more, Hemp would say, so hushed and awestruck his voice sounded like the foam on the shingle once all the waves had run back to the sea. In Dorana you could see Barl's Wall itself, that towering golden barrier of magic bedded deep into the sawtooth mountain range above and behind the City.

"See it?" the boys would gasp, unbelieving, no matter how many times they'd heard the story.

"Oh aye," Old Hemp assured them. "Barl's Wall ain't invisible, like the spells sunk deep in the horizon-wide reef that stops all boats entering or leaving the calmer waters between coral and coast. No, no, Barl's Wall be a great flaming thing, visible at noon on a cloudless blue day. Keeping us safe. Protecting every last Olken man, woman and child from the dangers of the long-abandoned world beyond."

That was when somebody would always ask. "And what about the Doranen, Hemp? Does it protect them too?" And Hemp would always answer: "Course it do. Reckon they're like to build a wall as won't save their own selves first and foremost?"

But he always said that quietly, as though they could hear him, even though the nearest Doranen lived over thirty miles away. For Doranen ears were magic ears, and they weren't the sort of folk who took kindly to criticism.

Unsettled and suddenly homesick, Asher shook himself free of memories then looked up and over the marketplace into the distance beyond the City, where Barl's Wall shimmered in the morning sun. Ole Hemp had been right about that much, any road: there the Wall was, and there it would stand, most like until the end of time itself.

A laughing group of Doranen sauntered by. Asher couldn't help himself: he stared.

They were a tall race, the Doranen. Hair the colours of silver and gold and ripe wheat and sunshine, looped and curled and braided with carelessly expensive jewels. Eyes clear and fine, glass hues of green and blue and grey, and their skin white, like fresh milk. Their bones were long and elegant, lightly fleshed and sheathed in silk, brocade, velvet, linen, leather. They carried themselves like creatures apart, untouched, untouchable, and wherever they walked the dust of the marketplace puffed away from them in deference.

That was magic...and they wore it like an invisible cloak. Wrapped it around their slender shoulders and kept it from slipping with the haughty tilt of their chins and the way they placed their fine-shod feet upon the ground, as though flowers should spring blooming and perfumed in their wake.

Down Restharven way, you'd hardly see a Doranen from one end of the year to the next. The king, at Sea Harvest Festival. The tax collector. The census taker. One of their fancy Pothers, if a good old-fashioned Olken healer couldn't fix your gripes or your broken bones for you. Other than that, they kept themselves to themselves on large country estates or in the kingdom's bigger towns and here, of course, in the capital. What they did to amuse themselves, Asher had no idea. Farmed and fished rivers and grew grapes and bred horses, he supposed, just like his own people. Except, of course, they used magic.

Asher felt his lip curl. Living your life with magic...it wasn't *natural*. These fancy yeller-headed folk with their precious powers to do near on everything for them, to make the world bend to their wishes and whims, who'd never raised the smallest blister in all their lives, let alone an honest sweat...what did they understand about the world? About the way a man should be connected to it, should live steeped in its tides and rhythms, obedient to its subtle voices?

Nowt. For all their mysterious, magical powers, the Doranen understood nowt.

With an impatient, huffing sigh, he moved on. Standing about like a shag on a rock wasn't going to get him any closer to finding a job.

With his elbows tucked in and one hand hovering protectively over his purse, he navigated the crowded spaces between the market stalls, asking each stallholder for work. The little girls back home, picking winkles at low tide, put fewer shells in their gunny-sacks than the rejections he collected now.

His heart was banging uncomfortably. This wasn't the way his dreams had gone at all. He'd reckoned finding a job'd be a damn sight easier than *this* . . .

Scowling, he stopped before one of the few Doranen stalls in the marketplace. The pretty young woman tending it smiled at him and snapped her fingers. The cunningly carved and painted toy dog prancing among the other toys immediately barked and turned a somersault. With another Doranen finger-snap a jolly fat clown dressed in spangled red began juggling three yellow balls. The little dog yapped and tried to snatch one out of the air.

The stall's other onlookers laughed. Just in time, Asher caught and swallowed a smile. Snorting, he turned his back on the dog and the clown and the pretty young woman and stumped away through the streaming crowd. Bloody Doranen. Couldn't even flummery toys to amuse spratlings without reaching for a spell.

At the heart of the marketplace stood a fountain, spewing water like a whale. Its centrepiece was a carved greenstone statue of Barl, with arms outstretched and a thunderbolt grasped in one fist. Beneath the bubbling surface, trins and cuicks winked and flashed in the sunshine. Asher fished a single precious copper cuick from his purse and tossed it in.

"It's a job I be needin'," he said to the silent face above him. "Nowt fancy, and all in a good cause. Reckon y'could see your way clear to helpin'?"

The statue stayed silent. Moisture slicked its carved green cheeks like tears . . . though what Barl had to cry about, he surely didn't know. Turning his back, Asher slumped onto the lip of the fountain's retaining wall. Not that he'd expected the statue to actually *speak*. But he'd half hoped for some kind of answer. An inspiration. A bloody good idea. For sure he wasn't the most *regular* of chapel-goers, but like everybody else in the kingdom, he did *believe*. And he obeyed the Laws. All of them. That had to be good for something.

He refused to accept his dream was dead before ever it drew breath. *Somewhere* in this noisy walled City there had to be an Olken in need of an honest young man with a strong back and a willingness to put in a long day's toil for a hot meal, a soft bed and fair pay at the end of it. Some kind of working man, or woman. No point botherin' with any of the fancy Olken. They were almost as bad as the Doranen. Fancy City Olken with fancy City houses and soft City hands and more money than sense, they'd be wanting workers—no, *staff*—with references and posh accents and clothes worth a year's catch of mackerel. He had no use for that malarkey, and the folks that did would have as little use for him.

No. He was a Restharven fisherman born and bred and he knew his worth. Somewhere in this City he'd find someone else who did too. Statue or no statue, he was going to get hisself that job.

He had to. He had a fortune to make and promises to keep.

Cutting through the babble of noise in the square, the indignant bellow of a cow. Asher snapped out of his slump. Of *course*. The Livestock Quarter. *Fool*. He should've tried there first, 'stead of traipsing from stall to stall getting nowt but a fistful of "no" for his trouble. In the Livestock Quarter he'd find farmers, cattlemen. His kind of folk. For certain sure there'd be somebody there wantin' the kind of service Asher of Restharven could provide.

He jumped up, hope rekindled. On the other side of the square, sound and movement distracted him. Shouting. Whistles. Applause. Glimpsed between the market stalls and crowding bodies, a flash of dark heads and blue and crimson livery: the City Guard, marching down the sloping road from the palace, which gleamed like a settled seagull up on the hill above the City.

Asher went to look. The Livestock Quarter wasn't going anywhere, and he was curious. Five minutes here or there weren't like to make a difference.

"Way now!" a stern voice shouted, carrying over the bubble and froth of the marketplace. "Make way for His Highness Prince Gar!"

Asher felt himself jostled and bumped forward with the rest of the crowd as it surged and seethed around him. He didn't understand the commotion. Why get so excited just because the prince was coming? The prince lived here in the City, didn't he, along with the rest of the royal family? Didn't City folk get to see him most every day of the week? Aye, they did. So why break a body's toes to lay eyes on him now?

But eyen as he muttered and cursed and shoved back, he had to admit to a breath of excitement. Not even Ole Hemp had laid eyes on a member of the royal family. This would put him one up, and no mistake. Da would be tickled pink.

With the roadway cleared of shoppers and stallholders, the prince was free to ride his bay blood horse with only one hand on the reins. It was a beautiful animal, mincing and dappled and harnessed in jewels. Asher felt his throat close in envy. That's what being a prince got you: a wondrous beast like that one, and a hundred more at home just like it, most prob'ly.

For the first time in his life, he was fleetingly sorry to be himself.

The approaching prince looked as well bred as his horse. His corn-silk hair, as long as a girl's, was caught in a tail at the nape of his neck. His green silk shirt and tan leather breeches were immaculate. The gloss on his black leather boots was blinding. On his head gleamed a beaten silver circlet of rank, studded with rubies. His thin face was lively with appreciation as he waved and smiled at the well-wishers to his left and right.

Thrust to the edge of the road by the heaving crowd, Asher eyed him up and down. So. This was His Royal Highness Prince Gar. Even down in distant Restharven they knew about *him*. Gar the Magickless. Gar the Cripple. Even, some whispered into their ale pots, Gar the Disgrace. Too blond to be an Olken, too magickless to be Doranen. That's what folks said about His Royal Highness Prince Gar... at least down Restharven way.

But from all the hooting and hollering of the City Olken around him it seemed they didn't mind the prince couldn't do magic. That he'd not be the one to take over the WeatherWorking once his father the king wore out. No, the City Olken seemed to think he was something to screech and dance for. Why? What use was a magician who couldn't do magic? About as much as a ship without sails, to his mind.

And it seemed he wasn't the only one to think so.

Barely a handful of Doranen had stopped to cheer their king's son as he rode off to spend a strenuous day in the countryside sniffing flowers, or whatever it was he did to amuse himself. A few had paused to smile and nod. A lot more, though, paid him no mind at all, or watched him pass with bland faces and judgement in their eyes. Did the prince see it? Did he care? It was hard to tell. For sure his dazzling smile didn't falter and his hand stayed steady on the reins... but mayhap there was a flicker in the green eyes. A momentary coldness, or stifled hurt.

Asher snorted. Catch him wasting time feeling sorry for a prince.

The king's son was drawing level now. In a moment would be close enough to reach out and touch if he'd had a mind to. Determined to remain unaffected, Asher stared into the smooth, careless face of royalty... and royalty stared back.

A frown. A jolt: of interest, or rejection, or something in between.

Then an Olken lass tossed a rose. It struck royalty's prancing horse on the neck. The horse shied, objecting, and the prince had his hands full.

Disconcerted, Asher stepped back from the edge of the road, heedless of the trampled toes and curses behind him. Despite himself, and despising himself for it, he was impressed. There *was* something about the prince. The king's son possessed an aura of authority. Of grace, even. Something inborn, of blood and bone and breeding, not circumstance. Something that made him...different.

Codswallop. The prince was rich, magic or no magic he was Doranen, and he was royalty; probably it was that and nothing more.

Asher shook himself, breaking the unlikely, unwelcome spell. All this standing about gawping at royalty. Da would've clipped him over the earhole long afore now. Time he took care of his own business.

He turned away. From six feet further along the road came a loud bang. A scream. Asher turned back to see a whirling, whizzing rush of light as the rockets in a fireworks stall erupted into blazing glory, shooting skywards in a shower of green and yellow sparks. The crowd shrieked.

Already unnerved, the prince's blood horse whinnied in fright and reared. His Royal Highness fell off backwards to land his royal arse hard and hurting on the dirty ground. Panic-stricken, preparing to bolt, the animal bunched its hindquarters and spun about, eyes wild. Foam flew from its gaping mouth.

"*Ballodair*!" the prince cried as the horse launched itself over his head in a great leaping bound.

"Catch him!" cried another voice, sharp and commanding, buried somewhere close by in the crowd.

Without thinking, Asher jumped into the path of the frightened horse. A lifetime of sailing boats in untamed weather had honed his reflexes and made him indifferent to danger. Catching those flapping reins was just like laying hold of a loose halyard in high winds; battling the beast to a standstill not much harder than wrestling with a net-load of fish reluctant to die.

And besides, it seemed a shame for a fine animal like that to break a slender leg just 'cause some royal folderol couldn't keep his arse in the saddle.

Shod hooves striking sparks, the horse plunged and spun. The screaming crowd scattered. Swearing as the horse's head collided with his own, seeing stars and shouting as an iron-clad foot ground his booted toes into the cobblestones, Asher struggled to keep the animal in one place. Blood from his split eyebrow blurred his vision. His sweaty hands slid on the leather reins as the horse grunted and thrashed and struggled for freedom.

In the end, Asher won. Defeated at last, the horse stood with all four feet on the ground, trembling. Its nostrils were red and wide open as ale pots as it huffed hot, hay-scented breath. Its eyes stared but no longer rolled, white-rimmed. Asher bent over, gasping.

Without warning the reins were plucked from his grasp and a shaking voice said, "Ballodair! It was just some fireworks! Are you all right, you fool of an animal?"

Head pounding, blood warm and sticky on his face, Asher straightened.

The prince, running an anxious hand down the animal's legs, was searching for damage. Paid no heed to the man who'd saved his wretched horse's hide. Offended, Asher cleared his throat. "It be fine, I reckon," he said, determined that this elegantly clad prince was a man, like him, who pissed and farted same as all men did, and had nothing more special to recommend him than an expensive tailor. "Don't seem like the beast's taken any harm, barrin' a fright."

The prince glanced up at him. A flicker of recognition lit his eyes and he nodded. Standing straight, he looped the reins over one arm then dusted his hands on his breeches. "So it would appear, Barl be praised." He kissed the solid gold holyring on his left forefinger. "He was a gift from His Majesty."

"A grand gift," said Asher. "Glad I could save 'im for you. I be fine too, by the way. You know. 'Case you were wonderin'."

The returning crowd gasped and muttered. A City Guard, his cheeks still pale from what might have been, frowned and stepped closer. The prince held up one hand, halting him, and considered Asher in unsmiling silence. Heart pounding, Asher lifted his chin and considered the prince right back. After a moment, the prince relaxed. Very nearly smiled. "Not so fine, I think. Your head is split open and your wits are addled from the blow. Have you taken any other hurt?"

The crowd buzzed its surprise, pressing to get a closer look at the ramshackle newcomer in such close conversation with royalty. Asher touched cautious fingertips to his eyebrow and shrugged as they came away red. "This ain't nowt. Reckon I've had worse shavin'." Then he scowled. "And my wits ain't addled, neither."

Horrified, the City Guard prodded Asher in the back. "Lout! Address the prince as 'Your Highness' and show some respect or you'll find yourself in one of Captain Orrick's cells!"

Again the prince lifted a hand. "It's all right, Grimwold. I suspect our reluctant hero isn't from around these parts." Smiling, he pulled a handkerchief from his shirt pocket, then unclipped a leather flask from his saddle and doused the fabric with its pale green contents. "Wine," he explained, offering it to Asher. "It'll sting, I'm afraid, but that's better than horse sweat in an open wound. Where are you from, by the way?"

With a grunt—and if the prince wanted to consider himself thanked, then fine—Asher took the handkerchief and dabbed his face with it. The alcohol burned like fire against his raw flesh; he couldn't swallow the pained hiss fast enough. "Restharven," he muttered. "Your Highness." Face clean of blood and dust, he glared at the soiled handkerchief. "Y'want this back?"

The prince's lips curved in faint amusement. "No. Thank you."

Was the king's son laughing at him? Bastard. "Got hundreds, have you?"

Now the smile was in full bloom. "Not quite. But enough that I can lose one and not repine. I've never been to Restharven."

"I know," said Asher. Then, prompted by the guard's glower added, sickly sweet, "Your Highness."

"How is it," asked the prince, after a thoughtful pause, "that you come to dislike me so thoroughly? And after I've given you a pure silk handkerchief, moreover."

Asher felt his face heat. Hadn't Ma always said to him, *Asher, that unruly tongue of yours will land you in such trouble one day*... "Never said I dislike you," he muttered. "Don't even know you, do I?"

The prince nodded. "That's very true. And easily remedied, what's more. Grimwold?" The silently scandalised guard snapped off a salute. "I believe we've provided enough entertainment for now. Move the people about their business. I'd like a private word with this gentleman." He turned to Asher. "That is unless you've pressing business to conduct elsewhere?"

Asher bit his tongue. Stared into a fine-bred face vivid with amusement, and a challenge. He cleared his throat. "No. Your Highness."

"Excellent!" declared the prince, and clapped him on the shoulder. "Then I shall steal a few minutes of your time with a clear conscience! Grimwold?"

With an obedient nod Grimwold did as he was told. The crowd dispersed in dribs and drabs, murmuring... and Asher was left alone with the Crown Prince of Lur.

CHAPTER TWO

Asher spared the grudgingly moving townsfolk a scathing glance. "Load of ole mollygrubbers. You fell off your horse, I caught it for you. Ain't no need for fuss. Ain't none of their business, I reckon."

Arms folded, head on one side, the prince regarded him with fascination. "Do you know, not even my enemies are as rude as you. At least not to my face."

Asher stared. Enemies? Since when did a prince have enemies? Then he scowled. "Rude? I ain't rude. I'm just me."

"Is that so?" said the prince, and laughed. "And who would 'me' be, exactly?"

It took Asher a moment to realise the prince was asking his name. Smart-arse. "Asher."

"Well, Asher—from Restharven—it's certainly refreshing to make your acquaintance. What brings you all the way from the coast to the City?"

Asher stared. Questions, questions and more bloody questions. Next time he'd let the horse bolt and break all its legs, he surely would. "A private matter," he said. Then added politely, because say what you like, Ma never raised her sons to be *rude*, "Your Highness."

"I see," said the prince, nodding. "Anything I can help with?"

Asher shrugged. "Prob'ly not. I be lookin' for work."

"Work?" The prince raised his pale eyebrows. "Hmm. So tell me, Asher. Since you come from Restharven, am I right in thinking you're a fisherman?"

"Aye."

The prince pushed aside his horse's questing nose. "Ah. Well, I can't say I've noticed a lot of fish in Dorana, unless you count the ornamental ones in the palace garden fishponds, and I don't think my mother would approve of you netting those." Another smile, reminiscent this time. "Besides, I ate one when I was four and it tasted disgusting."

"I can do other things aside from fishin'," said Asher, goaded.

"Really?" The prince considered him. "Such as?"

Such as...such as...sailing. Except there weren't no boats in Dorana, neither. Damn the man. "Lots of things. I can...I can..." Punch you in the nose for askin' damn fool questions. Which most likely would earn him a night in a cell. Oh well. It'd save him the cost of a room at Verry's if he had no luck in the Livestock Quarter. "I can—"

A voice, polite but with a brisk air of confidence, said, "Your Highness?"

Asher turned. A woman. Middle height. Maybe a year or three older than himself. Thin. Sharp-faced, sharp-eyed, with an intensity about her that could never be restful. No feminine frippery about her, makeup or jewellery or suchlike. Slung over one bony shoulder a string bag half filled with packages. She glanced at him, an air of disinterest behind the good manners, then returned her attention to the prince.

He was smiling again. "Dathne."

She offered him a scarecrowish curtsey, all knees and elbows. "Forgive me for intruding, sir, but I saw what happened. I trust Your Highness is unharmed?"

"Aside from the odd bruise to my posterior—and my pride," said the prince, rubbing one hip. "I should know better than to go tumbling off like that."

She shrugged. "Accidents happen. Sir, if I may be so impertinent... Matt was saying only last night that what with young Tolliver going back to his family's farm, he could do with another pair of hands about the stables."

"Was he indeed?" The prince turned to Asher. "Well?"

Asher stared. "Well, what? Sir?"

"My stable meister is a good man. Strict, but fair. All the lads like him." When Asher didn't reply, the prince added, impatiently, "I'm offering you a job."

"I were goin' to ask around in the Livestock Quarter."

"Well then," said the prince, grinning, "I've saved you some shoe leather, haven't I? So. Are you interested?"

Careful, careful. Only a fool dives headfirst into strange waters. "What if I am?"

The prince shrugged. "Then you're hired." He nodded at the woman, pleased. "A lucky coincidence, Dathne."

Her lips curved in a faint smile. "Yes, Your Highness. Would you like me to see him safe to Matt? You're on your way somewhere, I think."

"On my way and horribly late," said the prince. "So yes. You could take him up to the Tower. Thank you, Dathne." Gathering his reins, he slipped one booted toe into the stirrup and swung himself into the saddle with a lithe grace. "Tell Matt to get Asher settled in, and have him send for Nix to see to that cut. You can start your duties proper in the morning, Asher. All right?"

Taken aback by all the brusque efficiency, Asher nodded. "Aye. Sir."

"Certainly, Your Highness," said the bony woman.

"And after you leave the Tower, Dathne, you could stop by the palace and see if the queen is free to speak with you. I believe there's a book she's looking for."

Another curtsey. "It would be my pleasure, Your Highness."

"Excellent," said the prince, and nudged his horse forward.

Asher stared after him, mouth agape. "Wait a minute! You can't just give me a job and then ride off without so much as a—"

"I can, you know," the prince said over his shoulder. "It's one of the few advantages of being royal."

"*Wait* a minute!" Asher shouted, and hustled after him, ignoring a handful of staring bystanders and the distantly hovering Grimwold. "You ain't said how much you'll pay me!"

The prince swung his horse round. "Twenty trins a week, plus suitable work clothes, bed and meals."

Asher choked. Twenty trins? *Twenty trins?* Da had only ever paid him seven, and nearly not that, what with all of brother Zeth's complaining about him being the youngest with no family of his own to feed. He took a deep breath. "Thirty!"

The prince laughed. "*Thirty?*"

"I saved your precious Ballodair, didn't I? Sir?"

Another laugh. "And I can see your act of derring-do is going to cost me dearly. Twenty-five, and not a cuick more. Tell Matt. Anything else? Say no."

"No," said Dathne, who'd joined them. "Good-day, Your Highness."

Asher watched the prince ride out of sight, dumbfounded, then turned to stare at the skinny, interfering woman who'd just got him a job in the Prince of Lur's stables for the unheard-of sum of twenty-five trins a week, plus clothes and bed and board.

She grinned. "Well, well. It looks like I'm stuck with introducing you to Matt, so let's get it done, shall we? I'm a very busy bookseller and I don't have all day." She snapped her fingers under his nose and turned on her heel. "Follow me."

The wine-soaked, bloodstained silk handkerchief was dry now. Asher shoved it into his pocket and followed.

For all that she was a good head shorter than he, Asher found himself scuttling to keep up with the woman's impatient haste along the rising High Street that led, apparently, to the palace. The roadway was lined with shops; he would've liked to stop for a minute, have a stickybeak through their sparkling windows, but the sinkin' woman just kept forging ahead as though a shark had plans to swallow her for supper.

"So what's this Matt like then, eh?" he asked, hitching his knapsack back onto his shoulder for the fourth time.

"You heard His Highness," she replied. "He's an excellent fellow. You'll like him." She spared him a sidelong glance. "The question is, will he like you?"

That stung. "Ain't no call for him not to be likin' me! Reckon I be as good a man any day as some fancy prince's stable meister."

Her eyebrows lifted. "Well, that remains to be seen, doesn't it?" Taking him by the sleeve she tugged him off the main thoroughfare and down a quieter side street lined with balconied private dwellings. Just as Hemp had claimed, they were toweringly tall and painted all different colours. "This way."

Asher stopped staring at one high, narrow house painted yellow— *yellow*—and stared at the skinny woman instead, suddenly distrustful. He pulled his sleeve free and slowed, almost halting. "Where are we goin'? I thought we were headin' for the palace."

"We are, more or less," she replied. "His Highness hasn't lived in the palace itself since his majority. He has his own separate establishment in the palace grounds now. Going this way saves time." She favoured him with a sly grin. "Mind you, if I weren't in a rush I *would* take you the long way round. Make sure you were in a suitably humbled frame of mind before meeting Meister Matt."

Asher scowled. "What did the prince say your name were again? Mistress Clever Clogs?"

Surprisingly, that made her laugh. "It's Dathne," she said, and bustled on.

"Ha." With a leap he blocked her pell-mell progress along the quiet street. "And why would you be interested in doin' a favour for me, eh, Mistress Dathne? You don't know me from a hole in the ground."

Eyebrows raised again, she looked him up and down. "Who said the favour was for you? I thought to help Matt out—but if you're going to be this disagreeable, could be I'll think again."

"Y'can't!" said Asher, alarmed, feeling those precious twenty-five weekly trins trickling through his fingers. "The prince said—"

"Whatever he said can as easily be unsaid. He doesn't interfere with Matt's running of the stables, so long as he's happy with how the horses are looking. And trust me, His Highness is very happy. If Matt says he won't have you then you'll be out on your ear, Meister Fisherman, and all for the sake of a little civility. Is that what you want?"

After a struggling moment, Asher shook his head. "Never said that. I just like to know where I stand, Dathne. That's all. Don't like owin' folk. Especially strangers."

She favoured him with an enigmatic smile. "But we're not strangers, Asher. And as for owing me...well." Pushing him to one side, she started walking again. "I'm sure if I put my mind to it, I'll be able to come up with some way for you to pay me back."

Asher stared after her, mouth open. Did she mean...? He hoped not. Skinny lemon-tongued shrews weren't his catch of mackerel, not by a netful they weren't. And then he pushed the thought aside, because she was turning another corner and in a moment he'd have lost her, and what kind of an impression would that make, eh, with his twenty-five trins still hanging in the balance?

Hoisting his knapsack to safety yet again, he hurried to catch up.

The palace grounds were enormous. Stretching the entire width of the walled City, they were girded by an impressive pale cream sandstone wall with a number of entrances each guarded by a pair of liveried Olken resplendent in crimson and gold. The two sentries decorating the gates that Dathne led him towards straightened at their approach, smiling.

"Morning to you, Mistress Dathne," they murmured, waving her under the stone archway with a single, disciplined glance for the unkempt stranger tagging at her heels.

"And to you, Pamfret, Brogan," Dathne replied. Taking Asher's elbow again, she hustled him along a raked blue gravel pathway that wound through lavish garden beds.

After the hubbub of the market square and their breathless rush up the sloping High Street, the garden's tranquillity was like a cool draught of ale. Asher reclaimed his elbow and slowed, sucking in the perfumed air. Took a moment to consider his surroundings. To his far right rose the pure white walls of the palace, and to his left, just visible behind a belt of massive oak trees, a single column of midnight blue stone pointed fingerlike to the sky.

Dathne caught him staring at it. "The Prince's Tower."

"You mean he lives up there?"

"And works. Why? What's wrong with that?"

Skin crawling, Asher stared at the stone spire. "Houses ain't s'posed to be *tall*," he muttered, remembering Restharven's cosy stone cottages. "It ain't *natural*. What if it fell down?"

Dathne laughed. "It's nearly three hundred years old, Asher. If it was going to tumble it would have done so long before now. Besides, the Doranen don't build anything without stitching it up tight with magic. Trust me, it's perfectly safe."

"You've been in there?"

"Of course I have." She started walking again, fingers plucking at his sleeve to keep him with her. "Dozens of times. I often have books the prince finds interesting. He's probably the finest scholar in the kingdom, you know. Reads the original Doranen texts as fluently as if they'd been written yesterday."

"Oh aye?" said Asher, profoundly uninterested. "Good for him."

She looked at him sidelong, one eyebrow raised, a gleam of mischief in her eyes. "Do you like books?"

He'd never owned a book in his life. He could read, after a fashion; Ma had insisted on enough schooling for that, at least, before the wasting sickness whittled her to bones and eyes and put her in the ground. Once she was dead and gone, though, the sea had swallowed him whole and school had become a haphazard affair, his days there as scattered as flotsam on Bottlenose Beach. He shrugged. "Books? Don't think on 'em much one way or the other."

"Of course," she said. "Too busy fishing, I expect."

Was she laughing at him? He glared. "Fishin's a grand life. I ain't found one grander."

"Did I say it wasn't?" She raised her hands in mock surrender. "You're too easily prickled, Asher of Restharven. I don't know anything of where you come from. Could be you're the most important man in the village, and if that's so then I'm pleased for you. But a word to the wise now. Here you're the new boy and Matt won't stand for brangling. It upsets the horses, and in his eyes there's no greater sin. Is your skin so tender you can't take a little teasing?"

Asher felt himself burn. With six brothers unloving and Da pickled and stewed and blinded with grief, he'd learned early to meet aggravation with greater aggravation or pay a heavy price. He scowled. "Any brangling won't be 'cause I started it. A body's got a right to earn a livin' without havin' to sleep with one eye open 'cause some iggerant shit-shoveller can't leave well enough alone. And if your precious Matt ain't a man to see that, then I'll turn round right now and find m'self a different job."

She stopped and swung about then, bony fingers closing hard on his wrist. In her face, a riot of uncertainty. Her eyes, plain brown and piercing, searched his face over and over as though looking for answers to a question she didn't care—or dare—to speak aloud. Her brows were knitted and her teeth pinched her lower lip bloodless. There was a blazing ferocity in her he didn't understand...but the heat of it backed him up a pace.

And then she smiled, the heat snuffing out of her like a wind-blown candle. Stepping back again, she let go of his wrist. "I expect you're right," she said lightly. "It never hurts to let people know you won't be trifled with. Now come on. I really don't have all day."

At length the gravelled path led them to another wall, this one of rough-hewn bloodrock speckled with some kind of crystal that winked and flashed in the sunshine. An elaborate cast-iron gate stood wide open in welcome; passing through it, Asher saw the blue tower much closer now, yet still partly obscured by the oaks standing tall around its base. Straight ahead, though, was a grand curving archway of cream and ochre sandstone connecting two long, low ochre brick buildings. There were windows ranged at intervals along their walls, the open shutters painted a rich dark green. Through several of them horses poked long faces of brown and chestnut and grey, nostrils quivering, ears pricked, dark eyes wide and curious. Ringing into the surrounding quiet, a hammer struck echoes from an anvil.

"And here we are," said Dathne. "Matt's little kingdom." When Asher looked at her askance she added, "You think I'm jesting? Trust me, I'm not. The horses are his heart, and he protects them as keenly as any king does his subjects. Keep that fact pinned to your mast in plain sight, Meister Fisherman, and you'll not go far wrong."

"Ha," said Asher.

They passed beneath the sandstone archway and into the rich-smelling world of horses. The stables were arranged in a large square, each box opening onto an expanse of herringboned brick and dark red gravel. The yard was immaculate, swept and raked and clean as a cook's kitchen. At its centre gloried a lavish, bee-buzzed flowerbed.

The sound of hammering was louder in here, but had changed. Off to the left in a covered, open-fronted alcove a massive grey horse stood snorting with displeasure. A young Olken lad gripped its plaited leather lead hard in both hands. A giant of a man, Olken and mountainously muscled, crouched over one of the horse's raised hind legs, cradling the fetlock and hoof between his bent knees. His black hair was clipped neat as a hedge. One large hand held a hammer and pounded nails into the horse's hoof with such precise power that Asher, staring, had to wonder what it might feel like to be felled by a punch from him.

Be best, prob'ly, if he never found out.

Beside him, Dathne made a pleased sound. "There he is." She raised her voice. "Matt!"

Matt took a moment to tap the nail-head home with one final metallic blow, then shuffled carefully back to front, hand supporting the horse's hoof, so he could finish off securing the shoe. Settling into his new position, hitching the hoof high onto his thigh, he glanced up. Saw Dathne, saw the stranger with her, and froze. His brown eyes widened, and his lips parted, sucking in an astonished rush of air. Then his expression smoothed, became completely noncommittal.

"Dathne." His voice was deep and instinctively soothing. "Be with you directly." He glanced at the lad clutching the horse's lead rope. "Make sure you've got a good grip there, Boonie, he's tensing up." He made a hissing sound and jiggled the horse's leg gently. "Settle down, old son, it's nearly over."

Quickly, with an economy of effort and a minimum of fuss, the stable meister resumed his task. Asher, watching closely, was impressed. You could trust a man who knew his job and did it well, without boastful flourishes.

Finished at last, Matt guided the horse's hoof back to the ground and nodded at the lad. "Put him in his paddock now, Boonie, and mind he doesn't kick you when you turn him loose."

The lad bobbed his head. "Aye, Meister Matt," he said, eyes aglow with respectful worship, and led the grey horse away. Matt watched them for a moment, eyes warm, then stuck his hammer through his belt and crossed the yard to Dathne and Asher.

As he opened his mouth to speak, Dathne said brightly, "Matt, this is Asher of Restharven. His Highness has hired him to replace Tolliver."

Matt looked at her. "Oh he has, has he?"

"There was an incident in town, you see. Ballodair—"

"Ballodair!" Matt exclaimed. "Dathne, if you—"

She clapped her hands under his nose. "The horse is fine, Matt! Stop fussing!" She rolled her eyes at Asher. "Now do you believe me?"

Matt took a deep, steadying breath. "Just tell me what happened," he said with gritty patience.

Asher decided he'd had enough of other people speaking for him and deciding his fate. "Some fireworks went off, the horse took fright, tipped the prince onto his arse and tried to bolt. I caught it, and the prince offered me a job."

Matt was staring at Dathne, the warmth in his eyes chilled now. "Fireworks?" His voice was ominously quiet.

"One or two rockets," she told him, equally ominous. "No harm done."

"This time."

Asher scowled. From the looks of them, these two were set to start brangling like cats any tick of the clock. Something was going on here, some kind of lovers' spat, most like, and he wanted no part of it. Let 'em tussle on their own time. "Who do I see about recording my wages? Twenty-five trins a week I'm to get."

"Twenty-five?" Startled, Matt turned. "That's—"

"What the prince said he'd pay me," said Asher, truculent.

"He did," agreed Dathne.

"That's as may be," said Matt, still glowering, "but is he worth twenty-five trins a week?"

"Why should you care?" Dathne replied. "It's not your money, is it?"

"No," said Matt, "but it's my yard and my headache if the other lads hear—"

Her hand lifted, silencing him midsentence. Turning to Asher she said, "Are you going to blab to the other lads how much you're being paid?"

Asher snorted. "Course not. What kind of a fool d'you take me for?"

She turned back to Matt. "There. You see? He's the soul of discretion."

Matt gaped at her for a moment, then closed his mouth with a snap of teeth and glared at Asher. "What do you know of horsekeeping, any road? You've not the look of a horseman, that much I can tell."

Asher glared right back. "Reckon I know enough. His Highness went and hired me, didn't he? Don't reckon I need to give you more of a recommendation than that. Why don't y'wait and see what kind of a fist I make on the job afore you count me no good, eh? Mayhap you'll get yourself a pleasant surprise."

Matt shook his head. "Oh, I'm already surprised, Asher of Rest-harven." His scowling gaze snapped sideways to Dathne, and the air fairly sizzled between them. "Whether or not it's pleasant remains to be seen."

Definitely, something was going on there. Asher took a small step to one side, putting distance between himself and the bookseller. "Y'won't regret hirin' me on," he said. "I ain't a wastrel, nor a shimshammery tyke neither. If I take a man's money, I give 'im proper weight for it."

Matt looked at him then, really looked at him. In his piercing regard there was a strange echo of the way Dathne had stared at him earlier. After a long moment, the stable meister nodded. "So you say. But words are cheap. I'll judge you on deeds, if I judge you at all."

"And I'm sure nobody could ask for better than that," said Dathne briskly. "Now, Matt, once Asher's settled in His Highness wants Nix to have a look at that cut on his head. Your precious Ballodair did that, so probably you owe Asher an apology. I must be off, I've to go see the queen, and then it's back to my little shop before I lose any more business today!" She waggled her fingers at them and turned on her heel.

Matt took a thunderous step after her. "*Dathne!*"

Striding away, she called back to him, "Tonight in the Goose, Matt, remember? No later than seven or you'll be paying!"

Matt stared after her, face stormy. Then he raised his fisted hands, stamped one booted foot to the gravel and exclaimed in heartfelt tones, "Barl save me! That *bloody* woman!"

"Aye," said Asher, and shook his head. "She be a slumskumbledy wench and no mistake."

Matt blinked and lowered his fists. "*Slumskumbledy?*"

"Brangling," explained Asher. "Contrariwise." He shrugged. "A pain in the arse, if y'must know."

Matt shoved his hands in his pockets and stared at Asher. Asher stared back. Abruptly, spontaneously, they exploded into a duet of baffled, rueful laughter.

"A pain in the arse?" Matt echoed, eyes bright. "Asher of Restharven, I doubt I could've said it better myself!"

And just like that, though Meister Matt was the boss, and a handful of years older than his new stable lad, they were friends.

At five after seven that evening Matt shouldered his way into the Green Goose Inn, favoured watering hole and gossip mill of many royal staff, whether they served in the palace or the Prince's Tower. The Goose was a popular meeting place for several reasons: it was only a short walk from the palace grounds, useful for when a body's legs were all unsteady from an excess of cheer; the ale was cool and tasty, the food hot and plentiful, and their host, Aleman Derrig, could be sure to keep out any nuisances hoping to importune favours of a royal nature.

Though his name was called a dozen times as he ducked his head under the lintel, Matt just raised an acknowledging hand and did not stop to dally. All his attention was on Dathne, wedged comfortably in a corner booth with an ale-foamed tankard and a steaming bowl of soup keeping her company.

Sliding onto the bench opposite, he planted his elbows on the scarred, smoke-soaked table between them, leaned forward into the fragrant waftings from the broth bowl and said, his voice shaking with outrage, "That's him, isn't it? What in Jervale's name d'you think you're *doing*?"

"Keep your voice down. There's no need to tell the world and all his cousins what we're about."

Matt looked around the crowded inn. Humperdy's Band was racketing away in the far corner, fiddle and pipe and tambourine and drum filling the spaces between floor and rafters with raucous music. Many of the evening's rowdies were singing along, in tune and out of it. Heels banged away under benches and tables, more or less in time with the ditty, tankards thumped in counterpoint, and above that was the cheerful bellowing of friends gathered in good-natured banter. He doubted anyone standing even two feet away had overheard him.

He glared. "Stop trying to change the subject."

Dathne sighed and shook her head. "I did what was needful, Matt. No more, no less. I'm sorry to fret you. It wasn't my intention. But I must act when the push comes upon me, you know it, so don't sit there like a frog on a log pulling faces. We have him under our noses now, which is exactly where he should be. What's the rest of it compared to that?"

Matt bullied his face straight and stared at his freshly bruised knuckles, where one of the yearlings had tried its teeth that afternoon. "The rest of it?" He lifted his gaze to look at her. "Fireworks and bolting horses and all those people watching? Dathne—"

She waved an impatient hand. "Nothing happened that shouldn't have. And if you've a mind to bleat about your precious damned Ballodair again, I swear I'll throw this tankard of ale in your face then get the price of it off you straight after!"

That made him scowl again. "It's my job to worrit on the horses, Dathne."

She leaned close, eyes slitted with temper. "Your job is to do what I tell you and see that all runs as it should. What we're about here is worth a hundred Ballodairs, and our lives besides, and hating me for saying so doesn't change it. So you'd best make up that flitterbug mind of yours once and for all whether you can stomach the task or not. I can't do my part without a second pair of hands I can trust. If they're not to be yours then I need to tell Veira so she can find me another."

Stricken silent, Matt looked down. Around him the room heaved with laughter and eating and generous drinking. His friends, for the most part, folk he'd known half his life and longer. Simple, hardworking

Olken, blissfully ignorant of the secrets he'd kept for nearly ten years. Good people who were set to suffer and die if he and Dathne and the others of the Circle failed. His stomach rolled over, thinking on it, and the room disappeared in a blur of anguish.

Cool strong fingers on his wrist brought him back.

"Jervale's Prophecy is fulfilled, my friend," said Dathne. The sharp edges were gone from her voice: she sounded sad and tired and not like herself. "The Innocent Mage is come, and we stand at the beginning of the end of everything. I know you hoped the Final Days would pass you by, that the folk called after us would be the ones to face the fire, but that hope's dead and buried now. Digging it up and crying fresh tears on it won't change the truth. Like it or not, Matt, you and I are the ones born to the days Jervale foretold."

"How long have you known?"

"Long enough."

"And you're sure?" he whispered. "There's no doubt? No chance you might be mistaken?"

She shook her head. "Visions don't lie."

"They might."

"That's fear talking. Strangle it before it leads us all to disaster."

Matt winced as his guts cramped. "You may be Jervale's Heir, Dathne, but that doesn't make you perfect. You could be wrong!"

"I could be, but I'm not. I was three days short of my tenth birthday the first time I dreamed Asher's face. The next afternoon I was told some cousin I'd never met had died overnight and it was my duty to take his place as Jervale's Heir. And then I was told what that meant. I haven't had an easy night's sleep since."

There was pain in her, fiercely denied. Matt wanted to reach out, to touch her, comfort her, but he didn't dare. Something deep and dark and implacably cold inside her stopped him. He felt his heart break. "Dathne..."

Her chin came up, and in her eyes glittered a scornful self-derision. She mocked her own pain, even as she mocked his pain for her. "Since that first time I've dreamed Asher... oh, more times than I dare think of. Him, and other things."

"What things?"

"Things," she said, and shivered. "They're not important now."

"I say they are. I want to know."

Hollow-eyed and direly foreboding, she stared at him. "No, Matt. You truly don't."

He had to persuade her. She shouldn't have to bear this burden alone. "Tell me. Please. I've got broad shoulders, Dathne. I can help. Even the best of us make mistakes when we're tired. Sad. Besieged."

"Not me. I'm never wrong, Matt. Not about this. Call my dreams visions, call them warnings, call them echoes of Prophecy. It's all just words, whipped to nothingness on the wind. I am Jervale's Heir and I *know*. Asher is the Innocent Mage. The Final Days are coming. And I am the last living of Jervale's descendants, born to guide our ignorant fisherman to victory...or fail, and doom our world to death and despair."

His chest was so tight he could hardly breathe. "And me? What am I?"

She looked away, frowning. "My compass. My anchor. My candle in the dark."

Warmed and angered at once, he lowered his voice. "Then if I'm all those things, why did you never tell me any of this when we met? Barl save us all, Dathne, I could've done more, I could've—"

"No. You couldn't," she said gently. "Besides, I didn't know you then."

"You know me now! You've known me for years! You should've told me!"

Her smile cut him like a razor. "Matt, Matt. Why would I weigh you down with such cruel knowledge a heartbeat before you needed to know it?"

He could've wept. "I still say you might be wrong. We should talk about this properly, we should—"

"There's nothing to talk about." The iron was back in her voice, her eyes. "I am the Heir. You swore an oath to follow wherever I might lead. So I ask you here and now, Matt, and on my oath to the Circle I will never ask you again: are you with me?"

Helplessly he stared at her. Was he with her? He'd been with her from the moment they'd met, when he was new to the king's stables and she was setting up her bookshop, and word had come from Veira that he'd been chosen to stand by Jervale's Heir and do his duty however she saw fit.

Was he with her? He was with her even as he despaired of her, when she rode roughshod over his cares and concerns, acted out of impulse or instinct or sheer bloody-mindedness, when she danced down pathways that he, unsighted, could never glimpse.

Was he with her?

He was with her till the bitter end, whatever that might be.

He brought his other hand to rest lightly on the fingers that still held his wrist with a desperation she'd die before admitting, and nodded. "Aye, Dathne. With you, for you, behind you. Always."

For a moment he thought he might see her shed a tear, for the first time ever. Her lips softened, and her gaze, and the fingers on his wrist tightened hard enough to tingle. And then she laughed and let go of him, the mocking light returned to her eyes. "Good. Now put a smile on old Derrig's face and fetch yourself an ale, Meister Matt. Fetch me another one while you're at it, too, for I think I've a mind to get drunk."

Almost he opened his mouth and asked if she thought that was wise. Just in time, though, he caught the words behind his teeth. Swallowed them. Said instead, "As my lady commands."

There was, after all, more than one way of crying.

CHAPTER THREE

Asher's days trotted briskly by, filled sunup to sundown with the exacting business of horses. Aside from Barlsday mornings in the palace chapel, and those times when the prince came into the stable yard to discuss stud business with Matt or fetch Ballodair to go riding, he scarcely saw his employer.

Which suited him just fine. What did a fisherman and a prince have to talk about anyways, eh? Nowt, save for the weather. And once you got past "That were a nice drop of rain your da organised for last night, eh?" "Oh yes, wasn't it?" there wasn't much left to say. So let the prince keep hisself to hisself up in his fancy Tower. Asher of Restharven was happy to perform his horse-keeping duties untroubled by princes, count twenty of his twenty-five hard-earned trins into his own personal and private chest at the Royal Treasury at the end of each week ... and gloat on the thought of returning home to Restharven the same time next year a rich, rich man.

At first his nights were tossed and turned by dreams of the life he'd left behind. The sweet salt air, and the slap and suck of the tide against the hulls of the fishing fleet in the harbour. Jed's mad giggling. The wheeling, whirling gulls and the music of the village's menfolk come singing home from sea. Da's cracked baritone, butchering another ditty and making them all laugh.

Barl save him, there were mornings he'd wake with the memories so fresh it would be several pounding heartbeats before he knew where he was, and why the world smelled of horses. Before he remembered the names of the lads roused grumbling from their dormitory beds by Matt's merciless cowbell, and why they weren't his brothers.

Then he'd have to wait, hands fisted in his blankets, treacherous face hidden in the pillow, until he could greet the sunrise uncaring.

Those mornings were hard.

But the choice had been his. There was no point complaining about it, and no-one to complain to any road. This was his life now. Best get on with living it.

In spare hours Matt taught him to ride properly on the prince's retired brown hunter Dauntless, because—the stable meister said, comically despairing—he couldn't stand to see a man so woeful ignorant of decent basic horsemanship.

It was a far cry from his bareback slipping and sliding on Dotte, the family's decrepit half-blind nag who pulled the fish cart to and from Restharven Harbour. At first he wasn't sure about the notion of learning fancy riding. Especially when Dathne shut up her bookshop and came to watch, and laugh.

Turned out, though, he was an apt pupil with a knack for staying put in the saddle. Pretty soon Dathne wasn't laughing much at all, nor the lads neither, Boonie and Bellybone and Rinnie and the rest. Pretty soon he could walk, trot and canter ole Dauntless in figure-eights with his eyes closed, his arms folded across his chest *and* no stirrups. Ha!

So Matt promoted him onto Folly, with a wicked glint in his eye that said *"Right then, Meister Fisherman. Think you're a horseman now, do you? Well let's just see about that..."*

Folly had a pigroot in her that could turn a body inside out and back again faster than a frog catches flies. But Asher wasn't going to be beaten. Not by her, and not by smirking Stable Meister Matt. The tricky chestnut mare's antics had him eating dirt four times on the first day, twice on the second and never again after that. So, with an admiring grin and a proud slap on the back, the stable meister pronounced him fit to be seen in public.

That meant he joined Matt and his string of lads riding out every morning on the prancing apples of His Highness's eye: blood horses bred and cosseted for the purpose of fetching a tidy sum of trins at auction, or commanding high stud fees from hopeful folk with promising mares, or winning the races run every week for the entertainment of Olken and Doranen alike.

Within weeks, the sea dreams dwindled and life settled into a comfortable, comforting routine. In the evenings after work he tramped down to the Green Goose with Matt and the other lads. There they hobnobbed with other royal staff, supped ale, threw darts and swapped tales taller than the tallest house in the City. Often he'd argue amiably over a game of knuckles with Matt, then work up an appetite dancing with a comely Olken lass. Or Dathne.

In the softening light of the inn's lamps, when she let her hair loose onto her shoulders and a tankard or two of ale had smoothed the knife edges from her face, the bookseller was...well, not ugly. And she wasn't such bad company, either, once she'd blunted her sharp tongue on the hide of whoever was handy.

He learned soon enough to make sure it wasn't him.

Same as the other lads, he was only required to work five days out of six. So he spent his day off each week exploring the City on foot, or its surrounding countryside on borrowed horseback. Swam bare-arsed in River Gant. Fished for silver spotties off Dragonshead Bridge with a homemade rod and line, sometimes alone, more often with one or more of his new-made friends: the stable lads, a few of the junior City Guards, a handful of palace staff. Sometimes he even rode with Dathne in her wagon when she trundled off to investigate reports of old books for sale in other towns and villages.

Not that he was interested in old books. Or her. It was just nice to enjoy a change of scenery once in a while. To see how other Olken lived. To talk about things nowt to do with colic and fetlocks and worming elixirs. And if he came back from those occasional outings with a smile on his face, so what? Weren't no law against smiling, was there?

Riding. Swimming. Playing darts and sinking a few pints here and there. Dancing with pretty barmaids and aye, right, flirting with 'em too. All that on top of making fists of money without breaking too much of a sweat over stable yard chores.

If there was a better way to occupy a year of self-imposed exile from the ocean, Asher was hard put to imagine it.

So he didn't even try.

He was on his own in the yard one sleepy afternoon, pottering with bits and bobbery while Matt was out on errands and the other lads minded their own business mending harness, polishing carriages and collecting manure from the pastures, when a tingle between his shoulderblades told him he was no longer alone. He stopped sweeping the brickwork outside the currently empty sick box, and turned.

Prince Gar. Leaned against a convenient hitching post watching his fisherman stable hand earn those twenty-five weekly trins. Wearing his official ruby and silver circlet, what's more, which meant he was off to somewhere important. His clothing was officially flash, too: a crimson silk shirt under a gold and black brocade weskit and indigo fine wool britches, with his boots like polished black glass. Asher pulled a face. Fancy that for a job, eh? Primping a prince's boots till you could see your face in 'em. Poor bastard stuck with that chore must be near out of his skull with boredom by now.

"A touch of indigestion, Asher?" enquired the prince kindly.

Asher straightened his expression. "No, sir. Afternoon, sir. Somethin' I can help you with?"

Still leaning, still considering, the prince let his gaze stray around the immaculate stable yard. "Perhaps. How's the job working out?"

"Fine, sir," Asher said cautiously. "Thanks for askin'."

"No problems adjusting to your new life?"

"I been here nigh on two months, sir. Reckon if there were goin' to be problems I'd have stumbled across 'em by now."

The prince's lips twitched. "Yes, I reckon you would have." He sobered. Nodded. "That looks nasty. What happened?"

Asher looked down at his bare left forearm, revealed by the rolling up of his sleeve, where a thick white scar like old rope wound from elbow to wrist. "Cut m'self."

The prince blinked. "No. Really? How?"

Taking Jed up on a damn fool drunken bet was how. He'd pinched Young Mick's solo sailer and skimmed the waves all the way out to Dragonteeth Reef, intending to snap off a bit of coral and bring it back as proof, and a trophy.

Dragonteeth Reef had pretty near snapped off his arm instead.

Which wasn't the kind of thing he felt like telling this pretty prince, so he shrugged. "Just an accident. Fishin's a chancy life. Accidents happen all the time."

"Do they?" murmured Prince Gar. "Remind me not to take it up as a hobby in that case."

He kept a straight face, just. "Aye, Your Highness."

If he knew he was being laughed at, the prince didn't show it. Instead he smiled. "Matt says you've settled in well. It seems the horses like you as much as you like them."

Unsettled, Asher started sweeping again. Matt and the prince had been discussing him? He didn't much care for the sound of that. "Aye. Sir."

"Do you have a favourite?"

"S'pose," said Asher, with a one-shouldered shrug he'd picked up from Dathne. "I like Cygnet. He's a good horse."

The prince grinned. "Good? He's the best I've ever bred. You've a keen eye, Asher."

Asher shrugged again. "I'm learnin'."

"It's an admirable trait."

Still sweeping, Asher frowned. Something wasn't right here. Princes didn't make a habit of wandering about stable yards paying compliments to minions with brooms, did they? Not bloody likely. So. Time to land this fish and see what he'd caught. "Your Highness—"

The prince didn't let him finish. "Listen. I've seen for myself that you're quick in a crisis, and brave. Matt says you're a competent if reluctant reader, and your handwriting is legible, although a trifle undisciplined. He also says the rest of the lads look up to you, you're a cheerful drunk, you ride like a man born in the saddle even though everyone knows you weren't, you know when and how to hold your tongue, you never have to be told anything twice and you don't suffer fools gladly." A small smile. "Well. At all."

"He does, does he?" His fingers were clutched so tight around the broom handle he was getting splinters. Bloody Matt and his great big mouth. There'd be words down at the Goose that evening, oh aye, and none of them complimentary.

"Yes," said the prince. "He does. Is he right?"

Sweeping could wait. Asher leaned the broom against the nearest wall and scowled. For all his negligent post-leaning, the prince was... edgy. Like a colt with one ear cocked for the sound of wind and an excuse to helter-skelter madly with its heels kicking the air.

"Right enough," he admitted. "And what if he is? What's all that malarkey got to do with how well I shovel shit? Sir?"

The prince shook his head and smiled again. "Nothing. How old are you?"

"Four month older'n you." He'd surrendered to curiosity about the prince's age after a week and asked Dathne. "Why?"

The prince didn't answer, just stared into the distance instead, lost in thought. Waiting, Asher reached for the broom again and tipped it upside down to pick out two dirty bent stalks of straw from between the bristles. Matt surely went spare if his precious brooms weren't put away prissy like unmarried maidens. To hear him go on, you'd think the bloody Wall itself would tumble down otherwise.

"Do you have something to wear that's a little less...industrious?" the prince said abruptly.

Asher looked down at his green cotton shirt, brown cotton trews and sturdy brown leather boots. "No use blamin' me for how I look. Some ole biddy up at the Tower gave me this clobber."

"Mistress Hemshaw. My housekeeper. I know. But do you have anything else? Anything—I don't know...smarter?"

Asher scowled. Over his bitter protests Dathne had made him squander half his precious first week's pay on outfits that were neither fishermen's homespun nor Tower-provided working clothes. Not silk, ha, or leather, or superfine wool either. Lawn for the shirt and second-card wool for the trousers. Expensive enough. He'd only worn them twice. Didn't want to wear them out completely before he got home again to show them off.

"Smarter? Aye," he said reluctantly. "Sir. Why?"

"Good." The prince pushed away from the wall to stand with his hands on his hips. "Go and get changed then. Quickly. The carriage will be here any moment."

Asher gaped. "Carriage?"

"Yes. I always travel to Justice Hall in His Majesty's carriage. As the Lawgiver I speak with his voice. Arriving in his carriage sets the proper tone for the proceedings."

"Justice Hall?" Asher stepped back. The broom in his hands lifted, a flimsy barrier between himself and the might of royalty. "*Court*, y'mean? You be takin' me to court? Why? I ain't never broke the law and whoever said I did be a drowned liar!"

The prince raised a calming hand. "Peace, Asher. You're not in trouble. I want you to witness today's hearing, that's all."

"Why? Sir?"

"We can discuss that afterwards. Now go and change, quickly." The prince grinned. "We don't want Justice Hall smelling like a stable, do we?"

"And what about Matt?" said Asher, retreating slowly. "If he comes back and I ain't done with—"

"Matt knows you'll be absent this afternoon."

Oh, did he? Bloody Matt. No wonder he'd been so insistent that the stable yard be swept and raked again, even though Bellybone had done it well enough that morning. Wanted to make sure the prince'd have no trouble finding poor ole mushroom Asher.

And now he was off to Justice Hall? With the prince? In the king's carriage? *Why?* What in Barl's name was going on?

"*Asher*!" said the prince, all patience fled. "*Now*!"

Asher took the hint. Dropped the broom and ran for the dormitory, swearing under his breath with every pounding step.

Bloody Matt! Bloody Matt! Bloody bloody bloody Matt!

They were nearly halfway to the main palace gates, the king's magnificent enclosed carriage riding smooth as melted butter, when they heard a pounding tattoo of hooves approaching from behind. Scant moments later one of the smartly trotting carriage horses whickered and a young, feminine voice cried: "Hold up there, Matcher! I want a word with His Highness!"

As the coachman shouted a reply, Asher looked at the prince. Gar's face was pinched with displeasure and his manicured fingernails were drumming on his knee. "Barl save me," he muttered. "What does she want now?"

The carriage slowed. Stopped. The prince pulled down the sliding window beside him. "I'm in a hurry, Fane! Whatever it is will have to wait!"

Fane. Her Royal Highness the Princess Fane. Prince Gar's younger, only sister. A prodigious magical talent, so the gossips down at the Goose said, and the king's undisputed heir. Beautiful, too. Asher had never met her, or seen her even. He wriggled a little on his seat to get a glimpse.

"It can't wait!" retorted Princess Fane. Mounted on a panting sweaty brown pony, dust marring her rose silk tunic and crimson leather leggings, her annoyed face was almost level with her brother's. "Do you think I'd have galloped all this way like a madwoman on some servant's inferior plug if it was something that could wait?"

"You gallop everywhere like a madwoman, Fane," the prince replied, sighing. "On anything with four legs. Why should this time be any different?"

They looked eerily alike, the princess and her brother. Slender. Fair, even for Doranen. The same elegant eyebrows, the same straight nose, moulded lips, firm chin. Her eyes were blue, though, her lashes extravagantly long and darkened with something. She was exquisite, just like the gossips had said. But that beauty was marred now with temper; her grip on the reins was so tight the pony's lips had curled back and its eyes were rolling in protest.

"Just be quiet and listen!" she snapped. "I absolutely must have that copy of *Trevoyle's Legacy* you borrowed from Durm. I'm being examined on the Schism the day after tomorrow and—"

"I told you this morning, Fane, I returned it to the Master Magician last week."

"He says he doesn't have it."

"Then I don't know what to tell you."

The pony grunted as Her Highness bounced in the saddle. "*Gar*! You were the last one to see it. There isn't another complete copy of that text in all the kingdom and I *need* it! Do you *want* me to fail my examination?"

"What I want, Fane, is for you to go away. I'm due at Justice Hall and I can't be late. Have you tried a seeking spell?"

The princess's cheeks flushed. "Yes, I tried a seeking spell."

"Oh." Her brother bit back an unwise smile. "Well. Even I know they're unreliable. Why not ask Mama? She's the best in the kingdom when it comes to finding lost objects."

"Mama is locked up all day with a bunch of stupid women talking about stupid things like flower fetes!"

"Can't Durm do a seeking spell for you? Or Father?"

The princess's blush deepened. "Durm won't, and he's told Father not to either. I'm supposed to find it for myself."

"Well," said the prince, one hand on the windowpane ready to push it closed again, "let me know how you get on. I certainly wish you luck. And now I'm leaving. Goodbye."

Ignoring her outraged shriek he shoved the window shut, then tugged on a short blue bell-rope overhead. There came a musical jangling, the sound of a whip cracking, then the carriage rocked gently and rolled forward as the harnessed horses sprang into their knee-snapping trot.

"My sister," said the prince as they continued on their way. "Princess Fane."

Asher nodded. "I figured as much."

Arms folded over his chest, the prince considered him broodingly. "Do you have a sister?"

"No. Brothers."

"How many?"

"Six."

"*Six*?" the prince said, startled. Then he relaxed. "Of course. The restrictions don't apply to the fishing community." He shook his head. "Six brothers. I can't imagine it. Do you miss them?"

Asher was hard-put not to laugh out loud. "Not at all. Sir."

The prince looked surprised. "No?"

"We don't get along."

"Really? Why not?"

Asher scowled. Nearly said, *Prob'ly the same reason you can't stand your sister*, but thought better of it. Prob'ly that'd be a good way to get tossed out of the carriage on his arse.

"Lots of reasons," he said instead, shrugging. "They reckoned six brothers in the family was enough. Split a business six ways and you ain't lookin' at much on your plate. Split it seven and it be that much less. And I were a bit sickly as a spratling. Made Ma soft on me. Da, too."

"You don't look sickly now."

"I ain't," said Asher. "I be strong as an ox now. Just I had fevers and the trembles when I were little. My brothers never had a day sick between 'em. Thought I was makin' it up. I weren't ... but they'd never believe it. And they didn't much care for the cossetin' I got, when they never did."

The prince nodded. "That seems unfair. I'm sorry."

Another shrug. "Don't matter. That's them and here's me and there's an end to it."

"Indeed," the prince said briskly. "Now tell me, Asher, how familiar are you with our kingdom's laws?" He grinned. "You must know something of them, since you were so certain before that you'd not broken any."

"Well," said Asher cautiously, "I s'pose that depends on what you mean by 'familiar.'"

The prince waved an impatient, dismissive hand. "Oh, never mind. Just pin your ears back and listen while I explain what you should know before we reach Justice Hall. You'll find the whole experience much more interesting if you have a vague idea of what's going on."

Asher swallowed a sigh. Justice Hall interesting? Not bloody likely. But he'd better not say so; like it or not this folderol princeling was the source of his twenty-five weekly trins. Only a fool would risk the loss of such bounty.

And Da's little boy Asher might be a lot of things, but a fool weren't one of them.

Justice Hall sat cheek by jowl between Dorana City's public Barl's Chapel and the City Guardhouse. Together, the three impressive buildings made up one entire side of the central market square. A typically tall Doranen building, with walls of pale cream sandstone and roof tiles of blue clay, Justice Hall's narrow window frames housed panels of stained glass in every colour magic could imagine. Each panel depicted a momentous event in the kingdom's history: the coming of the Doranen, the holy covenant between the Olken and Doranen peoples, Barl's great sacrifice, the horrors of Trevoyle's Schism, the Healing Treaty's signing on the place where now bubbled Supplicant's Fountain.

The Hall's enormous oak front doors were bound and studded in polished brass and flanked either side with a sculptured relief. On the left stood blessed Barl, smiling benevolently down on those who entered seeking justice. On the right hung an unsheathed sword, reminding justice seekers that the truth cut two ways...and that the penalty for wrongdoing was both swift and merciless.

Asher had barely noticed the building on his first day in the City. He'd been too busy looking for work and then, amazingly, finding it. On one of his early days off he'd stood on Justice Hall's sandstone steps and marvelled at the place, listening to Dathne explain what each carving and stained-glass panel meant, but he'd felt no need to go inside.

Yet now here he was, riding in a fancy royal carriage on his way to doing just that. And he *still* didn't know why.

The prince said, "Asher! Are you listening?"

Asher jerked his wandering attention back to the present. "Aye. Sir. Of course."

"Good. Now, you're perfectly clear on the differences between Olken and Doranen legal jurisdictions, are you? You wouldn't like me to run through them again? Only once we're in the Hall I'll have to leave you to your own devices."

"No, sir. Reckon I got it straight," said Asher. It took an effort to keep his teeth ungritted. Did the prince think he was a knucklehead? "All criminal and civil matters Olken to Olken, up to and including malice *and* grievous damage inflicted with intent, stay in the Olken district courts. Any charge higher than that, like murder—not that we wander about killin' each other much—goes to the Olken central court." He pointed out of the carriage window. "That's over yonder, three streets behind the Grand Theatre, on the other side of the square. Next door to the City Library."

"Indeed it is," agreed the prince. "Visit the library often, do you?"

"No. Leastways not for me. Picked up a book for Dathne once or twice." He sniffed. "Don't see what she's wantin' borrowed books for. Got enough for sale in that shop of hers, ain't she?"

"Some knowledge is priceless," said the prince. "And must be made available to anyone who desires it, regardless of their personal wealth.

Or its lack. Go on. That's the Golden Cockerel Hotel we've just passed. We're nearly there."

Asher strangled a groan. When was he ever going to need to know about the law? This was such a load of bollocks...

"All civil and criminal matters Doranen to Doranen get judged at Justice Hall, before the Master Magician," he recited dutifully, "along with any branglin' between Olken and Doranen, no matter where they live. Any civil or criminal matters Olken to Olken what can't be sorted between ourselves go to Justice Hall, and you decide."

"Which is why we're going there today," said the prince. "Exactly. And cardinal crimes?"

Asher shuddered. There'd been no cardinal crime committed in Lur for years. You had to go back to when his long-dead great-grandpa was a spratling for the last one.

But that wasn't so odd. No fool in his right mind, Olken or Doranen, went about committing cardinal crimes. Not if he wanted to keep on breathing, any road.

"All cardinal crimes are tried before the king," he said as the carriage slowed and turned into a side street off the main market road. "Or queen. Whichever it is. And their Privy Council. Whether the trial be made public or not depends on circumstances."

The prince was staring at him. "Remarkable."

"What?" said Asher. "That I got a good memory? No it ain't. Your Highness. My ma, Barl save her, she had herself a memory twice as nimble as mine."

The carriage drew to a halt. As waiting attendants hurried to stand by the horses' heads and open the doors, the prince said, frowning, "Your mother is dead? I'm sorry."

Asher shrugged. "Happened a long time ago. Reckon I'm past grievin' now." Then, because that felt disloyal, he added, "Not that I don't miss her, like. Just...you get used to it, I s'pose. Sir. I mean, what other choice is there?"

The prince nodded. "So, you're a practical man, Asher of Restharven."

"Practical be my middle name." Asher gestured at the open carriage door. "After you, sir."

The rear of Justice Hall was, in its own way, as imposing as the front. There was a stable block to house the horses and carriages of those involved in the proceedings, complete with liveried Olken staff to take care of them. There were three separate entrances to the Hall, each with its own set of steps, each barricaded by its own pair of uniformed

Olken City Guards. There were neat gardens, trimmed trees, and an ominously well-trodden path leading into the grounds of the guard-house next door. Another path led in the opposite direction, towards the public chapel. Despite its location in the heart of the City, the atmo-sphere was hushed. Reverent, almost. As though the weighty matters decided inside the Hall discouraged unmannerly noise outside.

After greeting the various staff by name, and receiving smiles and greetings in return, the prince headed towards the Hall's middle entrance. Asher trailed in his wake, feeling like a barnacle in a bed of roses. The surprised, curious stares of the stable hands and guards burned his back. He knew that as soon as he was out of sight they'd be whispering.

Well, let 'em whisper.

The chosen entrance's decorative wooden surround was painted in crimson and gold. Above the lintel sat a carved relief of the Weather-Worker's crown, embossed with gold and silver leaf and set with chips of ruby and diamond. As the prince approached, the door's guards rapped their ceremonial pikes smartly on the ground and stood aside. The prince nodded and smiled and Asher followed him, into the cool splendour of Justice Hall.

As they passed from sunlight to illuminated shadow his first impres-sion was one of space. The floor, empty of furniture, was tiled in green and gold, with an enormous mosaic of an unsheathed sword in the middle. Gold-framed paintings covered the sandstone walls; past tri-als, Asher guessed, seeing as how there was a crowned and robed king or queen in each, and somebody smiling, and somebody else in chains, surrounded by guards and looking like their best boat had just sunk. There were two wooden staircases against the back wall, leading up to crimson velvet curtains, each one door-shaped. Between them, set into the rear wall, was a single wooden door. There were two more in each of the side walls. As the prince crossed over the mosaic sword one of the right-hand doors opened and a Doranen woman emerged. She was middle-aged, smothered in sombre blue silk and brocade.

"Your Highness," she said in a soft, calm voice, and offered a small bow. "Both parties, complete with speakers and witnesses, have arrived and await your adjudication."

"Excellent." The prince turned to Asher who was hovering in the background. "Marnagh, this is Asher. He'll be observing the proceed-ings today. Could you find him an inconspicuous chair in the Royal Gallery?"

Marnagh swept Asher up and down with a single shrewd look.

Whatever she thought of him stayed locked tight behind her pale grey eyes. "Of course, Your Highness."

"Asher."

Asher stepped forward, hands clasped tight behind his back. "Your Highness?"

"This is Lady Marnagh. She keeps order in Justice Hall. Without her we'd all be hopelessly lost and I wouldn't look half as wise as I do, or know a quarter as much about the law."

Marnagh laughed. "Your Highness is too kind."

"Better that than too green, which is what I was scant months ago. And don't bother trying to deny it."

Asher managed an awkward bow. "Lady Marnagh."

She acknowledged him with a nod that made him feel six years old again. He scowled. She smiled.

The prince started for the staircase on the right. "I must prepare for today's session, so I'll leave you in the Lady Marnagh's capable hands, Asher. If there's anything you need to know, she'll tell you."

"Aye, sir," said Asher, and watched him run up the staircase and disappear behind the crimson curtain. "I don't bloody believe it," he muttered. "He's gone and done it *again*."

"Done what?" asked Lady Marnagh mildly.

"Dropped me in it, then left me in the clutches of some woman I don't know!" said Asher, unthinking.

"Indeed?" said Lady Marnagh. "Well, if that's the worst thing royalty ever does to you, young man, I'd be eternally grateful!"

Abruptly aware of his audience, Asher flushed. "Sorry. Never meant no disrespect."

Her severe lips softened. "Yes. Well. If you'll come with me?"

He followed her up the left-hand staircase. Behind the shrouding red velvet was a screened gallery complete with comfortable chairs and an excellent view of the Hall.

"You can observe from here," said Lady Marnagh. "Please remain absolutely silent while the hearing is in session. It would be best if you stayed seated once His Highness has commenced the proceedings. To all intents and purposes anyone in the gallery is invisible to the Hall, but movement can be distracting." She frowned. "In fact, choose a seat now and don't leave it again until His Highness gives you permission."

Disconcerted, Asher stared. "And how long'll that be? I mean, what time's all this malarkey s'posed to end?"

"That depends entirely upon the matter at hand," said Lady Marnagh, her plucked eyebrows raised.

"Well, but, what if I need to...you know..."

The eyebrows rose higher. "Then I suggest you cross your legs—Asher, is it?" She smiled; he'd seen friendlier sharks. "Now I must attend to my duties. I trust you will find this afternoon's..." She paused and looked down her nose at him. "*Malarkey*, educational. Certainly I hope you know how privileged you are, being invited to watch the hearing from the Royal Gallery, as His Highness's personal guest."

Oh aye, he was privileged all right. Stuck in a box halfway up a wall with no way down again till the prince had finished his business, being told to cross his legs—ha!—if nature called, all for reasons that nobody saw fit to tell him! Privileged? Put upon, she should've said. Used and abused and taken advantage of, and what Matt was going to say when he came back to find none of the mangers scrubbed clean, like he'd ordered, and the yard only half swept and raked, and the lads doing evening stables without him...

Lady Marnagh was waiting for an answer. Her eyebrows had climbed so high they'd nearly disappeared into her pale yellow hairline, and her lips were thin with disapproval.

Asher sighed. "Aye, Lady Marnagh. Reckon there ain't been a body so privileged as me in all the history of Lur."

Lady Marnagh left the gallery. The way she twitched the velvet curtain closed behind her suggested that she wasn't amused. Oh well. Too bad. The prince wasn't paying him near enough to cover extra duties like keeping snooty shark-impersonating Doranen women smiling. He heaved another sigh and leaned his arms along the screened gallery's railing so he could get a decent look at what was happening down below.

Justice Hall was split down the middle by a wide aisle, and from side to side two-thirds along with a solid wooden barrier, maybe waist high on a man. Behind the barrier there was nothing but rows and rows of benches. For the public, Asher guessed, seeing the smattering of folks, mostly Olken, dotted about the Hall. The few Doranen all looked young. Students, most likely, from the university. They had an older Doranen with them, wearing a chivvying face. Asher grinned. Poor bugger. Be a good bet he'd happily change jobs with the prince's boot polisher, any day. Everyone, Olken and Doranen, was dressed up in their holyday best. Most of them wore hats, plain and flat for the men, tall and nodding with flowers and feathers for the women.

In front of the barrier there were chairs, and a wide wooden table on each side of the aisle. There were Olken sitting there, too, and seeing how serious they looked, he supposed they were the—what had Lady Marnagh called them?—the parties, their speakers and witnesses. So. The folks doing the brangling.

At the top end of the Hall, set into the wall, was a door. On the other side of it, he suspected, was the chamber where he and the prince had come in. Set some six paces in from the wall was a crimson dais. On it stood a high-backed wooden chair, padded and covered in crimson and gold velvet. Beside it, a slender wooden stand bearing a golden bell and hammer. On the wall behind the dais hung an enormous tapestry of an unsheathed sword. Just in case folks forgot what they were doing here, most likely.

Aye, right. As if *that* was like to happen.

Off to the right side of the dais was a small desk and a plain unpadded chair. The desk had a pile of paper on it, but no inkpot or pen. Asher couldn't see the point of that. He shrugged; the mystery would surely be explained sooner or later. And if it wasn't he could always ask the prince later.

Although whether the prince would *answer* him was another matter entirely. Too bloody secretive by half, was His Royal Highness Prince Gar.

The sound of hushed conversation rose from the floor of the Hall like the rolling of waves onto a distant sandy shore. Filtering through the stained-glass windows, sunlight from the world outside splashed a palette of colours over every face and turned the attending City Guards' uniforms into patchwork quilts. Asher counted twelve pike-wielding, po-faced officials: one on each side of the main doors, four along each wall, and the last two flanking the raised platform beneath the hanging sword. None of his friends was among them. Pity, that. He could've amused himself pulling faces at 'em.

The Royal Gallery he occupied in such solitary splendour ran almost the full length of the Hall. There was a similar gallery directly opposite, but it was completely filled in. A private place for the prince or the king or the Master Magician to gather his or her thoughts before hearing folks go on about their troubles, he guessed.

The door in the Hall's rear wall opened, then closed behind Lady Marnagh. Her silk and brocade tunic had been smothered with a plain robe of dark green. She crossed to the small table and stood behind it. The guards on either side of the dais rapped their pikes onto the tiled floor hard and sharp, three times. At the Hall's entrance, the guards flanking the open doors swung them closed with a muffled thud. Silence fell like an axe.

Then everyone seated in the Hall stood, eyes turned towards the end of the private gallery. A moment later a section of the gallery floor detached and descended with slow majesty. Asher felt his jaw drop. No ropes or mechanical devices guided the platform's progress: it moved by magic.

Of course.

Inch by inch, the unsmiling form of the prince was revealed. He was draped neck to knee to ankle in a gold and crimson brocade robe. His silver circlet had been replaced by a heavy, plain gold crown. His expression was grave. Thoughtful. He looked ... older.

The platform stopped a mere whisper above the floor. The prince stepped down and took his seat on the dais. Then he lifted the hammer from its hook and struck the bell three times. The air inside the Hall chimed. Shimmered. Asher felt something cool and invisible dance across his skin.

"We are gathered today, by His Majesty's authority and in his name, for the purposes of justice." The prince's voice carried effortlessly to every corner and listening ear. "Barl give us grace and wisdom and honour in its seeking." Bowing his head, he kissed his holyring.

"As you ask," murmured the crowd, "Barl mote it be." All round the Hall, lips were pressed to forefingers, ringed or not.

The prince replaced the hammer, then rested his hands on the arms of his chair. "Be seated. And let us hear the vexatious matter that brings us hence today."

With a sigh and a rustle and a scraping of the petitioners' chair legs on the tiles, everyone sat.

Intrigued despite himself, Asher waited to see what would happen.

CHAPTER FOUR

Who seeks my judgement in this matter?" asked the prince.

A young woman seated at the right-hand table stood. She was short and plump, her dress an unflattering shade of custard yellow. "I do, Your Highness."

The prince nodded. At the small desk Lady Marnagh closed her eyes and twice passed her left hand across the stack of paper before her. Orange sparks ignited, flared and faded. She returned her hand to her lap and glanced at the prince.

"State your name and place of residence for the records," he said.

"Mistress Raite of Deephollow Vale, Your Highness."

Asher pressed his face to the gallery's screen. Just barely, he saw orange fire dance across the top sheet of paper. A single line of words glowed for a moment then winked out.

So. Who needed pen and ink when magic could be had at the snap of the fingers?

"Thank you. Be seated," said the prince. "Who contests your claim?"

At the other table a middle-aged Olken man leapt to his feet. "Me, Your Highness! *I* contest my cousin's ridiculous, ungrateful complaint!"

He was tall and broomstick thin. His satin suit, frothed with lace at neck and wrists, was a bilious pea-green. Asher pulled a face; looked like colour blindness ran in the family.

The prince frowned. "I requested your name and place of residence, not your legal opinion."

Even from halfway up the wall and behind a screen, Asher could see the man's face turn tomato red. He grinned. So the king's son had a bite in him, eh? That was interesting. He'd been thinking all that silk and velvet might've softened the prince's sinews.

Useful to know that wasn't the case.

And what kind of a sinkin' fool was the pea-green man, to set up the prince's hackles against him in the first few minutes?

"Meister Brenin, Your Highness," the cousin said. He sounded perilously close to sulky. "From Tolton-by-the-Marsh."

As the man sat down again, whispering to one of his cronies at the table, the prince turned his attention to the young Olken woman. "Very well. Mistress Raite, for the record, state your complaint."

Flustered but resolute the woman stood again. The man seated beside her—husband? brother? too young to be her da, any road— reached for her hand, squeezed it tight, then let go. Asher leaned back in his chair, propped his heels on the railing inside the gallery's screen and prepared to be entertained.

The trouble had started when word was sent to Mistress Raite of her Uncle Vorlye's mortal illness. He was dying, and there wasn't a herb or potion in the kingdom to save him. Would she be able to nurse the poor soul in his fading days? Cousin Brenin was a busy man, with no wife at hand to shoulder the burden. Of course it meant three hours a day of travel, but they were family, weren't they? A good woman mindful of Barl's Laws would surely ignore a little inconvenience for the sake of a dying man.

What of the hospice in Salting Town, a mere half-hour from Tolton-by-the-Marsh? the prince wanted to know. It was a fine facility; he had attended its dedication by Her Majesty and Royal Barlsman Holze just last summer. The Barl's Brethren there were devoted to nursing the sick and dying. Uncle Vorlye would have been well cared for, and Mistress Raite not put to so much hardship. Meister Brenin?

Blustering, Meister Brenin pointed out that the Barl's Brethren, doubtless holy folk to the youngest novice, couldn't be held the same as a man's family, Your Highness.

Not to mention family wouldn't ask for a donation of fifteen trins a week towards the costs of ministering to a dying man, was the prince's dry observation. Asher snickered approvingly; he liked a man with a sense of humour.

Next, Mistress Raite became a trifle agitated. It seemed that dear Uncle Vorlye, who remained well in his right mind up to the very end, was so touched by her tender care that he saw fit to leave her a little something in his will.

"A *little* something?" her cousin snarled. "The bloody woman addled his wits, Your Highness! Tricked him into leaving her half his fortune! A scurrilous villainy of wickedness it was, sir, and the District Magister agreed! He overturned that poxy will in a matter of moments and fined the wretched woman accordingly. Only by a miracle did she escape a harsher penalty!"

"Peace, Meister Brenin," the prince said coolly. "Your turn will come." He turned to Mistress Raite. "You have good reason for refusing to accept Barl's Justice in this matter?"

Mistress Raite's chin lifted. "Yes, Your Highness. I'm innocent. The legacy was two hundred trins, not half his fortune, and I never asked for a cuick of it."

"Yet the District Magister upheld your cousin's claim."

"Yes, he did, Your Highness," she agreed. "And that would have nowt to do with how the District Magister and my cousin hunt regular together every week through winter, or play catch-ball in the lighter months, or race each other to the bottom of a wine barrel three nights out of six, now would it?"

Asher dropped his feet to the floor and leaned forward, impressed. Convicted and custard yellow she might be, but Mistress Raite was a persuasive speaker. He couldn't see a skerrick of guile in her. Just honest distress.

Staring down at the prince's shuttered face he tried to figure what the king's son was thinking. Was he convinced by Mistress Raite's tale of woe, or not? There was no way of telling; all thought and feeling were locked tight behind his Lawgiver's mask.

The prince was silent for long moments, considering. Then he looked at Meister Brenin. "Mistress Raite speaks the truth? You and this District Magister are friends?"

Meister Brenin looked down his nose. "We are, Your Highness." His lips curved into a thin, self-satisfied smile. "I have many friends, sir. I am a man of influence and standing in Tolton-by-the-Marsh."

The prince's answering smile glittered like a naked sword. "We are not in Tolton-by-the-Marsh, Meister Brenin."

Asher swallowed a hoot of amusement as Meister Brenin flinched. "I was unaware that such a friendship was frowned upon, Your Highness," the man said stiffly.

"Friendship is never frowned upon, Meister Brenin." The prince's faint emphasis on the word "friendship" wasn't lost on his audience; Meister Brenin wilted. The prince let his cold gaze linger a moment longer on the man's downcast face, then looked at Mistress Raite. "You have speakers present who will attest to the truth of your claims?"

"I do, sir."

The prince nodded. "Then let them be heard."

One by one, Mistress Raite's speakers rose and confirmed her version of events. When they were done, excited whispering from the audience drowned the silence and had to be quelled by the guards.

Called upon to answer the accusations, Meister Brenin lost his temper and swore at Mistress Raite. The prince cautioned him. On second thoughts, Meister Brenin's speakers declined to exercise their tongues on his behalf. Meister Brenin swore at them, and was given a final warning. Meister Brenin subsided, cowed at last.

"This hearing will pause while I withdraw and consider the charges and evidence laid before me," announced the prince. "Due to the sensitive matters raised this afternoon, the City Guards will prevent the withdrawal of any person here attending, until my judgement is rendered." Taking the hammer, he struck it against the golden bell three times.

On cue, the guards on either side of the Hall's double doors took two steps towards each other and extended their arms. There was a thunk of iron against iron as their pikes met in a cross between them. The exit was barred.

Asher grimaced. The way things were going, there'd be a whole lot of folks sitting with their legs crossed before this day was done.

Lady Marnagh, released from monitoring the magically recorded proceedings, pushed her chair back and stood. In response, everyone followed suit. Once the last man had found his feet the prince stepped down from his dais. As the platform lifted him to seclusion, Asher whooshed his lungs empty of air and sagged in his seat.

Well, sink him bloody sideways. If anyone had told him an afternoon in Justice Hall could be *exciting*, he'd have laughed.

Abruptly tired of sitting, he leapt up and marched the length of the gallery, arms swinging. Below, the hearing's captive attendees buzzed like bees in a stick-poked hive. A wise decision, to keep them penned until a judgement was reached. They'd be off and prattling on this in a heartbeat, given half a chance, embroidering and embellishing the plain facts like a pack of ole biddies in a sewing circle.

"Well?" said the prince's cool voice behind him. "What do you think so far?"

Asher turned. "What are you doin' here, sir? Ain't you s'posed to be cogitatin' your decision?"

The prince considered him, the faintest of smiles warming his eyes. He was still draped in the gold and crimson robe, but the heavy crown had been set aside.

"You're not in the least bit in awe of me, are you? Even now."

Fidgeting, suspicious, Asher said, "Is that another way of sayin' I'm rude? Sir?"

"Not...exactly. Perhaps forthright would be a better word. Or independent."

"I don't know about that. I was just surprised to see you, is all."

The prince nodded. "I'm here because I'm interested in your opinion of how I should rule in this matter."

Heedless of protocol, Asher dropped into the nearest chair. It was that or fall down completely. "*My* opinion?"

"Yes." If the prince cared that Asher sat while he was standing, he didn't say so. "Why should I believe Mistress Raite over her cousin Meister Brenin?"

"Aside from the fact he's a fartin' fool, y'mean?" said Asher, grinning. "And not a one of his fine friends'll stand up for him?" When the prince's grave expression didn't alter he sobered, and tried to think of a sensible answer. "Well…he's rich, and he reckons that makes him better than folk who ain't. He used drinkin' and sportin' with the Magister to do down a woman who nigh on killed herself, I reckon, lookin' after his da, when his da should've been his concern, *and* he disrespected his da's wishes when he did it." He snorted. "Just to snatch back two hundred trins, which from the sound of it would mean nowt to him, and all to her."

"I see," said the prince, nodding. "So even if he were in the right, and she were in the wrong, it wouldn't matter because he's rich and he'll never miss two hundred trins?"

"I never said that," Asher protested. "Don't you go puttin' words in my mouth. Sir. Point I'm tryin' to make here is he's mean, as well as twisty."

"Twisty?"

"He turned the law into a pair of hobnailed boots, and then he kicked her with 'em," said Asher slowly, scowling with concentration. "That ain't what it's for. The law's for helpin' folks do the right thing by each other, so's we can all live side by side without bangin' each other in the shins over piddlin' trifles. Or takin' what ain't ours just 'cause we want it. And if it can be bought for the price of a wine barrel, it ain't worth nowt at all."

"Then if not the price of a wine barrel, Asher, what? What monetary value can we assign to the law?"

"Well…y'can't," said Asher. "The law's priceless. That be the whole point of it. I thought. Sir."

The prince took a moment to adjust the folds of his robe. Then, as he turned to leave, he said, "This business shouldn't take much longer. You'll be home in time for supper."

"Oh," said Asher, bemused. "Aye. Right. That's good, sir. Sir? What—"

But the prince was gone.

"Sink the bloody man," muttered Asher, and jumped up to resume his pacing.

He'd marched there and back along the gallery five more times when the prince, once again wearing the crown, returned to the Hall and the hearing continued. After thanking the audience for their forbearance, the prince declared himself ready to render judgement. Mistress Raite and her cousin Meister Brenin stood and waited. The Hall was so silent Asher could hear a trapped fly battering at a nearby window, and voices in the street outside.

Judgement, said the prince sternly, fell in favour of Mistress Raite of Deephollow Vale. She was free to leave the City with her good name intact; all findings previously rendered against her were expunged, and fines made void. The bequest of two hundred trins accepted in good faith would be restored to her forthwith.

As for Meister Brenin, he was to remain in Dorana, in the custody of the guardhouse, while further investigations into matters arising from this hearing were undertaken. He could expect charges to be laid against him in due course. A summons for his friend the District Magister was even now on its way to Tolton-by-the-Marsh; they would be sharing a cell by sunset tomorrow.

The golden bell rang out three times. And that was that.

The prince withdrew to his private gallery. His departure released every trapped tongue in the Hall. As a score of excited conversations dinned the air, two guards took possession of a shocked and silent Meister Brenin. Mistress Raite took a step towards him, hands outstretched, face creased with concern. Her cousin's soundless snarl scurried her to the shelter of her companion's arm—husband for sure, Asher thought—and the congratulations of her witnesses and friends. Meister Brenin was escorted from the Hall through the door in the wall behind the dais.

Lady Marnagh approached Mistress Raite and her husband. After a brief conversation they followed her through the same door. A moment later a young Olken man entered, retrieved the official record from the small table, and left again. With the Hall's double doors once more unbarred and open, the still excited, still voluble crowd of onlookers dribbled out. The doors were closed behind them, and the remaining City Guards left through the door that had swallowed their fellows.

Asher was alone.

He waited. When nobody came to collect him from the gallery, he made his own way back behind the red velvet curtain and down the wooden stairs to the rear of the Hall. There he found the prince in deep and solemn conversation with Lady Marnagh. Both had removed their ceremonial robes. The prince glanced at him, held up a finger, and continued talking. Asher couldn't make out what he was saying.

Eventually he finished. Lady Marnagh nodded, bowed and without so much as a glance in Asher's direction returned to the room she'd been in when he and the prince arrived. The door thumped shut behind her.

"Home," said the prince. He looked tired.

The carriage was waiting for them. Sunk in thought, scowling out of the window as it carried them back to the Tower, Asher was only reminded of the prince's presence when his employer cleared his throat and said, "Well?"

He sounded amused. Startled, Asher pulled his gaze away from the passing faces and buildings. "Sir?"

"Do you agree with my decision or not?"

Feeling suddenly cautious, Asher examined his knees. "Don't reckon it be for me to agree or disagree."

"Asher!" The prince appeared shocked. "Please, *don't* go getting shy on me now."

"Shy? I ain't shy. I just reckon there's one of us in this carriage as shovels shit for a livin' and there's another what wears a crown in Justice Hall, and last time I looked I didn't see no crown in my boot-box."

"That doesn't mean you're not possessed of an opinion," the prince replied. "I'd like to hear it."

Perplexed, exasperated, Asher sat back and stared. "And I'd like to know what's got you so interested in the opinions of a fisherman stable hand. Sir."

The prince grinned. "That's more like it. I'll tell you what. You answer my question and I'll answer yours. Fair?"

"Fair," Asher said grudgingly. "Right then. My opinion, for what it be worth, is it were right to find in Mistress Raite's favour."

"But?"

"But I don't know why you said she were to get the two hundred trins and nowt more. That miserable bloody cousin of hers be a rich bastard, and where he's goin' he won't be needin' a pile of money. Not to mention he caused her a right load of heartache, one way and another. Reckon he should be punished for that."

"And he will be," the prince said quietly. "Meister Brenin and his friend the Magister conspired to pervert the course of Barl's Justice. I promise you, Asher, when this is over they'll be sorry they ever met."

"So where's the harm in makin' him give her more than the two hundred trins? That sort needs punchin' in the purse, if you reckon to drive the message right home. I know. We got one just like him back in Restharven."

The prince sighed. "Remember what you said about the law being priceless? It's the same with justice. The uncle wanted his niece to receive two hundred trins. The cousin took that money away, and I restored it to her. I also restored her good name in the eyes of the kingdom. That is justice. But to give her more than that would be to flout her uncle's expressed desire. Worse. It would be to say there is money to be made in defending Barl's Laws. I can't condone or encourage that. The Laws must be honoured and upheld because it's right to do so, not profitable."

"Huh," said Asher. "Good point, that."

"I'm glad you agree." The prince sounded sincere.

Pleased, and determined not to show it, Asher shrugged. "Still reckon it be a right shame you didn't get to kick 'im in the purse strings, though."

"Yes, I imagine it would've been fun," the prince said gravely.

Asher glared. Was that a joke at his expense? The prince's expression was politely patient, so...prob'ly not. He grunted. "All right. I answered your question. Now you can answer mine. Sir."

"Why do I care so much about your opinions?"

"Aye."

The prince looked out of the carriage window. They'd turned into the palace grounds. The Tower wasn't far away. Reaching up, he tugged on a red cord dangling above his head beside the blue bell-rope. A hinged flap fell open.

"Matcher?" the prince called through it.

From above them, the coachman's startled voice said, "Your Highness? Is owt wrong, sir?"

"No, nothing. But you can stop the carriage here and let us out. We'll walk to the Tower."

"Right you are, sir," said the invisible Matcher.

"Walk?" said Asher, scandalised. "Why? It'll take forever, and I got chores—"

The prince closed the ceiling flap. "No, you haven't. I told you, Matt knows you're with me. Are you suggesting he'll presume to tell me I can't borrow one of my own employees?"

"No, but—"

"Then that's all right, isn't it?"

The carriage slowed to a halt. The prince opened the door and stepped down, Asher at his heels, then closed it and thumped on the side with his fist. "Off you go, Matcher!" As the carriage pulled away, he turned to Asher and grinned. "That's better. We'll have time to finish our conversation now."

He started walking. Asher stared after him, dumbfounded. He was beginning to think he had no idea who this man really was. In the market square, the day they met, he'd been...almost an equal. In Justice

Hall, dressed in all that legal finery, weighed down by the solid gold crown and duty, the prince had been remote and unreachable. Stern. Frightening, almost. Had seemed years and years older. Now, whistling his way into the distance, he seemed as young and foolhardy as Jed.

Regular folk picked 'emselves a person to be and stuck with that. Trust royalty to be different.

Huffing in annoyance he undid a couple more shirt buttons and rolled up his sleeves. Then he jogged after the prince, caught him up, and fell into step beside him along the crushed and pounded blue gravel road that led straight to the palace. The wide thoroughfare was lined both sides with statuesque djelba trees. Their branches met overhead in a dappling canopy. Waxy pink blossoms the size of dinner plates soaked the cooling dusk air in sweetness.

"I'll start," said the prince, as though they'd never stopped talking, "by answering your question with a question of my own. How would you like to work for me, Asher?"

Asher glanced at him sideways. "I am workin' for you."

"Indirectly, yes. Directly, you work for Matt. I want to know if you'd be willing to work for *me*. With me. As my assistant."

"Assistant to what?"

"The announcement has yet to be made public, and I expect you to hold your tongue until it is, but His Majesty has appointed me the kingdom's first Olken Administrator. In many ways, it's just a formality. Practically speaking, I've been fulfilling the position's duties for nearly a year. Ever since my majority. Until now they've been tasks traditionally performed by the reigning monarch, so I've been performing them in His Majesty's name. In a nutshell, it means I attend to matters of concern that touch both our peoples, wherever they arise throughout the kingdom. It's like being a living bridge between Doranen and Olken. The title 'Olken Administrator' may be new, but the work itself began the day Barl and my ancestors came over the mountains and into this land."

"Oh," said Asher cautiously. "Sounds like a bloody big job, sir. Why don't the king want it?"

"'Want' has nothing to do with it," the prince snapped. "It's a question of how best can His Majesty's resources be used for the good of the kingdom. He is consumed by the WeatherWorking. My sister studies night and day to become his worthy successor. Her Majesty and the Master Magician also have their duties, with no time to spare for extra burdens, whereas I—"

Asher watched the prince's lips whiten with pressure. He didn't need to hear the sentence finished. Gar the Magickless needed something to do with himself, and his da the king had found it for him.

For the distance of two and a half trees, they walked in silence. Then the prince finished the sentence anyway. "Whereas I," he said carefully, "am in a unique position to be of use, not only to His Majesty but to all the people of Lur, Doranen and Olken alike. I consider it a privilege...but I can't do it alone."

"Alone? You got y'self a whole Tower full of folks, ain't you, all fallin' over 'emselves to do what you want?"

"I have a staff, yes, and they are invaluable," agreed the prince. "But I've learned a great deal since I started this work, mostly about how much I don't know about your people. I find myself needing something more than secretaries and clerks. Some*one* more. I need an Olken to work hand in glove with me, Asher. Someone who can help me be that bridge between our peoples. Someone who is unimpressed with the trappings of royalty, the seduction of court life, the social advantages of an elevated position. Someone with an instinctive sense of justice, who I can trust to be my right hand, my eyes, my voice, who won't be swayed by the flattery of those seeking favour and who I know will always tell me the truth, whether I want to hear it or not. In short, Asher, I need you."

Asher couldn't help it: he laughed. "You need your head read, more like."

"Really? Are you going to tell me I'm wrong about you? That you do care for all the pomp and circumstance and fawning flattery that royalty so often inspires?"

"No, sir! I couldn't care less for all that codswallop!"

"Well, then?" said the prince. The way he said it was a challenge.

Asher shook his head. "Well then, I don't want to do it."

"Why not?"

"Why d'you reckon? You'll be wantin' me to wear fancy clothes, won't you? Shirts with lace on 'em and little bits of ribbon and embroidery and suchlike. You'll expect me to stop soundin' like m'self and talk like a posh City Olken instead, won't you? Aye, you will! And I'll have to hobnob with folk who can't eat a meal less they use seven different forks, and think an honest workin' Olken man like me be good for nowt but opening doors for 'em!"

The prince was nodding. "I see. You're afraid."

"I ain't no such thing!"

"No?" The prince's expression darkened. Became grim. "Well, I am."

"What of?" said Asher, surprised. "Seems to me y'be doing a bang-up job. The way the folks cheer you in the streets. How you sat in Justice Hall today, as grand as the king hisself, you—"

"Don't." The prince stopped walking. "Don't ever compare me to the king. It's not...proper."

Asher swung round to face him and shrugged. "All right. But still. Y'can't be bollocksin' things up too bad or he wouldn't be making all this official, would he?"

They'd reached the turn-off that led away from the palace to the Tower. The prince started walking again, along the narrower road, and beckoned Asher to keep up. "I'm muddling through, Asher. I'm treading water, and so far I've managed not to drown myself, or anybody else. But I can trust to luck no longer. I've known for months now I needed Olken help to do this job properly. I was beginning to despair of ever finding the right person to be that help."

"And you reckon the right person is *me*?" said Asher. "You must be runnin' a fever, I reckon. Or else that crown you had on today's gone and bent your brain."

The prince frowned. "I love my father, Asher, as doubtless you love yours. I cannot fail in this. If I do, the king will be forced to resume those responsibilities I've assumed. At all costs, I must prevent that."

"Why? You said all this bein' a bridge malarkey usually got done by the...the reigning monarch. Why can't the king do it?" He watched the prince's face go very still, and his heart boomed hard against his ribs. "All right, sir. I reckon it's time you and me started rowin' this boat in the same direction. What ain't you tellin' me, eh? What's so sinkin' important about *you* doin' this Administrator stuff, and not the king?"

For the first time since Asher had laid eyes on the man, the prince looked uncertain. "Can I trust you?"

Asher sighed. "What kind of a daft bloody question is that? One minute you're askin' me to be your right-hand man 'cause I be so upright and incorruptible, and the next you want to know if I can be trusted? Reckon you need to make up your mind. Sir."

Temper flashed lightning-fast across the prince's face. "I'll thank you to keep a civil tongue in your head, Asher. The fact that I'll permit you a certain amount of leeway is hardly the same as allowing you to—"

"I see," said Asher. "So when you said you wanted someone who'd tell you the truth whether you wanted to hear it or not, *sir*, what you *really* meant was—"

"*All right!*"

Silence as the prince collected his thoughts and feelings. Asher pushed his hands into his pockets and amused himself by humming one of Da's favourite ditties under his breath. When he was done, and the prince still showed no sign of moving, he said, "If we stand around here much longer, some bird's goin' to think we're statues and shit on us."

The prince stirred. Looked at him, all uncertainty banished. "What do you know of WeatherWorking?"

Asher shrugged. "Nowt beyond what any spratling knows. The WeatherWorking and the Wall march hand in hand. Without Weather Magic we'd go back to the old days, when the weather was unchancy. We'd be at the mercy of storms and floods and droughts and famine. WeatherWorking feeds the Wall, keeps it strong. If it fails, the Wall fails, and there'd be nowt to keep us safe from all the evil that lies beyond the mountains. It's our duty to live our lives according to Barl's Law, so that never happens."

Lurking humour resurfaced, briefly. "A neat summary. Which means you can't have slept through *every* Barlsday sermon you ever heard."

Asher winced. Damn. How could the prince have noticed that? The royal family sat up the front of the palace chapel, while he always made sure to find the most shadowy corner right down the back. "Sir?"

"Relax. I won't tell. Holze is a good man, but even I have to admit his sermons are a trifle longwinded. The trick is to doze with your eyes open."

"Oh," said Asher. "Right." He'd be sure to try it, very next Barlsday.

"Anyway. About WeatherWorking. The thing is, it's very difficult and requires enormous amounts of energy. His Majesty gets tired." The prince frowned. "Exhausted. And before I assumed these extra duties, he would deplete his reserves of strength attending to them. At first he resisted the idea of relinquishing the obligation, but in the end Her Majesty, the Master Magician and I prevailed."

So. Not so much a case of "find the poor magickless prince something to do," mayhap, as a matter of necessity. Or both. Two fish caught with the same hook. Asher thought of his own da. The arguments they'd had about slowing down. Taking care.

"Reckon fathers don't take too kindly to their sons reminding 'em they ain't as young as once they were."

The prince sighed. "No. Mind you," he added sharply, "this in *no* way suggests that the king is unfit. Let me make that abundantly clear. He is as capable today as he was at his coronation. The kingdom could rest in no stronger hands."

"I never said otherwise. You just want to do the right thing by your da. Help him, like a good son should. Reckon I can see that. Reckon I admire you for it."

"So you do see, then, how important it is that I not fail as Olken Administrator? Failure would mean he'd resume those duties. Tax his strength, when all his strength must be given to WeatherWorking. And failure, *my* failure, would be used against him to—"

Another silence. The sun was sinking fast now. Long shadows crept across the manicured grounds on either side of them, through the trees, across the road. Asher swallowed.

"What d'you mean, used against him? Who'd want to use you to hurt the king?"

CHAPTER FIVE

Nobody," said the prince eventually, not looking at him. "It's complicated. Just tell me you'll change your mind, Asher. Tell me you'll take the job."

Feeling cornered, pressured, Asher stamped his heels into the roadway. A flock of nightbirds flew overhead, their harsh cries scraping the sky.

"This be politics, eh?" he said accusingly. "You be askin' me to mucky myself with politics. That ain't my job. My job's fishin' and sailin' and shit shovellin'. *Honest* dirty work. I leave politics to the likes of...of..."

"Me?" said the prince, smiling faintly.

"You're different," muttered Asher. "You got born to it without a say-so. You want me to *choose* it. On *purpose*." He released a hard-held breath. "Look. There's got to be a hundred Olken out there who'd lick the road clean from the City gates to your front door to get a job like this."

"That's true," said the prince. "Which is just one of the many reasons why you're perfect for the position. As my right hand, you'd be advising me on a wide range of Olken matters. Customs. Ways of thinking and experiencing the world that I, as a Doranen, might never understand. No matter my good intentions or willingness to learn. It means that in some cases I'd be letting you make the decisions altogether if I thought you were the better qualified to do so. Most people would eventually be overcome by that much power. They'd abuse it. But you're not most people, Asher. In all honesty, you're not like anybody I've ever met before. Olken or Doranen."

"And that's what today were all about, eh? Checkin' to see if I thought about things the right way?"

The prince hesitated. "Partly. Partly it was to see if you thought about things at all. Not everybody does."

Asher felt his lip curl. "And especially not fishermen turned stable hands?"

"Don't be ludicrous," snapped the prince. "Some of the biggest fools I've ever met in my life can boast a university education and blood lines that trace back to the Founding Families. If I thought like that, Asher, we wouldn't be standing here in the middle of the road discussing this, would we? You'd be in the stable yard shovelling shit and I'd be...somewhere else."

Fair point. "So why are we standin' here in the middle of the road discussin' this? Sir?"

"Because I started thinking about appointing an assistant a week after His Majesty agreed to let me take over from him, and nearly a year later you're the only man I've met who I can imagine trusting to do the job!"

Asher stared. "You're stark staring bonkers. You don't hardly know me from a hole in the ground."

"I know enough!"

It was impossible not to feel flattered. Hating himself for it, Asher scowled. "And what about all the other palaver? Clothes and—"

"Naturally," the prince said carefully, "you'd need to dress a little more formally than you do now. But there's no law that says you have to wear lace. As for your accent..." He smiled. "I confess it could do with a little citifying. Not because there's anything wrong with it, as such," he added, holding up a hasty hand, "but because, like it or not, first impressions count and you'll want people to be impressed with your abilities, not distracted by the way you speak."

"Huh." Asher sniffed. That didn't sound *too* bad. "All right. Say I agree. How much'll you pay me? 'Cause I don't reckon to be gettin' myself all hot and bothered over politics for a miserly twenty-five trins a week."

The prince's expression was a mingling of relief, hope and amusement. "What about fifty trins a week, plus all meals and a suite in the Tower, plus a wardrobe more fitting to your new station. And a horse. Say...Cygnet? Is that recompense unmiserly enough?"

Asher nearly swallowed his tongue. Cygnet? For his own? And fifty trins, every week? Forget about buying a lone modest, second-hand smack. He'd be able to buy a whole *fleet* of fishing boats, every one of 'em brand new, when he went back home to Restharven with that kind of money.

The dizzying thought stirred his conscience to life. He sighed, and shook his head. "Reckon it's more than enough, sir. But I can't do it. Sorry. Thanks for askin', though. I be right flattered."

Taken aback, the prince stared. "Why can't you? Don't try to tell me you're not interested. You're not that good a liar."

Asher scowled, hating to turn his back on all that money. Hating the prince for offering it to him. "'Cause I weren't plannin' on stayin' in Dorana longer than a year, all right? And this job you want me to do, that's the kind of job as goes for longer than that. For life, maybe. I mean, if your da's tired now he ain't goin' to be less tired this time next year, is he? You're goin' to be Olken Administrating till your hair's gone grey and your teeth've all dropped out. And you'll be needin' yourself an assistant as can go grey alongside you. That won't be me. I got other fish to fry."

"It's true I'll be Olken Administrator for as long as His Majesty reigns," said the prince. "And I pray Barl grants him many more years to pursue his sacred calling." His lips pressed hard against his holy-ring. "But no man lives forever. Our Doranen magic can do many things, Asher, but it can't make us immortal. What my sister will want of me once she becomes WeatherWorker is anyone's guess. It might well be that both I and my assistant will find ourselves without a purpose the day after she ascends the throne."

"All right, so mayhap you won't be Olken Administrating without your teeth. But the thing is, I made a promise to *my* da, see? I promised him I'd be away one year and not a day longer. I ain't about to go back on my word, not even for fifty trins a week and a horse like Cygnet. You can't expect me to. And if y'do...well..." He glared, defiant. "Then I reckon you ain't the man I thought you were."

The prince ignored that. Stared at the ground instead, thinking. "Of course you must keep your promise," he said at last. "But that doesn't mean you can't accept this offer. You can still make a valuable contribution, Asher. And when the times comes, I won't stop you from leaving. You have my word."

Oh. So that was one objection down, a score more to go. Politics. The claptrap that went with royalty. The ruckus of change. He had hisself a good life in the stables. The work wasn't demanding, it wasn't beyond him, and he had friends there. Even more important, he had no enemies.

None of that, he suspected, could be said of being the prince's Assistant Olken Administrator.

"And what happens if I say I'll do it, and after a week of workin' hand in glove we be hatin' each other's guts?"

"Then you can go back to the stables for as long as you like, and I'll find somebody else to assist me."

Or he could just find somebody else now and be done with it. Let them worry about the politics and the polite conversation and the sorting out of a hundred people's problems day in day out...

Except it were *fifty trins* a week. And *Cygnet*.

"Look," said the prince. "It's a lot to consider, I know. And I've sprung it upon you without warning. Why not take the night to think it over? You can give me your answer in the morning. I'll be exercising Ballodair first thing, you can tell me then. All right?"

"All right," said Asher, relieved.

The prince nodded. "Good. Now we'd best be getting along before somebody panics and sends out a search party."

In silent accord they continued along the road. At the entrance to the Tower forecourt they parted, the prince disappearing into the tall blue building, Asher breaking into a jog to reach the stables before Matt lost all patience and had his guts for garters. It was almost dark by then, and clouding over. The warm air pressed damp and heavy against his skin.

Though the inside of his skull was battered with conflicting thoughts and feelings, within the chaos he felt a fleeting moment of curiosity about the king. Borne the WeatherWorker, decreed by Barl to carry the weight of the Wall and their world upon his flesh-and-bone shoulders. Even now, while the rest of Lur busied itself with heedless living, in the secret place where all such wild magics were conjured the prince's father prepared to offer himself in the service of his people, Olken and Doranen alike.

Prepared to call the night's rain.

Exhausted, the prince had called him.

Asher shivered, and jogged along a little faster.

The stable yard was a puddle of light in the gathering gloom. Unheeded, he stood in the shadow of the sandstone archway and watched the other lads as they bustled back and forth across the lamp-lit gravel, carrying feed and hay and rugs, scoffing and laughing and tossing jokes to each other in passing. He watched the horses, too, his other new friends. Stared hungrily at Cygnet, gleaming like a pearl.

"In case you hadn't noticed," an exasperated voice said behind him, "we've already got ourselves a scarecrow. And the last time I looked we didn't need a guard dog. So what d'you think you're doing standing there with your thumb up your arse while all the lads are running their feet off for evening stables? Which are late as it is, seeing how we were short-handed all afternoon. Where've you been, anyway?"

Matt.

Asher turned. "Justice Hall."

"Justice Hall?"

"Aye, and it be all your fault. What did you want to go witterin' on to the prince about me for, eh? All that guff about me bein' so reliable and hardworkin' and clever? I never asked you to praise me to royalty, did I? Never said I were lookin' for work other than what I got here? If y'had to say somethin', why not that I'm no better or worse than I should be? Eh? It's the truth."

Matt walked past him and into the yard proper. "Prince Gar offered you another position?" His voice was calm, conversational, but there was tension in the set of his shoulders and the way his fingers held tight to his belt.

"Aye." Asher took a step forward himself so he could see Matt's face. "Some blather about bein' his right-hand man up in the Tower. He's bein' announced as the Olken Administrator, see. Says he wants me as his official assistant." Too late, he remembered. "Oh. Damn." He pulled a face. Lowered his voice. "Weren't s'posed to mention that. Don't tell anyone, eh?"

"I won't," said Matt. "I'm good with secrets."

"Aye, well, so'm I s'posed to be, if I do this job. And there's me blurtin' out the first one he trusts me with!"

Matt half smiled. "I wouldn't worry over-much. It gets easier as you go along." The smile faded, and his gaze shifted until he was staring far into the distance at the mellow golden glow of Barl's Wall rising out of the mountains. For a moment some strong and secret emotion bleached the colour from his tanned face so that all of a sudden he looked old and weary. Then the moment passed and he was himself again, wry and purposeful and full of spirit. "What he's offering you... it's a big compliment. And a big step. Did you accept?"

"I said I'd think on it," said Asher, shrugging. "And I will. But I don't know, Matt. Aye, the money's bloody good and the work sounds interestin', I s'pose, but... I'm happy here. I ain't one of them fancy folderol Olken as works up in the Tower, like Darran or that pissant Willer. Reckon I'll stick out there like an eel in a bowl of goldfish. I mean, I don't want to go makin' a bloody great fool of m'self, do I?"

"I reckon it's only natural to feel a little fear when a prince makes you an offer like this. There's a lot at stake."

"This ain't got nowt to do with fear!" said Asher, offended. "I be weighin' the fors and againsts, is all, like any sensible man should." He kicked at the raked gravel. "Like I said, this be all your fault. Reckon he never would've thought of me if you hadn't flapped your lips at him."

Matt took a deep, considering breath and let it out with care. "If His Highness is as good a judge of a man as he is of horseflesh, Asher, and I suspect he is, then he knows the right one for a job when he sees him. I doubt I had much to do with this at all. Some things are just... meant to be."

The mosquitoes were starting to whine; Asher slapped one to death against his bare forearm and scowled at the smear of blood it left behind. "So y'reckon I should say yes, eh?"

"I reckon," said Matt, unsmiling, "you should talk it over with someone else. Could be I'm not the best person to ask."

"Who?"

"Who else do you trust?"

Asher tugged at his bottom lip, thinking. "Reckon I trust Dathne," he said reluctantly. "She drives me near to distraction with her pokin' and proddin' and expectin' me to widen my horizons, read all those books she keeps on givin' me and then answer bloody questions after, but I trust her. She may be slumskumbledy but she's got a good head on her shoulders, I'll give her that."

Matt looked away. "Yes. You could talk to Dathne. I'm sure she'll tell you..."

"What?"

"What she thinks," said Matt, and looked back again. "She'll be down at the Goose in an hour or so. And you'll be finished around here by then."

"Huh," said Asher. Confide in Dathne, eh? Dathne was so sharp it was a wonder she didn't cut herself twice a day. Sharp, and never short of an opinion. She'd surely have an idea or three of what he should do. What all this could mean. And over the weeks she'd become an unlikely friend. "Mayhap I will ask her at that."

Matt clapped him on the shoulder. "Good. Now help the lads finish off evening stables, will you? It'll be raining any minute, and I've got the red mare to physic, a loose buckle to sew back on a rug and an order for feed to write up. I don't have time to stand around gossiping, and neither do you. Even if this does look to be your last night getting your hands dirty with the rest of us." He smiled, then, just a little, to take the sting out of his words... but Asher could sense a chill beneath it. Where it came from he didn't know.

And he wasn't sure he wanted to find out, either.

Two hours later he was sitting in a booth opposite Dathne, spooning the Goose's fragrant mutton stew onto slabs of fresh brown bread and telling her all about the prince's remarkable offer, this time without a mention of what the job was actually called.

Like Matt, Dathne was impressed. Unlike Matt, she was admiring too.

He liked that.

"And you didn't say yes on the spot? Asher!" Reaching across the benchtop, she pressed the back of her hand to his forehead. "You must be fevered."

Despite the stomach-growling goodness of the stew, he scowled. "Reckon I be the kind of fool what jumps into new water without testin' the depth first, do you?"

Dathne shrugged. "No. But are you the kind of a fool who turns down fifty trins a week just because he thinks he's a better man than a prince in pretty clothes?"

He tossed his spoon into the stew pot and banged his fist beside it. "I never said I thought I were better. Reckon he's all right, for a Doranen."

"If he's willing to pay you fifty trins a week, would it matter if he wasn't?"

Asher pulled the pot close again and shovelled in the last few mouthfuls. Buying some time. "It might."

"So you do *want* the job?"

"Don't reckon as I've decided one way or another yet." He brooded into the empty pot. "It does matter, him bein' a good man. And he is. Y'could see Justice Hall were important to him. Getting it right. Being fair. He cared about that. Y'could see he takes it serious."

"Well, that's good, isn't it?" she said encouragingly.

"Aye!" he retorted. "But that ain't really the point, eh? I only just got m'self settled good and proper in the stables. All this choppin' and changin' be enough to make a body seasick, I swear!"

Dathne took a deep draught of ale from her tankard, smacked her lips together and considered him with her head tipped to one side. "So do you really want to know what I think, or am I just here to be shouted and banged at?"

Asher felt his cheeks heat. "I ain't shoutin'. Might've banged once or twice. Whole thing's took me by surprise, all right?"

"I'll take that as a yes," said Dathne, rolling her eyes. "If it's living in the Tower that's got you worried, don't be. For a prince, His Highness maintains a remarkably informal household. I'm sure you'll fit right in. Of course Darran won't like you, but who cares? He won't be paying you."

Asher's jaw tightened aggressively. "Who said I be worried? And I don't care if that ole Darran likes me or not."

She smiled. "Good for you. So...is it you're afraid you'll fail?"

"No, I ain't afraid I'll fail! I ain't failed at a single thing I ever put my mind to, startin' with lacin' my own boots when I were a spratling of three. Why's everybody thinkin' I be afraid?"

"Well, it's only natural, isn't it?" Dathne eyed him over the top of her tankard. "A rustic young fellow like you thrown in the deep end with Doranen royalty. Put in charge of all kinds of important, secret things. Surely it'd be odd if you *weren't* afraid."

A hot bubble of outrage swelled in his chest, then burst into angry words. "Rustic? You reckon I be *rustic*?"

Dathne's eyebrows lifted. "Me? Of course not. But then I know you, don't I?"

He banged the benchtop again and leaned close. A few heads turned at nearby booths, curious. He ignored them.

"You know bloody nowt if y'reckon I be afraid to do this job just 'cause I were born in a small fishing village days and days from this here fancy big city!" he said hotly. "Let me tell you a thing or two about *fishin'*, missy."

"By all means," said Dathne, and put down her tankard. "I'm all ears."

Her gentle sarcasm was lost on him. Eyes burning, fists braced on the benchtop, he leaned even closer. "The coast of this kingdom be the only place left what sees weather the way it used to be. The way it were afore the Doranen came. Uncalled. Untamed. *Wild*. The spells Barl put in Dragonteeth Reef keep us invisible, and that be all. They don't stop nature. We get storms along the coast, blowin' in from the open ocean, blowin' over the coral and teeth-first into our faces. Water twisters what can suck up a whole boat and all her crew to the last man or boy and spit 'em out again in pieces. Hailstones big as your head. Giant waves just itchin' to slap you down like a hand of iron. Winds that'll blow you right clean out of your boots, and sleet to slice y'to the bone."

"It sounds terrifying," murmured Dathne.

"Aye, it bloody well is! But it don't stop us. We respect it, but we ain't afraid." He jabbed a pointed finger at her. "And *that* be why the WeatherWorker comes to us every year for Sea Harvest Festival. 'Cause the WeatherWorkers know we be different from other Olken. Aye, and from all the Doranen too. The WeatherWorkers know us fishin' folk face the weather their precious magic can't tame, *and* we survive it."

She stared at him, her intensity so fierce it fairly crackled in her hair. "You're proud of that, aren't you? Proud that your people are the closest to what we all were before the Doranen came."

"Course I am," he retorted. "Who wouldn't be? The storms what blow inland run smack bang into the Weather Magic no more'n half a mile from the water, and it kills 'em stone dead. They never reach the next nearest town or village. So aside from us fishin' folk, there ain't a man, woman or child in this whole kingdom knows what wild weather be like. What Lur used to be. Those folk livin' close enough to the coast to find out, Olken *and* Doranen, they hear thunder on our horizon and hide 'emselves under their beds till it's gone."

"You're scornful...but can you blame them?" said Dathne. "Is it their fault they weren't born fishermen? Thanks to Barl and the WeatherWorkers, the people of this kingdom have lived for more than six hundred years in peaceful prosperity, looking upon the weather as a friend. A gift. As a tool to be used, like any hammer or nail or needle. Not as something unsafe, or lethal. Even if you could, would you change that? Give the kingdom back its wild weather? Break the chains of magic and abandon us all to chaos? To hurricane and earthquake? Famine, flood and drought?"

Scornful. Frowning, all pent-up indignation released, Asher sat back and rubbed the tip of one forefinger across the grain of the wooden benchtop. "Don't be daft. Why'd I want to do a thing like that?" He looked up. "And I don't blame no-one for nowt. I'm just sayin' it ain't right to go around disrespectin' folk 'cause they ain't all City-born and sophisticated, like."

"I never said I disrespected you. And it's good to know you don't disrespect yourself either. Asher..." Dathne hesitated, her dark eyes sombre. "The day we met, I said you were too easily prickled. And you were. Has that changed? Because there'll be people who say, to your face and to your back, that they could do this job better. That the prince should've asked them. That you're an upstart rustic who should've stayed in the stables or, better yet, on your da's leaky little boat far away from here. And instead of shouting, or thumping tables or even, Barl forbid, thumping *them*, you'll need to smile and walk away. Can you do that?"

He glowered at her. "My da's boat don't leak. And I don't care two tubs of fish guts what other folks say. I be good enough for the prince, and that's all I care about. I can do whatever he asks."

Considering him thoughtfully she said, "Does that mean you'll say yes?"

He shook his head. Shrugged. "I d'know..."

Reaching across the table, she patted his arm. Her touch through his thick cotton sleeve was warm and familiar. It shivered him, somewhere deep inside. "Oh, come on," she coaxed. "At least give the job a *try*. All bluster aside, you know you want to. If only to prove to all those folk you don't care about that they're wrong. And he said you could go back to the stables if it didn't work out, didn't he?"

He sniffed. "Talk's cheap."

"I'll agree that nothing is certain save sunshine and rain," she said carefully, "but for what it's worth, Asher, I believe Prince Gar is a man of his word. And I think you do, too."

He couldn't deny it. "I s'pose."

She sat back again, eyebrows raised. "Look at it this way. If you *don't* give this new job a chance you'll spend the rest of your life wondering what might have been. *And* you'll be a lot poorer while you're wondering it. Fifty trins a week? That's not a sum to be sneezed at."

"Huh," said Asher. "Easy enough for you to say. You ain't the one lookin' at lace on his collar and seven forks to eat a bowl of soup." He scratched his chin, then shoved his emptied stew pot to one side. "Reckon I'm done here."

She smiled. She had a nice smile, when it wasn't pretending to be an unsheathed dagger. "You're welcome."

With a nod, he slid out from behind the benchtop and shouldered his way across the Goose's crowded dance floor.

Dathne watched him go. *"Missy?"* she said to herself, remembering, and laughed.

Asher opened the door and was lost to the mizzling night. He didn't see Matt lurking nearby in the shadows, waiting for him to leave.

Dathne looked up as the stable meister approached her habitual corner. Her eyes were triumphant.

"*So.*"

"Just tell me," said Matt, easing onto the seat Asher had abandoned, "that you had nothing to do with it."

Her straight black eyebrows shot up indignantly. "Of course I didn't! But at least now you have to admit that what I *did* do turned out to be the right thing. He's about to enter the House of the Usurper. Prophecy continues."

Matt sighed. "He said he'd take the job, then?"

"No. But he will. I told him he should, and he wants to. All that lovely money." She laughed softly, and swallowed some more ale. "And though I suspect he'd die before admitting it, he's proud as punch the prince has asked him. In fact, my friend, I'd say nine-tenths of that young man's backbone is nothing *but* pride." She paused, her expression thoughtful. "Which isn't such a bad thing, provided it's put to good use."

Matt rubbed his eyes. "There'll be folks none too pleased to see a stable lad elevated so far above the rest of us. He's bound to lose some friends over this. Or worse, make enemies."

Dathne shrugged. "He's not here to be popular. He's here to fulfil Prophecy."

"It doesn't bother you?"

"What? That I told him what would serve my purposes before his?" Another shrug. "I'm not here to be popular either, Matt."

He couldn't meet her eyes. "I feel like muck." His voice was so low he could barely hear it himself. "He's my friend, and we're using him. Without his knowledge, or his consent. It's wrong."

Her hand snapped out to close about his wrist, ink-stained fingernails biting deep between tendon and sinew. "*Look at me.*"

Reluctantly, he lifted his gaze.

"Saving kingdoms is a mucky business. We can soil our hands a little now, you and I, or we can see them soaked in blood later. Either way, we get mucky."

"And what if I don't like getting mucky?"

Dathne bared her teeth in a fierce smile. "Then I'd say sorry, bucko, but it's a bit late now." The smile disappeared and all that remained was ferocity. "You listen. He's not your friend, Matt. He's a pawn, just like you and me. Prophecy's tool. You don't make friends with a tool. You use it, and you keep on using it until the job it's designed for is done."

"That's cold," Matt whispered.

Her teeth bared again. "You mean *I'm* cold."

"I mean there might be another way. A better way."

She shook her head. "There isn't."

"But—"

"*There isn't.*" With a visible effort, she controlled herself. "There's a reason Prophecy calls him the Innocent Mage. He doesn't get told a thing, Matt. Not one *thing*. Not until he has to be told. Not until there's no turning back. Understood?"

A fraction more pressure from the fingernails on his flesh and she'd draw blood. He sat motionless, heart pounding, and endured her flame-filled eyes. Then he nodded, feeling scorched to his bones' marrow. "Aye. Understood."

She nodded sharply and released him. "Good. Now go fetch yourself a mug of ale and wash away that mopey look before somebody thinks you asked me to marry you and I said no."

"Ha!" said Matt, and shoved away from the bench. He didn't want a mug of ale. If he drank so much as a mouthful, his quivering guts would heave themselves onto the floor at his feet. "Ask you to marry me? That'll be the day!"

He saw his words strike home. Saw them hurt her.

To his shame, he wasn't sorry.

CHAPTER SIX

Darran, Private Secretary to His Royal Highness Prince Gar and self-appointed Guardian of the Tower, reached for his cup and took a genteel sip of his morning tea.

Gulping was for peasants.

"Darran?"

Darran replaced the cup in its saucer with a faint chink of porcelain. "Yes, Willer?"

His assistant and protégé was staring vexedly at a sheet of official parchment topping a pile of official parchments teetering untidily before him. "I think we have a problem."

With a sigh, Darran drummed his manicured fingernails on his pristine desktop. "Willer, *how* many times must I say it? In this office we do *not* have problems. We have interesting developments. We have challenges. If we absolutely *must* we may, on occasion, have a slight difficulty. But under *no* circumstances whatso*ever* do we have *problems*. Now. What is it?"

As befitted his subordinate position, Willer's desk was small and situated between the door and the bookcase, which was neatly filled with publications detailing the genealogies of all the kingdom's Doranen families, plus sundry other reference works such as *Dorana City By-Laws*, Fabrit and Delbard's *A Short History of Lur* and, of course, the indispensable Polger's *Etiquette, Precedent and Protocol*.

Squirming round in his chair—really, the boy ate *far* too many pastries, Darran thought—Willer held up the offending document, his expression trepidatious. "It's His Highness's diary for next month."

"Yes? What of it? How many times must I remind you, Willer? Above all else, a good private secretary is *lucid*."

With a grunt Willer shoved his chair back, got up and marched across the circular office's plush carpet waving the parchment in question. "Well, Darran, he's *lucidly* gone and declined all of next month's invitations except the one to the Brewers' Guild banquet."

"Don't be ridiculous." Darran held out an impatient hand for the diary. "He can't have. Declined Lady Scobey's soirée? Refused to attend Lord Dorv's hunting party? *Again?* Turned down the chance to go boating on the Gant with the Council? Tut! You've misread his— oh. Oh dear." Staring at the list of social engagements to which His Highness had been invited, noting with despair the decisive pen strokes through every invitation bar the least prestigious, he felt a sudden stab of pain between his eyes. "Barl preserve us!" he cursed, and thrust the parchment back into Willer's waiting hand. "What is he *thinking*?"

Wisely, Willer didn't reply.

"Lady Scobey is going to be furious! I've had her wretched cook in and out of here a dozen times this week, wanting to know His Highness's favourite dishes. He *can't* say no to her, I'll never hear the end of it!" Scalded with outrage, Darran snatched the diary back again and stared at it with loathing. "The *Brewers*" Guild? Is he out of his mind? That motley assortment of inebriated reprobates? There's not a man among them who knows how to tie a cravat properly! In fact, I doubt there's even one who knows what a cravat *is*! Barl *preserve* us!" He tossed the diary onto his desk and went so far as to stand and pace towards the window and back again. "Well. Clearly this is unacceptable. Willer, present my compliments to His Highness and request the indulgence of a short—"

There was a smart *rap-rap* on the closed office door.

"*What*?" cried Darran.

The door swung open to reveal His Royal Highness, and behind him a disreputable-looking Olken wearing deplorably scruffed shirt and trews and boots clotted with mud, or something worse. He looked vaguely familiar, was some kind of manual labourer about the place, possibly, but what he was doing here, in the ordered beauty of the Tower, with the prince...

His Highness smiled, that sweet, mischievous smile the hardest of hearts could not withstand. "Don't tell me, Darran. Let me guess. Willer's just shown you my acceptance list for next month's social engagements."

"Your Highness!" gasped Darran. "Oh sir, *forgive* me."

His Highness, sauntering into the office, waved a dismissive hand. After a slight hesitation the disreputable Olken followed him over the threshold. "It's all right. I didn't expect you to be happy about it."

Mortified at being discovered raising his voice in disarray, Darran took a deep, calming breath and reached for the diary. "As it happens, Your Highness, I did wish to consult with you on the matter of next month's engagements. I'm sure it's just an oversight, but—"

"Sorry," said His Highness. "No oversight."

Darran felt his heart plummet. "Your Highness, forgive me, but is this..." He hesitated. "...*wise*? To say no to all of these important Doranen personages, your peers, and then accept an invitation from the...the...Olken Brewers' Guild?"

His Highness shrugged. "I like the Olken Brewers' Guild."

"You do?" said Darran faintly.

"Well, I like the members. Their meister is best sipped in half-pints only. But yes." The prince sighed. "And clearly you think that's inappropriate."

"I do not presume to have an opinion," said Darran, avoiding Willer's gaze. "But I would be doing you a grave disservice did I not remind you that as the king's son you have social obligations and a duty to—"

"Be bored out of my mind in the name of politics?" said His Highness dryly.

"Well..." Darran ventured the very slightest of smiles; a little judicious sympathy went a long way in greasing the wheels of appropriate princely conduct. "Please don't mistake me, Your Highness. I do understand that sometimes it's difficult."

"Difficult?" murmured His Highness. "I think the word you're looking for is impossible."

"Yes, sir. I imagine it is. But, sir, if you could please bring yourself to reconsider...find a way to accept *one* other invitation...just one... it would be the politic thing to do."

His Highness sighed. Held out his hand. "Show me then."

Darran gave him the diary, stepped back again and cleared his throat. "If I might make a suggestion, sir?"

His Highness glanced up. "Short of gagging you, is there any way I can prevent it?"

"Oh, sir!" Darran protested with a deprecating laugh. "So amusing."

"I'm glad one of us thinks this is funny. Your point, Darran."

Darran nodded. "Of course, sir. My point is this: I happen to know that Lady Scobey has gone to great lengths to design her soirée in such a way as can only be highly pleasing to your palate."

"Lady Scobey," said His Highness, frowning, "is hoping against hope that I'll succumb to the dubious charms of her youngest daughter and offer myself as a husband. Lady Scobey, shrewd mama that she is, seems to have reached the flattering conclusion that my lack of magical ability is outweighed, just, by the fact that my father is the king and my sister heir to the crown. I suppose I should be grateful..."

There was an embarrassed silence. After a moment Darran cleared his throat. "Well, if the idea of Lady Scobey's soirée displeases you, sir, then perhaps—"

The prince's face twisted with a repressed and violent revulsion. "*Displeases* me? Why would it displease me? Lady Scobey's eldest daughter has just announced her engagement to Conroyd Jarralt's firstborn son. Now the good mama thinks to get her feet under both our tables and who can blame her? She's only thinking of her family. No, no, what *displeases* me, Darran, is—" And then he stopped. Shook his head and managed a rueful smile. "I'm sorry. You can't possibly be interested in Doranen romantic gossip. And of course you're right. I can't attend only the Brewers' banquet. Privilege has its price, after all. Give me a pen."

Darran nodded sharply at Willer, who inked a quill and handed it to the prince. His Highness scrawled a circle around the notation for Lady Scobey's party, crossed out his original rejection and wrote in the neat hand that Darran admired so much: *Invitation accepted— under protest.* Then he handed both diary and pen to Willer.

"Thank you, Your Highness," said Darran, scrupulously neutral. "Lady Scobey will be delighted, I'm sure."

That made the prince laugh; a mirthless sound. "Only until I make it quite clear that I've no intention of marrying her daughter."

The pain in him, imperfectly masked, was painful to see. To endure, without offering comfort. But Darran knew that while His Highness might, on very rare occasions, refer to his...imperfection... such references were never *ever* to be ratified by comment, or even acknowledgement.

"Is there anything else Your Highness requires?"

His Highness's expression cleared. "As a matter of fact, Darran, there is." He beckoned to the swarthy Olken, still silently loitering just inside the doorway. The ruffian hesitated then stepped into the office proper. "Asher, this is my private secretary, Darran. I believe you've heard of him. Darran keeps my life in order whether I want him to or not. And the young gentleman there in the startling pink weskit is his assistant, Willer."

The Olken nodded. Darran waited for him to speak, waited a little longer...then realised with an unpleasant jolt that an abrupt jerk of the chin was the only recognition he was going to receive.

How...offensive.

He looked this Asher up and down. A rough, unprepossessing fellow. Capable enough, most likely, in a purely brutish fashion. His face was scarred: a faded white line ran irregularly along his right cheekbone. It gave him a threatening, brawling air which was echoed in the muscled breadth of his shoulders and the blunt, square power of his hands, hanging relaxed by his sides. How old was he? Hard to say... Contemporary to His Highness, it was safe to assume, but with a wealth of dubious experience in his dark, calculating eyes. His complexion was weathered, suggesting a lifetime's exposure to a climate harsher than most in the kingdom. The chin was firm. Stubborn, even. And in him raged a crackling vitality, a brooding force of personality that hummed the air around him like an invisible dynamo.

Darran, who prided himself on being a swift and accurate judge of character, felt his spine stiffen.

Here was trouble.

His Highness placed a hand on the ruffian's shoulder. "Darran, this is Asher of Restharven. He's the man who caught Ballodair for me after I fell off in the market square, you recall? I offered him a job as thanks, and he accepted."

Slowly, Darran nodded. "Yes, sir. I do recall the incident." He shifted his gaze a fraction, let it rest on the ruffian's calm face. Was that dumb insolence he could see lurking behind the mask? He thought it was. The hairs rose up on the back of his neck.

Oh yes indeed. Here was trouble all right, and everything that trouble implied.

The prince slid a sidelong glance at the fellow. "Well, I've decided he was being wasted in the stable yard, so I've invited him to work with me here, in the Tower."

Willer made an incautious, strangled sound in his throat. Darran burned him with a look. "Really, sir?" he said, fighting the impulse to clench his hands into fists. "How interesting. If I may ask, sir, in what capacity will this—will Asher be working here?"

Again the fleeting, mischievous smile. "*Well*," said His Highness, "once upon a time he'd have been known as the Prince's Champion."

That startled a reaction out of the ruffian. "Eh? Champion? You never said nowt about me bein' a champion. Sir. Champion of what anyways? Folderol and footlin' about?"

Darran shuddered. Barl save them all, that *accent*! Thick enough to cut with a knife! And the disrespect. *Appalling.* He felt his stomach roll queasily. His world was unravelling right before his eyes and he had the most awful suspicion he was powerless to stop it.

The prince laughed. "Don't you like it? I do. *Champion.* I think it sounds quaint."

"Quaint," the brute echoed, voice dripping with disgust. "Ain't no call for quaint, I reckon."

"No? Well...perhaps not," His Highness said regretfully.

"Champion," the dreadful man said again. Then he smiled, a scornful twist of his lips. "Got that from one of them books Dathne's always fetchin' you, eh?"

His Highness appeared completely unperturbed. "As a matter of fact, I did. We had champions prancing all over the countryside a few hundred years ago, particularly during that bad patch after King Trevoyle died without an heir. But once the dust settled and all the bodies were buried it was decided we'd do without them for a while, and that was that. So, in deference to the past, we won't actually call you my champion. Not in public, anyway. I reserve the right to use the title in private, though, if ever I'm in a mood to irritate you. Instead, we'll call you my..." He fell silent, thinking.

Mistake! Darran wanted to shout. Call him your mistake, come to your senses and toss him back on the dung heap where he belongs! It's not too late!

The prince stirred. "Do you know, I believe I've a mind not to worry about the past and its refined sensibilities after all. Trevoyle's Schism was a long time ago. A champion's job was to stand at his lord's right hand, defending him from all harm. He spoke with his lord's voice in matters of local dispute and calumny and was relied upon to provide his lord with intelligence, information and advice whenever it was required." Again, the mischievous grin. "He was also expected to die on his lord's behalf ... but probably we won't need to worry about that."

The jumped-up stable hand was staring. "Oh, aye? Reckon that's a relief. Sir. But if you got to call me something, Assistant Olken Administrator'll do. Reckon the lads are goin' to give me a hard enough time about this as it is, without you taggin' me as a champion."

Darran swallowed an anguished cry. Assistant Olken Administrator? His Highness had decided to appoint himself an assistant—without consultation? Without guidance? Had appointed this man, this *awful* man, to the post? What was he *thinking*?

The prince frowned for a moment, then nodded. "Yes. I hadn't considered that. Very well. Darran ..."

Feeling ill, Darran said, "Sir?"

"As of today, Asher is the kingdom's Assistant Olken Administrator."

He flinched. Hearing it said like that, baldly, with no suggestion of doubt or equivocation, not even a hint of needing a wiser opinion, a moment to think ... the effort of controlling himself would likely give him a hernia. Driven to desperation he said, delicately, unwisely, "Sir, does His Majesty ... ?"

The prince's answering look was dangerously bland. "Does His Majesty what, Darran?"

Know? Approve? Permit? Darran cleared his throat. If he wasn't extremely careful, the next sound he heard would be that of thin ice cracking. He took a prudent step back to safer ground. "Well, sir, it's just your official appointment has yet to be announced."

"The news will be made public on Barlsday," said the prince. "Along with the announcement that I have chosen an Olken to work with me in this important undertaking." He smiled, but his eyes remained chilly. "As one who pays such close attention to politics, Darran, I thought you of all people would appreciate the gesture."

"Yes! Yes, sir, naturally I do!" And would appreciate it even more had the chosen one been anybody but this smirking lout. If the prince had thought to ask his vastly experienced private secretary who best would fill such important, such political shoes ... But the boy could be so *impulsive*. As surely as Barl came over the mountains, this would end in tears and tantrums, he could feel it in his bones.

"I'm pleased that you agree," said the prince. "And now, if there's nothing else that can't wait, I'll give my new assistant a guided tour of the Tower."

Darran throttled a gasp. "You, sir? Surely that is something more properly done by—" The protest withered and died in the face of His Highness's cool gaze. "Yes, sir. Certainly, sir. I have no further pressing business for you at this moment, sir."

"Good. I, however, do have some for you," said His Highness. "Reschedule the remainder of today's appointments and then inform my tailor and my bootmaker that I shall want to see them here as soon as possible, for Asher's fittings. Oh yes, and advise the palace provisioner that Asher and I will come and see her at some point this afternoon about furnishing the Tower's Green Floor to his tastes."

Darran nearly moaned aloud. His Highness was lodging the brute *here*? In the *Tower*? But *nobody* lived in here, saving His Highness. Staff lodged elsewhere, mainly the palace, and walked to work.

Lodging the ruffian here was an unprecedented mark of regard.

His Highness was staring. "Darran?"

"Yes, sir. Of course, sir."

"Naturally, you won't refer to Asher by his new title. Yet."

After a quick glance to make sure Willer was taking notes, Darran nodded. "Certainly, sir."

The prince frowned. "You'll need to inform the kitchen, too, so we all have enough to eat. And something else—oh yes." He stopped his headlong rush towards disaster and looked at the lout. "You've not changed your mind about Cygnet, have you? You'd not prefer another horse?"

Darran choked. A *horse*? On top of everything, His Highness was giving this peasant a *horse*? Worth an absolute *fortune*? Oh dear Barl preserve them.

"No, sir," the lout said. "Cygnet'll do me just fine."

"All right then," the prince said, nodding. "Darran, let Matt know he's just lost himself a stable hand, and that Cygnet henceforth belongs to Asher. Now, is that everything? Yes, I think it is."

"Wages," said the lout, scowling.

"Ah, yes. How could I forget that?" Taking the pen back from Willer, His Highness found a scrap of paper, scribbled on it, folded it in half and held it out. "Here is Asher's revised wage, Darran. It's a confidential matter, you understand?"

Darran took the proffered note with numb fingers. "Of course,

Your Highness," he said woodenly. "Your Highness, a question, if I may be so bold."

The prince frowned. "Of course. Since when do you need my permission to ask a question?"

Since you foisted this uneducated braggard upon me and called him your champion! Somehow, Darran managed a deferential smile. "I'm sorry, sir. It's just that I find myself a trifle confused as to the correct etiquette involved. To be blunt, sir, does this—your—does Asher report to me? Or do I report to him?"

"Neither," replied the prince. "You both report to me. On occasion, Asher will have cause and leave to speak with my voice. You will know when he does so. Otherwise I expect you to work together as equals with separate duties. Is that clear?"

Darran inclined his head. "Quite clear, sir. Thank you. And just one final point, a very small point I know, but it's best to be clear on these things from the beginning, don't you agree?"

The prince sighed. "What?"

"Where, precisely, does Willer fit into these...new arrangements?"

"Willer?" His Highness said blankly. "He doesn't. Willer's your assistant. Asher's mine. But if he should require any help, of course Willer will give it to him happily. Won't you, Willer?"

Willer flushed. "Yes, Your Highness. Of course, Your Highness."

The prince nodded. "Excellent. Well, we'll leave you now to get those messengers organised. Thank you for your time, Darran."

Darran bowed low, despite the scarlet ache in his middle. "Not at all, sir. My time is yours to command, as always."

The office door closed with a thud behind the prince and his boorish companion.

Willer, choking, spewed forth a laugh laced with horror and spite and collapsed into his chair. "Darran, I can't believe it. Can you believe it? His Highness has gone *mad*! Should I send for Pother Nix?"

Because the situation was so dire Darran decided not to flay Willer for his undisciplined outburst. In truth, it was something of a relief to know that his feelings were so perfectly shared. Heart pounding, mouth dry, he opened the slip of paper the prince had handed him and looked at the amount of money His Highness was prepared to throw away every week on the loutish ruffian he had, so incredibly, so inexplicably, taken into his employ.

Fifty trins.

Only twenty-five trins less than he earned himself after a lifetime of loyal service and immense personal sacrifice.

Hot thick hatred stirred. Who was he, this ruffian, this lout, this *stranger*, to march into all their lives and turn them topsy-turvy in such a fashion? Prince's Champion? Champion troublemaker, more like. Champion disturber of the peace. Champion error of judgement, and if he could say so he would, save that he knew his prince well enough to recognise the signs of an unwise idea firmly rooted. Knew, to his everlasting despair and from bitter personal experience, that no amount of wisdom or sage and loving advice would breach the determined certainty of royalty bent upon indulging an intemperate whim.

"Darran?" said Willer.

He refolded the scrap of paper into a tiny lump with swift, furious precision. "What?"

"Pother Nix. Shall I send for him?"

"Of course not! His Highness isn't ill, he is merely...enthusiastic. That ill-bred lout won't last a week."

Willer chewed his lip. "But what if he does? What if he lasts, I don't know, forever?"

Darran felt his stomach lurch. "Nonsense. I can assure you, my dear Willer, that he won't last anywhere near that long. You and I will see to that."

"We will?" said Willer, a delighted smile lighting his pasty face. "Excellent!" Then the smile collapsed. "Um...how?"

With a contemptuous flick of his fingers, Darran disposed of the little paper wad into the rubbish basket. "I don't know, precisely. Not yet. But I'll tell you this, my friend: if we give Asher of Restharven enough rope you can be sure that sooner or later he'll hang himself."

As he climbed the spiralling Tower staircase behind the prince, Asher chuckled. "Dathne were right. Reckon that Darran don't care for me at all."

The prince sighed and glanced over his shoulder. "Don't take it personally. Darran doesn't care for anybody overmuch; he was born under a disapproving star. But he's served my family all his life and he really is very good at his job, so I bear with his foibles. You'll just have to bear with them too." A sudden chuckle. "Do you know, I think this is going to be *fun*."

Asher snorted. "Well, I reckon it's goin' to be *somethin'*. Don't reckon I'd swim a long way to call it *fun*." He frowned with sudden thought. "Eh. What am I s'posed to call you, anyways?"

The prince swung about, walking backwards. "Well, in public you continue to call me 'sir' or 'Your Highness.' Around here, and whenever it's just us, you'll call me Gar, of course. Why? What did you think you'd be calling me?"

"Mad," said Asher cheerfully. "As a gaffed fish."

By the time the late-setting summer sun had sunk into shadow, a bewildering array of things had happened. Asher had an entire floor of the Tower to himself, acres of space, with a bedchamber and his very own privy closet and a sitting room and library—a right waste of space, that—and an office even, since Gar seemed to think he'd be up to his eyebrows in work soon enough.

More than that, each room was now filled with furniture chosen from a vast array of beds and tables and sofas and desks and cup-boards and whatnots stored in an entire wing of the palace. Even as the last stick of it huffed and puffed its way upstairs on the stout backs of various servants, there were maids with dusters and polishing cloths and sheets and pillows and towels and who knew what else rushing in to make his new accommodation fit for a prince.

Or, in his case, a prince's champion.

He grinned at the thought. Though he'd drown himself before admitting it aloud, he quite liked the sound of the title. For certain sure it'd make Da smile when he found out.

After the cheerful, crowded disorder of the stable lads' dormitory the solitary splendour of the Green Floor was nearly too much to take in.

And that wasn't all.

Much to his dismay the summoned tailor had arrived as bidden, breathless with excitement and rushing, with a whole school of under-lings in his wake. Before Asher could open his mouth to protest they had him stripped down to his drawers and were crawling all over him with tape measures and fabric samples, cotton and lawn and brocade and wool and linen and velvet and silk and leather, most of them in colours he wasn't exactly sure a man should wear. When he started to say this the tailor, a small man with busy fingers and a voice like the crack of a bullwhip, rapped him on the knuckles with his shears and told him to hold his tongue, what did a brawny musclebound bubble-head know about the finer points of fashion, pray?

Knuckles stinging, temper seething, he'd held his tongue.

Gar, drat him, had nearly fallen over with laughing before being diverted by a disapproving Darran to deal with a newborn crisis somewhere in the City.

By the time the tailor and his scurrying minions were done there were plans for some twelve different changes of clothes, plus extra shirts, weskits and trews and two sets of riding leathers. Even as he stood there being poked and prodded and stuck with careless pins, three of the sweating underlings had set up two treadle sewing machines and a portable cutting table, rolled out bolts of brown and black and blue and green and dull bronze fabrics and, following some quick sketches by their employer, somehow produced three shirts and two pairs of britches for him to be going on with.

When they were done, Asher dressed himself in blue and black and gazed at his unfamiliar reflection in the mirror, shocked to silence. Such fine clothes! He looked practically posh. If his brothers could see him now, they'd *puke*. He grinned. Well, see him they would in a year's time. He'd make sure to wear the fanciest weskit he still had left, just for the pleasure of their slumguzzled faces.

While the tailor and his underlings were making their last-minute adjustments the bootmaker arrived. More measuring. A servant was sent to his shop with instructions to bring back some on-hand boots and shoes that would do, at a pinch, until the made-to-measure items were ready. Asher, slipping his feet into butter-soft dark blue leather, couldn't imagine any boot could be finer. But the grimacing boot-maker said that while such journeyman items might be fine for an Olken off the street, for a personage as grand as—as—the prince's assistant, well, they were barely up to snuff.

Asher stared. It was his first inkling that perhaps his life was going to change in a lot more ways than he'd bargained for.

Eventually the last bowing and scraping body left and he was alone in his grand new apartments. A message was delivered from the prince: family matters would keep him at the palace that evening; he should feel free to dine whenever he felt hungry.

"Ha," said Asher, staring at the hastily scrawled note. Now what was he supposed to do with himself? In reply his stomach grumbled demandingly, so he went down to the kitchen for his dinner. There, the scandalised cook sent him away with a scolding lecture about the dire consequences of important personages running their own errands.

Suitably chastened and thoroughly educated on the uses of Tower lackeys, he went back upstairs and amused himself by rearranging furniture until his supper arrived.

After his meal, a delectable chicken casserole with baked leeks, and a raspberry fool for dessert, he sat back in his solitary sitting room and sipped the last of the crisp white wine that had accompanied his dinner. Some bright spark had left a pile of books on his bedside table—Gar, most like, being funny—but he couldn't begin to care about *Olken Law as it Pertains to Equal Weights and Measures in Commerce* tonight... or, possibly, *ever*.

Adrift, chartless and lost in unsailed waters, he headed for a familiar port.

As he'd hoped, he found Matt doing the rounds of his stable yard, quietly checking each horse, making sure no rugs had slipped, no bellies were colicking, no legs had filled with heat and swelling unnoticed. Hearing the crunch of boots on gravel, Matt turned. The flickering lamplight from outside each stable shadowed the look on his broad face into a mystery.

"Cygnet's a fine animal," he said. "He'll take good care of you."

"Aye," said Asher, and headed for his new mount's stable. The horse, a shimmering silver grey with eyes like blue glass, shifted in the straw and poked a cautious nose over the stable door. Rippled velvet-soft nostrils and nickered, a flirty little sound inviting apples.

Matt reached into his pocket. "Here," he said, and tossed Asher half a Golden Dewdrop. Catching it one-handed, Asher let Cygnet lip it from his fingers. Inhaled the rich scent of horse and crushed apple, and for the first time thought that perhaps he hadn't made such a blundering great mistake after all.

"I keep thinkin' I'm dreamin'," he said, tickling his horse under the chin. Cygnet's lower lip drooped, wobbling, and his eyelids half closed in simple pleasure. "One minute I'm muckin' out stables and the next..." Baffled, almost afraid, he shook his head. "And I still don't see how I'm s'posed to make a success of it."

There was an upturned bucket outside Ballodair's stable. Matt eased his way over to it and sat down, elbows braced on his knees, fingers laced to cradle his chin. The prince's stallion came to investigate. Blew in Matt's close-cropped hair, lost interest, and returned to eating hay.

"I think," Matt said, slowly, "by being the prince's friend."

"His *friend*?" Asher stared. "Me? Why? He's got hisself scores of friends, ain't he?"

"I don't think so." Matt's expression was sober, his voice melancholy. "He has... hangers-on. Toadies. Opportunists who see in him their own advancement and royal favour. But friends? No."

"Why not?"

Matt looked at him. "You know why not."

"Asher tugged gently on Cygnet's forelock, frowning. Yes, he knew. "How'd he get hisself born without magic anyways?"

In the flickering lamplight Matt's expression echoed the sorrow in his voice. "Nobody's sure. It just happens. Not often, though, and never before in the royal family."

"Still, it ain't his fault. And he ain't contagious."

"No. But he reminds the other Doranen that they and their magic are not invulnerable, or invincible. And they hate him for it."

"*Hate?*" said Asher, startled. "But he's the king's son."

Matt lifted one shoulder. "Which is why their enmity is subtle, Asher. A handshake released too quickly. A smile that doesn't quite reach the eyes. Nothing a body could point to and say, see? But it's there, and he knows it. He's no fool, Prince Gar. He knows it." He shook his head. "You watch your step, my friend. Like it or not you're in their world now...and there's more than one kind of shark swimming in the sea."

Asher snorted. "I grew up with sharks, Matt, and six brangling brothers besides. Reckon I can take care of m'self."

"Yes," said Matt, and once again his face was shadowed. "Yes, you probably can. Now I'd best say goodnight, for I've more stables to check and other work besides."

"I'll help," said Asher promptly. "I may be *important* now, Barl save me, with folk bowin' and scrapin' and fallin' over 'emselves to put a smile on m'face, but I ain't too pretty or proud to lend a hand."

"No, there's no need, you shouldn't—" Matt began. Then he stopped. Looked to be making a decision. "All right then," he said, and smiled. "Can't say I won't appreciate the company. Thanks."

Asher grinned. "That be thanks, *sir*, I reckon," he said. And laughed as Matt threw an apple at him.

CHAPTER SEVEN

So," said Dana, Queen of Lur, as her gathered family shared the evening meal, "was I imagining things, Gar, or did I hear one of the maids say that you'd hired a young Olken man to replace Darran?"

Her husband's fork stopped halfway to his mouth. "What? You've pensioned off Darran?" King Borne demanded. "Barl's nightcap. He'll be heartbroken!"

"I do wish you wouldn't swear," Dana complained gently. "At least not at the dinner table. And not in front of Fane."

"Oh, Mama," Fane protested. "Honestly. That's not swearing. *Swearing* is—"

"Inappropriate for the heir presumptive," said Durm. "Exercise a little self-control, madam." The Master Magician's fleshy face, carved with deep lines of experience and the trials of containing strong magics, reflected his displeasure. Beneath sparse grey eyebrows his eyes snapped and sparked, seething power never far from the surface of his skin.

But Fane was not afraid of power. "Well, if it's inappropriate for me, why is it all right for Papa? *Papa* swears all the time, and he's the king!"

A lively debate erupted. Gar sighed, sat back in his chair with his goblet of red wine and waited for the storm to pass. Once, just once, it would be nice to dine with his family without some trivial matter starting a battle royal. No pun intended. But Fane had been born under a quarrelsome star and it seemed a day could not go by without her living up to that birthright with a vengeance. Pity the poor fool who ended up marrying her.

After some five minutes of his sister's vigorous opinionatedness it was their mother, as usual, who held sway.

"Well, I don't care if Barl herself rushed about the countryside shrieking *rot my toenails*, I won't have that kind of language at the dinner table!" she declared. "Do I make myself clear?"

Borne took her hand in his and raised it to his lips. "As crystal, my love." His expression rearranged itself into sombre contrition. "We are duly chastised."

"Ha!" said Dana, and tugged his beard. "If only I thought you were!"

Gar hid his grin in his goblet. Fane groaned. "Oh, must you? *Flirting* at the dinner table is—"

"The prerogative of your parents," said Borne, affectionately severe. "Stop being tiresome, brat." As Fane subsided, pouting, he considered Gar and added, "Well? Have you?"

"Have I what?" said Gar. "Pensioned off Darran? No, of course not. Much as I'd like to." He shrugged. "But I have hired myself an assistant."

Fane speared a minted baby potato and nibbled it from her fork.

"An assistant?" She was looking especially pretty this evening, with her silver-gilt hair loose and gently curling round her face, and her soft skin glowing in the glimfire light. Her tunic was the particular shade of blue that brought out to perfection the diamond clarity of her eyes. "What for? You don't do anything."

Gar watched his father's gaze sharpen and shook his head, fractionally. There was no point. Fane was Fane, and he'd long grown used to her viperish tongue. Voice determinedly light he said, "And now I'll be able to do even less. Aren't I lucky?"

Borne frowned into his wine. "What kind of assistance are you expecting this person to provide?"

"The Olken Administrating kind." Borne looked up. Gar met his eyes steadily, and added, "I thought you might have it mentioned on Barlsday. Two announcements for the price of one, so to speak."

Dana, spreading butter on a fresh piece of bread, smiled at him. "You always were an economical child. So who is this person? Do we know him? Her?"

"Him," said Gar. "No. You've not met. His name is Asher, of Restharven."

Borne's frown deepened. "The fisherman you hired on as a stable hand?" Fane choked back laughter, and he raised a swift hand, silencing her. "Gar, is this wise? Surely Darran—"

"Darran has more than enough to do already," said Gar. "Besides, he's not suitable for my purpose."

Borne's eyebrows lifted. "And a stable hand is?"

"A man is not merely his employment, sir. Were you to start mucking out stables tomorrow, still you'd be who and what you are."

"Yes, dear, that's true, but even so..." Dana hesitated. "You must admit, it's rather a leap. There'll be a bees' hive of gossip once the appointment is made public. It's unusual to say the least, to elevate a stable hand so high. You can't think there won't be some... consternation."

Gar shrugged. "People will talk no matter who I choose. Since it's impossible to please everyone I decided to please myself and let the rest of the beehive buzz itself to strangulation."

Fane turned to the Master Magician. "What do you think, Durm? Gar's mad to hire some smelly ruffian he barely knows anything about to be his personal assistant, isn't he?"

"My opinion is irrelevant," said Durm, politely smiling, "given that this matter is unrelated to magic."

"Huh," said Fane with a toss of her head. "Well, I think he's utterly deranged. I mean, what could a fisherman stablehand possibly know about anything besides horse manure and fish guts? Gar's going to be a laughing stock. Which means *I'll* be a laughing stock too, because it's my stupid brother who hired this—this—"

"Darling..." said Dana, shaking her head.

Ignoring Fane, Gar stared at his father. "I assure you, sir, my decision wasn't made upon a whim. I've given this matter a great deal of thought. I chose Asher carefully, and for good reason."

The king sat back in his chair, one finger tracing the etched base of his wine goblet. "Indeed. And while you were ruminating on your choice did you happen to consider the reaction of a man like Conroyd Jarralt, once the news got out?"

"There you go being rude about Conroyd Jarralt again," said Fane, pulling a face. "I wish you'd explain why you don't like him. *I* like him. I think he's very charming and terribly good-looking. Even if he is old enough to be my father."

Gar turned on her. "Charm and good looks being in your tiny little book the most important attributes for leadership!"

She flushed and her eyes glittered dangerously. Lips curved in a poison-sweet smile she said, "At least he's not a cr—"

"*Fane!*" said Borne. His fist crashed on the tabletop so that all their goblets and the silverware jumped. Wine splashed, scarlet, on the white damask tablecloth. Fane retreated into sulky silence.

"It's all right," Gar said, his voice low. "It doesn't matter. Father, I'm truly sorry if I've displeased you. That wasn't my intention."

Borne's expression thawed. "Then why did you proceed without first asking my advice? You've not even been officially declared, Gar. If you must have such an unlikely-sounding assistant, and I'm still not convinced you should, why not at least delay announcing him until—"

"Because it wouldn't make any difference, sir," said Gar. "A few days, a week, a month, even: in the end it would be the same. Regardless of how long I wait to announce Asher's appointment, Jarralt will still carp and cavil at the idea of an Olken elevated to such a high position. So I choose to announce it now. And in proceeding as I have, without your involvement, his censure will fall solely upon me."

"You think so?" said Borne with a smile that did not quite reach his troubled eyes. "You give him too much credit. He'll say your poor judgement and want of conduct reflect a shabby discipline and a sad lack of upbringing."

"He may indeed say that," said Durm, stirring in his chair. "But not with impunity."

Gar watched his father and his father's best friend exchange swift grins. Opposite him, his mother sniffed.

"At any rate," she said, "I'm sure I don't see what concern it is of Conroyd Jarralt's if Gar decides to appoint an assistant. If Con does complain, Borne, tell him to mind his own business and be done with it." Another sniff. "Besides, his real problem is that he's never forgiven you the fact your great-great-great-grandfather bested his in the Crown Trials after Trevoyle died."

"I think you'll find," Borne replied, "that his pique springs from a more...domestic source. If he is unforgiving, my dear, it's because I won the prize he so desperately desired for himself."

"I neither confirm nor deny your theory," she said, dimpling. "Instead I would point out that poor Conroyd carries a grudge like a dog with a very old, very smelly bone. Somebody needs to smack him on the nose and tell him to drop it, once and for all."

"By all means," said Borne, his face alight with love and laughter. "Provided it's not me expected to do the smacking."

Dana smiled back at him. "Oh no. I'll do it. Barl knows I smacked him often enough when he was courting me."

Borne pressed a kiss to her palm. "It delights me beyond words to hear it."

"By the Wall," moaned Fane, spirits revived, and dropped her napkin over her face like a veil. "I'm going to be indelicately ill."

Laughter banished the last of the lingering tensions. The remains of the main course were cleared away, a careless word from Durm removed the wine stain from the tablecloth, and dessert was served. Pushing aside his berry compôte and cream scarcely touched, Borne tapped his fingernails on the table.

"If I may briefly and, I promise, sweetly, return to this matter of your new assistant, Gar..."

Gar nodded, masking his wariness with a smile. "Certainly, sir."

"I simply wonder why you'd choose an unsophisticated labourer to aid you in your duties when there must be dozens of polished, trustworthy Olken eager to serve you, and their people, in the position."

Gar hesitated. How to explain a feeling? A tickle in the brain that said, illogically, irrationally, that in Asher he'd found a man who could be trusted with any secret, any sorrow, any task no matter how trivial or tremendous.

He couldn't. At least not here, in front of Durm and Fane.

He said, obliquely, "Matt speaks very highly of him. He's courageous, hardworking and forthright, with a refreshing lack of

obsequiousness." Leaning over the table towards his father, Gar
willed him to understanding. "Sophistication, sir, is an overcoat that
any man may put on, but it can't hide the flaws beneath. I'll take honest unrefinement over sophisticated flattery any day."

Dana laughed. "Gracious, Gar. This young man sounds a positive
paragon!"

"Darran doesn't think so," said Gar, grinning. "Darran is more
appalled by him than Conroyd Jarralt could ever be, I promise you.
Nor do I think he's a paragon, either. But I do believe Asher of Restharven will be invaluable to me as I seek to deepen my understanding of his people, so that I may serve them, and His Majesty, more
diligently."

Fane sighed and rolled her eyes. "They're Olken, Gar. What more
is there to understand?"

"That is an ignorant observation, madam," said Durm, his expression heavy with disapproval.

Fane turned to him, flushed and resentful. "That's not fair! You've
no opinion of them either, you know you don't! 'A race with little to
recommend them save their muscle and a degree of business acumen.'
That's what you think, you said so not a week ago!"

Gar stared into the cooling remains of his berries and cream,
unwanted now, for fear Durm should see the look on his face. It
shamed and embarrassed him to hear his people disparage the Olken
like that. How much worse did it sound, then, such sentiments coming from the kingdom's Master Magician? It set a bad example. He
wished he could say as much to Durm, point out to him the unfortunate impression he was making...but of course, that was impossible.

Once, long ago, he and Durm had been master and pupil, and
friends of a sort as well. But then had come the dawning realisation
that the king's precious heir was, incredibly, devoid of magic, scarcely
better than an Olken, and their circumstantial friendship hadn't survived the ensuing frustrations and disappointments, the battles to
wring from him even the smallest hint of magical ability. Bitter days.

Then the unthinkable happened. The WeatherWorker sired a second child. And with Fane barely walking and already showing promise of a talent unimaginable, he'd been discarded entirely. Left to the
devices of mere scholars and bookmen. The pain of that abandon-
ment had been shot through with a sobbing relief.

Now he and the Master Magician were courteous strangers whose
paths crossed in Council, during official functions and at family din-
ners like this one. Because Durm was the king's best friend and closest

confidant after the queen, they maintained a superficial cordiality...
but it was a sham, and they both knew it. He could not forgive Durm's
lack of understanding and compassion, and the Master Magician
would not forgive his former pupil's failure.

Durm said now, his full face glowering, "It is true that I described
the Olken thus in private, because it is my private opinion and I make
no apology for it. But I have never said the like in public. Nor have I
ever said, madam, publicly *or* privately, that the Olken were not to be
understood. One day, Barl grant it be long hence, you will be this
kingdom's WeatherWorker, charged with the sacred duty of keeping it
safe. Therefore it is imperative that you comprehend the Olken's place
in Barl's great design. Granted it is insignificant, but that is not the
point. As WeatherWorker, every life in the kingdom will depend on
you. *Every* life, Olken as well as Doranen."

Eyes brilliant with tears Fane said hotly, "I know all that! You tell
me almost every day! All I meant was—"

Durm raised his plump hand, silencing her midsentence. "Your
meaning was lamentably clear. You are not interested in the Olken,
and therefore you dismiss them as unimportant. But if they were
unimportant, Barl would have deemed them so and she did not. You
and I may fail to understand her reasoning, but we must never question it. That is blasphemous ignorance, and an ignorant monarch is to
be abhorred. You know as well as I that your father relies upon your
brother's counsel and commitment in matters concerning the Olken.
In due course, if you are wise, you will find yourself relying upon
them too. Especially if you persist in this scandalous refusal to recognise what is important and what is not."

Choking back sobs, Fane shoved her chair away from the table and
stumbled out of the dining room. As the door banged shut behind her
Dana favoured the Master Magician with a furious glare.

"Why not send for a stick to beat her with while you're about it,
Durm? For certain she can't be properly chastised until she's bleeding
on the outside as well as within!"

It was Durm's turn to flush. "Majesty—"

"Oh, never mind," she snapped. "I'd tell you to remember that for
all her talent she's still a child, but I'd be wasting my breath."

Borne reached his hand out to her. "My love—"

She shook him free. "Yes, yes, you defend him, Borne, just as you
always do. Are you as blind as he, then? Barl save us all! Why can't
you see her as she is, here and now, instead of what she'll become one
day? I'm not saying she was right. She was wrong, we all know that.

She knows that. But there was no need to tear her down in such a fashion, not in public. Not in front of you."

Borne sighed. "Dana, my heart, you must accept the truth. Fane is fifteen years old and the days of her childhood are dwindling. There is little time left for indulgence and excuses."

Now the queen's eyes were bright with unshed tears. "But I don't accept it," she whispered harshly. "I shall never accept it. *Never.*"

Borne's face twisted with a sudden grief and he reached for her again. His hand trembled. "Dearest—"

"No," she said. "I'm sorry. I must go to her." Pulling away from him a second time she followed her daughter from the room, waving the doors open and then closed behind her with an impatient hand.

"It is I who should apologise," Durm said into the stricken silence. "Perhaps I was too harsh. But Fane is so talented, so rare. When she says such ill-considered things I—"

"It's all right," said Borne wearily. "Fane has never been one to take a rebuke lightly, you know that. As for the queen, well..."

"Indeed," said Durm.

"You are dear to her, old friend, never doubt it," Borne insisted. "But she worries, and it makes her short of temper." With a barely stifled grunt, he got to his feet. "So I think, if you'll excuse me..."

Durm shook his head and stood. "No, Borne. You and your son doubtless have more to discuss on this matter of his assistant, and any soothing of ruffled feathers is best done by the one who ruffled them."

Slowly, Borne sat down again. "If you're sure..."

Durm smiled. "I am always sure." He pressed a hand to his heart and bowed, favoured Gar with a noncommittal nod and withdrew, closing the dining room door quietly after him.

"Well," said the king with a short laugh. "So much for our jolly family dinner."

"Mama has a point." Gar reached for the wine carafe so he could refill his goblet. "Fane is still young."

"There have been kings and queens of Lur younger than she." Borne massaged his temples, and between his closed eyes the skin was pinched with pain. "Weather Workers all. She needs to grow up."

"And so she will, in time," said Gar. "But youth isn't the only pebble in her shoe."

Borne's mouth set in a thin, mulish line. "You're wrong."

"Of all the reasons there are to admire you, sir, your loyalty is the greatest. But loyalty needn't be blind. Indeed it mustn't be, for blind loyalty is no kindness at all. It's a curse."

"I don't wish to hear this from you," said Borne. "Fane is your sister. She loves you."

Gar sighed. Fortified himself with a long swallow of wine. "My sister knows precisely why she was born, and what will be forever denied her, and given her, because of it. There are few things more wearing, Father, than an unwelcome obligation. Were Fane's feelings for me contained in a coin, and were you to flip that coin, there's no saying which side would land face up: love, or hate."

Borne's head jerked at that, and his eyes blazed. "That is a monstrous thing to say!"

Gar nodded. "I know. But it's true."

"You are *wrong*."

"Father—"

"She is young. Too young for the burdens placed upon her shoulders, too young for the knowledge Durm burns into her morning, noon and night."

"But not so young she doesn't understand conversations overheard in corners, the scurrilous speculations repeated by those who should know better than to speak in the presence of a child." Gar tipped the rest of his wine down his throat.

"You babble like a brook," said Borne, his face turned away, his fingers knotted on the table. "You make no sense."

"You think I've not heard the rumours too? The stories? The gossip?" said Gar, knowing he failed to banish all bitterness and hating himself for it. "They say her talent is unnatural. They say she received the magic that should have come to me, as well as her own share. They say—"

"'They' are fools, Gar! And Fane doesn't believe the ignorant ramblings of—"

"Yes, she does, Father," Gar said quietly. "You know she does. Even though she understands the tales are rumour, half-truths, distortions of fact. Deep inside she thinks she's a thief. The sight of me is a knife in her heart, pricking."

"You are wrong."

Gar shook his head. "No. You simply wish I was."

Borne stood, his back turned, his head bowed. "It must stop, Gar. The bickering, the blame. It must *stop*."

"How? Will you tell her she can't feel? She was born to correct a mistake and for no other reason. Every waking moment of her life is dedicated to that end. If you forbid Fane her feelings, Father, what does she have left that belongs to her and her alone?"

Slowly Borne turned. "And if you were not as you are? If you had your birthright? Would you feel as she does? Trapped and prisoned and born for a purpose not of your own choosing, but mine?"

Gar shrugged. "How can I know? I'm not the WeatherWorker-in-Waiting."

Borne seized the back of his chair, gripping it with a white-knuckled ferocity. "Do you wish you were?"

Gar flinched. Reluctantly he met his father's burning gaze. All his life a conspiracy of silence had shrouded this, his family's festering wound. The wound he had caused by being born incomplete. That had only partially been healed by Fane's birth and the discovery that she was a prodigy whose powers might one day rival those of Blessed Barl herself.

He said, very carefully, "You've never asked me that before."

His father nodded. "I'm asking you now. Do you wish you were my heir?"

Gar stared at the tablecloth. Did he wish it? Did he envy Fane the birthright that should have been his? Covet the power that danced at her fingertips and lit her eyes like lanterns? Did he want to one day be the kingdom's WeatherWorker, even though he knew better than almost anyone breathing what that meant? The sacrifices and the savagery?

Oh yes. A thousand times yes. He wanted it so badly the desire ate his belly like an acid, churned in him and welled unbidden from his eyes in the hollow privacy of the night.

He looked up and smiled at his father, seeing in the tired face a maelstrom of dread and hope. He shook his head. "No, sir, I don't. I'm content with the life Barl has seen fit to give me."

And because he'd had a lifetime of practice in concealment, or because the need to believe was so desperate, or both, his father believed him.

Fractionally, Borne's whitened knuckles eased their grip on the back of the chair, and some of the strain eased. "I'm glad," he said, and sat down again. A small sigh escaped his pale lips. "And not because I fear the king you would have made, Gar. In truth, I think you'd be a king without peer, for reasons having nothing to do with magic. Reasons that Fane must learn if she's to be the queen this realm deserves and requires."

Another thing that had never before been said. It was long moments before Gar could trust his voice again. "Thank you, sir. I value your opinion above all others."

"You must help her see," his father said. "Durm can teach her everything there is to know about magic and the uses of power. Your mother can advise her on protocol and the womanly arts. I can explain from sunup to sundown the intricacies and hidden traps of government...but only you can help her see the richest crop in all our kingdom. The Olken, Lur's original children. You possess in abundance the one thing Fane lacks. The common touch. The Olken love you."

"And you!" Gar said swiftly.

Borne smiled and shook his head. "After a fashion, perhaps. Though I think it's more reverence than love. The functions I perform on their behalf, rather than myself. But you? You they hold in genuine and heartfelt affection and I thank Barl for it. I wish Fane were held in half as much respect."

"Give her time," said Gar. "Her life is circumscribed by study. She has yet to come to know them as I have these past months."

"Perhaps," Borne agreed. "I hope it is that and nothing more. She'll be queen soon enough and then it will be too late..."

Gar felt his heart constrict. "Again you raise the spectre of a diminishing hourglass, sir." His voice sounded harsh, almost accusing. "What haven't I been told? I wish you'd confide in me. I'm no longer a child. Are you unwell?"

Startled, Borne lifted his head to look at him, then smiled. "Unwell? Why, no. No more than usual. Did I frighten you? I'm sorry. I didn't mean to."

"You look tired," said Gar, his voice low.

"I am, a little," Borne admitted. "It's summer, and nearly time for harvest. The magic is strong now. Difficult to contain. Less a matter of subtlety, and more of brute strength. Today's WeatherWorking has given me a headache, that's all. It's nothing. There's no need to fret on my behalf."

But Gar, staring at him, thought there was. He looked weary. Worn down. "I wish I could help you," he said, his throat tight and hurting.

"You help me every day," his father said firmly. "You do as much as any member of either Council. More. Sometimes I think you do too much. When was the last time you went out riding with friends, hmm? Frolicked on a picnic? Asked a pretty girl to dance?"

Discomfited, Gar shrugged. "I've been busy."

"Yes, I know!" Borne retorted. "It seems of late that every time I see you your nose is in a book or you're rushing off to yet another meeting somewhere. You're a young man, Gar, with a lifetime of meetings and books ahead of you. There's more to living than work, my son. You must make time for entertainment, for amusement." He smiled, an anxious upturn of lips. "For romance."

"Father..."

Borne slapped the table with the flat of his hand. "If you tell me once more you're determined to deny yourself a wife and children, I promise I'll become angry. Gar, you can't—"

"*Please*, Father!" Gar flung himself away to stand with his back turned, so he didn't have to see the look in his father's eyes. "I beg you, not again. The choice is mine and it's made. Please respect my right to make it, even if you don't agree with the decision."

"How can I agree with it?" Borne cried. "It's the wrong one!"

Gar turned around, made himself stare steadily into his father's face. "For you. Not for me."

Borne's imploring hands reached out across the dinner table towards him. "But Nix says—"

"That he can give no guarantees. A child of my body might well be fully functional...or it might not. I can't take the chance. I won't. Besides, there's still Fane. She'll give you grandchildren. She'll continue House Torvig's line."

Borne surged to his feet then, on a roar of anger. "Unfair! *Monstrous* unfair! Do you think I care only for the line?"

"If you didn't care," said Gar, distantly, "you never would've fought with the Privy Council for the right to conceive her. You and Durm would've chosen the next WeatherWorker from amongst the foremost Doranen in the kingdom. It's all right. I understand. It's why I've chosen this path." He held his father's gaze and added, gently, "You know I'm right, Father."

The king's eyes were bright with anguish. "I do not!"

Gar smiled. "Yes, you do. As things stand, I'm just...an unfortunate aberration. Inconvenient, but not threatening. Could you say the same if I were to have a child, and that child were...like me? That would no longer be considered an aberration. It'd be seen as a pattern and a shadow would fall over Fane. Before we knew it men like Conroyd Jarralt would be arguing that our line is tainted, that it's grown weak, that the crown would be safer on a different head. *His* head. Even though some would argue his line has a taint all its own. And so it would begin again: the nightmare of dynastic warfare, the struggle for the throne, and who knows where it would end? The last such war brought us to the brink of disaster and the Wall nearly to ruin. You didn't raise a son so selfish that he'd drag a whole kingdom to the edge of that abyss just to spare himself a little loneliness."

Silence, then, as Borne struggled...failed...to find an argument he could stand against his son's austere logic. "You've never told me any of this before. Never explained why..."

Gar bit his lip. "Talking about it doesn't change anything, it only—"

"Makes things harder," Borne whispered. "I'm sorry." He turned away then, pressing his sleeve to his face.

"Don't be," said Gar, his voice a hair's-breadth from breaking. "It's not your fault. It's not anybody's fault. It's just the way things are."

"Is there something I can do? Tell me what I can do."

"You can accept my decision. And promise me you'll never question it again."

Silence. Gar waited, holding his breath.

At last his father nodded, his back still turned, his shoulders bowed.

Gar released the air from his aching lungs. "Thank you."

His father straightened and turned around. In his face nothing but determined good humour, all lingering traces of pain vanished. Banished. As though their last exchange had happened months ago. Or not at all. He sat.

"So. You're set on having this fisherman fellow as your assistant, are you?"

Weak with relief, Gar eased himself back into his own chair. "I took him with me to Justice Hall yesterday. For—an unsophisticated labourer, was it?—he demonstrated a remarkably keen grasp of legal niceties and a fine sense of right and wrong. Not to mention he saw through my motives for taking him there as though they were glass. Asher will grow into the task, Father, and not let me down. I'm sure of it. What's more, I think you'll like him too. Though he's rough around the edges, still there's a quality to him I know you'll recognise, and approve."

His father was frowning. "Justice Hall," he murmured. "A bad business, that. We were lucky to catch the rot before it spread any further. You did good work yesterday, my son. I'm proud."

"Thank you," said Gar, and let his warm pleasure show.

Pleased by that, smiling again, his father summoned the carafe closer with a snap of his fingers and refilled their goblets. "So. When do I get to meet this roughly likeable Asher, that I may judge his virtues for myself?"

Gar grinned. It only felt a little forced. "Actually I thought I'd bring him to the next Privy Council meeting."

His father snorted. "*After* he's been publicly announced as your assistant, you mean? In other words, you're putting off dealing with Jarralt's inevitable tantrum for as long as possible."

"You don't approve of the tactic?"

"On the contrary," Borne replied. "If you hadn't suggested it, I would've." He took another mouthful of wine and rolled it savouringly over his tongue before swallowing. "You do realise you're throwing your assistant into the deep end?"

"Well," said Gar, shrugging, "he is a fisherman, Father. I'm sure he knows how to swim."

"Is that so?" Borne lifted his goblet in salute, and warning. "Let us hope you're right, my son . . . for his sake, and the sake of us all."

CHAPTER EIGHT

With a sigh of satisfied weariness Dathne closed her accounts book and put down her pen. Recordkeeping was a tiresome chore but it had to be done. And there were times, especially after a brisk day's trading, when she almost found it pleasant. Although the bookshop was little more than an excuse for her presence in the City, she did enjoy running it, was relieved she had a knack for business. Closure of the bookshop would lead to awkward disruptions and, worse, would interfere with her breezy access to both Tower and palace—access that was vital now that Asher had arrived to usher in the Final Days.

The Final Days. It was at once a terrible and irritating phrase, raising questions without answers, fears without remedy. For one thing, how many of them were there? A month's worth? A summer's? A whole year? Was Lur living them now or were they not due to arrive until this time next year, perhaps? Could it be that Asher's arrival in Dorana was merely . . . Prophecy clearing its throat?

She had absolutely no idea. Prophecy didn't say.

In the Final Days shall come the Innocent Mage,
  born to save the world from blood and death.
He shall enter the House of the Usurper
He shall learn their ways

He shall earn their love
He shall lay down his life
And Jervale's Heir shall know him, and guide him,
   and enlighten him not.

That was it. That was all she had to help her, enlighten her, those few lines she'd been gifted with on her first day as Jervale's Heir.

Obscure didn't begin to describe it. What a shame her revered ancestor hadn't left a calendar complete with helpful hints and important dates marked in red to go with his damned foretelling.

Every night since Asher had at long last tumbled out of her dreams and into her life she'd gone to bed with the same prayer on her lips, in her heart: Jervale, send me another sign. Guide my steps. Show me what to do next.

But Jervale remained stubbornly silent.

A whisper from the shadows of her mind said: What if your prayers go unanswered because Jervale is as blind as you? What if he knows nothing beyond the verse he scribbled down all those centuries ago, when the Olken and the Doranen made their fateful pact? Or...what if he can't even hear you?

Shuddering, Dathne shoved her accounts book into the till and slammed shut the drawer. *No.* She wouldn't believe that. *Couldn't* believe that. Couldn't even let herself wonder. The kingdom of Lur depended on her remaining cool and controlled and confident.

There was no place in her life for doubt.

With the last of the day's shopkeeping duties seen to, habit sent her back to the front door, to double-check the locks. Not that theft was likely. The penalties were severe and the City Guard vigilant, but when young men drank an ale or three too many, as they were sadly wont to do, what might seem inadvisable in the sober light of day often became a rattling good idea in the tipsy rollick of the night.

Approaching the front window display of Vev Gertsik's latest romance she felt the tingle of magic, a breath of invisible power, breeze over her exposed skin. She frowned, shivering. It was the only drawback to her chosen, necessary profession: the constant whispering hum of Doranen books.

The Doranen disdained the use of ink and roller, the painstaking assemblage of type by industrious, un-magickal fingers. Not for them the sweat of laborious effort, the rattling, banging cheer of the type-setting workshop where Olken men and women used nimble skill to transform manuscripts into books that wore the badge of their imperfect creation proudly, like a flag.

No. Doranen books were sleek and polished and perfect. No misaligned letters, no smudging, no bleeding of colour on cover or frontispiece. Doranen books were birthed by spells and charms woven in a seamless song to call forth smooth pages and immaculate bindings. They attained a symmetry that the Olken Bookmakers' Guild could admire but never match.

As she checked the locked front door Dathne eyed askance the Gertsik book's cover with its languishing blonde heroine and stalwart blond hero locked in an unlikely embrace. The author's romances flew off the shelves almost as fast as they were unpacked. Gertsik was the darling of the Doranen, and a good many Olken readers as well. But Dathne couldn't bring herself to read them or approve of those Olken who did. Even though it wasn't their fault they were ignorant of all the other stories that could be, should be, told. Their own stories. Olken stories.

Vev Gertsik wrote soppy tales of Doranen love set in their Old Days, centuries dead and gone now and thus ripe for romanticising. The Old Days, when Doranen magic was limitless, when Barl and her lover Morgan had kissed, not killed, and war was as unthinkable as exile.

The Old Days, before civil strife and the desperate pitting of mage against mage had riven the long-lost land of Dorana with bloody lightning and given birth to a monster for whom no repression was too harsh, no punishment too cruel, no dark magic unimaginable. The Old Days, which had seen Barl and the other survivors of that terrible conflict stumble from their ruined cities in search of peace and freedom and a land where the monster Morg could not find them.

Before the coming of the Doranen the Olken had called Lur their own. They'd lived in thriving rural communities bound together by a dedication to the rhythms of life in all its tempestuous beauty and stark danger. The Olken of those long-dead days had lived small lives, true, but that didn't mean they were without value. On the contrary, those Olken lives had been priceless because they were theirs and wholly theirs. Untouched by foreign hands. Uncorrupted by an alien magic.

But there were no books written about the Old Days of the Olken. There couldn't be. Almost no-one alive in these modern times knew that once, before the coming of the fair-haired Doranen with their brash and brutal magic, the Olken had possessed power of their own. A soft and singing earth magic that bound them to the land and to each other without the need for mastery or control.

The only Olken who still recalled that magic, the way things used to be, belonged to the Circle. Sworn to secrecy and the scant words of a prophecy they didn't understand but were willing to die for, they remembered. In silence and sad dreams they kept the buried truth alive.

The loss of her people's heritage wrung Dathne's heart, though it had happened centuries ago. She would *never* accept that what they'd lost—no, what they'd given away, surrendered, sold—was worthless, no matter how glittering the gift in exchange. How safe and secure the life that had replaced it. And she'd sworn a fierce vow that one day every last Olken man, woman and child would learn their true heritage, reclaim their power, and that the bookshops of Lur would abound with stories of *their* Old Days.

If, after the Final Days were ended, there were still bookshops. If there was still a Lur.

Impatient, Dathne turned away from the locked front door and the book display, tugging at her haphazardly braided hair. That was enough maudlin sentimentality for one day. She had dinner to prepare yet, and after that orders to wrap ready for the morning's mail coach. With a swish of her skirts she headed out to the back of the shop and the staircase that led up to her small apartment.

The vision smote her halfway to the apartment door. Tripped her and sprawled her face down against the wooden stairs. She tried to rise. Failed, limbs leaden. She felt a tightness in her chest, heard a moan die in her throat. Her head moved restlessly against the scuffed timber, scraping her cheek. Her clutching fingers found splinters.

With her eyes shut tight and her mind a soundless scream of protest, she saw the future she'd been born to kill.

Hailstones of fire raining down from a sky the colour of clotted blood. Strong proud trees split asunder by spears of lightning. The River Gant rising, rising. Funnels of green cloud reaching thin, cruel fingers to pluck whole houses from the earth and fling them stone by stone by human bone into the howling winds. The Wall, pulsing, writhing, great holes like some gross leprous disease turning it to tatters. Broken bleeding bodies flung heedless into piles, into holes. Discarded. Disdained. And pressing down upon her an enormous smothering weight, crushing the air from her lungs and strangling the pulse in her veins. Within it a baleful intelligence: malevolent, insatiable and infinitely patient, squatting like a toad. Watching. Waiting.

Gasping for air, Dathne wrenched herself free. The effort sent her sliding backwards down the stairs till she came to a bruised and spreadeagled stop on the floor of the bookshop's workroom. Head and heart pounding, she stared at the worn blue carpet inches from her eyes and struggled to breathe, to forget, to remember. She felt befouled, her skin and soul smeared with the unspeakable detritus of evil.

When at last her heartbeat and breathing slowed she sat up, pushing sweaty strands of hair out of her eyes.

"Well," she said aloud, needing to hear her voice, any voice. Even a thin and frightened one. "They do say be careful what you wish for..." Breathy laughter shook her. Threatened to collapse into sobs. She pressed the back of her hand against her mouth, hard.

She'd always known the end would be terrible. For years she'd glimpsed snatches of it. Received scanty images bad enough to wake her sweating in the middle of the night. The knowledge of their possible future, the ultimate culmination of the Final Days, had dogged her like a shadow, visible only from the corner of her eye. But now she knew precisely the taste and sound and smell of what she and the others fought to prevent. Knew exactly *how* terrible, to the last drop of blood and the final, fading cry, Lur's death would be. The fear of that fate was merciless: a serpent coiled in her belly, waiting to strike.

Cold, Matt called her.

He didn't understand, and she could never explain it to him. There was only one way to defeat the serpent. Sheathe herself in ice. Freeze the tears that threatened when she thought of what would happen if she failed in her duty as Jervale's Heir.

Freeze her heart.

Panting, she closed her eyes. A mistake. Images of death and destruction flared. Her stomach churned. Sour saliva flooded her mouth. Lurching to her feet she scrambled upstairs to her tiny privy and emptied her spasming belly of the stewed rabbit and poached greens she'd eaten for lunch. Bile burned her throat, searing tears from her eyes. When at last she was empty she pressed her face into a damp towel. Swilled water round her mouth and spat it out.

Veira must know of this. She must be told that what they faced, what they and Asher must fight, was an intelligence. A person... or something pretending to be a person. It was unclear, and too terrible to dwell upon, at least so soon after enduring its foetid touch. Nevertheless, Veira must know.

Somewhere beyond the fragile safety of Barl's great Wall something... some*one*... was waiting. Not that Veira could do anything about it, of course, but it would be better if somebody else knew.

Less lonely.

Because she still felt unnerved and desolate she drank two full glasses of strong green wine, one straight after the other. Then, with warm lamplight dancing shadows on the walls of her small living room, she knelt by the fireplace and rummaged in the blanket box her mother had given her as a leaving-home gift. Buried at the bottom, beneath papers and letters and shawls with holes in she'd get around to mending one of these days, and frayed cushions she didn't want to throw out, was her precious Circle Stone. Gently withdrawing the blanket-shrouded treasure she unwrapped it, put it on the low wooden table by the window and sank cross-legged to the floor.

To anyone unknowing it was just a lump of rough quartz crystal, cracked and crazed and more dull than shiny, but to her it was priceless, her link to Veira and, through her, the rest of their Circle: a conduit to comfort and sanity when the weight of being Jervale's Heir grew too great for bearing. Her crystal and Veira's were twins, halves of a whole, forever joined no matter how vast the distances between them.

Using the Stone was at once simple and challenging. She was Olken. Her secret magic was a subtle thing, a matter of insinuation and gentle cajolery, soft as a whisper amidst the drowning shouts of brash and bossy Doranen incantation. Finding a quiet place in the chatter and noise of their magic was never easy: down the centuries its raucous echoes had soaked the City right down to the cobblestones. If she went deaf tomorrow she'd still feel its thrum against her skin and hear the racket of a thousand thousand charms ringing inside her skull.

The only good thing about the Doranen's loud magic was that it made detecting her a virtual impossibility. Somebody would have to be looking, and even then it was unlikely they'd hear her hushed voice in all the din.

Despite the evening's warmth, she shivered. "Don't be a fool, Dathne," she said aloud. "How can anybody be looking? No Doranen alive or dead knows you exist."

Which was just as well, given the consequences of discovery.

Closing her eyes, letting the lingering tension drain out of her neck and shoulders like rain sieving through sand, Dathne conjured Veira's face before her inner eye. Round and wrinkled like an ageing apple. Framed in a tangle of salt-streaked hair. Long bony nose. Dimpled chin. Eyes the colour of moss, which shimmered and shifted with her mercurial moods, now snapping with temper, now softened with sympathy.

Her fingers caressed the crystal, seeking the subtle vibrations that would lead her to the inner road, the pathway her thoughts would travel across the unknown miles that lay between her and Veira. The old woman's whereabouts were a secret... just in case.

Perfect peace. Perfect harmony. Breathe in. Breathe out. Thoughts like thistledown, floating on a breeze. *Veira...*

And Veira was with her. In the crystal, in her heart and mind, a warm, quizzical presence that never failed to calm and encourage. Or scold, if it seemed that scolding was called for.

It's been three days, child. I was beginning to worry.

Dathne felt her lips move, framing each word as it winged its way along the invisible connection joining her crystal to Veira's. "I'm sorry. I didn't mean to concern you, I—" She stopped. Was shamed by a sudden rush of emotion at the sound and touch of the old woman's voice.

Child, is aught amiss? There's an echo of something wicked and wild in you tonight. What's happened?

Haltingly, Dathne told her. Reliving the vision broke sweat upon her brow and clenched her fingers around the crystal. "I've never been given images like that before, Veira. I've been praying to Jervale, asking him for guidance, but I never thought..."

You have no doubts? It was the Final Days you were given?

"What else could it be?" She shivered. "Veira... it was terrifying. How can I hope to prevail against such evil?"

Prevailing isn't what you're here for. That's the Innocent Mage's destiny, child. Yours is to see him safe to the moment when the battle is joined.

"And how will *he* prevail? The mind I sensed, Veira, it was terrible! An evil beyond speaking! Asher's untried, untested, completely unprepared!"

Then we must prepare him, child, to the best of our abilities. Stop fretting, it does no good. The cup is pressed to our lips now. All we can do is sip and swallow.

"And if that's poison in the cup? What then?"

Then, child, we die.

"Veira!"

Hush. I can hear your bones rattling from here. If there was no hope of victory we would not know what we know, or have been given the tasks that bend our backs and break our hearts. You are Jervale's Heir, child. It is your duty to resist despair. Tell me of Asher. What news?

Reprimanded and comforted both at once, Dathne wrenched her mind away from the vision and thought instead of Asher. "It was announced in chapel yesterday. His Highness is officially named Olken Administrator and Asher is appointed his assistant. Although apparently it pleases the prince to tease him with the title of Champion."

And does it please Asher as well?

Dathne felt herself smile. "From the look on his face when he told me, no, I don't think it does. A gaggle of royal heralds rode out this morning to spread word of the appointments to the rest of the kingdom. Asher's about to become the most famous Olken in Lur...and I don't think that much pleases him either."

The link hummed with Veira's fat satisfaction. *But it does please me. So. He is taken into the Usurper's House. Prophecy continues.*

"Veira...I don't know what to do next. How to proceed."

You must do nothing.

She felt impatient anxiety ripple through her. "I can't do nothing."

Then wait. Waiting is not nothing. Waiting is what the Circle has done for six hundred years. Waiting has brought us safely to the here and now. It will serve.

"But I'm not the only one waiting! And I can't see what comes next. There must be a way forward from here, I just can't see what it is, or how I should arrange matters."

What makes you think you are the one to arrange matters?

"Of course I am! The vision—"

An irritated snort. *The vision is but part of the mosaic, child. It is important, I grant you. But so is Asher important, and the prince, and any number of puzzle pieces yet to be revealed. You must not let yourself be intimidated by dreams. They are sent to guide and inform you, not render you helpless with fear. Forewarned is forearmed goes the saying, and so, now we are forearmed. We know now something of the taste and texture of that which will oppose us, and this is all to the good. Be content with that, child. Doom rushes towards us fast enough without we raise the dust in hurrying to greet it halfway.*

Dathne felt her ribs expand and contract in a sigh. "I know."

Now tell me, what of our good friend Matthias?

The thought of Matt made her frown. "He holds. Just."

You sound uncertain.

She shook her head, even though Veira couldn't see the gesture. "No. Not of him. Not exactly."

Then what, exactly?

"He refuses to abandon this unwise friendship with Asher. I've told him it's madness but he won't listen. He's going to be hurt, I know it, but nothing I say will sway him. I tell you, Veira, I'm sorely tempted to take his hammer and hit him over the head with it until he sees sense!"

Are friends like pebbles on the road, child, so numerous they can be kicked aside uncaring?

Dathne let her own tone sharpen to match Veira's. "The butcher who befriends the lamb is a fool, and worse than a fool, for might not a family starve if for love he can't use his knife at the appointed hour?"

True. But consider this...what if we talk not of butchers, but shepherds?

"The shepherd delivers his lambs to market, knowing it's the butcher's money he'll put in his purse when they're sold. In the end, it's the same."

Veira sighed like a ghost, frost in the invisible air. *Be not harsh with good Matthias, child. Can you say for certain he is wrong in this? I know I cannot. You are not the gatekeeper of wisdom nor the sole one among us with a purpose. Until the song is sung and the musicians have all gone home, not even you can tell which notes made the melody.*

Rebuked again. Not harshly, but even so. Stinging, Dathne felt her head bow. "You are wise, Veira."

A whispering chuckle. *I am old. Sometimes it amounts to the same thing. Will you tell Matthias of this new vision?*

Dathne hesitated. She'd seen Matt weep for a dead baby sparrow dropped out of its nest. His heart was too soft: try as he might, he couldn't freeze it.

"No. There's no need. It's enough that I've told you. And besides, he won't have any more idea than I do right now how we're supposed to stop it from happening." Fear chilled her all over again. "Veira—"

Child, do not fret. We have trusted Prophecy so far, and so far it has not led us astray. I think we can—Wait, the Basingdown crystal calls me. Do you stay indoors tonight?

Dathne felt her heart leap; in Veira's thoughts, a discordant chiming of alarm. "Basingdown? You said that problem was behind us..."

Perhaps I spoke too soon. Stay within reach of your Stone, child. I will call you when I can.

Before she could reply, the connection was broken. The severance was so abrupt, the echo of Veira's alarm so jangling, that behind her eyes pain bloomed like blood in water.

Dizzied, adrift, she bumped from wall to wall like a bird encaged, unable to settle, nerves thrumming. She didn't know the exact nature of the Basingdown trouble any more than she knew the name of the Circle members who lived there. Only Veira knew each individual of the group. It was safer that way.

But something terrible had happened, she knew that much: every instinct she possessed was shrieking and her stomach clenched and unclenched like a fist.

Just when she thought she must go mad with waiting her crystal flared, and from its heart pulsed a soft white light. Deep in her mind, the insistent tug of Veira's thoughts to her own. Dathne flung herself to the living room carpet and feverishly sought the connection. Three heartbeats and she had it, hot and humming with alarm.

"What is it? What's happened?"

Calamity and woe, child. One of our number is revealed.

If she hadn't already been on the floor she would have fallen. Struggling for air she pressed her palm against her chest. "Revealed? How? Veira, what *happened*?"

The link between them vibrated wildly with the old woman's distress. *Four months ago Edv—*

Shocked, Dathne interrupted. "No *names*, Veira!"

Peace, child. It matters little now.

Dathne smothered her rising fear. Never in all their long years of friendship had she heard Veira sound so defeated. So heartsick, or afraid. "Sorry. Go on."

Edvord of Basingdown judged the time was ripe to bring his son Timon into the Circle. Edvord has a canker. He is dying. He was afraid to leave it any longer lest his failing wits desert him before what is needful could be completed. Timon is talented, but proud and impatient. Edvord told him he must wait, be guided, and so did I, but wise words fell on deaf ears. An hour ago Edvord's son was taken by the Town Magisters for the illegal practisings of magic.

Dathne knuckled a moan back behind her teeth. "He was seen?"

Yes.

"In Jervale's name, what was he *thinking*? Veira, we're undone!"

Veira rallied; through the link, Dathne could feel what it cost her. *Perhaps not. He was caught attempting Doranen magic.*

"*Doranen* magic? Why? Wasn't he told—"

Of course he was told, child! Did I not say Timon is proud and impatient? He refused to believe it is a song we cannot sing. He thought to prove his father wrong and be a hero.

Dathne swallowed a fresh rush of bile. Shut her eyes tight and willed her hands to stop shaking. "At least there's something to be thankful for. If he'd been caught casting Olken spells it would mean the end of everything."

Yes.

She smashed a fist against the floor. "Barl's *tits!*"

Edvord swears his son will die silent.

"Edvord is hardly unbiased." Another rush of bile. "This Timon must be dealt with, Veira. If he should attempt to save himself by betraying us..."

He hasn't yet. Besides, he is beyond our reach now. The magisters are taking him to the City as we speak. They'll be there by sundown tomorrow. A rider has gone on ahead, to alert the king.

"And the prince. As Olken Administrator he'll be up to his pretty green eyes in all of this. Which means that Asher will be too."

Through the link, Veira's mind echoed with sorrow and dread. *Once news of this disaster spreads, the people of Lur will bay for Timon's blood like hounds in the hunting field. He has broken cardinal law. It will mean an execution. How will that affect Asher, child? He is destined for magic.*

Dathne chewed her lip. "I...don't know."

You must find out, then. And you must repair any damage caused by Timon of Basingdown. Should the Innocent Mage refuse his destiny we are all of us doomed.

Dathne felt suffocated. *Hailstones of fire...* "What if I can't repair it? What if Asher himself leads the baying pack?"

You are Jervale's Heir. You must.

Just like that. The old woman made it sound as easy as sewing a new button on a shirt. It wasn't...but she had no choice. "I will. But Veira, there's a more immediate danger to consider. You know what will happen now."

Yes, child. I know.

The last breaking of cardinal law had been over a century before. Trial and execution a matter of one day's examination and five minutes with the royal headsman...but the seeds of suspicion and mistrust sown that day had taken root to flower and poison the air with an ill-smelling perfume equal parts fear, anger and blame. The aftertaste had lingered for months, years, the lifetimes of those who had seen the head fall.

A repeat of those unfortunate days was the very last thing they needed. Doranen eyes, woken from trusting sleep, would be newly sharpened by this violation of cardinal law, would look twice and more than twice at every harmless Olken gesture, every blameless Olken gathering, every thoughtless Olken laugh. Even on a good day the Doranen were apt to be jealous of their magics...and the days ahead promised to be anything but good.

Worse still, the Olken of Lur would be twice as vigilant, twice as suspicious as the Doranen. Eager to prove their devotion to Barl, to the Law, to their own preservation, they'd report the smallest doubt to show the world they could be trusted.

And in their midst the secret Circle...and Asher, the Innocent Mage.

Damn this wretched Timon of Basingdown and damn his dying father, too, for putting them all in danger, for risking the Circle and everyone in it and all that it meant for the future of Lur. What fools they were, like father like son, and did this now mean the end of all the Circle's hopes and plans and painstaking sacrifices?

The end of Lur?

Reading her mind, perhaps, Veira spoke. *There is yet hope. Hopeless though things appear. This is not the first storm the Circle has weathered. And I have known Edvord longer than you've been alive, child. If he says his son will hold true to his oath I believe him.*

"Well, you know him, Veira. And you know I trust your judgement," Dathne replied. "But if this fool does look like talking out of turn then I'm well placed to hear so. Asher is in the habit now of confiding most things to me. I swear I'll pluck Timon's wagging tongue from between his teeth before he can do us damage."

Vengeance will not serve us, child.

Dathne took a deep, rib-creaking breath. Let it hiss out again between her clenched teeth. "Our survival, Lur's survival, rests on the nerve of an idiot whose arrogant recklessness has brought us to the brink of disaster. We hang by a thread, Veira. At all costs, the damage must be contained. Vengeance has nothing to do with it."

Perhaps not. But anger does. Do not let it lead you astray.

"Are you saying I have no right to be angry?"

Of course not. Nor should you think yourself alone in your fury.

Which was true. Through the link, beneath the muffling pain for an old friend's agony, she could feel Veira's rage. Though frightening it also gave her a strange measure of comfort. Allowed her to step away from her own feelings and focus on what was most important.

"We can't allow this to distract us from our purpose, Veira. No matter the public outcry, the increased scrutiny, the fear and doubt this will rouse in the rest of the Circle...we must hold firm. Tonight's vision was sent to me for a reason. It's a warning, a harbinger of the evil yet to come. We ignore it at our peril and the ruin of every man, woman and child in this kingdom. *Nothing* can be allowed to sway us from the path upon which we toil, or failure and death are certain."

You speak wisely, as befits the Heir of Jervale.

Dathne didn't know if that made her feel better or worse. All she knew for certain was she could easily fold flat to the floor, crushed by the increased weight of her responsibilities. "As soon as I know anything, Veira, I'll contact you so you can keep the Circle calm and focused. That must be our priority if we're to survive the coming days."

Indeed, child. I shall await your sending.

The connection between them broke. Exhausted, Dathne wrapped her Circle Stone once more and replaced it at the bottom of the blanket box. Though her empty belly was growling she had no heart for food. All she wanted now was sleep. Her mind and body cried out for it. Even Matt would have to wait; she'd tell him about Timon and his mad foolishness in the morning. There was nothing he could do about it tonight. Nothing he could do at all, so why worry him?

Stripping herself naked in her tiny bedroom, letting her skirt and blouse and stockings and underthings fall where they liked, she crawled between cool cotton sheets and closed her eyes. Her last conscious thought was a prayer:

Please, Jervale. Let me not dream.

CHAPTER NINE

A sher stood in his underclothes and stockinged feet in front of his open wardrobe door, filled to the gills with the fine breakfast he'd shared with Gar in the Tower solar. Washed and shaved and smelling faintly of spice, he stared at the clothes dangling from their hangers. What to wear, what to wear? Not the blue shirt or the black britches, since he'd worn them yesterday. The green was good, a sea colour, reminding him of home. But on the other hand the bronze was a fine strong shade for a man. And it would go well with the chocolate-brown britches, snug and soft and cut to fit him like a second skin.

He'd never given much thought to clothes before, except as useful coverings for bare skin. Never considered himself much above average-looking. But now, buttoned up in his whispery silk shirt and his lined wool britches, stamping into shiny black boots that came right up to his knees, he thought he looked mighty fine. In fact, once he'd finished tugging his forelock to all the fancy lords in the Privy Council Chamber he just might wander down to town and see if there was some kind of book or other he could bring hisself to buy from Madam Hoity Toity the bookseller. Not that he wanted to spend any of his precious trins on books... but what other reason was there to go into Dathne's bookshop?

A pity none of the weskits was ready yet. A fine brocade weskit would finish him off just perfect.

Downstairs, waiting for Gar in the Tower's ground floor foyer, Asher winked at a scurrying chambermaid, what was her name again? Cluny? A blush tinted her cheeks, and he grinned. Oh yes indeed. *Mighty* fine.

"And what do you think you're doing, loitering about the place like a reprobate?" a snippy voice demanded.

He turned. Darran, all sour lemons and spite, coming down the Tower's spiral staircase. Experimenting, Asher discarded his first, instinctive response and smiled instead. "Mornin'," he said expansively. "As it happens, I be waitin' for Gar. We're off to see the Privy Council any tick."

Darran crossed the foyer's gleaming tiled floor silently, like a cat who's lost its collar and bell. "You are attending a Privy Council meeting?"

"Seems so," said Asher with exaggerated cheer. In truth he felt as incredulous as Darran sounded, but he'd not be admitting that any time soon. Off to the Privy Council to hobnob with the king...could his strange life get any stranger?

Darran sniffed. "I see." From the way his Adam's apple bobbed furiously in his scrawny throat it looked like Gar's secretary wanted to say a lot more than that, and none of it complimentary. After a short, silent struggle the ole crow nodded. "Well. I'm sure you'll find the experience educational. Have you ordered the carriage?"

"Carriage?" echoed Asher. "To go from here to the palace? Why would we be wantin' a carriage? Our legs ain't broke. We'll walk."

Darran's lips curved in a thin smile. "Oh dear. You do have a lot to learn, don't you? His Highness does not *walk* to official duties. He travels in a manner commensurate with his position." Crossing to a marble-topped display table he picked up a small shiny handbell and tinkled it sharply. "If you can't arrange even this small matter without supervision, I don't imagine you'll be remaining as His Highness's assistant anything for long. Observe."

Seething, Asher watched as a young boy dressed in black and green livery darted out of an adjacent room, skidded to a halt before Darran and bowed. "Sir?" he piped.

"His Highness shall be leaving the premises shortly. Kindly repair to the stables and—"

"No, don't bother," Gar called out as he descended the staircase. "Off you go, Remy. I won't be needing a carriage this morning."

The lad Remy bowed again and scuttled back into his messenger-boy bolthole. Scandalised, Darran turned to the prince, offered a punctiliously correct bow of his own and protested. "No carriage? But, Your Highness—"

Gar had changed from his casual breakfast attire of shirt, loose trousers and bare feet into a gold-beaded tunic of stiffened dark green brocade, dull black silk britches and black leather half-boots. His hair was caught back from his face in some kind of gold and green enamel clasp, and a gold and emerald circlet bound his brow. To Asher's eyes he had the air of a man preparing to ride into battle. That wasn't a good sign...

Smiling, the prince touched one hand lightly to Darran's shoulder. "It's a fine morning for a walk. Besides, after the copious amount of bacon Asher ate for breakfast he needs the exercise."

Ha. Very funny. But then so was the look on ole Darran's face.

"I see, sir," Darran said limply. "You know your own mind, of course. Shall I send a carriage to fetch you then, once your business at the palace is concluded?"

"Let's see, shall we? If I want one I'll let you know."

Darran bowed. "Certainly, sir. You can send Asher with a message."

Asher held his tongue, just. Gar sent him a sidelong glance, brimful of repressed hilarity. "I might just do that, Darran. Now don't let me keep you from your business."

In other words, buzz off, busy little bee. Busybody. Still experimenting, Asher sent the secretary on his way with a wide, wide smile, and was rewarded with a venomous flash of temper, swiftly smothered.

"Y'know, he really don't like me at all," he said happily. "But I don't mind. I don't like him neither. Starin' down his snooty nose at me just 'cause I ain't all flash and folderol."

Gar sighed. "Don't be difficult. I've told you, he does me valuable service."

"Ha," said Asher.

Now Gar was looking him up and down. "You seem presentable at any rate. Now come on. We can't afford to be late."

Instead of taking the road to the sprawling splendour of the palace, Gar chose a grassy pathway winding through carelessly scattered gardens and past older, abandoned apartments and residences that once had been home to other kings and queens of Lur. Long dead now, they were all laid to rest in tombs on the far side of the palace grounds.

Asher stared at the forlornly empty buildings and shook his head. "Seems like a bloody great waste to me. Perfectly good rooms and whatnots, ain't they? Why don't folk live in 'em any more?"

"I don't know," said Gar, shrugging. "Too many ghosts, perhaps. All those memories, pressing down. Sometimes people just want a fresh start...and who can blame them?"

Aye. Maybe. And speaking of which... "Thanks for not havin' me mentioned in the dispatches to the coast," he said as they left the old palace behind. "Reckon I'm grateful for that."

Gar's sideways glance was curious. "That's all right. I still think you're mad, but..."

"You wouldn't if y'had my brothers," Asher said flatly. "This news'll keep just fine till I'm home again."

"Yes. Well. As I said before, it's your decision." Gar waved a dismissive hand. "Now, about this Privy Council meeting...there's no need to be nervous." Another sideways look. "*Are* you nervous?"

Asher flicked a fly away from his ear. "Well..."

"Don't be. They won't bite. At least not while I'm there." Gar pulled a face. "Or not very hard anyway."

"And that's s'posed to make me not nervous, is it?"

Gar grinned. "Of course."

"Ha!"

"Besides, this is really just a formality. As my assistant you'll have more to do with the General Council, which takes care of the day-to-day business of running the kingdom. Guild issues, common legal matters, that sort of thing. Privy Council meetings are more... rarefied. You won't often be required to attend."

Asher hid his relief. Last thing he wanted to do was front up to the king and his personal advisers on a regular basis. "Suits me."

"I know the privy councillors are the most powerful men in the kingdom, but they're still men. Not ogres. That being said, however..."

"Oh aye?" sighed Asher. "Here we go. What?"

Gar was frowning. "His Majesty has many virtues but they don't include a wink and a shrug at inappropriate informality. No matter what happens this morning, remember that you are addressing the king or one of his chosen confidants. You may not..." He hesitated, searching for the right words. "Our interactions, Asher, are characterised by a degree of familiarity that would never be tolerated by His Majesty. Whatever you do, don't make the mistake of confusing us."

Like there were much chance of *that* happening. Asher rolled his eyes. "Don't worry, I won't." Then, as they took a short cut through yet another arrangement of perfumed flowerbeds, he added, "You sorry you hired me now, are you?"

"Don't be ridiculous," Gar said, flushing. "I just want your introduction to the Privy Council to proceed smoothly. You must realise that whatever I do reflects upon the king. And whatever you do reflects upon me."

That was fair enough. But... "If that's true, then how come you don't care if I speak my mind around the Tower and everywhere else? Folks ain't deaf, Gar. They'll hear what I think, and they'll hear I ain't one for mincing my words. And they'll flap their lips about it too."

"That's entirely different. All my people know I encourage—insist upon, in fact—open, honest and vigorous debate. But the Privy Council is different. Privy Council meetings are...political. Even when they're not. Every word, every gesture, can be interpreted in a variety of ways, and some people will always interpret things in the harshest light possible."

Asher considered that. "You sayin' it ain't just you that's got enemies?"

This time Gar's glance was chilly with warning. "No. His Majesty is beloved by all his subjects."

"Come on, Gar," said Asher, gently derisive. "Y'reckon the Doranen are the only folk with a taste for playin' politics? My da used to represent Restharven in the Coastal Alliance. I'd lay odds on the West-wailing Fishermen's Board agin your precious Privy Council any day of the week. So, who's the rotten fish in the barrel?"

That made Gar smile, if only briefly. He hesitated, then said, "Keep your eye on Conroyd Jarralt. In Privy Council and out of it. If he can do you a bad turn, he will."

"Why?"

"Because he's Conroyd Jarralt."

"And?"

"And that's all you need to know. For now. Asher—" Gar slowed, and stopped. Asher stopped beside him. "Think of Privy Council meetings as an elaborate game. One in which waving the flag of your indifference to almighty Doranen prestige will *lose* you points. Not win them, as it does with me. I'm asking that you watch your step. That's all. If you don't, well, chances are we'll both be sorry that I hired you."

So. The prince was nervous about the Privy Council meeting too. Mayhap even more than just nervous. Resisting the urge to clap Gar on the shoulder, Asher started walking backwards, arms outstretched. "Don't worry," he said. "I ain't about to let you down." He pressed a hand to his heart. "My solemn word." Which he'd keep, sink or swim. No way was he about to lose those fifty trins a week.

"Good," said Gar with a brief smile. "I knew I could count on you."

They hurried on, and five minutes later reached the newest section of the palace where Gar's family lived and worked. The pure white sandstone gleamed in the sun like freshly fallen snow. Some twelve storeys high, it was topped with blue and crimson roof tiles and sparkled at regular intervals with elaborate stained-glass windows. A grand sweeping courtyard, scattered thickly with blue and white gravel, stretched from the base of the centrally placed white sandstone steps and ground-level balcony, down to the mouth of the winding tree-lined driveway that led towards the City.

Side by side Asher and Gar ran up the steps, past the ceremonial guards and into the royal residence.

The palace's interior shocked Asher to a standstill. All height and breadth and radiant stained glass, it made Justice Hall look...*plain*. Cut flowers in ceramic vases splashed colour over every flat surface and sweetened the cool air. Exquisitely carved crystal birds wrought in shades of rose, sapphire, ruby, amethyst and emerald, tipped in gold, adorned indigo-marble display stands.

Two wide and winding polished timber staircases reached like arms to left and right of the grand entrance, embracing visitors, inviting exploration. The floor beneath Asher's feet was a riot of tiny blue, white, crimson and gold tiles in patterns his eyes could barely take in. The walls were papered in dull gold and bronze stripes. Breathtaking oil paintings, portraits so lifelike he'd swear their subjects were breathing, glowed at eye level, demanding admiration.

He had to guess they were members of the royal family, because there was Gar, years younger, with his arms round the neck of a fat black pony. A man and a woman—the king and queen? Had to be, 'cause there was Princess Fane. Maybe just six or seven years of age, but still beautiful. Bronze lamps jutted between the precisely placed frames, blazing with the same strange light he'd noticed in Justice Hall. Not candles. Not oil.

"Glimfire," said Gar. "It's magic, which is why you won't find it in the Tower."

Asher scarcely heard him. "Sink me bloody sideways!" he breathed. Recalling his own family's stone cottage back home, all shabby shadows and crowded cosiness, he shook his head in wonder. He'd easily fit his bedroom in here three times over. "You used to *live* here?"

Mellow laughter spun him to his right. Descending the staircase was a tall Doranen man, lean and proud, with lines of experience—or pain—carved deep into his face. His ceremonial likeness hung on the wall scant feet away. In the flesh, though, he was simply clad in a dark blue silk tunic and trousers. His eyes were green, like Gar's, but older. Seasoned by years and sights unseen by other men. An immaculately trimmed beard framed his strong jaw. A crown of twisted gold announced his rank. The royal house's emblem, a lightning bolt crossed with an unsheathed sword, was stitched in gold thread onto his collar points.

Asher swallowed. He'd seen the king before, down in Westwailing at festival time, but only from the arseend of a huge crowd. Gar's da had been little more than a blond stick-figure then, waving indiscriminately at the thousands of fisherfolk gathered to celebrate Sea Harvest. Up close, he was magic made flesh. The aura of raw power surrounding him dimmed everything beyond it to tawdry tarnishment.

Gar bowed. "Your Majesty. Good morning."

Somehow, Asher managed his own inadequate bow without falling over. "Y'Majesty," he muttered.

King Borne approached and stretched out one ringed hand. "You must be Asher of Restharven. My son has spoken most highly of you, and of his hopes that you'll prove invaluable to him in his work. Welcome to Dorana City."

Asher stared at the king's hand. Now what? Was he supposed to kiss it? Shake it? What?

Gar chuckled. "Barl save me. I believe my new assistant is lost for words."

"No, I ain't," said Asher, rallying. He took the king's hand and shook it. To his surprise it felt cold and thin, with something close to a tremble deep between the slender bones. All that power, and in the end Lur's monarch was still only human. Somehow he hadn't expected that. "Thank you, Y'Majesty. Reckon I be about the luckiest Olken in Lur. I won't do wrong by His Highness. Or you. I promise."

The king withdrew his hand. "I'm sure of it, Asher." A glance passed between himself and his son and his pale lips softened into a smile. "Now, shall we make our way to the Privy Council chamber? We have a full morning's work ahead of us."

Gar extended his arm towards the left-hand staircase. "By all means, sir. Lead the way. Asher and I are ready."

That earned him another swift look from the king. "You think so? Well. By all means let us see, shall we?"

Conroyd Jarralt was an outrageously handsome man even when flushed with anger and shouting. A Doranen in his glorious, powerful prime, dressed in purple silk brocade and seed pearls, with his falcon house-emblem emblazoned on his chest in silver and jet. His aristocratic face was as perfect as a carving in marble, his athletic vigour overwhelming. In contrast, despite his magical power, the king looked pallid and drained of all vitality. Like a moon dimmed by the sun.

Jarralt banged his fist on the chamber table. "This is *insupportable*, Prince Gar! An *Olken*? With unfettered access to this Privy Council, its members, its decisions? I think not, Your Highness. Barl's mercy, what possessed you to do such a thing without gaining our permission? To have this reckless appointment announced in chapel without first doing us the courtesy of discussion? And then to refuse an accounting of yourself until now? Insupportable, sir! Insufferable!"

Exquisitely polite, Gar said, "I discussed the matter with His Majesty, my lord. As for declining your invitation to discuss it further... as I said, I felt it to be a topic best reserved for the privacy of this chamber."

"Indeed." Jarralt's burning gaze turned on the king. "So. He discussed the matter with you. And you said *yes* to this insanity?"

"I did," said the king. "Obviously."

Jarralt clenched his jaw. "I see. Well. One is forced to wonder what will come next. Olkens marrying into the Founding Families, perhaps?"

"Now, now, Conroyd..."

Asher, seated beside Gar on the other side of the table from the raging Doranen lord, slid his gaze to Barlsman Holze, on Jarralt's left. The elderly cleric's expression was pained, his lips pursed in disapproval. Steepled forefingers tapped against the tip of his bony nose. Voice mellow, reproving, he continued: "I think we must—"

Jarralt silenced him with a white-hot glare.

At the end of the rectangular table, sitting directly opposite the king, Master Magician Durm contemplated the plain white ceiling with a vast, unnerving indifference.

And the king? Well, the king was smiling. Not nicely, but in a guarded way that hinted at possible unpleasantness should Jarralt travel any further down his current path. Asher winced.

"Intermarriage between our peoples is strictly forbidden, Conroyd," His Majesty said, deceptively mild. "Gar knows that as well as you do. Surely you're not suggesting he advocates the breaking of Barl's Second Law?"

"Of course he isn't, Your Majesty," said Holze, one thin hand resting on Jarralt's rigid forearm. His once blond hair was mostly silver now, and thinning. Cut unfashionably short for a Doranen. A single braid, tightly wound with Barlsflowers to denote his devotion, dangled to his frail left shoulder. "Conroyd was merely expressing an understandable concern for this—forgive me, Your Highness— potentially rash decision."

"Rash?" Conroyd Jarralt snatched his arm free. His dark gold hair was unbound and fashionably long, with just the hint of a curl. Beautiful hair. Girl's hair, thought Asher, then quickly discarded the thought in case it showed on his face. "Rash is too kind a word, Holze," the lord continued. "I'll thank you to answer for your own utterances, sir, not mine."

He had the most amazing voice, like magic given a tongue. It was a voice to drink deep of, as a thirsty man swallows water. Instinctively Asher stiffened his spine against it. He didn't trust a man who could say something wrong yet make his listeners swear black and blue it was right because the way he said it sounded nice.

Holze, defeated, dipped his head. "As you say, Conroyd. You must speak for yourself."

"And I do!" said Jarralt. "I want to know what the king was thinking, to approve this ridiculous appointment. To foist this Olken upstart upon his Privy Council without so much as a by-our-leave!"

The king did not answer immediately. Hands clasped loosely before him on the tabletop, he considered the demand for a moment, then said, "Are you saying you doubt me, Conroyd?" His manner was surprisingly calm, but there was a dangerous glint in his eyes. Jarralt saw it, and coloured faintly.

So, The king could bring Conroyd Jarralt to heel when he wanted. That was good to know. Beside him, Asher felt Gar twitch. The prince's gaze switched abruptly to the other end of the table, where Durm continued to inspect the ceiling for spiderwebs or inspiration or whatever it was he hoped to find there. Feeling eyes upon him he slowly lowered his own regard. Considered Gar in speculative silence for a moment, then returned his attention to matters seemingly above the heads of everybody else in the room.

"All I doubt," said Jarralt, "is the wisdom of the decision. Ordinary, uneducated Olken have never concerned themselves with the running of this kingdom and I see no reason for that to change. They should tend to their farming and their shopkeeping and leave important matters of government to those who can best address them."

Patronising bastard. Asher cleared his throat. Lowly Olken or not it was time he let certain folk know he wasn't some kind of deaf mute simpleton. Or a horse to be sized up and debated on, complimented on the strength of his back or criticised for the knockiness of his knees.

"Y'Majesty?"

The king looked at him. "You have something to add, Asher?"

Heart thudding, Asher nodded. Under the table, Gar kicked him. He ignored the warning. "Yes, Y'Majesty. I just wanted to say it be an honour and a pleasure to sit at table with you and these other fine lords. And, beggin' your pardon, Lord Jarralt, I reckon you be gettin' y'self all knotted up over nowt. I ain't come here to fret and fust you. His Highness be after an extra pair of hands on the halyards, is all, and I reckon if there be somethin' I can do to help him and His Majesty, here, then sink me if I won't."

Silence. Then: "I'm sorry," said Conroyd Jarralt, staring around the table and sounding not the least bit sorry at all. "*What* did he say?"

Another kick under the table, harder this time. "Asher merely assured you, sir," Gar said quickly, "that he has no intention of causing any problems for this Council."

"Did he?" retorted Jarralt. "How can you be sure? The man is scarcely comprehensible! But if that *is* what he said then I'm bound to point out to you, Your Highness, that the assurance comes too late! His very *existence* is a problem!"

"I disagree," argued Gar. "Anyone who can help me do my job as Olken Administrator more efficiently can only benefit His Majesty *and* this Privy Council."

"You expect this…this…*Olken* to improve your efficiency?" said Jarralt. "How? You'll be spending all of your time translating for him!"

"Asher has recently arrived here from the coast." From the look of him, Gar was only just keeping hold of his temper. "Olken fisherfolk are wont to speak in a colourful vernacular, it's true, but I have every confidence he'll soon adjust to the more measured speech of the City."

Shifting in his chair a little, moving his still-smarting ankle out of Gar's reach, Asher frowned. Speaking slowly, trying to mask the effort of mimicking the likes of Darran, he said, "Prince Gar has employed me to be his assistant, Lord Jarralt. As an honest man I'll do my best not to disappoint him, the king or this Privy Council. I may be just a magickless Olken, but that don't—doesn't—mean I ain't trustworthy." Well pleased with himself, he sat back in his chair and smiled.

Jarralt leapt to his feet. "*What*? You have the gall to *mock* me?"

"Mock you?" said Asher, bewildered. "I weren't mockin' you, I were just tryin' to explain how—"

Now Jarralt was leaning across the table, pointed finger stabbing. "I am the head of a Founding Family! My house is second only to that of the royal family! I will *not* be mocked by an ignorant Olken fisherman! Your Majesty, surely you can see this appointment is folly! Madness! This Privy Council is a solemn gathering of learned men whose sacred duty is the protection and governance of this kingdom. How in Barl's holy name can we be expected to uphold our oaths if we must constantly consider what we say before this...this interloper! He cannot be granted membership of this Privy Council! It is an affront to everything we stand for!"

"Asher, for the love of Barl *hold your tongue!*" hissed Gar, then turned to Jarralt. "My lord, it appears we are at cross-purposes. It was never my intention that Asher should join the Privy Council. I apologise if that's the impression I've given. As my assistant he'll be helping me—helping us all—continue this august body's ongoing dedication to the betterment and prosperity of Lur. Naturally he will not be concerned with the making of policy or interpretation of law or any other Privy Council duty. I merely wished you to meet him. That's all."

Unappeased, Jarralt bared his teeth. "In other words, you are incapable of carrying out your duties as Olken Administrator without help from an uneducated labourer. If that's the case, perhaps the matter of your appointment to the position should be revisited?"

The king looked at him through narrowed eyes. "Have a care, Conroyd. And take your seat."

As Jarralt obeyed, lips thinned, Gar raised a hand and turned to his father. "It's a fair question, sir, if ungraciously framed." He turned back to Jarralt. "My lord, I've learned many things since assuming the responsibilities of Olken Administrator, but the most important is this: that nothing but good can come from a deeper Doranen understanding of Olken society. History shows us a score of examples where unpleasantness and discord might well have been avoided if only we truly knew each other better. Can you at least agree with that?"

Asher smothered a grin as he watched Jarralt's expression congeal. "Agree?" the lord echoed suspiciously. "Possibly. But that doesn't—"

"Good," said Gar. "And surely we can also agree that nobody is in a better position to occasionally advise this Privy Council upon matters important to the Olken than one of His Majesty's Olken subjects?"

Jarralt glowered. "Yes. I suppose. In *theory*. However—"

"So if," Gar continued ruthlessly, "by appointing Asher as my assistant I can facilitate future harmonious Doranen and Olken relations, then it must logically follow that this Privy Council—as the decision-making instrument of our kingdom—can only benefit. And if *that's* true, I'd say I've proven my fitness for the position of Olken Administrator, not undermined it. Wouldn't you?" Spreading his hands wide, he appealed to the table at large.

Holze's smile was gentle and approving. "Well said, Your Highness. Above all, Barl desires Doranen and Olken to live peacefully side by side in the paradise she created. If this is indeed your objective, I see no reason to thwart this young Olken's appointment as your assistant. Can you, Lord Jarralt?"

Jarralt snorted. "Oh, to be sure, it *sounds* well and good. But what of practicalities? How often can we of the Privy Council expect this incomprehensible addition to grace us with his dubious presence? How much credence are we to lend to his profoundly experienced observations of good government? Tell us, Prince Gar, is it your intention that we allow your fisherman to lecture us? Instruct us? If it is, then I'm afraid I must decline the honour. The day some upstart Olken can march in here and presume to tell me my business—"

Durm cleared his throat. Jarralt swallowed the rest of his objection. Eyes narrowed, the Master Magician lowered his piercing gaze and considered the now silent lord. "You are raising a storm in a teacup, Conroyd. And that, I believe, is solely His Majesty's prerogative."

Jarralt stared. "Does that mean you *approve* of this..."

Durm shrugged. "It means, Conroyd, I have been given no cause to *dis*approve of him." His cold glance flickered. "Yet."

Seared by that swift look Asher stared at the table. Suddenly he knew how a mouse must feel when the shadow of the hawk passes over it.

"So," said Jarralt. For the first time, he sounded subdued. "Your mind is made up...Your Majesty?"

"Yes, Conroyd," said the king, his voice and face implacable. "And not to be unmade. I have complete faith in my son's choice of assistant."

"As have I," added Holze. "His Highness has proven himself a most capable Administrator. Isn't that so, Conroyd?"

Conroyd Jarralt laced his fingers and frowned at them. "Most capable."

Gar said carefully, "Your Majesty, my lords, I thank you. It was never my intention to take up so much time with this trifling business. I merely wished you to know that should there be anything of an Olken nature you wish to discuss or have clarified, Asher shall henceforth be at your disposal."

"And on behalf of this Privy Council," said the king, "I welcome his knowledge and assistance, wherever and whenever it may be extended to us."

There was an expectant pause. Asher, feeling the weight of all those Doranen stares, coughed. "Like I said," he muttered. "Reckon it be an honour to serve the Privy Council."

"Indeed," said the king. "Then I declare this subject closed."

"Well done," Gar murmured in Asher's ear as Jarralt and Holze exchanged whispered comments and looked at their paperwork to discover the next problem for discussion. "Now I think it's best if you go back to the Tower. Ask Darran for a copy of next week's scheduled appointments and be ready with your thoughts when I return. Don't forget to ask His Majesty's permission to withdraw."

Half out of his chair, Asher straightened and offered the king an awkward bow. "Y'Majesty. His Highness has work for me back at the Tower. Can I get on with it?"

Was that a smile, strictly denied? Maybe. And if so, what did it mean? That he had the king's support, or that he was little more than a joke? He couldn't tell and he didn't much care. He just wanted out of the small, crowded chamber. He could feel Conroyd Jarralt's eyes on him, staring.

The king nodded. "By all means, Asher. Return to your duties. Doubtless I shall see you again in the fullness of time."

"Y'Majesty."

Straightening from his farewell bow, Asher looked square into the frozen fury of Conroyd Jarralt's gaze. The force of it made him step back. Thudded his heart and stole his breath. That was *hatred* in the Doranen lord's eyes...

"Well go on, then," said Gar, nudging him. "Don't stand there with your mouth open, catching flies. I'll see you later."

Deeply disconcerted, Asher headed for the door. But as his hand reached for the handle it opened all by itself. An agitated young Olken in City Guard livery shoved him aside and barged into the chamber. He rushed to the king, dropped to one knee and held out a rolled parchment.

"Forgive the interruption, Your Majesty," he gasped. "An urgent message from Captain Orrick."

Frowning, the king accepted it. Untied the scroll's binding scarlet ribbon. Unrolled the message, read it, read it again, and blinked. Asher, looking closely at his face, thought he was in sudden pain.

"Very good," the king said quietly. "Return to the captain. Tell him to make the appropriate preparations and await further instructions. And tell him also—discretion is paramount."

The young City Guard nodded. "Yes, Your Majesty."

As the chamber door banged shut behind the guard, the Master Magician spoke.

"What is it, Borne? What has happened?"

CHAPTER TEN

Something bad, Asher judged, if the king's face was anything to go by. It had lost all its washed-out colour, leaving him as grey as the paper in his hand. He looked a score of years older, just as Da had looked a heartbeat after Ma exhaled her last rattling breath.

Gar was on his feet, one hand reaching out. "Sir, what is it? Mama? Fane? Are they—"

The king shook his head. "No. It's not family. It's worse." Lifting his gaze from the message he stared the length of the Council table and locked eyes with Durm. "Barl's First Law has been broken. The man is in custody and being brought to the City as we speak. He will be here by this evening."

Asher bit his tongue. What? Some bloody fool Olken had been caught pissin' around with magic? *Why?* Olken couldn't do magic, everybody knew that. And everybody knew that to try, to muck about mouthing words of Doranen power overheard in passing even, was as bright as jumping off Rillingcoombe Cliffs when the tide was out.

As bright...and as fatal.

It was Holze who shattered the shocked silence. "Your Majesty, there must be some mistake. Perhaps a misunderstanding..."

"No," said the king, still looking at the message. "No misunderstanding."

Holze shook his head, his blue-veined hands tight-clasped and trembling. "I find this quite incredible. There must be an explanation."

Lord Jarralt laughed, crudely amused. "Of course there is. They're jealous of us, any fool knows that. It's not enough that we provide them with a perfect world to live in. Predictable weather that is never too hot or too cold, too dry or too wet. Heat, light, plumbing...a veritable cornucopia of domestic comforts. They want more. They want to subvert the proper order of things. Usurp power that does not belong to them."

Well, that was just a lie, pure and simple. Asher opened his mouth to put Jarralt straight, caught Gar's glare and swallowed his angry denial. A curt nod directed him away from the door and against the wall, where he could observe unnoticed. Gar sat down again, his expression unreadable.

"No, no," protested Holze. His voice shook with distress. "Barl's Laws are taught throughout the kingdom. I cannot believe any Olken would willingly break the first and greatest of them!"

"Advancing age has withered your brain, Holze," Jarralt sneered. "This isn't the first attack on our most sacred law and unless we show no mercy to this blasphemous criminal it won't be the last!" He turned to the king. "You must make an example of this vile traitor. Every Olken man, woman and child must be shown, once and for all, what happens when Barl's sacred edicts are transgressed."

Holze reached out an imploring hand. "Conroyd, please! Curb your wrath! As our precious kingdom's most senior caretakers we must remain calm. We must seek Barl's guidance."

"Holze, you amaze me." Jarralt's tone was one of utter contempt. "As Barl's holiest representative among us you should be leading the outcry!"

Holze drew himself upright and stared at Jarralt with wounded dignity. "My lord, nobody knows better than I what duties are owed by me to our blessed, beloved Barl. Shame on you for implying otherwise!"

Jarralt flushed. "I imply nothing. I merely suggest—"

"Your suggestion offends me, Conroyd. And it hurts me too. I thought you knew me—respected me—better. I do not say this man should go unpunished. But you make it sound as though every week sees a new Olken transgression of the laws! You mustn't be so intemperate or unfair. It is a hundred years at least since this crime was last committed!"

"One hundred and thirty-eight," said Durm. "During the reign of Ancel the Red. The criminal was a woman named Maura Shay. She was beheaded, as will this man be."

The king sighed. "Yes. He will." His fingers convulsed around the message, crushing it. "The fool."

"So *now* will you reconsider your son's impetuous elevation of this Olken fisherman?" Jarralt demanded. "Clearly this is not the time for any Olken to be seen wielding power, no matter how meagre."

"You're wrong, Lord Jarralt," said Gar. "When news of this unfortunate business spreads, and it will no matter how discreetly Captain Orrick handles the matter, tensions in the Olken community will escalate. They'll feel vulnerable. Examined. Guilty by reason of association. This man's short-sighted—"

"Short-sighted?" said Conroyd Jarralt. "You consider this blasphemous, criminal act to be nothing more than a lapse in judgement, do you?"

Asher watched Gar's lips pinch tight. "Of course I don't. I'll thank you not to put words in my mouth, sir. What this man has done is unforgivable. His actions will have dire repercussions for all of us, Doranen and Olken alike."

Jarralt snorted. "They'll have dire repercussions for him, I know that much. In fact, I say a private beheading is too good for him. He needs to be broken. Literally and publicly, to drive the message home once and for all: Olken disobedience and blasphemy will meet with no mercy."

Gar leaned across the table. "You can't possibly be such a fool. The test here isn't how we deal with this stupid Olken, it's how we conduct *ourselves*. Even you must see that!"

The king raised his hand. "Gar, please..."

"But, Your Majesty!" Gar pleaded, ignoring Jarralt's salt-white fury. "Lord Jarralt is wrong. If we wreak vengeance instead of justice, what message will we be sending then? That the purpose of this Privy Council is to mete out heavy-handed retribution. That the Doranen hold all Olken accountable for the actions of one. If that's the message we send, sir, we'll undermine all trust between—"

"Trust?" said Jarralt. "What trust, when an Olken has been caught breaking Barl's First Law? Attempting magic. This short-sighted act has risked all of our lives, Your Highness. It has threatened the peace of your father's kingdom, sir, and jeopardised Barl's Wall."

Gar banged the table with his fists. "Hardly that, Lord Jarralt. Barl's Wall has stood unwavering for centuries. It took Trevoyle's Schism to weaken it, and that went on for eight months. One thoughtless, reckless act by a single Olken can't possibly have done any real harm."

If he could have Asher would've slapped his hand over Gar's mouth then, because Jarralt's eyes were shining like a shark's scenting blood in the water and all his teeth were on show. "So. You're questioning Barl's Laws now, are you? Your Highness?"

Too late, Gar realised where his passion had led him. Asher closed his eyes briefly, wincing, as the prince snapped back in his chair. "No."

Now Jarralt was all mock sorrow and solicitude. "Forgive the contradiction, sir, but I think you were. Barlsman Holze?"

The old man's sallow face was troubled. "I'm sure His Highness has nothing but the deepest respect for the laws. He knows, as do we all, that they form the foundation of this kingdom. They are the warp and weft of our existence, and have been for over six hundred years. Barl said: *Let no Olken raise his voice in magic, for it is not their way or their right or their purpose in this land. And let the Olken who does so pay with his life, as all would pay if my Wall were to be disturbed by such a lawless act.* To this first law must we all hold true, or pay a terrible price in blood and tears. Is that not so, Your Highness?"

"Yes, sir, it is," said Gar. His clasped hands rested on the table before him, white-knuckled with pressure. "With all my heart I believe it, and I challenge anyone here to dispute my faith. But one can be a man of faith and still question. There's more to the warp and weft of this kingdom than Barl's Laws, important though they are. *People* are the true fabric of Lur, gentlemen. Olken and Doranen. And if we don't handle this matter with tact we'll tear the fabric of this kingdom apart." He turned to his father, naked appeal in his temper-flushed face. "Am I not right, Your Majesty?"

Asher looked at the king. His expression was remote, chilled; stare as he might, Asher could see no softness there. No mercy. No sorrow even, for the death that would soon come to one unthinking Olken. For all the similarity of bone structure, the arch of an eyebrow, the curve of a lip, he and his son looked no more alike than did ice and a flowing river.

"If you're in any way suggesting that this act can be excused," said the king, "then—"

"Excused? No, sir, not excused," said Gar. "I know that's impossible."

At the other end of the table the Master Magician stirred from his silence. "What, then? What would you have us do?"

Gar turned to him. "Lord Jarralt is...mistaken. Yes, this man must be punished, but not publicly."

"Why not?" Durm's eyes were hooded, his expression smooth as glass. "His crime was public."

Gar took a deep breath and let it out slowly. "Because, sir, it can't seem that we take any pleasure in his death. If we turn his execution into a spectacle, as though it were...were street theatre..." His voice was shaking. "For the same reason, his punishment can't be cruel. If he's truly guilty of this crime then he should die as precedent dictates. But that death must be swift, sure and with all the mercy we possess. And Asher *must* remain as my assistant. What better way is there for this Privy Council—for His Majesty—to show all the kingdom that the Olken people will never be held responsible for the actions of one misguided man?"

Jarralt's lip curled. "You seem inordinately concerned on this point, Your Highness."

"*Inordinately* concerned, sir?" Gar echoed. "You wouldn't say that if you'd bother to study your history. One hundred and thirty-eight years ago, when Maura Shay was found guilty of the same crime, innocent Olken were dragged from their beds, locked up and terrified, and for no other reason than fear. That was a crime too. We may be Doranen, sir, we may have magic..."

Asher winced as Gar hesitated. As Jarralt raised an eyebrow at him, imperfectly hiding his scornful smile. Pale now, Gar continued.

"But having magic doesn't make the Doranen impervious to flaws, my lord. Speaking plainly, as Olken Administrator it's my duty to ensure this business doesn't interfere with the good name or wellbeing of the Olken community."

Air hissed between Jarralt's white teeth. "So. Now we come to it. You would place their welfare above ours, Your Highness. Isn't that so? You would side with *them* against your own people."

"Why must you talk of sides?" demanded Gar. "There are no sides here, Jarralt. As His Majesty's subject and a child of Barl I want the law upheld. As Olken Administrator I want it upheld justly. Why would you criticise that?" He turned to the king. "Your Majesty?"

Asher, barely breathing, stared at the king. Was he going to let this argument rage unchecked forever? Who did he side with, his son or his enemy? After a long silence Borne stirred and lifted his heavy gaze. Considered Durm.

"I think I would know what my Master Magician has to say."

All eyes turned to Durm. A large man, generously fleshed, he seemed to Asher not the least bit put out by the hot and anxious stares.

His vast robed shoulders lifted in a shrug. "And I, Your Majesty, would know the opinion of our newly appointed Assistant Olken Administrator."

The king's pale eyebrows lifted. "Would you, indeed?" He turned. "Well, Asher? This business concerns you as much as any of us. Satisfy the Master Magician's curiosity. And mine."

Asher bit his lip. Now everyone was staring at him. He didn't like it, not one little bit. His grand new trousers fit too tightly for him to shove his hands in his pockets, which was what he wanted to do. Instead, he crossed his arms over his chest and scowled.

"What do I reckon?" He glanced at the Master Magician then looked back at the king, because it was easier. "I reckon I ain't to blame for what this sinkin' fool's gone and done, Y'Majesty. And I reckon y'should chop the stupid bastard's head off five minutes after he gets here. That'll teach him to go muckin' about with things as don't concern him, eh?"

Barlsman Holze leaned forward. "You are harsh, young man."

"Am I?" said Asher, chin lifting. "Look. Sir. I ain't the most religious man you'll ever see in your chapel, but I reckon I know right from wrong. Olken don't do magic. And if they try, and they get caught, then too bad. They can't snivel they didn't know it were wrong, or what would happen. Everybody knows."

The king said slowly, "The idea of an Olken dying such a horrible death doesn't distress you?"

Asher shrugged. "No. It's only what he deserves."

"So," said Conroyd Jarralt. "You have no loyalty to your own people."

Asher sneered, just a little. "Sure I do. But my first loyalty be with the king. And the law. Ain't yours?"

"Leave him be, Conroyd," advised the Master Magician as Jarralt's face clenched with fury. "You provoked that. Your Majesty..."

The king smiled, the very faintest softening of his cold face. "Durm?"

"His Highness is right. There can be no repeat of what occurred the last time we had a conviction of this kind. I see no detriment in this Asher remaining as your son's assistant. Let him be seen freely by His Highness's side as we prosecute this law-breaker. Let the Olken of Dorana City know by word and deed that we cherish them as we have ever cherished them and grieve as they grieve at this gross betrayal of Blessed Barl by one of their own."

The king nodded. "As ever, old friend, we are thought and echo. It shall be handled as you suggest," He turned his attention to Asher. "Leave us. Attend to your duties as my son has requested and hold your tongue on this unfortunate business until he gives you leave to speak publicly."

Swallowing relief Asher bowed, to the king and then the rest of the Council. "Aye, Y'Majesty," and escaped the chamber before something else could go wrong.

On returning to the Tower he collected his copy of the next week's appointments from a prune-faced Willer, ordered himself an early lunch from the kitchen and settled down in his office to eat and work until Gar returned.

The prince walked in three hours later, looking tired and on edge. He threw himself into the nearest armchair and propped his dusty boots on the edge of the desk. "What are you doing?"

Asher shoved his pen back in its ink pot. "What you asked."

"Oh," said Gar. His fingers drummed on the arm of the chair. "Are you finished?"

"Just about."

Still drumming, Gar nodded. "Good."

"I had a question, though, on—"

Gar lifted his hand. "Tell me. Did you mean what you said?"

Asher considered him warily. "About what?"

"Chopping off this man's head. Did you mean it?"

Oh. That. With a sigh, Asher shoved aside his laboriously scrawled notes, leaned back in his chair and kicked his own heels onto the desktop. If it were good enough for a prince...

"Course I meant it," he said. "Did you think I didn't?"

Gar frowned. "No. At least...I thought...I wondered—Jarralt was being so difficult..."

"Aye. He's a right bastard that one, eh?" Remembering, Asher scowled. "You said he might do me a bad turn. You *never* said he'd hate my guts. If he had his way, Gar, I'd be a slimy red—"

"Don't worry," Gar said flatly. "It's nothing but bluster. Ignore him. Politely." He brushed a smudge of dust from his knee, still frowning. "Asher...I hope you know we're not all so arrogant. About your people. Doranen like Jarralt, like..." He hesitated. "It's just that some Doranen hark back to the days when our magic was less...restrained. They're fools, of course. That kind of magic destroyed us. Brought us here and changed a lot of things forever. Besides, most if not all of the incantations are centuries lost. But even if they weren't, Barl's Laws are clear. It's prohibited, with penalties as severe as any the Olken face."

Asher snorted. "Oh aye? So if one of your lot were caught pissin' about with magic as didn't concern 'em, would you turn y'self inside out worryin' for 'em?"

"No, I suppose not," said Gar, sighing.

"Then why fret me on not carin' what happens to this Olken fool in custody now, whoever he is?"

"His name is Timon Spake," said Gar. "He hails from Basing-down."

"Never heard of him. But even if I had—"

"Yes?" Gar stared at him. "If you had? If you knew him? If it was Matt, say, who'd been caught breaking the law and not this stranger? Would you still be so eager to see his head struck from his shoulders?"

"Well, for a start I ain't eager to see *anybody's* head struck off their shoulders," Asher pointed out. "I just want to know it got done. And Matt would never break Barl's First Law. He ain't a fool like this Spake man."

"You know what I mean."

Asher sighed. Yes, he did know. "Gar, it's the law. What are you tryin' to say? That the rules should be different for your lot and mine? Or we should forget about 'em if we happen to know the law-breaker?"

Gar thumped his boot heels to the floor. "No! No, I just—I wish—"

"'Cause y'know that'd never bloody work. The only reason your lot and mine rub along as well as we do is 'cause everybody's livin' under the same rules and nobody plays favourites. You start muckin' about with that and the next thing y'know we're all in the water and some of us is drownin'."

With his elbows on his knees, Gar pressed his face into his hands. "I know that," he said, muffled.

"Well, then," Asher said bracingly. "Now we got that settled, how's about we get started on all these appointments you got lined up, eh? I been thinkin' on 'em, just like you asked. Even got some ideas. I'll tell 'em to you, so long as you promise not to laugh."

It took a moment, but Gar finally looked up. "I promise I'll try," he said, with a faint smile. "But that's as far as I go."

Their discussion of the next week's calendar took the rest of the day. Gar had meetings scheduled with the Sheepgrowers' Association, the Miners' Guild, the Bakers' Guild, the Vintners and more. Asher's head whirled. He didn't have hardly a clue what any of them did or what they thought their problems were. So Gar had to give him a quick history of each guild, who their meisters or mistresses were, what they wanted, who they were feuding with and how each one impacted on all the others. By the end of it he wasn't sure whether he was horrified at all the things he was going to have to learn or impressed by the fact that Gar knew them so well already. Most of the ideas he'd already come up with had to be thrown overboard, which meant he'd have to come up with some new ones, quick smart.

He started to think that at fifty trins a week, he'd be *under*paid.

Dusk was fast approaching by the time they finished. Groaning, Asher slumped against his chair-back and rubbed his eyes. "Don't reckon I can see how you been managin' on your own. Did the king have all this claptrap to go on with as well as his WeatherWorkin'?"

Just as slumped. Gar nodded. "A lot of it, which is why I stepped in. Of course since I made myself available for consultation and assistance the workload has gradually become heavier and heavier. Hence you."

Asher grinned. "No good deed goes unpunished, eh?"

"Something like that." Gar fought a yawn, and lost. "I hope you're not too alarmed. Most problems can be solved by sitting down and talking them through. A lot of the time people just like to know they've been listened to. Once you're familiar with who's who we can—" A knock at the door interrupted him. It was young Remy, carrying a note. "Yes?"

Remy bowed. "'Scuse me, Your Highness, but this just come from the palace."

Gar took the note and dismissed the lad with a nod. He read it and sighed. "Timon Spake has been delivered to the guardhouse. There's to be a preliminary enquiry before the Privy Council in the morning."

Asher sat up. "What does that mean?"

"It means he'll be asked formally, under oath, if he's guilty of the crime. If he says no we proceed to a full and public trial."

"And if he says yes?"

Gar's expression was bleak. His fingers worried at the note and his gaze was distant. "Then he'll not see another sunrise."

"That fast?" said Asher, surprised.

"There's nothing to be gained by prolonging the agony. Asher, I want you to do something for me. Go down to the guardhouse and make sure this Timon Spake is well situated. He must be decently housed and fed and not subjected to unnecessary restraint. At this moment he's only accused, not convicted, but the crime is so heinous I fear for his safety."

Asher stared. "In the guardhouse?"

"Captain Orrick is an honourable man and an excellent officer," Gar said carefully. "But feelings will be running high. I want it made clear to him and his subordinates that regardless of personal outrage and the severity of the accused's crime, we mustn't run ahead of the verdict."

Slumping again, Asher swallowed a groan. "You want me to go right now?"

"Yes." Gar reached across the desk and pulled paper and pen towards him. As he scrawled a quick note he said, "I can't go myself, for obvious reasons. As my assistant, however, you'll be speaking with my full authority." Finished with his writing, he folded the note and held it out. "Give this to Orrick. It'll ensure his complete cooperation."

Asher took the note and studied it. "Only if he believes it's come from you. What if he accuses me of makin' it up or somethin'? Decides I'm in cahoots with this Timon Spake? He might, seein' as how he's so diligent and he don't know me from a hole in the ground. I mean, he knows someone called Asher's your new assistant, but he don't know for sure that's me."

Gar frowned, took the note back again and headed for the door. Asher scrambled after him and they hurried downstairs to Darran's office.

"Your Highness?" the ole crow squawked as they marched in. "Is something wrong?"

As Gar sealed the note with crimson wax and pressed his house ring into it he said to Darran, "You'll need to send messengers out at once cancelling all my appointments for tomorrow."

"Yes, Your Highness," Darran said faintly. "May I ask, Your Highness, what reason I should—"

"No," said Gar. Ignoring Darran's offended shock and Willer's fish-faced goggling, he handed the sealed note to Asher. "Be thorough but don't linger. Report to me the minute you return to the Tower."

"Aye, sir," said Asher, and tucked the note into his pocket. "What d'you want me to do if I find—"

"Whatever you deem appropriate," said Gar. "Bearing in mind I shall have to answer for it to the Privy Council."

"Aye, sir," said Asher, glumly, and withdrew. Not even the look on ole Darran's face had the power to cheer him up. Damn. If this was what bein' Assistant Olken Administrator were all about, then he was *definitely* underpaid.

The last person Dathne expected to see come riding down the High Street from the direction of the palace was Asher. But there he was, scowling and unimpressed on top of his precious silver Cygnet, making his way through the crowd in the City's central square. When he saw the milling, muttering Olken as they bumped and gathered around Supplicant's Fountain and stared across the square at the guardhouse entrance, his scowl melted into dismay, then returned more ferociously than ever. She saw his lips move and imagined the cursing.

She didn't blame him; she felt like cursing, too.

Pushing her way through the bodies she called his name and waved. "Asher! Asher!"

Startled, he drew rein and stared down at her as she reached him. "Dathne? What are you doin' out here?"

"I could ask you the same thing," she said.

He nudged his horse sideways until they were pressed flank and knee against the Golden Cockerel Hotel's front wall. "Official business. Now what's all this rabble-rousin' about?" He leaned over Cygnet's wither as she crowded close and lowered his voice. "You got any idea what's amiss?"

She nodded, one hand steady against the grey colt's warm, sleek shoulder. "I know exactly what's amiss. And so does everybody else here. With or without an official announcement from the palace, by this time tomorrow I expect every man, woman and child in the City will know."

"That some fool's got caught messin' about with—" Stiff-faced with angry surprise, Asher glanced at the mob and reconsidered. "How did you find out? The king only got word this mornin'."

"And Timon Spake was taken yesterday afternoon," she replied, shrugging. "Enough people here have family in Basingdown, Asher. The dressmaker two doors down from my shop has a sister there. Are you forgetting messenger pigeons? It only takes one or two, and after that it's running feet and gabbling tongues. Did you really think you'd keep something like this a secret?"

Asher frowned. "The king did."

"The king was wrong then, wasn't he?" She glanced over her shoulder. Moment by moment the crowd was growing, and as it grew the muttering swelled to an ominous rumble. "I don't like the look of this."

"You and me both," said Asher with another worried look at the gathered Olken. "What are they all doin' here? What do they want?"

She shrugged. "Reassurance. Revenge. The last time this happened a lot of innocent people were hurt. That's not been forgotten. I think the Olken of Doranen want to make it perfectly clear from the outset where their loyalties lie." She shivered. "I'd say if Spake walked out here now they'd tear him limb from limb." Another shiver. "This is going to get ugly."

Even as she spoke, a stream of guards flowed out of the guardhouse, each one armed with a long pike and a short truncheon. They took up positions along the front of the guardhouse railings and planted the butts of their pikes beside them. Their faces were grim. All around the square and along the City streets glimfire flickered into life inside the public lanterns that sat atop light-poles, dangled from gates and shopfronts and hung suspended from wires over street corners. The light threw long shadows, painting the world with danger.

Asher was staring at the thickening crowd. "Wonder if the king knows about this?"

"If he doesn't, he soon will," she said. "What are you doing here anyway?"

"Gar sent me. He be worried about this man Spake. Wants to make sure he ain't gettin' treated unfairly in there." He nodded at the guardhouse. "Reckon he wants to be more worried about this mob out here. Dath, I got to get goin'. You should go too, back home. Might not be safe out here much longer if these folk take it into their heads to get rambunctious."

Dathne nodded, her mind racing. Asher was going into the guardhouse? To see Spake? *Perfect.* Here was a gift unlooked for. A way to salvage this sorry situation. To save her life's work and a kingdom besides from the folly of one heedless idiot. She put her hand on his knee. "Asher, let me go with you."

Dragging his frowning gaze away from the crowd, he laughed. "Don't be daft."

"I mean it. I need to get in there. I must see this Timon Spake."

"Why?"

Because I have to stop his mouth before he talks or there won't be enough empty cells in all of Dorana to hold the victims of his arrogance. "Because he's by way of being family," she said with all the wide-eyed sincerity she could summon. "Only indirectly, a cousin of a cousin of a cousin. You know how it goes. I've never actually met him, but no matter how distant the connection he's still family. If I could just see him, make sure he's—"

"No, I said!" snapped Asher. "I'll tell you how he is, and you can tell whoever asks. But you ain't comin' into the guardhouse with me. If Gar—"

"I'm sure the prince wouldn't mind. He knows me. And I won't be a nuisance. I won't even speak, I promise. I'll be as quiet as a mouse."

She tried a winning, winsome smile. "Please, Asher? You wouldn't even have this job if it wasn't for me. A favour for a favour."

"Dathne!"

Clearly her winning, winsome smile needed some work. "Look, you say you're here to make sure this Spake is all right? Well, I can promise you he's not. He's in that guardhouse, locked in a cell, probably terrified. Probably being fed on pig slops because he'll have no friends in there. After what he's done he's got no friends anywhere. I could run back to my place, it won't take long. I've sweet cakelets I baked just this morning. He's welcome to them. And a book to take his mind off things. I'm sure the prince would approve of that, showing mercy to a condemned man. It's why he's sent you, isn't it? I'd just be helping. Who could object?"

Asher let out an angry huff of air. Chewed at his lip and banged his fist on his thigh, thinking. "Run fast then," he said at last, grudgingly. "Ten minutes I'll wait, and after that I'll be goin' in there without you."

She bolted. The cakelets were on the kitchen windowsill; after setting three onto the benchtop she rummaged in the back of a cupboard. Found the small glass vial she was after and the thin hollow straw she needed. The sickly-sweet smell of tinctured draconis root made her blink. With the straw she cautiously sucked the poison out of the bottle, then dripped it with immense care into the heart of each cakelet.

It wasn't murder. He was going to die anyway, so you couldn't call it murder. And his silence, ensured, would save the lives of hundreds. Maybe thousands. Maybe everyone alive in the kingdom. Veira would be angry, but so long as the old woman was angry after the fact that didn't matter. As Jervale's Heir she had a duty to ensure the smooth passage of Prophecy...and she would do whatever she had to, no matter the cost.

She felt a brief, burning hatred for the man who was making her do this. Forcing her hand to take his life. Who had sworn the same oath she had, to silence, to the Circle, to death before betrayal...

The bastard should have killed himself.

When it was done she wrapped the cakelets in a clean tea towel, put them and a book into her string bag and bolted all the way back to Asher.

"Just in bloody time," he muttered, eyeing the packed square uneasily. "Stick close now. I reckon this mob's goin' to start a riot any second."

Fingers wrapped tight around his stirrup leather, holding hard against Cygnet's trembling side, she pushed with him through the surging crowd. The air was thick with ugliness, with fear and fury. Looking around her she couldn't see a single fair head anywhere, only dark ones. Only Olken. The press of bodies parted reluctantly, complaining, and they continued forward until a guard standing at the entrance to the guardhouse lowered his pike point-first and challenged them.

"Let me pass," said Asher curtly. "I'm Asher, the Assistant Olken Administrator. I've come on the prince's business."

Dathne watched the guard's tense gaze flicker over the expensive horse, its rider's expensive clothes and lastly his face. The pike's point dropped, fractionally. "The woman?"

"Is with me. Now stand aside." Asher touched his spurs to Cygnet's flanks. The horse snorted, ears pinned back, and danced a little.

"Pass," said the guard, and stepped sideways.

Asher eased his hand on the reins and Cygnet jumped forward. "Easy, you ole fool." He glanced down. "You be all right there, Dathne?"

She took a deep breath. Her heart was booming and her mouth was dry. She could still smell the draconis. "I'm fine. Let's just get this over with, shall we?"

"Aye. Let's," said Asher, and together they walked through the gates of the Dorana City guardhouse.

CHAPTER ELEVEN

Captain Orrick of the City Guard was a lean, hatchetfaced man of middle years who wore his plain crimson uniform like a second skin. His dark, silver-threaded hair was clipped even closer than Matt's and his grey eyes were cool and calculating. He stood in front of the guardhouse lobby desk and twice read the note Asher handed him. Then he looked up.

"I'd heard someone was appointed His Highness's Assistant Administrator."

"Aye, well, that someone'd be me," said Asher.

"So you say." Orrick considered him. "But we've not been formally introduced."

Asher shrugged. "It only just happened. Reckon His Highness'll get around to officially tellin' you it's me in his own good time. Mayhap he's been too busy trimmin' his toenails to think of it."

Orrick's thin lips tightened. If they hadn't been surrounded by the captain's nervous subordinates, all looking out of the windows and muttering about the gathered crowd outside, Dathne would have trodden on Asher's toes, hard. Pellen Orrick was the last man in Dorana to be amused by an eccentric sense of humour.

"His Majesty has charged me straight to keep the prisoner isolated," Orrick said. "Do I understand you expect me to disobey a lawful order from the king?"

"Look," said Asher, sighing. "I don't know nowt about that. All I know is Prince Gar sent me hotfootin' it down here to have a quick gander at this Spake from Basingdown. You be holdin' his note of authority in your hand. If you want to get in a brangle between the prince and his da, that be your business. Mine's doin' as I'm told by the man payin' me a fat sum of trins every week not to stand around arguin' about every little thing. Right?"

Orrick's chill gaze shifted. "You're not mentioned in His Highness's letter of authority, Mistress Dathne."

"No, but I am," said Asher. "And she's with me. Brought a mite of comfort for the prisoner. You sayin' you ain't goin' to let a condemned man have a mite of comfort in his last days? That's hard, that is."

Unprompted, Dathne held out the string bag. Orrick took it from her and inspected the contents. "It's not much," she said. "But a little is better than nothing."

"You know what crime it is this man stands accused of?" said Orrick, handing back the bag.

"Yes, Captain. Word's got about, it seems."

Orrick's face tightened. "And knowing it, still you'd bring him comfort? This blasphemous traitor?"

"As you say, Captain, he is but accused," she said, keeping her gaze discreetly lowered. "And Barl believed in mercy as well as swift retribution. If guilt is proven he'll be punished soon enough."

Orrick made a disgusted, impatient sound. "Very well. You have five minutes to satisfy your prince's concerns, Meister Asher." Turning to one of his guards he snapped his fingers. "Bunder. Take the prince's assistant and Mistress Dathne here along to see the prisoner Spake. Stay with them while they count his fingers and toes and bring them back smartly thereafter."

Bunder saluted, then took the brass ring of keys Orrick handed him. "Yes, Captain!"

Dathne favoured Orrick with her best smile. "Thank you so much, Captain. I'm sure His Highness will be well pleased, won't he, Asher?" When Asher scowled she did tread on his toes.

"Oy!" he said, annoyed, then took the hint. "Aye, he'll be tickled pink." He glanced out of the nearest window, then looked back at Orrick. His expression softened. "Reckon you got a bit on your plate tonight as it is, Captain. We'll be out of your hair directly."

Orrick's eyes lost a little of their chill. "I would appreciate it. Bunder?"

There was a stout wooden door to one side of the main desk. The guardsman opened it for them, let them pass, then closed it and led them along a corridor towards the rear of the building. The cells on either side of the passageway were empty. Dathne wasn't surprised; the guardhouse tended to fill up only at the end of the working week, when an excess of cheer and ale and lost bets on the horses caused trouble. As she followed Bunder's stiff spine and squared shoulders, the string bag bouncing on her shoulder, Dathne felt her heartbeat booming louder, faster.

It was a terrible thing she planned to do, terrible and dangerous. Draconis was not an obvious poison. It acted slowly, weakening the blood vessels in the brain. Some hours after consumption it induced violent seizures, mimicking the natural effects of a stroke. After suffering a series of convulsions, the victim lapsed into a stupor from which he could not be roused, then faded away over two or three days. Twice to her knowledge it had been used in other, equally dire circumstances and in neither case had the Olken healers or Doranen pothers summoned for aid detected its presence. Like so many other things, the knowledge of draconis root had slipped into darkness.

Still, she was taking a dreadful risk. Captain Orrick was a diligent man, jealous of his authority and jurisdiction. There was a chance he might on principle suspect foul play, even though she knew it most likely the brainstorm would be blamed on an Olken's tampering with magic. If the stakes hadn't been so high she never would have contemplated such a dangerous act. But if this fool Spake's nerve failed and he attempted to save himself by implicating others...

She felt vilely sick, with nerves and revulsion for what she was about to do. As poisons went draconis was relatively painless, but even so... *Jervale forgive me, I have no choice. Either I soil my hands a little now, or see them soaked in blood later.*

At the end of the corridor there was another door. Bunder selected a key from the ring he carried and unlocked it. Swinging the door open, he ushered them through.

The room beyond was small and windowless. Most of it was a cell, partitioned from the small front section by floor-to-ceiling metal bars in which a narrow door had been set. It was heavy with padlocks. The cell contained a bench, a bucket and a man. Its floor was strewn with fresh straw. Two small barred vents high up on the rear wall allowed fresh air to flow into the restricted space, but it wasn't enough to mask the stench of recent vomiting.

Hearing the door open, the prisoner looked up from his hunched squat over the bucket. The first thing Dathne thought on seeing him was: *Veira! Why didn't you tell me he was so young?*

Young, slight of body and plain with it. His face was unremarkable, his chin a trifle weak, his eyes mud brown and his black hair cut unbecomingly above his ears, which stuck out ever so slightly. There were freckles on his nose. It was hard to imagine him shaving. Harder still to imagine him whispering the words of forbidden magics.

She glanced at Asher, solid and silent by her side. His expression was smooth, unflustered; she was beginning to learn that it meant some deep consternation. Behind them Bunder closed the door and stood before it, feet wide and arms crossed over his chest. Fingers tight around the neck of the string bag, Dathne took a deep breath to calm her roiling stomach and waited.

"Is Hervy coming? Hervy Wynton?" Timon Spake asked uncertainly. He had a pleasant voice, deep for a young man, and it shook only a little. "He's a family friend. He said he was coming."

"I ain't the one to tell you that," said Asher. "I'm from the prince, to make sure they're treatin' you fair."

Spake's shoulders slumped. "Oh. I see." With a grunt and a grimace he got to his feet, one hand pressed to his middle.

"Well?" said Asher. "Got any complaints, do you?"

"No," said Spake.

Asher glanced over his shoulder. "Sure you ain't just sayin' that cause he's listenin'?" He jerked a thumb at Bunder.

"No," Spake said again. He was very pale, and there was a twitch beside his right eye. "I'm all right."

"Hungry?"

Spake shuddered and glanced at the bucket. "No. They gave me something a while ago but it's just made me sick."

Dathne felt a wave of despicable relief. Surely that would help muddle the cause of death, hint at something wrong before ever she got there...unless the cakelets made him ill, too, before the draconis could do its work. She tried not to frown. It couldn't be helped, she'd just have to hope for the best. *The best*, as she stood here face to face with the man—the boy—she was plotting to kill. She could easily have been sick herself. Not for the first time she wished she'd been born anything, anyone, other than Jervale's bloody Heir.

Asher said, "Well, there's some cakelets here for you, and a book anyways. It's bound to be a long night, you might as well have somethin' to take your mind off things. And Dathne's cookin's got to be better than prison slops. But then you'd know that, eh, what with her bein' family."

Spake stared, clearly puzzled. "Family? I'm sorry, I don't think I—"

Damn. "Distant family," she said quickly. "Cousins of cousins, several times removed. You've probably never heard of me except in passing mention." She took a hard breath then, and let it out again softly, instinct warring with caution. "Although...I think we both know Aunty Vee..."

The young idiot didn't make the connection. With a kind of hopeless courtesy, Spake raised a hand. "No, no. Thank you, but—" He blinked. "Did you say *Aunty Vee?*"

"Aye, y'fool. Be you deaf as well as gormless?" Asher said roughly. "Go on, take 'em, whether you know her or you don't. She needn't have brought anythin' for you, Spake. And you might be glad of somethin' in your belly afore the sun comes up."

She wouldn't, she couldn't, raise her voice to cajole the boy further. She'd done enough, invoking innocent Veira's name. But she held up the string bag, of a size to slide between the prison bars, and took a step forwards. Just then somebody hammered on the door behind them and burst through it, shouting. Unprepared, bellowing, Bunder rocketed forward and sideways. Crashed straight into Asher, who yelled and crashed into her. She went down hard beneath his weight. Landed on the string bag and the cakelets and the book, crushing them all together in a sticky mess.

The guard whose fault it was stood panting and redfaced in the doorway. "Captain Orrick says you're to come at once! There's folks barged into the guardhouse and he says he wants the prince's man to send them away again or he'll fill the cells to bursting and a pox on all their guildmeister heads!"

Winded, groaning, her ribs bent almost double and her thoughts in shrieking disarray, Dathne lay on the cell floor as Asher and Bunder found their feet and cursed the stupid guard who'd skittled them.

"Bloody idiot, Torville!" Bunder raged. "You might've broken all our bones!"

Asher reached down a hand and pulled Dathne to her feet. "You all right?"

"I'm better than the cakelets," she said, and didn't know whether to laugh or cry. This had been her one and only hope of saving the Circle from Edvord Spake's arrogant son. Now all their lives were in his foolish, trembling hands...and she didn't know how she felt about it. She kicked the string bag with the toe of her shoe. "They're fit for nothing but rubbish now."

He patted her on the shoulder. "Never mind, Dath. It were a kindly thought, and that's what counts."

Picking up the string bag she took out the book, which had escaped the worst of the mess thanks to the tea towel she'd wrapped around the cakelets. After swiping her sleeve over it she thrust it through the prison bars. "Here."

"Thank you," said Timon Spake, taking the book. He looked at its cover and read the title. "*Heroes of the Old Days.* I've never read this one."

"It's very good," she said, and fixed her grim unblinking gaze upon him. "It's about brave men facing dire consequences with courage. Men who keep to their oaths despite all danger and temptation."

"Oh," said Timon Spake. Nothing showed in his face, but in his sad, troubled eyes questions were dawning. "It sounds...inspirational."

"It is," said Dathne, still holding his gaze. "It surely is." She lowered her voice. "You could do worse than follow their example."

"You must come now!" Torville insisted in the doorway, sounding shrill. "Captain Orrick insists!"

So they left the prisoner to his book and his thoughts and hurried back to the guardhouse lobby, where pandemonium ruled. Somehow a great gaggle of well-dressed City Olken had forced their way past the guards in the street outside and were now all shouting and stamping their feet and banging their fists upon the desk. Captain Orrick was standing behind it on a chair, trying to make himself heard above the din.

"Here!" he shouted as Torville practically shoved them through the door. "Here is Asher, His Royal Highness Prince Gar's Assistant Administrator! If you damn fools refuse to listen to me, then listen to him! For if you don't I swear I'll see you all locked up for a month of Barlsdays!"

Dathne dug her elbow into Asher's ribs. "Go on then, introduce yourself. After all, they had to meet you sometime, didn't they?"

"Ha. Don't reckon Gar had this in mind when he mentioned me gettin' to know a few people."

The largest well-dressed Olken pushed to the front of the crush around the desk. "*Who* do you say he is? I have never seen this man before!"

Cornered, Asher shot Orrick a dagger-drawn look then lithely leapt on top of the desk. "You heard 'im! I be Asher, Prince Gar's Assistant Administrator, as was newly appointed and announced last Barlsday. Who are you?"

The large man swelled inside his velvet and furs. "I? I, sir, am Norwich Porter, Meister of the Brewers' Guild!"

"Ah," said Asher. "Got yourself the prince's acceptance to the banquet, have you?"

Norwich Porter goggled at him. "What? Well...yes...as a matter of fact it arrived—"

"Well, you can set an extra place for me. I'll be there, and so will His Highness—provided you quit all this caterwauling and get on home where you belong!"

Norwich Porter's face flushed dark red. "How dare you, sir! We are going nowhere, *nowhere*, do you hear, until we get satisfaction! We represent the will and the wishes of all the Olken guilds and we demand—"

"You ain't in the right place to be demandin' nowt!" said Asher. "Who do you think you are, eh, come bargin' into the City guardhouse, blusterin' and bossin' Captain Orrick, here, who's doin' the job your taxes pay him for. The job His Majesty King Borne told him to do just this mornin'. In Privy Council. Where I heard him with my own ears."

Dathne, smothering a smile, thought Norwich Porter was going to fall to the floor in a foaming, spluttering heap. All around him his fellow guild meisters and mistresses gasped and protested and waved their fists. Asher, bless him, was supremely unimpressed.

Norwich Porter said, incredulous, "You dare—you dare—by what right do you stand there and insult—"

"What insult? I'm just tellin' you what's what."

"No, sir," Porter retorted. "I shall tell *you* what's what. It is rumoured that Captain Orrick has in custody a vile, treacherous, *evil* law-breaker. We will have him brought to justice! We will see him for ourselves! We—"

"Will end up in the cell next door if you don't quit flappin' your lips and listen!" shouted Asher. "Aye, there be a man here. He's accused—only accused, mind you—of a terrible crime. First thing tomorrow he'll stand afore king and Privy Council and then we'll know the truth of it. Until then he ain't standin' afore anybody, least of all a rabble what comes in here over lawful restraint tryin' to usurp the king's privilege!"

A shocked silence fell. After a moment, Norwich Porter cleared his throat. "I can assure you, sir," he said stiffly, "that nobody here intends to usurp the king's privilege."

"No?" said Asher, one eyebrow raised. "You could've fooled me."

Norwich Porter deflated a little further. Glanced uneasily at the guild officials on either side of him and took a small step back from the desk. "You say this man is to stand before His Majesty and the Privy Council?"

Asher smiled, fiercely. "Aye. Unless you got an objection, which I'd be more than happy to pass along to the king."

Behind Norwich Porter, the other guild meisters and mistresses exchanged furtive looks and began unobtrusively inching towards the front doors. Facing defeat, Norwich Porter rallied himself for one last blow. "And you, sir. Asher, you call yourself? Precisely how are we to know you are who you say you are?"

"Aside from bein' introduced by Captain Orrick here?" Asher smiled again, and Norwich Porter winced. "Come and say hello at your banquet next month. I'll be the one sittin' next to His Highness. Chances are I might remember you."

Dathne had to turn away, the urge to laugh was so strong. She doubted Guild Meister Porter had ever received so public a set-down in all his life.

Giving ground, Norwich Porter tried to gather the shreds of his dignity. "You are rude, sir. I shall be sure to mention that to His Highness the next time we speak."

"Well, you can if you want to," said Asher. "Only I figure he's noticed already. Ain't stoppin' him from payin' me, mind."

As the guild meister, by this time almost completely deserted by his peers, gasped and gobbled a string of incoherent threats and imprecations, Orrick got down from his chair and came round to the front of the desk. "Guild Meister Porter, these are fractious times. I appreciate your concerns but the City Guard has everything under control. Do your duty, sir, you and your fellow meisters and mistresses, and tell your members outside to go home. There is nothing to be done here this night."

With a final glare at Asher, Norwich Porter and the handful of remaining guild officials with him departed.

With a pleased smile Asher leapt down from the desk. "So," he said cheerfully. "That be what they call public speakin', eh?"

Orrick favoured him with a considering look. "Public bullying, more like."

Asher shrugged. "Silly ole farts, the lot of 'em. Ain't they the ones s'posed to be settin' an example for the rest of us?"

Orrick's lips twitched. "That's the idea."

"Well, a fine bloody example that was."

"Yes," said Orrick. His grey eyes were warm with amusement. "It certainly was." To Dathne's surprise, he held out his hand. "Well done, Meister Asher of Restharven. Welcome to Dorana. I'm sure you'll do very well here."

Despite her protests, Asher insisted on walking Dathne home, Cygnet clip-clopping at his side, even though the gathered crowd had mostly dispersed by the time they left the guardhouse. She bade him goodbye at her bookshop door and for a few moments watched him climb onto Cygnet and trot away up the street, back to the Tower.

Once inside her small apartment she put the string bag and the ruined cakelets in the hearth and burned them. Then she made herself a solitary supper and after that went straight to bed. She wasn't going to tell Veira what she'd almost done that night. It was one secret she'd take to her grave. Because she didn't wish to hurt her friend and mentor. Because she didn't want to argue the merits of an action that in the end was not taken. And because if she never spoke of it, ever, she might one day be able to forget what she'd found herself capable of doing.

Asher found a note pinned to his bedroom door when he finally got back to the Tower. *See me.* Cursing under his breath, he climbed the spiral staircase up to Gar's suite. Bloody worry-wart of a man. Spake wasn't going anywhere, was he? Couldn't this have waited till after he filled his empty belly?

"Spake's fine," he said, wandering into the prince's library. "Scared spitless, but fine. So—"

Gar's raised hand stopped him. "*Deverani, deverani,*" he murmured, staring at an unrolled parchment on the desk before him. He glanced up. "Contextually speaking, which is the closest modern Doranen word, do you think: *undone* or *released*?"

Asher blinked. "You're askin' *me*?"

"Well...yes," said Gar, and shook his head. "Though I don't for the life of me know why. Did you want something?"

"Aye," replied Asher, and thunked his shoulder against the nearest handy bookcase. "Dinner. But there's this note on my door, see, and—"

Gar's expression clouded. "Oh. Yes. Sorry. I was deep in the Fourth Century."

"Huh," said Asher. From the look on the prince's face he wished he was still back there. "Spake's fine. I saw him, spoke to him. He ain't complainin'."

"Did he say anything at all?"

"Not really."

"He didn't...I don't know, confess? Explain *why* he'd want to—" Breaking off, Gar pinched the bridge of his nose.

"No," said Asher. "But then I didn't ask him, did I? Don't see what difference it makes any road. Who cares why? *Why* ain't goin' to change things, is it?"

Gar sighed. "No. I suppose not."

"All that matters now is Orrick's doin' his job fair and proper. You got nowt to fret on where that's concerned."

"Good," said Gar, again staring at the parchment. "That's... good."

Asher sniffed. "Mind you, things got a mite interestin' for a moment, seein' as every guild meister and his best friend was crammed into the guardhouse tryin' to drag the fool outside and hang 'im from the nearest lamppost..."

Gar's head snapped up. "*What?*"

"It's all right," Asher said quickly. "Me and Orrick sorted 'em out."

"Which means, I suppose, that by lunchtime tomorrow I'll be up to my armpits in outraged Olken guild meisters?" Gar stifled a groan. "How in Barl's name did they find out?"

Deciding not to take offence, Asher shrugged. "You weren't never goin' to keep it a secret."

"Not a secret, no, but I'm sure His Majesty would've liked at least one day's grace!" Gar pressed ink-stained fingers to his temples. "I know I would." He sighed. "Oh well. What's done can't be undone. And you're *sure* Spake is comfortably situated?"

Briefly, Asher debated telling him about the small cell and the prisoner's sickness and his terror, barely leashed. About how young he was and how unlikely, how pathetic, a criminal. But what was the point? Gar couldn't change any of it. And he'd see for himself soon enough, when the boy was brought before the Privy Council for examination.

"I told you," he said, pushing away from the bookcase, "he's fine. Now, if there ain't anythin' else, I'll see about my dinner. Reckon I be halfway to starved and—"

"Wait," said Gar. "There is something."

Caught in the doorway, Asher swallowed an impatient groan and swung around. "Aye?"

"I want you there tomorrow. At Timon Spake's hearing."

"Me? Why me?" Asher demanded, incredulous. "I don't need to be there. That's Privy Council business, it's got nowt to do with me. Besides, that Lord Jarralt—one look at me and he'll shout the guard-house down."

Gar's eyes were cold, his expression unyielding. "He can shout till his head falls off for all I care. By this time tomorrow there's a very good chance Timon Spake will be dead. Executed by command of the Privy Council. I want an Olken witness. Justice must not only be done, it must be seen done. I want someone there who can tell who-ever may ask that this man's life wasn't taken from him lightly. I want you, Asher. And I won't take no for an answer."

Silence. Staring at Gar, Asher knew he stood at a crossroad. If he refused this order it was all over. He might as well hitch a ride on the next wagon back to Restharven because nobody would hire on a man who walked away from His Royal Highness Prince Gar. And if he accepted it...

If he accepted it, there'd be no turning back. Whatever else he became in the future, however rich he was when he finally returned home or how many boats he bought and sailed and sold, he'd always be the man who once had served the son of a king...no matter what was asked of him. A man whose dreams of independence were paid for, in part, by the blood of a guilty fool.

Question was, could he live with that?

Well, Timon Spake was doomed, whether Asher of Restharven was there to see him die or not. And Gar was right about one thing, sink him. They did need an Olken witness to Spake's trial, someone who could stand on top of the tallest building in the kingdom and shout for every Olken man, woman and child to hear: *See? See what muckin' about with magic gets you?*

That was important. It might mean the end, once and for all, of such mad foolishness. Could be that by being there, by seeing first-hand how fair the Privy Council dealt with such a blasphemous criminal and then telling what he saw, he'd *save* lives. That was a good thing, right?

Besides, if he did walk away, who would profit? Who'd be saved then? Timon Spake would be just as condemned. Asher of Restharven would be forced home poor, back to the bruising domination of his brothers. And Da would go to his grave never knowing the comforts he deserved.

With a sigh deep enough to make his ribs creak, he nodded. "Right, then. Seein' as how you're so set on it, reckon I'll see you in the mornin'. What time?"

If Gar was relieved or sorry he didn't show it. "Be downstairs by nine. Make sure you're dressed... soberly."

Asher nodded. "Soberly. Right."

Their eyes met. There was such angry despair in Gar's face Asher had to look away.

"You can go now," the prince said. "I won't need you again this evening. Close the door behind you."

Dismissed, and glad of it, Asher left him to his rage and his reading and headed back downstairs to his own rooms.

All of a sudden, he wasn't hungry any more.

CHAPTER TWELVE

Barl have mercy," King Borne exclaimed, shocked. "This Timon Spake is practically a *child*! Why did no-one inform me?"

As Captain Orrick rummaged through the paperwork piled on the table before him, Asher avoided Gar's accusing gaze. The prince'd thank him for not saying anything. Eventually. From the looks of him Gar had barely slept a wink the night before. If he'd known just how beardless a youth it was they had in custody he'd have fretted himself to a standstill, with nothing to show for it by sunrise save a face fit to curdle cream.

Weighed down with chains, his face half hidden as he stared at the flagstoned floor of the guardhouse examination room, Timon Spake of Basingdown knelt in silent disgrace. A City Guard stood on either side of him, strong hands pressing hard on each shoulder as though at any moment he might sprout wings and fly away from the fate that awaited him.

Orrick looked up from his parchments. "The prisoner is sixteen, Your Majesty. Under the law he is a man, and as a man must stand trial for his crime."

The king nodded. "Very well. In that case let the examination commence. Barlsman Holze?"

Holze lowered his head until his single silver-yellow braid dangled, and pressed his hand to his heart. "Let all here now entreat Blessed Barl's guidance, that we may know the truth and speak it unreserved to the glory of she who made the Wall and the comfort of all her children. O Blessed Barl, we stand before you in this place and at this time to hear the grave charges laid against your son, Timon Spake of Basingdown..."

Asher swallowed a sigh. If he'd known there'd be Holze sermonising he'd have found himself something to sit on. Now he had to stand and wriggle his toes so his legs didn't fall asleep while the ole cleric prosed on and on and on...

After surviving a single scorching glare from Jarralt as they arrived at the guardhouse he'd wedged himself into one unobtrusive corner of the examination chamber while the hearing's preparations were concluded. From there he could witness the proceedings as commanded without actually getting involved.

The more he thought about it the more *not getting involved* seemed like a very good idea. This grim stone room was a far cry from the beauty and splendour of airy, stained-glass Justice Hall. In Justice Hall, though important matters were daily decided, there was still a kind of brightness. An unstated recognition that even though the hearings were serious there yet remained light and laughter in the world.

Not so in here. Light and laughter had no place in this plain, crowded place. In here, without beauty or splendour, the lives of men were stripped bare and judged, and if found wanting...ended.

The examination chamber was full of people: the king and his Privy Council, a wall of disapproval and dire consequence implacably ranged against the grubby miscreant cowering at their feet. Lady Marnagh from Justice Hall, seated at the table beside Orrick and once more acting as justice's official record-keeper. Two more faces Asher couldn't put a name to. Speakers for the accused? Or against him. He couldn't tell. There were three other guards as well, one on each side of the prisoner's entrance to the chamber and one at the examiner's entrance.

In keeping with his royal authority Borne was seated on a tall gold and crimson chair set upon a raised platform that ran the length of the bleak examination room. Austere in black velvet, his crown flashed green and crimson fire in the glimlight. At his left hand stood Master Magician Durm, sombre in a black brocade robe. Gar stood at his right hand, equally grave in midnight blue silk. Droning Holze, wrapped in white as befitted the Royal Barlsman, stood next to Gar with Conroyd Jarralt, magnificent in peacock blue, beside Durm.

Asher stifled a curse. So many bodies: surely they'd soon breathe up all the air in the stuffy, windowless room. Already he was sweating, trickles down his spine, behind his ears, stinging his eyes and soaking his armpits. At this rate his suitably sober green shirt and brown weskit, sent along from the tailor yesterday afternoon with all his other clobber, would both be ruined with stink and salt.

Holze's prayer still showed no sign of ending. Asher stared at the king. Could be it was his imagination but he thought Gar's da looked even more stripped clean of flesh than he had the previous morning. As though some terrible fever had rushed rampaging through him overnight, stealing meat and muscle from his bones unopposed. His clear green eyes, Gar's eyes, had sunk deep into his skull, and the unguarded moment of surprise at first beholding the prisoner, which had flushed his hollow cheeks, was vanished without a trace. Now Borne's face looked like a winter snowfield, cold and clean, with all emotion frozen.

Gar's face was a bonfire in comparison; leaping behind his eyes the flames of passionate revolt, their shadows flickering, their heat washing his cheeks red with reflected warmth. Though he stood motionless at his father's side, it seemed to Asher that the prince was shaking, so extreme was the tension in every line of his body.

As for Durm and Jarralt...they more closely resembled the king. Their expressions were chilled, their gazes laden with ice. Even Holze, praying, appeared unsympathetic. Timon Spake of Basingdown had but one friend on that platform, and Gar would never prevail in such company, even if he wanted to.

Barring intervention from Blessed Barl herself, Timon Spake of Basingdown was doomed.

Sixteen years of age, and never to see seventeen. Never to kiss another girl or fondle a woman's breast or dandle a milk-sucking son upon his knee. No more springtimes. One last sunset.

What a waste.

At long last Holze's prayer ended. The king said gravely, "Read the charge, Captain Orrick."

Orrick bowed and unrolled crackling parchment. "On this day, the sixth day in the second month of summer in the year 644 After Barl, it is alleged that the prisoner, one Timon Spake of Basingdown, did upon the fourth day in the second month of summer in the year 644 After Barl wilfully and absent coercion break Barl's First Law: to wit, that before witnesses he exhorted magic in the full knowledge that he is Olken and thus forbidden to do so on pain of death." He looked up then and stared stonily at every face in the chamber. "Whosoever does dispute this charge speak now or be hereafter silent."

When nobody spoke, Borne nodded. "Thus is the charge heard and ratified and entered into record. Who speaks against the accused?"

One of the men Asher didn't know stepped forward. Serious in dark brown velvet, draped in chains of office with a feather nodding in his cap, he bowed to the king then again to the rest of the Council.

"Your Majesty, I am Bryne Fletcher, Mayor of Basingdown. It was my daughters who did come upon this man in the woods and so espy his blasphemous and criminal conduct."

Borne's hands rested quietly on his knees. His keen, cold gaze considered the Basingdown mayor in silence. When he spoke his tone was level, his manner dispassionate. "And where are your daughters now, Mayor Fletcher?"

"At home with their mother, Your Majesty. They are but maids, eleven and thirteen years of age. I have given the guard captain their sworn and witnessed statements, as prescribed by law."

"It is so, Your Majesty," said Orrick. "I have the statements here."

A shadow of disquiet crossed Borne's brutally sculptured face. "And are your daughters sure beyond doubt of what they saw, Mayor Fletcher? In capital matters tender years are no defence against a false accusation. Children have fanciful imaginations, sir. I know, I have two of my own. Before we proceed in this matter I ask you most strictly: do you stand by the witnessed statements of your offspring? Knowing that should this charge be challenged and a full, public hearing be demanded by the accused, as is his right, you and your wife will be held equally accountable for their claims should they be proven false?"

The mayor's florid face lost its colour, but his forthright gaze held steady. "I stand by my girls, Your Majesty. Their mother and I have raised them to honour Barl, to obey the law, to daily do right by their neighbour and without exception turn away from wrongdoing. Your Majesty, they have nothing to gain from this and much to lose. They know Timon and are fond of him." The mayor hesitated. Glanced once at the prisoner and cleared his throat. "We are all fond of him. But my daughters know their duty and have done it. My wife and I are proud of them, sir."

"I see." Borne held out his hand. "The statements, Captain."

Orrick presented them to the king. Borne read each one, pale brows drawn low. When he was done he gave them to his Master Magician, who read them also, and from him they passed in turn to the other Council members to be read and considered.

Gar was the last to see the witness statements. When he was done he passed the papers back to the king. Borne read them a second time then gave them back to Orrick, who returned to his seat beside Lady Marnagh.

"The statements are in order," Borne said. "And therefore stand in evidence against the accused. Thank you, Mayor Fletcher. Your duty is done. You may commend your daughters on our behalf."

"Yes, Your Majesty," said Fletcher, breathless. "Thank you, Your Majesty." Dismissed, he stepped back again, visibly relieved.

The king said, "Who now speaks for the accused?"

The second man unfamiliar to Asher presented himself. After an unsteady bow he clasped his hands to his drab woollen chest. "Your Majesty." His voice was scarce above a whisper; a gently ageing man, he seemed overcome. "My name is Hervy Wynton. I am friend to the Spake family. Edvord Spake, father of the accused, was too ill to make the journey from Basingdown. He has a canker and is dying. He asked me to speak for him in this matter."

Borne nodded. "And what would the accused's father have you say on his behalf?"

Hervy Wynton licked his dry lips. His troubled gaze rested briefly on his friend's son, chained and kneeling, then returned to the stern figure of the king. "Your Majesty, Timon is a good boy. A loving son. He is all that my friend Edvord has left to him in the world. Whatever Timon has done it was never with malicious intent. He is no blasphemer, Your Majesty. Just a rash youth who thought to amuse himself with something he did not understand. Edvord knows his time is short, Your Majesty. He implores your mercy, that his last days be not spent in bitter grief and ceaseless tears."

If the king was moved by the old man's plea there was nothing to show it. "And do you or the accused's father challenge the charge as it stands? Can you show evidence of false accusation? Of wilful slander? Of any dark design intended to bring harm to Timon Spake of Basingdown and thereby benefit the accuser?"

"No, Your Majesty," whispered Hervy Wynton. "We accept... that the girls saw what they saw."

Borne nodded. "Very well. You may tell your friend Edvord Spake that his words were heard by king and Privy Council."

Hervy Wynton bowed again and shuffled back to stand beside the mayor. Now all eyes turned to the accused. Borne's thin fingers tightened once upon the arms of his tall chair, then relaxed. "Timon Spake of Basingdown, you have heard the charge levelled against you. What now have you to say for yourself? Are you guilty or falsely accused? Say you guilty and sentencing shall follow. Say you falsely accused and a public trial shall be held, with no shadowed corner left unlit until this matter is illuminated to the full."

For the first time since he'd been brought into the chamber, forced to his knees and held in silence as his life was pulled to pieces around him, Timon Spake of Basingdown looked up.

Asher saw Gar's face contract, saw him flinch as though someone had struck him a painful blow. He scowled. So the blaspheming lawbreaker looked no more dangerous than a half-grown hound. So what? He'd still shown his teeth, hadn't he? He'd still put a kingdom— a people—at risk. His own people, if this whole disaster had got out of hand. He looked pitiful now, aye, but that didn't change what he'd done. On purpose. With not a man there to twist his arm and make him cry if he didn't.

Da always said, *Talk is cheap and so be a sorry smile.*

"Answer the question, Timon Spake," the king said coldly. "Your life depends upon it. Are you guilty or falsely accused?"

The chains that bound him looked heavy. They must be hurting him, Spake's thin muscles must surely be shrieking beneath their weight by now. And his knees, pressed unpadded into the unforgiving stone floor, had to be hurting too. Grudgingly, Asher had to admit he admired the fool's nerve not to show it.

Mayor Fletcher's head bowed low, awaiting the answer. Beside him, Hervy Wynton cried out.

"Dispute the charge, Timon! Give yourself a chance! Think of your father, boy! Must I go home without you and break his dying heart?"

"Be silent, man," the king commanded. "We have heard from your own lips your belief that this is a true and lawful charge untainted by deceit or ulterior motive. Do not encourage the prisoner in dishonesty lest justice turn its eyes upon you."

Reprimanded, Hervy Wynton shrank back against the wall and turned his face away. Solitary and splendid in his tall chair King Borne leaned forward, hands braced on his knees, and bent a piercing gaze upon his prisoner. "I ask you a third time, Timon Spake of Basingdown, and give you fair warning: I will not ask again. Are you guilty or falsely accused?"

Timon Spake of Basingdown's weak chin lifted and his chained shoulders braced themselves. When he spoke his voice was calm. Resigned. "Your Majesty, I am guilty."

Borne turned his head to left and right, raking his winter gaze along the faces of his privy councillors. "Gentlemen, you have heard the accusation and the prisoner's reply. Out of his own mouth is he convicted and therefore public trial is rendered moot. Before sentence is pronounced, is there any one of you who would raise his voice in mitigation? If so, raise it now."

One by one Asher looked at the men of the king's Privy Council. He could read nothing in Durm's fat face; it was as smooth as a bladder of lard. Barlsman Holze looked unsurprised and gently sorrowful. Conroyd Jarralt was smiling, a small fierce flashing of teeth. And Gar...

All the flames behind Gar's eyes had died, the passionate hope crumbled into ash. He looked ill and tired and unspeakably sad.

Not one of them answered the king's call.

Borne sat back in his chair. On his head his jewelled crown danced colour across the grey stone walls. "Timon Spake of Basingdown, you have been heard by king and Privy Council in strict accordance with law. By your own admission and the unchallenged statements of honest witnesses you are found guilty of the charge laid against you. The penalty is death. Therefore I, King Borne, by Barl's grace named WeatherWorker of Lur, do declare your life forfeit and claim it in recompense for the crime committed. Captain Orrick?"

As Timon Spake stared blankly at the floor and Hervy Wynton's harsh sobs punctured the silence, Orrick stood up from his chair and bowed. "Your Majesty?"

"Have you a headsman at hand?"

Orrick nodded. "Yes, Your Majesty."

"Is his axe sharp?"

"Sharp and waiting, Your Majesty."

"Can you think of any impediment to the immediate culmination of this proceeding?"

Now Orrick was frowning, the merest hint of concern. "No, Your Majesty. Everything is ready."

Borne's fingers laced themselves tightly in his lap. His eyes were hooded, his face untouched by any human feeling. "Then let it be done, and done swiftly."

Orrick hesitated. "You mean now, Your Majesty? In here?"

The king considered him. "The kingdom is not served by a public spectacle, Captain. Or unwarranted delay."

"Of course not, Your Majesty." Orrick bowed again. "If Your Majesty and the Privy Council would care to withdraw to my office, then—"

"Withdraw?" said Borne. "For what reason? Justice must not only be done, Captain. It must be seen done or it is not justice at all."

"Your Majesty, I will be here. The guards will be here. Justice—"

"Demands that those who pass judgement shall witness judgement," said Borne. "And if not justice then surely conscience. No more discussion. Captain. Proceed."

Orrick nodded. "Yes, Your Majesty. There will be a short delay. Certain items that—"

"See to them. Quickly."

Orrick turned and flicked a commanding finger at the guard standing alert by the prisoner's entrance to the chamber. The man nodded, opened the door and went about his business. The mayor covered his face with his hands and turned away from Timon, who knelt unmoving, as though in a trance. Heedless of any personal danger Hervy Wynton cried out again and flung himself forward to land on his hands and knees at the king's feet.

"Have mercy, Your Majesty!" he begged, his voice rough with tears. "Give me an hour alone with the boy, give him one more night, at least let him see another sunrise, oh please, *please*, Your Majesty—"

For the first time, Durm spoke. "To what end, Wynton?" He stepped down from the platform and pulled the man to his feet, away from the king. "What can Timon Spake do between now and another sunrise that will make the least bit of difference?"

Wynton's face was ravaged with grief. "But...but..."

"It's all right, Hervy," said Timon. "Don't fret. This is my doing, not yours. Take my father a message, would you?"

As Durm stepped back onto the platform Wynton stumbled two steps towards his friend's son, then halted as the guards raised warning hands. "What message?" he asked brokenly. "I swear I'll deliver it."

Now there were tears on Timon Spake's white cheeks, and his lips were trembling. "Tell Papa he was right. Tell him I'm sorry. Tell him I did the right thing at the end, when it mattered."

"I'll tell him," Wynton whispered. "Dear boy, I'll tell him."

"Hervy Wynton," said Borne, and beckoned the man to him with a single raised finger. "It is not necessary that you stay and see this matter concluded. If you would care to wait outside..."

Wynton shook his head. "No. No, Your Majesty. I'll stay. I owe his father that much, having failed him."

For a moment Asher thought the king might touch Hervy Wynton. Lay a hand upon him. Pat his shoulder, or hold his thin wrist briefly. The impulse was in Borne's cold face, he could see it, the swift desire, the fleeting need. Then it passed. "You did not fail him, Wynton. Timon Spake has failed himself. Failed all of us who labour night and day for the greater good of Lur."

Slowly, the old man nodded. Dipped his head in a bow. "As you say, Your Majesty," he replied, and stepped back.

The king looked at the mayor of Basingdown. "And you, sir?"

Fletcher's face was the colour of skimmed milk. "I—my wife—my girls—"

"You may go," said Borne.

Then came a flurry of activity as Orrick's paperwork was removed along with the table and chairs. Lady Marnagh took her records and departed. Mayor Fletcher went with her. More guards entered the chamber, carrying armfuls of straw and a roughly shaped wooden block and a basket. The king turned his head. "Holze."

"Certainly, Your Majesty," murmured Holze, and went to the prisoner.

Asher, disregarded and disbelieving, watched as the Barlsman knelt beside Timon Spake. Rested a gentle hand against his cheek and began to speak softly in his ear. Whatever he was saying seemed to give the boy a measure of comfort. He began to nod. To cry more freely. Holze sang a hymn and the boy joined in, haltingly, his forehead lowered to Holze's white silk shoulder.

Asher looked at Gar. Wasn't it about time he spoke up? Said something along the lines of, "Well done, Asher, you can go"? His da had just pronounced sentence of death on that stupid, beardless youth. Any minute now they were going to chop off his stupid head, right in front of them, in front of *him*, and when he said he'd witness the hearing that didn't include the head-chopping bit afterwards.

As though reading his mind Gar looked at him. Shook his head, the very slightest of motions. Spoke not a word, but instead let his face do the speaking for him.

You wanted him dead. You can watch him die.

Stunned, furious, Asher felt his sweaty hands clench into fists. This wasn't *his* fault. Timon Spake was the criminal here, not him, so why was he getting punished? Why did he have to see poor bloody Timon Spake get his head hacked off? That wasn't fair. Well, one thing was bloody certain. Fifty trins a week didn't cover *this* kind of aggravation.

No amount of money covered this kind of aggravation.

The prisoner's entrance door opened again and a tall man in black, wearing a black mask and carrying a wicked-looking axe, stepped into the chamber. Asher felt his stomach heave, all his partly digested breakfast rising hot and acid into his throat. He was sweating in earnest now, rivers of horror pouring down his back, his chest. He could hardly breathe, and there were little red spots dancing before his eyes.

The straw had been spread on the flagstone floor to the far right side of the chamber. Well beyond spraying distance of king and Council, Asher realised. The wooden block squatted in the middle of that yellow, absorbent sea and the basket waited on one side. Now Holze was kissing Timon Spake on the forehead. Was helping him to his feet so he could take the faltering steps that would place him within reach of that block, that basket. Now Spake was kneeling again, Holze's tender hands helping him down, down, to the thick and golden straw. The headsman was taking his position. The boy, bound in chains, convicted out of his own mouth, bent over. Lowered his head. Stretched across the wooden block. It was rough. He must be getting splinters in his throat. Holze withdrew. The room was hushed, no speaking, no sobbing. Time stood still.

The headsman looked at the king. The king nodded.

The axe came down, a single strong and steady stroke. The blade bit through flesh and bone and deep into the rough-hewn timber of the block. Timon Spake of Basingdown died. The golden straw around him turned red, the airless chamber filling with the rank iron smell of fresh blood. Hervy Wynton vomited.

Asher didn't, but only just.

The king rose from his tall chair. His hands were steady, his face untouched by tears or anything else. He went to Hervy Wynton, who was wiping his mouth with a handkerchief. "You may take Timon home now, Meister Wynton," he said softly. "Lay him to rest with kindness. He wasn't a bad lad. He lacked judgement. But Barl's Law must hold for all of us, the wise and the foolish alike. My sorrow to his father."

"Yes, Your Majesty," whispered Hervy Wynton. "Thank you, Your Majesty."

Borne turned away from him. "Captain Orrick?"

Orrick, seemingly unmoved, bowed. "Yes, Your Majesty?"

"Assist Meister Wynton. Then see that word is spread throughout the City. Justice is served. Barl's Law is upheld. This business is done, and done. The king's mercy on Lur's people and Barl's blessings as well."

"Yes, Your Majesty."

Borne and his Privy Council left the chamber. Asher, his legs unsteady, followed them out of the guardhouse and into the fancy courtyard out the back, where all their carriages were waiting. The air was clean and fresh. Unbloodied. The sun was shining. There were people in the streets beyond, perhaps the same people who last night had gathered and muttered and called for vengeance. They were bustling now, preoccupied, going about their daily business. As though nothing had changed. As though no-one had just died. When they found out, would they be sorry? Or would they dance with delight?

Gar turned to him. His expression was cold. Distant. "I'm returning to the palace with His Majesty. You can take the carriage back to the Tower if you like. I won't need you again today."

Dumbly Asher stared at him. Took a deep breath and rediscovered his voice. Even to his own ears it sounded strange. Thin, and unfamiliar. "I don't want the carriage. I'm goin' to walk for a bit."

"Suit yourself," said Gar, shrugging. "I'll send it back to the stables then."

As Gar turned away, Asher reached out his hand. Brushed his fingertips against the prince's elbow so that he looked back. "Did you know that were goin' to happen?" he demanded harshly. "Did you know Spake were goin' to be killed right then and there?"

Gar's glance flickered towards the king, who was climbing into his carriage. Durm, dismissing the groom, held the door open for him. Holze and Jarralt were already tucked neat and tidy into their own carriages, waiting for Borne to take his leave so they could retreat as well. The prince shook his head.

"No. Of course I didn't. But Durm was right. Today. Tomorrow. What difference did it make? He was always going to die."

Asher watched him wave their carriage away, climb into the king's carriage and pull the door shut. Watched the dark brown horses respond to Matcher's whip, and trot away.

He turned on his heel and started walking.

As the bookshop door closed behind another customer Dathne let her head drop to her hands and groaned aloud. It was tempting, so damned tempting, to hang her "closed" sign in the window and shoot home all the bolts, even though it was barely an hour past lunchtime. And she'd do it, she really would, if one more person rushed in to her today and gasped, "Have you heard? There's going to be a trial. They say he planned to bring down the Wall! Barl have mercy, what is the world coming to? I hope they hang him from the top of the guardhouse. I hope they beat him first. I hope they make him pay. To bring such shame on innocent Olken. To make the Doranen question our loyalties. Our gratitude. What a wicked man. What an evil deed."

Her head was pounding with their fear, their indignation, their fervent desire for swift punishment and an even swifter return to normality. A pretence that none of this had ever happened. Her mouth was sour with it, her insides knotted. As if she didn't have her own fears. As if she weren't on tenterhooks, waiting. Wondering. Dreading. Every time the shop door opened she looked up expecting to see a City Guard with her own death in his face.

When it did swing wide again and the little warning bell jiggled and rang, the noise scraped her raw nerves like fingernails down a plaster wall. Swallowing a scream she pinned a smile to her lips and looked up.

Asher. Smart as new paint in a fancy weskit and brand-new shirt and breeches, although, looking more closely, they seemed a little the worse for wear. Something dreadful lurked in his eyes. She slid out from behind the shop counter, one hand reaching for him. "What is it? What's happened?"

He looked at her and her heart twisted. "It's over," he said. There was an undercurrent of savagery in his voice. "He's dead."

It was like a fist to the stomach, violent and unexpected. "Spake?"

Ignoring her outstretched fingers he began to pace, hands shoved deep into his breeches' pockets, stretching them all out of shape. "He confessed. The king had his head cut off on the spot."

She had to sit down. Groping her way back behind the counter again she bumped herself onto the shop stool and tried to steady herself. "Oh."

Adrift, staring at the bookshelves but seeing something else entirely, Asher shook his head. "There was so much blood. Didn't expect that. Spent most of m'life beheading fish, y'know, and pullin' their guts out for good measure, but they hardly bleed at all. Don't know why." He shuddered. "Spake bled. He bled everywhere. All over the floor. Up the wall, even. Made a right bloody mess. Ha." Frowning, he shook his head. "Weren't like he was a big bloke, either. Scrawny little runt really. Hardly fair to call 'im a man, even though he was sixteen, and legal."

She remembered to breathe. Timon Spake was dead, and the Circle lived. "I know."

Asher's dark expression melted into something softer. Sorrier. "Stupid bastard. Why'd he want to go fartin' about with magic anyways? Stupid, stupid bastard."

A little colour was seeping back into his face. Going to him, she took his hand. It was like ice. "Tell me what happened," she coaxed, tugging him towards the little sofa by the window where customers liked to sit and browse and chat. "Tell me *everything*."

After he'd finished she poured a glass of brandy down his unresisting throat. Then she poured one down her own. He said, vaguely, "I never asked you what you thought."

"About what?"

He waved his hand. "Spake."

"It doesn't matter what I think," she said, cramming the cork back into the brandy bottle. "He's dead. It's over. Life goes on."

Brooding, Asher stared into his empty glass. "Bloody Gar. I didn't need to see that. Bastard. Reckon I've got a good mind to—"

Dathne went cold. "You can't," she said, snatching the glass from him. "You have to stay. We Olken need you here working with the prince, now more than ever. You can't quit, Asher."

He glanced at her and his lips twisted in a lopsided smile. "I know. I need the money, don't I?" He stood. "Thanks for listenin', Dath. I needed it."

"You're going?"

He shrugged. "Got some more walkin' to do, I reckon. Got to see if I can't leave what happened a bit further behind me."

He bent to kiss her cheek, and she let him. "If you need to talk more, you know where I am."

"Aye," he said. "Reckon I do."

She locked the door behind him then dashed upstairs and contacted Veira.

You have news, child?

She took a deep breath to calm her racing heart. "It's done, Veira. Timon Spake is dead, and we are safe."

Dead? Already? How?

Quickly she explained. "I'm as surprised as you. I never dreamed it would be dealt with so swiftly."

Poor Edvord. This will finish him. He was only hanging on for the boy. For us.

"It seems he knew best in the end. His son kept the faith. Prophecy will continue."

Edvord can take comfort from that, at least. But what of Asher?

"What of him? He's shaken, but he'll be all right."

The link between them fell to humming silence as Veira considered. *Tread softly, Dathne,* she said at last. *This may go deeper than you know. He's seen first-hand the consequences of what we do. When the time comes for him to join us...*

"He'll join us," she said. "Prophecy says so."

Another silence. *Is that Seeing, child, or hoping?*

"Seeing," she said, with far more confidence than she felt, remembering Asher's revulsion and his milk-white face.

Jervale grant it be so. Thanks, child, for the news. I'd best be with Edvord now.

"Veira!"

Yes, child?

"We are going to be all right now, aren't we? With Timon dead, the Circle will be safe?"

There was another, longer silence. Shocked, through the link Dathne thought she could feel Veira weeping.

"I'm sorry," she whispered. "I forget sometimes. You knew him. You know us all. This must be so hard for you..."

It is hard for all of us, child. Prophecy is a cruel master. As to your question... yes, I think we are safe. Our secret is unspoken, our existence still unknown. But I'll warn the others to have a special care. You tread lightly, too, and Matt.

"We will, Veira. I promise."

With the link severed, Dathne went back downstairs, reopened the shop and let business and the swiftly spreading news of the blasphemer's just desserts crowd out all her other clamouring concerns.

They were safe. Prophecy continued. Now all she had to do was wait.

CHAPTER THIRTEEN

When Asher finally wandered into the Tower stable yard, his feet blistered from walking so far in new boots and his guts still burning from the brandy Dathne had bullied him into drinking, Matt came to greet him. All around them the lads scurried about their afternoon chores as the horses hung their heads over their stable doors, whickering hopefully for food. Butterflies danced above the flowerbeds.

Seeing him, the lads laughed and waved. Bellybone catcalled, grinning, and wagged a rude finger. Asher wagged back but couldn't quite manage a return grin. Suddenly, sharply, he missed the rough simplicity and uncomplicated companionship of the stables.

"Where've you been?" said Matt, looking him up and down with appraising eyes. "The carriage got back from town ages ago."

Asher scraped a line in the gravel with his heel. "Walkin'."

"For three hours?"

"So? Ain't no law against it last time I looked."

Sighing, Matt hooked his thumbs into his scarred leather belt. "You've been avoiding me lately. Why?"

Asher shrugged. "Didn't want to talk about Spake."

"Who says I did?"

"You sayin' you didn't?"

Matt pulled a face, admitting defeat. "Word is Spake's dead. Executed."

"I know. I was there."

Matt's expression changed. "You all right?"

Asher smiled, tiredly. Was he all right? No. Not really. "Y'know, you be the first one to ask." He sighed. "I'm fine. Just...when I got up this mornin' I surely didn't count on..." He shrugged again and shoved his hands deep into his pockets. *"That."*

"Who would?" said Matt, one eye on the lads. "Bellybone!" he called sharply. "You're dropping hay all over the countryside!"

Bellybone stopped. Looked. "Sorry, Matt!" he shouted, grinning. His skinny arms clutched a hastily stuffed sack of dried grass like it was his last hope of true love. "I'll pick it up directly!"

Despite the cold lump of miserable anger in his gut, Asher smiled. Bellybone was contagious. Always grinning, no matter what, infecting everybody around him with smiles. Even Matt was fighting to keep his face stern.

"Mind you do!" the stable meister retorted. "Or you'll find it on your dinner plate tonight and that's a promise!" As the other lads hooted and whistled he turned back to Asher. "Timon Spake was a fool."

The brief amusement died. "Well, he be a dead fool now," said Asher grimly.

Matt's hand came to rest on his shoulder. "It had to be done."

"I ain't sayin' it didn't. Just..."

"Saying it and seeing it are two different things?"

"Aye."

Letting his hand drop, Matt stared over the treetops and into the cooling blue sky. Towards the mountains and the indirect cause of Timon Spake's lonely death.

"The Wall's all there is, Asher, keeping us safe. You can't let misplaced mercy put a whole kingdom at risk. Not after six hundred years. It's sad a man died, but if his meddling had brought down the Wall, how many more deaths would there be? It's one life against tens and tens of thousands, my friend. And anyway, Timon Spake knew the price of law-breaking, just like the rest of us do. Now he's paid it."

Asher nodded. "That's pretty much what Dathne said."

"Did she? Well, then. You should listen to her. She's right. And so am I."

He was really very tired. "I know, I know. You're right, she's right, the king's right. Everybody's right. And that poor bastard's dead. And Gar..."

Matt picked up an errant stick of straw and began shredding it with his strong, blunt fingers. "What about him?"

"He's...sorry."

The stick of straw disintegrated. Matt tucked the tattered remains in his shirt pocket and considered him. "And you're angry."

Bloody oath he was angry. Despite hours of walking and silent swearing, still angry. He turned away, simmering resentment hunching one shoulder. "I agreed to witness the hearing. Nowt more. Weren't me passing judgement on Spake, eh? Weren't me had the power to speak up for him and didn't. That was Gar. He should've let me leave with the others. *Bastard*."

Matt frowned. "Do I have it wrong? Was Spake's guilt not certain after all?"

"No. It was as certain as I be standin' here. He admitted it. And there were sworn witnesses. Two little girls...but sworn, all the same. Their father's a mayor. He vouched for 'em."

"So. Spake was guilty. And you agree the law's got to be upheld?"

Now what was Matt getting at? "Course I bloody do! What's your point?"

"Then you judged him, didn't you?" Matt said gently, using the voice he saved for especially fractious colts. "And if you judged him you owed him witness of his death. That's only fair."

Because it was Matt, whose opinion he'd come to value, he didn't swear and stamp off back to the Tower. "I s'pose," he muttered grudgingly.

"Tell me something. You say Gar wouldn't let you leave? Fair enough. You were stuck there. But he couldn't force you to watch, could he? When the moment came you could've closed your eyes. Or looked away. Why didn't you?"

"How d'you know I didn't?"

Matt's smile was melancholy. "It's written all over your face, Asher."

He glared at the ground. "I couldn't. The stupid little bastard had guts, didn't he? Never begged. Just owned up. He...he put his head on that bloody chunk of wood like he was in bed and that were his feather pillow!" It was an image he knew would haunt him for nights to come. Maybe forever. "Sixteen, he was. Not a man, I don't care what the law says. And he knew he was goin' to die. But he sang a bloody hymn with Holze and he knelt in all that damn straw and he let 'em cut his head off with an axe...and he never once said they shouldn't or begged 'em not to."

"He was brave then."

"As brave as he was stupid! And Barl knows he was as stupid as they come. If y'want the truth, Matt, I don't know if I could've been so calm. So I s'pose I—I felt like I owed it to 'im not to look away."

"Despite everything then, Spake was a good lad." Matt's voice was thick with feeling. Shocked, Asher saw tears in his eyes. Matt turned away, embarrassed. Plucked a faded bloom from a nearby rosebush and crushed the wilted petals in his fist. "His death's a stupid, shameful waste. If he'd lived, he might've been..." Unheeded, the ruined rose petals drifted to the ground. His voice fell to a whisper. "He might've been anything."

"Aye, well," said Asher once the silence had stretched a good ways beyond comfortable, "it's all over now any road, and a damn good job too. Reckon I've had enough blood and death to last me a lifetime."

Matt stared at him, frowning. "Well...it's not *quite* over," he said, and nodded at the other side of the stable yard. "Cygnet's saddled and waiting for you."

Following the nod Asher saw his horse's bridled head poke over its stable door, ears pricked. "Why?"

Matt met his challenging stare with a challenge of his own. "His Highness rode out of here nearly an hour ago and I didn't much care for the look of him. I think he was—" He reconsidered. "He'd been drinking. Said he was going out to Salbert's Eyrie. You know where that is?"

"Aye. Bellybone and Mikel took me to see it my second week here." Asher thought about that. "The Eyrie? And he's drunk, you say? Sink me bloody sideways! Matt, you don't reckon he'd do somethin' daft like—"

"Would I be standing here if I did? What I think is you should go after him. Forget you're angry. Forget what you saw. Just...go after him. Now."

Asher went. Even though it meant leaving dinner behind, Cygnet was glad of the gallop; his enormous strides ate up the eight miles between the Tower and the popular picnic park and lookout over Lur's deepest, wildest valley gorge.

Nobody was picnicking there now. The Eyrie was deserted save for Gar's horse Ballodair, tied to a safely distant sapling and dancing at Cygnet's arrival...and Gar himself. The fool had blithely, stupidly ignored the safety railings and the warning signs and perched himself on a rock several feet distant from the official viewing platform. Sighing, Asher tied Cygnet next to Ballodair and joined the prince in his folly.

"If you be thinkin' of jumpin' don't expect me to follow you down," he remarked. "I ain't got no head for heights."

Gar glanced at him sideways then returned to his contemplation of the bone-breaking drop below them. The valley floor was hidden. All that could be seen was a sharply sloping terrace of boulders, bare dirt, scrubby saplings and tangled undergrowth, then nothing but tree after tree after tree, spreading for miles like a green and leafy ocean.

"What are you doing here?" asked the prince. His expression was remote. Uncaring. If he was in his cups the excess alcohol hadn't spilled out of him yet.

Asher hunkered to his heels cautiously. Peered over the edge of the precipice and pulled a face. "Buggered if I know." He shrugged. "Came to talk, I s'pose."

"How...convivial...of you."

Moving at a snail's pace, mindful of the merciless drop mere inches away, Asher sat down. "But not prince to fisherman, mind. I'll tell you straight, I ain't in the mood for that kind of conversation just now."

That earned him a dark look. "Are you ever?"

So. His Royal Highness was a surly drunk, was he? Well sink that for a load of mackerel. "Look. If you don't want company, Gar, just say so. I ain't—"

"Stay," Gar said. "Please. And we'll talk like fr—like two men in plain clothes with not a crown in sight."

Asher stretched out his legs again. "Fine."

"Good." Reaching inside his black tunic Gar pulled out a silver flask inlaid with mother-of-pearl, unscrewed the lid and trickled something smelling of old peaches into his open mouth.

After a moment, Asher said, "My ma always said it were polite to share."

Gar tipped the flask upside down. It was empty.

Asher snorted. "Ha. That'd be bloody right."

Contemplating the wild and unforgiving valley, the flask discarded beside him, Gar said, "It'll be night soon."

Asher looked at the fading sky, the swiftly sinking sun. "I noticed. Reckon we should think on headin' home in a bit, eh? That ole Darran's like to be piddlin' his panties, worryin' on where you've got to."

Frowning now, Gar picked up a handful of pebbles from the rock beside him. Juggled them in his palm. "I've been wondering. Would it've hurt, do you think, to have given Timon Spake one more sunrise?"

Asher shrugged. "I don't know. Would it?"

The pebbles trickled slowly through Gar's spreading fingers. "I think I'd want another one."

"And another one, and another one..." Asher picked up a fist-sized chunk of loose rock and threw it over the edge of the Eyrie. Listened for a moment as it bounced from boulder to boulder below them, rousing echoes. "It had to be done, Gar."

Gar looked at him. Beneath an icy surface his eyes reflected all manner of uneasy things. "You can still say that? Even now? Even after seeing... what you saw?"

"Even after. Though I reckon I'd say the same even if you hadn't made me stay and watch."

The prince stared at his booted toes. "You're angry about that."

Asher sighed. "I was. I ain't so much now."

"Why not?"

"Matt and me had some words. He made sense."

"Don't you want to know why I made you stay?"

"I know why."

Gar looked at him. "Oh?"

"Aye."

"Well then, don't stop there. Tell me. Explain. Elucidate. Show me," said Gar, savagely, "to myself."

"All right. Only I ain't best pleased with you just now so don't say I didn't warn you."

"I won't."

Asher took a deep breath and hissed it out between his teeth. "Well then. Why is because misery loves company. Because law or no law you didn't want Spake to die and I did. Because that made you angry.

Because even though you're a prince and the very important Olken
Administrator and you were up on that platform alongside all the
most powerful men in this whole bloody kingdom, you were as
chained-up and powerless as stupid Timon Spake. And you didn't like
how that felt one little bit. So you turned around and you chained *me*
too. To prove you do have power. To prove you ain't helpless after all.
That's why."

Very slowly, Gar turned to look at him. "You *bastard*."

"Aye." Asher raised an eyebrow. "But that don't mean I'm wrong."

Gar's eyes glittered. "You are if I say you are."

"Oh, here we go." Asher pulled an obsequious face. "Deary me,
Your Highness, *that's* a pretty crown. A present from your da, was it?"

With a wordless cry of rage Gar snatched up a nearby shard of rock
and flung it into the valley. Sudden fury lent him strength, so that the
rock tore through the tops of distant trees and sent birds shrieking
into the fading light. "It's Barl who's wrong! It's a *stupid* law!" he
shouted. "Olken can no more do magic than I can! They—*you*—can't
possibly damage the fabric of the kingdom or Barl's Wall! It's a stupid,
senseless law! And today a man *died* because of it!"

Behind them the horses' bits jangled as they threw up their heads,
protesting the noise. Asher glanced over his shoulder to make sure
they were still secure, because it was a long walk back to the Tower
and he had enough blisters to be going on with. Then he looked at
Gar. Risked a kindly mocking smile.

"Prob'ly you shouldn't go round sayin' things like that where folks
can hear you."

Breathing heavily, Gar stared. Accepted the mockery and managed
a twisted smile. "Yes. Well. You're folks."

"Aye, but I'm different."

"You certainly are." He glanced longingly at his empty brandy
flask, then dragged a hand over his face. "He was so brave."

"I know," said Asher. "So what?"

"So what? So we'll never know now, will we, what he might have
given this kingdom? All his unfulfilled promise has gone to feed the
worms!"

"I know what he gave this kingdom," Asher said roughly. "Fear
and uncertainty and mobs in the street. He was a traitor. He betrayed
you, your da *and* his own people. Your folk and mine might be chalk
and cheese, Gar, but we got one thing in common. Lur. Keepin' it
safe. Keepin' that Wall standin' strong and shinin'. Where all that's

concerned there ain't no you and me, there's just us. Timon Spake? He were the enemy. And you don't cry for enemies. You kill 'em."

Gar stared down into the valley. "Yes. We do." His face spasmed. "*I* do. Well. It's nice to know there's one Doranen thing I'm good at anyway. Seems I'm not a complete cripple after all. Although it's fortunate we used an axe. I couldn't have killed him if magic was part of the proceedings." He laughed. "Now why didn't I think of that before? *Damn*! I could've gone to the king and said, you know, sir, since we Doranen presume to have the right of life and death over our lesser Olken brethren, why not go the whole hog and show them how superior we *really* are? Why don't we kill Timon Spake with *magic*? That'd make those pesky inferior magickless natives sit up and take notice, wouldn't it? Conroyd would *love* that. He'd be your new best friend. Oh, and since I'm nothing but a useless cripple, what you might call a walking talking birth defect, I'll leave the whole trial and execution with magic details to you. All right?"

Appalled, Asher stared. Walking talking *birth defect*? Where was this coming from? Was it the brandy putting wild words in his mouth or did he really *believe*... "Gar, you're ravin'! You can't—"

"Blessed Barl save me!" Gar lurched dangerously to his feet. "I'm the Olken Administrator! I'm supposed to *help* your people, Asher, not *kill* them!"

This was getting out of hand. If Gar wasn't careful he really would go over the edge of the precipice. Asher stood, slowly, and took the prince by the arm. "You do help, Gar," he said, and inched him backwards towards safety. "You be a fool to think otherwise. That woman in Justice Hall, remember her? She'd be in prison today or ruined or both if it wasn't for you. Stop frettin' on stupid Timon Spake! You didn't kill him. He bloody well killed himself, near enough!"

"I know!" Gar shouted. "I know, I know. But I had a chance to speak for him and I didn't. I'm the Olken Administrator, it's my job to take care of your people. I could've said *something* in his defence and I didn't."

"*What*? What could you have said? In front of your da and his precious Privy Council? Pellen Orrick, and all those other Olken? Knowin' that every word in that chamber was bein' recorded by Lady Marnagh? What could you have said to help Timon Spake when he was doomed by his own words?"

Suddenly boneless, Gar folded at the knees and slumped to the ground. "I don't know..." he whispered. "Something."

"Oh, aye? Something like, 'Barl was wrong, it's a stupid law'? And what would've happened then d'you think, you mad fool! Don't you know Conroyd Jarralt's just *waitin'* for you to make that kind of a mistake? Grow up, Gar! You may not have magic but you're still Doranen. *Royal* Doranen. And this is what bein' royal is all about. Protectin' the kingdom. Keepin' it safe and sound...even from the people who live in it. Even when it hurts like murder."

Gar's voice was stark with pain. "That's what I mean, Asher. What happened today. What I did in that chamber. It may have been lawful. It may have been necessary. But it still feels like murder."

To Asher's dismay Gar's voice broke on the last word. "Don't," he said, horrified. "Don't do that. What's the use of cryin', eh? What's the bloody use, Gar? Ain't goin' to bring that Timon Spake back, is it? Ain't goin' to help his poor bloody father?"

Gar was beyond hearing him. So he stood, staring over the shadowed gorge, and waited until the harsh, gasping sobs faded into silence. Stars came out overhead and the first sharp cries of hunting owls pierced the gloom in the valley.

Face hidden behind one muffling hand, Gar said, "I received two letters about you this morning, before we—" He cleared his throat.

"Two letters afore the sun's properly up?" said Asher, determinedly bracing. "Ha. You'd think folks'd have better things to do with their time, now wouldn't you?"

"The first one was from Guild Meister Norwich Porter, castigating you for, among other things, your rude, high-handed and disrespectful tone towards him during a trifling misunderstanding at the guardhouse last night."

Asher snorted. "The only misunderstandin' that puffed-up ole geezer had were in thinkin' I could be knocked arse over eyeballs by a fancy title and some bits of dead animal hair nailed to his weskit. Who were the other letter from, then?"

Gar raised his head. "Captain Orrick. He wished to compliment me on my recent choice of an assistant. He found you efficient, decisive and of great help in breaking up a nasty confrontation at the guardhouse last night."

"Ha," said Asher, pleased. "He's a good man, that Pellen Orrick."

"Yes," agreed Gar. "He is. While Norwich Porter is a puffed-up ole geezer with a fancy title and—and—"

"Some bits of dead animal hair nailed to his weskit," Asher said helpfully.

"Yes. Thank you. The rest of the guild is all right though. I'm sure we'll have a wonderful time at the banquet next month."

"Aye, sir. If you say so."

Silence. The last thin line of light on the horizon died. Gar said reflectively, "Asher? I think I'm drunk."

Asher sighed. "Aye, well, I think you are too. Reckon you can ride or do I send back a carriage for you?"

"I can ride." A pause as Gar tried and failed to stand. "It appears I can't get up, but I'm sure I can ride. Assuming of course I can find where I left my legs."

Leaning down, Asher took him by the forearm and hauled him to his feet. "Don't worry, we'll go nice and slow and that ole Darran can just find himself a dry pair of panties to put on, eh?"

Gar started haphazardly brushing dirt from his fine clothes. "I have the nasty creeping feeling that tomorrow, when I wake up with a terrible headache, I'm going to remember I made a fool of myself here this evening."

Holding his breath, trying to forget the sheer drop somewhere ahead, Asher retrieved Gar's silver flask and gave it back to him. "No, you won't. Nowt happened here today but two friends havin' a bit of a chinwag. Where be the foolishness in that?"

Gar tucked the flask back inside his tunic. Stared at Asher, unsmiling. "Is that what we are? Friends?"

Asher blinked. Were they? Did he want them to be? He thought maybe...yes. Why not? Gar wasn't Jed, or Matt even, but he wasn't bad company. For a Doranen. And if he'd ever met a man who needed a friend it was Gar, just like Matt had said. Sink him. Trouble was, the decision weren't up to him. "You tell me. Your Highness."

"I thought you said this wasn't a prince to fisherman kind of conversation," said Gar, eyebrows lifting.

"It ain't."

Gar grinned. "So there's your answer. Come on...friend. It's time we went home."

Side by side in the silent star-pricked darkness, letting the horses follow their noses, they rode back to the Tower stables where Matt was patiently waiting and all the lamps were lit.

PART TWO

CHAPTER FOURTEEN

Honestly," said Princess Fane in an undertone to her mother, "I don't see why we have to suffer through all this nonsense just because Papa is another year older. It's all right for Gar, it's not as if he's got anything better to do with his time, but Durm and I are right in the middle of a very difficult sequence of incantations. It's *stupid* for me to be stuck here in this stuffy pavilion with people I can't stand watching silly men prancing about on their ponies and attacking defenceless bits of wood. Not when I could be getting important work done!"

Her mother sighed. "I know you don't believe me, dear, but your father's birthday celebrations are work too, equally as important as your arcane studies. You'd do well to be guided by Gar in this. Your brother understands the importance of such occasions."

"Well, being decorative is the only thing he's good at," Fane said impatiently. "And since he does it so well, why do you need me?" She knew she was being petulant. She didn't care. A private family dinner to celebrate her father's birthday would have been a much better idea. She hated all the froth and bubble of public occasions. Despised the feeling of being on show, paraded like one of Gar's wretched horses in the sale ring. All those looks and whispers everybody thought she was too young to notice or understand.

Too young. Fools. She was sixteen, not stupid.

Her mother's expression was a blend of exasperation and affection. "Oh, Fane. Gar's royal duties involve a great deal more than being decorative and you know it. Besides, do you think Durm would be here if participation in this event weren't as vital to the well-being of Lur as the most perfect calling of rain?"

Fane pulled a face and snatched a pastry from a passing silver platter. Around a mouthful of crabmeat and mayonnaise she replied, "Durm is Papa's best friend. He doesn't want to hurt his feelings."

Dana sighed again and reached out a slim finger to coax a wisp of

Fane's silver-gilt hair back into place. "Whereas you, being merely his daughter, are above such trifling considerations?"

Fane blushed. "That's not what I meant."

"Then be more careful when you speak," her mother said with an edge to her mellow voice. "It's one day, Fane, out of an entire year. Tell me I haven't raised a daughter so selfish that she can't spare her father one single day from so many."

"That's not fair! All I want to do is get back to work!"

"I know." Her mother looked suddenly sad. "But the work will always be there, darling."

As Fane opened her mouth to argue, a roar went up from the enormous crowd of spectators crammed shoulder to knee in the tourney field beyond the royal pavilion. King Borne turned aside from watching his Birthday Games, and with laughter smoothing the lines grooved deep in his face called, "Come along, you two! Have done with your gossiping and join us! Asher has just gone one up over Conroyd and looks in fine enough fettle to win the competition!"

"Please, Fane…"

Fane met her mother's cool blue gaze and felt some of her heated impatience cool in return. With a pang she realised that Dana was looking tired, worn. Older now than even a few short months ago. Heart-wrung, she pulled her mother close and kissed her on one smooth, violet-scented cheek.

"I'm sorry," she whispered. "I don't mean to be awful. I'm just a little—I'm feeling—" She swallowed. "Durm told me last night I'm ready for my first WeatherWorking."

Her mother's eyes went wide. "Oh," she said. "I see."

"I promise I won't spoil Papa's day."

"I know you won't, Fane." After a moment, her mother smiled. "And besides, you've still got your surprise present to give him. I can't wait to see what it is, you've been so mysterious."

Fane grinned. "Yes. I have." She laughed, then whirled in a kaleidoscope of silk and brocade and joined her father on the pavilion's flower-strewn balcony. "What did you say? *Asher* win the King's Cup? Darling Papa, exactly how many birthday toasts have you drunk today? He'll never wrest it from a horseman like Conroyd Jarralt!"

Seated with her father were her brother, Durm and sundry obscure lords and ladies who for whatever reason had been deemed worthy of the honour. As the sundries laughed politely, Borne raised amused eyebrows at her, Durm smiled and Gar looked down his brotherly nose.

"Don't be so certain. Asher's been practising his javelin skills for weeks."

"Really? Then for his sake I hope you found somebody halfway decent to help him. Your aim is so bad you couldn't hit the side of a stable with a shovel of wheat! How many strikes did you manage to score in the first round? One? I could've beaten that blindfolded."

And would have, if they'd let her compete. But no. That was too dangerous a pastime for the Weather Worker-in-Waiting. She might take a tumble and break her pretty neck, and then where would they be?

Gar was smiling. "I don't doubt that." In his eyes, understanding. Pity. She felt rage scald her. She'd have no pity from a cripple. For a moment she wanted to claw her fingers into talons and scratch out those green eyes of his that saw so much. Too much.

And then she remembered her birthday surprise and her fingers relaxed. She smiled. Talons could come in many different shapes, after all.

Still watching the competition, her father said, "Young Asher has proven himself an object lesson to all of us, I think, not just Conroyd, in how dangerous it is to judge a man on looks and bearing alone."

Gar glanced at him sidelong, smiling smugly. "If these weren't your birthday celebrations, sir, I'd be tempted to say 'I told you so.'"

"I think you just did," Borne pointed out, and laughed. Patting his son's arm he added, "But that's all right. I'm more than happy to be proven wrong on this occasion. I like him very much, you know. He's a man of uncommon good sense, hard-working, honest and refreshingly forthright. And he's a good friend to you, I think."

"An excellent friend," said Gar. "I doubt I'd have achieved anywhere near as much this past year without his shrewd counsel on Olken matters."

Borne let his considering gaze roam the faces of the lords and ladies, and Durm, before resting it again on his son. He lifted his voice slightly, making sure everyone could hear him. "Yes. The Olken are lucky to have him working so hard on their behalf." Another pat on the arm. "They're lucky to have both of you, Gar. And so am I. This precious kingdom would be poorer without you."

Gar flushed. "Thank you, sir. It's good of you to say so."

"Nonsense," the king said briskly. "It's nothing but the plain, unvarnished truth. Isn't that so, Durm?"

"Indeed," Durm agreed. "As ever, Your Majesty has the right of it."

Pretending to stare over the tourney field where Conroyd was so majestically defending Doranen honour, Fane rolled her eyes. Of course Durm would agree in public. In private, though, they felt the same way about useless crippled Gar, and Asher and the rest of his lumpen, magickless brethren. Not even her tutor's vast affection for her father could change that.

Another throat-ripping roar went up from the crowd. Rising above the excited clamouring, the competition adjudicator's amplified voice: "And Lord Jarralt makes a perfect run to score three targets out of three! We have a tied match! Fresh targets, if you please!"

Fane laughed. "There you are. Your precious Asher hasn't won anything yet, Gar. My money is still on Conroyd."

"Or it would be if you were allowed to bet, which of course you're not. Goodness, it is exciting though, isn't it?" Dana said brightly, scooping Fane into the guardianship of one encircling arm and easing her away from Gar to a spare seat on the other side of Durm. "I can't remember the last time the competition ran so close. Now tell me, Borne my dear, who do you honestly think has the best chance of winning your beautiful Birthday Cup?"

As befitted his social stature Darran watched the king's birthday celebrations from the royal household enclosure, where palace and Tower staff enjoyed some of the best seats available and were liberally plied with sweetmeats and chilled ale by the servants roaming among the spectators. Beside him sat Willer, as was only right and proper. Why should he suffer alone, after all?

He released a lugubrious sigh. This was the last place in Lur he wanted to be. Not because he resented spending his time helping to celebrate His Majesty's latest birthday. Not at all. No, what he resented was being made to celebrate it by watching that wretched Asher make a spectacle of himself in public.

Willer shifted irritably in his seat. The boy looked like a pudgy peacock in his shiny blue and gold satin. He was dusted with sugar powder, soaked in scent and querulous with pique. "For the love of Barl, can't we please go? Five minutes more of this rubbish and I'll fall down dead of a brainstorm, I swear."

Darran permitted himself another discreet sigh and rearranged his long legs. "We leave when His Majesty leaves and not before. Now stop fidgeting or I shall have your pay docked for impertinence."

Willer scowled. Fixed his glowering gaze on the crudely muscular figure of their employer's indispensable assistant and said viciously, "Who does Asher think he is anyway? Competing for the King's Cup.

Presuming to ride against the Doranen nobility. He's just an Olken like us, no better than you or me. In fact he's a damned sight worse."

Darran glanced around the enclosure, full of Asher's friends, and rapped his knuckles on Willer's soft knee. "Keep your voice down. You and I may know the truth of him but we are lone voices crying in the wilderness."

Willer snorted. "We certainly are, Darran, and I for one am getting a damned sore throat! How much longer must we suffer his presence? It's been over a year now! Give him rope, you said, and he'll hang himself. Well, we've given him so much rope he could knit a blanket big enough to cover the kingdom and he's *still* here. Basking in His Highness's affection, wallowing in the ignorant adoration of the masses, making our every waking hour a misery!"

Darran's meagre lips stretched in a thin smile. "Patience, Willer. Even a long road must eventually come to an end."

"I know, Darran, but when? I've been patient! I've been patient till I'm practically choking! I don't think I can go on being patient for very much longer!"

"You must," Darran replied, and summoned one of the roaming servants with an imperious finger. It was hot and he was thirsty, and he feared that only more ale would sustain him to the end of this lamentably tedious affair. "Have faith, Willer, Patience is always rewarded, sooner or later."

Down on the tourney field, Asher ran a reassuring hand along Cygnet's sweating neck and turned to smile at Dathne. She was sitting on the grass by the roped-off tourney field, Matt at her side.

She nodded back, all cloudy dark hair, brown skin and gleaming cat-slanted eyes, and waggled congratulatory fingers in her typically offhanded way. He felt his heart race at the sight of her, and cursed. *Never you mind about that now, fool! You got a cup to win!*

Matt raised his clenched fists high over his head and hollered cheerfully. Seated on the grass with them, Mikel and Bellybone and some of the other lads shouted and whistled too, oblivious to the Doranen looks their loud support attracted.

A short distance away Olken lackeys scurried back and forth across the turf, pounding in fresh rows of wooden pegs ready for the final bout between himself and Conroyd Jarralt. A silly sort of game it was they were playing. Sticking the pointy ends of long javelins into tiny wooden targets. What his sensible da would have to say on it when he told the tale, Asher didn't like to think. But there was a pleasure in aiming true and holding fast, and if it meant knocking Jarralt off his lofty perch, well, where was the harm?

Swallowing impatience, he waited. The enormous mixed crowd of Olken and Doranen spectators buzzed and hummed like a tame swarm of bees and the royal band played loud and hard enough to break their strings and bend their brass. Perched in his official seat, the tourney adjudicator blew foam off a fresh mug of ale and Conroyd Jarralt shouted at his Olken servants as they struggled to saddle a fresh and fretful horse for the ride-off. Asher felt his lip curl and turned away before his lordship noticed the disrespect. The bastard always made sure to pay back any slights, real or imagined, and he had a vicious, inventive tongue.

Fresh horse…Asher snorted, and gave Cygnet's damp silver neck another pat. Even if he owned another horse—and he could if he wanted to now, aye, more horses than a body would need in a lifetime—he'd not insult Cygnet in such a fashion.

With the last wooden peg secured the lackeys scurried off to stand on the sidelines. The adjudicator swallowed the dregs of his ale and strutted to the middle of the field. Beneath the pomp and ceremony of his adjudicator's scarlet regalia he was Ruben Cramp, Meister of the Butchers' Guild. Asher knew him well now, and liked the unpretentious ole fart.

"Attention, please…might I have your attention, my lords, ladies and gentlefolk!"

Heaving a weighty sigh, Asher eased his leather-clad buttocks in the saddle. Talk, talk, talk. Couldn't they just get on with it?

The buzzing crowd hushed. Into the sudden silence the stamp and jingle of impatient horse as Jarralt's fresh mount objected to restraint. Jarralt jerked his hand and the chestnut threw up its head, eyes rolling in protest against the sharp bite of the bit.

Asher scowled, and Ruben Cramp continued his address. "And so, Your Majesties, Your Highnesses, Master Durm, my lords, ladies and gentlefolk, the bout be tied, with Lord Jarralt and Meister Asher on six strikes each!"

The tourney ground exploded into applause. Asher bowed towards the royal pavilion, punched the air with a clenched fist then blew Dathne a kiss. She pretended not to see it. Always playing hard to get was Dathne. Drat her.

As the cheering subsided, Ruben concluded: "Therefore the winner of the King's Cup will be decided by a tie-breaker, the best out of three runs. Gentlemen, be you ready?"

Asher raised his lance in reply, and was echoed by Jarralt. Their eyes met, and Asher smiled at the fury and hatred burning in the Doranen lord's gaze. Fool of a man. As if it mattered. It was a game, just a game, with some poxy ole tin pot the prize. How could it possibly matter?

The band blew a flourish of mellow notes into the high blue sky. Ruben reached into the folds of his fancy overcoat and pulled out a bright scarlet pennant. "Gentlemen, make ready!"

Asher closed his calves on Cygnet's silver sides and the horse pranced to the starting mark. In a flourish of spurs and flying foam Jarralt galloped to the far end of the target run and took his mark.

Ruben raised the pennant high overhead. "On three, sirs, and may the best man win! One...two...three!" He opened his fingers and the scarlet cloth fluttered to the ground like a wounded bird. A roar went up from the crowd. Sudden thunder rolled around the tourney field as iron-shod hooves hammered the green grass.

Asher forgot everything: Jarralt, Dathne, the stupidity and futility of the game he played. He forgot the watching king and queen and prince, unlikely friends; the princess, the Master Magician and other enemies. Forgot that this life would soon be left behind, and that the difficult leaving of it still lay ahead. All that existed in that moment was the pounding horse beneath him, the outstretched lance before him and the driving need to pierce a tiny wooden target through the heart and win himself a golden cup.

"First pass, and it be a peg to Meister Asher, a miss to Lord Jarralt!"

As the crowd greeted Ruben's announcement with excited shouting Asher lowered his lance for the lackeys to remove the speared and splintered wooden target and kept his fierce eyes far away from Jarralt. His lordship was cursing his horse, which was only to be expected. Didn't Da always say: *It's a bad workman as blames his tools, boys, and let that be a lesson for you.* Privy councillor or no, there was far too much of the bad workman in Jarralt. It was an ongoing wonder to Asher that the king kept the man on the Council or listened to him when he spoke.

Within moments it was time for the second pass. Time to win the cup and get down to some serious celebrating with Dathne and his friends down at the Green Goose.

Except that when he reined Cygnet in at the end of their second thundering run, it was Jarralt who waved a wooden-tipped lance in the air and he who was left looking a fool, his target abandoned on the turf.

Damn.

He kicked Cygnet into place and waited, breathing quietly, for Ruben to drop the pennant a third and final time.

"...three!" the butcher bellowed. *"Three!"* the crowd bellowed with him as the scarlet scrap of cloth drifted on an errant breeze and Jarralt buried golden spurs in his horse's bloodied sides and Cygnet pinned his ears back, no need to be told what to do.

Out with the lance, Asher, down with the tip, aim for the heart, strike, pierce, hold, lift, lift, stay there, you beauty, you bastard, stay there, you're dead, you're mine, where's Jarralt, he's dropped it, he's dropped it, I win, I win, Da, ain't this somethin', I win—

Buoyant on the crest of the band's joyous music and the crowd's shrieking admiration, Asher rode his victory lap with head and lance held high. Pink-cheeked Olken lasses threw him their flowers and giggled behind their hands. Mikel and Bellybone and the lads pulled faces and pretended they weren't impressed. Matt hopped and hollered, and Dathne speared his heart with a smile as Cygnet cantered dulcetly by.

Those he worked with in the Prince's Tower were dancing on their chairs in the royal household enclosure. He stood in his stirrups as he pounded by them, waving one fist in the air. Laughed when he spied Darran and Willer, looking as though they'd swallowed curdled milk. A pox on the pair of them, the mouldy ole crow and his jackdaw lackey.

In passing the royal pavilion he eased to a slow trot and brandished the lance in a salute to the king, who stood on his balcony and applauded, laughing. On Borne's left stood the Master Magician; Durm spared him a spurious smile, grey-green eyes warm as glass. On Borne's right and grinning like a split melon, Gar. They pulled a face at each other. He nodded and smiled at the queen, and her Most Royal High Snootiness Princess Fane, and then the royal pavilion was behind him and it was time to collect his prize. He passed Cygnet over to young Jim'l for a rub-down and a cool drink, then waited for the king to join him, Ruben and a glowering Conroyd Jarralt in the centre of the tourney field.

Borne took his hand and shook it as though they were equals, or old friends. "An impressive display, Asher. Congratulations."

He bowed. "Thanks, Your Majesty. It's an honour."

Borne grinned. "It's a cup, actually," he said and gave it to him, a glittering golden affair studded with a few careless gemstones and not much good for anything except maybe a daffodil or two. As the prize changed hands the band struck up a lively jig, the crowd cheered and Jarralt accepted the king's commiserations and made his escape. Onto the tourney field danced a troupe of gymnasts, acrobats and clowns, and under cover of diversion Borne leaned close and said, "Come. My son wishes to congratulate you in person. A short delay, and then you'll be free to celebrate with your friends."

Matt and Dathne would be waiting for him under the Cobbler's Tree, as arranged last night in the Goose. But work always came first. "Aye, sir. Of course."

Together they walked towards the royal pavilion. One jewelled royal hand found a place on his shoulder; surprised, Asher slowed a little to match the king's easier pace. Without warning, Borne stumbled. For two strides and a heartbeat Asher carried the king's full weight. Then Borne regained his balance and held up his other hand to silence concern. His face was marble white and sheened with sudden sweat.

"I'm fine, Asher," he said curtly. "Perhaps a touch too much wine at luncheon. All those birthday toasts. Our little secret, yes?"

Asher opened his mouth to argue. The king looked abruptly unwell. His clear green eyes were fogged with discomfort, his tightly gripping hand palsied with strain. "Your Majesty—"

The king frowned and removed his hand. "*Asher*. I am fine."

He lowered his eyes. Nodded. Clasped his hands behind his back lest anyone presume to think they hovered in case the king should misstep himself a second time. "Aye, sir," he murmured dutifully. He'd mention it to Gar, once they were safe inside the pavilion. Gar wouldn't get tossed into one of Pellen Orrick's prison cells for arguing with his own father.

He scowled as his entrance into the royal pavilion was met with a hailstorm of applause. Lords and ladies, who'd be hard put to give him the time of day anywhere else, crowded forward to congratulate him, to proclaim his prowess, exclaim his skill, to reassure themselves and any royal personage who happened to be watching that they had nothing but respect and admiration for the lowborn Olken who rode so high in the royal estimation.

Well used to it by now, he accepted their compliments as though they meant something. Caught sight of Gar's amused face, imperfectly hidden behind a glass of wine, and rolled his eyes.

Elegant in azure and silver brocade, fine gold hair swirled and savaged with gemstones, the queen came forward to greet him. She passed the King's Cup to a servant to mind, took his hands in her own and pressed a sweet-smelling cheek to his sweat-grimed and stubbly one.

"Dear Asher," she said, ocean eyes sparkling. "And to think that a year ago you didn't even know one end of a lance from the other."

Borne laughed. "Or a horse, for that matter." He still looked pale. Surely somebody would notice?

Not Gar, too busy scoring points. "I confess he's been an adequate pupil."

Despite his concern for the king, Asher grinned. "And Stable Meister Matt's been a damn fine teacher!"

Amidst the dutiful laughter Dana protested, "Really, Gar! The least you can do is say 'Well done, Asher.'"

Gar offered him a mocking bow. Hidden beneath it was genuine admiration. "Well done, Asher."

He bowed back. "Thank you, sir. You owe me a hundred trins."

Gar groaned. "I know. That'll teach me."

"Aye, sir. It will."

"Well," said Dana, still holding his hands, "I think it was a thrilling competition. We're all so pleased you won, Asher." Around the silk-walled pavilion, blond Doranen heads nodded their vigorous agreement.

"Thank you, Your Majesty," he said, and raised her fingers to his lips: the queen was a fine liar and he loved her for it. Kissing her thus was a daring gesture, almost improper, but she was smiling and so was the king, so what did it matter if Durm looked thunderous? Then Lord Jarralt entered the pavilion and politics demanded that the queen greet him in a scented cloud of sympathy. As the noble lords and ladies gathered around their fallen comrade Asher stepped aside and lost himself amongst the fernery along the far wall.

A razor voice dipped in honey said sweetly, "Well, well, well. Who's a clever little Assistant Olken Administrator, then?"

Fane.

Concealed in a high-backed chair drawn out of the mainstream, she sat straight-spined and elegant in gold silk, her slender white fingers juggling three balls of glowing glimfire. Her blue eyes watched him sideways and carefully over and around the spinning magical spheres. She was so beautiful, the way splintered ice and a new harpoon and sea storms were beautiful, and just as dangerous. What she'd be like once grown out of adolescence and crowned Weather-Worker, Asher didn't like to think.

He raised his eyebrows. "Jealous, Your Highness?"

Anger danced beneath the surface of her face, but her voice was placid and bored as she replied, "Desperately. It is my life's ambition, Asher, to stick sharp metal spikes into eensy teensy bits of wood."

He was impressed with the juggling, even though he didn't want to be. Glimfire was unchancy stuff. Useful if your candle snuffed out, to be sure, and you were Doranen and able to conjure it, but in the last year he'd seen more than one nasty burn when some humour in the air ignited a flare-up.

She was her mother's daughter in some things, Fane, and could read in his face what he was feeling. "Now who's jealous?"

"Of parlour tricks?" he retorted, and thought *ha* as her eyes sparked fire. She hid the lapse quickly, smoothed over the annoyance with a spurious, friendly smile and leaned a little closer to him, confidingly.

"Come now," she encouraged him. "You can confess to me, Asher. I won't tell. Have you never been tempted, even the tiniest bit?"

"To try my hand at magic?" Deep-sunk memory surfaced, flashing like the belly of a breaching fish. *Timon.* He felt his expression freeze. "No."

She leaned closer again and lowered her voice. "I'll bet you have."

Slapping her would be a mistake even if she did deserve it, so he swallowed the impulse and shook his head. "Sorry. I like my head where it is, Your Highness."

She pretended surprise at that; the glimfire balls danced a little, echoing. "Asher! You don't think my brother would let someone cut off his best friend's head, do you? Even for breaking Barl's First Law?" She laughed, a tinkly little sound with shards of ice in it. "I don't think even the *king* would let it happen!"

Now what was the little minx playing at? There was a glitter in her he mistrusted to his marrow. "With respect, that's a foolish thing to say. His Majesty holds no man above the law."

She pursed her pretty pink lips. "I'm not so sure. You should've heard him singing your praises before, Asher. Do you know, if he could I think he'd embrace you as a second son. Barl knows you've more in common with Gar than I could ever have."

Bitch. With an effort he kept his expression bland and offered her a bow. "A man could do a lot worse than have qualities in common with your brother. Now, it's been delightful chatting with you, Highness, but I got some friends outside tappin' their toes, so if you'll excuse—"

In other, maybe more important ways she was her father's daughter.

Discarding one line of attack, she chose another. It was in the shining of her eyes and the set of her chin. "Oh no, Asher, you musn't leave!" She blew on the balls of glimfire with her mint-scented breath; they turned into little dancing butterflies and fluttered away. "Gar and I have a special gift for the king." Leaning around the edge of her chair, she searched the room for her brother, found him, and raised her voice: "Gar!"

In the midst of conversation, Gar lifted a hand in apology to his audience and turned a little in her direction. "Yes, Fane?"

"I need you!"

Gar excused himself and threaded his way through the talking, laughing, eating throng to stand a cautious pace from her side. "What do you want?"

Fane's eyes glowed with anticipation. She leaned closer to her brother. "Did you find one?"

"Yes," said Gar, "but—"

"Excellent," she replied. "Fetch it."

"This is ridiculous," muttered Gar, but he went to his official chair, dropped to one knee and groped beneath it. A servant paused and offered help; Gar waved her away and came back a moment later clutching a dead brown stick.

"Show me," said Fane. Took the stick, inspected it, and handed it back with a glowing smile of approval. "Perfect."

"For what, exactly?" Gar said, exasperated. "I wish you'd stop being so mysterious and just tell me—"

"If I told you," said his sister severely, "it would ruin the surprise." She unfolded gracefully from her chair, wrapped her skilful fingers around his wrist and tugged him after her. "Come on."

As brother and sister cleared a path to their father, Asher stepped further into the fernery and chewed his lip. Whatever she had planned, he wanted no part of it. Bad enough he'd have to cope with Gar afterwards. The prince always came off second best in Fane's little schemes. Why Gar allowed himself to believe she'd ever mean him anything but hurt, he never knew. He'd long since given up arguing about it.

With one overhead sweep of her arm Fane ignited a starburst and effectively silenced the room. Every eye fixed itself upon her, and she smiled. "Your Majesties. Master Magician Durm. My lords and ladies. On this day of celebration my brother and I would honour the king with a special gift. Gar?"

Bemused, Gar stared at her. Asher watched the assembled nobility, searching for the expressions that were too still, for lips that twitched or eyes that shone with sudden, undimmed hilarity. Noted faces, and names, and held his breath as his friend trembled on the brink of a new disaster.

Gently, Fane prompted her brother. "Our gift, Gar. You're holding it."

Gar stared at her. At the stick. No escape. "Happy birthday, Your Majesty."

Borne took the offered stick. "Thank you, my son. I don't quite know what to say."

"Please," said Gar, cheekbones sharp beneath the skin, "don't say anything."

Fane broke the anguished silence. "That stick, Your Majesty, represents our lives without you. Dead. Dry. Lifeless. Gar chose it himself. Now, if I may?" She took the stick from her father. Held it between her hands, closed her eyes and concentrated.

At first nothing happened. Then the stick shivered. Rippled once along its dry, brown length. Rippled again. A flush of green rolled along it, as though someone had upended an invisible beaker of paint and poured it from end to end.

"Ah," breathed her spellbound audience, and crowded a little closer.

Gar curved his thinned lips in the semblance of a smile and kept his unclenched fists forcibly relaxed by his sides. Asher groaned under his breath and closed his eyes briefly.

The dead brown stick, now green and supple, swelled with buds. The buds blossomed. Delicate leaves unfurled. One end of the stick swelled, larger and larger, until it exploded into petal and drenched the room with a glorious perfume. Silver and gold and shimmering, it glowed with vibrant life and bloomed in perfect symmetry.

As Fane's audience erupted into wild applause she held out the living miracle to her father and curtsied. "And this sweet rose, Majesty, represents all that we have with you as our king."

Borne took the vibrantly alive flower, his green eyes dark with emotion. "Well. Now I truly am speechless. Thank you, daughter. And you, too, Gar. Thank you both."

"It was nothing, sir," said Gar. And stepped back as Fane entered their father's embrace, trembling with triumph.

"I was so afraid it wouldn't work!" she exclaimed, watching as the rose was passed from hand to eager hand and the gathered nobility chorused its admiration. "Durm and I have been practising for weeks, haven't we, Durm?"

The Master Magician was smiling, his habitually stern expression softened into something more approachable. "I never doubted your skills as a student, Highness."

Borne punched him lightly on one elaborately robed shoulder. "Or your own as a teacher, you old rogue! Thank you! It is the most beautiful gift."

Under cover of exclamation, Fane turned a little in the proud circle of her father's arm and smiled at her brother. Then she caught sight of Asher's face. He couldn't have said exactly what she saw there but it killed her smile stone dead. For a moment an unfamiliar blush of shame stained her cheeks. Then her chin lifted, her eyes cooled and she turned her back on them both. The voluble crowd closed in around her, around the king and Durm, and mercifully hid them from sight.

Asher made a move towards Gar then, his own breath painful in his lungs. The prince held up a hand, sharp as a blow.

"Don't," he said. His voice could have shattered ice.

After more than a year, Asher was impervious. "Smile, or she wins," he said, barely above a whisper.

"She's won already," Gar replied distantly. He was very pale. "As always."

"Only if you let her. Only if you show that it matters."

Gar shrugged. "It does matter. Pretending otherwise only makes me look more foolish."

"And not pretendin' makes her happy!" Asher retorted.

Gar looked him up and down. "A churlish brother I would be, to begrudge a sister's happiness."

"*Gar—*"

"Enough," said Gar. "You don't understand. I doubt you ever will."

Scowling, Asher looked elsewhere for help. Captured the queen's stricken gaze with his own. She understood. Dana took a step towards her son, her eyes stormy—and was halted by a cry.

"Help here! The king! The king!"

It was Durm's voice, almost unrecognisable in its dismay. The clustered nobles staggered backwards, aghast, to reveal Borne, ashen-faced and swaying on his feet. Clutching at his chest. With the stunned room watching he collapsed at Durm's feet.

"*Majesty!*"

As Gar leapt to his father's side and Durm fell to his knees to take Borne in sheltering arms, Dana turned to Asher.

"I'll find the pothecary," he said.

Her eyes were enormous, and brilliant with fear. Her voice was faint. "Quickly."

He looked back once from the door of the royal pavilion. Borne was unconscious, grey and slimed with sweat. Durm held him in a close embrace, furious with fear. Fane wept on her father's still chest. Gar supported his mother, or she supported him. They were too closely entwined to tell. The servants clustered together against one wall, wide-eyed and horrified. Their expressions were mirrored in the faces of the noble guests.

Well. Most of them anyway.

And abandoned on the floor, crushed and trampled and broken, the beautiful birthday rose.

Asher let the heavy curtain drop down behind him and ran.

CHAPTER FIFTEEN

The palace runner caught Willer as he was going out to lunch.

"A message for His Highness," piped the child. "From the Master Magician."

Willer snatched the rolled letter from the boy's hand and waved him away. Curse it, now he'd be late, and if you didn't get a luncheon table at Fingle's within the first ten minutes you might as well not bother getting one at all.

He cast an unenthusiastic glance up the Tower staircase. Even worse, he'd have to go and disturb His Highness with this missive, which doubtless meant he'd have his head bitten off for daring to put his nose across the library threshold. There'd been shouting and banged doors already this morning, and Darran disappearing into their office in a secretarial huff. For a whole week now, ever since the poor dear king's collapse, His Highness had been a positive *bear* to live with.

Not that one could complain, or would. His Highness was beside himself with worry for the king, which he supposed was only to be expected. But the gloom and despair were infectious. Even the Tower maids kept dashing into linen closets to cry. And if he tripped over one more snuffling boot-boy he really was going to scream. Or take off his belt and give someone a thrashing. Or both. Really, it was so unnecessary. Hadn't Pother Nix announced officially that the king would make a full recovery? Yes, he had. So what was the point of all this temperament? There wasn't any, but it had Darran in as fractious a mood as the prince. Really, between the pair of them life was hardly worth living.

Willer heaved a put-upon sigh. He did hope the king would make his full recovery *soon*, so that life could get back to normal.

Behind him the Tower's heavy oak front doors banged open. Swallowing a startled shriek he whirled, the message clutched protectively to his velvet-swathed chest.

Asher grinned as he sauntered into the lobby, stripping off his sweat-stained gloves as he came. "What's that then, Willer? Not another love letter? Does Darran know?"

Hot with dislike and humiliation, Willer uncrumpled the rolled parchment. "*You*," he said with awful disdain. "And where have you been?" As if he didn't know. Carousing. Gallivanting. Prancing about on personal business when his duty lay at the feet of their prince. *Reprobate*.

Asher tucked his gloves into the waistband of his disgusting leather britches and looked down his crooked nose. "Out."

Willer sniffed. It was beneath him to rise to such obvious provocation. Instead he held out the Master Magician's message. "This has just come from the palace for His Highness. Take it up to him."

Insolence informing every grubby line of his face, Asher snorted. "Take it yourself, Willer. I ain't your servant."

A gentleman never resorted to violence, no matter how justified it might be. With rage thick in his throat Willer retorted, "No, you're *his*, and more's the pity for it too! I swear you'd know the meaning of good manners if you were answerable to *me*. If that were so you'd no more dream of entering His Highness's official residence dressed like—like a *highway rider* than you would of flying over the Wall! Barl save us! Couldn't you at least have *bathed* before coming in from the stables? You reek of sweat and horses!"

Asher smirked. Oh, how Willer longed to wipe that look from the upstart's face! "Better than reekin' of lavender water," was the insufferable reply. "Or rosewater or old tea leaves or whatever it is you douse yourself in every mornin'. No wonder you're gettin' love letters, eh? Or is it just your smelly recipes they're after?"

With a restraint that nearly caused his veins to burst, Willer swallowed his instinctive reply. Darran had made himself abundantly clear on many, many occasions: the prince would brook no disrespect to the kingdom's Assistant Olken Administrator. So instead he clung to his precious talisman, Darran's promise: *give him enough rope...*

Such dreams he had, such pleasant dreams, of a stretched brown neck, and feet vainly kicking the indifferent air!

"I am very busy with work for Darran," he said through stiff lips. "Be so good as to take this message to His Highness immediately. It's from the Master Magician."

A little of the arrogance seeped from Asher's face. Even his monumental pride faltered before the mention of the kingdom's second most powerful magician. "Fine," he muttered and held out his hand. "Give it here then."

With silent contempt Willer handed the message over, waited till Asher was round the first bend of the Tower staircase, then hurried out of the side door. If he walked *very* fast, he might just reach Fingle's in time after all.

Asher took the winding staircase two treads at a time, scowling. He'd happily live with the honest stink of sweat and horse in his nostrils, but leave him for five minutes in that prissy sea slug Willer's company and he was itching for hot water and soap.

Gar was working at his library desk, surrounded by towers of ancient books, piles of yellowed and crumble-edged parchment and pages of notes. Ink-stained and harassed, he muttered under his breath and streaked his blond hair blue with dragging fingers. Asher paused in the doorway and frowned. This was getting beyond a joke.

Without looking up from his jottings Gar snarled, "Darran! For the love of Barl, man, I said I didn't want to be—"

"Mind now," Asher interrupted mildly, entering the room. "You'll hurt my feelings, and we wouldn't want that." As Gar sat up, blinking, he threw himself into the nearest comfortable armchair and slung a leg over one side.

Gar pulled a face. "Sorry. He's been pestering me all morning."

"Try tellin' him to turn into a bug and beetle off then."

"I did in the end," Gar admitted. "Although not quite in those words. Look, amuse yourself for a moment, would you? I just need to finish this..."

Asher sighed. Books, books and more books. Ever since the king's collapse Gar had buried himself in parchment and ink pots. Fool that he was. At this rate he'd work himself into a bed right next to his ailing da, and then three guesses who'd get the blame for it? By his reckoning, Gar hadn't set foot outside in six days. Ballodair was so short of work he'd bucked Matt off that very morning; the bruised and limping stable meister wasn't amused.

And Gar was looking short of work too, or at least fresh air. His thin face had grown thinner and there were lines of temper and worry engraved around his eyes and mouth. All this time and he'd still not seen his father. The strain was wearing him down, winding him tight as a lute string ready to snap.

This whole bloody mess was a pain in the arse and no mistake. Just as he'd *finally* been set to tell Gar it was time and past time he packed his bags and went home to Restharven...

He'd been meaning to do it for nigh on a month now, but unforeseen circumstances kept getting in the way. First off, right on the anniversary of his arrival in Dorana, a tricky dispute had arisen between the Brewers and the Vintners and it had taken a week's worth of persuasion from both him and Gar to avert an alcoholic disaster. Hard on the heels of that excitement there'd been the Barlscoming Anointments; it would've been cruelty to dumb animals if he'd left Gar to cope with all that religious fervour on his own. And after *that*, the king's birthday celebrations.

Which he *easily* could've missed, and should have, except he'd made the mistake of drinking one glass of wine too many and accepting Gar's bet that he couldn't make the final four of the King's Cup competition. After all, there was nowt to it. He'd seen Conroyd Jarralt win the cup the last King's Birthday holiday, and if Conroyd Jarralt could do it, *well...*

Naturally, he'd had to stay on and defend his honour. Da would understand that. Course he would. It had meant spending every spare waking hour on horseback learning the hard way how not to skewer himself or his mount with a stupid steel-tipped javelin as he tried to stab stupid bits of wood at a passing amble.

He'd done all right in the end, though.

Thinking of the gold cup, now sitting in his bathroom holding his razor and shaving brush, he smothered a grin. Actually, he'd done more than all right. Conroyd Jarralt still wasn't speaking to him: two prizes for the price of one.

But he'd promised himself that would be the end of it. The birthday celebrations would be his private going-away party. Once all the bunting was put away for another year he'd bid his farewells to Dorana

City and go back to where he truly belonged. The coast. Restharven. Home.

And then what had to happen? The king had to go falling over sick with a fever, didn't he? Now Barl alone knew how long it would be till His Majesty was hale and hearty again and he could in good conscience quit the City for home. At this rate he'd have to send a reassuring message ahead of himself, damn it, and ruin the surprise.

Scratch scratch scratch went Gar's inky pen over the paper as he translated yet another of his precious bloody parchments...

Although, if he were being dead honest with himself, turning his back on Dorana wasn't looking to be as easy as once he'd expected. In his first weeks here, with homesickness a blight, the year of self-imposed exile from Restharven had seemed a length of time without mercy. Now, though, *now*...He swallowed a sigh. Truth be told, he'd almost welcomed all those very good reasons for delaying his departure. Without ever meaning to he'd made a lot of friends in the City. Amongst the guilds. The guards. In the royal household and the Tower, especially. Well, not Darran. Or Willer. But Matt. Definitely Matt, and the rest of the lads down at the stables. The housemaids and cooks, like a bloody great gaggle of sisters and aunties and well-meaning grannies.

Gar.

Asher rubbed at a mud spot on his knee, frowning. If anyone had told him a year ago that one day he'd look on a Doranen prince like a brother he'd have laughed himself sick. Yet a year later here he was. As fond of Gar as he'd never been of Zeth or Wishus or any of the others.

Damn it. That hadn't been part of his plan...

Bloody Gar, with his mercurial moods, his devotion to family, his courage in the face of magic and its lack in himself. His besottedness with horses and books and history. His sly sense of humour, and his imperfectly hidden pain.

In the aftermath of Timon Spake's execution, feelings in Lur had run high and wild. Fear, both Olken and Doranen, tainted the sweet air of City and countryside alike. During those dangerous, difficult days he'd watched the prince work himself near to a standstill, mending fences, building bridges, soothing the turbulent kingdom and preventing any echoes of long-past unrest sounding in the streets of her towns and villages. Watched him lay flowers on the grave of Edvord Spake, who'd followed his son into death three days after receiving his boy's body home from the king's justice.

And the hard work hadn't stopped there. Long after the stormy waters of Timon Spake's death had calmed, Gar laboured on behalf of his father's magickless subjects. Laughed with them when their babies were born, wept when their mothers died, danced at their weddings and calmed their quarrels in guild meetings all over the kingdom. Listened to them in Justice Hall and agonised afterwards in case he'd not heard their hearts correctly.

Thanks to Gar, Asher of Restharven had been a part of all that. He'd helped solve those disputes. He'd danced at those weddings. Held meetings with the most important Olken in the kingdom and stood before the king in Privy Council to speak his heart and mind on things that had come to matter. *And* he'd been listened to. Plus he was a rich man now, a different, cannier, wiser man, and that was also thanks to Gar.

Some folk would say leaving was a sinkin' poor way to repay such a debt. He might even say it himself. Might not go at all, at least not just yet, not this year, if it weren't for Da.

But he'd made his father a promise, so that was that.

And then . . . there was Dathne.

How did a body know if they'd fallen in love if they'd never been in love before? And of all the women he'd ever met, at home and here in Dorana, that he could've fallen in love with . . . why *Dathne*?

In body and mind she was an angular woman, all sharp corners and flat, hard planes. Not even when drunk could he ever call her beautiful. And yet she stirred him, deeply. Her secretive eyes. The curve of her lips. The long smooth column of her throat. The way her hands shaped the air when she talked. She provoked him beyond bearing. Teased him. Challenged him. Made him laugh. Made him think. He'd learned as much in a year of knowing her as he had working with Gar. And that was saying something, because sometimes he thought his head would burst like an overripe melon with everything he'd learned working with Gar.

But how could he be certain sure it was love, not . . . something else? Was it because whenever he was with her he felt strangely whole? Because he looked forward to seeing her the way he'd used to look forward to sailing? Or did he know because the thought of leaving her behind when he went home raced his heart and dried his mouth? Made him feel ill and panicked and all of a jitter?

That could be it. A lifetime without Dathne in it? He might as well say he'd settle for a lifetime without the sea.

He didn't think he could do either.

So. He'd just have to say something, wouldn't he? Not that she'd ever given him a sign, as such, nor what most men would call encouragement even when they were both tipsy in their cups. But she liked him. He was sure of that much. They saw each other three or four times a week without fail, and she was always asking how he was, what was happening in his life. Inviting him on jaunts about the countryside. Giving him books to read and asking him what he thought of them afterwards. Showing an interest. Listening, with her eyes as well as her ears. A woman didn't do that if there wasn't *something* going on.

Still: He'd be happier if she'd said something... dropped even the smallest of hints...

Of course it could be she was shy, like him. Uncertain. Unwilling to risk a rebuff. To be fair, he'd not exactly shown his hand either. But then he'd seen Dathne rebuff other would-be suitors: it wasn't a pretty sight. So he'd sort of... let it slide. Told himself he had plenty of time. That some women weren't for rushing. Had put off declaring his feelings again and again and again, waiting for the perfect moment to declare his love.

Well, he was fast running out of moments, wasn't he? Perfect or otherwise. He'd have to risk speaking soon or he might never see her again.

He imagined telling her, at long last. Imagined the feel of her hands tight in his. Her gasp of sweet surprise. The blush on her cheeks and the warm glow of pleasure in her eyes. He imagined kissing her...

"What are you smiling at?" said Gar.

Startled, Asher blinked. "What? Nowt. Nothing, I mean. I was just thinking."

Gar returned his pen to the ink pot and leaned back in his chair, groaning at the tug of stiff muscles. "Careful. You might sprain something." His lips curved briefly, the closest he was coming these days to a smile. He took in Asher's dishevelled appearance and lifted his eyebrows enquiringly. "You've been out?"

"Aye," said Asher, and grinned. "Takin' care of the Guigan brothers."

Gar considered him. "And?"

"And I reckon they've seen the error of their ways." Asher flexed reminiscent fingers. "Once they realised we were onto 'em they changed their tune right enough."

"Excellent. The carters have enough to contend with at this time of year without being short-weighted on their fodder. Penalties?"

Asher shrugged. "Thirty percent discount to all their regular customers until the end of Fall. I got a good long list of deservin' names that'll need checking, double-checking and, like as not, checking again. Be nice and say I can give it to Darran, eh?"

Frowning, Gar said, "Thirty percent's a little harsh, isn't it? If I recall correctly we discussed twenty."

"And twenty it would've been, right enough, except they got themselves a little mouthy. Couldn't let 'em get away with that now, could I?"

"I suppose not. Although I imagine they're not very happy."

Asher grinned. "Not very happy at all, no. But as I said to 'em, they could do things my way and be unhappy in the comfort of their own shop, or their way and be unhappier still standin' afore you in Justice Hall explaining what they'd been up to and why. Funnily enough, they decided to do things my way."

"Ah," said Gar. "Thus showing that greed and stupidity don't necessarily go hand in hand. Good job." Then he noticed the rolled letter balanced in Asher's lap. "What's that?"

Asher tossed the scroll at him. "A message from Durm."

Gar's expression changed. "Idiot," he said curtly. "You think the Guigan brothers are more important than this?" Ripping off the neatly tied ribbon, he yanked the letter open and devoured its contents with eyes gone suddenly opaque.

"Well?" said Asher, fingertips drumming on the arm of his chair. "What's the ole spell-crow want now?"

Gar opened his fingers and let the paper rustle to his crowded desktop. "The king wishes to see us," he said distantly. Shifting in his chair, he stared out of the library's stained-glass window into the gardens below. His lips, unsteady, pressed tight together.

"So he's feeling better," said Asher. "That's grand." Then he paused, and listened again to Gar's pronouncement. "Wait a minute. He wants to see *us*? As in you and me? Why?"

Gar pushed free of his chair and headed for the door. "I must make myself presentable. You'd best do the same. Bathe and change, for Barl's sake. You reek of sweat and horses. I'll meet you downstairs in ten minutes."

"All right, all right," Asher grumbled, following him out of the library. "But make it fifteen. And you ain't answered my question, neither. What's the king need to see me for?"

No reply. Swearing lustily under his breath, Asher hurried to his apartments.

Now what?

*   *   *

Master Magician Durm was waiting for them in the anteroom to Their Majesties' private chambers. A light, bright, airy room it was, but dragged down to dirt level by Durm's heavy frown and the way his plump lips tucked in tight at the corners, forbidding smiles. His glossy brown robe hung on him with less grace than it would on a coathanger, its heavy folds mimicking the bloated lines of his body. Following in Gar's hurried footsteps Asher hung back a little and let the prince be the first to feel the embrace of Durm's warm welcome.

"You took your time," the Master Magician announced, sharp white teeth snapping the tail from his greeting. Cold grey eyes, tinged green like wet slate touched with lichen, slid briefly sideways to notice but not acknowledge Asher. "His Majesty is waiting for you. Be brief. Pother Nix and I are satisfied with his progress but he is still swiftly wearied."

For Gar, a lifetime of the man had blunted his impact. Indifferent to censure, thrumming with anticipation, he said, "Has Nix decided yet what caused the fever?"

"As I suspected," Durm replied, soft hands folded across his comfortable girth, "it was a matter of exhaustion and overwork. The king's crown weighs heavy, Your Highness. Even the strongest of men will stumble from time to time."

Gar gnawed his bottom lip. "There must be something I can do."

"We have discussed this. His recovery is in hand, Your Highness."

"You should have let me see him before now." Gar's voice was bladed, his eyes no longer opaque.

Durm unfolded his hands, spread them wide. "To what purpose? Nix, Her Majesty and I are doing all that can be done. He finds other visitors fretsome."

Gar glared. "You're saying he'd find me fretsome? I am his *son*, Durm."

Now the hands reached out, patted Gar's shoulders in a gesture doubtless meant to reassure. Asher, watching from a safe distance, mistrusted the paternal smile that accompanied the gesture. "And as a good son you've held his best interests highest. Now shall we be about our business? It will soon be time for His Majesty to sleep."

Gar nodded, turned his head far enough to meet Asher's neutral gaze and flickered an eyelid. Stride for stride, they made their way towards the closed chamber door.

Durm stepped forward and reached out, catching Asher's passing elbow between finger and thumb. "Where do you think you're going?"

He pulled his elbow free. Not roughly, never roughly, but with a polite, restrained violence. "The message said His Majesty asked for me too. Sir."

Durm shrugged. "He asks for many things, as unwell men are wont to do. He may not be strong enough to see you. Wait here until—"

"Asher!"

Gar, calling impatiently from his mother and father's private room.

A dangerous grin. An apologetic shrug. Don't see the venomous look in the spell-crow's eye. "If you'll excuse me, then," he said with awful courtesy, and slipped out of harm's way into the king's inner sanctum.

Borne sat up in his bed, swaddled in blankets and buttressed with pillows. The ravaging fingerprints of fever were plain upon him. Thin, pale, his eyes sunken to depths Asher hadn't seen since the day of Timon Spake's trial, he was decently robed to the throat in finest linen. His silver-blond head looked naked without a crown, yet somehow he still managed to look like a king.

An open fireplace roaring in the chamber's far corner billowed heat into the shuttered, curtained room. Something scented had been cast into the flames; the stifling air hung heavy with perfume. Glimfire cast fuzzy pools of light from sconces on the walls. Seated on a chair by his side, the queen demurely embroidered some folderol stretched tight in a sewing hoop. She looked up as Asher entered and bowed, and gifted him with a smile. Then she put aside her amusement and her stitching, kissed her husband and stood.

"There, now. I'll leave you fine gentlemen to your plottings. Don't tire yourself, my dear. Remember what Pother Nix said."

Borne pulled a face at her. "How could I forget, beloved, when his words are engraved upon my liver?"

They exchanged a private smile, then Dana turned to her son. "Come see me in my parlour when you've finished, Gar. It seems an age since we've talked."

Two paces from her side, Gar stood and stared at his father as though at a stranger. Asher could see the shocked dismay locked safe and tight behind his eyes and the small half-smile that curved his lips. Stirring, the prince turned away from the altered man in the bed and reached for his mother's hand to kiss it. "Of course, Mama. I'll be with you shortly."

In return she kissed his cheek. Smiled again at her husband, gathered her silk skirts about her and left. As the door was closed behind her, Gar moved nearer to the bed. Asher drifted sideways, to conceal himself in shadows.

"You sent for me, sir," said Gar.

"I certainly did. Sit, sit." Borne patted the arm of the chair by the bed, then glanced into the shadows at the foot of the bed. "And how are you, Asher?"

Asher cleared his throat and stepped forward into flickering light. "Very well, thank you, Your Majesty. It's a great relief to see you looking better."

"Rubbish," said Borne. "I don't look better, I look like the walking dead. Or I would, if Nix would let me walk. But your kind dishonesty is appreciated nevertheless. I'll talk with you in a moment. First I must speak with Gar."

"Yes, Your Majesty."

He returned to the shadows as Gar slid into his mother's chair and laid the back of his hand briefly against his da's forehead. "How are you feeling, sir?"

"I'm fine. Really. This is naught but a storm in a teacup."

"That's not what Durm says."

Borne pulled another face, deepening the newly mined hollows in his cheeks. "Durm's as bad as Nix. I am fine. Or I would be, if it weren't for the pills and potions I'm made to swallow."

Gar hesitated, frowning. "Durm says there's nothing I can do to help you while you're convalescent, but I don't believe that. There must be something. I wish you'd tell me."

"It's funny you should ask," said Borne after a small pause. "There is one important thing I can't do. It would ease my mind considerably were you to do it for me."

"Name it," Gar said promptly. "I'll do anything."

"You can take a trip to the coast."

Asher twitched. The coast? Why the coast? And why now? Then he saw it. Damn. Of course. Borne was going to send Gar south to West-wailing for the annual Sea Harvest Festival. Well, well, this was going to make things tricky. He'd thought to go home via the festival himself. All those thousands of people. They could hide him from his brothers. Let him find Da and smooth things over without trouble from Zeth and the rest of them.

Well, *damn.*

Gar was frowning. "The coast, sir?" Then his expression cleared. "Oh. I see. It's coming up to Sea Harvest Festival time, isn't it? But surely you'll be—"

Borne shook his head. "I am forbidden to put so much as a toe out of bed for another week. And it's to be a full three weeks of naught but gentle strolling after that. Someone needs to go to Westwailing in my place, Gar. I thought you might enjoy the experience. Besides, it's past time the Olken of Lur's south met you."

Asher bit his tongue. *Gar*? Sing the *festival*? Was the king mad? Gar couldn't sing an uncracked note to save his life. Fever must have addled Borne's brains.

To be fair, Gar was looking just as surprised. "I don't know, sir. I'm not sure I'm the right person for this. Surely Fane is the obvious choice. Especially since—"

Borne's lips thinned in displeasure. "Magic has nothing to do with this, Gar. Sea Harvest isn't a ceremony of power. It's a symbolic event honouring the ancient pact between the Olken and ourselves. Celebrating the ocean's bounty, Barl's reward for the dutiful observance of that pact. A royal presence is what matters, not whether your voice is good enough for public display. Or whether you have magic. You couldn't possibly—"

"Spoil things?" Gar finished for him, his expression twisted. "Of course not. You wouldn't be asking me to do this if there were any danger of that. Would you?"

The king's face flooded with hectic colour. "*Gar!*"

"Forgive me," Gar said distantly. "But we both know it's true."

"What's *true*," the king snapped, "is that I thought to have you take my place in Westwailing. You are the Olken Administrator, Gar. Important in your own right. You should be seen by—"

"And Fane is Lur's next WeatherWorker."

"Your sister is full occupied with her studies," said Borne, plucking at his blankets with impatient fingers. "And even if she weren't I'd still want you to do this. I don't understand your attitude. What makes you so prickly? Has something happened I should know about?"

Asher sighed quietly. Had something happened? Only his father seemingly at death's door, his sister poised to be made WeatherWorker and Durm barring the king's only son all access to his grievously ill parent.

Hardly anything really.

Gar shoved out of the chair and moved to stand with his back half turned to the bed. "I'm sorry if I appear ungrateful. It isn't my intention. You must know, sir, this has been a trying week."

In the king's face was all the anguish that his son, prideful to the marrow, would never willingly show. "And I'm sorry, too, for worrying you with this foolish fever. Truly, it looks much worse than it is. I'll be up and about in no time, I promise. Please, Gar. Sit. Let us discuss this matter like men of good sense."

Put that way, by a man who looked to have his left foot planted firmly in the grave, refusal was impossible. Gar resumed the chair by the bed and managed to unknit his brow. "Of course, sir."

"I would not force you to do anything you mislike," Borne said, his hand reaching out to rest on Gar's knee. "If the idea of representing me in Westwailing displeases you so greatly, just say so and—"

"It doesn't." Gar's voice was unsteady. "It shames me to think I've given you that impression. When do I leave?"

"You're sure?"

Gar nodded. "Sure. As well as humbled, and honoured."

"Good. I'm glad." Borne's tired eyes sparkled with vicarious excitement. "You'll leave next week. I suggest you meet with Darran on this, and be guided by him. He knows to the last detail what's involved in the festival. In fact I think it would be best if you took him to Westwailing with you."

Gar grimaced. "Must I?"

"Oh, come," Borne said. "He's not so bad as all that."

"Of course he's not," agreed Gar, faintly smiling. "After all, you loved him so well that on the morning of my majority you gave him to me as a gift."

"He knows his business, my boy, and was exactly what you needed in setting up your own affairs. Admit it. Your office runs like clockwork, doesn't it? You never miss an appointment or find yourself unprepared for a meeting or at a loss when important men come to call?"

Gar sighed. "I know. I know. But he fusses. And he hovers. And he refuses to wear anything that isn't black."

"And he'll tell you all you need to know about the Sea Harvest Festival," Borne added, "and the part you'll be playing in it. Including all the words to the Sea Harvest Hymn."

"Can't Asher do that? He used to be a fisherman, after all. Who better to teach me what I need to know than him?"

Borne's gaze flickered to the shadows, then back again. "I have no doubt Asher will be of invaluable service to you during your journey and time in Westwailing. Indeed I'm counting on him to be your strong right arm, as usual. But Darran knows the protocols and procedures from our perspective, Gar. Trust me, you will need him."

Gar sighed. "Oh, all right. I'll take him with me." And added, uncertain, "Tell me. You are sure about this? If I should give you cause to regret your offer, sir, I—"

Borne lifted his hand. "*Never*," he said, voice thickened with emotion. "You could never make me regret, Gar. You're my son, and I love you."

Gar nodded. Took his father's hand and tightened his fingers. "I won't let you down, sir. I swear it."

"I know." The king cleared his throat and adopted a bright smile. "Now run away and visit your mother while I have words with your assistant here. She misses you."

"Yes, sir," said Gar, and withdrew from the chamber, giving Asher a hard glance in passing. *Don't tire him. Be polite.*

Asher rolled his eyes and stepped out of the shadows to meet with the king.

CHAPTER SIXTEEN

Borne indicated the chair by the bed, inviting Asher to sit. "The queen tells me you were a great help to her the day I fell ill. I wanted to thank you."

Perching on the edge of the comfortable armchair, Asher shrugged. Politely. "I didn't do much, Your Majesty."

"I think the queen would disagree. She says you—" Borne broke off, squinting with pain.

Asher leaned forward, alarmed. There was a sudden sweat on the king's brow and his pale face had turned a sickly yellowish green. "Majesty!"

Weakly, Borne indicated the crystal jug of water on his bedside table. Asher poured him a glass. Slipped his arm around the king's shoulders and held him off his pillows to drink.

"Thank you," Borne whispered after three sips. Asher laid him gently back against the pillows and put the glass aside. "If you could stir up the fire for me, Asher? This cursed fever—I'm afraid I feel the cold."

Asher's shirt was sticking to him in the heat, but he lumbered another huge log into the fireplace and stirred the flames to bolder life, choking a little at the cloying wave of scent that wafted around the room.

That done, with fresh rivulets of sweat pouring down his spine, he sat down again and waited for Borne to say whatever else it was he wanted to say. A year in the service of this family had taught him one important thing: there was regular time, and there was royal time, and it did a body no good at all to get the two confused.

Eventually Borne stirred, and sighed. "I love my son, Asher. Not a day passes that I don't regret..." He stopped. Folded his thin fingers in his lap. "I love my daughter, too, misunderstand me not. If there has been any good arising from Gar's affliction it is that I have her to love as well. Fane will make a strong WeatherWorker when I am gone. The Wall will hold fast, never fear, once it comes within her care."

"Aye, sir," said Asher. And added, riskily, "But Gar has the love of the common folk."

"Fane is young, yet," Borne replied, smiling gently. "Just sixteen. She will learn. Gar has had six more years than she to polish his manners."

Asher kept his expression unremarkable. Six years, six decades, six centuries even. He doubted it would make any difference. Fane might be a magickal prodigy but there was more warmth in an icicle than the whole of her regal little body. And there were no point at all in telling that to Borne. Fathers could be strangely blind to the faults of their children. Hadn't he grown up seeing it first-hand for himself?

"Aye, sir. As you say."

"I will confess, Asher," said the king, lightly frowning, his thin fingers smoothing the blankets, "it caused his family no little surprise to learn that Gar had hired himself a champion."

Asher blinked. He'd been summoned to the king's bedside to chat about things a year and more old? "Aye, sir. Reckon it might have done, at that. But you know, I ain't really his champion. He only calls me that to rile me up."

The frown became a smile. "And does it 'rile you up'?"

Another polite shrug. "Not really. Not any more. But I let him think it does. Gives him a laugh."

That made Borne laugh, but his amusement ended in more coughing and another sip of water. When he could speak again: "Making no bones about it, Asher, I wasn't sure Gar hadn't made a mistake, in the beginning. But I've been watching you, perhaps more closely than you know, and he was right. You've done an admirable job as his assistant. And, moreover, you've been good for him."

"Oh, aye?" said Asher cautiously. Something was coming, he could smell it like rain in the wind. "That's good to hear, Your Majesty."

Borne nodded. "My son is less solitary now than once he was. Less inclined to live inside duty and books. He smiles more. I think you've shown him that a life lacking magic can still be a life filled with joy. In your company he forgets he is a cripple."

"Barl bloody save me!" snapped Asher, unthinking. "He ain't a bloody *cripple*!"

Melted with fever, wan and reduced, Borne stared at him in silence.

Appalled, Asher stared back. "Your Majesty," he added, wincing. Then thought, *sink it*. He was leaving, wasn't he? When would he get another chance to put Gar's father straight on a few things? "He ain't a cripple, Your Majesty," he said again, this time remembering his manners. Keeping his tone moderate. Suitably deferential. "I know there's folk think he is. *He* thinks he is. But he ain't. He's a good man who works hard for you and everybody else in Lur. He'd kill himself for this kingdom, I reckon, if he thought it'd do any good."

"I know that," the king said quietly. "He is my son. Do you think I don't know that?"

Asher gestured helplessly. "Well, then...?"

"Well then, Asher, you may say he's not a cripple. And so, in the privacy of my bedchamber, may I. But the truth remains that he is without magic. And a Doranen without magic is no true Doranen, just as a bird without wings is not truly a bird. *If* you accept that the base property of birds is the ability to fly. Do you?"

Asher stared at the carpet. "Aye," he muttered. "But I still reckon it ain't fair."

"You say it's not fair? *You* say? He sprang from *my* seed, Asher! He is the fruit of *my* loins. And yet you sit there and say *you* think it's not fair?"

"Codswallop to that!" retorted Asher. "It ain't no more your fault than Gar's, Your Majesty. It ain't anybody's fault. It just happened. And sayin' otherwise, thinkin' it even, well that just adds more grist to the mills of folks like Conroyd Jarralt. And what bloody fool would want to do that, eh?"

With a grunt of effort, Borne sat himself more upright against his raft of pillows. His lips twitched. "Well. Not this bloody fool, certainly."

Asher put his head in his hands. "Sorry, Your Majesty. I'm sorry. I'm so used to Gar, we shout and we brangle and we call each other names and I *forget*—"

The king's hand brushed against his knee in a brief benediction. "Gar told me once that above all else he treasured your honesty. He said he could trust you, as he trusted nobody else, to always tell him the truth. Whether he particularly wanted to hear it or not."

Slowly, Asher lifted his head. The king's eyes were kindly and his lips were curved in a smile. "Don't see the point of tellin' him anythin' else, sir."

The smile faded. "Can I trust you'll always do the same for me?"

"Of course, Your Majesty."

Borne slumped a little. Let his head fall back against the pillows. "He also told me you'd said you wouldn't be staying in the City above a year. That you had plans beyond that."

Mouth dry, Asher nodded. "Aye. I said that."

"But it's been more than a year now, and you're still here. Have your plans altered?"

It was hard, but he made himself meet the king's gaze squarely. "No, Your Majesty. In fact I were thinkin' on it just this mornin'. How I'd have to be makin' arrangements in the next few days for gettin' back home to Restharven."

Borne stared at his lacklustre hands. "What can I say, what can I do, to make you change your mind? There must be something you want..."

"I want nowt, Your Majesty. Except my home."

With his tired gaze still averted the king said, "I could command you to stay."

Asher felt his heart leap. Ignored it. "Aye, sir. You could."

"I don't understand." Borne looked up again. "Are you unhappy here? Have you been mistreated? Are your duties as Assistant Olken Administrator no longer to your liking?"

"No, Your Majesty. I like 'em just fine. I like everythin' about bein' here. And that's the truth."

"Then why leave? You must know it will make Gar unhappy! If you are truly his friend you would avoid doing that at all costs. He depends upon you daily to help him with his work. In truth, *I* depend upon you in that regard. As do your fellow Olken, in the City and beyond it. You aren't a fool, Asher. You must know you've become a man of influence. What does a small life in a small fishing village have to offer that your current life here in the capital does not?"

Helplessly, Asher stared at him. "My da lives in that small fishing village, Your Majesty. And he's waitin' for me to come home."

Borne stared. Sighed. "I see."

"I made him a promise," said Asher, leaning forward. "And I aim to keep it. I know it'll hurt Gar but I ain't got a choice. This is family. D'you think I'd hurt him for anything less?"

"No," said Borne. "And if your father needs you then of course you must go."

He should have felt relieved. He should have felt like turning cartwheels. Instead he felt like some kind of traitor. "I'll never forget what the prince has done for me, Your Majesty. I'm a wealthy man, thanks to him. I got a wardrobe full of fancy clothes. Books to read. A fine horse. I know things now I never knew I didn't know, if that makes any sense. And I've made a lot of good friends. Never would've had any of that without Gar."

"When do you plan on telling him?"

"Soon. I thought—"

"Wait," said the king. "Wait till you're in Westwailing and the festival is done. I want you to guide him through it safely, Asher. He's never seen the festival. Never even seen the ocean. As a child he used to beg me to take him with me to Westwailing but the queen and I..."

Didn't want to parade their magickless son in front of a gawking crowd. Asher nodded. "Aye."

"Wait," Borne pressed. "Don't give him anything else to fret about. After everything you say he's given you, it's not so much to ask, is it?"

Asher chewed at his lip. He didn't want to wait. With his mind made up to go didn't want to keep the decision secret. It'd been hard enough these past few months, knowing his time was running out, making plans with Gar for various projects, discussing ideas. He'd felt like a liar and a cheat because all the time he'd known he wouldn't be there to see them through.

"Asher?" said the king. "Please. As a favour to me, and to his mother."

A king was begging a favour of him. Of all the strange things that had happened to him since setting foot in Dorana City this had to be the strangest. Asher frowned. "But he'll guess, sir. He'll know somethin's in the wind when I start packin' all my—"

"Then don't pack. At least no more than you'd take if you were going down to Westwailing and coming back again. I'll make arrangements for all your possessions and your money to follow you safely down there a day or so after you leave. You'll not be short-changed by so much as a single cuick."

Asher sighed. So he'd spend a few days feelin' uncomfortable. He'd survive. He'd felt the same way in the weeks leading up to his departure from Restharven, hadn't he, and that hadn't killed him. "All right, Your Majesty. I'll wait till the festival's over and done."

Relief washed some colour into the king's white face. "Thank you. And speaking of the festival..."

"I'll help him every way I can," promised Asher. "If that ole Darran'll let me." He pulled a face. "Are you sure he has to come with us?"

That made Borne chuckle. "I'm sure. You never know, Asher, you might even find yourself learning something of the festival from him."

"From *Darran*? And me a fisherman born and bred?"

"Well, perhaps not," conceded the king. "But you'll humour me and let him think it's possible, won't you?"

Asher rolled his eyes. "Yes, Your Majesty."

The brief amusement in Borne's face died, leaving him tired and sad. "I'm sorry to see you leave us, Asher. I hope some day you'll come back to the City, and bring your father with you."

"Your Majesty..." Asher slid off the chair and knelt beside the king's bed. "I don't know what to say except thank you. Reckon if I were leavin' Dorana with less money than I had when I got here, and that'd be bloody near impossible, I'd still be leavin' a wealthy man, 'cause I had the luck to know you. And your son."

"The luck runs both ways, I think." Beckoning Asher close, the king pressed dry and burning lips to his forehead in a kiss. "Barl's blessings go with you, Asher. Your father is a fortunate man."

"Aye, sir. Thank you, sir," said Asher, and made good his escape.

Gar was waiting for him outside the chamber. "Done at last?" he said as they headed for the door. "What did he want to see you about?"

"Makin' sure you don't make a muck of the Sea Harvest Festival," said Asher, after the briefest hesitation. "I'm to hold your hand every step of the way."

Gar snorted. "Not where anybody can see us, you won't be."

"Course not. Don't want to make that ole Darran jealous, do we?"

Gar choked. "Or Willer." He burst out laughing, all the strain and despair of the last week draining from his face.

Relieved for the moment, dreading the future, Asher laughed with him.

In the aftermath of the announcement that His Majesty had that very morning been pronounced once more fine and dandy by the royal physician Pother Nix, the Green Goose was crammed to the rafters with celebration and a damned fine tune from Humperdy's Band. No sooner had the sun gone down and the last shop shut its doors than the inn began to fill with cheerful Olken ready to raise a mug or many to the king's good health and the Wall's longstanding.

Not that there'd been any fear for the Wall, of course. Everybody knew the king was a powerful strong magician who'd never let that Wall fall down. And anyway, there was always Princess Fane, ready to be WeatherWorker as soon as was needful. And if that wasn't a reason for celebration, then just what bloody well was?

Dathne waited and watched as Matt fought through the heaving, hilarious crowd to the bar for a fresh mug each of ale. Despite the good news about the king she was in no mood for smiling.

After a year without visions, Prophecy was back.

She'd dreamed last night of evil eyes, waiting, and a wind of fury blowing every tree in the Black Woods bare. Of stars bleeding scarlet as they fell from the sky, and the sound of women weeping.

The stubborn silence had continued for so long since her last vision she'd begun to doubt all that had at first felt so clear and certain. If Asher were truly the Innocent Mage, why had Prophecy abandoned her, Jervale's Heir, leaving her ignorant and blind? Where was calamity? What had happened to the Final Days? Had she been wrong after all?

Wait, Veira had counselled her. *After six hundred and forty-four years, what is one more? Prophecy unfolds itself according to its own desires, child. Not ours. You were not wrong. Asher is the one, and his time will come. Wait.*

So she'd waited. Waited and waited and *waited*, filling her days with work and her nights with schooling Asher as best she could, without revealing anything, in whatever arts and knowledge she thought might help him in the hidden days to come. And after a little while had got well used to waiting. To laughing. To his company. So that waiting had stopped feeling like waiting...and instead began to feel like happiness.

Now at long last the waiting was over, and all she could do was long for the silence and nights empty of dreams. For after the dream that had woken her screaming into the dark, there burned in her mind a new knowledge. An understanding that *here* now were the Final Days, counting down to chaos. That the last year had been a kind of gestation, and bloody childbirth waited hungrily, its time almost come. The knowledge sat on her shoulder like a midnight crow, cawing and chittering its fears and foretellings into the dark secret places of her mind where there was no hiding, no kind forgetting, no respite from care.

And to think she'd hoped that maybe, just maybe, the Final Days had somehow passed them by...

But she forbade her rediscovered weariness and fear to show in her face as she crunched garlic-roasted nuts and waited for Matt to return with another mug of ale. Still stuck fast in the raucous crowd he turned his head to smile at her, shoulders shrugging an apology. She smiled back, but it was an effort. Then Humperdy's music changed from gleeful laughter to a sweet, slow lament and a bracelet of fingers closed tight about her wrist.

"This be my favourite," Asher announced, his breath tickling her ear, stirring the wayward curls that escaped the confinement of her practical plait. "Dance with me, Dathne."

She hadn't seen him come in. Before she could protest, demur, distract or simply slap him down he'd dragged her into the swaying, close-packed press of bodies on the Goose's tiny excuse for a dance floor. His arms were loosely on her, gathering her close. The smell of him was all around her, clean and male and vaguely redolent of horse, and it was wrong, so wrong, he wasn't for her, couldn't be for her, there was no-one for her. She'd been chosen for other things, and so had he...

Wickedly, she let her forehead drop against his broad chest, and for one chorus and half a verse allowed the music to move her as it willed. His arms tightened, and for the first time in a long time...ever...she felt safe. Secure.

Fool! her inner self screamed and the moment shattered.

She stepped back, easing a proper distance between them. Lightly, brightly, in the bantering tone she'd taken with him from that first day in the bustling marketplace, she said, "So you've come out slumming, have you? Am I to be honoured or should I just fall over in surprise?"

He scowled. "Ha ha. I been stuck up in that bloody Tower for a week, haven't I? Taking care of all the bits and bobs that Gar forgot about, seeing as how the ceiling were going to cave in if he didn't finish translating some stupid ole story or other."

"Oh well," she said. "He's been worried about his father." And so had she, and Veira. Remembering anxiety, she asked: "His Majesty's really better?"

Asher nodded, and slyly pulled her closer again. "Oh, aye. At least he seemed well enough when I saw him this morning. Tired but on the mend, just like Nix said."

"You saw the king? This morning?" She stared at him. "In his bedchamber?" And stared a little harder, as some memory chased across his face. "Is something wrong? What did he want?"

He chewed his lip a moment, hesitant, then said, "Gar's going down the coast, to Westwailing. It's nearly Sea Harvest Festival time, and since the king's still too poorly to sing it, Gar's going to. I'm going with him. We leave in three days."

"Oh, I see. Well, it sounds very exciting. I'll look forward to hearing all about it when you get back."

"Thing is..." said Asher, after another silent moment. "I ain't coming back."

There were too many people dancing. All the breathable air had been sucked from the smoky room. Bumped and jostled she stood there, and he stood there with her, staring down, anxiety and excitement and a kind of foolhardy bravado lighting him from within.

"I'm sorry?" She almost didn't recognise her own voice, so breathless and uncertain did it sound. "*What* did you say?"

"I'm leaving Dorana. Going back to Restharven. Mayhap I'll stay there, mayhap I'll shift along to one of the other fishing villages. Depends on Da. And my brothers. But—"

"Does the prince know?" she demanded, a little strident, a touch querulous. Be easy, her saner self counselled from a great distance. But easiness was nowhere to be found.

Asher shrugged, uncomfortable. "Not yet."

That made her stare. "You haven't *told* him?"

At least he had the grace to look abashed. "I been meaning to. Now the king's asked me not to. But Gar's always known I were never going to stay in the City much above a year."

"I never knew that. You never told me."

He pulled a face. "Figured it were easier all round if I kept that to myself. Nobody but Gar needed to know."

She wanted to slap him. Wanted to scream, *I did*. She said, "And if he says no, you can't leave?"

"He won't. I got his word. I can leave whenever I want to."

"And now you want to." There was a pain in her chest like hot coals, burning. "I can't believe you've never told me. I thought we were friends."

"We are," said Asher unhappily. "You and Matt, you be the best friends I ever had, along with Gar."

She lifted her chin. "And this is how you treat us?"

"Don't be angry, Dathne..." Asher brushed her cheek with his fingertips.

She took him by the arm, ungently, and hauled him through the dancers and the drinkers, heedless of the catcalls and the laughter, outside to the empty street which glowed gently in the golden light from the distant, magic-soaked mountains. Dominating the night sky, Barl's Wall soared effortlessly upwards, losing itself amongst the stars.

"You can't leave," she said fiercely. "Gar needs you."

He pulled his arm free. "My da needs me more."

She took a deep, steadying breath and let it out. Careful handling, always careful, that was the key to Asher. For many more reasons than one. So she calmed her frightened heart and sweetened her voice and said, persuasively, "You can't be sure of that. But even if it's true, your father has other sons. Gar has only one of you. How will he get on if you leave? You're his strong right hand, Asher. The most important Olken in the kingdom. If you're worried about your father, send for him. You can look after him here as well as there."

Asher shook his head. "He'd hate it here, away from the ocean. All this dry land, no salt air, no rolling waves. It'd kill him."

"You can't just walk away!"

"Watch me," said Asher, eyebrows knitted, jaw tight. Stepping close again, she rested her palms flat to his chest. "Please. Don't go."

He stared down at her, his broad and weather-beaten face clouded with unhappiness. His mouth opened and she could see the denial in him, the rejection, the stubborn, ignorant undoing of them all...and then he looked at her hands, resting on him, and his expression cleared, vivid as a crack of lightning. Suddenly there was hope in him, and wonder, and a kind of terrified joy.

"Come with me," he countered, and covered her hands with his own.

Noise and light spilled through the alehouse's open door and windows, painting the cobblestones and the cool night air. His hands were warm, the skin callused, working hands, a man's hands. His unexpected touch goosebumped her, shivered the tiny hairs on the back of her neck and stoked the fires banked low and deep within. Harshly, with a piercing reluctance, she pulled her own hands free.

"Asher, be serious."

His face was eager now, smiling. "Just listen, eh? Hear me out. I know you've got the bookshop and all, and they don't be much for reading down Restharven way, but you could change all that. I'm pretty nigh rich now. I could set you up all fine and dandy with another little bookshop and I reckon it'd be only a month or two afore you'd have 'em all eatin' out of your hand, just like you do here."

She stepped back again, shaking her head. "You're drunk."

"Or, or," he continued, heedless, all tangled up in his bright and futile dreams, "you could just come for a visit. For a while. And if you like it, and I know you will, *then* you could stay."

"Oh, *Asher*," she said, torn between tears and temper.

"You work too hard, Dath, and you're always so serious. As if the weight of the Wall rested on your shoulders. It don't. That be King Borne's problem, and Fane's after him. Come with me. I...I...care for you, Dathne. I don't want to leave you behind."

"You're drunk," she said again, and pressed her fingers to her face. "Or I am. Or I should be. Are you mad? I can't just drop everything and run away to the coast with you, even for only a week or three. What are you doing? Why are you asking me this *now*? What possessed you to say it at all?"

He was blushing. How boyish. How charming. The pillock. "Don't know," he muttered, staring at his expensive shoes. "Been wanting to for a while. Just never could get up the nerve."

She could have hit him. Her fingers clenched to her palms, making fists. Oh, how she wanted to hit him. "I'd say you've got plenty of nerve, Asher of Restharven! I can't come with you. Not next week, or the week after, or the week after that. Not *ever*."

"Why not?" he said roughly. "Ain't I good enough for you?"

Good enough? *Good* enough? Oh, if only he knew. She gentled her voice. "That's not the point. I have work to do that can't be done anywhere else. My place is here in this City, Asher. I'm sorry. I can't do what you want."

"Can't?" he echoed. "Or won't? You're a bookseller, Dathne. You could sell books any ole place. If you wanted to."

She was filling with furious tears. He'd weakened her, damn him. Made her vulnerable in a way she'd never been before. "I'm sorry," she said harshly. "I don't mean to be unkind. I don't want us to part in anger. I don't want us to part at all! But what you want is impossible."

He nodded, slowly. Stared thoughtfully through the Goose's open door. "Is it Matt then? Are you in love with him?"

That surprised her into laughter. "*Matt*? Now you're being ridiculous. Of course I don't love Matt. Asher—"

"Then it's me." His eyes hardened, and he stepped away from her. "Go on. You can say it. I'll not break into tiny pieces and run screaming into the night. Say it."

And now she'd hurt him, truly hurt him. Oh, why hadn't she seen *this*, as well as all the other things? What should she do? Lie and say he meant nothing to her? Or should she defy Prophecy? Break her vow, her solemn oath, and tell him the real reason behind her refusal of him? Tell him the terrible truth of himself, long before it was time for him to know? Risk everything, risk a kingdom and everyone in it, all for the sake of one man's bruised heart? Even if the man was Asher?

Or was she supposed to go with him? Jervale's Heir will guide him, Prophecy said. Did that mean she should abandon her shop and Matt and traipse all the way to Westwailing with him? She would if she had to, but it made no sense. Asher's place was in the Usurper's House. In the Tower, the palace. He didn't belong on the coast, not any more. Restharven was his past, not his future.

Closing her eyes, she looked into that hidden part of herself that all her life had guided her, ruled her, brought her here, to this place, this time, this terrible moment…

Let him go. He will return.

A hesitant voice behind them said, "Eh up. What's going on?"

Matt.

She turned, eyes wide, willing him to go away. "Nothing."

Asher said, "I'm leaving."

"Already? You only just got here. What's the rush? There's a barrel of ale in there with your name on it, you know."

"I mean I'm leaving the City," said Asher, and his expression was cold and distant. "Going home."

Matt was staring, aghast. Joining them in three swift strides he said, "For *good*? No, you can't. Asher, you can't leave. Dathne, *tell* him, tell him he can't—"

She sank her fingertips into his arm, making him wince. "It's his life, Matt. His choice. There's nothing I can say that will make any difference." She looked again at Asher and managed a smile. "I'm sorry. Truly I am."

He didn't smile back. Just turned on his heel and walked away.

"*Dathne!*" said Matt explosively. "What are you doing? Go after him! *Tell* him!"

She stared up the street, at the shrinking shadow that was Asher. Felt the knowledge in her, the certainty, the sorrow yet to come, and slowly shook her head. "It's not time."

With a quick glance over his shoulder to make sure they were alone, Matt pointed one scarred, accusing finger at the shimmering mountains and lowered his voice to a scalding whisper. "I think it is. That damned sorcerer's Wall is all that's standing between us and chaos,

Dathne. When it goes, when whatever it is waiting beyond those mountains comes crashing down on all our heads, our only hope will be Asher. He *has* to know."

"And he will," she said steadily. "But not yet."

"Really? Seeing as how he's leaving for good? Dathne, you're wrong. He has to know. And if you won't tell him, I will." Reckless with fright he turned and stamped his way up the rising cobbled street.

Oh, Matt. Dear Matt. Often blind and sometimes foolish Matt. She raised her voice and snapped it at his heels. *"Don't."*

He stopped, as she knew he would. Waited for her to join him. "He thinks he's leaving for good, Matt, but he's not," she told him. "What he wants isn't there. He'll be back."

Matt's inner turmoil reflected in his face. "Who says? Dathne the bookseller? Or Jervale's Heir?"

"Both of us." She said it quietly, confidently, hiding the hurt. "Matt, just trust me, all right? He will be back."

"*Trust.*" Matt raked his fingers through his close-cropped hair. "It's a little word for a big thing, Dathne. Sooner or later we're going to have to trust *him*, you know. With the truth. With us, and himself." With a jerk of his dark-stubbled chin he looked up the empty street that led to the rarefied air of the palace, and the Tower, and Asher. "With Prophecy."

"Yes," she agreed, knowing it in her bones and in her aching heart. "But not yet."

"Not yet! Not yet!" he shouted in sudden rage, fists clenched. "You keep saying that! You've been saying that for a year now, Dathne! We've been lying to him for a whole damned *year*! When is it going to stop? When will *not yet* become *right now*?"

If she cried nothing would ever be the same again. Her own hands fisted, the blood in her veins on fire, she stared at him. Said coldly: *"Not yet."*

For long moments he glared back at her. Hated her. Then the angry resistance in him melted, as it always did, and he rubbed his large horseman's hands over his despairing face. "Oh, Dath. I'm sorry. I don't mean to question you, I know you know what's best. I just..." He groaned. "Damn. How'd I ever get mixed up in all this anyways?"

She smiled, because he needed to see it, not because she felt like smiling, and stepped close. Eased her arm around him until it lay across his defeated shoulders. "The same way as me and Asher, my friend. You were born for it. And in case you were wondering...yes. It's far too late to turn back now."

CHAPTER SEVENTEEN

"I can't believe you're really doing this."

With a deft flick of his wrist Asher tipped another forkload of manure onto the muck sack. "Why not? Ain't like I never mucked out horse shit before."

"You know what I mean," said Matt, and kicked the stable door he was leaning over.

Gently pushing Cygnet aside, Asher slid his fork under another pile of manure. In the yard behind him the bustle of afternoon stables half drowned their conversation. Why he'd felt the need to come down here and shovel shit he wasn't sure. Mayhap 'cause this was the last chance he'd ever have to do it. The last chance here, any road. In this stable. In this yard, where it had all begun. It was, he supposed, another good-bye that needed to be said. He glanced up at Matt, then kept working.

"Aye."

"Have you seen Dathne since—"

"No," said Asher, disposing of the manure. He didn't want to, either. Just the thought of what he'd asked her, how she'd answered, could flood him hot with angry embarrassment. Seeing her was impossible. The faster she faded into memory, the happier he'd be.

"Are you going to?"

There were three more piles of manure to collect. Bloody Cygnet; the horse was nowt but a pretty silver shit-maker.

"No."

Another bang as Matt kicked at the stable door again. "Why not? You're leaving tomorrow. She'll be hurt if you don't."

"I doubt it."

"Asher!" Matt's laughter was baffled. "She's your friend. How can you not—"

"Easy!" he shouted, glaring. "Because I don't bloody want to, all right? Because—because—" He couldn't say it. Couldn't make the words leave his mouth. If he didn't say it, maybe that meant it didn't have to be true.

Matt's expression changed. "Oh." In his voice, a sudden understanding. "Oh, Asher. Why didn't you say something?"

Savagely he scooped up another pile of manure and dumped it with the rest. "Because I didn't want to. Anyway, it don't matter."

"Of course it matters. When did you—I mean, how long have you known you..."

Asher sighed and let himself collapse against the stable wall. Moodily he poked at the straw with the tips of the fork tines, and watched the lazy swish of Cygnet's tail as the horse nibbled hay. "I don't rightly know. Seems it kind of snuck up on me." He glanced at Matt, then glanced away, not wanting to see the sympathy in his friend's face. "I asked her to come with me."

"Oh," Matt said helplessly. "Asher, I'm sorry. Damn, I wish you'd said something. I could've told you she'd never agree to leave Dorana."

Oh, could he? "It's all right," Asher said curtly. "She told me herself."

"I had no idea you felt that way. No idea at all."

"Why would you?" said Asher, pushing away from the wall and forking up the remaining manure. He needed to get out of here before Matt said something they'd both regret. It looked like he was parting badly from one good friend; he didn't want an argument with Matt to make it two. Not when he had Westwailing looming on his horizon.

"It's what I do," Matt said, almost to himself. "I see things."

Asher snorted. "Around here, maybe, but only 'cause it's your job. And I ain't a part of it, not anymore. Not for a long time. Here," he added, and held out the fork for Matt to take. Then he gathered up the corners of the laden muck sack and dragged it towards the stable door. Cygnet huffed through his nostrils and pretended to be terrified. "Let me out."

Matt opened the stable door and stood aside to let him pass. "Still, I wish I'd realised."

"Why?"

"I would've said something," said Matt, bolting the stable door closed again.

Young Fulk scurried past empty-handed. Asher grabbed him by the scruff of the neck and gifted him with the muck sack. "Said what?" he demanded, once the lad was safely on his way to the muck heap. "No offence, Matt, but I don't reckon as it's any of your business. Unless you got an idea I'd be poaching." Scowling, he watched Bellybone slosh water buckets across the yard. "Is that what this is about?"

"No." Matt spoke absently, as though he'd barely heard the question, or didn't care what it might mean. "Look, I'm sorry you've been hurt but if you had told me I could've spared you some of it. There's no use having feelings for Dathne. She's not that kind of woman."

That snapped his head round. "And what's that s'posed to mean?"

"It means..." Matt stared at the ground. "She's not for home and hearth, Asher. Her life is in the bookshop. Business. She belongs here, in the City."

Something else he didn't need Matt to tell him. "I know that now."

"And even if you stayed, it wouldn't make any difference."

He shoved his hands into his pockets. "Well, I ain't staying, am I, so there you are."

"I know, but..." Matt shrugged. "Even if you were, Asher. She still wouldn't—well, her answer would be the same. That's all I'm saying."

All this bloody interfering. Friends, eh. Who needed 'em? "Y'know that for a fact, do you?" He sounded waspish. He felt it. Right this moment he could sting, and sting, and sting.

Matt rested a hand on his shoulder. "If you mean has she ever said as much to me, no. She didn't have to. I know her, Asher. We've been friends a long time, and sometimes—not often, but sometimes—she confides in me. Dathne's a...a racehorse. Not a broodmare."

Despite the anger and pain, he laughed. "I wouldn't go round callin' her a horse where she can hear you, Matt. Not less you fancy yourself as a gelding."

"I just wish you'd not told her," said Matt unhappily. "It only makes things harder for her. It's not that she doesn't care, you know. She just doesn't care like that."

"For me?"

"For anybody."

"So, this ain't about you bein' jealous?"

Matt gaped. "No! Me and Dathne, you mean? Barl save me. *No.*"

Asher stared, suspicious. "You're sure?"

"Bloody sure. I promise."

Stepping sideways so that Matt's hand was pulled free, he scowled. "Well. Anyways. I did speak to her, didn't I, and I reckon I'm paying dear enough for the mistake without you chewing on my ear for good measure. Now were there anything else? Only I've got to meet with bloody Darran to make sure there's been nowt forgotten for tomorrow."

"Anything else? I don't know. No. Yes. Asher, if going home doesn't work out for you..."

Asher began inching towards the gate that led to the Tower. Bloody Darran would start squealing like a hog in the slaughterhouse if he didn't turn up soon. Even worse, if he was late he'd have to apologise, and apologising to Darran gave him indigestion. "Of course it'll work out. I got it all planned, Matt. Had it planned for years, not just since I came here."

Matt took a step after him. "Yes, but you've been away a long time, Asher. Things change."

He laughed. "Not that much, they don't."

"I know. I know. But if they do. If they have..."

The urgency in Matt's voice and face made him stare. Matt as a rule was a placid man. Urgency was saved for important matters like lameness and difficult foalings. He stopped inching towards the gate. "What's going on, Matt? Is there something you ain't tellin' me? D'you know something I don't, and should?"

"No." Matt's expression cleared of everything save a gentle concern. "Of course not. What could I know? I'm just trying to be a good friend."

Damn, he hated saying goodbye. He had to wait a moment before he could trust himself to speak. "You've always been a good friend, Matt. Always, from the first day I got here. I ain't likely to forget it."

Matt smiled. His eyes were melancholy. "I hope not."

He was late. He had to go. "I'll see you in the morning, eh? I need Cygnet saddled by seven, mind."

"He'll be ready."

And there wasn't anything else to say after that. Slipping through the stable-yard gate, he started running for the Tower.

"Ah. Asher," said Darran, poisonously polite. "I'm afraid you've missed most of the discussion."

"Sorry," muttered Asher as he slid into Darran's office. "Got held up."

"Indeed." Darran looked down his bony nose at him. "Well, I'm not inclined to waste time by repeating everything we've already agreed upon. I'll give you your instructions once we're done."

Willer sniggered. He was seated beside the Tower's housekeeper, Mistress Hemshaw, who in turn was wedged into the chair next to Trundal, the palace provisioner.

"Fine," said Asher, burning, and propped himself against the nearest bit of wall.

After confirming with Trundal that everything necessary for the long journey was assembled ready for loading into the wagons, Darran turned to the housekeeper. "Mistress Hemshaw, have you anything else to add?"

She fluffed herself like a broody hen. "No, Darran, save for the matter of His Highness's wardrobe. He's still not made up his mind as to exactly what clothes he wishes to take with him so I can have them properly packed and ready for loading."

Darran's nostrils pinched shut. "I see."

"Don't look at me," said Asher, already bored to sobs and staring out of the office window. "I ain't his nursery maid."

"For the sake of efficiency, shall we pretend otherwise?" said Darran. "Just this once?"

Asher sighed. "Fine. I'll take care of it."

"All that remains, then," Darran continued, "is one final announcement. After due consideration and the proper consultation with His Highness I have decided to allow Willer to accompany us on this historic trip to Westwailing. He shall be our official chronicler of the expedition, charged with the solemn duty of keeping a daily diary and accurately recording every moment of His Highness's triumphant procession."

Willer sat bolt upright and squealed like a girl. "Oh, Darran! Really? Oh, thank you, *thank* you!"

Aye, thought Asher sourly, as Mistress Hemshaw and Trundal dutifully congratulated the little sea slug. Thank you very much, Darran. And Gar. Barl bloody save him. With Darran and now Willer along for the ride, it looked like this was going to be the longest, most tedious trip from Dorana to Westwailing in the history of Lur.

An hour after dawn the next morning Gar's entourage was in the last throes of its preparation to quit the City. Four large covered wagons and a travelling coach crammed nose to tail around the outer edges of the Tower's forecourt. Darran stalked along their length, interrogating the drivers and any menial who couldn't scurry away fast enough. Asher, in counterpoint, crisscrossed the scattering gravel on horseback, barking orders, contradicting Darran, chivvying and bustling and scuttling folk out of his way.

Still put out about Willer being included in the expedition, Gar decided, and swallowed a smile. Oh well. It served him right for being so rude about people who had so many fancy bloody clothes they couldn't make up their mind which three shirts to throw into a suitcase, and did he really think the folk down Westwailing way *cared* whether his britches were blue or crimson? Because, you know, it was damn near certain they didn't.

Every spare inch of the forecourt not occupied with last-minute baggage waiting to be stowed or grooms holding horses or messengers bearing sundry forgotten items was packed shoulder to heel with palace and Tower folk and townspeople, eager to send him on his way with a smile and a wave. Even the surrounding gardens were peppered with grinning faces. Seeing them went some small way to warming the cold hollow space in his chest.

If he wasn't very careful he'd find himself feeling terrified of the job that lay ahead. Terrified of doing something wrong, of looking a fool, of letting his father down when the only thing that mattered, in the end, was making him proud.

Reading his mind as usual his mother said, "It's a shame this expedition doesn't appear on the official calendar. I know the Olken on the coast hold the event close to their hearts. But, for reasons that doubtless seem sanguine to the Privy Council, you must depart without their auspices. When it comes to the Sea Harvest Festival not even your father warrants a goodbye wave from Conroyd, you know." She flickered a smile at him. "Are you so very disappointed?"

They were standing together on the Tower's front steps, pretending to be bored by all the hustle and bustle. With a lifetime of practice behind her, his mother was much better at it than he was. He, lowering though it was to admit, was feeling pretty damned excited.

It was, he supposed, marginally better than feeling terrified.

"Disappointed? Not at all. It was the first thing Darran told me so I've had ample time to recover from my devastation," he replied dryly. "You know as well as I, the minute the Privy Council gets involved in anything the protocol quotient trebles and it takes five times as long to get anything done. On the whole I'm as happy as they are that they're still snoring sweetly in their own little beds."

His mother chuckled. "And of course I needn't mention how sorry your father is that he can't be here to give you his blessing. But Durm and Nix were adamant, and I confess I'm glad of it."

He closed his fingers around hers and squeezed gently. "I would've been cross beyond measure if I'd seen him here this morning. Joining us for dinner last night pushed him to the limits of his recovery. All that needed to be said between us was said then, and I'm content."

She kissed his cheek. "Good."

"Still," he added, shattering all his excellent intentions, "I thought Fane might come to see us off. And Durm."

His mother hesitated. Smoothed his embroidered linen sleeve with a troubled hand and said, "She's busy with her studies, Gar, and of course needs Durm beside her."

"You mean she's jealous and he's excusing her. As usual."

His mother made a small noise of distress. "Oh, Gar. I thought you'd forgiven her that business with the stick and the rose. I know it was unkind. I've spoken to her most severely on it, she knows—"

"You're mistaken, Mama. I don't care about that," he said impatiently, even though he did. Even though the memory could still freeze his blood. He still didn't know which was worse: that she could have done it or that he could have been so blind, so stupid, as to have let her. She was his only sister. He wanted so much to love her. And even though he knew why she had to make it so difficult, there were times he found it almost impossible.

Now it was his mother's fingers that closed, comforted. "Darling, I—"

Scattering pebbles, Darran appeared before them at the base of the carved sandstone steps, harried, harassed and voluble.

"Your Majesty, Your Highness, please forgive me but I must bring to your attention a catastrophe of—"

"What is it, Darran?" Gar sighed.

"I can't find Willer," said Darran, almost wailing. "He's not in the coach where he's supposed to be, he's not in the office, I can't see him anywhere in the forecourt or its environs and—"

Gar lifted an impatient hand, cutting off the spate of words midflow. Turning to search the crowd in the forecourt he saw his target and raised his voice.

"Asher!"

Asher stopped interrogating a groom and nudged Cygnet sideways with knee and heel. "Yes, Your Highness?" And added, with his first smile of the day, "Morning, Your Majesty."

The queen smiled back. "And to you, Asher."

"Do you know where Willer is?" Gar demanded.

"Were I supposed to?" Asher jerked his head at Darran. "That's his job, ain't it?"

Gar permitted himself a barbed smile. "As of now it's yours. Find him."

Asher scowled, then offered a short, sharp bow. "Yes, sir."

"Thank you, sir," said Darran as Asher rode away.

Gar frowned. "If you kept a better eye on your people, Darran, there'd be no need of thanks. Now hurry up. Call me eccentric but I'd like to leave before noon. Today."

"Yes, Your Highness." Darran bowed. "Your Majesty. Your Highness."

Gar watched him retreat then glanced at his mother and shrugged. "I know I shouldn't show it but he does get on my nerves. If I wasn't afraid it'd bring on a relapse I'd leave him behind with strict instructions to wait hand and foot on Father, just the way he used to."

He expected a short, not wholly undeserved lecture on the importance of keeping one's temper with the staff, but instead his mother took his arm and drew him four paces back from the forecourt, close to the blue curving brick of the Tower wall. In her eyes was a look he'd never seen before.

"What?" he asked, alarmed. "Mama? Has something—is Father—"

"Hush, Gar, and listen to me." Her voice was low, insistent, her fingers like a vice through his shirt sleeve. "You make jokes, but I'm afraid I can't laugh at them."

He stared. "What do you mean? Are you saying he *is* in danger of relapse? Durm said—Pother Nix said—"

"I know what they said. And they're right, in their own limited fashions. He is recovering well enough from this fever. But, Gar, my dear, the situation is more complicated than that."

"Complicated how?"

She released his arm. "The Weather Magic is a double-edged sword and every time you wield it, you cut yourself a little. Your father has been bleeding to death drop by drop since the day he called his first rainfall."

"*Mama!*" If they'd not been in public he would have pressed his fingers to her mouth. He didn't want to hear this. Not now. Not ever. She'd voiced concerns before, fretted his father's dedication to duty at the expense of his own health many times, but never like this. Never so bleakly or with such cold despair. "Mama, why are you—"

"He's changed, Gar. He's not been the same since that business with the young man from Basingdown. You don't know. You don't live with him. You don't wake to the sound of his weeping in dreams, as I do. You haven't had to watch him shrink from himself, as I have, all because of that one brutally necessary act. He may be your father but he's my husband. And a wife sees things..."

He reached for her hand. "I see more than you think, Mama. And I, too, have dreams."

She pulled away from him. "He is weary, Gar! Sick at heart. And the WeatherWorking grows harder and harder with every sunrise. I have asked him to abdicate, *begged* him, but he won't. Fane is still too young, he says, and I know he's right, of course he's right, but even so..." With an effort she collected herself. "When the day comes for her to ascend the throne—however that day comes—there *must* be a clean succession. There can be no hint of doubt as to her readiness. Do you understand?"

"Yes, of course, but—"

His mother's eyes were fierce. Pain and brute determination

burning there. "No matter what Fane does, Gar. No matter how unkind she may be, it can't matter. Your father isn't blind, he can see when she hurts you, and he mustn't be given any more reason for worry. So you'll have to hide it. However deep the wounds your sister inflicts, he must never see the blood. Now I know you're pained because she's not here this morning to wish you well. I don't care. The more hours she spends in study the sooner she can take the burden of WeatherWorking from your father. And that could mean his life, Gar. His *life*. What are your bruised feelings compared to that?"

He was finding it hard to breathe. "Nothing, Mama, they're nothing, but—"

"Your sister will be the greatest WeatherWorker this kingdom has ever known, but only if she's ready when the time comes. If she's not, if she's forced to it before Durm has tempered her, she could break. And then what? We look to the likes of Conroyd Jarralt? Pray Barl not, Gar. For then the Wall would surely crumble and the horrors that lie beyond it will overcome us all."

Taking her cold hands in his, holding them tight, he said, coaxingly, "It's been six hundred years since Barl and our ancestors fled Morgan—Morg and his tyranny, Mama. He is long since dead and gone to dust. Nothing but a name used to frighten naughty children. He can't hurt us. In truth, we don't know there are *any* horrors still beyond the Wall."

Again, she pulled her hands free. "We don't know there *aren't*! A man like Morg. A magician of his unspeakable powers and unbridled lust for domination. Who knows what legacy he left behind him? Who can say how far his hand stretched? He may have spawned children. He may have founded a dynasty of tyrants that has stretched from his time to ours. All that stands between us and the fruit of those diseased days, their savagery and their slaughter, is the Wall. Would I stand idly by as your father kills himself by inches to protect it if I didn't believe the sacrifice was necessary? Would I give up a child of my body to the same cruel fate?"

Another word, another syllable, and she would have him in tears. "I know you wouldn't," he said, his voice unsteady. "I wish you'd told me this sooner. I wish I could do more to spare him. I wish—"

She wrapped her arms around him then, and held him close to her breast. "Forgive me!" she breathed, her own voice breaking. "I am all to pieces, dearest. It was wrong of me to speak on it. Especially now. Your father is making a fine recovery and I fear he'd be vexed indeed to learn I'd made you worry!"

She felt as frail as a sparrow. "Don't, Mama. Don't treat me like a child. When I come back we'll speak more on this. We'll find a way to spare him, I promise. You—"

A ripple of laughter, rising to a wave, ran through the crowd that had gathered to see him depart for the coast. His mother loosened her grip and they stepped apart to see what was causing the commotion.

Asher, the thrown stone, jogged his horse down the path from the storehouses at the rear of the Tower. Slung over the front of his saddle was Willer, plump rump quivering like a satin-covered jelly, short legs kicking the innocent air. He was shrieking.

"Put me down! Oaf! Cretin! Barbarian! Put me *down*!"

Ignoring him, Asher jogged on through the crowd's swelling mirth. Reached the foot of the Tower steps and lifted his reins, signalling an indignant Cygnet to stop. He was grinning. "Found 'im," he announced, and slid Willer to the gravel-strewn ground.

Gar sighed. "So I see. Willer? I take it you have an explanation?"

His secretary's assistant, scarlet-faced and puffing like a bellows, staggered in a ragged circle and nearly upended himself in a bow. His blotched face streamed sweat despite the early hour. "Your Hi-Highness! Your Majesty! Your Highness!" Then he turned on Asher. "*You*! You did this on purpose!"

Asher rolled his eyes. Darran, squawking up to join them like an enraged hen, attacked from the rear. "Depend on it, Your Highness, Willer is telling the truth! From the day he arrived Asher has failed to show me and my staff the veriest *breadcrumb* of respect! He—"

Forgetting his place entirely, Willer interrupted. "He locked me in that storeroom so he could shame me before everyone!"

Asher heaved a vastly put-upon sigh. Ignoring Willer and Darran he looked to his prince. "I didn't."

Abruptly weary of the lot of them, Gar lifted a dismissive hand. "We'll discuss it later."

Willer squeaked. "But, Your *Highness*—"

"Later, I said!" Gar snapped. "It's time to leave."

Willer deflated. Bowed. "Your Majesty. Your Highness."

Ungently manoeuvred by Darran, the assistant secretary withdrew. Gar, still watching, smiled a little at the glare with which he scorched an impervious Asher; a degree or two more heat and his irritating friend would be stone dead on the ground and doubtless smoking. Turning his back on them all, he laid a hand against his mother's thin cheek. "Tell the king I shall not fail him. Tell him to rest, and get well. The kingdom needs him."

Her hand came up to cover his and she met his gaze with her restored and customary cool strength. "Barl's blessing on you, my dear. You carry your king and queen's full confidence." She kissed him and stepped back, a determined smile on her lips. Only if he looked deep into her eyes could he see her smothered distress.

"I'll see you in a few weeks," he promised, not daring to say more. Kissed her hand, beckoned for his horse and swung himself into the saddle.

Asher grinned. "No need to fret, Your Majesty. I'll keep a close eye on him, make sure he don't catch cold or stub his toe."

"I know you will," said Dana. "Goodbye, Asher."

For some reason, Asher started. A flea bite, perhaps, thought Gar. If so then serve him right, with a fulminating Darran still to come.

Asher's grin faded. "Goodbye, Your Majesty." He bowed, a fisted hand pressed close to his heart.

Which was odd, Gar thought, and not the least like Asher, who disdained all public protestations of affection.

As the rumbling cavalcade set forth with himself and Asher in the lead, and the people cheered and the horses tossed their bright heads and jingled their bits, gently excited, he turned to his assistant and said, "So, we're off. Excited?"

Asher was barely paying attention, his frowning gaze scouring the rows of wellwishers left and right. "Not really."

He raised his eyebrows severely. "Not really. The first chance to see your precious ocean again in more than a year, and you're not excited. Asher, I declare, there is no hope for you."

"No," said Asher vaguely, still searching the crowd. "Prob'ly there ain't." Some of the ladies were throwing flowers; absently, out of habit, he caught a dethorned rose and tucked it behind one ear. The black-haired girl who'd tossed it subsided amongst her friends in a flurry of giggles.

Goaded, Gar kicked Asher's ankle. "Looking for somebody special?" he asked in a tone of voice guaranteed to irritate.

Asher snapped his head round. "No," he said shortly, and after that did not let his gaze stray from the straight road leading out of the City.

Gar grinned. *Yes*. Happy that he'd repaid at least a part of the debt he freshly owed Asher, all too aware of the sibilant dissatisfaction in the coach behind him, he patted Ballodair's warm brown neck and looked forward to the journey ahead.

*   *   *

In her tiny rooms above her bookshop Dathne gathered the tools of her secret business and laid them out on the table by the window. A breeze stirred the curtains and wafted the scent of fresh-picked jasmine through the cramped and book-crammed living room.

A large shallow silver bowl, filled to the brim with untainted rainwater.

Three glass vials, unlabelled, and stoppered against leakage.

A sprig of dried tanal leaf, known also by another name, never to be spoken aloud.

The leaf was bitter, flooding her mouth with sharp saliva. She chewed and chewed and chewed again but did not swallow, for that would lead to madness. When the shiny golden foliage was a pulped mass on her tongue, all its properties extracted, she spat the dregs of it into a scrap of rag for later burning. Tipping her head back, closing her eyes, she swilled the acrid saliva around and around her mouth, sieving it through her teeth and over the avid mucous membranes of her gums and palate. Then, giddy with the potency of it, she spat what was left onto the rag with the leaf pulp, and waited.

In time the room grew dim to her sight, even as the sun's bright light flooded through the open window. When it looked to her as though midnight were upon the world, she reached for the first vial, plucked free its stopper, and dribbled a scant three drops of vervle into the silver basin.

The water bubbled and swirled and turned the colour of blood.

Carefully she put the first vial aside and reached for the second. Cloysies' tears. Four drops this time, and this time the water heaved in fury, spitting forth a burned ochre steam. It was pungent, smelling of the grave.

The last vial, its potion the most virulent. Moon-rot. One drop only. The muddy water stirred and seethed, thickened like a porridge and belched a sour, sickly smell. Dathne flared her nostrils to catch it like a horse scenting home, and smiled. The steam thinned, thinned some more, disappeared, and now the water in the basin was black like glass. Reflected on its surface her eyes glowed back at her, gold around the edges, fathomless and wise. She spread her hand above the bowl and spoke aloud the name of he whose image she summoned.

"*Asher.*"

The shiny black water waited motionless in its basin, like a cat before the mouse hole. Breathing in through her nose, and out through her nose, Dathne waited with it, hands loosely resting palm down on the table, head drooping a little as the magic bubbled in her blood.

A small bright light, brighter than a diamond in sunshine, pierced the darkness in the water. Slowly it blossomed, bloomed, opened like a window onto another world. Hazily a picture formed, bleary, the way a woman's sight is bleary upon opening her eyes to the morning after a long hard night.

Dathne eased a sigh from her lungs and leaned a little closer over the basin.

The picture rippled, then coalesced into focus.

Asher. And Gar. And the rest of the prince's troupe, clattering their way over the City's cobblestones, waving to the townsfolk who'd forsaken their beds to wish them good journey. Gar was smiling, laughing, waving left and right. Asher waved too, and smiled after a fashion, but it didn't reach his eyes.

For a long time she sat before the basin, breathing in and breathing out, and watched him. Knowing he rode towards heartbreak and shattered dreams. The exact nature of the pain awaiting him she could not tell, but she felt it as though it were her own. Like a knife in her heart.

Soon after reaching the coast he would return. And she would be waiting for him, whether he wanted her there or not. Because she had to be. Because he needed her, even though he didn't know it.

And Prophecy, her cruel master, would continue.

In sudden anger, sudden fear, her hands plunged into the silver basin of water. Asher's image shattered. The water cleared, became just a jug's worth of rainwater once more. Her heavy head ached. She lowered it into her wet hands and wept.

CHAPTER EIGHTEEN

Without mishap, Gar's mostly cheerful cavalcade made its stately way along the City Road, over the bustling River Gant and away from Dorana and its Home Districts. Leaving the Home farms and orchards in their wake they climbed up the gentle Saffron Hills and down the other side, where the Flatlands spread before them in a tapestry of green and blue and yellow and brown. Tiny birds like bright winged jewels danced among the flowering grasses, flitting from stem to nodding stem. Butterflies floated indolently on the perfumed breeze, and rabbits, startled and scudding, caused the horses to dance on restive hooves.

Just past noon they stopped for luncheon. Two cooks prepared the food while other servants pitched a silk pavilion to protect their prince from the unfettered sun, trapping the wild Flatland grasses beneath carpets of hand-woven splendour. The fresh bloom-laden air turned savoury with the spitting smell of venison roasting.

But before food came business. Wedged into a folding chair plumped comfortably with cushions, and appeased with a goblet of wine, Gar reluctantly admitted a poker-backed Darran to his presence. The man was looking even more desiccated than usual. Pique, probably, sucking him dry of life's joy.

"Before you say anything, Darran," he said tersely, "I've spoken to Asher and he assures me that Willer being locked in the storeroom was an accident."

Darran's nostrils pinched tight. "I have no doubt he does, sir."

"Do you imply Asher is lying, Darran? To *me*?"

Darran laced his fingers across his middle and considered the pattern of the carpet beneath his feet for a long moment. "The alternative, sir," he said at last, lifting his gaze, "is to say that Willer is lying to me."

Of course it was. Damn. Gar tossed back the remains of his wine and held out the empty goblet. With only the merest hesitation, his secretary refilled it from the carafe on the sideboard and handed it back.

"I grant you," he said, after another deep swallow of spicy Brosa red, "that Asher mishandled the business. As you very well know, at times he has a ... dubious sense of humour."

"Dubious, Your Highness?" Darran sniffed. "I submit, sir, that 'dubious' is too mild a word for it."

Barl save him. "That'll do, Darran. I'm not in the mood for semantics."

Stung, Darran dipped his head. "Sir."

Gar glared at his dusty boots. Despite some lingering misgivings, he'd been looking forward to this expedition. Over dinner last night his father had called it "a wonderful adventure. An experience to be savoured." And had added, grinning, "So get out there and savour it." Which, all nerves aside, he'd had every intention of doing. But then there'd been his mother's fraught confession, and now *this*.

Damn Asher anyway. And Willer. Idiots, the pair of them. After all this time you'd think they'd have found a way to get along. Or at least squabble in a way that didn't inconvenience *him*. He swallowed another mouthful of wine.

"Frankly, Darran, I see no point in prolonging this unfortunate business. Least said, soonest mended, and so forth."

Clearly Darran didn't agree. His sparse eyebrows lowered and his lips pursed. "Naturally, sir, if you prefer to declare the incident closed—"

"I do."

"I see, sir."

Struck with conscience—after all, Darran did have a point—Gar softened his tone. "Look. Rightly or wrongly, what's done is done. We'll just have to keep them apart as best we can until Willer's bruised pride has mended. And it's not as if he were *hurt* or anything. A trifle bounced, perhaps. But nothing life-threatening."

Darran favoured him with a frosty smile. "As you say, sir."

Unaccountably, it made him feel defensive. "For the love of Barl, Darran, we both have better things to do than concern ourselves with such trifling matters. I'm bored with the whole stupid affair. Don't trouble me with it again."

Darran bowed. "Your Highness."

"Just...go and relax, Darran. You've been run off your feet the last few days and it's only going to get worse once we reach Westwailing. Take a moment to enjoy the fresh country air. You deserve it."

Another bow. "Your Highness is too kind."

"Not at all," he replied, teeth gritted. "Now don't allow me to detain you any longer. Given our early start and brisk pace, I'm sure you're hungry and thirsty."

As dismissals went, it was mild. Darran offered him a third bow, meticulously calculated to convey respect laced with a deep and grievous disappointment, and withdrew.

A scant moment later Asher entered. "You settle the ole crow then?" he asked, pouring himself a goblet of wine.

"Yes. And for Barl's sake, stop calling him that!"

Asher shrugged. "If you say so."

"I do. And as for Willer—"

"What about him?"

"I want you to apologise."

That snapped Asher's spine straight. "What? Why? How many times do I have to tell you, Gar, I never locked him in that bloody storeroom!"

"I'm not saying you did."

"Fine," said Asher, truculent. "Then I ain't got anything to apologise for, have I?"

Gar's fingers tightened on the stem of his goblet, but he refrained from throwing it: the wine was too good to waste. "It was unkind and unnecessary of you to make him a public laughing stock. I don't care how annoying you find him, you're the Assistant Olken Administrator. People look up to you. You can't go around indulging intemperate whims like that. There are repercussions."

Asher was staring. "Gar... it was a *joke*."

"A bad one. Willer is a member of my staff. When you embarrass him, you embarrass me... or had you forgotten that?"

"What are you talking about? I was just poking fun at him. It was harmless."

Snapping, Gar put down his goblet. "A year in my service, of dealing with the meisters and mistresses of the guilds and Conroyd Jarralt and *still* you haven't... Nothing you do is without the potential for harm. Now find Willer and tender him your apology. Or else get back on your precious Cygnet and return to the Tower. I don't care which. The choice is yours."

Asher collapsed into the other chair. "You're serious."

"Congratulations! Light dawns at last!"

"Gar..." Asher sat back, his face a mask of baffled concern. "What's got into you? What's going on?"

Damn. After a year of working together Asher knew him too well. The urge to confide, to share the burden of his mother's fears, was almost overwhelming.

What's going on? Not much. My mother's falling to pieces, my sister's a selfish bitch and my father's committing slow suicide for the sake of his kingdom. That's all.

He couldn't do it. Not only was it unfair to Asher, to crush him with such knowledge, it would be in some strange way a betrayal of his father.

Forcing a smile, he shook his head. "There's nothing going on. I've got a headache. From hunger, probably. Please... do as I ask. Apologise to that tiresome prat so I'm not forced to spend the next few weeks enduring a pissy Darran and a whinging Willer. I'm not asking you to declare undying devotion! Just say you're sorry. I hardly think it's going to *kill* you."

"Ha," said Asher, standing. "I ain't so sure about that."

"Well, if I'm wrong and you do drop dead at his feet, I promise there'll be a lovely funeral."

"And don't think I won't hold you to it!" retorted Asher, glaring. Then he sat again, abruptly, his expression softening into concern. "Look. I'm sorry, all right? I never meant to raise a ruckus. I thought it were funny. Thought it might give you a laugh. Things've been a mite fraught lately, and..." He shrugged. "Guess I were wrong."

The unexpected apology disarmed Gar. Doused his anger and stirred guilt. "I'm sorry too," he replied, frowning at his fingers. "I know I've been short-tempered lately. Unapproachable. This business with the king...it frightened me." He managed a faint smile. "And I don't much care for being frightened."

"Who does? But your da's on the mend now. He'll be right as rain in another few days. So you can relax, eh?"

He made himself smile. "I'll relax after you've said your sorries to Willer."

Asher pulled a face and stood again. "Aye. You'll relax and I'll lose my bloody appetite." He shook his head. "Apologise to Willer. Ha! The things I do for you..."

With a meaningful grimace he took himself off, wine goblet dangling negligently from his fingers and splashing vintage Brosa red to the carpet like fat drops of blood.

Gar sighed. Reached for his own goblet and drank deep. Asher and Willer and Darran on the same expedition...three spiky peas crammed into the same small pod. Barl save him from temperament. And then, suddenly recalling Willer's plump satin buttocks, upended over Asher's saddle and wriggling like two pigs in a blanket, he snorted into his wine. Choked. And laughed till he was breathless.

Asher stamped his way over to where Flavy Bannet was guarding corn cobs boiling in a tub of water and licking his greasy fingers. Five enormous platters of carved meat steamed on the bench beside him, and loaves of bread wrapped in hot cloths sat next to bowls of salad greens.

"Oy," he said, stomach rumbling. "Never you mind shoving food down your own gizzard, Flavy. The prince is nigh to fainting with hunger. How long afore this lot's ready?"

Flavy gave a guilty start and smeared the rest of the grease down the front of his apron. "Five minutes, Asher."

"Aye, well, if it's five and a half, you and me'll be having words, right?" He filched a slice of venison and slouched off to find Willer.

The prissy little sea slug was in the travelling coach, writing in a big leather-bound book. His hysterical account of the historic expedition, most like.

"What do you want?" Willer snapped, pen poised and dripping ink. Noticing, he hissed and fumbled with salt and blotter to undo the worst of the damage.

Asher scowled. "I don't care what you say, it wasn't me who shut you in that bloody storeroom. Like as not you shut yourself in there by accident when you went poking about for biscuits to stuff in your pockets."

Willer sat up. "How dare you! I am no thief! I went into the storeroom to—"

"D'you think I care why you went in there?" said Asher impatiently. "Just shut up and let me apologise, would you?"

"Apologise? *You*?" Willer's voice was curdled with contempt. "You don't know the meaning of the word. And why should I accept? You don't even—"

"One more squeal out of you afore I've finished," threatened Asher, "and you know what you can do with your bloody apology. Right?"

Willer sneered. "I know what *you* can do with it. We both know you're not sorry. The only reason you're grovelling to me now is because His Highness is making you do it."

Asher felt his fingers tighten on his goblet almost to breaking point. "And how would you know that, eh? Been spying again, Willer? Been creeping and crawling like a little rat, listening to conversations that ain't none of your business?"

Willer flushed a blotchy red. "I don't know what you're talking about."

Ah ha. Now this was more like it. This was a damned sight better than apologising. Grinning, Asher propped one foot on the carriage's unfolded bottom step, rested his elbow on his knee and trapped Willer inside the carriage.

"Thought I never noticed you, eh?" he said conversationally. "Must reckon I'm as blind as a bat and deaf as a post to boot. I'll give you this much, Willer. You're a persistent little slug. A year now you've been tryin' to get me in trouble with Gar, haven't you? Or Darran, or the guild meisters, or the Council, or anybody else you reckon'll listen to your lies. Hanging round meeting rooms once everybody else has gone. Chatting up the guild meisters' assistants. Sneaking little looks at messages and letters not addressed to you. Accidentally on purpose eavesdropping over conversations that ain't none of your concern. Looking and looking for something what'll get me fired, or worse. All the time thinking yourself so clever, 'cause nobody ever noticed. Well

I noticed, Willer. I'd have to be thick as two short planks not to and, trust me, I ain't."

Willer's face had drained from blotchy red to sickly white. "*You're* the liar. You always lie. That's what you are. A rotten born liar."

Still grinning, Asher downed the last half-swallow of wine and dangled the goblet thoughtfully. "You must think I'm as stupid as you are, Willer. Ain't you worked it out yet? You can't hurt me. Not today, not tomorrow, not ever. And not just "cause Gar's my friend, although he is and that's a part of it. Mainly you can't hurt me "cause you're a piss-weak little sea slug, and the only reason I ain't squashed you afore now is "cause I don't care for slug slime on my boots."

Willer leaned close, his writing forgotten. The inkpot tipped, spilling blue all over the plush red velvet carriage cushions. Willer didn't notice. There was spittle in the corner of his down-turned mouth. His eyes gleamed brimful of hate and his soft hands were clenched tight as a tantrum by his sides.

"You'll mind your step if you know what's good for you, Asher. You think I'm the only person who despises you?" he hissed. "A lot of people despise you. They're just not brave enough to come out and say it. And do you know *why* they despise you? Because you think you're untouchable." His voice was shaking, virulent, and his pink skin shone damp with spite. "And you think you're as good as His Highness. Well, you're not. You're still one of us. You'll *never* be one of *them*."

Asher laughed. "I don't want to be one of them. That's your problem, Willer. Not mine."

Willer recoiled as though he'd been slapped. "That's *blasphemy*! You take that back, Asher. *Take it back!*"

Shaking his head, Asher straightened and took his foot from the carriage step. Stared at Willer, who was breathing in such harsh, strangled gasps he looked near to suffocating.

"You're a sorry little man, Willer."

Willer lunged off the carriage cushions. Book, pen and inkpot went flying. Wheezing, trembling, he clutched at the carriage doorway as though his fingers were round Asher's throat.

"Not as sorry as you'll be one day, I promise you!"

Stepping forward again, Asher reached up to Willer's smooth, soft cheek. Patted it gently. "Don't threaten me, Willer. It's a waste of breath, "cause you ain't got the brains or the balls to see it through." And laughed as Willer jerked away from him. Losing his balance, the slug fell to the carriage floor, where he stuck tight between the seats like a sausage in a bun.

Whistling, tossing his empty goblet from hand to hand, Asher sauntered back to the prince's pavilion, where Gar was wolfing down meat and bread and hot buttered corn. The food was neatly laid out in dishes and platters on a cloth-covered table. At the rich, heady aromas Asher's empty insides contracted and saliva flooded his mouth. He was bloody famished. He nodded to the little pot boy doing double-duty as a serving man and watched greedily as a plate was piled high with food for him.

"So," said Gar around a mouthful of venison, "you saw Willer? He's all sorted out now?"

"Oh, aye," said Asher, taking his plate from the pot boy, hissing as he burned his fingertips on a fat yellow corn cob. "He's well and truly sorted."

Gar, holding out his goblet for another serving of wine, wasn't paying attention. "Good. Now eat quickly, would you? We have to get back on the road."

Asher rolled his eyes. "Yes, Your Highness. Whatever you say, Your Highness."

And laughed as Gar threw a bread crust at him.

Luncheon concluded, they packed up their wagons and continued on their way. The Flatlands unrolled behind them as they chased the sinking sun. As the last of the dusk surrendered to the stars they reached the hamlet of Flat Iron and the Hooting Owl Inn, where it was arranged they'd spend the night. For the first time in his life Gar went to bed without the glow of Barl's Wall gleaming through his bedroom curtains. Strange, it felt, and unsettling, but the long day's riding took its toll and he fell into a weary sleep.

He woke again, hours later, to the sound of rain thrumming the slate roof overhead. For a moment he was confused. How could it be raining? The king was still too weak to WeatherWork. Durm had forbidden it for at least another week; his father had groused about it last night over his invalid's dinner of steamed chicken and mashed carrots.

Then he realised. *Fane.* Of course. This was the perfect opportunity, wasn't it, to get her feet wet, no pun intended. She'd had the Weather Magic for three months now, had undergone the Transference ceremony amid much excitement and celebration and private gloating. Once she'd recovered from the exhaustion that followed the acceptance of such strong magic they'd had a special dinner, just the family and Durm. His father had glowed with pride and his mother had wept. At the time he'd thought that was pride too but now, after their conversation on the Tower's front steps, he wasn't so sure.

"Your father has been bleeding to death, drop by drop, since the day he called his first rainfall."

One day, perhaps sooner than ever he'd imagined, there'd be no blood left for his father to shed. The thought terrified him. Pounded his heart and stifled the air in his lungs. His mother was wrong. She had to be. She was panicking for no good reason. The king was perfectly fine. Well on the mend. Hadn't Nix said so? And Durm? Surely Durm, his father's trusted friend and adviser, wouldn't lie. Not about that.

But then...

If his mother was wrong, why had Durm put Fane through the punishing Transference ceremony a full year earlier than planned? Why would she be up in the Weather Chamber now, bleeding, proving her worth, making it rain, if not to hurry the day when she could be named WeatherWorker in truth? When she could take the crown from their father's head, the burden from his shoulders, and in doing so save his life.

Save his life, and spend her own.

As Fane's gentle rain whispered down the chamber windowpanes, Gar tossed on his pillows, racked with doubt and dark imaginings.

Her first WeatherWorking. He should be pleased. Proud. She was his only sister, and despite everything he did love her. Sometimes anyway. As often as he could. As often as she'd let him. Already she'd sacrificed so much for the good of their father's kingdom. Slain her childhood, slain whatever dreams she once might have had about her life. He should remember that instead of dwelling on the wounds she inflicted. Should be desperately grateful that her imminent elevation to WeatherWorker meant their mother's dire predictions would never come true.

He was so jealous he could vomit.

Exhausted, he lay in the dark and listened to the rain until it died and the sun broke free of the horizon.

Within half an hour of breakfast the next morning they were on their way once more. Headed for the long road that led, eventually, to the narrow stretch of coastline supporting the fishing towns and villages of Westwailing, Restharven, Dinfingle, Bibford, Chevrock,

Rilling-coombe, Tattler's Ear and Struan Caves. All of Lur's fisher-folk were to be found in those eight places. Nowhere else along Lur's three-sided coastline was habitable. For mile upon mile the land stopped abruptly, falling away to the water in sheer cliffs jagged as broken glass. According to Asher, not even a madman would risk a boat and his life in the savage surf that battered itself to foam and ribbons on the rocks that ringed the kingdom.

Gar, not disbelieving exactly, still found it hard to credit. He was the product of an orderly existence. The promise of such excessive disorder was breathtaking. He began to feel truly excited by the pros-pect of seeing for himself the wild and untamed water that had some-how managed to produce a man like Asher.

The second night of the journey saw them safely bedded down in the town of Chillingbottom, commercial hub of the prosperous horse-farming region known as the Dingles, although nobody, not even Darran, seemed to know exactly why. The third night saw them welcomed with parade, brass band and flatteringly excited locals into the paper-making town of Slumly Corners named, apparently, for the paper-pulping mill around which the township had grown. On the third and fourth nights they camped in the middle of Grayman's Moor. Darran complained that his pallet was lumpy.

After that, Gar found that some of the novelty and excitement wore off, and then some more, and then pretty much all of it, so the journey became little more than a blurred succession of towns and villages and more towns and villages and lots of scenery and waving people and aching buttocks and too much food which he couldn't politely refuse because somebody's wife had always gone to so much trouble to prepare it, sir.

His father had somehow forgotten to mention that aspect of the adventure.

He started running beside Ballodair for part of each day instead of riding him, and not just to give his backside some rest. His leather rid-ing breeches were starting to feel a little tight.

Asher thought it was very funny, and said so. At length.

Nobody else, of course, dared say so much as a word but he could feel them looking. And smiling.

Roll on Westwailing.

One thing did have him puzzled, as they got closer and closer to their destination. He and Asher hadn't discussed it, partly because he'd been drowning in the preparations for the festival, and partly because Asher wasn't the kind of man who waxed lyrical about anything of a personal nature, or welcomed questions—but still, he'd expected *some* comment, some mention, even in passing, of the fact that after more than a year away his friend was returning to what used to be his home.

But no. Asher hadn't said a single word about it. Not back in Dorana while they'd made the preparations for the journey, and not in the last days on the road. Even worse: the closer they got to the coast the more silent and withdrawn he became. Sullen, almost, and annoyingly short-tempered. In fact, here they were scarcely an hour away from Minching Town and their final night's billet, with Westwailing practically close enough to smell, and Asher hadn't said so much as three words since luncheon, nor cracked a smile since sunrise.

It wasn't good enough. At this rate, by the time they did reach Westwailing Asher's mood was likely going to ruin his whole experience of the Sea Harvest Festival.

Well. He wasn't about to put up with *that*. It was time for some answers. Like it or not, Asher was going to be asked some pointed personal questions over dinner that evening. *And* he was going to answer them, whether he wanted to or not.

By the time they straggled to a halt in the cobbled stable yard of The Juggling Crow, Minching Town's best inn, Asher was close to cross-eyed with weariness. For all the riding he'd done since his arrival in the City, after near on two weeks across country his buttocks and thighs were a shrieking anguish and his back felt beaten with red-hot pokers. Mayhap if he slept in a bathtub tonight, and a serving wench got herself assigned to topping him up with boiling water every half-hour or so, he could stomach the thought of one last day in the saddle tomorrow...

The Crow's beaming landlord, Meister Grenfall, and his beaming wife and his seven beaming children were waiting for them as they arrived. Beyond any kind of pleasantry save a surly smile, Asher left the social chitchat to Gar, Darran and Willer. Instead he swung himself groaning to the ground and got busy organising the stabling of the horses and the stowing of the coach and wagons and the securing of the various valuables they were carting all the way to the coast.

The inn's head groom was a bent-backed old gaffer, seen it all, done it at least twice, and not the least bit impressed by princes and their hangers-on or anything about them except, perhaps, the quality of their horseflesh. That had him nodding and smiling, as well it might. Asher, pleased, handed Cygnet and Ballodair to the ole man's underlings without a qualm. There'd be no suggestion of second-best oats and not enough hay here. Not that there had been anywhere else but it never hurt to check. Folks were unchancy at the best of times. The trick was never to let them think they could sell you sardine for shark.

Letting himself into the inn through the back door he heard the now familiar sounds of excitement at Gar's presence under the innkeeper's humble roof. Rightly speaking he ought to follow the laughter and join the prince and Darran and Willer and the rest of them, but he was too damned tired to face it. Instead he asked a passing maid for directions to the prince's private parlour, declined her offer of an escort and climbed the stairs, hopefully to find brandy and a comfortable chair.

Westwailing tomorrow.

The parlour was blessedly unoccupied, and there was indeed brandy and armchairs. Also a spinet, a polished mahogany dining table and a cheerfully crackling fire in the hearth. He dragged off his boots, poured himself a generous slosh of comfort, slumped into the nearest chair and stretched his stockinged feet towards the leaping warmth.

Westwailing tomorrow.

Imagine. A year and more of dreaming, of planning, of looking forward to seeing Da again, seeing his pride and pleasure in a son's job well done—and now that the moment was almost upon him, he was afraid.

Afraid of Da thinking what he'd accomplished this past year wasn't enough. Of thinking him changed. Of his brothers ruining everything out of meanness and spite. Afraid that he hadn't saved enough money after all and that somehow all his plans of boats would come to nowt.

But that was just him being foolish. He had more than enough money. It was on the road behind him now, along with all his other bits and pieces. Had to be, because the king had promised he'd see to it.

And then there was Gar. He'd long since started to wish he'd stood up against Borne, fought for his right to tell the prince he was quitting his position before they left the City. Then he could have made his own way home in his own time, with a clean break behind him. He wouldn't have had to spend the last long days pretending. Keeping up appearances. Dreading Gar's disappointment and demands that he stay. Because there would be disappointment. And argument. Shouting, probably, and things thrown in anger.

Not even his brothers could start him throwing things the way Gar could.

The parlour door opened and Gar came in. "There you are." He thanked the maid holding the door open for him and headed for the brandy. The maid curtseyed, pink-cheeked, and quietly withdrew. "I was wondering where you were."

Asher sat up a little straighter. "I got a bit of a headache. Couldn't face all the botheration downstairs."

Brandy balloon in hand, Gar turned to consider him. "A headache, eh? I should've thought of that one. Do you know, before this expedition I never would've thought a man could be *welcomed* to death."

Asher grinned, briefly. "They're excited to meet you, is all."

Gar sipped his drink, pulled a little face then took a thoughtful turn about the room. Took a seat at the spinet and tinkled the keys idly. Cheerful chiming music filled the air. Smiling, he swallowed another mouthful of brandy then put down his glass and began to play properly, some highfalutin' fancy tune you'd never hear down at the Goose. "I know," he said, his voice lifted above the intricate music. "I should be flattered, but it's so damned exhausting."

"It ain't just the locals excited, either," said Asher. "Everyone is. Westwailing tomorrow. Reckon those pot boys won't get a wink of sleep tonight. Worse than magpies, they are, chattering."

"Everyone?" said Gar.

"Okay, well, maybe not Darran. But then he ain't the type to be frisking and gambolling like a spring lamb, eh? That ole crow couldn't kick up his heels if his life depended on it, I reckon."

"I wasn't thinking of Darran."

Oh. Guardedly Asher stared at Gar across the top of his brandy. Now what? "Me? I ain't the frisking type either."

Gar changed tunes, started playing a popular tavern ditty instead. "I don't know about that. I've seen you kick up your heels once or twice. That memorable evening at the Vintners' ball leaps immediately to mind..."

Asher grinned, remembering. He'd never been so drunk in all his life. It had been a grand fine night, all things considered. Even the next morning's murderous headache had been worth it. Dathne had danced with him, all dressed up in silk and ribbons...

"What?" demanded Gar. "Your face just fell a thousand feet. Asher, I wish you'd abandon this mania you have for secrecy and tell me straight out what's bothering you. And don't try to tell me nowt, because we both know lying to me is a waste of time. You've been worried about something for days now. Do you not want to see the coast again? See your family? Is that it? If so, why didn't you say something? There was no need for you to come if you didn't want to. Barl knows I've nursemaid enough in Darran. Did you think I'd be unsympathetic? That I'd force you to come on this trip if you didn't want to?"

As the music flirted in time with the flames in the fireplace, Asher stared at the floor. Damn. For days he'd wanted to break the news. Tender his resignation. Now the chance was handed to him on a silver platter by Gar himself, and he didn't want it. There was going to be such a fuss...

"No," he said. "That ain't it."

"Then what?"

Wait till after the festival, the king had said. Don't give him anything else to fret about.

He shrugged. "Nothing."

Gar's warm concern chilled. He stopped playing the spinet and stared. The sudden silence was uncomfortable. "You're lying."

"Nothing important," he amended. "Nothing that can't wait."

"And what if I don't wish it to wait? What if I wish to know right here, right now?"

"Then I'd say it ain't for you to decide. This is my problem, Gar, not yours."

Gar got up from the spinet stool. Paced to the window, then thumped his fist against the wall. Spun around. "Don't you understand, you fool? I'm trying to help!"

"I didn't ask for your help! And anyways, there's nothing you can do."

"You don't know that." Gar pushed away from the wall and threw himself into the nearest armchair. "I spend most of my waking life helping people, one way or another. Why should you be any different?"

Exasperated, Asher glared at him. "Because I am! Because some things can't be helped! Because if you want the truth, Gar, this ain't none of your bloody business!"

Gar looked down his nose. "I'm making it my business."

Stalemate. Asher took a deep breath and unclenched his fists. Losing his temper now would only make things worse. "Don't. You'll only regret it."

Gar laughed, incredulous. "Was that a *threat*?"

Too late, Asher realised his mistake. He should have told a different lie. Instead of denying a problem existed he should've invented a less explosive one. Spun some malarkey about a wobbly wagon wheel, or loose horse shoes. Bleeding piles. Something. Anything. Instead he'd roused Gar's rampant curiosity...which nothing but the truth would satisfy.

Well. No point fretting about it now. That boat had well and truly sailed.

"Fine," he said flatly. "You want to know what's bothering me? I'll tell you. But I give you fair warning: you ain't going to like it."

"Anything's preferable to you sitting there telling me bare-faced lies. I deserve more than that, I think."

"Aye," said Asher, sighing. "You do. So here's the thing. Once we're done with the Sea Harvest Festival, I'll not be going back to Dorana with the rest of you. My year's well and truly up, Gar. I'll be going home. To Restharven."

CHAPTER NINETEEN

Silence, as flames crackled in the hearth and somebody's heels thudded along the corridor outside. Then Gar laughed.

"Very funny, Asher. What's the idea? Give me a false shock then ease me into the actual bad news? Don't waste your time, or mine. Dinner will be here shortly. Come. You're not usually so coy. Just tell me the problem and together we'll work it out."

Asher put down his glass. "I ain't being coy, Gar. I'm moving on. Sorry."

Another silence, longer this time. Gar released a shuddering breath. "You bastard."

He held up his hands. "Gar—"

Gar sat back. His face had lost its colour and the look in his eyes was unbearable. "Well, well, well. You know, I pride myself on being something of a judge of character, but you certainly had me fooled. Congratulations. A whole year as my trusted assistant, my indispensable right hand, and you never talked about your brave little plan to go home and buy fishing boats. Not once. Not even in passing. Instead you insinuated your way into the Tower. Into the City. Into my plans. And smiled, saying nothing, as I gave you more and more responsibility. More and more...*trust*. As I increased your wages. Twice. Days turned into weeks, weeks into months, and now here we sit a year later. And in all that time, Asher, with all the opportunity in the world, you said not a single, solitary word about leaving."

"I never thought I had to! I told you when you first gave me the sinkin' job, I *told* you I'd not be staying in the City above a year!"

"But you have stayed above a year." Gar's eyes were glittering and he spoke with great care. "Quite some time above a year, as it happens. The anniversary of your arrival in Dorana came and went, Asher, unremarked by you. So what was I to think? That you'd perhaps forgotten? Or changed your mind?"

"Well if that's what you thought, why didn't you say somethin'? Why didn't you ask me?"

"Why should I? It was for you to speak, Asher. Or stay silent. And you did stay silent, even as you continued to accept my money. Naturally I drew my own conclusion. What's more, you continued to stay silent as we looked to the future of Lur. Why, not three days ago we were making plans for the new Thatchers' guildhouse cornerstone ceremony. Remember? The ceremony where you were to make the speech, instead of me?"

"Of course I bloody remember," Asher snapped, slamming his glass onto the table beside his chair. "And if *you* remember, I didn't want to talk about it! It can wait, I said. We got enough to worry on with this bloody festival, I said. But no, you wouldn't leave it alone. You had to talk about the bloody cornerstone ceremony then and there. Just like you had to talk about *this*, even though I made it clear I didn't want to!"

"Were you even going to tell me? Or were you intending to slip away while my back was turned?" Gar was still holding his brandy balloon. If his fingers tightened any more he'd smash it to pieces and slice all his fingers off too, most like. Well, wouldn't that just serve him right? Poking and prying and not taking no for an answer...

"Of course I was going to tell you! What kind of a man d'you think I am?"

Gar smiled. "I don't know. But I'm beginning to find out."

Bastard. Asher shoved himself out of his chair and started pacing. It was that or smash his fist into Gar's face. "I meant to tell you weeks ago. But things kept happenin', I kept puttin' it off. And then your da—"

Gar's lips tightened dangerously. "His Majesty, you mean?"

"Aye," said Asher, glaring. "The king."

"What about him?"

"That day he wanted to see us. See me. He asked me straight out, were I stayin' in Dorana or goin' home. And when I told him *goin'*, and soon, he made me promise not to say anythin' to you till after Sea Harvest."

Slowly, precisely, Gar put his brandy balloon down on the floor. "I see."

Cornered, Asher turned on him. "*You* should have bloody asked me, Gar. You should have bothered to find out if my plans had changed. I would've told you. I never been anythin' but straight with you. But no. You just sat back and drew your own conclusion. Assumed my plans had changed, even though I never said so. What did you reckon, eh? That your fancy City and your fancy Tower and all my fancy clothes and gewgaws had somehow seduced me into staying? That I'd forgotten about my da back home in Restharven? Forgotten the promise I made to take care of him now he's gettin' on in years? Is that what you thought of me? Well, shame on you!"

Thinly, with fireshadows dancing over his face, Gar said, "And what about the promise you made me?"

Asher kicked the nearest chair, hard enough to shift it. Hard enough to hurt. "I bloody well kept that too and you know it! A year I'll give you, I said. And so I have. A year and then some. And I never once shirked a day of it. I've worked my arse off for you, Gar. I may have taken your money every week, aye, taken it gladly, but there ain't a single trin of it I didn't earn honest, fair and square!"

Gar's eyebrows lifted in delicate derision. "And yet you seem to have left it all behind. An unfortunate oversight, surely?"

"Course I haven't bloody left it!" he shouted. "Think I'm stupid, do you? It's on the road behind us. Your da—no, excuse me, His Majesty the king—saw to it for me."

Gar flinched as though he'd been struck. "Did he?" His voice was a whisper. "Did he indeed? How very considerate of him. Well...damn him. And damn you too, Asher. Damn you both beyond the—"

A brisk knock sounded on the parlour door and then it opened, admitting a capped and aproned maidservant pushing a trolley laden with an uncorked wine bottle and covered dishes trailing delicious aromas. Seeing the prince, she bobbed a breathless curtsey. "Your Highness, sir, the meister and mistress's compliments, sir, and here's dinner for you and your assistant, just as you requested."

Gar nodded stiffly. "My thanks to your meister and mistress."

With a nervous sideways glance between the two of them the maid-servant began unloading the trolley onto the parlour table. First the food, then the wine, and then a place setting of glass, knife, fork and spoon. That done, she began on the second setting.

"Thank you," said Gar. "I'll be dining alone. You may go."

Her startled gaze flickered from him to Asher and back again. Her cheeks flushed deep pink. "Yes, sir, Your Highness. Enjoy your dinner, sir."

Once the door was closed behind her, Gar seated himself at the table. Poured himself a glass of wine then lifted the cover on the first chafing dish, revealing lightly poached salmon in a dill sauce.

"I believe staff meals are served in the kitchen."

Asher dragged his hands over his face. Well, hadn't this turned into a fine mess of fish guts? Bloody Borne and his damned bloody meddling...He bit his lip. Took a step closer to the dining table and cleared his throat.

"Gar. I never said this job was for good. I never said that."

Gar savoured a bite of the fish. Explored the second chafing dish: roast duck. In the third, garden fresh vegetables swimming in herbed butter. He helped himself to both.

"My meal is getting cold."

Asher scowled. So the prince was going to sulk, was he? Spoiled, stupid pillock that he was. Trying to make out he was the injured party. Conveniently forgetting—and oh, wasn't that just like royalty—that other people had lives and plans and promises that mattered just as much as theirs.

"You sure the servants' hall ain't too grand for the likes of me? Maybe I should go out to the kennels, eh? See if the hounds have left some bones for chewin'? Would you like that better? Sir?"

Gar speared a mushroom on his fork. Chewed. Swallowed. "It seems to me, Asher, that what I like doesn't interest you in the slightest. I suggest you please yourself. It appears to be what you're best at, after all."

Asher slammed the parlour door behind him so hard it was a wonder the hinges didn't spring free of their housings. Stamped back into his boots and banged his way along the corridor, down the stairs and back out to the stables where he knew he'd be welcome. He didn't care about dinner. He'd lost his appetite. For food, for friendship, for everything else except getting home...and leaving all things Doranen behind him, once and for all.

*   *   *

Once the parlour door closed and he was alone, Gar pushed his laden plate away. His stomach was churning. If he ate another mouthful he'd be sick.

That his father could *do* such a thing. Could conspire behind his back with Asher like that. That Asher would keep such a secret. It was so demeaning. So patronising. So painful.

In his mind's eye he could see them: heads bent close together as they plotted his unnecessary protection. "Poor Gar," they must have whispered. "He's the only choice for the festival, we have to send him, but Barl knows it's a risk. So let's not tell him you're leaving, shall we? He might get all upset and ruin everything. We'll keep it our little secret." "Certainly, Your Majesty. Anything you say, Your Majesty." "Excellent, Asher, and here's a little something extra for your trouble..."

How could they do this to him? How could his father do it? Treat him like—like a *cripple*?

In silence he stared at the dining table and its burden of abruptly unwelcome food. The old inn creaked around him, settling for the night, and the fire slowly crumbled into glowing cinders. But still he sat there, because it occurred to him that Asher might come back to argue some more or state his case or beg for pardon or hurl abuse, or even plates. Barl knew they'd had their disagreements over the past year. Loud, long and heated disagreements, some of them. But in the end they'd always worked things out. In the end they managed to find their way back to common ground and even laugh about whatever it was that had set them fighting.

They'd never walked away without shaking hands, even if it meant agreeing to disagree.

But Asher didn't come back. The food grew cold, then colder, then congealed into pig food. The fire went out and the candles burned down to their sockets.

Eventually, he went to bed.

Standing by the touring coach the next morning, waiting for the signal to leave, Willer glanced left and right, made certain no underling's flapping ears were close enough to hear, and said eagerly to Darran, "Well? What did you find out?"

Darran looked down his long nose. "Really, Willer. You make me sound positively clandestine."

"No!" he protested. "No, not at all, Darran. Discreet. Politic. Tactful."

Instead of answering, Darran snapped his fingers at a passing servant and nodded at the coach door. The servant opened it, pulled down the little steps then stood back so that his superior might enter. Darran acknowledged the courtesy with a nod and took his place inside. Willer, ignoring the servant, climbed in after him.

Seated in safe silence within the coach, Darran arranged himself comfortably against the cushions. Unfolded his working desk from the panel in the coach siding, extracted a sheaf of papers from the cunningly hidden pocket beneath it, perched his glasses on the end of his nose and began reading.

Just barely, Willer stopped himself from screaming. It was a game, Darran's favourite game, Tease the Assistant, and he'd kiss Asher's fingers and call him "sir" before he'd give Darran the satisfaction of another question. Instead he poked around in his own satchel of papers and pulled out the order of events for the festival. He'd already memorised it, of course, but it was just another part of the game. The more eager he appeared, the longer Darran would wait before sharing what he knew. But his eyes, skimming over the notes, scarcely saw them and his mind was filled with things other than the Great Gathering and the Sea Harvest hymn.

Through the carriage's window, he watched as Asher had scowling words with a groom, all the while tugging at his horse's girth straps and waving his hands about. Temper hung on him like a mantle, thick and black and red.

Movement from the inn's rear entrance caught his attention. The innkeeper, that provincial rustic Greenhill or Grimfulk or some such name. And His Highness. Looking, Willer saw with dawning delight, as mantled in bad humour as Asher. So perhaps the gossip was true. The prince and his ill-chosen personal assistant *were* at odds. At last, at longest, longest last, the first cracks in that Barl-forsaken alliance were beginning to show.

The urgency of preparations escalated sharply as the bustling servants caught sight of their royal master. Willer, all pretence at reading forgotten, leaned forward to better see the look on Asher's face. At first sight of His Highness the upstart froze, mid-complaint. His spine stiffened and his chin came up, all arrogant defiance, no proper humility, no deferential awe. Just pride and consequence and him nothing but an uneducated pedlar of fish carcases when he'd first arrived in Dorana, to fall into luck and attach himself to His Highness like a leech from Boggy Marshes.

Heart pounding, hands clenched, Willer waited for the prince to notice the scullion. When their eyes met it was like the clashing of boulders, the grinding of ice floes in winter River Gant. Asher was the first to look away. Throwing his reins at the chastened groom he busied himself elsewhere as His Highness showed his back to the courtyard, pretending an interest in whatever the innkeeper was squittling about.

Pleasure, warm and liquid, bathed Willer's skin in a languorous, golden glow.

"You're being obvious, Willer," said Darran, chilly with disapproval.

Caught, Willer felt his cheeks burn, and his hands scrambled on the forgotten paperwork. "No, you misunderstand, I—"

Darran raised sparse eyebrows. "I rarely misunderstand anything. Do cultivate a little self-control, dear boy. The man who controls himself controls the world."

"Yes, Darran," he muttered, and smoothed his creased paperwork back into its carry bag.

"Come, come," Darran chided, thin lips curved in a smile, eyes alight with an unfamiliar fire. "This is no time for sulking. Our patience has at last been rewarded, just as I said it would be."

After a long moment's puzzling, Willer shook his head. "I'm sorry, Darran, but I don't know what you mean."

Darran's smile broadened, revealing crooked teeth. "Asher has resigned."

The shock of it stole his breath, so that for several heartbeats all he could do was gape like a country halfwit, mouth slack with disbelief. "No," he managed at last. "*No*! I don't believe it! There must be a mistake!"

Darran looked at him. "I am not in the habit of being mistaken. I had it from His Highness himself who, I suppose you will allow, has some inkling of his own business."

Resigned? Asher had *resigned*? But that wasn't the plan. That wasn't it at all. Asher was to be found out, brought down, revealed to all the world and reviled by it. He wasn't supposed to just...just... walk away. Not unpunished. Not whole. How could that be?

Darran said, clearly put out, "He will remain behind in Westwailing once the festival has concluded." And when Willer could still do nothing but stare, snapped, "What is the matter with you? Our dearest wish has at last been granted! Asher's ruffian, unseemly influence will soon be gone from court. He will rapidly become nothing more than the memory of a bad taste in the mouth, and I, for one, am highly pleased by this turn of events. If you are wise, Willer, you will be highly pleased too!"

"Yes, Darran," said Willer, discarding with a sharp pain between his ribs his daydreams of Asher's public downfall. "Of course, Darran. As you say. It's for the best. Of course I'm pleased. I'm *very* pleased." And he smiled, a brave smile, as though he weren't sick with disappointment at all.

In the courtyard Asher's voice rose above the general hubbub. "Right-ho! Mount up, climb up and all aboard! We got ourselves a hefty stretch of travellin' yet and the sun ain't standin' still."

Willer settled himself more comfortably against his cushions and pulled out a book. It was, he discovered with faint surprise, some small comfort that from the sound of it Asher was just as unhappy about impending unemployment as *he* was about his lost hope for revenge.

Good, he thought, and snapped over the page with a vindictive thumb. And what's more, after all this riding I hope he gets piles.

The journey continued in silence. Word had spread, as word always does, that there was something seriously amiss between the prince and his assistant. Even if it hadn't, the chilly unaccustomed silence, their haughty, aloof faces, and the way they rode apart and alone would have shouted as much to anyone who knew them even a little. The grooms, the cooks and the pot boys all exchanged swift, eloquent glances, raised their eyebrows, shrugged their shoulders and in the shorthand of discreet employees everywhere said: What's up with them, then, eh? Dunno. Mind yer step, though, for himself's in a temper and no mistake.

The subdued day dragged on. They reached the Coast Road and got their first look at the ocean an hour and a half after leaving Minching Town. At any other time the breathtaking sight would have stopped them all in their tracks, had them gasping and pointing and begging stories from Asher to match the heart-stopping, impossible stretch of ceaseless blue water.

But Asher was hardly even looking at it and neither was the prince, so that was that. The cavalcade trundled on: overheated, overtired and unhappy.

Luncheon was a brief and acrimonious affair on a sparse stretch of salty open heath land. Strange, ugly bushes writhed low to the ground as far as the jaded eye could see; agonised outcroppings of deep purple and red rock clotted the barren landscape. The horses were unhappy, lashing their tails at stinging flies and snapping yellowed teeth at anybody daft enough to stand too close. Gar ate in solitary splendour beneath a parasol. Asher savaged a heel of bread and a hunk of cheese in the shade of the supply wagon and was wisely left alone. From the look on his face, the horses and flies weren't the only creatures in a biting mood.

They didn't rest for long; Darran had them back on the road within the hour, fussing about punctuality and reminding all and sundry that they would have to stop again before reaching Westwailing so that everyone could change into the fresh clothes kept aside for their official arrival and welcome.

After two interminable, buttock-bleeding weeks on the road, the journey was nearly over.

Westwailing welcomed them with open arms, smiling faces and a raucous brass band, whose five burstingly proud members were crowded at the foot of the mayor's beribboned dais, strategically placed at the top end of the High Street. All the gathered fisherfolk of Lur were there, lining the long, downward-winding thoroughfare, perched precariously in trees and on rooftops, dangling daring from open windows, and every one eager for a glimpse of the flaxen-haired prince from that unimaginable place, the City. The air was brisk and laced with salt, flavoured with fish. There was a speech from the mayor, mercifully short, and then the brass band played in earnest as His Royal Highness Prince Gar and his royal party minced their recently washed and meticulously reclothed way between the cheering spectators. The mayor and his wife and various other local dignitaries tucked in behind, basking in royalty's reflected glory.

Face schooled firmly into an expression of gratified pleasure, hand raised and waving impartially left, then right, Gar slid his gaze sideways to his scowling companion and said, "Smile. You owe me that much."

Asher manufactured an obedient, empty smile.

Smothering the hurt, Gar looked to the crowd again. Released a sigh, soft as the briny breeze. All these people. All this excitement. They meant nothing. Nothing. They'd cheer a dancing bear just as hard. Cheer harder if it fell on its fat, moth-eaten behind. Would he fall on his tomorrow, during the Sea Harvest Festival? And would they cheer if he did?

Dear Barl, if you can hear me, he said to the vaulting, cloudless sky, lips pressed hard to his holyring, don't let me fall. Please. If you love me...don't let me fall.

*   *   *

That night there was a banquet, and the whole town was invited. The Westwailing market square was reserved for the mayor and his important guests but the streets belonged to Lur's fisherfolk. Coloured lanterns draped the trees, hung from windows and shop signs, lit the shiny cobbled streets in garish rainbows. Trestle tables and benches marched end to end between the pavements and the air was soaked to the gills with the smoky smells of roasting meat. Hogsheads of wine and ale stood open on every corner, and on this one night alone it was no shame to be merry with grog. Laughter was music, and music was music, with the warring shrill and pipe of a dozen different strumming bands and voices raised in discordant song.

The daily grind of life had been packed away in its battered box, not to be looked at or sighed over for a day, or even two. For now only merriment counted, and ale, and fat roast pork, and the cheerful gossip of those lucky enough to have a caught a glimpse of the Prince from Up Yonder.

In the market square the celebrations were more refined but just as enthusiastic. The same brass band played valiantly in the centre of the square, the edges of which had been lined with trestle tables covered in donated best tablecloths and garlanded with scentwax and ruby gloss-glows and pale purple bugles.

The official table stood above the rest, as was only fitting, and was waited on by the self-important few who'd been honoured and schooled and reminded and teased and resented on it until they were thinking that mayhap their friends and relations carousin' in the streets had the better bargain after all. For certain, serving the likes of that bossy long streak of cat's piss in black who called hisself "sir" when he caught sight of his face in the mirror, most like, and went by the name of Durgood or some such, well, servin' the likes of him weren't a minute of fun ... nor the fat, overdressed little creature who followed him around like a bad smell.

But take no never mind of them. There were the prince and the Mayor and Mrs. Mayor and the seven other town and village leaders, and they were gracious enough. Oh, aye, and that other fellow. The Olken. Used to be a local, someone said, vaguely recognising him, and how had he managed to climb so high above the rest of them? Sitting there in his fancy clothes, with a fancy gewgaw in his ear and silver rings on his fingers flaming blue and red and purple fire in the guttering torchlights. And not hardly speaking a word, neither, black thunderclouds in his face. Who was he? Who were his kin, and what village or town did he once call home?

Busier than seagulls among fish guts, the serving lads and lasses scurried from table to carvery to wine barrel to bread bins and back again, and looked and wondered, and raised their eyebrows at each other as the banquet continued beneath a crystal clear vista of stars.

Asher buried his face in a fresh mug of ale and cursed himself for the greatest fool breathing. They were all staring at him, sink 'em. Even when their heads were turned or they gobbled a plate of food or swallowed an ocean of wine, still they were staring. The minute he opened his mouth he'd branded himself a local, and what a fool he'd been not to have thought on that possibility.

Aye, he had a City accent now, though he'd never noticed it creeping up and would be glad to lose it fast enough, but still he was one of their own and they knew it. And of course Ole Sailor Vem, Restharven's village adjudicator, had took one look at him and nearly fallen over backwards with shock. He was fair worn out with the effort of avoiding the ole codger. Last thing he wanted was to have to tell Vem what he'd been up to. Turned out protocol was good for something after all. Vem would never get up from his table before Gar, and Gar was too busy troughing to be going any place any time soon.

In his ear a familiar voice, laced now with unfamiliar spite. "Stop sulking," Gar advised, a lying smile on his lips. "Did I say you couldn't stay? Stay, if that's what you want. Stay and be damned."

Dumbstruck, he could only stare. What did Gar want him to say? Never mind, it was only a joke, of course I'm coming back to the City with you? Got no life of my own, no plans, no ambitions. The only promise that counts is the one I made to you. So I'll just tag along at your heels until I be old and grey and all my teeth be in a jar. Was *that* what the prince expected?

Then more fool him.

He opened his mouth to say so but was drowned by the renewed vigour of the band, striking up a lively dance tune.

Gar turned away, offering his arm to the lady mayoress. She blushed and dimpled, the silly cow, as though royalty wouldn't tread on her toes just like her husband, and accepted his invitation. As they ponced their way to the clear space in the middle of the market square other couples joined them, and soon the cobblestones rang beneath jigging feet and stamping heels.

Sailor Vem, safe on the other end of the table, put aside his crumpled napkin and stood.

Asher pushed back his chair, abandoned his barely touched food and slid silently into the night. He thought he heard a disappointed shout behind him, but didn't look back.

Westwailing Harbour was wide of mouth and deep of bottom. Draped over the stone wall separating the general public from the business of catching fish, Asher sucked in a deep double lungful of heady ocean air and marvelled at himself for staying away so long.

A wide stone pier jutted from the main wharf, pointing like a finger towards the horizon...and the foam and break of the huge, magically protected reef. As a boy, Asher had sat atop a headland at sunrise and watched the morning light glint off the ferocious coral construction and wondered, achingly, what might lie beyond that meeting of sea and sky. Nobody knew. Hardly anybody cared. What did it matter, so long as the fish found their way through the reef and into the harbours, that they might end their days on a dinner plate somewhere?

Their lack of curiosity had enraged him. But that was people for you. They were the same in the City. Day in, day out, that bloody great Wall gleamed and towered and cut them off from whatever lay beyond it, but they didn't care. It was just the Wall, it had always been there and it always would. Anyway, what other kingdom could possibly be better than Lur? Lur was perfection. Let beyond the Wall look after itself.

Not even Dathne cared. Not even Gar. He supposed he didn't even care all that much himself. Just sometimes, looking, he'd be struck with wondering.

Just like he was struck now, gazing out at the serene, silvery waters of Westwailing Harbour, with the sounds of celebration loud still behind him, and the softer slosh and slap of waves before, and a full moon riding high overhead.

The beauty of it seared him. That afternoon, as they travelled the winding road down to the headlands and the salt wind blew off the water and they'd got their first dazzled, dazzling glimpse of the ocean, his eyes had stung with tears. He'd known then that leaving the City, coming home, was the only right thing left for him to do. All the aggravation, now and to come, was worth it, had to be worth it, because there was the ocean. There was his heart, whose muffled beating in a dry city had gone on long enough.

Tomorrow, after the festival, he'd find his father. Kneel at the old man's feet and beg his forgiveness for being away so long. For staying silent. Da would be angry at first, but he'd come round soon enough. They understood each other, he and Da, as his brothers had never understood either of them.

And after that, their new life would start.

Before that, though, he'd try to mend fences with Gar. It would be a damned shame, after a year of friendship, if they parted so bitterly at odds. Gar wasn't a mean man. He'd just been thoughtless. Was disappointed. Angry that this wasn't a decision he could overturn or overrule. But, just like Da, the prince would come round.

Or if he didn't, it wouldn't be for want of trying.

A giggling couple, courting and fuddled with ale, weaved their arm-in-arm way down the sloping street to the stone wall. They were young and in the full bloom of love. She was short and sweetly plump, he a hand span taller, with the close-cropped hair and muscled arms of a working man. Her eyes were starry for him, her lips red with his kisses. He was peacock proud, walking on a fine cushion of air for all to see.

Asher, caught unprepared and opened to beauty by the night, watched their bodies melt one into the other as they murmured breathlessly into each other's mouths. His heart hitched. *Dathne*.

He must have said something, or made a noise, because the couple broke apart, charming in their confusion. Then, laughing, they drifted away into shadow and the all-consuming fire of private passion.

Asher shook his head, fingers tight on the sharp stones of the harbour-mouth wall. Fool, he cursed himself. There was no point in pining. He'd asked, she'd answered. If he couldn't share his life with Dathne, then mayhap there'd be someone else he could share it with. That could take care of itself too. All that mattered now was he was home, beside the ocean, and he'd never leave it again.

From the direction of the square the sound of footsteps on the pathway, coming closer. He didn't need to look: he knew that slovenly gait. "You followin' me, Willer? Have a care. Folks'll talk."

Willer's snide and snivelling voice said: "So. We're finally rid of you. I must say it took long enough."

He sighed. "Piss off."

"The question everyone's asking, of course, is did he jump or was he pushed?"

"In case you hadn't noticed, we're standin' on the edge of a tidy drop into deep water," said Asher. "So I wouldn't be talkin' so much about jumpin' and pushin' if I were you. The amount of food you shovelled down your gullet tonight, reckon you'd sink faster than a stone."

Laughing softly, Willer drifted forwards until his fat belly met the stone harbour wall. Asher noticed he kept his distance.

Smart man.

"I do hope, Asher," he continued conversationally, "you weren't expecting any public displays of grief over your long-awaited departure. Impassioned pleas for you to stay. A going-away party, or any such thing." He paused, considering. "Although now I come to think of it I could name one or two people who'd happily pay large amounts of money for a 'Praise Barl he's gone' party."

Asher took a deep breath. Let it out, throttling rage and the desire to silence the vomitous sea slug once and for all. He turned his head and looked at Willer, baring his teeth in what wasn't exactly a smile.

"Fancy that. Here's us workin' together all this time and I never knew you for a man who liked livin' dangerous."

Willer laughed again. "You're wasting your breath. You don't frighten me. You never did." He pushed away from the harbour wall. Drifted backwards, and was swallowed by shadows. "Goodnight, Asher. Goodnight and good riddance."

Back in the town square the partying continued. Snatches of music and laughter floated down to the harbour, and drowned in the sighing of the sea. Propped up by the ancient stone wall, Asher listened.

It was a long, long time before he finally turned away from the moonlit water to make his way back to his bed in the mayor's house, where he could sleep away the scant hours before the great event of the morning: the Sea Harvest Festival, and the end of Asher, Assistant Olken Administrator of Lur.

CHAPTER TWENTY

"Tell me again," said Gar, reaching for the damp towel Darran held out to him, "whose spectacularly clever idea this was."

"His Majesty's, I believe," Darran replied. His smile was sympathetic. "If it makes you feel any better, sir, His Majesty also became... indisposed before his first Sea Harvest Festival."

Sitting on the edge of a chair, his emptied stomach churning, Gar blotted cold sweat from his forehead. He was shivering, even though the Mayor of Westwailing's very best guest room faced full into the morning sun and the chamber's air was warm against his bare chest. Less than an hour before he was due to lead the procession down to the Harbour...to lead the Sea Harvest Festival...and he was puking his guts into a chamberpot like a virgin on her wedding night.

Perfect.

He spared Darran a sour glance. "You're just saying that."

"I assure sir, I am not," Darran said blithely. "As it happens I was in a position to perform for your dear father the same service I perform for you now."

"Really?" Gar considered him. "That's very dedicated of you, Darran. Surely there must be something more edifying you can find to do with your time?"

"Not at all, sir," said Darran as he tidied away the pot and the soiled facecloths. "I consider this opportunity a great honour."

The roiling queasiness was easing. Overcome, possibly, by sheer, fascinated horror. "You think watching me vomit my breakfast into a chamber-pot is an honour? Darran, you really need to get out more."

Darran laughed politely and relieved him of the damp towel. "Your Highness, I have served your father's house since before he was born and I was a small boy, of an age to be trusted with running messages. Serving him once he ascended the throne...serving you, now, in whatever capacity I can...well, there isn't another Olken in the kingdom who can claim such continuity. Who has been gifted with such trust. How could I be anything but honoured?"

Tentatively, Gar straightened. When his stomach didn't revolt, he took a cautiously deep breath. "I suppose."

Darran bowed. "Indeed, sir. Now, as you can see, I've laid your clothes out for you. Of course, if you've changed your mind, then—"

"No," said Gar, glancing at the grass-green silk shirt, the deep blue, gold and crimson brocade weskit embroidered with bullion thread, the sea-blue woollen breeches he'd selected last night. They were as respectable as anything else he'd brought. "Well, not about the clothes anyway. Are you sure I can't change my mind about leading the festival?"

"You are a prince, sir," Darran reminded him with a discreet smile. "You are at liberty to do as you please. But I wouldn't advise it."

"Neither would I. The king would skin me alive." Gar frowned, briefly, the thought of his father still a small, stinging hurt. He banished the pain. There'd be time enough to deal with that upon his return. For now he had to concentrate on the matter at hand. "But even so, I can dream, can't I?"

"Certainly you can, sir," Darran said. "But if I might suggest that you dream and dress at the same time? We are due to leave for the harbour within the half-hour."

Nodding, Gar reached for his shirt. Buttoning it, careful to keep his eyes on the task, he said, "Have you seen Asher this morning?"

Darran stiffened. "Yes, sir. He took breakfast with the rest of the staff in the servants' kitchen."

"And did you convey to him my displeasure at his leaving the banquet so peremptorily last night?"

"I did." Darran's voice was frigid. "He saw fit to inform me that his whereabouts were none of my concern."

Gar glanced at Darran. Noted the burning spots of colour in his sallow cheeks. "But not quite as politely as that?"

Darran sniffed. "Not quite, sir. No."

He felt his jaw tighten. Felt the simmering rage surge. "I see."

"If I may be so bold as to suggest it, sir," Darran continued, "you might be best served by dispensing with Asher's services at the festival ceremony this morning. His attendance can achieve no useful purpose and his recent behaviour clearly demonstrates a distressing want of conduct and appreciation for his position. Without wishing to cause you further perturbation, I would remind Your Highness that in a short while you shall be the cynosure of all eyes. It would be regrettable indeed should Asher's deplorable conduct in any way reflect poorly upon yourself or His Majesty."

With the last button successfully captured, Gar turned his attention to pulling on his breeches and tucking his shirt tails into their waistband. "No," he said. "He is sworn to me until the end of our stay here and I shall hold him to that oath." Not least because clearly it was the last place Asher wanted to be.

Vindictive? Him? Never.

After a short pause Darran said, "Certainly, sir. If you say so."

Gar shot him a look. "I do. Hand me my weskit."

Darran gave him the brocade vest and adjusted it across his shoulders after he'd shrugged it on. "Your Highness is naturally free to do as you see fit."

"Yes, Darran, I am," he snapped, and eased his feet into his boots. Damn the man; criticising and judging and never a word out of place... "And as I said before, I'll have no gossiping on this, do you hear me? It's between me and Asher and nobody else."

"Sir," said Darran, grossly offended. "I do not stoop to *gossip*."

Gar held out his hand for his circlet of office. The plain one, which had been passed down from father to son since the days of Barl herself. "And there's no point getting huffy with me either."

Lips thin with disapproval, Darran removed the circlet from its velvet-lined case and with a soft cloth began to buff it to a glowing lustre.

"People talk," Gar added as his secretary's careful hands coaxed highlights from the beaten white gold. "It's to be expected. I'd just better not hear about it, that's all I'm saying."

"Sir," said Darran with awful dignity, and handed over the gleaming circlet. "If you will excuse me, Your Highness, I shall ensure that the rest of the party is ready and awaiting your pleasure."

Gar nodded. "As you like. I'll be downstairs shortly." Ignoring Darran's straight-spined departure he laid the circlet on the bed, found a brush and put his hair in order. Then, staring at his immaculate reflection in the chamber's full-length mirror, settled the circlet of office on his head. Behind him, the door opened again. Asher.

The circlet wasn't quite straight; damn thing was always a horror to get right. "Yes?" he asked, fingers cool and steady on the gold.

"Just checking to make sure you be all set." Asher was dressed in dull purple and dark blue, all silk and brocade and leather, thick black hair freshly washed, polished half-boots on his feet. There was nothing of the fisherman about him.

"Of course I'm all set," said Gar. "Do you think I can't get myself dressed for some half-baked country yodelling session without assistance?"

Asher sighed. Came further into the room and kicked the door shut behind him. "Look. Let's not leave it like this, eh? Not when we'll likely never lay eyes on each other again after today. You want me to say I'm sorry? Then I'm sorry. You want me to say it were wrong of me not to drop a hint every now and then? 'When I get back to Restharven,' that kind of thing? Fine. It were wrong. And I know I should've said something the minute I knew my mind was made up to go. But, Gar, I didn't. And you poutin' and stampin' and pullin' faces like a frog on a log over it ain't goin' to change that now. What's done is done. And you did say I had leave to quit you after a year. So can't we just shake on it, eh, and part friends?"

One final nudge and the thin strip of ancient gold was perfectly aligned. It clasped his skull lightly. Only his imagination made it heavy. Gar took a step back from the mirror and eyed himself up and down one last time. He looked fine. Better than fine. He looked every inch a prince. Doranen royalty. Keeper of Barl's Law. Defender of the

Realm. Morg's Scourge. Pity about the magic, but there it was. You couldn't have everything, could you?

Letting his gaze slip sideways, he met Asher's uncertain, reflected eyes. "Change your mind."

Across Asher's face, a skittering of emotions: sorrow, anger, an impatient compassion. "I can't."

And there it was. Final as a door slam. Part friends? Not likely. "You're making me late," he said. "Go downstairs and wait with the others."

Correct to a hair's-breadth, Asher bowed. "Yes, Your Highness." The door closed softly behind him.

Gar snatched off his circlet and threw it at the door. Part *friends*? Not likely.

But he wasn't going to think about it. Let Asher toss his life away. Let him wade chin deep in fish guts and end his days scarred and shrunken and seasoned with salt, like all the old men of Westwailing. He'd had his chance and turned his back on it. More fool him.

His Royal Highness Prince Gar had more important things to worry about. It was Sea Harvest Festival time, and very soon now he would stand before thousands of the king's subjects and lead them in song and celebration.

Asher? Asher who?

Miles and miles and days away the king disobeys his keepers and calls a fall of rain. The power writhes through his weakened body, finding all the sorry places, and he cannot help but cry. Too soon, too soon, his keepers were right, but the choice was not theirs to make. Was never theirs to make, and the fault was his, to let them make it. Is he not King Borne of Lur, the WeatherWorker? Bound and sworn to solemn duty unto the bitter end? He is. His daughter was not ready for the blade. Had bared her throat to its edge before the proper time... and now pays dearly for the privilege.

The ceiling of his Weather Chamber is solid glass. Early autumn sunshine spills across the timber floor, his shaking hands, the map of Lur that guides his heart and mind and tells him where to send the rain, sing the seeds, chill the earth with snow and ice.

But pain shouts more loudly than magic. Drowns it in a scarlet flooding tide. He falls to his knees. To his hands. Stares hotly at the map on the floor, sweating. Stares at Westwailing township, down on the coast. Thinks of his son, serving him, serving Lur, and smiles. Power seethes and surges through him, turning his blood to bubbles.

His long silver hair, lank with recent ill health, stirs of its own accord on his shoulders. Crackles with blue sparks that arc and dance and ignite the air.

"Gar," he whispers. "Sing for me, my son. Sing the harvest. Sing the festival. Sing the health and happiness of the people. Sing well, and make me proud."

Beyond the naked chamber ceiling, the blue sky trembles...and across the glowing golden sun a cloud, like gauze.

"Gar!" the king cries, fingers clawed and clutching, his head crowned with a nimbus of unspeakable power. "Barl save me...save me...save him!"

And then darkness, as the sun goes out.

The festival fishing boat danced on the end of its mooring, sprightly as a lass at her first grown-up party. Mouth dry, heart pounding, Gar imagined himself upon it, upon the ocean, which was vast and blue and very, very deep. He couldn't remember Asher ever saying it was deep.

Yesterday, still seething with anger at the ingrate's intentions; he'd scarcely noticed the immensity of water stretching from the coastline to the horizon. Even though it was the first time he'd ever seen it. Rage had blinded him.

Now, though, *now*...

He imagined himself at the mercy of all that wild water, which not even a WeatherWorker's might could tame, and felt a tremble in his bowels.

Fear was unbecoming. Ruthlessly he throttled it. Throttled imagination too. Instead glanced at Asher, who stood at his fisted right hand. Who stared at the ocean and the boat, his unknowable eyes alight with avarice, and who thought both were more important than anything he'd ever achieved...had yet to achieve...in the City of Dorana.

The Mayor of Westwailing cleared his throat. "Your Highness?"

Gar nodded. Turned his face away from the water. "Of course, sir. We are ready?"

They were standing on a dais that had been erected at the township end of the harbour's pier. Darran and Willer stood behind them in the second row, along with the other dignitaries who represented their local communities. An enormous crush of bodies filled every inch of space along the harbour front, the promenade, the streets winding down to the water. Men, women and children, bright and shining in their once-a-year festival shirts and skirts and hats and trews and painfully polished shoes. And their faces, glowing with anticipation.

Eerily silent, like one vast, indrawn breath, they waited for the ceremony to begin.

A flag waved. The mayor bowed to Gar. "We be ready, Your Highness."

And so was he. He thought. He hoped. He'd spent enough time studying for this moment. If he wasn't ready now he had no right to call himself a prince, or the Olken Administrator, or anything but a witless fool. He nodded to the mayor.

"Then let us celebrate the harvest, sir. And Barl's blessings on us all."

The mayor smiled. "Barl's blessings, aye indeed, sir."

Raising his arms Gar took a deep breath. Then, throwing back his head, eyes closed, expression ecstatic, pierced the waiting air with a single, singing word:

"*Rejoice!*"

Like a curlew's cry the sound unwound into the faultless blue sky. And then the cloudless ceiling cracked as thousands of voices, united, replied in heartfelt joy and wonder:

"*We rejoice!*"

The Sea Harvest Festival had begun.

In the king's bedchamber, restrained pandemonium. "You said he was making a fine recovery!" the queen rages at the royal pothecary. "You said we were out of the woods!"

"We were, Your Majesty!" Pother Nix replies. "But that was before he took it into his mad head to go and make it rain!" Then he grunts as one flailing royal arm collides with his ribs. Turning on a hapless assistant he snarls, "Hold him still, I told you! This is not the king, this is a patient! Hold him!"

"Gar!" the king cries, struggling against the loving hands that crush him to the mattress. "Sing, my boy! I know you can do it!"

Beyond the chamber's curtained windows, a tempest. Hail rattles the glass like rocks thrown by a rampaging giant. Fane, newly risen from her own sick bed, clutches at her temples. "It hurts!" she sobs. "The energies are all wrong, they twist like snakes and cut like knives! Make it stop, Durm, make it stop!"

Durm shakes his head. "I cannot. He has the Weather in his hands and he'll do with it as he wills. As the fever wills." Looming over Nix, he says, "Break it, man. Break the magic's hold on him or it shall break us, and all to tiny pieces."

Nix quails. "I shall do my best, Sir."

Durm's lips bare his teeth in a snarling smile. Overhead, a crack of lightning sears pain through every head. "Do better," he advises. "Or you'll be midwife to the end of the world."

Drowning in music, Gar clutched the dais railing and marvelled at the glorious sound. He'd long since stopped singing, just so he could listen more perfectly. So many voices…a harmony he'd never dreamed of. There were tears on his cheeks. The fresh salt air couldn't dry them fast enough, his eyes were over-run with emotion. Why had his father never *said*? "Off to the festival," he'd groan with a smile, and ride away and long days later ride back and never once had he *said*.

There were tears on Asher's cheeks too. He was still singing, his hoarse baritone melding roughly with the mayor's rich tenor, the lady mayoress's true soprano and the motley choir of the other officials. In his face, a fierce exultation. This was his moment, his heritage, his future. He was a sudden stranger.

Beneath the blazing sun the crowd's united, uniting voice made magic of the air. "*Rejoice*," the fisherfolk sang, in descant and harmony, each voice a thread in the marvellous tapestry of sound. "*Prepare*," they sang, and "*Praise the bounteous ocean*"; "*Strength to the fishermen*," they sang. "*Plenty to the harvest. Clear skies and calm seas.*" Even the trees bent to listen, or so it seemed. And in the harbour the fish leapt to hear it. Singly at first, a rainbow flash of fin and scale. Then in pairs. In triplets. Flinging themselves boldly towards the sun.

"*Behold they come!*" the fisherfolk proclaimed, as they raised their hands in welcome and thanks. "*The ocean's bounty, our lives, our living!*"

Slowly, slowly, the harbour began to boil.

As the king thrashes insensible upon his pillows the queen anchors her fingers to Pother Nix's arm. "Do something! He cannot continue like this much longer!"

Princess Fane slumps in a corner, her face blotched with tears, her eyes slitted with pain. Durm sits with her, an arm about her shoulders. In his set face rages a promise of death, or worse. Nix turns away from the mage's terrible eyes, shuddering, and rests trembling fingers on Her Majesty's hand. Another second and her nails will draw his blood.

"I dare not give him more heartsease, Majesty!" he protests. "As it is I have exceeded the proper dosage by some half again…one drop more and it may be fatal!"

"Whereas these seizures are a very bromide?" Her Majesty retorts. Her face is frightening. "What good will your caution do us if he dies in delirium?"

Nix presses a hand to his sweaty forehead. They are all looking at him: the queen, the Master Magician, the princess, his apprentices, all desperate for an answer, an ending in smiles and laughter. The stout palace windows rattle and shake as the king's storm lashes without mercy. "Majesty," he implores, "we must wait a little longer before we essay more potions! In conscience I cannot allow otherwise."

The queen draws breath to argue, but before the hot words can scald forth an ominous rumbling fills the air, shaking the weathered stones of the palace walls. Princess Fane leaps to her feet, a startled fawn.

"What is that?" she whispers.

Now the furniture itself is dancing, and the hand-woven rugs beneath their uncertain feet ripple as though afflicted with unnatural life. The small table beneath one window jumps, pinpricked, and beyond the closed chamber door the sound of screams and unbridled fear. Nix flings out an arm for balance, is steadied by an underling, who must needs clutch a twitching curtain to keep them both upright.

"Barl save us!" the queen says, and takes her child into her arms. "Is the Wall falling down around our ears then?"

Durm staggers to a window and looks outside. "No," he replies, and even he cannot quite mask his fear. "But the ground moves as though it were alive...never before have I seen the like."

Drawn like magnets, every gaze swivels to the epicentre of their lives.

Oblivious and sweat-soaked in his bed the king shakes and shakes, and all around him fair Dorana echoes his wild trembling.

In all his life Gar never imagined he would see a sight like it: the harbour seething with fish, thousands of Olken united in song and hope, the air itself alive with the strength and joy of it. He thought his heart might burst from the beauty.

The Harvest Hymn reached its crescendo. Soaring on wings of worship the massed choir of fisherfolk opened its glorious throat and exalted the final note, the final word, in a multitude of harmonies, the men, the women, the children, hands joined, hearts joined, eyes clear and wide and focused on the future...*Rejoice*...the music poured forth, unstoppable, inexhaustible, to fill the sunbright space between sea and sky...

Nix cowers as the Master Magician raises clenched fists to his face.

"Fool!" he thunders as the windows crack and splinter to the floor and dislodged roof slates smash to smithereens on the heaving ground outside, so far beneath them. "Must I lay hands upon His Majesty and choke him to stillness before the fabric of the world is torn to pieces and the Wall itself comes tumbling down?"

The queen is bruised and bloody from being thrown against the fireplace. "Do something, Nix!"

Wild rain drives into the chamber, guttering the glimfire and ordinary candles. Nix cries out in pain as razor-edged hail lays open one blanched cheek. "Do what?" he snaps, nerveless fingers fumbling through his box of remedies. "This fit is beyond anything I—"

"Master Nix!" an apprentice shouts. "The king!"

Thrashing in his tangle of blankets and sheets, Borne opens his eyes. His mouth stretches wide, split lips peeling back. He looks demented.

"Rejoice!" he bellows, voice cracked and desperate, rising in a wild despairing scream. "Rejoice rejoice rejoice rejoice rejoice—"

Beyond the jagged gaping windows green and purple clouds writhe in mortal combat. Scarlet lightning spears the ground. Hailstones like hens' eggs pulp the streaming gardens and the felled trees' foliage, gouge great holes in the lovingly tended lawns of the palace grounds. Unleashed rivers pour from the sky.

"Rejoice!" the king commands.

His Majesty's bowed body lifts off the wrecked bed. In concert the palace seems almost to lift off its very foundations in one final upthrusting convulsion. The queen, the Master Magician, the princess, Pother Nix and his three witless apprentices are thrown to the heaving floor.

"Gar!" the king screams. "Gar!"

A mighty crack of thunder explodes directly overhead. A flash of white and scarlet light blinds every uncovered eye. The king collapses unstrung to his waiting blankets. The restless earth is stilled.

Stunned almost to gibbering, Nix raises himself on one throbbing elbow to look outside. He sees the clouds streaming south like a river in springmelt flood, leaving innocent blue sky in their wake. Sunshine glitters on rain-washed grass and shattered glass. A warm and gentle breeze stirs the curtains. His ears ring with silence. Smothering a small sob of pain, Nix gathers his scattered wits and climbs to his feet. He is a man of medicine. There are patients...

Chalk-white, stone-still, the king sprawls in a welter of limbs. Bright scarlet flecks his lips, his beard, the rumpled, tangling sheets.

"Your Majesty?" Nix whispers. Around him the stir and mutter of the others as awareness returns. "Your Majesty?"

The king does not reply. Beneath his white skin a delicate tracery of blue. His eyes, heavy-lidded and almost closed, stare without comment at one limply folded hand.

Nix begins to tremble. His fingers flutter, helpless as limed birds. The room is swimming before his eyes.

"Your Majesty...!"

Loud enough to crack the sky, the gathered multitude of fisherfolk erupted into raucous cheering. Hats sailed exuberantly into the air, and feet stamped the cobbled ground in excited liberation.

Battered with exhilaration Gar caught Darran's eye, remembered his protocols and gestured for the mayor to lead them off the dais and on to the next stage of the festival. Puffed with pride, the three-man crew for the festival boat was waiting for them at the end of the pier. Introductions were made, hands were shaken and greetings exchanged, and then it was time.

Gar took a deep breath and hoped against all hope that he appeared, if anything, slightly bored. Sailing? Oh yes. Nothing to it. He sailed all the time back home in Dorana.

"After you then, Captain Kremmer," he invited. Kremmer, a grizzled veteran of some forty festivals, touched his salt-stained cap, collected his crew with a nod and boarded the perilously fragile-looking fishing boat.

"All aboard who be comin' aboard, Yer Highness," Kremmer called. "They fish'll be leavin' the harbour directly!"

Tradition mandated that the reigning king or queen—or an appointed representative—joined the festival fishing crew in collecting the harvest's bounty from the ocean. Heart pounding, Gar looked at Westwailing's politely attentive mayor and his colleagues, at Darran and Willer but not at Asher, then finally at the plank of wood linking the pitching boat deck to the solid pier.

It was so *narrow.* Couldn't they have found a fatter tree?

Asher said under his breath, "You'll be fine. A jaunt about the harbour, is all, fetching up a few net loads of fish. You'll be back on dry land afore you know it. And I won't let nowt happen to you on board, I promise."

Diverted, he glanced at Asher. "And what makes you think you're coming?"

Asher blinked, and the edged sympathy in his eyes froze. He leaned close. Whispered. "Only a petty man'd make me stay behind."

He whispered back. "You'll pay for that."

As Asher's eyebrows rose, derisive, Captain Kremmer rang his shiny ship's bell. Darran cleared his throat. "Your Highness..."

He got on the damned boat. And so did Asher, along with all the fishing village mayors. Darran and Willer stayed behind. Within moments of boarding, the fishermen had their sleeves rolled up and were doing incomprehensible things with ropes and anchors and tarry, stinking fish nets, their salt-scoured faces alight with vigour and purpose and a pure uncomplicated joy.

"Set yourself here," said Asher, pushing him without ceremony to stand by a stout mast, "and don't touch *nowt*."

As if he needed to be told that. What did Asher think, that his prince harboured secret ambitions to dance about the deck of this tiny wooden bath tub singing jolly sea songs? Ha! It was all he could do not to throw his arms tight about the mast and bellow for his mother like a foal at weaning...

...but after a few minutes that urge mercifully passed and he stopped thinking about the fathoms of water beneath his unsteady feet and the rapidly retreating harbour behind them and the fact he was on a *boat*, on the *ocean*, Barl save him. Began instead to notice the sharp, clean tang of the snapping breeze and the laughter in the fishermen's faces, in Asher's face, as they shouted in their foreign fishermen's tongue and tossed the nets overboard with practised ease and an enviable springiness of wrist and arm.

One of the crew squeezed past him to haul on a lever. The middle section of the deck unhinged and dropped inwards, revealing the boat's dark belly and releasing a stomach-rolling whiff of old fish. He felt his face contract in horror and slapped an appalled hand over nose and mouth. The man laughed at him, and he found himself laughing back.

"You be right there, prince?" the fisherman asked, still chuckling. "Fine day for sailin', eh?"

"Oh yes, fine, fine," he replied, answering both questions, and laughed again. "I'm having a wonderful time."

"Course you be," said the fisherman. "Sailin's a wonderful thing. Mind yerself now, "cause we be bringin' in the catch."

And so they were. Muscles straining, the crew hauled the nets back on board, bulging with flapping fish. It was like a dance the way they moved together in unison, perfectly poised, perfectly balanced on their toes and heels, no need to ask questions or look to see where the next man was or what he was doing. Seamless, bred and born in their bones and perfected over years and seasons.

Stabbed with jealousy, wrenchingly reminded of the solitary life from which Asher's friendship had rescued him, and to which he must now return unwilling, Gar leaned against the mast, heedless of stains, of splinters, of everything except this extraordinary brotherhood of which he could never be a part.

But Asher could. Asher was. This was his life, his true life, the life he'd been born to and wanted back again. And who in all honesty could blame him? To be sure he had a fine and fancy life back in Dorana City. He had a good job, one with purpose and value. He had friends. But he didn't have *this*. And this was Asher's blood and breath, as any fool with eyes could see.

The first takings of the festival catch streamed into the boat's hold, four net loads in all. Sweat-streaked and panting, hilarity lighting his face in a way Gar had never seen in twelve months and more of dry City living, Asher wiped tarry fingers on his good breeches and called over, "You be right there, sir?"

He couldn't speak, could only nod and offer a smile, because he knew now he had lost the battle, if it was a battle at all, if one man's life and the way he wanted to live it could actually be fought over.

Jinking in a strong gust of wind, the boat swung suddenly about so he had to grab at the mast to stay upright. "Hang tight," called Asher, grinning wide enough to split his face. "You bloody landlubber!"

He opened his mouth to say something insulting in return, something to show that he understood now, that it was all right, really, and no grudges at all... but there was another gust of wind and a sudden convulsion of the deck beneath his feet. On the wind, a terrified crying of voices.

"Barl save us! Look!" Captain Kremmer shouted, and pointed a shaking hand back to port.

Staggering, sea legs nonexistent, Gar shuffled around till he could see Westwailing Harbour, so far behind them. "The Wall protect us," he whispered, and felt his heart seize fast in his chest.

The cloudless blue sky over Westwailing was gone, consumed by a terrible writhing of purple and black. Scarlet lightning flickered like a snake's tongue. The shrieks and moans of panic-stricken fisherfolk swarming desperately to reach shelter carried over the agitated harbour. As Gar and the crew watched, dumbstruck, thunderbolts tore gaping holes in the tumultuous storm clouds and struck the unprotected ground below. A moment later they heard the booming concussion and the agonised screams of people unable to escape.

Aggressive with fear, Asher navigated the lurching deck to grasp Gar's arm. "This ain't a sea-born storm, it's come from inland. What's goin' on?"

Gar pressed a fist to his lips. "I don't know."

"We got to get back there," said Asher, and let go of Gar's arm to turn on Kremmer. "Captain! Get us about! We got to help those folks!"

"Help them?" Kremmer demanded. The boat plunged through a wave and he was thrown to one knee. "How? Reckon we'll not help ourselves now! Reckon we won't make it off these waters alive! *Look!*"

As one, they turned to look back at the township. Gar felt his mouth suck drier than summer. "Father..." he whispered. "Father, what are you doing?"

The lurid clouds were streaking towards them, blown by a howling malevolent wind. The harbour waters churned and rolled, great waves whipping up, dashing foam, blotting out the terrible sky. Thunderbolts rained down, hissing and spitting as they struck the turbulent water.

"Do something, Your Highness!" Westwailing's mayor bellowed. "Or we'll all be drowned for certain sure!"

"I can't!" Gar shouted back. Hating himself. Hating the mayor for asking.

A cold hand closed over his wrist. Asher. "You're sure? You can't even try?"

Gar snatched his arm free. Swallowed bile. "You can ask me that?" he hissed, even as rain sharp as glass began to drive through the murky air to strike flesh without mercy. "After a year in the City, you can ask me *that?*"

Asher stepped back. "Sorry," but the word was whipped out of his mouth and shredded on the rising wind, ominously howling, bansheevoiced and battering. The inadequate fishing smack pitched and tossed, helpless in the face of the climbing waves. Gar and Asher and the rest flailed about the boat, catching hold of whatever could save them from falling, as their vulnerable flesh bruised and split and streamed rain-diluted blood.

"I can't save us!" Gar screamed into the teeth of the wind, into their blank and fear-blanched faces. "I'm *sorry!*"

And then there was no more time for talking, as the storm fell upon them in all its immediate fury.

CHAPTER TWENTY-ONE

Splinters flew as hailstones like rocks battered the deck beneath their feet. Ear-splitting thunder claps exploded in time with the scarlet lightning that rent the sky. Green and purple fingers of cloud stretched down to the white-whipped harbour, sucking up whirlpools of water. Fish plucked from safety spun and spun and spun apart. Flaming thunderbolts sizzled the air and pounded the boat. One struck the Mayor of Chevrock's head clean off his smoking shoulders. Gar felt his stomach heave, tasted acid as he vomited into the howling wind. Then the boat stood on end and he was sliding face down along the deck, collecting splinters and fish scales, tearing his fingernails as he clutched in vain at the weathered timber beneath him. He cried out in pain as his soaked and suffering body collided with some hard wooden surface at the far end of the boat, then again in alarm as the shuddering vessel tipped the other way and he careened back the way he'd come, only just avoiding a plunge into the hold. The other men were shouting too, he could hear them, barely, through the savage noise of the storm.

Something wet and warm ran down his face; he touched his fingers to it, expecting rain, and they came away red. He was bleeding.

"Gar!"

Muzzy, confused, he turned towards Asher's anchoring voice. Pain pulsed in time with his hammering heart.

"Stay down!" Asher bellowed as he kicked himself free of a tangling net, blood dripping down his chin. "You'll be safer that way!"

That made him laugh. Safer? There was no safer, not any more. As though to prove the point, a giant wave punched the fishing boat like a fist, rolled it half over so that he had to throw his arms around the nearest solid something and hold on for his life. Somebody tumbled past him, yelping, to plummet head-first into the fish-laden belly of the boat.

With a snapping crack the sail tore loose, sending the boom swinging wildly out of control. The boat plunged again with a twisting shivering shudder. Tossed into the air like so much soggy kindling, Gar found himself somersaulted to his feet, where he swayed and tottered and tried to get his bearings. Somebody screamed *"Look out!"* and he turned, too late. The swinging boom with its madly flapping canvas caught him across the chest with a dull thud. Drove the gasping air from his lungs and swept him contemptuously into the air. Over the side of the canting fishing boat he tumbled, and into the unruly sea.

An icy coldness closed over his head. Stinging salt surged into his mouth, up his nose, burned out his eyes and swamped his ears. Deaf, dumb and blind he tumbled inside out and upside down, insignificant and unremarked within the vastness of the ocean and the might of the storm. For one heartbeat he struggled, and another, and another. There was a roaring in his head that might have been the storm, or might have been all his trapped cries of protest dying for lack of air. I am drowning, he thought, and could feel only a mild regret. I wonder if Fane will cry at my funeral. I wonder if she'll even bother to come. Then he stopped struggling altogether. Stopped thinking, because it was simply too hard. Instead he surrendered to the water and the dark and waited for death to come on slinking seaweed feet.

A sharp and sudden pain wrenched him out of complacency. He grunted, eyes slitting open. What the—somebody had him by the *hair*, there were fingers in his *hair*, tangling, tugging...

Struggling anew he ploughed his leaden arms through the oppressive ocean, struck something soft and yielding. No. Some*one*. He wasn't alone. There was somebody in the water with him, there was an arm around his chest, legs kicking behind him, he could see flashes above him through the watery prism of the heaving waves. His head broke the surface and he sucked in great gasps of air, coughing, sneezing.

"I got you!" said Asher, rasping in his ear. "Hang on tight now, I got you!"

Teeth chattering, ice-cold to his marrow, Gar dragged his hair off his face and looked up into the whirling storm clouds overhead. Asher was a fool, he never should have bothered, the waves towered above them like Barl's mountains, waiting to fall, eager to smear them into red stains on the surface of the sea—

The purple and green sky lit up then, with an eye-searing flash brighter than the sun. He cried out and tried to hide from the whiteness of it. With the flash came a crack of sound like the end of the world. For a moment he lost consciousness.

Then he thought he must be dreaming, because he could feel gentle sunlight on his salt-sticky skin and his ears were empty of the howling wind.

Bemused, he opened his eyes.

The storm was gone. Overhead, a limpid blue sky, cloudless. All around them gentle water, flat and calm as a pond. No scarlet lightning. No sizzling thunderbolts. Just out of reach the fishing smack floated like a duck, lightly, on top of the tranquil sea. Someone called, shakily, "Asher! Be that you? D'you got the prince?"

The arm around his chest tightened, relaxed. Asher called back, sounding a little shaky himself, "Aye! We be here! Come get us in, eh?"

"Hang tight, lad, we be comin'!"

Limp as a neck-wrung chicken, Gar stared up into the pristine sky. Sharp pain stung him as his eyes filled with tears. "*Father!*" he cried inside his head, his heart. "*Father...*"

Soon after that the sky faded and, with it, all awareness.

He wasn't sorry.

Dorana City was in a screaming uproar. Those streets and alleyways not choked with fallen roof tiles, with shattered glass, broken flowerpots and all other manner of debris, seethed and heaved with bodies, Olken and Doranen alike, as they stumbled about in consternation and full-throated dishevelment. Captain Orrick and his City Guards, as shocked as everybody else, struggled to maintain a semblance of order in the face of flooding due to cracked and gushing water pipes, fires and indiscriminate rushing about in a panic.

Dathne, bruised and battered by shelves of falling books, escaped her upheavalled shop and joined her dazed neighbours in the street. Once sure her friends were for the most part unharmed she made her struggling way to the Tower stable yard to find Matt, and see if together they could make sense of this unexpected calamity.

Prophecy hadn't warned her about *this*. If she weren't so shaken up she'd be furious.

There were no guards on duty at the gate into the palace grounds. Hurrying through unhindered she saw where the earth had lifted and buckled through the garden beds and lawns, tearing the turf to shreds and revealing rich brown dirt like scars. Some trees had fallen; their roots scrabbled at the sky.

Ahead, beyond the gap-toothed circle of oaks, the prince's Tower still stood sentinel. It wasn't till she saw it there, untouched, that she realised the depth of her terror, her fear that it might have come down, pulping everything around it beneath gigantic blocks of blue stone.

The Tower stable yard was buzzing with lads, some bruised and bloody, some whole, all intent on nurturing the nervous, wide-eyed horses who whickered and whinnied and kicked their stable doors in protest.

"Where's Matt? Where's Matt?" she asked them, and they pointed their trembling fingers at the path leading to the pastures beyond the yard. Picking up her skirts, she ran.

And found him sprawled in one of the fields nearest to the stables, his face smeared with blood from a cut along his hairline. In his arms he held the limp body of a young man. There was blood on his hands too, she realised. And down the front of his shirt. Before she could ask if he was all right—

"It's Bellybone," he said numbly, staring up at her with huge, hurt eyes. "He was trying to bring in the colts. One of them kicked him— look…"

His stained hand parted the blood-soaked hair on the back of the man's head. Bellybone? Ah yes. She remembered. At eighteen, one of Matt's senior stable hands. A charming rogue, forever pestering her to play a hand of Cock Robin with him down at the Goose. She nearly always refused; her money was too hard-earned to go losing it at cards with a young man who'd made an artform of winning. She leaned a little closer. Frowned.

"He's dead, Matt. His skull's been crushed."

He nodded. "I know."

"I'm sorry."

He turned his head. Following his gaze, she saw a group of gangly young horses huddled in one corner of the field. Another was stretched ominously still on the buckled green grass. There was the faint sound of many flies, buzzing.

"That's Thunder Crow," he said. "He broke both front legs. There was nothing I could do for him, I had to…had to cut his throat…"

Which explained the blood. Crouching, her eyes hot, she touched her fingertips to his shoulder. "Matt, we have to talk."

Shuddering, he dragged his eyes away from the dead horse. "What happened, Dathne? Is it the end then? Has the Wall begun to crumble? Is the king dead?"

"I don't know. They're not saying anything down in the City. There's been no announcement. It's madness there right now. But I think he must be. The Wall still stands for now, but I think this is the beginning of the end."

"Asher?"

Her fists clenched, echoing her frustration. "I don't know that either. I don't know how far the storm extended or what other districts were struck. The coast is so far away, you'd think he'd be safe… but I just don't know. I tried to scry him but the energies are all over the place. I couldn't find a path to him. I couldn't reach Veira either. Perhaps later tonight, when everything's calmed down."

He nodded again, slowly. Looked down at dead Bellybone, then back up at her. "You didn't see this coming, Dathne. Did you?"

She lowered her face to her knees, perilously close to breaking. "No, Matt," she said, her voice muffled in her skirts. "No, I surely didn't."

"What do you think it means?"

"I don't know." She lifted her aching head. "But I expect we'll find out soon enough. Maybe Veira can tell us, once I can reach her."

"Yes," he said. "Maybe she can." Then he frowned. "And what about you? Are you all right?"

She waved a hand. "I'm fine. Which is more than I can say for my poor shop. It's a mess, all the books off the shelves. Windows broken. Half the floorboards have sprung loose. Unless I can find a Doranen willing to lend me a magickal hand it'll take days and days to—"

"But you're all right," said Matt, with his dead stable hand cradled against his chest. "No bones broken. No need for a healer."

He was in shock, she realised. Ridiculously, it was the last thing she'd expected. Matt was her rock, her foundation, the shoulder she leaned on, the hand that she held in moments of quiet desperation. She *needed* him.

And he needed her, at least for the moment.

Kneeling, disregarding his uncoordinated resistance, she gently prised Bellybone from his grasp. Hoisted the limp form over her shoulder and got to her feet. He hadn't been a big man, most stable hands weren't, but still he was heavy enough to make her back and shoulders ache. But that was all right. She could manage.

"Come on, Matt," she said gently, looking down at him. "We need to lay poor Bellybone somewhere cool and quiet and you need to get back to your horses. The other lads will be looking for you. It's Meister Matt they're needing now, more than they've ever needed him before."

Wincing, Matt stood. Without a word took Bellybone from her, turned, and started walking back to the stable yard. After a moment she fell into step behind him. She could just make out the dead youth's eyes, half closed, as his head rested in the hollow between Matt's neck and shoulder.

Damn you, Asher, she thought as a shiver ran through her from head to toe. Damn you, damn you, damn you. You'd better be all right...

*   *   *

Hands trembling, Darran added mustard powder to the bowl of freshly boiled water in front of him. The steam spiralling into his face turned abruptly acrid, stinging runny mucus from his nose and tears from his eyes. Well, at least he'd have an excuse now. *Old fool*, he scolded himself, and stirred the browny yellow water with a wooden spoon anxiously provided by the mayor's cook. He's not dead. You've not failed Their Majesties this time. He's not dead. Think on that, not on what might have been. He added more mustard to the mix and sloshed it vigorously, blinking and sniffing.

In the deep armchair behind him Gar shifted inside his enveloping blanket. Was that a cough? Had the prince caught a chill, or worse, from his fearful immersion in the ocean? You should have stopped him, Darran. Who cares what tradition dictates? You should have put your foot down. You knew it was foolhardy for him to risk himself on all that open water with only that Asher for protection. You know what he's like. Any dangerous thing, he'll do, and has done, ever since they told him he was—ever since he realised he would always be... different.

Oh, how he remembered that day. Seared into memory, it was, and even into nightmares sometimes. Five, the prince had been, tall for his age and splendid, just like the early paintings of his mother that hung in the palace's Hall of Memories. Silver-gilt hair and eyes that mirrored every blossoming hope, every dead dream. "No," he'd screamed. "I'm not a cripple, I'm not I'm not I'm not!" Then he'd run away from his parents, from the Master Magician, from his unbearable life, to the stables. "Let him go," the king had said, his deep voice ripe with sorrow and regret. "The sooner he learns he'll not outrun this, the better." And had punished the prince only for galloping his pony into the ground.

He'd been a junior secretary then, and privy to the calamity only by accident and a handful of urgent letters. For himself he'd have cut the pony's blue-black throat and drunk the steaming blood for breakfast, if it could have changed the terrible truth. If it could have given the prince his magic.

From the armchair, another ominous throat-clearing sound. Barl knew the prince was hardy enough, not in the least prone to distempers and ill humours and the like. But this was different. This was a near drowning and something more terrible besides... a bad chest, or even worse, was a distinct possibility.

His innards clutched again, fear yammering at him, twisting him. *Old fool! He needs you! Control yourself!* He took a deep breath and then began to cough himself, from the mustard fumes. The prince's footbath was thickening nicely. Perhaps a drop more water...

When it was just so, and perfect, he blotted his face and hands dry with a towel, picked up the bowl and turned a bright and resolutely calm smile on his employer. "Here we are, sir. A nice hot mustard bath to ward off any chills."

The prince's face still lacked colour, the bruises and scrapes he'd suffered standing out like spilt ink on snow. The minute they'd brought him up from the harbour, battered and bloody and stiffening with salt, he'd been put in a hot bath and ruthlessly scrubbed clean. Darran cast yet another prayer of thanks Barlwards, that the prince had been largely insensible throughout the entire unpleasant ordeal.

Inside his nest of blankets Gar lifted heavy-lidded, glowering eyes. "Where's Asher?"

Years of training kept his expression unchanged. "He's fine. Now if you'll just put your feet in the bowl, sir, you'll feel much better."

"I don't want a damned mustard footbath, Darran!" the prince snarled. "Unless you want to drink it, take it away!" On his marked face a look all too reminiscent of the Master Magician's, when that terrible man was not pleased with the chaff that served him.

Darran put the bowl back on the table. He's upset, he's just upset, of course he's upset. His hands were shaking again. He doesn't mean it, you know he doesn't, he never does. He hasn't thought, he doesn't understand...

"I failed them, Darran."

He turned. "Failed who, sir?"

The prince was staring out of the chamber window. His expression was desolate. Disconsolate. "Asher's people. On the boat. In the town. As the storm hit us the mayor begged me to do something. To save them. I couldn't. I failed. Useless, useless *cripple*..."

"I'm sure you're no such thing, sir!" Darran's heartbeat stuttered in panic. "I'm sure not even Master Durm himself could have stopped that dreadful storm."

But the prince wasn't listening. "And I lost the heirloom circlet. It's somewhere at the bottom of Westwailing Harbour."

"Never mind, sir. I'm quite sure that given a choice Their Ma—" He stopped. Breathed deeply for a moment. "The queen would much rather have you back safe and sound than a circlet."

"The king presented it to me on my twelfth birthday." There was grief in the prince's face now, and in his voice, raw as an open wound. "I swore to him I'd look after it. I swore—"

"It doesn't matter, Your Highness," said Darran, trying to soothe. It was hard; he felt jagged with his own distress. "Not compared to—"

"Of course it bloody matters, you stupid old man!" Gar shouted. "That circlet was a treasure, a priceless part of Lur's history. It was a gift from my *father*! How can you stand there and say it doesn't—"

"Because you matter more!" Darran shouted back. "Don't you understand that, you foolish, foolish boy?"

Shocked silence. Horrified, Darran turned away, fists pressed against his chest. Behind him the prince shifted in his blankets. "Darran..."

He'd promised himself he wouldn't speak. Had reminded himself over and over that his was the privileged place of servant to the royal family. The creed, unbreakable, was see all and say nothing. He was a man in the autumn of his life, this prince young enough to be a grandson. The onus was on him to behave as was proper, to indulge the hot blood of youth, to wave an indolent hand at intemperate outbursts. To understand and forgive, no matter what the provocation. That was maturity. That was the code.

Without permission his body turned and his mouth opened. His voice emerged, sounding thin, frightened, not his voice at all.

"I remember the day you were born. Your gracious mother placed you in my arms with her own fair hands. You were so tiny. You smiled at me. I know you don't remember, but you did." Memory curved his lips into the answering smile he'd blazed at the little thing.

The prince stared, startled and discomfited. Uncertain, and in need of a wiser man's guidance though he couldn't see it. "Darran..."

It was the vulnerability that shattered the last of his resolve. "I thought you were drowned!" he cried. "I thought I would have to take your broken body back to your mother! Or worse, tell her—tell her you were lost beneath the waves, not even your body to—"

The hot tears behind his eyes burst forth, unstoppable. Flooded with shame he turned away again, hands pressed to his face. Disgraceful, this was *disgraceful*...but oh, how dreadful it had been with the storm upon them and the screaming and the howling and the clouds and rain and lightning and thunderbolts, the hail, the blood, the shrieking children, the waves as tall as trees and taller, pounding them to the ground, pounding them to pieces on the cobblestones, and the prince alone out there on the unprotected ocean! Moaning, he pressed his thin fingers to his lips and willed away the raw and recent horror.

"Darran, you musn't," the prince said, his voice strained. "I'm not drowned. I'm not even hurt, not to mention. Just a few bumps and bruises. I know you had a nasty shock, we all did, but we can't go to pieces now. There's too much to do."

He could only nod, couldn't trust his treacherous voice.

The prince said, shifting inside his blanket, "You know what that storm means, Darran. You know what must have happened."

No, no, no. It wasn't true. *Couldn't* be true. Fresh tears brimming he turned, looked at the king's son, whose own eyes were brilliant with unshed grief. "We don't know anything for certain," he whispered.

"*I* know," the prince said starkly. "Barl save me, Darran. I *know*. Such a cataclysm can only be the result of…it has happened before, twice—I fear only one conclusion can be drawn! His Majesty is… His Majesty has…" His expression fractured then, exposing a wasteland of loss. A hand came up to cover his face, fingers white and pressing.

On a choked sob Darran went to him, heedless of protocol, of propriety, of every rule he'd ever followed, every boundary he'd never crossed. He put his arms around the prince's shoulders and held him. "There, there," he said, helpless, washed in his own tears. "There, there."

At length the prince withdrew, pain banished, a new and harder resolve in his eyes. "How bad is it in the township, Darran? The truth."

Oh, how he'd dreaded that question. Prevaricating, he stood and moved away. Smoothed his rumpled vest, his limp collar and sagging sleeves. Took deep, mustard-scented breaths until his heart was racing only a little.

"Bad enough," he replied, and on another breath turned and faced his prince again. "Perhaps half a hundred dead. There seems to be some difficulty in agreeing on a final tally. Some drowned, some struck with debris. Some…trampled underfoot in the panic to escape the foreshore." Despite himself he shuddered, seeing again an old woman crushed to a pulp in the first mad stampede. "Injuries, of course. Aid stations have been established in several locations. Doranen healers have been sent for, but Barl alone knows how long they'll take to reach us, even if any are to be found. This is an Olken part of the world, sir. They have their herbalists and their pothecaries, fine people, doing all they can. Of course it's not the same as having a proper Doranen physicker, but they seem to be managing tolerably well."

"What of damage to property?"

"As you can imagine, sir, it is extensive. Trees down, roof tiles blown off, windows shattered. Boats sunk to the bottom of the harbour."

"The Crown will see them right," the prince said, and pulled his blanket closer. "Whoever has lost what is dear in this calamity, he or she shall be recompensed."

Aching, Darran passed a shaking hand across his eyes. *My boy, my boy, and who will recompense you?* His heart broke anew at the thought. "Of course, sir," he said. "I have set Willer to starting the tally in anticipation of such a commitment."

Incredibly, a faint smile. "Your efficiency does you credit, Darran." Then the smile faded. "I must return to the City. Tomorrow, at first light. The rest of today I will inspect as much of the damage as I can. Pay my respects to the bereaved. I'll need you to work with Asher to ensure my speedy leave-taking come the dawn."

"Leave *tomorrow*?" Aghast, he stared at the prince. "But that's impossible! Recall that you nearly drowned, Your Highness! You mustn't exert yourself before a proper medical inspection, by a proper Doranen pothecary! You need rest, sir, and embrocations for your bruises!"

The prince waved an impatient hand. "Don't be ridiculous. The pothers are for those with real injuries. You're making far too much of a few cuts and scrapes. I've had worse falling off my horse out hunting and you know it."

Grimly determined Darran straightened his spine hard and said, lips pinched with disapproval, "I cannot support such behaviour, sir."

The prince lurched to his feet, blanket clutched haphazardly about his chest, eyes blazing. "I haven't asked you to support it! I'm telling you what I intend to do! My mother needs me and I will go to her, is that clear?"

Somehow he stood his ground in the face of royal anger. "You are needed *here*, sir."

"I know," the prince replied. "But the queen takes precedence. You will act in my stead, with my voice, my hand. Do whatever needs to be done. I'll support any decision that you make, without reservation. But I am returning to Dorana at dawn."

He was beaten and he knew it, so he bowed, punctiliously. "As you wish, Your Highness."

"No," said the prince, and his face was bleak as winter. "As I must. Now. Where's Asher? I need to talk to him."

"I don't know where he is, sir," he said, scrupulously neutral. "He left the premises against my express request. Something about making sure his family was all right."

The prince paused in midscowl. Let out a deep sigh. "Of course. I should have thought. *Are* they all right?"

Darran lifted an eyebrow. "I'm sure I don't know, sir. All I do know is he had no business leaving without your permission. He has duties, obligations—"

"Oh, for Barl's sake!" the prince snapped. "He has *family*, Darran. For all we know one or all of them could be among the injured. Or the dead. Of course he went to see if they're all right!"

Well, naturally the prince would say that. His judgement was woefully suspect when it came to that ruffian. The prince was a good lad with a kind and lonely heart, ripe pickings for the unscrupulous, the callous and the calculating. "Yes, sir."

The prince sighed and thumped back into his armchair. When he looked up again his expression was wry and cross and irritatedly patient. "You know he saved my life, Darran."

Saved his life. That was how Asher would tell the tale, for certain. Like as not it had been an accident; like as not he'd been flung into the ocean himself and just happened to latch onto His Highness in all the confusion. Circumstance. Serendipity. To suggest that an uncouth savage like Asher could be *heroic*?

With a bow and smile he humoured his prince. "Yes, sir."

The prince flicked him a sharp look. "Darran, he did. I was drowning and he saved me."

Prickled by sudden doubt, by the new shadow in the prince's eyes, Darran stared at him. "Drowning?"

"A few more seconds and I would've been dead. Don't let your dislike blind you, Darran. You're a better man than that. I owe Asher my life."

"Yes, sir," he said faintly.

With a dismissive wave of his hand the prince slumped inside his blankets. "Now leave me. Find one of our pigeons and get a message to the queen. Let her know I'm all right and that I'm coming home. And when Asher returns send him to me immediately."

Another bow. He could try arguing some more, but what would be the point? "Certainly, sir. Can I send up something from the kitchens, sir?"

The prince shrugged. "No. Yes. I don't know. Do what you like. Some soup, maybe."

"Yes, sir."

"And Darran?"

Fingers on the door handle, he turned. "Yes, sir?"

The prince was scowling again. "You might as well give me the damned mustard bath. Seeing as it's just sitting there, getting cold."

"Yes, sir," he said, killing the fatuous smile that threatened to spread over his face. "As Your Highness commands. As always."

"Watch out!"

Asher looked up, saw the slithering roof tiles and leapt aside just in time. With a crash and a splintering spray of clay shards the red squares hit the cobblestones beside him. Peering downwards, a pale face mottled with bruises, eyes wide with alarm.

"Be you unhurt?" the man shouted.

"Aye," he called back, but didn't stop, kept on hurrying. If he stopped for every man, woman and child that needed help in these demolished streets he'd not reach the Dancing Dolphin till the middle of next week. That's where he'd find his family. Year in, year out, without alteration, at festival time they stayed at the Dancing Dolphin.

It wasn't a fashionable inn, which was why Da liked it so much. Good food, better ale, soft beds and no gapesters forever goin' on about how they saw the king and what a mighty upstandin' man he be and weren't they lucky to have such a king to help sing in the harvest. *Lucky.* When everybody knew their festival weren't nowt to do with any Doranen. An Olken matter, it was, and the king bein' invited no more than a courtesy when you got right down to it.

Skirting more debris he turned his face away from a woman standing in a doorway with a mute wrapped bundle in her arms and tears pouring down her blanched and sunken cheeks. Ducked up Lickspittle Lane and into Baitman Alley, which ran along the back of the houses and shops facing onto Seaswell High Street and came out almost opposite the Dolphin at its far end. The damage wasn't so bad along here. The storm seemed to have cut a straight path down through the township and over the water, as though it were alive, as though it knew exactly where it wanted to go and didn't care what it went through to get there.

He didn't want to think about what that might mean. Couldn't be distracted by Gar's problems right now. Right now he had his own.

Heart hammering, uncaring of his cuts and bruises and the pains they caused, he jogged along the alley until he reached its end. Then he stopped, one hand clutching the corner of the building beside him, and stared.

The Dolphin's sign was half torn from its moorings, dangling tipsily groundwards. Two windows on the top floor were broken. Somebody, probably Hiram the innkeeper, had already boarded over the holes.

There were a few tiles missing here and there. By the side door, the old pittypine tree he'd played in as a spratling was half blown over, gnarly roots clotted with dirt and tangled like an old man's fingers. Apart from that, the inn seemed to still be in one piece. Absurdly, his heart lifted. Brothers aside he had good memories of the Dolphin.

Dodging carts and timber-laden packhorses he crossed Harbourmaster Street, made his way through the gate and along the path that led to the Dancing Dolphin's front door and banged both fists on it, hard. His heart was beating so violently he thought he could feel his eyes jumping in their sockets.

"Asher!" Hiram exclaimed, his vast belly swathed in a dark green apron and his wiry hair a little greyer than the last time they'd met. Standing back, the innkeeper swung the door wide open. "Sink me with a rusty anchor! Hepple said he'd seen you ridin' alongside that namby-pamby prince they sent down from the City, and a course I arsked your fambly and they said they knew nowt on it, said you'd took yourself off a year ago and nobody knew where you were, so I reckoned Hepple'd made a head start on the ale this year, but now here you be and by the looks of your fancy togs you ain't a fisherman no more so Hepple were right then, were he?"

"Hiram," said Asher, trying to see round the innkeeper's bulk, "be my family here? Be they all right? Da—"

Hiram shook his head and stood back from the doorway. "Sorry, lad, sorry, here's me gabbin' like a barmaid and you all worrited about your fambly, and speakin' of fambly let me be the first to tell you how bad me and ole Mistress Hiram did feel when we got the news about—"

"Hiram. Stow that gabble afore I slice out your tongue and roast it for dinner."

Silenced midsentence, Hiram turned his head to look at the speaker.

Asher didn't need to look. He knew that voice. Had known it all his life, and the fists that went with it. With a nod and a grim smile at Hiram, he stepped over the Dolphin's threshold and prepared to meet his brothers.

CHAPTER TWENTY-TWO

Warily, Hiram shifted sideways to reveal the inn's modest staircase and a pack of men, descending. Their boots on the uncarpeted treads were loud in the sudden hush. In the lead, of course, as always, lean and mean and warm as midwinter...

"Zeth!" Hiram said. "Look who be here!"

Standing still now, scarred fingers taut on the banister, Zeth nodded. "I got eyes, Hiram. I can see."

Hiram cleared his throat. "Aye. Well. I'll just be gettin' on then, eh? You boys have fambly business to take care of, I reckon. Don't need no outsider puttin' in his three cuicks worth, eh? Good to see you again, Asher. Mind you say goodbye, now!"

"Aye," said Asher, his eyes not leaving Zeth's cold face. "That I will, Hiram."

With a last nervous smile, Hiram retreated. Asher closed the inn's front door behind him then stared at his brothers. Coming down the stairs one after the other, oldest to youngest, the way they went everywhere. Zeth. Abel. Josha. Wishus. Niko. Bede. All grimly staring and not a bump or bruise between them. Despite everything, he was relieved. He took a step forward. Shoved his hands in his pockets and shook his head. "That wasn't very polite, Zeth. It's Hiram's inn, you know."

Zeth bared his teeth in a smile. "Come home to lesson us in manners, boy?"

Asher swallowed a stupid reply. At Zeth's back, his other brothers muttered. "There's no need for trouble, Zeth. I just want to see Da."

Zeth's sharp smile widened. He started down the stairs again, the pack of brothers at his heels. He looked... older. There was grey in his hair and a new scar on his face, a pink and puckered line slicing through his left eyebrow and down his cheek, making his eyelid droop.

"That be a fancy tongue you got in your head, boy. And fancy clothes on your back too. Where'd you come by them, eh?"

Asher stood his ground. It was an old game this, one they'd played him at all his life. Standover bully-boy tactics. Raised fists and whispered threats. Well, he wasn't in the mood for games and he wasn't afraid of them any more. Realising that, he nearly laughed out loud. He wasn't afraid of them any more. After a year of Lord Conroyd Jarralt and Master Magician Durm, who was Zeth? Who were any of 'em?

"Don't piss me about, Zeth. Where's Da? I want to see him."

"Curly Thatcher said he saw you ridin' into town alongside the prince," said Zeth, conversational, at the foot of the staircase now and leaning a negligent shoulder against the newel post. Silent and staring, the others spread out behind him. "Sailor Vem said you were troughin' slops with 'im. That where you been this past long while? Hobnobbin' with blondie?"

Asher let the air hiss softly from his lungs. "I don't answer to you, Zeth. Not any more. Now for the last bloody time, I want to see Da. Where is he? Upstairs? Then let me past. You got no right to keep me from him."

Zeth turned his head, swept their brothers with a measuring gaze. Then he looked again at Asher. "No. No, he ain't upstairs."

An icy splinter of fear pierced him. There was something in their faces. A memory in their eyes. "Then where is he, Zeth? I want to know. Now."

Zeth sighed. Inspected his chipped fingernails. Lifted his unfriendly face and said, with all the brutality in him, "Why, he's right where you put 'im, Asher dear. Deep in the cold dark ground."

Boom, boom, boom went Asher's heart. "What d'you mean, in the ground?"

"What d'you reckon I bloody mean!" said Zeth, suddenly savage. "Da's *dead*, boy. Eight months gone. Mast cracked and fell on 'im. Split 'im in half like a rotten apple."

"No," he said. But not because he disbelieved his brother. Not because it wasn't true. The truth of it was raw and bloody in the air between them, in Zeth's voice, his face. In all his brothers' faces. *"No."*

Zeth heaved another sigh. "'Fraid so. But don't you go feelin' too bad about it. He died screamin' your name." He shrugged. "Course, his heart were already broke long afore the mast felled 'im. You could say he were a walkin' dead man, really. Ain't that right, boys?"

Shoulder to shoulder his brothers nodded and muttered, thunder on the horizon.

"Over and over the same old questions," said Zeth. "What's happened to my Asher? Where's he gone? Why did he leave me? I'll tell you, boy, it grew a mite wearisome after a while, and that's for sure. Afore long Da weren't altogether right in the head no more. My word, it was the saddest sight I ever saw. That proud ole man, weepin' night after night into his ale pot and sobbin' your name."

"No," whispered Asher. "That's wrong. I left a message. I asked—"

"Message?" said Zeth. "Don't know nowt about any message, boy. Now just you keep your mouth shut, why don't you, and let me finish? As I were sayin'. Day after day, for weeks on end, Da fretted on you. Drove us all mad. Then one night a storm blew in from beyond the reef. Howlin' and wailin' and peltin' us with ice. Da swore he could hear your voice on the wind, callin'. He got to the boats afore we could stop him. Sailed out to find you. Wishus and me, we went after him, but there weren't nowt we could do with him in one boat and us in another. He were sore distracted lookin' for you, Asher, and distraction on a boat be an unchancy thing when there's bad weather about. Prob'ly you might remember that." Zeth's cruel gaze raked him up and down. "Then again, dressed so fancy like a Doranen, might be you don't."

Asher swallowed. There was a roaring in his head, as though the killing storm had returned. "I don't understand. The night I left I gave Jed a message for him. Jed swore blind he'd deliver it so's Da wouldn't worry."

"The night you left, boy, Jed fell down drunk and cracked his head like a hard-boiled egg." Zeth's eyes were wide with mock sorrow. "There be nowt for Jed these days but sittin' on street corners, droolin'."

No. No, not Jed. Childhood friend. Partner in many a crime. Freckle-faced and easygoing and always game for a lark...."You're lying. You'd say anything you could to hurt me, Zeth."

The mock sorrow gone now, Zeth straightened out of his comfortable slouch and took a step closer. His eyes were empty of everything but hate. "I got better ways to hurt you than words, little brother. You should've told us yourself what you had planned."

Asher held his ground, just. "You would've stopped me. Or tried anyways."

"Course we would've!" Zeth snarled. "You got no business leavin' the family. You owe your life to the family, your breath and your body belong to us. *We* say what's to be done with 'em. *We* say where you go and what you do. Them's the rules."

"*Your* rules," said Asher. His voice sounded strange, as though it belonged to somebody else. "Not mine. Not anymore."

"Da's dead 'cause of you, boy," said Zeth. "You might as well have stuck a guttin' knife in his heart. You should've. Would've been cleaner. Kinder. Quicker. But no. You had to kill him *slow*."

The air in his lungs had turned to ice. He couldn't breathe. "I ain't killed nobody. I'm goin'." Turning his back on them, he reached for the inn's front door.

Zeth growled. "Boys…"

Like wolves in the Black Woods they were on him. Clenched fists pummelled him. Vicious kicks felled him. Fingers snarled in his hair, his clothes, dragged him across the floor and tore the fine vest and shirt off his back. Face down they hauled him up the hard wooden staircase and pinned him to it like a bullock to the slaughter block. There were too many of them and they were too strong, he couldn't escape; nothing had changed, he might as well be a child again and helpless before them as their grieving father drank away all memory of his dead wife, deaf to his youngest son's cries for help as his brothers paid him back for eight years of their mother's love and their father's careless indulgence.

The sound of Zeth's copper-studded belt sliding free of his trousers closed Asher's teeth on his battered lip. Drew blood. Amid his other brothers' eager encouragement, the first blow fell.

When at last their fury was sated and there was nothing left in the world but torn flesh and pain, they dragged him outside and threw him and his stripped-off clothing into the gutter. It was dusk and Harbourmaster Street was empty.

"From this day on," said Zeth, standing over him, panting down on him, "you be no kin of ours and Restharven ain't your home. Don't look for shelter anywhere else neither, for we'll be bannin' your name up coast and down. Your fishing dreams are over, little man. Go back to the City and your new blond friends. You be not wanted here."

Asher stared up at his hateful, hating brother. Hot words crowded his throat, clamoured for release. *You can't* and *By what right?* and *He were my father too!*

All he could do was moan.

One by one his brothers spat on him to seal the sentence. Then they went back into the Dolphin and slammed the front door behind them.

Floating on a scarlet sea, Asher barely felt the spittle as it trickled through his hair, down his cheeks, between his parted lips.

Da, he cried, though no more sound escaped him. *Da…*

Ages later he sat up beneath a starry sky, inch by painful inch, and pulled on his torn shirt. The weskit was beyond saving so he left it in the gutter. Then, wincing at every step, he dragged himself to the nearest ale house. Sat in a dark corner, ignored by the other patrons who'd gathered to share wild stories and lucky escapes, and spent all his money on glorious cider and beer. Once his purse no longer jingled, the barman pushed him into the street and locked the door behind him.

It was late. So late it was early. He laughed aloud at his own clever wit; the harsh sound bounced off the nearest stone wall, echoing. The streets were deserted. All the windows he could see were dark and cold, no friendly lamplight, no warm waiting welcome. Ah, well. Best he got back to the mayor's house. There was a bed there for him at least. For now. And now was all that mattered. He couldn't think past now. Couldn't think at all.

Weaving his way along the uneven pavement he stopped twice to empty his belly onto the cobblestones. Bending over made his head pound like a galloping herd of horses. After the second heaving he had to sit down for a while. Standing up again was...interestingly difficult. There was pain in him somewhere but all that lovely cider and beer kept it far, far away. He'd need to drink some more soon, to sternly discourage its approach.

After a wrong turn or three he found the servants' entrance to the mayor's house. The door was locked. Of course. He didn't have the strength to knock, so he kicked instead. Bang, bang, bang. Eventually the door creaked open. Maggoty Darran stood there, nostrils all pinched in, eyes slitted and beady. What a welcome. Maybe he could be sick again, all over the ole crow's shoes. Would that make him go away?

"Where in Barl's name have you been?" Darran hissed. "It's the middle of the night! His Highness has been worried sick!"

"Suck on a blowfish and die," he said, and pushed his way into the house. Tripped over something. A chair. Fell down. Oooh. That hurt. Def'nitely he needed another drink.

After a couple of false starts he found his feet again. Bed. He wanted his bed. There was a staircase in front of him. He didn't like staircases. With a grunt, he started upwards. Behind him came Darran, wittering.

"How *dare* you come back here in this condition! After everything His Highness has been through, how dare you insult him in this fashion!"

At the top of the stairs, turn left. No, right. No, left. Along the corridor, what a nice wall, holding him up. If he fell down now he'd never stand again. He needed a bloody *drink*...

"—*disgusting*, that's what you are—"

If he hit Darran, would that shut him up? He'd get into trouble but what did that matter? What did anything matter any more? He swung around, fist clenched. "Shut your trap, you manky ole maggoty man!" he growled. "Shut it afore I shut it for you!"

"How *dare* you!" Darran gasped. "You should be flogged for this!"

He grinned. "Too late."

Darran wasn't listening. "You should—" He swallowed the rest of the sentence. Collected himself, and bowed. "Your Highness."

Asher shuffled round a bit and looked blearily behind him. Gar, tying the belt of his quilted blue dressing-gown as he walked towards them, scrapes and bruises stark on his face, expression grim.

"Hey!" he said, and waved. "Blondie!"

"He's drunk, sir," said Darran.

Gar raised his eyebrows. "No. Really?" Then he sighed. Dragged a hand over his face. "Go to bed, Darran. I'll deal with this." Darran hesitated. Mouth all pruned up. "Go, I said!" Gar snapped, and Darran withdrew.

"Nighty-night!" Asher called after the ole scarecrow.

Gar grabbed him by the shirt front. Shook him. It was a wonder his head didn't fall clean off his shoulders. "Shut up," said Gar. "And come with me."

Stumbling, protesting, he fumbled along the corridor at Gar's heels until they reached the prince's room. Gar opened the door, pushed him inside and closed the door behind them. "You stink of vomit and beer," he said. Curt. Clipped. Eyes and face as hard as a brother's.

Asher shrugged, adrift between the chamber door and the window. "Aye. Well. S'what happens when you spend the night drinkin' ale and pukin'."

"I'm not interested. Get yourself cleaned up and sober. We leave for the City at first light."

"What d'you mean, 'we'? I don't work for you no more, remember?"

"You work for me until I say otherwise."

Asher blinked at him, swaying gently. "Why go back to the City? We only just got here."

There was a muscle leaping along the side of Gar's clenched jaw. "The king is dead."

Asher winced. He really needed another drink. The pain was getting closer and his mouth tasted vile. "How d'you know he's dead? Did Zeth tell you?"

Gar said, "I don't know any Zeth. Now be quiet and listen. We—"

"Cause if Zeth didn't tell you, then—"

Gar shoved him, hard. "I said *be quiet*! What's the matter with you? Didn't you hear me? My father is *dead*!"

That was funny. That was so funny, he had to laugh. "He is? Well, what d'you know? So's mine! You an' me finally got somethin' in common, eh? Aside from the no magic business, I mean. Fancy that."

Gar hit him.

Well. Now he *really* needed another drink. He touched his fingertips to the corner of his mouth. Found blood. Stared at it. Wiped it off on the front of his shirt and headed unsteadily for the door.

"You're not leaving," said Gar.

"Watch me."

As he reached for the door handle Gar pushed him aside, hands flat to his shoulderblades. Pain flared, roared, drove the air from his lungs in an anguished grunt of protest. He fell against the wall, clutching at it to stop himself from falling. Eyes screwed tight shut he pressed his bruised cheek to the pretty wallpaper and waited for the flames to die down.

"What is this?"

Reluctantly he opened his eyes again. Looked at Gar. The prince was staring at his hands. There was blood on them.

"Nowt." He was tired all of a sudden, so terribly tired. "Nothing."

Gar looked at him. "Show me your back."

"No."

"Show me your back or I'll call Darran in here to help me make you!"

And he would, too. Bastard. Wincing, Asher peeled off his once fancy fine silk shirt. Dropped it to the mayor's expensive carpet. Closed his eyes and leaned against the wall for support.

Gar sucked in a quick, sharp breath. "Who did this?"

"Nobody."

"*Asher.*" Gar's voice demanded instant obedience. Ha. "An assault on you is an assault on me. I want his name."

He never should have come back. Not to this house. Not to West-wailing. "Leave it be."

"His name, Asher."

Somehow he opened his eyes. "I fell down."

Gar stared, incredulous. "I don't think so."

"I fell down."

"That's a lie!"

"*I fell down!*"

Infuriated, Gar shoved him a second time. He toppled like a stack of bricks, like the roof tiles on the storm-shattered houses of West-wailing. Landed hard, half on his back, and it hurt so much he started laughing because it was that or cry, and he didn't want to cry.

Gar stood over him, fists clenched. "*This isn't funny!*"

"I know," he said, and hid his face against the floor, and kept on laughing.

The sound of bare heels stamping across the carpet. The door, wrenching open. "Darran? What are you doing out here? I told you to go to bed!"

"I know, sir, I'm sorry, sir. Sir, is everything all right?"

"No. I need a pothecary. Find one, wake him up and bring him to me. Now."

"Yes, sir."

The door, closing again. Thump thump of heels. A slithery swish and a bump as Gar slid down the wall to sit on the floor beside him. A quiet voice. "Your father's dead?"

He stopped laughing. "Aye."

"In the storm?"

"An accident. Eight months ago."

"I'm sorry. How did you—"

"My brothers told me."

"Your *brothers* did this?"

"They blame me."

And they weren't the only ones. *He died screamin' your name.* From somewhere beyond the chamber door, the muffled buzz of voices. Gar said, very quietly, "Your brothers did this..."

The carpet smelled of dust and salt. "This is nowt, I'm shunned, Gar. Zeth and the rest of 'em, they've banned me. No fishing boats for Asher. Not in Restharven. Not anywhere in Lur." And what was the pain in his flesh compared to that?

A sharp intake of breath. Tense silence. Then: "For how long?"

"Forever."

More slithery sounds as Gar shifted against the wall. "Can they do that?"

Not only could, but had. It was done, and by common fisherfolk law not to be undone. "Aye."

"No. It's not right. Fishing's a dangerous life, how many times have you told me that? Whatever misfortune befell your father, Asher, it wasn't your fault. Don't worry. I'll fix this."

In the cavernous coldness within, a small warm flame. "You can't. It's Olken business. Fishermen's business. You'll make no friends stirrin' that pot. Leave it be."

"Even though they beat you half to death?"

"It ain't that bad," he said, lying. "Reckon I've had worse."

"Really?" Gar scoffed. "When?"

He sighed, even though breathing hurt like fire. "Leave it, Gar."

"How can I? Here you are, beaten to a bloody pulp, denied your heritage, the means by which you choose to make your living, exiled from your home...and by your own damned *family*, Asher! *Leave* it? How can I possibly do that?"

"Because I'm asking you to."

Gar muttered something under his breath. He sounded angry. Resentful. "I don't like it."

"You don't have to."

Silence. "Well..." Gar's voice was laced with doubt. "If you're sure."

"Damned sure."

"In that case...what will you do now?"

Stay curled up on the floor forever and ever. Drag his sorry carcase to another alehouse and drown it in an ocean of alcohol. Find a Doranen magician to turn back time so none of the past year had ever happened. So Jed wasn't a drooling gapwit and Da was still alive.

"I don't know," he said roughly, swallowing tears.

Another silence. Then: "I really do have to leave at first light. Her Majesty will need me."

"Aye."

"I'll take Mishin with me. Or Fitch."

"You'll take me."

"Asher, you can't—"

With a grunt and a groan he rolled over. Sat up, teeth gritted. "You'll take me," he said again with all the force he could muster. He sounded like a half-drowned cat, mewling.

Gar was shaking his head. "You're out of your mind. *Look* at yourself. You *can't* ride all the way back to Dor—"

Despite the pain he reached out and grabbed a handful of Gar's dressing-gown. Bunched it in his fist and shook as hard as the dregs of his strength allowed. "*I have to!*" he said raggedly. "*I can't stay here!*" Perilously close to breaking, to begging, he loosened his fingers and let his hand fall. "I can't stay here."

Gar hesitated. Nodded. "All right. All right, you can come. Provided the pothecary says you're fit."

"Sink the pothecary. I'm fine."

Gar sighed. Shook his head. "Of course you are." Then added, hesitantly, "You don't have to stay in the City afterwards. Not if you don't want to. I gave you my word you could leave my service after a year and of course I'll keep it. I'm sorry I was so angry before. It was unjust." He frowned. "Unprincely."

If he leaned against the wall his back would burst into flames. Pulling up one knee, he rested his aching head. "No. You were right. I should've said something. Anyway. It don't matter now." He sounded bitter. He couldn't help it, and didn't much care.

"You are welcome to stay, of course," Gar said, abruptly formal. "I still need an Assistant Olken Administrator. If you stayed it would save me a lot of work, showing someone else the ropes."

Face hidden, Asher smiled, a sarcastic twist of lip. *If* he stayed? What choice did he have now but to stay? Where else was there for him to go? He couldn't be a fisherman any more. Assistant Olken Administrator was the only work he was fit for now. A dry life the only one that wanted him.

He lifted his head. "I'll stay. You're mad if you think you'll find anybody else to put up with Darran and Willer."

Gar made a small sound of amusement. "Probably that's an exaggeration but...good. I'm glad."

With a groan Asher let his head drop again. If he didn't get another drink soon he'd have to start climbing the walls. He glanced at Gar. Saw trenched hollows beneath his eyes, the scouring grief within them.

"You're sure about the king?"

Gar nodded, bleakly. "I'm sure."

When, exactly, did a body fill up with so much pain it couldn't feel any more?

Soon, he hoped.

Gar looked...destroyed. He should say something, but the words wouldn't come. And then the door opened and manky ole Darran bustled in with the pothecary. After that the only pain that mattered was the clean, physical kind.

A pity it wasn't likely to stay that way.

Scant hours later, in the cold dawn of the mayor's stable yard, drugged and dour in the saddle, Asher waited as Darran flapped and fuddled over Gar.

"Oh, sir, I do wish you wouldn't do this!"

Gar frowned. "So you've said. And said. Don't say it again."

Darran's lips pressed tight. "No, sir." He looked like he wanted to scream.

Asher knew the feeling.

"You've plenty of coin in your saddlebag, sir," Darran continued. "And as much bread and cheese and sausage as I could pack." He chewed his lip for a moment. Turned abruptly and glared at Asher. "Make sure he sleeps in a decent bed every night, you. Not rough under a hedge by the side of the road or in an open field. You're to look after him, do you hear?"

Asher didn't have the energy to bite. "Aye."

Willer, lurking behind Darran, glared daggers through puffy, bloodshot eyes. Spite and thwarted triumph roiled in him like snakes in a vat of rancid oil. Asher looked away, biting the inside of his cheek. Willer's bitter disappointment was the only good thing about his forced return to Dorana.

Gar hissed through his teeth, impatient. "Thank you, Darran. Asher knows his duty...and so do you. Remember, you are my voice here now. Speak softly and with charity to all."

Darran nodded unhappily. "Yes, sir. Safe journey, Your Highness. And my..." He flicked a glance at the mayor and his wife, huddled inside their best coats, blinking bleary eyes at the sunrise, "...regards, to Her Majesty."

"Yes." Gar turned to his hosts. "My thanks to you and your good lady, Mr. Mayor. I regret that I'm forced to take my leave in such an unseemly fashion."

The mayor bowed. "Aye, Your Highness."

"If there's anything you need, *anything*, don't hesitate to tell Darran. He'll provide it."

"Thank you, Your Highness."

With a final nod at his secretary, Gar nudged Ballodair over to Cygnet. Lowered his voice. "You can do this?"

Asher nodded. Gar's saddlebags may be bulging with food but his own were crammed with little pills and potions from the pothecary. "Aye."

Still Gar stared at him. "I won't spare you."

"I never asked you to."

"I can't," said Gar, anguished. Uncertain. "If the ride is more than you can manage—"

"It won't be."

"But if it *is*..."

Asher glanced at the nearby treetops, tipped with light. "Sun's almost up. Are we leavin' or ain't we?"

Side by side they wheeled their horses round and started the long journey back to Dorana.

They followed the wreckage-strewn path of the storm.

If Gar had any opinions regarding the gouged earth and splintered trees, the flattened crops, the houses peeled like oranges, he didn't share them. Nor did he offer aid or comfort to the grieving Olken they encountered as they rode. He stopped only when necessary: to drink, eat, piss or rest the horses. As far as Asher could tell, nobody recognised them. The prince wore plain brown leathers and a hood. With his bright head covered, from a distance he'd easily be mistaken for Olken, like Asher.

As the sun slid up the sky then down again the miles unrolled behind them. Mindful of all the miles still waiting, Asher hoarded his treasure of pills and potions and accustomed himself to pain.

They were stranded between villages when at last Gar was forced to admit it was time to stop riding. The sun had set and the moon was a remote sliver of light, high and to the west. They halted and considered their choices.

Squinting in the dark, Asher pointed. "There's a barn still standin'."

"That'll do," said Gar. Turning Ballodair's head he kicked the weary horse into a walk. "I won't tell Darran if you don't."

There were rats in the straw and holes in the roof but it was better than nothing. After unsaddling the horses and leaving them to eat a mean double-handful of oats each, they sat in the dark and devoured their own meagre dinner of sausage and cheese. They had candles and a flint box but didn't dare use them.

"You all right?" asked Gar for the first time since leaving West-wailing.

Asher started to shrug, then stopped. "I'll manage."

Rustling and dust as Gar shaped straw into a makeshift mattress and pillow and lay down. "Barring disaster," he said, stifling a sneeze, "I think we might reach Dorana inside a week."

"Aye. Barring disaster. We want to watch the horses, though. Matt'll never speak to us again if we founder 'em."

"I know."

Asher rummaged in his saddlebag, found one of the pother's vials and drank its foul contents, grimacing. After a few moments the raging fire in his flesh faded to a warm glow. Praise Barl. With a sigh of relief he eased himself onto his side and pulled his saddle a little closer for a pillow.

He was so tired he could see purple blotches dancing in the air in front of his face, even without candles. He closed his eyes. One by one, protesting, his muscles relaxed. Sleep beckoned.

In the darkness Gar said softly, "I was five when Durm confirmed what had long been suspected. When I learned I was...what I am. Once the first shock wore off I lived in daily fear that my father would no longer love me. I thought I might be farmed out somewhere, perhaps to an Olken family where lack of magic didn't matter. I don't know why I thought that. Children have strange fancies, I suppose. Even at that young age I knew I meant trouble for my parents. Maybe even for the kingdom. Unlike other Doranen families I knew that kings and queens were allowed only one child, one heir...and that my father's precious legacy had been squandered on a magickless cripple."

"Sounds daft to me," Asher said drowsily. "Reckon there should be an heir and a spare, at least."

"You're forgetting your history. Trevoyle's Schism. This kingdom was nearly destroyed by brothers and sisters fighting for the right to be named WeatherWorker."

"Didn't anyone think of drawin' straws?"

A breath of brief, wry amusement. "Three months after my true nature was revealed my father took me riding. It was a great treat. He'd been so busy of late, so troubled. I'd heard raised voices. Crying. Somehow I knew it was because of me. We rode for, oh, ages, until we were quite alone, right at the foothills of the mountains. There we stopped and he told me Barl was giving me a sister. I was confused. I thought I wasn't allowed a sister because of who we were. He said I needn't worry about that. All I had to do, he said, was be my new sister's big brother. It was a very important job. I had to love her and take care of her and help her to one day become the greatest WeatherWorker in the history of Lur."

Asher grunted. "Lucky you."

"I remember my father leaned down from his horse, cupped my face in his hands and kissed my forehead. There were tears in his eyes. On his cheeks. He said, 'I will always love you, Gar. I don't know why you were born without magic but I know there must be a reason. Barl has a destiny for you, my son. In my heart I know this is true. All we need is patience, until it's revealed.'"

"Did you believe him?"

"I believe he loved me."

"And what about the destiny thing? Don't s'pose Barl's dropped any hints, has she?"

"He was a father trying to ease his child's pain. What do you think?" Gar said roughly. Then, whispering: "Blessed Barl save me. He's gone, he's gone... and I don't know how to bear it..."

Outside the barn a hunting owl shrieked. The horses lifted their heads and shuffled the straw uneasily. Further away a fox barked. Barked again. Another fox answered it.

I don't know either, thought Asher, but didn't say it. There was no point. Frowning, he felt memory rise like a mist, blotting out the present. Smothering him in the past. "The only time I saw my da cry was the day we buried Ma," he said, almost to himself. "It was a bad day. Not rainin', just a cold, miserable, mizzly drizzle blowin' in from beyond the reef. After they put her in the ground and said what was needed, folks went home. My brothers went home. But Da stayed. Sat in the dirt beside the hole that swallowed her and said her name, over and over. Amaranda. Amaranda. His face was wet. I told myself it was the drizzle but deep down I knew different. I knew it was tears."

"How old were you?"

"Eight, just gone. A spratling. When he wouldn't get up I sat beside 'im. He put his arm around me, which didn't happen often. I said, 'Don't be sad, Da. We'll be right. One day when I be a man growed, and rich, I'll buy us a boat, and we'll call her *Amaranda*. Paint her green and blue, Ma's favourite colours. And nobody but us'll be allowed to sail her. Zeth and the others, we won't let 'em so much as look at her. That boat'll be just for us. I promise. You and me, Da. Together and laughin', eh? You and me.'"

In the soft silence Gar sighed. "I am sorry. About your father. And your friend, too, what was his name—"

Asher felt his fingers close around fistfuls of old straw. He'd wanted to find him, see him cared for, but there'd been no time. "Jed."

"Yes. Jed. Look... Asher..." Now the prince sounded hesitant. "You must realise, you *must*, none of what happened is your—"

"I know," he said, hard and fast. To shut Gar up, not because he believed it. "Now I reckon that's enough talkin' for one night. We ought to be savin' our strength for tomorrow, and the day after, and the day after that. We got a long road ahead of us with nowt but heartache at the end of it. So if it's all the same to you I'll go to sleep now. You'd be smart to do the same."

He thought Gar might argue, but he was answered with silence. After a time the prince's breathing slowed and deepened. Hours later he said his father's name but didn't wake.

Eventually Asher escaped into sleep himself... and dreamed.

Dawn didn't come soon enough.

CHAPTER TWENTY-THREE

"Well?" Matt leaned over Dathne's shoulder. "Have you got him?" She pushed him back with a crooked elbow. "Don't crowd me. And be quiet. I need to concentrate."

Beyond her living-room window dusk softened the edges of the City. If only it could soften her too. Flinty, she felt, and rough, like scratched glass. Five days since the storm and still she'd not managed to find Asher in her scrying basin. Twenty times at least she'd tried, tried till her head throbbed to splitting with too much tanal leaf. No luck. First it was the leftover effects of the catastrophic weather, and after that the waves and waves of Doranen magic flowing in and over and round the City as all efforts were made to repair the damage done by wind and water and heaving earth. Even her precious Circle Stone had been affected. She'd finally reached Veira that morning, a quick brush of mind to mind to make sure the old woman was safe. To assure her that she and Matt had escaped calamity unscathed.

Well. Mostly unscathed. Matt still grieved for Bellybone and the dead colt. There was nothing she could do about that, though, so she kept herself focused on what she could do. Find Asher. Confirm that he was safe too, and returning to the City where he belonged. Where Prophecy needed him.

Where she needed him.

"Come on, Dath," said Matt, fretting. "Get on with it. I've got to get back to the yard. There's poultices and dressings to change. Willem's a good lad but he's not quite ready for that on his own just yet."

She swallowed curses. "You were going to stay for dinner. We've not talked decently since the storm, Matt, there's things we must—"

He turned away from her. "I can't. Maybe tomorrow."

"Tomorrow?" she echoed, temper rising. "Are you mad? Look around you, Matt! Think of what's happened! The storm—the king—what do you think is going on? What do you think it all *means*?"

He'd lost weight these last days. His eyes were hollow, his cheeks sunken. The scrapes on his skin had healed but the wounds to his spirit, his soul, still pained him. There was doubt in him now, where once there'd been only blind, stubborn faith.

"I don't know what it means," he said. "All I know is if everything you've seen in your visions is true, Dathne, then this storm was nothing, *nothing*, compared to what's coming. And this storm shook us like a cat with a mouse. Folk *died*, Dath. Children died. And what did we do about it? What could we do? *Nothing*."

"It's not our job to do, Matt! You know that. Our job is to watch. Wait. Follow Prophecy and guide Asher. *He's* the one born for the doing of great things. Not us."

Trembling, he flung himself away from her and paced the room. "Then *find* him, would you? Stop lecturing me and bloody *find* him, Dath! Make sure he ain't dead or broken to pieces in a ditch somewhere! Because if he is—if that's what's happened to him—"

The effort nearly choked her but she held her tongue. Lashing out at Matt would be too easy, not just thanks to the excess of tanal leaf but because he was giving a voice to her own doubts, her own fears, and she didn't want to hear them spoken aloud. In case speaking them made them come true. Lashing out might make her feel better, if only for a moment, but it would hurt him. Hurt them. Their oathsworn bond, and their friendship. The mood she was in, it would be so simple. Undoing the damage would be far more complicated and they didn't have the time.

So instead of shouting back at him, instead of stamping her foot and slapping him, she gentled herself. Went to him and rested her hand on his arm. "Dear Matt. Don't you think I'd know if he were dead? Don't you think Prophecy would've told me?"

His eyes were stark. "Would it? I don't know. Seems to me there's a lot going on that Prophecy's not talkin' about."

Her fingers closed on his shirt sleeve and shook him. "He's not dead," she said fiercely. "Come. Sit down. Hold your tongue. Let me work and I'll prove it to you."

She tugged him towards the table. With a stifled groan he dropped into a chair. She sat beside him, smiled at him briefly then took another pinch of tanal. Chewed it, spat it out and began again the ritual to open her mind, send it winging through the world in search of her heart's desire.

This time she found it.

Asher rode into the sinking shadows, towards the towering might of the Wall. All around him the countryside was laid to waste. Trees felled. Crops ruined. Grim endurance was in his face and the way he sat his stumbling horse. The set of his slumping shoulders and the bloodless hold he had on the reins.

Dreamily, held deep within the tanal's insinuating grasp, she took Matt's hand and pressed his fingers with her own. "He's coming," she murmured. "I see him."

"Praise Barl," said Matt, his voice unsteady. "He's all right, then?"

No. There was pain. In the muscle and the mind. The heartbreak she'd foreseen for him had struck deep. She could feel it. But it didn't matter. Nothing mattered save that Prophecy was served once more.

Asher was coming home.

She stirred the basin's water. Broke the link. "Yes. He's fine."

Sitting back, Matt dragged one hand over his face, breathing heavily. "Praise Barl." He looked at her. "Praise Prophecy." His expression altered. "Dath..."

"It's all right," she said. "I was nervous too. I think we'd be fools not to be. These are nervous times, Matt. A kingdom's at stake."

He nodded slowly. "Nervous. Aye."

She started rolling up her diminished pouch of tanal leaf. "He's not so far away. They've travelled fast. Tomorrow night, maybe, or early the morning after that, will see them in the City."

"They?"

She frowned. "The prince is with him." Impatiently she shook herself free of the melancholy she'd felt from both men resonating through the scrying spell. "So, you can rest easy now. Go, if you're going. See to your precious poultices. I'll call if I need you." Reaching across, she tugged at the small calling stone on its leather thong around his neck. "And if I call, come. I worry when you don't answer me. Ignore me again and I'll tell tales on you to Veira, I swear."

He had the good grace to flush. As well he should. Twice since the storm she'd used the crystal to signal she needed him, and twice he'd put his precious damned horses before her.

"I will," he promised. "Dathne..." His hand rested on her shoulder. "You look so tired."

And so she was. Tired, and more than tired. Her recent days had been spent fixing the bookshop, helping neighbours, and her nights were twisted with dreams. Not Prophecy, not precisely. Just dark forebodings and uneasy intuitions, riding her hard till morning dragged harsh fingers across her face and she woke, bathed in pale yellow sunshine and sweat.

"I'll stay," said Matt. "You're right. The horses won't die for lack of a poultice. I'll stay and make us soup and we can talk, Dathne. All right?"

Perversely, it wasn't all right. With the last lingering tartness of the tanal on her tongue, her sight just tinged with its golden potency, all she wanted now was to be left alone. To slide between cool sheets in the rose-scented darkness of her bedroom and surrender to sleep.

With luck, she wouldn't dream tonight.

She shook her head. "No. You go. There'll come a time soon when you'll need to leave the horses behind without a second thought. Don't abandon them till you have to. I'll be fine."

His callused hand moved from her shoulder to her cheek. Rested there. "You're sure?"

She stood and moved away from the table. Towards the door. Hinting. "When have you ever known me not sure?"

He laughed, as she'd intended. Collected his coat from the arm of her dilapidated couch then paused in the open doorway. "I'll stay around the stables and call the minute he gets back."

"Good," she said, and closed the door firmly behind him.

Blessedly alone, she stripped off her skirt and blouse and underthings and bathed in a basin of warm water. Then she fell into bed, too weary for even one page of a book. Blew out the candle. Sank into sleep.

And dreamed.

"Look!" said Gar, and lifted an unsteady hand to point. "Dorana."

Anchored to his saddle by habit and exhaustion, Asher blinked groggily and squinted into the distance. Everything looked bleary and his head hurt. Ha! His head? His head, his back, his legs, his toenails... "Where?"

"There! See it? That glittering beyond those far trees? It's the sun setting on the palace windows. We're nearly home, praise Barl. Just a few more miles."

"Aye," said Asher, and dragged a filthy sleeve across his dirty, unshaven face. "Good." For him, any road. Gar was nearly home. As for himself...

But it was the City, right enough. And about bloody time too. The muddy track they travelled now linked with the great City Road, and that would lead them all the way to the main gates. And through Dorana. And up to the palace, and the Tower, where he'd have to sleep tonight and tomorrow night and the next and—

His blistered fingers tightened on Cygnet's reins; the horse half raised his head, grunting. Poor beast. He was exhausted too. Matt would be furious when he saw how much condition his precious animals had lost. They'd need a week at least of stable rest, and all the grain and mash they could eat, after the punishing ride from Westwailing.

Come to think of it, he could do with a bit of that himself.

"Let's trot a bit," said Gar, his pale voice humming with tension. He looked rough as guts too. Dark gold stubble sandpapered his cheeks and chin. His bloodshot eyes had sunk into their sockets and his dirty hair hung limp and lank. If Darran could see him now he'd most likely faint.

"Trot?" Asher groaned. "Barl bloody save me. Do we have to? My damn spine's near to jolted through the top of my skull."

"And you think mine isn't?" snapped Gar, glaring. "Come on. We can try, at least. If we can I want to—" He stopped, coughing like a man with lungrot. The fit passed eventually, leaving him milk-white and gasping. Waving away Asher's concern he pressed his fingers to his eyes, hard, then let his hand drop. "I'm all right." Glancing at Asher, he frowned. "Which is more than I can say for you. You look worse than I feel, if that's possible. You shouldn't have come. I was mad to let you talk me into it."

"I'm fine," said Asher, then laughed, unamused, because it was such a lie, and he knew it, and Gar knew it, and truly, what was the point? "Don't fret on it. Like you say, this mad ride were my decision, not yours. Besides, what good would not comin' have done me? If I'd stayed behind I'd have killed that ole Darran by now. Or if not him, then def'nitely bloody Willer. And anyway, I've got nowhere else to go, have I?"

The words scalded, bitter as bile. Damn. He'd never meant to say that out loud. Gar's expression was shocked. Hurt. Bewildered.

"What do you mean?"

"Nowt. Nothing. Forget I said it," Asher replied, inwardly cursing. "I'm tired, is all. Not thinkin' straight. And that bloody pother's pills and potions ran out two days ago. You want to trot? We'll trot."

Gar bullied his horse forward, blocking the path. "I thought I made it clear to you, Asher, I wasn't forcing you back here. I *offered* to fix—"

"I know!" said Asher, raising his voice. "It's all right. I didn't mean it. I don't mind comin' back to Dorana. If I can't have the coast, it's as good a place as any to—"

Gar wasn't listening. "You saved my *life*, Asher! Do you think I'd repay that by making you do anything you didn't want to? Is that the kind of man you think I am?"

"Of course it ain't, you bloody fool."

"You saved my life," Gar repeated, and this time it was a whisper. In his scratched and dirty face a memory of wild water, and drowning. "Barl forgive me. Can you believe I *forgot*..."

Asher heaved a sigh. "Don't fret on it. Reckon you've had a bit on your mind this last little while."

The uncertainty in Gar's face hardened into resolve. Reaching out he clasped Asher's shoulder, his fingers like a vice. "I can never fully repay you. But if ever you're in need, come to me. Ask, and no matter the favour it will be granted. My word as a prince."

Embarrassed, Asher looked away. "Aye, well..."

Gar's fingers tightened to the point of pain. "I mean it."

Asher looked back again. Nodded. "I know. I'll remember. Now if it's all the same to you, can we get on? I'm halfway desperate for a beer and a bath. And Her Majesty must be lookin' out every window for you by now."

Gar released his grip. Backed Ballodair up a pace and dragged the horse's head round till they were facing the City again. "Yes," he said flatly. "You're right. The queen will be waiting."

They stirred the reluctant horses with their spurs and jogged along in silence, too tired to talk further, too full of separate griefs that couldn't be eased with sharing. Rounding a bend in the track they joined the City Road. It crossed open countryside, and the great storm's passage was less evident here. In the distance ahead was the City itself, somnolent in the sinking sunshine.

On they jogged, bringing Dorana closer stride by stride. They travelled the road alone.

After a time they could make out the City walls. They looked intact. So did the enormous City gates, standing wide in welcome. "Reckon the storm left Dorana alone?" asked Asher, shading his eyes and staring. Cygnet dropped into an ambling walk. He didn't have the heart to spur the horse again. Beside him, Gar loosened his reins and let Ballodair follow suit.

"Unlikely. Durm would have organised a Working. Teams of mages to repair the damage. However bad it was in there, I expect it's all back to normal by now."

The City, maybe, but nothing else. With the poor king dead there'd be a new WeatherWorker. Queen Fane. And that was like to make life very, very interesting indeed...

Asher scowled at Cygnet's ears. He'd never asked for interesting. He'd never asked for much at all, really. Just some money, and a boat, and a little peace and quiet. And yet it seemed as though he'd asked for more than fate thought right to give him.

It wasn't bloody fair.

Gar said, "Without wishing for another argument, I want to say this. Once we know how things stand in Dorana, once...the new order has been established, I think you should take some time to consider your future. I don't want you to feel obliged to continue in my service. You've come a long way from the fisherman turned stable hand I hired a year ago, Asher. I should think you could do anything you wanted now."

Oh, aye. Of course he could. Anything except the only thing that had ever truly mattered. He glanced at Gar sideways. "What did you have in mind?"

Gar's lips quirked in the smallest of smiles. "Oh, I don't know. Perhaps Dathne needs an errand boy in her bookshop."

Asher's stomach clenched. *Dathne.* Damn Gar. He'd been working so hard at not thinking about Dathne.

"I wasn't imagining things, was I?" Gar continued. "You and she—"

"We're friends," he said flatly. "At least we were. Then I left. I ain't sure what we are now."

"You parted badly?"

Asher sighed. "We parted."

"I like Dathne," Gar said thoughtfully. "She's an uncommon woman. Too good for you really. Take my advice, Asher, and as soon as you can seek her out and ask her—hold on. What's that?"

It was a carriage, flying recklessly towards them. The sound of hooves pounding the hard road carried clearly on the cooling evening air, and the snap of the whip as the driver cracked it over the backs of the galloping horses.

Despite their bone-deep weariness Cygnet and Ballodair broke into a sidling, head-tossing jog. Exchanging looks, Asher and Gar urged them on. The carriage came closer, closer, and they could see it was an open touring model, and that there were two people in the back behind the reinsman. Closer still and the carriage's passengers were on their feet, standing, a dangerous thing to do in a speeding vehicle, holding each other tight and waving. Shouting. Closer again, and they could see that one of the passengers was the queen, was Dana, her long blonde hair streaming behind her, and the other—the other—

"In Barl's blessed name..." Gar whispered. He dropped his reins, forgetting entirely to kiss his holyring, and swayed in the saddle. Trained to a hair's-breadth Ballodair skidded to a halt. Asher stopped beside him and stretched out a steadying hand. Heedless, Gar sat and stared as though turned to stone.

The carriage was slowing, Coachman Matcher leaning back and

hauling on his lines, shouting at the horses to whoa, whoa. Before it stopped scant feet away the passenger door flew open.

"Papa?" Gar cried, and slithered to the ground. "Papa! *Papa!*"

They ran to each other, father and son. The king was staggering; not strong, but desperate. They collided. Embraced with abandon, laughing, weeping. They pounded each other's shoulders and touched each other's cheeks with trembling fingers. Their joy was incandescent.

Silent as death, Asher watched the ecstatic reunion.

"Where's Da, Zeth? I want to see him."

"Why, he's right where you put 'im, Asher dear. Deep in the cold dark ground."

Stumbling in her haste, the queen joined her husband and their son. Three people tangled into one, and they all cried togther.

Time passed. At length the king, the queen and the prince disentangled themselves and, still exclaiming, walked to the carriage. Climbed inside. Closed the passenger door. Matcher clicked his tongue and picked up his whip. The carriage turned around and the horses, encouraged, broke into a spanking trot. Its passengers continued to hug and hold and never once looked back.

Asher watched them go. Leaned over and picked up Ballodair's abandoned reins. "Come up then, boys," he said, and nudged Cygnet into a reluctant walk. Ears pinned flat to his head, eyes rolling and mouth agape as he leaned against his bridle, rebellious, Ballodair followed.

Together they travelled in the carriage's wake all the way back to the City.

PART THREE

CHAPTER TWENTY-FOUR

By the time Asher finally made it back to the Tower stable yard, it was dark.

The royal carriage had swiftly left him and the horses behind. Suddenly unable to face the City and the welcome he knew he'd receive from its citizens, he decided to ride the long way round to the Tower. Even though he was tired almost beyond bearing and his body hurt so badly the thought of one jolting step more than strictly necessary was a torment. Even though he was freezing cold and dripping sweat at the same time.

Halfway around the City wall's fat circumference he stumbled across Pellen Orrick, who was inspecting the joins between the huge blocks of stone with a lamp strung on the end of a long pole. Dorana's Captain of the City Guard looked immaculate, as usual, but grim and tired around the eyes. There was a smudge of dirt on his cheek and half-healed scrapes on his knuckles.

"Meister Assistant Administrator," Orrick said, and raised his eyebrows. "Welcome back. You look somewhat the worse for wear, if I may say so."

"Only 'cause I am, Captain. What're you doin'?"

"Looking for cracks. The wall's been mended thrice over and passed sound by the Master Magician and Lord Jarralt, but I like to be thorough. So, if you're back, and leading Ballodair, can I take it the prince has also returned?"

Asher nodded. "Aye." He stared at the City's stone wall, because it was better than meeting Pellen Orrick's sharp, considering gaze. "The storm do much damage here, then?"

"Enough."

"Any deaths? Injuries?"

"Too many."

"And are the people behaving 'emselves? Namin' no names, I can think of one or two as might see in all this woe and wail a chance to line their own pockets with somebody else's misfortune. Certain tradesfolk, for instance."

"The same thought had occurred to me," said Orrick, an appreciative glimmer in his dark eyes. "Don't fret. I've my eye on one or two... opportunists. Naming no names, of course."

"Good," said Asher. "So there be nowt I need to take care of straightaway?"

Orrick shook his head. "Not straightaway. I've a report on its way to the Tower for you, as it happens. It can wait a day or two, before we meet on it."

"Can it wait a week?" said Asher hopefully.

"Perhaps," said Orrick, smiling. "Now ride on, Meister Assistant. It's an offence to interfere with a guardsman doing his duty, you know."

"Y'don't say," said Asher. "Fancy that." With a gentle kick and a tug on the reins he urged Cygnet and Ballodair into a shambling walk and kept on riding. After three strides he turned his head, just a little, and added over his shoulder, "Glad to see you're all right, Captain."

Orrick's laughter was soft in the descending dusk. "And the same to you, Asher. The same to you."

Cheered, Asher continued the long way round and entered Dorana through the private royal gate high up behind the palace. The startled guards waved him through; he lifted a hand to them, nodding, but didn't dawdle. The horses picked their way along the bridlepaths and in between the flowerbeds by starlight and the Wall's golden glow, heads drooping almost to their knees. Ballodair still dragged sullenly against his bridle, so that Asher thought his arm must soon pull free from his shoulder.

An energetic chorus of whinnies greeted their plodding entrance into the Tower stable yard. A few of the lads tumbled downstairs from their dormitory to see what all the fuss was about. Matt, who was sitting on an upturned bucket mending a head collar by lamplight, leapt to his feet. Leather, needle and waxed thread fell unheeded to the ground.

"Barl save us," he breathed, coming forward to stare at the filthy, overwrought horses. "Asher, what have you *done* to them?" A wave of his hand brought a gaping lad over. "Duffy, take Ballodair. Into his stable with him, quick, and mind you handle him gently. You know what to do."

As Duffy obeyed, still gaping, Asher wriggled his fingers in greeting. "Hey, Matt."

Matt swore. His hand rested on Cygnet's trembling shoulder, soothing, stroking. "*Damn* it, Asher. Get off that bloody horse now, before you fall off."

It was an enticing notion. He'd had enough of saddles and horses to last a lifetime. But the ground looked a long way down. He wasn't sure he could reach it safely. The last of his strength had drained away; the stables, the whispering lads, the pools of lamplight and Matt's frowning face all blurred together. The world faded.

"*Asher*!"

He dragged his eyelids open. "I'm right here," he muttered. "Don't shout."

"Where's the prince?"

"Up at the palace, I s'pose." Asher's eyes drifted shut again. "King and queen met us in a carriage, on the road. He went with them."

Matt snapped his fingers at the nearest lad. "Mikel! Off to the Goose with you and bring back a jug of strong cider. On my chit, tell Derrig. Now! Run!" The lad bolted, and Matt came closer. Punched Asher's knee with a light fist. "Reckon the horses aren't the only ones pushed over the line. Can you get down all right?"

The rough, kind voice was almost his undoing. "Course I can!" he growled. "What d'you take me for, some namby-pamby City Doranen?" Leaning forward, swallowing a groan, he half slithered, half fell out of the saddle. Only Matt's strong arm saved him from humiliation.

"Steady now," his friend said. "I've got you."

On a shuddering, indrawn breath, he managed to straighten. Stared after poor footsore Cygnet as Jim'l led him away. "Sorry about the horses, Matt. We thought the king was dead."

Matt pulled a face. "You weren't the only ones."

"We rode back as fast as we could. Cross-country nearly all the way."

"The storm reached all the way down to the coast?"

"Damn near flattened Westwailing. We were out on the harbour when it hit. Gar almost—" He shook his head. Flaming thunderbolts. Scarlet lightning. Waves towering overhead and the boat standing on end. Gar smashed over the side into the raging ocean. Another memory he wanted no truck with. Not for a good long while, any road.

Matt's fingers tightened on his shoulder. "What is it? What happened?"

"Nothing. It don't matter. Matt..." He could feel his knees shake, threatening to buckle. "Reckon I need to sit down."

"Lie down, more like," said Matt, snorting. He slid his arm around Asher's back. "Let's get you—"

No, no, no. That wasn't going to work. Pain streaked his vision blood red. "I can walk," he gasped and managed, just, to pull free.

"There's a cot in the yard office," said Matt, one hand hovering. "We had a horse or two hurt in the worst of it."

He rolled his eyes. "Nursemaid Matt. Horses all right?"

"They will be. Are you walking or talking?"

He took a tentative step forward. "I can do both."

"Maybe, but do you have to?"

The short distance to the office felt almost as long as the ride from Westwailing. Matt shadowed him every inch. Sent the remaining lads back about their business with a barked command. Opened the office door for him and guided him to the cot.

"You had it bad up here too?" he asked as he lowered his abused and shrieking body to the rough bed. Laid his head on a pillow for the first time in days, and closed his eyes. The glory of it stole his breath.

"Bad enough," Matt's voice said above him. He hesitated. "Dathne's fine...if you were wondering."

He prised his eyelids open. Was he wondering? No. Maybe. "What about you?"

Matt shrugged. "I'm fine too. Glad you're back."

He wasn't. "And the king's all right then, is he? Not dead, I saw that, but—"

"There was some kind of crisis. That fever. Word is he's well on the mend now. Asher, did you know there's blood on your shirt?"

"I'll survive."

"That's not what I asked." Matt turned away, opened a cupboard and took out a stoppered clay pot of something that smelled potent. "This'll do till we can get Pother Nix to see you."

He groaned. "I don't need that ole bone-botherer fussin' and fartin' all over me."

"Didn't ask you that either," said Matt. "Just hold your tongue for once, if you can, and let somebody help you."

"Nursemaid bloody Matt," Asher muttered, then hissed as Matt pulled his shirt up.

"Well," said Matt eventually, after a humming silence. "Good thing I made up a new batch of ointment, ain't it?"

The first touch of the salve on his wounds had him gasping. Face pressed into the dark anonymity of the pillow, hands fisted by his sides, Asher chewed his lip bloody as Matt's gentle fingers woke fire in his battered flesh. Then, mercifully, the burning faded and instead there was blessed numbness.

Dimly he heard the office door open. Heard Matt say, softly, "Well done, Mikel. Put it on the table there and close the door behind you. Tell Duff and Jim'l I'll be out directly to check on those horses."

The quiet thunk of a stone jug on wood. The door closing again. A sloshing sound as liquid was poured from the jug into something smaller. Then Matt was helping him up. "Drink this." He pressed a mug into his hand. "Derrig's best."

The cold cider slid easily down his dry throat, welcome as a lover's kiss. He emptied the mug in two swallows. Emptied it again. And again. Then he lowered his head to the pillow once more. Was aware, just, of a thin blanket settling over him. Of Matt, staring down at him. Of the yard office receding like a wave from the shore.

He let the waters close over his head and surrendered to sleep.

Two hours later, startled by a sound, Matt looked up from his sleepy vigil in the office to see Gar standing in the open doorway. The prince looked as tired as Asher. Fading bruises marked his face. Some cuts and scratches. Shadows under his eyes.

He stood. "Sorry, Your Highness, I didn't—"

Gar held up his hand and moved to the cot. "It's all right." He was whispering. "How is he?"

Matt shrugged. "I've doctored him as best I can, sir, but it's Pother Nix he's needing."

Gar was frowning down at Asher. "He'll have him. Did he tell you what happened?"

"No, sir."

Gar told him. Briefly. Brutally. "From the day he got here he was planning his triumphant return to Restharven. Imagining his father's pleasure. Daydreaming the boat they'd sail together. And for the last eight months..."

Wrung with horrified sympathy, Matt stared at his sleeping friend. "Damn. Sir."

The prince's expression was cool. Guarded. "So long as his brothers live he can never go back to the coast."

Damn. This was what Dathne had foreseen then, when she said so confidently that Asher would return. Not for the first time he felt relief that he was not Jervale's Heir, cursed with foresight and Prophecy.

The prince said, "How are the horses?"

Anger and duty warred. Duty won, just. "They'll do, sir. In time."

Gar wasn't fooled. "I'd have spared them if I could, Matt." He nodded at the cot, where Asher lay on his stomach like a corpse. "I'd have spared him, too."

"Yes, sir."

"He can't stay here."

"I know, sir. I'll see him safe to his own bed once he wakes."

Gar considered him. "You're a good man, Matt. A good friend."

The words twisted his guts like a knife. "I try to be, sir."

"He'll need his friends, I think, in the next little while. He's lost his whole family." The prince shuddered. "I can't imagine..."

"No, sir," said Matt. Then added, hesitantly, "Sir, if you don't mind me saying so, you should be in bed too. You've ridden as far and as hard as Asher. If you want the truth of it, you look fair worn out."

Gar smiled. "Do I?" Stirring, he turned. "I suppose you're right. Show me the horses, quickly, and I'll be on my way."

After the prince had seen his Ballodair, and Cygnet too, fed them carrots and petted them, he left the quiet stable yard. Matt watched him go, then hesitated. He'd thought to wait till morning to tell Dathne of Asher's return. There'd seemed little point in summoning her to the stables at night-time only to show her his sleeping body. But now...

His calling stone lay hidden in his pocket, twin to the one Dathne carried. Closing his fingers hard around the small crystal he opened the link between them. Sought her fierce, unquiet mind with his and whispered her name.

Half an hour later she arrived, crackling with excitement. He met her under the stable yard archway. "Where is he?" she demanded. "How long ago did he get back?"

If there was any unease in her, any sense of awkwardness given the manner of her parting with Asher, she didn't show it. But then she wouldn't. "He rode in a short while ago. Dathne..."

She was frowning. She knew him so well; it was getting harder to decide if that was a good thing, or a bad. "Tell me."

He repeated what the prince had told him. Watched her closely as she absorbed the news, looking for some small sign of sorrow. Looked in vain. Her eyes glittered. "So. His ties to the past are broken. He belongs to us now."

Sometimes the hardness in her hurt him. "Is that all you can say?"

She met his hot gaze coldly. "It's all that matters."

He tried to turn away from her, tried to hide his eyes. She wouldn't let him. "His father's *dead*, Dathne!" he cried. "Doesn't that mean anything to you?"

"Not what you want it to mean. There'll be a lot more dead fathers in this kingdom if we fail in our duty, Matt." She let go of his arm. "I'll see him now."

"I don't think he wants to see you, Dathne. Not yet, anyway."

She shrugged. "And if he's sleeping, he won't."

He had to wait a moment before he could trust himself to follow her quietly, calmly, into the yard office. She was kneeling beside the cot. Either Asher had rolled himself onto his back, or she'd done it. Her left hand was on his unresponsive wrist and the fingers of her right hand pressed against his forehead.

"What are you doing? He needs to rest."

She looked up. There was the faintest spark of alarm in her eyes. "He has a fever, did you know?"

He realised then that Asher's breathing was loud. Laboured. Saw that his face had flushed from pale to hectic. His lips were dry and his head tossed uneasily on the cot's pillow. Taken aback, he clutched at the door. "He was all right when he got here. Exhausted and in pain, but not—"

Her glare scalded him. "Well, he's not all right now!"

No, he wasn't. Matt laid his hand on Asher's burning forehead. Heard the rattle in his chest. Pressed cold fingers to the pulse point in his throat and felt the echoes of his friend's thundering heart. "I'll send for Pother Nix and alert the prince."

She stood, and pulled her shawl tight. "Yes, you do that. I'll tell Veira Asher's back. The Circle can help here. I'll ask her to link with the others in a distant healing."

Matt chewed his lip. "How can that work? They don't even know him."

"They know of him," she snapped. "And it's better than doing nothing."

She'd slap him if he argued, so he nodded and stood aside to let her leave. As the door slammed shut behind her and the sound of her running feet faded, he looked again at Asher.

Then he throttled fear and went outside to rouse the lads.

Dathne was breathless by the time she reached home. Flinging herself up the shop stairs to her apartment, dragging her Circle Stone from its hiding place, dropping to the floor with it in her sweating hands: blind panic consumed her, crowding out all sense and cool collection.

He cannot die, he cannot die, he cannot cannot must not die...

She'd never make the connection to Veira like this. Linking the Circle Stones required a peaceful, meditative state. A calm heart. Her hands were shaking.

Setting the crystal aside she lay flat on the floor. Closed her eyes, and made an effort to breathe out the fear.

He cannot die, he cannot die, he cannot cannot must not die...

His father was dead. What a cruel thing. What a harsh way to serve the will of Prophecy. But then Prophecy had no father, no mother, no child, nor even a heart to break. It just was. Implacable. Unknowable. A spear tip lodged deep in the mind. No matter the pain, however the heartbreak, Asher would survive his loss. Prophecy needed him. And what Prophecy wanted, Prophecy got, one way or another.

He will not die.

Dathne sat up. Reached for her Circle Stone and called to Veira. "He is returned."

The old woman's relief shuddered through the link between them. *It is soon, then.*

"Yes. The waiting is almost over. The air itself oppresses me, Veira. My skin crawls like an anthill and my nights writhe like a nest of snakes. We are wounded, we are wounded, and soon the blood must flow."

And he is ready?

"He is ill. Prophecy has used him harshly. Body and heart are bruised, and will take time mending. I thought the Circle might—"

A wise suggestion, child. Share him with me now, that I might call for a healing.

So she thought of Asher. Unchained her memory and opened her heart. When it was done:

Oh, child. Child. Dathne...

She felt impatience. Stifled it. "I know. It can't be helped. It doesn't matter. It makes no difference."

No difference? Not to you, mayhap, but—

"Not to him, either. I won't let it. He'll never know."

So far away, Veira sighed. *I pray you're right. Child, the Circle will hold him safe. I have said so. Be at peace now, for as long as peace can last.*

Which wasn't long, thought Dathne, breaking the link, if foresight served her. Which most likely it did.

It always had before now.

Gar was standing in the Tower lobby, sorting through the pile of mail and messages that had been delivered just before breakfast, when his father came through the open doors.

"Demoted to post boy, are we?" Borne asked, grinning.

There was clean, fresh colour in the king's face. A vitality to his demeanour Gar hadn't seen for...well, come to think of it, not for a very long time. To see it now, to see him whole and happy: it was a joy as sharp as pain.

"Apparently," he replied, grinning back. "It seems I miss Darran more than I anticipated."

"Never mind. He'll be home soon."

Gar pulled a face. "Not soon enough. But please, I implore you, don't ever tell him I said so."

"Your secret is safe with me," his father promised. "Is there anything urgent? Matters that must be tended to immediately?"

He glanced again at the accumulated correspondence. "No. Another report from Darran, as it happens. Things proceed well, he says. I thought to discuss the matter at length at this afternoon's Privy Council meeting."

His father nodded. "I look forward to hearing the details." Then he glanced sideways, up the Tower's spiral staircase. "And how is your assistant this morning?"

Gar followed his father's gaze. Frowned. "There's no change. Nix has been and gone already. He assures me Asher's prolonged stupor is nothing more serious than the protest of an overstrained mind and body. The fever has abated somewhat and his wounds are healing cleanly. He just won't wake up."

"Perhaps he doesn't want to."

"I thought of that," said Gar unhappily. "I can only hope you're wrong. One life is dead to him, it's true, but he's spent the last year making a new life here in Dorana. That life still lives and breathes. Awaits him. He's needed."

Borne nodded. "He knows that. And when he's ready to face that life again, he'll wake. Have faith in good Pother Nix. I'm living proof he's a miracle worker, after all. Without his passion for herb lore, for combining Doranen healing magics with old Olken remedies..."

"You'd be dead, like King Drokas and Queen Ninia." Gar shivered. The mere thought made him ill. Calamity had come too close this time. He dropped his voice to a whisper. "WeatherWorking is so cruel. Sometimes I wonder why Barl—"

His father smiled, sadly. "Because she had to. There was no other way. The natural energies her magics control are vast, Gar. Intricate. And the paradise they've bought us must be paid for."

He could no longer hide his pain. Even though he'd sworn never to reveal it. These last days had been too hard. "Paid for with your blood?"

"Yes," his father said simply. "It's our side of the pact, my son. Our way of thanking the Olken people for giving us a home when our own lay in ashes behind us."

"I know, I know, but—"

"Gar, I'm not here to debate history or its consequences," his father said firmly. "I have news. Something's been discovered. Something I think you might find...intriguing."

Smothering sorrow, Gar stared at his father. In that ascetic face, excitement. "What?" he said. "What have you found?"

The king crooked his finger. "Come, and I'll show you."

Largely uninhabited since the massive building works undertaken by Queen Antra at the turn of the last century, the Old Palace baked its crumbling stoneworks in the autumn sunshine and dreamed of its glory days, dead and gone.

Looking around the abandoned west wing's deserted central courtyard, Gar recalled the solitary childhood games he'd played here. The empty chambers and echoing corridors had been his private kingdom. Such fantastic dreams he'd woven, fashioned out of rooms piled high with discarded furniture, chests of fabulously outdated clothing, statues and knick-knacks and all manner of mysterious, grown-up things. He'd not been back here in years. The place looked sad now, not alluring. Weeds had long since taken over the flowerbeds he'd once so industriously tended, growing roses and snapdragons for his mother, and creeping wartsease slowly strangled the little row of plumple trees he'd raised for fruit, crisp and juicy and all his own. There were even some gaps in the courtyard walls, where bricks had tumbled as a result of the recent earth tremors.

"It's just through here," said the king. "In the old kitchen courtyard. Mind your step now, the ground is uneven in places."

Gar stared at his father. "What in Barl's name were you doing poking around the Old Palace grounds?"

They squeezed through a half-rotten doorway in the central courtyard wall. "I wasn't. One of the palace cooks made the discovery while searching for her runaway cat. Instead of finding the wretched creature she found this."

This was a huge, gaping hole in the middle of the old kitchen courtyard. The sunshine shafting into it over the roofline of the surrounding buildings revealed, faintly, some kind of chamber far below their feet. It seemed to be lined with shelves. More shelves crammed side by side across the space beneath the ruined ceiling. And on every shelf, books. It was impossible to tell exactly how large the chamber was, but Gar suspected it was a goodly size; the free-standing bookcases stretched beyond the edges of the breach. Aside from that obvious damage, the rest of the old kitchen courtyard appeared intact.

"Barl save us," Gar said as he and his father skirted the hole to join the queen, Durm and Fane, who were standing together a prudent distance from the lip of the rent in the ground.

"Extraordinary, isn't it?" said the king, jubilant. "And to think—"

"At last!" the princess cried. "Durm was just saying you must have found another hole and fallen into it."

Smiling indulgently, the Master Magician rapped her on the head with his knuckles. "I most certainly was not, madam."

She grinned at him. "Well, you were thinking so. Don't try and deny it, I know you too well!"

As the others laughed, Gar sighed. He and his sister had hardly spoken since his return from Westwailing. Partly it was because he'd been immersed in emergency meetings with his father and both Councils. Also he'd spent a great many hours asleep, recovering from the gruelling cross-country ride. Some of it was because, whenever he could, he'd been sitting with Asher hoping his friend would grow tired of the history book he'd been reading aloud and sit bolt upright, demanding that Gar give over natterin' afore his bloody ears fell off in self-defence.

It hadn't happened yet, but he remained cautiously optimistic.

But he couldn't blame all of the silence between him and Fane on work and worry. More and more, it seemed of late, they simply had less and less to say to one another...and they'd never had a great deal in common to start with. The distance between them was troubling. If in truth the king had perished, his sister would now be his queen. And their strained relationship would have made his life a hundred times harder than it already was.

It was time and past time that he found a way to cross the abyss that separated them. One day, Barl pray long hence, she would be the kingdom's WeatherWorker and he would have to bow his knee to her in solemn obedience. Between now and that day he had to find a way to her goodwill. Because if he didn't...

She was frowning at him. "What are you staring at?"

"Nothing," he said, with a lightness he was far from feeling. "You look most becoming in that dress. The colour suits you."

"Doesn't it?" said the queen, smiling. "I must order a bolt of the fabric for myself."

Fane twitched her skirts of deep primrose silk. She appeared pleased by the compliment...and suspicious too. Typical. "There's something you want?"

Gar stifled his mother's protest with a glance, and smiled. "Yes, actually," he said, seizing the moment. "Lunch."

"With me?"

"No, with your lap-dog. Of course with you."

Her eyes narrowed. "Why?"

He kept his tone light, though his fingers itched to shake her. "Can't a man ask his sister to lunch without first facing a stern interrogation?"

"Of course he can," said Dana before Fane could answer. "What a lovely idea, Gar. You can make it a picnic. I'll have the kitchen prepare a special basket for you. Would you like chicken, or—"

"My love," said the king, slipping his arm around her shoulders, "I think if we don't turn our attentions to this mysterious chamber at our feet, Durm is going to erupt with impatience."

Dana laughed. "Of course."

Ignoring the calculating looks Fane was shooting him from beneath her carefully lowered lashes, Gar inched a little closer to the edge of the hole and peered downwards. "It looks like a study. Or a library. But what's a library doing here, practically smack bang beneath the Old Palace kitchens? Beneath *anything*?"

"You're the historian of the family," said his father. "You don't recall any mention in palace archives about this study or library or whatever it may be?"

"No," said Gar after a moment's furious thought. "Nothing comes to mind."

"Don't you think it's strange," Fane said suddenly, "that despite this enormous hole in the ground there's no rubble or dirt down there? Or in the courtyard. At least, nothing that looks fresh."

"I wonder," Dana said slowly. Moving sideways to the nearest stretch of courtyard wall she picked up an ancient, moss-covered lump of rock. Took aim and tossed it at the hole in the ground. There was a vicious crack of sound, a flash of brilliant blue light and a noxious puff of smoke as the stone exploded.

"A shield," said Durm, his eyes glittering. "Barl's eyeteeth, the chamber has a *shield*."

For once, Dana made no complaint about swearing.

Borne stared at his Master Magician. "Why would a library needed shielding?"

"It's obvious," said Fane. "Because it isn't an ordinary library." She was lit up from within, on fire with excitement. "Papa, Durm—do you know what this is? Do you realise what we've found?"

Gar sighed. "Fane...no. I'm sorry, but it can't be."

She turned on him. "Why not?"

Helplessly he looked at her. For all her powers she was still a child, and subject to a child's flights of fancy. The last thing he wanted to do was hurt her, but... "Because the idea is nothing more than romantic nonsense," he said as kindly as he could. "A fairy tale. At best it's completely unsubstantiated rumour. There's no proof, none at all, that Barl's so-called 'lost library' ever existed."

"It wouldn't matter to you even if there was proof," his sister retorted. "What use would a library filled with arcane magical texts be to you? For all we know you've come across hundreds of references and you've ignored every one of them because either you don't care or you couldn't understand what they meant. Both, probably."

Gar took a deep breath and kept his tone reasonable. Academic. Adult. "Fane, I know what this means to you. I know you want it to be true. You've been fascinated with Barl and Morgan and the doom of the Doranen ever since you were a little girl and I used to read you your bedtime story. But no documents from the time of the Great Flight or the Arrival have survived to the present day. All we've got are oral accounts, recorded years after the fact. A friend of a friend of a friend of a servant who used to clean Barl's boots told me. That kind of thing. We don't know that Barl left behind so much as a note for the kitchen, let alone books of ancient and powerful spells. Certainly not a whole library's worth of them."

Fane pointed at their feet. Her face was flushed with temper. "You don't call that proof?"

"I call it a hole in the ground. Beyond that we don't know anything."

"Nor will we," said Durm sharply, "until we enter the chamber itself and make a thorough examination of its contents."

Borne nodded. "Exactly. My love..." He turned to Dana. "You've a knack for finding things. Would you care to nose out the way into this mysterious library for us?"

The queen lowered her unhappy gaze from Gar and Fane to the breached courtyard. Sadness gave way to a sense of purpose. "I can certainly try." She managed a small smile. "No promises, mind." Stretching out her palm, she closed her eyes and whispered under her breath. The air above her hand quivered. Thickened. Coalesced into a small orange ball of energy.

For a moment the questor hovered there, like a hunting dog uncertain of the scent. Then it leapt upwards, swooped over the hole at their feet, circling, buzzing like a bee—and darted through the main door opening onto the kitchen courtyard.

"After it!" Borne cried.

Acrimony forgotten, they hurtled in pursuit.

The queen's questor led them through deserted kitchens, along dusty corridors and down rickety staircases. After a few minutes Durm conjured glimfire to light their way. On and on they hurried until they reached an enormous echoing meat larder where once, years and years before, whole sides of beef and mutton and venison, plucked pheasants, ducks, geese, swans and peacocks had hung from polished hooks dangling from the ceiling. The hooks remained, tarnished and dulled by age.

"Oh no! It's lost!" Fane cried, almost stamping her foot with frustration as the orange ball bumped blindly along the larder's far wall, humming faintly.

"Wait," said Durm, hand lifted.

With a triumphant chime, the questor plunged through what appeared to be solid whitewashed bricks and disappeared.

Fane rushed to spread her palms flat to the old, cold stone. "No! Durm, do something!"

"I have a better idea," the Master Magician suggested. "You do something. Unlock for us the key to this hidden door."

"But I..." Fane began. Glanced at Gar, then nodded, her expression hardening. "All right. I will."

Fingertips lightly searching, she explored the section of wall where her mother's seeking spell had disappeared. Lightly frowning, lips pursed and eyes closed, she teased at the stonework.

Gar, watching, felt a familiar stab under his rib cage. When I'm fifty, he thought, despairing, will I still be jealous? Will I never outgrow this useless, unspeakable resentment?

As though reading his son's mind Borne rested a hand on Gar's shoulder and squeezed. Gar smiled at him, a brief, wry quirk of lip, self-mocking. Borne's answering smile was approving, his raised eyebrow a compliment, of sorts.

"I think I have it," Fane murmured indistinctly, with her cheek pressed hard against the stone. "It's a masking incantation all right. So old. So faint. Like a song carried on the breeze over distant water. If it was just a little louder, I could sing it..."

Dana was frowning. "Durm, you do this. Please. She's still not fully recovered from her first WeatherWorking, and unravelling another magician's lock-and-key spell is hardly—"

"I'm fine, Mama," said Fane, opening her eyes. "Stop fussing. Anyway, this spell is so old it's practically nonexistent. I just need to—ah. There." She stepped back. Struck the wall above her head three sharp blows. *"Impassata."*

The stone rippled. Melted away, to reveal a door-shaped space.

"Well done," Durm said quietly. He turned to the king. "Indulge me, Borne. It may not be safe beyond this portal. Let me take the lead."

"You are far less expendable than I," Borne objected.

Dana took his arm. "Let him."

"My love..."

"*Let him.*"

Borne sighed and waved an inviting arm. "Very well then, Master Magician Durm: lead on."

Conjuring fresh glimfire, tossing it into the air, Durm stepped through the unbarred doorway and into the unknown.

CHAPTER TWENTY-FIVE

There was a narrow passageway beyond the meat larder, hung with old cobwebs and starved of clean air. Sneezing, breathing heavily, Gar and his family followed Durm along it. The glimfire illuminating the gloom cast elongated eldritch shadows on the floor and up the walls.

"There," said Durm at last. He pointed. "The questor, do you see it?"

The little ball of orange light hovered further along the passageway, glowing faintly. "What's it found?" said Fane, peering.

With a wave of his finger Durm increased the power of the glimlight. "A door," he said. He nodded at Dana. "My compliments. Your Majesty. We appear to have reached our destination."

Warily, they approached the end of the passageway.

The door barring their progress seemed to be made from solid wood. The dark timber was intricately carved in patterns alien to their eyes. In its centre was a seal of faded crimson wax, shot through with green and blue and fashioned into a complicated woven knot. It shimmered in the glimlit air.

"A ward," said Durm, and looked at Dana. "Your Majesty?"

With a snap of her fingers she sent the seeker spell forward, encouraging it to travel through the carved door. The moment it touched the timber the questor exploded in a shower of sparks.

"So," said Borne. He glanced at Durm, eyebrows lifting, and together they stepped up to the door. "The rest of you stay well back," he added over his shoulder. "Any ward that can survive untold centuries and retain any level of potency at all is not to be trifled with."

"Then pray do not trifle," said Dana tartly. "Explaining an exploded king to his kingdom may prove somewhat awkward."

Borne grinned. "Yes, my love."

In cautious unison he and Durm stretched out their hands to the knot of wax centred on the door. "Can you feel the skill, Borne? Magnificent," the Master Magician murmured. "A work of genius."

"But weakened, yes?" breathed Borne.

Durm nodded. "Yes. Weakened enough to break, I think. Not easily. Not without danger. But it can be broken."

They lowered their hands, stepped back a pace and soberly regarded each other. "The fashioning of that seal," said Borne. "Do you recognise it?"

"I do," said Fane, shrugging aside her mother's restraining hand and crowding forward. "It's Barl's." She spared Gar a look. "That *is* on record. In the *Magia Majestica*. Durm showed it to me." Then, her attention back on the door and her father, she said, "I was right, wasn't I?" She was quivering. "This is Barl's lost library."

"I concede," Borne replied after a pause, "that the door appears to have been sealed by Barl. Beyond that we don't know."

"And we won't until we get in there and look," she replied. "I could do it. I could break the seal. Can I?"

"No!" Borne and Durm spoke together, a single peal of thunder. Borne continued, "Be silent a moment, Fane. I need to think."

"She's right, Borne," Durm said. "We must know what lies beyond this door."

"Must we?" Borne pressed his fingers to his temples as though his head were aching. "Think, Durm. Think what this might mean, if... if fantasy were to become fact. If we have indeed found Barl's lost library."

"It could mean the discovery of a lifetime." Durm's eyes were fevered. "After six long centuries we could bridge the gap between ourselves and our ancestors. Once we Doranen were a proud and mighty race of warrior mages. But what are we today? To what ends do we employ our skills? Plumbing. Glimfire. Bookbinding." The contempt in his voice was searing. "We open doors. Close windows. Bloom pretty flowers and keep our clothes clean without soap and water. Domestic comforts and rustic pursuits are our purview now.

WeatherWorking aside, that is the length and breadth of our magic. Yet our ancestors had knowledge of spells and incantations that we, pale reflections of their former glory, can only dream of!"

Slowly, Borne nodded. "My friend, that's what frightens me."

"Frightens, Borne?" Durm shook his head. "Why?"

Borne stared. "How can you ask me that? Barl and our ancestors faced a mage war of such cruel violence it was either flee into the bitter unknown or face destruction. That is what might await us beyond this door. After six hundred years of peace, would you loose such evil upon our people again?"

Durm frowned. "You know me better than that."

"I thought I did."

"Majesty..." Durm sighed. "Forgive me. In truth, it's most unlikely that this chamber contains books of arcane lore. I fear that great knowledge is long lost to us. But I beg you to consider this. If it is not lost, if we have indeed discovered a buried treasure trove of ancient Doranen magic...can you truly contemplate not unburying it?"

"To keep my kingdom safe?" Borne's eyes were stark, haunted. "I'd burn it."

As his father and his father's best friend stared at each other like strangers, Gar cleared his throat. "But, sir...what of our history?"

"Our history, Gar, as you damn well know, is blood and terror and exile!" Borne replied. "We came to this land in desperation and in desperation we conquered it. Only Barl's great sacrifice and the willing aid of the Olken people have kept us safe since then. This kingdom's prosperity owes everything to the partnership of mutual trust and obligation between its two peoples. I will not be the one who teaches the meaning of desperation to the descendants of those first Doranen and the Olken who joined with them to make a better world for all."

"But, Papa, nobody's asking you to!" said Fane. "All we're asking for is the chance to see what's behind that door!"

"Borne, dear friend," said Durm. "Your love for this kingdom and its peoples is beyond question. And so, I had thought, is my love for you. Let us cease this profitless speculation and instead uncover the truth. If we find anything you mislike, anything at all, we can destroy it."

Borne stared at him searchingly. "You could do that?"

Chin lifted, shoulders braced, Durm nodded. "If you told me to, yes. I could. I would. You are my king. I live to serve you, and your kingdom." Stepping close, he rested one hand on the king's shoulder. "Borne. All our long lives have you trusted me. Tell me now, and tell me truly: have I ever failed you?"

Borne shook his head. "Never."

"Then please. I entreat you. Trust me now."

Borne looked at the queen. "My love?"

Dana was pale. "I think we must. Even if you buried this place again and swore us all to silence, who can say how long it would remain secret a second time? And if in the future it was discovered again... by someone less scrupulous than you... who knows what might happen? For better or worse, we are here now. I think we must act."

Borne took a deep breath and let it escape, harshly. Looked at Durm. "Very well," he said, voice and face grim. "Breach the chamber, Master Magician."

Durm bowed. "Majesty."

Borne glanced at his family. "The rest of you stand well back."

Dana reached for his sleeve and tugged. "And you."

For a moment Gar thought his father might argue. Then the king sighed, and nodded, and urged them all away from Durm and the sealed door.

In the flickering light Durm's expression was grave. Facing the wooden door he spread his hands wide above the ancient wax seal, tipped his head back, closed his eyes, and sank into a deep meditation.

Gar glanced at his father. Borne looked calm enough, but there was doubt in the droop of his eyelids, and disciplined fear in the tightness of his lips. He reached out a hand and brushed his fingertips against his father's forearm.

"Even if your worst fears are realised and we do find books of magic in there," he said, keeping his voice low, "the danger is remote. Until they're spoken, spells and enchantments are nothing but words on paper."

Borne nodded. "I know. But even so..."

"I am ready," Durm announced. "Go further back, all of you. This ward may be breakable but there yet remains enough power to crisp the hair on all your heads, or worse."

"Be careful, Durm," said Borne, shepherding his family to safety.

"And when, old friend, have you ever known me to be otherwise?" Durm raised his right hand and waved it over the seal from left to right, then traced an intricate sigil in the air with his right forefinger. A twisted thread of green glowed briefly in midair, then faded. With his left hand he waved from right to left, and with his left forefinger traced the empty air. A blue thread glowed and died. Three more times to left and right he unwove the seal's bindings, until the faded red wax was untouched by other colours. "There," he said, as the last glow of blue died. "So much for the peripheral wards. Now for the heart ward."

He raised both hands and spread them over the dull red seal of wax. Shoulders hunched with concentration, head tilted forward, he began to breathe heavily, groaning. A thin keening, faint at first, then gaining in strength, reverberated in the musty air.

"Stay here," said Dana as Fane tried to wriggle free of her mother's restraining arm.

"But how can I see what he's doing from way back here?" Fane argued. "If I can just get—"

Borne took her other arm. "Be quiet. Is this a parlour trick for your idle amusement? Hold your tongue and don't distract him. He risks his life for all of us."

Chastened, Fane fell silent.

The keening was loud enough to be painful, drumming against their ears, driving iron nails into their heads. Higher it rose, louder and more shrill. From the seal pulsed a vibrant red light; Durm became a silhouette of fire. He was shuddering.

Then, with a blazing flash of heat, amidst a shriek of surrender from the wax and a cry of agonised triumph from Durm, the ward exploded.

The air in the sealed library smelled peculiar. Faded. Stretched. It tickled Durm's nose and his throat. He stifled a cough and stared around the chamber as the others spread out, exclaiming. The room was larger than he'd imagined, and every square foot of it was crammed with laden bookshelves. Taller than Borne, they marched in rows, formed little alcoves, lined every available inch of wall. Squashed to the side of the crowded room was a desk with three drawers and a lumpily padded chair. On the face of it, an unremarkable place...especially when one considered the remarkable nature of that ward.

Durm fought a shiver. His teeth were still vibrating from its residual power and his skin felt lightly scorched. On the whole, an unpleasant experience.

But worth it.

I have broken Barl's Seal. The Seal of Blessed Barl herself, greatest magician in the history of Dorana.

And I broke it.

"Are you sure you're all right?" the king asked, turning back to him. "The residual power in that ward was...well, I can scarcely believe it, and I saw it with my own eyes. I can't imagine what it felt like."

No, Borne, you couldn't. He waved a deprecating hand. "I'm fine, Your Majesty."

"Are you certain of that?"

"I admit to a moment of discomfort, but only a moment, and it passed swiftly." Unlike the triumph, which would last a lifetime.

"You never cease to impress me," Borne said, shaking his head. Then his smile faded. "Durm—you know it was never a matter of not trusting you."

Dear Borne. A good man, right to the marrow of his thinning bones. Racked always with cares and concerns and a duty that overwhelmed his strength. Haunted by the ghosts of old decisions. Forever doubting. "I know," he replied. Just as he knew, with sorrow, that in this matter, where the king's judgement was concerned, trust was something in short supply. Kings came, and kings went, but magic... magic lived forever. And it was up to the kingdom's Master Mage, keeper of the *Magia Majestica*, guardian of the Weather Orb, to ensure it. To give his or her life, if necessary, to its jealous preservation.

So Borne would burn Barl's books of magic, would he?

Over my dead body, old friend. Over my dead and rotting body.

"It's incredible!" the queen exclaimed, running hesitant fingers along the spines of the books before her. "As though the door were closed on them only yesterday. There's been a strong preserving spell cast here. Can you feel it?" She glanced at him. "But I think it's fading, Durm, don't you?"

He shut his eyes and stretched out with that part of his mind concerned with all things magical. Felt the weft and the warp of the incantation. Where it held, and where it was threadbare and unravelling. "Yes," he agreed, as he marvelled at the power of an enchantment that could last more than half a millennium. Let there be spells here, oh, let there be spells. We have laboured too long in ignorance. "I shall cast another before we leave, to be certain nothing here can be damaged."

"Yes, you must," said Gar, horrified. "This place, these books, are a find of monumental significance. Whatever we need not destroy must be protected."

Borne stared at the gaping hole in the ceiling. The spilling sunlight cast his fever-wasted features into sharp relief. For all his remarkable recovery, still he had meagre strength. Durm watched him marvel at the feat of magic used to keep the chamber hidden for so long, and felt a flood of affection. He needs me now more than ever before, to ease his burden. To make the difficult decisions for him. That terrible illness has cost him dearly. He is lost in a wilderness and cannot see the way. But I can. I can.

"We've some six hours before I must go up to the Weather Chamber," Borne said. "Let's see what we can find in that time, hmm?"

Ever headstrong, Fane objected. "I don't see why we should stop exploring just because you're called to the night's WeatherWorking, Papa."

"Because I wish it. Fane..." Borne softened his tone. "This library cannot become an obsession. I have duties. You have your studies. Six hours is a long time. Do you really want to waste them in argument?"

"But, Papa, even with four of us we won't be able to check every last book today. There must be hundreds! Why don't we send for help? Lord Jarralt, or—"

"No!" Borne took his daughter's chin between his fingers and tilted her face upwards. Blazed his eyes into hers. "There will be no discussion of this place or what we find in it, is that clear? Not until I'm sure it's safe. Not until I know precisely what we've found."

Fane jerked her chin free. "But the Privy Council—"

"Answers to me," Borne said. "Not I to it. I bear the ultimate responsibility here, Fane. The final authority is mine."

"Father's right," Gar told her. "The last thing we need is politics complicating matters."

With an ease perfected by years of practice, Durm hid his contempt. As though a cripple's opinion were relevant, or required. He was here on sufferance, nothing more.

"Come," said the queen, and touched her daughter lightly on the shoulder. "We can work along this shelf together."

"Trust me, Fane," Borne said, and kissed her forehead. "I know I'm only your father, but I do know what I'm doing, truly."

She looked to him, then. To her beloved mentor, Durm. Just the smallest flick of her eyes and the merest twitch of one eyebrow. His precious Fane. The child of his heart, the daughter of his mind and magic. A perfect blending of her parents, yet moulded in his image. Trained and tutored and steeped in the ways of enchantment, the lore of *Magia Majestica*. Soon she would be a queen unsurpassed in the history of Lur. In the history of all magical kingdoms, wherever they might be. If any existed beyond the Wall.

He nodded at her, frowning lightly, and she sighed. Pulled a face at her blood-and-bone father. "All right," she answered both of them. "If you say so. But let's get *on* then! Time's wasting!"

Again they separated, each taking a different direction. Gar pulled a book from a shelf above his head and opened it. "It's written in the Old Tongue. Pure as the day Barl came over the mountains."

Fane glanced over her shoulder. "Can you read it?"

He gave her a dark look. "Yes."

"Well, then, what does it say?"

Give the cripple his due, he was an excellent scholar with a talent for language and history. He'd even made a study of the original Olken tongue, though why anyone would bother Durm couldn't fathom. Such endeavours doubtless endeared him to the likes of that repellent Asher, of course, and the native populace in general. Made him feel...important. Lacking magic, doubtless he needed something to fill the void. It was a harmless enough pursuit and it made Borne and the queen happy. For himself he didn't much care, really. Once the boy's impediment had been identified, the prince had ceased to be of the least interest to him.

Gar was frowning over the book's first few pages. "The print is very small," he muttered. "A Doranen typeface I've never seen before..."

"You can't read it," said Fane, and turned away.

"I think it's a story," he said, and turned more pages. "I think it's— it's a *romance*." He laughed.

"What?" Fane cried. Took three steps to join him, reached out and plucked the book from his unresisting fingers. "It can't be. You're making it up. Papa, tell him to take this seriously!"

"Let me see," said Dana, and looked for herself. "Well, I'm nowhere near as accomplished as Gar in reading Old Tongue but I think he might be right. Never mind. I was wanting something new to read and I've always been partial to romance. This will make a nice change from Vev Gertsik. I find her a trifle florid, I'm afraid."

"Stop fretting, Fane," Borne advised. "And keep searching. If you find anything of a less frivolous nature I suggest you put it on the table there so we can look at it more carefully in due course."

"Huh," said Fane. "*Romance*." Complaining under her breath, she turned back to the bookshelves.

A muttering silence fell as they began to search the shelves in earnest. Gradually the pile of books on the table grew as they each found something to spark interest or excitement.

For himself, Durm was circumspect. Closing his senses to the brief laughter, the exclamations of triumph, the cries of wonder, he quested silent and single-minded for his heart's desire. To maintain appearances he chose volumes at random and added them to the collection on the table. Histories. Fairy tales. Folklore. Of a certain interest, to be sure, but of little value compared with the treasure he sought. That he *knew* must be here somewhere. *Nobody* sealed a room for six centuries to protect fairy tales. Certainly not a magician like Barl.

Fane balanced her latest find on a crowded corner of the table and pouted. "No magical treatises yet," she said sadly. "And it's been nearly three hours."

"There are still a lot of shelves to investigate," the queen consoled her. "You mustn't be so easily discouraged."

Fane slumped onto the chair with a disconsolate sigh. "But what if we don't find *anything* useful?"

Gar laughed. "Only you could be so short-sighted, Fane. Most of these books in some way or another deal with the original Dorana. The land of our ancestors. Our home, in a way."

"I couldn't care less about what happened six centuries ago in a country that probably doesn't exist any more," she retorted. "The only place that matters now is Lur. And the only thing that matters is finding a book that tells us more about the enchantments our ancestors knew. The ones we've lost. The ones we never knew existed. Durm's right," she added, and glanced at him, bestowing approval. "That's our true heritage. The only heritage that counts. Not that you'd understand." To emphasise her point, she pulled out the desk's top drawer and banged it shut again, hard.

Something inside the drawer rattled. Rolled. Curious, she slid it open again and put her hand inside. When she pulled it out her fingers were clasped tight about something clear and round and the size of an orange.

Gar, tight-lipped and smarting—though she'd only spoken the truth and it was past time he accepted the facts and stopped spitting in the wind—put aside the book he held. "What's that?"

"I don't know," she said, and unfurled her fingers. "A portrait."

Another tedious squabble averted. Borne and the queen exchanged relieved glances and joined their children around the table. Dana caught a proper look at the sphere, and her face contracted in disgust. "Barl's mercy! Get rid of it, Fane. Put it back in the drawer."

Fane ignored her. Instead lifted the sphere until it was level with her eyes and stared intently at the face contained within it. A coldly handsome face, it was, with ice-blue eyes and hair so pale it looked silver. Extravagant cheekbones. Imperious nose. Lips too full and sensuous for a man.

"It's *him*, isn't it?" she breathed. "Morgan. Morg. I always wondered what he looked like."

"Heed your mother," Borne said harshly. "Put it away. Better yet, destroy it. He was a monster."

"No!" said Fane, and curved her hands protectively around the sphere and the face within it. "It's only a portrait, it can't hurt anybody. It must have been Barl's. She must have kept it. Why would she keep it if there was any danger?" She loosened her grip and stared again at the haughty face of evil. "He was so handsome. None of the history books ever mentioned he was handsome."

With a cry of revulsion Borne pulled her round to face him. "What does that signify? Fair of face he may have been but he was even fouler of heart, which is all that matters! Barl *died* to keep this kingdom safe from him, and for six hundred years the kings and queens of Lur have spent their lives ensuring her sacrifice was not in vain. I have spent my life upholding that sacred trust. My *life*, Fane. And next it will be your turn to stand alone in the Weather Chamber with the weight of the Wall crushing your bones to powder. To spend your life in Barl's service in the full knowledge that if you fail you condemn a kingdom to catastrophe. All because of *him*. Because of Morg. You know this. You *know* this. And yet you can sit there and simper and say he was *handsome*?"

As Fane shrank before the king's outrage, pale and brimming with tears, he wrenched the sphere from her loosened clasp and hurled it at the shielded ceiling.

In light and in sound, the sphere vanished.

The queen caught Borne's trembling hands between her own, carried them to her lips and kissed them. "She meant no harm, my love. She doesn't understand yet. How can she?"

"She's not a child any longer!" Borne retorted, and pulled his hands free. "She is the Weather Worker-in-Waiting, and childhood is yesterday's dream. Durm! What say you to this? I thought you had taught her more than just the right words in the right order at the right time!"

The rebuke, although unjustified, was expected. Pain and fear had made Borne short-tempered of late. Clasping his hands behind his back Durm offered the king a shallow bow. "Majesty. You are right, of course. But while it is true that Morg, in his dedication to dark magics and his unquenchable quest for power, split asunder our ancestral land and drove our forbears into exile and suffering, he was also Morgan, the beloved of our beloved Barl. Perhaps it's not such a bad thing that Her Highness reminds us of that. Certainly it serves to show just how great was her sacrifice, and how even love cannot overcome all."

"We must agree to disagree about love," the queen said, reaching again for Borne's hand, "but as for the rest…you make your point, Durm."

As always, Borne's anger died as quickly as it ignited. He put a contrite arm about Fane's shoulders and held her tightly. "Forgive me, daughter. Illness has left me out of sorts. I know you meant no harm. But think on what I said and you'll discover that I am right."

"I know you are," Fane replied, still shaken. "All I meant was that it's sad. She loved him but she had to run away to be safe from him. And then she had to die, to make sure."

"Yes," said Borne. "Yes. It is sad."

"Do you think he ever loved her?" asked Fane. "Really? Truly?"

Borne shook his head. "I don't know."

Gently, the queen said, "It's likely that he did. Once. Before his soul was warped by the black magics he embraced. You see, my darling Fane, even the purest heart cannot withstand such evil. Magic isn't always benevolent and kind."

Durm had to bite his lip and turn away at that. Such sentimental drivel! She and Borne were as bad as each other. Magic was a tool, nothing more. It served whatever purpose its wielder decreed and was no more benevolent or evil than...than...a chair!

With a strained smile Borne said, "Come. Let's keep looking. I admit, though I know you're disappointed, Fane, I find the failure to discover any magical treatises encouraging. Not all knowledge is a blessing."

And there, sad to say, was the difference between them laid bare as bones. There could be no meeting of minds and hearts in this matter. With that simple declaration Borne showed himself to be unfit, as a mage, to caretake the secrets Barl had hidden somewhere in her lost library.

Fear not, brave lady. I shall find your books of magics and protect them from the well-meaning blunders of my friend. Our heritage will be saved, I swear on my oath as Master Magician.

He returned to the search, and an hour later was rewarded.

It was some strange, unrecognised instinct that drove him into the rib-crushingly small alcove tucked away in one dark corner of the library. A tickle in the mind that enticed, beckoned. Sang with promise and set his heart to racing. Startled, he glanced at Borne, the queen, Fane. Were they suddenly deaf and numbed, then, as crippled as the prince, that they did not feel it? How could that be? It was a mystery...

Or was it? Perhaps this was meant. Perhaps this was a simple case of one Master Magician speaking across the centuries to another. Perhaps he was the only one capable of sensing the presence of such spells. Borne was a powerful magician, but his talents had been trained to the weather, shaped and fashioned for a single purpose. Other buds, other shoots, had been ruthlessly pruned years ago. The queen, well, she had talent enough but used it for womanly pursuits only. Hers was a decorous and dainty application of magic. And Fane, for all she burned bright with a raw power unseen for generations, she was still a student. Inexperienced. Her palate had potential, yes, but was yet too broad for subtle flavours.

So Barl's magic sang for him, and him alone.

Unhurried, maintaining his air of scholarly distraction, he eased himself into the small, book-lined space and conjured glimfire to banish the shadows. The light danced along the spines of leather-bound journals pressed cover to cover in the awkward alcove. He trailed his fingers along them and felt the magic sizzle beneath his skin.

Somewhere in here...somewhere...

Finding the book was like kissing a lightning bolt. He bit his lip to blood to stop from crying out.

It was a slender volume. Cloth-bound, and tucked between the pages of some obscure text on falconry. Trembling, he freed it from captivity and opened the cover. A diary. Handwritten, the ink faded but legible, a collection of notes, a recitation of deeds accomplished, and yes! oh yes! a listing of incantations, pages of them, and they were completely new, had never been heard of before in this kingdom. And all in a handwriting he knew so well, from the WeatherWorking notes and strictures she'd left behind.

This was Barl's diary. These were her secrets. This was what had called to him.

He could have moaned his excitement out loud.

Beyond the alcove, the prince was saying, "—a lifetime's work, Father. I don't know whether to laugh or cry."

I believe I am familiar with the feeling, boy.

"It's certainly a miraculous collection of books, Gar," Borne agreed. "I must say, given the wide range of subject matter and its relative mundanity, I'm at something of a loss to understand why Barl and her followers made such efforts to take this collection with them when they fled."

"Oh, but Father!" the prince said. "Don't you see? They were trying to preserve an entire civilisation. To encapsulate untold centuries of lore and learning in a single haphazard collection of books. It's an extraordinary ambition. When I think of them struggling to decide what to take and what must stay behind...it breaks my heart."

Borne laughed. "Spoken like a true historian. And you're right, too, about how much work it will take to properly catalogue and translate what's here. It must be done with care, and reverence, and most importantly with an eye to the potential dangers such knowledge carries with it. It's not a task to be awarded lightly."

"No," the prince said, his voice sober. "You're right, of course."

"So when can you begin?" his father added.

"Sir?"

"Yes, Royal Curator? That is, if you'd like to be."

As the prince stammered his delight, his surprise, his protestations of faithful duty, and the queen laughed, and the king laughed too, which was good to hear, and Fane muttered sarcasms under her breath, he held Barl's diary in his trembling hands and gave thanks.

"Durm!" the king called, and stood behind him. "The afternoon fades and WeatherWorking time draws near. We should go."

Half turning his head, keeping the diary hidden close against his chest, Durm said, "By all means, Majesty, you go. I am happy to stay working unaccompanied."

"I know," Borne said affectionately. "Given the chance you'd work yourself to a collapse searching for anything remotely magical. I'd rather you didn't. Aside from the deleterious effect on your health, I'd prefer we didn't draw any more attention to this place than is absolutely necessary. Besides, there's always tomorrow."

Argument, however mild, was too dangerous. "That's true," he agreed.

"We'll leave the place warded. It'll be safe enough. And tomorrow we'll finish what we've begun, then decide what next to do." With a glance that encompassed them all, Borne added, "Apart from ourselves, the only person who knows of this place is the servant who discovered the breach in the courtyard. When she told me what she'd found I commanded her to hold her tongue. Tonight I shall fuddle her to make sure she loses all recollection of her little adventure. This library *must* remain a secret. Not a word is to be said to anybody. Is that understood?"

The others nodded and murmured obedience. "As you say, Majesty," Durm agreed again, and slipped Barl's diary inside his robe where it could lie against his ribs, hidden and protected. He loved Borne like a brother but that didn't blind him to the sober truth: the king could not be trusted with this discovery. Not tonight. Perhaps not ever. The thought pained him...but never before in his life had pain stood in the way of duty. Nor would it now.

"Durm?" said Fane as she stood back to allow him and her parents to lead the way out of the library. "Is everything all right?"

He smiled at her, Barl's diary a warm and promising weight against his skin. "Foolish girl," he said, and shook his head indulgently. "Of course it is."

CHAPTER TWENTY-SIX

Much later that night, after dinner, having eased Borne down from his WeatherWorking jitters and wrapped him safe in a robe before a roaring fire, with the rest of the palace retired to bed and only a handful of servants scurrying like mice about the corridors, Durm locked himself into his private study and opened Barl's diary.

The book-lined room was hushed. A modest fire crackled in the hearth, scenting the warm air with the spicy freshness of pine. Candles scattered shadows. He'd left one window uncurtained; the glow of Barl's Wall splashed prismed gold light on the carpet as it filtered through Borne's soft rain and the thin glass panes.

Comfortable in robe and slippers, a tankard of mulled wine by his side and his belly groaning pleasurably with food, he crossed his ankles on a hassock, propped his elbows on the arms of his chair and held the book as tenderly as he would a lover, had there ever been one.

"Speak to me, brave lady," he breathed, and began to read.

Hours later, he stirred. The candles were burned down almost to their sockets. The fire had dwindled to ash and cinders. His half-drunk wine sat cold in the tankard, and the remnants of Borne's rain barely trickled down the windowpanes.

"Barl save us," he said aloud; the sound of his voice was a startlement.

The contents of the diary were...unspeakable. Borne had been right about one thing: were it to fall into the wrong hands the potential for catastrophe was limitless. Appalling. All their lost powers, in one slim, innocent-seeming volume. Spells of war. Spells of enslavement. Incantations to sear the guarded truth from a captive's mind. Enchantments to suck a soul from its body and trap it for all time in crystal. Summonings to bring forth beasts the like of which he'd never imagined could exist as flesh and blood: dragons, horslirs, trolls, werehags. Incantations of death and destruction that would see Lur laid waste within hours. She had even recorded the most terrible words of all, the words of UnMaking, designed to unknit a man's flesh from bone and undo his place in the world as though he had never been. A desperate spell that would undo the speaker, as well as his victim. Until this moment that incantation had been mere myth. Passed down in secret whispers from Master Magician to Master Magician and never spoken of beneath an open sky. What breed of magician could labour to bring forth such horrors? What man could bend his gifts to birth such monstrosities? Would want to?

Morg.

Praise Barl he was dead then, his like never to be seen again.

The diary wasn't all horror, though. Threaded through the incantations of insanity were more useful applications of magic. Ways of translocating animate matter. Methods of transmuting base metals to gold. Tricks of transcendence. Devices of enhancement.

And a way to see beyond the Wall.

In the Old Tongue, Barl had written:

> *So it falls to me, as I knew it would, to keep this place safe for all time. I have made a beginning, with the banishment of all dark and greedy magics from my people's hearts and minds, but that is not enough. There is still Morgan. His shadow has not touched us yet but I fear it will come, sooner rather than later, and only I can prevent it. There is a way. I believe the natural harmonies in this land, combined with our more militant magics, can be fused into a barrier that will never be breached, so long as it is nurtured most diligently and forevermore. Using some new magics that I have devised I will anchor this Wall in the mountains and a reef around the coastline. Sink its strength into the bowels of the world and feed it daily with the weather magic I will create. I will make this place a paradise, so that our children need cry out in fearful dreams no more.*

Rereading the hastily scrawled entry Durm felt unexpected tears prick his eyes. The heart of her. The passion, and the courage. The *mastery*. She was the last of the great magicians, the last to create new magic out of old. For six centuries the Master Magicians of Lur had followed the strictest guidelines, first and most sacred of which being *No new magic*. It was too dangerous. New magic, untried and untested, might disturb the precarious balance between the Weather and the Wall. Might bring it down and so unleash chaos. In the early days, according to judicial records, certain magicians had thought the rule did not apply to them.

Their deaths had been slow and spectacular and were recited into memory and repeated in a litany unto this very day by the new generation of Doranen magicians in their schoolrooms.

No new magic.

He agreed with the rule, of course he did. But sometimes he dreamed, he wondered, of what freedom would be like. To experiment. To risk. To create that which had never before existed. To be another Barl. But for that he would need to stand on soil that was not of Lur.

Mouth dry, heart tolling like the Great Bell on Barlsday, he opened the diary again and continued to read what she had written.

But while a locked room is safe, without a key it is also a trap. So I have fashioned one and in time I will use it to open a window in the Wall, that I may see what has become of the world beyond. And if it be safe, then we will go home. I swear it, I swear it on my life. One day we will all go home.

"Poor Lady!" he cried to the glowing barrier beyond his window. "You didn't know the making of your Wall would kill you!"

Home. Somewhere out there, beyond the mountains, lay home, Dorana, the birthplace of their race. Their true cradle. Somewhere beyond the mountains there was a land where magic flourished, where incantation was an artform and not a survival mechanism or a toy, where great men could labour their lives in its mysteries, untrammelled by rules and dire punishments in the breaking of them.

And in his hands, his trembling hands, he held a way to find it.

Six centuries ago Morgan, become Morg, had plunged his people into bloody war. He was dead now, dust and ashes on the wind. A frightful phantom, a legacy well remembered, a lesson never to be unlearned. But he was dead. And the living cried out to be set free.

Hesitantly he turned to the next page of the diary, and looked at the sigils and syllables of the incantation that would allow him the first glimpse beyond the Wall in more than six centuries.

If I tell Borne of this, he will say no. He will burn this book for fear of what might be. The crown has clipped his wings. For him the sky is forever out of reach.

For him. But not for me.

And when it is done and we stand atop the mountains and survey the world made new, he will know I did the right thing, and thank me.

With the spell committed to memory Durm stood in the middle of his study. Prepared to start the incantation—and hesitated.

What he was about to do was extremely dangerous, even for a magician of his talent and experience. There was a chance...a small, slim, unlikely chance...that something might go wrong. And if it did, and his study's sanctum was invaded by strangers, or even friends, they would discover Barl's diary.

Which would be a disaster, for many reasons.

His study was full of books. He selected one remarkable for its age and loosened, misshapen leather binding, summoned a narrow-bladed dagger from its drawer and carefully unpicked the back cover's stitching. Slid Barl's slender diary between leather and backing, conjured a needle and painstakingly stitched it whole again.

There. Should worse come to worst, nobody would suspect the book had been tampered with. No magical residue would adhere, and there was no sign of fresh stitching. Barl's secret diary would remain a secret.

Misgivings allayed, he put the book back on its shelf and returned to the business of making history.

Raising his left hand, he traced the first sigil in the warm air. Trailing fire, burning with promise, it hung before his face, waiting. And so, turning half a pace to the left, the second sigil. Another half-pace, and then the third. All with the left hand. With the right, he traced three more, with a half-pace turn between each so that at the end he stood within a wheel of burning sigils, each and every one foreign and thrilling to his eye.

Now for the next step.

"*Elil'toral*!"

In the marrow of his bones and the running of his blood, magic stirred. The sigils bloomed with fresh fire and he felt his skin scorch with the heat.

And the next step.

"*Nen'nonen ra*!"

The sigils quivered. Then, incredibly, began to drift counterclockwise, pirouetting midair like dancers freed from bondage. Slowly at first, then faster, and faster still, until their single shapes were lost and all were a unified burning blur.

And the last.

"*Ma'mun'maht*!"

The spinning wheel of fire snapped in two. Unfurled. Plunged into his chest and transformed him into a living pillar of molten magic. Mouth wide and soundlessly screaming, eyes staring, he glared transfixed at his reflection in the window overlooking the Wall. His bones were melting, his blood boiled, it was pleasure and pain and fear and wonder and power the likes of which he'd never dreamed, never *dreamed* ...

And then he was streaming out of his body, leaving it behind, an abandoned ramshackle of excess flesh. Riding the arrow of fire he plunged through the windowpane, flew over the City, through the gently dwindling rain, above the fields beyond and the Black Woods at the foot of Barl's Mountains...and through the impenetrable Wall as though it were nothing but mist.

It was dark beyond the mountains. A darkness not just of night but of something else as well. Something unseen, yet palpable to his questing mind as it flew over tangled forests and heath-land. In the small distance, lights. Dim. Sallow. But lights, all the same.

With a thought, his arrow of light aimed true towards them and he left Barl's Mountains behind.

A town. Small. Narrow streets, deserted. Iron-barred windows. Doors locked and uninviting. A central marketplace. Wooden gibbets, dangling crow-feasted bodies. Bones gleaming in the sickly moonlight.

What did it mean?

Onwards he flew, his mind seeking, seeking. Somewhere there was fear and a terrible foreboding, but he pushed the feelings aside.

More open countryside. Dispirited trees. Sickly crops. The land looked poisoned. Beaten to its knees. Another town, bigger than the last but shrouded in the same aura of dread.

Something caught his attention. Movement in the empty streets. He swooped closer.

Horror. A patrol of...of...beasts. Men with the mouths of animals, their eyes black and merciless in their dead white faces. Demons. They carried torches. Set fire to a house. The inhabitants ran screaming, burning. The laughing demons butchered them.

Sickened, he fled the dreadful scene. This could not be all. There was still Dorana, shining bright light in the midst of madness.

More woodland ahead. Thick. Black. Menacing. Out of its creeping darkness a shadow, rising. Man-shaped, with eyes that glowed like the sun and a mouth opened to swallow him alive...to swallow the world. It stank of evil incarnate.

Through the whisper-thin link that anchored him to his body he heard himself scream.

The shadow lunged, eyes flaming fire. Words formed in his gibbering mind: *Who are you?*

Terrified to the brink of unreason Durm turned tail and fled. Away from the woodland. Over the countryside. Over the second township, the first township, flying faster than thought for Barl's Mountains and the Wall and the inviolate safety of home. The magic parted before him and he was through the golden barrier once more, flying over the City rooftops and into his study, back in his body where he belonged.

Housed safely once more in his cage of blood and bone he fell to his knees, retching. Pain windmilled behind his eyes. Shuddering, gasping, he lay on his face, fingers clawed into the carpet, and waited for the world to stop spinning.

At length, when he thought he could trust his legs, he lurched to his feet and stumbled into his little washroom. Splashed water into the basin and sluiced the sweat of fear from his skin. Slowly, slowly, reason returned. With shaking hands he reached for a towel, blotted the water from his face and looked up to meet his stunned reflection in the mirror.

He wasn't alone.

Behind him stood a man, shadowy and insubstantial, with eyes that glowed like the sun. Coldly handsome, with hair so pale it looked silver. Extravagant cheekbones. Imperious nose. Lips too full and sensuous. The man smiled.

Durm screamed. Turned. Raised a hand in self-defence: to no avail. Morg's shade lunged for him. Was on him. In him. Melted into his flesh like sunlight through snow. Durm's curdling shriek died mid-breath. For a single frozen moment he wore two faces: his own, and that of the man stealing his body.

And then time ticked forward...and there was but one face in the mirror. Durm's.

But the mind and the soul behind the eyes belonged to Morg.

"Master Durm? Sir? Where would you like the tray put, sir?"

Morg, studying his outstretched hands intently, nodded to the table by the window. "There."

The servant bobbed its head. "Cook said to tell you, sir," it said, uncovering steaming plates and bowls of food and laying them neatly on the blue tablecloth, "we run right out of chinchi eggs so she flipped a couple of bunties instead, seeing as how you like them almost as much, and hope that's right as rain with you."

What was it babbling about? "Yes," he said. "Now get out."

The servant darted him a startled glance. "Yes, sir."

The door clapped shut behind it and he was alone again. Alone with his host...and his body.

"I have a body," he marvelled to the room at large, and laughed, and laughed, and laughed. And the pleasure of that made him laugh all the more.

Seated at the table, knife and fork held lightly in remembering fingers, he took a deep breath—lungs! I have lungs!—and felt his head swim with the rich aromas. Eggs. Mushrooms. Beef. Gravy. Porridge, with cream and honey. Crusty warm bread soaked in butter. Spiced wine.

Durm ate all this for *breakfast*? No wonder the fool was fat.

Four hundred years had passed since last he'd tasted food. It was a memory. Less. The memory of a memory, discarded along with all other physical considerations and the inconveniences they entailed. No sacrifice was too great in the service of his higher purpose. So it could not be regret turning down the corners of this borrowed mouth. Could not be longing, remembered. It was the shock of finding himself corporeal once again after so long without flesh or form.

There was no regret. No longing. These emotions were nothing but the taint of the mind that even now gibbered inconsequentially from its cage deep within. Above all else he was an intellect, a necromancer powerful beyond the dreams and imagination of this wittering Durm and the others, the traitorous descendants of treacherous forebears, soon to be returned to the fold.

Soon to be punished.

But until that glorious moment he was also a body. And his body was hungry. Saliva pooled behind his teeth, under his tongue. His belly rumbled. His nostrils flared.

He ate.

The tastes! The textures! Sweet...soft...runny...crunchy...it was too much. Too much. After so long, an assault on the senses almost past bearing.

Of course, there were certain drawbacks to being housed within flesh once more. For one he was enslaved to that flesh, was bound by its limitations, would have to tend its needs, dance to its desires—not all of which were as delightful as eating. But no matter. For the short time he'd be lodged here, he could manage.

Of greater concern, but still no serious impediment, the matter of his reach and influence. He knew his own mind. He knew the captive Durm's mind. All others were closed to him. After nearly six centuries of unfettered access to every thought, every whim, every dark dream of the men, women, children and demons in his domain, the stark silence had been, in the first hours of his occupation, distressing. But he was adjusting now to the ringing empty echoes. To the knowledge that in this place his powers were circumscribed. That any attempt to use them, to channel the vast arsenal of magic at his disposal, would melt the meat from Durm's bones and in doing so destroy himself as well.

And that was hardly part of the plan.

It meant he could not afford to be overconfident. He would have to proceed cautiously. Carefully. Housed within this fleshy prison he was, for the first time in centuries, vulnerable. To accident and perhaps more than accident if he raised an unwise suspicion, or misjudged the temperature of a moment.

Not that he rated the danger highly. These feeble halfwit child's-play magicians were so far beneath him he had no need to read their minds to know their hearts. Their capricious faces would tell him everything he required to bring them to their knees before him.

And bring them to their knees he would. Soon he would have the means to chastise these unruly children of Lur. To ripen this sweet plum of a place, that he might pluck it neatly from its nourishing branch and thereafter swallow it whole.

So.

Licking egg-yolk from his fork, he chuckled. Really, this was turning into something of a—now what was the word? Ah yes...a holiday.

With his borrowed body bathed and dressed in a fresh robe, he went to the cupboard and withdrew from it an ancient wooden box hasped with silver. Placing it on the table by the window, he sat and considered it. Allowed himself a brief moment of gloating. Deep inside he felt Durm's impotent fingernails, scratching, scratching, desperate to be let out. With a casual swipe of his will he silenced the fat fool and flipped open the box's lid.

Inside, a pearly white globe nestled on a bed of blue velvet. Swirling deep within its heart a flux of colours: gold and green and crimson and purple. One might even call it beautiful, if beauty mattered.

"Barl, Barl, did you truly think you could defeat me? Six years... six hundred...six thousand...you should have known I would never let your treachery go unpunished."

Her fingerprints were all over the thing. Inside it, where the magic dwelled. He could smell them. Taste them. Feel them, like a breeze across his mind, an invisible caress. For six hundred years he had dreamed of confronting her. Vanquishing her. The discovery of the secret to prolonging life and intellect beyond a mere body had been theirs. All these long centuries he'd dreamed of meeting her face to face once more and bringing her to book for her narrow-minded rejection of the greatness he'd planned for both of them.

But even there she had denied him. Spurned their great discovery. Spurned him. Instead of transmuting herself as they'd planned, as they'd promised, she'd squandered her own life in the making of this perfect little kingdom.

In the creation of her damnable Wall, which had held him at bay for longer than any mortal had ever lived.

And in doing so had cheated him, again. Rejected him, again. Defeated him...

"Or so you thought, my love. Yet here I am, and here shall I stay, and here will I pull down your Wall and everything behind it you tried so hard to protect."

Ransacking Durm's memories and devising his plan of conquest had been ridiculously simple. The key to the Wall's destruction lay in the magics that held it together, that fed upon themselves and the ordered management of the weather within the kingdom. It was an endless, self-perpetuating cycle: the power of the weather lent power to the magic, just as the strength of the weather helped maintain the invisible bonds that held the Wall inviolate.

Snap one link in the chain and Barl's precious Wall would come tumbling down.

All he had to do was take the Weather Magic into himself, find that one link, the one point that would yield most meekly to his coercion, and then he could just sit back and watch as Barl's defiance unravelled and her defence of this place crumbled. And then he would stretch forth his hand upon the land...and his victory would at last be complete.

It had come as something of a surprise to learn that Durm did not possess the Weather Magics. He was their guardian, sworn to the tedious task in an unbroken line from Fuldred, the first Master Mage, appointed by Barl herself. Only the WeatherWorker, and the Weather-Worker-in-Waiting, were permitted to absorb the Weather Magics from the Orb. Not that more people couldn't possess the magic. They just wouldn't. Because Barl told them not to. The idea astounded him. Revolted him. Slaves. These lost Doranen were nothing but slaves who had placed the chains about their minds with their own hands and then had willingly swallowed the key.

Well. Now he would swallow them.

The Weather Magics were absorbed from the Orb intact and self-fulfilling. Whoever had them could immediately use them. Call rain and wind and sunshine and snow, with only a thought. Amazing. Hate her though he might, he conceded that Barl had created a miracle. But even so he would defeat her. After all, he was something of a miracle himself.

With a great surge of satisfaction he removed the Orb from its box. It felt warm, peculiarly alive, all that vibrant, violent magic humming within its fragile shell. Helpless to resist, Durm had given him the words of the Transference spell. He summoned them now. Cupped the Orb in both hands, closed his eyes, spoke them aloud—

—and was thrown across the room in a soundless explosion of heat and light and barrier magic. It seared his mind and scorched his skin and sent his disordered senses reeling. Echoing in his stunned mind, a whispering voice not heard for six hundred years.

No, Morgan. This is not for you. This is never for you. Never... never...never.

Gasping, retching, he barely made it to Durm's small private privy before he lost his extravagant breakfast down the boghole. From a great distance deep inside he heard the fat fool laughing.

When he was again himself, could stand on steady legs and walk, he returned to the study and stared at the discarded Orb, unsullied, undamaged, unplundered and abandoned on the floor. Barl had anticipated him. Assumed that somehow he would reach this place... or at least that he might. And because she knew him as no other body or mind had ever known him, she had devised a way to keep her precious Weather Magics away from him. Safe from him.

A tidal wave of thick red hatred surged within him, robbed him of sight and hearing, clawed his fingers and tore at his throat.

"Bitch! Slut! Treacherous whore! You think this will stop me? You will never stop me! I am Morg! I am invincible and your defeat is a foregone conclusion!"

He picked up the Orb. Put it back in its box. Put the box back in its cupboard, and closed the doors.

So. If he couldn't bring down the Wall this way, he would bring it down in another. In the end the manner of its destruction wasn't important. All that mattered was that he saw it destroyed.

Slumped in a chair, he let his scheming thoughts wander. The key to his victory lay in manipulating the Weather Magics. In using them—their wielder—to bring down the Wall. The king was unassailable. Pointless to try and corrupt the girl, or take her over. Fane's power was extraordinary, perhaps as fine as Barl's had been, and she believed in protecting Barl's Wall as fervently as the rest of them.

Which left only the cripple...

Frustrated, he paced Durm's untidy study. There was a way to use the boy, yes, at least in theory, but it would take so *long*. He'd not thought to spend more than days in this place and now he'd be here weeks. The notion was intensely irritating.

But he could sustain a little irritation. Especially when the reward for patience was so great.

And he was in no danger here, provided he remained undiscovered. The greater part of himself that he'd left behind the Wall would wait for his return, their rejoining. Soon enough he would be Morg again. Would slough off this binding vulnerable flesh and once more become immortal, invulnerable spirit.

Soon enough, Barl's Wall would come down.

Some time later, after a second round of bathing and dressing, and fortified with his new plan, he ventured outside to find the king and queen. Thanks to Durm he knew every twist and turn of the palace, every face that passed him. This place was as familiar to him as the contours of his own mind.

Their Majesties—*Majesties!*—were in the palace solar, lingering over breakfast. A pleasant room, with birds and flowers and spilling sunshine. Pink and cream and gold. Pretty colours. Pretty furnishings, too, plump and fringed and tasselled and sparkling in the warm light. How soft they were, in this place, in the delusions of their safety.

"Durm!" the king said. "Come. Sit." There was something vaguely familiar about him. Chances were he was descended directly from Ryal Torvig; the nose was the same, the mouth, and a trick of the eye. Ryal, who'd promised loyalty and delivered betrayal. Ryal, who'd died screaming amidst his own entrails. But it would seem his whore had survived after all, to breed on. A pity.

"Have you eaten?" asked the queen.

"Thank you, yes." He sat. "Forgive the interruption but I needed to speak with you. I have been thinking."

The king plucked a hothouse strawberry from its bowl. Plump and ripely red, it looked delicious. "About?"

"Barl." He felt his emptied stomach spasm. The bitch, the slut, the treacherous whore. "And her library."

"Durm?" the queen asked, teacup paused at her lips. "Are you all right?"

On a deep breath he relaxed. Unclenched his fingers. "Of course. A touch of indigestion."

The king favoured him with a wicked grin. "Shall I call for Nix? He has so *many* potions..."

Durm would smile at that, so he curved his lips. "That won't be necessary. But I am touched by the thought."

"I thought you might be." The king bit into another succulent strawberry: pink juice dribbled down his chin and the queen, laughing, dabbed him clean with her napkin. "So, you've been thinking about the library. And?"

"And I fear that yesterday I allowed my zeal to over-ride my better judgement," he continued, and assumed a suitably apologetic expression. "Your better judgement."

"How so?"

"Blessed Barl in her infinite wisdom hid that chamber, and those books, for reasons we cannot fathom. I fear we were wrong to ignore that wisdom."

"I don't know what to say," said the king after a lengthy silence. "What's brought about this abrupt change of heart?"

"The thought that we may yet discover treatises of ancient Doranen magic."

Exchanging glances with the queen, the king leaned forward. The hothouse strawberries were forgotten now. "I thought you wanted to find them."

"I did. In truth, part of me still does. But the danger of doing so far outweighs the benefits. If such magics were discovered...if they were to fall into the wrong hands...the Wall itself may be destroyed, Borne, and that is unthinkable." For them, at least. For himself, he'd been dreaming, plotting and planning little else for centuries.

The king frowned. "Whose 'wrong hands' concern you the most?"

"My own," said Morg. Seasoning Durm's voice with a rueful, courageous honesty, he continued, "I'm afraid that if I found such magics, if I discovered a book with our arcane heritage writ large upon its pages, I would not resist the temptation to use it. I fear that my zeal and, regrettably, my arrogance—"

"Arrogance?" the king protested. "Durm, what—"

"Please, old friend!" he said, shaking his head. "Can you truly sit there and smile in my eye and say I am not arrogant? I am, and we both know it. And *I* know that my arrogance would indeed overrun my more temperate self, and that in so doing I would bring about calamity and woe."

"This is arrant nonsense!" the king retorted. "You would never, *never*—"

He lifted a hand to halt the passionate spate of words. "It is an unwise man, Majesty, who claims 'never.' I think you told me that once."

The king's pale face was flushed with temper. "I grant you're a passionate man, Durm. Confident in your abilities, as well you should be, because they're prodigious. But you would *never*, and yes I use the word, not unwisely, *never* betray me or my kingdom. And if you think I'm going to sit here and listen to you malign yourself in such a fashion, you—"

"Borne," said the queen, and laid a gentle finger on his wrist. "Let him finish."

Which was interesting. Little ranting Durm knew the queen did not like him overmuch but kept her peace for the sake of her husband. For himself, he found her reservations amusing, springing as they did from her unreasoning love of that mewling monstrosity she called a son and a suspicion that Durm had no real respect for her at all.

And there, little magician, do we find ourselves in agreement, and nobody is more surprised than I to discover we share a toehold of common ground! This queen is no queen at all; your king is blinded by love. And not just for her. For the cripple, too. But let's not be too harsh towards our little princeling, eh? He is, after all, the tool of your destruction and is to be cherished. At least for now.

The king said, subsiding, "He can talk until crows grow on corn stalks, Dana. It still won't make him right."

"Do you say he doesn't know his own heart?" she countered. "Why then have you called for his counsel all these years if you so easily mistrust what he says?"

There was a dangerous glitter in the king's eye. It made him look more than ever like long-dead Ryal. "I think you'd best speak plainly, madam."

"Plainly, then, you should stop bellowing and hear him out," the queen snapped. "Yesterday you were the one saying the library should remain unbreached. Now Durm is agreeing with you, a little late perhaps, but still. Tell me what there is in this to mislike!"

"I mislike," the king said dangerously, "that he would sit there and accuse himself of foul, unspeakable treachery. Even more do I mislike the fact that you don't defend him, even from himself!"

How tedious. As if he had time for wedded spats. "Dear friends," he raised both hands placatingly. "Please do not disagree on my account. Your loyalty moves me almost to tears, Borne, but in this the queen has the right of it. Allow me to know myself and my personal demons a little better than you."

"You are no traitor," said the king. "My life upon it. I cannot believe you would ever put your own desires above the welfare of this kingdom. I *will* not believe it, even if Barl herself should come back from the grave to tell me in person."

"Well, I expect you're right," said Morg, as deep within the darkness trapped Durm wept, inconsolable. "But can you understand I prefer not to put that belief to the test?"

"Yes," the queen said. "Of course we can understand. We do understand. The library will be sealed and the secret of its existence will die with us."

Well, that much was certainly true. He turned to the king. "Borne?"

"I confess," the king said slowly, "that I spent an uneasy night. I had bad dreams. *Not* because I mistrust you. Every argument you made yesterday holds true in the light of a new morning. And yet..."

"Precisely," he said, smiling. "In the harsh light of day, doubts outweigh daring. Countless thousands of lives depend on us. You were right all along, Borne. The risk is too great."

"So be it." The king grimaced. "Fane will be desolate."

Ah yes. The magical prodigy. He was looking forward to meeting her: Durm considered her quite amazing. "I will deal with Fane," he said. "As WeatherWorker-in-Waiting, she will understand that we act with the kingdom's best interests at heart."

"And what of Gar?" said the queen. "Borne, he'll be devastated. All those books. You said he could study them, you named him—"

"I know," said the king. "It can't be helped."

"A compromise, perhaps," Morg suggested. "It's clear that what we found yesterday is harmless. His Highness could safely take those books and translate them to his heart's content. If it's made known that those texts comprised the extent of the discovery, all should be well."

"An excellent idea," approved the queen.

The king nodded. "I agree. And it would be a shame to come away from this empty-handed." Sighing, he frowned at the bowl of strawberries.

Finally succumbing to temptation Morg reached for one, though his purged belly was still uneasy. The flavour exploded on his tongue, sweet, so sweet. He almost moaned aloud. When he could speak: "Might I make another suggestion?"

"Of course," said the king.

"Let me be the one to tell the prince of this decision. It will distress him, and since I'm the one responsible for it, it's only fair that I bear the brunt of his displeasure."

"Like Fane, he will understand," the queen said sharply. "Gar is no fool."

A matter for debate, surely. But he smiled at the queen, and spread his hands wide. "That was not my meaning, Majesty. Forgive me if I was unclear."

"Doubtless it's cowardly of me but—very well," said the king. "By all means, break the bad news to Gar."

"Excellent," said Morg, and smiled. "If you'll excuse me, Majesty, I'll do so directly. When a plan is decided there seems little point in delay. Don't you agree?"

"Certainly," said Borne. And smiled. And flicked his fingers in fond, unsuspecting farewell.

The fool.

CHAPTER TWENTY-SEVEN

He found the cripple in the Tower's foyer, conversing with Nix. No fool, the pother excused himself and withdrew. Since protocol dictated that Durm bow to the prince, Morg lowered his chin, briefly. "Good morning, Your Highness. I hope your health remains robust?"

"Certainly," replied the cripple. He looked wary. "Nix was here to see Asher."

Ah yes. The Olken hero. Morg smothered a sneer; it was important he gained the weakling's trust. "Still not recovered, then? I'm sorry to hear it. The kingdom owes him a great debt."

The cripple's wariness eased. "Indeed. And when he's on his feet again—Barl grant it be soon, now—the debt shall be paid. Durm, what brings you here? Is something wrong?"

He smiled. "Not...precisely. Shall we walk?"

To his and Durm's surprise, the cripple took the news well. "I'm sorry, of course," he said as he was circumspectly guided towards the Old Palace. "Sorrier than you'll ever know. But I can't say I wasn't expecting it. A discovery like this—it's too dangerous. His Majesty is absolutely correct in his decision. I consider myself fortunate to be left with any books at all."

"Which is why I have brought you back here now," said Morg, halting before the door that would lead them, eventually, to his bitch lover's long-hidden chamber. "I thought perhaps you and I might take a few moments to look over one or two more shelves. See if there's not something particularly splendid for you to add to your collection."

"Are you sure? Does His Majesty know that—"

"His Majesty trusts me, Your Highness," said Morg. "And so should you. You used to, once upon a time."

"Once upon a time," the cripple replied, "you thought I was my father's son and that together we'd work great magics." Then he shook his head. "I'm sorry. That was uncalled for. Of course I trust you, Durm."

In silence, they continued to the library.

"It's such a pity," the cripple sighed, wandering among the bookshelves, touching their spines with foolish, doting fingers. "Who knows what grand histories of old Dorana are hidden here? What fabulous tales of those glorious long-dead days I'll never get to read. I'm going to spend the rest of my life wondering. Mourning, really."

Morg swung the chamber door shut with a nod. "No, you won't. Eunuch."

The cripple stopped. Stared. "I'm sorry...*what* did you just call me?"

"Eunuch," he repeated politely. "It means 'impotent one.' A man bereft of the means by which to perform. Agreed, there is a slight contextual difference, but the spirit of the word still applies. Magically speaking, little princeling, you are *limp*."

The look on the cripple's face was worth quite a lot of the aggravation his treacherous slut was causing him. "I think you must be unwell," the prince said with great care. "I suggest you see Pother Nix immediately, and I'll forget this ever happened."

"Well...you're half right." With a casual flick of his fingers he froze the witless natterer where he stood. "Grand histories of old Dorana. You *cretin*," he sneered, and felt contempt twist his borrowed face. "There is nothing grand about those long-dead days! The dynastic squabbling, the interhouse rivalries, the needless shedding of blood. Politics for its own sake. No thought for the purity of our people, no consideration for the future. All they cared about was power for personal aggrandisement. The greatness of our race, the fulfilment of our destiny, meant nothing to them. *Nothing*! They were fools, your ancestors, every last one of them, and Barl the most foolish of all. Did she think I would stand idly by and watch our race tear itself to pieces like a pack of rabid dogs? She said she loved me. How could she love me, yet know me so little?"

The cripple did not answer. Empty of thought, of feeling, a blank sheet of parchment waiting patiently for the pen, it stood tranquilly before him.

"And *you*," he went on, bile and spite scalding. "You think you're safe here? You think it couldn't happen to you? Are you deaf, then, to the growls in the throat of that dog on the Privy Council? You think Jarralt and the rest of his relatives are without ambition? That they don't nurse dreams of crowns and palaces and the crackling fire of Weather Magic? Hah! Of course they do...thanks to you. You blotted the family copybook, boy. You're the crack in your father's armour. The lever by which Conroyd Jarralt would tilt your world on its axis if he could. Tilt and tilt and tilt until it tumbled, and the sky rained fire on all your pretty heads. You think Trevoyle's Schism was bad? Little eunuch, it pales in comparison with the bloodshed I've seen. I stood on top of the tallest tower in all of old Dorana and watched your forebears melt the flesh from each other's bones. Boil brothers' eyes in their cracking sockets. They turned their mansions into charnel-houses and their children into charcoal. *That* is your grand Doranen history. Your glorious past. Your grim future. It's a good thing I'm here, little crippled princeling. I've come to save you from yourselves."

It came as a shock to realise that he was panting. That there was sweat on his brow and his borrowed hands were trembling. He took a deep breath, then spat it out.

"Your precious Wall is offensive to me." He closed in on the cripple to rest Durm's reluctant fingers upon his waiting shoulders. "The time has come for it to fall."

Leaning close, he pressed spittle-flecked lips to the cripple's smooth forehead. Breathed words into the lax body beneath his hands. He felt the muscles leap. Felt the sizzle and swish of the magic as it breached the body's shield, the skin, and raced through blood and sinew.

Brighter than any glimfire ever conjured; colder than any winter ever called: the imprint of Durm's lips burned blue above the bridge of the prince's nose. Burned...burned...and faded.

Morg turned away. Began sorting through the books piled on the chamber's old desk. A moment later, the cripple stirred.

"I'm sorry, did you say something, Durm? I'm afraid I wasn't listening."

"It was nothing, Your Highness," said Morg, and gently smiled. "Nothing at all."

*   *   *

When Asher finally drifted to the surface of his dreamsoaked sleep it was to see Dathne sitting in the chair beside his bed. She looked almost serene. Her hair was briskly restrained in a plait, laying bare the pure, sharp lines of her face. She was knitting. Something pink and fluffy, which was so unlike her he thought for a moment he must still be lost in fancies.

He felt his heart crack open and all his throttled feelings for her come pouring out.

Glancing up, she saw his open eyes. "Well, well, well," she said, tart as fresh lemon. "If it's not Prince Lazybones himself." Without waiting for an answer she put down her knitting and picked up a little silver bell from his bedside table. Then she went to his bedchamber door, opened it and tinkled the bell into the corridor.

A maid appeared. Cluny. "Yes'm?" she asked.

"Go and tell whoever needs to know it that Asher is awake."

Cluny squealed. "Oh, *yes'm*!"

Dathne closed the chamber door on the sound of Cluny's feet pounding down the spiral staircase and tinkled her way back to the chair by his bed. Replaced the bell on his bedside table but didn't pick up her knitting. Instead she sat with her hands folded neatly in her lap and frowned at him.

"We parted badly, Asher, you and I," she said in that brusque, forthright way he'd come to treasure. "As much my fault as yours. You took me by surprise. More than a year we've known each other, and you never once said anything about...feelings."

He found his voice: it felt tentative. "You expecting an apology?"

"No. We all have our secrets. But here's the thing." Still frowning, she smoothed her blue wool skirt over her knees. "I don't love you, Asher. I don't love anyone. But that doesn't mean we can't be friends."

He laughed, though he was anything but amused. How many different pains were there in this world? And was he going to have to feel all of them? "Don't it?"

"Not to me. Of course I can't speak for you, but I'd like to think you felt the same. We've been good friends till now, haven't we? I see no reason to lose that." She hesitated then, and for once looked uncertain. "I don't want to lose that."

His breathing hitched, air catching in his chest. He wanted to reach his hand to her. Touch her. Friendship wasn't nearly enough, but if it was all she had to give him...and mayhap in time he could convince her otherwise. Teach her to trust his heart...and her own. "My da died."

Her frown softened. "And you're shunned. Forbidden the coast and all eight fishing communities. I know. I'm sorry."

He didn't know what to say to that. Was afraid if he tried to speak, tears would drown the words. "How long since I got back?" he asked when enough time had passed.

"This is the seventh morning since you fell ill." She skimmed his skin with her cool hand and nodded, satisfied. "Do you still hurt?"

For a moment he was confused. Why would he hurt? Then he remembered. His beaten back. His punished body after all that desperate riding. Great waves of furious heat and freezing cold, sweeping him from head to toe as fever claimed him. Closing his eyes he searched himself, and discovered nothing but a lingering lethargy. "No."

She nodded, smiling. "Good."

He looked at her again. Devoured her face with his eyes. She flushed, a small tide of colour washing over her cheeks, but she didn't look away. He lifted an eyebrow. "So. Have I missed anythin' exciting?"

She told him. Details of the damaged City. All the repairs, and the official Day of Thanksgiving: wasn't he sorry he'd slept through that? No, not really. The books discovered in the deserted Old Palace. His Highness was like a pig in mud. "Aye, I'll bet," said Asher, rolling his eyes.

"And Westwailing?" he asked when she was finished. "Is everything all right there now?"

"It is according to Darran," she said. "He and Willer got back safely the day before yesterday. The rest of the expedition is following on."

Asher scowled. Bloody Willer. Now if *he'd* gone arse over earholes into the harbour...

She smiled. "And your things, and all your money, which the king sent down to the coast for you—they're safely back."

He could only shake his head. "How do you know so much?"

"I make it my business."

"So what caused the storm in the first place?"

Dathne shrugged. "In a nutshell, the king's illness. He was lost in fever. Worried about the prince. The Weather Magics followed the path of his thoughts. And because he was delirious and couldn't control his own power or the way it manifested, we got a storm. It's tragic, but it's nobody's fault." She pulled a face. "The king has been distraught. The minute he was allowed out of bed he went to the City Barlschapel and spent the night on his knees, praying for those who died, and after that he joined in the repairs. I hear Pother Nix was furious, and the queen, but His Majesty refused to yield."

Asher shifted on his pillows. "He's a grand man, is Borne. We're lucky he didn't die."

"You'll get no argument from me," Dathne agreed. Then she grinned. "There's something else as well. Although probably I shouldn't tell you. Probably the prince will want to tell you himself when he gets here."

There were suspicious glints of mischief in her eyes. He mistrusted Dathne's mischief, heartily. "You tell me now."

"No, no," she said, laughing. "He'll be cross as two sticks if I spoil the surprise."

"*Dathne*—" he started, but broke off because the chamber door flew open and Gar strode into the room. Dathne slid off her chair and curtseyed.

"Barl save me from all that goes bump in the night!" the prince exclaimed, stopping at the foot of the bed. "It's about damned time you woke up!"

For a moment Asher couldn't speak. Hollow-cheeked and feverish, Gar looked like a man driven to his limit. His crumpled silk shirt was splotched with ink stains and his fine wool breeches had a tear across one knee. "Barl save you, all right! You look bloody dreadful, Gar. What've you been doing?"

"Fretting for you," said Gar, and laughed. There was a shrill edge to the sound and his eyes were wild. "No. Sorry. I've been working my fingers to the bone fulfilling your duties as well as mine and I have to say I'm well sick of it. When are you getting up?"

Asher worked his way upright and rested his shoulderblades against the bedhead. "Dathne said you found some mouldy ole books? Bet you've had your nose stuck in 'em day and night without resting and that's what's got you lookin' like death on a toasting fork."

Another grating laugh. "All right, all right. I confess," Gar said. "I have been burning a smidgin of midnight oil translating some mouldy ole books, as you so disrespectfully call them." He turned to Dathne and pretended displeasure. "Stealing my thunder, are you, Dathne? I hope you didn't tell him about that other matter!"

Dathne curtseyed again. "No, Your Highness."

"I should think not!" Gar rubbed his hands together as though he were trying to start a fire.

"When was the last time you slept?" asked Asher.

"Who needs sleep?" said Gar, derisive. "Besides, you've been snoring enough for the both of us. Now let's stop bleating about me, shall we? Asher, I have a surprise for you. You'll never guess what it is."

Asher pulled a face. "Don't think I want to."

"All right then, I'll tell you. There's to be a parade in your honour."

He stared at Dathne, horrified. She shrugged. He stared at Gar again, still horrified. The silly prat was grinning like a loon. "A *what?*"

"If you don't stop scowling like that your face is going to shatter," said Gar. "And anyway, nothing you can say will make a difference. Their Majesties insist upon a parade so a parade there will be. Darran's been sweating blood over the final details ever since his return. We've just been waiting for you to wake up. It'll start here at the Tower and go all the way through the City, along every main thoroughfare. What do you think about that, eh?"

"I think you be clean out of your pretty yellow head!" said Asher, choking. "A *parade?* I don't want a bloody parade!"

"Well, want it or not, you're getting one," Gar replied. "So I suggest you start practising your smiling and waving."

Asher slid back down the bed and pulled the blankets over his face. Pulled them away again and said, despairingly, "But *why?*"

Some of the frenetic animation died out of Gar's expression. "Why do you think? Because you saved my life, you fool."

With the dregs of his dwindling strength Asher tugged a pillow from behind his head. "Well, if I'd known it'd mean a bloody parade I'd have damned well let you drown!" And he threw the pillow as hard as he could at Gar's fatuously smiling face.

Shortly afterwards Pother Nix interrupted the ensuing lively discussion by arriving with his basket of pills and potions and demanding privacy for himself and his patient.

"Waving and smiling, Asher, remember?" said Gar, retreating. "Both must be perfect. Darran insists upon it."

Asher glowered. "Ha."

"Come and see me later, if you're able. I'll be working in the library."

"*Ha.*"

"I'm glad you're mended," said Dathne as she stowed her knitting in her string bag. "I'll look for you in the Goose at week's end, same as usual, shall I?"

"Maybe," said Asher.

She smiled, hefting the straps of the bag onto her bony shoulder. "Definitely. Unless I see you in the parade first, of course."

And then she was gone, laughing, and it was just him and the damn bone-botherer. Nix pronounced him sound in wind and limb, which he knew already, then made him drink another damn potion that put him right back to sleep.

When he woke again it was late afternoon and he was alone. For some small time he lay there unmoving. Thinking. About Da. Jed. His brothers. His life. About decisions, and choices, and who controlled who.

About how that was all going to change.

Zeth and the rest were due a few unpleasant surprises.

And with that settled he realised he was suddenly sick of pillows and blankets. Cautiously, expecting his legs to fold like a newborn foal's at any moment, he clambered out of bed. His legs held. Amazing. Somebody had left a bowl of fresh fruit on the table. He ate a couple of teshoes and an apple as he wandered around his apartment, just to see if his legs would still take him from here to there and back again without collapsing. They did. He felt fine. Whatever Nix had put in that potion, it had worked a treat. His head was clear, his body free of pain, and he was ready to brave the world beyond his bedchamber. So he found some fresh clothes, pulled them on and left his rooms.

The first person he saw when he reached the Tower lobby was Darran. Looking like a stork on its way to a funeral, same as usual, all black plumage and long spindly legs. He halted abruptly as Asher stepped off the last staircase tread.

"Asher." He moved closer, knobbly fingers clasped in front of him. "You have Pother Nix's leave to be out and about, do you?"

Asher rolled his eyes. "Aye, I be feelin' ever so much better, Darran. Thanks for askin'. I be touched. Honest." He headed for the doors.

"Asher, wait!"

Sighing, Asher waited. "What?"

Darran darted a quick, hunted look about the empty lobby and came closer still. The ole fool's wrinkly throat was working like he'd swallowed an orange whole and couldn't get it down. "I want a word with you."

"About?"

"You saved His Highness's life."

Asher raised his hands palm out. "Darran, if this is about that stupid parade, you're wastin' your breath. I were asleep when Gar and his folks dreamed up that little bit of madness so you can't blame me."

Darran's pinched face was stiff with dislike, and something else. Something Asher couldn't place. "Asher, be quiet. I am perfectly aware that the parade in your honour was requested by Their Majesties. That's not what I wanted to talk to you about."

"Then what?" said Asher impatiently. "I'm tryin' to get out for a breath of fresh air, Darran, in case you haven't noticed. Feels like I ain't seen nowt but the inside of my own eyelids for six months, not six days."

Darran's thin cheeks stained red. "You really are the most impossible man it has ever been my misfortune to know," he snapped. "I merely wanted to say that in saving Prince Gar's life at the risk of your own you demonstrated a courage and sense of honour I heretofore did not suspect you possessed."

Asher thought about that for a moment. "Am I still dreamin' or was that a compliment?"

Darran nodded. "Apparently. Though I'm beginning to wonder why."

"That makes two of us," said Asher, grinning. "Ain't no need for compliments, Darran. I didn't save him for you."

Darran's clasped hands clenched bloodless. "Nevertheless. You saved him."

With a small shock Asher realised then that this wasn't Darran somehow doing him a backhanded bad turn. The ole fool meant every word he was saying. And that was the thing in Darran's expression he'd not been able to place: the bitter taste of swallowed pride. *Bastard*. He sighed. "I had to."

Darran considered him in silence for a long time. "I see," he said at last. "Very well, then." He turned away. Paused, and turned back. "You realise, of course, this in no way implies that I suddenly approve of you, or have changed my opinion that at heart you remain a lawless ruffianly reprobate."

"Of course. Same as it don't imply I reckon you're anything but a dried-up old dog turd."

Darran's lips thinned in a smile. "Precisely."

Honour mutually satisfied, they parted company.

Without making a conscious decision Asher found himself heading for the stables. The autumn air was crisp, the leaves on the trees all around him dying in a riot of crimson and gold. He took a deep, lung-filling breath and was overwhelmingly glad to be alive.

Of course, whether he was glad to be alive here, and not down on the coast, was another matter. Fresh grief stabbed him. *Da*. And Jed. Would there ever be a time when he could think of his father and his friend and not feel pain? It was hard to imagine. Da was dead…Jed was addled…and he was to blame.

"Barl save us!" Matt cried when Asher entered the stable yard, and dropped the bucket of feed he was carrying. "Look what the cat's dragged in." All around the yard Matt's lads shouted and whistled and catcalled. Matt strode to meet him and, to his extreme surprise, folded him in a ribcracking embrace. "Damn it, Asher, you scared fifty years out of me!"

Warmed, Asher returned the hug. "Sorry."

With a final thump between the shoulderblades, Matt stepped back. "Dath said you were looking fine," he said, eyeing him critically. "And so you are. I heard there were people thinking healing thoughts for you. Barl must have been listening."

Asher stared. There'd been City folk *prayin'* for him? Damn. That was even worse than a bloody parade. "Cygnet all right?"

Matt laughed. "Cygnet's fine. Ballodair too." Then his smile faded and he stared intently into Asher's face. "I'm sorry about your father. It comes to all of us in time, no escape, but it's still a bad blow."

Especially when you helped it happen. "Aye." He shrugged. "But it's happened. No point fratchin' on it. I'm fine."

Matt looked as though he didn't believe him. One of the drawbacks of friends. "And what about staying in Dorana?"

So. Matt knew the whole of it. Somebody's tongue must be tired of wagging. Gar. Dathne. Fools. Didn't they have nowt better to do than sit around gossiping? Asher felt his expression harden. "I'm thinkin' I might have a quiet word with my brothers on that score."

Matt stared at him, uncertain. "What? You're going back to Restharven? But I thought—"

"You thought right, for now. But only for now. Fishin's in my blood, Matt, same as horses are in yours. I ain't givin' it up. Not on Zeth's say-so. It'll take time, I know, but that's fine. I'll wait."

"For how long?"

He grinned, feeling savage. "A few months. A year. As long as I have to. Sooner or later the tide always turns." He shrugged. Stared around the immaculate stable yard. "And in the meantime, if I can't have the ocean I s'pose Dorana'll do."

Looking relieved, Matt slung an exuberant arm around his shoulders and shook him. "That's the spirit."

"Get off me, y'great lummox!" said Asher, fighting free. "Stop hangin' round my neck like a girl and show me my poor bloody horse!"

"Heard about your parade," Matt said as they headed for Cygnet's stable. Asher speared him with a look. Matt looked back, innocently smiling. "It's so exciting. Going to wear tinsel in your hair, are you? That should look pretty."

"There'll be tinsel up your arse if you ain't careful," said Asher darkly.

Matt mimed shock. "Asher! Now is that any way for the Hero of Dorana to talk?"

Asher stopped. Stared. "The *what* of *where*?"

Matt's broad, weathered face split into a delighted smile. "That's what they're calling you, down in the City. Haven't you heard?"

Asher hung his head. "I'm goin' to kill Gar for this, I swear. I don't know when, and I don't know where, but I'm goin' to bloody kill him."

Matt just laughed, and laughed, and laughed.

Returning to the Tower after half an hour of feeding Cygnet and Ballodair enough carrots and apples to rupture their guts, Asher could think of nothing but food and putting his feet up. But first he thought he should pay a call on Gar. The prince hadn't looked well, and the last thing anybody needed was him flat on his back with a fever. For one thing it'd mean *he'd* have to take over all the work, and he wasn't in the mood for that at all.

He banged on Gar's library door for five minutes before it opened the width of three thin fingers. "What do you want?" said the prince. "Can't you see I'm busy?"

Asher winced: the words were slurred, spat into his face on a cloud of bad breath. "Let me in, Gar. I need your ear for a minute or so."

Gar grinned, a ghastly revelation of teeth. "Give me a knife and you can have both of them, provided you go away afterwards and never bother me again."

"*Gar!*"

"Just joking."

"Do I look amused to you? Open the bloody door, would you?"

Gar scowled, resisting. Then he stood aside grumpily. "One minute. Then I'm calling a guard."

Just as grumpily, Asher shoved the door open and marched into the library. "What's goin' on, Gar? I mean, I know you like your books and all, but this is plain ridiculous!"

Gar returned to his desk, which was layered inches deep in paper and parchment and towered with piles of ancient-looking volumes, whose faded titles Asher couldn't read. More books were piled row after row on the floor so there was hardly any space to walk. The library curtains were drawn. Just one lamp was lit. The room looked like a manky bear's cave. Stank like one too, the air thick and overused. Fumbling through the mess, Gar withdrew a single sheet of paper and held it out.

Asher stared suspiciously. "What's that?"

"A list of people you're to see tomorrow. I'm too busy. Find out what they want, give it to them if you can, tell them they'll have to wait to see me if you can't."

Asher ran his eye down the list of names. Mistress Banfrey of the Milliners' Guild. Meister Glospottle of the Dyers' Guild. Captain Orrick—"What's Pellen Orrick want?" he asked, looking up.

"I'm not sure," said Gar, pawing at his damned books again. "Something about crowd control for the parade, I think. It's your parade, you sort it out."

"How many times do I have to say it, Gar? I don't want a damned bloody stupid parade!"

"It's to be held the day after tomorrow by the way," Gar continued, pen raised. "Speak to Darran about the particulars. There's no use asking me, I'm—"

"Too busy," said Asher in disgust. "I'm gettin that. Gar, when were the last time you saw yourself in a mirror? You look like—"

"I'm afraid you'll be taking on quite a lot of extra responsibility for the next good while," said Gar, oblivious. "These books we've found are extraordinary, I can't begin to tell you." He dipped the pen into the inkpot: it came up dry. "Oh." Discarding the pen, he picked up the pot and held it out. "I seem to have run out of ink. Would you mind—"

Asher snatched the pot from him and threw it across the room. "Yes, I'd bloody mind!" he shouted. "Gar, what's the matter with you?"

The prince stood so fast his chair tipped over. "With me? Nothing's the matter with me! I'm busy, that's all! Can't you understand that? Has everyone become very stupid all of a sudden? First Darran, then Nix, now you?" He waved his arm wildly at the room. "Look at all these books, Asher! They are the greatest find in the history of the kingdom! I have to catalogue them, I have to translate them, I have to—"

"You have to stop. Afore you fall to pieces entirely." Shoving the list of appointments inside his shirt, he picked up the upended chair and pushed Gar into it. Stared down into his hollow-eyed, hollow-cheeked face. "You're halfway there already."

For a long time Gar said nothing, just sat bolt upright on his chair wrestling with demons only he could see. Arms folded, expression as mulish as he could make it, Asher waited.

"I do feel...a bit strange," Gar confessed at last, slumping a little and rubbing his hands up and down his arms. "Like my skin is crawling with invisible ants. As though there are hundreds and hundreds of tiny fire-crackers going off inside my head. If I close my eyes I can see the explosions."

"See? I was right!" said Asher. "Too much readin' *does* rot your brain. Did you tell any of this to that ole bonebotherer?"

"Nix?" Gar shook his head, a kind of convulsive shudder. "No."

"Good. He'd prob'ly just give you something disgustin' to drink." With a silent sigh, Asher hitched his hip onto the corner of the desk. "You're a damn fool, Gar. You said already you ain't been sleeping. When was the last time you ate something?"

Gar waved a vague hand. "Oh. I don't know. I'm pretty sure I had a boiled egg yesterday."

"Look. I don't care how bloody special these mouldy ole books are, no book is worth you workin' yourself into a collapse over. You've got to get some rest now, or it'll be your turn to spend a week in bed and then you'll miss the damn parade. And if you think I'm goin' through all that malarkey on my own, then you really have cracked."

"Miss the parade?" Gar managed a small smile. "And the sight of you smiling and waving and wishing you were anywhere else in the kingdom? Hardly."

"Then you'd best have a bath and a bowl of soup and a good night's sleep, eh?"

Gar turned back to his desk. Brushed his fingers across the nearest open book. "Yes. You're right. I know. I'll just finish this page and—"

Asher slammed the book shut. "*Now.*"

As he closed the library door behind them, one hand on Gar's shoulder to prevent an attempted escape, Asher glanced through the banisters. Darran was standing on the staircase below them, halfway between floors, hands clasped neatly before him. His face was pinched into a worried frown. On seeing Gar the frown eased, just a little. Then he looked at Asher, and raised one eyebrow.

Asher rolled his eyes and kept on walking.

It was late when Dathne was at last able to contact Veira. After the visit with Asher there'd been shop business and errands, and supper with Matt to discuss where they were along Prophecy's mysterious road.

The fact that she still didn't know, and he couldn't help her find out, was something she refused to dwell on.

"Asher is woken, Veira, and taken no harm from his trials. Tell the Circle their healing was a success."

It will lift their hearts to hear it, child.

"Beyond that, I've nothing more to tell."

Nothing? Veira sounded disappointed.

Well, so was she disappointed. Disappointed and guilty and stuck like a cow in the mire. "I'm sorry! If I could force matters, I would. I pray and I pray for Jervale to show me the next step, but there's nothing. Just forebodings and unease."

You knew Asher would return. We must satisfy ourselves with that for now.

"No, Veira, I can't. It's not enough!" The link between them trembled with the violence of her thoughts, her feelings. "Night after night I rack my brains trying to see the way forward, trying to understand how Asher can be the Innocent Mage. What it means that he is in the Usurper's House. How it's possible for the Wall to be brought down when not even the king's cataclysmic fever disturbed it. We are in the Final Days, Veira, I know it in my bones, in my heart. Yet all remains unaltered. Life jogs along, just the same as ever it did. Now that they're safe and the City is healed of damage and things are returning to normal, people have even started making jokes again. *Jokes.* As though any of this was funny!"

Hush, child. You'll make yourself ill with such fretting.

She was already ill. Churned up and quivering. "I feel like I'm somehow suspended between breaths," she said, fists pressed against her chest where her heart was racing. "As though the storm was an inhalation. Any moment now the world will need to exhale again, and when it does…when it does…" Cross-legged on the floor before her Circle Stone, she began to rock. "I need to be ready. I need to know what to do, how to react, and I don't, Veira. I don't. And I'm so afraid it will mean the ruin of us all. What if I'm wrong about him, Veira, and he's not the Innocent Mage after all? What if I've been wrong about everything?"

Foolish. You are foolish, Dathne. These are but the fancies of an overtired mind. He is who you have named him. And when the time comes you will know exactly what to do and how to react. Why else would you be Jervale's Heir?

There were tears in her eyes, welling, burning, flowing down her cheeks. "I don't know. I don't know."

I do. Trust me, if for the moment you cannot trust yourself.

Angrily she smeared her cheeks dry. "It's hard. Even with Matt, even with you…I feel so alone."

You are not alone, child. You are never alone. The Circle stands with you always.

A rolling wave of love flowed through the link between them. Dathne gasped, feeling it fill her, feeling it smother the strident voices of fear and doubt. Her eyes stopped burning. Her racing heart slowed. Her distress eased, so she could sit still once more with her hands quiescent in her lap. "I wish I could meet you, Veira," she whispered. "On the outside, I mean. In the flesh."

Warmth. Pleasure. *When the time comes, child, you will. Now go to bed. Get some sleep. Trust Prophecy.*

Breaking the link, Dathne did as she was told. Went to bed, tried to sleep…and found she couldn't.

Instead she lay awake staring at the ceiling. Waiting for the sound of the world exhaling.

CHAPTER TWENTY-EIGHT

Morg reclined in the royal touring carriage in the company of the king, the queen and the princess and considered the excited, flag-waving natives that lined the street on either side of them. A sturdy people, these Olken. Little more than peasants, of course, dirt-grubbers and third-rate merchants, magickless as rocks. But sturdy. And he liked a good sturdy peasant. They made excellent raw material for demons.

The ranks of his demon armies would swell like the belly of a pregnant sow once all these cheering Olken were put to better use.

"Asher! Asher! Barl's blessings on Asher!" cried the crowd.

Riding at the head of the official procession, directly in front of the touring carriage and marching band and the other coaches carrying the rest of the Privy Council, was the prince, all decked out in his best silk and leather, with the sunshine glinting off a silver circlet rammed onto his unworthy head. As they'd gathered before the start of the parade he'd overheard the cripple bemoaning the loss of some other pointless trapping of rank and had been hard put not to hit him. You're a *cripple*, he'd wanted to shout. Don't you understand? This crown or that one, it makes no difference. Dip you head to toe in molten gold and stick rubies big as hen's eggs where your eyes used to be, you'd still be nothing but *dross*.

But he'd held his tongue. There'd be time for harsh truths later.

Beside the cripple rode his brutish peasant friend, object of the crowd's adoration. Reason for this ridiculous procession through the streets of Dorana. Although, to be fair, he couldn't really begrudge the lout his moment of glory. For one thing, without him the cripple would surely be dead and his own plans of conquest severely disarrayed; and for another, this was likely to be the last glorious moment of the peasant's life. Feeling magnanimous, Morg smiled. Let him savour it while he could.

"Enjoying yourself after all, Durm?" said the king, his voice raised to carry over the exuberant blasting of trumpets. "I told you it wouldn't be so bad."

"You did indeed, Your Majesty," Morg replied. "And as usual, you were right. May I say it's a beautiful day for a parade?"

The king offered him a small mocking bow. "I do my humble best."

The crowd continued to shout. "Hail Asher! Hail the Hero of Dorana!" they chanted, and threw flowers and streamers and handfuls of rice.

"Poor Asher," said the queen, stifling an unbecoming giggle and nodding at the lout as he sat his horse ahead of them. "Even the back of his head looks embarrassed. Perhaps we should have thought of another way to thank him, Borne."

"Nonsense, my love," said the king robustly. "This parade is a perfect antidote to the lingering tensions in the City. Look at the people's faces. They're loving it. The very last thing on their minds is the fright I gave them with that unfortunate storm. Besides, what Asher did was heroic and it would be churlish of us not to show our public appreciation."

The princess, barely managing to conceal her lack of enthusiasm for their outing, spoke for the first time since leaving the palace. "Since you mention the storm, Papa, Conroyd Jarralt has done a wonderful job with the restoration effort. Don't you think so?"

The king's lips tightened but he had no choice other than agreement. Thanks to Durm, Morg knew as well as the rest of them that Jarralt had worked ceaselessly for days, alone and in concert with other Doranen magicians, to heal the storm-damaged City and send more teams of magicians into the surrounding districts to effect repairs there as well. Looking at the City now, pristine and sparkling beneath the blue and sunlit sky, a visitor would never believe the wrack and ruin left behind by the lashing force of the king's fever-blasted mind.

"Yes, Fane," the king said curtly. "Jarralt has done his duty, as have all my subjects. I would expect no less."

She wasn't a stupid girl: she knew when to hold her tongue. Pouting, the princess sank once more into silence. The king and queen waved at the gathered masses. So did Fane, after some sharp prompting.

He would have liked to wave himself, simply for the delicious irony of the gesture, but Durm wasn't the hand-waving type, so he kept his fingers folded in his lap and instead took advantage of the opportunity to see Dorana City for the first time since his arrival.

It reminded him of the old Doranen capital, Manitala, where once he'd lived and loved as a mere mortal thing. Lost Manitala, long since destroyed by war and fallen into crumbled decay. That city had looked just like this one, with its brightly coloured houses trimmed with flowerboxes and carved frameworks, its bold shopfronts and broad, cobblestoned thoroughfares. With its wide open Central Square, its bubbling fountains, its treeshaded gardens and its flocks of wheeling songbirds.

Barl had transplanted memories here, as well as magicians.

Wrenching his mind from that unprofitable destination he once more paid attention to the king and queen. She was speaking: "—threatened to take those wretched books away from him if he didn't take better care of himself."

"Oh, Mama," said the princess. "Gar's a grown man. He doesn't need you fussing over him as though he was still three years old."

"A mother never stops fussing no matter what age her children are!" the queen replied. "Rest assured, Fane, I shall be fussing over you and your brother when your hair is grey and your eyesight has grown dim. It's a prerogative of motherhood. You may roll your eyes now, young lady, but you'll be agreeing with me fast enough once you're a mother yourself."

As the princess begged to differ, groaning and laughing, and the king added his own opinions, Morg stopped listening. Drivel, drivel, drivel. Family and its attendant sentimental slop. Yet one more mortal bond he'd left behind without the smallest whimper.

He looked over the heads of the marching band and considered the cripple, still waving to the mawkish crowds. Closing his eyes, he extended his senses and quested for the shape and smell and taste of the spell he'd kissed into the runt's brain. It must be grown and close to bursting by now...

With the sun on his face and the sweet scent of autumn roses blowing on the breeze, he smiled. There it was. Squatting in the depths of the cripple's compost mind like a pustuled toad. Black and bloated and ripe with promise.

It was time.

We have been dragged along on this parade today to celebrate one peasant and his transitory moment of glory, he thought, gloating. May I suggest we celebrate this, instead?

With a single, searing thought he triggered the spell—and His Royal Highness Prince Gar fell from his saddle to the cobblestoned road like a poleaxed bullock in the slaughterhouse.

Everybody screamed: the crowd, the queen, the shocked marching trumpeters at whose stumbling feet the cripple landed. The king shouted and even the princess squealed, just a little. The touring carriage stopped in a clatter of hooves. The lout threw himself from the back of his horse, snatched the reins of the cripple's fine beast and shoved them and his own into the hand of a City Guard who'd come running.

Behind them, the remainder of the Privy Council had tumbled from its halted coach and was milling at the door of the touring carriage. Holze, the religious sot, was crying, "Barl save us, Barl save us," as though his life depended on it. Which it did, though he was wasting his breath. Barl was long past helping anybody now. Conroyd Jarralt's expression was harder to read; was that true concern or just a polished mask for public consumption?

Morg considered him carefully. A mask, he decided, crafted to hide an interesting face. In many ways it was a pity he'd been forced to take Magician Durm's body. Conroyd Jarralt was a man much closer to his taste and temperament.

The king got out of the carriage, then the queen close behind and the princess soon after. Morg, mindful of Durm's dignity, followed at a discreet distance. At his heels trailed Holze and Jarralt.

The lout was sprawled in the middle of the road, the cripple dragged across his lap. "I don't understand it!" he panted at the king. "One minute he were makin' a joke, laughin' at me, and the next he just went over! I don't understand it! Someone ought to fetch that bonebotherer Nix, quick!"

Restrained and muttering on three sides was the crowd, flags and flowers forgotten. Ignoring them, the king dropped to his knees and pressed his hand to the cripple's forehead. Morg watched, lending him Durm's apparent, silent support. "He's quite cool," said Borne, fear coated with calm. Leaning close, he patted his son's cheek. "Gar. Gar. Can you hear me?"

"He's been working himself to bits over those mouldy ole books," the lout said. "But we had words on it and yesterday he seemed right as rain."

The king spared him a brief smile. "It's all right, Asher. Nobody's blaming you."

"*I'm* blaming me!" retorted the lout. "I'm s'posed to look out for 'im!"

"And you do," said the queen, coming close. She held Fane's hand in hers, tightly. "Why else are we all here?" She glanced at the staring, muttering crowd, then at the king. "We should get him back to the palace, Borne. The carriage will be best, we can—" She stopped, gasping. The cripple's eyes were open, their pupils shrunk to pinpoints, and in their green depths burned an inky flame that flickered and darted like a black toad's tongue. "Durm! Durm, look at this! Have you ever seen anything like it?"

No, Durm hadn't. Neither had Morg, since this was the first time he'd ever artificially induced magic in another person. The effect was certainly impressive. He bent over to get a closer look and cleared his throat. "Your Majesty, we must proceed with care. I have a suspicion as to the root cause of this matter, and if I am proved correct..." He paused dramatically, and waited for the unfolding enchantment to finish the sentence for him.

The unfolding enchantment obliged.

With a series of cracks like an exploding string of fireworks the cobblestones beneath the cripple's body and all their feet rippled and split asunder. Pale green shoots erupted from the earth below them, rushing towards the sun. As those in the crowd close enough to witness the miracle shrieked aloud their surprise and consternation, and the lout cursed, and Holze began begging Barl's mercy again, the green shoots darkened their colour, increased in size then burst into flower. Within moments the cripple and everyone within ten feet of him were surrounded by a riot of hollyhocks, roses, tulips and snapdragons.

"No!" cried the princess. "No, he can't do this!"

Morg swallowed a smile. Oh dear. Well, he'd never expected her to be happy about it. But then he wasn't doing this for her, was he?

At his feet, the cripple stirred. His mouth opened. His arms lifted, slowly, until his fingertips were pointing at the sky. "*Ni'ala do m'barra. Tu-e. Tu-e.*"

A hush, reverent and waiting. Then sighs, as a golden rain began to fall.

Gar was dreaming. He knew he was dreaming because he was doing magic, and that only ever happened in dreams. These dreams were particularly vivid, though. Visceral, in a way he'd never before experienced. He was bursting flowers from the ground and squeezing raw magic from the sky in fat golden drops. He could feel the crackle of magic at his fingertips, smell the burned-orange tang of discharged energy, as real as anything waking could be. But it wasn't possible. Was it?

He opened his eyes.

"Welcome back," his father greeted him. There were tears in his eyes.

"Sir?" he said, and was staggered by the sound of his own voice. Rusty as nails in a bucket, and thin, as though he'd poured too much of it from his throat and was now left with only dregs. "What happened?"

"You don't remember?"

He felt so empty. And light. As though he'd float right off the bed and out of the open window if the blankets weren't pinning him to the mattress. Remember? Remember what? "What day is it?"

"Still today," his father said, and straightened the edge of his sheet. "You fell off your horse three hours ago."

"Where's Mama?"

"With your sister. She'll be here directly."

The dream lingered, fresh in his memory. The tang of burned orange. Within his mind, a difference. Intangible, but *there*. It was impossible, of course. Grown and magickless men did not spontaneously burst into flower.

Impossible or not, he had to ask. "Sir, when you perform magic..."

His father leaned close. "Yes?"

You fool, you fool, it was only a dream... "Do you smell anything afterwards? Say, burned orange?"

"No," said his father.

He had to close his eyes, turn his head to the opposite wall. For one brief and burning moment he'd actually believed the dream.

"For me, it's a sharp kind of lemon smell," his father said. "Your mother swears it's fresh baked bread. Fane won't tell us what she smells. It's different, you see, with each of us. Nobody knows why. Something individual in the blood reacting with the energies. Whatever it is, it's personal. Certainly it's not discussed outside the family circle, so I don't recommend you run around asking everybody you meet what they smell when they perform an incantation. It might lead to unpleasantness."

His heart pounded, booming like a drum. "It was a dream. I was only dreaming."

"Were you?" his father whispered.

With fear like an anvil on his chest he lifted one arm from the bed and held out his palm. Recited, silently, the words to conjure glimfire, the first incantation a child is taught. The one Durm had tried to teach him a hundred times, a thousand, and could not. Failure had seared the syllables of the spell into memory.

His flesh crawled. His fingertips tingled. His nose wrinkled: burned orange. He opened his eyes...and there was glimfire.

Durm said, "I told you, did I not, that the spell was an easy one?" He'd been shadowed in a corner, unnoticed. Now he came forward to stand by the bed next to the king. He was smiling, one hand on the king's shoulder. It was the face he'd worn all those years ago, before the truth had soured them both. With the snap of his fingers he plucked a dead, dry stick from thin air and held it out. "Make me a rose, Your Highness."

The king stared. "Durm, are you mad? Four hours ago he couldn't even make glimfire! He can't—"

"Can't?" said Durm. "Who are you to say what he can't? We have no idea what his capabilities may be. For all you and I know, Borne, for Gar there *is* no 'can't.'"

As his father and Durm locked gazes Gar took the outstretched stick. It was rough and dry to the touch. Truly dead. "I don't know how to—"

"Use your imagination," Durm suggested. "Close your eyes and think of a rose."

Gar shrugged. It couldn't be that simple. Even Fane had found the translation a challenge, and Fane was gifted beyond living memory. But he had nothing to lose by trying; it wasn't as though he were a stranger to failure, after all. He closed his eyes and thought of a rose.

Burned orange. His blood like boiling wine. Searing. Intoxicating. Power, filling him in an unstoppable wave, rolling through him and over him, dragging him under, flinging him high.

"Ow!" he said, and opened his eyes. There was a bead of blood on the tip of his thumb and a rose in his hand. He laughed, a harsh expulsion of air. "I forgot about the thorns."

Durm said, very quietly, "Fane practised that translation day and night for a month to get it right."

His frowning father reached out and took the rose from him. "There is no precedent for this."

"There is," said Durm. "And then again, there is not. Records show that a late assumption of powers is not unknown."

"Records show that before today the oldest Doranen to finally exhibit his magical heritage was twelve and a half years old!" retorted the king. "Gar is almost twice that!"

Durm shrugged. "Nevertheless...it is not unknown."

"So," said Gar. He thought he should be screaming. Dancing. Laughing...or crying. He could do none of those things. With the taste of burned oranges still lingering on his tongue and the memory of a power so grand and grim thrumming yet through his bones, all he could do was breathe. "I am a true Doranen after all."

The idea was obliterating. In the blink of an eye his world was filled with possibilities. A wife...a family...the right to stand equal with the rest of his race...

Smiling, weeping, his father leaned forward and kissed him on the cheek. "Yes, my son. Yes. You are a true Doranen."

If one more person tried to squeeze into the Goose, thought Dathne, the walls were going to split asunder and the roof would crash down on all their heads. Matt had to press his lips against her ear and shout to make himself heard above the din.

"But what does it *mean*, Dathne? It don't make any *sense*. One more magician in the Usurper's House makes the Wall safer, doesn't it?"

"I don't know what it means, Matt!" she shouted back. "I told you, I'm stuck. Can't see any further forward than around the next corner, and that's only if I stick my neck out. Looks like we're back to waiting."

"Waiting!" said Matt, disgusted, and drained his tankard dry. "I hate bloody waiting!"

She had to grin. "You sounded just like Asher, then."

"Aye, well, reckon I—" Matt began, imitating, then broke off and pointed at the door. "Speaking of..."

A huge clamour from the Goose's patrons rattled the rafters: Asher had arrived. The walls and roof remained intact, just. Aleman Derrig's customers mobbed their man; hands stretched to pluck at his shirt sleeves, to tug at his elbow, to hold him fast and make him answer their quarrelsome questions. He withstood it for a minute then shoved all the shovers aside to climb up onto the bar.

"Shut your damned cakeholes, all of you!" he bellowed. "Shut up and I'll tell you what's the business! Or at least as much as I can!"

A ragged silence fell. Dathne exchanged a raised-eyebrow look with Matt and sat back in her seat, waiting.

"Right," said Asher. He was still dressed in his parade finery, though it was looking a little the worse for wear. He was looking the worse for wear, too, strained about the eyes and tense in the shoulders and back. "His Highness is fine. The king's seen him, the Master Magician's seen him, Royal Pother Nix's seen him. If they thought it'd help they'd get in a vitinery to see him. He ain't dyin'. He ain't even sick. He's just got his magic, is all."

A fresh wave of clamouring questions. Asher let it rage for a moment, looking tired, then lifted both his hands till the racket died down.

"That's all I got to say. There'll be a royal announcement presently, I reckon. In the meantime you could put yourselves to good use and start spreadin' the word."

Laughter, protests and a few jeering catcalls. Asher ignored them. From her booth up the back, Dathne caught his eye. Crooked her finger at him and beckoned. He hesitated, then shook his head and indicated the Goose's door.

"He wants us to meet him outside," said Dathne, and pulled at Matt's arm. "Come on."

The street was almost as packed with people as the inn. Every second one of them recognised Asher and stopped to beg him for news. "This is bloody ridiculous," he muttered, and led them round the back to the Goose's service alley. It stank of stale beer and rotten cabbage.

"The prince is really all right?" said Matt. "You're sure?"

Asher glowered. "No, I just said that 'cause I felt like lyin'."

Dathne shoved Matt with her elbow. "What happens now, do you know?"

"With Gar?" He dragged his fingers through his hair. "Don't have a bloody clue. But I'll tell you what's about to happen with *me*. Come tomorrow I'm goin' to be the only body in that whole bloody Tower workin' as any kind of Olken Administrator. I'm goin' to be up to my bloody eyeballs in Meister Glospottle's piss problems and Mistress Banfrey's lace shortages and Barl bloody knows what else!" His eyes widened in horror. "*Sink me*! I might even have to sit court at Justice Hall!"

Indeed a horrifying thought. Dathne took a deep breath, choked on it, and said, "What about Gar? This magic, it's unprecedented. Do you know how, or—"

"Why no, Dathne, I'm afraid I don't," said Asher with exaggerated care. "My best friend Durm and I ain't had time for today's cosy little chat over afternoon tea."

"All right," she said, recognising incipient revolt. "Clearly this isn't a good time."

"No, clearly it bloody well ain't!" said Asher.

"Don't shout at her," snapped Matt. "None of this is Dathne's fault."

"Well it ain't my bloody fault either!" shouted Asher. "But who cares? Reckon I'm about to get covered in shit anyway! First Westwailing Harbour, then him and his mouldy ole books and now this! Barl bloody knows where we'll end up with this! You should've seen the look on that Fane's face when all those flowers started sproutin'.

I'm tellin' you, if looks could kill I reckon we'd've had a head start on a bloody funeral!"

"So..." Dathne tried a sympathetic smile, to see if that would calm things down. "You're going to be fairly occupied in the next little while."

The smile worked; Asher deflated, and kicked at the dirty ground. "Looks like."

She patted him on the arm. "Well, you know where I am if there's anything I can do. He must be pleased."

He gave her a blank look. "Who?"

"The prince. He must be pleased that at last he's found his magic."

Asher shrugged. "S'pose. I ain't seen him yet." He sighed. "I'd best get back. That ole Darran's flappin' about like a chicken with its head cut off and bloody Willer's no use at all."

Dathne stared. "Since when have you been so concerned about Darran?"

"I ain't bloody concerned," said Asher. "But if the ole crow does hisself a mischief while he's flappin' you can bet your arse he'll find a way to blame it on me!"

As he stomped off down the alley, Dathne let her head fall against Matt's shoulder. "Jervale protect us."

He nodded. "Dathne, I don't like this."

She stepped away from him. "It's not for you and me to like or dislike. It's Prophecy working itself out. All we can do about it is be patient and see what happens next."

Matt turned away, hands fisted on his hips. "This can't be natural. Magic comin' on a Doranen so late in his life."

"It's unusual, I grant you. But unusual doesn't mean unnatural, Matt. You know as well as I their magic is a spiky thing, abrupt and uncomfortable. We can't ever hope to fully understand it."

He wasn't convinced. "These past days...I haven't felt right."

"How do you mean?"

"Don't know, exactly," he said, shaking his head. "Not sure I can put it into words. But I feel the world around us, Dathne, and something's changed."

"Changed how?"

Frustrated, he tugged at his weskit. "I don't *know*, I tell you. Look, I ain't a Seer, like you. I'm not Jervale's Heir. I don't have visions and I can't scry to save myself. All I'm good at are horses and...and... feeling the way the world is."

"And you think it feels different?"

"I *know* it does. Different, and worse than different. *Wrong*. I just don't know *how*, exactly."

"Why didn't you say something before now?"

He shrugged. "I thought I was imagining it. I thought it was just jitters, after the storm. Losing Bellybone, and Thunder Crow. Worrying about Asher. It's not like I can prove anything. How can you prove a feeling?"

She sighed. "I'll be honest with you, Matt. I've not felt what you have. But then, as you say, we've all got different talents. You've always been especially tuned to the natural world." She thought hard. "It could be you've sensed Gar's blossoming. Whenever a Doranen child manifests his or her powers it changes the tune magic sings in this place. Being so much older, with his Doranen magic repressed for so long... perhaps that's it."

"Perhaps," Matt said after a moment. "But what if it's not?"

Unfairly, she felt a stab of anger at him. As if she didn't have enough to be losing sleep over. Then common sense reasserted itself. No point in having a voice of reason to hand if you stoppered its mouth every time it said something you didn't like. "I'm going to sound like a corncrake, jabbering the same old song over and over again," she sighed. "But—"

"I know," he said glumly. "We just have to wait. Well, like I said before—I hate bloody waiting."

"And so do I hate bloody waiting," she snapped, losing patience. "But we're like a woman with child, Matt. We've had a long gestation and a false cramp or two and now we're eager for our waters to break. Well, they'll break when they're ready and not before, and sticking a knife between our legs to hasten matters won't do much beyond making us bloody and putting the whole damned business at risk. Is that what you want?"

He was glaring. "Of course it ain't."

"Well, then. It's getting late. Best you go and tend your horses and leave me to decide when we've waited long enough. Seeing as how I am Jervale's Heir."

That earned her an even dirtier look. "Fine." He bowed. "As madam desires."

She let him go unhindered. His ruffled feathers would smooth soon enough. In the meantime, she'd take some time to sink herself in meditation and see if she couldn't sense for herself whatever it was he had felt... and been so unnerved by.

In the end Gar sent everyone away. His parents. Durm. Nix. Especially Nix. Yes, it was amazing. Yes, it was a miracle. But dear Barl save him, he needed *solitude*. Time. A chance to breathe and come to terms with this tumultuous reshaping of his life. He couldn't imagine feeling any more shocked and disarrayed than if he'd woken one day and looked in the mirror to find himself female.

Escaping to his private garden, where he could be sure of undisturbed privacy, he sat on a carved wooden bench in the late afternoon sunshine and let the perfumed air caress his skin. Let the birds in the trees around him sing and soothe his overwrought mind.

I am a magician. A true Doranen. My father's son, at last.

He wasn't sure if it was safe to feel so much joy at once. Could mere flesh contain it? Surely not. Surely any moment now his skin must burst and all his joy come pouring out, as golden and as glowing as the magic that burned and bubbled in his blood. In a heartbeat, in the blink of an eye, he was remade. Reborn. And nothing would ever be the same again.

As though to prove it he snapped his fingers and conjured a glowing ball of glimfire. Obedient, opalescent and *there*, right before his eyes, simply because he wished it, the coalesced magic bobbed on the breeze.

Suddenly, one just wasn't enough.

He conjured a second ball. Then a third. Conjured more, until twenty balls of glimfire hovered in the air above him. Enchanted, he conjured them different colours. With a thought, nothing more. The ease of it stole his breath anew. Then he made them dance. Simply, at first, as he sought to find the balance of energy that would keep them under his control. Then more daringly, and more daringly still, until they looped and swirled and flirted like live things, butterflies or birds or some other, magical creatures, celebrating his great good fortune.

Then, without warning, the multicoloured balls of glimfire exploded into black smoke. He cried out in shock and protest and sudden fear as through the drifting remnants of his dancing glimfire Fane crossed the close-clipped lawn towards him, her crimson cloak billowing about her like blood. Her face was obdurate, carved in stone. There was no joy in her at all.

He leapt to his feet, furious. "Why did you do that?"

"You think magic's game? Is that what you think?"

Heart pounding, he watched her halt before him. "No. Of course I don't."

"You think it's all pretty lights and showing off?"

There was pain in her eyes, as well as fury and disgust and something else he couldn't define. He let his own pain show in return. "I don't understand you, Fane. Why can't you be pleased for me?"

She laughed. "Are you truly so stupid?"

"I must be. You'll have to explain it to me. Explain why my own sister, my only sister, whom I love, though sometimes she makes it hard, could so resent my miracle."

She didn't answer him straightaway. Pushed past him to the garden bench and sat on it, arms extended along the back, face tipped back to drink the sunshine. He stood there, watching her. Waiting.

"On my fifth birthday," she said at last, eyes closed, "Durm took me to watch Papa work the Weather Magic. The blood and the pain scared me so much he had to take me out of the Weather Chamber and slap me into silence. When I finally stopped screaming, do you know what he said to me?"

Aching, Gar shook his head. "No."

"He said, 'You are this kingdom's only hope. One day it will be your duty to call the rain and the snow, to sing the seeds in springtime and slumber the earth in winter. In doing this you will keep the Wall strong so that no harm can come to us from beyond the mountains. But if you fail, or deny your destiny, the Wall will fall and with it every man, woman and child in the kingdom. Abandon your childish dreams and desires, Fane. You are no ordinary girl, and your life has never been your own.'"

"That was—" He stopped. Cleared his throat. "That was cruel. He shouldn't have done that."

She opened her eyes; they were sharp with derision. "Of course he should. He was right. I was born to be a WeatherWorker. So every day since that one I have sweated and bled and wept, learning how to be one. How to be this kingdom's only hope." She slid off the bench, sinuously, and in her pellucid eyes stirred something dark and dangerous. "I tell you this, brother. I did not sweat and bleed and weep in vain."

He stared at her, helpless. "Fane, you have to believe me, I'm not interested in usurping your place. I don't want to be the next Weather-Worker."

Her tapering fingers became talons and her beautiful face twisted into ugliness, contorted with hate and despair and a lifetime of remembered whispers. "*Liar*! You think I don't know what you're planning? Of course I know. There's only room for one cripple in this family, Gar, we both know that. And now that you're got your precious magic you're going to make sure I'm it! Well, it's not going to happen. Do you hear me? I won't let you cripple me! I'll *kill* you first!"

Gar felt sick, all joy congealed into sorrow. "Fane, this is ridiculous. You don't want to kill me. And even if you did, you couldn't."

"No?" she spat. "I think you'd be surprised at what I can do, *brother*." Clapping her hands hard she conjured glimfire. No pretty coloured sphere, but a brute red thing pulsing scarlet with her pain and untamed fury. She aimed it at him, pelted it, and the air sizzled in its wake.

Startled, he raised a hand in self-defence. Thought desperately of shields and barriers and quenching rain. It wasn't enough, or he lacked the skill. Her glimfire scorched him, blistered flesh and singed silk before exploding into a shower of blood-red sparks. "*Hey*! Fane, stop it! You know this is against the law! You know the penalty for duelling with magic! Do you want to cause a scandal? Do you want to bring the king down here?"

Clap clap, went his little sister's hands. Clap, clap, clap. "No," she cried as balls of scarlet glimfire erupted into life around her. "I want everything to be the way it was! You bastard, you *bastard*! Why couldn't you have stayed a bloody cripple! Why didn't he let you drown?"

His heart broke. "Fane! Fane, listen to me—"

"No, I won't listen!" she screamed. "Why should I listen? What can you say that I could *possibly* want to hear?"

He tried again to reach her. Not because he thought he could, but because he had no other choice. "Fane. Please. I'm begging you, stop now before it's too late. Before you go too far. It doesn't have to be like this. I love you. We can work our problems out..."

She screamed again, a wordless outpouring of vitriol and hate. Her hands flung wide, her eyes blazed blue in her chalk-white face...and suddenly the sky was raining fire.

CHAPTER TWENTY-NINE

Somehow Gar deflected her flaming rage. Managed this time to explode the balls of glimfire she hurled at him before they could touch his exposed and vulnerable flesh. Given no choice he hurled his own fire back at her in wild self-defence. He had no idea where the magic came from, it just welled out of that secret place inside him that nobody, not even Durm, had ever suspected he possessed.

"Fane, for the love of Barl, *stop this*!" he shouted as the air filled with noxious smoke and exploding glimfire, his and hers. The sound of it boomed around his small walled bower, rocketed from brick to brick and sent the songbirds screaming into the sky. "Fane! Are you mad? There are laws!"

But she was beyond reason, beyond hearing. Almost, he realised, staring heartsick into her venomous eyes, beyond sanity.

Her wild attack intensified. It was impossible to destroy all the fireballs she flung at him; those he failed to extinguish engulfed trees, garden benches, flowerbeds. The smoke thickened till she was reduced to a crimson nightmare shadow spewing hate and fire. He defended himself as best he could but she was much more practised than he. Raw talent was no match for years and years of training.

If this didn't stop soon one of them was going to die.

He thought he heard distant voices, shouting. The madness had to end now, before death and scandal overtook them. The sweat of desperation and fear poured down his face.

She was the most powerful magician born since Barl, or so Durm said. How in the name of their blessed saviour was he supposed to stop her?

"Imagine a rose," Durm had told him, and he had, and in his hand he'd held a rose. Now he imagined a whip of glimfire, snapping and curling at his command.

"Bastard!" Fane shrieked as it lashed around her ankles and tugged her flailing to the grass. She retaliated with a whip of her own and, unburdened by scruples or any kind of reason, aimed for his hands, his throat, his eyes. He couldn't deflect all her strikes.

Soon he began to sting, to burn, to bleed. Began to lose his temper as a lifetime of buried resentments boiled to the surface of his carefully cultivated facade. Spoilt brat. Rotten bitch. Never happy unless she was humiliating him. Taunting him. Hurting him. Whatever had he done to her to deserve such unkind treatment? *Nothing*. All he'd ever done was try to love her. Understand her. Forgive her. Defend her to their mother, their father, even though her words and deeds were so often indefensible.

With a supreme effort he evaded another strike and wrapped his lash of glimfire round her body, pinning her *arms* to her sides. She cried out, fingers spasming, and her own whip fell from her fingers to dissolve on the ground in a puff of acrid smoke. She cried out again as he hauled her towards him across the charred and stinking grass. As he seized her by the shoulders and forced her backwards against the rough trunk of the nearest tree. She kicked and cursed him as he framed her face in his hands, palms flat and pressing, holding her so she could look nowhere but into his anguished eyes.

"*Bitch*!" he panted. Sobbed, nearly. "What is *wrong* with you? All I ever wanted was for you to care like I cared! To be my sister as I was your brother. Why is that so hard? Why is that so much to ask? Why in Barl's name do you *hate* me so much?"

She was crying, her contorted face screwed up with rage and hurt. "Why do you think, you stupid bastard? Because they never wanted me! Not for me. Not for myself. Only because you were a failure! The only reason I exist is because you were born *defective*! And now here you are, reborn a magician...so what's to become of *me*?"

Her mewling self-pity was his undoing. His fingers tightened on her face, nails digging into her soft flesh. "Who cares?" he hissed. "So you're not the only one with magic, so what? Do you think the world will cease its spinning? Do you expect the Wall to shatter and our lives to end in blood and fire, all because of me? Because at last, *at last*, Barl has delivered me my magic? My *birthright*? Do you think what I now have diminishes you? Little sister, you preen yourself too proudly!"

Her eyes were wide, the pupils cavernous. Flooding tears washed the soot and smoke from her ice-white cheeks. Through distorted lips she choked, "Gar—let go—you're hurting me! You're *hurting* me!"

"Merciful *Barl*!" he shouted, blind and deaf to her pleading. "You are the most selfish creature alive! Have you even given one minute's thought to what *I'm* going through? To what I've gone through my whole life? No, of course you haven't. Because no matter what happens, no matter who is suffering, at the end of the day you're the only one who matters. You! You! You! And you have the temerity to complain that *I'm* hurting *you*?"

Untrammelled at last, his rage would have overpowered him, would have clutched his fingers round her throat and shaken her till she wept her penitence and begged for his mercy, or suffocated.

They were saved from disaster by Asher.

"You damned bloody idiot!" his friend bellowed, hauling him bodily away from Fane, one strong arm anchored round his chest and arm. "Are you out of your mind? What are you doin'? You tryin' to *kill* her?"

Gasping, swearing, he struggled free of Asher's grasp. "Keep out of this! Go away! It's none of your business and you wouldn't understand anyway!"

"*I* wouldn't?" said Asher, glaring. "Me? With my bloody brothers?"

Panting, Gar dragged his charred sleeve across his gritty, sweat-stained face. The rage was still in him, burning, yearning. He throttled the impulse to flatten Asher where he stood. "That's different!"

Asher's expression was profoundly sceptical. "Aye. Right. I forgot.

Royalty's got a better class of family strife." He shook his head. "What were you *thinkin'*, Gar? Half the bloody Tower's heard the two of you goin' at each other like alley cats! Darran's pissed his panties twice over! What's got into you? Has all that newfangled magic gone and burned up what little common sense you were born with?" He flung out a hand towards Fane. "She may be sixteen and a pain in the arse, y'fool, but she's still little more than a child! *And* she's your bloody sister!"

As though waking from a nightmare Gar turned and looked at Fane. She'd slid down the tree trunk and was folded at its base, face pressed into the battered ground, weeping fit to break a brother's heart. Fury fled, and sanity abruptly returned. Flooded with sudden shame and self-loathing he went to her. Fell to his knees at her side and gathered her into his arms. For one searing moment she resisted him...then crumpled against his chest.

"No, no, don't cry, Fane," he whispered, rocking her. "I'm sorry. I'm sorry. Don't cry. It's all right. Everything will be all right. We'll work this out. I don't know how, but we'll think of something. You're my sister and I'm your brother, and even though you drive me to distraction I love you. Nothing either of us can say or do will ever change that."

She was hidden from him, her voice muffled. "So you say."

"So I promise." He gently shifted her so he could see her tear-stained face. "And I promise something else, too, and Asher will be my witness." He raised his voice. "Won't you, Asher?"

"Aye," said Asher, keeping a discreet distance. "Provided you promise it fast so's we can get out of here."

Ignoring that, Gar took his sister's chin between his fingers and stared unguarded into her face. "The crown is yours, Fane. Only yours. Always yours. You are the WeatherWorker-in-Waiting. On my life, I will never take that from you."

He watched the doubt shift behind her eyes. "On your life?" She shook her head, frowning. Rejecting. "I don't believe you."

She sounded uncertain, though. As though she wanted to believe him but couldn't quite bring herself to make that leap of faith. Despair threatened. He couldn't let this happen. He couldn't allow his miraculous magic to tear their fragile family apart. Not when they should be celebrating.

Inspiration struck. A memory from distant childhood, a time when he and Fane had not yet learned to hate. Holding out his hand he dribbled saliva onto his palm and showed it to her. "You have to believe me. See? I've spit on it. Now. Your turn. Come on."

Her eyes widened. Filled with a brief, incredulous laughter. "No. That's disgusting."

"Spit on it," he insisted.

She shook her head. "It doesn't mean anything."

"Doesn't it?" He bit his lip, thinking. "It meant something when I didn't tell about the gardener's flowerpots. It meant something when you fell off the stable roof that time you thought you could fly. It meant something when—"

"All right!" she cried, torn between laughter and temper. "Shut up. My memory's as good as yours. Better, probably."

"Come on, Fane," he murmured coaxingly. "You know you want to. You know I mean it. Just spit and we can put all this behind us. Start over, on a whole new page. My magic won't change anything for you. I swear it."

She stared at his spittled hand, her dirty face screwed into a frown. Holding his breath he willed her to accept the challenge. Join him halfway. End the destructive, corrosive feud poisoning their family.

She said, still frowning, "Mama doesn't like it when we swear."

His laugh was half a sob. "Mama's not here."

She spat. Pressed her hand on top of his and shook. Then she looked up at him, a little shy, a little defiant. "I'm not really selfish. I'm just focused."

"Focused?" he said, grinning. Light-headed with relief and hope. "So that's what they're calling it these days." Fishing a handkerchief out of his pocket he wiped the tears from her face, then smeared both their hands dry of saliva.

Asher said, agitated, "All done then? All finished swearin' and spittin' and tryin' to kill each other? Good. Then best the pair of you make yourselves scarce. Ain't no tellin' who that ole Darran's gone flappin' to."

Gar nodded. Got to his feet and pulled Fane upright beside him. "You're right. As usual. And then we're going to have to come up with an explanation."

Fane was staring around them, her expression awestruck. "It's going to have to be a pretty good one, Gar."

For the first time he gazed at their erstwhile battleground. His glorious bower was a smoking ruin, splintered and scarred and shredded. Hardly a flower was left untouched. Beneath the smashed branches of one blackened tree, four charred and feathered corpses. The air stank of magic and death, smudged still with drifting smoke.

"Barl save me," he said quietly. Tiredly.

Asher was staring over his shoulder, his face grim. "Well, somebody bloody better. 'Cause here comes trouble times three."

Gar felt his heart plummet. Wrapping his fingers around his sister's trembling hand, he turned. Took a deep, shuddering breath and prepared to face his father and his father's best friend... and his father's bitter enemy.

"*Barl's sacred bones*!" roared Conroyd Jarralt as his fist crashed down upon the Privy Council table. "This is *your* fault, Borne. *You* are to blame for this appalling state of affairs!"

"Now, now, Conroyd—" Barlsman Holze began, his expression pained.

Jarralt turned on him. "Hold your tongue, Holze, you pandering old fool! Don't think I've forgotten *your* part in this!"

Morg had to bite the inside of his cheek to stop himself from laughing aloud; the look on the pandering old fool's face was priceless. But Durm would not have let such an affront to dignity pass unchallenged so he arranged the magician's face into a frown. "Mind yourself, Lord Jarralt. We will swiftly achieve nothing if we cannot control our choler."

Jarralt continued unchastened. "And why should I control my choler, Master Magician? We are facing the gravest crisis this kingdom can know: a divided succession. Not since the days of Trevoyle's Schism have we seen such a barbarous display as provided by Prince Gar and Princess Fane! Control my choler? No, indeed! Rather I should be shouting my outrage from the rooftops of the City. The rooftops, sir!"

Pale and rigidly composed the cripple stirred in his council seat. "Lord Jarralt, you are gravely mistaken. There is no divided succession. When the time comes I have no intention of challenging my sister for the crown. She has worked for it her whole life. Sacrificed every joy of childhood in service to the goal of serving this kingdom as its queen. As a prince of the ruling house I have my own duties and I am well satisfied with them. Fane will be WeatherWorker hereafter. I do so swear it, in this place at this time before you, my witnesses."

"So you say now," retorted Jarralt. "And it sounds well and good in theory. But a man can change his mind, Your Highness. Especially when lured by the promise of power." Turning his back on the cripple he glared again at the king. "I said this day would come, Borne, didn't I? Do you remember? I said it was a mistake for this Privy Council to side with the General Council and sanction the birth of a second child to your house... and a mistake it has proven to be!"

The king lifted burning green eyes to his accuser's face. "Sanction? You imply there was some kind of rule-breaking, Jarralt. We broke no rule."

"You birthed a second child! Trevoyle's Legacy states clearly and unequivocally: *The ruling house shall spawn but one heir, lest discord and strife once more tear the land asunder. One* heir, Your Majesty. And now you have two."

"If you're going to quote law, my lord, do me the courtesy of quoting it accurately," said Borne. "The Legacy goes on to say: *Should the ruling house be robbed of its heir by death untimely, then—*"

Jarralt struck the table again. "But it wasn't, was it? That is precisely my point! Your heir did not die, he—"

"He was magickless!" cried the king. "And what is that if not death, to a Doranen?"

Silence. Morg watched, mildly fascinated, as Jarralt and Holze looked anywhere but at the cripple. The king reached out his hand and laid it on his son's shoulder. "Gar—"

Face white as milk, the cripple shook his head. "It's all right, sir. Your point is valid."

"Hardly!" said Conroyd Jarralt. "Magickless or not you lived. There is no provision in Trevoyle's Legacy for a Doranen heir born without—"

"There wasn't then," interrupted Holze. "There is now. You helped make it so, Conroyd."

Jarralt bowed his head. "Yes. To my everlasting shame, I did. In a moment of weakness I stopped my ears to the counsel of my heart and allowed myself to be swayed against my conscience by you, Holze, and you, Durm, and you, Your Majesty. When we all know you should not have had a voice in the matter at all."

The king smiled thinly. "Because I had a vested interest in the outcome? Whereas you, who would have nominated your house to succeed mine, naturally had nothing but the welfare of the kingdom in mind."

Conroyd Jarralt's handsome face was blotched with venom and spite. "That would have been the proper order of things! The law made no provision for the birth of a cripple. You know it! But you pleaded and you cozened and you convinced us to make an exception. And now look at the result. Your two charming children at each other's throats. Attacking each other with magic. This kingdom poised on the brink of anarchy. And all because of your overweening arrogance and pride. You were ever thus. All your life whatever or whoever you wanted you took, heedless of anybody's best interests but your own."

The king was on his feet. "*Silence!* You go too far, Conroyd!"

"Too far?" Jarralt kicked back his chair and lunged, thrusting his face into the king's. "I think not! I think we've a distance further yet to travel, Borne, you and I. This kingdom's two Councils made a ruinous mistake in letting you and your precious, persuadable queen birth a second child. Blinded by love or seduced by sympathy or simply shouted down, we indulged your intemperate ambition and now the kingdom is asked to pay the price. Well, I say it is too high. The time has come to—"

Holze slapped his palms on the tabletop. His normally mild face was vivid with displeasure. "*Enough*, my lord! Your Majesty! This unseemly brawling will cease immediately! Are we cur dogs in the gutter, to snap and snarl in such a fashion? In Barl's name I tell you to be silent and mindful of your stations!"

Shocked, shamed, the king and his councillor sank back into their seats. Vastly entertained, Morg watched them gather their tattered dignity and studiously examine their fingertips.

Holze glanced at the cripple, sitting in pallid, mortified silence, and said with utmost reason, "No mistake was made. Laws must change to reflect the current reality. When Trevoyle's Legacy was first laid down, centuries ago, there was no record of a magickless heir ever being born. With His Highness incapable, His Majesty was to all intents and purposes childless. He was well within his rights to breed up a new heir to his crown. And since we settled this some seventeen years ago I fail to see why we must revisit the matter now!"

"Why?" said Jarralt, looking up. "Because now it appears we were a trifle premature in our proclamation of Prince Gar's *technical* demise. Now it appears he is a magician of power equal to, if not greater than, his sister. Now we must contemplate a world in which they attempt to burn each other to cinders! And that returns us to my original assessment of the situation: our kingdom faces the dire prospect of a divided succession."

The cripple sighed. "This afternoon's unfortunate incident will not be repeated. You have my solemn word. Besides, it was merely a... misunderstanding."

"So you say. But I say we can afford no more 'misunderstandings.' The next one might well do more than char a few trees and rose-bushes and kill a handful of birds!"

"Did you not hear my oath, Lord Jarralt?" the cripple snapped. "Do you wish me to open a vein and write it in blood for you? *I will not contest the crown.*"

With a happy, inward sigh Morg cleared his throat. "I'm afraid, Your Highness, the matter is not quite so easily dealt with as that."

Caught unawares, the cripple stared. "Why not?"

"Because this kingdom must be served by the magician best suited to become the WeatherWorker. Family sentiment cannot play any part in the choosing. Once, before your miraculous transformation, Fane was the obvious WeatherWorker-in-Waiting. Now…" He shrugged. "The matter is less clear. You must receive the Weather Magic, so that I may properly assess who is most fit to follow in your father's footsteps."

"But—" The cripple turned to his father. "Your Majesty, I can't. The law—"

"Was designed to serve us, Gar," the king said. "And not the other way around. Durm is right. There is only one way to settle the question of who will succeed me."

"No!" the cripple protested. "I won't. I refuse. Not only am I not qualified or prepared or willing, I gave Fane my word I wouldn't usurp her inheritance."

"That promise wasn't yours to give, Gar," the king said heavily. "It's possible that Fane is still the best magician to wear the crown once I am incapable. But it's equally possible that you are the one destined to be Weather Worker after me. We *must* know. Soon, before uncertainty can undermine the kingdom's stability."

The cripple flinched. "She'll think I've betrayed her."

"I shall speak to her. Make her understand."

"You can try," the cripple said. "But I'm afraid—"

With an abruptly raised hand, the king silenced his son. "She will understand."

Jarralt was scowling. "And if His Highness is right and the Princess Fane refuses to accept her displacement? Then I'll be proven right. Your children will come to daggers drawn, and that will lead to civil unrest at the very least. The people have yet to fully recover their faith after your fever-born storm, sir. Once word spreads of today's altercation—"

The king looked grim. "There was no altercation. It was an unwise experiment that got out of hand. His Highness has yet to refine his magical control. Master Magician Durm will be working most closely with him to ensure such an accident does not occur again. That is the explanation to be given, should anybody ask. If I hear of a different explanation…I will know where to look." His gaze touched Jarralt with frost.

Impervious to cold, Jarralt sneered. "You expect that sorry tale to hold water?"

"I expect everybody here to make sure it does."

Morg watched, bubbling with private mirth, as the king and his rebellious privy councillor again locked gazes. The cripple and the religious sot held their breaths. Sadly, Jarralt this time gave ground. Lowered his eyes and nodded. "Yes, Your Majesty."

The king slapped the table. "Then we are adjourned, save for one last matter. Until further notice, while Gar devotes himself to arcane study, Asher will be the Acting Olken Administrator. As such he shall enjoy all powers and duties previously ascribed to His Highness Prince Gar in the same capacity. He will attend these Council meetings and raise his voice with impunity wheresoever he deems it appropriate. I trust, gentlemen, that when he makes his first appearance in his new position you will make him feel right welcome."

Jarralt was displeased. "Are you certain that's wise? I was told he's been traipsing from tavern to tavern telling anyone who'll listen that His Highness is now a 'proper' Doranen. One wonders what kind of Doranen he considered the prince to be before today."

As the cripple and the king exchanged startled glances, and Holze tut-tutted his disapproval, Morg smothered a smile. Obedient Asher, following the Master Magician's suggestion. And in doing so, possibly—hopefully—weakening his inconvenient friendship with the cripple.

That was important. The sooner Prince Gar relied solely on the warmth and support of his tutor—kind, patient and understanding Durm—the better.

The cripple said, "There must be some mistake. Asher wouldn't—"

"No mistake," said Jarralt. "I had it from my groom, who was in the tavern at the time. If this is an example of how the Acting Olken Administrator intends to conduct himself, then perhaps—"

"You give unexamined credence to servants' gossip?" replied the cripple. "You surprise me, sir."

"And you surprise me, Your Highness! To place your unquestioning trust in a man who would—"

"If Asher did in fact make this announcement—"

"*If?*" Jarralt stabbed a pointed finger at the cripple's flushed face. "So now you accuse me of lying? To the Privy Council? To *His Majesty?* How dare—"

The king seized his son's wrist with crushing strength. "Let be. Both of you. Conroyd, Gar's unexpected transformation is hardly a secret, seeing as it took place in front of half the City. If Asher did speak on the matter it's hardly a crime. Surely we have more urgent matters to attend to. This Privy Council session is ended. Go about your own business, my lord. Leave Asher to my son."

Jarralt departed, a silent snarl in his eyes. Breaking the uncomfortable silence, Holze turned to the cripple with a gentle smile. "Do you know, in all the unpleasantness I did not think to say how pleased I am for you, Your Highness. I know you'll use this unexpected gift wisely. Barl's blessings upon you, sir."

"Thank you, Holze," the cripple replied, flushing. "You can be sure I'll look for your guidance in the days to come."

As soon as the old dodderer had gone the king released his son's wrist and pulled a face. "Well. That proceeded as I imagined it would."

"I am so sorry, sir," said the cripple. "To have exposed you thus to Conroyd Jarralt and his—"

"He was always going to scream about a divided succession," the king said wearily. "That at least is not your fault. As for the other business..." He frowned. "It's over and done with. In the past, and best left there. I need not ask that it never be repeated?"

"No, sir," the cripple agreed, subdued. "You needn't. Sir, might I beg a favour?"

Fingers exploring a flaw in the wooden table, the king sighed. "What?"

"While I accept—reluctantly—that for now at least I must be considered as a potential Weather Worker-in-Waiting, need Fane be informed immediately? For the first time in years, if ever, she and I are truly talking to one another. I want to give this fledgling bond between us time to strengthen before she learns I am indeed a rival."

Troubled, the king looked to his best friend for advice. Morg seethed. More delay? He was tired of delay, tired of waiting. He wanted this petty kingdom beaten *now*. Crushed *now*. Subordinate to his sublime domination *now*.

But fat Durm would counsel caution. Would side with the cripple, not for any care of it or its feelings but to protect his precious protégé Fane from distress.

He would have to follow suit.

Nodding Durm's head, pursing Durm's lips in a considering smile, he agreed. "Perhaps it would be wise, Your Majesty. Indeed, until I have had time to fully assess His Highness's breadth and depth of skill, it might be prudent to delay any announcement. If it should prove that Prince Gar is, after all, the moon to your daugher's sun we might well avoid any unnecessary unpleasantness."

"Very true," said the king. "All right. We stay silent for now. But the minute you're sure, Durm, we must proceed. This kingdom cannot afford any more body blows. One way or another the question of the succession must be settled to my satisfaction. Soon."

Morg smiled again, and bowed. Thinking, and so it will be settled, little king. So it will be. But to no-one's satisfaction save my own.

* * *

In something of a self-flagellating mood, Gar headed from the Privy Council chamber to his ruined private garden. With most of it comprehensively destroyed perhaps he should take the chance to consider redesigning its layout. This time he could include a small shrine to Barl, for the offering of penance after transgression.

He found his mother there, making repairs.

Not turning at his approach, keeping her attention on the resurrection of a garden seat, she said, "I suppose this was inevitable really. It's not just your world turned topsy-turvy, it's hers too. But we were so elated for you, your father and I, I'm afraid we neglected to consider that." She sighed, and with a snap of her fingers completed the transformation of charred cinders into carved wood. "No doubt that makes us bad parents."

Gar slipped his arms around her waist from behind and kissed her hair. "It makes you nothing of the sort, Mama. You might as well say this ridiculous eruption between me and Fane makes us bad children."

She covered his hands with hers and squeezed. "Who says I don't?"

Laughing, he slid away from her to sit on the newly restored garden seat. "Ouch, Oh well. I can't say a little scolding is undeserved. I'm sorry, Mama. I should never have let it get so out of hand."

She sat beside him. "No, you shouldn't," she said with mock severity. "Nor should she have used her magic as a weapon. It's strictly forbidden, and nobody knows that better than your sister. But what's done is done, Gar. Best that we all look to the future now." She patted his knee. "Tell me; how are you feeling? Truthfully?"

"Truthfully? Truthfully, Mama, I'm scared spitless. My blood has turned to sparkling wine. My bones are made of molten gold. Every time I open my mouth I'm afraid I'll breathe a cloud of butterflies into the air. The birth of magic is a grim and glorious thing." He hesitated. "Was it like that for you?"

"No." Her expression softened and her tired eyes gazed into the past. "For me, magic crept like the tide upon a beach. Softly. Gradually. Lapping further and further into my life until I looked around and saw only water. I suspect it's much the same for other Doranen. But your magic has crashed upon you violently, like a storm. And like a storm it's left the landscape a little the worse for wear. But we can fix that, Gar. With time. With patience. Most importantly, with love."

Gar considered the wrecked garden. "I hope so." They exchanged a brief smile. "Where's Fane?"

"In bed. Sleeping. I had Nix give her a draught. When she wakes we'll talk sensibly, mother to daughter. We'll work this out, Gar. We must. The kingdom depends on it. Your father depends on it." Something implacable stole into her voice. "Now, more than ever, we can't let him down."

Gar felt a catch in his throat. Had to blink a few times to clear his blurring vision. "We won't, Mama. *I* won't. I swear by Blessed Barl herself." He kissed his holyring hard enough to hurt. "No matter how this turns out, no matter what I have to do, His Majesty's kingdom will be safe."

She took his hand and pressed her lips to his knuckles. "My darling boy," she whispered, then released him. "Now run away. I want to have this garden tidied up by dinnertime and I'm sure you've got things to do too."

He looked at her, uncertain. "Well...that's very generous of you, Mama, but surely I should help you..."

She shook her head. "No, Gar. I think you've done more than enough gardening for one day."

Shocked, he stared at her. She stared back. A gurgle of laughter escaped her firmly pressed lips.

"*Mama!*" he protested. "It's not *funny!*"

She struggled for control. "I know, dear. I know. Only...look at it!" Her arm swept wide, encompassing every last sorry inch of the ruined bower. "And you were always such a *tidy* boy!"

Stricken, trying to stifle their shrieks, they fell against each other, shoulders shaking. "Oh dear, oh dear," his mother moaned through muffling fingers. "I can't think what's come over me..."

Sitting up again, Gar sobered. Dragged his shirt sleeve over his face and heaved a sigh. "Neither can I. I can't imagine what Darran would say if he saw us."

His mother shuddered theatrically. "I can. Thank you, Gar. I'm now perfectly sober." She kissed his cheek. "Off you go. Will you come to dinner?"

"How about breakfast?"

"All right. Till the morning then."

With a smile and a wave he left her to the garden and returned to the Tower, where duty waited.

The first person he saw was Darran.

"Good," he said brusquely, a raised hand silencing the old meddler before he could start asking questions or offering advice. "I wish to address the staff. Have everyone—Tower, grounds and stables—assembled in the foyer ten minutes from now. Where's Asher?"

"Sir?" Darran said faintly. "Yes, sir. Asher's upstairs, as far as I am aware. Sir, if I may just—"

"No," he replied, and turned for the staircase. "You may not."

He found Asher sitting disconsolate at his desk, the week's appointment diary unrolled before him. "That Darran reckons we should cancel *all* your meetings for the week," he said, looking up. "But if we do it means—"

"Never mind that for now." Gar leaned against the nearest chair. "Why did you go from tavern to tavern discussing my condition without first asking?"

Asher sat back. "Well, to start with it were one tavern, the Goose, and to finish, because Durm said to. He wanted me to 'calm the fears of our good City Olken.'"

"*Durm* said?" Gar frowned. "Are you sure?"

"Of the two people in this room, Gar, which one's more likely to have a clear recollection of recent events? Me, same as ever and not a whit changed, or you, the man who spent the morning rollin' around on the cobblestones spontaneously sprouting flowers?"

Eyebrows lifted, Gar stared. "'Spontaneously sprouting flowers'?"

"Don't look at me," said Asher, scowling. "You're the one who said I should read more books."

"Feel free to stop at any time," Gar retorted. "So Durm told you to—"

"*Aye.* Why? Is there a problem?"

Puzzled, Gar shook his head. "No. It's nothing. It's just odd he didn't mention it when—" He shrugged. "Never mind." Then he frowned. "Was it only this morning? It feels like a lifetime ago."

"It was," said Asher darkly. "Reckon I've aged fifty bloody years in the last six hours."

Gar smiled. "Well, I wouldn't let that worry you. I promise you don't look a day over sixty. Now come downstairs, would you? I'm about to address the staff."

There was barely enough space for his assembled people to fit in the Tower foyer. He stood on the fourth step of the spiral staircase, Asher at his right hand, and looked at all their expectant faces as they crowded knee to hip to shoulder inside the room's circumference.

"My friends," he said, smiling, "as doubtless you all know by now Barl has, in her mysterious and infinite wisdom and despite my advanced years, chosen to bestow upon me the Doranen gift of magic. As I'm sure you can imagine I am both honoured and humbled by this momentous event."

"Praise Barl!" said Darran, and started clapping. "Praise Barl most mightily!" The rest of the staff joined in.

After a moment Gar raised his hands. "Thank you. Barl is indeed worthy of our praise and appreciation. Now, I expect you also heard about a little trouble in the garden a while ago."

No applause this time, just shuffling feet and surreptitious glances. He produced a shamefaced smile.

"It galls me to admit, friends, that while Barl may indeed have gifted me with magic she has yet to bestow the wisdom required to use it properly. Both I and the gardening staff would appreciate a mention of this slight omission when next you're in the chapel."

Relieved laughter. A slapped back here and there. Good. Soon the explanation would be running all over the City. As the laughter died down:

"I'm sure you know this will mean some important changes for us all. From tomorrow I shall be consumed with arcane study so that I might learn how best to control and apply my new talents. Therefore Asher shall become our kingdom's Acting Olken Administrator. You know him well now. You trust him, as do I, without reservation. Take your problems to him, no matter how large or small they may be. He will help you, as I have helped you. As one day soon I will help you again, in whatever manner Barl sees fit. Thank you all, for your affection and your service. Barl's blessings be upon you, my friends."

From the rear of the crowd, his stable meister's voice rang out. "Three cheers for the prince, lads and ladies!"

As they cheered and stamped and hooted their approval Gar felt his throat close with tears.

His loyal loving people...his newly reconciled sister...his magical birthright, burst upon him...truly, truly, was ever a prince of Lur so blessed?

He'd never felt so happy in all his life.

CHAPTER THIRTY

No, no, *no!*" shouted Durm as the wobbling pile of coloured wooden blocks tumbled into disarray. "The alignment must be *exact*, that's the entire *point* of this exercise!"

Swallowing rage, choking on humiliation, Gar glared at him. "I'm trying."

Durm bared his teeth. "Not hard enough. Now. Pick up the pieces and we'll start again."

He reached for the nearest block; Durm cuffed the back of his head. "Not with your *fingers*, you fool! With *magic!*"

Gar leapt back from the workbench, shaking. "Hit me again, Durm, and Master Magician or not there *will* be consequences!"

For long moments they seethed silently at each other. Then Durm sighed, deflating, and shook his head. "Forgive me, boy. I know you're doing your best. Magic is hard work. And it must be difficult, trying to reconcile a lifetime's deprivation with a mere month's bounty."

Gar unstiffened his spine. "Durm," he said ruefully, "you have no idea..."

A month and still he hadn't quite accepted his new self. It had been a week before he was able to open his eyes in the morning and not call glimfire even before emptying his urgent bladder. And while that panicked need to reassure himself was now past, still the pleasure of his newfound power was so piercing he was sometimes hard put not to embarrass himself by weeping.

Look at me, I made a flower. Look at me, I locked the door. Look at me. Look at me. Look at me.

The wellspring of magic within him was sweeter than wine. It fed his mind, his heart, his soul. If there'd been a way for him to dive headfirst into it and stay there forever he would have.

Sometimes, dragging himself into bed at night so tired after a day of Durm he could hardly raise his arms, he amused himself by conjuring tiny balls of glimfire and dancing them in the darkness like fireflies.

Harmless tricks like that came as easily as breathing now. But *this*... the exercises Durm had him working at day after day...the struggle to encompass his power, shape it, refine it, control it drop by miserly drop when it thundered through his veins like a waterfall of fire...

"You must," his father had said in a moment of privacy. "For the Weather Magic is like a hundred hundred waterfalls and it will crush you to oblivion if you don't learn control."

Remembering, Gar exhaled sharply. Braced his shoulders, lifted his head and met Durm's piercing gaze unflinching.

"Right," he said. "Let's start again."

This time he succeeded. Briefly. The blocks stayed balanced in their tower for a full three seconds before clattering onto the workbench.

"Better," said Durm, and patted him on the shoulder.

"Much better. I'm going to leave you to practise now. I have other matters to attend to for the next little while. I'll rejoin you here after lunch, and once you've demonstrated to my satisfaction your mastery of this exercise we shall proceed to the next level."

Dismayed, Gar stared at him, then at the scatter of blocks on the bench. The sweat of effort was still wet on his skin. "The *next* level?"

Durm laughed. "And now you begin to understand, Your Highness. The reward for conquering one challenging task is another *more* challenging task. Welcome to the world of magic, boy."

Sourly, Gar watched him leave. Pretty soon, something would have to be done about all this "boy" business.

Fane appeared at the open doorway. Gar's frown vanished, replaced with a tentative smile. She wandered in, casual in green silk tunic and trousers, and laughed when she saw the tumbled wooden blocks on the bench.

"I remember those," she said, pulling a face. "Bloody things. I used to have nightmares about them."

Cheered, Gar grinned. "Really? That's reassuring. And don't say bloody."

"I will if I want to," she retorted, and poked her tongue out. "Bloody, bloody, bloody. See?"

"Mama doesn't like you swearing," he reminded her, fighting another smile.

"Mama isn't here. Besides, swearing is better than blowing things up."

"What things?"

She shrugged. "Anything I could find, when I couldn't make the magic do what I wanted. Why do you think this work room is so empty?"

He hadn't really noticed. He'd had other, more pressing concerns than a critique of the décor. Looking round the small room, though, seeing it properly for the first time, it did suddenly strike him as a bit on the austere side. Two workbenches, three stools and a cupboard for all of Durm's training knick-knacks. There was a series of shelves on the wall beside the window, but the only thing on them was dust.

"You always did have a temper," he said, reminiscent. Then he hesitated. Dithered for a moment, and decided to plunge in and take his chances. "I don't suppose you've got any useful advice, have you?"

She didn't answer straight away. Instead took a slow turn around the room, one finger upraised and trailing a thin streamer of dark purple smoke. It swirled and scented the room's heavy air. "About?"

He waved his hand in a vague attempt to encompass his new life. "*This*. Magic. Durm. Surviving my arcane education. I'm just beginning the journey, Fane, and you're almost at its end. There must be *something* you can tell me."

She lifted one eyebrow, head turned a little over her shoulder. Her lips curved in a complacent cat's smile. "I'm sure there is. The question is, why should I?"

"It's not a competition!"

"So you say." She draped herself across the other workbench, chin propped winsomely in her hands. "Your promise still stands then, brother dear? My birthright as WeatherWorker remains unchallenged?"

He kept his face blank, just. "My heart remains unchanged. I have no desire to wear His Majesty's crown."

It wasn't a lie. It just wasn't the...exact...truth.

Eyes narrowed, she stared at him. "I'm not sure I believe you."

"I confess," he said carefully, "to curiosity, and a little envy. WeatherWorking is the most sacred, most revered act of magic in the kingdom. If I said I hadn't wondered what it would be like to work the weather, how it would feel to serve the people in that fashion, then yes, I'd be lying. So I freely admit to you: I have wondered. A part of me does...regret. Is that the same as betraying my oath to you? I don't think so. But perhaps you see it differently."

Still she stared, nibbling her lower lip. He held his breath. The newborn bond between them continued tenuous, their common ground still stony. If he lost her now...

Sliding off the workbench, Fane twirled a gently curling strand of hair around her finger. "The trick with the wooden blocks," she said severely, "is in balancing the push and the pull of the energies. As I'm sure Durm explained, the blocks have been individually enchanted to repel each other. *Your* job is to subdue the antithetical elements and forge a fluid alliance between the competing vibrations so they can oscillate in harmony, not discordance. Only when you've achieved that will they remain balanced one upon the other."

He rolled his eyes. "Is that all? And here I was thinking it was difficult!"

Her smile was kindly condescending. "Gar, don't be dense. You're a musician, how can you not see the way it should go?"

Frustrated, he glared at the blocks of wood. "What's music got to do with it? I'm not plucking lute strings here, Fane, I'm—"

"*Think*!" she insisted, and clipped him on the back of the head. He winced. Like master, like protege. "How do you play music? One note at a time! How do you balance the blocks, control the energies? One vibration at a time!"

And suddenly it all made sense.

He closed his eyes, sought in the velvet darkness for the sounds, the colours, the tastes of each block's singular identity. Still with his eyes closed, his fingers drifted, his magic unfurled like a seed from its pod. Vibrant with life but at the same time tamed. Only the echo of waterfalls now, waiting for his command. With his mind's eye he saw the tower of blocks whole, cohesive, compliant. Heard the song they should be singing and coaxed them into a choir. The first block—the second block—third, fourth, fifth, sixth...

He opened his eyes.

"See?" said Fane. "Simple."

Sturdy as a tree, the wooden tower block sat on the workbench before him. Pleasure like pain suffused him.

"Thank you," he whispered. "Thank you, thank you, thank you."

Unthinking, he hugged her...and for the first time since her innocent infancy, she hugged him back.

Asher put down his pen, linked his fingers behind his neck and tugged. All the muscles went *pop-pop-pop* and for a moment the room swam. Groaning, he rolled his head around and around, trying to ease the persistent, nagging ache that had settled at the base of his skull and down into his shoulders.

All day he'd been stuck indoors, working, just as he'd spent nigh on the last six weeks stuck indoors, working. Or stuck indoors taking meetings with guild meisters, with Pellen Orrick, with concerned citizens. For the life of him he couldn't see any hour soon when he *wouldn't* be stuck indoors, working. Reading letters. Writing letters. Reading affidavits. Responding to affidavits. Preparing for meetings. Attending meetings. Reading notices. Drafting notices. Five more minutes of this and he was going to scream. Like a girl.

It hadn't been so bad when he was Gar's assistant. He'd done a lot of going around talking to people, and he'd enjoyed that. Enjoyed poking his nose into other people's businesses, other people's lives. Solving their problems or, if he couldn't, making sure somebody else did. Seeing how the brewers roasted their hops and the cheese makers waxed their wares and the cartwrights made their wheels so round. Especially enjoyed the respect and the welcome and the way they were so proud, because he was one of them elevated near as good as royalty, eh, and sitting in their parlours, taking tea.

But now, with Gar all magically afflicted and everything so up in the air, he'd had to leave all that pleasurable visiting behind. Instead of talking to people he was either listening to them complain in formal meetings or else bloody writing to them and he *hated* writing. It made his fingers ache and his brain buzz and he kept getting ink all over himself. The laundry maids were complaining. And if all that wasn't bad enough he wasn't getting out to the stables. He wasn't riding or sharing a morning mug of tea with Matt or mucking about with the lads. At this rate Cygnet and the stable meister both were going to forget what he looked like.

Worst of all, his once regular visits down to the Goose had been severely curtailed. With no assistant of his own, and trying to carry his own responsibilities as well as Gar's, his free time had disappeared faster than a jug of ale down a thirsty field-hand's throat.

His nights down at the Goose were *useful*, damn it. All sorts of gossip and titbits he picked up down there. That's how he'd found out about the Guigan brothers and their shifty dealings in stock feed. How he'd put a stop to a right old bust-up between the candle makers and the beekeepers practically afore it started. How he'd throttled more than a dozen brewing storms. If he couldn't get on down to the Goose nice and regular, who was going to nip all those pesky little problems in the bud, eh?

A nasty, sneaky voice in the back of his mind said: *you could always ask Dathne.*

Scowling, he told the voice to shut its trap. The only good thing to come out of any of this was him not having much time to lay eyes on Dathne. The thought of her was a raw wound, scabbing over. Last thing he needed was to go pickin' and pokin' and scratchin' at that little embarrassment.

I don't love you, Asher. I don't love anyone.

The razor-sharp memory of her cool voice, so controlled, so brisk and matter of fact, made him want to throw something. Hit someone. He didn't know whether to be relieved that he didn't have a rival or appalled that he couldn't break down the wall she hid behind and reach the warm and beating heart of her.

He only knew that he missed her, and he never wanted to see her again.

She'd offered her help. If he took her up on that, if he pretended he was happy to be nothing but friends, if he bided his time, like any good angler, and baited his hook with patience and undemanding good company...

Codswallop.

Time to face facts. Dathne wasn't interested. The sooner he stopped pining, the better. Starting right now.

Abruptly, savagely sick of his office and his desk and the endless stream of problems he was expected to solve like—ha!—magic, he threw his pen at his inkpot and headed for the stables.

Where he found Matt and Dathne, damn her, sitting in the yard office amusing themselves with cards.

"Thought you had yourself a shop to run?" he demanded from the doorway, not caring overmuch that his sour temper showed.

She exchanged an arched-eyebrow look with Matt, took a moment to consider her hand of cards, put one on the table and slid a replacement from the pile between them, then said, "Poppy's after some extra pocket money so I left her to mind the till for the afternoon. Is that all right with you?"

Her sweetly poisonous tone galled him. "Poppy?" Slouching into the tack room, he pretended to care what was bubbling on the coal-fed burner in the corner. Barley and linseed mash: the fuggy steam of it hit him full in the face, stealing his breath. Out of habit, and because he didn't want to look at bloody Dathne, he grabbed the old wooden stirring spoon and slopped the horse porridge from side to side in its pot.

She was staring at him; he could feel her gaze smouldering his spine. "Aleman Derrig's youngest. Poppeta, commonly known as Poppy. The one who insists on giving you lovelorn glances and free ale when her father's not looking."

He put the spoon aside, the lid back on the porridge pot and turned round. "I know who Poppy is."

Dathne sniffed. "You could've fooled me."

"Aye, well, reckon the village idiot could fool you, Dathne," he sneered, folding his arms across his chest.

There was a half-eaten apple on the table beside her. Flushed with temper she threw it at him, hard, as Matt said protestingly, "Hey now, hey now! What's all this, Asher? There's no call to fratch at Dathne like that!"

He caught the apple, demolished it in three angry bites and lobbed the core into the waste bucket by the sink. "Sorry."

"My, *that* sounded sincere," said Dathne, rolling her eyes. She sounded just like her spicy, spiky self...except there was a hint of hurt surprise in her face and the cards in her clutching fingers shook ever so slightly.

He felt like a murderer. "Sorry," he said again, and this time meant it. He crossed to the camp cot against the wall and collapsed onto it. "Don't mind me. I been penned up in that Tower for what feels like three lifetimes, tryin' to come to grips with Meister Glospottle's piss problem."

"Eh?" said Matt. "I thought you had that solved a week ago."

"Aye, well, so did I," said Asher. And added, darkly, "It came back."

"What... like a persistent bladder infection?" suggested Dathne delicately.

Matt guffawed. Dathne grinned. And then they were laughing, all three of them, like the good and true friends they were.

"Come on," said Matt, wiping his eyes. "Forget Meister Pissy Glospottle for a bit and play a round of cards with us, eh? We've not laid eyes on you for days now, and we've missed your ugly face. Haven't we, Dath?"

"Speak for yourself," said Dathne, but she was smiling and shoving out the table's third chair with her foot.

He sat down and waited while Matt took back all the cards. As he shuffled them with casual expertise the stable meister said, "How's His Highness getting on then?"

Asher shrugged. "Buggered if I know. Hardly lay eyes on him from sunup to sundown these days. Every time I do catch a glimpse he's rushin' off to practise turning toads into toadstools with that ole Durm. Or his sister, if you can believe that."

Matt started dealing. Dathne, waiting for all her cards to arrive before picking them up, said, "Is he any good?"

Asher laughed. "Don't ask me. Still..." He thought for a moment. "Reckon he can't be exactly *bad*, I s'pose. If he were bad he'd be in a worse mood than me, but every time I see him he's smiling."

Dathne and Matt exchanged glances. "Well," she said brightly, and turned her cards over, "isn't that nice for him? I'll start, shall I? Ladies first, and all that horse manure. I wager... three cuicks to a demi-trin I'll see full house in seven switches."

Grinning at Matt, who was throwing a theatrical fit at the outrageous wager, Asher sat back in his chair and stared at Dathne while pretending to consider his own cards. For the first time in a long time he felt something approaching happiness.

Friendship was less, far less, than his heart's desire, but if it was all he could get, at least for now, perhaps it wasn't so bad after all.

Morg wrote the note in Durm's cramped and crabby cursive: *Come to my study at dawn.* Sealed it, and gave it to a servant to deliver to the prince.

Duly summoned, the cripple presented himself at sunup the following morning, agog with curiosity. "Durm? Is something wrong?"

Inviting him in with a beckoning finger, Morg closed and warded the suite's double doors and guided him into the library to a seat at the round velvet-covered table by the window. On it was the ancient wooden box housing the Weather Orb.

"What's this?" asked the cripple, examining the box with interest.

Morg sat in the other chair and waved his hand. "Why don't you see for yourself?"

The cripple raised an eyebrow and reached for the box. Went to slide free the pin securing the lid and yelped as the lightly applied ward spell bit him.

Morg laughed. "Did you think I would make it easy? Undo the ward spell."

"I would if I knew how." There was an edge to the cripple's voice.

"You don't need to know how," he countered. "The 'how' is within you, Your Highness. As it was the day your magic revealed itself and I asked you to make a rose. Remember?"

The cripple gave him a look. "I remember that just yesterday you told me I was a cretin and a fool and a disgrace to the memory of my ancestors."

"Academic hyperbole." Morg dismissed the complaint with the wave of one hand. "It was merely enthusiastic encouragement, I assure you."

"Perhaps *over*enthusiastic would be a more accurate description," muttered the cripple. "To be honest, I think I've been doing exceptionally good work of late."

"And so you have, Gar, so you have," Morg soothed. "Why else do you think I've summoned you here this morning?"

"I don't know why you've summoned me. I'm still waiting for you to tell me."

"And I will," Morg promised. "Just as soon as you deactivate the ward spell."

After a single, searching glance at him the cripple reached out to the box and dissolved the lock's guarding enchantment. He laughed. "I did it!"

"Of course you did, Your Highness. I believe there is nothing you can't do, provided you put your mind to it."

"It was so simple!" the cripple exclaimed. "So natural. Just like... breathing."

"Of course," agreed Morg. With my help, you deformed monstrosity. "That is how magic should be. The reason you've found it so hard during our lessons is because I've been forcing you to think about it. To analyse it. To apply your powers consciously when in reality they flow most easily from the subconscious part of your mind."

"Then why do it?"

"Because it is necessary. Trust me."

The cripple smiled. "You know I do. Implicitly. Durm..."

"Yes, my boy?"

"How is this possible?" the cripple whispered. "How could I have had all this power inside me for so many years and never once *imagined* or suspected or felt so much as a hint of it?"

He smiled and spread his hands wide. "That, I'm afraid, is likely to remain a mystery. Let's just put it down to another of Blessed Barl's miracles, shall we, and continue with our current business. Open the box."

The cripple obeyed, revealing the box's contents. His face stilled. "That's the Weather Orb. Fane described it once. Why are you showing it to me?"

"Why do you think?"

Shoving his chair away from the table, the cripple retreated. "No. It's too soon. Durm, my powers woke from their slumber scant weeks ago! And now you want me to undertake the Transference? Fane studied with you for *years* before—"

Morg shrugged. "You are not your sister. Her powers are great, I don't deny that. But they grew as she did. Matured as she did. I had to wait until she was ready to face the immense tides and tests of the Weather Magic. But your circumstances are very different. Your power has sprung forth fully developed. With you it's not a case of maturation but exploration. And while your power is formidable, Gar, it might yet be that Fane is still the better WeatherWorker. Receiving the incantations is but the first step on the way to determining who ultimately shall be named your father's heir. Even I cannot tell how long it will take you to master their complexities. Or even if you can. Don't you see? The sooner you're given the magics, the sooner can we begin to explore your aptitude for controlling and applying them."

"I understand that," the cripple said, still staring at the Orb. Fascinated. Repelled. "But what would a little further delay matter? I need more time, Durm. Time to fully grasp what's happened to me. How I feel about it. What it means, for my future and the future of the kingdom. That's all. Just a little time."

Morg sighed. Lowered his voice and let Durm's face assume a sorrowful, portentous expression. "Your Highness, unwittingly you have put your finger on the very pulse of the matter. Time is the one thing we may not have. To be brutal, and forgive me but there is no other way, we don't know how long your dear father will remain the WeatherWorker. The bulk of his life now lies behind him, spent lavishly in the service of Lur. For the sake of our kingdom we must ensure the succession. If we don't, we give Conroyd Jarralt more grist for his mill. And then he will grind and grind and grind until the flour comes out to bake a bread of *his* liking. Not ours.'

The cripple had lost all his colour and in his eyes, tears. Stupid, sentimental fool. He'd do better saving his woe for the days to come. Soon he'd have something truly worth weeping for.

"You're certain of this?"

Morg spread his hands. "Alas."

"And once the decision is made, between Fane and myself? What then? Only one can hold the Weather Magic."

Ah. So his little worm was hooked, and wriggling. Morg swallowed a smile. "There is an incantation for Transference reversal. Unpleasant, to be sure, but the effects aren't permanent. Please, Your Highness." He gestured at the empty chair. "I promise, this is how it must be."

The cripple returned to his seat at the table. "You're absolutely certain...?"

"Absolutely, Your Highness. After all, as loyal subjects and men who love our king, we have our duty."

"Duty..." The cripple sighed. "Yes. In the end it always comes down to duty, doesn't it?"

Yes indeed. Duty was the magic word. "It does, Your Highness. And like your father you have never shirked your duty, no matter what the personal cost."

The cripple straightened his spine. "Then let's proceed...on one condition."

He kept the smile pinned to Durm's lips. "Yes?"

"When it's over I want to be the one to tell Fane. I want to explain to her that I had no choice. That this doesn't mean I'm breaking my word. If I explain, I know she'll understand."

Morg laughed. Did he truly know his sister so little? "Of course, Your Highness. I have no objection. Now. Remove the Orb from its box and hold it lightly in your hands. Clear your mind. Quiet your soul. Look deep into its heart and breathe in...out...in...out..."

The incantation of Transference was a complicated one, with five different levels culminating in a single trigger word. As the cripple prepared himself for the assumption of powers, Morg plucked the words of the Transference from Durm's memory and rolled them on his tongue like a gourmand tasting truffles. Yes...*yes*...it was all so ludicrously simple. All he had to do was change *this* word—and *this* word—and finally *this* one—and all would be well.

For him, at least, if for nobody else in this doomed kingdom.

He looked up. The cripple was ready: centred and silent and waiting, oblivious.

With a smile so wide it felt he could engulf the world in a single bite, as tiny Durm screeched and scrabbled impotent in his cage, Morg triggered the spell.

The cripple screamed. Inside the pulsing Weather Orb the magic writhed like a living thing in torment. The Orb began to glow, brighter and brighter until it burned like a multicoloured sun. A shadow touched it: Morg held his breath. Would Barl's magic detect his handiwork in the cripple's mind? Would it reject the prince as it had rejected him?

The shadow faded. Disappeared. Morg released the trapped air from Durm's aching lungs and leaned forward. Watched avidly as the cripple's fingers convulsed around the Orb, blind staring eyes reflecting gold and green and crimson and purple.

It was working.

The radiant light spread from the Orb and over Gar's fingers like butter, melting. Flowed *into* his fingers, his hands, his wrists and through his entire body until he glowed like a lantern made of flesh.

And then the light died, suddenly extinguished. With a moan the cripple collapsed across the table, emptied of incandescence. The Orb rolled from between his lax fingers to rest quiescent against its drab wooden box.

Morg let out a long, shaky breath. Reached for the cripple's lax wrist and felt for a pulse. It was there: scudding, erratic. His chest rose and fell quickly, shallowly.

He'd survived.

As he waited for the cripple to wake from his stupor he stared longingly at the Orb. More than anything he wanted to destroy it, crush it, spill Barl's trapped magic to the floor and smear it into nothingness beneath his victorious, contemptuous heel.

But he couldn't. So he put it back in its box and returned it to the cupboard. Briefly he considered sealing the doors with a killing ward, but discarded the notion. To do so might arouse unwanted curiosity; they were trusting fools, these lost Doranen. The king came here often, and was used to rummaging at will amongst Durm's things. Going to another cupboard he extracted an empty glass globe and its stand and put them on the table. Then he sat back, gloating, and waited.

At length the cripple stirred. Sat up. "Durm." He pressed his fists to his temples. "You should have warned me it would hurt like that.

Fane said it was exhausting, but not that there'd be pain. I thought it would tear me apart...or turn me to ash."

Morg shrugged. "Such warnings are pointless. One man's pain is another man's pleasure, after all. Each Transfer is different."

The cripple shook his head. "I feel so *strange*. Did the Transfer work? For a moment it felt almost as though the Weather Magic wanted to...to reject me. Why would that be?" He laughed, shakily. "Am I still not good enough?"

"You are perfect," Morg said sharply. "But to put your mind at rest, let us try a small experiment. Here is an empty vessel. Cast your mind within the void and make it rain."

"I'm afraid," the cripple whispered.

"You are a prince of royal House Torvig!" thundered Morg. "Honour your father and make it rain!"

The cripple reached for the clear globe. Held it before his eyes in silence, gaze unfocused as he searched the new knowledge within. Then he stirred. Stared into the globe's vacant heart and spoke. The air within it churned. Thickened. Turned white. Grey. Black.

Wept.

"Look, Durm," the cripple breathed. There were tears in his eyes. On his cheeks. There was blood, a tiny trickle, but he didn't heed it. "I made it rain..."

The servants he passed in the corridors on his way to find Fane spoke to him, but he couldn't hear them. He said something in return, "Good morning" most probably, but he couldn't hear himself. Could barely see their faces or remember their names.

He'd made it rain.

Blessed Barl preserve him, he'd made it rain, and his life would never be the same again.

He found Fane in the palace solar, eating a solitary breakfast. The hovering servant bobbed a curtsey. He dismissed her and crossed the marble floor towards his sister.

Without looking up from her plate she said coldly, "Go away."

He stopped. Frowned. "Fane..."

She reached for her teacup. Sipped. Swallowed. Put it back in its saucer with a faint *plink*. "Did you think I wouldn't know? Did you think I wouldn't *feel* it?"

He went to her and dropped to one knee beside her chair. "Fane, I'm sorry. It wasn't my idea. I didn't want the weather magic. I *begged* the king to let my promise stand. But the day we fought there was a scene in Privy Council. It was...awful. Accusations were made. Conroyd Jarralt—"

"He made you break your word?" Her face was pale, composed. She spoke calmly, with a vague air of disinterest. As she sliced a hothouse teshoe with her sharp little fruit knife her eyes never left his face. "What a bad man."

"I argued. I did. I told them I'd made you a promise. But it was all of them against me. Even Father agreed it had to be done. In the end, it came down to what's best for the kingdom."

She popped a slice of teshoe into her mouth. Chewed. Swallowed. "I'm sure it did."

He put his hand on her arm. "Fane, I wasn't lying. I didn't ask for this. I didn't break my promise willingly. I had no choice."

She reached for a bread roll. The movement broke the contact of his fingers against her sleeve. "So you'd abdicate, would you, if it was decided you'd make the better WeatherWorker? You'd refuse the throne for my sake? Is that what you're saying?"

"Yes!" he cried. Remembered the rain. Cursed. "Perhaps. I don't know." Frustrated, he stood and began to pace around the solar. "It might not be as easy as that. This can't be about what you or I want, Fane. Our personal desires are *nothing* compared to the welfare of the kingdom. It all comes down to duty. You understand that better than anyone."

Fane finished tearing the bread roll into tiny pieces, selected one and smeared it with sweet butter. "Now I'm confused. It's a simple question, Gar: would you abdicate, yes or no?" Still watching him, she ate the bread.

Gar stopped pacing. Returned to her side and again knelt on the chequered tile floor. "I...don't think I could. Not if I were truly chosen. But, Fane, I swear, it won't come to that. You are the superior magician, I have no doubt of it, you—"

Fane sat back in her chair. Her eyes were very...polite. "So when you swore to me the crown was mine, only mine, always mine, what you really meant was, unless you decided you'd rather it was yours?"

Barl save him. "*No.* I meant what I said, Fane. You have to believe that. I spat on it, remember?"

She smiled. "I remember." Leaning forward, she spat on him. As the hot saliva trickled down his cheek she said, "And now we're even."

He pulled a handkerchief from his pocket and wiped away the spittle. "Please, let's talk about this. I want us to be close, Fane, I want us to be friends, I want—"

"I don't." She picked up her sharp little fruit knife and pointed its tip at him. Sunlight flashed upon the blade. It was a small knife, hardly lethal, but somehow it was worse than a hundred balls of flaming glimfire. "What I want is for you to go away. Now."

He stood. Tucked the soiled handkerchief back in his pocket. The knife was still pointing at him. "I can't leave it like this, Fane."

Her eyes were glittering. With tears, with temper, with implacable hate. "I can."

He reached out his hand to her. "Fane...*please*..."

With a shriek like a falcon swooping for the kill she lunged across the table. The knife caught him. Cut silk and skin. Spilled blood.

He fled the solar, his wounded arm tucked inside his weskit where no-one could see it. The memory of her face chased him all the way back to the Tower.

CHAPTER THIRTY-ONE

D'you *mind*?" said Asher as his inkpot floated gently past his nose for the third time.

Gar grinned, briefly. "No."

"Well, I do!" Asher snatched the pot to safety. "I got work to finish here. Reports for Pellen Orrick don't write 'emselves and—"

"Would you like them to?"

"What are you hangin' around here like a bad smell for anyways? Ain't you and Durm s'posed to be goin' on a magical field trip or some such shenanigans?"

"He's been delayed. He'll be along in due course."

Asher groaned. "Then why don't you wait for 'im downstairs? No muckin' about, Gar, I'm bloody drownin' here."

Gar looked at the desk crowded with papers and parchment. "So I see."

With a sigh, Asher sat back in his chair. "Truth is, I don't reckon I'll manage much longer without a proper assistant. And *not* that bloody Willer! He's as much use as tits on a bull."

Gar's lips twitched. "All right. Find yourself an assistant you can work with, if there is such a creature. Offer them thirty trins a week."

"Twenty-five," said Asher, scowling. "No point givin' a body ideas above his station, eh?"

That made him laugh: something of a miracle. "Fine. I don't really care. Just deal with it."

After a considering pause Asher said, "So. Is she talkin' to you yet?"

She. Fane. Gar rubbed the half-healed cut on his forearm and shook his head. "No."

"Aye, well...give her time," said Asher. Trying to sound confident. Failing. "She'll come round."

"No, Asher," he replied sadly. Remembering her face. The knife. "Somehow I don't think she will."

Time for a change of subject. "Well," said Asher, "now you've got your floatin' inkpot trick down a treat, when d'you reckon they'll let you out in public to impress the locals?"

Gar shrugged, feigning indifference. "Soon."

"Which means when? Tomorrow? Next week? Next month?"

"I don't know exactly. All Durm will say is *soon*. I think he wants to be certain I'll not disgrace him."

"Bugger what he wants," said Asher, snorting. "Do you feel ready?"

Gar laughed nervously. "Good question. Sometimes I think yes, and other times..." He shook his head. "Durm's right. I must be ready. I must have complete control of my power. Revealing my transformation prematurely would be disastrous. This isn't just about me, Asher. You know the political ramifications of this change. For most of my life I've been an object of pity. Of scorn. An embarrassing aberration. For most of my life I've been more or less invisible, at least to my own race."

"You're forgettin' Lady Scobey."

Gar shuddered. "If only I could. You know, if there's a drawback to my miracle it's knowing she's going to redouble her efforts to match me with her wretched daughter."

Grinning, Asher nodded. "Never mind. She won't be the only one. You'll have your pick of blonde beauties now, I reckon. Lucky bastard."

"Yes," said Gar, his smile sly. "I confess the thought isn't entirely unpalatable. But my search for a bride will have to wait, I'm afraid. First I must leap the hurdle of my past and gain the confidence and trust of my peers. They know me only as a magical failure. As a cripple. I'll have one chance to show them that's no longer true. One chance...and if I stumble, I'll not get a second."

"You worried about that?"

Gar hesitated, then flicked his fingers. "Of course not. Not really. I just—"

He was interrupted by a sharp knock on the open office door. Willer. Stiff-necked and stuffy, as usual. "Your Highness," he said, bowing. "Their Majesties are here, and desirous of speaking with you."

"Very well," said Gar. "Show them into the library, then, and—"

"Forgive me, sir. They're outside. In a carriage."

"Oh. All right. Thank you, Willer." Willer bowed and retreated, and Gar raised his eyebrows at Asher. "Coming?"

"You don't listen, do you? All that bloody magic's bunged up your lugholes worse than earwax. I got *work* to do."

Gar clapped him on the shoulder. "It'll still be here five minutes from now. Come on. You need some fresh air. In case you hadn't noticed you're getting as persnickety as Darran."

The royal carriage was halted at the Tower's front entrance. It wasn't one of the official carriages, enclosed and groaning beneath the weight of gilt and hand-carved curlicues, but the open touring affair used on the day of Asher's parade. Sprawled on its crimson leather seats were his father, his mother and Fane, splendid in brocades, leather and wool. His parents were talking, laughing; Fane was silent, her expression as smooth as glass. Gar tried to smile at her as he came down the sandstone steps but she refused to meet his gaze. He felt a small pain between his ribs, but kept it from his face as he turned the smile towards their parents instead.

"There he is!" said Dana, and beckoned him closer with a gloved hand. "Gar, my love, we're off to Salbert's Eyrie for a family picnic. Just us, nobody else. We had the whole area closed so we could enjoy some privacy. Conjure yourself a warmer coat, because the weather's definitely getting chilly. One for Asher, too. There's more than enough room in the carriage for him and, besides, he's practically family as well."

Gar tried to catch Fane's eye again, and again was unsuccessful. Thwarted, he glanced at the cloudless sky. A family picnic? It was a perfect day for it, certainly. He wished he could go; behind his mother's bright smile and determined gaiety there was strain and a feverish unhappiness.

"Mama, it's a charming idea, truly, but—"

"Come on, Gar," the king said coaxingly. "The snow will be here before long and there'll be no more picnics for months."

"Yes, sir, I realise that, but—"

With a roll of his eyes, Borne turned to Asher. "Well, sir? What about you?"

Asher bowed. "I'd surely come if I could, Your Majesty. Trouble is,

Meister Glospottle's still got problems with his piss, y'see, and he's waitin' on me to fix 'em for him."

"And can you?" said the queen. "I'm most anxious for his difficulties to be resolved, Asher."

Another bow. "I be doin' my best, Your Majesty. But it seems there be more to Meister Glospottle's piss problem than meets the eye."

"I see," said the king after a pause. "Well, far be it from me to come between you and Meister Glospottle's..." A wicked grin. "Problems. Gar, must I make this a royal command?"

"Even if you did, I'd have to refuse. I'm due to meet with Durm at any moment. My studies—"

"Are swallowing you alive," said Borne. "Barl knows we've hardly seen hide nor hair of you these past long weeks, Gar. There's more to life than magic. Family is important too."

Gar couldn't help himself. For the third time he looked at Fane. This time she let a spasm of emotion cross her face. His heart sank. "Yes, I know that, sir, but—"

"But pleasure," a new voice said urbanely, "needs often take a back seat to duty."

"Durm!" said Borne, startled, and craned his neck. "Where did you spring from? I swear you move more and more like a cat every day."

Standing beside the carriage horses' heads, Morg smiled. Glossy brown beasts, they were, with perfect paces and gentle eyes. Reaching up a casual hand he stroked the nearest soft nose. "Did I hear you aright, Majesty? You're bound on a picnic?"

"To Salbert's Eyrie," said Dana. "Before the snows come. Will you join us?"

"Nothing would give me greater pleasure," said Morg, fingers sliding up and down the horse's nose. Perfect, perfect, so wonderfully perfect. "Salbert's Eyrie is an ideal place for a picnic, but alas, I must decline. His Highness and I still have much work to do. Another day, perhaps. But don't let us detain you any longer on such a superb morning...and do think of us slaving away as you quaff your wine and nibble the dainties you've brought in your picnic basket." He sighed. "Life is so cruel, isn't it?"

There was laughter as he pulled a mock-sorrowful face. Lifting his other hand, smiling, he ensured he was touching both horses. Power flowed through his fingers. The horses' liquid brown eyes flared scarlet. He stepped back. "Mind your animals, driver," he admonished the coachman as the horses snorted and pinned their ears back, heads tossing.

Borne looked from the cripple to the lout and shook his head in sorrow. "I can see your minds are quite made up. I confess I'm disappointed, but not surprised. I warn you, though, next time we really won't take no for an answer."

"As His Majesty commands," said Morg, and moved to join the prince at the foot of the Tower steps. "Next time."

"Drive on then, Matcher," said Borne. The coachman picked up his reins and shook his whip and the carriage rolled forward as the horses leaned into their harness.

Morg looked around as Asher came down the rest of the steps. "You should go," the lout said to the prince in an undertone. "When you thought he was dead you'd have given anythin' to spend just one more day with him. Now here's a day bein' handed to you on a silver platter and you're turnin' it down. For what? For *magic*? That's mad. He ain't goin' to live forever, Gar. Go."

Frozen, the cripple stared at the gravel beneath his feet. "You're right," he whispered. "I'm a fool."

"Just remember," the lout added, "you got that meetin' with Matt this afternoon, about this season's two year olds. So don't go gettin' carried away with the scenery and whatnot."

The prince looked up. "It's a picnic, not an expedition. I'll be back in time, don't fret. And tell Darran where I've gone, will you? He'll fuss, otherwise." He turned and pulled an apologetic face. "Sorry, Durm. Studies are cancelled for today." Then he sprang after the carriage, shouting. "Wait! Wait!"

As the carriage stopped and the king turned round in his seat, Morg rested speculative eyes on the lout. "Well, well, well," he murmured. "What a meddlesome young man you are." And could have *killed* him with such pleasure...

Defiant, stiff-necked, the lout stared back. "It's only one day. He can put aside his studies for one day. Sir."

"As you say," he said, smiling thinly. "It's only one day."

Seated now in the carriage, the cripple leaned out and waved an arm. "Durm! Come on!" he called. "There's no point in you staying behind now!"

"No," Morg agreed under his breath. "There's no point at all." He waved an acquiescent hand. "I surrender, sir! Your persuasive powers have overcome my better judgement. To Salbert's Eyrie we go!"

Walking slowly, because above all things Durm was a dignified man, Morg closed the distance between himself and the royal carriage, his mind turning over and over as he rearranged his important plans.

Again.

Soon, very soon, he would have to arrange a special reward for the Olken lout Asher.

The carriage bowled along through the lush open countryside, heading for picturesque Salbert's Eyrie lookout. As the horses shied, plunging, Borne spoke over his shoulder to the coachman. "The team seems fresh today, Matcher!"

"That they do, Your Majesty," Matcher replied, forearms rigid as he grasped the reins. "Don't know what's got into them and that's a fact."

"Must be all this crisp autumn air," Borne said. "Mind how you go, won't you?"

"Certainly will, Your Majesty."

Seated opposite him, the queen tipped her face to the sun and sighed. "Oh, it feels so good to be outside. Do you know I've done nothing but chair committee meetings for nearly a week? I declare I don't know how those women can be so staid. That Ethienne Jarralt—"

"Ha," said her husband. "I'll gladly swap you the lord for the lady."

Dana sniffed. "No, thank you."

The cripple considered his father. "He's not still complaining, is he?"

"No more than usual," said the king with a dismissive flick of his fingers. "It's all right. Conroyd can't help himself. He's exactly as your mother described him: a dog with a bone. Either he'll bury it and forget where it is, or he'll chew it to pieces and there'll be an end to the discussion."

"With any luck," said the cripple, disdainful, "he'll chew it and choke."

"I think," his sister said distantly, "you should be kinder to him. I don't care what any of you say, he's not a bad man." She was seated with her back to the coachman, beside her mother, curled up in the corner of the wide touring carriage. Her hair was knotted in loops and braids on the top of her head and she was staring with intense concentration at the countryside flashing by. "It's not his fault his ancestor lost Trevoyle's Trials and his house never got to breed up kings. He's a powerful magician. He might have made a very good Weather Worker."

There was an awkward pause, filled with the pounding of hooves on the roadway and the bouncing creak of the carriage. Morg let his eyelids droop and watched the girl from under his lashes. She was looking very beautiful this morning. A pity the smooth perfection of her forehead was marred by a frown. Tension, arising from resentment of her brother. Foolish child. Life was far too short to waste in petty squabbling. It was a shame she'd never realised it.

As the carriage picked up a little more speed, Borne again spoke up. "For the love of Barl, Matcher, must I repeat myself? Slow those damned horses down!"

"Yes, Your Majesty," said Matcher, and once more hauled on the reins.

Morg let his gaze drift over the greenery by the side of the road and smiled. Beside him, the cripple shifted on the red leather seat then leaned forward a little, trying to catch his sister's attention. "I've not seen you for days, Fane," he said. "How do your studies progress?"

She sat there like a maiden carved from ice. "Satisfactorily."

Her brother nodded. Morg could feel the effort in him as he tried to chip away her frozen façade. Fool. Didn't he know by now he was wasting his time? The girl was just like Barl: a beautiful heartbreaker. "That's good," the cripple said, trying to sound encouraging. "What incantations are you working on?"

"My own."

The queen tried to smile. Took her daughter's hand in hers and squeezed. "Come, darling, you can tell us more than that, can't you? I'd like to hear what you've been doing, too."

Fane pulled her hand free. "I thought we were leaving work behind today."

"Don't be rude, Fane," the king said, mildly enough, but with an undercurrent of warning.

The girl's eyes flashed cold fire. "I'm not rude. I just don't want to talk about it." Her gaze flickered to the cripple, then elsewhere. "Why don't you ask Gar what he's been doing? I'm sure that's much more exciting."

The king's tired face contracted. "Stop it. I'll have no quarrelling, is that clear? This is a family outing, something to be enjoyed, and I won't have your tiresome jealousy spoiling it."

The cripple lifted one hand. Placating, as always. Pathetic weakling. "Father. Please. She's a right to be hurt. Angry. Willingly or not, I broke my promise to her and—"

Fane sat up. "I don't want you defending me."

"Please," said the queen. "Please can we just—"

"*Enough*!" Borne snapped. "How many times must I say it? I won't tolerate a divided house! I refuse to leave that as my legacy to this kingdom. Not after a lifetime of sacrifice and service. Gar, Fane—one of you will be WeatherWorker after me and the other won't. If you refuse to accept this then anarchy will again stalk this land. In days long hence, once a new generation's blood has soaked into the soil, they'll call it Borne's Schism. Or Gar's. Or Fane's. Is that what you want? Is that how you wish our house to be remembered?"

"Oh, *please*, let's not argue," cried the queen. There was a treacherous break in her voice and her eyes were sheened with tears. "It's such a lovely day. Can't we leave politics behind us for a few hours and enjoy each other's company? I'm so tired of magic and WeatherWorking and worry! Of late I find myself profoundly sorry that Conroyd Jarralt's wretched ancestor *didn't* win Trevoyle's bloody Trials! Then he could be the one with the weight of the kingdom on his shoulders and I could look forward to night after night of sleep unriven by nightmares!"

After a short, stricken silence: "My love..." Borne took his wife's hand and pressed it to his lips. "Forgive me. Forgive us all. These past weeks have been hardest on you, I think. You're so busy being strong for everyone around you...and we're so used to counting on that strength...it's selfish and unfair and we should all know better." He kissed her hand again. "*I* should know better."

"As should I," the cripple said quietly. "I'm sorry, Mama."

"So am I," his sister added, thawing slightly.

Dana put her arm around the girl and hugged her, hard. "I know, darling. It's all right. We've had a lot on our plates lately. That's why today is so important. We must smile. Laugh. Model ourselves on ladies best not mentioned and be frivolous!" She flashed a teasing look at her husband's Master Magician. "Even you, Durm! I am determined that before the day is out I shall see a daisy chain around your neck!"

Morg smiled. "I very much doubt it, madam."

She smiled back, refusing to believe him. Foolish woman. A cautiously companionable silence fell; at length they reached the gated turn-off for the Eyrie. Slowed. Stopped to greet the guards on duty, posted to turn away lesser mortals who might interfere with royalty at play. The horses tossed their heads and fretted, straining in their harness. When the coachman released his hold on their bits they leapt, and the carriage rattled onwards.

"Look," said Fane, pointing. On their left, flashing by as the horses' long strides ate up the road, a painted sign. *Welcome to Salbert's Eyrie.*

"Nearly there," said Dana, and threaded her arm through her daughter's. "Oh, we're going to have a wonderful day. I can feel it in my bones. How long is it since we picnicked together at the Eyrie? It must be nearly a year!" Turning a little, she raised her voice. "Matcher, Matcher, do slow *down*! The countryside is whipping past at such a rate we can scarcely see it, let alone enjoy it!"

"Yes, Your Majesty, sorry, Your Majesty!" said Matcher, and

leaned back hard against the horses' iron mouths, grunting with the effort. Morg stared at his straining back, his heaving shoulders. He was wasting his time. The horses' minds were a ferment of madness now. No power under the sun could stop them, save his.

It was nearly time. Shifting a little in his seat, Morg readied himself. Regretted, briefly, Durm's fleshy and ponderous body. Still. He had power enough to overcome the minor impediment. He had power enough for anything...

Out of patience entirely, Borne raised his voice. "The Eyrie isn't far from here, Matcher. Stop the carriage and we'll walk the rest of the way. It's a view to be savoured, not rushed at. You can take the team back to the stables and return for us this afternoon. Perhaps the extra mileage will cool the heat from their heels."

"Yes, Your Majesty," said Matcher, and signalled his team to drop out of their spanking trot and back to a suitably sedate walk.

Nothing happened.

"Matcher!" Borne said sharply. "I said stop here!"

The coachman fetched a desperate glance over his shoulder. "I heard you, sire! It's the horses that ain't listening!"

And just as though the words were a signal the spanking trot became a lurching canter, and then a pounding gallop.

"For Barl's sake, Matcher, what are you doing?" Borne shouted. "The Eyrie, man! The *Eyrie*! Stop those bloody horses *now*, before it's too late!"

"I'm trying!" Matcher sobbed. "I can't!"

"Then turn them off the road! Break all their bloody legs if you have to! Barl's sweet love, you fool, do you want to kill us all?"

Matcher gasped. "I can't—they're too strong—"

On a muffled oath, Borne tried to climb up and over the coach railing. Struggled to reach Matcher, to reach the reins, to lend his strength to the coachman's desperate hauling on the demented horses.

The cripple let out a cry and flung himself to the other side of the carriage to join his father and the coachman. Morg shoved him back into his seat.

"What are you doing?" the cripple raged as the king and the coachman wrapped the reins round their forearms and pulled, shouting aloud with the effort. "I have to help!"

"You can't," said Morg. "You might hurt yourself."

Now the king was trying to save them with magic, shouting at the horses at the top of his lungs. Spells of somnolence. Spells of obedience. Even a spell to snap the harness so the carriage could break free.

Spell after spell after spell...Morg destroyed each and every one with a thought. The carriage swept around the final bend and Dana, staring along the roadway, screamed. Directly ahead was the famous lookout. Spectacular. Untamed. Between disaster and safety, nothing but a stout wooden railing. The roadway curved to the right, intending to guide visitors to the genteel security of picnic grounds and nodding bluebells, of brilliant sunshine and dappled shade.

The carriage hurtled on.

"Durm, *do* something!" screamed Fane, clutching her mother, all beauty consumed by terror. "There *must* be a spell—"

"Oh, there is," Morg said, smiling, and stood.

With a flourish and a single word he froze them all: Matcher, Borne, Fane, Dana and Gar. With another word and the snap of his fingers he sent Gar flying out of the carriage and onto the grassy side of the road. The prince hit the tussocked turf hard, sliding, to fetch up against the trunk of a spindly tree.

With arm upraised Morg opened his mouth to send himself to safety and leave the carriage plunging towards its destruction. But one wheel hit a half-buried rock on the side of the road. Shattered. The carriage leapt into the air and before he could save himself Morg was thrown out. Striking the road hard, splintering fragile bone, tearing vulnerable flesh, he rolled and rolled and rolled until his head struck another rock and his pell-mell progress halted.

By which time the magic-maddened carriage horses had galloped the king, the queen, the princess and their coachman clean through the wooden safety rail and over the edge of Salbert's Eyrie. As though they had wings. As though they could fly. Their screams, falling, echoed the skirling of the eagles that rode the thermals high above the hidden valley floor. Then the screams stopped, abruptly, and a fusillade of echoes rang out as the carriage and its passengers and its horses shattered on the slopes of the unforgiving Eyrie.

And after that: silence.

ACKNOWLEDGEMENTS

Where to start? This has been an epic journey: thanks are owed to so many people...

Stephanie Smith, for believing in me even though the early work was—exceedingly early. And drafty.

The entire HarperCollins Voyager team, for helping the dream come true.

Australian Literary Management, for taking me on.

Mary, for her keen and critical eye and years of friendship. One serendipitous phone call and a mutual love of "The Sandbaggers." Who'd've thunk it, eh?

Carol, who said it'd happen a long time before I really believed it would.

Jenn, Cindee, Sharon, Gill and Ellen, for being.

My fellow Voyager authors, and the Purple Zoners for the warmth of their welcome.

The Infinitas Writers' Group, and Elaine and Pete and Melissa, for their input and encouragement.

The folk at the original Del Rey Online Writers Workshop, who gave me hope.

Terry Dowling and Kim Wilkins, for the right words at the right time.

The booksellers, for championing Australian writers.

And last, but never least, you...the reader...for putting your money where my mouth is. Here's hoping your trust hasn't gone unrewarded.

BOOK 2

THE AWAKENED MAGE

PART ONE

CHAPTER ONE

With one callused hand shading his eyes, Asher stood on the Tower's sandstone steps and watched the touring carriage with its royal cargo and Master Magician Durm bowl down the driveway, sweep around the bend in the road and disappear from sight. Then he heaved a rib-creaking sigh, turned on his heel and marched back inside. Darran and Willer weren't about, so he left a note saying where Gar had gone and continued on his way.

The trouble with princes he decided, as he thudded up the spiral staircase, was they could go gallivanting off on picnics in the countryside whenever the fancy struck and nobody could stop them. They could say, "Oh look, the sun is shining, the birds are singing, who cares about responsibilities today? I think I'll go romp amongst the bluebells for an hour or three, tra la tra la."

And the trouble with working for princes, he added to himself as he pushed his study door open and stared in heart-sinking dismay at the piles of letters, memorandums and schedules that hadn't magically disappeared from his desk while he was gone, damn it, was that you never got to share in that kind of careless luxury. Some poor fool had to care about those merrily abandoned responsibilities, and just now that poor fool went by the name of Asher.

With a gusty sigh he kicked the door shut, slid reluctantly into his chair and got back to work.

Acridly drowning in Meister Glospottle's pestilent piss problems, he didn't notice time passing as the day's light drained slowly from the sky. He didn't even realise he was no longer alone in his office until a hand pressed his shoulder and a voice said, "Asher? Are you dream-struck? What's her name?"

Startled, he dropped his pen and spun about in the chair. "Matt! Y'daft blot! You tryin' to give me a heart spasm?"

"No, I'm trying to get your attention," said Matt. He was half grinning, half concerned. "I knocked and knocked till I bruised my knuckles and then I called your name. Twice. What's so important it's turned you deaf?"

"Urine," he said sourly. "You got any?"

Matt blinked. "Well, no. Not on me. Not as such."

"Then you're no bloody use. You might as well push off."

The thing he liked best about Matt was the stable meister's reassuring aura of unflappability. A man could be as persnickety as he liked and all Matt would ever do was smile. The way he was smiling now. "And if I ask why you're in such desperate need of urine, will I be sorry?"

Suddenly aware of stiff muscles and a looming headache, Asher shoved his chair back and stomped around his office. Ha! His cage. "Prob'ly. I know I bloody am. Urine's for gettin' rid of into the nearest chamber pot, not for hoardin' like a miser with gold."

Matt was looking bemused. "Since when did you have the urge to hoard urine?"

"Since never! It's bloody Indigo Glospottle's got the urge, not me."

"I know I'll regret asking this, but how in Barl's name could any man have a shortage of urine?"

"By bein' too clever for his own damned good, that's how!" He propped himself on the windowsill, scowling. "Indigo Glospottle fancies himself something of an *artiste*, y'see. Good ole-fashioned cloth dyein' like his da did, and his da's da afore him, that ain't good enough for Meister Indigo Glospottle. No. Meister Indigo Glospottle's got to go and think up *new* ways of dyein' cloth and wool and suchlike, ain't he?"

"Well," said Matt, being fair, "you can't blame the man for trying to improve his business."

"Yes, I can!" he retorted. "When him improvin' his business turns into me losin' precious sleep over another man's urine, you'd better bloody believe I can!" Viciously mimicking, he screwed up his face into Indigo Glospottle's permanently piss-strangled expression and fluted his voice in imitation. "'Oh, Meister Asher! The blues are so blue and the reds are so red! My customers can't get enough of them! But it's all in the piddle, you see!' Can you believe it? Bloody man can't even bring himself to say piss! He's got to say *piddle*. Like that'll mean it don't stink as much. 'I need more *piddle*, Meister Asher! You must find me more *piddle*!' Because the thing is, y'see, these precious new ways of his use up twice as much piss as the old ways, don't they? And since he's put all the other guild members' noses out of joint with his fancy secret dyein' recipe, they've pulled strings to make sure he can't get all the urine he needs. Now he reckons the only way he's goin' to meet demand is by going door to door with a bucket in one hand and a bottle in the other sayin', 'Excuse me, sir and madam, would you care to make a donation?' And for some strange reason, he ain't too keen on that idea!"

Matt gave a whoop of laughter and collapsed against the nearest bit of empty wall. "Asher!"

Despite his irritation, Asher felt his own lips twitch. "Aye, well, I s'pose I'd be laughin' too if the fool hadn't gone and made *his* problem *my* problem. But he has, so I ain't much in the mood for feelin' amused just now."

Matt sobered. "I'm sorry. It all sounds very vexing."

"It's worse than that," he said, shuddering. "If I can't get Glospottle and the guild to reach terms, the whole mess'll end up in Justice Hall. Gar'll skin me alive if that happens. He's got hisself so caught up in his magic the last thing he wants is trouble at Justice Hall. Last thing *I* want is trouble at Justice Hall, 'cause the way he's been lately he'll bloody tell me to take care of it. *Me!* Sittin' in that gold chair in front of all those folk, passing judgement like I know what I'm on about! I never signed up for Justice Hall. That's Gar's job. And the sooner he remembers that, and forgets all this magic codswallop, the happier I'll be."

The smile faded from Matt's face. "What if he can't forget—or doesn't want to? He's the king's firstborn son and he's found his magic, Asher. Everything's different now. You know that."

Asher scowled. Aye, he knew it. But that didn't mean he had to like it. Or think about it overmuch, either. Damn it, he wasn't even supposed to be here! He was supposed to be down south on the coast arguing with Da over the best fishing boat to buy and plotting how to outsell his sinkin' brothers three to one. Dorana was meant to be a fast-fading memory by now.

But that dream was dead and so was Da, both smashed to pieces in a storm of ill luck. And he was stuck here, in the City. In the Tower. In his unwanted life as Asher the bloody Acting Olken Administrator. Stuck with Indigo bloody Glospottle and his stinking bloody piss problems.

He met Matt's concerned gaze with a truculent defiance. "Different for him, but not for me. He pays me, Matt. He don't own me."

"No. But in truth, Asher, the way things stand for you now—where else could you go?"

Matt's tentative question stabbed like a knife. "Anywhere I bloody like! My brothers don't own me any more than Gar does! I'm back here for now, not for good. Zeth or no Zeth, I were born a fisherman and I'll die one like my da did afore me."

"I hope you do, Asher," Matt said softly. "There are worse ways to die, I think." Then he shook himself free of melancholy. "Now. Speaking of His Highness, do you know where he is? We've a meeting planned but I can't find him."

"Did you look in his office? His library?"

Matt huffed, exasperated. "I looked everywhere."

"Ask Darran. When it comes to Gar the ole fart's got eyes in the back of his head."

"Darran's out. But Willer's here, the pompous little weasel, and he hasn't seen His Highness either. He said something about a picnic?"

Asher shifted on the windowsill and looked outside. Late afternoon sunshine gilded the trees' autumn-bronzed leaves and glinted off the stables' rooftops. "That was hours ago. They can't still be at the Eyrie. They didn't have that much food with 'em, and it only takes five minutes to admire the view. After that it's just sittin' around makin' small talk and pretendin' Fane don't hate Gar's guts, ain't it? Prob'ly they went straight back to the palace and he's locked hisself up in the magic room with Durm and forgotten all about you."

"No, I'm afraid he hasn't."

Darran. Pale and self-contained, he stood in the open doorway. Nothing untoward showed in his face, but Asher felt a needle of fright prick him between the ribs. He exchanged glances with Matt, and slid off the windowsill. "What?" he said roughly. "What're you witterin' on about now?"

"I am not wittering," Darran replied. "I've just come back from business at the palace. The royal family and the Master Magician are not there. Their carriage has yet to return."

Again, Asher glanced out of the window into the rapidly cooling afternoon. "Are you sure?"

Darran's lips thinned. "Perfectly."

Another needle prick, sharper this time. "So what're you sayin'? You sayin' they got lost between here and Salbert's Eyrie?"

Darran's hands were behind his black velvet back. Something in the set of his shoulders suggested they were clutched tightly together. "I am saying nothing. I am asking if you can think of a reason why the carriage's return might have been so severely delayed. His Majesty was expected for a public park committee meeting an hour ago. There was some...surprise...at his absence."

Asher bit off a curse. "Don't tell me you ran around bleatin' about the carriage bein' delayed! You know what those ole biddies are like, Darran, they'll—"

"Of course I didn't. I'm old but not yet addled," said Darran. "I informed the committee that His Majesty had been detained with Prince Gar and the Master Magician in matters of a magical nature. They happily accepted the explanation, the meeting continued without further disruption and I returned here immediately."

Grudgingly, Asher gave a nod of approval. "Good."

"And now I'll ask you again," said Darran, unimpressed by the approval. "Can you think of any reason why the carriage hasn't yet returned?"

The needle was stabbing quick and hard now, in time with his pounding heart. "Could be a wheel came off, held 'em up."

Darran snorted. "Any one of them could fix that in a matter of moments with a spell."

"He's right," said Matt.

"Lame horse, then. A stone in the shoe, or a twisted fetlock."

Matt shook his head. "His Highness would've ridden the other one back here to get a replacement."

"You're being ridiculous, Asher," said Darran. "Clutching at exceedingly flimsy straws. So I shall say aloud what we all know we're thinking. There's been an accident."

"Accident my arse!" he snapped. "You're guessin', and guessin' wrong, I'll bet you anything you like. What kind of an accident could they have trotting to Salbert's Eyrie and back, eh? We're talking about all the most powerful magicians in the kingdom sittin' side by side in the same bloody carriage! There ain't an accident in the world that could touch 'em!"

"Very well," said Darran. "The only other explanation, then, is... not an accident."

It took Asher a moment to realise what he meant. "*What?* Don't be daft! As if anybody would—as if there were even a reason—y'silly ole fool! Flappin' your lips like laundry on a line! They're late, is all. Got 'emselves sidetracked! Decided to go sightseeing further on from the Eyrie and got all carried away! You'll see! Gar'll be bouncing up the staircase any minute now! You'll see!"

There was a moment of held breaths, as all three of them waited for the sound of eager, tapping boot heels and a charming royal apology.

Silence.

"Look, Asher," said Matt, smiling uneasily, "you're most likely right. But to put Darran's mind at rest, why don't you and I ride out to the Eyrie? Chances are we'll meet them on their way back and they'll have a good old laugh at us for worrying."

"An excellent suggestion," said Darran. "I was about to make it myself. Go now. And if—when—you do encounter them, one of you ride back here immediately so I may send messages to the palace in case tactless tongues are still wagging."

Scowling, Asher nodded. He didn't know which was worse: Darran being right or the needle of fright now lodged so hard and deep in his flesh he could barely breathe.

"Well?" demanded Darran. He sounded almost shrill. "Why are you both still standing there like tree stumps? *Go!*"

Twenty minutes later they were cantering in circumspect silence along the road that led to Salbert's Eyrie. The day's slow dying cast long shadows before them.

"There's the sign for the Eyrie," shouted Matt, jerking his chin as they pounded by. "It's getting late, Asher. We should've met them by now. This is the only road in or out and the gates at the turn-off were still closed. Surely the king would've left them open if they'd gone on somewhere else from here?"

"Maybe," Asher shouted back. His cold hands tightened on the reins. "Maybe not. Who can tell with royalty? At least there's no sign of an accident."

"So far," said Matt.

They urged their horses onwards with ungentle heels, hearts hammering in time with the dull hollow drumming of hooves. Swept round a gradual, left-handed bend into a stretch of road dotted either side with trees.

Matt pointed. "Barl save me! Is that—"

"Aye!" said Asher, and swallowed sudden nausea.

Gar. Lying half in the road, half on its grassy border. Unconscious...or dead.

As one he and Matt hauled against their horses' mouths and came to a squealing, grunting, head-tossing halt. Asher threw himself from his saddle and stumbled to Gar's side, as Matt grabbed Cygnet's reins to stop the horse from bolting.

"Well?"

Blood and dirt and the green smears of crushed grass marked Gar's skin, his clothes. Shirt and breeches were torn. The flesh beneath them was torn.

"He's alive," Asher said shakily, fingers pressed to the leaping pulse beneath Gar's jaw. Then he ran unsteady hands over the prince's inert body. "Out cold, though. Could be his collarbone's busted. And there's cuts and bruises aplenty, too." His fingers explored Gar's skull. "Got some bumps on his noggin, but I don't think his skull's cracked."

"Flesh and bone heal," said Matt, and dragged a shirt sleeve across his wet face. "Praise Barl he's not dead."

"Aye," said Asher, and took a moment, just a moment, to breathe. When he could, he looked up. Struggled for lightness. "Bloody Darran. He'll be bleating 'I told you so' for a month of Barl's Days now."

Matt didn't laugh. Didn't even smile. "If the prince is here," he said grimly, his horseman's hands white-knuckled, "then where are the others?"

Their eyes met, dreading answers.

"Reckon we'd best find out," said Asher. He shrugged off his jacket, folded it and settled Gar's head gently back to the cushioned ground. Tried to arrange his left arm more comfortably, mindful of the hurt shoulder. "He'll be right, by and by. Let's go."

Remounting, he jogged knee to knee with Matt round the next sweeping bend. Battled fear and a mounting sense of dread. Cygnet pinned his ears back, sensing trouble.

They found Durm next, sprawled in the middle of the road. As unconscious as Gar, but in an even bloodier and broken condition.

"Busted his arm, and his leg," said Asher, feeling ill as he ran his hands over Durm's limbs. The Master Magician's body was like a wet sack filled with smashed crockery. "Damn. Make that both legs. There be bits of bone stickin' out everywhere. And his head's laid open like a boiled egg for breakfast. It's a miracle he ain't leaked out all his blood like a bucket with a hole in it."

Matt swallowed. "But he's alive?"

"For now," Asher said, and got wearily to his feet. Looked further down the road for the first time—and felt the world tilt around him.

"What?" said Matt, startled.

"The Eyrie," he whispered, pointing, and had to steady himself against Cygnet's solid shoulder.

Not even approaching dusk could hide it. The splintered gap in the timber fence at the edge of the Eyrie—wide enough for a carriage to gallop straight through.

Matt shook his head. "Barl save us. They can't have."

Asher didn't want to believe it either. Sick fear made him more brutal than Matt deserved. "Then where's the carriage? The horses? The family?"

"No. No, they *can't* have," Matt insisted. He sounded years younger, and close to tears.

"I reckon they did," Asher replied, numb, and dropped his reins. Obedient, resigned, Cygnet lowered his head and tugged at the grass verge, bit jangling. Asher broke into a ragged run towards the edge of the lookout.

"Don't," said Matt. "We're losing the light, you fool, it's too dangerous!"

The voice of reason had no place here. He heard Matt curse, and slide off his own horse. Shout after him. "Asher, for the love of Barl, stay back! If they are down there, we can't help them. If they went over the Eyrie they're dead for sure! *Asher!* Are you listening?"

Heedless, he flung himself to the ground and peered over the drop. "I can see somethin'. Maybe a wheel. It's hard to say. At any rate there's a kind of ledge, stickin' out." He wriggled backwards and sat up. Stared at Matt. Now standing behind him. "I don't reckon they went all the way to the bottom. I'm goin' down there."

Appalled, Matt grabbed his shoulders, tried to drag him to his feet. "You *can't*!"

He wrenched himself free and stood. "Get back to the Tower, Matt. Tell Darran. Get help. We need pothers, wagons, ropes. Light."

Matt stared. "I'm not leaving you alone here to do Barl knows what kind of craziness!"

Damn it, what was wrong with the man? Couldn't he *see*? "You got to, Matt," he insisted. "Like you say, we're losing the light. If they are down there and they ain't all dead, we can't wait till mornin' to find out. They'd never last the night."

"You can't think anyone could *survive* this?"

"There's only one way to find out. Now what say you stop wastin' time, eh? Might be they are all dead down there, but we got livin' folk hurt up here, and I don't know how long that maggoty ole Durm's goin' to keep breathing without a good pother to help him. I'll be fine, Matt. Just *go*."

Matt's expression was anguished. "Asher, no...you can't risk yourself. You mustn't. I'll do it."

"You can't. You're near on a foot taller than me and two stone heavier, at least. I don't know how safe the ground is on the side of that mountain, but a lighter man's got to have a better chance." Matt just stared at him, begging to be hit. "Look, you stupid bastard, every minute we stand here arguin' is a minute wasted. Just get on your bloody horse, would you, and ride!"

Matt shook his head. "Asher—"

Out of time and patience, he leapt forward and shoved Matt in the chest, hard. "You need me to make it an order? Fine! It's an order! *Go!*"

Matt was beaten, and he knew it. "All right," he said, despairing. "But be careful. I've got Dathne to answer to, remember, and she'll skin me alive if anything happens to you."

"And *I'll* skin you alive if you don't get out of here," he retorted. "Tie Cygnet to a tree so he don't follow you. I ain't keen on walkin' back to the Tower."

"Promise me I won't regret this," said Matt, backing away. His scowl would've turned fresh milk.

"See you soon."

Matt stopped. "Asher—"

"Sink me, do I have to throw you on the damned horse mys—"

"No, wait!" Matt said, holding up his hands. "*Wait*. What about Matcher?"

He lowered his fists. "What about 'im?"

"He's got a family, they'll worry, start a fuss—"

Damn. Matt was right. "Stall 'em. Send a lad with a message to say he's got hisself delayed at the palace. That should hold his wife till we can—"

"You mean *lie* to her? Asher, I can't!"

Barl bloody save him from decent men. "You have to. We got to keep this as secret as we can for as long as we can, Matt. *Think*. If we don't keep her fooled for the next little while—"

"All right," said Matt. "I'll take care of it. I'll lie." His face twisted, as though he tasted something bitter. Almost to himself he added, "I'm getting good at it."

There wasn't time to puzzle out what he meant. "Hurry, Matt. Please."

He watched his friend run back to the horses, anchor Cygnet to a sturdy sapling then vault into his own saddle. The urgent hoof beats, retreating, echoed round the valley. Then, under a dusking sky lavished lavender and crimson and gold, Asher eased himself over the edge of Salbert's Eyrie.

It was a sinkin' long way down to the hidden valley floor.

Don't look, then, you pukin' fool. Take it one step at a time. You can do that, can't you? One bloody step at a time.

The rock-strewn ground at first sloped gradually, deceptively. Beneath his boot heels gravel and loose earth, so that he slipped and slid and skidded, stripping skin from his hands as he grappled stunted bushes and sharp-sided boulders to slow his descent. His eyes stung with sweat and his mouth clogged dry with fear. The air was tangy and fresh, no crowded City smells tainting, flavouring. It struck chill through his thin silk shirt, goosebumping his sweat-sticky flesh.

Further down into the valley he went, and then further still. Every dislodged rock and pebble rang sound and echo from the vast space below and around him. Startled birds took to the air, harshly protesting, or scolded him invisibly from the Eyrie's dense encroaching foliage.

He reached a small cliff, a sheer-faced drop of some five feet that looked to give way first to a sharply sloped terrace and from there to a natural platform jutting out over the depths of the valley. Most of the platform itself was obscured by shadow and rocky outcrops, but he was sure now he could see the edge of a wheel, tip-tilted into the air.

If the carriage had landed anywhere other than the hidden valley floor, it would be there. Beyond the edge of the platform was nothing but empty space and the shrieking of eagles.

Five feet. He'd jumped off walls as high without thinking twice. Jumped laughing. Now, belly-down and crawling, he eased himself feet first and backwards over the edge, tapping his toes for cracks in the cliff face, burying his ragged, bloody fingernails in the loose shale as he scrabbled for purchase.

If he fell...if he fell...

Safely down, he had to stop, still holding onto the cliff edge, sucking air, near paralysed with fright. That sharp little needle had returned and was jabbing, jabbing. His ribs hurt, and his lungs and his head. All the cuts and scratches on his fingers, his palms, his cheek and his knee burned, bleeding.

Time passed.

Eventually recovered, the needle withdrawn and his various pains subsided, he let go of the cliff. Turned inch by tiny inch to press his shoulderblades against the rock and look where next to tread...and felt his heart crack wide with grief.

So. His eyes had not misled him.

It was indeed a wheel, and more than a wheel. It was two wheels, and most of an ornate, painted carriage. It was a brown horse, and sundered harness, and a man, and a woman, and a girl.

He closed his eyes, choking. Saw a broken mast and another broken man.

"Da," he whispered. "Oh, Da..."

Ice cold to the marrow, shaking, he continued his descent.

*   *   *

There was blood everywhere, much of it spilled from the shattered horse. Splashed across the rocks, pooled in the hollows, congealing beneath the stunted, scrubby bushes that clung to life on this last ledge before the dreadful drop to the valley floor, it soaked the air in a scarlet pungency.

Staring over the platform's edge Asher saw treetops like a carpet and the white specks of birds, wheeling. There was no sign of the second carriage horse or Coachman Matcher. A fine fellow, he was. Had been. Married with two children, son and daughter. Peytr was allergic to horses and Lillie had the finest pair of hands on the reins the City had ever seen.

Or so said Matcher, her doting father.

Despairing, he turned away from the pitiless chasm yawning at his feet and faced instead the death he could see. Smell. Touch.

Borne was pinned beneath the splintered remnants of the carriage. His long lean body had been crushed to a thinness, and one side of his face was caved in. He looked as though he wore a bright red wig. Dana lay some three feet to his left, impaled through chest and abdomen by branches smashed into javelins. The impact had twisted her so that she lay half on her side, with her fine-boned face turned away. It meant he couldn't see her eyes. He was glad.

And Fane...beautiful, brilliant, impossible Fane had been flung almost to the very edge of the narrow rock shelf; one slender white hand, unmarked, dangled out into space, the diamonds on her fingers catching fire in the sun's sinking light. Her cheek rested on that outstretched arm, she might have been sleeping, only sleeping, anyone finding her so might think her whole and unharmed...if they did not see the jellied crimson pool beneath her slender torso, or the eerie translucence of her lovely unpowdered face. Her eyes were half open, wholly unseeing; the lashes, darkened by some magic known only to women, thick and long and bewitchingly alluring, as she had been alluring, lay a tracery of shadow upon her delicate skin.

There was a fly, crawling between her softly parted lips.

For the longest time he just stood there, waiting. *In a moment, one of 'em will move. In a moment, one of 'em will breathe. Or blink. In a moment, I'll wake up and all this will be nowt but a damned stupid ale-born dream.*

In a moment.

He came to understand, at last, that there were no more moments. That not one of them would move, or breathe, or blink again. That he was already awake, and this was not a dream.

Memories came then, glowing like embers at the heart of a dying fire. "*Welcome, Asher. My son speaks so highly of you I just know we'll be the greatest of friends.*" Dana, Queen of Lur. Accepting his untutored bow and clumsy greeting as though he'd gifted her with perfumed roses and a diamond beyond price or purchase. Her unconstrained laughter, her listening silences. The way her eyes smiled in even the gravest of moments, a smile that said *I know you. I trust you. Trust me.*

Borne, his sallow cheeks silvered with tears. "*What does my kingdom hold that I can give you? He is my precious son and you saved him. For his mother. For me. For us all. You've lost your father, I'm told. I grieve with you. Shall I stand in his stead, Asher? Offer you a father's words of wisdom if ever you need to hear them spoken? May I do that? Let me.*"

And Fane, who smiled only if she thought it might do some damage. Who never knew herself well enough to know that beneath malice lay desire. Who was beautiful in every single way, save the one that mattered most.

Dead, dead and dead.

Bludgeoned to tearless silence, he stayed with them until to stay longer would be foolish. Stayed until the cold and dark from the valley floor crept up and over the lip of the ledge and sank icy teeth into his flesh. Until he remembered the last living member of this family, who had yet to be told he was the last.

Remembering that, he left them, reluctantly, and slowly climbed back up the side of the mountain.

CHAPTER TWO

There were hands to help him over the broken railings at the top of Salbert's Eyrie.

"Easy does it," said Pellen Orrick, holding his elbow with firm fingers. "Catch your breath a moment. Are you all right?"

Bent over and heaving air into his lungs, aware of stinging scrapes and strained muscles, Asher nodded. "Aye. Where's Matt?"

"Minding his own business back at the Tower." Orrick frowned, and released his grasp. "You know, Asher, some folk might say you were mad to climb down the side of the Eyrie. I might even be one of them. Was it worth the risk?"

Breathing easier, he slowly straightened. Some Doranen or other had conjured glimfire; a floating flotilla of magical lights turned the new night into a pale imitation of day. He looked into the Guard captain's shadowed, hatchet face and nodded again. "Aye."

Orrick's expression tightened. Then the tension left him and he sagged, just a little, and only for a heartbeat. "You found them."

There was nobody else within earshot. Orrick had set a line of guards to keep everyone away from the Eyrie's treacherous edge and further calamity. Beyond them, by the side of the road, clustered a group of agitated Doranen. Staring, Asher recognised Conroyd Jarralt and Barlsman Holze; Lords Daltrie, Hafar, Sorvold and Boqur: Jarralt's General Council cronies. No sign of Gar or Master Magician Durm, though. Doubtless they'd been rushed back to the palace and the eager bone-bothering of Pother Nix.

Further along the road stood two wagons, a fancy Doranen carriage and one of Orrick's men guarding coils of rope. With a pang of relief he saw Cygnet, still safely tied. An uneasy silence muffled the scene, broken only by the stamp of a hoof and snatches of sharp speech from the gathered Doranen lords.

"Asher?" said Orrick.

"Aye," he said. "I found 'em. The family, any road. Coachman Matcher's lying at the bottom of the valley, I reckon, along with one of his precious horses."

"And you're certain they're dead?"

He laughed. Was he certain? *Red blood and white bone and black flies, crawling...* "You want to go see for yourself?"

With a deep sigh, Orrick shook his head. "Can their bodies be retrieved?"

He shrugged. "Maybe. Reckon it'll take a hefty dose of magic and some luck, though."

"Their position is precarious?"

"They're on a bit of a ledge stickin' out over the valley. You tell me if that be precarious or not." Swept by a sudden, obliterating tide of exhaustion, Asher felt all the blood drain from his face and staggered where he stood. "Damn," he muttered.

"Easy now," said Pellen Orrick, once more taking his arm. "You've had a nasty shock."

The captain's kindness was almost his undoing. Grief and rage and a hot swelling helplessness blurred his sight. He could feel his heart's brutal beating, solid blows against his ribs like the tolling of a funeral drum. The cold night air seared his struggling lungs and his teeth began to chatter like bones in a breeze. He felt wetness on his cheeks and looked up. Was it raining?

No. The starry sky was clear of cloud. And anyway, how could it be raining? Lur's WeatherWorker was dead. Furious, he blinked back the burning tears. *Tears?* Fool. Tears were for folks with time on their hands...

A shout went up from the cluster of Doranen dignitaries. Lord Hafar had spotted him. Pointing, he tugged at Conroyd Jarralt's brocade sleeve. Jarralt turned, frowning, mouth open to snap or snarl. Then he saw too. His chin came up, his shoulders braced and his teeth clicked closed. Vibrating with angry self-importance he broke away from the group... and so revealed its centre.

Revealed Gar.

Awoken to a fragile consciousness, the prince—no. Not any longer. Not after today. The *king* was sitting on a cushioned stool at the side of the road, draped in a blanket with a hasty bandage wound tight about his head. His left arm had been bound hard against his battered body to safeguard the broken collarbone. In his right hand he held a mug of something steaming, and stared into its depths as though it contained all the secrets of the world.

Conroyd Jarralt took another step forward, his jewelled fingers fisted at his sides. "Asher!"

The sound of his name rang like a chapel bell calling for silence. The lords' muttering voices faltered. Stumbled. Stilled, as step by step Asher shrank the distance between himself and his friend. His king.

Gar looked up. One pale eyebrow lifted, seeing him. And he realised there was no need for anything so crude as words. The truth was in his tears, still drying amidst the dirt, and the telltale pallor of his cheeks, nipped as cold as frostbite.

He reached the tangled knot of Doranen lords. Reached Gar, who looked into his rigid face with an air of calm enquiry. A polite patience. An absence of anything more powerful than a mild curiosity. He stopped and dropped to his knees. There was pain as his bones met the unyielding road. It scarcely registered. Hands by his side, shoulders defeated, filthy with dirt and sweat and little smears of other people's blood, he bowed his head.

"Your Majesty."

From the watching lords, gasps. A cry, quickly stifled. A sob, smothered.

Somebody snickered.

Asher snapped up his head, disbelieving.

Gar was laughing. His face was mirthless, and his eyes, but still he laughed. The blanket around his shoulders shivered free. The scarce-touched contents of the mug slopped over its sides to splash dark stains on his ruined breeches. His nose began to run, and then his eyes, tears and mucus reflecting glimfire, glittering like liquid diamonds. And still he laughed.

Jarralt turned on him. "Stop it!" he hissed. "You disgrace yourself, sir, and shame our people! Stop it at once, do you hear?"

He might as well have saved his breath. Ignoring him, Gar continued to laugh, not stopping until Barlsman Holze came close to touch his unhurt shoulder with gentle fingertips.

"My boy," he whispered. "My dear, dear boy. Hush, now. Hush."

Like an Olken toy running down its clockwork, the giggles bumped erratically into silence. Asher dragged a kerchief from his pocket and held it out. For some time the former prince just sat there, staring at the square of blue cotton. Then he took it and wiped his face. Handed back the soiled kerchief and said, "I want to see them."

The lords broke into a babble of protest.

"Don't be ridiculous," snapped Conroyd Jarralt. "It's out of the question."

"Conroyd's right," added Holze, and tried to lay a calming hand on Gar's arm. Gar shook him free, heedless of the pain, and stood. His expression was ominous. "Truly, the idea is most unwise!" Holze persisted. "Dear boy, think of the danger. You heard what Pother Nix's assistant said! You need warmth. Rest. More rigorous physicking. We must get you indoors, immediately. Come now. Listen to your elders, Your Hi—Your Ma—Gar. Be wisely guided, and leave this unfortunate place."

The other lords echoed the demand. Asher, aware of Pellen Orrick now standing close behind, grunted to his feet and exchanged uneasy glances with him as the lords closed ranks about Gar and raised their voices in ever more vehement argument.

Gar let the storm of words rage unchecked. Seemed almost not to hear his clamouring subjects. His frowning gaze was focused somewhere distant, pinned to something only he could see. Then, at last, he stirred. Lifted his hand.

"Enough."

Ignoring him, the lords continued their clamour.

"*Enough*, I said!" The lords fell back, shocked. Stared at the glim-fire flaring from Gar's fingertips as his newly focused gaze swept all their dumbfounded faces. "Is this how you speak to your king?"

Conroyd Jarralt stepped forward. "You presume a title not yet con-ferred, Your *Highness*." He turned to Asher. "You."

This was no time for lord-baiting. Asher bowed. "Sir."

"Borne's death is not in doubt?"

He shuddered. "No. King, queen and princess. They're all dead down there."

Grief rippled through the Doranen. Jarralt, the only one unmoved, stared at him with eyes like frozen silver. Then he glared at Gar. "Even so. Until both councils have met and the proper ceremonies been observed, you are yet a prince, sir. Not king."

Gar clenched his fingers and the glimfire died. "You challenge my claim?"

"I challenge your presumption. Scant hours have passed since your father's death. Before the succession is settled there are questions to be asked, and answered, in the matter of His Majesty's destruction."

"What questions?"

Jarralt waved an impatient hand. "This is neither the time nor the—"

"I disagree," said Gar. "It is the only place, and if you don't ask here and now I swear you never will."

Holze insinuated himself between them. "Gar, Conroyd, please. This is unseemly, the bodies cannot yet be cold. Desist, I implore you, in Barl's—"

"No," said Gar. "I would hear Lord Jarralt's question."

Jarralt's lips thinned in an angry smile. "Very well. Since you insist. How is it that you survived the accident barely touched when the rest of your family is so dreadfully perished?"

Gar's answering smile was winter cold. "You forget Durm."

"Our esteemed Master Magician is unlikely to live through the night. Come the dawn, I warrant, there will be only you."

"You accuse me of *murder*, Lord Jarralt? Of killing my father, my mother, my sister—"

"Your unloved sister," said Jarralt. "Who scant days ago tried to kill you." He nodded at the edge of bandage peeping beyond Gar's shirt cuff. "I believe the wound is yet unhealed."

"So, Conroyd. You are a man who listens to servants' gossip," said Gar. "How...disappointing."

Jarralt's face darkened. "It pleases you to insult me. Very well. But how long will your arrogance last once I have undertaken enquiries as to precisely how this accident unfolded? When I—"

"As to that, my lord," said Pellen Orrick, "any investigation into these deaths falls to me. As Captain of the City it is my right, and my responsibility."

"Indeed?" said Jarralt, skewering Orrick with contempt. "And why should I trust your impartiality? Or your competence?"

"Because the late king trusted them, sir," Orrick said quietly.

"And if you discover foul play, Captain?" said Holze. "What then?"

Orrick's hatchet face sharpened. "Then I will pursue the murderer to the ends of the kingdom. He or she will find no escape and receive no mercy...regardless of rank, social status or privilege."

Gar nodded. "Satisfied, Conroyd? Good. Now if you'll move aside, I intend to visit awhile with my family!"

Alarmed and helpless, Asher watched Gar take two staggering steps towards the edge of the Eyrie. Unbidden, Lords Daltrie and Sorvold reached for his arms in an effort to restrain him.

It was a mistake.

"*Let be!*" Gar shouted. A golden light shimmered into life around him. The lords unwisely touching him cried out and snatched their hands away.

Conroyd Jarralt's hand went to the sheathed knife on his hip. "You see?" he demanded. "He uses magic as a weapon! Prince Gar is unfit for any kind of authority! He knows nothing about being a true Doranen! He is a precocious, undisciplined child who cannot be trusted with the power so newly come upon him!"

"You're the one who can't be trusted!" Gar spat. "All your life you've coveted my father's throne and now he's dead you think to take it! Well, think again, Conroyd. There was more kingship in my father's little finger than you possess in all your body. I'll see this kingdom a smoking ruin before ever I see you on its throne!"

Jarralt raised a shaking fist. "Just like your father, you overstep all bounds. Magic or no magic, you're not fit to rule! You're nothing but the unnatural offspring of a selfish and short-sighted fool!"

Gar's golden aura deepened. Flared crimson, like a fire fed fresh fuel. Jarralt was forced half a pace backwards. "Stand in Justice Hall and say that, Conroyd," Gar whispered. "I dare you. Stand in Justice Hall and see what the people reply."

Conroyd Jarralt sneered. "*The people.* That undisciplined rabble of Olken? That's who you'd call for your support? You wretched boy, if they are all you can rely upon then—"

Dismayed, Asher jumped as Pellen Orrick leaned close and whispered urgently, "Do something, Asher, quick, before the fools go too far."

"*Me?*" He stared. "Why *me?*"

"Because you're the only one here the prince'll listen to."

Gar was shaking, his face screwed up against every kind of pain. "Is this disaster your doing, Conroyd? Is your appetite for power so ravenous you'd *kill* to feed it? My father, my mother—"

"*Kill your mother?*" Heedless of Gar's crimson mantle of power, of his torn flesh and broken bone, Jarralt grabbed him by the shirt front and dragged him to his toe-tips. "You pathetic little worm, I *loved* your mother!" he cried. "I love her still! If she'd married me she'd be alive this minute! If she'd married me I'd have given her a *real* prince! A son she could be *proud* of!"

"My lords!" shouted Asher, and threw himself at Jarralt. Snatched at the incensed man's hands and dragged them free of Gar's shirt, then shoved Gar in the chest, heedless of the danger, sending him staggering back two paces. "For *shame*, sirs, both of you! The royal family dead and you brawling like drunken sots in an alehouse!"

Jarralt turned on him, snarling. "Lay hands on me again and I'll see you strung from a gibbet before sunrise!"

Holze chimed in, parchment-grey with distress. "No, Conroyd, no, the boy's right. You must control yourselves—this dreadful business—set an example—" The elderly cleric's eyes were full of tears. Behind him the other Doranen lords dithered, paralysed by protocol and surprise. "His Highness is overwrought, he spoke out of grief and shock, you can't think he'd believe that you—that *anyone*—would deliberately harm our king and his family! And you, Conroyd, you spoke unthinking too. This terrible tragedy—we are all of us in dreadful disarray. Your Highness—"

The crimson glow around Gar was fading fast. His face had emptied too, of fury, of passion, leaving only pain. He looked confused. Bewildered. "My lords—I don't—I feel—" An enormous shudder racked him head to foot, and he blanched dead white. "Barl help me," he murmured as his eyes rolled back in his head.

Asher leapt and caught him before he thudded to the road. "Gar!"

The prince was a sprawling dead weight, he had to let him go, let him sag to the ground despite his wounds and broken bone.

"His Highness shouldn't be here," Asher said to Holze as the cleric knelt and took Gar's unharmed wrist to chafe. "He needs to go home."

"He needs a good physicking first," said Holze, and looked about him. "Conroyd...?"

Without a word, Jarralt came forward. Dropped to one knee, slipped his arms beneath Gar and stood easily, the prince cradled against his chest.

"Into the carriage with him, Conroyd," said Holze, regaining his feet with Asher's help. "He must be seen by Nix as soon as possible. The rest of us will have to make do in one of the wagons. I'm sure the experience won't kill us." Realising what he'd said, he flinched.

"You ain't goin' back with him?" said Asher, surprised.

Holze shook his head. "No, no. There are things to do here first. A shrine. A prayer candle. I brought all the necessaries with me."

Asher nodded. "Reckon Gar'll appreciate that. And the king."

"Yes, well..." For a moment, fresh grief threatened. Then Holze mastered himself and flapped a hand at Jarralt. "Don't just stand there, Conroyd! Go!"

Trailing after them, Asher waited until Gar was stowed safe and silent in the lushly upholstered vehicle with Conroyd Jarralt by his side. "Take His Highness to the palace infirmary, my lord," he said as the carriage door was pulled shut between them. "I reckon Nix must be waiting for him on pins and needles."

Jarralt's handsome face was all sharp lines and smooth planes. Cold. Remote. Like the Flatlands in the depths of winter. "Yes. I expect he is."

"My lord..." Asher hesitated, then plunged on. "I can't believe this weren't a terrible accident, but if Captain Orrick finds otherwise... you have to know. Gar ain't the one responsible."

For a little while Jarralt sat in continued silence. Then he turned his head, just enough, and met Asher's gaze directly. "Nor am I."

Asher nodded. Lied. "I believe you. Sir."

Jarralt's look was icy enough to freeze a man solid where he stood. "And what makes you think I give one good damn about what you do or don't believe?" His hand slapped the carriage door's painted panel. "Coachman! To the Tower!"

Pellen Orrick patted Asher's shoulder as he joined him in the middle of the road. Together they watched the glimlit carriage disappear around the first bend. "Well done, Asher," he said. "A nasty moment neatly turned. If ever you get tired of life in the prince's employ I'm sure I could find a place for you in the Guard."

"I got to go," said Asher. His head was aching so badly he thought it might explode. "There's folks back at the Tower wondering what's amiss, and prob'ly ready to raise the roof by now. What are you goin' to do about the bodies?"

"Tonight?" Orrick shrugged. "Nothing. Even with magic and

glimfire it's too dangerous to retrieve them in the dark. I'll leave the lads here to keep watch and return with help at first light."

Cautiously, Asher nodded. "Just one problem with that. You're forgettin' Matcher. We got his wife and family sittin' at home as we speak, expectin' him to walk through the door any minute. And then there's the lads at the palace stables. They'll miss the horses."

"Damn," said Pellen Orrick. "Yes. All right. Leave it to me. I'll send senior officers. Make sure the news doesn't spread."

"Fine," he said, relieved. "So I'll be off, then. See you tomorrow some time."

Orrick nodded. "Yes. You will."

Asher trudged away. Cygnet was anxiously pleased to see him, all snorts and whickers and impatient stamping. Holze conjured a small ball of travelling glimfire to light his way home and blessed him with unsteady hands.

"You served Barl well tonight, young man," the cleric said as Asher hauled himself into the saddle. "I shall remember you in my prayers."

Looking down at him, Asher nodded. "Reckon we're all goin' to need prayin' for by the time this mess is sorted."

"Indeed," Holze said soberly. "Indeed." And stood back as Asher clapped his heels to Cygnet's sides and bounded away.

It wasn't till he was long past Jarralt's sedately travelling carriage and almost back at the Tower that Asher realised he'd spent the last little while giving orders to some of the most powerful Doranen in the kingdom... and the Doranen had obeyed him.

Arrived at last in the Tower stable yard, after handing Cygnet over to Boonie for a rubdown and his mash, he found Matt tending a colt that had kicked its way out of a transport cart and was pincushioned with splinters for its trouble. A look and a headshake were all he needed to give the bad news. Matt's face lost some colour, and his hands shook a little as he eased another spike of wood from the injured colt's neck.

"Barl bless them," he said, dropping the splinter into the basin at his feet. "We'll talk later?"

"Aye," said Asher, turning away. "Later."

It was a short walk from the stables to the Tower. Hollow, dreading the confrontations to come, he dragged his feet through the pathway's raked gravel and thought it might be nice to drop down dead of a seizure just about now. So he wouldn't have to open the Tower's front door. Wouldn't have to go inside. Wouldn't have to see the faces

of the people he knew were waiting there, for him, for news. Waiting
to be told not to worry, it were all a false alarm.

Waiting in vain.

The Tower's front doors stood slightly ajar. He took a deep breath.
Wrapped his fingers around each brass handle. Pushed hard and
stepped inside.

"I sent everyone home," said Darran, rising from his chair at the
foot of the staircase. "It seemed pointless to keep them loitering about
here for hours on end."

"Pointless," Asher said slowly, shoving the doors shut behind him.
"Aye."

Fingers laced precisely across his concave middle, Darran took
three steps forward then stopped. "Well?" Anyone who didn't know
him would think he was in complete control of his emotions. "Is he
dead?"

Adrift in the middle of the empty foyer, Asher blinked. "No." All
of a sudden he was feeling very tired. He needed a chair. Hadn't there
been more chairs in here this morning? "Just banged up a bit. Jarralt's
takin' him to see Pother Nix now."

"*Lord* Jarralt," said Darran automatically. "Asher?"

He dragged his sagging eyelids open. "What?"

"Is anybody dead?"

He turned away. The maggoty ole fool was goin' to go *spare* when
he heard.

"*Asher.*"

Turning back, he shoved his hands into his pockets. Forced himself
to look into Darran's haggard face. "Not Durm. Durm's alive. Or he
was when I saw him last." He shrugged. "Just."

"I don't care about Durm," said Darran.

"You should. 'Cause if he don't pull through and speak up for
Gar's magic I reckon we're all in a mess of trouble."

Darran hardly seemed to hear him. "Who else? You said not Durm.
Very well. Who else lives...aside from him and Gar?"

It was the first time he'd ever heard the ole scarecrow refer to Gar as
anything other than "the prince" or "His Highness." It frightened
him. "Nobody," he said, brutal. "All right? His whole family's dead.
Oh, and Matcher too. And the horses. Better not forget the poor
bloody horses, eh? All of 'em dead. Lyin' in bits and pieces on the side
of Salbert's Eyrie. Now, were there anythin' else you wanted to know?"

A thin, disbelieving moan escaped Darran's alarmingly blue lips. His
fingers unlaced. Clutched at his chest. He began to sag at the knees.

Asher leapt at him. "Don't you dare! You fart, you bugger, you silly cross-eyed crow! Don't you bloody *dare*!"

Grunting with the effort he lowered Darran to the tiled foyer floor and wrenched open the sober black coat and the weskit beneath. Scrabbled at the old man's plain cravat, loosening its knot, then tugged open the pristine white shirt. The old fool's chest heaved for air, thin as a toast-rack covered with a tea towel. There were tears in his eyes, welling and welling like a magic fountain. He needed a pillow or something to rest on. Asher looked around, grabbed a cushion from the solitary foyer chair and rescued Darran's head from the floor.

Then, helpless, he chewed at his lip. Now what? He weren't a pother, he had no idea what to do next. Dimwitted ole fart, sending away all the staff, even the messenger boys. He grabbed Darran's right arm, shoved back the coat and shirt sleeves and chafed the blue-veined wrist, thin and pale and knobbly.

"Come on, now," he said desperately. "There's been enough death around here for one day, you ole crow. Gar won't thank you for peggin' out on him. He's to be king now, he'll need you for that. If you ain't here to keep him organised they might ask Willer, and that little sea slug couldn't organise a piss-up in a brewery!"

Darran tried to frown. His lips worked soundlessly for a moment, then he whispered, "Willer—my assistant—you show respect—"

"That's more like it," he said, grinning with relief. "Just you lie there and breathe, Meister Scarecrow. In and out, in and out, and don't you dare think of stoppin'."

Darran's eyes fluttered closed, but his chest continued to rise and fall. Asher released the old man's wrist and sat back on his heels. He could feel sweat trickling down his spine and gluing his hair to his scalp. He needed a bath. And food. His empty belly growled at the thought. But bloody Darran had sent the cook away. He'd have to risk her wrath and raid the kitchen for whatever was lying about. And he would, too... just as soon as he could be sure Darran wasn't going to cause him even more trouble than usual by dying.

Then he looked up, because the Tower doors were swinging open. It was Gar. On his own two feet and walking. A step behind him, Conroyd Jarralt. They saw Darran and halted.

"Barl save me," said Gar. Looking and sounding like a man who'd lost his last hope of happiness. "Is he—"

"No," he said, scrambling off the floor. "What are you doin' here, you're s'posed to be on your way to see Nix!"

"I came to tell Darran what happened."

He spared Jarralt an accusing glance, then said, "Aye, well, I already told him. Can you get him to Nix? Now?"

Not looking at Jarralt, Gar nodded. "My lord?"

In searing silence Jarralt helped Asher get the groggy old man out to the waiting carriage. Gar followed behind, somehow managing to keep his own self upright.

"You need me?" said Asher, once Darran was settled against the plush velvet cushions and Gar had climbed in beside him.

"Yes," said Gar.

"Ride with the coachman," said Jarralt curtly, and climbed into the carriage.

Biting his tongue, Asher obeyed.

The Royal Infirmary was located in a wing off the palace's main building, with its own driveway and entrance and courtyard for privacy and peace. Willing hands assisted Darran inside. Offered to help Gar and were coldly rebuffed. No longer required, Jarralt departed with little more than a correct bow. Gar nodded austere thanks, Asher heaved a sigh of relief and the infirmary assistants barely noticed.

A carry-chair was produced for the ailing old man to rest in and a couple of servants summoned to do the carrying. A spare pother, hastily produced, took one look at Darran and Gar, tut-tutted, and trotted them off to the person who knew best how to handle difficult patients.

Asher, hovering close by Gar in case of another collapse, prayed hard under his breath for strength. The smells in this place were making his head swim. If he didn't get out of here sooner rather than later the infirmary's manky bone-botherers were going to have one more patient on their hands.

After a short trip along narrow, quiet corridors they found Nix standing in some kind of three-sided reception area, complete with desk and chairs and several potted plants. There was a closed door in each wall, each painted a different colour: blue, green and deep crimson. The Royal Pother stood before the crimson door, washing his bloodied hands in a basin held by one assistant, while dictating notes to another.

"—twice hourly, with a goodly compound of urval, goats-foot and stranglepus rubbed well into the unstitched wounds," Nix recited, his eyes half-closed in thought. Reaching for the towel draped over the basin-holder's forearm, he pursed his lips. "For the stitched wounds, dust every four hours with powdered grassle. In an hour we'll—" Suddenly aware of a wider audience, he stopped drying his hands and refocused his attention. Saw Darran slumped in the carry-chair, tossed aside the towel and went to him.

"Well?" said Gar.

Nix looked up from his gentle examination. "He'll do."

"And Durm?"

Nix turned to the basin-holder. "Wulf, fetch Pother Tobin." To the chair-carriers he said, "Take His Highness's secretary into the green chamber."

"Tobin?" said Gar, watching Darran's departure. "No. I want you to—"

"Tobin will see your Darran right, never fear," said Nix. "He's had a heart spasm but he's in no immediate danger."

"Very well," said Gar after a moment. "Then take me to Durm."

Nix shook his head. "Not yet."

Beneath the churning pain in Gar's eyes, a flare of heat. "It wasn't a request, Nix."

"Not yet," said Nix stubbornly. "He needs quiet, not company. Think of him, sir, not yourself."

Asher risked a touch to Gar's rigid, uninjured arm. "Durm's in good hands. Get yourself seen to. You're set to fall arse over eyeballs any moment."

Gar's glance was like a whiplash. "Did I ask you?"

"No," said Asher, holding his ground. "Don't mean I'm wrong, though."

Nix held out his hand. "Come, Your Highness." His voice was gentle now. Coaxing. "Let me heal you. And then I'll take you to Durm."

Swaying on his feet, Gar capitulated. Allowed himself to be led away like a docile child.

Uninvited, Asher followed.

CHAPTER THREE

Nix led the way to his book-lined, herb-infested office. The chamber's air was thick with hints of potions past, reluctantly swallowed. Cheerful flames leapt in a small fireplace; the room was stiflingly warm.

"Right then," he said, planting himself between desk and scarred workbench. "Now that we're beyond sight and sound of nuisance, let's see the truth of the matter, shall we, Your Highness? Time to strip, please, down to your skin."

Too battered and weary for further protest, Gar let Nix and Asher between them ease him out of his hasty bandages and ruined, blood-stained clothes. With memories of his own past hurts resurfacing, Asher was as gentle as he could be, wincing as the full extent of Gar's injuries were revealed. Breathing unevenly, Gar cradled his left arm with his right hand and waited for the ordeal to end.

"Hmmph," said the pother, inspecting the prince like a man at a horse auction. A frown pinched his bushy grey and yellow eyebrows together as his blunt fingers skimmed the surface of Gar's insulted body, marking each cut, each scrape, each ripening bruise. Air hissed between Gar's clenched teeth as Nix's fingers lightly traced the irregular line of the broken collarbone.

He felt Gar's skull, took his pulse, listened to his heartbeat and breathing, checked the coating on his tongue and the clarity of his eyes. "Any idea how long you were stunned out of your senses?"

"No," said Gar. "I remember—I think I remember—flying through the air. Hitting the ground. I know I woke twice. Tried to get up, go for help...I couldn't even stand."

"It were mid-morning when you left," said Asher. "And dusk when me and Matt found you."

"Hmmph," said Nix. "A goodly brain rattling, then. You'll need a day or three in bed, to guard against conniptions."

"Bed?" Gar pulled a face. "I think not."

"Did you know I've an excellent cure for an argumentative patient, sir?" Nix asked, eyes narrowed. "It involves needle, thread and meals sucked through a straw."

"Spare me your dubious wit!" retorted Gar. "Your king is dead and his heir with him! It falls to me now to continue his legacy. Do you tell me I can do so from my *bed?*"

Suddenly pale, and with tears in his eyes, Nix jabbed Gar's chest with a pointed finger. "I tell you, sir, that as Royal Pother I am charged with the gravest responsibility: the care of this kingdom's physical wellbeing in the body of its Weather-Worker. With Borne's death, may Barl keep him, that body is now yours. From this day forth you belong to Lur, first and foremost. And in the pursuit of my sacred duty as your pother I will allow you no secrets, grant you no privacies, spare you no shame and brook no argument. If I say you must rest you *will* rest. For upon your health depends the welfare of Barl's Wall and the kingdom it protects. The lives of every last man, woman and child. Because of this your health is *my* kingdom and in this room *I* am king. Do you understand?"

As Gar stared at Nix in silent shock, Asher sighed. "He's right. And no, you didn't ask me."

"I didn't have to," said Gar. His voice was a strangled whisper. "Of course he's right."

Gentle again, Nix lightly touched Gar's shoulder. "Sit, sir, while I collect what's needful."

There was a chair close by. Asher helped Gar into it, then stood back. More than anything he wanted to drape himself over the desk or lean against a handy stretch of wall, but protocol dictated otherwise. And Nix would probably throw something at him for making a mess.

The pother went to his office door, pulled it three inches wide and barked through the opening: "Kerril! Fetch me a quarter-cup of janja-vet with two drops of dursle root essence added after pouring. Also a measure of bee-blossom. Quickly!"

While he waited for his subordinate to bring him the requested potions, Nix rummaged in a cupboard and withdrew four cork-sealed pots, a bluestone mortar and pestle and a small clear vial of something green and viscous. After depositing them on the crowded bench he rolled up his dangling sleeves and got to work. The smell as he pounded each ingredient in the pestle was vile.

Gar stirred and looked up, his expression apprehensive. "You expect me to swallow that?"

A tap on the door indicated Kerril's return. "No," replied Nix as he pushed the door shut and handed Gar one of the cups Kerril had given him. "This."

Gar sniffed the liquid suspiciously. "What is it?"

"Something to dull the pain while I fix that broken collarbone," said Nix, standing over him. "Bone-knitting's not the gentlest of healing magic."

The pother's expression was sympathetic but unyielding. Gar spared him a single burning look then shuddered and tossed the potion down his throat.

"Barl's mercy!" he gasped, and started gagging. "Are you trying to poison me?"

"I'd advise you not to vomit, sir," said Nix, returning to his mortar and pestle. He added the bee-blossom and resumed pounding. "You'll only have to drink another lot and I'm told it tastes even worse the second time. Now just sit quietly while it takes effect and I finish this ointment."

Still gagging, Gar dropped the cup and hunched over, fisted fingers pressed to his mouth. A few moments later, Nix was ready.

Eyes closed, words whispering under his breath, the pother laid his hands on Gar's broken collarbone. At his touch a spark of light ignited. Became a flame. His fingers began to dance up and down the bone's irregular length, drumming lightly, and the flame danced with them.

Asher had never seen a Doranen bone-knitting before, although he had friends who'd required it after a squall off Tattler's Ear Cove rattled them like thrown knucklebones from bow to stern in their fishing smack. "Hurt like blazes," Beb and Joffet had told him with identical grimacing shudders.

Clearly, Gar would agree. Even with the pain-dulling potion his face was salty white and shiny with sweat, and his breathing came hard and harsh. Small grunts escaped him, and his right hand spasmed on the arm of the chair.

"Nearly done," Nix murmured. The flame beneath his fingers was a furnace now; Asher imagined he could feel the heat of it in his own flesh, and winced. "Take a nice deep breath," said Nix. "And hold—hold—hold—"

With a final burst of light and a sharp command the broken bone beneath the pother's hands snapped back into place. Gar shouted, and would have flung himself out of the chair if Nix hadn't restrained him. Flinching in sympathy Asher watched the healer cradle Gar hard against the magic's tormenting aftermath, patting his back and clucking like an old hen.

"There now, there now, that's the worst over, I swear it."

Slowly, Gar recovered. Straightened, and pushed Nix away. "I'm fine, stop fussing," he muttered.

Nix returned to his bench and retrieved the mortar of stinking ointment. "Stand up for me, Your Highness. We'll just test that arm first, then take care of your bumps and scrapes."

His breathing still a little unsteady, Gar stood. Lifted his left arm above his head, waved it in circles, clenched his hand to a fist and pulled his elbow tight to his side.

"Excellent," said Nix. "Another day and you'll never know it was damaged. Now for the rest of you."

In swift silence he daubed his pungent green concoction onto Gar's hurts. Seconds after touching the damaged flesh it melted out of sight. The dried blood faded, and with it the ointment's eye-watering smell. A thin protective film now coated each wound.

"There," said Nix at last. "Better?"

Gar touched cautious fingertips to his cut forehead. Pressed them against his torn hip, thigh, ribs. "Better." He let his hand rest on Nix's arm for a moment. "My thanks."

Nix nodded. "You'll take the ointment with you. Apply it morning and night for three days. You'll be healed by then."

"Yes," said Gar. "I'll do that. But as for staying in bed, Nix..."

The pother heaved a disgruntled sigh. "I know. I know. The burden of kingship cannot be laid down." He turned to Asher. "I charge you to keep a close eye on him. Send for me at the slightest suspicion of weakness, or collapse."

Asher nodded. "I will."

"And now," said Gar, "I will see Durm."

Asher looked at him sidelong. "Dressed like that?"

Gar's reply was to close his eyes, frame four silent words with still-colourless lips, and with the fingers of his left hand trace in the chamber's warm air a complicated sigil. Two heartbeats later he was holding shirt, trews and a weskit in his arms.

The effort dropped him back to the chair.

"You didn't let me finish," said Nix, reproving. "No magic for a week."

Stippled with sweat, Gar shook his head. "I must. The Weather Working—"

"Will wait. Schedules can be adjusted. Performing magic in your condition could cripple you."

Cripple. It was a word laden with bitter memory.

"Fine," Gar said curtly. Shakily he stood again and, with slow deliberation, began to dress.

Nix busied himself emptying the rest of the mortar's ointment into a small jar. "And you, Asher," he said. "There's blood on your hands."

Asher looked. True, there was. Not all of it his, though. Most of it not his. But how could he say that, in Gar's hearing? He shrugged. "Scraped knuckles. I'm fine."

"Show me."

He shoved his hands under Nix's nose. The pother ran his experienced gaze over the cuts, dabbed them with ointment, then stoppered the jar with a cork and held it out. "There's enough here for you, too. Both of you use it, or I'll know the reason why."

Asher looked up from his tingling hands. "Yes, sir."

Behind them Gar fastened the last button on his weskit. "Durm," he said. His face and voice brooked no opposition. "Now."

*   *   *

Pother Tobin was waiting for them in the reception area. When she saw Gar, she bowed.

"Your secretary is resting comfortably, Your Highness. He's been given a good strong dose of heartsease and should be well enough for visitors come the morning."

Gar nodded. "My thanks." As the pother bowed again, retreating, he turned to Nix. "Where is Durm?"

Nix nodded at the reception area's crimson door. "In there. But before you see him, I must caution you. His injuries are grave, his appearance...unsettling. I have done all I can for him. What happens now is up to his constitution, and Barl's mercy."

Gar didn't reply immediately. His gaze wandered round the hushed reception area for long moments, touching on the bright-painted doors, the windowless walls, the potted plants. His expression was distant. Unmoved. "Will he live?"

Nix pursed his lips. "I'm a healer, sir. Not a soothsayer."

There was a pother in Durm's room, seated in a chair beside the patient's bed. She stood as they entered the windowless chamber. Glimfire sconces threw small shadows onto the cream-coloured walls and a fire kept any chill at bay. At a signal from Nix she left them, closing the crimson door behind her.

Supported by mysterious pother magic, Durm floated some eight inches above a high, wide platform fitted on all four sides with wooden railings. To Asher it seemed there wasn't a single square inch of the man's naked skin that wasn't stitched or stained or stretched with splints. Indeed, the massive head wound was embroidered so thickly his hairless scalp looked infested with caterpillars. His eyes, once as cold and piercing as spears of ice, were now invisible, consumed by the bloated purple flesh of his face.

Gar checked when he saw him, one hand coming up in a fierce denial. "Barl have mercy," he whispered, a small wounded sound in the silence. "If I didn't know it was him..." He managed a step closer. "Why haven't you knitted his bones, Nix? You can't leave him broken like this!"

"Bone-knitting would most likely kill him," said Nix. "We'll get to that, in time." *If he lives*. The words hung unspoken between them.

"His stupor..."

"A result of the head injury. It is...severe."

"Will he wake?"

"Perhaps."

"With his wits?"

Nix shrugged. "Unknown."

"How long? Before he wakes? Before you do know."

Nix frowned, but answered. "Days, certainly. Most likely weeks."

Reluctantly, Gar dragged his gaze away from the monstrosity hovering over the bed. "But not months. It can't be months, Nix. The Weather Working. My succession. This kingdom needs him! *I* need him!"

"I know that," said Nix. "And if he can be healed, sir, I will heal him and return him to you."

"*If?*"

Nix sighed, and clasped his hands behind his back. The unspoken words would have to be spoken. "You must forgive my plain speaking, Your Highness, but I see no point in prevarication. To be blunt, I hold little hope."

Gar's face was chilled and chalk-white. Staring wide-eyed at Durm he said, "But little is not the same as none."

"No," Nix replied after a cautious pause. "No, it's not."

Asher watched as Gar moved to Durm's bedside like a man entranced. When the prince spoke, his voice was the merest thread.

"I loved him once, and then I hated him. Now I don't know what I feel..." He fell silent, struggling for words. "Except fear. I've known him all my life. He is as much my family as my father, my mother, my sister. If he dies...I am truly alone."

He sounded bereft. Knifed to the soul.

Nix stepped forward and rested his hand on Gar's shoulder. "No, sir," he said, his voice rough with tears. "Not alone. Never alone while there is breath in my body."

Asher cleared his throat. Banished tears of his own. *Da. Da.* "Nor mine," he added. "Gar...let's go. There ain't nothing you can do for Durm...and you need sleep."

Gar's stricken gaze continued to feast on the unconscious Master Magician. "No. No, I can't leave him."

Nix's fingers tightened. "You can't stay," he said gently. "Indeed, your presence might well hinder, not help. I will send for you the moment there is any change."

For a moment Asher thought Gar would fight them. Then the prince—the king—sighed deeply. Touched two fingertips to his lips and pressed them lightly to Durm's cheek.

"Come back to me, Durm," he whispered. "I can't go on without you." Then he let Nix shepherd him to the chamber's crimson door.

Asher followed them out, and didn't look back.

*   *   *

Trapped in his prison of spoiled and spoiling flesh, Morg screams and screams. Wherever he is, he is not alone. There are voices somewhere close, nearby, but they click-clack on the edge of hearing and he cannot reach them or understand what they say. Struggling like a spider tangled in its own web he battles to make sense of this new reality.

Durm's body is broken and bleeding. Only his own indomitable will keeps the fat fool's flesh alive, his spirit from oblivion. The sluggish blood is soaked in drugs, enveloping and deadening and holding him fast, but still he is assaulted by pain. It is centuries since last he felt such a sensation. It is insulting.

His predicament is insulting.

He is Morg, far beyond the pettiness of physicality in all its incarnations, yet he is caught. Against every expectation, and in the face of all his power, he is bound to this lump of sundered meat. Shackled to its fate. Slave to its destiny. If Durm dies, he dies.

The shock is enough to threaten his reason.

How can this be? he wails. I am Morg! I am invincible!

Death, his bitter and once-beaten enemy, is laughing at him. Waiting in the shadows and laughing. It rubs its greedy hands with glee as it waits for the fat fool's body to die. For the spell to fail, and so release Morg's spirit to destruction.

No, cries Morg. You have not won. I will not die. I am Morg and my name means Victory! You cannot defeat me. You will never defeat me. There is a way. There has to be a way. Am I not immortal? Immortal beings cannot die! I cannot die!

Yes, you can, says Death. In this place and time, you can.

Morg knows Death speaks the truth, and despairs. For the first time in centuries, he is desperate. Faced with circumstances he did not create and cannot control. For the first time in centuries, he feels fear. The damage done to this borrowed body is dire. Even with his vast powers it still might plunge into Death's greedy abyss, taking him with it.

And if not—if he does manage to keep the fat fool alive—what if Durm is permanently crippled? His faculties deranged? If the pothers cannot mend this broken frame it will be no use at all. What then? Will he be forced to endure eternity inside Durm's ruined body?

Morg howls at the thought, twisting and turning and beating the bars of his cage. Durm's sickly flesh rebels at his fury. The failing heart fails further, and the labouring lungs deflate. Panicked, Morg abandons profitless emotion and focuses his will. Beat, heart! Breathe, lungs!

Resentfully, dying Durm obeys him.

Morg reflects. He is in this place for one reason only: to tear down Barl's Wall in all its golden glory and grind her treacherous heart's descendants into the dirt so he might claim the last square inches of the world for his own. To do that, he needs a host. And if Durm can no longer serve that purpose, he must find another host who can.

Another host . . .

He has no idea if such a transfer is even possible.

I will make it possible, vows Morg. I am limitless, and I will finish what I started. After that, fat Durm can die, and welcome. Along with all his friends.

Time marches, and with it the events he has set in motion. Soon the black toad magic planted within the cripple's mind will warp, and shrivel, and die. He must be there to see it. He must be alive to savour the moment, nectar on the tongue, and birth the bloody days that will usher in the end of the world as these poor fools have known it.

I am Morg, he sighs. Immortal and invincible. I feel no pain. I feel no fear. Reaching out his mind, he wraps the fraying thread of Durm's life around his fisted intellect and bends his will towards eternity.

Live, Durm, he croons into the echoing spaces around him. Live, fat fool. For I am Morg, and I'm not done with you yet.

Matt sighed, then stretched his back. It had taken far longer than he'd thought, but at last the injured colt was plucked free of splinters, sticky with ointments and drowsing in the deep straw of its stable. Finally done with physicking he smoothed his hand down an unspoiled length of dappled grey neck, then leaned against the nearest wall. He was alone now, and waiting, all the lads dismissed for the night. It was just him and his horses, the way he liked it best. The colt flicked its ears at him and he stroked it again, seeking comfort in the warmth of living flesh beneath his hand.

Pushed far away where he couldn't feel it, pain lurked like a wolf in the woods. All the royal family save Gar was dead, and tomorrow the City would wake to a world unimagined. What this meant for him and Dathne, for Veira and the rest of the Circle, for Gar, for Asher, he had no idea. He was too tired now to think of it. Too tired, and too afraid. The shadows in his life had crept much closer, were touching him now with chilly darkness and surprise. He'd been looking for them, and still they'd caught him unawares.

Silence settled inside the stable and out. Matt closed his eyes and let himself settle with it. Let himself breathe, just breathe, and sought out the subtle shift and sway of the energies swirling invisible through the night air. Unfurled his gift and asked it to taste the flux and flow of magics in the world.

Something was different. Something was...missing.

Frowning, he tried to pin down the sensation. What was its cause? Not death, though the death of King Borne was momentous. Powerful Doranen had died before now and he'd not detected any great change in the world. The silence their passing created was soon smothered by the voices left behind.

No. This had something to do with the other change he'd felt. The one that had stood the hair on the back of his neck in a kind of creeping horror the first time he'd noticed it. The one he couldn't begin to explain, to Dathne or himself. A single discordant note in the choir of Lur's magic, thin and sharp and sour. Poison, to a man with his knack of feeling the world.

That note had fallen silent. After weeks of hearing its soft, malevolent voice he'd almost grown accustomed; its sudden absence now sounded louder than a shout.

But *why*? Why had it disappeared, as abruptly as first it arrived? Entirely disconcerted, he stretched his senses to their limits in an effort to find the answer.

An edgily amused voice said, "You look like a man sniffing milk to see if it's gone off."

Matt sighed and opened his eyes. "Dathne."

Small and straight in the stable doorway, her head and shoulders covered in a green wool shawl, she raised her eyebrows. "Your call through the crystal sounded shrill. What's happened?"

The colt stirred, disquieted by their voices. Matt soothed it with a touch and a murmured reassurance then eased his way out of the stable. The lamplit yard was hushed, just the normal sounds of horses in their beds and owls in the surrounding trees, hooting. His lads were upstairs in their dormitory, sleeping or playing cards. It was safe to talk.

Even so, he kept his voice down. "Borne's dead. The queen, too. And Fane. Durm as good as, and might not last the night."

Shocked silence. In her face a wealth of surprise, which meant she hadn't dreamed this. Strangely, he was comforted. If she'd known and kept it from him...

"Jervale defend us," she said at last, her voice a fervent whisper. "*How?*"

"An accident."

"And what of Gar?"

"He's injured too. But in no danger."

She seemed unable to grasp the enormity of it. He was having some trouble there himself. She said, still stunned, "They're dead? You're certain?"

He shrugged. "Asher is. He saw them for himself and told me."

"*Asher* saw...?" Her thin face blanched. "He was there? Involved? Is he injured? Is he—"

He put a hand on her shoulder to calm her. "He's fine."

She shook her head. Tugged her shawl tight. "Tell me everything."

When he was finished she stepped closer, her face flushed with angry colour, and shoved him hard in the chest. "You *fool*! What were you thinking, letting him do anything so rash, so dangerous? Climbing into Salbert's Eyrie? That's madness! What if he'd fallen? What if he was lying there dead like the rest of them? What then?"

He caught her hands as she lifted them to shove him a second time. "I tried to stop him. But he was determined and I had no good reason to keep on arguing. Not one I could share. You bade me hold my tongue, remember?"

She pulled free. "So it's my fault? Why didn't you go climbing down there yourself?"

"I offered to but he wouldn't listen. Dathne, why are we fighting? He isn't dead."

"No, but he could be! You had no right to risk him!"

"And you haven't risked him?" he retorted. "By not telling him what he should know of himself? And that business with the fireworks and Ballodair the day we first met, you don't think *that* was risking him?"

"That was different and you know it. I had to put him in the prince's way, I had to get him into the Usurper's House!"

"And I had to let him see if any of the royal family were left alive," he said. "Or risk stirring his suspicions. Asher was beside himself, Dath. Ready to go right through me. What would you have done if you'd been there instead of me?"

Furious, resenting his logic, she glared up into his impatient face. Then, without warning, her hot gaze shifted. Focused somewhere behind him. Melted into relief and sorrow and something else. Something he didn't want or dare to think about.

He turned, knowing already who it was he'd see. Asher. Trailing into the yard like a man at the end of a week's marching over unforgiving ground.

He heard her gasp. Stepped aside and watched her go to him. Stand before him, thin and worn with worry. "Matt's told me," she said. "Are you all right?"

The question seemed to surprise Asher, as though the last thing he expected was concern for himself. He shrugged. "Aye."

"And the prince?"

"He'll live. I've put him to bed up in the Tower."

"Praise Barl." She looked at her feet, and then into his face. "And it's true? They're really dead?"

"Aye," he said again. "They're really dead."

As though speaking the words out loud were some kind of catalyst, his stolid composure fractured. His face crumpled, lost years, became the face of a boy in unbearable pain. Matt felt his own face twist in sympathy.

Dathne held out her arms and welcomed Asher to her breast. He went to her gladly, fiercely, holding her like a man in fear of falling. Her holding of him was no less desperate.

The sight of their embrace sank Matt's untouched heart, and roused a host of fears. Dathne's face was hidden from him, and he was glad, because he could see Asher's...and it told him everything he needed to know. More than ever he'd wanted.

"Jervale have mercy," he said aloud...but softly, so they wouldn't hear him. "Please. And then tell me what to do now."

CHAPTER FOUR

Asher woke the following morning fully clothed and sprawled face down across his bed. For long moments he just lay there, groping for his bearings. His head felt heavy, wooden, and his mouth tasted like barnacle scrapings. His hair was tacky with dried sweat, making his scalp itch. There was dirt under his chipped fingernails. Dirt on his shirt sleeves too, along with dried blood. His back ached, and his shoulders, and his hands were scabbed with cuts. What the—

And then a wave of memory crashed over him, tumultuous with fragmented images. *Borne. Dana. Fane. The dead brown carriage horse. Gar's face. Dathne...*

He groaned, rolling over to stare at his pale blue bedchamber ceiling. Groaned again as muttering pains roused to a roar. Everything hurt. The room tip-tilted about him and he clutched at his blankets, waiting for it to steady right side up so he could think more clearly.

After the stables, and Dathne—*the way she'd held him, soothed him, the warmth of her hand against his cheek and the tickling rush of her breath across his skin*—he'd staggered back to the Tower. Gar had demanded to be left alone, insisting he was all right, but he'd wanted to make sure. Nobody could lose their entire family in one blow and still be all right, not even a man as habitually cool and self-contained as the Prince of Lur.

But Gar had locked his suite's main doors and wouldn't answer no matter how hard the bell rope was pulled or how loudly the carved wood was banged upon. Truth be told, he'd not been sorry. He'd had his fill of grief for one night.

So he'd gone all the way downstairs and underground to the deserted Tower kitchen and filled his empty belly with this and that from the cook's precious pantry. Then he'd staggered up to his room, intending to sit awhile and try to think this calamity through. Unravel all its implications and decide what it might mean, to himself and the kingdom.

Instead, he must have fallen asleep.

No reason to feel guilty, he told himself sternly. The dead were dead. The living still had to sleep, didn't they? Aye, and eat and work and fight and love...

Love.

Dathne.

Pushing the thought of her aside, because he didn't begin to know what last night might mean and lacked the energy right now to untangle the puzzle, he sat up. Swung his still-booted feet to the floor, twitched open the bedside window's curtain and looked outside.

It was late. Maybe half-nine. From this high up he could just make out the tail end of the morning's second exercise string: six immaculate horses heading out from the stables towards Spindly Copse. Looked like Willem bringing up the rear; the boy always liked to ride Sunburst, and he'd know the chestnut colt's broad backside anywhere.

In his imagination he heard the stable lads' laughter and scoffing catcalls as they rode out to the Copse, and was greenly envious. Lucky bastards. What he wouldn't give to be one of them again, far from the glare of public service and the intimacy of lives shattered by disaster.

A battering of fists against his apartment's outer doors startled him. Then came a voice, raised in impatient demand: "Asher! Asher, get out here at once!"

Willer. *Bastard*.

For one single, luxurious moment he contemplated deafness, or insensibility, or even self-inflicted death. Any or all were better than dealing with Willer at half-nine in the morning on a growlingly empty stomach after a day and a night like the ones he'd just lived through.

But no. Somebody had to take charge of the Tower till Darran was released from Nix's clutches, and if he didn't do it Willer would. Which meant that by eleven o'clock he'd have *everybody* running around killing themselves.

Scowling ferociously he flung wide his apartment doors. "Keep the noise down, you bloody great fool! You want to wake the prince?"

Blinding in purple satin, Willer stared at him, took one horrified breath and immediately fished for his kerchief. "Barl preserve me!" he said through pale mauve silk. "You *stink*! And you're filthy! What is going on? And where is Darran? He sent all the staff home yesterday over my strenuous objections and now he's nowhere to be found and the maids are milling about like hens!"

"Darran's been taken poorly. He—"

"Poorly?" Willer dropped the silk kerchief and lunged. "What do you mean? What have you done to him? I swear, Asher, I *swear*, if you've harmed so much as a hair on Darran's head I'll—"

With some difficulty Asher fended him off. "I ain't done nowt to the ole crow! Now shut your trap so's I can tell you what's what, or I'll push you head first down my water closet!"

Willer hurriedly stepped back. "Lay a finger on me and I'll have you arrested."

"You could try," he said with an evil, relishing grin. "Now listen. Seein' Darran's in his sickbed you'll need to stand in for him today, Barl save us all."

"Of course I shall stand in for him!" Willer snapped. "Who else could be entrusted with such an important task? Certainly not you."

He throttled the impulse to kick the little pissant where, on reflection, it wouldn't do much damage. "Look, you, stop flappin' your bloody lips and *listen*. There's an important announcement to be made on another matter. Get the staff together in the foyer while I—"

"Announcement? About what? Asher, I *demand* you tell me—"

"*Listen*, I said! Or are you deaf as well as a dimwit? Get the staff together, grounds folk and stable as well as Tower, while I see how the prince wants to proceed. All right? Understand? Or do I have to draw you little pictures?"

"And who are you to give such orders?"

"I'm the man who's goin' to punch you in the nose if you don't do as you're told!"

The sea slug's eyes narrowed in fury. "You have no authority over me."

"Want to bet? If you don't about-face right now and get the staff assembled, I'll see you dismissed and chucked out of here on your pimpled fat arse. And don't think for a moment Gar won't back me up, 'cause we both know he will."

"You arrogant, insupportable *bastard*. One day," said Willer, wheezing with rage, "there will be a reckoning for you! One day I shall strip you naked before the world and you'll be seen for the rotten, pernicious, power-hungry—"

Closing the door in Willer's face made him feel a lot better. A hot bath and some food for his empty belly would've made him feel better still but there wasn't time for that. So he washed quickly out of his privy basin, haphazardly scraped the bristles off his face with a razor one stropping short of sharp, brushed the worst of the sweat and dirt from his hair, hauled on clean clothing and went upstairs to rouse Gar.

This time when he knocked on the royal suite's front doors they swung open on soundless hinges. There was nobody on the other side.

"Smartarse," he muttered, and entered. Crossed the empty sun-striped foyer and took the stairs up to Gar's bedchamber. With a brief knuckle-rap on the closed door he opened it, and was confronted with darkness.

"Gar? You in here?"

All the bedroom's curtains were drawn: only the merest sliver of sunshine slid between them to leaven the gloom. Asher banged and bruised and cursed his way to the nearest window and pulled back the brocade hangings.

"If I'd wanted light," said Gar, "I would've made some."

He was slumped in an overstuffed armchair, still dressed in the clothes he'd pulled on last night in Nix's office. His pale hollow cheeks were stubbled with gold; grief was smeared into dark shadows beneath his half-closed eyes. The sumptuous bed was unslept in.

Asher crossed his arms and bumped his backside onto the windowsill. "When Nix said rest, I think he meant in a bed."

"And if I'd wanted company," Gar added, eyebrows lowering, "I would've sent for someone."

He shrugged. "Darran says a good servant anticipates his employer's wishes."

Gar let his bruised, unbandaged head fall against the padded chair back. "I'm sure he does. But since when do you give a fat rat's fart what Darran has to say?"

"I don't. How are you feelin'? Collarbone all right?"

Gar lifted his left arm. Waved it overhead, and let it drop back to his lap. "Fine."

"Your bumps and bruises?"

"Also fine. Nix is an excellent physician."

"Good."

An awkward silence fell. Asher took refuge in it, frowning at the carpet. Gar looked bad. Brittle, as though one word too many, one breath too deep, would shatter him.

But he couldn't say nothing.

He looked up. Felt his eyes burn, his throat tighten. With eyes wide open saw again the blood. The bodies. He took a deep breath and let it out, shakily. "Gar. About yesterday. Your family. I—"

"*Don't*," said Gar, one hand swiftly raised. "I can't afford your sympathy, Asher. Not now. Not yet."

He blinked. "Oh."

"If you want to help...then help me stay strong."

"I can do that."

A little of the bleakness eased from Gar's face. "Thank you." He pushed to his feet. "Now I must make myself presentable. The staff—"

"I got 'em waiting downstairs. Will you make the announcement, or d'you want me to—"

"I'll do it. Tell them I'll be with them shortly, would you?" He pulled off his weskit and tossed it over the back of the armchair. "Give me ten minutes."

Nodding, Asher slid off the windowsill. Started for the chamber door, hesitated, and turned back. "Gar..."

Impatient, Gar glanced at him. "What?"

Still hesitant, he took another step closer. Brittle or not, grieving or not, there were things Gar needed to hear. Things that couldn't wait. "Nix may be a good pother, but he ain't got the power to make a man live if his body's hurt past healing. Or mend a mind that's broken. I know this is hard, but—"

Gar paused in the middle of undoing his buttons, his eyes abruptly cold. "No."

"You don't know what I'm goin' to say yet!"

"I know exactly what you're going to say," Gar replied, and returned to his unbuttoning. "The answer is no. I have a Master Magician."

"Gar..." He closed the gap between them a little more. "I know Durm's your family now, but you can't let that make your choices for you."

Gar stripped off his shirt and threw it at the chair. Despite Nix's stinking green ointment, his torso looked like a mad painter's palette. "I'm not."

"You are! You got to look at this the way the people will," he insisted. "All your life they've known you as Gar the Magickless. Gar the Cripple. And it never mattered because there was your da, and your sister, two of the best magicians this kingdom's ever seen. The smallest spratling in Restharven knew the kingdom was safe, because of them."

"The kingdom is still safe!" retorted Gar, stung. "I am Gar the Magickless no longer!"

"I know, but it's only been weeks! *Weeks*, Gar, after all those years. Folks have barely got used to the idea that you're a magician, and now you want 'em to see you as king? As *WeatherWorker?* You may be as powerful as Fane ever was, but you're not trained. Not the way you should be. You said it yourself, Durm still had so much to teach you!"

"And he shall teach me," said Gar, eyes bright with temper. "As soon as he recovers."

"You don't know he will!"

"And you don't know he won't!" snapped Gar. "Unless we are now to number physicking amongst your many talents!"

Asher shoved his hands in his pockets, sorry he'd ever opened his mouth. But he had, and it was too late now to take back what he'd said. "I ain't the one holdin' out little hope, Gar. That's Nix. His words, not mine. You can't pretend otherwise just because—"

"I'm not pretending anything!" said Gar, and turned his back. "And neither am I continuing this conversation. The subject is closed."

Asher reached out, grabbed Gar by the arm and spun him around. "No, it ain't. Like it or not, you have to face facts. You need a Master Magician. You can't leap into WeatherWorking on your own, without some other trained magician to guide you. It's too difficult. Too dangerous! You can't—"

Gar raised a warning finger. "Say 'can't' to me one more time and I promise you'll be sorry!"

"Sorrier than if you charge pig-headed into WeatherWorking and bring the Wall crashing down around our ears?" he said, ignoring the raised finger, and the dangerous light in Gar's eyes, and everything save the need to make the fool see sense. "I don't think so."

"I have no intention of destroying Barl's Wall!" retorted Gar. "Or of appointing Conroyd Jarralt my Master Magician!"

"You have to! Who else is there powerful enough to manage the job? You have to appoint him Master Magician, even if it's only for a while! Until Durm gets better, since you're so sure he won't die or wake up an addled wreck. 'Cause if you don't, if you try Weather-Working alone, without help, and somethin' goes wrong, that more'n likely means you'll be dead and Jarralt'll be king and then what'll the rest of us do?"

"Are you deaf?" cried Gar. "I will not do it! I have a Master Magician!"

"No, Gar! What you've got is a lump of bloody meat held together with catgut and pothering and prayers and you can't—"

"*Enough!*" Gar shouted, livid with pain. His arm came up, fingers fisted—and the room was filled with furious power.

Asher felt the magic hit him. Felt it lift him and toss him like a bundle of kindling on fire from the inside out. He flew backwards. Hit the bed. Bounced off it again, slammed into the wall, then slid into a crumpled heap on the carpet. Every sleeping bruise woke and started screaming. Deafened, he lay there feeling warm blood trickle from his nose, his mouth. Smelling scorched air. Beneath the pain there was fear.

Bleached white and still as stone, Gar stared back at him. Watched as he groped his way to his feet and half sat, half collapsed onto the bed. Watched as he touched the blood on his face and considered his crimsoned fingertips.

"Asher," he said at last. "I—"

Asher lifted a hand and Gar fell silent. Turned on his heel and disappeared into his privy closet. There came the sound of water running into a basin. The opening and closing of a cupboard. Then he came out again carrying the basin and a soft white cloth. Closed the immeasurable distance between them and waited.

Silently Asher took basin and cloth and cleaned his face of blood. The sharp pounding pain subsided, but the fear remained. Translated slowly into anger. Still unspeaking, he handed back the basin and stained white cloth, stood and pushed past Gar to stand once more at the window. His bones ached. Looking outside he saw a horse and rider draw to a halt in the Tower's front courtyard. Saw a liveried servant—Daniyal—appear and take the animal's reins.

He knew that horse. Knew its rider, too.

"Pellen Orrick's here," he said, not turning around.

"Asher..."

"I'll go down and see what he wants while you finish tidying yourself ready to speak to the staff. After that you'd best get over to the infirmary. See how Durm's doin' this morning. And Darran. The ole man'll howl like a girl if you don't make a fuss over 'im, take him some flowers and a box of sweetmeats."

"*Asher...*"

Still he refused to turn round. Couldn't trust what his face might show. "Reckon that'll be the first and last time you ever raise a hand to me, Gar. Reckon you do it again, with magic or without, and that'll be the end of that."

Subdued, his voice small in the large round room, Gar said, "Yes. Asher, I'm sorry. Forgive me."

Now he risked revealing his face. Looked at Gar for long moments and saw that the prince's contrition was genuine. He nodded. "You're grievin'."

"That's no excuse."

He didn't want to talk about it. Wanted to forget it had happened, forget that this Gar, magician Gar, wasn't the man he'd made friends with in Dorana's market square a lifetime ago. That this man was about to become a king, and contained in his fingertips the power to kill. "Anythin' you need me to say to Orrick?"

Gar shook his head. In his eyes understanding and a reluctant acceptance. "No. Not that I can think of."

"Fine," he said, and headed for the chamber door.

"Asher!"

He slowed. Stopped. Waited.

"I'll think on what you said. About Durm. And Conroyd Jarralt."

"Good."

"And I truly am sorry. It will never happen again, I swear."

He nodded, and kept on walking.

Pellen Orrick was waiting halfway down the Tower's front steps. Immaculate and self-contained as ever, the Guard captain looked at him closely and said, "Are you all right?"

"Aye," said Asher, meeting his sharp gaze full-square. "Why wouldn't I be?"

"No reason," said Orrick after a brief hesitation. "Beyond the obvious, that is." Beneath the spit and polish he looked weary. Sick at heart. "We got the family up safe and sound, just after dawn. Barlsman Holze took them to the palace directly. The infirmary."

With an effort, Asher blotted out memory. *Red blood and white bone and black flies, crawling.* "No sign of Matcher, I s'pose?"

"I'm sorry."

He'd known before asking. Had to ask anyway. "So, what now?"

Orrick shrugged. "Now we wait for the results of the physical examination. Holze, my men and I combed the accident site before retrieving the bodies, looking for any sign of tampering. Anything that could suggest that someone somehow sent the carriage over the Eyrie on purpose, with or without magic. We found nothing."

"That's good. Ain't it?"

Another shrug. "That depends. People like explanations for things, Asher. That's their nature."

"I s'pose. Nix is lookin' at the bodies now, you say?"

"Nix and Holze."

"And they really can tell if there's been magic used?"

"Holze says so," said Orrick. He was silent a moment, inspecting the nearby treetops. Looking for crimes? Probably. The law was Pellen Orrick's bread and butter and blankets. "He kept vigil all night. He's a good man. A holy man. If we can't trust his findings, and Nix's, we're all in trouble."

"D'you reckon they will find anythin'?"

"No," said Orrick, grimacing. "Borne was a great king. Revered by everyone. The queen was loved. Princess Fane respected, and accepted by all as the WeatherWorker in Waiting. There's not a soul in Lur who'd want them dead."

Asher looked at him sidelong. "Gar might."

"*What?*"

"Don't tell me you ain't considered the idea, Captain. Gar's got his magic now. Might be he decided he'd make a better WeatherWorker than his sister and didn't want all the folderol and kerfuffle of a schism over the matter."

Pellen Orrick fell back a pace and stared at him, his expression a mixture of disbelief and horror. "Asher, are you serious? Do you truly want me to consider His Highness responsible for this tragedy? Is it what *you* believe? Don't forget, it's only by Barl's grace that he and the Master Magician survived!"

"Could be it was planned that way."

Orrick seized his arm. "Asher, I charge you straight: if you have any proof or knowledge that this was no accident, you cannot stay silent. *Was* it deliberate murder? Tell me!"

Pulling free, he said, "I ain't got the first idea, Captain. I don't reckon so. But even if it was, there's no way Gar were involved."

"*Not* involved?" Orrick glared. "Then why in Barl's blessed name would you—"

"Because I can think of at least one man who'll say it's possible!" he said. "Maybe even likely. Can't you?"

Some of the angry colour faded from Orrick's face. His eyes narrowed and he folded his arms across his chest. "Lord Jarralt."

"Exactly. And you need to be ready for him, Captain. He'll stir up trouble if he can. Claim the kingdom needs a seasoned magician as WeatherWorker. And without Durm to stand behind Gar as the heir, things could get real nasty real fast."

"What do you mean, without Durm? I'd not heard the Master Magician was dead."

"He ain't. Not yet, any road. But between you and me and the anchor, it ain't lookin' good. And Durm dead'd suit Conroyd bloody Jarralt right down to the ground. So I'm just sayin', Captain. Keep your eye on him. Don't let him bully you into makin' a findin' that suits him more than you or the kingdom."

Now the faintest of smiles was curving Orrick's thin lips. "For a fisherman, Asher, you display a remarkable grasp of politics."

"Aye, well, I'm a fast learner," he said, scowling.

"Speaking of His Highness," said Orrick after an appreciative pause, "how is he this morning?"

He shrugged. "Fine." Orrick's eyebrows lifted. With an effort, silently cursing the Guard captain's instincts, he smoothed his tone. "Grievin', of course. Looks a bit the worse for wear, which is only to be expected. But he's fine."

"I'm glad to hear it," said Pellen Orrick. "Because the kingdom needs stability, Asher. There's nothing a man in my line of work likes less than a lack of stability. It tends to make people...frisky."

From inside the Tower came a loud lamentation, voices male and female raised in disbelieving shock and pain. Daniyal, still holding Orrick's horse at a discreet distance, looked around, alarmed.

Asher winced, then sighed. "He's told 'em. Now we're in for it."

Orrick clasped his shoulder briefly. "I must get to the palace. With luck Holze and Nix will know by now if there was magical foul play. Will you tell His Highness the bo—his family is safely retrieved?"

Asher nodded. "Aye."

"He'll want to see them, of course. Tell him that provided Holze and Nix have finished their examinations, I have no objection." Orrick frowned. "I hope Nix thinks to...put them to rights. His Highness shouldn't have to see them...like that."

"No," he said after a moment. "He shouldn't."

"Good morning then," said Orrick. He collected his horse, mounted neatly, economically, and trotted away.

Daniyal came slowly up the Tower steps, looking to Asher for instructions.

"Go inside," Asher told him. "The prince has news for you."

Daniyal ran. Asher stayed on the Tower steps, letting the sunshine soak into his bones. Willing it to melt the shards of ice still chilling him to the marrow. Familiar footsteps sounded behind him and he turned.

"So. That's done," Gar said grimly. Dressed head to toe in unrelieved black, his hair had been confined in a tight plait. Black ribbon was threaded through the braiding. "What did Orrick want?"

Asher told him. Gar took the news in silence.

"You goin' along to the palace now?" said Asher.

"Once I've eaten. You'll join me?"

"S'pose," he said, shrugging.

Gar's icy expression fractured, revealed a churning of emotion. "I've said I'm sorry. I've sworn it won't happen again. What else do you want from me?"

What he wanted, Gar couldn't give him. Nobody could. The dead were dead and couldn't be brought back to life, nor an unfamiliar world made trustworthy once more. Gar was staring at him. Angry. Fearful. Uncertain. He shook his head. Smiled, just a little. "Griddle cakes, berry syrup and hot buttered toast."

Gar's face flooded with relief. "I think I can manage that. Come on. We'll eat in the solar, quickly, and then go to the palace. There's a lot to be done today."

Aye, there was. And none of it pleasant. In silence, he followed Gar back into the Tower, where the housemaids were weeping and even Willer's tongue was stilled.

One of Nix's myriad assistants came forward to greet Gar and Asher as they entered the Royal Infirmary's reception room. She bowed low then clasped her hands behind her back. The green badges on her collar, denoting her status as a fifth-year apprentice, winked in the bright glimlight.

"Your Highness." Her voice was calm, her face smooth, polite, but there was a horrified sympathy deep in her eyes. "I'll tell Pother Nix you're here."

She withdrew, and some moments later Nix joined them. He looked exhausted; Asher realised that the sagging, wrinkled blue robe he wore this morning was the same one he'd worn last night.

"Your Highness," said the pother, and offered a perfunctory bow. "How are you this morning?"

"Well enough," said Gar. "How is Durm?"

"Still with us, sir. His will is extraordinary. I think any other man would have succumbed to his injuries by now."

Some of the tension eased from Gar's face. "Not if he had you as his pother. May I see him?"

"Perhaps later. To be truthful, there was some agitation during the night. We've got him quiet again, well dosed with calming herbs. I wouldn't like to see our good work fly out the window quite so soon."

"Agitation? Do you mean—"

"I'm sorry, Your Highness," Nix said, and pressed a hand to Gar's arm. "No sign of awareness, as such. Just an excitation of the nerves. It's to be expected, with this kind of injury."

"I see," said Gar, and cleared his throat. "Well, you know best, Nix. And you have my complete confidence."

"Thank you, sir. I'll do my utmost to ensure it's not misplaced."

Gar nodded, and banished the last betraying emotion. "So. If I can't see my Master Magician, can I at least pay a visit to my secretary?"

"Certainly you may," said Nix, and smiled his relief. "Indeed, you'll make the old gentleman's morning."

"He is well?"

"Well enough to leave us soon, I believe. If you'd care to follow me?"

As Nix moved towards a nearby corridor, Asher touched Gar's elbow. "I don't need to see Darran too, do I? Like as not one look at my face'll drive the ole crow straight into a relapse and Nix'll have my guts for garters. Why don't I just go and—"

"No," said Gar. "I've got something important to say to both of you, and I want you in the same room when I say it. Don't worry. I'll protect you from Nix. Now come along. We don't want to keep the good pother waiting."

Swallowing a groan, Asher fell into step.

Darran had been removed to a small private chamber a short walk from the reception area. Propped up in bed and looking ridiculous in a pale pink nightgown, when he saw the prince the faint colour in his cheeks faded altogether.

"Oh, sir! Sir!" he cried, struggling to throw back his blankets.

As Nix withdrew, closing the chamber door behind him, Asher propped himself against the wall and Gar moved to the bedside. "Lie still, old friend. Nix tells me you're doing well and might even escape confinement later today—provided you do nothing foolish."

"I fancy I've been foolish enough already," murmured Darran, sinking back against his pillows. One thin veined hand stole out, fingers brushing against Gar's black silk sleeve. His expression was beseeching. "Oh, sir. Dear sir. Tell me it isn't true. Tell me your ruffian friend there has played a cruel trick on me. It would be like him, after all. Tell me anything...except that they're dead."

Gar shook his head. "I wish I could. I'm sorry."

Darran burst into gulping, gasping tears. Gar sank to the edge of the bed beside him and opened his arms. Clutching, coughing, Darran continued to weep, his face buried against Gar's shoulder.

"I'm sorry—I'm so sorry—"

Gar patted his back, stroked his hair. "I know, Darran. I know."

Skewered with pity, Asher looked away. He had no time for scarecrow Darran but even so...the ole fool's grief was genuine. Was a knife, opening half-healed wounds. *Red blood and white bone and black flies, crawling...a friend, addled and drooling...a tired old man broken by a mast, alone and abandoned and calling his name...*

Imagination lashed him like a whip. Smarting, he shoved his hands deep into his pockets and set his jaw. He wasn't going to cry, he wasn't, he wasn't. Tears were nothing but a waste of good saltwater.

At last the old man stopped his ragged weeping. Stared into Gar's tearless face and whispered, "Oh, sir. Sir. What are we going to do?"

"What we must, Darran. Go on without them."

"Without them?" Darran echoed. Fresh tears spilled. "Dear sir... I'm afraid I don't know how."

Gar reached into his tunic, withdrew a black handkerchief and held it out. Speechless, Darran blotted his sallow cheeks dry and let the damp crumpled silk fall to his lap.

"In truth, Darran, neither do I," Gar said. "But there must be a way. And if there isn't, we'll have to make one. The kingdom needs me, and I need you. More than I ever have before. Can I count on you?"

"Sir!" said Darran. "As if you need to ask!"

Gar smiled and patted his hand. "I don't want to take you for granted. Darran, I have a huge favour to beg of you. One that will tax your loyalty and endurance to their very limits, I fear. But I wouldn't ask such a sacrifice of you if I didn't think it was important. Will you hear me out? Please?"

The old man flushed faintly pink, like a maiden at her first Festival dance. "Well, of course, sir. You must know there's nothing I won't do for you."

Asher rolled his eyes. Silly ole fool...

"Thank you, Darran," said Gar. His pale face was settling into new and unaccustomed lines. He looked years older now, and grim. "Asher?"

Suspicious, he took a reluctant step towards the bed. "Aye?"

"I know there's scant love lost between you two," Gar began carefully. "That you take great delight in puncturing each other's consequence, as often and as publicly as possible. There is fault and provocation on both sides, though I think you'd rather die before admitting it. But I also know you both love me, and I hope you know that love is returned, as for a crusty old uncle, say, and an irascible brother."

Asher raised an eyebrow. "We s'posed to guess which one of us is which?"

"Hold your tongue, you impertinent guttersnipe!" snapped Darran. "His Highness is speaking!"

"*Please!*" said Gar, glaring.

Instantly contrite, Darran lowered his head. "Your Highness."

"Sorry," Asher muttered.

Darran snorted. "*That* was convincing."

"Barl save me!" cried Gar. Overhead, the air beneath the chamber ceiling thickened. Darkened. A flickering tongue of lightning licked the underbelly of the looming cloud and the chamber's glimfire lamps sparked and sputtered. "Must I find bandages to stuff in your chattering mouths? *Listen* to me! This kingdom faces its gravest crisis since Trevoyle's Schism. *I* face the darkest, most demanding days of my life, and I'd rather not face them alone."

"You are not alone, sir," said Darran, offended. "You have me, for as long as there's breath in my body."

"I know, but it's not enough!" Gar slid off the bed and began to pace the small chamber. "Don't you understand? I need *both* of you! I've always lived a public life, but this will be different. As Weather-Worker I will be scrutinised as never before. I may be my father's legitimate heir but my journey has been, to say the least, unorthodox. With every eye upon me I can't afford the slightest stumble. For if I fall, not one Doranen hand will reach out to help me to my feet. Instead they'll clutch the sleeve of Conroyd Jarralt, the only other magician we have who's capable of wielding Weather Magic. It is the last thing my father would've wanted. I *can't* let Conroyd win! If he wins—"

"Er...Gar?" said Asher.

Gar turned. "What?"

He considered the cloud-obscured ceiling. "Are you s'posed to do that?"

"What?"

"That," he said, and pointed.

Gar stopped. Looked. "Oh." He frowned. "Probably not." He snapped his fingers and the incipient thunderstorm vanished. "Asher—"

Damn, damn, damn. This was going to give him ulcers, he just *knew* it. "I get it," he sighed. "You need a united household. Me and Darran singin' the same song."

Gar's expression softened. "Precisely. I don't ask you to love each other—I'm not that much of a fool—but I do ask you to support each other, at least in public. Because in supporting each other, you support me. And Barl knows, in the weeks and months ahead I shall need all the support I can get!"

Asher heaved another sigh. "No need to fret yourself. Reckon I can stomach playin' nice with Darran here, at least till all this upset's settled down. Provided we ain't talkin' years."

"Not exactly a ringing endorsement, but I'll take what I can get," Gar murmured, faintly smiling. He turned his head. "Darran?"

Darran had the look of man who had bitten into an apple and found half a worm. "Your Highness?"

Returning to the bed, Gar rested a hand on the old man's blanketed knee. "Please. I know he's a ruffian and a reprobate and a thorn in your side...but he's not all bad. Would I have him for a friend if he was?"

Darran's thin fingers hovered for a moment, then curled around Gar's hand. "Of course not, sir. Never fear. I will do precisely what you ask, no matter how difficult—" He flicked a dark look sideways. "—or painful—the task proves to be."

Leaning down, Gar pressed his lips to Darran's forehead. "Thank you."

"I want to return to work," said Darran. "Will you tell Nix to release me?"

"No," said Gar. "You'll stay in that bed until you're quite recovered."

Defeated, Darran slumped against the pillows. "Then can you at least do something about his dreadful medicine?"

Gar nearly laughed. "No, Darran, I'm sorry to say I can't. I can call lightning from a clear sky, snow from a sunbeam and rain from a red dawn, but I am powerless in the face of those bloody awful potions."

Darran heaved a lugubrious sigh. "That's most unfortunate, sir."

"It is, isn't it?" said Gar, smiling, and touched his fingers to the old man's cheek.

Nix was waiting for them in the reception area. "Your Highness."

The warmth and brief amusement had disappeared from Gar's face. "I understand my family was brought here for examination by you and Barlsman Holze."

"Yes, Your Highness."

"Your examination is complete?"

"Yes, sir."

"I wish to see them."

"Certainly, Your Highness. Allow me to—"

"No need," said Gar. "I know the way."

Asher swallowed a groan and started after him. As Nix fell into step beside him he glanced sidelong at the pother and muttered, "You sure? They weren't exactly portrait material last time I saw 'em."

Nix's face spasmed in an uneasy mix of anger and understanding. "To the best of my ability, that has been rectified. What do you take me for?"

Asher grimaced. "A good pother," he admitted, and let Nix hurry him along in Gar's impatient wake with an imperious wave of his hand.

CHAPTER FIVE

The palace's dead room was located underground, two floors below the infirmary wing. The chill was pronounced, the silence complete. Two City guards stood sentinel by the double-doored entrance. They stepped aside as Gar approached and bowed as he and Nix swept past unseeing. Asher, who shared a weekly pint at the Goose with both of them, acknowledged each with a nod and followed Gar into the dead room's antechamber, where he drifted into a cold white corner and held his tongue.

Holze was lighting the Barlscandle in the chapel nook cut into one stark white wall. Dressed in his most dignified crimson, cream and golden robes, he looked wan of face and grossly old, almost transparent with grief and weariness. As though his cape of office was too heavy to bear. He turned at their entrance. "Your Highness!" With an effortful puff he blew out the taper, discarded it on the floor and approached Gar with outstretched arms. "My dear, dear boy. How are you this sad morning?"

Gar suffered Holze's embrace of peace without protest, but stepped back once the elderly cleric released him. "Well enough, sir. Yourself?"

Tears welled in Holze's red-rimmed eyes. "Indeed, my heart is heavy."

"What did your examination of my family's bodies reveal?"

Holze exchanged a discomfited glance with Nix. "Ah...yes. The examination. Pother Nix...?"

Nix cleared his throat. "Captain Orrick has charged us to keep our findings secret until his final report is complete."

Gar nodded. "Asher. Send to Captain Orrick and command him to make his report to the existing Privy Council two hours hence. I'll want you there too. Dress appropriately."

"Me?" he said, startled.

Gar ignored him. "Nix," he continued, "as far as the conduct and findings of the examination are concerned, Holze will speak for you both. Your duty lies at Durm's bedside. Return to him now, and do not leave him again unless it's to tell me he's awake and ready to fulfil his role as my Master Magician."

Struck dumb, Nix gaped. "Your Highness," he said at last, faintly.

"I would have privacy now," said Gar, raking his cold gaze over all their faces. "Leave."

There was only one other door in the dead room's antechamber. Gar opened it, entered the chamber beyond and thudded the door shut behind him.

In the silence that followed, Pother Nix blew out his cheeks and said, "*Well!* Of all the high and mighty—"

"Poor boy," said Holze, shaking his head. "He's clearly undone with grief. Careful handling, that's the key. Barl knows he's a fine young man but he does have a temper, though he's seldom shown it. I wonder how best we can convince him to..."

As one, they exchanged glances then turned and stared at Asher.

He folded his arms across his chest and stared back, unimpressed. "Don't you go lookin' at me," he advised them sourly. "I ain't got a death wish. You're his spiritual advisor, Barlsman Holze, and you're his official physicker, Pother Nix. Those are sacred callings, ain't they. Me? I just work here. Now I suggest you do like the good prince said, eh? Unless you're looking for new positions and a change of scenery."

And with that sage advice he left them to their business, so he might attend to his.

Privy Council? *Privy Council?* Ha! *Now* what was Gar up to?

The dead room was cold. Well, it had to be, didn't it? Dead flesh rotted. Even when magically preserved, in the end it still rotted. Best not to give nature a head start, then. Best to beat back the ravages of decay for as long as possible, with whatever weapons came to hand.

Cold was the first.

Shivering, Gar stood with his shoulderblades pressed to the chamber's heavy door and kept his eyes closed. One glimpse of those three shrouded figures had been enough. They were here in the dead room, laid out on plain wooden tables. What else did he need to know? To see?

Their unsmiling faces. Their unmoving lips. Their still, unbreathing bodies.

If he didn't, would he ever believe this nightmare was real? Or would he spend the rest of his life waking each and every morning to think, no, no, it's all right! It was just a dream!

The idea was unbearable. He had to look. No matter how dreadful, how haunting, how unspeakable the images might be, he had to look his fill until truth overcame hope. Until he could begin to accept the inescapably altered landscape of his life.

Slowly, he opened his eyes. The first thing he truly saw was colour. Vases of sweet pink pamarandums stood in niches cut into the whitewashed walls. Their scent danced in the air. Tickled his nose. Cloyed in his mouth.

He was going to be sick.

Somehow he swallowed the flooding bile, just as last night he'd swallowed Nix's gross potion. Ah, the things one did when one was a king.

Was nearly a king.

"I know you never believed me, Fane," he said to the smallest of the shrouded shapes before him, "but I really don't want to be WeatherWorker. I wish there'd been time to convince you I was telling the truth. Do you believe it now, wherever you are?"

Silence.

He stepped away from the door. Folded his arms across his black silk chest and tucked his fingers into his armpits. Taking another step, then another, he found himself standing not quite an arm's length away from his family, lying so still beneath their kindly covering sheets. As part of his ritual offices Holze had laid a twisted strand of Barlsflowers on each breast. That each small bouquet sat undisturbed and unmoving hammered home, like a nail through his heart, the fact that they were dead.

"I don't know what to say to you, Father. Mama. Little sister. You died and I didn't. What can I say, faced with a truth so ugly? 'Sorry'? It hardly seems adequate."

There was something...wrong...with the shape of his father's hidden body. From the shoulder region down it looked strangely flat.

Imagination stirred. Recoiled. He wasn't going to think about that.

"Durm survived too," he said. "Nix says his hopes are slim, but I don't think he'll die. I'd have to appoint Conroyd his successor if he died and Durm won't want to give him the satisfaction. I know I bloody don't."

He held his breath, then, waiting to hear his mother's loving, scolding voice. "*Don't swear, darling. It isn't nice.*" The silence persisted. He stared at her shrouded silhouette, willing her to speak. A lock of her hair had escaped the confining sheet. It shimmered in the dead room's glimlight, just as once, only yesterday, so long ago, it had shimmered in the sunshine as she laughed. He longed to touch it. To wind that gentle curl about his fingers and tug, teasing, as once he'd tugged and teased as a boy.

He couldn't. What if that glorious golden hair felt dead, as she was dead? What if it came away in his hand like straw severed from the living earth? It would be a desecration...

His lungs were clamouring. He let out his pent-up breath in a sobbing rush and sucked in cold pamarandum-tainted air. The scarlet spots dancing before his eyes dimmed, and his frantic heart eased.

He knew then he couldn't look at them unshrouded. Couldn't bear to poison living memory with dead flesh. All he could do was accept their passing. Be true to their hopes and dreams for him, for the kingdom they had loved their whole lives, and pledge his own life to its ceaseless service.

"Pellen Orrick is investigating, but I think this was just a terrible accident," he told them. "Barl would never let it be otherwise. For six and a half centuries she's watched over us. Protected us. There's no reason she'd abandon us now. This was an accident."

Faintly, through the room's solid door, he heard voices. The heavy tread of booted feet. The City Guard, changing over. Four souls among the thousands now resting in the palm of his hand. But was his palm big enough to hold them all safely? Heart pounding anew, he examined that palm. Every line of it. Every crease. And thought... *perhaps not.*

The palm became a fist, shaking. In his blood the power burned, yearned, yammered for freedom.

It was big enough. It had to be.

"And it *was* an accident," he said. "Wasn't it?"

The shrouded figures before him didn't answer.

He sighed. Relaxed his fist and tucked his cold fingers away again. The hunger in his blood receded and, with its siren song silenced, he was able to think more clearly.

He wasn't crying.

This was his family, laid out like butcher's kill for housewifely perusal. Why was he so calm? So detached? Surely that couldn't be right. Shock didn't last this long, did it? Here he was, face to face with his family's broken bodies, decaying even as he stood there watching. Shouldn't he be feeling *something*? Something other than physical, fleshly cold?

And oh, dear Barl preserve him, he was cold. Cold to the fingertips, cold to the marrow. Cold to the centre of his heart.

Is that what had happened to his tears? Were they frozen? Unable to flow? He'd wept, surely, the last time he'd thought his father dead. He was certain he remembered weeping then. In that barn. Buried in straw. Yes, yes, he'd wept then. Quietly, so Asher wouldn't hear him.

So shouldn't he be howling now, like a dog? With his father and mother and sister smashed to pieces on a mountain, scraped piecemeal off the rocks, brought here to this cold white room of death, shouldn't he be *howling*?

"I'm sorry," he whispered to his rotting flesh and blood. "I don't know what's wrong with me."

In less than two hours' time he would face Conroyd Jarralt in the Privy Council. Lay the matter of these deaths to rest so that his family might rest too. In peace. Forever. In less than two hours' time he would be named the next king of Lur.

So soon. So dreadfully soon. Fear, soft and secret, fluttered in the pit of his belly.

"Can I do this, Father? Am I even a shadow of the man you were? If not, the fault is mine. All that's good and true in kingship I learned by watching you. I'll do my best not to betray that legacy. I promise."

But what if it was a promise he couldn't keep? What if his best efforts proved inadequate to the task? What then? In his imagination he heard Fane's laughter, scornful and scouring.

"Then, brother dear, our parents and I won't be alone for long."

Shuddering, he dropped to his knees. Grasped the end of his father's wooden table with desperate fingers.

"No," he whispered. "You're wrong, Fane. You were always wrong. I will not fail. As Barl is my witness...*I will not fail.*"

In the sun-shafted Privy Council chamber, Conroyd Jarralt looked at Pellen Orrick with guarded dislike and an imperfectly disguised disappointment. "An accident? You're certain?" His tone implied that only an idiot could believe such a thing.

Asher let his gaze march along the council chamber's velvet-burdened curtain rails. Poor bloody Orrick. His back was so stiff and straight you could snap a tree trunk across his spine with a single blow, and his face was blank, battened down like Restharven Harbour in a storm. Seemed like the captain enjoyed Privy Council meetings just as much as he did.

"As sure as I can be, my lord. Certainly I've found no evidence or proof of deliberate malice," Orrick replied.

Asher looked at him then, marvelling how he could stay so calm in the face of Jarralt's hostility. Just a little something in the eyes, mayhap. Some flash or flicker of distaste.

Jarralt sneered. Of them all he seemed to be the only one who'd enjoyed a tranquil night's sleep. Still handsome, still arrogant, wrung by neither grief nor despair, even his clothing was ostentatiously bright: forest green instead of black. There was lace at his throat and a diamond winking like a strumpet in one ear. "How hard have you looked? It's not quite a day since it happened. I find it difficult to believe you could have reached your conclusion of 'accident' so swiftly."

"My lord, I have exhausted all avenues of enquiry," Orrick replied evenly. "There are, after all, only two possible explanations for what happened. Either it was an accident or a murderous attack. Quite apart from the fact that nobody in his or her right mind would attempt to slaughter our entire royal family, the Eyrie was closed to the public yesterday. There is only one road in or out and two of my guards were posted at the turn-off to warn away the general citizenry. Nobody approached them."

Holze said, "Why didn't they raise the alarm when the family failed to return in good time?"

"Because Her Majesty dismissed them, sir," replied Orrick.

"The criminal, or criminals, might already have been hiding at the Eyrie, or somewhere close by," said Jarralt.

Asher cleared his throat. "I don't reckon so, my lord. The picnic was decided on the spur of the moment. Nobody knew ahead of time."

Jarralt burned him with a look. "So you say."

"And I," said Gar. "If that is of any interest to you, Conroyd."

"Everything about this business interests me," said Jarralt. Then added, after a pause just long enough to be insulting, "Your Highness."

Pellen Orrick cleared his throat. "Furthermore, both Barlsman Holze and Royal Pother Nix assure me that no trace of arcane interference can be found in or on the bodies."

"That's exactly so," said Holze. "Nix and I examined them most rigorously. No taint of magic was present."

Jarralt scowled. "I wish to examine them myself. As a Privy Councillor, I have the right."

A frozen pause. Asher didn't dare look at Orrick, or Gar. Then Holze rested admonishing fingertips on his colleague's indecently decorative sleeve. "It may well be your right, Conroyd, but I doubt it would be wise. Or well received."

Face darkened with blood, Jarralt snatched his sleeve free. "Is that an accusation?"

Holze sighed. "No, old friend. It's a warning."

"Of what? For what?" demanded Jarralt. "Am I a Privy Councillor or not? Do I have the right to satisfy my concerns or don't I? The king is *dead*, Holze!"

The cleric flushed. "I know that, Conroyd. I held his poor broken body in my own two hands! Kissed his cold brow with my own lips! I know that he is dead!"

"Then you of all people should want this matter investigated thoroughly!"

"I'm sure it has been," Holze said wearily.

"But I—"

"*Think*, Conroyd! There are only two people in all the kingdom who can be considered worthy of the WeatherWorker's crown. You and Prince Gar. Surely you see it's impossible for you to involve yourself in any investigations. Instead you must trust that I, Pother Nix, and our good Captain Orrick here, have ascertained the truth of the matter. Without any fear or favour."

Asher glanced sideways at Orrick. The man's hatchet face was sharper than ever as he watched the confrontation with eyes that drank in every gesture, every hesitation, and gave away not a single thought of his own. Crafty bugger.

Jarralt's teeth were clenched, muscle leaping along the line of his sculptured jaw. "Holze—"

"Conroyd, *please!*" said Holze, so moved that he thumped a fist to the tabletop before him. "Do you think I'd not be thorough? I assure you, I was. While at the Eyrie I examined the remains of the carriage horse *and* what was left of the carriage. I also did a casting of the area around the lookout. Now while I'm the first to admit I'm no Durm, still I fancy my skills are sufficient for these tasks. Not to mention the fact I am Barl's devoted servant, dedicated to truth and justice. I would solemnly swear on my chapel's altar in front of all the kingdom, neither the horse nor the carriage nor any of the royal family were tampered with, and I support wholeheartedly Captain Orrick's findings. This dreadful event was caused by a caprice of fate, and not by any malignant human agency. Barl, in her infinite, unknowable wisdom, has called Their Majesties and Her Royal Highness home. It is not for us to question why."

Jarralt's lips twisted. "I'm sorry, Holze, but I find that hard to believe."

"Nevertheless," said Gar, stirring in his dead father's seat, "you will believe it. Unless you wish to accuse Barlsman Holze, Pother Nix and Captain Orrick of corruption and conspiracy? Perhaps even murder? If so, I hope you have the proof. Barl's Laws are pointed in the matter of baseless allegations, sir. Some might even say unforgiving. As you well know."

"What I know," said Conroyd Jarralt, "is that this matter is far too serious for sweeping under the nearest convenient carpet with a havey-cavey enquiry and a mouthful of religious platitudes."

"Meaning, my lord?" asked Orrick, scrupulously polite.

Jarralt spared him a scant look. "Meaning the account of yesterday's...accident...is incomplete."

Gar regarded him through narrowed eyes. "Conroyd, how many more times must I tell you? You asked me last night if I remembered what happened and I said no. You've asked me here, twice, and still the answer is no. Can you honestly believe a third asking will magically elicit a different answer? Perhaps Durm will be able to satisfy your curiosity when he—"

"When?" scoffed Jarralt. "Don't delude yourself. The man is—"

"Alive," said Gar softly. Dangerously.

Jarralt smiled, an unpleasant baring of teeth. "But for how long?"

"Nix tells me there's hope."

"Nix is a fool who tells you what you want to hear," said Jarralt.

Asher stirred. "That ain't true. He's a good man with the kingdom's best interests at heart. If he says there's hope for Durm, you can believe it, my lord. And even if there ain't, it's the prince's decision who gets made Master Magician next. Nobody else's."

The council chamber fell utterly silent. Jarralt turned his head, eyes glittering with rage. "You dare? You *dare* to speak to me like that?"

Before Asher could answer, Gar said, "He speaks as my friend... and a member of this Privy Council."

"*What?*"

Horrified, Asher looked at Gar. "Wait a minute. Sir. I never—"

"I need you," Gar said, his eyes not leaving Jarralt's furious face. "As I need you, Conroyd. And Durm."

With an effort everyone could see, Jarralt thrust aside the issue of an Olken on the Privy Council. "I've seen Durm," he spat. "It's a miracle his brains weren't spilled on the road as well as half his blood. Even if he lives, you can't think he'll be of any use? That he can continue as the kingdom's Master Magician? If he lives he'll be nothing but a witless fool and you know it."

Still reeling, Asher caught his breath. Felt his heart constrict and heard a distant echo of tipsy laughter. *Jed.* Pellen Orrick looked at him, one eyebrow raised in query; he shook his head. Forced himself to breathe again, quietly, and made his fingers unclench in his lap. Orrick looked away.

Gar said, "I said I need you, my lord. I didn't say in what capacity. I have no intention of appointing a new Master Magician today."

"I wasn't aware we'd decided you had that authority," retorted Jarralt. "Orrick has yet to satisfy me that we are indeed dealing with an accident."

Gar shoved back his chair, stood and began to pace the chamber. "Barl give me strength, Conroyd! Do you truly believe I murdered my family? If so, say it. Here and now, with these good men as witnesses. And then perhaps you can explain how I managed to do so while nearly getting killed myself!"

"Even the best of plans can go awry. Or... perhaps it's that you had an accomplice!"

"An *accomplice?* What madness are you pursuing now, my lord? Who in this kingdom would—"

"Who do you think?" cried Conroyd Jarralt, and flung out an accusing arm. "*Him*, of course! Your upstart Olken!"

Asher leapt out of his chair so fast he nearly fell over. "*Me?* Are you raving? Me, kill the king? The queen? Princess Fane? Not to mention poor bloody Matcher and his horses, who never hurt a soul in their lives! You got no call to go accusin' me, nor no proof of anythin' neither! The only things I ever killed in all my days were fish and fleas! You take that back, Jarralt! You take that back right now!"

Jarralt slid from his chair like a well-oiled eel. Swallowed the distance between them in three swift strides and backed Asher into the nearest wall. One elegant manicured hand, its fingers laden with rings, flattened itself to his chest. "*Lord* Jarralt, you vermin-ridden interloper," he corrected, his voice a virulent whisper. "You misbegotten whelp. You stinking piece of Olken offal. You're behind all this, aren't you? How did you do it, hmmm? Who did you suborn with promises and lies to perpetrate this foul deed? The palace staff? A greedy minor Doranen lordling? Or was it the prince himself you bewitched into this murder? And what, in the name of all that's good and holy, did you hope to achieve by doing it? And did you really think I'd not *discover* you?"

Speechless, gaping, Asher stared into Jarralt's eyes, into bottomless blue wells of such obliterating hatred he thought he felt his heart stop beating. "You are mad, Jarralt. You're stark bloody raving."

"That'll do, my lord," said Pellen Orrick. His hand came down on Jarralt's shoulder and his fingers tightened in a warning, and a threat. "Let's all draw breath and talk like the calm custodians of the kingdom we are. Or should be."

With a wordless snarl Jarralt stepped sideways, breaking the captain's grip.

Asher looked at Orrick. "I never hurt 'em," he said. "My life on it."

"I know," said Orrick. "I have a dozen witnesses to place you at the Tower when the carriage went over the Eyrie."

"Witnesses?" He didn't know whether to be relieved or outraged. "You mean you *checked* on me?"

Orrick sighed. "Of course. I checked on you all. Even Barlsman Holze, may Barl excuse me." One by one he looked at them, his expression exasperated and uncompromising. "Gentlemen, I am Captain of this City. It is my sworn and sacred duty to uphold Barl's Laws and bring miscreants to justice. If I thought a man had done this thing I wouldn't rest until I had him in my hands. Not if he were the lordliest lord in all the kingdom. Not if he were a king himself." His hard gaze rested on Gar. "Nor even a king's son."

Gar nodded. "As well you should not. This kingdom expects no less of you, and the men who serve under your command. Orrick, you've said you think these deaths came about by misadventure, not murder. Upon peril to your very soul, I'll ask you for the last time: do you still stand by that conclusion?"

Orrick squared his shoulders and clasped his hands behind his back. "Your Highness, I do."

"Very well," said Gar. "You have the gratitude of this Privy Council for your swift and thorough examination of these events. Be advised, however, that should any new facts come to light and cause you to rethink your conclusion, we expect to hear of them immediately."

Orrick nodded. "You will, sir."

Gar turned to Jarralt, a series of thoughts shifting behind his cold green eyes. When at last he spoke his tone was mild, polite, but with an undercurrent of ice. "My lord, it's no secret we've had our differences. But I believe that honest dissent is no bad thing. If our decisions cannot withstand scrutiny then we don't deserve the authority to make them. I have accepted Captain Orrick's finding in this matter. The tragic deaths of my father, my mother and my sister—this realm's king, queen and WeatherWorker in Waiting—did not come about by any human agency. If ever I did impugn your honour in relation to this, I say now I was in error. And I offer you my hand in token of a new beginning between us."

To accept the prince's apology Jarralt had to step closer. Yield his position. Asher held his breath. If the bastard didn't do it, if he persisted in his mad claims of conspiracy and murder, the kingdom'd go up in flames, near enough...

"A new beginning," said Conroyd Jarralt, as though the words were broken glass in his mouth. He stepped forward and grasped Gar's forearm.

His fingers tight on Jarralt's sleeve, Gar smiled. "So you accept Captain Orrick's conclusion? Neither I, nor my assistant Asher, nor any man, woman or child associated with or known to me or him, did plan or execute the murder of my family, or the attempted murder of Master Magician Durm."

Jarralt's answering smile was complicated. "I accept Orrick has no evidence or proof of it. I accept he made a genuine attempt to uncover the truth of the matter. I accept...the role of honest dissenter."

Gar stared at him. "And do you also accept I am my father's true and lawful heir to the throne of Lur? To the title of WeatherWorker? Speaking bluntly, sir: do you, Lord Conroyd Jarralt, in this place and at this time, before these witnesses, accept that I am, by Barl's great mercy, your king?"

CHAPTER SIX

Jarralt's head went back, as though bracing for a blow. Asher stared, holding his breath. If Jarralt chose to fight...

But he didn't. Instead he offered Gar a curt nod. "Yes. In this place and at this time, I accept you as king. Your Majesty."

The challenging light in Gar's eyes faded. Releasing his grip on Jarralt's arm he let his lips soften into a reserved smile. "Excellent. It seems we understand one another at last, sir."

Asher nearly swallowed his tongue. Was Gar suntouched? Did he think one brief arm clasp and a grudging admission meant the end of Jarralt's opposition? Of his enmity, and his likely crusade for the crown? Did *any* of them here think that?

Bloody Holze clearly did... or wanted to. He was beaming like a maiden aunty at the birth of a new nephew. Orrick? Well, who could tell? Orrick's inscrutable face revealed nothing except, perhaps, a smidgin of grave approval. For himself, he'd as soon believe he could vault straight over the Wall. And as for Gar—

Gar was still smiling. Self-contained and seemingly satisfied. No warmth in his eyes, though. He wasn't fooled, not he, after a lifetime with these people. For there was no warmth in Jarralt's eyes either, if ever there had been or could be. This was just a breathing space in the battle. A momentary pause in hostilities. Because Conroyd Jarralt would no sooner give up his dreams of a crown than—than—the late and unlamented Princess Fane would've kissed a commoner in the street, and Gar knew it.

"And now we have that settled," he said, "we must turn to other pressing matters. Gentlemen, let us resume our seats."

Asher waited for Gar to sit, then Jarralt, before sliding back into his own chair. Was it a trick of the light or did Captain Orrick spare him the merest hint of an approving nod as he, too, sat down again? Uncertain, he folded his hands primly on the table before him. Lowered his eyelids to half-mast and let his gaze discreetly rest on Gar's face as he tried to work out what was coming next.

Gar sat in silence, collecting his thoughts. He looked remade. Gone was the magickless prince, fallible and vulnerable and endearingly human. In the space of a few scant hours tragedy had remoulded Gar into a portrait of untouchable, unreachable monarchy, as distant and unknowable as any daubed onto canvas in the last six hundred years. Asher thought it was like looking at a stranger, and felt a chill shiver through him.

"Obviously, the first order of business is to inform the kingdom of yesterday's tragic events," Gar said. "I will need you all to assist in this difficult task."

Jarralt was asked to inform members of the General Council. Barlsman Holze would see that the kingdom's Barlsmen and women were told and encouraged to offer all words of comfort to their grieving chapel districts. Asher was appointed the task of telling the palace staff and helping to coordinate the dozens of couriers and heralds required to spread the news throughout the City and the rest of the kingdom. Pellen Orrick was commanded to assist Asher in that detail, and also see to it that strict law and order was maintained in Dorana once the sad news broke.

"What about Matcher's widow?" said Asher. "She's been sittin' at home under guard since last night."

For a moment Gar looked nonplussed, as though he'd never heard of the royal coachman. Then: "Yes. Of course. Dismiss the guards and present yourself to the lady, Asher. Extend to her my deepest sympathies for her bereavement. Assure her she need have no fears of hardship; there will be a generous pension. And thank her for her discretion in this delicate matter."

Asher swallowed a groan. More grief, more tears... "Aye, sir."

With Durm indisposed, Gar continued, Barlsman Holze would announce his ascension to WeatherWorker that afternoon on the steps of Justice Hall, once the Barl's Chapel bells had tolled for the late royal family. "While there is no question of my fitness or right to assume the throne," he said, not looking at Jarralt, "the last Weather-Worker to die without first publicly declaring an heir was Queen Drea. That was more than two centuries ago. Therefore, above all, we must forestall any misgivings amongst the population: they should know their lives will continue in safety and prosperity, no matter whose head supports the crown."

"An excellent idea," Holze approved. "And what of your coronation?"

Gar frowned at his laced fingers. "Tradition dictates a Weather-Worker be crowned in the presence of his or her Master Magician."

"Then it would appear," said Conroyd Jarralt, smoothly, "we have a problem. Your Majesty."

"Not yet we don't, Conroyd."

"But as you rightly point out, you cannot be crowned Weather-Worker without—"

"Yes, I can," said Gar, glaring. "It's tradition, not law."

"That's true," conceded Jarralt. "At least as far as the coronation is concerned. However, it is stated in law that a WeatherWorker cannot rule without the guidance of a Master Magician. And while Durm draws breath today, each moment might be his last. Admit that much, at least. Your Majesty."

"I'd be a fool not to consider the possibility," said Gar, his voice thin with leashed temper. "But that's all it is: a possibility. For the good of the kingdom I shall be crowned WeatherWorker at midnight on Barl's Day after next, whether Durm is revived or not. Two weeks after that I shall reconsider his position."

Hungry as a hunting cat, Jarralt leaned forward. "Against all urgings and advice, Durm has neither named nor trained his successor. The choice will be yours."

"He felt that to prematurely appoint his own heir would be to invite...unrest," said Gar coldly. "There is historical precedent for his concern. My father was satisfied with the decision, therefore—"

"Your father did not foresee the current crisis. If he had, then we wouldn't—"

"Conroyd!" said Holze, shocked. "Please!"

Gar raised a quelling hand. "It's true our lives would be simpler had Durm made his choice before now. He didn't. And as he still breathes I have no intention of replacing him or usurping his right to name his successor. At least not until I must. His life rests in Barl's hands now, gentlemen. I suggest we wait and see what she intends to do with it before we visit this matter again."

Holze cleared his throat, breaking the charged silence. "There is one other thing we should touch upon, if only briefly."

"The funerals," said Gar. "Yes. My family shall lie a month in state, Holze, in the palace's Grand Reception Hall, so that all in the kingdom who wish to do so might pay their final respects. After that time they shall be interred privately in our house vault. Asher—"

He sat up. "Sir?"

"I'm charging you, Darran and Captain Orrick with the responsibility of arranging the public viewings."

"Sir," he said, and swallowed a sigh. He didn't mind the prospect of working closely with Orrick. But with *Darran*? "What about the actual interment? You want me to—"

Gar shook his head. "I'll worry about that. Holze, you and I will meet to discuss the matter."

"Certainly, sir," said Holze. "At your convenience, naturally. And your removal to the palace? When can we expect that?"

"The business of good government does not require my nightgown to be hung in a palace wardrobe," said Gar. "When I am more accustomed to my new estate I shall revisit the matter of leaving the Tower. Not before."

Holze, no fool, could recognise a door when it was slammed shut in his face. He nodded. "Certainly, Your Majesty."

"And the Wall, Majesty?" asked Jarralt. "The weather, and its Working?"

"Aren't matters you need be concerned with, my lord," replied Gar. "Thanks to Durm's prudence and foresight I have the necessary skills at hand."

"But lacking a Master Magician, sir, and yourself...unpractised, in the art of Weather Working, surely—"

"I am my father's son, Conroyd," said Gar. "I need no more qualification than that." He stood. "Gentlemen, you have your assigned duties. Apply yourselves to their commission without further delay."

Scrambling to his feet with the rest of them, Asher watched Gar leave the Privy Council chamber like a slender, haughty cat. Watched Conroyd Jarralt frown, wait a moment, then leave and turn out of the doorway to walk in the opposite direction. Watched Holze sigh, and smooth his unadorned braid with unhappy fingers, and follow Jarralt.

"So," said Pellen Orrick once they were alone. "Meister Privy Councillor now, eh?"

He swallowed bile. "It weren't my bloody idea!"

"I know," said Orrick. "I saw your face when he said it."

Resisting the urge to spit sour saliva on the chamber floor, he said, "About yesterday. Your findings. Was it really an accident?"

"Why?" said Orrick. "Do you doubt my competence now, along with our good Lord Jarralt?"

He scowled. "Course not. Just...it seems wrong, somehow, all those powerful magicians brought low by an *accident*."

"I see," said Orrick, amused. "Feeling a touch mortal, are you?" He shrugged. "Doranen die, Asher, just like we do. Their magic can't protect them from everything. I've known Doranen who choked on a fishbone. Broke their necks falling down a flight of stairs. Drowned in their bathtub. Death has no rhyme or reason. It comes for us all, making up its own mind as to when and how."

Still scowling, Asher scuffed at the chamber floor with his boot heel. "I know, but—"

"But you want it to make sense." Orrick laughed. "I was right last night. You do have a guardsman's mind." Sobering, he stared out of a chamber window. "If you're asking whether I think these deaths out of the ordinary, then yes, I do. But beyond that? I have neither reason nor proof to question Pother Nix and Barlsman Holze's findings. Nor your innocence, or His Majesty's, or even that of Lord Conroyd Jarralt, though as a man I find him...distasteful."

Surprised, Asher stared at Orrick. "That ain't very discreet of you, Captain."

Orrick stared back. "Why? Are you a tattle-tongue?"

He just snorted and shook his head. "Gar—His Majesty, I mean— he seems—"

"He's a king without warning, Asher. A young man whose whole family has just died in violent, sudden circumstances. He wears his royalty like a suit of armour, to keep emotion at bay." Orrick smiled then, mockery and sympathy combined. "Are you feeling slighted?"

"No," he said, affronted. "Reckon I'm feelin'..." *Sorry. Scared. Uncertain. Overwhelmed.* "Hungry."

"Then eat."

"Ha. Who's got time, Captain?"

"Call me Pellen. Since it seems we're to be working hand in glove, for a while at least. And speaking of which—"

"Aye?" he said.

"I'd like to sit down with you, once I've prepared my men for what's coming," said Orrick. "Look at calling an urgent meeting of all the guilds' representatives. When this sad news breaks, the streets will be awash in tears, I think."

Asher nodded. "And the guilds are in a better position than we are to keep their members under control. That's good thinking, Cap—Pellen."

"When you've a moment to scratch yourself send a runner down to the guardhouse," said Orrick. "I'll come up as soon after as I can."

"Provided you ain't had to lock me up for throttlin' that ole biddy Darran. 'Cause I'm tellin' you, Pellen, it ain't beyond the bounds of possibility."

"Well, don't hold back on my account," said Orrick, straight-faced. "We could meet in your cell, then, which would save me a trip to the Tower."

It took him a moment to realise the joke. Who'd have thought it? Hatchet-faced Orrick with a sense of humour.

"Ha!" he said, warmed, and headed for the door. "Very funny."

Pellen Orrick fell into step beside him. Smiled, swiftly and with a dry amusement. "I thought so."

Undisturbed by customers, Dathne was tidying shelves when she heard the first faint, wailing cries from the street outside her bookshop. Turning, she looked through the display window to see her alarmed neighbours spilling out of their premises like ants from a stick-stirred nest, pushing and shoving in a cluster round Mistress Tuttle from the bakery five doors along. Mistress Tuttle was flapping her hands in a frenzy as she spoke, her oven-flushed cheeks streaked with tears.

Dathne felt her breath catch as relief warred with sorrow. So. The news was out then. Which meant she could put down one burdensome secret, at least, and worry instead about what next Prophecy would send to try her. Not more death, she fervently hoped. Three lives—well, four if you counted poor Matcher—and five if you included Asher's father—had already been sacrificed for the sake of an uncertain future. To ensure that whatever must come to pass would come to pass, so Asher might be reborn as the Innocent Mage.

Why, Veira? she'd asked the old woman the previous night, after telling her of the royal family's fate. *Why would Prophecy need to kill so many?*

Veira's reply through the Circle Stone had been typical. *We don't know it is Prophecy's doing, child. But if it is then you should know there is a reason. Even if we can't see it for shadows.*

As the uproar in the street outside intensified, Dathne starting shoving a new shelf of books into line. Reason or not, it seemed to her that Prophecy was being needlessly harsh. Surely events might have been managed without bloodshed, and suffering, and the look on Asher's face as he fell into her outstretched arms.

Snared in memory she felt again the weight of him against her, his bone-deep trembling beneath her spreading hands. Heard for the thousandth relived time the way he exhaled her name like a prayer and drank her face down with his eyes. Fresh longing rose sharp within her like sap in the trees after winter...

No. He was the Mage and she was the Heir. It was true they walked the same path at the same time, but they must journey alone, their hands never touching, their hearts unentwined. What she felt was sentiment, pure and simple, and Prophecy had no time or use for sentiment. *She* had no time or use for it. Sentiment would kill a lot more people than Prophecy ever could.

But oh...how hard it was to deny him. Hard, and day by day getting harder, for now she knew him. *Really* knew him, not simply as the living embodiment of Prophecy but as a man.

She knew he liked malt ale better than hop. Roast chicken, not sauced duck. Liked to sing, but out of mercy refrained in public. His favourite colours were green and blue. He thought play-acting in the theatre was a ragtaggin' bloody great waste of time but would stand in front of a puppet show for an hour and never notice the time fly past. He was impatient of pretension, self-opinion and the puff-and-ruffle of guild meisters and their lackeys, yet gave his time, favours and sometimes money freely to those guild members he found in need. Complained bitterly if asked to read any kind of history book, but snuck peeks at the brightly illustrated fairy tales left lying about the shop for children to discover.

He was rude and crude and caustic and compassionate. Loyal, implacable, honest and fair. His skin against hers was a benediction, his voice at her doorstep a song.

"*Damn* you, Asher! Why couldn't you have been hateful? Or—or married, or ugly, or old? Why couldn't you have been anyone but yourself?"

"Who are you talking to, dearie?"

Startled, Dathne turned. Pushed her hands into her skirt's capacious pockets and blanked her face. "Meister Beemfield! I'm sorry, I didn't realise I had a customer. Can I help you?"

Meister Beemfield's hat was askew on his head and there were tears in his faded blue eyes. "Oh, dearie," he quavered, lost, bewildered. "Have you heard? It's the king, lass. And the queen too, and that pretty daughter of theirs. Dead, dead, all dead. The heralds are crying it throughout the City!"

"No!" she gasped, suitably shocked, and tried to squeeze out a surprised tear or two. Failing, she groped for her handkerchief and hid her face. "How awful!"

Meister Beemfield was shaking his head. "You'd best shut up your shop for the day, dearie. There'll be nobody buying books this afternoon. The heralds say there's to be an announcement at five o'clock on the steps of Justice Hall. If you like I'll escort you there now. The streets are fair thronged and there's no saying what could happen when folks are ramshackled with dismay."

He was the one who wanted to go, she realised. Wanted, and was perhaps afraid, feeling frail and overwhelmed by tragedy. Certainly he wasn't wrong about the streets. One glance through the window showed her a solid mass of townsfolk streaming along in the direction of the City's central square. One misstep, one stumble, and the old man might well be thoughtlessly trampled. For herself she could easily miss the gathering. Whatever the announcement she'd learn of it soon enough. But it meant so much to Meister Beemfield, and he was an excellent customer...

And there was a good chance Asher would be there.

"That's a very kind offer, sir," she said. "Let me get my shawl."

Lady Marnagh had been weeping. Her pale grey eyes were bloodshot and puffy and her lower lip persisted in trembling. Every so often, when she thought Asher wasn't looking, a finger crept up to capture an errant tear. He would've offered her a kerchief but still felt in awe of her. Besides, she probably had her own. Probably, she was trying to be discreet.

They stood with the rest of Justice Hall's staff inside the building, as Barlsman Holze graced the steps beyond the open double doors and prayed before the gathered multitude in the square. The mood in the hall was sombre, the silence almost complete. A muffled sob here, a shuddering sigh there: they were the only sounds aside from Holze's measured, stately voice. Magic carried his words through the air and into the hearing of the City's inhabitants, who'd crushed themselves into the square so tightly Asher doubted you'd fit even a feather in there with them. More folk crowded at the windows of the various buildings lining the square. He thought they might even have tried crowding into the guardhouse, if Captain Orr—Pellen had let them.

Staring at all those listening people he found himself counting heads. So many yellow, so many black. From up high like this he could see they formed a pattern. A lot of the yellow heads were gathered right up the front, around the base of Justice Hall's wide marble steps. Others were thick around the edges of the square, so it looked like a pie: golden pastry edges with a thick blackberry filling.

It occurred to him he'd be hard-pressed to put a name to most of the Doranen faces out there. The only Doranen he could claim to know, even slightly, were Barlsman Holze and Conroyd Jarralt. Lady Marnagh. And a few of the Doranen on the General Council. Jarralt's cronies. And only then because he couldn't avoid them. Beyond that, Doranen society was a mystery to him. Like oil and water his folk and Gar's sloshed around inside Dorana's walls, touching frequently but never quite mixing. Even as Assistant Olken Administrator he'd never had to deal with the City's Doranen. On the rare occasions over the past year or so when a Doranen was involved in Olken business, Gar had taken care of it. And when one of them invited Gar to dinner they never saw fit to include an Olken fisherman at the table. Even one who'd learned the hard way which fork to use when.

With an unpleasant shock he wondered if *Gar* could put a name to all their faces. The only times the prince mixed with his own folk was when duty or royal protocol meant he couldn't escape the encounter, or when Darran's protests and pleadings wore him down and he grudgingly accepted one of those invitations to dinner or the races or some other kind of exclusive Doranen entertainment.

Now though, thanks to disaster, that was about to change. Magickless Prince Gar could avoid his peers, but WeatherWorker King Gar was suddenly one of them. About to go sailing into strange and unfamiliar waters. And, like a rowboat tethered to a smack, Asher of Restharven was about to go sailing into them with him.

Asher bit his lip in dismay. How would the Doranen react to the notion of their almost invisible prince upon the throne of Lur? To a once-crippled outcast, more at home with the Olken than his own people, suddenly become the beating heart of all their lives? And how would they react when they realised he expected to marry one of their daughters so he might breed himself an heir?

Before the accident Gar had felt nervous at the thought of unveiling himself to them as a prince reborn. So how would it be now? He was an untried, untested magician, famous for all the wrong reasons, and now he was the king. The WeatherWorker. All that stood between Lur and the unknown dangers beyond the Wall. And not one of his own people knew if he was up to the job. To be honest, even Gar didn't know. And if he stumbled, even once, even slightly, Conroyd Jarralt and his cronies would be on him like cats on a mouse.

Asher felt his heart sink like an anchor. *Barl bloody save me! I ain't a bloody guard dog!*

Holze had finally finished entreating Barl's mercy and protection. Now he waited as the echoes from the crowd's final response died away. Feeling Lady Marnagh's disapproving gaze, Asher wrenched his attention back to the moment at hand and managed to mutter something appropriate at the tail end of the Hall's employees' heartfelt murmuring. Then he took a small step forward, the better to see the crowd and waited, hardly breathing.

"Now, good people of Dorana City, it falls upon me to answer the greatest question of all," said Holze. He wore his finest vestments; the lowering sun struck multicoloured fire from threads of gold and silver, from rubies and emeralds and deep purple amethysts. There were so many fresh blossoms tied into his braid he could've opened a flower shop. "Tradition dictates it is the Master Magician who names our next WeatherWorker. But our dearly beloved Durm still recovers from his injuries, so it falls upon me to stand in his place. Barl, in her infinite and mysterious wisdom, has decreed we must live our lives henceforth without the loving guidance of King Borne or the expectation of his glorious daughter Fane's reign thereafter. But in her magnificent adoration of us, her children, Barl has yet kept the promise made to our forebears and ensured our continued peace, prosperity and safety. Therefore in her great name I give you His Majesty King Gar, WeatherWorker of Lur!"

As a swell of sound surged from the crowd, Asher heard shocked gasps behind him. He turned and there was Gar himself, walking through the gap between the gathered Justice Hall staff. Still dressed in unrelieved black, his bruised head bare of circlet or crown, his face was pale and set in grim lines. As though completely alone he passed between his staring subjects, straight by Asher, out through the open doorway and onto the steps of Justice Hall.

When the crowd saw him the noise threatened to shatter the sky. Shrieks. Shouts. Great cries of welcome, and of woe. Somewhere in the gathered press of flesh a man's voice screamed, "King Gar! King Gar! Barl bless our King Gar!"

Another voice echoed him. Then another. And another. Then two voices in unison. Three. Ten. Thirty. Fifty. Louder and stronger, man, woman and child, the chant leaping from throat to throat like flames in a wheatfield.

"King Gar! King Gar! Barl bless our King Gar!"

There were Doranen voices raised out there, along with Olken. They were raised in here, too, Asher saw. Not as loudly as the folk outside, but with the same amount of passion. In the faces of the gathered staff he saw love, relief and a transcendent joy. Lur had a new WeatherWorker. They could go to bed tonight feeling safe, protected, knowing the world could continue unchanged, and for that they gave thanks. Which was all well and good and a nice way to finish the day, but how long would joy and gratitude last if Gar wasn't ready?

Holze had dropped to his knees, head bowed to his chest in homage to the new king. Gar left him there for three heartbeats, then bent and drew the elderly cleric to his feet. Embraced him. The crowd's chanting doubled in fervour and volume. Asher could feel his bones vibrating. The noise was so loud he thought it might bring the roof of Justice Hall down on all their heads and tumble the City's buildings into rubble and dust.

On the steps outside, Gar released his hold on Barlsman Holze and turned to face the crowd. His hands lifted high overhead and a stream of golden light burst forth from his outstretched fingertips. Up and up and up into the air it poured, and suddenly the world smelled of freesias and jasmine and all sweet things. The crowd fell raggedly silent, watching, as the raw magic coalesced over their heads, becoming a thick golden cloud.

Gar clenched his fingers into fists. The golden cloud shivered. Shuddered. Collapsed into thousands and thousands of flower petals that rained onto all the upturned faces of his people. As the crowd gasped in wonder, Asher swallowed his own surprise. It was hard to get used to Gar doing magic. It was like watching a crippled bird spread its wings and fly effortlessly, casually, the way it should've flown from birth.

"Citizens of Dorana!" Gar cried. "Yesterday there walked among you a man known in this kingdom as His Royal Highness Prince Gar of Lur. Yesterday that man died, along with all his family, and today is reborn as your king. Your servant. Barl's instrument in the world, whose only ambition is to maintain and nurture the strength of her Wall. Whose only reason for living is to keep you as you are: loved and safe and obedient to her will. Yesterday I was a prince with one father, one mother, one sister. Today I am a king with more fathers and mothers and sisters than I can count. Yes, and brothers too, aunts and uncles and cousins and children. For the people of Lur are my family now. And I will love my family unto death, and defend them from any who would wish them harm. In Barl's name I swear it, and may magic desert me if my heart and oath are not true!"

A breathless hush. A quivering silence. Then:

"King Gar! King Gar! King Gar!"

Asher felt the small tight knot in his gut unravel just a little. Gar had sounded calm. Confident. At peace with himself and the burden Barl had placed, for no good reason, on his unready shoulders.

He'd sounded like his dead father. Like a king.

As Asher watched, weak-kneed with relief, Gar started down the steps of Justice Hall. Holze reached out a hand to him, saying something in an alarmed undertone; the words were lost in the crowd's cries of adoration and acclaim. Gar ignored him. Asher pushed forward to the doorway, incredulous. Was Gar mad? He couldn't just saunter into that mob on his own! Not that he was in danger, not from any deliberate unlawful act. But all those people! The unbridled emotion! They'd want to touch him, talk to him, he'd be overwhelmed.

Horrified, Asher stared at Holze and Holze stared back, his hands spread in helpless disbelief.

"Do something," he hissed. "Start up another prayer or a hymn, quick! We can't let him—"

But it was too late. Gar had reached the bottom of the marble steps. Was stepping into the crowd. The Doranen before him fell back, pushing against the people behind them. A hesitant middle-aged Doranen man in blue brocade spoke to him. There were flower petals caught in his unbound yellow hair. Gar replied, then nodded and rested a hand on his shoulder. The man stared at Gar, speechless, then burst into sobs. Gar embraced him. Held him close for a heartbeat, then let go.

The simple gesture broke the stunned silence and the crowd's uncertain stillness. Suddenly Gar was surrounded by eager, reaching hands, Doranen and Olken both, seeking to touch their miracle king. To comfort and be comforted in this time of pain and loss and new beginnings. His aura glowing like a candle, Gar moved through the press of bodies in the square, embracing and being embraced, and his people made way for his progress. Welcomed him into their arms and their hearts and laid the ghosts of his family to rest.

Asher watched in silence for a time, then turned again to Holze. "Well. Seems he knows what he's doin' after all."

There were tears on Holze's seamed cheeks. "He is indeed his father's son," he whispered, hungry eyes following Gar's slow progress through the square. "For the first time since I saw that terrible gap in the Eyrie's fence, I am not afraid."

Asher bit his lip. "Don't s'pose you know where Lord Jarralt is, do you? Thought he'd be here for this."

"I have known Conroyd Jarralt all his life, Asher," Holze said softly. "He is many things, not all of them comfortable, but a heretic and a traitor he is not. Conroyd loves this kingdom. He would never do anything to harm it. If you believe nothing else, believe that."

There was no point arguing. Asher nodded. "Aye, sir."

"I'll return to Barl's Chapel now, and pray for their late Majesties and Her Highness. If His Majesty should need me for any reason, send a runner."

"Aye, sir," said Asher again, and stood aside to let Holze pass. Before following him back into the hall, he cast a last look over the crowd and his king. Likely Gar would be out there for hours yet, the way every last Olken and Doranen was trying to lay a hand on him. Which meant it looked like another late night for one Meister Asher, formerly of Restharven.

Hooray.

A cleared throat behind him distracted his frowning attention. He turned.

"Is the staff dismissed then, Asher?" asked Lady Marnagh. "May I send them home?"

She'd never deferred to him like that before, not in all the time he'd known her. Yet he wasn't the one who'd changed. Was this what he could expect from everybody now? Some of Gar's kingly lustre rubbed off on him? He nodded. "Might as well, m'lady. Ain't no work to be done, and they'll be wanting their families, most like."

"What about you?"

He shrugged. "Reckon I'll be stayin' on for a bit, till that crowd out there's seen its fill and gone home. Might be something the king wants doing."

"Yes, of course." She hesitated, and fresh tears brimmed in her eyes. "Will you tell His High—His Majesty how sorry I am? How sorry we all are."

"Aye."

She brushed her fingertips across his sleeve. "Thank you. Good evening to you, Asher."

"And you, Lady Marnagh."

He watched as she gathered her staff together and herded them towards the rear doors. Outside, voices in the crowd swelled and crested like the restless, roaring ocean. Abruptly reminded, suddenly homesick, he turned on his heel and followed the tail end of Marnagh's staff out of the Hall.

CHAPTER SEVEN

In the Hall stables where Cygnet had been left to browse on hay, Asher found Ballodair dozing in the box beside Cygnet, and a single stablehand polishing brass.

"You can go, Vonnie," he said. "Since there ain't no other horses to mind. I'll wait here till His Majesty returns and see the horses come to no harm."

Shy Vonnie nodded his thanks, lit the stable-yard lanterns against the creeping dusk and scarpered. Asher found an empty water bucket, upturned it and sat with his back braced against the wall between the two occupied stables. Passingly curious, Cygnet whuffled in his hair. Asher patted his nose. With no apples forthcoming the horse lost interest and withdrew to doze in the deep straw. Asher stretched out his legs, folded his hands in his lap and followed suit.

He woke some time later when somebody kicked him in the ankle. "Ow!" he said, and opened his eyes. It was dark and he was cold. "Where's Gar?"

"He's still out there," said Dathne. She was buttoned into a black woollen jacket and carried a cloth-covered basket in one gloved hand. "Hungry? I brought dinner."

He creaked to his feet. "What time is it?"

"Nearly half-seven." She put down the basket and uncovered it. The air filled with the scent of hot cornbread; he sniffed appreciatively, suddenly ravenous.

As Dathne busied herself with the basket's contents she added, "The square's still straggled with people. They won't go home till they've touched their new king, and he won't send them away, even though he must be exhausted by now. People are singing his praises up street and down. If they were afraid before, or uncertain, they aren't any more."

He held out his hand and took the napkin-wrapped food she was offering. "How'd you know I was here?"

Her smile was brief and affectionate. "Where else would you be but nearby, waiting for him?"

He shrugged, his mouth too full for speaking. The cornbread was soaked in butter; he nearly moaned aloud at the taste. She smiled again, enjoying his enjoyment, and took a dainty bite of fried chicken wing. He had melted butter running down his chin and inside his sleeve. He didn't care. She'd thought of him and brought him dinner.

She said, "Tell me, if you can: how is Master Magician Durm? Really?"

"Not dead," he replied, reaching for a plump seasoned drumstick. "Were you out in the square then? When Holze announced Gar king and he gave his pretty speech?"

"It was a pretty speech. It made a lot of people cry."

He sucked butter and chicken fat from his fingers, watching her face. "You?"

"Would you like more?" she asked, and bent to the basket. "There's plenty."

He held out his napkin and she filled it again. Bloody woman. If she had cried, she'd never tell him. Did that mean she'd never be his, if she couldn't even share that much of herself? He thought it might. Despair chilled him. He could feel his dreams and desires for her, for them, fading like mist in the morning. Once, just once, he wished he could know her true heart.

"What?" she said, staring.

He shook his head. "Nowt. This is good," he answered, and filled his mouth with more hot sweet cornbread before he said something else. Something he could never take back and would go to his long-distant grave regretting.

"Everything's going to change now," she said, bending again to fuss with the basket. "Have you thought about that?"

Every bloody moment, waking and sleeping, since the horror of Salbert's Eyrie. "A bit."

"He'll have no time for Olken administrating now. The Weather-Working will swallow him alive, just like it swallows all of them." She straightened. "I imagine he'll ask you to take over for him for good. Olken Administrator Asher. Asher of Dorana, instead of Restharven."

The words were a harpoon between his ribs. "You sound like bloody Matt," he said, more roughly than he intended, or wanted. "So I'll tell you what I told him. Dorana's my home for now, not forever."

"Fine. But while it is 'for now,' what are you going to do?" she demanded. "If the king asks you to serve him as his Olken Administrator, what will you say?"

He dropped his chewed chicken bone and the butter-stained napkin into the basket. "What d'you reckon? I'll say what I always say when he asks me to do things," he muttered. "I'll say yes."

She reached out and touched his hand. Smiling now, temper forgotten. A shock blazed through him, lightning in a hot sky. "Don't be so gloomy. There are worse ways to pass the time."

"No, there ain't," he said, fighting the urge to take the fingers that had touched him and hold them captive till the end of time. "'Cause it means I got to work hand in hand with that bloody ole Darran like he and I never wanted to kill each other every day from the first day we met. And since we did—we do—"

She laughed. "Oh dear. Sounds to me like you need an assistant. Somebody to save you from him...or him from you."

"Of course I need a bloody assistant!" he said, glowering. Reaching again to the basket he helped himself to more hot cornbread, luke-warm now, and chewed savagely. "I've needed one ever since Gar got his magic and I been left to pick up the pieces of everything else."

"Will I do?"

It took a lot of red-faced coughing and a few well-placed blows on his back to dislodge the cornbread that had gone down the wrong way. Eyes streaming, chest heaving, he stared at her. "*You* be my—ha! That's very funny, Dath!"

Her smile was unsettling: cool and contained and faintly challeng-ing. "It's not a joke."

He looked more closely and realised, no, it wasn't. "What about your bookshop?"

She shrugged. "What about it? I can hire someone to sell books for me. I've been selling them myself for a long time now, Asher. Perhaps I'd like to do something different."

He wiped his hands up and down the front of his breeches, heed-less of grease stains. If she'd sprouted hooves and a tail he doubted he'd feel more surprised. Dathne as the Assistant Olken Administra-tor. *His* Assistant Olken Administrator. It was crazy. She'd want to run back to her books inside of a week. All that pettifogging detail and dealing with the guilds. She'd lose her temper and bite them on the nose at the first sign of contrariness...

"I handle people as much as I handle books, Asher," she said, read-ing him. Drat her. "You're not the only one who has to deal with the guilds, you know. And flibbertigibbet shillyshalliers who couldn't make up their minds if their lives depended on it. Plus I'm an excellent record keeper, and well known in the City. Not to be immodest, but I'm well liked too. I could be very useful to you, in all sorts of ways."

She meant it. She really was offering herself as his assistant. "It ain't great pay," he warned her. "It's long hours and lots of argy-bargy and aggravation and no matter how hard you try you almost never please everybody. And nobody thinks you got a life of your own, they think you're there to listen to all their problems any hour of the night or day and then fix 'em with a snap of your fingers. And when you can't, or won't, they pout and whinge and threaten to lay a complaint."

She grinned. "Don't you think I know all that? After a year of lis-tening to you moaning into your ale down at the Goose, Asher, don't you think I know exactly what this job entails?"

"And you still want to do it?" When she nodded, he threw up his hands. "See? You are mad."

"If you don't want me, you can say so. But don't think I'm not serious."

"What does Matt say?"

"What's Matt got to do with it?"

He grimaced. "Seems to me you talk to him about practically everything. Seems to me every time I turn around there's you and him nose to ear in a corner somewhere, whispering. Thought you'd've asked his opinion on this afore scarin' the life out of me with it."

"This has nothing to do with Matt," she snapped. "It's about you and me, and whether or not you want me as your assistant administrator. So. Do you?"

Did he want her? Barl save him, he wanted her so much he sometimes feared his bones would melt. The thought of working with her ... of having her with him every day ... hearing her voice, smelling her hair, watching her glide through a room, dividing the air like a beautiful knife. It meant he'd have all the time in the world, then, to learn that secret heart of hers. To coax it out of her close keeping and hold it in his careful hands.

"What?" she said as he cloaked intemperate desire in a fresh fit of coughing. "What's wrong, are you all right?"

"I'm fine," he said, and banged his chest. Grinned. *Every day ... every day ...* "Indigestion. Must be somethin' I ate."

That made her laugh, and smack the side of his head. "Ungrateful lump! That's the last time I—" And then she stopped, the smile vanishing. Sober, serious, she dropped to the ground in a deep curtsey. "Your Majesty."

He spun about. Gar. Looking exhausted and exultant and subtly not himself. "Sir," he said, and bowed.

"You waited," said Gar.

"Course I bloody waited. You all right?"

Gar's eyebrows lifted. "Shouldn't I be?"

Dathne took a hesitant step forward. "Sir, if I may—if it's not presumptuous—I'm sorry. Your family was deeply loved, and will be sorely missed. I know you'll make a fine king, I don't mean—it's just—oh dear—"

It was the first time Asher had ever seen her tongue-tied. Disconcerted, he watched as Gar stepped close, kissed her gently on the cheek and said, "I know. Thank you, Dathne. Now you should go home. It's late, and I have more work for Asher."

She curtseyed again, then snatched up her basket. "Yes, sir. Thank you, sir. Asher, we'll speak again soon?"

"Aye," he said. "Soon."

In silence they watched her hurry away. With his head still turned, Gar said, "Do you know the worst thing about all this?"

He folded his arms across his chest. "No."

"Everyone is so sorry. In such pain. For me, for themselves. I tell you, I've been wept on so much tonight my tunic is soaked right through. They tell me how their hearts are broken, they tell me how wonderful my family was, they think they're giving me comfort but what they really want is for me to comfort them." Gar laughed softly. Ballodair stuck his head over the stable door and whickered. Crossing to him, Gar smoothed a tangle from his forelock and gently tugged one curving ear. "So I do. I hold them in my arms, even though I know Darran for one would faint at the thought, and I let them weep against my chest and tell me how hurt they are that my family is dead. And then I give them the kiss of peace and promise that no harm will come to them or their children now that I am king. And they smile at me, because that's really what they came to hear, and they go back to their living family and someone else steps forward to take their place."

"The *Doranen* do that?" he said, staring.

Gar's sideways smile was derisive. "What do you think?"

After an uncomfortable pause, he cleared his throat. "You know I'm sorry, right?"

Gar nodded. "Of course."

Another pause. He inspected his shirt cuffs, wondering what Gar was waiting for. "That were quite the show you gave them out there tonight."

Gar shrugged. "I had to do something. They had to see I'm a cripple no longer. But sparkly lights and flower petals won't hold them forever, Asher, Olken or Doranen. They believe in me now because they're shocked and grieving and, as you say, I put on a convincing show. Unfortunately their belief won't last long. Not without something more...tangible...to back it up."

He pulled a face. Gar was right, drat it. "Ain't much you can do about that."

"On the contrary," said Gar. "I can call rain. And not just here in Dorana, but all over the kingdom."

He choked. "All over the *kingdom*? Are you mad? You ain't never even called rain in a teacup!"

"Not in a teacup, no. In a test globe. The principle is the same, it's just a question of degree."

"Of degree? Have you lost your wits? Not even your da made it rain over an entire kingdom! You'll kill yourself! Why not wait a day or so? See if Durm comes round. If he does, you can ask him what—"

Gar's look was dagger sharp. "I can't afford to wait that long. I can't afford to wait at all. If I don't do something definitive the people will cease to believe in me and Lur will crumble into chaos and despair. Conroyd Jarralt will make his move and I'll lose the crown my father spent his life serving. I'm calling rain, Asher. Tonight. And I want you with me when I do."

"*Me?*"

"Who else?"

He stepped back a pace, aghast. "Anybody but me!"

"You'll be quite safe, I promise."

"You don't know that! You ain't never done this before!"

"True," Gar conceded after a lengthy silence. "But for all things there must be a first time. For me, for WeatherWorking, tonight is that time. Asher, I can do this alone. I just don't want to."

And what about *me*? he wanted to shout. What about what *I* want? He half turned away, hands clasped to the top of his head. As usual, what he wanted was about to go overboard with the fish guts. He turned back. "All right. Just this once. But you better not think I'll be makin' a habit of it, 'cause—"

"Good," said Gar. "Now let's hurry. I want the sky full of rain within the hour."

In silence they rode back to the palace, but instead of continuing to the Tower they branched off towards a wooded expanse in the old palace grounds, where gardeners and lawn keepers no longer toiled and nature ran riot. Washed with pale travelling glimlight, the horses picked their cautious way along a narrow path that led directly into the heart of the tangled trees and undergrowth.

"Here," Gar said at last, and drew rein. "It's best if we go on foot the rest of the way. The path is narrow and the trees grow quite thickly. Besides, horses are sometimes—disturbed—by the Weather Chamber."

"Oh, aye?" said Asher, sliding to the ground. "And what about fishermen?"

Gar flung his leg over the pommel and jumped. "I wouldn't know."

"Well, I bloody would," he said, and tied Cygnet's reins to the nearest sturdy tree branch. "Fishermen are even more disturbed than horses. And don't dismount like that, it's dangerous. You could break your bloody neck."

Gar sighed. "I've been dismounting like that for years, Asher. Does my neck look broken to you?"

"No, but there's a first time for everything," he retorted. "Or so I been told."

Gar tugged on Ballodair's knotted reins and gave the horse a brisk pat. "Come on. The night's not getting any younger."

Side by side they hurried along the narrow grassy path. The thin air had sharp nipping teeth, but Asher didn't feel them. Noticing his shivers, Gar had conjured a coat for him right out of his wardrobe in the Tower and handed it over with such a look of self-satisfaction he'd had to grin, even though circumstances dictated that amusement was in pretty poor taste.

Of course, so was arguing with the recently bereaved in pretty poor taste, but some things couldn't be helped.

"I still ain't convinced this is a good idea."

"Of course it is. You said it yourself just this morning. I shouldn't attempt WeatherWorking alone."

"But what if something goes wrong?"

"You'll fetch help, of course."

"Help. Right," he said slowly. "Only, I reckon there might be a problem with that."

Gar looked mystified. "A problem?"

"Aye! 'Cause after they've helped you, it's *me* they'll be helpin', right into the nearest empty cell down at the guardhouse." Still Gar looked mystified. Asher could've hit him. "It's forbidden for Olken to meddle in magic, or had you forgotten that? I mean, has the name Timon Spake completely slipped your mind? 'Cause I'll tell you right now it surely ain't slipped mine!"

Gar stopped. "I forget *nothing* about that day. And it offends me that you'd think I would."

"Well, I'm offended by the idea of gettin' my head chopped off!" he retorted, wheeling round to face his idiot king.

"Barl save me!" Gar snapped. "Nobody is going to chop your head off! And you won't be meddling in magic, you'll be protecting me while I perform my sacred duty as Lur's WeatherWorker. You fool, you're more likely to be awarded a medal!"

"Tell that to Conroyd Jarralt!"

With an impatient hiss Gar grabbed Asher's arm with one hand and with the other pointed upwards. "Look at the gift Barl gave us. Go on. *Look* at it."

Heaving a sigh, scowling, Asher tilted his head back and looked up at the Wall. At the great and glowing wash of gold soaring into the star-studded sky beyond the treetops. Remote. Mysterious. Magnificent.

"All right," he said sourly, and tugged his arm free. "I'm lookin'. So what? It's the Wall, Gar. Same as it's always been."

"Yes. The same, for more than six hundred years. And you've grown completely used to it, haven't you? Hardly give it a thought from one week to another. And do you know why? Because you've never had a reason to doubt it would be there when you looked for it, any more than you doubt there'll be air to breathe when you open your eyes after a good night's sleep."

"Gar—"

"What does the Wall mean to you, Asher? What do you see when you look at it?"

"I don't know," he said, baffled. "Safety. Prosperity." He shrugged. "Magic."

Gar stared up at the golden mountains. "I see the altar upon which my father sacrificed his life. Upon which all of Lur's WeatherWorkers have sacrificed themselves, generation upon generation, all the way back to Blessed Barl herself, whose life was given in the making of it. I see a sword, which starting tonight will cut me and bleed me one day at a time, until I have no blood left to shed. I see my life, and my death, and the pain-soaked days in between, offered as payment for the taking of a land that wasn't ours, and the visitation of a danger that should have passed your people by and didn't. Because of mine." His gaze slid sideways then, before returning to the Wall. "That's what I see, Asher."

Asher frowned. Again, abruptly. Gar was a stranger. An unfamiliar spirit housed in prosaically familiar flesh. He shoved his chilly hands into his coat pockets. "D'you really reckon you can make it rain all over the kingdom?"

With an effort, Gar tore his gaze away from that glowing wash of gold. "I reckon that if I don't try, we'll never know." He started walking again and Asher fell into step beside him.

Half a mile later the path ended, spilling like a riverlet into a small clearing...at the centre of which stood the kingdom's Weather Chamber. Seeing it, Asher felt his feet stumble and his heart thud hard.

According to history, Barl herself had built it from her own design and spent her last living days there as she invented and perfected the Weather Magic and the Wall that would keep Lur safe from predation until the end of time. Made of the same stone as Gar's Tower, it was crowned with a domed glass roof and an uninterrupted view of the sky. There was no other palace building within sight or earshot. Light from the Wall seemed nearer here, brighter and more dense, as though the Chamber had some power to call it close. It splashed over the ancient bluestone blocks, roaring them to midnight life.

He looked around. "There ain't any guards."

Gar shook his head. "There's no need. The Chamber's steeped in magic. My father used to say it feels...alive. Somehow it knows when it's not alone. If any visitor comes here with ill will the door won't open and no magic known to us can make it otherwise."

He stepped into the clearing. Asher took a deep, shuddering breath and followed.

The chamber's door was plain, unvarnished wood. No handle, no knocker, no keyhole or lock. Gar frowned, dredging memory.

"I was just a child the last—the only—time I came here," he murmured. "Durm had intended to bring me back soon, to expand my education..." His lips tightened and he wiped his palms down the front of his black tunic. "Another plan smashed to pieces, along with everything else." Throwing his head back he slapped his hands to the timber and pushed.

The door remained shut.

"It's just stuck," said Asher, breaking the white-hot silence. "Damp's got it or somethin'."

"What damp?" said Gar through clenched teeth. "I haven't made it rain yet."

He pushed again, harder. Again the door resisted him, creaking a little. Releasing a sobbing breath, Gar stepped back. Stared at the door, perplexed and angry and a little afraid. "Give way, damn you! I am the king and I *will* be admitted!" He struck the timber a blow with his fist. "*Admit me!*" And then he stepped close once more. Rested his forehead against the door and stroked his fingers down the weathered grain like a coaxing lover. "Please," he whispered. "Please...let me in..."

Discomforted, Asher laughed. "It's a door, Gar. Wood. It ain't really alive. And even if it is, I don't see any ears stickin' out anywhere, do you? No way it can bloody hear you. I'm tellin' you, it's the damp." To prove his point, he shoved against the closed door himself.

It opened.

"Bloody thing," he said, scowling. "Playin' hard to get, that's all. If it is alive, I bet it's female."

Gar tugged at the hem of his tunic. "No. It was some lingering damp, as you say."

Asher looked up. "How many stairs to the top, do you reckon?"

"One hundred and thirty."

"Oh, my achin' legs."

Gar sent the travelling glimfire ahead of them into the chamber's entryway, and in muscle-burning silence they climbed to the solitary glass-domed chamber at the top of the tower. Gar opened its door unhindered, nodded Asher through and followed him inside. The bobbing glimfire cast their shadows on the floor in long thin lines. With a wave of his arm Gar swung the door closed again, then ignited fresh glimfire in the sconces attached to the curving walls. Shadows vanished and the chamber was revealed.

The room was clean and cold, smelling faintly, lingeringly, of rain. The parquetry floor gleamed a dark red-brown, hundreds of timber strips laid end to end and side by side in a subtle, intricate pattern. Perhaps some fifty couples dancing would fit beneath the domed glass ceiling...that was if the centre of the floor had been empty.

It wasn't. Directly beneath the domed ceiling sat something that to Asher's fascinated gaze looked like an overgrown child's toy.

"The Weather Map," said Gar, his expression avid. Hungry. Tinged with awe, and fear. "Barl's incredible power laid bare. It's a magical representation of the kingdom, down to the last hamlet and village."

Cautiously approaching, Asher saw he was right. There were Barl's Mountains, with the Black Woods clustered at their feet. There was Dorana with its high, encircling wall, and the River Gant spreading silver fingers. The Saffron Hills. The Flatlands. All the places he and Gar had visited or passed through on their trip to Westwailing, as well as the kingdom's other towns, villages, farms and hamlets, its orchards, vineyards and fields of wheat and barley, re-created in perfect miniature. He leaned closer and felt his stomach clench. There, exquisite and touchable and utterly out of reach, was his beloved Restharven.

Without looking up, not wanting to tear his eyes away from even this small taste of home, he said, "How does it work?"

"To be honest, I'm not exactly sure," Gar admitted.

Now he did look up. "You ain't *sure*?"

"Not about the how, no," said Gar. He sounded defensive. Looked annoyed. "Durm and I didn't get this far."

Too bad. "But you're sure it works."

Gar walked around the edges of his inherited kingdom, his gaze greedy. "Oh yes. It changes, even as the kingdom changes. Newly cultivated fields spring up, fallow fields fall into slumber. Land is sold, boundaries change, and you'll know it just by looking here. Whatever happens in the land is reflected in this map." Annoyance forgotten, his fingers skimmed the air above the toy towns, the wheatfields, the open meadows and the wooded glens. "Isn't it magnificent?" he whispered.

There was something so naked in his face Asher felt embarrassed. Love...longing...avarice...desire...or some strange alchemical blending of all those difficult emotions. It was too intimate a moment for observance.

He looked up. Whether it was his imagination or some trick of the crystal-clear glass arching overhead he didn't know, but the stars looked close enough to touch. The Wall too. Silver and gold, crushing him with beauty. He had to look down again, it was too much to bear. Gar still circled his little kingdom like a cat contemplating a bowl of cream, lost in a private reverie with his soul stripped bare, so he found something else to look at.

The Chamber's curving walls had long ago been soothed smooth and white with plaster, and fitted from floor to waist-height with sturdy cherrywood bookshelves and a single, double-doored cupboard. The shelves were burdened with leather-bound books, some thick, some slender, some ancient, some nearly new. The space between the ceiling and the first crammed shelf was covered like a child's scrapbook with calendars, charts, diagrams, hand-scrawled notes on yellowing scraps of parchment, sketches, jottings...

Skimming their circular surface, he saw they were all in some way connected with the weather. Rainfall patterns, wind patterns, seasonal guides, planting guides, snowfall indicators. Notes concerning what crops were harvested when, and where, and how, and what each farmer needed to get the job done in a timely fashion. How much rain was needed to lush the grass in the horse-breeding Dingles district. How much snow the icegrape growers felt was just enough to nurture their precious vines. How deep down the River Gant should freeze for the very best of winter skating, and what was the best temperature for its careful melting come the spring. Not a single facet of Olken or Doranen life was missing. Everything thought of, everything cared for.

When he'd come full circle, he looked at Gar. Shook his head. "I had no idea..."

"Why should you?" said Gar. He'd stopped prowling round the map and was watching him instead. His face was comfortable again, all private feeling decently tucked away. "WeatherWorking isn't an

Olken concern. It's not even a Doranen concern. Only the Weather-Worker is required to shoulder this burden. To know its weight and import in the world. The balance is too delicate, the scope for disaster too great, for it to be otherwise." He smiled. "A boat is less likely to capsize with only one hand on the tiller."

"It's too much," said Asher. "Too much for one man. Or woman." He waved his hand at the crowded wall. "You thought Fane could do this? Little Fane? She never would've been strong enough. I could've near snapped her in half with my bare hands!"

Gar's pale face stilled, so it looked like a mask of marble. Asher, realising what he'd just said, cursed under his breath. "Gar—I didn't mean—look—"

"It's all right. In the end she did break easily, didn't she? But that was just flesh and bone. What we have here is a matter of power. And Barl knows, Fane had more of that than most."

"More than you?"

Gar shrugged. "It's moot. The only question that counts now is do I have enough?"

"And do you?"

"That's what we're here to find out, isn't it?"

Again Asher looked at the Chamber's wall with its burden of knowledge, of history. Of expectations. "You got any idea what all this means?"

"Some," Gar admitted. "But I'm not so worried about that. See those books in the bookshelves? They're the diaries of every Weather-Worker who ever lived, all the way back to Barl herself. Contained in those pages is everything I need to know about the weather, and the Wall, and how they work to keep each other strong. All I need to do is read them and remember. And we both know I'm very good with books."

Asher looked away. Books, aye. Gar had never had trouble with books. But this? This was different. This was all their futures, their health and their happiness and the ordered life of Lur...and it rested in the hands of a man not so far past his majority and only recently come into his magical birthright. A man alone, bereft of an older, experienced voice to guide him when he doubted, to support him when he stumbled.

To save him if he failed.

Suddenly he was feeling sick again. "Maybe Jarralt's right. Durm should be here. What help will I be if something goes—"

Gar's face tightened with impatience. "How often must I say it?

Nothing will go wrong! This is my *destiny*, Asher. How can I be doomed to disaster when Barl herself has placed me on her throne?"

"I don't know," he said unhappily. "But there's more than one fisherman who's set out to sea under clear skies and never come home again. Sometimes storms break without warning, Gar."

"Westwailing was an accident," Gar said curtly. "The unfortunate result of illness. I am meant to be here. Nothing will go wrong."

Asher shoved his hands in his coat pockets. "Why couldn't you stop the horses?"

"*What?*"

"There were five magicians in that *carriage*, Gar. You tryin' to tell me one of you couldn't have used magic to stop the horses from gallopin' over the edge of Salbert's Eyrie?"

Gar stared at him. "The art—if you can call it that—of magically influencing another living thing is long lost to us. Barl forbade it, and with good reason. Can you imagine what might happen if one magician could crawl inside another's mind and work his will unhampered?"

Asher turned away. He could imagine it, aye, and bloody well wished he couldn't.

Gar's voice pursued him. "What are you really trying to say? I thought the accident was behind us. I thought we had moved on from uncertainty and suspicion. Was I mistaken? Do you still have doubts? Do you doubt *me*?"

CHAPTER EIGHT

"No!" said Asher, turning back. "But it's all happenin' so fast! This time last night we're standing at the edge of Salbert's Eyrie. I've just crawled up from seein' your poor dead family, and you're there tellin' the world it was Conroyd Jarralt who killed 'em. A day later it's all decided what happened were an accident, you're proclaimed king and here we are in the most secret, sacred place in the kingdom ready for you to make it rain and me to save you if it all goes arse over eyeballs! I'm dizzy, Gar! I just want to *stop*, just for a minute, so's I can get my bearings! Sink me, I'm a *fisherman*! I never came to Dorana for *this*!"

Gar's face was riven with stresses he'd never asked for. Never deserved. "And I never expected to be king. Barl have mercy! Don't you think I'd sacrifice every last drop of magic in me if it would turn back time and save them? Do you think I *wanted* this?"

"Of course I bloody don't! Nobody in his right mind would want this."

"But I have it," Gar said grimly. "Want it or not, it's mine."

"But not mine!" he said, and thumped his chest. "I'm Olken, your magic's got nowt to do with me. And if this does go arse over eyeballs I don't want to be the one left behind to explain what you're doing lyin' stone dead on the floor!"

A ringing silence. Then Gar flicked a finger and the chamber door swung open. "Of course. I should've realised. I'm sorry."

Expecting argument, or rebuke, Asher blinked. "Gar—"

"No. It's all right. Only fools never feel fear." A bleak smile. "I'm so afraid right now I could vomit. But that's not your concern. You're right. This Weather Chamber is no place for an Olken."

Torn between relief and guilt he shoved his hands back into his pockets. "See, Gar, you got to be careful now. Jarralt could use me bein' here as a way to undermine you."

With a flash of unfamiliar arrogance, Gar lifted his chin. "He could try."

"That's the point. He would. He will."

"No. The point is that I've been selfish. In the time since we first met, I've come to think of you as the brother I never had. I suppose I hoped—thought—you felt the same way."

Gar his *brother*? Asher stared. He had enough damned brothers to last him a lifetime. Did he really want another one? One with blond hair, a crown and enough trouble trailing in his wake to start a dozen fistfights down at the Goose?

The answer came slowly, but with certainty. Yes. He did. Because, despite all the aggravation and the irritation, the heart-stopping catastrophes and the niggling spats, in a little over a year Gar had given him more, trusted him more, leaned on him more, laughed with him more and cared about him more than his flesh-and-blood brothers had in a lifetime.

The realisation must have shown in his face because Gar smiled. "I'm glad. Now go."

"Go?" he echocd. "But—"

"Brothers don't burden each other unfairly," Gar said. His expression was contrite. Earnest. "Get some rest, you look exhausted. But before you retire send a message to Conroyd Jarralt asking him to join me. I'll wait till he arrives."

Asher cleared his throat. Good. This was good. He didn't belong here, in the fiery heart of Doranen magic. No Olken did. "You're sure?"

Gar nodded. "Yes. It has to be Conroyd."

He took a hesitant step backwards. Battled his better judgement, lost, and said, "If you really want me to stay, I'll—"

"What I want isn't important. Go, Asher. I'll see you in the morning."

Guts churning, he turned and walked towards the open door. He was relieved, he was affronted, he was thrilled, he was furious. *Bastard*. Why couldn't Gar have argued? Why did he have to be so—so—understanding? So *reasonable*. Did Gar think he *couldn't* do it? That he wasn't strong enough to take whatever WeatherWorking could dish out, even as a bystander? Somewhere deep inside did Gar think the Olken were *weak*?

That *he* was weak?

He reached the door, fingers touching the unpainted timber. He stopped.

Was he weak?

"*Damn* it!" he shouted, and slammed the chamber door closed in his own face. Whirled around to glare at watchful, waiting Gar. "You always know what to say, don't you! Always know which strings to pull so's you can get your own way! I should've known—I've watched you do it day in day out as the bloody Olken Administrator! Mind you, can't say I ever expected to find you administratin' *me*!"

Gar flushed. Folded his arms across his chest. "Well? Did it work?"

"Of course it worked, you devious bastard! I'm on this side of the bloody door, ain't I?"

The first true, unfettered smile since the accident lit Gar's face. "Don't expect me to apologise."

He snorted. "Don't worry. I'm dumb, but I ain't that dumb."

"I know I'm asking a lot," Gar said, the bright smile fading. "It seems I'm always asking a lot from you. But don't expect me to apologise for that either. You're a man with many gifts, Asher. Gifts best used for the good of this kingdom, and if you think I'll stop using them just because the idea makes you uncomfortable, or me, then you really should walk away now."

"No. I already got one friend harmed for life 'cause I walked away." *Jed*. Asher folded his arms against the bruising memory and thudded his shoulderblades to the door. "I'm stayin'."

Gar nodded. "Good." He returned to the map of Lur, his expression now revealing uncertainty. Caution. A wary hope. "It's like a dance," he whispered. "One with a set pattern that hasn't changed in over six centuries, that's been passed from WeatherWorker to WeatherWorker since the Weather Magics were born. All I have to do is find the right place to join in..." He frowned. "The transfer of incantations from the Orb was...difficult. Painful. Durm said it was to be expected, but..."

"You think it didn't work?"

"No, no, it worked," said Gar. "The Weather Magics are in me. If I close my eyes I can see their shapes. Taste the words. The sigils tingle my fingertips, eager for release."

Asher shrugged. "Then let's not keep 'em waiting."

"No. Let's not." Stepping slowly, walking widdershins around the map, Gar raised his right hand and traced a figure in the air. Its shape glowed, burned bright as fire, then faded. At the same time he pronounced a single word: "*Luknek*." Another shape, with the left hand this time. Another word: "*Tolnek*." Bright fire burned, and faded. Right hand. Word. Left hand. Word. Right hand. Word. Left hand. Word. Out of nowhere a wind, rising. It centred around Gar, stirred his clothing as he walked and spoke and drew burning patterns in the air.

Still leaning against the closed door, Asher felt his skin prickle and saw a faint blue shimmer dance along his forearms, then disappear.

The power was building.

As he watched, caught between fear and fascination, small clouds thickened over the map's model Dorana City. Touched by a shadow he glanced up and saw clouds through the glass-domed ceiling, spinning into life out of the clear night sky.

Buffeted more strongly now, Gar continued to circle the map, sweating as he traced more sigils in the air and uttered the words of power, faster and faster. The wind increased in strength, began to howl like a live thing trapped and tortured. Three more turns around the table and he could walk no further: the wind was too strong. The power too great. So he stood, braced against its might and fury, arms raised, fingers battling to make the signs that would call the rain. His eyes were screwed tight closed and his mouth was open in a silent gasping, as though he were being torn apart.

The writhing clouds above the map billowed outwards to cover the entire recreation of Lur. Tiny forks of lightning flickered in their depths, to be echoed a heartbeat later in the clouds above Chamber and City. Thunder rumbled, inside and out.

Blue light like little fingers of flame danced the length of Gar's body. Unravelled his disciplined hair and whipped it round his face as though the long blond strands were alive and in torment.

At its raging peak the power ignited into a wild blue firestorm, roaring and crackling and feeding on itself, with Gar at its greedy heart. Blood burst from his eyes, from his nose, his ears, his mouth, and his whole body flailed and shook. He opened his mouth and screamed like a man on fire. Horrified, Asher started forward then stopped, indecision a knife at his throat.

"Gar!" he shouted. "Gar, are you all right? Is this normal or not? What should I do? For Barl's sake, tell me what to do!"

But Gar was far beyond hearing. In the nightmare leaping of blue flame and golden glimlight his blood-slicked face looked inhuman. Unreachable. Unknown.

Then, as had happened at the height of the storm in Westwailing, an enormous explosion of sound rent the air. Asher cried out and clapped his hands to his ears. Gar echoed him, screaming as though he'd been pierced by a sword...

...and overhead the blotting clouds wept their summoned rain like a benediction over Dorana City and all the lands of Lur.

Conroyd Jarralt was entertaining friends to dinner. Only the heads of the best houses, naturally. Those closest in status to his own. The Doranen might be illustrious by nature, but still, some families were more illustrious than others. Sorvold. Boqur. Daltrie. Hafar. Direct descendants of the great exiles from Old Dorana, those wise magicians who'd seen the way the wind was blowing and fled before Morgan's madness destroyed them as it destroyed hundreds of other, less perspicacious magicians. They were names to be proud of. Histories that would embarrass no one, most particularly their host. And they were all senior members of the kingdom's General Council too, with their busy fingers pressed against any number of pulses.

A man could be a friend and useful at the same time. In fact, it was better if he was.

Of course, Council service or not, none of those names was as illustrious as his own. Conroyd Jarralt of House Jarralt, founded by Lindin Jarralt, one of the finest magicians the Doranen race had ever produced. Only the royal house could boast a better pedigree, more exceptional magicians, and even that was subject to debate. After all, would House Jarralt have bred up a cripple as heir to the throne?

No. It most certainly would not.

Were it not for the treachery and mischance his family had suffered during the turbulence of Trevoyle's Schism, it would be WeatherWorkers born of House Jarralt, not Torvig, who ruled the Kingdom of Lur. Dusty memory had power still to boil his blood; the degree of kinship between his ancestor and the madman Morgan had been slight. Hardly worth mentioning. Good for the merest footnote in the annals of history, if that. More importantly, there had never been so much as a breath of an allegiance between the insane sorcerer and his twice-removed cousin Lindin. As Barl was his witness, Lindin had been one of the first to voice concern over Morgan's experiments! Could Borne Torvig have claimed the same of his own ancestor? No, he could not.

But that, seemingly, counted for nothing. Morg's shade haunted them all. Tainted him still in some eyes, though no one would dare say so to his face.

Only now, with the near extinction of House Torvig, did blighted House Jarralt have a chance to assume its rightful place in Doranen history. Why, if Gar had been killed along with his family, or if the miracle flowering of his magical birthright had never happened, it would be Conroyd Jarralt who stood today as king.

But Gar wasn't dead, and his late-born powers appeared formidable. Which meant that yet again House Jarralt was to be denied its proper place in the world.

Fate could be monstrously unfair.

Not for the first time, Jarralt regretted his lack of a daughter. He could have married a daughter to the fate-favoured scion of House Torvig and died less unhappily, knowing his blood flowed through the veins of Gar's child, the kingdom's next WeatherWorker. But no. Even that small consolation was denied him. Two children he'd been granted, like most citizens of Lur. Even if dispensation could be arranged for the birth of a third child it was far too late now and just as likely his dull and dutiful wife would waste the effort on another son.

Still. Where the prospect of rightful glory was concerned, not *all* hope was lost. Fat Durm's hold on life was yet precarious, or so discreet enquiries informed him. With the Master Magician's successor carelessly unnamed, Gar would be forced to make the appointment himself. And it was clear that in all the kingdom there was no one better bred, better qualified or more deserving of the honour than Lord Conroyd Jarralt.

"My dear," a voice beside him murmured. "The wine."

Jarralt blinked and watched his surroundings swim back into focus. His dining room, lavishly appointed. His wife, lavishly jewelled. His friends, waiting patiently for his next unimpeachable pronouncement. "Wine?"

The immaculate Olken servant standing at his elbow bowed and held out a bottle for his inspection. "As requested, my lord. Vontifair Icewine, vintage 564. Chilled for precisely forty minutes."

Nole Daltrie wagged a finger. "564? Cuttin' it a bit fine there aren't you, Con? Icewine don't hold its bite for more than eighty years. Any longer than that and you might as well pour us a glass of piss and vinegar."

Con. Jarralt hid his irritation behind a bland smile. "Don't worry, Nole. The eightieth anniversary of this vintage's bottling isn't until tomorrow."

Daltrie hooted and slapped the table. "Vintage icewine and vintage Conroyd! What an evening!"

Jarralt nodded at the servant, who broke the bottle's dewarded seal and splashed a mouthful into the next course's wineglass. The icewine's thin, snow-laden tang sliced through the dining room's lingering redolence of honey-baked lamb, muscatel venison and spiced pork; Jarralt's guests sighed and licked their lips. He rested the rim of the glass against his teeth, subduing greed, and permitted a trickle of clear blue indulgence into his mouth.

It cleansed his jaded palate like magic.

"Perfect," he said, lowering the glass, and nodded again at the servant. The other glasses were scrupulously burdened with three inches of icewine, not a hair's-breadth more; the disappointment-laced avarice in his guests' eyes almost made him laugh out loud. Waiting, he travelled his gaze around all their guzzling faces. When the servant had withdrawn and they were again alone, he remarked, "So. A new day dawns for our beloved kingdom."

As though invisible cords had been cut his fellow diners let out silent sighs of relief and relaxed in their chairs. Morel, Sorvold's robustly handsome wife, fluttered her jewel-crusted fingers. "I must say, Conroyd dear, it's all terribly disconcerting. I mean, the boy's a *child*. In magic, at least, if not in fact, and even there he's still young. What kind of a king will he make? Does anybody know? Does anybody know *him*? I certainly don't!"

Iyasha Hafar was nodding her vigorous agreement; her diamond pendant earrings prismed the chandelier's glimlight and scattered rainbows across the tablecloth. "Exactly! Why, he's practically a stranger! I think he's only ever attended one of my garden parties and I'm sure even then it was under sufferance! I'd swear you could count on the fingers of one hand the number of invitations he's accepted in the last year."

"Doranen invitations," her husband added dryly. "As far as I can make out, he's always available for carousing with the Olken."

Tobe Boqur replaced his emptied wineglass on the table and belched. "Don't be too hard on him, Gord. For a start it's been his job to mix with Olken society, and for another—"

"For another," said Madri Boqur, smiling at her husband as she finished his sentence for him in her irritating little-girl whisper, "I don't imagine he ever felt comfortable around his own kind. Not while he was—" She blushed. "You know."

"I think the word you're avoiding is 'crippled,'" Jarralt replied. "No, no, my friends, please don't look like that. I assure you, he applied the term to himself often enough. Borne's son is nothing if not a realist."

"You'd know, serving with him on the Privy Council," said Payne Sorvold. "What else is he, do you think?"

"Our king," said Lynthia Daltrie. Her sharply jutting chin looked more stubborn than ever. Nole had long since lost the battle to control her; such a pity. "As ordained by Barl and therefore above reproach. I have to say I liked his speech in the square today. It showed heart. Courage. I think his father would've been proud."

A reflective silence fell. Jarralt waited for his wife to break it: Barl save him, she was a woman who couldn't abide a room without words in it.

"All I know," Ethienne said peevishly, "is that it will feel most peculiar, addressing that unfortunate young man as 'Your Majesty.' He's younger than both of my boys!"

"I suppose he's got what it takes to *be* king," Madri said uncertainly. "I mean to say . . . Barl wouldn't allow an incompetent to inherit the throne. Would she?"

Almost as one their gazes flicked to the glass balcony doors through which gleamed the Wall's distant golden haze. Jarralt hid a smile at the sight of their apprehensive expressions. Even tediously devout Lynthia had her doubts. As well she should have. Lur was in greater danger now than ever before, even during the schism. How lucky for his friends and their children that Conroyd Jarralt was at hand. Watching their silent dismay, the way they tried not to look at each other or reveal unflattering fear, he again wanted to laugh out loud.

Ah, dear. They were good enough people, these friends of his, but as transparent as his dining-room windows. Lacking any kind of real ambition or inner fire. They represented the best that Doranen society had to offer, yet not one of them was strong enough to wield real power. To balance the kingdom in the vital role of Master Magician, or wear the crown of the WeatherWorker.

Only he was. And praise Barl for that. For if Gar's power should prove insufficient…if the strain of WeatherWorking killed him sooner rather than later, as had happened more than once in the past…if he should fail to produce an heir or sired one as crippled as he himself had used to be…

Well.

Thunder boomed over their heads, rattling the windowpanes and the emptied wineglasses on the table. Jarralt's secret smile died. "What was that?" he demanded, pushing to his feet.

Ethienne pointed at the sky beyond the doors. "Look! Clouds!"

"And lightning!" added Tobe Boqur. The words had hardly left his mouth when the room strobed a second time as, outside, spears of blue-white fire streaked earthwards from the rapidly thickening atmosphere. Even as they watched, the Wall's golden glow dimmed, dimmed, and disappeared.

Gord Hafar stood and crossed to the doors. Flung them open and thrust his hand outside. He looked back over his shoulder. "It's going to rain," he announced. "The air's alive with it. You never told us Gar had been given the Weather Magics, Conroyd." Gord sounded accusing. In his eyes, a shadow of hurt surprise.

Fool. Just because he shared his icewine did Gord think he'd share his secrets, too? "You didn't need to know," he replied brusquely. "Before the accident there was still a question mark over the succession. There was no way of telling who would prove to be the stronger WeatherWorker, Fane or Gar, without testing them first."

Payne Sorvold cleared his throat, his expression disapproving. "You took a risk, Conroyd. The law is clear on the matter. Only two people might possess Weather Magic at the same time: the Weather-Worker and the WeatherWorker in Waiting. Such action was a recipe for another schism. As Privy Councillor you should have stopped it."

Jarralt spared the man an impatient glance, inwardly seething. Who was Payne Sorvold to task *him*? "Exceptional circumstances require the taking of risks and the bending of law. As Privy Councillor it's my duty to recognise that. Besides, the danger of schism was Borne's doing, not mine. If he hadn't bullied his way into a dispensation for a second child we never would've faced a divided succession in the first place. If you're going to criticise anyone, Payne, why not start with the General Council for weakly acquiescing to—"

"The General Council," Nole said loudly, his flabby cheeks reddening, "weakly acquiesced to nothing! We did what had to be done for the good of the kingdom. We acted according to law *and* with Barl's blessing!"

"And why we're arguing about it now, nearly twenty years later, I cannot begin to understand!" added Lynthia. "The point is moot!"

"As is the question of Gar receiving the Weather Magic," said Jarralt. His gaze remained fixed upon the curdling sky. "With the death of his sister he is once more an only child. The line of succession is clear, and the law stands."

"On a sprained ankle, if you ask me," muttered Nole.

"Nobody did, dear," said Lynthia, and patted his arm. "Never mind. As Con says, what's done is done. All that really matters is we have a WeatherWorker and the kingdom is safe."

As if to punctuate her words a thunderclap like the end of the world boomed over their heads. The women shrieked. The men shouted. Jarralt laughed. Beyond the open glass doors the murky cloud-covered sky gushed rain like a woman whose waters have broken.

King Gar, WeatherWorker of Lur, was born.

Jarralt eased away from his dining table. Crossed to the doors leading out to the uncovered balcony. Stepped over the threshold and into the rain.

"What are you doing, Conroyd?" Ethienne demanded breathlessly. "You can't stand out there, you'll be soaked! All your clothes will be ruined! Come back inside. Conroyd? Conroyd, are you listening? *Conroyd!*"

He ignored her. Ignored the surprised protests of his dinner guests. Walked to the very edge of the balcony, six tall storeys above the ground, braced his widespread hands on the balustrade and looked out across the City. Looked further, beyond the City's encircling wall to the invisible horizon. The view was exactly the same: rain, rain, rain. The weeping clouds went on forever.

His new silk brocade tunic was sodden, a dragging weight against his shoulders. Rivulets of water ran down his arms, his chest, his legs, and pooled in his brand-new shoes. Yes, Ethienne, all ruined.

He tipped back his head and felt more water from his soaking hair run down the back of his neck. Eyes open, mouth open, he lifted his face to the pouring rain. Drowned himself, blinded himself, in the miracle of Gar's calling.

Every droplet was a needlepoint of acid etching him with bitterness and despair, in his flesh, his bones, his bowels. In his heart, and the secret places of his soul.

Borne ... you bastard. You bastard. You've beaten me again.

Released at last from the Weather Magic's merciless grasp, Gar swayed drunkenly, bloodily, then collapsed unstrung to the floor beside the map of Lur where the little clouds dropped tiny vanishing raindrops from the mountains to the sea. Groaning, retching, shaking, he began to laugh.

Asher dropped to his knees beside him. "It ain't funny!" he shouted, fright shattering his voice. "You maniac! You great ravin' *lunatic*! What are you laughin' for? It ain't bloody funny!"

Flopping like a landed fish, Gar stared up at him through a mask of blood. "It worked!" he gasped, spitting scarlet bubbles. "Did you see? It *worked*! I made it rain! *Everywhere!* Fane never managed that!"

"Aye, aye," Asher muttered, scrabbling in his pockets for a handkerchief. "You made it rain and you made a mess and you took ten years off my life, you daft bastard. Hold still!"

"You know...that hurt," Gar wheezed as Asher mopped the worst of the gore from his face. "A lot. But it was incredible! The *power*. I never knew—I never *dreamed*—oh, Asher! Aren't you sorry you'll never know what it's like? That you'll never command a power like it? Aren't you...I don't know...jealous? You can tell me. I won't mind. I'll understand."

Asher stared down at him. At his shivering, shuddering, pain-racked body. "Oh aye. I be so jealous I could spit."

Gar grinned redly and stared up at the glass-domed ceiling, enchanted. "Look," he whispered. "*Look* what I did."

"Aye," he said as the rain fell from the quietly clouded sky. The sound of it striking the transparent ceiling woke gentle echoes in the chamber below. "Look what you did. Now shut your trap while I find somethin' to clean you up proper. 'Cause if you go back to the Tower lookin' like this and Darran sees you, sure as sharks the ole crow'll find some way to make this all *my* fault." And then, relenting, added roughly, "Your da'd be proud right now, I reckon. And your ma too."

Fresh tears gathered in Gar's bloody eyes. "I hope so," he whispered, triumph extinguished, lurking grief ascendant once more. "Oh, I hope so."

Asher cursed. *Fool. Damned fool. Just when you got him smilin' again...*

"Come on," he said. Slipping an arm beneath Gar's shoulders, he levered the exhausted king upright. "Scoot yourself backwards and lean against the wall till you're feelin' better." Looking around the chamber, he scowled. "Why ain't there any chairs in here?"

"I don't need a chair," said Gar, sliding by inches across the parquetry floor. He reached the wall, slumped against it and groaned. "I'm fine."

Asher stood. "You don't look fine. You look like shit."

Eyes half closed, Gar raised a finger. "Now, now. Remember to whom you speak."

"Excuse me," he said. "You look like royal shit."

Gar's lips twitched. "That's better."

"Does it still hurt?"

"Oh, Asher..." Gar blinked his eyes open again. "You have no idea."

But he did. Some idea anyway. He'd heard Gar's screams, after all. Watched helpless as his friend writhed inside the power. Convulsed. Wept blood even as he laughed.

"Well..." Uncertain, he folded his arms. "For how long? For always? I mean, is this your life now? Nowt but blood and pain?"

With an effort, Gar pulled his knees up to his chest and wrapped his arms around them. "Yes."

"But...you can't do this every day," he said, appalled. "You can't bleed and hurt like this every day. How will you stand it?"

Gar shrugged. "The same way my father did, and my grandfather, and my great-grandmother, back and back and back till the dawn of our days here."

"But you *can't*!"

"I must. What's the alternative? Shirk my duty and hand the crown to Conroyd Jarralt?" Gar pulled a face. "I don't think so. Besides, it's not every day. Well. Not always. As I recall, my father sometimes had two days' respite at a time, between Callings. Three even, in winter." He smiled, remembering. "Winter is good."

"Gar, nowt happens in winter. What about spring?"

The remembering smile faded then and Gar frowned at his knees. "Oh, spring. Yes. Spring is...not so good."

"You fool, spring'll *kill* you if this is just a taste of what's to come!"

Gar shook his head. "No, it won't. You're forgetting this wasn't a normal Working. Tonight I made it rain from one end of the kingdom to the other, and that's not the way it's usually done. Not even in the spring. You're worrying over nothing. I'm fine, or I will be soon enough." He stretched a hand out in front of him and flexed his fingers with only a small grimace. "See? The pain's easing already."

Asher snorted. "Even if you poked my eyes out I could tell you were lyin'. Gar—"

The outstretched fingers became a fist. "*Don't.*" Then Gar's icy gaze melted and the fist became a hand, became vulnerable fingers, trembling. "I am who I am, Asher. I was born for one reason and one reason alone. You can't change that."

Asher kicked one boot-heel against the floor, scuffing the polished parquetry. "All right," he muttered grudgingly. "If you say so. You're the king."

"Yes," said Gar. "I am." In his voice, echoes of pain and a tired, replete satisfaction. "And now the king says, time to go home."

"Not till I clean up the rest of that blood. You look like a slaughter-house apprentice." His gaze fell on the Chamber's single cupboard. On impulse he crossed to it, opened the doors and inside found a pile of soft rags, a bowl and a stoppered vial. Looking back at Gar he said, "Seems like your da kept himself prepared."

"Or Durm," agreed Gar. "Bring them here."

"There ain't any water."

Gar smiled. "Give me the bowl. I'll take care of the water."

He handed it over, then sank cross-legged to the floor and watched as Gar closed his eyes, spread his hand above the empty vessel and whispered something under his breath. A blue spark ignited in the space between clay and flesh. Gar grunted, his face contracting against new pain. The blue spark briefly danced then died...and the bowl began to fill with water from the bottom up, as though an invisible spigot had been opened.

Asher laughed. "How'd you do that?"

Gar gave him back the bowl. "Do you really want to know?"

Abruptly, he remembered who he was, and where he was, and what the penalties were for asking those kinds of questions. "No."

"It's all right," said Gar. "I'll answer. If you want the truth, it'll be a relief to talk about it. With Durm...unwell, there's nobody else to listen."

Asher dipped his fingers in the water. It was warm. Wetting one of the soft cloths, wringing it out, he said, "Holze'd listen."

Gar shook his head. "I can't talk to Holze. Not about this. Not about any kind of magic. I can't talk to any of them."

He held out the cloth. "I s'pose not."

"Holze may be a cleric, but he's also on the Privy Council and friends with Jarralt," said Gar, his voice muffled as he cleaned his face. "With all the prominent Doranen. If there was even the smallest suggestion I was unsure about the WeatherWorking, about *anything*..."

He sighed. "I know. Goodbye King Gar, hello King Conroyd." With a grunt, he unstoppered the vial from the cupboard. A pungent, eye-stinging stink wafted into the chamber. He spat out the cork, choking.

"I'm not drinking that," said Gar.

Cautiously, Asher sniffed. "One of Nix's little concoctions. It pongs a bit like the one he gave me after gettin' back from West-wailin'. Your da must've kept it here, for afterwards." He held out the vial. "You might as well. I mean, you're so weak right now I could just pinch your nose shut and tip it down your throat, but that'd be a mite undignified, I reckon. You know. Seein' as how you're king and all."

Glaring balefully, Gar held out his hand. "I don't know when, and I don't know how, but I swear I'll get you for this."

Asher grinned. "'Course you will. Just one swallow, mind. We got no idea how strong that muck is."

Gar swallowed. Gagged. Thrust the vial blindly in Asher's direction and scrubbed at his mouth with the bloodstained rag. "And after I've got you," he panted, spitting and hawking, "I'll bloody well get Nix too!"

Asher restoppered the vial then inspected his friend. Whatever was in the pother's vile sludge it was doing the trick. A little colour was returning to Gar's complexion and his hands were steadier. "Better?" he asked.

Gar grimaced. "Yes."

Into the fallen silence, as the magic rain clouds thinned into memory over the map of Lur, he said, "So. Seems you are a Weather-Worker, just like your da."

The faintest of smiles ghosted over Gar's face. "Yes. And you know what that means."

Asher let his head drop. Here it came. "I got a sneakin' bloody suspicion."

"There's no one else I'd trust to be Olken Administrator," said Gar. "And no one else I need more on my Privy Council. But I promise you this, Asher. When Durm is well again and I am settled into my rule, when I am married and the succession is assured, if you want to go back to your precious ocean I'll make no attempt to stop you. And when you do leave, it will be as a fabulously wealthy man."

Asher turned his head to stare at tiny Restharven, where tiny boats made of magic danced in the tiny harbour. With money and power and King Gar's blessing his brothers would never stand in his way again. He'd return home inviolate, able to dictate his own destiny without interference.

And Dathne had offered to be his assistant...

He grinned. "Ah, sink it. Restharven ain't goin' anywhere."

"Does that mean you accept?"

"Aye," he said. "I accept."

CHAPTER NINE

From her privileged position as a member of the elite royal staff, Dathne sat on her cushioned seat in Justice Hall and watched Barlsman Holze crown Gar as Lur's new king.

A temporary dais had been erected at the front of the Hall, where usually the Law Giver sat and pronounced sentence. Draped in gold velvet, it shimmered richly in the glimlight called for the occasion.

Hands meekly clasped before him, Gar knelt on a crimson cushion at Holze's feet as the Barlsman prayed over his bowed head. In contrast to the cleric's jewel-crusted green and gold and crimson brocade robes, his gold-laden cap and the various holy rings clasping his fingers, Lur's almost-crowned king was dressed starkly in white. He looked like a sapling willow stripped bare of bark. Young. Vulnerable. Unready for the burden fate had thrust upon him.

Beside her, dressed in the finest silks and brocades she'd ever seen him wear, Asher watched the ceremony in anxious silence. Fretting, she suspected, on things going wrong at the very last moment. Worrying that all his hair-tearing work with Darran would somehow come to naught. She let her fingers drift to his arm and lightly squeezed. Smiled when he glanced at her. He smiled back, but without enthusiasm.

Holze spread his arms wide and tipped back his head. "O Blessed Barl, look down upon this man, your child in magic, and hear now his solemn oath, sworn in this place before you and all his people. Anoint him with your beneficence, pour your strength into his heart and guide him to truth and wisdom all the days of his life."

Gar looked up then. Folded his hands across his heart. "Blessed Barl, from whom all life flows, I solemnly swear to serve you and the kingdom you gave us, Doranen and Olken alike, unto my last living breath. I will keep your children in peace and prosperity, Working the Weather, keeping your great Wall strong and upholding your laws without exception until my last drop of blood is shed. May magic desert me if I am untrue."

Holze nodded at a waiting acolyte. The robed assistant stepped forward, bearing the WeatherWorker's crown. Handed it to him. Dathne held her breath as the intricately wrought silver and copper and gold was lowered onto Gar's bowed, waiting head.

Booming from the square outside, the City's great Barl's Clock tolled the stroke of midnight. Signalling the end of night...the start of day.

It was all very *symbolic*.

A great sigh went up from the gathered witnesses: City guild meisters and mistresses, Captain Orrick, the General Council's Doranen lords and ladies, mayors and mayoresses from the kingdom's larger towns, select royal staff. Dathne saw in their faces the raw relief bubbling like stew in a lidded pot. *Praise Barl, praise Barl, now life can get back to normal...*

She felt profoundly sorry.

Barlsman Holze began reciting the traditional WeatherWorker's Blessing above the head of still-kneeling Gar. Glancing sideways, she saw Darran wipe away a surreptitious tear, dear old fusspot that he was. A stickler for protocol, inevitably irritated by someone like Asher, but a good man.

Not like Willer.

Further along the pew in which they sat, Willer hunched in his finery like a dyspeptic peacock. Still sulking, the repellent little tick. Everything Asher had ever said about the slug was true. That he could actually think he'd be named Olken Administrator, or even the assistant! Was he mad as well as horrible? And the way he'd acted ever since the announcement of her appointment. Snide. Sneering. Uncooperative. He'd better get over his snit soon or Asher would dismiss him no matter how many more excuses Darran found for him.

Sick of the sight of him, she let her gaze wander elsewhere. Darran wasn't the only one moved to tears: royal staff who'd known their new king as a babe in his cradle, as a toddler tumbling about the corridors of the palace and getting into mischief like any normal small child; guild officials who'd come to know him so closely this past year, and maybe mourned his loss to magic; noble Doranen, perhaps regretting that late-blossoming power and the madcap dreams it killed...or dreaming instead of a nubile daughter's chances of being crowned queen. They all had tears on their cheeks.

So many faces. So many hidden thoughts. So many lives that would wildly unravel once Prophecy was fulfilled.

Her grim musings were interrupted as Holze reached down and drew Gar to his feet. Turned the new king to face his silent subjects. Raised his arms and cried: "Behold a miracle! Behold our virtuous king, by Barl's great grace, Gar the First, WeatherWorker of Lur!"

Now the assembled witnesses were getting to their feet, cheering. Well. Mostly cheering. Dathne scrambled to copy them.

Beside her, clapping along with everybody else, Asher leaned close.

"Barl bloody save me," he said as, moved almost to tears, King Gar stood before them and accepted the rapturous acclaim. "*Now* life's goin' to get interesting!"

The unkempt, ill-favoured denizens of the Green Goose were in diabolical form, rollicking and carousing and tipping their mugs of beer over their shrieking neighbours' heads then laughing as though they'd just done something terribly clever and hysterically funny.

Funny? Willer sank further into his obscure corner seat, hugged his fourth tankard of ale closer to his chest and sneered. It wasn't in the least bit funny. It was puerile. Juvenile. No, no, that was far too old for this unruly mob. It was infantile. Yes. Infantile and...and... mortifying. These rowdy sots were royal servants. His colleagues, loosely speaking. *Very* loosely. Supposedly they were the cream of Lur's Olken population. Yet here they were carrying on like ignorant farmhands at a barn dance, getting drunk and singing bawdy songs out of tune and generally making fools of themselves.

Morg smite them all, was this any way to celebrate the crowning of a king?

And what was there to celebrate anyway? The day Gar's family had carelessly fallen off the side of a mountain more than just a carriage had been wrecked. More than people had died. He hadn't realised it at the time, but he knew it now. His future had been wrecked too. His dreams had died, as bloodily as any king.

Quivering with overwhelming indignation, Willer swallowed another mouthful of his admittedly excellent ale.

He couldn't understand it. How could Barl have *done* this to him?

Another inebriated toast to the new king rattled the inn's smoke-soaked rafters. He winced. What in Barl's name had brought him into this den of iniquity? He didn't belong in here, he belonged in the Golden Cockerel where the only interruption one ever experienced was the gentle throat-clearing of the waiter, asking if sir required more wine. There was violin music in the Cockerel. There was an exquisite silk-swathed soprano in the Cockerel. There was cut glass and polished silverware and fine dining in the Cockerel. What had he been *thinking*, coming here?

A sly little voice inside his head answered, *You were thinking that in here you'd be safe. In here, you wouldn't have to laugh, and smile, and wear a brave face. In here, you could be invisible.*

Which wasn't the case at the Cockerel. He was well known there.

Lauded and fawned on and minced after, importuned and flattered and visible. Anonymity there was impossible. Worse, waiting for him in the refined atmosphere of the Cockerel were his genteel royal colleagues, the other secretaries and assistant secretaries and undersecretaries and junior royal apothecaries who also frequented Dorana's most fashionable establishment.

The ones who even now were saying:

"Poor Willer. Passed over twice. First in favour of the fisherman and then for that odd woman—you know the one, all skin and bone, hangs on the stableman's sleeve, the bookseller. Yes, her. Without even his own precious superior to argue his case."

"No! You mean to say Darran supports the appointments? Gracious! Ah well. They do say every man finds his level, and it seems poor Willer has found his. But who'd have thought it would be so low?"

Moaning, he took another deep swallow of ale.

Of course it was foolish to feel hurt by Gar's decision. He should have expected the slight; *everyone* knew that where Asher was concerned, the pri—the king had all the perspicacity of a newborn babe.

What he *hadn't* bargained for was Darran's betrayal. After three years of faithful service, of uncomplaining drudge-work and utterly reliable discretion, of forgone private pleasures and curtailed private plans, to be publicly humiliated like that. To be ranked as just another dispensable pen-pusher. To see Darran standing shoulder to shoulder with that unspeakable Asher, their mutual implacable foe, and hear him praise the lout without stint or sarcasm. *"Our good friend Asher, who'll serve His Majesty and the kingdom superbly as Olken Administrator."*

Trembling with rewoken outrage, Willer tried to drown tormenting memory with more ale but instead spilled the tankard's remaining mouthfuls down his shirt front.

"Damn!"

He tried in vain to catch the eye of one of the Goose's three slatternly barmaids, but the useless wenches were too busy inviting Matt's stable lads to ogle their dubious charms. Defeated, he slumped further in his seat and brooded into the emptied depths of his ale pot.

Somebody squeezed into the corner booth with him. Without asking. The cheek! "Kindly find another place to sit," he said haughtily, not looking up. "I do not care for—"

A full tankard of ale thudded onto the benchtop before him. Now he did look up, into a face unknown to him. Long, thin, middle-aged. Olken. Unpleasant. The face smiled. "Evening to you, Meister Driskle."

He frowned at the impertinent oaf. "Do I know you, sir?"

"No," said the man. His clothing was covered by a long grey cloak, and in one hand he held a matching tankard of ale. "But I know you."

"Many people know me. I am a well-known man."

"You are," agreed the stranger. "And an honour it is to be sitting here with you." He nodded at the tankard he'd placed on the bench. "Will you share a toast with me, Meister Driskle? To our new king, may Barl bless his days among us!"

Well. One could hardly refuse to toast the king...

"And to the memory of his family, Barl give them rest!"

Or his late parents and sister...

"And to the swift recovery of our revered Master Magician!"

Not even Durm, though life was surely more peaceful without him.

Feeling a trifle bleary, Willer squinted at his new friend. "Who *are* you?"

The man smiled. "The servant of someone who'd like a word or three, Meister Driskle. If you've the time just now."

He sniffed. "If this is some clumsy attempt to weasel a favour from a man with royal influence, then—"

"Oh no, Meister Driskle," the man in grey said. His eyes were amused.

"Then what does this 'someone' want? Does he have a name? I'll not set one foot outside this wretched tavern if you won't tell me who—"

The man smiled. Lifted a finger and pulled down the edge of his cloak to reveal his collar. It was embroidered with a black and silver falcon: the emblem of House Jarralt.

Willer thumped backwards in his seat. "What is going *on* here?"

The man smiled more widely still and winked. His finger crooked, beckoning. Dumbfounded and mizzled with ale, Willer struggled from behind the bench and followed House Jarralt's grey-cloaked servant out of the rackety inn and into the street, where a dark, discreet carriage drawn by four dark, discreet horses stood by the kerb. The servant opened the carriage door, and Willer peered inside the curtained, glimlit interior.

There was only one occupant.

"Lord Jarralt!" he gasped. Snatching off his hat, he hastily offered an awkward, unbalanced bow. "How may I be of service, sir?"

Lord Jarralt was dressed in sober greys and blacks. He waved one ringless hand, indicating he desired his visitor to join him. Awed, Willer clambered up the carriage steps and bumped himself onto the empty black velvet seat opposite the Privy Councillor. His heart pounded painfully beneath its muffling layers of flesh.

"You may leave us, Frawley," the lord said to his grey-cloaked servant.

Willer flinched as Frawley clicked the carriage door shut. There came the crack of a whip, the slip-sliding clatter of shod hooves on wet cobbles, and the carriage moved off. To where or in what direction it was impossible to tell.

"My lord," he said, breathless, "I don't understand. Is something the matter? The king, is he—"

Jarralt lowered his upraised, silencing finger. "For the moment our beloved king is unharmed, Willer. And may I say how well it becomes you, that your first thought was for him and his safety. I am...impressed."

Willer nearly swallowed his tongue. He didn't know which was more exciting: that Lord Conroyd Jarralt knew his name, that he was sitting in the grand man's carriage or that he'd just been paid an extravagant compliment by one of the most powerful and prestigious Doranen in the kingdom.

He cleared his throat. "Thank you, my lord. How may I serve you? Your man was most circumspect..."

"I am pleased to hear it," said Lord Jarralt. "Our business is of a private nature. I wouldn't like to think of it as...food for public consumption."

Was that a warning? Yes. Yes, of course it was. "Oh, sir, you may rely on my complete discretion! I know the value of silence, I assure you. Why, in my capacity as private secretary to His Majesty, I—"

"Silence," said Lord Jarralt. "Yes. Silence is often useful and so frequently underrated. It can even be a weapon, if wielded wisely. Do you follow me, Willer?"

He snapped shut his teeth and nodded eagerly.

Lord Jarralt smiled. "Excellent."

Questions crowded Willer's mouth like pebbles. Why am I here? Where are we going? What is it you want of me? Why are we meeting in secret? He was choking on curiosity, could barely breathe. His hands clutched the brim of his hat so tightly he thought his knuckles would crack.

Lord Jarralt said, "You don't like Asher, do you."

It wasn't a question. Still unspeaking, he shook his head.

"You're not alone. Tell me...were you asked to describe him, what would you say?"

What would he say? What *wouldn't* he say? Feeling oppressed by all the savage words clamouring to be set free, he tittered. "I'd say he's—he's a bilious headache, my lord."

That made Lord Jarralt laugh out loud. "A bilious headache! Yes. How true. But he is more than that. He is a noxious weed grown rampant and unchecked in our garden, this precious Kingdom of Lur. I'm told he's been appointed Olken Administrator. A tragedy, to be sure."

Willer swallowed. "Yes, my lord."

"To be truthful," Lord Jarralt mused, fingers tapping idly on one knee, "I thought it might be you, but...alas. Doubtless Asher is to blame. He's poisoned the king against you."

A pang of hope seized Willer's heart. He leaned forward, his crushed hat falling heedless to the carriage floor. "Oh, my lord," he breathed. "I'm so afraid. His Majesty is so good, so kind, so trusting. I fear he has nurtured a viper in his bosom unawares. While Darran thought as I do I had some hope of Asher's villainy finally coming to light, but now *Darran* has fallen under his spell too. I don't like to seem immodest but I think I am the only one who can see—"

"Modesty is best reserved for those who have much to be modest about," said Lord Jarralt. "For men like us, Willer, men of accomplishment and vision, it is a pointless conceit. You have no need to fear. You are not the only one who sees Asher for what he truly is."

Willer released a silent sigh of ecstasy and sat back in his seat. The cold void within him was gone now, filled to overflowing with a bubbling warmth. *Men like us.* "My lord, I am relieved beyond words to hear you say so. But what can we do? We are two lone voices, crying in the wilderness."

"I know," said Lord Jarralt, and smiled so sadly Willer thought his heart might break. "It is a lonely road we walk, Willer. I take it you love our new king?"

Willer gasped. "Of *course*!"

Lord Jarralt twitched aside the curtain from the carriage window and for a long moment stared through it into the night-dark landscape beyond. Where they were now, Willer had no idea. The horses' hooves no longer pounded cobblestones, he could tell that much. It meant they must have travelled beyond the City. Did it matter? Not at all. This incredible conversation had already taken him further than he'd ever gone in all his life.

"Gar is of an age to be my own son, you know," said Lord Jarralt, sounding almost wistful. "It's how I've always thought of him. And like any father, I worry. Imagine a host of dangers that might at any moment befall him." His gaze flickered. A warning, or an invitation?

Willer took a deep breath to calm his booming heart. "You think the king is in *danger*, my lord?"

Jarralt let the curtain fall again. "What do you think?"

Willer stared. "I—I don't know."

"I think you do. You said it yourself. A viper in the bosom."

"Yes...I did..." He frowned. "But Asher saved his life in West-wailing."

Lord Jarralt smiled. "Or so we're told."

"I suppose," Willer said slowly, "the story could be untrue. We only have Asher's word, after all. The king's recollection can't be relied upon, he was drowning at the time. And the truth is a mirror, isn't it? What you see in it depends very much on who's looking, does it not?"

Lord Jarralt sighed. "I am a plain man, Willer. Plots and puzzlings and devious designs are foreign to my nature. Therefore allow me to speak plainly, in the hope that you will speak plainly in your turn."

"I will, sir."

"Speaking plainly, then, I am afraid Asher wields an undue influence over the king. I am afraid His Majesty has been duped. Deceived into believing the lout is harmless. On the contrary, he is baleful. He holds the Doranen, Barl's own people, in contempt. And now that his power is unparalleled in the kingdom I am afraid he will use it to manipulate our gentle, trusting new king for his own ends."

"What ends, my lord?" he said, trembling.

Lord Jarralt shrugged. "What is the ambition of every noxious weed?"

The question seemed to suck all the air out of the carriage's interior, so that Willer struggled to keep his lungs inflated. He felt hot and cold, terrified and vindicated, brave and confronted, all at the same time. "To take over the garden," he whispered.

"Exactly."

"But, my lord..." He was anguished. "We have no proof."

"What is proof, my friend, but a coat of paint required by fools who cannot see that a house unvarnished is still a house?"

"I know...I know...but His Majesty will never believe us without it."

"That's true," Lord Jarralt admitted. "So we must find it. Or, should I say, you must find it."

He sat back. "Me, my lord? How? I have no magic, no authority. I'm a mere Olken, a cog in the royal wheel, I—"

Lord Jarralt smiled. "Willer, Willer...don't sell yourself so short. You are far more than that. You are brave. Wise. Dedicated. Most importantly, you are *there*. Within the royal household. In the right place at the right time to do what must be done. To discover the proof that will rescue our dear king from this monstrous Olken. I know it will be difficult, torture even, but you must slay your pride. Swallow your repugnance for Asher, mask your legitimate loathing of him, and stay as close as you can so his actions might be observed. Can you do this, my friend? Tell me you can. Tell me I am not mistaken in your nobility, your dedication to doing what is right no matter the personal cost."

He could scarcely breathe. "You are not, sir, I swear you are not!"

"You will report every discovery, every suspicion, to me and me alone," Lord Jarralt cautioned. "No one else can know what we are about. In time, Asher's true nature will be revealed, of this I have no doubt. But for now he has the king—indeed the kingdom—hoodwinked."

"Hoodwinked and bamboozled," Willer agreed. "To my daily pain."

"But not forever," said Lord Jarralt. "One day, Barl grant it be soon, Asher will stumble and you will be there to witness it. You, Willer, will save our king and kingdom from disaster and so earn the love of all men unto the end of time. But only if you say yes. If you don't, we shall see calamity unknown since the days of Morg and you will be known throughout eternity as the man who helped to kill a kingdom. As Blessed Barl is my witness, I know this to be true. So now we come to it, Willer. Now we reach the point of no return. Will you serve our beloved Lur, my friend? Will you join me in this holy quest to slay the monster Asher?"

"Yes, my lord," said Willer, still breathless with emotion. "Oh, *yes*. I will!"

PART TWO

CHAPTER TEN

Drifting on a drug-soaked sea, Morg cradles Durm's fragile life tenderly, like a mother her babe in arms, and sings to it a song of survival. The fat fool's flesh is reluctant to heal. With every laboured breath Durm fights him, willing himself to die. Morg sweats and strives to deny him the victory.

Pother Nix is his unwitting ally, as determined as Morg to see this ruined carcass claw its way back from the brink. The tiny part of Morg not consumed by the battle is amused; would Nix fight so hard if he knew who it was he struggled to save?

Little King Gar is also an ally. Every day he comes to sit with Durm. Pours love and hope and healing into Durm's slumbering ears and prays out loud for a miracle.

Morg prays with him, and hopes dead Barl is listening.

Durm is listening. Durm weeps, even as he hardens his weakened heart against the king's entreaties and continues to strive for death.

Nix says to his king, Do not give up, sir. For where there is life is also hope.

Morg devoutly hopes that he is right. Marshals his strength, and continues his war.

With a shuddering sigh Gar released Durm's flaccid hand. Sorrow and despair were weights on his chest, pressing his lungs flat and crushing his heart. "Sometimes I think coming here is a waste of my time, Nix."

The pother pressed his shoulder briefly. "Not at all, Your Majesty. I believe our good Durm draws strength from your loving presence."

"But he's struggling. Isn't he?" he said, frowning at the Master Magician's waxy, fallen face. "Why? Why must he fight so hard? I thought you said his injuries were healing."

Nix fussed at a vase of mixed lilies and sweetums on the window-sill. "They are. Slowly."

The man's evasiveness was a naked flame to dry grass. Anger ignited, consuming royal restraint. "*Too* slowly!"

"Everything that can be done is being done, sir. He is dosed on the hour with the freshest, most potent herbs from the infirmary garden and hothouse. All of my magical skill is dedicated to his recovery."

"Then why is he not *healed?* Why does he lie here day after day in this stuporous daze, never once speaking to me or even opening his eyes!"

Nix spread his hands wide. "If I could answer that, sir, I'd be the greatest pother in history. But he *is* making progress. It just takes time."

Gar pushed out of his chair and began to pace Durm's small and airy chamber. "I'm being pressured, Nix. My Privy Council would have me decide Durm's fate sooner rather than later. He was my father's dearest friend. Is a Master Magician beyond compare. I need him. Already I've stalled my advisors twice. I can't procrastinate forever. My kingdom requires a Master Magician in more than name. When will I have one?"

Nix crossed his arms and tucked his hands into his sleeves. His expression was disappointed and reproving. "Your Majesty, you know better than to ask me that."

Stung, Gar folded his fingers into fists and stared through the room's small window. In the gardens outside men and boys toiled amongst the flowerbeds, laughing in the early morning sun. How he envied them their untroubled lives. If he couldn't at least point to a tangible, touchable improvement in Durm's condition by the end of the week he'd have no choice but to abandon all hope of keeping Conroyd out of the Weather Chamber.

Even worse, it would be the right thing to do.

"I'm sorry, Nix," he sighed. "I don't mean to slight you. I know you can't make that kind of pronouncement, or give me promises Durm's body might not be able to keep."

The pother's severe expression eased. "If I might presume on a life-time's acquaintance, sir?"

"Presume away."

"Don't let yourself be bullied by men who have a vested interest in Durm's slow recovery. Or by those whose honest concern is the kingdom's welfare, but who have yet to fully accept your new status. *You are the king.* Sanctified by Barl, blessed with the Weather Magic. Don't forget that... or let those who are sworn to serve *you* forget it either."

Surprised into silence, Gar stared at Nix. Then, as the pother's words sank slowly home some of the crushing weight eased and he could breathe more comfortably. "No," he said at last. "I won't."

"You should get some rest," Nix said abruptly. "I spent more years than you've been alive watching what WeatherWorking did to your father. It's a cruel business. Be miserly with your energy, sir, or you'll not live to see your own child follow in your footsteps."

Gar closed his teeth on a stinging rebuke. The man was obeying the impulse of his own sacred duty...and he was right, damn him. WeatherWorking was proving to be everything his mother had complained of, and more. Despite the pother's revolting restorative his head ached all the time and his bones felt strangely friable. Likely at any moment to crumble into dust. If not rigorously disciplined, his thoughts floated like thistledown on an errant breeze, impossible to catch. And he trembled inside, as though a thin cold wind blew ceaselessly beneath the surface of his skin.

"It's only been three weeks," he said. "In time I'll adjust, as my father adjusted before me, and his before him. Barl would not have given me the crown without also imparting the strength to wear it."

Expression circumspect, Nix nodded. "Indeed."

Gar let his gaze drift to Durm's still body. Rested it there, aching. "I must return to work. If he should in the smallest way stir..."

"Of course," said Nix, and opened the chamber door for him. "At once."

As he made his way through the palace to Durm's desolately empty apartments, he thought: *Let him stir soon, Barl. I'm running out of time.*

It felt strange, almost...indecent...to be sitting in Durm's hushed, private study, holding one of his jealously hoarded magic texts. This room so belonged to the Master Magician he felt like a trespasser. He could almost hear Durm's deep and disapproving voice demanding to know what he thought he was doing...

The book he balanced so carefully in his lap contained the spells he needed to shape the marble effigies destined to grace his family's coffins. There were Doranen in the City who could do it, of course. Who performed the magic for any citizen with the money and a need for such reminders. Where the royal family was concerned, though, tradition dictated the task be reserved for the Master Magician.

With Durm insensate, he'd do it himself. A last, loving service for those he had capriciously survived.

He let the book fall open and searched through its age-mottled pages until he found the incantation. Read the words, felt the sigils unfold, and marvelled anew at the difference within him.

Years ago he'd studied nursery spells, struggling to make them come alive in his mind. Had failed, because without magic he'd been as successful as a deaf child trying to hear music by reading a score. Now incantations sounded in his head like a choir and the magic in his blood danced to hear them.

Banishing exhaustion, lost to the slow march of daylight past the curtained window, he sank himself beneath the surface of wonder and let the magic sing.

According to the notices outside the palace hall where the royal family lay in state, public viewing stopped at six o'clock. Asher stood in the shadow of a deep-set doorway and listened to the plaintive protests of stragglers as Royce and Jolin, the guards on duty, kindly but firmly chivvied them out. It was nearly half-past the hour. After a day locked up in consultations he was tired. Hungry. Worn to frazzlement with other people's problems and dreading the night's Weather-Working to come. He could think of at least three other places he'd rather be.

And yet, here he was.

Tear-stained and still complaining the stragglers wandered past him, unseeing. He waited till they'd left the palace completely, then stepped out of concealment.

"Leave that," he said to Royce and Jolin as they started to close the hall's double doors. "Go home. I'll stand watch till the next shift arrives."

Surprised, they stared at him. "You sure?" said Royce.

He made himself grin. "When did you know me not sure, eh? Go on. Scarper. Or I'll report you to Orrick for insubordination."

Jolin grinned back. "No need. We're away. Why not join us down the Goose later for a pint or three? Or are you too grand now, Meister Olken Administrator?"

"Not too grand. Just too busy. Have one for me."

Laughing, they agreed to suffer on his behalf and departed. He watched them for a moment, envious, then entered the huge hall where Gar's family lay in all their silent splendour.

The room was gently glimlit, casting shadows, softening death. Three velvet-draped biers stood end to end in the centre of the room: Borne, Dana, Fane. Crimson ropes formed a cordon around them, protecting them from extravagant grief. Their faces were uncovered, serene; their bodies buried in a riot of hothouse blooms whose scent tinted the air with summer.

He shivered, suddenly cold. Closed the distance between himself and

Borne and made himself look into that blank, unihabited face. The king's hair was gold again. Washed clean with soap, or magic. Flooded with relief, he realised some part of him had expected blood. Stupid.

He took a deep breath. Released it slowly through gritted teeth. "Well, Your Majesty, here's a thing. You dead. Durm still makin' up his poxy mind. Gar figurin' out your fancy Weather Magic as he goes along. And me...me seein' and doin' things no Olken's got business stickin' his oar into. It's all a bloody mess, ain't it?"

The hall's ceiling was so high his voice echoed. His throat felt sore, his chest tight. A tic in the muscle beside his eye twitched wildly.

"So. Dead or not, sir, you got to do something. He's my friend but he's your son and I'm tellin' you straight, I don't know how to help him. I can't tell if he's doin' your magic right or not. I mean, it rains. It snows. Freezes where it's s'posed to. I think. At least nobody's complainin'. But it's *killin'* him. He says it's s'posed to hurt, it's the price he has to pay, but *this* much? I can't believe that. It's like he's burnin' alive. Bein' cut with a thousand knives. He bleeds and bleeds. At this rate I don't reckon he'll last *one* year, let alone a lifetime. And I ain't any use to him, all I can do is watch. You asked me to take care of him, and I'm tryin', but...you need to tell me *how*!"

No reply. He shifted slightly. Looked instead at Dana and Fane. Beautiful once more, all cruel deformities hidden beneath sweet petals of pink and blue and yellow and mauve. Burnished with glimlight, preserved with powerful magic, their pale skin glowed, lifelike.

Revolted, despairing, he flung himself away.

Silhouetted in the doorway Dathne said, "I thought you weren't going to come here."

His heart was pounding. "Changed my mind."

She came forward, slowly. The day's hard work showed clearly in her tired eyes. She looked pale. "Why?"

Because Gar's killin' himself with magic and I don't know how to stop it. But he couldn't tell her that, so he chose a different truth. "Thought if I saw 'em like this, all clean and covered in flowers..."

"You'd be able to stop seeing them all broken and bloody?"

He nodded. Who'd've thought he'd start bad dreams at his age? "Somethin' like that."

"And is it working?"

Without warning her face blurred and he was looking at her through a prism of tears. "No."

"Oh, *Asher*..."

He wrapped his arms so tight about her he thought he heard her ribs creak, but she made no complaint. Didn't pull away. Just threaded her long thin fingers through his hair and murmured nonsense words of comfort against his skin. Pain was a rising tide he was too weary to hold back.

"I miss my da," he whispered into her hair. "I never got to say goodbye. My damn brothers—they wouldn't even tell me where he's buried..."

Her warm hands framed his face. "They're bastards. *Bastards.* Don't think of them."

"I don't. I didn't. Not until now."

"Let it go, Asher. Your father was mortal. He was always going to die."

Her sudden brutality shocked him. Prising her hands free he nodded at Gar's perished family. "Like them?"

"Yes! Like them. We're none of us immortal, Asher. Death lies at the end of every journey. What matters is how we travel the road." Then her fierce eyes softened, and her fingers touched his cheek. "This isn't just about your father, is it? Something else is troubling you. Can't you tell me what it is? We're friends. I can help."

He closed his eyes. If only he could tell her. Share the burden. The weight of it was crushing him. The fear that something terrible was happening to Gar and he was powerless to prevent it. "It's...complicated, Dath." Reluctantly, he stepped away from her. His skin where her fingers had rested was warm; the rest of his body felt like ice. "Maybe one day."

"You look exhausted."

"I am."

"Then stop tormenting yourself in here. Go home to bed. You've another full day of appointments tomorrow, you'll need your wits about you."

He shuddered. "Don't remind me. I got a last-ditch meeting with Glospottle and the Dyers' Guild. If I can't make 'em see sense it's all goin' arse over eyeballs into Justice Hall."

A glimmer of amusement amid the concern. "Do you need me?"

If he told her how much, he'd frighten her away. "I'll be fine. You got enough on your plate as it is."

"I can reschedule my meetings, I can—"

He pressed a finger to her lips. "No. The Bakers' Guild can't wait, or the Vintners', or Lord Daltrie's taxation committee. You want to help me? Keep the whole bloody pack of 'em far, far away and I'll love you forever."

Love. The unguarded word fell between them like a rock. Silently he cursed himself and took his finger from her lips. She turned away. Fumbled at her tunic.

"I'll do my best."

"Dathne—"

"I should go," she said, glancing at the open doorway. "I'm meeting Matt in the Goose. Did you want to—"

His turn to look away. "Can't. Somewhere to be."

Her relief was imperfectly disguised. "Another time then."

"Aye," he said, heart heavy. "Another time."

She was smiling, but her eyes were troubled. "If we don't cross paths tomorrow between meetings, good luck with Meister Glospottle."

"Thanks. I'll need it."

She left him then, and he watched her go with his fists clenched hard at his sides. Fool. *Fool.* Of all the stupid things to say ...

Please, Barl. Please. Don't let me have chased her away.

Not long after Dathne's abrupt departure, Colly and Brin arrived for their turn at guard duty. He left them to it and made his brooding circuitous way on foot to the Weather Chamber. Entered, and waited upstairs for Gar to arrive. Stood helplessly by, again, as Lur's king screamed and bled and fed the land its rain and magic.

Sickened, shaking, he held the dose of restorative to Gar's blue and bloodstained lips, coaxing it into his mouth. "Send for Jarralt, Gar! Make him Master Magician before this kills you and he takes it all."

Feebly, Gar pushed the cup away and slid sideways down the wall until he was prone on the parquetry floor. His shirt was soaked through with the sweat of his efforts. Convulsive shudders racked him from head to toe. He looked like a man in the last stages of some desperate illness.

"No."

He threw the cup across the room. "*Damn* you! What am I s'posed to *do*?"

Gar closed his sunken eyes. "Nothing. I am my father's son. This cannot kill me."

"Well, it's bloody near killin' me!"

The faintest of smiles touched Gar's face. "Poor Asher. I'm sorry."

Abruptly ashamed, he dropped to the floor. "No. No. Don't mind me. I'm scared for you, is all."

Grimacing, Gar forced himself to sit up. Leaning against the wall, chest heaving, he gave Asher's shoulder a clumsy pat. "Don't be."

Don't be? What kind of sinkin' stupid thing was that to say? Fear transmuted to fury. "*Gar*—"

"You should go," Gar said. "We don't want—" He broke off, coughing harshly, a terrible tearing rasp of sound suggesting lung-rot. "Go," he whispered. "I'll be fine. I just need to rest awhile."

"No, Gar, you—"

"Shall I make it a royal command? *Go!*"

He stood. "You're mad, y'know that? Stark staring crazy."

Gar just shook his head. "I'll see you tomorrow."

The long walk back to the Tower was chilly, and haunted with ugly images. What to do? Perhaps a confidential hint dropped in Pother Nix's ear...

Willer, a satchel hugged under one arm, was leaving the Tower just as he arrived. "Asher!" The sea slug's face contorted into a peculiar expression of nervous ingratiation. "Fancy meeting you this late. Don't tell me you've not stopped working yet?"

Mindless chatter with Willer was the last thing he needed. "No."

Willer stepped a little sideways, blocking him. "Me, either. Darran needs these papers delivered to the palace as a matter of urgency. You know, I thought we worked hard when Gar was just a prince, but—"

Asher raised an eyebrow. "Gar?"

"I mean His Majesty," said Willer hastily. "Sorry. No discourtesy intended."

Sorry? What the— "Willer, was there somethin' you wanted?"

The pissant's fat pink cheeks flushed. "No. Well, yes. Nothing imp— that's to say—look. Asher. I've been thinking. I know we've never quite seen eye to eye." An embarrassed titter. "As much my fault as yours, I expect. I'd like to start over. Show you I'm not such a bad fellow after all. In fact, I'll show willing, shall I? Darran's got me working from sun-up to sundown and beyond, but I'd be happy to place myself at your disposal. Work alongside you, as another assistant. Who knows? We might even turn out to be friends!"

Barl save him. His night was going from bad to worse. "Friends? You and me?"

"Yes. After all, lots of people get off on the wrong foot to start with and then realise they were wrong about each other. Why not us?"

Why *not*? He didn't know whether to laugh or vomit. "Willer—"

"Oh, please, Asher. At least think about it. Consider the idea of us making a fresh start."

"Sure. I'll consider it." *Once I'm dead and buried...*

Willer beamed. "Oh, that's wonderful. Thank you. I promise you won't regret it."

He was regretting it already. "Fine. Grand. Goodnight, Willer."

He left the little slug babbling his gratitude on the Tower's front steps and took himself up to bed. Sent down for a supper of soup and hot bread then sat stubbornly in his cosy parlour, fighting sleep, until he heard Gar's ragged footsteps on the staircase beyond.

Only then did he crawl into bed himself.

Gar woke late the next morning, grudgingly. The merest sliver of light between his drawn bedchamber curtains was like a scythe slicing through his head. His chest hurt and his screwed-tight eyes. His skin. His bones. His whole body overflowed with a grinding, remorseless pain.

Which was nothing compared with the exquisite torment of last night's WeatherWorking.

Asher's right, damn him. This really does have to stop...

Tentatively, he uncurled his clenching of limbs beneath the blankets and eased his eyelids open. The room tilted. Spun like a top. His empty belly heaved, spasming. Good thing he'd forgone dinner or he'd be thrashing in its stinking remains right now...

With infinite reluctance, the violent nausea passed. Drenched in sweat he lay in his tangle of bedclothes and stared at the light-dappled ceiling until he could no longer ignore his nagging bladder.

His face in the privy closet mirror was horror enough to give little children nightmares.

Haphazard bathing and an unsteady shave lifted his spirits, marginally. More than anything he wanted to crawl back into bed and blot out the world for a day... a week... forever... but he had a sacred duty to perform.

No matter how ill and old he was feeling.

Breakfast was out of the question, so he dressed and went downstairs. Bad luck crossed his path with Darran's in the Tower's empty foyer. His secretary looked up from perusing some newly delivered message and didn't quite stifle his shocked gasp.

"I know," he said, forestalling a spate of consternation. "Death warmed over and so on and so forth. Consider it said and the conversation closed. Where's Asher?"

Darran cleared his throat. "In meetings all day, sir. Did you wish me to—"

"No. No. Doubtless I'll catch up with him in due course."

"And you, sir? Where will you be, if you're needed?"

"The family crypt. I'm going to create their effigies today, Darran. Immortalise them in marble. Assuming of course that the templates have been delivered?"

A reflection of his own pain shimmered in Darran's eyes. "Yesterday, sir. While you were otherwise engaged. I did leave a note for you on your library desk, did you not—"

"I haven't set foot in there for weeks." After all this time he'd hoped to have made a start on the precious few books saved from Barl's lost collection, but events had galloped past him.

"Never mind, sir," said Darran gently. "Your books and scrolls aren't going anywhere. When you're ready, they'll be waiting for you."

He was so tired an old man's kindness could touch him to tears. He patted Darran's arm in passing and left him to his duties.

House Torvig's crypt had been built in the grounds of the palace just after Trevoyle's Schism. Its architect was his first royal ancestor, King Cleamon, who'd won the right by Duel Arcana for himself and all his descendants to call themselves WeatherWorker, live in the palace and inter their dead in an opulent marble sepulchre crowned with the newly redesigned house emblem: a thunderbolt crossed with an unsheathed sword.

The chamber he'd chosen for his family's final resting place was small. It seemed... fitting. They'd been close in life, after all. Why not rub shoulders in death, too? He bumped around it now like a fly in a honey pot, heedless of bruising his hip on the corner of one open, waiting coffin. Trying not to look at the three templates the undertakers had left here, propped on wooden sawhorses, ready for magical moulding. One male figure, suitably kinglike. One female, dressed like a queen. And of course the lovely young girl's body, representing Fane. He shuddered. These marble approximations were even more unsettling than his family's actual bodies.

Abruptly tired, he dropped onto the bench seat cut into the chamber's far wall and hid his face in his hands.

He was afraid.

The task awaiting him, a magical creation of their living faces in lifeless stone, was the last thing he'd ever do for them. Years from now, when he too was dead and sleeping beside them in this small cold place, strangers yet unborn would look upon what he wrought here today and believe that what they saw was true.

He lifted his head to stare at the effigy that would become his sister. Its marble face was a blank white expanse, a clean slate, a held breath. The features he gave it here and now would *be* Fane, forever;

he could give her a hook nose, bulbous lips, beady eyes or a lumpen, misshapen brow. He could pouch her cheeks like a greedy squirrel's. Reduce her chin to a querulous afterthought. He could make her as ugly on the outside as she'd been on the inside and nobody could stop him. She certainly couldn't. She was dead.

Vivid as a crack of lightning he saw her: silver-gilt hair gleaming in the sunshine, limpid blue eyes sparkling with mischief, or maybe malice; the sound of her laughter rang in his head more clearly than any silver bell.

He stood. Moved to the lump of carved rock that must become his sister and, ignoring all pain and illness and bone-deep fatigue, summoned the transformation spell.

Untamed, untrammelled, the words surged through his mind like a storm tide, burst from his mouth like snow melt released, sweeping aside all fear. Power cascaded from the secret place inside, raged through his bloodstream, poured out of his fingertips and into the chilly waiting marble. Stone turned to cream beneath his hands, softened and slipped and slithered as memory and magic transformed rock into remembrance.

When at last it was done and Fane lay sleeping before him, beautiful and whole, he pressed his cold flesh lips to her warm stone forehead. Let his cheek rest against hers, and whispered into her immaculate ear.

"I could have made you ugly and I didn't. Remember that, little sister. Remember I still love you, and this as well: you haven't won. The magic remains mine. I did not seek this power and yet it came to me. I did not yearn to be WeatherWorker, but that is who I am. All of it Barl's doing, not mine. I'm sorry you're dead but I won't betray our father by rejecting her gifts just because you couldn't bring yourself to share."

The pain behind his eyes was fierce now. Unforgiving. Feasting on the flickers of remaining magic in his blood. He ignored it. Glory was in him, and triumph, and a burning determination to see this sacred duty done.

His mother's face came less glibly, exhaustion threatening her defeat. Grimly he beat back the scarlet tide even as he felt his face distort in a rictus of torment. When at last she lay before him, eyelashes curling, lips curved in a secret smile, he pillowed his aching head upon her breast and let his trembling fingers caress her hard white hair. In the crypt's swaddling silence he thought he heard her singing, an old sweet lullaby of love and loss. He could have stayed there forever, except his task was not complete.

Stern and joyful, gentle and bold, his father waited.

This time the magic came forth snarling, like a cur dog dragged from the gutter. No riotous gushing but a mean trickle, dregs dripped from a guzzled keg. Panting, sweating, that thin keen wind beneath his skin howling now like one of Asher's sea storms, he wrestled his reluctant power, screamed at it, cozened and commanded and demanded its obedience. The marble beneath his frenzied fingers seethed and surged, and in his mind's eye the memory of his father's face refused to stand still. Slipping and sliding and shifting its focus, it wouldn't let him see, wouldn't let him remember, wouldn't let him offer this last loving gesture in honour of the man he'd adored.

"I will do this! I *will*!" he shouted. "*Electha toh ranu! Ranu! Ranu!*"

The ancient words of compulsion shuddered the crypt's glimlit air. He felt the magic sear his veins like acid, excoriating his flesh. Something deep inside him twisted, tore, ripped his thoughts asunder with monstrous claws. In their place an endless emptiness, unfurling like a fledgling seed.

A profound silence. Then a fist of darkness crashed upon him and the world ended.

CHAPTER ELEVEN

Halfway up the stairs to her apartment after double-checking Poppy's bookwork for the day, Dathne heard the banging on the back door and groaned.

"Go away!"

The banging continued. Cursing, she started down the stairs again.

"I'm coming, I'm *coming*!" she protested, and flung open the door. "*What?*"

Asher, resplendent in green velvet and dull gold brocade. She felt her heart constrict as betraying colour flooded her cheeks.

"Oh. It's you."

He carried a sealed wine jug. Holding it up, tightly smiling, he said, "Care to help me drown my sorrows?"

For a moment she didn't follow. Then, remembering his last meeting of the day, his meaning dawned. "Oh no."

"Oh yes," he replied. "Glospottle refused to see sense, and so did his poxy guild. So it's arse over eyeballs and tits over toenails all the way to Justice Hall."

It wasn't funny, it truly wasn't, but she had to press her lips hard together for a moment. "I'm so sorry."

He shoved the wine jug at her. "Not as sorry as me. Just don't laugh."

"I wouldn't dream of it." She took the jug then looked past his shoulder into the small yard behind her shop. "Where's Cygnet?"

"Snug in his bed. I walked. Needed the exercise, and the time to think."

"I'm not surprised."

"So you goin' to ask me in then, or just take my wine and shut the door in my face?"

Again, she felt her cheeks heat. Stepping back, she said, "Sorry. Of course. Come in. Have you eaten?"

"Not lately," he said, crossing her threshold. "Is that an invitation to dinner?"

"Yes," she said after a moment. "I suppose it is."

Three steps inside her tiny living room he stopped and stared around him, unabashedly curious. He'd never been inside her home before. Keeping him at a friendly arm's length had always been her best defence.

It didn't seem to be working any more.

The tiny dining table was set for one, so after putting the wine jug in her equally tiny kitchen she fetched cutlery for him and a napkin.

He sniffed appreciatively. "Somethin' smells good."

"Rabbit stew," she said, trying not to notice how easily he fitted into her home. "Not as fancy as the meals you're used to these days, but—"

"It's perfect," he said. "Want me to pour some of that wine?"

She wished he wouldn't smile like that: warmly, intimately...lovingly. "Why not? You've got those sorrows to drown, after all. Glasses are in the cupboard beside the sink."

He went rummaging. "I'd rather drown Indigo bloody Glospottle."

How many times could she straighten a knife and fork before she looked ridiculous? "In a big smelly vat of his own urine."

That made him laugh, but the sound trailed off into a groan. He reappeared in the doorway, holding two glasses of palest green icewine. "Don't bloody tempt me." He shook his head. "Barl save me, Dath. I'm goin' to *Justice Hall*."

She took the glass he offered her. "And not in chains, which is the biggest surprise of all."

That made him laugh too. It felt good to know she had the power to amuse him. *Careful, careful*, her inner self warned. But she didn't want to be careful. The icewine was superb, tart and full of fruit. She took a second swallow then put the glass on the dining table. "Have a seat. I'll dish up."

It felt odd, sitting opposite him at the table she usually shared with no one. Circumspectly, from beneath her lowered lashes, she watched him eat. Even that had changed about him. So much polish he'd acquired. He wore his expensive clothing now as though it was just another part of him, like his hair. Once, she vividly remembered, he'd walked around inside velvet and brocade as though at any moment he expected them to bite him. He'd never seemed to her precisely young, just rough... but not any more. Grave responsibilities had aged him. Seasoned him, like green timber long soaked in sunshine and rainstorms. She didn't know whether to be pleased, or to feel sorry for the fisherman stranded so long on dry land.

Upon closer examination, sorrow won. The Glospottle crisis had intensified the strain she'd sensed in him yesterday evening, not replaced it. Whatever had bothered him then continued to bother him now. He was being gnawed by a secret; the pain of it was in his eyes, his voice, his stubbled face.

She dabbed her lips with her napkin. "And how is our new king? He's not been seen in public since his coronation. You must know people are starting to wonder."

Asher tipped the last of his wine into his mouth. "He's fine."

"Are you sure?"

He shrugged, an irritated twitch like a horse dislodging flies. "You think I'm lying?"

"I think you're withholding the truth, which is lying's kissing cousin."

"*Damn* it, Dathne!" Shoving his chair back, he let his knife and fork clatter to the plate and went to her curtained window. Twitched the faded coverings open and stared into the street. "I told you last night, it's complicated. Stop bein' such a...a...slumskumbledy wench!"

"I do know what that means," she said primly. "Matt told me."

"Matt wants to keep his tongue between his teeth."

Appetite stifled, she folded and refolded her napkin. "I'm only trying to help you."

"You can't."

"How do you know if you won't let me try?"

"Don't you understand? I'm tryin' to *protect* you!"

Damn him and his quaint notions of decency. She had to *know* ...
"I never asked for your protection."

"You would if—" He turned back to the window, hiding again.
"This ain't a game, Dathne. We're talkin' laws and consequences and
things best left alone. I'm grateful for your friendship. I enjoyed your
rabbit stew. I can't repay that by puttin' you in danger."

He sounded so torn. So tempted to confide and make her part of
his secret. Here then was the moment. If she could break him now,
he'd truly be hers. She slid out of her chair, joined him at the window
and let her palms rest flat against his back. He flinched, tension
thrumming through him. The flesh beneath her hands was as hard as
marble.

"It's my choice, Asher," she whispered. "My decision. If you can
risk this danger, whatever it is, then so can I. Let me help you. *Please.*
No one should be this alone."

He sighed, a deep and shuddering breath. Broke away and went
back into the kitchen. When he came out again he was drinking from
the jug of icewine.

"Don't know if I can do this sober," he said, almost apologetic, and
held out the jug to her. "Don't know if you can either."

She set the jug aside. "*Tell me.*"

Eyes stricken, expression agonised, he dithered like a horse on the
edge of a ditch too wide to safely jump. "Dathne ..."

She smiled, as invitingly as she knew how. "It's all right. I'm not
afraid."

He leapt. "I been goin' with Gar to the WeatherWorking."

"Oh," she said, after the silence between them had stretched
beyond bearing. Clasped her hands behind her back so they wouldn't
start beating him about his stupid wooden head. "And whose bright
idea was that?"

"His—at first."

"But then you adopted it as your own?" Try as she might, she
couldn't keep the acid sarcasm from her voice.

"Someone's got to be there," he said, stung. "You got no idea what
it's like! The bloody magic *guts* him, Dath. He bleeds like a butchered
hog, he ain't able to walk for an hour after. Sometimes longer. He
can't face that alone."

She wanted to shake him till his teeth fell out. Centuries of waiting dribbled down to these last weeks and days and he was risking

everything the Circle lived for, *everything*. "And you can't face it with him! It's death to dabble in their—"

"I ain't dabblin'!"

"But you're *there*, Asher!" she cried. "Witness to their most secret, sacred magic! To everyone else it'll mean the same thing. If this comes out—"

"How can it come out? I ain't tellin', Gar ain't tellin.' Are you about to—"

"No, of *course* not!" Hammered with fear, she wrapped her fingers round the end of her plait and tugged until her scalp screamed for mercy. She hadn't seen this coming. Why had she not seen this coming? All of Prophecy's plans at risk because of his friendship with Gar! "Asher—"

He flung himself away from the window and began a ragged pacing. "You reckon I *want* to be there, holding the bowl as Gar vomits his guts out night after night? You reckon I enjoy washing all the blood off him, and me? That I like having to sneak about the Tower prayin' like a Barlsman that bloody Willer don't stumble across me comin' when I'm s'posed to be goin', or goin' when I should already be gone?"

"But it's not fair, what the king's asking. How he's putting you at risk. I don't believe there's not a single Doranen he can't call upon to aid him until Durm either recovers or is replaced."

He stopped then, and dropped into her shabby armchair like a deer struck with an arrow. With his elbows braced on his knees he let his head fall heavily into his hands. "Who? Not Nix. That sends the kind of message Jarralt's just itchin' to read. Not Holze. He'd see it as his moral duty to say somethin' *for the good of the kingdom*. There's nobody, Dath. Nobody he can trust to see him like that, except me."

He sounded so defeated. She sat on the arm of his chair, fighting the urge to thread her fingers through his hair. He wore it longer now than once he had. "I'm sorry I shouted," she said softly. "I'm glad you told me."

"It's the only way I can help him, Dath," he said, and slumped sideways a little to lean against her. "I don't know what else to do. All he ever talks about is avoiding another schism. How that'd be a betrayal of his da. He's convinced that if Conroyd Jarralt ever learns how hard it is for him to control the Weather Magic, the bastard'll challenge him as unfit. And he would too. Jarralt couldn't care less about a schism if it means stickin' the crown on his own head after."

"But if Gar truly isn't strong enough—"

He jerked away. "We don't know that! Look what's happened to him in the last two months! First he gets his magic, then he's nearly killed gettin' thrown from a runaway carriage. And losin' his family on top of it—there ain't been a WeatherWorker in history who's come to the throne like that. It's a bloody miracle he can do it at all."

He slumped again, anger spent. Unbidden, her hand drifted to rest on the nape of his neck; he made a pleased little sound deep in his throat and closed his eyes. She let her hand stay where it was, thinking hard.

Another schism. That would surely usher in the Final Days foretold by Prophecy. Indeed, for a time the Circle in Trevoyle's time had thought *they* were the ones to face the fire. The idea made sense. Fitted all too neatly with her visions of death and destruction. A battle between mages for the crown, for the control of Barl's Wall, would swiftly see the magical balances of the kingdom upset. And Asher would be in the middle of it, standing at Gar's right hand as he fought to keep control, to stay king. Yes. It all made horrible sense.

What she couldn't see was how Asher was supposed to stop it from happening. Not with Olken magic, which was a soft and subtle thing, cajoling and persuasive. Not when he hadn't even discovered its existence within himself yet.

The not knowing was killing her. *What about a hint, Jervale*, she silently pleaded. *Just a little hint...*

No reply, and none truly expected. She'd have to learn the truth of things another way. Since Gar seemed at the heart of the mystery, and Asher was close to Gar, then she'd have to get closer to Asher. In the name of duty. In the service of Prophecy.

Yes, yes, she answered the critical voice within. *And because I want to.*

Beside her, Asher stirred. "I should go," he muttered.

"Why? Is there a WeatherWorking tonight?"

"No. But he was all set to create his family's effigies today. He'll take it hard. I should—"

"Leave him be," she advised. "Let him grieve without an audience."

He pressed his fingers to his eyes. "Aye...maybe...but you don't want me clutterin' up your livin' room. I'll—"

She drifted her hand from his nape to his shoulder, almost caressing. "Did I say that?"

Dark colour flushed his weathered skin, and in his face she saw the deepening, the maturing, of all the feelings she'd seen there that night outside the Goose when he'd asked her to leave Dorana with him and go gallivanting off to Restharven. Uncertainly he said, "I thought—"

"You need to ease your mind, Asher. Like it or not you aren't a fisherman any more. You're a man of power and responsibility. A solver of problems, even unlikely ones drowning in piss. Gar's not the only one who needs a friend to look out for him. Stay. Rest. Forget about Gar's problems, and Justice Hall, and all the other worries weighing you down. Stay. Your company's no hardship to me."

She watched hope flare in his eyes. Felt guilt, and a wicked flaring of her own, and smothered them both. Some of the strain eased from his face. He smiled and her heart turned over. "All right," he said. "I'll stay. But only for an hour."

In the end he stayed two hours, and took his leave in a far better mood than when he'd arrived. He hadn't chased her away. If anything she seemed closer to him now than she'd ever been before. As though something inside her had surrendered to the feelings she fought so hard to deny.

He didn't know why, and he didn't much care.

She's mine, she's mine, and soon I'll hear her say it.

He jogged back to the Tower, invigorated. Made it all the way up to his suite, had his fingers on the door handle, damn it, when a peremptory voice called out: "Asher! A moment if you please!"

Swallowing a groan, he turned. Darran stood on the landing below him, a frown pulling his face into tight lines of concern.

"Darran, it's late," he said, looking down through the staircase railings. "Whatever it is, can't it wait till morning? I'm fair bloody knackered. What are you still doin' here anyways? Nix'll have your guts for garters if you keel over again after all his pills and potions. He'll say you're makin' him look bad."

"I'm not interested in Pother Nix's reputation," replied Darran. "And if it's all the same to you I'd rather not stand here bellowing like a fish-monger in the markets. Kindly come down to my office where we can converse like civilised men." Forestalling argument, he disappeared.

Swallowing another groan, Asher trudged downstairs. Just to prove a point he didn't actually enter Darran's office but leaned against the doorjamb instead. "You must be feelin' poorly, callin' me civilised."

Darran looked up from behind his desk. "I was being polite."

"No need to bother on my account."

"Clearly not," said Darran snippily. "Now do stop being obstreperous, at least for five minutes. Or is that too much to ask?"

Despite his crushing weariness, Asher grinned. "Prob'ly." Then, to avoid a tongue-lashing, he did as he was asked. Kicked the door shut behind him and dropped into the nearest chair. "Well?"

Darran steepled his fingers against his chin. "I'm worried about His Majesty."

He could've screamed. "Gar's fine."

"He is *not* fine," said Darran. "He needs a Master Magician."

"He's got one."

"The one he's got is broken. He needs a new one."

"He doesn't want a new one!"

"This isn't about what he wants, Asher! It's about what's best for him!"

Asher got up and started pacing, his heels thumping the carpet as though he were killing cockroaches. All the lovely lingering glow of pleasure from Dathne's company was vanished. Now he felt prickled and badgered and shoved in a corner, hot and bothered and bullied.

"In case you hadn't noticed, Darran, I ain't a Doranen. I can't snap my magic fingers and make everything all right."

"Perhaps not, but you can talk to him. Use your dubious influence. Make him see he must—"

"Don't you think I've *tried*?"

"Then try harder!"

"How? What d'you want me to do, Darran? Lock him in a room alone with Willer till he begs for mercy and promises anything to be let out again?"

Darran slapped his desk. "If that's what it takes, yes! Asher, are you blind? Have you seen how dreadful he's looking?"

"Of course I bloody have."

"Then *do* something. Don't you understand? You're the only person he'll listen to! In short, I fear you are his only hope!"

"I don't want to be his only bloody hope!"

"And that makes two of us!" Darran shouted back, surging to his feet. "But what we want is irrelevant! All that matters is our king!"

Asher threw up his hands. "All right! All right! I'll do it! Anything to shut you up! Barl's mercy, you bang away like a bloody woodpecker, don't you?"

Darran's lips curved in a mocking smile. Slowly, he sat again. "Given you possess all the sensitivity of a tree stump, I thought it the wisest tactic."

"Oh, ha ha," he muttered, and threw himself back in the chair. A fresh headache was building behind his eyes, thunderous as a storm.

Now Darran's smile was mordantly amused. "I hear you're to preside in judgement at Justice Hall. Extraordinary. I must say Barl has a strange sense of humour."

"You're tellin' me."

"Such an undertaking will involve a great deal of preparation. You'll require assistance."

"I got assistance."

Darran pulled a disapproving face. "As a legal expert I'm sure Mistress Dathne makes a very fine bookseller."

He felt his face heat. "I never said it was Dathne."

"You didn't have to. And while I'm sure she performs her duties as Assistant Olken Administrator quite adequately, clearly this is a very different situation. Therefore, in the interests of not disgracing His Majesty, *I* shall coach you in the duties and protocols expected of you in the matter of Glospottle and the Dyers' Guild. No, no," he added, lifting a hand. "There's no need to thank me."

"Trust me," Asher said grimly. "I weren't about to."

"Have you set a date for the hearing?"

"Not yet."

"Best to make it sooner rather than later. This ridiculous Glospottle business has dragged on for far too long," said Darran with a severe sniff. "We can begin work tomorrow morning. After you've spoken with the king. Yes?"

He glared. Darran smiled. Still glaring, he stumped out of the ole crow's office and slammed the door as hard as he could behind him.

The loud bang of timber against timber didn't relieve his feelings, or help his headache, in the slightest.

He tried to speak to Gar first thing the next morning. But Gar wasn't in his apartment suite, or the solar, or anywhere in the Tower. Mildly disconcerted, he wandered out to the stables, where he found Ballodair eating breakfast. Which meant the king wasn't out for an early ride. So where was he?

"What's amiss?" said Matt, behind him.

He rearranged his expression and turned. "Nowt. Just stretching my legs."

Matt was grinning. Pulling on his gloves, ready for riding. "I hear your little meeting with Glospottle and the Dyers' Guild nearly came to blows. Make sure you save me a seat in Justice Hall, eh? I wouldn't want to miss the sight of you in your crimson robes."

"Sink me bloody sideways! Who told you?"

"It was the talk of the Goose last night. If you weren't famous before, my friend, you will be after! An Olken sitting in judgement at Justice Hall? You're a man of hidden talents, Asher."

"I'm a man of many headaches, is what I am. I'll see you later, Matt. I got some business to attend to."

As he left the stable yard, frowning, a nasty thought occurred.

Yesterday Gar had gone to his family's crypt to create the effigies. But that wouldn't have taken all day and night. Not unless—

—unless something had gone horribly wrong.

Brisk walking turned into a fast jog, then an all-out run as he headed for House Torvig's private burial vault. He was panting, streaming sweat, by the time he reached it. Glimfire still burned in the passageways; not a good sign. He took four wrong turns before finally stumbling into the small glimlit room Gar had selected to house the coffins.

He found his king sprawled face down on the flagstoned floor.

"Gar!"

There was a pulse, praise Barl, and slow, measured breathing. Gar's skin was dry, cold, his eyes gently closed. Even as Asher poked and prodded and shouted his name he stirred. Coughed. Woke and stared around him, confused.

"Asher?"

"Barl bloody save me," Asher muttered, and helped him to sit up. "Are you all right? What happened? Don't tell me you decided to *sleep* in here! 'Cause that's takin' reverence for the dead just a—"

"No, no," said Gar, and pressed a hand to his head. "I was moulding the effigies and—I can't remember—there was pain, and a bright light, and—" His expression changed, confusion to caution to sudden fear. "Help me stand."

With a grunt Asher hauled him to his feet. Gar swayed for a moment, finding his balance, then looked at the three coffins. Sucked in a great gasp of air and blanched fish-belly white.

"Barl bloody save me," Asher said again, and this time it was a prayer. Serene, peaceful, exquisite: the faces of the queen and her daughter slept side by side, a song and its echo. But Borne's face was a monstrosity.

On the left side it was perfect. An immaculate representation of the man. The right side, though, was twisted. Melted. The stone eye in its socket had boiled and burst, dribbling marble tears down the sunken cheek. It was as though the effigy were made of wax, not stone, and some mad magician had breathed on it with fire.

"What happened? What went wrong?"

"I don't know," Gar whispered. "It's all a jumble. Barl have mercy, Asher. His *face*!"

Asher stepped between Gar and the dead king's coffin. "Don't look at it. Just listen. This happened 'cause you're coming apart at the seams, Gar. Nix's bloody potion ain't fixing you, it's just been keepin' you glued together. Except now even that ain't working. And folk are startin' to notice."

"What folk? What are you talking about?"

"Darran's been on at me. He can see how poorly you're looking, and so can everyone else."

Gar frowned. "Don't. Not in here."

"Where then? Gar, it's time you came to your senses. Durm's no closer to gettin' out of bed today than he was three weeks ago and a blind man can see you need a Master Magician *now*."

"Must I make it a royal command? I said I won't discuss it!"

"You have to." Heart thudding, Asher shoved his fists in his pockets. "You're so bloody worried about betraying Durm. What about him?" He stepped aside, revealing Borne's disfigured face. "If you work yourself unconscious or worse, into a fit that *kills* you this time, you'll be givin' this kingdom giftwrapped to Conroyd Jarralt. And if that ain't a betrayal of your da I don't know what is!"

For a moment he thought Gar was going to hit him. Then fury faded, and Gar turned away. "I know."

"You need help. With the WeatherWorking, your magic. You need someone who understands what it means to be Doranen. I can hold your coat for you while you make it rain, and mop you up with cloths and water afterwards, but I can't tell you how to control your power."

"I know that too," said Gar, and turned round again. He looked shattered. "I know I've been postponing the inevitable. And I know it has to stop." He looked again at his father's ruined effigy and flinched. "This is a sign from Barl, I think. A warning."

"Then take the hint."

Gar nodded. "I will. Tomorrow. Today I must rest. There's Weather-Working tonight and I need to regain my strength. If what happened here should happen while I'm in the midst of a Working..." He shuddered.

"Fine," said Asher, and started backing towards the chamber door. "Tomorrow. And don't think I won't hold you to it. That bloody Darran'll never let me hear the end of it otherwise."

Pale again, and sombre, Gar followed. As he passed his father's coffin he paused, bent low and pressed his lips to the cold, marred stone of his brow. "I'm sorry, Father. I'll return soon and make this right. I promise."

"Course you will," said Asher, waiting in the doorway. "It only happened 'cause you're tired."

"Yes," said Gar, still staring at his father's face. "I expect so."

Something in the way he said it prickled Asher's skin. He took a step back into the chamber. "Gar?"

"I'm fine. It's just—"

"Gar, don't. Magic ain't like the spotty blisters. You don't catch it then get over it. Even I know that much. If you start thinkin' like that—"

"Like what?"

"Like maybe...maybe..." He couldn't say it. If the words remained unspoken...

Gar's lips twisted. "Like maybe my magic is failing?"

Damn. "No! That's daft. How can magic fail? It's magic. I mean, you're the historian, Gar. Has there ever been a case of a Doranen's magic failing? Running out? Drying up?"

Slowly, Gar shook his head. "No. But then there's never been a case of it manifesting at such a late age either."

"So now you're not just studyin' history, you're makin' it," he said, itching to shake sense into him. Shake out fear, and doubt. "You're *tired*, Gar. That's all. For the love of Barl, don't you start lookin' for things to fret on! We got problems enough as it is."

Gar sighed. "You're right. I'm sorry."

"Aye, well, don't be sorry. Just be walkin', eh? Some people have got work to do."

That made Gar laugh. "You are so rude."

He grinned, flooded with relief. "I ain't rude. I'm just me."

"Yes, you are," said Gar. "And praise Barl for it."

CHAPTER TWELVE

After seeing Gar safe and sound to his apartments, and narrowly avoiding both Darran and Willer, Asher lost himself in yet another day crammed top to bottom and side to side with meetings. Decisions. Authority. Things he was getting used to, but slowly. He saw Dathne only in passing. She smiled at him, her eyes warm, and his spirits lifted. Telling her his secret was dangerous but he couldn't be sorry. Nothing would make him regret feeling closer to her.

The day ended, at last. He ate his dinner down at the Goose, suffering with as much goodwill as he could muster the whooping and hollering and ribtickling about his upcoming appearance in Justice

Hall. Matt's lads promised to fill his boots with manure for good luck. Behind all the joshing and jibing, though, was genuine admiration. A kind of rough-spun awe. He was one of them, one of their own, and yet he was different. Not better. Just...special.

The idea made him laugh. *Tell that to my brothers.*

With several hours to go before he was due to meet Gar for Weather-Working he distracted himself playing darts with Matt and a few of Pellen's lads. Hoped Dathne might stop by for a pint, but she didn't show. Just before closing he paid out the money he'd lost in wagers, said his goodnights and made his circumspect way to the Weather Chamber.

Gar arrived some ten minutes after he did, brisk and rested and uninviting of personal enquiries. "Any crises occur today I should know about?" he asked, conjuring pale gold glimfire.

"None I couldn't handle."

"Darran told me about Glospottle," Gar said with a sly smile. "Don't worry. I'll see you through Justice Hall."

Asher nodded. "Appreciate it. What's on the menu tonight then?"

"Rain on the Flatlands. Snow in the Dingles. And the River Tey is overdue for freezing."

So. A long hard night then. Wonderful. Swallowing a sigh, Asher settled himself in the armchair conjured for his comfort and waited for the show to begin.

Braced for the coming onslaught, Gar raised his left hand. Closed his eyes, murmured a brief prayer and traced the first sigil on the waiting air. The magic ignited, feebly. Asher frowned.

"Gar...that were the wrong sigil."

Gar's look would have burned stone. "It was not."

"You just drew the third sigil for the right hand. Not the first for the left."

"I did *not.*"

He sighed. "I've watched you call rain enough times now that I could teach the incantation in a classroom. That were the wrong sigil. And you didn't walk widdershins."

"Asher!"

He sat back. "Fine. You're the king."

Walking this time, Gar started again. Waved his hand through the incorrect sigil, dispelling its energy, and this time drew the proper one. "*Tolnek.*"

He winced. *Luknek*, Gar was supposed to say *luknek* first. "Gar..."

"*Be silent!*"

Asher bit his tongue.

Breathing heavily, Gar raised his right hand and drew the fifth sigil, not the second. Instead of burning brightly it hung wraithlike for mere seconds, then faded. On a stifled curse he tried again, and this time managed the correct sign.

Increasingly uneasy, Asher watched Gar stumble through the rain-making incantation. This was *wrong*. By now the power should be rising, but the atmosphere in the chamber was unstirred. Instead of painting the sigils smoothly on the canvas of waiting air, Gar's fingers clawed the shapes without grace or commitment. All his precision was gone, and with it his accuracy. His confidence. This Working was a mishmash of meaningless gestures, a litany of misremembered words. A travesty.

At last he could bear it no longer. He got to his feet and moved to intercept Gar's disjointed procession. Held out his hands and said, rough with compassion, "Stop. Gar, just stop."

"No," Gar said, and shoved him aside.

Stepping in front of him a second time he said, "You ain't rested enough. Leave it. The rain can wait."

"It can't wait. Without the Weather Magic the Wall will fall."

"In one night?"

Gar dragged a shaking hand down his face. "You'll have to help me."

"*What?*"

"The words are in here!" said Gar, rapping his forehead with his fingers. "And the sigils. But I can't quite see them...grasp them..."

"Me, help?" He tried to swallow, but his mouth was too dry. "With magic? Are you mad?"

Impatient, Gar looked at him. "You said it yourself: you know the incantations back to front and inside out. Guide me through them. Say the words and draw the sigils so I can copy them."

"You are mad," he whispered.

"Weren't you *listening*?" Gar's eyes were feverish. "I can't remember the incantation's proper sequence! If you don't help me then it won't rain tonight and that will be all the provocation Conroyd needs to challenge my fitness as WeatherWorker."

"And if I do, and he finds out, that's *my* head usin' a wooden block for a pillow!"

"How would he find out?"

Asher opened his mouth. Closed it. Glared.

"I'm not asking you to break Barl's First Law," Gar said with quiet intensity. "I'm asking you to help your king."

Shit. *Shit*. He could just see the look on Dathne's face if he told her about *this*. "I don't know."

"Please."

Stomach churning, he took refuge in movement. Stamped back and forth across the chamber, anger fuelled by resentment. He could feel Gar's eyes on him. His tension and barely controlled fear. Echoing in memory, a promise to an unwell man. *I'll look after him.* He stopped.

"All right. I'll do it, on one condition."

Gar couldn't hide his wild relief. "Name it."

"First thing in the morning you go see Nix and tell him you're sickenin' for something. You drink whatever disgusting muck he puts in your hand. And then you pay a visit to Conroyd Jarralt and congratulate him on his promotion."

A long silence. A reluctant nod. "Very well," said Gar.

He looked as though his heart was breaking. Asher didn't care. "Then let's get this over with. Before I come to my bloody senses."

"How do you want to do this?" said Gar, frowning. "Longwinded explanations won't work."

He shrugged. "You ever play a mirror game?"

"When I was three!"

"You got a better idea? 'Cause I'm all ears!"

They stood face to face beside the Weather Map, arms outstretched and fingertips touching. Torn between fear and feeling stupid, Asher closed his eyes. "You ready?"

"Yes. When the power ignites, be sure to get out of the way."

He snorted. "Like I need tellin'."

Stepping slowly sideways they began the WeatherWorking dance. Not exactly meaning to, with his inner eye Asher saw the Flatlands in full sunshine. The rolling hills and the nodding grasses, burdened with tiny birds. Tasted the clean tang of open air and heard the curlews crying. Closing his eyes he commanded from memory the exact sequence of signs that would summon the rain. Then, hesitantly, he raised his left hand. Gar's hand lifted with it. Together, they drew a picture in the air. His voice whispered, *"Luknek."* Gar echoed him. Walk, walk, walk. Raise the right hand. Draw the second sigil. *"Tolnek."* Another echo. Walk, walk, walk. Raise the left hand. Draw the third sigil. It was getting easier somehow. *"Luknek."* Again, the echo. Asher frowned. Was it his imagination or did his fingers just tingle? No. It was nothing. The blood not getting to his fingertips properly, that was all. *"Tolnek."*

Gar cleared his throat. "Asher..." His voice sounded strange.

"Shut up, I'm trying to concentrate," he growled. What was the next sigil? Oh. Aye. Confident, now, he drew it. *"Luknek."*

A rising breeze trailed hot fingers across his face and his silk shirt whispered. Deep in his blood, a seething sizzle. *"Asher!"* Gar said urgently. *"Look!"*

Sweating, he halted and unclenched his eyelids. Gar was untouched, but blue fire was dancing over *his* hands and up his arms. Even as he watched, Gar let his fingertips drift away. Let his arms fall by his sides. Stepped back.

But the blue fire kept on dancing.

"Sink me bloody sideways!" he choked out, and stumbled away from the map until he hit the wall, hard. It was the only thing that stopped him from falling.

Silence. The thickened air above the map slowly uncurdled. Asher stared at it.

"What was that?"

"Start the incantation again," said Gar, his voice thin and strained. "By yourself this time."

"No bloody way!"

"Please."

"No! No more please, no more help! I'm gettin' out of here!"

He headed for the door, but Gar got there first. "Asher. Start the incantation again."

He was so afraid he thought he might suffocate. "Get away from the door, Gar. Or so help me I'll knock you on your arse and step over you on my way out."

"Asher . . . I think there's magic in your blood."

"No, there ain't!"

Gar pointed at the map. "Then how do you explain what just happened?"

"I don't! And neither do you! It didn't happen. I ain't never been here. I'm goin' home to bed and I ain't never comin' back!"

He shoved Gar aside and wrenched wide the chamber door. Gar's cold, unfriendly voice said, "Leave and I'll have you arrested."

He stopped. Couldn't turn round. "You're *threatenin'* me?"

"I'm asking you to stay. I'm telling you we have to learn the truth. Here. Now. Don't you understand? If you have power, *everything* changes!"

He felt dizzy. "I don't want it to!"

"Our personal private desires don't count. Asher, on the night of Timon Spake's death—"

He turned. "I don't want to remember that!"

There was no colour in Gar's face now. No emotion either. He looked as human as one of those marble effigies in his family crypt. "On that night," he said, relentless, "I called Barl's First Law stupid and senseless because Olken couldn't do magic. But it seems you can. And that explains everything. Why Barl made that law, why your people must die if you break it. Because there's only room for one race of magicians in this kingdom. Mine."

"That's fine with me."

"But not with me! Don't you understand?" said Gar, entreating. "We stole more from you than land! We stole your magic! For six hundred years your people have been living a lie! One that my people forced upon you somehow."

"And do we look like we're sufferin' because of it?" Asher demanded. "No. Gar, it don't matter. Who cares what happened six hundred years ago?"

"*I* care! And so should you!"

"Well, I don't. I ain't you, a romantic in love with the past. I'm a practical man livin' in the here and now. Let this go, Gar. Pretend it were a dream. If you don't it'll only end badly for both of us."

"I can't," Gar whispered. "Please. Try the spell again. Perhaps I'm wrong and you don't have magic. Perhaps it was just an odd kind of Transference, because our fingers were touching."

He nodded. "Fine. That's what it was. Problem solved. Good—"

Gar put his arm across the open doorway. "But if I'm right... Asher, you say you can forget this but we both know that's a lie."

Damn him. Damn *everything*. Why had he come to this wretched bloody City? Why hadn't he just left well enough alone, stayed in Restharven and worked something out with his brothers? Or he could've upped stakes and shifted to Rillingcoombe. Bibford. Tattler's Ear. What had possessed him to abandon his safe life on the coast for *this*?

He had *magic* inside him? How could that be?

It had to be a mistake.

Damn it. Gar was right about one thing, the bastard. Until he knew for sure, he'd never get a good night's sleep again.

Cursing, terrified, he returned to the Weather Map.

This time he kept his eyes open. Felt an odd kind of tugging sensation, drawing his mind and imagination to the map's recreated Flatlands. He watched his shaking fingers draw the sigils as a voice he scarcely recognised as his own recited the rain-calling incantation. Watched the sigils burst into fiery life. Saw blues flame dance up and down his arms. Felt magic's wind rise, gently at first, then stronger and stronger till it buffeted him like storm breath racing inland over the open sea. His blood bubbled with an unfamiliar power that remembered the ocean. He couldn't have stopped even if he'd wanted to.

Barl save him, he didn't want to. How was this *possible*?

The air above the map began to thicken. Darken. The unwanted power he'd raised gave tongue in rumbling thunder and tearing cracks of lightning. He was hot and cold all at once. Shaking and utterly still. His body tingled, like the kissing of a hundred pretty girls. His hair spat sparks, and his fingers, and all the world shimmered bright and blue.

Then the rain burst forth...and the world washed blue to red in a heartbeat as his blood exploded through the confines of his flesh, poured burning from his eyes, his nose, his mouth. And everywhere he turned there was pain.

He fell, screaming. Consciousness receded on a scarlet tide. When it flowed back again he was propped against the chamber wall. His face was tacky with blood and Gar was pressing a cold cup to his lips.

"Drink. It will help."

Dazed, confused, he swallowed. Gagged. Then opened his eyes as Nix's foul concoction burned through the fog in his aching head. "Tell me I'm dreamin'," he whispered. "Tell me I didn't just do that."

Gar put down the cup. "I wish I could."

Humiliatingly, he wanted to whimper. "Sink me, that hurt."

"I know."

Yes, he knew, but so what? It was *supposed* to hurt him, he was Doranen. The WeatherWorker. *I'm a bloody Olken, I'm s'posed to get hurt stubbin' my toe, not workin' magic!*

"Gar, this ain't right. It can't have happened. We *have* to be dreamin'!"

Gar shook his head. "Sorry. It was no dream." He grimaced. "A nightmare, perhaps..."

"But..." He struggled to sit up. "Barl bloody save me. What do I do now?"

"Now?" Gar straightened out of his crouch and looked down at him, all emotion buried. "Now you drop snow on the Dingles and freeze the River Tey."

The words stole his breath like a gut punch. "I can't."

"You must."

"I *can't*, I—"

"If you don't there'll be questions. I can't afford questions, Asher. Not until I've had time to think."

He never knew fear could make a body physically sick. Sweet-sour saliva flooded his mouth, and his belly churned. Now Gar looked almost...angry. "This ain't my fault. I never asked for this."

"I never said you did. Just...finish what you started, Asher."

"And then it's finished?"

Gar nodded. "Yes. Then it's finished."

His body still thrumming with pain, he clambered to his feet and did as he was told. He called the snow, and he froze the river, and when it was done he was a twitching, blood-spittled heap of unstrung bones on the floor.

He felt Gar's hand press his shoulder. "I'm sorry. I'm sorry. Thank you."

He couldn't have opened his eyes if his life had depended on it. But even with them shut he could feel the warm golden wash of Barl's Wall through the chamber's glass ceiling. The touch of it made him want to vomit.

"Go away."

Gar went. Alone at last, he surrendered to tears.

"Barl bloody save me...who am I? *What* am I? And why did this happen to me?"

"Damn!" Pother Nix cursed explosively. "And he was doing so well!"

Beside him, young Kerril gasped as a writhing Durm banged a violent fist to his forehead. The blow reopened an almost-healed wound. Blood spattered his hand, his face, the sheets.

"Now, now, Durm, that's enough," Nix grunted, pressing his palms to the Master Magician's heaving shoulders. "Tincture of ebonard, Kerril, quickly, before he breaks his bones a second time!"

She obeyed, fumbling a little in her haste. At the door to Durm's chamber crowded the other pothers on duty, the ones who'd come screaming for help when the Master Magician's convulsions first started.

The ebonard fumes from the cloth Kerril pressed to Durm's nose and mouth were taking effect. His thrashing slowed, became more feeble. His eyelids flickered. A crescent of white showed, rolling.

"Good girl," said Nix. "Now a lozenge of ebonard and tantivy. You can administer it. Use a spatula or you'll lose your fingers."

She was an excellent student. Deftly she slid the wooden stick between Durm's teeth and tucked the dark green drug under his tongue to dissolve. As they waited for the soporific to calm him completely, Nix looked again to the gaggle of pothers in the doorway.

"Well? Your duty's done here. Be about your business."

They retreated in silence, but their exchanged glances said it all. Even staunch Kerril looked doubtful.

"Go," he told her. "I'll sit with him till I'm satisfied he'll stay sleeping."

She nodded and withdrew and he sat there with his fingertips pressed to Durm's erratic pulse, his mouth bitter with the taste of impending failure. He couldn't maintain the charade any longer; this fit had stripped him of all final, fading hope.

Durm was dying. It was merely a matter of time now, before the Master Magician's weakening will succumbed.

"I'm sorry," he sighed, and patted Durm's slack wrist. "I tried. Please believe me, I tried."

So close, so close to breaking free, Morg feels the drug seep into his prison of blood and bone and cries aloud his fury and despair. Barl's Weather Magic burns him like a brand. It means the cripple still has his unnatural magic ... but how can that be? Gar's artificial powers should have failed him by now! They were explicitly designed to fail!

Thrust into the shadows, Durm the dunghill rooster crows his temporary triumph. Morg snarls at him, revealing all his terrible teeth, and Durm wisely shuts his beak and cowers.

Satisfied, Morg bends his mind and will towards victory. He must escape this fleshy cage. He must discover why the cripple's magic still holds sway. He must bring his exile to an end.

Let me out! Let me out! Let me out!

Matt felt the change roar through the world like fire. The ferocity of it sat him bolt upright in his bed, shattering sleep, scattering dreams. Heart pounding, he lit his bedside candle and stared around his tiny bedroom.

Everything looked exactly the same.

There was sweat on his face, stinging his eyes, trickling through his stubble. Dragging up the sheet he blotted himself dry and waited for his thundering pulse to ease.

Was it Asher? Had something happened to him? He couldn't tell. Sight wasn't his gift, and for the first time in his life he regretted its lack.

As always when he was troubled he sought solace in his horses. Safety lamps burned throughout the night beside each stable, casting shadows. Overhead, the cold stars shone like chips of living ice and the Wall glowed gold as steadily as ever. He trod across the yard softly, slippers whispering, mindful of every step. His lads were good lads, well trained; they'd wake at the first sign of upset or the sound of unexpected feet crunching gravel.

Poor neglected Ballodair roused from dozing and chumbled sleepily over his stable door, curved ears flicking. Patting him, petting him, Matt promised to make sure the king rode him more often or else let him go away for a time to the countryside, where a horse could be a horse and kick up his heels at will.

Wheeling like rooks disturbed, thoughts and questions crowded his aching head. Something momentous had just occurred. The balance of Lur's magic was changed, upset, disordered. Turned arse over eyeballs, as Asher would say.

He frowned, letting Ballodair's tidy forelock thread through and through his busy, distracted fingers.

Was it Asher behind this change? And if so, did that mean they'd truly reached the end of waiting? In the last year there'd been so much tension. Anticipation. He felt as though he'd been holding his breath forever beneath a lowering sky, watching lightning flicker, listening to the thunder roll, expecting it to rain now...now...now...

Was *this* now? Had the first hard raindrops finally fallen? Had the Innocent Mage lost his innocence at last?

"Matt!" a soft, breathless voice called from the shadows. "*Matt!* Did you feel it?"

Dathne, as though summoned by his questioning thoughts.

He hurried to her, mindful of how clearly voices carried on the cool night air. "What are you doing here?" he whispered, hustling her out of the stable yard proper and into the gardens beyond. "Are you mad?"

She was panting, as though she'd run all the way from her apartment to his stables. Even in the palest of moonlight he could see her wildly shining eyes. "Did you feel it?" she said again, her fingernails digging into his arm. "Like an explosion of fireworks! A hundred times stronger than when I felt him first arrive! Do you know what this means? Asher's power has woken!"

So. The Final Days were upon them at last. "Then it's time to tell him the truth."

She shook her head. "No."

"*No?*" He took hold of her. In his grasp her shoulders felt so breakable. "*Think*, Dathne! We might not be the only ones who felt him wake. If the Doranen learn of him they'll kill him within the hour and tell everyone he died in his sleep. Then they'll turn on the rest of us.

We *have* to tell him! Tonight. He must've felt it too, he must realise something's changed in him. We have to explain before he does something stupid out of fear or ignorance. What if he reveals himself before we're ready?"

Frowning, she held up a silencing hand. Matt felt his heart thud: he knew that look. She was searching within, listening for that small voice that only she could hear. That spoke to Jervale's Heir and no one else. These were the times she became a stranger. Her hair was unruly, loosened for bed. It billowed round her sharp face in a soft cloud. Made her look younger than her years... and she was hardly old to begin with.

"No. We have time yet," she said at last, stirring.

He wanted to shake her till her teeth fell out. "Please, Dathne, *please*. For once in your life be guided. He's the *Innocent Mage*. This kingdom's only hope. We can't risk him, we can't leave him ignorant any—"

"I'm Jervale's Heir!" she hissed at him, like a cat. "I can do whatever I see fit!" She pointed to the Wall, their silent golden witness. "Does the damn thing look unsteady to you? Trembling on the brink of destruction? No. Which means Prophecy is incomplete. I still have time."

"To do *what*?"

She looked away. "To convince Asher he can trust me with all his innermost secrets. With *this*."

He decided to take a risk then. "You know he's still in love with you."

She wasn't a stupid woman. She heard the silent criticism. The implied accusation. Her jaw tightened and she folded her arms across her narrow chest. "Of course. Why else do you think he'll tell me what I need to know?"

A hundred words, a thousand protests, clamoured for release. He beat them back. Took another risk and let his hand return gently to her shoulder. "Be careful, Dathne. You think you're oh-so-clever— and in some ways you are—but he's not the only one in love."

He'd shocked her. Her mouth opened. Closed. Opened. Her sharp eyes dulled with surprise and all the passionate colour fled from her face. "My feelings are none of your business, Matt. I'm Jervale's Heir. I know what I'm doing. And anyway, I don't have any feelings."

Defeated, as always, he shoved his hands in his pockets. "If you say so."

"I say so. And this too: don't question my judgement again."

"All right. If that's what you want."

Her eyes were cold. "Yes. It's what I want."

He thought she knew herself well enough to understand it was a lie. And that she knew him well enough, too, to realise he had no intention of holding his tongue if he thought he had to speak. This was a matter of saving face, of soothing hurt. She thought she'd kept her love hidden and was angry to discover she was wrong.

"Fine. I'll go back to bed then," he said. "If that's all right with you."

"More than all right," she snapped. "If anything else happens, I'll let you know. Probably."

"Aye, Dathne," he said, walking away. "You do that."

The memory of her pale, furious face chased him into sleep. Worry and dread made sure it wasn't peaceful.

Gar walked back to the Tower in the dark, without benefit of glimfire. He was too afraid of what might happen should he attempt its conjuration. His chest felt tight, hooped with iron bands. His palms were sweaty, his eyes hot and dry.

Asher made it rain. Asher made it snow. Asher froze a river.

And I couldn't.

Some sound caught in his throat then. A sob, or another expression of distress. Breathing was suddenly painful, as though the air had turned to knives.

He'd fallen into the habit of visiting his unburied family of a nighttime, once the public were safely elsewhere. He couldn't face them tonight. Not after such a catastrophic failure. Fane would jeer at him and call him names and his father... his father...

He stared at Barl's magnanimous Wall, serenely shining in the distance. Emblem of his sacred oath. Victim of his inadequacy.

"Sweet lady, Blessed Barl," he whispered, dropping to his knees beneath the indifferent sky. "Tell me how I've failed you. Show me how to make amends. From earliest boyhood my only desire has been to serve you. Why did you gift me with magic if not to make me your voice in Lur? Why did you take back the gift? Is my service now distasteful? Did I falter, or did you?"

Holze would say the question flirted with blasphemy, and perhaps it did. Too bad. He still wanted—*needed*—an answer.

None came.

A different question then. "Where does Asher's magic come from? You? Or was it always in him? Is it in all his people? If so, what does it mean? And what should I do about it? If Conroyd Jarralt ever finds out Asher is a dead man and perhaps all his people with him. Is that what you want? The Olken dead? *Asher* dead?"

Still no answer. A sudden wave of fear and fury drove him to his feet. "Well, I won't have it! I won't let you kill him!" he shouted to Barl's last lingering presence, her Wall, implacable and uncaring. "I defy your First Law, madam! I defy *you*! No matter how I came to it, I am Lur's king and I shall do what I must to protect it from harm. To protect the Olken from harm. From you, if I have to. Do you hear me, Barl? I would even protect them from *you*!"

He returned to the Tower. Stripped and fell into bed to dream wildly of flood and fire and women weeping. Exhausted, he woke hours later to daylight and a dreadful understanding that needed nothing so crude as manifested proof.

Once more, he was empty. His magic was gone.

CHAPTER THIRTEEN

Willer had already been hard at work for nearly three hours when his prey finally deigned to come into the office. Ever since his... arrangement...with Lord Jarralt, that was how he'd thought of Asher. And of himself as the wily hunter, poised to bring him down.

But as prey, damn him, Asher was proving elusive.

Hidden in the false bottom of the right-hand drawer in his desk were his notebooks, filled cover to cover with the lout's transgressions. He remembered them all. He'd practically crippled himself these last few weeks, painstakingly listing each and every crime. Just as soon as he could he was going to pass them along to Lord Jarralt. Lord Jarralt would find them fascinating reading, he was sure. They'd go a long way to seeing that Asher got his deserved comeuppance, he was certain.

Almost certain.

Because while they were damning, they weren't precisely...treason.

What he *really* needed was to catch Asher in the middle of committing an act so heinous, so treacherous, so clearly illegal, that not even his nauseating friendship with the king could save him. It was the only way to save His Majesty.

Tragically, though, catching the bastard red-handed was proving harder than he'd anticipated. Asher was slippery, and disinclined to let anyone close. He doubted now if his offer of assistance would get him where he needed to be. Perhaps he'd have better luck working on the stupid bookseller; a woman that plain and unapproachable would surely be grateful for the attentions of a well-set-up and influential young man.

He did know one thing for certain. If he didn't soon come up with some kind of evidence to seal Asher's fate, Lord Jarralt would turn elsewhere for aid. Someone else would be the key to Asher's destruction. Someone else would get the glory.

He thought he'd rather die.

Some twenty minutes later Asher finally made an appearance in the office, looking ill and strained and altogether drained of his irritating arrogance and energy. He moved as though his head might topple from his shoulders at any moment. As though every muscle pained him, separately and in chorus. Willer felt his pulse quicken. The bastard had been drinking. To excess, to look as poorly as this. And now here he was, determined to make vitally important decisions that would affect hundreds of lives.

Splendid.

"Gracious me," he said, unctuously concerned. "Are you quite well, Asher? You look positively *green*."

Asher barely glanced at him. Eased himself by inches into the nearest chair and scowled. "When's Darran meetin' with the market committee again?"

"Tomorrow."

Asher grunted. "Make sure I get a copy of last month's figures by end of day then."

Willer swallowed a scream. "Certainly."

"Have you seen Dathne?"

"I believe she had a meeting with the Midwives' Guild this morning. I'm so sorry, I thought you knew."

Asher's expression was filthy. "Midwives' Guild. Aye. That's right. Course I knew."

Liar. Willer knocked a pen to the floor and dived beneath his desk to retrieve it. When he could trust his face again he sat up. "Is there anything else I can help you with? Preparations for the upcoming hearing in Justice Hall, perhaps?"

"No."

Watching the bastard screw his thumb tips into his eye sockets, watching him wince, Willer felt his fingers tighten to crushing point around the pen. Rude, ignorant, arrogant...

Hurrying footsteps sounded on the staircase outside. Then a junior messenger, pink-cheeked and breathless, appeared in the open doorway and bowed. "Meister Asher, sir, His Majesty's compliments and you're to join him in the stable yard. Dressed for riding, he said."

"Riding?" said Asher ungraciously, lowering his hands. "Now?"

The messenger darted a glance at Willer. "Yes, sir."

Asher cursed under his breath. "Go back and tell him I can't, Toby. Tell him—" Another curse. "Damn it. Tell him I'll be there directly."

"Sir!" squeaked the shocked messenger boy, and fled.

With an effort, Willer schooled his face to solicitude. "I'll tell Mistress Dathne you've been called away, sir, shall I? When she returns? And Darran? They'll need to rearrange your appointments."

"Rearrange 'em?" snarled Asher, hoisting himself to his feet. "For all I care they can—" He stopped himself, just. Favoured Willer with a look of intense dislike, and headed for the door. "Aye. Do that."

Willer waited for the sound of his feet on the staircase to fade into silence, then indulged in a gust of silent, excited laughter. Refusing a royal summons. Was there no end to Asher's arrogance? How perfect for his purpose. And before a witness, too! Messenger boys' tongues waggled faster than their knobbly little knees did when they ran. This story would be all over Tower and palace by sundown.

Lord Jarralt was going to be *thrilled . . .*

Swearing viciously, Asher yanked off his fine indoor clothes and pulled on his riding leathers, boots and a second-best shirt. Meet Gar in the stable yard! As if he had time for riding! As if he felt well enough, with every inch of his body still screaming bloody murder after—after—

He could scarcely bring himself to think it. When he'd woken a scant hour before sunrise, cold and stiff on the Weather Chamber floor, his face crackling with dried blood and his fine shirt ruined, he'd snivelled like a spratling, a girl, so monstrous was his fear and confusion and dread.

And now Gar wanted to talk about it.

Well, he didn't. What was there to talk about? Nobody could ever know what had happened last night. They must never speak of it, not even when they were alone. That's what he'd tell Gar while they were out riding through the poxy countryside.

And that would be the end of it.

The horses were saddled and waiting in the stable yard. Matt was holding them, chatting with Gar. Seeing Asher, his eyebrows flew up and his lips pursed in a soundless whistle. "I've seen healthier-looking drowned cats. What's amiss?"

Smoothly, Gar answered for him. "Asher is proving himself my most hardworking and loyal subject." Beneath the surface pleasantry, Asher saw he was brittle as sugar-glass.

"That's our Asher," Matt agreed, handing over Ballodair's reins. "Dedicated to a fault. Now you have a good ride, Your Majesty, and mind yourself, because he's feeling a bit fresh this morning."

Proving the point, Ballodair humped and cow-kicked when Gar swung himself into the saddle, then bounded stiff-legged across the stable yard. As Gar fought to control him, gasping, Matt turned to Asher.

"You do look bloody awful," he said, grabbing hold of the offside stirrup leather to keep the saddle steady.

Asher pulled himself aboard his patient Cygnet and nodded his thanks as Matt slid his boot home in the stirrup iron. "Too many meetin's, not enough fresh air."

"Ready?" Gar called out, Ballodair momentarily subdued.

Matt stepped back, frowning. "Come see me when you've done riding. We'll talk."

"Ain't got time for talkin' these days, less it be with poxy guild meisters and the like," Asher replied, giving Cygnet a nudge with his heels. Then he dredged up a smile, because Matt was looking right down in the mouth. "But thanks."

And he followed Gar out of the yard.

They cantered side by side for miles along the barren Black Wood Road, not speaking, until they reached the turning for Crasthead Moor. Gar kicked Ballodair onto it, urging the stallion to go faster, faster. Standing in his stirrups, Cygnet's long silver mane flogging his face, Asher pounded in their wake. Under clean blue skies, with cold air whipping their cheeks to colour, they rode into the heart of desolation. When at last the rock-strewn moor spread bleakly in every direction, Gar lifted his hands and eased Ballodair back to a canter, then a trot, then a walk and finally a steaming halt. Panting, sweating, Asher gentled Cygnet to a standstill opposite, keeping his distance.

A wary silence filled the space between them. When it became unbearable, Gar spoke.

"We can't pretend it didn't happen."

Asher blinked away wind-whipped tears. "I can."

"No," said Gar, his expression as cold and remote as the moor. "You can't. You see, we have a problem."

"You reckon?" he said, and laughed. A pluming of breath echoed his derision.

Gar's gloved fingers tightened on his reins. "If you laugh again I'll pull you from your horse and beat your head to a bloody pulp with a rock."

He looked Gar up and down. "You could try."

With a cry of frustration Gar wheeled Ballodair in a churning of mud and small stones. The horse snorted, resenting the rough treatment. "Asher. Don't. It doesn't help us."

He settled his gaze on the distant horizon. "True. There's only one thing can help us. Me leavin'."

Ballodair pawed at the wet ground, grunting his impatience. Gar jerked the reins hard. "You can't."

"I can," he said, fear stirring. "I will. I—"

"Asher, I've lost my magic."

Somewhere in the distance, a faintly crying curlew. Beneath him, Cygnet snorted and swished his tail. He cleared his throat. "I don't know what that means."

Gar's eyes were terrible. "Yes you do. We both do. Gar the Magickless has returned."

"That ain't possible." A dreadful premonition was beating black wings about his head. He tried to fight it off with words. "You're just exhausted. Imagining things."

"*Imagining* things?" Gar shouted. "How dare you say so? How *dare* you after all I've lived through? Do you think I could forget what twenty-four years of barrenness felt like after a mere few *weeks* of magic? I am *empty*, Asher. Devoid of all power, and even its memory. Whereas you—*you*—"

Asher flinched as Gar's furious glare burned him. Jerking up his hands, closing his calves against Cygnet's sides, he backed the horse two paces. "Don't say it."

Gar was implacable. "I must. And you must hear it."

"*No*. I can't—you can't ask me—expect me—"

"But I can, Asher. I do. I may not in conscience be king any longer, but I'm still my father's son. Custodian of his legacy. The last living link to House Torvig, caretakers of this kingdom for nearly four centuries. I have a duty and I will fulfil it. Regardless of the cost, or consequences."

"To you?" Asher laughed, unamused. "There ain't no cost or consequences to you! Cost and consequences are for ordinary folk like me and Timon Spake!"

Gar just looked at him. "Last night, Asher, you made it rain. So don't you sit there and prate to me of ordinary folk. You are anything but *ordinary*."

"I am if I say I am!" At the tone of his voice Cygnet tossed his head, ears pinned. "You think I *want* this? Magic? Ha! If there was a way to get rid of it right here and now I would!"

"Really?" said Gar, taunting. "Are you sure? Don't tell me you didn't feel magic's glory last night, as well as its agony. I saw your face, Asher. I know *exactly* what you felt."

Shocked speechless, shaking with outrage, he could only stare. The thin wind blew chill and bitter in his face, biting all the way to bone. Cygnet jittered, haunches swinging left and right, ready to bolt. "That ain't my fault. I never asked for it."

Gar's lip curled. "Maybe not. But you've got it."

"And you're so jealous you could spit, ain't you? Well, damn you, Gar," he said at last, and wheeled Cygnet away.

Gar spurred Ballodair forward, blocking his escape. "I'm sorry," he said harshly. His face was filled with a monstrous pain. "You must understand. I thought I was my father's son in more than name, but I'm not. Oh Asher, don't you *see*? You *have* to help me. If it's discovered I've lost my magic, there'll be chaos!"

"And if it's discovered I found it, there'll be chaos anyway! Not to mention an execution!"

Gar shook his head. "That won't happen."

"Why?" he sneered. "Because you'll protect me?"

"Yes."

"Ha! Like you protected Timon Spake?" It was a low blow, but he didn't care. As Gar recoiled, silenced, he jerked Cygnet back a pace. "Don't ask me to use Weather Magic again, Gar. I can't do it. I *can't*."

Recovered, Gar ignored him. "Barl's Wall cannot survive without it. And if the Wall falls this kingdom and all the innocent people in it will be destroyed. Is that what you want?"

"I ain't the only one who can do it! There's Conroyd Jarralt, for a start. And he's Doranen. He's *supposed* to!"

Gar's face twisted. "Oh yes. King Conroyd: a thought to ice the blood. But there are others, too, with sleeping dreams of majesty. If my failure is made public wild ambition will rule the day and we'll be wading hip-deep in blood before the week is out. Trust me, Asher. I'm an able historian and I know what the promise of power can do."

Asher's fists were clenched so hard on the reins that his gloved fingers were going numb. "So...don't tell me. Let me guess. You want to go on wearin' the crown while I take care of the WeatherWorkin'? Is that the plan?"

Gar looked him full in the face. "I'm desperate."

"Well, *I* ain't! And I ain't scraddled in the head neither! You'd never keep this secret, Gar! Sooner or later folks'll notice you ain't doin' magic in public any more. There'll be talk. Questions. Polite at first, but in the end they'll be demands. The truth'll come out, and when it does I won't be the only Olken in strife! You can't ask me to put all my people at risk. You can't!"

Silence. Gar stared again at the bleak and dreary moor. Asher, slowly freezing to his marrow, tucked his fingers into his armpits and waited. A sparrowhawk soared overhead, wings outstretched. Spying something amongst the grassy tussocks below, it abruptly halted, feathered wingtips snatching at the clear bright air. A plummeting dive, a shriek of triumph and it wheeled away again, death dangling from its talons.

"You're right," said Gar at last, rousing from reverie. "We can't keep it secret forever. But we can keep it secret for a month."

"And what good'll *that* do?"

"Asher, your people weren't safe during Trevoyle's Schism. Hundreds died. And if the kingdom schisms again, hundreds more will join them. Maybe thousands, this time. You can stop that. In a month I should be able to read every medical and magical text we have, to see if there's a cure for what afflicts me. There might even be something in Barl's lost library. I never got the chance to look through it completely."

"So you're saying there's a cure now?"

Gar shrugged. "There might be."

"And if there ain't?"

Another shrug. "If by the end of a month I've failed to find a remedy, or if Durm is still unconscious—or dead—and can be no help at all, I'll go to Conroyd and Holze. Tell them my magic has failed. Name Conroyd king and Holze the new Master Magician. Conroyd will receive the Weather Magic, undertake his first WeatherWorking and then be publicly presented as king. No uncertainty. No schism. No death."

A month. Rain and snow and blood. *Magic.* "Don't wait," he said, his belly churning. "Do it now."

Gar shook his head. "Not while there's even the slimmest hope I might still keep this kingdom from Conroyd."

"Then choose someone else!"

"There is no one else."

"Barl bloody *save* me!" he cried, and spun Cygnet about so he wouldn't have to look at Gar's quiet despair a moment longer. "I wanted to be a fisherman, Gar. I wanted nowt but a boat and the ocean and an open sunlit sky—"

"And I wanted magic," said Gar. "Not every man gets what he wants, Asher. Most men just get what they're given."

Asher stared over the moor, unwilling to trust his voice. Afraid that a single word might shatter him entirely.

Gar said distantly, "I was going to be married. I was going to be a father. It's funny, isn't it, how you can tell yourself you don't want something so often you actually begin to believe it."

Crasthead Moor blurred. Anguished, he blinked it clear again. Found his voice. "How can you ask me to do this?"

"How can I not?" said Gar.

It was a demand. A plea. A millstone round his neck.

He slipped his feet free of the stirrups and slid from the saddle. Dropped his reins and walked away, head down, boots squelching in the wet.

He'd always lived a dangerous life. A man went out at dawn, there was no saying he'd come back at sunset. Fishing was an unchancy way to spend your days. He'd grown up with that. Accepted that. He understood fishing.

But this? How could he understand this?

I got magic in my blood.

Where had it come from? How did it get there?

How do I get rid of it?

One sip of Weather Magic had been enough. No man should have that much power, not for any reason. Not even to do good. His bones still ached with the memory of it. With the glory, and the pain.

Behind him, the sound of boots thudding to the muddy ground. The slap and squelch of Gar approaching. A familiar, frustrating presence at his back.

He didn't turn around. "What if I ain't the only one, Gar? What if there's other Olken like me?"

"Then I pray they stay safely hidden."

"I'm *scared*!" he said, and felt his gloved hands become fists.

"So am I."

Asher turned, then. Took a deep, hurting breath and let it out. Gar didn't look scared. His face was a mask, all feelings smothered.

"If this goes wrong—"

Gar shook his head. "It won't."

"It *might*! And if it does—"

The mask slipped. "Then they'll have to kill me too," Gar said. His voice was low and shaking. "They'll have to kill me first. I swear it, Asher. On the bodies of my father and my mother and my poor misguided sister. They will have to kill me first."

Stirring words, honestly meant. He wanted to believe them. Gar believed them. But was that enough? If the unthinkable happened and this mad scheme was discovered, would the oath of a magickless king be enough to save him?

When he'd asked Gar's dead father how best he could help, this wasn't what he'd had in mind...

Gar said quietly, "Please, Asher. Do this. I think our kingdom is doomed if you don't."

For one long moment he forgot how to breathe. A terrible interior pressure swelled and swelled, dancing black spots before his eyes and threatening to crush his lungs. The desolate moor smeared red and orange and gold. He flung away from his tormentor, his friend, his king. Bent double, closed resentful fingers around a wet grey rock and hurled it into the melting distance. Hurled another, and another, and another, his bones vibrating with an incoherent rage. When he could stand it no longer he opened his mouth and screamed, bellowed, vented all his fear and fury into the wide, uncaring sky. And then stood there, his head bowed to his chest. Emptied and resigned.

Gar's gentle hand came to rest on his shoulder. "Thank you, Asher. I promise you won't regret it."

The return ride from the moor to the Tower stables was completed in silence. Back in the stable yard, Gar threw Ballodair's reins to young Boonie and walked away. Asher watched him go, not the least sorry they were to be separated for a while.

He needed time to think.

Jim'l offered to take care of Cygnet, but Asher refused. Good honest labour, that's what he was after. Distraction, and sweat born of muscles, not magic. He returned Cygnet to his stable, untacked him, then collected a spare grooming box and busied himself with the soothing task of making the silver stallion beautiful.

Solitude didn't last long.

"Have a good ride then?" Matt asked, leaning over the stable's closed half-door.

He glanced up from untangling Cygnet's tail hair by hair. "Aye."

"You should go out more often. Cygnet needs the exercise, and you need the fresh air."

"Aye, but when? Ain't enough hours in the day as it is."

"Early," suggested Matt. "Before breakfast. It'll give you an appetite."

"Give me a heart spasm more like," he said, briefly grinning.

Matt frowned. "That's not funny. Asher, what's wrong?"

He freed the last tangle in Cygnet's tail and reached for a dandy brush. "Nowt."

"Why don't I believe you?"

Damn. Too sharp by half, was Matt. He made himself look up. "Nowt you can help with."

"It's a big job you've taken on, this Olken administrating," Matt said after a moment. "Before, you could hide in the prince's shadow. Now he's king and you're in full sunlight. If you're not careful you could get burned."

An observation too close for comfort. He swapped the dandy brush for a soft-bristled body brush and started scrubbing at the dried mud on Cygnet's flanks. The horse swished its immaculate tail, and he thumped its rump in warning. "I'll be fine."

"I'm sure you will," said Matt, looking unhappy. "Just mind your step, will you? Don't do anything stupid."

What, like make it rain? To hide the thought he swapped sides from Cygnet's left flank to his right. "Fuss, fuss, fuss. Ain't you got work to do?"

Matt slapped the stable door. "Yes. I just wanted to tell you the horses to pull the royal hearse arrive sometime today."

"His Majesty'll want to inspect 'em. Let me know when they get here."

"Of course," said Matt.

Alone again, Asher indulged himself in another half-hour of horse-primping then surrendered to the promptings of duty and returned to the Tower. Where Darran was waiting, armed with a four-foot-high stack of legal books and an evil smile.

In his weaker, less honourable moments, Asher found himself wishing that Darran had . . . all right, maybe not *died*, but remained ill enough after his collapse for Nix to have made him retire. To the country. At the other end of the kingdom. And forbidden him long carriage rides.

"You got to be bloody joking," he said, stopping in his office's open doorway. "And that's *my* desk you're sittin' at, in case you hadn't noticed."

Darran unfolded himself from the chair. "I've taken the liberty of conferring with Lady Marnagh. Given the vexatious nature of the dispute between Indigo Glospottle and his guild brethren, and despite the fact you're a jurisprudential ignoramus, we thought it wise to gazette the hearing for early next week. That's after the funeral, and should give me enough time to prepare you adequately." He sniffed. "Now kindly take a seat. We have a great deal of work to get through before—"

Asher slouched into his office. "Not we. Me. I can read, Darran, and I don't need you turnin' the pages for me. If I run into trouble I'll ask Gar."

Darran's eyebrows lifted. "You can't possibly bother His Majesty at a time like this! *I* will—"

"Mind your own business," he said, and tugged Darran out from behind the desk. "He's burying his family this Barl's Day, Darran. Don't you reckon he might welcome somethin' else to think on?"

An expression of grudging acknowledgement crossed Darran's face as he pulled his arm free. "Perhaps."

"Glad you agree. Now if there ain't anythin' else—"

"There is. Apparently there are several matters pending at Justice Hall that require the attentions of a Master Magician. Lady Marnagh feels the issue is becoming...urgent. If you could mention as much to the king?"

Coward. "Aye," he said, and sat down. "I'll mention it. Now close the door on your way out."

Alone at last, he eyed the pile of legal books with weary distaste. After the madness of Crasthead Moor he couldn't be less interested in Glospottle's pissy piss problems.

Barl save me. What have I done?

The office door opened, admitting Dathne. "I've finally settled that business with the Midwives," she said, hanging her cloak and satchel on the corner coat rack. "I doubt we'll have any more trouble now."

He couldn't remember what the problem was but smiled anyway. "Fine."

"Oh—and His Majesty asked me to give you this."

He leaned across his desk and took the note she held out to him. Cracked the crimson wax seal and read it.

See me. The crypt. Two hours after sunset.

Barl save him, what now? What else could there be for him to sacrifice on the altar of Gar's desperate dedication to Lur?

Dathne was watching him closely. "Trouble?"

"No," he lied, sliding the note into his pocket.

She dropped into the chair opposite his desk and nodded at the pile of books Darran had left behind. "A little light reading?"

"More like a recipe for headaches," he said, and let himself look at her, just look at her. Since joining the Tower staff she'd unwillingly exchanged her comfortable bookseller cottons and linens for the stiffer formality of silk and brocade. The expensive fabrics suited her. Brought out the sheen in her thick black hair and softened her lean angularity. Damn, she was so beautiful...

Even when she was frowning. "You've got a headache now, haven't you?"

He rubbed his throbbing temple. "Does it show?"

"Only to me." Returning to her satchel, she rummaged for a moment and withdrew a small stoppered pot.

"No potions!" he protested. "You're as bad as bloody Nix. Just you keep away from me with that muck."

Affectionately scornful, she moved to stand behind him. "Gossoon. It's a salve, not a potion. Now be quiet."

The smell from the pot as she unstoppered it was almost pleasant, hinting at mint leaves and honey and other things, unknown but soothing to the senses. Her ointment-smeared touch on his skin was a benediction, a tingling taste of what could be. Should be.

Would be, if fate just once was kind.

Kneading, stroking, her strong and supple fingers smoothed his temples, his neck, slipped inside his shirt collar to flirt with his shoulders. "You're so tense," she murmured. "No wonder you've got pains..."

He sighed and let his head fall back to rest against her blue brocade chest, soft and welcoming: a pillow long desired. Her fingers roamed freely, wandered upwards to dally through his hair.

"You'll make me smelly," he complained, drowsy and only a little serious. "Like that pissant Willer."

A soft chuckle. Slender fingers waking fire. "Barl forbid. Now—"

A sharp rat-tat of knuckles on the office door. "Asher!" said Matt, barging in. "Those horses are—oh." Foolishly he stood in the middle of the office, staring, and foolishly Asher stared back. Behind him he could feel Dathne stiffen.

"Asher's busy, Matt," she said, all amusement fled from her voice. "Go away."

"Busy," said Matt, still staring. "Yes. I can see that."

Asher sat forward, a tide of heat washing through him. "I had a headache. Dathne was helping."

The strangest look passed over Matt's abruptly pale face. "Yes, well, she's a very helpful woman."

"Matt!" said Dathne sharply. "Don't you—"

Asher raised one finger and she fell silent. A miracle, of sorts. He stood. Stared Matt full in the face. "That'll do. Horses in good fettle?"

Matt nodded. "They are."

"Good. The king'll come see 'em directly. Anything else?"

"No."

"Fine. Then you can go."

Another nod. "Very good. Sir."

Dathne broke the awkward silence Matt left in his wake. "I should go. More meetings. You know how it is. I'll leave the ointment here, shall I? You can rub it in yourself if the pain returns."

No, he wanted to cry. *Stay. Tell me what you meant by this, tell me I ain't dreamin', tell me if you felt what I felt when you touched me.*

"All right," he said. "You have any trouble, you let me know. I got to make a start on these bloody legal books."

Her smile was fleeting, and impish. "Good luck. If I finish my meetings in time I'll help you with them, shall I?"

He shrugged. "If you like."

"No promises, mind," she warned.

No promises.

For some reason, the comment made him shiver.

CHAPTER FOURTEEN

The day dragged on, and at long last died in a fiery sunset. Dathne didn't come back. He wasn't hungry but he ate dinner anyway. Cluny would read him a lecture if he didn't, then for good measure badger the cook into serving him a dessert of offended complaints and insulted imprecations. He didn't have the stomach or the energy to hear them. His headache had returned with a vengeance.

See me.

Hiding in his private sitting room, he stared through the uncurtained window and watched the world outside dwindle into dusk, into darkness. Even the glow of Barl's Wall seemed faded. Tarnished. Or was that just fear, pulling a deadening veil across his eyes?

See me.

When it was time he fetched a coat from his wardrobe, shrugged it on and let himself out of his apartments. The Tower was hushed. The faintest murmuring of voices drifted downwards from the staircase over his head: Cluny and her hardworking housemaid friends tending the stairwell candles. A door banged. Someone laughed. Someone else shouted two floors down, sounding disgruntled. He thought it was

Willer. With a sigh, needing support, he took hold of the handrail and began his reluctant descent. Slipped unseen from the Tower and made his way to the palace grounds.

Gar was outside the crypt, holding a candle-lantern and looking annoyed. "At last. Two hours, I said. Have you forgotten how to count?"

"I ain't that late."

"Late enough. Come on."

He pushed open the crypt door and went inside. Asher stared after him, apprehension like a sea swell rising to swamp all other, harsher emotions. Then he followed.

In the royal family's chamber three more candle-lanterns had been lit and placed around the small, chilly room. Flickering shadows danced up the white walls and over the flagstone floor. Balanced on Borne's incomplete effigy was a creamy-white globe.

"What's that thing?"

Gar glanced at it. "The Weather Orb. Come in, would you?"

Fascinated, repelled, Asher took half a step closer. "There're colours in there..."

"That's the Weather Magic," said Gar, withdrawing a battered, ancient-looking book from a satchel on the floor.

Asher nodded at it. "And what's that?"

"A collection of spells and incantations specific to the role of Master Magician. I took it and the Orb from Durm's study this afternoon. The rest of his books and papers are being boxed up and delivered to the Tower tonight. One month isn't long, Asher. I don't intend to waste a minute of it."

He felt his guts cramp. "So you pinched Durm's stuff. What's that got to do with me?"

"Everything," said Gar, impatient. "If you're going to preserve Barl's Wall you have to take on her Weather Magics. Or try to, anyway. I've no idea if the Transference will work with you saying it instead of a Master Magician. I've no idea if it'll work on you at all, given you're Olken. Still, we don't have a choice. The attempt must be made. And in secret...hence us meeting here."

Mouth dry, heart racing, he stared at the Orb. "And if this Transference don't work? What happens to me?"

Gar shrugged. "I don't know that either. But these magics come from Barl herself. I can't believe she'd let them hurt someone. Kill them."

Beneath the fear, a spark of anger. "She's six centuries dead, Gar, and you never knew her. You got no idea what she would or wouldn't let happen."

Gar frowned at the floor, then looked up. "Are you having second thoughts?"

"Wouldn't you?"

"Probably."

He tried to smile. "What about third?"

"Asher—"

"Ah, sink it!" he said, and scrubbed a hand across his face. "Let's just get it over with, eh?"

Gar nodded. "Agreed."

They sat facing each other on the flagstones. Gar held the Weather Orb and balanced the open spell book in his lap. "It's only fair to warn you ... this might hurt."

He rolled his eyes. "Now he tells me."

"Since you can't read Ancient Doranen I'll recite the spell and you can repeat it after me. If what happened in the Weather Chamber holds true, that should trigger the Transference."

"And if it don't?"

A wintry amusement touched Gar's face. "Then it's hail King Conroyd."

Asher glared at the pretty pearl-white Weather Orb. "Hurt how much, exactly?"

"I survived," said Gar, and gave him the Orb.

It felt peculiarly heavy. Almost alive. Or aware. The colours swirling beneath its skin made his senses swim. Without conscious thought his fingers formed a cradle.

"That's right," said Gar. "Hold it just like that. No tighter, no looser. Close your eyes. Breathe. Good. Now ... are you ready?"

Asher felt the crypt's cold air catch in his throat. Ready? No, he wasn't bloody ready. How could anybody be ready for something like this? He grunted.

"All right," said Gar, softly. There was a rustling of pages, a slithering of leather, as he picked up Durm's book. "Repeat after me: *Ha'rak dolanie maketh ...*"

Heart booming, head spinning, Asher licked his dry lips and repeated the tongue-twisting words. "*Ha'rak dolanie maketh ...*"

As he whispered the last syllable the Orb trembled in his grasp. He felt warmth. A humming energy. He opened his eyes, stared down at the maelstrom of gold and green and purple and crimson magics he held between his hands ... and fell headlong into it. From some impossible distance he heard Gar's voice and he echoed it, repeating the words he had no hope of understanding.

Deep within, some secret place he never knew existed seemed to... open. Unfold, the way a rose unfolds its petals at the first kind kiss of the sun. The Orb was glowing so brightly he shouldn't have been able to look at it, but he could. He could see right into the heart of it, and it felt like staring into the heart of magic itself. Images poured into the newly opened space within him, and with them came words...knowledge...

Power.

He could feel his chest heaving, his breath rasping. The Orb's heat and light burst free of their shell, rushed through his skin like hot sweet wine through cheesecloth and now he was the Orb, glowing with magic, his bones were burning with it and the world had turned crimson and gold.

There was no pain.

Gar was still speaking; standing on the rim of this brand-new world he could hear his friend's voice, drifting towards him from a vast distance. He let the words float into his ambit. Breathed them in and breathed them out again as though they were incense, or the smoke from one of Dathne's scented candles. The power pouring into him swelled like a wave racing in from the ocean, deep and strong and impossible to control. He felt like a child again. Remembered the time Da tossed him over the side of their fishing boat and into the water, so he'd learn how to swim.

"Don't fight her, boy! You'll never win! Let go, just let go! She'll hold you like a woman if you let her! Let go..."

He let go now, as he had then. Let the wave of power take him, lift him, drag him deep under and throw him up high. He heard himself cry out, a sound of wonder and despair. A fountain of words welled into his mouth and he shouted them for all the world to hear. A final surge of magic speared him like a javelin of fire. For one brief, exulting moment he knew himself invincible...

...and then the fire faded. The power snuffed out like a pinched candle. He was a man again, not magic made flesh, and the Orb in his trembling hands was nothing more than a bauble.

He could have wept.

When at last he stirred, Gar was staring at him as though they'd never met. "There was no pain for you...was there?"

He shook his head. Slowly, awareness returned. That was a lantern. He sat on the floor. Above him lay the quiet stone faces of dead people. He felt light enough to fly. Weighed down with impossible knowledge.

"Do you know that at the end you were saying the last words of the Transference spell with me, not after me?"

Carefully, he returned the Orb to Gar. "If you say so. I can't remember...it's a blur."

Gar stood. His face was cold, all emotion smothered like a river under ice. "There's one more thing we have to do."

He slumped against the nearest coffin, groaning. "What? Gar, I don't want to do anythin' else. Not tonight. I'm knackered. All my insides are turned upside down and my head's near to burstin' open there's so much stuff been crammed in it."

Gar's answer was to look in his satchel and remove a small pottery bowl filled with damp soil. "There's a seed in here," he said, holding it out. "Make it sprout."

"Make it sprout?" Asher stared. "Why?"

"As a test. We need to be sure the Transference worked."

"I ain't a bloody gardener! I don't know how to—"

"Yes, you do!" said Gar. Leaned down, grabbed him by one arm and hauled him to his feet. "It's *in* you now, as it once was in me."

"Ow! Leave off!" he protested as Gar tapped him ungently on the side of the head to make his point.

"Just think of the seed, Asher. Imagine it bursting into life. Magic will do the rest."

Scowling, he snatched the dirt-filled bowl and glared into it. His mind was blank. *Think of the seed.* He held his breath, screwed up his face and imagined green and growing things. Words floated to the surface of his mind and flirted there like sea foam on the ocean.

Talineth vo sussura. Sussura. Sussura.

He parted his lips and let them escape.

Melting heat. A javelin of fire. A flaring of crimson and gold. The bowl vibrated. Even as he gasped in pain, felt something warm and wet trickle from his nostrils and over his lips, the moist dirt shivered. Shimmered. Erupted like a waterspout. Something slender and green unfolded from the dark earth, leapt to life in a riot of yellow and blue. He cried out. His fingers lost their tenuous hold of the bowl, let it slip and fall. It shattered on the crypt's stone floor, spilling dirt, spitting shards of clay.

The flower he'd given birth to kept growing. Breathless and disbelieving he watched as its stem broadened, budded, as the buds opened, as the blue and yellow petals uncurled and doused the air with perfume, as its tangle of roots tangled further. At long last it stopped growing and instead lay like a miracle at his feet.

"Barl save me," breathed Gar. "Germinate the seed, I said, not turn the crypt into a greenhouse." He shook his head in wonder, and envy. "Who are you, Asher? *What* are you?"

Asher stared at the flower, feeling such a brangle of things—fear, elation, horror, joy—that for a moment he forgot how to speak. "You're the history student," he said when his tongue at last obeyed him. "You tell me."

Gar's face tightened. "I wish I could."

He busied himself collecting the Orb and the book and stowing them safely back in the satchel. Turned then to picking up the shards of broken pottery and putting them in there too. His movements were savagely self-controlled.

Asher bent to help him. Gar struck his hand away. "I'm not helpless."

He stepped back. "I never said you were."

"But you thought it!"

"I never did. Gar—"

"Helpless! Useless! Defective!" On the last word Gar's voice cracked, his face twisted and he turned away.

Knotted with unwanted sympathy, all Asher could do was wait. Gone was the proud and powerful king who'd walked amongst his people in the market square, comforting and being comforted, wearing his magical birthright like a mantle of crimson and gold. In that man's place this born-again cripple, brought low by grief and fate and a bewildered anger that his life could take such an unkind turn. That against every belief and expectation an Olken could possess the magic he'd longed for so passionately all his life. That had manifested without warning then deserted him without rhyme or reason, leaving him emptied, hollowed, not even a shadow of his other, grander self.

At long last Gar regained his self-control. "I'm sorry."

Asher patted Gar's shoulder, feeling awkward. "Don't be."

"It's late. We should go. But first..." Painfully, Gar looked at his father's mutilated marble face. "The effigy. If I gave you the incantation would you...I don't want anyone to see...it's dangerous. For both of us. And disrespectful to him."

Asher sighed. He didn't want to. The less magic he used, the happier he'd be. But—

He let Gar give him the words he needed and remoulded Borne's disfigured features as though they were made of butter, not marble. Then he banished the spilled dirt and the riotous plant he'd created into the woods that ringed the crypt.

"Thank you," said Gar. Subdued. Withdrawn. "I'm grateful."

"Prove it," he said. "Find me a way out of this."

Gar nodded. Touched his fingertips to his father's perfect effigy. "I'll try."

*   *   *

Deaf to all of Darran's entreaties, Gar had decided upon a private interment for his family. Six sober City guards removed the bodies from the
palace's east wing, watched by Conroyd Jarralt, members of the General Council, Pellen Orrick and a host of palace and Tower staff who'd
gathered in silent respect on the lawn bordering the gravel driveway.

Asher, standing with Dathne and Darran and Willer, chewed on
his lip and bullied his face into some semblance of stern discipline.
Bloody funerals. He hated them. He and Dathne had attended Coachman Matcher's four days after the accident as official representatives
of the king, and what a weeping and a wailing that had been. The
dreams he'd had that night. His mother's funeral. His father's death
and the funeral he'd been denied. Poor addled Jed, as good as dead.

Now this.

Holze walked behind the sad procession of coffins, weighted down
with his most ornate robes of office, offering his prayers for the dead roy-
als in a clear, carrying voice. Beside him walked Gar, silent, swathed head
to toe in deepest black. For the first time since his ascension to the throne
his clothes were embroidered with the sword-and-thunderbolt symbol of
House Torvig. On his collar points, his shirt cuffs and over his heart.
Another battle with Darran, that had been, one Gar had wisely lost. The
reigning monarch always wore his or her house insignia. *Always.*

Even if it did make him feel like a fraud.

As the lowering sun threw shadows across the surrounding gardens,
Pellen's boys slid the three coffins neatly into the back of the glossy
black hearse, closed its rear doors, then fell into place well behind Gar
and Holze. Matt picked up the black horses' reins and his whip and
soberly moved away from the palace, down the tree-lined drive that
would lead them, eventually, to the crypt. Equally sober, Gar, Holze
and the guards followed in its wake. Holze was still praying.

As soon as they were gone from sight, sobs broke out amongst the
crowd. Asher glanced around, saw weeping Olken, weeping Doranen.
Not Jarralt, of course. Even if he was genuinely grieved he'd never
lower himself to show it in public. But the Doranen members of the
General Council, they seemed not to have such scruples. They grieved
without reservation, as did the Olken guild leaders. There were even
tears on Pellen's cheeks. Of course the royal staff were awash with
misery. Beside him, Willer had surrendered to soggy hiccups and Darran was practically howling into his handkerchief.

Dathne, her eyes bright, touched his sleeve. "They're sheep in
search of a shepherd, Asher. You should say something."

He didn't want to. Hated drawing attention to himself, especially with Conroyd Jarralt watching, but she was right. And Darran was in no fit state, blubbing like a baby.

"My lords and ladies, good guild meisters and mistresses, gentlefolk all," he called, raising a hand to attract their attention. "This sad day sees the end of an era in our kingdom. As His Majesty goes to bid his private farewells, let us remove to the palace's Hall of Meetings to partake of refreshments and shared memories in honour of King Borne, Queen Dana and the Princess Fane."

A moment of surprised silence, of exchanged looks and lifted eyebrows. Then those nearest the palace began to drift towards it. Darran, damply composed now, plucked at his elbow. "That was well said, Asher. Very well said indeed."

"You sound surprised."

Darran's chin lifted. "I am. Now—"

"Asher," said Conroyd Jarralt, suddenly at his elbow and icily civil. "A word."

He bowed. "Of course, my lord."

"In private."

"Certainly." He turned to Dathne. "I'll see you inside."

She withdrew, taking Darran and Willer with her and sparing him a swift, sympathetic smile over her shoulder. He didn't dare acknowledge it. Instead he surrendered to Jarralt's frigid scrutiny.

Contemptuous of social niceties, Jarralt said, "When does the king intend to appoint his new Master Magician?"

"My lord, he has one already."

Jarralt's colour heightened. "Durm is nothing but a breathing carcass." His voice was pitched low, for intimacy. "And Gar's sentimental attachment to him places all of us in danger. You have his ear, fisherman. Bend it. Advise our king that further delay in the matter of Durm's replacement will lead to questions I'm sure he'd prefer weren't asked."

Asher clasped his hands behind his back, so Jarralt wouldn't see fists. "Is that a threat?"

"A warning," said Jarralt, and smiled. "I will not see this kingdom imperilled by a boy whose judgement has already proven...questionable. He gave an undertaking before witnesses that this matter would be resolved."

"And it will be, my lord. In his time. Not yours."

The smile widened. "Indeed. But time is not infinite. Time...runs out. Listen carefully, Meister Administrator. That sound you hear is the swift approach of a last chance."

Bastard. *Bastard*. Asher manufactured a smile of his own. "Really? Seems more to me like the sound of a man puttin' a noose round his own neck."

Jarralt laughed. "Were I you, Asher, I'd not be so swift to speak of nooses and necks. You have my warning. Do with it what you will... and be prepared to reap the consequences."

Fighting nausea, he watched Jarralt saunter across the manicured lawn and into the palace.

It was some time before he could bring himself to follow.

Flickered by candlelight, Gar listened to Holze's footsteps retreating. To the crypt's inner door banging closed. To the faint echoes of the heavy brass-bound outer door booming shut. He crossed the small, crowded chamber and pushed its heavy oak door until it thudded home against the jamb. Then he turned and slumped against it.

"So. Here we are then. Alone at last."

Someone giggled. After a startled moment he realised it was him. He slapped a hand across his mouth to stifle the shocking sound.

The cold stone coffins, full-bellied now with bodies, graced with those beautiful marble effigies, sat silent before him.

"I won't stay long," he said after a little while. "I know you want to sleep. It's just...there's something I'd like to ask you. Just a little matter I'd like to see cleared up. Now that you're safely here, in your new home, and we're sure not to be overheard. You don't mind, do you? No, I didn't think you would."

With an effort he pushed himself away from the door. The chamber shimmered softly in the candlelight. No glimfire now, not unless he asked Asher to conjure it for him. He felt his guts twist. *Like a child, running to its nurse for sweetmeats. Please, Asher, may I have some glimfire? Please, Asher, can you make it rain?*

Fane's stony sweet face mocked him...and all his rage broke free.

"I don't understand it!" he shouted at them. "Did you *know* this could happen? Asher made it rain, he made it snow, he fixed your face, Father! And you'd have me repay him with *death*?"

Unmoved, unmoving, his father's face slept in the gently flickering light.

"I helped you murder Timon Spake! I forced Asher to watch! *Why*? To make sure we maintain our stranglehold on power in this land? To keep the Olken ignorant of their magic? To continue this shameful legacy of lies and deception? We didn't *save* Lur, we *stole* it. Conquered it. Somehow managed to bury the truth of the Olken's own magical birthright. Robbed them of their heritage and history. Do you know what that makes me? The inheritor of a criminal crown, no better than the monster Morg!"

No one answered him.

"And now we are punished. *I* am punished. What do I do next? How do I proceed? My magic is extinguished. Vanished as though it had never existed. Durm remains unconscious, teetering still on the brink of death, and Conroyd..." He took a deep, shuddering breath. "Conroyd is circling and he won't wait forever. All that stands between your kingdom and disaster, Father, is an uneducated Olken fisherman! How did this happen? Why did it happen? Tell me, please, *what does it mean?*"

His anguish echoed in the small stone chamber, bounced from wall to floor to ceiling in concentric circles of grief.

Flinging himself to the floor beside his mother's coffin, he seized her cold stone shoulders in his hands and willed her spirit to hear him.

"Mama...Mama...I grew to manhood watching you treat everyone you met with grace and courtesy, no matter who they were or how they lived. Baker, butcher, nobleman or nurse, Doranen or Olken, they were all the same to you. Everything I know of living Barl's legacy, of honouring her teachings and upholding her laws, I learned from you! And now I've learned it was likely all a lie. So what do I do now, Mama? Guide me, I beg you! I swore an oath to protect this kingdom and its sacred laws with my life! If I hold true to that oath I have to kill Asher. And in killing him I'll kill our kingdom with him. So no matter what I do, I'm forsworn! Is that what you want for me?"

Releasing his mother, he turned again to Borne. "You were never ambitious for ambition's sake. If you'd wanted this kingdom's future placed in Conroyd's hands, if you'd trusted he'd do right by *all* the people, not just our own, you *never* would've bullied the Councils into giving you Fane. You'd have named him heir, to us if not to the population. But you didn't. I know you don't want me to abdicate. I know you don't want Conroyd as king." He stared into his father's marble features, searching for answers. For hope. "I suppose I could be wrong. It could be that Asher is the only Olken who can do magic. And if that's so, isn't it some kind of miracle? That he's with me now, in my darkest hour? Doesn't it mean he was born special for a reason? Don't I have to keep him secret, and safe, even if it means breaking Barl's Law myself?"

He glanced over at Fane. "I know what you'd do, sister dear," he said, derisive. "You'd say the risk was too great. You'd round up every last Olken and put them in prison. Or send them to the axe, just in case he's not the only one. You'd say it was what Barl wanted but I won't believe that. How can he be Barl's enemy, our enemy, and also be the key to the kingdom's survival?"

Fane stayed silent. She always did, when the questions proved not to her liking. Exhausted, he let his body slump against her coffin. His head was aching badly. "And if Durm does wake, what then? Where will his loyalty lie? With Barl? The kingdom? With the memory of a dead king he loved like a brother...or with the crippled failure his friend left behind as heir?"

He pressed his hands to his face. "I'm so tired, Father," he whispered. "I'm confused. Afraid. I've no one to talk to. Asher's the only man I can trust now and he's more frightened than me. Barl save me, I wish you were here. I wish I knew what you wanted me to do...what *you* would do..."

His father didn't answer, which might have meant any number of things.

At length, chilled and hungry and empty of answers, he returned to the Tower where, mercifully, people left him alone. After a half-hearted meal he crawled into bed, fell asleep...and dreamed of Fane, laughing. Of a scarlet sky bleeding red rain. Of the Wall's demise.

Try as he might, he couldn't wake.

CHAPTER FIFTEEN

Pother Nix sat in an easy chair, rereading his notes on the applied uses of lorrel seeds. A peculiar piece of flora, lorrel, good for gangrene and bloody flux. Found only along Lur's savage east coast, where it clung precariously to life along the barren cliff tops; just one of many unique Olken plants. Without magic, their healers relied on natural remedies and for that he was profoundly grateful. Like it or not, and most Doranen abhorred it, magic could only do so much. Olken herb lore had saved many a Doranen life, and praise Barl for it.

In the bed beside him, wasted and wan, Durm shifted, sighing. Nix glanced up, anxious, but it was dreaming only. No new fit or seizure. He released a grateful breath.

Praise Barl for herb lore indeed. He thought it was the only thing keeping Durm alive, for his healing magics had long since reached their limits. Durm stirred and sighed again, bald head rolling on the pillow. Nix reached out an absentminded hand, intending to check his patient's pulse—

Durm's fingers curled around his own.

"Barl save me!" cried Nix, and leapt to his feet. Durm's eyes were open. Unfocused, but open. "Kerril! Kerril, to me!"

The chamber door flew open and Kerril practically fell into the room. "Sir? Are you—"

"He's awake! Barl be blessed, he's awake! Fetch me a wet cloth, quickly!"

As Kerril fled, Nix sought the pulse point in Durm's throat. It thrummed beneath his fingertips, fast but strong.

"Mmneeugh," said Durm, struggling to speak. "Hwheee..."

"Hush, hush," he soothed. "You're safe, man. Lie still."

Despite their best endeavours, Durm's lips were dry and chapped with flaking skin. When Kerril returned, followed by the inevitable gaggle of colleagues, Nix took the cloth she handed him and pressed its wetness to the Master Magician's mouth.

At its touch Durm's gaze sharpened. Breathing harshly, he tried to sit up. Nix restrained him. "No! Durm, no! You must stay still!"

Durm frowned, tugging his scars into tangled new shapes, and his lips framed soundless words. He stared around the healing chamber, searching for something, or someone. "Borne," he gasped, his voice harsh, guttural. "Borne!" Tears leaked from his bloodshot eyes.

"Somebody fetch the king," said Nix.

As Kerril bolted, scattering pothers like so many skittle-pins, Durm spoke again. "Nix? Nix, help me!"

"I'm trying," Nix told him, and felt tears of joy, of shock, pricking his own eyes. "But you must lie *still*."

Durm shuddered, a mighty convulsion that lifted his shoulders from the mattress. His eyes opened wide, and his mouth, and the most extraordinary expression of triumph and ecstasy and virulent relief washed over his face. "*Awake!*" he roared. "At last, at last, *awake!*"

"Yes, awake, but poorly yet!" said Nix. "You must—"

"Let me up," Durm demanded, and struggled to throw aside his blankets. "I have wasted too much time here, I have spent more of myself than I can spare, healing this rotten carcass. Let me *up*, I say! Or be blighted where you—"

Heedless of newly knitted flesh and bone, Nix threw himself across Durm's chest. "Fetch me ebonard! *Now!*"

As someone scuttled to do his bidding, he spread his right hand flat and pressed it against Durm's thundering heart. "*Quantiasat! Boladuset!*" It was a calming invocation, useful when a patient was conscious but agitated. "*Boladuset*, Durm, Barl curse you with hives! Be *still*!"

The invocation caught, and Durm flopped back against his pillows. Somebody thrust a vial of ebonard into Nix's hand; he tossed the contents into Durm's gaping mouth and slammed closed his jaw for good measure.

Durm swallowed. Gagged. Snorted. His staring eyes rolled, fogged, and a foolish smile melted over his face. Nix sagged, then turned to scowl at his goggling underlings.

"Be off with you! His Majesty will arrive soon."

But it wasn't the king who answered his summons.

"What's amiss?" demanded Asher, striding into the sick man's chamber as though he owned it. Nix, staring, remembered the rough-spun young Olken he'd once treated for a split eyebrow and thought he'd not have achieved a more perfect transformation with magic.

He stood. "I requested His Majesty's presence."

"His Majesty ain't available. Why do you need him?"

In the bed between them, momentarily forgotten, Durm shifted and sighed and said, "Borne..."

"He's *awake*?" said Asher, incredulous.

Nix smiled. "Awake, and seemingly with all his faculties."

Still staring at the recovered Master Magician, Asher said, "I'll fetch the king," and left as abruptly as he'd arrived. Nearly half an hour later he returned, this time accompanied by His Majesty.

Gar looked worn to the nub and ripe for dropping. Not surprising, perhaps, since he'd interred his family only yesterday. Still...

Nix bowed. "Your Majesty."

Gar barely acknowledged him. Pushed straight past and dropped into the chair beside Durm's bed. Snatched up Durm's fleshless hand and pressed it to his lips.

"Durm. Durm, I'm here." When Durm didn't respond, Gar looked up, displeasure unhidden. "What is this? You said he was *awake*!"

Nix exchanged a glance with Asher and cleared his throat. "He became agitated, sir. I was forced to gentle him with ebonard. He'll stir again presently, I'm sure."

Unmollified, Gar turned back to Durm. "You had no business drugging him, Nix. You *know* I need him alert and—"

In the bed, Durm sighed. Stirred. Dragged his eyelids open. "What...what..."

Breathing hard, Gar leaned close. "Praise Barl. Durm, can you hear me? Do you know me?"

Durm smiled into Gar's anxious, waiting face. "Of course," he said. His voice was soft and slurring. "You're crippled Gar, Borne's runting regrettable offspring."

Nix stepped forward. "Ebonard is a powerful soporific, sir, and oft tickles the tongue to unfortunate utterances. It would be unwise to—"

Gar's face was bleached of blood. "You think I'd hold a sick man's words against him?"

Another exchange of glances with Asher. This time the king's friend frowned and shook his head. Nix abandoned remonstrance. "Of course not, Your Majesty."

Durm stirred again, querulous now. "Borne? Where is Borne?"

Subdued, Gar leaned close. "He can't be here at the moment. But he sends you his love."

Durm smiled. "Borne. My friend. Give my love to him. Tell him I shall see him soon." He sighed and slid again into sleep.

Gar released Durm's hand, stood and moved to the window. "He has no memory of the accident?"

"It's too soon to say for certain," replied Nix. "But given his injuries...likely not. Once he's strong enough I'll—"

"No. I will tell him."

"As Your Majesty desires."

"How soon before he can return to his duties?"

Nix hesitated. Everything about this grieving young man urged caution. "Sir...it's a miracle Durm lives at all. Perhaps it's not wise for us to look too far into the future."

Gar glanced over his shoulder, a cold look. "You know I need him, Nix."

Caution was all very well, but he'd not be bullied into harming a patient. Not even by a king. "I know that whatever your needs may be, Your Majesty, Durm's will always come first."

"The king knows that," said Asher. His tone was conversational, his eyes sharp. "Just do your best, eh, to bring Durm about as fast as possible. That's all we're askin'."

We. Nix felt the faintest stirring of unease. "Your Majesty?"

Gar turned. "That's right. Of course you must protect his health. Protect, but not coddle. I'm asking for him as much as myself, Nix. Durm is not an idle man. He'll heal faster knowing there's work to be done. Knowing he's needed."

It was a fair observation. Still, Nix felt unsettled. Some new stress was carved into Gar's face. Something apart from Weather Working. "To be sure. And how does Your Majesty? You seem to me a trifle... peaked."

"I'm fine."

To satisfy himself, Nix reached for Gar's wrist and laid a palm to his forehead. The king suffered his swift, impersonal touches with a thinly veiled impatience. When he was done, and grudgingly satisfied, Nix retreated. "You should rest more. I warned you, these first weeks of Weather Working will break you if you let them."

"I'm fine, I told you," Gar snapped. "Save your energies for Durm."

He risked a smile. "I have enough energy for both of you, sir."

Gar stepped forward, furious. "You think this *amusing?*"

"Majesty, no. I—"

"*Heal him*, Nix! Or I'll not be answerable for the consequences!"

Shaken, Nix watched him leave. Frowned, affronted, as Asher, on the king's heels, gave him a look of filthy disgust.

In his bed Durm slept on, smiling like a babe.

Conroyd Jarralt was in his bath when the message arrived. *Durm has woken and is in his right mind.* So great were his rage and disappointment that the cooling water began to bubble with heat and he had to leap out naked before he scalded himself.

"Tell Frawley to wait in the library," he told the flustered maidservant. "I'll see him directly."

"Sir!" she gasped, and fled.

He wrapped himself in a rich brocade robe, dried and ordered his hair with an impatient finger-snap, then descended the stairs to meet with his henchman.

"My lord," said Frawley, bowing low. Wrapped in his customary grey cloak, hat pulled low to his forehead, he looked, as ever, usefully nondescript.

"Our fat friend sent you a note, I take it?"

Frawley shook his head. "No, sir. He tracked me down to the Whistling Pig and accosted me in the privy."

"Were you observed?"

Frawley looked hurt. "My lord."

He couldn't care less about Frawley's feelings. "Is that all he said?"

"Yes, my lord."

Jarralt sat at his desk and drummed his fingers. "Willer is laggardly in his task."

"I did mention you were eagerly awaiting good news, my lord," said Frawley. Uneasy now, he pulled off his hat and let his fingers nibble at the brim. "I made a point of telling him."

"I think it's time he was reminded of his mission's urgency," said Jarralt. "Where is he now?"

"His lodgings, most like, sir, this time of night."

"Find him. Escort him to the west gate of the City Barlsgarden. I will meet you there."

"My lord," said Frawley, and took his leave.

Ethienne was amusing herself at her spinet in the music room. "I'm going for a walk," Jarralt told her.

"A walk?" she said, astonished. Mercifully she stopped playing and stared at him as though he'd sprouted wings. "At this hour? But you've just had your bath."

"Please don't distress yourself in staying up till I return. I feel a trifle restless this evening. I might well walk for some time."

She stretched out a hand to him. "Oh, Conroyd. Are you still so very sad?"

"We live in sad times, my dear." For many reasons, and one more just added to the list.

"But you got over loving Dana years ago," she said, pouting just a little. "And you never had a fondness for Borne. Not as a man, I mean. As our king, of course, you revered him, as did we all."

She'd have to know, sooner or later. "Durm has woken. I just received word."

And now his second-best wife understood. "Oh, *Conroyd!*"

"Yes," he said softly, and indulged in the thinnest of smiles.

Ethienne rallied. "We cannot despair," she announced, rising from her music stool. "Awake is one thing. Unimpaired and able to function as the Master Magician is quite another. My dear, do not abandon hope. You will be Master Magician one day, I know it."

She had no idea of his true ambition, of course. He would never dream of confiding in a woman like her. She was challenged enough to keep her mouth shut on his supposed desire to take Durm's inferior place at Gar's side.

He shrugged. "Whatever happens, it will be according to Barl's will."

Flushing, she fingered the holy medal on its chain around her neck. "Of course."

"Pray continue with your music-making, my dear," he added, nodding at the spinet. "And I shall see you in the morning at breakfast."

He escaped her enthusiastic butchery of a popular dance tune and exchanged brocade robe and slippers for sober-hued tunic, trousers and boots. Muffled in a black cloak, with a low-brimmed hat to encourage concealing shadows, he left his townhouse and made his brisk way out of the exclusive Old Dorana residential district and towards the City Barlsgarden.

The night was clear, with no rain set to fall. According to the current Weather Schedule—Borne's last—there'd be no rain in the City for another five days. The temperature was due to start dropping, though. Gar would need to take care of that soon, or the River Gant wouldn't freeze over and there'd be no skating parties. He'd not stay popular long if that annual delight was unforthcoming.

The idea made him smile.

Amusement faded swiftly, however. His window of opportunity was fast sliding shut. Ethienne's optimism was little short of wishful thinking. If Durm had survived this far it would be just his luck for the man to make a full recovery. And if that happened any hope of discrediting Gar would disappear. Durm would safeguard his dead friend's son to the death. Even to the extent of protecting that miserable Asher.

No. If he was going to strike...seize the throne...seize his destiny, it would have to be soon.

He passed a pair of patrolling City Guards. They stared hard, recognised him, and nodded their heads politely as they continued on their way. He ignored them.

The Barlsgarden wasn't far on horseback or by carriage; on foot, it took him over half an hour and he was sweating by the time he reached the west gate. So much for his bath. The flower-infested patch of ground lay in the City's somnolent religious district. No shops or taverns or restaurants here, just the sprawl of Barl's Chapel seminary, hospice and modest accommodation for clergy too old or infirm to continue their religious duties abroad in the kingdom. It was the perfect place for a meeting best kept private. No foot traffic, no inconvenient horses or carriages carrying people who had no need to know his business. All the little novices and Barlspeakers would be safely tucked into their beds or on their bony knees by now, praying. He was safe.

The Barlsgarden had a high wrought-iron fence all round it, punctuated with four gates, but to the best of his knowledge they were never shut. He slipped into the grounds through the west gate and waited.

"My lord! My lord?"

Frawley. Panting at his heels pudgy Willer, streaming sweat and stinking of garlic. The reek of it warred with the Barlsgarden's sweet winter jasmine, and won. Jarralt resisted the urge to press a kerchief to his nose and mouth, and stepped into the faint pool of light cast from a distant glimlamp.

"Lower your voice, Frawley," he ordered. "Sound carries. You extracted Meister Driskle without comment?"

"Sorry, sir. Yes, sir. Nobody saw me take him."

Willer, his expression a distasteful conglomeration of anxiety and eagerness to please, bowed untidily. He was still struggling for air. "My...lord! How can I serve you? Frawley says he passed...along my message. I'm afraid I don't know any more than that, concerning...the Master Magician's condition."

Jarralt looked down his nose at him; it was a useful technique for intimidation. "Yes. It is your lack of knowledge that brings us here."

The fat little Olken paled. "My lord?"

"When we first met, Willer, you gave the impression of a man urgently desirous of saving our precious kingdom from calamity," he said, letting his displeasure show. "Yet all I have received from you so far are vague hints, unsubstantiated suspicions and a list of transgressions that, while they may perfectly illuminate Asher's unsatisfactory character, hardly advance our cause of proving he's a danger to the crown. Can it be I was mistaken in you, sir?"

"My *lord*!" the little man squealed. "I'm doing my best, I swear it! But it's not easy. Asher's so damned secretive!"

Jarralt allowed his expression to ice over. "So. When you assured me you were perfectly placed to uncover Asher's misdeeds, you were in fact..." He stretched the pause to screaming point. "Exaggerating?"

"No, no! And I wasn't lying either! I *am* perfectly placed, my lord! My life on it!" the Olken protested in a gasp. "It just might take a little longer than I—than *we*—thought. But I'll do it. I swear I'll do it!"

"Neither my time nor my patience, Willer, are infinite."

Cringing like a whipped cur, the Olken dared to touch a fingertip to Jarralt's sleeve. "My lord, I'm sure I could learn more if only I could get access to Asher's private papers. To his office and all his desk drawers."

"You suspect Asher of hiding incriminating evidence in his office?"

For a moment the fat man struggled with his reply. Then he shrugged unhappily. "My lord, I can't in honesty say so for certain. But if he keeps it anywhere, I'm sure it's there. Or in his private apartments. If only I could get inside when he wasn't around, I know I could find the evidence we require. But he keeps all his doors locked and I don't have keys. Darran does but he won't let me—"

The flowerbeds were lined with small round river pebbles, black and white in turn. Jarralt stooped and selected one of each colour.

Enclosing the black one in his right fist, he whispered an incantation against his folded fingers and waited for the humming buzz against his flesh that would signal the spell's success. A flash of heat, a sizzling thrill, and it was done.

"This will unlock any door or drawer," he said, holding the pebble out to his pawn. "Use it wisely. I will know where it has been."

With eyes like a greedy child's the Olken took the pebble and slipped it into a weskit pocket. "My lord."

Next he enchanted the white pebble and held it out. "This one will give you an hour's feeble glimlight. Enough to see by, but not be seen. Rap it once against a hard surface to activate the spell, once again to turn it off. When you have found what it is we require throw both pebbles into the nearest well and send to Frawley immediately, no matter the hour. Is that understood?"

The white pebble disappeared into another pocket. "My lord, I will not betray your trust," fat Willer promised. "We will apprehend this miscreant, you have my solemn word. The kingdom will be saved."

Clearly, he was expecting some kind of response. A compliment, possibly, or a heartfelt declaration of faith and gratitude. Jarralt looked at Frawley. "Escort him back to his lodgings by a different route. Avoid the guards and any other late-night pedestrians."

Frawley bowed. "My lord." Taking the repellent man's black woollen sleeve, he hustled him away.

Jarralt watched them go, waiting till they'd rounded a corner out of sight, then pulled his own cloak a little closer and struck out for home. Smiling, he allowed a little of Ethienne's optimism to warm him.

Soon. Soon now, despite Durm's tiresome attachment to life, he would have Borne's wretched son and the inconvenient Olken at his mercy. A brief unpleasantness, a minor upheaval. A short period of public mourning, and then a new day would dawn.

Bow down, you people of Lur. Make way. Pay homage. Here is your new liege, King Conroyd the First.

Dathne propped her elbows on her dinner table and frowned. "I thought you liked my cooking," she said. She sounded puzzled. Maybe even a little hurt.

Seated opposite her, Asher looked at the muddle of carrot, spinach and spicy mince on his plate and pulled a face. "Sorry. Guess I ain't got much of an appetite."

She reached for the bread, tore off a fresh hunk and mopped up her leftover gravy. "What's wrong?"

He loved to watch her eat. Such swift, precise movements. All her formidable personality focused on taste and texture. "There's a WeatherWorking set for tonight."

Displeased, she wiped her fingers on her napkin. "If it disturbs you so much, don't go."

"Dath..." He sighed. "Don't."

"I won't pretend to like it just because you want me to," she said tartly.

"You'd rather I lied?"

"I'd rather you stayed here!"

"Aye, well, so would I, but we both know I can't."

She pushed away from the table and began clearing the plates. "Won't."

Damn. He'd come here for respite, not reproaches. He stood. "I can't do this, Dathne. Not tonight."

She beat him to the door. Pressed her back to it and held her palms out. "Wait. Wait." Her hands came to rest on his chest. "I'm sorry. Don't go. Not until you have to. I didn't mean to nag. It's just—I worry about you."

His heart beneath her hands beat hard and fast. "I know. But with any luck I'll not be involved much longer. Now Durm's turned the corner—"

"Is it certain? Nix thinks he'll make a full recovery?"

"He's...hopeful."

He watched the doubt shift behind her eyes. Saw her take a breath, ready with more pesky questions he couldn't answer without telling more lies. He stopped her mouth in the only way he could think of: with his own.

Shocked, she tightened her fingers on him, clutching at his shirt. He heard her muffled protest. Felt her stiffen and begin to pull away. Giddy, he put his arms around her, crushing her close. She tasted of wine and spices and surprise. Just as he thought he'd misread her entirely, ruined everything, she surrendered. Became pliant in his arms. Kissed him back, with passion.

When at last they parted she stared at him, panting. He managed to smile. "Not goin' to hit me, are you?"

Her soft lips curved in a smile. "I should."

"For takin' liberties? Aye. Prob'ly. Specially since I ain't sorry." He felt his own smile fade then. "Are you?"

She answered him with a kiss that stole his breath as completely as he'd stolen hers. Then she released him, and reached up to frame his face with her hands. Her eyes were fierce. "I understand why you do it, Asher. Gar's your friend and you love him. But don't let love blind you to danger. Or lull you into false security. He may be your friend but he's the king first and he'll not forget that. Don't you forget it either."

Her words cut too close for comfort. To hide his face from her he pulled her to him in another embrace. Sighed as her arms slid around his neck and her fingers ran through his hair. "It's all right, Dath," he whispered. "I know what I'm doing." And hoped she'd believe him. Wished he could believe himself. For the briefest, maddest moment he wanted to reveal his impossible secret.

She pulled away, half smiling, half frowning. "What? What is it?"

No. It was impossible. To tell her would be monstrous. Selfish. Unkind, and dangerous. How could he love her and risk her life? He shook his head. "Nothing. I should go. Rest up a bit, before the Working."

"Rest here."

"Dath, if I stayed I doubt either of us'd get much rest."

She punched him. "Speak for yourself! I know what's right and what isn't."

He rubbed his smarting chest; she had a hard fist when she felt like it. "No. I meant that sooner or later you'd start on at me again about Gar and then we'd be branglin' and I don't want to spoil things." He traced the sharp clean line of her cheek with his finger. "Spoil this."

Capturing her hand in his, she touched her lips to his knuckles. "You won't."

"I know I won't, 'cause I'm leavin'," he said. "I wanted to see Matt any road. Clear the air after the other day. We been avoidin' each other."

"Don't worry about Matt," she said, pulling a face. "He'll get over it."

"Aye, but I won't. I'm a sensitive flower, me," he said, and laughed when she punched him again. "Ow. See?"

She pulled free of him and opened the door. "Fine. Off you go then, Meister Flower. I'll see you in the morning."

"What, you ain't goin' to walk me out?"

"I would if you deserved it."

He kissed her again for that, swiftly, and let the expression of shy pleasure on her face warm him all the way home. Where, since he'd been telling the truth about Matt, he went straight to the stable yard.

Matt was still at work, mending a broken bridle in his office. The pot-bellied stove in the corner belched heat and bubbled a kettle on its lid. Asher kicked the office door closed and went to the cupboard. Fished out a mug and the tea jar and set about brewing himself a cup. Matt threaded his needle with a fresh length of waxed thread, mute as a swan.

He sighed. Added a dollop of honey to his tea and said, stirring, "You told me you weren't in love with her."

"I'm not," Matt answered, after a moment.

"Then why does it matter if I am?"

"Did I say it matters?"

Exasperated, he threw down his spoon. "You didn't have to! It was written all over your face. So d'you want to tell me what's goin' on?"

Still Matt stared at his stitching. "Nothing's going on."

"Is that so?" Carefully, he put down his mug. "Then why won't you look at me, Matt? What are you scared I'll see in your eyes when you say 'I don't love her'?"

Matt did look at him then. Stabbed his needle into the ball of waxed harness thread and stood. "Nothing. It's none of my never-mind, Asher, you've made that clear. Now why don't you go about your business and leave me to—"

A crashing from the stable yard spun him about, last words forgotten. As one they leapt for the office door. Matt reached it first, wrenched it open. All the horses were jostling now, roused to whickers and kicking by the panicked banging and thrashing in their midst.

Matt swore. "That bloody animal, it's been nothing but trouble—grab the long line, Asher. I'll need your help."

The grey colt that had hurt itself on the way to Dorana was cast in its stable. As the startled lads rushed downstairs into the yard, hauling on boots and jackets as they came, Matt caught the rope Asher threw him and led the way to its box.

"Stand back, boys," he ordered the lads. "We don't want to panic him further."

Asher looked over the stable door. The colt had rolled up against the wall. Legs half folded between belly and timber, it was trapped and half mad with terror. He could see blood already. Horses had killed themselves like this; they didn't have much time.

Without speaking, not needing to, he and Matt entered the stable. The colt began to thrash again. He went to its head, held its cheek to the straw with one hand and pressed its neck flat with his knee. Restrained, the colt grunted and groaned but couldn't move. Swiftly Matt looped one end of the rope around the colt's front legs, the other around its hind. With the knots secure, he looked across and nodded.

"On three. One—two—*three*!"

He pulled, and Asher guided the colt's head and neck, rolling it over and away from the wall. As soon as it was clear Asher pinned the colt down again and Matt untied the rope. Young Jim'l, always fast on the uptake, slid the bolt on the stable door and held it open just wide enough. Then they threw themselves out of the stable as the sweaty colt lurched to its feet, then bucked and reared and stamped its rage.

Safe in the yard, blotting sweat, Matt said, "Thanks. Damn bloody thing."

Asher grinned. "Me or the horse?"

Matt's answering grin was...complicated. "What do you think?"

They had an audience of goggling stable lads; it was no place for a private, painful conversation. "I think I need to get goin'. We'll talk later, eh?"

Coiling up the rope, again Matt wouldn't look at him. "If you insist."

Baffled, hurt, he shoved his hands in his pockets. "You sayin' there's nowt to talk about?"

Then Matt did look up. His face was weary. Sad. "I'm saying I doubt it'll make much difference."

Stung, Asher turned on his heel and started walking. Said over his shoulder, "Aye...well...don't do me any favours, Matt."

Despite his anger, he hoped Matt might come after him. Call after him, at least. Make *some* kind of effort.

Nothing.

So—sink it. If Matt wanted to play the sore loser, let him. He had other friends, and other things to worry about.

Like WeatherWorking.

CHAPTER SIXTEEN

Two hours later, as the burning magic faded, Asher let his legs fold beneath him and thudded to the Weather Chamber floor. Through barely open eyes he watched gentle rain tumble onto the fallow apple orchards of the Home Districts, and snow feather itself over the ice-wine region of Fairvale.

"Here," said Gar, and held out a cup of Nix's disgusting potion. Hand shaking, Asher took it and drank the vile sludge of herbs and vinegars concocted to keep body and soul together. His belly heaved, protesting, but he managed to keep it down.

Gar reached for him with a damp cloth. "Now your face—"

"I can do it," he mumbled. "Don't need a bloody nursemaid."

He could feel Gar's worried gaze on him as he dabbed at his blood-sticky skin. "You shouldn't try to do so much at once," Gar said. "Olken aren't meant to endure this kind of power."

He dropped the stained cloth and dragged himself to his feet. He couldn't stand unaided, though; the Weather Magic still ate him like acid. He shuffled sideways and leaned against the chamber's circular wall, his head viciously pounding. "I got no choice. Can't afford to spend all night on it. I still got work to do, back at the Tower."

"Can't it wait?"

"No."

Gar busied himself shoving cloth, basin and potion back in the cupboard. Slammed its doors. "I know this is hard," he said, his voice low. "But what would you have me do? I'm reading Durm's books. I'm searching for a cure."

He pulled a face. "Read faster."

"I can't! The books are *old*, Asher, recorded in ancient dialects, obscure codes! If I translate them incorrectly, if I let haste overcome scholarship, I'll make a mistake, one that will kill you or me or everyone in Lur! Is that what you want?"

"I want this to be *over*!" he retorted, goaded to desperation. "I want my life back the way it was before!"

Gar turned on him. "Before what? Before when? There is no 'before,' Asher! There's only now, from this minute to the next, holding on tight and hoping the sky doesn't fall on our heads."

Asher stifled a groan. His bones were chalk, ready to snap at the smallest exertion. He'd left exhaustion behind days ago. "When we said a month, I thought: that ain't such a long time. I can do that. But now I ain't so sure. Right now an hour feels like forever."

"I know. I'm sorry," said Gar. He was stricken with guilt. "Look. I'm supposed to draft a new Weather Schedule soon. There might be some arrangements I can change. Stretch things out a bit, give you more time between Workings."

"You'll have a queue of farmers and suchlike bangin' on the door with complaints."

Gar frowned. "The WeatherWorker's word is law. If I can adjust the rain and snowfall frequencies without adversely affecting the crops..."

"Try," he said. "Please?" It shamed him, begging; but the magic was breaking him. He could feel the fissures spreading.

The gentle shush and splash of snow and rain on the relief map was easing. With a sharp, deep breath he pushed himself away from the wall. Made himself stand up straight.

"I'll do, now. You should get on back. I'll wait a bit, then follow."

Gar shook his head. "You're in no fit state to walk alone. And we shouldn't risk you falling asleep in here. We'll go back together. It's late enough now that no one should notice."

It wasn't a good idea, but he didn't have the strength to argue. "Fine," he said. "You're the king." And even let Gar help him down the stairs, one arm strong and steady about his shoulders.

They returned to the Tower in silence. Gar went on up to his apartments and Asher, reluctant, headed for his office. The worst of the pain and nausea had passed, he was mostly tired now, and light-headed. An hour longer, he'd work, and that should keep nagging Darran satisfied.

Light spilled from beneath his closed office door. He opened it, and there was Dathne. "What are you doin' here?"

"You and that damned WeatherWorking. I couldn't sleep," she said, apologetic and truculent at once. "And there was work to do. I didn't think you'd mind."

He came inside and closed the door. Shrugged out of his jacket and hung it on the coat rack. "No. I don't mind."

"Good," she said, and smiled. Then relief faded as she looked more closely at him. "Asher—there's blood on your weskit."

He looked down. Damn. So there was. "It's nowt."

"Nowt?" She came round from behind her desk. "Since when is blood nowt?"

Barl save him, he was too tired for this... "Dath, don't fuss. I got a bit too near to Gar when he was WeatherWorking, is all; I told you, it's a bloody business."

"*His* bloody business. So how is it *you're* the one looking half dead?"

"I'm *fine*," he insisted.

She stepped back. "No. You're not. There's something you aren't telling me."

The hurt in her eyes was like a knife wound. "Don't do this, Dath," he whispered. "Please. Can't you understand? I've made promises."

She was silent for a moment. Staring. Thinking. Then she moved close to him again and touched her fingertips to his weskit, where blood had turned cream to crimson like magic. "You should go to bed. You really do look dreadful."

He felt dreadful, all his sleeping pains rewoken. "Can't. Glospottle's hearing is the day after tomorrow and I ain't nowhere near ready. I still got a pile of books to read through and make notes on."

"Then I'll stay and help," she said, smiling. "Two heads are better than one."

A tempting offer, but it was late and his defences were weakened. If she asked him again to confide in her, he might not have the strength to resist. Especially since he was feeling so desperately alone. "Dath—"

She rested her palm above his heart. "Let me stay. Please?"

He shouldn't... he shouldn't... "All right," he said. "But only for a while."

At her suggestion they took the books he needed up to his apartment library, which had sofas on which they could comfortably recline. She took one half of the pile, he took the other, and they settled down to reading.

Time passed. Soon he forgot about "just an hour" and "only for a while." It didn't matter that he was weary or that his eyes felt gritty. Scented pine burned cheerfully in the fireplace and it was so cosy, so domestic, to be sharing silence with her in his private apartment, working.

Curled up on the other crimson leather sofa Dathne sighed, used a finger to mark her place in the book she was studying and scratched some more notes on the already crowded piece of paper beside her. Her expression was one of grave concentration. The very tip of her tongue poked out from the corner of her mouth as she wrote, and there was an ink smudge on the end of her nose. He felt his heart turn over.

She looked up, sensing his regard. "What?"

He couldn't say it. Said instead, "I been thinking. Don't reckon I can do this."

"What? Preside over the hearing?" She returned to her notes. "Of course you can."

"No, I can't. It's *Justice Hall*, Dathne! Legal folderol and footlin' about! I don't understand that claptrap!"

She grinned. "Which is why we're sitting here in the small hours of the night studying when all sensible people are in their beds. Have you finished *Tevit's Principles of Jurisprudence* yet?"

Tevit's tedious bloody Principles of Juris-bloody-prudence lay open and abandoned on his chest. The first three paragraphs on page one had given him a thumping headache and it had gone downhill from there.

"No."

"*Asher...*"

He pushed the book to the carpeted floor, where it landed with a satisfying thud. "Can't I just throw Glospottle and the rest of the Dyers' Guild into prison instead?"

Another grin. "I'm sure Pellen Orrick would love that."

"I know I bloody would," he said, glowering. A yawn overtook him; when it was done twisting his face inside out he let his head thud onto the sofa's padded arm roll and closed his eyes. Exhaustion was like a blanket of warm snow, weighing him down. "I just reckon the world's gone mad if a no-account uneducated fisherman from Restharven can sit on that throne in Justice Hall and tell folk he hardly knows what they can and can't do with their own urine."

"You don't give yourself enough credit," said Dathne, her voice coming closer. "Next to our king you're the most important man in Lur." She was bending over him. He could feel her soft breath fanning his face. "I thought you'd realised that by now."

"What I realise, Dathne, is that I—"

Her warm, soft lips suffocated the rest of his sentence. Shocked silent, he lay there drowning in exquisite sensation. After an age she released him, and he breathed again. He opened his eyes.

"Now who's takin' liberties?"

"Me," she whispered and kissed him again, smelling of passion and perfume. Tasting of the honey-mints she liked to nibble when she thought no one was looking. He lifted his hands to the nape of her neck and unpinned her thick black hair. It fell about his face in lavender-scented disarray. Her fingers were framing his face, holding him, caressing him. Shivering his skin and setting it on fire. Even through a barricade of brocade and silk he could feel her breasts against his chest. All the blood left his head in a dizzying rush, making a beeline south.

"Asher? What is it? You're not enjoying this?" she murmured against his mouth.

"Yes! Yes!" he whispered frantically.

Her fingers tightened. "Then kiss me back, damn you!"

He was her obedient slave. His arms crept around her back, encircling the fragile ribcage, home to her thundering heart. At last they broke apart, sobbing for breath. Her stunned eyes were enormous, her lips wet and swollen. He pressed his fingertips against them and shuddered as she touched him with her tongue.

"Don't," he groaned, and captured her hand in his. "If you do that again I might—"

"What?" she whispered, and trailed her other fingers across his bare chest. Bare? When had his shirt come unbuttoned?

"You know what! Dathne, we can't *do* this!"

"But I want to do this," she said, and kissed him yet again.

Head swimming, senses blazing, he let himself respond. Let the whirlwind take him, blind him to sense and reason. Her skin was silk and cream beneath his questing fingers. She moaned his name, trembling at his touch. He felt like a king.

They slid from couch to carpet and she fell beneath him, crying aloud as he kissed her breasts, a small shocked sound of pleasure.

He stopped, panting. "We can't. We mustn't. We're not married, Dathne."

Her scented skin was damp, her hair the wildest tangle. She smiled. "Then marry me."

Disbelieving, he stared into her passion-blurred face. "*What?*"

"There must be a Barlsman awake somewhere in this City." She smoothed his cheek with her fingertips. "Let's go find him."

She was serious. Closing his fingers around her wrist he tugged her free. "You said you didn't love me."

She wouldn't look at him. "I lied."

"Why?"

"I was afraid."

"Of what?"

She sat up. Buttoned her blouse, her fingers unsteady. "Nothing. Everything. It doesn't matter now."

"It matters to me."

She touched her lips to his, lightly. "It shouldn't. What's important is that I've come to my senses."

"Why now?"

"I realised I could lose you."

"*Lose* me?"

Her gaze flickered sideways. "Don't tell me you've not noticed all the fond Olken mamas as you ride through the City. They point you out to their unmarried daughters and tell them to smile as you pass by. You could start a florist's shop ten times over with the roses that get thrown at you on public occasions. There must be a hundred girlish hearts breaking in Dorana, all for love of you."

He didn't know whether to kiss her or shake her silly. "Dathne, since when have I noticed fond mamas or their husband-hunting daughters? For one thing it ain't been nowt but work, work, work ever since I got to this bloody place, and for another..."

"Yes?" Her voice wasn't quite steady. "For another?"

"Yours is the only girlish heart I'm interested in."

Tears spilled down her cheeks. This time their kiss was delicate, dulcet. When it ended he folded his fingers around hers.

"But it don't mean I can marry you. At least not yet."

Her eyes widened in pained surprise. "Why not?"

She was a fiercely bright woman. Married to him, living with him, she'd discover the truth. If things went wrong and he couldn't protect her… "The kingdom's only just out of mourning, Dath. And Gar—"

"Must marry soon himself," she said. "Haven't you heard Darran on the subject?" She pulled a face. "Why should the king care if we stand before a Barlsman and exchange our vows? Or is he so churlish he'd begrudge you a marriage born of love instead of duty?"

Right now, with his own hopes for love and family cruelly blighted. Gar might well begrudge any kind of marriage. And even if he didn't, it would be equally cruel to flaunt happiness under his nose.

Something else he couldn't tell her. "Dathne…it ain't as simple as that."

"It could be," she said, and withdrew her fingers from his. "Perhaps you don't love me after all."

He answered her calumny with a kiss that stole all the air from their lungs and left them gasping. "Believe me now?"

With her head on his chest and one hand crept inside his shirt to lie against his ribs she said, "Yes. But you'll put duty first."

Ever since they'd met she'd been his sympathetic sounding board, his sage advisor, his blunt and brutal mirror. It cut him to the quick, repaying her honesty with half-truths and lies. "I'm sorry," he whispered.

She smiled painfully. "Don't be." Bending low, she kissed the ropy scar along his forearm. "I know a little about duty myself."

He didn't deserve her. Couldn't believe he'd won her. What a courtship he'd endured…

She kissed him again. Soaring, he lost himself in sensation. Kissing was so much better than thinking. Or worrying. Or trying to come to grips with *Tevit's Principles of Jurisprudence*. Who'd have thought a floor could feel so comfortable? Or a spare and angular body so soft? Kissing Dathne was a homecoming.

Breathing hard, they sat on the floor in tangled silence. Then Dathne stirred. Her fingernails traced circles on his chest, raising goosebumps. "Do you know how we Olken married before the Doranen came?"

He rested his cheek on the top of her head. "No."

"We stood together, witness for each other. We declared our desire to be handfast and faithful. And we were married."

"Just like that?"

She nodded. "Yes, my love. Just like that."

My love. Dizzy, he tilted her head back with a finger beneath her chin and gazed into her heavy-lidded eyes. "That were a long time ago, Dath. There were reasons things changed."

She pouted. "I know, I know. Marriages need to be recorded, babies can't be born willy-nilly. We must never outgrow the land we have here. But I'm not saying we won't ever stand before a Barlsman, Asher. When you think our public happiness won't hurt the king we can have our marriage entered in the registry. But why should we deny ourselves our private joy till then? If we were any other people, living anywhere else in Lur, we could marry in a heartbeat. I'm sorry for the king's sorrow, truly, but why must we suffer because of it?"

Her words struck a deep chord. Unbidden, buried resentment stirred. Why indeed? He was already sacrificing so much for Gar. Risking so much. He deserved something in return, didn't he? Some small spark of happiness. He and Dathne couldn't live together of course. Not at first. Maybe not for months. Might only have a handful of stolen moments, like this one. But the moments would be theirs. Joy would be theirs. And in her arms he could mercifully, hopefully, forget his other, unjoyful secrets.

Harsh practicality doused his daydream. "But what about babies? You know there can't be any babies, Dath, not until—"

"Hush," she said, and pressed a finger to his lips. "Babies are women's business. Leave that to me. We'll have no babies till the time is right."

Relieved, he gathered her close. "Even married, you know there'll be things I can't tell you. Private business 'tween Gar and me that can't go further. It don't mean I ain't mad in love with you. I am. Reckon I always have been. But—"

She kissed him. "I know. I understand."

"And we'd have to be bloody careful. There'll be folks around all the time. Noticin' types like Darran and pissant Willer. They can't suspect a thing. Can you live a secret life like that?"

Tears welled in her eyes. "I think so."

He frowned, then. "And you can't tell Matt either."

"Don't worry," she said. "Matt's the last person I'd want to tell."

Jealousy stabbed. "So he *is* in love with you."

"No. *No.* But he'd...disapprove. We'd argue. And this is my choice, not his." She kissed him, hard. "Matt is a friend, Asher. You're the only man who's ever moved me."

The simple declaration stunned him. "You really want to do this?"

Her answer was to break away from him. Bemused, he watched her lock the library door, pad to the fireplace and heave fresh logs into the dying flames, then retrieve a pale gold silk-weave scarf from the depths of her satchel.

"Hold out your hand," she said, so he did. She sank to the carpet before him and matched his move, palm kissing palm, and laced her fingers with his. Then, frowning lightly, she bound their flesh together with the scarf. He said nothing, feeling giddy, feeling dreamlike.

They were getting married.

The ritual binding complete, she sat on her heels and considered him. The heat of her hand was like magic in his blood. "I am Dathne Jodhay, a maid of good conscience and unsullied name. I take this man, Asher, to be my husband and swear to him my love and loyalty until I die." She smiled then. "Your turn."

"I am Asher of Restharven," he replied. In his own ears his voice sounded...breathless. "I'm a man of good conscience and unsullied name, except if you ask Darran or Willer or Conroyd Jarralt and why would you? Dathne Jodhay is my woman, my wife, and if anybody looks so much as sideways at her I'll knock their bloody block off."

Dathne was shaking with silent laughter. "Oh, Asher, you're such a romantic!"

"Sink romance," he growled, and pulled her to him hard enough to make her gasp. "Are we married?"

"Oh yes," she said, and toppled him to the floor. "We're married."

And then there was no more talking, as clothes peeled from flesh like shedding skin. Laughing, groaning their mutual needs, hands roamed, tongues touched, fingertips coaxed forth bonfires of delight.

Suddenly disconcerted, lost in a wilderness of pleasure, Asher fumbled to a halt. Lifting his lips from her breast, he gazed into her chaotic eyes. "Uh, Dath. You know I ain't never..."

More laughter. Wicked hands, holding. "It's all right," she promised him, trembling. "Neither have I. But I reckon we'll work something out."

The minute he laid eyes on them, Matt knew. Stepping back into the shadows between the stallion stables and the feed room, watching them creep into the stable yard like conspirators, he felt his heart turn over.

Dathne, Dathne, what have you done?

It was early yet, not quite a half-hour past dawn, and the lads were only just rousing from their beds. Smeary with sleep, he'd abandoned his own blankets nearly two hours ago to check on the grey colt, and stayed up to finish mending that broken bridle. To worry about Asher and the rift sprung up between them that he didn't know how to close. Now his stomach was growling for breakfast and there was a pain behind his eyes and all he wanted was hot tea and sizzling bacon and a moment just to sit, and rest, and not think about anything.

What he *didn't* want was another argument with Dathne. But now, having seen her, seen Asher, how could he stay silent? Pretend he'd not seen anything? She'd lost her mind. The strain of being Jervale's Heir must've upset her judgement, tipped her right over the edge of reason. And while he owed loyalty to her, and paid the debt gladly, there was an even greater claim on his conscience. He had a duty to the Circle. To Prophecy.

And somebody had to save her, even if it was from herself.

They weren't holding hands, not exactly. But their fingertips were touching as they tiptoed to the tack room and she was looking into his face with her unlocked heart in her eyes. He was grinning, happier than the City had ever seen him.

She waited as he slipped into the tack room and emerged a moment later with Cygnet's saddle, saddlecloth and bridle. The horse had recognised his step and was hanging over its stable door, ears pricked, nostrils fluttering a welcome. He saddled up and she draped herself over the door, watching. Giggling softly. *Dathne?* It was hard to believe. When he was done, she swung open the door for him and stood aside as he led Cygnet into the yard.

"Ride carefully now," she admonished him, her voice hushed. "The kingdom needs its Olken Administrator in one piece." Her hand was on his arm. There was something terrifyingly possessive about the simple gesture. She smiled, her expression wicked and suggestive and heartbreakingly intimate. "And so do I."

His hand slid round her waist, down to her hips, down even lower, and he pulled her to him with a grunt of satisfaction.

"Stop fratchin' at me," he said. "Cygnet and me've been out early every morning this week and ain't come to harm. It's the only time I get to m'self these days, and I ain't about to give it up." He nipped at the soft skin between her jaw and throat. "Not even for you."

Their kiss was molten, passion unleashed. Matt watched it, despairing. There wasn't enough common sense in all the kingdom to douse this. When they parted Dathne stepped back, unsteady on her feet, and Asher was flushed.

"Now get away from me, woman," he said, throwing the reins over Cygnet's head, "afore I go off like a rocket. I'll see you back at the Tower sharp at nine."

"Yes," she said. "There's the rest of Tevit to get through today."

"Sink Tevit and his bloody *Principles of Jurisprudence*," said Asher, grinning. He swung himself into Cygnet's saddle and sat there, staring down at her. "I love you."

"And I you," she replied. "Now go if you're going. Matt and the lads will be downstairs any minute."

She watched him ride out of the yard, then turned to leave through the main entrance's archway. Her face was shuttered again, closed down and self-contained. Matt took a deep breath and stepped out of the shadows.

"Dathne."

Startled into silence she stared at him. Then: "Matt. You're about early. And stealthy, too. You should mind where you creep, my friend. You might give some poor soul a seizure."

Closing on her, he took her upper arm in his callused fingers. "Are you mad, Dathne? Have you abandoned all sense? You're *futtering* with him?"

She jerked her arm from his grasp, glaring. "I'm married with him. It's not futtering when you're married, Matt."

"You're *married*..." Speech failed him. Aghast he looked at her, this sudden stranger, and struggled to find the words. "*Dathne*—"

The door leading up to the staff dormitory flew open and the chattering stable lads tumbled into the yard. "Not out here," she said grimly, and stalked to the office. He followed her inside and closed the door behind them.

"You're married with him," he said, despair reducing his voice to a whisper. "Does Veira know?"

"Not yet."

"*Why*, Dathne?" he asked her. "Why did you do it?"

"Because I had to. Because I need him bound to me, body and soul. He's holding something back, Matt. Something important. I must know what it is."

He collapsed into the office's dilapidated armchair and rubbed his hands across his face. "You *are* mad. You told Asher you loved him, Dathne. I heard you."

Her cheeks tinted pink. "That conversation was private."

"Dathne! Love won't save you when he finds out you've used him!"

Outrage and dismay churning through him, he pushed to his feet and began pacing the small office. Outside in the yard the horses were neighing and banging their stable doors, demanding breakfast. The lads laughed and joked, gravel crunching beneath their boots and buckets rattling as they crisscrossed from feed room to stables and back again. "When did you marry?"

She was watching him closely, chin up, arms folded across her chest. "Last night."

"Who witnessed? Holze?"

There was a moment's hesitation before she answered. "Nobody."

"*Nobody?*" he said, incredulous. "You mean you just exchanged vows with each other? No Barlsman? Whose crazy idea was that?"

The heat in her cheeks deepened. "Mine."

He wanted to scream. Stamp. Throw mugs at the wall and watch them shatter. "Of course it was. Dathne, you're a fool! If there wasn't a Barlsman then you *aren't* married and it *is* futtering and if anybody finds out—"

"They'll only find out if you tell them!" she retorted. "Save your breath, Matt. It's done and you can't undo it. And I was right. Whatever he's hiding, he almost told me last night."

"Before or after you futtered him?" he said bitterly.

She slapped him, hard enough to burst stars before his eyes. "Don't you dare."

His face throbbed, but he ignored the pain. "You say I'm your compass, but what good's a compass if you don't follow its directions? Ever since he came here I've said he should be told."

"And he will be!"

"But only when it's too late! After this, after what you've done, when he finds out the truth he'll spit on you and walk away!"

"No, he won't."

"Yes, he *will*. He'll walk away and Prophecy will fail and our lives will've been for *nothing*!"

There was fear in her face now, crowding out her defiant anger. "You're wrong. He understands duty, Matt. And sacrifice. He wouldn't be the Innocent Mage if he didn't!"

"He may be the Innocent Mage, Dathne, but he's also a man! He's a man before he's anything else, and if you think a man can so easily forgive this kind of betrayal then it wouldn't matter if you'd futtered a *hundred* Ashers, you'd still be an ignorant girl!"

He was ready for her this time and caught her wrist before her hand reached his face.

"Let go of me," she said, her voice a deadly whisper.

"Dathne—"

"*No!*" Her eyes were glittering. "It's over, Matt. You're no use to me any more. I'm telling Veira you've stepped aside. Can I trust you'll hold your tongue? Say yes. You must know by now there's nothing I won't do in the service of Prophecy."

"No," he whispered back. "Nothing. Not even strumpeting yourself."

The office door swung open and in walked Asher, talking all the while. "You in here, Matt? There's half a tree come down on the fence round Crooked Paddock and all the three year olds are out. Thought I'd best ride back and warn you, seein'—" He stopped, all friendliness freezing. "What's goin' on? Dathne?"

Before she could answer, Matt turned on him. "And *you*! Are you as mad as she is? You're the Olken Administrator! Don't you know what scandal there'll be if you're found to be futtering out of wedlock with your assistant? Not even the king will save you then!"

Incredulous, Asher stared at Dathne. "You *told* him?"

"He saw us."

"No, he didn't," said Asher, and slammed the office door. "He didn't see nowt. He don't know nowt. And if he values his bones unbroken he'll let go of you right now."

Matt released Dathne's wrist and stared at the livid white marks his fingers left on her flesh. "Tell him you made a mistake, Dathne. Please. Tell him everything."

"What everything?" said Asher. His expression was ugly. "What's he on about, Dath?"

She stepped forward, barring Asher's progress. "Nothing. It's nothing. It doesn't matter. We were just talking."

He didn't believe her. Gently he pushed her aside and came closer. Matt made himself meet his friend's unforgiving eyes. "I asked you once if you had feelings for Dathne," said Asher. "You said no. Seems to me you lied, Matt."

He turned to her. "For Barl's sake, Dathne—"

"I'm sorry, Matt," she said, and threaded her arm through Asher's. Her eyes were pitiless. "I wish I could care the way you want me to, but it's Asher I love. Not you."

"*Dathne!*"

"Look, Matt," said Asher, voice and face thawing slightly, "I'll make this easy on you. You're dismissed."

He stared, stupid as a scarecrow. "I'm what?"

"Dismissed," said Asher. "Let go. Relieved of your duties. I'm reas-signing you to His Majesty's stud farm down the Dingles. I'll get Gan-fel from over the palace stables to step in for now. He's a good man with horses, he'll see the place don't fall apart till I can decide who'll take over here."

He shook his head. "You can't—"

"I can," said Asher. "I have. It's done."

Still, he couldn't believe it. "But...but..."

"*It's done.*"

There was no fellowship in Asher's face now. No amusement or warm understanding. Matt wasn't sure he knew this man at all. "I thought we were friends."

Asher smiled. Stepped closer and lowered his voice. "We are. Which is why you're walkin' out of here on your own two legs." The smile vanished. "You put your hand on her in anger, Matt. Ain't another man in all this kingdom who'd do that and walk away." He stepped back again. "Now, why don't you go see to them pesky sight-seein' three year olds, eh? After that you can report to Darran. He'll help you with the particulars of gettin' resettled down to the farm."

Matt turned again to Dathne. "You're just going to stand there and let him—"

"I'm sorry, Matthias," she said. She never called him Matthias. "I do believe it's best this way."

Her denial of him hurt worse than Asher's anger. Almost, he opened his mouth and blurted out the truth and Jervale's Heir be damned. But he couldn't do it. He'd sworn a sacred oath to obey her...and he'd keep it, no matter what that cost.

"What if I fight you?" he said to Asher in a strangled whisper. "I could fight you."

Asher shrugged. "You'd lose. I never came to this dratted City lookin' for power, Matt, but it seems I ended up with it anyways. Ordinarily I ain't one for throwin' my weight around but for this I'll make an exception. Dath's right, even if you don't see it now. And you'll do fine down in the Dingles. Maybe you'll not be as high up the ladder there as you are here, but you're young yet. You'll manage."

You're young yet, from a man six years his junior. Feeling like he'd been turned to solid wood, he nodded again. "Yes, sir." He allowed himself a pinch of sarcasm. "Thank you, sir."

Asher's eyes narrowed. "Off you go then."

Without looking back, without saying another word, he went.

CHAPTER SEVENTEEN

Darran and Willer were already at work in their office when Asher returned to the Tower, his hopes of a morning ride dashed to pieces. Cluny and her housemaid friends bustled about the foyer, putting fresh flowers in the vases, straightening the paintings on the walls. They dimpled and curtseyed as he strode in. It wasn't their fault he was in a killing mood, so he smiled and nodded and pretended not to notice the wary surprise in their eyes.

"Asher!" Darran called as he pounded up the stairs on his way to change clothes. "A moment, please!"

"I'm busy," he called back without stopping. "I'll be down directly."

A scuttling of footsteps behind him. A plump hand, plucking at his sleeve. "Darran says it's urgent," Willer gasped. "It's about the weather."

He pulled his arm free. "What about it?"

There was definitely something...furtive...about Willer these days. He smiled too much, and in the wrong way. His familiar belligerence was drowned in sugar syrup and yet somewhere beneath the sticky sweetness a sharpened knife blade glinted, waiting. These days Willer put his teeth on edge in a whole new and unpleasant way.

"Please come," the sea slug said, his eyes wide and earnest. "Darran needs you."

And thanks to yet another promise to Gar, what Darran wanted Darran got, all in the name of nauseating bloody unity. Swallowing a string of curses, Asher followed Willer back down the stairs and into the secretary's office.

"What?"

Darran looked up from his desk. The sun had barely started its long slow crawl up the sky and there he was, crisp and shaven and immaculate in black, distressingly healthy, surrounded by ink pots and parchments and piles of important papers.

"As a matter of urgency I require the new Weather Schedule," he said. No "good morning," or "sorry to interrupt you," or any such common-and-garden pleasantries. Bloody ole crow. "And a firm idea of how often His Majesty intends to prepare one. The palace informs me the late king drafted the weather patterns some six weeks in advance.

Does His Majesty intend to maintain the same routine? Or does he anticipate an alteration? If so, I must know. I'm getting messages from all over the kingdom wondering when the next schedule will appear. People are agitating, Asher. I would much prefer they didn't."

"Ask Gar. It's weather business, that is," said Asher. "Ain't none of my nevermind."

"I'm making it your nevermind," said Darran, and not without a gleam of malicious pleasure either, the miserable geezer.

"Sink me bloody sideways," he muttered. His head was aching already and dawn was only five minutes ago. "All right. When I get a minute I'll—"

"Now," said Darran. "If you please."

Clearly, there was no escape. And anyways the ole crow was right, drat him: the last thing Gar needed was widespread agitation over a delayed Weather Schedule. That'd suit Conroyd bloody Jarralt right down to the ground, that would.

Willer was goggling at him, fat lips pursed in a smile. He scowled. "What are you bloody lookin' at, eh?"

Willer's smile widened. "Why, nothing at all, Asher. I promise."

"Well, go look at it someplace else. You're makin' me seasick!" And on that mildly satisfying note he headed for the door...only to turn back halfway, remembering. "Matt's transferrin' down to the Dingles stud farm, Darran. Draft me a letter of recommendation to sign, would you? Lots of compliments. And send a runner to the Treasury so's he can take his money with him, and one to the palace for Ganfel to take over just now."

Darran exchanged a surprised look with Willer. "Matt is leaving? Why?"

"Personal reasons. Nobody's business but his own. I'll tell the king. No need for you to bother him about it. He don't need to be fratched with anythin' else just now. Right? That means you too, Willer. Not a bloody word."

Frowning, Darran said, "Willer knows the meaning of discretion as well as I do, Asher. Matt's departure shall not be mentioned outside this room." He sighed. "But I think it a great pity. His Majesty's very fond of him."

Asher felt a stab of pain. *And so was I fond of him, before he laid hands on Dathne...* Then he shrugged, and continued to the door. "Folk move on, Darran. You can't hold onto 'em."

He overtook Cluny on the last flight of stairs up to Gar's suite. She was carrying the king's breakfast tray, and dimpled when she saw him.

"Morning, Asher."

The wafting aromas of bacon, fried potato, scrambled eggs and hot bread teased his empty stomach and doused his mouth with saliva. "Morning. Want me to take that up for you?"

"Oh, would you?" said Cluny, pink-cheeked and grateful. "Only we've a maid with the collywobbles and there's ever so much to do." She thrust the covered breakfast tray into his hands, dimpled again, enchantingly, and flew back down the stairs. Despite all his aggravations, he smiled after her. He liked Cluny. A lot. If it hadn't been for Dathne...

His blood stirred, thinking of her. *We're married...we're married!* Thinking of all they'd done the night before and soon would do again, he hoped. With that warm pleasure to sustain him, crowding out all dark thoughts of Matt, he headed on up the stairs.

Gar was in his library, barricaded behind towers of books. Asher kicked the door shut behind him and wandered over to stand in front of the desk.

"Breakfast."

Gar grunted and kept on working. Asher sat down, tray in his lap, uncovered a plate and filched a crispy slice of bacon. Kicking his boot heels onto a handy table he sat back with a sigh, crunching. Then noticed what was different about Gar's crowded, chaotic library.

There was a new painting on the far wall.

Well. Not new new. But new to the Tower. Sucking bacon grease from his fingers he studied the enormous portrait. The royal family stood beside a spreading djelba in full bloom; the velvet pink petals looked real enough to touch. Behind them the pristine white walls of the palace, jewelled windows glinting in the sunshine. And behind the palace Barl's Wall, soaring triumphantly into the cloudless sky. It was a masterful painting, commissioned from one of the kingdom's finest Doranen artists. Lord Someone-or-other. Short, skinny, busy fingers, temper like a sex-starved tomcat. *Bracan.*

He'd caught his subjects seemingly between breaths. Borne was smiling, Dana seemed ready to laugh. Fane looked so beautiful it broke a man's heart. Remembering them, he felt his throat close hard and tight. Painted Gar stood beside his sister, one hand resting on her shoulder. Posed by Bracan, doubtless. You'd never catch them touching on purpose, unless it was to slap or stab. Gar was smiling too, but his eyes were sad. As though he knew something the others didn't. As though he could see the future, and was sorry.

"We were a handsome family, weren't we?" said Gar.

Asher nodded, melancholy settling like a mist. "Aye."

Gar turned away from the painting. "I miss them so much," he said, his voice low. Unsteady. "Even Fane."

"I know."

"I just received word from Nix," Gar said, and flicked a discarded note with one fingertip. "Durm is awake again and much improved. He's asking to see me."

Damn. Unsettled, Asher drank some of Gar's teshoe juice. "You goin'?"

"Of course."

"When?"

"Soon."

He chewed his lip. "Durm know about your family yet?"

"No." Gar examined an ink stain on his finger. "When I tell him, and he learns I'm now the king, he'll ask about my magic. The Weather Working. And if he senses something's wrong—if my lies don't fool him—well. It doesn't bear thinking about." Then he frowned. "Is that my breakfast you're eating?"

"Aye." He held out the tray. "You want it?"

"Not anymore." Elbows resting on the desk, Gar considered him. "You all right? You had me worried last night."

He helped himself to a slice of toast. Bit. Chewed. Swallowed. "I'm fine."

"Really? You look...angry. Are you having second thoughts? I wouldn't blame you if you were. Last night's Working was hard."

Asher scowled at the breakfast tray. He had bigger problems than the Weather Working just now. If he told Gar about Matt, things would get very messy very fast. Doubtless Gar would order his stable meister's reinstatement, and Matt needed putting in his place. Deserved some punishment for so distressing Dathne. A month or two in the Dingles would serve him right. He could come back after that. After he'd had time to cool his heels and accept the fact that Dathne would never be his.

None of which he could tell Gar. Far better to let Matt slip away quietly and then tell Gar after the event. He shook his head. "Darran's been jawin' at me, is all. Wants the new Weather Schedule. Today."

"I don't have time today."

"Then make time," he said, scowling. "You said you'd fix things so the Weather Workin'd go a bit easier on me. Here's your chance."

Gar waved a hand at the books on his desk. Waved again at the books piled on the carpet beside his chair. "I know what I said. But Asher, I can do the Weather Schedule or I can keep on ploughing through Durm's library in search of the solution to our problems. I can't do both, and you're the one complaining I'm not reading fast enough."

With a rattle of plates and cutlery Asher dumped the breakfast tray on the floor. "Gar—"

"I'm serious!" said Gar. "With Durm awake again we could have less time than we planned. If his recovery proceeds swiftly—if he's able to return to his own apartments before our month is up—"

All the books would have to go back. And Durm, learning of their removal, might suspect something was wrong. Questions could be asked—secrets revealed—

Abruptly his pilfered breakfast curdled in his belly and hot fear rose in his throat. "Then we'll be in the shit, won't we?"

Gar sat back, regarding him steadily with narrowed eyes. "You *are* having second thoughts."

"One of us has to!" Restless in his chair, he stared through the nearest window. "With your da gone Durm's the strongest magician in the kingdom now, ain't he?"

"Yes."

"Pity you can't declare him king."

Gar shook his head. "It's against the law. No one can be Weather Worker and Master Magician both."

"Then give him the crown and find another Master Magician."

"It would have to be Jarralt," Gar pointed out. "Which doesn't help us much. Anyway, Conroyd would never accept the lesser prize. Not in favour of Durm. And Durm's not married, he's childless and has no prospect of an heir. It's grounds for a challenge, Conroyd knows it, and we're back to schism again."

Damn. It seemed every way they turned there was Conroyd bloody Jarralt standing in the way. He scowled at his boots, thinking. "Look," he said at last, "I know you don't want to hear this, Gar, but I don't reckon you got much choice. With Durm awake it's too dangerous for us to keep on the way we've been. Go to him today. Tell him what's happened, that your magic's failed."

"I can't tell him about you!"

"Of course you bloody can't!" he said, alarmed. "You'll have to lie, won't you? Say your magic failed last night. And if he can't fix you and Jarralt has to be named king, at least he'll be there as Master Magician to keep him in line."

"Only if he makes a full recovery," said Gar. "And if Conroyd is content for him to stay Master Magician."

"That ain't his decision, is it?"

"Technically, no," said Gar, pulling a face. "But in truth I'd not put it past Conroyd to push Durm from power. He knows too well Durm's opinion of him. And that Durm's loyalty will always be first and foremost to House Torvig."

"Durm knows that, though. He won't let Jarralt shuffle him off without a fight. And Jarralt won't raise a public ruckus over it—he'd lose support in a heartbeat."

Gar's expression was mulish. "I don't care. This is all speculation, Asher. So long as Durm doesn't know what's happened I still have a chance to find a cure on my own and remain king. The second we make my infirmity known, it's over. Now you promised me a month. Do you keep that promise, or walk away from it?"

Bastard. He'd never gone back on a promise in his life, and Gar knew it. "All right," he said, not caring how surly he sounded. "But here's fair warning. One month and not a day or even an hour longer. That's our agreement and that's what I'll hold you to. Even if you drop to your knees and beg."

"I won't," said Gar, unsmiling. "I have my honour, as you have yours. My word is my word and won't be broken. Do you doubt it?"

"No. Just want my position understood, is all."

Gar nodded. "It's understood. Now leave me so I can get back to these wretched books. If you want to be useful, go see Durm in my stead. Give him my regards. Find out from Nix how his recovery proceeds."

Asher stood. Drifted towards the door, eager to be gone. "And if Durm asks when he'll see you?"

"Soon," said Gar. Picking up his pen, he returned his attention to his parchments. "Tell him he'll see me soon. And, Asher?"

Hand on the door latch, he turned. "Aye?"

"Tell Nix to break the news about my family."

"Right," he said, after a moment. And closed the door gently behind him.

Morg glared at the gormless young pother attempting to foist upon him yet another dose of herbal muck. "Unless you desire ears like a rabbit I suggest you go away!"

The nitwit blanched. "I'm sorry, sir, it's Pother Nix's orders."

"Then fetch me Pother Nix so I might rescind his ridiculous orders!"

"Sir," the nitwit said faintly, and scuttled away.

Groaning, Morg lay back upon his raft of pillows. Damn this broken body. With Durm at last defeated, safely silenced and caged once more, he'd thought his mastery complete.

But no. Chained to the vagaries of a corporeal existence, he found himself still weak. Still hostage. Twice this morning he'd tried to rise and twice Durm's mangled remains had defeated him. The situation was intolerable. There had to be another way...

The chamber door opened, admitting Nix. He looked displeased. "Durm, I must insist you don't frighten my staff. They are merely acting upon my instructions. Do you wish to make a full recovery or don't you?"

Morg bared his teeth. He had no time for a full recovery. This body was old and weakened, first with excess, now with injury. And he had lingered in this place for far too long.

In the doorway behind the pother, unnoticed, lurked crippled Gar's pet Olken. He pointed. "What is he doing here?"

Nix turned. Saw the upstart and raged. "I told you to wait outside, Asher! The Master Magician is not ready for vis—"

"Sorry, but I got orders from the king," the upstart said stubbornly. "A message."

Because Durm was not supposed to know of Borne's death, Morg struggled against his pillows and let his voice tremble. "From Borne? I don't understand. Why does he not deliver his message in person?"

As Nix glared, murderous, the Olken stepped forward. "It's all right, Nix. Gar said to tell him."

Morg let his voice grow faint. "Tell me? Tell me what?"

Rage relinquished, the pother sighed and folded his hands. "I'm sorry, Durm. We kept the news from you for fear it would be too much to bear. Borne is dead. The queen, too, and Princess Fane."

"Dead?" Morg whispered, and let Durm's grief well into his eyes. Dribble down his cheeks. "No...no...may Barl have mercy..."

"Gar is our king now," Nix murmured. "The Wall stands strong in his stewardship."

Yes, but *why*? Morg raged behind his mask of tears. *How*, when his magic should have died long since? "Poor boy. To be orphaned and crowned in such swift, unkind succession," he said brokenly. "I must see him. I beg you, Nix, send for him at once. I will not rest until I can—"

"I'm sorry, sir," said the upstart Olken. "I'm here to give you His Majesty's regards and say he will come, soon."

"But not now?" Morg dashed Durm's tears from his cheeks and let himself sag, frail and pathetic, against his pillows. "Why not now? Is something wrong? Is the Weather Working too hard for him? Does his magic not hold?"

The Olken stiffened. Watching closely, Morg saw something flicker in his eyes. And knew that whatever words next fell from his lips would be a lie.

"Why would you wonder that, sir? His Majesty's magic holds strong and true. He's his father's son, right enough. He'll tell you so himself just as soon as he can."

Nix said sharply, "And if that is your message delivered, Asher, you may leave. The Master Magician has enough to contend with for now."

Gar's pet bowed. "Sir." Bowed again to Durm. "Sir. You got any message for the king? Reckon he'd be heartened by a word or two. No disrespect intended, but he's been frettin' for you somethin' fierce."

Morg squeezed out another tear. "The dear, dear boy. Tell him this, Asher. I love him, and grieve with him, and promise him this: that together we shall see our kingdom reach its glorious destiny, ordained on the day Barl came over the mountains."

The Olken exchanged a baffled glance with Nix and bowed again. "Aye, sir. I'll tell him."

He departed. Nix too, after more fussing. Ablaze with triumph, Morg allowed himself a raucous, silent crowing.

The cripple was failing. The time at last had come.

All he needed now was a way out of Durm's used-up, useless body...and the victory would be his.

Conroyd Jarralt walked downstairs to the musical strains of Ethienne berating a servant. "I particularly asked for *yellow* roses, you useless girl! Are you colourblind? Or just stupid, like the rest of your Olken friends?"

The servant was on the brink of tears: brimming eyes, flushed cheeks and a trembling lower lip. Ignoring her, he slid an arm around his ranting wife's shoulders and smoothly swept her with him along the hallway to the foyer and front door. "That's enough, Ethienne. They're flowers, not a matter of life and death."

She pouted. "But, Conroyd—"

He tightened his encircling arm, squeezing her to silence. "Like little starlings in their nest, my dear, Olken servants twitter. And with the Olken lout so close to the throne and wielding influence I would prefer he received no fourth-hand reports claiming I permit the mistreatment of his people under my roof. Understood?"

She wriggled and he let her go. Watched as she smoothed her hair with immaculately manicured fingers. Jewelled rings flashed in the afternoon sunshine filtering through their town-house's tall windows. Her ageing, perfectly made-up face was sulky. "Yes, Conroyd."

He kissed her scented cheek. Softened his manner, because Ethienne always responded most readily to coaxing. "I have business with Holze. Shall I bring you home some yellow roses?"

She reached up and flattened the folds of his silk cravat. Echoes of the flirting girl he'd married. "Very well. And don't be late! The Daltries and the Sorvolds are guesting here this evening, remember?"

He did. And with luck he'd have news for them that would add extra spice to the meal. "Of course, my dear," he said, and kissed her cheek again. "Till this evening."

He closed the front door on her simpering laughter and ensconced himself in his bright blue carriage, the one with his house emblem blazoned proudly on both doors. The horses drawing it were blood bays, caparisoned with equal pride.

This was not a day for stealth. At least, not overtly.

Dorana's mood was elevated, he noted, as the carriage rumbled briskly from his townhouse to the centre of the City. The gloom of the past weeks was gone, doubtless washed away by Gar's proficient Weather Working. The Doranen and Olken faces he passed were smiling, carefree. Relieved. Death's shadow had blotted out the sun, but only for a moment.

He let the carriage curtain fall back to cover the window and rested his head on the cushions behind him. Despite Durm's inconvenient recovery and Willer's failure to uncover malfeasance beneath Gar's roof, still he refused to abandon hope. There was one last weapon in his battle for power that he'd yet to lay his hands upon...

He found Holze in the cleric's Barl's Chapel study. It was a small room, unadorned save for the ubiquitous portrait of Barl hanging above a perpetual candle. Warm light flickered across the saviour's grave young face, her golden hair, the long plait that trailed over her left shoulder. The chamber's atmosphere bordered on the unpleasantly chill.

Holze was reading a religious text and making notes. "Conroyd!" he said, looking up from behind his plain desk as an acolyte ushered his visitor into the room. "Gracious. Am I expecting you? I don't recall—"

"Efrim," said Jarralt, deliberately genial. "No. I came in the hope you'd be free and able to spare me some of your valuable time." He threw a pointed glance at the acolyte. "On matters of state."

"Of course, of course." Holze closed his religious text, disposed of his pen and dismissed the acolyte with a smile and a nod. "Have a seat."

For reasons best kept to himself Holze didn't believe in comfortable chairs. Jarralt arranged himself in the uncompromising wooden stool-and-back arrangement beside the cleric's desk and folded tranquil hands in his lap.

"I realise any reservations I express regarding our kingdom's current circumstances will be seen by some as nothing more than the mouthings of an ambitious, embittered man. But I hope you'll see them for what they truly are: an honest concern for Lur's future."

Advancing age had failed to dull Holze's wits. His eyes were sharp and his expression astute as he said, "You're here about Durm. And the king."

Jarralt nodded. "Yes. And while you and I haven't always agreed, still I think you know me as a man who loves this kingdom, Efrim, and wants only what is in its best interests."

"Yes, Conroyd. I do."

"Please believe me, what I have to say gives me no pleasure. But to stay silent would be a betrayal of everything I hold dear." He kissed his holyring. "Of Blessed Barl herself."

Holze sighed. "Go on."

"I am trying to remember that His Majesty is young and recently bereaved," Jarralt said, frowning. "And that Durm has devoted his whole life to Lur's prosperity. But I am deeply worried and have no one else to whom I can, in confidence, turn to for advice."

"Unburden yourself, Conroyd," Holze said gently. "Share your misgivings with me and together we'll find a way to ease your troubled mind."

Jarralt resisted the urge to resettle himself on the uncomfortable chair, and instead schooled his expression to one of sober, sombre confession. "Borne was a great king. We weren't close, for obvious reasons, but I would never deny his power as a Weather Worker. Question his domestic decisions, yes. And the way he used his influence, his charisma, to further his dynastic ambitions. That in particular I deplored. But it was done, and ratified, and even I could see that Fane was something out of the ordinary."

"Gar is hardly mundane either," Holze pointed out.

"But for all the wrong reasons, Efrim. He was a cripple for most of his life. Magical as a rock. And then, without warning, his power burst upon him and nobody questioned it. Nobody thought it was odd. They were too busy celebrating the miracle." Hearing his own bitterness, he took a moment to moderate his tone. "And now with Borne dead, Fane dead, he's our Weather Worker. Charged with the most sacred magic in the kingdom. And nobody thinks to ask if he's suitable. Or stable. Nobody has thought to wonder if that capricious magic might leave him as suddenly as it arrived."

Holze's fingers stroked the rat-tail Barlbraid on his shoulder. "Durm said his legitimacy as a magician is beyond reproach."

It was no good. He could tolerate the chair no longer. Pushing to his feet, he paced the small, cool chamber. "Durm was the closest thing Borne had to a brother. Borne loved him uncritically and trusted him without question—feelings that were returned tenfold. I doubt there is nothing Durm wouldn't do if it meant protecting his dead friend's dynastic claim to the throne."

"That...is a serious accusation, Conroyd," said Holze. He looked and sounded troubled.

"Don't mistake me, Efrim!" he said, raising one hand. "Durm would never break the law or act against the interests of the kingdom. Not consciously, at least. But I have come to wonder whether his judgement is to be trusted where Borne's son is concerned. And now...with these terrible injuries...the ravages of grief...can we be certain there's been no permanent damage? Is it safe, or wise, to trust him without question?"

Holze nodded slowly. "I confess, Conroyd...these are matters I have myself been pondering."

Jarralt smothered unseemly elation. "And there is yet another matter. More disturbing even than Durm's precarious position. Asher."

Holze let his gaze settle on Barl's portrait. "You've never much cared for him. Or his people."

"Perhaps not, but that doesn't mean my concerns aren't legitimate. This Olken has the ear of our king, and the power to persuade him towards actions that might not be in our best interests. He's been made a Privy Councillor! Are you at ease with this? For I'm not!"

"No," said Holze eventually. Unhappily. "I, too, find Gar's deepening reliance on Asher...disturbing. Barl gave the Olken into our keeping. They are a simple people, ill-equipped to deal with matters of magic or high government."

Tasting victory, he crossed to Holze's side and dropped to one imploring knee. "Then, Efrim, we can stay silent no longer. You are Lur's most senior cleric. Both of us serve as Privy Councillors. Gar's fitness as ruler is demonstrably questionable. For the good of the kingdom we *must* act. We owe Borne's memory nothing less."

Holze's elderly face crumpled. "Conroyd, Conroyd, I fear you're talking about a second schism."

"*No!*" he said, and rested an urgent hand on Holze's reluctant arm. "I'm talking about saving our people from a compromised king and his questionable Master Magician before it's too late and our moral cowardice destroys us all."

Holze turned his face away, distress in every frail line of his body. "How do you suggest we proceed?"

"Then you're with me? When I take this matter to the General Council, you'll add your voice to mine?"

"Don't you mean, will I champion you as Lur's next king?" Holze said bitterly, his face still averted.

"Only if that is Barl's will. Perhaps you should ask her, Efrim."

Holze sighed. "I already have. Change is coming, whether we welcome it or not."

Heart singing, face grave, he again kissed his holyring. "Then may Barl's will be done. And thank you for your support."

"I don't see I have a choice Conroyd," Holze whispered. "Even though I fear we'll break two hearts with this."

He stood. "Better two hearts than a whole kingdom, Efrim. Remember that when your conscience pricks you." He adjusted his coat and cravat. "I'll go now to the infirmary. Speak with Durm and assess his condition. After that we'll talk further. Agreed?"

Reluctantly, Holze nodded. "Agreed."

Morg floated beneath the surface of awareness like a fly drowning in honey. Damned Nix and his damned potions, thrusting him yet again into helpless impotence. Rage was somewhere. Desperation too. And Durm. Gibbering witlessly now, the force of his personality diminished to a thinness, a shadow, a mere suggestion of his former self. How he longed to let the fat fool die...but the risk was too great. Body and soul were still tied, and if the connection were broken there was some small chance the carcass would vomit its unwelcome lodger into the ether, and death.

It wasn't a chance he was prepared to take.

He heard—felt—the door to his chamber, his prison, open. Footsteps. Voices. The door closed again. He tried to open Durm's eyes, struggled to impose his weakened will on the drugged flesh that enveloped him tighter than a virgin's body. The drugged flesh defeated him, again.

"There, my lord. You see?" The pother. Sounding irate. Affronted. "As I told you, the Master Magician is still sleeping. He cannot speak with you!" A wicked man, Nix, overflowing with pestilent herb lore. Interfering, meddlesome. There'd come a day soon when Pother Nix would choke himself to a bloody froth on a *banquet* of herbs...

"My apologies, Nix, if I appeared to question your competence, or honesty." And that was Conroyd Jarralt. Blood called to the memory of blood. Echoes of ancestry. Hope, stirring. The blossoming of a ger-minated idea...

"If it is so important that you confer with him, my lord, perhaps when he wakes I can ask him if—"

"Good pother," said little lord Jarralt. "May I speak my mind to you? Trusting of course in your absolute discretion?"

"You may, my lord."

"Your word as a pother on it?"

"Certainly!"

A sighing silence. Then: "It's no secret, Nix, to those of us whose business it is to know such things that Durm's injuries were savage."

"They were."

"So savage his survival is a miracle?"

"Yes."

"So savage that to think he might regain his former strength and power undiminished is...regrettably...little more than a daydream?"

A long hesitation. "My lord..."

"Say no more," said Jarralt, all sweet sympathy. "Your face answers all."

"Lord Jarralt—"

"It is a delicate matter. I understand." Such kindness in that warm molasses voice. "And painful. You answer to a king who perhaps has...lost perspective."

Struggling to surface, Morg thrashed feebly against the weight of Nix's damnable drugs. There was ambition here, he could smell it like a demon scenting birth-blood. Ambition and a ruthless will to win at all costs. *Splendid.* This Jarralt was strong...and now more than ever he required strength. Had been kept prisoner by weakness for long enough.

Jarralt was the answer to a prayer.

The pother cleared his poxy throat. "My lord, you know I am con-strained—"

"Of course," soothed his ambitious descendant. "I understand you perfectly. Be not alarmed, Nix. We are cut from the same cloth, you and I. Men of honour sworn to serve this kingdom above all else, even the bonds of personal attachment. Durm is my friend. We've served together on the Privy Council for many years and his fall from great-ness breaks my heart. Yet despite that, I'll do what's necessary to safe-guard Lur from harm. As will you, I'm sure. Now I wonder if I might have a little time alone with my friend? Affairs of state have kept me from his side and I would lend him whatever strength he can use."

"Certainly, my lord," said the mewling pother. "But I warn you, he's heavily sedated. If he should wake be good enough to send for me at once."

Morg heard the chamber door open. Close. Heard footsteps come closer to the bed. Heard Conroyd Jarralt laugh softly. Seductively. A man on the brink of conquest.

"Well, Durm. Now it is just we two alone," he whispered. "And I shall tell you how the story ends..."

CHAPTER EIGHTEEN

It wasn't the voice of a friend. It echoed with avarice, with deep dislike and ambition long denied.

Suddenly Morg realised he was in danger.

He thought his mind would twist apart then, so frantically did he try to break the stuporous bonds holding him prisoner. With outraged astonishment he recognised the acid emotion: fear.

Fear?

When was the last time he'd felt such a thing? Had he ever felt it? He couldn't remember. No, no. It wasn't possible. Morg—the supreme power of the world—*afraid*?

Never.

Or...never before now. But now he was helpless, trapped, at the mercy of this man who stank of a desire for death. Durm's death. *His* death, for so long as he remained in Durm's body. He'd thought to house himself in Jarralt next. In a day or two, once Durm was finally free of drugs and he could act unhindered.

But here was the vessel now, fattened with plottings of its own and suddenly there was no *time*...

There came the sound of timber scraping tile as a chair was pulled closer to the bed. A sighing creak of springs, a swish of silk against silk. Cool fingers touching fevered flesh.

"I never liked you, Durm," said Jarralt. The molasses was melting, revealing the naked blade within. "And you never liked me. Yet we continued to play our silly game of pretend, didn't we, in order to keep Borne happy. To keep the people happy and ensure unadulterated peace. You always thought I loved myself more than this kingdom, but you were wrong. If that had been true I would have challenged Borne's right to rule long ago."

With a greater force of will than he'd ever before exerted, Morg calmed his raging spirit. Experienced another unfamiliar emotion: shame, that he could so completely forget himself, if only for a moment. It was a contaminant, this flesh. It polluted the purity of the unfettered mind, shackled it to urges and impulses and infirmity.

He couldn't wait to leave it behind.

Jarralt was softly laughing. "Notice I'm referring to you in the past tense, old man. Broken man. Defeated man. Your tenure as Master Magician is over. Soon I will take your place, but not for long. Before the year is out I'll have the means to bring down brave House Torvig, brick by rotten brick. Then Conroyd will be king. As I should've been king twenty-five years ago. What do you think of *that*, Durm?"

In the depths of his cage, Durm was also struggling. Morg felt some fleeting sympathy. Focusing his will, drawing his weakened powers close about him like a cloak, he saw himself as a lance of fire poised to pierce the veil of Nix's cloying, thwarting drugs. The flame consumed itself, consumed the remaining strength he'd not used up in his fight to live despite Durm's mangled body.

"Were I so inclined I could smother you here and now," crooned Jarralt. "Shall I do it? Do I dare? The way your body's ruined it might even be a mercy. You were never one for weakness. You'd have smothered Gar if you could. Would Borne have loved you, I wonder, had he known? Had he seen in the depths of your eyes what I saw the day his son's crippledom was made public?"

Morg felt his spirit shudder. Heard Durm's sickbed creak as Jarralt leaned upon it. A warm, sweet breath fanned Durm's flaccid face. Soft, strong hands clasped close the hollowed cheeks. As he struggled to escape Durm's useless body he heard a gloating whisper.

"There's a shadow falling over you, Durm. Do you feel it? It's the shadow of House Jarralt, plunging you deep into an endless dark..."

The hands resting against Durm's face tightened. Thumbs hot as coals pressed hard against his eyeballs, burning through tissue-paper lids. Morg felt his spirit spasm, felt a great leap of power to power, like to like, a song of lust and greed and unslaked thirsts. From far away he heard Durm's dreadful wail of anguish.

"Look at me, you drug-soaked carcass!" hissed Jarralt. "Look at me and see how I have won!"

Blinding brightness, as Jarralt's thumbs forced open Durm's pain-sunken eyes. Morg gloried in it, revelled in it, felt the final surging flare of his strength and will break through the barrier between himself and the wider world. The clammy bonds of failing flesh snapped at last and he was free of Durm's broken body, free of that terrible prison, free to pour himself into a new host, a perfect host, a vital, vigorous, voracious host.

Jarralt opened his mouth to scream—and Morg poured into him. Flowed through arteries and veins, soaked skin and sinew, suffused Jarralt's muscle and bone and brain until no single cell remained that was not himself. Left Durm behind and dying, his tongue tied tight against utterances of *Morg*.

Pulling away from abandoned Durm like a man who has unwittingly handled offal, Morg strutted the confines of the infirmary chamber and revelled in the glory of his new host: a man in his prime, fit and lithe and fabulously handsome. At last, flesh worthy of his spirit! Captive deep inside himself Jarralt shrieked and scrabbled and clawed.

In the bed, propped up by pillows, Durm breathed slowly, heavily, dragging air into his lungs with reluctance.

Morg smiled. "Fat fool. A pity you'll not be here to see my final triumph." The sound of his words wrapped in Jarralt's exquisite voice was a shock. He'd grown used to Durm's unromantic gravelling. Reaching, he touched a slender finger to the ruined man's flabby, sallow cheek. Prepared to extinguish his sputtering life.

The chamber door swung open and Nix cleared his throat. "My lord, forgive me, but Durm is in need of further physicking. You may return tomorrow, if that's your desire."

Morg straightened. "I would like that, Nix. Affairs of state permitting."

"Of course, sir," said the pother. "I hope you derived some comfort from your visit, my lord?"

He gave Durm's pillows a hearty pat, as though he were concerned with the care and comfort of the patient, and swung about to smile at the pother.

"Comfort? Dear Pother Nix," he said, in that magical, musical voice, "you have no idea."

Feeling perverse, not even waiting for his palace replacement Ganfel to arrive, Matt packed up his small hoard of belongings, cleared out of his stable yard accommodation while the lads were busy elsewhere, and took a room at Verry's Hostelry. He needed time alone to absorb what had happened that morning and decide how best to go on from here.

Asher had dismissed him. And Dathne had stood by, letting it happen. Hadn't lifted so much as a *finger* to save him...

The pain of that calamitous confrontation was savage. Jervale save him, could he have handled matters any worse? He was a *fool*. He should've waited. Should've tackled Dathne somewhere, *anywhere* else. Should've given himself time to calm down. Think things through. "*She's a racehorse, not a brood mare.*" That's what he'd told Asher. And then, forgetting all his own sage advice, like the clumsiest clot-head apprentice stable lad he'd tried to ride roughshod over her. Knowing full well she was mad in love with Asher. Seeing with his own two eyes that she was newly risen from a night in his arms, all aglow with passion and in no mood for sober chiding.

And you wonder why sometimes she doubts your wisdom?

Well, the milk was all spilled now and the jug smashed to pieces for good measure. She'd made her decision quite clear.

"*Go away, Matt. You're not wanted any more.*"

Well, he might not be wanted but he'd damn well be needed. Forget Asher's high-handed decree. He couldn't bury himself down in the Dingles, it was too distant. Trouble was, he couldn't stay here in Dorana either. He needed somewhere else, somewhere safe, where he could watch over Dathne and her Innocent Mage without fear of discovery.

Feeling like a traitor he rummaged through his hastily packed belongings and unearthed the chip of crystal he'd never before had to use. Never imagined he'd need to use. That he'd never told Dathne he possessed.

Veira answered almost immediately. Her surprise was shot through with sudden alarm. *Matthias? Is that you?*

"Yes, Veira. It's me." And was surprised himself to feel the pricking of unexpected tears.

She sensed them, and her manner gentled. *What's happened, child?*

Quickly, stumbling a little with nerves and emotion, he told her.

I should have suspected it, Veira replied slowly. *I knew she loved him and of late she's been...evasive. Wound tight as tight, with Prophecy's slow progress. Can you not speak with her? Find your way back to understanding?*

"No. She's got the bit between her teeth, Veira. The only voice she hears right now is Asher's. If I stay, if I try and force a reconciliation, I fear I'll just drive her further away. And she needs me still, I know it."

As do I, child, and all our precious Circle. So you must come to me and together we'll wait for Prophecy's wheel to turn again. Don't despair, Matt. Jervale will not abandon us now.

Relief was so great it was almost like pain. He wasn't alone. He had somewhere to go. A job still to do. "All right, Veira," he said. "I'll make arrangements and leave at first light."

On a cherry blossom day in the Royal Gardens, Gar chases his giggling sister between and around the cultivated pansy beds, the rows of quiet peters, brilliantly blue, the sapling trunks of youthful flowering pim-pim trees. He chases, but not too closely. Her baby legs are chubby, her unshod baby feet stomp the grass with delight, but unsurely. In the radiant sunshine her hair is a crown of gold thistledown, suggesting another crown yet to come.

"Can't catch me, Gar! Can't catch me!"

He's not even trying, but she doesn't know that. He pretends to be winded and pants at her, "You're too fast for me, Fane!"

Somewhere close by, just out of sight, their parents are watching. He knows they worry about him. Worry he might not love his little sister for having in abundance the magic he was born without. They needn't, but he can't tell them that. They think he doesn't know why shadows lurk behind their smiles.

They're his parents, Lur's king and queen, but still, they are mistaken. He knows.

Up ahead, his sister stumbles. Her baby legs buckle and she tumbles headlong to the ground. Grass stains smear her pretty pink frock, her petal-soft skin. There is a moment of shocked silence and then she begins to cry.

He swoops. Gathers her up in his big strong nine-year-old arms. Cuddles her to his green and bronze weskit, brand new, a present from Mama. For why? Just because.

Because he is different...less...and not supposed to know it, or feel less loved.

Fane sobs against his chest in rage as much as fright. Her rosebud hands make small knobby fists and she beats them against the air. She's a feisty one, his little sister. She'll have the world her way or not at all. Two years of age just gone, she is, and everyone who knows her knows that.

"It's all right, Faney, please don't cry," he begs her, rocking and

jigging to lull her to laughter. "I'm here. I've got you. You don't have to cry."

She hiccups. Swallows furious grief. Tips back her small head, looks into his face and smiles...and smiles...and smiles...

"Fane," said Gar, and opened his eyes. His face was wet with tears.

Behind his bedchamber's heavy velvet curtains, a glow of mid-morning sun. A new day, beset with old problems.

Durm again was deeply stuporous.

Telling him yesterday evening, Nix had been nearly incoherent with despair and disbelief. He couldn't understand it. The Master Magician had been fine all morning. Had accepted, grudgingly, the need for more rest in the afternoon. Had swallowed his medicine and gone straight to sleep. Not even Lord Jarralt's brief visit had disturbed him. Everything about him appeared as it should...And yet he would not wake.

Most like would never wake now. It was time to accept the unacceptable: Lur's Master Magician would not recover.

Nix blamed himself, of course, but it wasn't anyone's fault. People died, whether you wanted them to or not.

Swaddled in a cocoon of blankets, Gar brooded at the pale green ceiling. If he could swallow that bitter pill he could swallow another one, too. Had to swallow it, because that's what kings did. They faced unpalatable truths.

His charade as WeatherWorker was over.

With Durm mere days—maybe hours—away from dying, he had nowhere left to turn. Conroyd would now demand he be made Master Magician and with no reasonable way of denying the appointment the truth of his magical blighting would come out. There was no way he could hide it any longer.

He'd gambled, and he'd lost.

Duty demanded he go to Conroyd this very morning, admit his magic had deserted him, and offer the man his crown. His kingdom. To do otherwise would not only be a betrayal of his sacred oath, it would put Asher in danger of discovery.

And that was out of the question.

Making Conroyd king. The merest thought of it was enough to close his throat, stifle his lungs, make him sweat and sweat. Everything within him resisted, strenuously, the idea of making Conroyd king.

Groaning, he rolled out of bed. Relieved himself—it reminded him of Indigo Glospottle, and coaxed a fleeting smile—scraped overnight stubble from his chin and cheeks, fumbled his hair into a rough-and-ready plait then found clothes to cover his nakedness. His belly rumbled but the thought of food made him nauseous. He sat in an armchair and returned to his brooding.

What would his father do, faced with this dilemma?

The answer came swiftly. *Fight.*

Borne would fight this, as he'd fought when his son's lack of magic could no longer stay a secret. The law was clear on the question of royal children. *One* heir to the throne. But Borne had known then what his son knew now: that to meekly submit to the law meant the ascension of House Jarralt and the fall of his own. Meant surrendering the care of the kingdom and its peoples to a man half convinced that Olken weren't people at all. Just slightly intelligent cattle. They weren't. And to treat them so would lead to civil war.

So Borne sidestepped the law. Fought with his councils, both Privy and General, until they saw things his way and gave him an heir, not an error.

Yes. Faced once more with the prospect of Conroyd as king, Borne would do anything, everything, to thwart the lord's burning ambition. But what? *What?* What could Borne's son do that might deny Conroyd the crown?

Shining in the darkness, a glimmering, ghostly idea.

Perhaps... risk a schism?

Chewing on a thumbnail Gar let his thoughts race along unfamiliar paths. He'd always assumed that, as the acknowledged, superior magician, Conroyd must be named king. And that to widen the field of candidates for the crown would be to invite disaster. His father had believed so. And he trusted his father's instincts implicitly. Accepted his conclusions without question.

But Conroyd had two sons. Give him the crown and he would have to choose his heir. Elevate one... disappoint the other. Be it now or later, schism was again the likely outcome.

Could there be another choice for Weather Worker? Someone other than Conroyd? Was there in his kingdom a Doranen of another house fit to wear the crown? A magician of sufficient power to wield and control the tormenting Weather Magic? Who might... just might... share Borne's affection and respect for the Olken and so preserve amity between the races?

He had no idea. Only Durm would know. As Master Magician he knew intimately the strengths and weaknesses both magical and personal of every Doranen living in Lur. It was from them he would appoint his own successor. It was his duty to know.

A pity he'd not also thought it his duty to record his conclusions for posterity in writing, so someone else might read them and use the information to avert disaster.

If he could find someone other than Conroyd...assure himself beyond all doubt that he or she was fit to rule...he could sidestep Conroyd altogether. Crown this unknown Doranen in private and present Privy Councillor Lord Jarralt with a king or queen he couldn't replace.

"I think I have it, Father," he said to his empty bedroom. "A solution that answers all dilemmas...and shows, perhaps, that I'm still your son."

It meant he'd have to see his Master Magician today. Bully Nix into rousing the dying man long enough to get some idea of where to find this Doranen paragon, this uncrowned monarch of Lur. Because one thing at least was certain. The longer he delayed taking action, the more likely it was that Durm would die unconsulted.

And that would be...unfortunate.

Fired with a desperate enthusiasm, but still mindful of what else was happening today, Gar went downstairs to find his Olken Administrator.

Asher was in his apartments, vomiting.

"I don't know why you're letting yourself become so overwrought," Gar told him, watching as he blotted his pale sweaty face with a towel. "You've been in Justice Hall a score of times. And it's not as if Glospottle's case is a matter of life and death. It's *piss*, for Barl's sake. The dispute never should've gone this far in the first place!"

Asher straightened, glaring. "You sayin' this is *my* fault?"

Gar raised a placating hand. "No. You handled the matter as well as anyone could have. Glospottle's a stubborn fool and the guild is just plain greedy. This was always going to end up in Justice Hall."

Pausing in the middle of changing shirts from green silk to blue, Asher snorted. "Wish you'd said so sooner. I'd've chucked it all in and gone back to Restharven."

"Why do you think I didn't?"

That earned him a sharp look. "What's amiss now?"

He didn't want to say too much in case his idea came to nothing. "I've had a thought. About how to extricate ourselves from the mess we're in without risking discovery."

"Aye? And?"

"I'll tell you later...if it works out. If it doesn't, I don't want to look foolish."

Asher's lips twitched. "Bit late for that, I reckon."

In all his life, nobody ever spoke to him like Asher. Like he was just another man. An equal. A worthy target for easy teasing. It made all the darkness...bearable.

He cleared his throat. "I received a note from Conroyd last night. Requesting an urgent meeting with himself and Holze in their capacity as Privy Councillors."

Asher finished pulling on boots buffed to an eye-searing shine. "Privy Council meeting? I weren't invited."

Gar smiled wryly. "I noticed. Which is why I'm yet to respond. I don't know for certain what they're after but I think I can guess. I'm going to ignore them for as long as I can."

"Ignore them forever!" said Asher, indignant. "Who's the bloody king around here, eh?"

"Yes...well...that's the thorny question, isn't it?" Gar allowed himself a brief and bitter smile, then changed the subject. "I'm sorry I can't be with you at the hearing today. I'm sorry I wasn't more use in helping you prepare."

"Don't fratch it," said Asher, shrugging into an opulent gold and peacock weskit. "You had more important things to think on, and I had help enough. Besides, Dathne weren't about to let me set foot in Justice Hall without I was stuffed full to indigestion with folderol and jurisprudery."

He saw the way Asher's eyes warmed at the mention of her name, and took refuge in a little gentle teasing of his own. "When are you going to do something about that woman? Declare your intentions? Sweep her off her feet? It's clear to anyone with half an eye you're as mad as maggots about her."

Asher flushed. "Don't know what you're talkin' about," he muttered, and dragged his best dark blue velvet coat off its hanger. "I got to get goin'. Bloody Darran's insistin' I ride in a coach all the way to Justice Hall. Silly ole crow."

"That was my idea," Gar confessed, and laughed out loud at the look on Asher's face. For a moment, just a moment, the ache in his chest eased a little. "It's an historic day, Asher. An Olken, Law Giver in Justice Hall. I wish we could celebrate it the way you deserve."

"Ha!" said Asher, rolling his eyes. "I'm bloody glad we can't. There's been enough botheration already."

Gar shook his head. Struggled for words that wouldn't sound maudlin but reflected how he felt. "I owe you so much. I doubt there's another man living who'd have done what you've done. Risked what you've risked just because I asked it. I want you to know it's appreciated. And one day—I don't know when or how—I'll back up my words with deeds."

He held out his hand. Asher stared at it, his expression a muddle of exasperated pleasure. Such a rough-mannered man, his fisherman friend. Brusque and bullish, impatient of so much, and so many. But with a heart as strong and as grand as his beloved ocean, and possessed of a courage as unbreakable as Barl's blessed Wall itself.

"Get away with you," said Asher and, to Gar's surprise brushed his hand aside to clasp him in a brief and rib-bending embrace. "Stop wastin' my time, eh? You want history to show I was late to my first big performance at Justice bloody Hall?"

Gar stepped back. "Of course not. Go. Good luck. You can give me a blow-by-blow account over a cold ale before dinner."

Heading for the door, Asher grinned over his shoulder. "Provided you're payin'."

"Just do me a favour. Make sure the blows aren't literal?" he added. "And Asher?"

Asher whirled. "*What?*"

"There's a Working tonight. Remember?"

All the warm amusement fled Asher's face. Stilled, chilled, he nodded. "You think I could forget?"

And then he was gone.

Abruptly sobered, harshly reminded of everything he most wanted to wipe clean from recollection, Gar returned to his apartments to prepare for his meeting with Durm.

Asher looked so resplendent in his Justice Hall finery it was all Dathne could do to stop herself from throwing her arms around him in front of all the Tower staff, shouting for everyone to hear: "He's mine, he's mine, all mine!"

Instead she allowed herself to meet his questing eyes with a single, burning look, and laughed to see it kindle fire in his face.

"Let me see now, let me see," fussed Darran, bustling to meet him at the bottom of the Tower's spiral staircase. "Olken Administrator or not, Law Giver or not, I won't let you set one foot outside if you're a disgrace to His Majesty."

To Dathne's surprise Asher bore the old man's wittering with unpolished good grace. Let him tweak at his weskit, smooth down his sleeves, repin the diamond at the centre of one expensive lapel. With half a smile and exaggerated patience he looked down his nose at Darran and asked him, drawling, "Well?"

Darran sniffed. Stepped back, thin hands folded across his black silk middle. "You're as gaudy as a popinjay, but I suppose you'll do."

The maids, the messengers and the extra clerks Darran had requested from the palace broke into enthusiastic applause. Willer just smiled a strange, frozen little smile and fluttered his fingers, which could have meant anything. Miserable little sea slug. For herself, Dathne clapped until her palms were stinging.

"All right, all right," said Asher. "Ain't you lot got work to do?" Pretending to be cross with them, but inwardly tickled pink. If he was hurt by the conspicuous absence of the stable lads he didn't show it. They weren't speaking to him, on account of Matt.

Briefly, sharply, she felt a pang of guilt. If only she hadn't lost her temper. If only Matt hadn't lost his. If Asher had stayed out on his ride, instead of returning unexpectedly and catching them in conflict.

She hadn't told Veira yet. Couldn't bring herself to expose her lack of judgement.

I am the Heir. I should've known better.

But it was done now, and too late for undoing. Matt hadn't left for the Dingles yet, she knew that much. His letters of recommendation were still with Darran, uncollected. She'd give it another day and then go see him. Mend their broken fences. Convince him to stay longer while she eased Asher back to the idea of him being here. He couldn't really believe Matt was in love with her. The idea was ridiculous. He'd see that himself, once cooled completely of temper. He had to.

And Prophecy would continue unhindered, taking its own sweet time as usual.

As the staff departed, chattering, Darran said, "The coach is waiting out front for you. Willer and I will see you in the Hall."

Asher stared. "I don't need you there."

"Nevertheless." Darran smiled. "We are attending."

"Fine," said Asher. "But don't think I'll sit still for a review after." He looked at Dathne then and held out his hand. "Coming?"

She wasn't expecting that. "Me?"

"To go over the last-minute details." His voice and face were proper and polite, but his eyes promised wickedness. Her blood became honey, warm and voluptuous.

Ignoring Willer's jealous glower and Darran's avuncular simper, she pretended to boredom. Waved away Asher's outstretched hand. "Very well. If you insist." And marched off without him towards the foyer doors.

He followed, laughing.

As the carriage rolled down the driveway, Asher drew the curtains tight closed and stole her breath in a kiss. She let him thieve from her again, just once, then pulled away and wrenched the curtains open. The carriage had just turned out of the main palace gates and was heading down the long slow street to the City centre.

"Oy!" he protested.

"There'll be time for dalliance later," she said severely. "For now, you look outside this carriage then tell me the curtains should stay shut!"

"Sink me bloody sideways," said Asher, awestruck, and stared at the passing pavements. "What d'they think they're *doin'*?"

It seemed there wasn't an Olken man, woman or child in the City not crammed on the pavements to see him go by. They were shouting. Waving. All the young girls brandished flowers. Reaching across him she slid down the window and the crowd's excitement poured into the carriage like a waterfall.

"Asher! Asher! Asher!"

"Don't just sit there," she scolded, laughing. "Wave to them. They're your people, they're proud of you. For the first time since the coming of the Doranen we have one of our own at the pinnacle of power."

"Did I say I wanted to be a bloody pinnacle?" said Asher, scowling. "Barl bloody save me!"

She watched him put his face to the window. Heard the roaring crowd roar louder, seeing him. Knew that this was right, felt it in her bones as she'd not felt anything so strongly since that morning—a lifetime ago now—when she'd woken to know that at last he was within her reach. The ties of blood and magic making her Jervale's Heir rejoiced.

The Olken in the streets scant feet from their carriage, the Olken shouting and laughing and calling his name, they adored Asher for being their Olken Administrator. How much more would they adore him when he was revealed as their Innocent Mage?

Suddenly she no longer cared that she couldn't see how that would happen. No longer cared that dreams and visions had fallen into slumber. Her desperate need to know had died. It was enough that she was here, beside him, in a royal carriage headed for Justice Hall where he would sit in the seat of the Law Giver and solemnly uphold the law. Enough to know that she had done her part in guiding him to this place, at this time, when the world trembled on the brink of change.

Enough that he was her husband and she his wife.

If Matt had been here he'd be moping. Frowning. Worrying that Prophecy had more to say than just there was an Innocent Mage. He'd be reminding her of danger, too. That Asher was born to face a fearsome darkness. That Prophecy was vague on what, or who, or how, and could be she should think on that.

She was tired of thinking on that. She'd thought on that for years of her life and what had it got her? Sleepless nights and a belly full of dread. A small and shabby apartment above a shop full of books and no one in the bed beside her.

Asher was here. Prophecy's child. Soon enough he'd confide the last of his secrets to her, because he loved her. Trusted her. It was meant. Prophecy unfolded and they would do its bidding.

Asher took her hand, shaking her free of reverie. "Pellen told me there'd be a ruckus but I didn't believe him. Now I owe him a beer, the bastard." He laughed. "There's even Doranen out there! Come to see *me*! What would my da say, eh, if he could see this?"

Daringly, she raised his fingers to her lips. "He'd say he was proud," she whispered. "As I am proud."

The carriage trundled onwards.

CHAPTER NINETEEN

I'm so sorry, Your Majesty," said Pother Nix unhappily. "I've seen this happen before, and there is no explanation for it that I or any pother can give. When a man is this grievously injured, logic oft disappears. For reasons known only to itself Durm's body has given up the fight to live."

Sitting close beside the bed, Gar chafed Durm's cold lax fingers; it was like rubbing a bundle of sticks. "And you're quite sure there's nothing more you can do to save him?"

"Sir, as I told you last night, I have fed him every herb under the sun, in more combinations than I thought were possible," said Nix. "And exhausted my supply of healing spells and incantations. Alas, for all his formidable skills, Master Magician Durm's injuries have proven greater than his ability to survive them."

Gar rested his gaze on Durm's sunken, retreating face. On the graceless folds of emptied skin draped across jutting cheekbones, the thinned and shrunken lips, the pouched, sagging jowls. He'd never been a handsome man, Durm, but there'd been power in his face. A blunt brutality of character. Now there was merely absence. A fast-fading reminder of the man who once had lived there.

"How long does he have, can you say?"

Nix spread his hands. "No, sir. He's in Barl's keeping."

"Is he like to wake again, before the end?"

"Perhaps. I cannot say for certain, Your Majesty."

Gar chewed at his lip. Now matters could become a trifle...difficult. "Nix, I must speak plainly. I'm sore in need of Durm's counsel before he dies. There's the question of who he wished to succeed him, and other matters I'm not at liberty to discuss. Is there a way of... encouraging his waking? Some stimulating herb or incantation you can apply, that will rouse him enough to speak?"

Nix's indrawn breath was loud in the hushed chamber. "Your Majesty! Such interference would violate every—"

"Nix." The pother flinched. Gar released Durm's quiet hand and stood. "I have all solemn respect for your calling, you know that. But I am king of a curious country. One whose balance may be disturbed more easily than any man can know. If these past weeks have taught me anything of kingship it's that there's no sacrifice too great it can't be made. No principle too inviolate it can't be slain in the service of the greater good. I have learned that there's theory and then there's practice, and a king who can't place pragmatism above all the other virtues is a king unworthy of his crown. *I need to speak with Durm.* Can you make that happen?"

The room was cool, but a bead of sweat trickled down Nix's cheek. In his face, a terrible struggle. "Your Majesty—I can try. If you can swear to me on the most holy thing you know there is truly no other way."

"Then on the stilled hearts of my family, I swear it."

Nix slumped and a deeply sorrowing sigh escaped him. "There is an herbal paste which should achieve your desired outcome. It will take me a moment to prepare."

"Go, then," Gar said, and sat again. "Durm and I will be waiting."

Nix departed, the chamber door closing softly behind him. Gar recaptured Durm's fingers with his own and squeezed. "I know you approve," he said, trying to smile. "All my life you've despaired of my softness. My easily bruised emotions. You should be proud now, old friend. Old enemy. For what could be more ruthless than taking a dying man by the heels and dragging him backwards from the brink?"

Only the fractional rise and fall of Durm's chest betrayed his fragile hold on life. Not by so much as a flicker of his eyelid did he show that he could hear or feel a presence by his side. Gar let go of the dying man's hand and pressed hard fingertips to his eyes. His head was aching. It always ached, these days. His head...his heart...

Behind him the chamber door opened again. Closed. Nix padded to the bedside, a small mortar in one hand. A stinging smell, sharp like the depths of winter and acrid as smoke, burned the air.

"I dare not use too much of this," Nix cautioned as he scooped a little of the stimulant onto the tip of a tiny wooden spatula and smeared it into the portal of Durm's left nostril. "I wish I dared not use it at all." He flicked a glance over his shoulder; in it Gar saw concern. Anger. The bitterness of necessity.

"You use it at my bidding," he said, gently. "There is no blame attached to you, Nix."

"If I were a knife in your fist, perhaps," retorted Nix. Now he was smearing more of the blue paste against the mucous membranes of Durm's lips and gums. "But I'm flesh, not steel, and I have a mind of my own and a conscience I must answer to." He hesitated. "Don't burden it with more than is necessary, Your Majesty."

Gar let his gaze ice over. "Rest assured, Royal Pother, that whatever your burdens they are minuscule compared to mine."

Rebuked, Nix dropped his gaze to the floor for a moment, then looked up again. "If the stimulant works at all, and I don't guarantee it will, you'll see a change in the next few minutes. If he does rouse then for pity's sake ask your questions quickly, don't press him further than he seems able to go and spare him as soon as you can."

"I will," he said. "Now go. Bolt the door behind you, and seal the chamber against sound." Seeing the surprise in Nix's eyes he added, "It's a question of solemn secrecy and the need to husband my powers for the WeatherWorking. I would not spend them except in that service."

Nix bowed. "Your Majesty." With a lingering, potherly look at Durm, he withdrew.

It felt as though centuries passed before Durm showed any response to Nix's stinking concoction. His shallow breathing deepened. His fingers twitched. His head shifted on the pillow. Heart pounding, Gar leaned forward.

"Durm," he whispered. "Durm, can you hear me?"

The faintest of moans, little more than a sigh. A gathering frown in the scarred face. A spindle of spittle, oozing from the corner of his lips. Beneath the translucent eyelids, a turgid roll of eye.

"Durm," he whispered again, more insistently. "Please?"

Now the moaning sigh became a groan, and Durm's chest rose and fell more vigorously. In his formless face surfaced some echo of the personality housed within his failing body. A grunt. A snuffling snort. Blue mucus oozed and bubbled from his nostril and over his parting lips.

"*Durm!*"

Durm's eyelids lifted, barely. His slitted gaze dragged through the air as though burdened by invisible anchors. "*Gar...*"

He pulled the armchair closer. Leaned further in till his lips were almost touching Durm's ear. On the tip of his tongue was the question he'd come here to ask.

Instead he asked something else, because not to ask it was impossible. He'd never have another chance. When Durm died his last hope of recovery, of keeping his kingdom, would die along with him.

"My magic's failed, Durm. Is there a cure? An answer in your library, or Barl's? Do you know a way to save me?"

In a gravelled whisper Durm said, "No."

The word was like a sword thrust in his side. His breath hitched. His eyes burned. "Are you certain?"

"No cure."

"Then who can I crown instead of Conroyd? I need a different heir!"

Durm coughed again, his face gathering tight in a monstrous frown. His bed began to tremble gently, echoing the larger tremors now racking his reunited limbs. He opened his mouth and screamed.

"No!" cried Gar, and leapt up to press Durm's shoulders to the mattress. "Not yet! Hold on, Durm! I need you!"

Another gargling scream.

He captured Durm's thrashing head between his hands and forced the maddened eyes to meet his own, even as the wasted, frantic body of his father's best friend struggled and writhed.

"Help me, Durm! *Help me!*"

"The diary!" Durm shouted, bucking and twisting beneath his blankets. "Barl's diary! Your only hope!"

Heart pounding, he leaned closer still, willing the dying man to hear him. "Barl left a *diary*? When? Where? Do you have it? *Durm!*"

A terrible convulsion shook the Master Magician. Blue froth bubbled between his lips and his eyes rolled back in his head. Panting, Gar pulled juddering Durm into a desperate embrace.

"Did you tell my father about it? Did you give it to him?"

A terrible sound, then. Durm was laughing. Wasting the last of his life. "He doesn't know...I hid it..."

"Oh, Durm...*Durm*!" Dying or not, Gar could have strangled him. "Where is it now? Where will I find it? Why is it our only hope? Hope for what? For me? Can it give me back my magic?"

Tickling his skin, a fading breath. In his ear, a failing whisper. "Conroyd...beware Conroyd..."

The convulsions ceased. He lowered Durm gently to the mattress, the pillows, and looked into the waxen face. "I know," he said sadly. "I do. Durm...where is the diary?"

Hollowed, emptied, Durm parted blue-stained lips. "Borne... forgive me. I couldn't stop him..."

He cupped his hand to Durm's fleshless face. "You're forgiven. Durm, where have you hidden the diary?"

But it was useless, and he knew it. He wept, despairing, even as Durm's chest rattled with air like a child's toy. The light behind the half-lidded eyes dwindled. Tears brimmed. Even as he watched, the final dregs of colour drained from Durm's cheeks, leaving them like living parchment, and his eyelids closed completely. Whatever strength Nix's stimulant paste had lent him it was failing fast.

"Never mind, Durm," he said softly. "It's all right. Go in peace, and Barl's great grace attend you."

Some dark shadow flitted over Durm's waxy face. "Barl," he murmured. "The bitch, the slut, the treacherous whore." His eyelids fluttered. Lifted. Revealed confused and clouding eyes. The rattle was in his throat now; an ominous portent. "Gar..."

A butterfly's shout would sound louder.

"Hush," he whispered. "I'm here. I'm with you."

The vivid personality behind Durm's eyes was utterly defeated. "*Forgive me...*"

He kissed Durm's cold and clammy forehead. "For everything."

Another inwards breath, rattling. A long pause. A bubbling exhalation.

Then nothing.

Gar called Nix into the room. "He's gone. Do what is needful, but make no public mention of his passing. Bind your staff to strictest secrecy on pain of dire retribution. I will announce this disaster in my own good time."

Nix bowed, his expression frozen. "Yes, Your Majesty. If I may ask—did you get what you needed, before...?"

"No," he said, after a moment. "No, I did not."

Outside the palace, the day continued cool and bright, just as Asher had ordered. Scarlet warblers whistled in the trees. Squirrels scampered. The Wall soared clean and bright and golden into the cloudless sky.

Carefully, so carefully, he made his way back to the Tower. Asher needed that new Weather Schedule. He could do that at least. And when it was done, he would look for Barl's diary ... for all the good it could do them.

Lady Marnagh pounced on Asher the moment he walked through the rear doors of Justice Hall. With his ears still ringing from the shouting, the shrieking, the screaming of his name—*Asher! Asher! Asher!*—and his lips tingling from Dathne's last swift kiss, he dived into the Hall's shadowed silence like a parched man finding water.

Marnagh escorted him up to the private screened Law Giver's gallery. Robed him in the Law Giver's crimson robe. Settled the Law Giver's crown firmly on his head. He closed his eyes, not wanting to see the thunderbolt. Still resistant to all it implied.

Then she guided him onto the magical platform that would deliver him to the madness waiting below. The minute his shiny black boots became visible the restless ocean of sound filling the Hall crashed into waves of fresh and unstinting acclaim. Shouts, applause, cries of "Praise Barl" and "Bless our Administrator" dinned his ears as the platform drifted downwards.

He opened his eyes and, for a heartbeat, let his mouth hang open. The hall was *packed*. Mostly with Olken, but there were some Doranen mixed in there as well. Conroyd bloody Jarralt, hoping he'd make some terrible mistake most like. Olken members of the General Council. Conroyd Jarralt's cronies, Daltrie, Sorvold, Hafar and Boqur, the ones who'd been with him that night at Salbert's Eyrie. Even Holze was there. The cleric saw him staring and smiled, his eyes watchful, his expression ambiguous.

Dathne had squashed herself into a front pew between Darran and Willer. She waved at him, just a little.

He fought the temptation to wave back.

There was Indigo bloody Glospottle, trouble's architect, tall thin streak of piss that he was. His face was the colour of piss, too, as though finally, *finally*, he realised what he'd got them all into. On the other side of the aisle from him the Dyers' guild meister, red-faced and bloated with consequence, not looking at all happy about being here.

That'd teach him to be greedy.

Amongst the clamouring Olken faces were dozens more he recognised. Cluny, and the rest of the house staff from the Tower. Some of the palace staff he was coming to know. Pellen Orrick, grinning like a loon, the bastard, and waggling his eyebrows like this was *funny*. Lads from the guardhouse, off-duty and mashed in shoulder to shoulder to watch their old drinking mate make a ninny of himself. Guild meisters and mistresses, some of whom he'd offended and others just mildly irritated. Many, though, who thought of him as friend. Aleman Derrig and his daughters. Folks he knew to smile at in the street, that he'd never met but who knew him because he was the Olken Administrator, and important.

No Matt, of course. He was sorry for that. Sorry for losing his temper, too. But he'd put it right soon enough. Go all the way down to the Dingles if he had to and set the matter straight. Long silences could easily get filled with calamity...and one Jed in a lifetime was enough.

The platform came to a stop, bumping him free of memory. The tumult of welcome intensified, vibrating his bones. He almost turned tail and ran. But then he saw Lady Marnagh at her Recording Table, glaring daggers at him from behind a polite mask. Reading his mind. He took a deep and gulping breath then stepped onto the Law Giver's dais. Sat in the Law Giver's chair and struck the golden bell three times.

He might as well have pissed into the wind.

So he stood, raising his arms for silence. His Olken audience only shouted louder. He waved his arms, burningly aware of Conroyd Jarralt, of Barlsman Holze, the Doranen General Councillors. Of what this looked like to them and how easily they might take it out on Gar. On him. On the Olken in general.

He looked at the nearest City guard, pulling a mad face. Stifling a grin, Jolin rapped his pike-butt on the tiled floor in warning. The other guards joined in.

His Olken admirers, drat 'em, ignored the summons to silence.

On a deep breath, his heart pounding, he jumped onto the Law Giver's red velvet seat. "Sink me bloody sideways!" he bellowed. The hall's magicked acoustics amplified the shout, delivering it sharply to every attendant ear. "Would you bloody well *pipe down*?"

Laughter. A few shocked gasps. A tail-ending of "Praise Barls" and "Hail Ashers." Then a ragged hush descended. He leapt lightly off the chair.

"Right," he said, tugging at his weskit through his crimson velvet robe. "So now *that's* sorted, let's get down to business."

Indigo Glospottle spoke first. Although most of the City by now must have known the bones of his complaint, given how his tongue wagged at every opportunity, even so the Olken in the audience hung on his every word as though they sat in the theatre, not Justice Hall, and this was a grand fine entertainment laid on for their amusement.

Asher supposed, swallowing a grin, that in many ways it was. The crimson velvet chair was comfortable. He sat back, chin sunk in one hand, and tried to look as though Glospottle's groanings were exciting news to him.

Eventually, after much huffing and puffing and hand-waving, Glospottle's tale of hard-done-by and persecution dribbled to an end. Which meant that Guild Meister Roddle rose ponderously to his feet and argued in the opposite.

Ten minutes later, Asher had had enough of the overdressed dyer's droning. He raised a warning hand. "Wait a minute. Just…wait. Seems to me this is all startin' to turn a bit hedgehog."

Roddle blinked. "*Hedgehog?*"

"Uncomfortably prickly," he explained, as yet another titter of amusement rippled round the crowded hall. He ignored it. "Now, Meister Roddle—"

"*Guild* Meister Roddle."

"For now," he said, and bared his teeth. "Provided you don't fall into the habit of interruptin' me. Now I just spent the last two days reading your guild's rules and statutes and chartered articles and what-not and I don't recall seein' mentioned anywhere as to how new techniques belong to the guild and not the man or woman who invented 'em."

Roddle cleared his throat. "The tradition is long-standing, sir," he said stiffly. "The actual amendment to ratified guild charters is more recent."

Asher narrowed his eyes. "How recent?"

Roddle's face flushed a dark purplish red. "This morning."

The spectators muttered loudly as Indigo Glospottle leapt to his feet. "That's *outrageous!*"

"Shut up, Indigo!" said Asher. "You've had your say." Indigo subsided, spluttering. "This morning, eh?" he continued. "That smacks to me of cheating, Roddle. Did you see the whacking big sword on the outside of the building as you came in? You recall Barl's opinion on little things like cheating?"

"We are not *cheating*!" the guild meister protested. "Indigo Glospottle is a *thief*, sir, he steals from his guild brethren, he—"

"And you can shut up too," he said, and waved his hand in dismissal. "Reckon I've heard all I need to. It's my turn to flap lips now." From the corner of his eye he caught the look on Lady Marnagh's face as she dutifully supervised the magical recording of the proceedings. He suspected she wasn't sure whether to hit him or hug him.

"Sir," said Roddle faintly, and resumed his seat. The spectators held their breaths and sat forward, waiting.

Asher slid out of his chair, stepped off the dais and began pacing back and forth the full width of the hall. Against every and all expectation he was enjoying himself.

"Our kingdom's a place of rules and regulations. We've got ourselves so used to 'em I reckon we've near forgot how many there are. Rules for marriage and for bearing children. Rules for schooling and religion. Where we work, how we work, what we work towards. What jobs the Olkens do, what jobs the Doranen do. Who uses magic and who doesn't." His voice dried up momentarily and he had to wet his lips before he could continue. He hadn't meant to say that last bit. "Any road. Lots of rules. And then we got the guilds. The guilds are important. They enforce a lot of our rules. Help keep this kingdom runnin' sweet and smooth just as much as any Weather Worker ever did. Without the guilds binding us all together, could be we'd find ourselves in a right mucky mess."

A murmur from the audience. Exchanged glances between Jarralt and his cronies. Holze, nodding in slow agreement. Pellen Orrick, his eyebrows lifted, watching everything and everyone with his melted-ice eyes.

"And for a long, long time now," Asher continued, still pacing, "nowt much has changed around here. The way we brew beer. The way we milk cows. The way we grow cotton and card wool. Harvest grapes. Raise horses. I reckon turn the clock back a hundred years, two hundred, and no one'd notice the difference." He stopped pacing then, right in front of a transfixed Indigo Glospottle, and shook his head. "But then along comes a man with an idea. An idea for bluer blues and redder reds, and the next thing you know the apple cart's turned arse over eyeballs and there's pippins all over the street. And here's me, s'posed to be pickin' 'em up without a one bein' bruised." Lifting his gaze, he swept it over the packed Hall. "Sorry, folks. That ain't about to happen. Nobody upsets an apple cart without there bein' a few apples spoiled."

"All right then!" a voice shouted from the midst of the throng. "So what're you goin' to do about it?"

He grinned. "Well now, I'm glad you asked me that question, Willim Bantry, and that'll be three trins in the Barlsbox if you please, for speakin' out of turn."

A gust of laughter. Asher's grin widened.

"So. Guild Meister Roddle wants the secret to Indigo Glospottle's superior piss handed out willy-nilly to every guild member, even though they did nowt to deserve the money they'll make off it. And Indigo Glospottle wants to keep his secret piss a secret and get rich off it all on his lonesome. And if they won't let him do that, he wants to leave the Guild." He sighed and shook his head. "Well, I can't be having that. The guilds keep us strong. I ain't about to weaken 'em, Indigo, by lettin' you run about on your own undermining the Dyers' Guild's authority."

Glospottle pouted.

"*But*," he added, with a burning look at Roddle, "I ain't about to sit back twiddlin' my thumbs as *you* get rich off another man's invention. So here's my ruling. Indigo gives the Guild his secret piss recipe, and for every bolt of fabric sold that was made with that same recipe the guild gives Indigo a tithe. Five trins sounds about right to me."

As Indigo Glospottle broke into excited laughter Guild Meister Roddle rose shouting to his feet. "I object, sir! I *object*!"

"You don't get to object, you whingeing bloody ninnyhammer!" roared Asher, closing on him. "If you'd stuck by the first agreement, that Indigo'd keep his secret to hisself and pay the Guild a tithe from every sale, we wouldn't be here now! But you didn't and we are and now I've made my ruling! So get out of my sight afore I knock you on your pimpled arse and make you drink a *pint* of Glospottle's secret bloody piss! *Hot!*"

The hearing concluded immediately thereafter, amidst much confusion, cheering and acclaim.

With her ribs still aching from laughter Dathne hovered at the rear of Justice Hall and waited for Asher to emerge. Half an hour after his riotous conclusion to the trial and still he'd not escaped. Guild Meister Roddle had come out, ashen-faced and spluttering, supported by a bevy of guild members, after signing the paperwork that entered the ruling into law. Indigo Glospottle had come out too and hugged her, weeping with relief. Pellen Orrick had come out briskly, raising his eyebrows at her in passing.

Pellen Orrick's risen eyebrows spoke untold volumes.

At long last Asher emerged, all alone. He saw her and smiled. "Take me away from here, woman," he said limply, and let her hustle him into the small, anonymous hired carriage she'd paid to wait round the side of Justice Hall. The official carriage she'd dismissed with a coin for the coachman and a conspiratorial smile.

"You fool," she said, and kissed him. "I'm afraid to imagine what you'll think of next."

They went back to her apartment over the bookshop and watched the sun go down from the rooftop. When hunger stirred she fetched them roast chicken and baked potatoes and soaking sweet honey cakes from Meister Hay's cookery down the street, and they gorged themselves to hiccups.

Then she took him by the hand and led him to her bedroom.

"You know I can't stay," he said. There was honey smeared in the corners of his mouth.

"Not the whole night," she agreed, kissing him clean. "But for a while."

Falling breathless into each other's arms, onto her creaking old bed, they let pleasure have its way with them. Afterwards he slept, and she sat up in the bed and watched him, marvelling. Eventually she drifted into dozing sleep and woke only when something cold and feather-light kissed her on the cheek.

It was snowing.

Heart-stopped and speechless she stared at the whirling ice flakes as they fell from the lacy white cloud beneath her bedroom ceiling. In the bed beside her Asher muttered and moaned, his eyes closed tight. The merest thread of blood trickled meanly from beneath his lashes, like a tear.

She nearly suffocated, she held her breath so long.

It was over soon enough. The snowfall stopped, the lacy cloud dispersed. He began to stir. Alarmed, she slid under the blankets beside him and pretended she was sleeping. She felt him slip from the bed. Heard the swish of silk and leather over skin as he pulled on his clothes. Shivered as his warm lips touched her mouth.

And then he was gone.

Alone and still shivering she lay in her bed and rocked like a child, stunned beyond the release of weeping.

Of all the things she'd ever imagined, she'd never imagined *this*.

CHAPTER TWENTY

Close to panic, Willer turned away from shuffling the papers and parchments on top of Asher's desk and began to rummage through its drawers instead. He *had* to find something incriminating tonight. This was the fifth time he'd crept into Asher's office, he couldn't fail again! Lord Jarralt was losing his patience, there'd been harsh words outside Justice Hall today after the Glospottle hearing and besides, the whole business was so *dangerous*.

Nothing in the first drawer. Or the second. What about the third...

Just as he reached for the last drawer he heard a pair of muffled voices. A key, scraping in the office door's lock. He swallowed a shriek. Snatched Lord Jarralt's lightstone from the desktop and smacked it against the timber until the tiny glow extinguished. Fumbling it into his pocket he made a dive for rat-faced Dathne's desk just as the office door swung open. Heart pounding, runnelled with sweat, he wrapped his arms about his head and waited for the axe to fall. A flare of conjured glimlight splashed shadows on the carpet and lit up two pairs of passing legs.

"—extraordinary discovery," the king was saying, voice hushed. "I can scarce believe Durm kept it secret. Who knows what might be in it? A cure, perhaps..."

"Then keep on bloody lookin' for it if you reckon it's so important!" said Asher, stamping across the carpet to his desk. "Or go back to readin' Durm's books. I told you, I don't need you there. I can manage for one night on my own."

"No, you can't," the king retorted. "It's too dangerous."

Shuffle, shuffle, as Asher searched through the papers scattered all over his desk. "It ain't no more bloody dangerous now than it was the night before last. I survived then, I'll survive tonight. All I want from you is a way out of this! I want to come back from the Weather Chamber and hear you say: 'That's it, Asher. That was the last time. No more Weather Working for you.'"

In the silence that followed, Willer stuffed his coat sleeve in his mouth to stifle a horrified cry. *Asher* was *Weather Working*? How could that *be*?

The king said, very quietly, "Don't you think I want that too?"

Asher's reply was swift and scathing. "Well, wantin' ain't enough,

Gar. We've gone a bloody long ways past wantin'. Durm can't help us now, he's dead. It's just you. One way or another you got to fix this, 'cause every day that goes by with you pretendin' to be king and me pissin' blood to make it rain and snow is one more day someone could find out the truth. How many bloody times do you need to hear it? I can't do this much longer!"

Willer was afraid they'd hear his heartbeat, pounding in his chest like a madman's hammer. Durm was dead? When? How? Don't say Asher had *killed* him!

"I promise," the king said after a long and tension-filled pause. "You won't have to. I know as well as you this has to stop."

The sound of Asher's palm slapping timber was so loud, so unexpected, Willer almost hit his head on the underside of Dathne's desk. "Are you sure you left the new Weather Schedule in here?"

"I put it on your desk myself," said the king. "Let me look." More slithery sounds of paper and parchment shuffling. "Here it is. You buried it under your notes for Glospottle's hearing."

"No, I didn't! I ain't been—oh, never mind!" said Asher, and Willer let out a sigh of silent fright. "Bloody Darran prob'ly snuck in here snoopin' while Dathne's back was turned. Now, you're sure you got this right? I ain't goin' to send snow where there should be rain, and ice where there ought to be snow?"

"It's right," the king said. "I may have lost my magic, but I can still read and count."

For a moment Willer thought he might faint dead away. King Gar had *lost his magic*?

"Glad to hear it," said Asher. "Now you get back to your books and I'll take care of this."

"All right then," said the king, reluctant. "But for Barl's sake, be careful. Don't overtax yourself. And make sure you drink Nix's potion after."

"Nag, nag, nag," said Asher nastily. Oh, he was *such* a nasty man...

There came the sound of parchment, rolling. Two pairs of booted feet, leaving. Willer held his breath until the door clicked closed behind them and Asher's key scraped again in the lock.

Alone again, and undiscovered, he stayed under Dathne's desk and shook so hard he thought his teeth would shatter like glass. Durm dead...the king unmagicked...and Asher of Restharven a criminal. The man who just that very morning had stood up in Justice Hall and dared, *dared*, to lecture on the welfare of the kingdom. The sanctity of Barl's great Laws.

He was *Weather Working*. Even more incredible, he was doing it with King Gar's knowledge! His blessing, even. How could that be? *Gar* wasn't evil. There was only one explanation: Asher must have bewitched him, somehow. Ensorcelled him into doing his wicked bidding. Perhaps even stolen his magic in the first place.

Monstrous. *Monstrous.*

And then horror slowly gave way to a dawning joy. How this had all happened was no longer important. It had happened, and that was more than enough.

Praise Barl! he wept in silent ecstasy. *Praise Barl and all her mighty works! My prayers at last are answered!*

Then, unexpected, within his transcendent triumph chimed a thin sharp note of fear.

When the kingdom learned all he knew—when Asher's perfidy and the king's blind foolish faith were revealed—there would be chaos. The uproar following Timon Spake would be nothing, *nothing*, to the crisis brewing now. It was inevitable: all Olken would in some way, large or small, pay for Asher's crime. Even though they were innocent. Even though this wasn't their fault.

Imagining it, he felt his courage falter. He held their lives in the palm of his hand. Would be, once he told Lord Jarralt of this discovery, the immediate cause of their unjust suffering. People would know it. And *blame* him. He swallowed more tears. Oh, how unfair. How *unfair.*

One more crime to lay at Asher's feet.

And yet, he had no choice. He had to speak. For the good of the kingdom, he could not stay silent. Asher must not escape punishment. The king must be freed from his pernicious, evil influence, no matter the cost. No matter that poor Willer, Barl's blameless instrument, would yet carry some of the blame. History would redeem him. In time, he'd be seen as a hero. A champion for right, and justice.

That's what I am, Barl. I'm your champion!

When he judged enough time had passed, he unlocked the office door with Lord Jarralt's magical key, crept unseen from the Tower and made his way towards the Weather Chamber. He didn't want to report this momentous news to Lord Jarralt until he'd witnessed with his own eyes the filthy stinking depths of Asher's crime.

He got lost twice. Royal staff knew in theory where the Chamber was located but none had cause to visit it. Snow began to fall just after his second wrong turning. When at last he stumbled onto the right pathway, he was cold, wet and out of breath, his pantaloons were torn and his left hand was scraped to blood from when he'd tripped over a tree root and gone ungainly sprawling.

The Weather Chamber was awe-inspiring. Terrifying. It was a wonder Asher dared stain it with his shadow, let alone defile it with his presence. A strange glow flickered at its very top, flashes of blue and silver-white and scarlet.

Willer crept closer, jumping at every whisper in the grass, every creaking in the trees. The mournful hoot of a low-flying owl nearly made him piss his pants. Hot-faced, gasping, he fell against the Chamber's door. He almost couldn't hear over the pounding of blood in his head.

To his surprise it was unlocked. He felt his lip curl. Sunk deep in arrogance, Asher thought himself inviolate. Undiscoverable. He couldn't wait for the look on the bastard's face when he realised how wrong he'd been.

He entered the Chamber. Not daring to use the lightstone he fumbled his way up the stairs in the dark, stubbing his toes and chewing his lip to stop himself from crying out at the pain. There were tight iron bands clamped about his chest. He was going to have a seizure, his legs were about to burst into flame.

Just as he thought he really would die the endless stairs came to an end and he was outside the Weather Chamber itself. The door was open the merest sliver. Through the hairline crack he could see a fierce bright light and hear strange and horrible sounds. Someone was screaming, a garbled gobbling of extreme distress, and buried within was a string of unintelligible words.

Willer felt the hair stand up on the back of his neck.

As he stood there, dithering, the screaming rose to a ragged crescendo and abruptly stopped, as though cut with a knife. A moment later came the thud of a body hitting the floor.

Trembling, hardly breathing, he pushed wide the door and looked his fill.

An austere room papered with complicated charts and diagrams. Shelves crammed with ancient books. In its middle a miraculous thing, a model of the kingdom, and above it tiny clouds twinkling snowflakes. Unmoving beside it, Asher. Smeared and dribbled with blood. Dead then? Please not. *Please* not, for he must live to face his crimes, to kneel at the feet of his vanquishing foe. To be stripped naked before all the City, the kingdom and seen for the monster he was, knowing full well who'd unmasked him.

He crept closer. Asher was breathing. Shallowly, groaningly, with lines of pain cut deep in his flesh. Blood caked his eyelashes, clogged his nostrils, glistened redly on his lips. He was deeply, gloriously insensible.

Stealthily, Willer withdrew. Used Lord Jarralt's charm to lock the door behind him and used it again on the door at the foot of the staircase.

And then he ran.

"Conroyd! Conroyd, wake up, dear, wake *up!*"

Morg opened his eyes. Who—ah yes. His gormless, wittering wife...at least for now. "Ethienne?"

"Oh, Conroyd!" she said, querulous and pouting. "There is a *dreadful* little Olken downstairs and he won't go away no matter *what* I say! He insists you must see him and he won't leave the premises till you do!"

Morg stretched, revelling in the oiled ease of his glorious new body. "Did he give you his name?"

"Willim. Or Wolton. Or something beginning with 'w,'" said Ethienne, still pouting. "Do make him go away, Conroyd, please? It's the middle of the night and he really is quite awful!"

Morg flung back the blankets. "*Willer?*"

"Yes, that's it. Willer. What in Barl's name have you to do with such a—"

He leapt out of bed, cursing. "Be silent, you ridiculous old hag!" And ignored her gobbling shock as he flung on Jarralt's dressing-gown and hurried from the room.

Willer waited in the foyer, dishevelled and bloodied and muddied and gross. "My lord!" he cried, and scuttled across the carpet to meet him at the foot of the stairs. "Oh, my *lord!* The Master Magician is dead, and...and..."

Morg seized him by the shoulders and shook him. "And what, man? Is it Asher? Tell me quickly, is it Asher?"

The fat little Olken's eyes were shining like stars. "Oh, my lord, yes, it's Asher! At last, sir, at *last!* Lord Jarralt, *we have him!*"

PART THREE

CHAPTER TWENTY-ONE

Pellen Orrick sighed and took another thoughtful sip of tea. Beyond the window of his guardhouse office, silent snow continued to drift through the air and settle on the sill, the garden, the gateposts and the street. The glow of glimfire from the City streetlamps turned white to gold, a constant reminder of magic.

Deep silence surrounded him. The guardhouse cells downstairs were free of guests, for the moment, and the lads on night call were sleeping peacefully in their cots. Business as usual, now that the City had emptied of mourners and life was slowly falling into its new rhythms. Gar on the throne. Asher the Olken Administrator.

The thought of Asher tipped his mouth into a smile. Outrageous. The man was outrageous. Today's—no, yesterday's—performance in Justice Hall would be gossip fodder for weeks. Months. He'd thought Guild Meister Roddle would drop dead of a seizure on the spot. He'd nearly had a seizure himself from trying not to laugh out loud.

Reprobate Asher had climbed onto the Law Giver's *chair*. The chair that had cradled royal law-giving rumps for years. But then that was Asher all over, wasn't it? Always climbing onto things. Yes, and over them too. Benches. Tables. Obstacles. Restrictions. Traditions. Shredding pomp and consequence with all the finesse of a cheese-grater.

A silent convulsion of laughter shook his bones. Indigo Glospottle's name would live on for generations now. Asher had seen to that. So much authority resting on those broad and brawny shoulders. If it had been anybody else standing on that Law Giver's chair he knew he'd not be laughing, but worried. Power like that could turn a man's head more easily than the lilting walk of a pretty girl passing by. But not Asher's. If ever he'd met a man entirely unimpressed with the trappings of power, it was Asher.

Sparks spat in the fireplace as a log broke apart, crumbling into coals and ash. The room was warmed with magic, of course, but he still kept a fire burning through winter. Most people did. Even the

Doranen loved the sound and smell of fresh burning pitty-pine. The romance of leaping flames.

Orrick stifled a yawn. Middle of the night, he should be sleeping, but paperwork couldn't tell the time and he'd let it lapse of late. Extraordinary. He was a man of strict and proper procedure. He couldn't remember the last time he'd left this office without the daily report being finished and filed for future reference. And here he was with a full week's worth of reports undone. It wouldn't do.

Sound and movement in the street below his window caught his attention. The hollow clopping of hooves on cobbles. A carriage, drawing to a halt at the guardhouse gates. Two cloaked figures alighting.

Pellen Orrick put down his pen and went to investigate.

"Lord Jarralt!" he said, betrayed into showing surprise. He stood back from the guardhouse front door. "Please, my lord. Enter."

The king's Privy Councillor was attended by Willer Driskle, from the Tower. The palace. Wherever it was he worked these days. A blameless man, but not well liked. Unpopularity wasn't a crime, though, so the guard had no cause to know him. Orrick nodded politely and closed the door behind them.

"Your office," said Lord Jarralt, stripping off his gloves. "Now."

Such a chilly man. Orrick bowed, taking no offence; it was pointless. "My lord." With a quelling look at young Piper, on overnight front desk duty and struggling not to gape, he led his visitors upstairs.

Jarralt refused the chair that was offered him. Willer almost accepted, caught the lord's cold eye and changed his mind. Orrick, not inclined to be intimidated in his own office, took his chair behind the desk and sat back, observing.

"Tell him," said Jarralt, slapping his gloves across one palm as though his flesh offended him. "All of it."

"Yes, my lord," Driskle said, and planted his fists on the desktop. There was something eager, *lascivious*, in the way his eyes were shining. Something predatory.

Disliking him, Orrick stared at the encroaching hands till the fat little man withdrew them and stood back. "Tell me what?"

"Captain Orrick, you must arrest Asher of Restharven at once. He has broken Barl's First Law and attempted magic!"

He laughed. "*Asher* has? Are you *mad*?"

"*Tell him*," said Lord Jarralt grindingly.

He listened in growing disbelief as Driskle spewed forth a tale as horrifying as it was unlikely. "I don't believe it," he said at last, once the man was done with his litany of accusations.

"I do," said Lord Jarralt.

Orrick shook his head. There was a hot buzzing in his ears and his eyes were fogged with shock. "But Olken can't do magic." He turned to Willer. "You *saw* him call the snow?"

"I saw the snow falling and went into the Weather Chamber. He was alone. Unconscious on the floor and covered in blood. And I heard him and the king talking about Weather Working. I *told* you," whined Driskle. "Asher's a criminal and he has to die!"

Feeling sick, Orrick ignored that. "How were you in a position to overhear anything of a private nature discussed between Asher and His Majesty?"

"That is not your concern," said Lord Jarralt.

He stood. "Forgive me, but it is. These are grave accusations. I won't proceed against Asher on nothing but the word of a man who, if I may be blunt, appears to have a personal stake in his downfall."

"You will proceed, Captain," snapped Jarralt, "or find yourself relieved of duty. Master Magician Durm is dead, and you are questioning the orders of his successor."

Jarralt's eyes were frightening. Pale, pale blue and colder than any winter ever called. Flickering in their depths, a scarlet thread. Or was that just his imagination? Orrick didn't know. It took every skerrick of strength in him not to cower beneath that burning stare.

"Dead, my lord? I had not heard so."

"The news is not yet public. You will consider it privy, and not to be repeated."

"Of course. My lord, His Majesty trusts Asher implicitly," he said, still fighting, even though he knew he was lost. "What Driskle suggests is madness. And as for this nonsense about magic, even if it were possible, which it isn't, to say that Asher would so imperil himself, this kingdom—"

Lord Jarralt smiled. "You speak most eloquently in his defence, Captain. Should I be questioning *your* loyalty?"

He felt his face bleach white. "I am as true a subject as ever lived."

"Really? I always felt you accepted the explanation for the late king and his family's unfortunate deaths somewhat readily, Orrick," said Jarralt. "Perhaps that is a matter which in due course would pay further investigation."

"My lord, I protest! I do my duty without fear or favour!"

Smile vanished, Jarralt's eyes were deadly. "Indeed? Then rouse your men, Captain, and tell them nothing of magic. That information you may regard as secret, on pain of death. Am I understood?"

"Yes, my lord," he said. His mouth was dry.

"You and your officers will accompany me to the Weather Chamber. Then we'll see how willing you are to yoke your future to Asher's short, bloody and painful one."

He was Captain of the City Guard. He had no choice. He bowed. "My lord," he said, and went to wake his men.

Tossing restlessly on the hard floor of the Weather Chamber, shot through with sizzling sparks of pain, Asher dreamed.

Sick and dying in her bed, Ma holds out her arms to him. Thin white arms, which once had been so plump and brown. "Give me a hug now, Asher, and promise you'll be a big strong boy once I'm gone," she says in her foam-thin voice, which only a month before had been as strong as the ocean itself. "Your da's goin' to need his little man soon and I know you won't do nowt to fratch or disappoint him, will you? You'll never let him down."

He cries, oh how he cries, as they lay her in the cold salty ground and sing the Farewell above her head.

Standing at the graveside in his best brown homespun shirt and trousers that Ma made, he can't believe the sun is shining and the sky is so blue, as blue as her favourite blouse that only last night Zeth cut up into pieces to grease the hinges on the fish trap in his boat. How can the sun be shining on such a terrible day?

As he weeps, dark clouds race in from all directions, tumbling and tearing and clogging the sky until all the light is gone, the bright yellow light, and it begins to rain.

"What be you doin', Asher?" his brothers angrily shout. "You ain't s'posed to make it rain! We'll have to give you a damn good straightenin' if you think it be your business to make it rain, a no-good Olken fisherman like y'self!"

And Zeth undoes his copper-studded belt. Slides it free of his narrow waist and cracks it double against his leathery palm. In his eyes such a yearning for blood...

"Stay clear of me, Zeth!" he says, backing away. "Da, don't let him! Don't let him, Da!"

But Da's not listening, Da's on the ground with a heavy great mast across him, split in two, and the rain's washing all the blood out of him, all Da's blood is running into the grass, onto the grave, soaking away to be with Ma.

The rain falls harder, bits of ice in it now, the clouds have turned as black as pitch and purple like bruises and there's thunder, thunder, boom boom boom...

Asher woke, gasping, to the hollow echoing tread of feet on the stairs leading up to the Weather Chamber. Mazed with dreaming, with woken pains both old and new, he was only halfway to his feet when the door burst wide and Willer gabbled in, pointing. At his heels were Pellen Orrick and Conroyd Jarralt.

"See? See? I told you he was here! *Now* will you believe me?"

Pellen's face was bloodless, his eyes narrow with pain. A truncheon hung from his belt. "Asher? What are you doing here? Don't tell me this repulsive little popinjay was *right*?"

A terrible wave of anger and despair crashed over him and he took a wild step forward, fists clenched. "You fool, Willer! You farting bloody *fool*! You've gone and ruined *everything*!"

Willer was grinning like a numbskull, dancing on the balls of his ugly flat feet. "Not ruined! *Saved*! I've saved the kingdom and soon everyone will know it!" he crowed. "There are guards downstairs with chains and rope to bind you hand and foot. It's over, Asher! You're done with!"

Asher leapt on him. "You sinkin' idiot!" he shouted, pummelling and kicking and clawing in fury. "You slime-ridden, shit-eating, runting, putrid *sea slug*, you—"

Pellen stepped forward and clubbed him on the head. Still fragile and vulnerable from the Weather Magic, he was brought to his knees by the blow, retching.

"Don't believe him, Pellen," he choked, red pain rolling through him. "You *know* me. I ain't a criminal *or* a traitor!"

A face carved from ice would look warmer. "How can I not believe, Asher? You're inside the Weather Chamber, where you ought not to be."

He groaned. "Send for the king. He'll explain everything, he'll—"

"What are you doing here?"

He was so afraid he wanted to vomit. "I ain't sayin'," he whispered. "I want to see Gar."

Pellen's eyes were devoid of hope, or pity. "Asher of Restharven, in the name of our king and by the authority granted me as Captain of this City, I arrest you for the capital crime of breaking Barl's First Law."

"Well done, Captain," said Conroyd Jarralt, and let one smoothly gloved hand fall on Pellen's shoulder. Beside him Willer still danced his little victory jig, shining like a greedy child on grand Barl's Day morning. "I can see I need doubt your loyalty no longer. Now call up your men and make sure this traitor's bound fast. There are many questions to be asked...and answered."

They locked him in the same cage Timon Spake had occupied in the hours before his death. When one ignorant Asher of Restharven had blithely said, "*Chop off the bastard's head.*" He swallowed black laughter, and tears.

I wanted nowt but a boat and the ocean and an open sunlit sky...

Gar's answer, echoing, taunted him from a distance of days that felt like years now.

"*Not every man gets what he wants, Asher. Most men just get what they're given.*"

Again, the threat of morbid amusement.

Fine. So can I give it back?

Stifling a groan he tried to ignore his body's insistent pains. The guards had ripped off the gag and choking hempen noose they'd thought was needed to get him here from the Weather Chamber but had left his arms tied to breaking point behind his back. His elbows thrummed, his wrists stung, his swollen hands throbbed and his shoulder sockets burned. His mouth tasted like ashes and dried blood. His head ached, and his ear, where Pellen's truncheon had clubbed him.

He was desperate to sit but they'd taken away the bench and straw that Timon Spake had enjoyed, and the floor held no attraction; even through his booted feet he could feel the flagstones' chill.

Even more desperate was his need for a pot: his bladder was full to bursting. But even if they'd left him one he couldn't unbutton his trousers, so when he couldn't hold it any longer he just let go; the hot piss running down the inside of his right leg was the only warm thing in the place. That and the shame that burned him like coals.

Shame, but not fear. He refused to be afraid. Gar had promised he'd be protected, and Gar was the king.

Time passed. He wondered why his release was taking so long; surely they'd wake Gar for this, even if it was still dark outside. Was it still dark outside? He couldn't tell.

When the outer cell door finally opened it was to admit Conroyd Jarralt, with Pellen behind him. Asher straightened. "Where's His Majesty?"

"Snoring sweetly in his bed, I presume," said Jarralt.

"You ain't *told* him?" He turned to Pellen. "You got to tell him, Pellen, you—"

"Captain Orrick."

"What?"

Pellen's expression was rigid. "You will address me as Captain Orrick."

He took a moment to breathe slowly, carefully. To subdue fear. "All right. Captain Orrick. I know how this looks but I swear if you rouse the king and ask him to come, he'll explain—"

"It's your explanation we're interested in," said Orrick. "Your presence in the Weather Chamber is a capital crime, punishable by death. Attempting to implicate His Majesty will not save you."

"I got nothing to say! Not till you get Gar down here!"

With a gentle sigh, Jarralt stepped forward. "You may leave us, Captain. I require private conversation with the prisoner."

Orrick shook his head. "No, my lord. He's in my charge and is my responsibility. Traitor or not he has certain rights. I must stand witness."

Jarralt's face spasmed with rage. "Need I *again* remind you, Captain, that I am—"

"With due respect, the Master Magician has no jurisdiction over criminal investigation," said Orrick, unflinching. "Only sentencing, once guilt is established."

Asher stared. Master Magician? Since when? "You're gettin' ahead of yourself, Jarralt. Durm ain't even cold yet, and Gar—"

"*Silence*," hissed Jarralt. He glared at Orrick. "Captain, I commend your diligence. But we deal with matters beyond mere law-breaking. This business strikes at the very heart of our kingdom and touches upon questions of magic, which are of no concern to you."

Orrick hesitated. Asher, fear flaring, pressed his face to the prison's bars. "Don't go, Pellen. Captain Orrick. Don't leave me alone with him. *Please*."

"Fear not, Captain," said Jarralt expansively. "I have no intention of cheating the axeman of his fee."

"Very well, my lord," said Orrick. "But I shall hold you to your word." The door closed behind him.

Jarralt smiled. The malice in him stepped Asher back three paces. "I ain't sayin' nowt till Gar gets here."

"Really?" Something deep in the Doranen lord's eyes flared scarlet. "*Pain*," he whispered.

And pain cut through Asher like a scythe. Doubled him over and stole his breath. "Barl rot your entrails, Jarralt," he grunted, still bent in half. "I ain't tellin' you *nowt*."

"Wrong, filth," said Jarralt. "You'll tell me everything."

And he did, in the end. Once he'd finished screaming. He couldn't stop himself. Jarralt's mind winnowed his like a grain thresher, reducing all thoughts of resistance to chaff.

Eventually, emptied of words, he fainted.

For the fifth time since his early arrival at the Tower that morning, Darran got up from his desk and poked his head through his open office doorway. Looked down. Strained his hearing for any sign of his tardy assistant. But no, *still* no Willer. Where could the wretched man be? They had *oceans* of work to swim through...

And then he heard the Tower's front doors open and Willer's imperious voice demanding, "Berta! Is Darran arrived yet? We have urgent business!"

We?

As the maid replied he caught a glimpse of Willer, and the man he ushered up the staircase before him.

Lord Jarralt.

He returned to his desk. When Willer flounced into the room on Lord Jarralt's heels he was busily reading the day's schedule. He stood and bowed. "My lord." Then he fixed his attention on his assistant. "You are fearsome tardy this morning, sir. Might I ask where—"

"At the guardhouse," said Willer. "Engaged on matters of state."

"At my behest," added Lord Jarralt. "I presume you have no objection?"

Matters of state? *Willer?* Darran bowed again. "Of course not, my lord." He cleared his throat. "Did you require something of me, my—"

"Asher of Restharven is arrested," said Lord Jarralt. Anyone would think the announcement was unexciting to him, provided they weren't looking at his eyes.

"Arrested?" Darran said faintly. "On what charge?"

"No charge, but proven treason!" said Willer. "His guilt is beyond all doubt! He—"

"Willer," said Lord Jarralt mildly.

Willer's mouth sprang shut like a mousetrap.

"I must see the king," Jarralt continued. "Take me to him."

Darran shifted uneasily. "My lord, His Majesty called snow last night. The WeatherWorking taxes him, he often remains late abed the following—"

"Now," said Lord Jarralt.

Clearly, argument was out of the question. "My lord," he said, then turned to eye Willer quellingly. "I shan't be long. Kindly prepare for me the notes for today's session with—"

"No," said Willer. He was grinning. "I don't work for you any more. I've accepted Lord Jarralt's offer of a position on his staff."

"You've done *what*?"

"You're a fool, Darran," Willer said spitefully. "Asher took you in along with everybody else. Even the king. But not me. *I* saw through him. I stayed loyal to Barl—and Lord Jarralt knows it. You'll have to find yourself another errand boy."

His hand itched to slap the insolent smile from Willer's face. "I see," he said thinly. "Congratulations. Make sure you remove any personal items from your desk before you depart."

Willer looked around the room, his gaze sticky with distaste. "There's nothing I want from here."

"Then repair to my townhouse," said Lord Jarralt, "and await my return."

"My lord," said Willer with an extravagant bow, and withdrew.

The pompous, ungrateful little—little *turd*. Darran watched him go with ill-concealed loathing, then stepped from behind his desk. "My lord? If you would follow me?"

Heart pounding, head awhirl with shock and speculation and a burning desire to know what Asher had done, he led Lord Jarralt up the spiral staircase to the door of His Majesty's suite.

Gar was woken from slumber by a rough hand shaking him and a dazzling assault of sunlight.

"Stir yourself, boy," said a curt, unwelcome voice. "Your sins have found you out."

He sat up, incredulous. "*Conroyd?* What is the meaning of this? How did you get *in* here?"

Outlined in sunlight Conroyd Jarralt stood beside the bed, his golden head a glowing nimbus. "Your secretary admitted me."

"Then he's dismissed. Darran, do you hear me? You're dismissed!" He screwed up his eyes and squinted round the room. "Where are you, you damned interfering old woman?"

"Not here," said Conroyd. "What I have to say is for your ears alone."

Sliding back under his blankets, he rested a forearm across his face. It felt as though he'd fallen asleep mere moments ago. Hours and hours spent searching through Durm's borrowed books, and not even a sign of Barl's diary.

"I'm not interested. Now get out." When Conroyd made no move, he sat up and shouted. "Are you deaf? Your king just gave you a command! *Get out!*"

Conroyd smiled. "Your tame Olken is arrested and sitting in a cell, and you are called upon to clarify certain matters arising from his apprehension."

He half climbed, half fell out of bed. Reached for his dressing-gown and covered his nakedness. "*Arrested?* On whose authority? Yours? How *dare* you? Free him! *Immediately!* And then take his place in the guardhouse!"

Conroyd considered him, unmoved. "You don't ask why he's arrested. Can it be you already know?"

Barl save them...Barl save them... "I don't care why! All that matters is you've laid hands on a fellow councillor without recourse to your king! You'd never have done this while my father was alive and you won't do it now that he's dead!"

"Asher has broken Barl's First Law," said Conroyd. "Where else should he be if not in prison?"

Conroyd knew. Stunned into silence, he felt his blood turn to ice. *Somehow, he knew.*

Conroyd sneered. "You puling cripple. Did you truly think you could succeed? Against *me*? Did you actually believe you could deny me my destiny? My rightful possession of this land? You're just like your father, a weakling and a—"

"*Don't you speak of my father!*"

Conroyd ignored him. "Criminal. Asher has confessed, boy. Magic has failed you and your complicity in his crimes is beyond doubt."

"Do you *hear* yourself, Conroyd?" he said, his voice low and shaking. His empty stomach roiled and bile burned his throat, his mouth. *Asher was arrested.* "'Your rightful possession of this land'? You arrogant bastard. Father was right: given the chance you and your heirs would elevate the Doranen to godhood and reduce the Olken to slaves! Is it any wonder I'd do anything, risk anything, to keep House Jarralt away from the throne?"

"You pathetic earth-sodden worm!" Conroyd screamed in a whisper, backing him into the wall. "Are you truly this blind, this *stupid*? You've given an Olken magic! Given a subhuman race of cattle *power*!"

"Let go of me, Conroyd," Gar said as fingers twisted in the brocade of his dressing-gown. "Let go and get out."

"How did you do it? Who was it helped you?" Conroyd hissed. "The filth didn't know. Was it one of my so-called *friends*? Is that how you did it? Did you promise Daltrie power, or Boqur? Sorvold? Hafar? Promise them riches in return for—"

"I promised nothing to no one!" he shouted, and wrenched himself free. "And that was assault upon your king—so now *you're* the traitor."

But Conroyd wasn't listening. Motionless, the hectic colour fading from his face, comprehension dawned behind his eyes. "It was *in* him?" he said slowly. Almost disbelieving. "The Olken has magic of his *own*?"

Heart thumping, Gar pushed past him. Stumbled against the corner of the bed and nearly fell. "Go home, my lord. Consider it house arrest. I will—"

"Do nothing!" said Conroyd, and laughed. "Little crippled king, do you not understand? It is *over*. Your secret is revealed, your failure discovered. Asher of Restharven is destined to die...and you are powerless to save him."

But I promised him...I promised... Fighting nausea, he made himself look into Conroyd's hateful, hating face. "Anything Asher did was because I asked it. Because he is my friend."

Conroyd smiled. "Then he is a fool. And his lack of discrimination will kill him."

Gar wondered if this was how his father had felt when the carriage hurtled over the edge of Salbert's Eyrie. "I'll make you a bargain, Conroyd." His voice sounded thread-thin and distant. "Release Asher and I'll give you the crown."

Conroyd laughed. "The crown is mine already, boy, and all the kingdom with it! Instead of bargaining you should get on your knees and *beg*!"

"For what? Asher's life?" he dropped to the carpet. "Very well, then. I beg." He winced as strong fingers, heavy with rings, imprisoned his face.

"Too late," said Conroyd.

Something dreadful was burning in the man's eyes. Gar forced himself not to quail before it. Made himself meet that incendiary gaze. "If you kill him, Conroyd, I'll shout from coast to coast that the Olken are as magic as we. I'll destroy the lie our people have lived here these past six hundred years. I'll tell the truth and let it cost me my life."

Conroyd's cruel fingers tightened to gasping point. "Breathe one word of Olken magic, cripple, just one, and I'll bring House Torvig down on your magickless head. By the time I'm done history will remember your father as an ignorant, impotent, cuckolded king. And your mother? Your mother will be known as the Strumpet Queen who sullied her marriage bed with some rutting Olken farmhand, your true father, and then foisted her blasphemous spawn upon an unsuspecting kingdom. Your house will be reviled, its crypt will be struck open and the corpses of your family cast into the wilderness. And your sister? I'll erase her from Doranen memory as though precious, precocious Fane never lived. When I am done with it all that will remain of House Torvig is the cuckold, the strumpet and the half-breed cripple. Is that the legacy you want to leave, boy? Shall that be the sum of your dynastic achievements?"

"You wouldn't," he choked, fighting the urge to retch. "You loved my mother!"

"*Loved* her?" echoed Conroyd. "Your mother was a bitch, a slut, a treacherous whore!"

Guts heaving, Gar knocked the grasping fingers aside and stood. "I promised Asher I'd protect him. To break that oath would be to destroy House Torvig myself. So do your worst, Conroyd. But be warned: my house stands stronger than you know...and you're not as loved as you think."

Conroyd's face twisted. "I could kill you, worm, before you had the chance to open your mouth."

"You could, but you won't," he retorted. "Without me to endorse your succession there will be a schism, Conroyd, with no guarantee you'd emerge victorious or even alive at the end of it. Be sensible. Spare Asher and I'll abdicate in your favour and keep secret his use of magic. Kill him..."

A moment of blazing silence. "Well, well, well," said Conroyd softly. "So the worm has a spine."

"How often must I tell you? I am my father's son."

Conroyd's eyebrows lifted. "And as your father's son how will you react, I wonder, when I declare a purge upon the Olken?"

"*What?*"

Now Conroyd was smiling. "Unless you abdicate *and* sign a proclamation publicly condemning Asher of Restharven to death as a criminal, a traitor and a breaker of Barl's Law, I promise he'll be but the first Olken to die. For the sake of the kingdom, and to uphold our sacred laws, I shall launch a purge the likes of which this land has never seen, and when I'm done if there are enough Olken left living to fill a single village then I'll say that I have *failed!*"

Bludgeoned to a disbelieving silence, Gar stared at Conroyd. "You're mad," he said at last. "The General Council would never let you. *Holze* would never—"

"Stop deluding yourself!" Conroyd said brutally. "Do you think there's a Doranen breathing who wants to see an Olken with magic? And if you think Holze would try to stop me, you've sadly mistaken the depth of his devotion to his precious Barl and her Laws!"

Abruptly, his legs would no longer bear his weight. Collapsing onto his bed Gar turned his head away so Conroyd wouldn't see his despair. His defeat.

"Is there no human feeling in you?" he whispered. "Does a king's word mean nothing? Asher *trusted* me. Trusted my promise I'd keep him safe."

"Then he is twice a fool. It was a bargain you had no business making. A promise you knew full well you could never keep, didn't you?"

No. *No.* At least...not a promise he thought he'd have to keep. Damn it, they'd been so *careful.*

"The choice is a simple one," said Conroyd, relentless. "Do as I say or drown in a flood of Olken blood."

Gar made himself look at his tormentor. "You'd truly do it, wouldn't you? You'd kill them all."

"I have said so," said Conroyd. "Do you at last believe it?"

Yes. He believed it, and wondered, sickened, if his father had ever once suspected the truth of this man. The hatred and the violence that slept behind his eyes.

"And what of me?" he asked dully. "What happens to me once I've signed my name to your filthy lies? A convenient accident?"

Conroyd shrugged. "Not unless you lose your senses and try something...unwise. You'll remain here in the Tower. In seclusion. Withdrawn from public life, your health sadly ruined by the loss of your family and your magic. By the betrayal of one you so stupidly trusted."

"The people—"

"Won't miss you for long. The Doranen barely noticed your existence before your mistaken elevation to king. And as for the Olken..." Another disdainful shrug. "They were never people in the first place."

Gar pressed a fist against his heart. There was a pain in him so dreadful, so deep, he thought he should die of it. He wished he could. Kill Asher...or kill a kingdom full of his innocent brethren. Whatever he decided, he'd be stained with blood forever.

Oh, sweet Barl, forgive me...

"Bring me your proclamation then," he said, and could hardly recognise his own voice. "I will sign it. And may Barl damn you, Conroyd, in this life and the next."

CHAPTER TWENTY-TWO

After a sleepless night, Dathne rose with the sun, washed and dressed and ate a half-hearted breakfast, then drifted downstairs to the bookshop. Dusting shelves was a mindless antidote to worry, and anyway it needed to be done. Young Poppy, hired to run the place day to day, was perfect with customers but seemed allergic to cleaning.

There was something soothing about books. Even the newest Gertsik romance calmed her riotous nerves. Made her smile. Safe amongst her silent shelves, pretending it was still her old life that she lived, she dabbed and drifted and tried not to remember the touch of snowflakes on her skin.

But memory would not be denied.

Asher made it snow.

Her hands shook, and she dropped her dusting cloth. She'd never dreamed his power would come like this. Weather Magic was Doranen magic. She'd never known of an Olken who could wield it.

"Fool," she berated herself savagely, retrieving the duster. "He's the Innocent Mage and born of Prophecy. What did you think he was? Just another Olken? Oh, Asher, *Asher*. If only you'd *confided!*"

Failure burned her. She'd been so sure that if she seduced his body his mind would surely follow.

She wasn't used to being wrong.

"I'm Jervale's Heir," she whispered to a shelf crammed full of histories. "I'm in the business of being *right.*"

Clearly, the time had come to tell him. To spirit him somewhere to safety and show him to himself at last. Reveal to him his destiny and purpose. Veira would know best where he could be hidden, which meant she could no longer avoid talking to the old woman. And if that meant a scolding for her silence, so be it.

Decided at last, Dathne tossed aside the dusting cloth, turned for the door leading back to her apartment—and was startled by an urgent tapping on the bookshop window. It was young Finella, Mistress Tuttle's apprentice, on her way to work at the bakery. The girl's eyes were popping-wide in her pale face. She waved her hand, pointed round the corner, then disappeared from view.

Frowning, Dathne unlocked the shop's back door and slipped into the tiny courtyard behind. "Yes, Finny?"

The girl was on the brink of tears. "Oh, Mistress Dathne, I saw you in there as I was passing and I thought perhaps I should tell you but now I don't know, I don't want to get in trouble, but you work with him, you're friends with him, and you've always been so kind to me..."

Asher. Resisting the urge to shake the wretched child, Dathne forced a smile. "It's all right, Finny. Take a deep breath and tell me what's amiss."

"Oh, Mistress Dathne!" Finny whispered. "Meister Asher's been arrested!"

"Arrested?" she said sharply. "Nonsense. Where did you hear such a poppycock tale?"

Finella shrank back. "From my brother Deek! He was street-cleaning in the alleyway opposite the guardhouse and he saw them bring Asher in. All tied up he was, with a cloth over his face and a noose round his neck! But the cloth slipped and Deek saw him. It was awful, he said! Captain Orrick was there, and Lord Jarralt too."

Arrested—and in such a skulduggery fashion. She could hardly think straight for the frantic pounding of her heart. "And did they see Deek spying there?"

Finny coloured, indignant. "He wasn't spying, he was doin' his job! But no, he says they never saw him 'cause he made sure to stay quiet as a mouse. Deek says a smart man who comes across that kind of business is deaf and dumb and blind!"

"And yet he told you?"

"I'm always the first one up, on account of starting so early in the bakery," said Finny, shrugging. "He said he had to tell someone, he was feeling all wobbly, and he knew I'd hold my tongue. And I will too! I'm only telling you 'cause I know you're Asher's friend!"

Trembling, Dathne hugged her. "And I'm right grateful, Finny. Now off you go to Mistress Tuttle's before you get docked for lateness. And, Finny—not a word about this to *anyone*. Promise?"

Finny nodded vigorously. "Oh yes, I promise. Mistress Dathne, is Asher going to be all right?"

She forced a smile. "Of course he is. I'm sure it's all a terrible mistake."

Reassured, Finny hurried away. Breathless with fear, Dathne contacted Veira.

Arrested? the old woman repeated. The link connecting them vibrated with her shock. *Do you know why?*

"No," said Dathne. "But, Veira...he has the Weather Magic. I fear he's been discovered."

Veira swore.

"I'm sorry!" Dathne wailed. "This is all my fault! I should've told him who he was weeks ago, I should've listened to Matt, I should *never* have—"

We can lay blame later. Pack all that might betray you, child, and leave the City at once.

"Leave?" she said. "Veira, no! I have to save Asher, I have to—"

You can't, child. Not on your own. And the City won't be safe for you now. Come to me and together we'll find a way.

Smearing the tears on her cheeks with a shaking hand, Dathne nodded. "All right. Where are you?"

The knowledge sped from Veira's mind to hers through the Circle Stone link. "The Black Woods? You're not so far away then."

Far enough. Don't risk a horse, for fear of attention. Cloak yourself and slip out of the City sideways. Walk as fast as you can. The Black Woods Road is lightly travelled this time of year. If you do see someone, hide till they pass. I'll meet you on the way.

She wasn't alone...the relief was overwhelming. And then she sat up sharply, remembering. "Matt! Veira, I have to warn Matt."

Leave Matthias to me. Think only of yourself, child. If you stay there much longer the next knock on your door could be a guardsman with inconvenient questions.

Numbly, she stared into the pulsing heart of the Circle Stone. "Asher will think I've abandoned him," she whispered. "He'll think I never meant a word I said."

Maybe he will and maybe he won't, said Veira. *That's not for you to say. Now hurry!*

Fat with satisfaction, Morg scattered salt on the wet ink of the proclamations that Gar would shortly sign then sat back in his chair. Beyond the closed door of Jarralt's private library he could hear voices as the lord's household bustled.

At last his plans were fruiting. And with inconvenient Asher soon to be dead, the cripple off the throne, and himself as king and free to tamper as he willed, Barl's cursed Wall would quickly be a memory.

Knowing how close he'd come to failure, fury stirred. First Durm's injuries, then the unexpected interference of that Olken filth. A tremor of hatred, of livid frustration, shook his fine-knit limbs. He was so *sick* of this place. Sick of this exile behind Barl's Wall. Of being cut off from his vast reservoir of power, trammelled and confined in these prisons of meat, vulnerable to mere *accident*. Forced to wait and plot and connive and scheme instead of reaching out his will and *taking* what he wanted the instant that he wanted it!

To be thwarted by an Olken? It was enough to make him vomit! He wanted to kill them all. Slaughter every last Olken and yes, the Doranen too. Rid this pretty kingdom of its cattle and renegades. Cleanse the land with blood and fire.

But no. As an infinite intellect trapped in finite flesh, he dared not risk it. Alarm and alert the kingdom's magicians and united they might defeat him. Caution was the key. The moment Barl's Wall was destroyed he could abandon this body and reunite with his larger, immortal self. But until then he had to be careful. Until then, Morg could still die.

A whisper from his deeply prisoned host. *Yes, yes, die!*

He smiled. Fool Conroyd, who'd fancied himself a mage to be reckoned with. Who only now began to understand the meaning of ambition. Of mastery. Of power.

The parchments dry now he rolled them, secured them with a ribbon from the desk drawer and tucked them under his arm. Fat Willer was waiting patiently on a bench outside the library door.

"My lord!" he cried, lumbering to his feet. "What now?"

A useful little toad, this. Disappointed poisonous men were always useful. "Return to the Tower. Inform that black streak of misery Darran that I wish him to announce an emergency session of the General Council for two o'clock this afternoon."

Willer bowed. "Yes, my lord."

Next Morg ordered Jarralt's carriage and directed it to the City Chapel, where he found wittering Holze in the midst of leading a morning service.

"Conroyd!" the Barl-sodden cleric exclaimed once the caterwauling was over and the congregation had emptied from its seats. "You look quite perturbed! Is something the matter?"

Morg arranged Jarralt's austerely beautiful face into lines of tragedy and woe. "Alas, dear Efrim, I'm afraid it is. Can we talk? Privately?"

"Of course! Come, we can speak in my office."

Smiling quietly, Morg followed him out of the chapel.

As they passed yet another portrait of his dearly beloved dead whore, he blew her a kiss.

When Asher roused from his stupor he found himself still on the floor of his cell in the guardhouse, unbound, and Pellen Orrick sitting in a chair outside it reading reports. The pain Jarralt had inflicted was gone but the memory of it dried his mouth and threatened to start him shaking all over again.

Unsteadily, he sat up. Leaned against the nearest bars. "I want to see Gar," he croaked. "I got a right."

Orrick looked at him. Nobody would ever describe the captain as forthcoming, but they'd fallen into the habit of easy, joking conversation in the last long weeks. He'd been halfway to thinking the man might become a friend. Now, though, the warm flicker of appreciation in Orrick's pale eyes was extinguished and his face was set like stone.

"Don't speak to me of rights, Asher. Not after what you've done. And don't go trying to change your tune now, either. You *confessed*, to Lord Jarralt and then to me! You're condemned out of your own mouth!"

He'd confessed to Orrick? He didn't remember that. Pain had stolen his last hour or so. "I only did what Gar asked me to do."

Orrick grimaced. "So you say."

"I'm a liar now, am I?"

"Asher, I'm afraid to think what you are," said Orrick and stood, turning away.

He wrapped his fingers round the cell bars and hauled himself to his feet. "Jarralt ain't told you, has he?"

Reluctantly, Orrick turned back. "Told me what?" he asked at last, grudging.

"Gar's lost his magic."

Another silence, longer this time. Then Orrick shook his head. "That's impossible."

"No. It's true."

"Then you stole it," Orrick retorted, "though Barl alone knows how."

"*Stole* it? Do I look brainsick to you?"

"You look like a traitor."

It was no good, he couldn't stand up any longer. Stifling a groan, he slid back to the floor. "Well, I ain't."

"You broke Barl's First Law!"

"And Jarralt broke the Second! He hurt me with magic, Pellen! Do you care about *that* law? Or doesn't hurting me count?"

For the first time a shimmer of uncertainty crossed Orrick's obdurate face. "I have no bias in the law, Asher," he said stiffly. "I agree Lord Jarralt was...misguided. But he was also sore provoked!"

"And so was I bloody provoked!" he shouted. "D'you think I did this *willingly*? Gar begged me, Orrick. You got any idea what that's like, being begged by a king? He was desperate to keep Lur out of Jarralt's hands and I was stupid enough to let him convince me. *Ask* him, Pellen. He'll tell you I ain't lyin', I *swear*."

Orrick ran a hand over his face. Listening, but not convinced. "You didn't steal His Majesty's magic?"

"*No.*"

"Then where did it come from?" Orrick whispered. He looked torn between fear and fury. "Olken are taught from the cradle: we don't have magic. So where did yours come from if not the king?"

"I don't know and I don't care! All I know is Gar swore to protect me if the truth came out. Well, Pellen, it's out. And instead of actin' like the City's Captain and askin' the king yourself whether or not I'm tellin' the truth, you're runnin' about like Conroyd Jarralt's lapdog! Takin' his word unchallenged—a man who tortures with magic. A man who's coveted this kingdom's crown for the best part of his life. Who'd do just about anythin', I reckon, to snatch it off Gar's head and put it on his own."

Orrick glared, seething. "I am no man's lapdog!"

Muscles screaming, Asher forced himself onto his knees. Hanging onto the bars, harshly breathing, he looked Pellen Orrick full in the face. "Prove it."

Orrick stayed silent as a thousand thoughts rolled behind the glassy surface of his eyes. Slowly, the outright rejection in his face faded to wary suspicion. "Why should I? You're the one in prison, not me."

"Today," Asher agreed, feeling ill. "But if you let this injustice stand without raising a finger against it there won't be a single Olken safe in all of Lur. Don't you see, Pellen? If Jarralt dares hurt *me* with magic, who of us won't he touch?"

Still suspicious, Orrick tapped a knuckle to his lips. "You must see, Asher. What you claim strains all bounds of credibility."

It was a struggle, but he kept his voice steady. He was so close to begging...and he'd never begged for anything in his life. "I can't help that. What I did was for Gar, and the kingdom. I swear it. Pellen, you know me. You *know* me. I ain't a traitor."

Like the first hint of sunlight on snow, Orrick's expression softened. "Before today, I confess I'd have laughed to hear you called one."

Asher swallowed. "And nowt's changed. But without your help I'll never prove it."

"Lord Jarralt has laid it strict upon me I'm to keep this coil a secret," said Orrick, frowning. "I'm not to step foot outside the guardhouse till he returns."

He'd never known hope could hurt so much. "Then send Gar a message. Private and sealed. If you ask him, he'll come. He'll fix this, I know it. He promised."

Orrick turned away from the cell. With his hand on the outer door's latch he said, not looking back, "I promise nothing."

"But you'll try?"

The longest moment of silence he'd ever lived through. A fractional dip of Pellen Orrick's head. White knuckles on the door latch. "Yes, Asher. I'll try."

When Conroyd Jarralt returned to the Tower and was shown into Gar's library, he wasn't alone; Holze stood at his shoulder. One look at him and Gar knew Conroyd had told all. Eyes grim, mouth pressed thin and unforgiving, there was little of the kindly, welcoming cleric about the royal spiritual advisor now. Instead he looked like a man made of iron, against which all gentle things must shatter.

Pinned to his chair by Holze's hard, heavy gaze, Gar felt himself diminish. Weaken. Falter.

In the time between his rude awakening and this moment he'd managed to gather his scattered wits. Smother dismay and bolster courage. Let Conroyd bluster and bully as he liked, he was not king. His threats were the rantings of a man unhinged by thwarted ambition, nothing more. No Doranen of conscience would stand by and let him slaughter innocent Olken. No cleric who followed Barl's merciful teachings would countenance such uncivil discord. Holze would never side with Conroyd. Holze would understand that what his king had done was done for the good of all.

Or so he'd told himself as he bathed and dressed and recovered his balance. But now Holze was here before him, with all his thoughts clear in his face.

"Your Majesty," he said. "I scarcely know where to begin."

Gar stood. There must yet be hope. "Holze. Efrim. I thought you of all men would understand."

"Understand what?" said the cleric, a whip-snap in his voice. "That you placed personal ambition above a sacred oath? That you suborned blasphemy in the pursuit of worldly power? That you conspired to pervert the course of law and justice, of Barl's holy word, which you were sworn to uphold? No, sir. I do not understand. I will never understand. And I praise Barl your father did not live to see the day his son committed such sins against the kingdom in whose sweet service he spent his life."

"How can the truth be blasphemous?" he demanded. "Holze, don't you understand? We've been living a lie, all of us. The Olken are possessed of magic. Learning this, how can we in good conscience—"

"The question of Olken magic is irrelevant!" said Holze. "The only arbiter of conscience is Blessed Barl and her Laws and they are crystal clear on the matter. Magic is reserved for the Doranen, custodians of Barl's kingdom. As king you but hold this land in trust. A trust you have grievously betrayed."

Gar looked from Holze to Conroyd Jarralt. Until now, he'd never thought hate could be a thing you tasted, like wine gone sour in the jug. "Congratulations, Conroyd. Somehow you've managed to convert a good man to your deceitful cause."

Conroyd smiled. "The only deceit was yours. Now hold your tongue. All we require from you is a signature on these proclamations. Your opinions have ceased to carry weight in this kingdom."

"Whilst yours have assumed all the heaviness of a crown?"

"In due course."

The bastard was unspeakably smug. Feeling sick, his ill-advised breakfast churning in his belly, Gar held out his hand to receive the first roll of parchment. Untied the ribbon encircling it. Read its contents.

He looked up. "I can't sign this."

Holze exchanged glances with Conroyd. "Why not?"

"Because it's a lie!" he said, and tossed the parchment aside. "Asher didn't steal my magic. There was no Olken conspiracy to dislodge me from the throne, or usurp Doranen authority in the kingdom. Asher did what he did because I asked him to and for no other reason! Isn't it enough that you want me to kill him? Must I kill his memory also, and all the good he did as well?"

"If you do not sign it, you leave open the possibility that some misguided Olken fool might question the validity of his condemnation," said Conroyd. "He is popular, this monster you created. To uncreate him you must paint him blacker than he's painted himself and so ensure he is remembered not with love but with loathing. His destruction must stand as a beacon till the end of time, a warning to any Olken who would dare disturb the quietude of this kingdom."

As well talk to a wall as to Conroyd Jarralt. He looked to Holze. "Can't you see this is wrong? How can you support it? Ask me to support it? I thought you loved me!"

"I loved a boy who loved his family," said Holze, unmoved. "I loved a man who loved this kingdom, who bore misfortune with fortitude and spent his life in service to others. I don't know the man I see before me today. And how can I love a man I do not know?"

Gar felt his legs give way, fold him once more into his chair. Suddenly it was hard to breathe. "I can't do this."

"You must," said Holze. "Asher is a canker, poised to kill a kingdom. He must be cut from its heart before his poison spreads. If you do not see it there is as little hope for you as there is for him."

He'd never imagined soft-spoken Holze could sound so harsh. "But he is innocent. Blameless."

"Hardly innocent," said Conroyd. "By your own admission he broke the law!"

Again, he looked to Holze. "Do you know what Conroyd threatened, to make me agree to this perfidy? Did he tell you what he swore he'd do if I refused to conspire with him in Asher's murder?"

Holze was shaking his head. "Lawful execution is no murder."

"He said he'd despoil my family's legacy!"

"You've done that yourself."

"He said he'd slaughter thousands of guiltless Olken!"

"If it's discovered there are other Olken—other traitors—with pretensions to a power denied them by Barl herself then certainly they will die," Holze replied. "But that is hardly slaughter."

Conroyd smiled. "Accept it, boy. Your reign is over. You threw power away when you yoked yourself to Asher of Restharven. Sign his warrant of execution and this, your intent to abdicate, then get down on your knees and praise Barl that for the sake of this kingdom's peace you're to be spared a more *rigorous* accounting of your actions."

Gar stared at the second roll of parchment and for one last mad moment considered defying them. Considered spitting in Conroyd's handsome, hateful face and trusting himself and Asher to Barl's mercy. To the love of his kingdom's people, both Doranen and Olken. To their forgiveness of his frailty, his failure as a magician, his desperation as a king.

Somehow, Conroyd read his mind. "They might—*might*—forgive you, boy. They will *never* forgive Asher. He is dead already. He was dead the moment you convinced him to defy Barl's First Law. And if you're honest, if you're even capable of honesty, you know I speak the truth."

He felt a peculiar inner breaking then, as though his bones were made of glass and Conroyd's words were hammers, striking. He nodded. "Yes. I know."

There was pen and ink in the desk drawer. He fetched them and signed the proclamations. Wrote carefully, with a steady hand, using all his names and titles. *Gar Antyn Bartolomew Dannison Torvig, Scion House Torvig, Defender House Torvig, Weather Worker of Lur.*

Traitor...betrayer...and breaker of oaths.

"Don't forget your personal seal," prompted Conroyd. "The finishing touch, so to speak."

A stick of sealing wax lay in another drawer. Conroyd melted it for him with a word, smiling just a little. He pressed his signet ring into each blood-red pool and completed his act of treachery. Watching, it was as though a stranger's hand did the deed.

Conroyd took the signed proclamations and rolled them swiftly. "As for the rest..."

"Rest?" he said, dully. "What rest?"

"My elevation to the throne. I've called an emergency General Council meeting at which you'll announce your abdication and withdrawal from public life. You'll declare me your lawful heir. Lur's new king and Weather Worker. Then you'll return to this Tower and not set foot beyond its grounds until such time as I give you permission."

This was a dream, it had to be. "Today? You want me to abdicate today?"

Conroyd was pulling on gold-stitched gloves. "Why postpone the inevitable? Without magic you cannot be king. And Lur needs its WeatherWorker. Barl only knows what damage was done by that creature you let meddle with the Wall."

"Asher did no damage."

Conroyd sneered. "How would you know? You're a magickless cripple."

He flinched. Felt corrosive self-hatred, like acid. His father would *never* so meekly submit...he *had* to keep fighting...

He made himself stand. "For all you know there might be a cure for me, Conroyd. I demand consultation with Pother Nix. I demand—"

"Nothing," said Conroyd. "Not now, not ever. And besides, there is no cure. Now, as to the dispersal of your household."

"Dispersal? What do you—"

Conroyd ignored him. "In keeping with your newly reduced role in the kingdom, and to minimise your burden on the royal purse, the majority of your staff will be reassigned. Only Darran will remain to take care of your modest daily needs. I hope he can cook. And clean."

"One man?" Gar said, incredulous. "To care for all this Tower? Darran is elderly, and recently infirm! You can't expect him to—"

"But I can," said Conroyd, smiling. "I do. Perhaps you could in some small way shift for yourself? Barl knows you'll have the time."

"Conroyd," Holze murmured disapprovingly. Standing to one side. Doing nothing, *nothing*, to stop this.

Unheeding, Conroyd continued. "Your stables of course will be emptied; horses and equipment sold off."

Fresh pain stabbed. "Sold? Ballodair? No! He was a gift from my father, you have no right to—"

"Your expenses must be defrayed somehow. And given you'll not be riding anywhere in the near future, what need have you of horses? The animal will be sold, along with all the rest." Conroyd stepped closer, pale eyes glittering. "You dare to complain? Don't. Mercy has its limits. You are free on sufferance, boy."

"Free?" he said, and laughed. "I'm your prisoner."

Holze cleared his throat heavily. "If this Tower has become your cell, then it's a cell of your own making."

"And as cells go, it's not without comfort," Conroyd added. "I'm sure your unfortunate Olken would be pleased to change places."

Gar felt his belly spasm. "He's not to be touched, Conroyd. You've got your wish. He's in prison and condemned to die. That should be enough even for you." When Conroyd stayed silent, he turned to Holze. "Barlsman, I'm begging you. Restrain Lord Jarralt. If not for me, then for the love you bore my father."

Holze's face twisted. "Your purse is empty of that coin, sir."

"Your purse is empty of all coin," said Conroyd. "Save the cuicks I let fall in your path. Remember that. Remember also the Olken stand hostage to your good behaviour and silent tongue. If word of Asher's exploits leaves this room, there will be consequences."

"I see," said Gar, when he could trust himself to speak. "I disobey and someone else suffers?"

Conroyd's smile was pure poison. "Exactly. Now, I suggest you spend the next while penning a short, crowd-pleasing speech for our esteemed General Council. As for the meeting, I'll return to collect you for it later this afternoon. Don't keep me waiting."

With an effort, he bit back a response. Instead looked to Holze. "About Durm—"

"I go now to the palace infirmary," the Barlsman said. "He shall be afforded all rites and respect. None of this mess is of his making."

Was that true? He wished he knew. Wished, desperately, that he'd had more time to quiz the dying Master Magician. To learn more of Barl's diary and what use Durm had made of it, if any, and how it was their only hope. He had to find the thing. If there was an escape from this nightmare, perhaps he'd find it there... "Thank you, Holze," he said stiffly. "For myself, and my father." He looked again at Conroyd. "You will need to choose his successor."

Conroyd shrugged. "Certainly. At some point."

"No. Now. The law is quite clear, you must—"

"Law?" Conroyd laughed. "You sit there and lecture me on *law*? Hold your tongue, brat. Remember your new position in the kingdom."

He stood, feeling most peculiar. Disconnected and likely to float right out of his body. "I shall. Are we done?"

"For now."

"Then get out."

Conroyd's golden eyebrows lifted. "Get out, *Your Majesty*."

He opened his mouth to say something catastrophic, but was stopped by Darran's flustered entrance. "Forgive me, Your Majesty, but an urgent message has come from the City Guardhouse. It's from Captain Orrick. The runner is awaiting your reply."

Conroyd held out his hand. "Give it here."

Darran hesitated. "My lord, it is addressed to the king."

"*Give it here.*"

Gar nodded as, uncertain and unhappy, Darran glanced at him. The message was handed over. Conroyd broke the seal, read the note. Refolded it and slipped it into his pocket. "Tell the runner to inform Captain Orrick I shall arrive at the guardhouse in due course."

Darran took a step towards him. "Sir...?"

Gar stared at the floor. "Do as Lord Jarralt says, Darran."

"Yes, sir," said Darran, and withdrew.

"What did it say?" he asked.

Conroyd shook his head. "Nothing that concerns you any longer."

Jarralt and Holze departed, taking the signed proclamations with them. Aimless, emptied of thought and feeling, Gar wandered around the room like a boat set adrift on a lowering tide. Darran returned and hovered in the open doorway.

"Your Majesty..."

"Leave me be."

Darran took a step forward. "Sir, Lord Jarralt is issuing orders. He says—"

"I know what he says," he whispered, and ran gentle fingers along a shelf-line of books. "Lord Jarralt is a voluble man."

Darran's lined face was a picture of confusion and dismay. "Sir... he says you're no longer the king."

"He's right. I've had a busy morning, Darran, though you might not think so to look at me."

"Your Majesty..."

"*Don't call me that!*"

A shocked silence. Darran crept a little closer. "Sir?"

"Do you know what I've done since opening my eyes?"

It was Darran's turn to whisper. "No, sir."

"Then I'll tell you. I've eaten breakfast, renounced the throne and murdered my friend. And look, it's not even midday! Quick, Darran, find me a baby and I'll strangle it before lunch!"

"Sir!"

It came as a shock to realise he was crying. Hot tears, falling from cold eyes. Springing from a cold and killing heart.

"Just get out, would you?" he shouted. "Get out of here, old man, old fool! Get out and leave me alone!"

Darran fled.

It felt like years had passed, but finally Orrick returned. When the cell's outer door opened again Asher grunted to his feet and stepped to his cage's locked door.

"Pellen!" he said eagerly, craning to see past the captain's shoulder. "Did you fetch him? Is he coming? Is it all sorted out? What's that scroll you got there? Is it my pardon?"

Pellen gave him a look so cold, so hard, it was like being struck in the face with a bar of iron.

"Be silent."

He felt his heart jolt. "Pellen? What is it, what's—" And then he stopped, because entering the outer cell was Conroyd Jarralt. He carried a slender poker, tapping it against one boot as he walked. At his heels Willer, bloated and shining with triumph. And behind him came two guards, manacles dangling from their fists. Ox Bunder and Treev Lallard, casual darts and drinking mates down at the Goose.

He felt the blood drain from his face, leaving him dizzy and sick, and stepped unsteadily backwards. "Pellen? What's goin' on?"

Ignoring him, Orrick looked at Jarralt. Jarralt nodded. Orrick unrolled the scroll and began to read.

"*Insofar as he has been apprehended in the midst of a blasphemous and criminal act, with witness unimpeachable, and insofar as this act is named the breaking of Barl's First Law: I, King Gar the First, Weather Worker of Lur, hereby condemn Asher of Restharven to lawful death.*"

Numbly disbelieving, he let the words wash over him like so much salty water. "*...suspicion of baleful influence upon his king...instigation of Olken conspiracy to usurp the throne...Furthermore, let it*

be known that said criminal Asher of Restharven has acted in a fash-
ion suggestive of further miscreancy...authorised to question by
whatever means necessary..."

Orrick stopped reading. Confused, Asher stared. "No. That ain't
right. Gar wouldn't—that ain't right! It's a forgery! Jarralt—"

Orrick stepped forward and flattened the parchment against the
cell bars. "*It is no forgery.*" His voice was harsh with rage and pain.
"Or don't you recognise the signature? The seal?"

They were Gar's.

"So what?" Asher said, starting to shake. "That don't prove nowt.
Gar wouldn't abandon me like this, make up that pack of lies about
conspiracies and usurping. This is Jarralt's bloody bastardry! Gar
would *never*—"

"That's *enough*, Asher!" Orrick shouted, snatching back the proclamation. "His Majesty has renounced you. It's over."

Conroyd Jarralt cleared his throat. "Well...not quite, Captain.
Before death comes discomfort. Unless of course Asher would like to
reveal here and now the names of those who helped him?"

"Nobody helped me," he said. "There was nowt to help with!
There ain't no conspiracy!"

"The king says there is," said Conroyd Jarralt. "And that's good
enough for me. Guards?"

The cell door was unlocked. Bunder and Lallard entered. Shackled
him with the manacles, fixed the chains to the sides of the cell and
stretched him out like a scarecrow in a field.

"Excellent," said Jarralt. "Now leave us."

"What about a trial?" demanded Asher as the outer door banged shut.
Already his shoulders were burning. He saw Willer step closer to the cage,
eyes alight with eagerness. "Don't I get a trial? Timon Spake got a trial!"

"You're not Timon Spake," said Jarralt. "The king himself has cor-
roborated your confession and condemned you out of hand."

"He wouldn't! He *promised*."

Jarralt ignored him. Instead turned to Orrick. "Captain, it's likely
this traitor's co-conspirators will be found amongst his intimate
acquaintances. Seek them out and arrest them quietly before they
have a chance to flee justice."

Dathne. Asher choked back a cry of protest. *No.* Oh, to be able to
warn her. There'd be a way with magic, if only he knew what it was.

Bloody magic. It had to be good for more than causing trouble.

Orrick was nodding. "Yes, my lord."

"Willer?"

"My lord?"

"Assist Captain Orrick. You'll know best who to look for and where they can be found."

Willer's disappointment was almost comical. "My lord? I wanted to stay, to assist you in—"

"*Willer.*"

Cringing, the slug retreated. "Yes, my lord. Of course, my lord."

"And Willer? Captain? One last thing." With the snap of his fingers and a softly spoken word, Jarralt froze Orrick and the slug where they stood. "Attend. Asher was apprehended attempting magic, not performing it. There is no power in him. This is what you know and will remember."

"That's a lie," said Asher. The blankness in Pellen Orrick's face made him feel sick. It was as though the man's soul had been wiped away. Willer's too... if the little turd possessed one. "I can do magic. I'd bloody kill you with it if I could!"

The look in Jarralt's eyes was frightening. "You couldn't. But in the short time remaining to you, dare hint to anyone that you could try and I'll kill them. Their families, too. Is that clear?"

Nauseous, believing him absolutely, Asher nodded. "Aye."

"Good." With another snap of his fingers, Jarralt released his frozen victims. "Carry out your orders then. And see to it I am not disturbed hereafter, Captain."

Orrick bowed. Seemingly he'd taken no harm from whatever Jarralt had done. "My lord." Without a backward glance he left the cell, a subdued Willer at his heels.

Asher watched Jarralt pass his hand before the outer cell door. Saw the air shiver blackly. Felt a brief pressure against his chest. Jarralt turned. Smiled. Approached.

"Alone at last."

Asher felt his lungs hitch. "Gar never signed that proclamation."

Lounging in the open cell door, Jarralt raised his eyebrows. "Of course he did."

"No. You faked it. You—"

"*Asher.*" Jarralt's smile twisted into something more complicated. "He signed it."

Asher believed him. For a moment he couldn't breathe at all. Rage...grief...terror...his heart was barely beating.

"You know I did this on my own," he protested. "You know there ain't a conspiracy. You were inside my head. You know *everything.*"

Jarralt raised the poker and eyed its slender strength. "True."

"Then why—"

"Because I want to. Because your simple axe death will not satisfy. You interfered, little Olken, and I brook no interference. So I'm going to punish you...the good, old-fashioned way."

There was sweat rolling down his back. His face. Asher blinked the stinging saltwater from his eyes. There was something...different about Conroyd Jarralt. He'd always been a smug bastard. Impatient. Contemptuous. Superior. Utterly unlikeable. But now he was something else. Something more. It rolled off him in thick stinking waves. Blood-curdling, stomach-churning...

Evil.

"Gar was right about you," he whispered. "Borne, too. You're bad. Rotten bad, all the way through. You can't hide it any more. And when your Doranen friends see the truth of you, they'll not let you keep your stolen crown. This kingdom'll tear apart, Jarralt. It'll die, and you'll have killed it. Is that what you want?"

"Yes. Now save your breath," Jarralt advised him kindly. "You'll need it for screaming. And when you're done with screaming—after I've reduced your throat to a raw and bloody wasteland—Orrick and his men will take you to the centre of the City Square, where you'll be chained in a cage for all the world to see and spit upon. And at midnight on Barl's Day next, a suitably dramatic moment you'll agree, before as large a crowd as can be contrived, your head will be hacked from your shoulders, your body will be fed to the swine, the swine shall be butchered and fed to the dogs, and the dogs will be shot dead with arrows."

Languid and unexcited, Jarralt strolled into the cell. Spoke a single, knife-edged word. The poker's brass tip caught fire. In his pale ice eyes pleasure flickered, and something else. Something dark and dangerous and soaked in blood. He smiled. Touched.

Asher's world disappeared in a scarlet sheet of flame.

CHAPTER TWENTY-THREE

With a small self-satisfied sigh Darran covered His Ma—His Highness's lunch tray with a damask napkin. The prince's silence since Lord Jarralt's abrupt departure and his own unkind ejection from the library had been absolute and ominous. Luncheon gave him the excuse he needed to make sure everything was all right.

Well. As all right as it could be, given recent appalling developments.

With a last look about the kitchen he picked up the tray and headed for the door. It was perhaps a good thing Mistress Hemshaw had been dismissed; if she could see the place now, after his distracted efforts at cooking, she'd have gone into strong hysterics.

He was tempted to go into strong hysterics himself.

How empty the Tower felt with all its people forcibly removed. Aching with sorrow and regrets he climbed stair by silent stair up to Gar's suite of apartments. Passing by Asher's floor, he shuddered. Closed his mind to a calamity of images and kept on climbing.

The prince was still in his library, sitting in the armchair he'd shifted to face the uncurtained window.

"I've brought you some luncheon, sir," Darran said, standing just inside the doorway.

"I'm not hungry."

"Hungry or not, you should eat," he replied, forcing his voice to a cheerful chiding. Hesitantly, he entered the room. "If you fall ill it'll be Pother Nix's potions you'll be swallowing, and while my cooking isn't perfect I can promise you it does taste better than that."

"Leave it on the desk then," said Gar. His voice sounded dull. Lacklustre. His left hand was just visible, dangling over the arm of the chair. It looked dead.

Darran frowned, and shook his head even though the prince couldn't see him. "Now, sir, you don't want it to get cold."

"I said *leave it on the desk!*" Gar shouted, and flung himself out of the chair. A sapphire-studded dagger dangled from the fingers of his right hand and his eyes were frightening.

Darran stepped back, his grip on the lunch tray tight enough to hurt. "Sir, the weapon isn't necessary. I assure you the chicken is quite deceased. I roasted it myself."

With a roar of rage Gar threw the dagger across the room. It struck the doorjamb and stuck there, quivering. "I care naught for your chicken, old man! Take it away! And if you can't do as I tell you, don't come here again!"

He would *not* look at the dagger. Instead he put down the tray on the nearest flat surface and approached his prince. "Enough, sir," he said, hands raised palm out like a man reasoning with madness. "You're going to hurt yourself."

Gar laughed. "Hurt myself? You old fool, I never hurt myself! Only other people! My parents—my sister—Durm—yes, he's dead now too." He groaned, and dropped slowly to the floor. "Asher..."

Darran knelt beside him, deaf to complaining muscles and creaking bones. "You're talking nonsense. You didn't cause the accident that killed your family and our poor Master Magician, Barl rest him."

"How can I be certain?" demanded Gar. "I don't remember what happened! It might have been me, Darran. It might have been my damned capricious magic. No physical agency for the accident was ever discovered, was it? And clearly my power was never right. It was flawed, as I am flawed. If I wasn't I'd still possess it. I'd still be the Weather Worker and Asher would... Barl's *tits*, Darran. I swore I'd protect him, I swore he'd be safe, and instead I signed his death warrant. I betrayed the only friend I've ever known, a man who saved my life, who tried to save my kingdom when I couldn't. I am *pathetic. Disgusting.* I wonder how you can bear to be in the same room with me."

Distressed by his distress and closing his ears to the blasphemy, he seized Gar's hand and held on tight. "Don't say such things, sir!"

"Why not? They're true. So what if Conroyd threatened me? I should've found a way to defeat him. To save Asher!"

He stared. Gar's hand felt so cold. *He* felt so cold. "Lord Jarralt threatened you? How? Why?"

Gar pulled his hand free and let himself sag against the armchair. "It doesn't matter. What matters is I've given our kingdom to that man. Handed it over without a fight. My father would be so disappointed..."

"No, sir! *No*," he said fiercely. "That's not true. Your father loved you and was proud of you every day of his life. He's proud now, I'm certain of it, as I am proud. And nor is it true that Asher is your only friend. *I* am your friend, sir, and will remain so till the day I die."

Gar looked at him. Tried to smile, and miserably failed. "Then in the name of all that's merciful, Darran," he whispered, *"leave me alone."*

He sighed. Clambered to his feet, frowning. "If I do, sir, will you promise me first that you'll eat?"

"I could," said Gar. "But my promises are a figment, Darran. Don't you know that yet? I shed promises the way a dog sheds fleas."

"And *that's* not true either!"

Now Gar stood, only to slump on the arm of his chair. As though standing were a task beyond his strength. "Isn't it? Ask Asher."

He sniffed. "I don't consort with criminals."

"He's not a criminal. He's a sacrifice."

"But he's arrested! Why would he be arrested if he's not a—"

"Darran..." Gar hesitated. Examined the carpet. "If I tell you what's happened, why I'm deposed and the Tower emptied, Asher condemned—"

"Oh, I wish you would, sir! I can't make head or tail of anything!"

Now the prince looked up. His face was solemn, his gaze intent. "You can never repeat it. Lives will depend on your silence. Not just yours and mine, but those of every Olken in the kingdom. Do you understand?"

Darran straightened. Let a little of his affronted pride show. "I have spent the best part of my life in royal service, sir. I think I know the meaning of discretion."

Faint colour washed into Gar's pale cheeks. "Of course you do. Forgive me."

"Certainly. Now please, sir. *Tell* me."

By the time the prince finished Darran knew the world he'd lived in was gone forever, or perhaps had never existed. He groped his way to the library's other chair and sat down.

"Barl have mercy," he whispered. "This is all my fault."

The prince stared. "Your fault?"

Hot with shame, he couldn't look at Gar. Stared instead at his manicured fingernails and longed hopelessly to be anywhere else in Lur, confessing anything but this. "You see...I always encouraged Willer in his antipathy towards Asher. Allowed him to know the depths of my own disliking. For a whole year, longer, we carped and criticised and complained of his existence to each other. And then, after you asked Asher and me to work together for the good of the kingdom, I failed to take Willer into my confidence or explain my change in attitude. Instead I reproved him for bad behaviour. When you became king I think Willer was expecting some kind of promotion. But it didn't come—and then I was so busy—oh, sir. Willer never would've turned to Lord Jarralt, never would've spied for him, if I'd handled the matter with greater tact!"

After a long silence Gar sighed. "You don't know that. I don't know that. And it hardly matters now. If it's any consolation, Darran, I don't blame you. I think Willer and Asher would've been enemies regardless. They're cut from different cloths."

Subdued, Darran folded his hands in his lap. "You're very generous, sir." He cleared his throat. "Is there nothing you can do for Asher?"

"No," Gar said tiredly. "I wish there was. I'd die in his place if Jarralt would let me. But the kingdom comes first, and your people must be protected. If Willer hadn't been set to spy on him—if our mad plan hadn't been discovered—we might have weathered this storm. Found a way to calmer waters, or a cure for my affliction. But it's too late now. I can't save Asher. I can't even save myself."

Darran shook his head. "It's beyond all comprehension sir. That an Olken could *do* such things..."

"I know," said Gar. "And now you must forget what I've told you. I should've held my tongue. Not burdened you with the truth. It's just—" His voice cracked. "I don't want him to die without another person knowing the good he tried to do. Knowing that no matter what is said of him once he's gone, he was *never* a traitor."

Darran moistened dry lips. "Yes, sir. I understand. It's been a shock, I won't deny that... but I'm glad you confided in me."

"Are you?" The prince shook his head. "Let's hope that doesn't change."

"It won't," he promised. "Sir... this is all indeed a tragedy, but nothing can be gained or changed by you making yourself ill. Please. Won't you eat?"

Gar sighed. "I'll try. But I make no guarantees, Darran. I've a speech to write and the thought of it makes me retch. Leave me be, and I'll do my best with your damned chicken."

"Yes, sir," he said, his heart all in pieces, and left the prince alone.

The palace's Great Assembly Hall was humming with a score of different conversations as Morg made his eloquent entrance, cripple in tow, a few minutes before two o'clock. Once passed through the hall's open double doors he paused, considering the scene before them. Filling the left-hand pews were Doranen lords and ladies of varying talents and influence, who fondly imagined that a seat on the General Council equated with having some sort of power. He smothered a smile; ignorance could be such a comfort. Clustered together, as usual, in the pew closest to the speaker's chair were Nole Daltrie, Gord Hafar and Tobe Boqur: Jarralt's deluded friends. How disappointed they'd be to learn they weren't the kingdom's next Privy Council.

Gord saw him and raised a discreet hand in acknowledgement. Noticing, Nole and Tobe followed suit. He nodded back, briefly smiling.

The hall's right-hand pews were the province of the Olken guild meisters and mistresses. According to Jarralt's plundered memories they were normally a noisy crowd, but this afternoon they sat in silence or conversed in low, uneasy voices. Their cattle faces were tight with worry, their eyes shadowed, darting uneasy looks across the hall at their Doranen betters. They were magickless, but not quite stupid. Word of loutish Asher's arrest had clearly spread. Dealing a cruel blow to their pretensions and raising a host of fears.

They were right to be afraid.

Directly opposite the hall's entrance was the speaker's chair and behind that the specially reserved seats for the king and his Privy Council, placed on a raised dais. How bare it looked now, with only one other chair occupied. No Borne. No Durm. Only Holze, who'd arrived earlier and sat now in silence, his bare head bowed in prayer or sleep.

Such a reduction of power. A thinning of the ranks. But they'd get no fatter. King Morg would have no Privy Council, no chorus of fools. His rule would be absolute. No dissenting opinions, no bleating naysayers. Now...and once the Wall was fallen. One king. One voice. It was the only sure way to rule. Six hundred years of absolute mastery had shown him that.

Jarralt's other dear friend, Payne Sorvold, the current Council Speaker, caught their arrival and met them halfway across the hall's central floor space. "Your Majesty. Conroyd. Welcome."

The cripple nodded. "Lord Sorvold."

"Forgive me, sir, but we had not expected you. It was Lord Jarralt here who requested this extraordinary—"

"I know. I desire a brief word with the Council," said the cripple. "Before you attend to...other business."

"Certainly, Your Majesty. Conroyd, if I might ask for an inkling of the matter you wished to raise, then—"

"Once His Majesty has had his say," Morg explained, gently smiling, "I think you'll find the other business self-explanatory."

Sorvold's pale green eyes narrowed and his thin lips pursed. "Indeed? All respect, but as Speaker I—"

"Should practise silence," he said.

Flushed, taken aback, Sorvold turned to the cripple. "Your Majesty, if I might have a brief word in private?"

"You may not," said Morg before the cripple could answer. "Call the Council to attention, Payne. We are all busy men."

As Sorvold withdrew, offended, the cripple said, "I'll thank you not to speak for me just yet. I'm still king here, Conroyd."

He smiled. "So jealous of your dwindling moments, little runtling?"

Leaving the cripple to make his way to the speaker's dais, Morg joined Holze. The Barlsman stirred at his arrival and sat up. His face was wan. Worn. Doubtless he'd come here direct from overseeing the disposition of dead Durm's body. There was grief in his eyes and in the way his hands clasped each other tightly in his lap. Such a wasteful emotion.

"Conroyd."

"Efrim."

Just below them, Sorvold picked up his little hammer and tapped it on the Assembly Bell. All around the hall surreptitious conversations ceased. Those standing assumed their seats. The air of restrained dread, of watchful curiosity, intensified.

With silence achieved, Sorvold sounded the Assembly Bell a further three times. Nodded to the young woman acting as secretary, so she might trigger the recording spell for the meeting's minutes, then cleared his throat.

"With the authority vested in me as Speaker of the Assembly I declare this meeting open. May Barl's mercy attend us, her wisdom guide us, her strength sustain us. All silence, please, as His Majesty now addresses this august body."

"Thank you, Lord Sorvold," said the cripple. His face too was wan, thoroughly bleached by the black tunic he continued to wear in honour of those dead fools, his family, and the thankfully abandoned Durm. "My good councillors, I appear before you today with a heavy heart, bearing news I know you will not welcome, as I do not welcome it. But I trust in your restraint and acceptance of Barl's will... no matter how hard acceptance may be."

Well, he certainly had their attention. Long denied a good piece of theatre, Morg sat back and prepared to enjoy himself.

"Firstly," continued the cripple, his hands resting before him on the speaker's lectern, "it is my sad duty to inform you that Master Magician Durm has passed from life and into Barl's mercy. I ask now for a minute's silence in honour of his greatness and a life spent in service of our kingdom."

The minute passed, tedious slow.

"Thank you," said the cripple. "Of his life and dedication, more shall be said in due course. Secondly, I must now tell you that due to irreparable health concerns I forthwith abdicate our kingdom's throne and withdraw from public life indefinitely. Be it known I have chosen my lawful heir and successor, Lur's new king and Weather Worker, and name him Lord Conroyd Jarralt."

Sensation. Cries. Lamentations. Shock, and a rising furore of voices both Doranen and Olken crying, "No! No! We do not accept this! You are our king!"

The cripple let them continue unchecked for a short time, then nodded at Sorvold, who again hammered his little bell. Gradually the uproar subsided.

"Good people," said the cripple, hands raised in supplication. "I can no longer serve you as your king. The magic that so lately flowered in my breast has withered and died. In memory of the love you bore my late and so lamented father—that you bear me, in his memory—I beg you to accept this decision without remonstrance and instead devote your loyalty to King Conroyd the First. And if anyone here should think to dally with notions of challenging his accession, be warned. It is my right and duty to name an heir and I have done so. A second schism hurts all and helps none. If you truly love me, be satisfied with my decision...and Barl's mercy on us all."

More buzzing. Tears, and consternation.

"Lastly," the former king said, raising his voice above the din, "I would touch upon the matter of my Olken Administrator."

And silence fell like the blade of an axe.

"As many of you doubtless know, Asher is arrested for crimes against Barl and this kingdom and soon will pay the price in full. I think I need not say how grieved I am. What I will say is this: that no matter how heinous they might be, the actions of one Olken must *never* be counted the actions of all. To do so would be a gross injustice and a violation of Barl's intentions in this land. Guard against revenge and retribution, my lords, my ladies and dear gentlefolk. Guard against it at the peril of your souls. I know King Conroyd will."

A ripple of whispers through the watching Olken. There were tears in the cripple's eyes now, leaking onto his cheeks. His hands were unsteady on the speaker's lectern.

"I hope you know how I have loved you," he added, his voice breaking. "Please believe that my actions today spring from that true devotion. Better that I should die than any harm come to you and yours through me. Barl bless you all and guide King Conroyd to wisdom and mercy."

One of the Olken leapt to his feet. "Barl's blessing on you, sir! Barl's blessing on Prince Gar!"

The cry was taken up at once, shouted by Olken and Doranen alike. Morg watched, amused, as all the councillors leapt to their expensively shod feet and roared their acclaim as Gar made his way towards the hall's exit. Beside him, Holze said grudgingly, "Well. He managed that quite acceptably."

He patted the cleric's arm. "Dear Efrim. Do you think so?" And left the fool staring as he descended to the floor of the hall, meeting the cripple by the large double doors. "Thin ice, runtling," he murmured. "Very thin ice."

"I'm glad you recognise your danger, Conroyd," said the cripple. "Are you a historian, sir? If not, I suggest you pick up a book. The past is peopled with unwise individuals who forgot that brute force leads to nothing but defeat. The name 'Morg' springs to mind."

Startled, he stared more closely at the runt. "And what do you know of Morg, cripple?"

Gar shrugged. "Only what any half-intelligent person knows. That he was a small man who tried to make himself larger with violence... and failed. I hope you learn from his example, for your sake."

He laughed. Laughed until tears pricked his borrowed eyes, then patted Gar sharply on the cheek. "The carriage is waiting. Return to your Tower, boy. When I want you again, be sure I'll send a lackey. And mind you remember the terms of your freedom, for I will not hesitate to change them. Defy me and I'll place guards at all your doors and grievously punish those who seek to aid you."

For long moments the cripple stared at him. Then he turned his back and left. Morg watched him for a moment, still vastly amused, then forgot him. Basked instead in the music of obedience and acclaim soaring upwards to the hall's distant rafters.

"Hail our King Conroyd! Hail our King Conroyd! Barl bless our King Conroyd, Weather Worker of Lur!"

Their desperate pleasure at his ascension floated him all the way to the dais the cripple had just vacated for the last time. Listening to their eager cries he felt a shrivelling contempt. They were all cattle, these peasants and their overlords. There wasn't a man among them worthy of anything but slaughter.

Standing before them, hands folded on the lectern, he let his gaze roam their animal faces as they continued to shout and stamp. Cattle? No. Even cattle had a semblance of purpose. The Olken and Doranen of this pallid kingdom were sheep. Willing to follow anyone who could promise them peace and an endless procession of magical days. It made him ill to see it. That a race as majestic and proud as the Doranen should come to *this*? This bleating, following, milling flock.

Whatever strength Barl's escapees had possessed it was bled to nothing here in their descendants. Their descendants were paper Doranen... destined all to burn.

He unfolded his hands and held them up in modest appeal. "Good people, good people, I beg you: enough!"

Ragged silence fell. Those fools who'd leapt to their feet resumed their seats. Like penned sheep who heard the rattle of the gate unlocking, they stared and waited, hoping for food.

"My dear councillors," he said, infusing his voice with sorrow. "These are dark days indeed. Our beloved kingdom has come to a pretty pass. Brought to the brink of destruction by the actions of one misguided man. I know—" He raised one hand in warning. "You loved your former king. Love him still as a prince and the sad representative of a fallen house. I commend your love, my subjects. I do. Your willingness to overlook his profound errors of judgement tells me all I need to know of your hearts. Good hearts. Stout hearts. But not, perhaps, as wise as Barl might wish them to be."

A muttering now, and a flurry of exchanged glances. He waited a moment then rode roughshod over their objections.

"Blind devotion is a dangerous thing," he told them. "It was blind devotion that handed power to the traitor, Asher, furnishing him with the means to dabble in forbidden magic." Another pause, as a gasp rippled its way through the flock. "Only Barl knows the true intent of his black, unloving heart. Only Barl knows what damage he has wrought in the paradise she died to create."

Nole Daltrie, always reliable, stood and cried out: "What are you saying, Conr— Your Majesty? Do you think the kingdom's in danger?"

"The kingdom was in danger from the day Gar elevated that stinking fisherman to heights he didn't deserve," he replied. Conroyd's belief was fervently and passionately felt. Shared. "Now I fear we face more than mere danger. I fear we face catastrophe."

Not muttering now but cries of consternation. Daltrie exchanged horrified looks with the rest of Conroyd's councillor friends. "Do you say the Wall itself is in jeopardy?"

The thought was so appalling it froze their voices in their throats. Stricken, Daltrie sank back slowly to his seat.

Morg nodded. "Hard as I find it to say so, Lord Daltrie, yes. I fear it might well be."

"*No!*" they shouted, thawed by terror. "*Save us!*" they begged him with tears in their eyes.

Holze stood, uninvited, and raised his voice above the lamentations. "Councillors, control yourselves! In Blessed Barl's name, I command you, have faith!" As the noise subsided, he continued. "Barl will not let her Wall be defeated. Has she not delivered us from Asher's evil and given us into the care of King Conroyd, in whom her power resides? Have faith, I tell you. And be guided by His Majesty."

Ah, Efrim. Barl-sodden, but useful. Morg nodded to the cleric then turned back to the assembled councillors. "I am your king," he said quietly as Holze sat down. "Of course I will save you. But I fear it won't be easy, Thanks to Asher's meddling, the balance of magical power in the kingdom is gravely disturbed. How badly the Wall is affected I don't yet know...but we must face the bitter truth. It is affected."

The Olken councillors were moaning. Covering their faces with trembling hands and rocking on their haunches. Every Doranen eye was upon them, and the looks were far from friendly.

"In his lust for a power that was never meant for him, Asher has endangered the life of every soul in this kingdom," said Morg. Letting his words bite now, like the tip of a lash. "And every Olken who encouraged him to think he was more than an Olken bears a share of his guilt. Fear not—I will not punish the undeserving. But I tell you here and now, guild meisters and mistresses of Lur: look hard at your people. Examine their behaviours. For henceforth I hold you accountable, and will see you answer for their sins."

Not a sound from the Olken. And if any one of them had harboured some lingering affection for Asher, the looks on their faces told him it was stone dead now. He hid a smile.

Holze said, "And what of the Wall, Your Majesty? What of the Weather Working?"

"History shows us we have a period of grace," he replied. "Some short time to live without Weather Working before we are undone. Therefore I shall withdraw from the public eye, that I might take into myself the Weather Magics and study how best to apply them. To undo the damage Asher has wreaked and avert a dire disaster."

Now it was Payne Sorvold who spoke. "You'll require a Master Magician... Your Majesty."

He nodded. "I shall appoint Durm's successor once this crisis is past, Lord Sorvold. For now all I need to help me restore our beloved kingdom is contained in his books and journals. Have no fear, sir. I shall prevail."

Sorvold nodded. "Yes, Your Majesty. And what of Your Majesty's Privy Council?"

He felt his expression harden. "It too must wait until the crisis is past." He unpinned his gaze from Sorvold's frowning face and swept it around the hall. "Good people, do you not yet understand? By the merest whisper have we escaped a disaster of Asher's making. Life as once we knew it has changed. Perhaps forever. Listen, now, as I explain more fully what I mean..."

Carted back to the Tower like so much lumber, Gar stifled a groan when he saw Darran waiting for him on his palatial prison's front steps. Even dredged up a smile as the old man bowed and insisted on opening the carriage door for him. The gesture came hard, though. Any brief satisfaction he'd felt in defying Conroyd before the General Council, of warning him to leave the Olken alone, had faded. All he felt now was ill, and tired, and desperately sad.

"Well, old friend, it's done," he said, as Conroyd's carriage rattled away. "I am again Prince Gar the Magickless."

There were tears in Darran's eyes. "Yes, sir."

He willed his own eyes to stay dry. Forced his voice to remain steady and strong. "It's for the best. What can any of this be but Barl's will, after all? My magic is gone, and that's hardly Conroyd's fault. In truth, none of this is his fault. I may hate him, but I can't blame him. At least not for being the best remaining magician in the kingdom."

"No, sir."

"I'm going to the stables now. To say goodbye to the horses before—"

Darran touched his sleeve. "I'm so sorry, sir. They're already gone. Men from the Livestock Guild. I couldn't stop them, they had written orders from Lord Ja—from the king. It was all I could do to hide the little donkey. If we keep it in a pasture down the back no one will know we have it. I just thought...well...it may come in useful. As a lawn mower, if nothing else."

Poor Darran. He looked so stricken, so brimful of guilt. "It's all right," Gar said gently. "Of course you couldn't stop them." *Ballodair. Oh, Ballodair.* "Well, if there's no point visiting the stables I'll go for a walk instead. Don't fret if I'm gone for some time, Darran. I have a lot to think about."

"Yes, sir," said Darran. And, as Gar turned away, said, "Sir?"

Gar looked back. "Yes?"

"Be careful. Don't...walk too far. Don't give that man an excuse to take anything else."

He smiled. "What is there left for him to take, Darran?"

Darran stepped closer, his face screwed up with pain and trepidation. "Your life."

"My *life*?" He laughed. "Ah yes. My life. Do you know something, Darran? I'm beginning to think he can have it, and welcome."

"*Sir!*"

Relenting, he patted the old man's shoulder. "It's all right," he said, and started to back away. "I was joking."

Darran shook a finger at him, just as he used to when he worked at the palace and was scolding a younger, happier Gar. "Really? Well, as jokes go it wasn't the least bit funny!"

Turning his back on Darran's disapproval he walked away and kept on walking, until his family's crypt appeared among the trees. Quite possibly he was breaking Conroyd's rules by coming this far but he didn't care. If Conroyd thought to keep him from his family he was very much mistaken.

As ever, the crypt was cool. Dark. Fumbling for lantern and matches, skinning his knuckles, he tried to forget that once light had been his for the asking.

The amplified candlelight cast attenuated shadows up the walls and across the faces of his family. He kissed his father, and his mother. Tickled his sister's feet. Arranged himself uncomfortably on the floor.

"I'm sorry," he said into the silence. "I'd have come sooner but...a lot has happened since you left."

His mother whispered: *That's all right, dear. You're a busy man.*

"Not as busy as you might think," he replied. "Father, I have a confession. I've lost the two best things you ever gave me: your crown and your horse. It seems you raised a careless son."

A father's disappointment. *Very. Can't you get them back again?*

Of course he can't. He's useless. A sister's angry scorn.

"I'm sorry," he repeated. "I did the best I could. Unfortunately my best proved inadequate to the task."

Silence. Were they really speaking, or was his mind at last unhinged? And if it was...did it even matter?

Typical, he heard Fane sneer. *Whinge, moan, sigh. It's a wonder you didn't die years ago, drowned in a butt of self-pity. Don't just sit there, idiot. Do something.*

Even imagined, the sharp words stung. He grabbed hold of his sister's stone foot and hauled himself upright. "Do *what*?" he demanded of her. "I am powerless. Exiled in my own City. Discarded, irrelevant and alone. What would *you* do, if you were me?"

The answer came not in words but as a spearing shaft of memory. Of intent, abandoned.

Barl's diary. If Durm was right, their only hope. How or why, he had no idea. But he trusted Durm. He had to. He had nowhere else to turn.

Damn it, how could he have *forgotten*? He had to find that diary. Had to go back to the Tower, now, and search Durm's books again before Conroyd discovered their removal and took them away. No matter he'd searched the collection twice, without luck. The diary *had* to be there. Cunningly hidden, as was Durm's devious habit.

Please, Barl, let me find it. Show me a way out of this disaster.

He dropped a grateful kiss on his sister's cold stone cheek and ran all the way back to the Tower.

CHAPTER TWENTY-FOUR

Blistered and weary, the knapsack on her back as heavy as an anvil, Dathne trudged along the empty road that led to the Black Woods. To Veira and her village, beating at their timber heart. There was dust on her face, turned streakily to mud by infrequent, unhelpful tears. She was chilled, she was hungry, she was eaten with despair. The sun had set two hours earlier, and weak moonlight was her only guide. She'd tripped and stumbled a dozen times, lost her footing completely and crashed to the roadway once. Her scraped knees and elbows stung viciously; her tired mind was one vast and aching bruise.

Asher. Asher. Asher.

She hardly recognised herself, so diminished felt her spirit. Misery was a crushing weight, compressing her bones to chalk. She never knew she could feel so small.

Asher.

That catastrophe seemed worse even than the now unstoppable onslaught of the Final Days. Asher was flesh and blood to her, he was laughter and whispers and callused fingers, touching. Pleasure like magic coursing through her veins. The Final Days were unimaginable. For all her frightened dreaming, she couldn't seem to make them real. But Asher was real. Asher was arrested. And unless some miracle intervened, Asher was dead...along with any hope for the kingdom's future.

The thought knifed pain through her whole body, so swift and severe she couldn't walk. Gasping, hurting, she braced her hands upon her thighs and waited for the torment to ease. A kind of wild rushing wind stormed through her mind, blotting out thought, obliterating memory.

She welcomed it.

Gradually the pain eased and reason returned. She straightened, inch by hesitant inch. The night stretched for miles around her, inhabited by stars, and trees, and small rustling creatures.

Then, carrying keenly on the thin cold air, new sounds. Horse-shoes ringing hollow on hard-packed clay, slowing from a brisk jog to a cautious walk. A wooden creak of turning wheels. Approaching round the bend ahead, a looming shape framed in dancing torchlight.

Heart pounding, she waited for the cart to reach her. Watched as the shaggy brown pony pulling it slowed, slowed then stopped in a puffing cloud of breath. She looked up into the hooded, mysterious face of the person holding the pony's reins.

Gnarled hands pushed the hood back onto rounded, slumping shoulders. "Dathne."

She nodded. Tried to smile. "Veira."

"Well, child," the old woman said, and sniffed. "If you were a few years younger and my joints a little less creaky I'd fling your skirts up over your head and put you over my knees for this."

Dathne stared at her, speechless.

In the torchlight Veira's face leapt and flickered with shadows. "But you're a young woman, and I'm an old one, and I don't suppose a pad-dling would make either of us feel any better. So don't just stand there gawking. Come up here beside me and let's get you home to bed."

They travelled in awkward silence for nearly three hours, along the narrow road that drew them deep into the Black Woods like a crooked, beckoning finger. At first the trees grew thinly, with spindly trunks and lacy foliage, but the further the pony ambled them into the gloom-ridden forest the more robust and vigorous the djelbas, honey-pines and weeping noras became. The air grew close and still as more and more of the star-strewn sky disappeared from view. Even though she was miles closer now to Barl's Wall and the mountains that anchored it, its golden glow was reduced to a smeary shadow. Anyone living within this sea of trees could easily forget the Wall existed.

She wished she could.

Her nose was tickled by the scent of rich rotting mulch. She caught the sound of trickling water somewhere to the left. Keeping herself distracted she let her gaze roam the encroaching forest as it rolled along beside her. Caught sight of a glowing orange fungus on a fallen tree trunk—newt-eye, good for enhancing concentration—and wished she could ask Veira to stop the cart. Newt-eye was hard to come by in the countryside round the City.

The City. Her home for six long years, but now a place of danger she could never visit again. At least not until...and always assuming there was anything left to visit afterwards. Was her absence noticed yet? Had anyone raised the alarm? Were they hunting for her even now? Well, let them hunt. Let them turn the City upside down. They'd find no clue to help them. No guiding trail of breadcrumbs. She'd escaped. She was safe.

She'd abandoned Asher behind her.

The passing forest blurred and she rubbed a hand across her face. If Veira saw it she didn't say so. All her attention was on the pony and the winding road ahead. Dathne pulled her coat more tightly round her ribs, wondering what would happen to her bookshop, that convenient mask she'd come to love, despite herself. And all her things, in her tiny rooms above it. Obeying Veira's command she'd brought with her only the items that might raise suspicion. Her Circle Stone. Her orris root, the tanal leaf, other herbs and simples not generally found in an Olken pantry. A few clothes, too, for necessity. A dragonfly in amber, gifted to her from Asher the first Grand Barl's Day after his arrival in Dorana.

She felt her heart hitch, and fisted her fingers in her lap. She *would not* think of Asher.

Beside her, Veira cleared her throat. "'Nother half-hour and we'll be there, near enough," she said.

Dathne nodded. "Good."

It was strange to hear the old woman's voice out loud, a sweet and solid sound, after so long with nothing but Circle Stone communication, mind to mind. Even seeing her was a shock. In the link she'd seemed younger. Smoother. Less... wrinkled.

Aware of the scrutiny, Veira chuckled breathily and glanced at her sidelong. "Told you I weren't no oil painting, child."

She felt her cheeks heat. "I'm sorry, I didn't mean to be rude, I—" Her fingernails were close to drawing blood, so tightly were they clenched against her palms. "I'm sorry." And not just for staring. She was sorry for everything.

"I know," said Veira, and patted her on one blanketed knee.

She blinked her vision clear. "You warned Matt all right? He's safe?"

"As safe as any of us," said Veira.

"I handled that badly," she whispered, pinning her fists between her knees. *The look on his face, as she sided with Asher...* "I handled it all badly. I've no business being part of the Circle. Prophecy is falling to pieces and it's all my fault!"

In the flickering torchlight Veira's expression was a mystery. "You don't know that, child. Best not to run ahead of ourselves. This business ain't done with till the Wall's fallen down, and last time I looked it was still standing."

"Then we're not lost? The kingdom can still be saved? Asher won't—" She couldn't finish the sentence out loud. Didn't even dare complete the thought.

"I hope not," Veira said at last. "We'll do our best to save him. Though I fear it will come at a terrible cost."

"You have a plan?"

Another long silence.

"I have an inkling of a possibility," said Veira without looking at her. "I'll not be speaking of it yet. I've others to consult, and hard thinking to do first."

And that sounded less than encouraging. Sounded frightening. Dangerous. Likely to fail. In Veira's comfortable voice, there tolled a premonition of sorrow.

She'd had enough sorrow for one day. "I can't imagine living in a forest," she said, staring at the branch-latticed sky.

Veira smiled, revealing crooked teeth. "I can't imagine living anywhere else. Not any more."

"Do you like it?"

"Well enough. A forest's cool. Quiet. And there's always fresh rabbit when the fancy takes me."

"Yes, but what do you *do*? How do you live?" In all the time she and Veira had known each other, she'd never once asked. Once, it hadn't seemed important.

"I'm a truffle hunter," said Veira. "Means nobody asks me why I live so far out from the village. Why I spend so much time alone with my pigs." A breathy chuckle. "Mind you, the pigs is more for company. I got easier ways of finding truffles than parading about the forest with a pig on a leash. Good listeners, pigs. Better than most people I know."

"And the other villagers? What do they do? Why would they choose to live in such isolation?"

Veira shrugged, and rattled the reins to keep the pony up to its bridle. "It's only isolated from the Doranen. The village is a happy, close-knit place. Lively. And there's a mort of things to do in the Black Woods, child. Berrying. Mushrooming. Trapping. Herbals and dye-plants. Sweetsap. Woodcarving. Clockmaking. Bees—some of this kingdom's finest honey comes from our bees, you know. Oh yes. The Black Woods are full of bounty for those who aren't afraid of the dark."

"Oh," she said, feeling ignorant. Feeling helpless. She should have brought some books to sell... "Well. I had no idea."

"No reason you should do, child," said Veira comfortably.

"Is the village large?"

"Large enough. A hundred and fourteen families, last count." Veira pointed ahead of them, to the right. "Over thataways, it is."

"And how will you account for me? I've always been told villagers are a curious lot. They'll want to know who I am, where I'm from..."

"No, they won't," said Veira. "I've done a tidy job of keeping myself a loner. Folks know me, but only as deep as I want 'em to, and only when I go to them. I discouraged visitors years ago." Clicking her tongue, she once more rattled the plump pony's reins. "Get on with you, Bessie. You ought to be smellin' home by now."

Not long after that they turned left onto a rutted grass-grown roadway. Followed it in silence, and at last reached Veira's thatched stone cottage all alone in the wooded vastness of the forest. Warm light glowed through a curtained front window. The night air smelled of jasmine and moonroses, the flowers' perfume mingling with the spicy sweet scent of honey-pine smoke drifting out of the cottage's chimney.

Veira eased the cart to a halt by the open front gate. "Bessie's bedroom's round the back. Get yourself inside, child, while I see the poor beast settled. Stir up the hob and put on the kettle like a good girl. I'm parched for some hot sweet tea."

Oh yes, yes, tea. Clasping blanket and knapsack Dathne clambered out of the wagon and made her unsteady way up the garden path. She felt stupid with tiredness. More than anything she wanted quiet, and somewhere to rest her aching head. Just as she reached the front door, it opened.

Matt. Tall. Frowning. Swallowing all the space in the small doorway. Here? In Veira's cottage? She felt the knapsack slip from her fingers. Heard a tinkling crunch as something broke inside it. Or did the sound come from inside her? She couldn't tell. Couldn't speak. Could only stare, and stare, and stare...

"Hello, Dathne," said Matt, unsmiling. "Welcome to the Black Woods."

When Asher groped his way back to reluctant consciousness he found himself in a different cage. This one was outside. On a cart in the middle of the City Square—just as Jarralt had promised. The straw beneath his huddled body was fouled and stinking. There were heavy iron manacles on his wrists and his ankles, connected by a short, heavy chain. The manacles' inner surfaces were rough and rusty. Chafing. The pain was small compared to the enormous hurting in the rest of his abused body. Jarralt had been thorough. And enthusiastic. *Bastard*. Who knew he'd wanted that damned King's Cup so bad, eh?

Pity I didn't just let the mongrel have it. Might've saved me a lot of grief.

It was dark. Late. Hovering glimfire splashed shadows and soft light. Standing at attention a few feet from the nearest corner of his cage, a poker-backed City Guard. If he'd wanted to he could've called the man's name out loud.

He didn't want to. Also as promised, his throat was raw and swollen. Only one thing kept him from surrendering to despair: they hadn't found Dathne. Orrick had returned to report his failure, refusing to look at Jarralt's bleeding, moaning victim hanging in his chains.

So. No Dathne, and no Matt either. It seemed that sulking out of sight somewhere after their quarrel had saved him.

Thwarted of more victims, Jarralt had been furious. Had returned to his vengeance with greater vigour. Asher shuddered, remembering. He would've died happily then, knowing she was safe—that they both were safe—but Jarralt knew to perfection how to hurt, and hurt, yet keep him on the wrong side of death's door.

He blinked, shivering, trying to clear his pain-blurred vision. Unfolded his arms and legs, needing to ease his cramped muscles. His putrid straw bed rustled, pressing against his filthy shirt and trousers, his burned and bloodied flesh. From somewhere quite close, a shout.

"He's awake! The blasphemous bastard's awake!"

He lifted his head. Four guards, not one. Four men who once had been his friends, matched to each corner of his cage. He strained to see past their blue and crimson uniforms. Slowly, achingly, the world swam into sharper focus. What he saw stopped his heart, or so it felt. Beyond the cage, beyond the guards, beyond the wavering circle of glimlight, a sullen shifting mass of silent faces.

The Olken of Dorana City had come to feast their eyes on the traitor.

Wincing, breathing harshly through pinched nostrils and gritted teeth, he made himself sit up, even though it hurt so much he thought he might vomit again. There were faces out there that he knew. Guild meisters he'd counselled. Guild members he'd helped. Turning his head, looking over his shoulder, he saw more friends. People he'd drunk ale with down at the Goose. People who'd laughed to see him. Thrown roses without thorns. Flirted. Flattered. Boasted that he knew them and smiled at his approach. Screamed his name as he'd travelled the road to Justice Hall. Who'd witnessed him sitting in judgement in that grand place and applauded as though he was their hero.

Nobody was applauding now. Now he wasn't anybody's hero.

"Filthy blasphemer!" somebody called from the crowd.

"Liar!"

"Traitor!"

Somebody threw something. An egg. It burst against the bars of the cage to drip stinking, rotten and slimy to the floor. The stench mixed with the reek of excrement and vomit, clogging his blood-caked nostrils, churning his stomach with acid and bile.

"I ain't!" he croaked, and felt the split skin of his face crack and ooze. "I ain't no more a traitor than you!"

As those in the crowd close enough to hear him burst into jeering laughter, the nearest guard turned and thrust his pikestaff into the cage in a single, economical jab. It caught him in the mouth, crushing his lip against his teeth, tearing his flesh even wider.

"One more word," the guard said, "and I'll cut out your tongue. Got it?" It was Dever. They played leapjacks together down at the Goose on the nights they found themselves there at the same time. Used to play. Dever wasn't grinning now, wasn't reaching out to slap him on the back, buy him a pint, bend his ear about the latest lady love.

Now he looked cold enough to kill.

Another egg came sailing out of the crowd. This one found its target. Hit him on the side of the head. The smell was gut-wrenching. Somebody else threw fresh cow shit. Lukewarm but still stinking, it burned his face where Jarralt had laid him open, searching for satisfaction.

The guards made no attempt to stop the rain of abuse. Only when something landed too close to them did they raise their pikestaffs and shout. There was no escape. All he could do was survive it, just as he'd survived Jarralt. In the end he curled up on his side and tried to ignore the shouts, the insults, the eggs, and everything else they threw at him. The pain. Concentrated instead on the one thing that would sustain him for as long as this ordeal endured. Hate. On the one name that fed his slow-burning fury.

Gar.

When he woke a second time it was again to glimlit darkness and the rise and fall of unfriendly voices, sibilant as the ocean, to the smoky scents of roasting meats as food merchants catered to the avid crowds of Olken still gathering to gloat and deride. So large had their numbers swelled that a barrier had been erected around the cart and cage, keeping the insomniac onlookers at bay; standing beyond it, pike-staffs at the ready, a different set of guards.

What was wrong with the bastards, eh? Didn't they have homes to go to? Children to care for? Did they have nothing better to do than stand around here feeding their faces on sheep fat and bile?

Well, no. Clearly not.

Groaning, swearing as all his hurts growled, biting, and colder than ever he could remember, he managed to force himself upright. "Barl's ti—" he began to curse under his breath, then stopped. Stared. Closed his fingers into fists.

Willer stood outside the cage, smiling in at him. In his pudgy hands a hot beef sandwich, dripping bloody juices down the front of his apple-green jacket. He didn't seem to notice. His bloated face was shiny with grease, with triumph, and his eyes gleamed in the lambent glimfire.

"I told you I'd make you pay," he said conversationally, around a mouthful of sloppily chewed bread and meat. "Didn't I?" The gloating smile widened, like a toad's. "This should teach you to disbelieve me."

"Go away," he said, even though he knew he was wasting his breath.

Willer shivered with pleasure. "The executioner was in the guard-house all afternoon, sharpening his axe. I went to watch. Zzzt, zzzt, zzzt. You'll never guess: the townsfolk are placing bets on how many strokes it'll take to do the job. They hate you, Asher. Thanks to you, Olken life is about to change for the harder. I'm hoping it'll take three strokes to kill you. Four, even. I'm hoping it hurts. A lot. You deserve to suffer. You deserve everything that's happening to you."

"You're a fool, Willer," he said tiredly. "Such a damned bloody fool. You got no idea what you've done."

"I know exactly what I've done," said Willer, eyes bright with malice. "I've helped bring a blasphemous traitor to justice." Dripping beef forgotten, he stepped even closer to the cage. "The guards say they heard you screaming. How I wish I'd been there to see it." His voice was laden with longing. "All those times you disrespected me. Abused me. Humiliated me. Insulted me with your very presence. Did you think I would forget? Did you think I would *forgive*? They say you shat yourself like a baby, that you—"

"Willer," said Darran, stepping out of the shadows. "That's enough. He knows you've won. Go home."

Startled, Willer spun about. "Darran! What are you doing here. You're supposed to be nursemaiding pathetic magickless Gar!"

Darran came closer. Smoothed out a wrinkle in the pissant's beef-stained coat. "When I think I once felt affection for you, I could vomit," he said, his voice low, shaking. "Go home. Before I forget myself and make a scene."

Uncertain, truculent, Willer knocked the age-spotted hand aside. "Why are you protecting him, Darran? You hate him as much as I do! You wanted him brought down as much as I did, don't try to deny it! 'Give him enough rope and he'll hang himself,' that's what you said. And then you preferred him over me, *me*, who served you like a son for years! *Why?*"

Darran shook his head slowly, like a teacher despairing of a backward student. "Because Gar asked me to. Because, like you, I swore to serve him with faith and loyalty. Because *unlike* you I kept my word."

Willer's jaw dropped. "Asher's a traitor. A blasphemer! He broke Barl's First Law!"

"Yes, he did," agreed Darran, nodding. "And for that he'll die. But even so, he's a better man than you'll ever be."

"Succouring a traitor is treachery in itself!" hissed Willer. "I could have you arrested for that. I *will* have you arrested! I'm not your dogsbody any more. Now I'm a man of influence and I won't be trifled with!" He turned away, searching for the nearest guard, and his wet pink mouth opened wide, to shout.

Darran's fingers closed about his arm. "I wouldn't, Willer, if I were you." His voice was soft. More dangerous than Asher, watching and for the moment disregarded, could ever have imagined. "For a man who prides himself on his memory you seem to have forgotten a thing or two. Even with all that's happened I'm not without influence myself. Remember Bolliton? I do. I also have proof. The right words in the right ear and—"

"*What?*" Sea slug Willer pulled free and backed away, his greasy face puce with fury, and fear. His elbow bumped the bars of the cage. "How *dare* you threaten me? I'll tell the king what you've said, I'll see you thrown in prison for it, I'll—"

The fat fool had forgotten where he was. Despite his chains Asher touched his fingers to the back of the pissant's collar. Seized it and twisted savagely, cutting off Willer's air with a gurgle.

"You'll do nowt or I'll kill you here and now," he whispered into Willer's ear. "Think I can't? Think I won't? What can they do if I wring your neck? Chop my head off twice?"

With a strangled shriek Willer wrenched himself free. The nearest guard, finally noticing the prisoner had visitors, turned. Scowling, his pikestaff at the ready, he approached. Then, seeing who they were, hesitated. "Meister Darran. Meister Driskle."

The ole crow bowed. "Good evening, Jesip."

"Meister Darran, you shouldn't be here," Jesip said unhappily. "You neither, Meister Driskle. We got strict orders to—"

"Relax, guardsman," said Darran with his oiliest smile. His hand fell on Willer's shoulder, fingers tightening. The sea slug closed his mouth, his expression pinched with pain. "I've orders of my own." Darran lowered his voice to a conspiratorial whisper. "Confidential. A matter of state. You understand?"

Asher held his breath. Jesip was new. Young. Easily awed. And Darran had a reputation.

"Two minutes, Meister Darran," said Jesip. "Orders or no, I can't give you more than that."

"Thank you," said Darran. "I'll make sure your cooperation is noted in the right circles."

Jesip flushed. "Just doing my job, sir." He looked at Willer. "And Meister Driskle?"

"Is with me," Darran said smoothly. His grasping fingers tightened further. Willer squeaked. "But he's not feeling well. A morsel of food gone down the wrong way." He spared the slug a reproving look. "One should never eat and speak at the same time, dear boy. There might be an unfortunate incident."

As Willer gasped like a landed fish, Jesip nodded, one finger raised in warning. "So it's two minutes, then. And only because you work for the palace."

"Exactly," said Darran.

"And once you're done, best mind you take care on your way home," Jesip added. "The mood's a mite unchancy round here just now."

Darran nodded, smiling. "Excellent advice. Thank you."

As Jesip withdrew, Darran released his fearsome grip on Willer's shoulder. "Run away now, Willer, and forget you saw me... or I swear there'll be a reckoning you'll not forget."

Tripping over his own feet, cursing, Willer fled. Asher looked at Darran. "Bolliton?"

Darran sighed. "Alas, an unsavoury business. I reimbursed the prince's coffers from my own pocket. Kept various receipts... hidden. Allowed Willer less leeway afterwards. It seemed the prudent thing to do. In hindsight, however..."

"Prudent would've been dismissing the little turd," Asher muttered. "Might've saved a lot of heartache." Without warning a fresh wave of pain assailed him. He slid down the cage bars again, into the filthy straw.

Darran didn't reply. Instead just stood there, silent, his eyes unreadable, his expression composed, as his measuring gaze took in the brutal evidence of Jarralt's displeasure. The dried manure and egg and other detritus, gifts from a grateful, adoring public. Asher looked away, not wanting to see his condition written plain in the old man's face.

"What are you doin' here, Darran? You come to gloat?"

The secretary shifted his gaze and stared at the crowd. "Look at them all. By now I doubt there's a cradle-bound babe anywhere in this City who doesn't know you're arrested, and why. Within days they'll have heard it even down on the coast."

Asher closed his eyes. "That'll put a smile on my bloody brothers' faces." Thinking of the coast, of the people there, he bit his lip. Made himself look at the ole crow. This was going to hurt worse than Jarralt's poker... "Darran. I need a favour."

Darran drew back. "A *favour?*"

"It ain't for myself," he added quickly. "Not exactly. I got a friend. Jed. We grew up together in Restharven. He's hurt, on account of doing something I asked, and won't ever get better. Since we got back from Westwailing I been sendin' him money. Makin' sure he was looked after. When this is over... when I'm—" He took a deep, painful breath. Let it out. "—dead, can you make sure what's left of my savings finds him?"

Darran's expression was a mingling of surprise and sorrow. "Asher, all your money's been confiscated. Your possessions too. You don't have a cuick or a shirt to your name."

He should have expected it. *Jed.* He swallowed anger. Thought of something else and sat up sharply, no matter the pain. His heavy chains rattled. "Cygnet? What about Cygnet?"

"I'm sorry," said Darran after a long pause. "The stables are disbanded. Someone said—I truly am sorry, but Conroyd Jarralt has your horse now."

It was a sharper agony than anything done to flesh and bone. He pressed his bloodstained hands to his face and felt salt sting the open wounds there. Felt his hard-pressed willpower break at last. His precious Cygnet, prey to that man's hands and heels, to cruel bits and crueller spurs.

Darran stepped closer. "You should know, Asher, I've been told everything." His voice was thinned to a whisper. "Is it true? That you can—you know?"

Wrenching his thoughts away from Cygnet, poor Cygnet, he lowered his hands. "What does it matter?"

"*Asher!* Is it *true?*"

He let his head rest against the cage. There was no point denying it now. "Aye. But I wouldn't go repeatin' it if I were you. Jarralt'll kill you."

Darran seemed torn between horror and fascination. "Then if you do have...*power*...can't you free yourself?"

He'd asked himself the same question. He supposed it was possible. In theory. He could call down a freezing on the City, say, that'd turn all its citizens into ice statues. Leave him free to break out of this cage and run. But long before they'd frozen the guards would have clubbed him unconscious. Or dead. And anyway, there was nowhere to run to.

"No. I can't."

Darran stepped closer still, so his face was near to touching the cage. "I know why you did it."

He let his eyes close. "'Why' don't matter. Not any more."

"You did it because you love him."

That made him laugh. He dragged his eyelids open. "*Now* you believe it?" He breathed hard, trying to dull the stabbing pain. "Gar was more a brother to me than Zeth or Wishus or Bede or *any* of 'em. A hundred times I could've walked away. Should've. Wanted to. But I didn't. And I broke Barl's Law 'cause he asked me to. 'Cause he promised to protect me and I believed him. I thought his word meant something." His hands fisted. "Better watch yourself, ole maggoty man. Better take a good long look at what's happened here and ask yourself twice what you're doin', staying with him. 'Cause this is where loyalty leads you."

Darran wrapped his fingers around the bars. "Asher, listen."

Beyond the cage Jesip and the other guards had drifted into a huddle round an open brazier to drink some ale and gobble meat pies. One of them stirred up the coals with a poker; the brazier's mouth glowed with a steady, scarlet heat. Searing memory stirred and he felt his muscles contract, his bowels loosen.

"Asher?"

Shame turned to anger. "Go away, Darran. Ain't nowt you can do here and I'm sick of your manky ole face."

Darran let go of the bars. "Not before you've heard what I came to say."

"I ain't interested."

"This wasn't Gar's fault."

He choked. "Not his *fault*? Of course it's his fault! He said he'd protect me and look where I am!"

"If you'd let me explain, then—"

"Explain?" he said, incredulous. "Explain *what*?" He wanted to howl, to scream, to tighten his fingers round Darran's scrawny throat and throttle him into silence. "That it turns out Gar's gutless? I know that already!"

"Please, Asher, you must see his position!"

"I do see it! He's alive and I soon won't be. He's in his Tower and I'm in this cage. I saved his *life*, Darran! He's only breathin' today 'cause of me!"

"I know that," said Darran, desperately whispering. "*He* knows that."

"Then he has to stop this! He *owes* me, ole man!"

"Oh, Asher," said Darran, his voice breaking. "Don't you think he'd save you if he could? He *can't*. His hands are tied, he—"

"Tied?" he said savagely, and raised his manacled wrists. "Well, mine are bloody *chained*!"

Darran stepped back, his face grey and drawn. "He knows that too. And he's sorry, Asher. You've no idea how sorry he is. But there's nothing he can do. There were threats made. Dreadful threats. Against him...against the Olken people. He had to sign that proclamation."

"He's the *king*, Darran! He can bloody *unsign* it!"

There were tears in Darran's eyes. *Tears.* "Not any more. Haven't they told you? This afternoon he renounced his crown in favour of Conroyd Jarralt. Our new king has confined him to the Tower and stripped him of authority. For all the good he can do you now—for all the good he can do himself—Gar might as well be in that cage with you."

Hope's last embers died. Despairing, Asher flung himself at the iron bars separating him from Darran and pressed his face against them.

"I wish he was! You tell him that, you stinkin' ole maggot! Tell him *he's* the traitor and it's *his* head they ought to cut off with their sharp and shiny axe! But since it'll be mine, tell him I hope he dies a long, slow death years and years from now, and that every minute of every day of every one of them years is *agony* and that every time he closes his eyes he sees my face! The face of the friend he *murdered*!" Exhausted, shuddering, he felt himself start sliding down the bars. "Go on, you bastard! *Tell* him!"

Jesip must have heard him then, because he left his fellow guards, marched back to the cage and poked his pikestaff between the bars. Asher barely felt its sharp tip puncture his skin.

"Watch your mouth, traitor!" Jesip growled, then turned to Darran. "I'm sorry, sir, but you've had more than two minutes and—"

"It's all right," said Darran. "I'm leaving now."

"Right then," said Jesip. He sounded relieved. "Goodnight to you, sir."

"Goodnight, Jesip," replied Darran, turning. "And...goodbye, Asher."

He summoned a skerrick of saliva and spat. "Piss on you, Darran. And piss on that treacherous shit in the Tower."

Jesip hit him. Hit him again, and again, until all he could do was lie face down on the floor of the cage, breathing in the stench of shit and egg and vomit, grunting with each blow. Moments later the other guards joined in. The sounds of their dedicated fury mingled with the shouts and applause of the crowd.

Not soon enough, the world went away.

CHAPTER TWENTY-FIVE

Morg stood before Conroyd's dressing-room mirror and admired the way his blue brocade dressing-gown brought out his eyes. Behind him, Conroyd's wife continued to wail.

"But you *can't* send me away!" Ethienne protested, perilously close to stamping her foot. "I'm the *queen* now, Conroyd! I belong in the *palace*!"

He sighed and smoothed his unbound blond hair. She belonged in a coffin buried six feet deep. "My dear, I know. And when the time is right the palace is where you'll be. Where we both will be, with the House Jarralt falcon flying proudly above it. But until that time I want you out of Dorana, safe on our country estate with our sons to look after you."

"How am I unsafe here? You're the king!"

"I know," he said, turning. Smiling. "But until the traitor Asher is dead, the City will be filled with Olken from every corner of the kingdom, come to see him die and all doubtless unhappy with the curfew and other restrictions I've had to lay on them in the wake of his wickedness."

She pouted. "Who cares if they're unhappy? It's their duty to obey you without question and if they don't they should be arrested!"

"And they will be, my dear. But you've told me yourself how this business has upset the staff, and it will only get worse before it gets better. There'll be no such upheaval on the estate. Besides," he patted her cheek, "I must concentrate on my new, important duties, and you know what a distraction you are."

That had her simpering, the silly cow. "Oh, Conroyd, dearest—"

"So, my pet, you'll go? To please me?"

"And what of my pleasure?" she retorted, folding her arms. "I only like the country in the summer and anyway, I want to see that dreadful Asher die."

Out of patience, he snapped his fingers before her petulant face. "*Obedience.*" All the lively argument drained away, leaving her pale and docile and, above all, silent.

What a shame he couldn't so ensorcel every other Doranen in the kingdom. It would make things so much easier. Unfortunately, that was impossible. He'd have to find another way. It was vital he get rid of as many Doranen from the City as he could; the fewer magicians he had around him the better, for even the most rudimentary practitioners would begin to notice the Wall's decline.

Provided, of course, he could achieve its demise. Unsustained by Weather Working it would fall, eventually, but that would take too long. And too many questions would be asked in the meantime.

The Doranen, sheep or not, would notice his lack of Weather Working. Holze would certainly begin to agitate. Demand proof of his proficiency and the appointment of dead Durm's replacement. And, if unsatisfied would doubtless rally the kingdom's magicians against him.

There was only one solution. He *had* to find a way to thwart Barl's will. To absorb her wretched Weather Magic into himself and unravel her Wall from within.

For if he didn't...

First things first, however. He turned again to Conroyd's wife. "You are leaving for the country, Ethienne. Willingly and with enthusiasm, eager to begin preparations for the creation of a new Doranen court." A happy thought occurred, and he laughed out loud. "What's more, as soon as you arrive at the estate you'll invite as many of the City's Doranen as can be accommodated to join you there, that they might assist you in those preparations. Make it a royal decree. You'll enjoy that, and they won't dare refuse."

Ethienne nodded, witless and smiling. "Of course, Conroyd. Whatever you say, my dear."

Not all the Doranen would go, of course. The damned councillors would stay, some of them, royal decree or not. Conroyd's friends, for certain. But many would obey the summons, greedy for the chance to make themselves indispensable to the new regime.

And that would give him the time and space he needed to devise a way around Barl's safeguards against him. To kill her Wall and her kingdom, once and for all.

Veira's kitchen was small and cosy. The walls were painted a buttery yellow. The drawn curtains were blue. The cupboards, the dresser, the table and chairs, all were crafted from mellow brown timber and carved with acorns and wheat sheaves and lambs. Dried herbs in bunches dangled invitingly overhead, scenting the air. Seated at the table, Dathne breathed in the muddled aromas of sage, of dilly-tip, rosemary, thyme and pods of tottle seeds, feeling oddly comforted. The stove in the corner wafted heat from its wood-filled pot belly. Standing before it, as though he'd grown up here, as though he belonged, Matt tipped fresh tea leaves into an old brown pot then filled it from a kettle boiling on the stove top. His back was to her, and he wouldn't turn around.

"I don't understand it," she said, slumping partly against the wall, partly over the tiny table. The cushion on the chair was a blessing after the hard bench seat of Veira's wagon. "Why didn't you tell me you were coming here?"

Matt said nothing. Veira, setting out plates, glanced at him. The look was as good as a poke with an elbow. He shrugged. Said, over his shoulder, "We weren't on speaking terms, remember?"

She frowned, not liking the reminder. "But how did you know where Veira lived? Even *I* didn't know where she lived! Not until she told me!"

"And I told him too," said Veira. She'd shed her hooded cloak since coming inside; plump and comfortable, she was layered in a patchwork of blue cotton and black felt and bright scarlet sheep's-wool; her long grey hair was coiled round and round the back of her head like an elderly sleeping snake. Slivers of silver-bound jet dangled from her soft earlobes and her fingers were burdened with rings. Her eyes, dark brown and lively, were narrowed now in sharp consideration. "Did you think you were the only one with a Circle Stone, child?"

Shocked, Dathne sat up. "Well, of course not...but I didn't think—" She stared accusingly at Matt's stubborn back. "You were *spying* on me?"

"Feh!" said Veira, disparaging. "*Spying*. Twice, I've spoken to Matthias since you and he fell in together. I called him, to make sure I could, and after that stayed silent, hearing not a whisper until he reached out and told me he needed to hide."

She let her gaze rest broodingly between Matt's shoulderblades. Wanted him to feel its weight. "And was that all you told her?"

He refused to turn. Pretended he had to guard the waiting mugs in case they sprouted wings and flew away. "I told her everything. I had to. You wouldn't."

She wanted to leap from her seat and beat her fists against him. "You had no right! I'm the Heir, not you. It was for me to tell, in my own time and in my own way! You've resented my feelings for Asher ever since you learned of them. Maybe he was right. Maybe you *are* jealous! You—"

He did turn then, his face white with temper and tiredness. "Jealous? Don't flatter yourself! Believe me, Asher's welcome to you, high-handed, self-opinionated slumskumbledy woman that you are! So convinced that you're invincible, just 'cause you're the Heir! Well, you're *not* invincible. You didn't see this coming. You didn't see he had their magic in him, and maybe none of ours. And you wouldn't listen when I said, over and over, he needed to be told. If we'd told him, he wouldn't be in this mess!"

For a moment she could hardly breathe. Matt *never* spoke to her like this. *Nobody* spoke to her like this. "You don't know that!" she spat back at him. "You don't know anything! Telling him might've made things worse!"

"How could they be *worse*?" he shouted. "Asher's going to *die*!"

"Now that's enough," said Veira, and slapped her palm down sharp on the table. "Both of you. I'm too old for all this brangling and besides, it won't change what's happened. There's been mistakes on both sides that can't be unmade now." Her kindly face was tight with disapproval. "Dathne, you've no business flying at Matthias. Yes, he told me all your muddleheaded doings, and then spent twice as long again making excuses for you. He's been a good and loyal friend, my girl. Better than you've deserved."

Hot with shame and angry embarrassment, Dathne stared at the knobbly pine-board floor. Couldn't bring herself to look at Matt. "I'm sorry," she muttered. Her voice sounded very small in the cottage's kitchen. Small, and unremarkable. Not the voice of an all-seeing prophet at all. She lifted her gaze. "I'm just tired, and worried. I'm glad Matt came to you, Veira. He'd have been in danger, else."

Veira sniffed. "Oh, he's still in danger, child. We're all of us in danger." She looked again to Matt. "That tea ready yet, my boy?"

"Nearly," he said, and pulled out a chair at the table for her. "Sit. I'll do the rest. Biscuits as well?"

Veira settled herself in the seat with a sigh. "Of course biscuits. Tea ain't tea without biscuits."

Briefly grinning, he opened a nearby cupboard and pulled down a large corked clay jar glazed red and blue. Took a crock of honey from another, teaspoons from a drawer and a pitcher of milk from a coolbox set under the sink, and placed them on the table.

Dathne stared. "Well! You've made yourself at home!"

Frowning again, he turned away to gently swill the tea inside its pot. "I had to, didn't I? Seeing I was kicked out of my own."

She flushed. "Matt—"

Veira rapped her knuckles on the tabletop. "No more, I said! Rivers don't flow backwards."

Reproved, Dathne closed her lips tight and looked at Matt instead as he busied himself with pouring the brewed tea. Despite everything it was good to see him, large and practical in Veira's little kitchen. He'd lost his scent of horses. Smelled now of honey-pine and beeswax. His face was thinner, though, carved with lines she'd never seen before. And there was a sadness in him that was also new. Her doing. She felt her throat constrict, and turned to Veira.

"So...you know everything?"

Veira's eyebrows lifted. "Everything Matthias knew, yes. Which I'll warrant's not the same as everything there is to know. I've no doubt there're things you kept from him as well as me."

There was a look in Veira's eyes that made her squirm. "Nothing important, I promise. Veira...what I did. It wasn't for me." Handing out the tea-filled mugs, Matt made a small, disbelieving sound. Her cheeks burned. "All right. Not wholly for me. I hoped that if Asher and I were...close...intimate...he'd believe he could finally trust me. Confide his secrets. Then I'd know how best to proceed. Prophecy's proven unreliable, Veira. Unclear, and even ambiguous. And it's never been constant. I couldn't see where it was leading us."

"So you told yourself it led to that young man's mattress," retorted Veira. "Which is where you've always wanted to travel."

"Veira!"

"She's right, Dath, and you know it," Matt said sharply. "We'll not solve a thing if we can't face the truth unflinching."

She didn't want to think about that. "You don't seem very surprised, Veira. That I—that we—Asher and me, that we—"

Shrugging, Veira peered into her steaming mug. Splashed in some milk and a dollop of honey. "It's true I ain't the Heir no more than Matthias, but I've still got a good pair of eyes in my head and a knack or three of my own," she said, stirring. "I could tell which way the wind was blowing."

"Then why didn't you stop me, if Matt's right and it was such a terrible thing to do?"

"Did I say he was right?" said Veira, and exchanged glances with him as he passed her a plate piled high with almond biscuits. "Did I say it was terrible? I don't recall saying that. We still don't know where this will end."

"We've got a pretty good idea," Matt said, glowering, and leaned against the kitchen bench.

Instead of answering, Veira dipped a biscuit in her milky tea and ate it with lip-smacking relish. "Drink up, child," she said mildly. "And then you'll do some scrying and we'll see what we can see."

Dathne felt herself shrink with fear. She had no desire for tea. "Scrying? For Asher? Veira, I can't. Not tonight. I'm so tired. Maybe tomorrow—"

"Yes, tonight," the old woman said, eyebrows pulled low. "Before sunrise. I've tried but I can't seem to find him. Matthias says you never fail, no matter what the distance."

She glared at helpful Matt. He shrugged, his eyes cool and contained as he took a sip from his own mug. There was an empty chair beside her; he could've sat down if he'd wanted...

Pain, quick and sharp. Such a gulf between them, greater than ever before. Could they cross it? Rebuild their bridges? Or was their friendship dead and buried, as Asher might soon be dead and buried?

Of course she wanted to see where Asher was. How he was. She was desperate to know...

She was terrified of what she'd find out.

"You must, child," said Veira, relentless. "Knowledge is power."

"All right," she said grudgingly, making no effort to be pleasant. "If you insist."

They finished their tea and their biscuits and Veira brought out her scrying basin. Prepared the water, the tanal leaf, vervle, cloysies' tears and moon-rot. When everything was ready Dathne looked at her and at Matt and said, still tetchy, "I'll make no promises in this. He might well be beyond me."

"All I ask is that you try, child," said Veira. "That's all I'll ever ask."

So she tried. A part of her so fearful, a part of her with hope. Deep in the tanal leaf's languorous grasp, she seasoned the scrying water and opened her heart. Sent forth her questing mind.

Asher. Asher. Asher.

Moments later she found him. Huddled. Hurting. Caged like an animal and abused by the very people he was born to save. Weeping, she told Veira and Matt what she saw in the basin and heard them gasp in turn. "We must help him," she whispered as the tears coursed down her face. "We must save him. Can we save him? Is there time?"

"That's a question I can't answer," said Veira as she put her arms round Dathne's shoulders. "Not yet. But I promise you this much, child. We'll try."

"We must save him. Can we save him? Is there time?"

Tossed and turned by Dathne's desperate questions, Veira rose before dawn and tiptoed into her little kitchen to make a cup of tea. How odd, to be creeping thief-like about the cottage she'd lived in solitary for twenty-seven years. But she knew already that Matthias was a light sleeper; years of living with horses and their capricious maladies had honed him to startling alertness. She didn't know about Dathne yet, but chances were the child slept just as shallow. And since just now she needed quiet and time alone with her own bleak thoughts, it was best she played the mouse.

She lit a single candle, then the fire in her stove to boil the kettle. Outside the window darkness mantled her yard, the forest, the mountains. Barl's Wall was a whisper of gold, lost amongst the stars. Sometimes it was easy to forget it was there. Or that she was here because of it, tied to a scattered group of not-quite-strangers whose lives she could end with one unthinking mistake. Who knew her but not each other and willingly lived with danger for the sake of an ancient prophecy and a life that had vanished centuries before they were born. Their courage had her weeping, if she let it.

Guardianship of the Circle had come to her three months before her thirty-sixth birthday. Married at twenty to a lovely boy whose face she no longer remembered, widowed childless at twenty-three, she'd not had the heart to woo or wed again. At least, for a long time she'd thought it was sorrow.

After her Great-Aunt Tilda had died, though, leaving her a mysterious box and a legacy she still had cause to curse, she wondered if that wasn't Prophecy working its will upon her. Dabbling its fingers in her private doings long before it needed her. Keeping her ready for the day when it did.

For this day, when dark decisions must be made so that an even darker future might not come to pass.

The kettle took a deep breath and started whistling. She whisked it off the stove top and made her mug of tea. Cradling it between fingers just beginning to feel the pinches of age, she sank into a chair at the table to rest her elbows and brood on matters likely to break her heart.

After sending Matthias and Dathne to their beds scant hours earlier, she'd reached out to another Circle member, Gilda Hartshorn, to confirm the truth of Dathne's scrying. A seamstress in Dorana City, Gilda sewed often for staff up at the palace and in the City guardhouse. She had a genius for gossip and inspiring confidences.

It's true, it's true, all true, Gilda had told her. *Asher's due to die at midnight Barl's Day. A proclamation from the new king, Conroyd Jarralt.*

Prompted by unfathomable instinct, knowing they'd need all the help they could find to rescue him, she'd told Gilda the truth about Asher. Shocked, then tearful, Gilda had demanded, *But he's guarded day and night and there's a crowd around him no matter what the hour! Veira, Veira, what shall we do?*

Gilda knew no more of Dathne and Matt than they knew about her, and still it was best things stayed that way. So she'd settled the seamstress's fears with a calm assurance three parts a lie, then climbed in her bed to sleep. She was sixty-three years old now, and nowhere near spry. And the journey to collect Dathne had shaken her bones to aching.

Sleep hadn't come, though. She'd told Dathne she had an inkling of an idea on how to save their Innocent Mage, and she did. But that idea was dreadful. Merciless. Uncaring of hearts broken, lives lost, futures trampled. Doubtless it came from Prophecy itself, which accounted for its coldness. It also might account for coincidence: that of all the people who could be the key to Asher's freedom, it was her flesh and blood. Her sister's son. A boy grown now to manhood who she'd brought into the Circle against her will. Against all bonds of family. Against the voice in her heart crying, *No. Don't. Choose another.*

She hadn't. Couldn't. Like Dathne, like her nephew Rafel, she'd been chosen as Prophecy's tool. She might rail against destiny from dawn till dusk but it made no difference. Rafel was part of the pattern. Part of Prophecy. And so she'd called him to her, and willingly he'd come. Listened to her fantastic tale of omens and promises and dead men's dreams, and smiled.

"Of course I'll help you, Veira. What am I meant to do?"

Then, not knowing, she couldn't tell him. Now, suspecting...she couldn't bring herself to think of it.

From the henhouse outside in the yard, a babbling of girlish chicken voices and the rooster's lusty crow. Lifting her head, she realised the sky outside had lightened. That tentative sunsingers in the forest's foliage were warbling in chorus. It was day, and she had chores to do. Decisions to make. Plans to devise.

Prophecy to obey.

She was sixty-three years old, and nigh on sick of Prophecy.

Her mostly untouched tea was cold now. Wrinkling her nose, she tipped it down the sink then crept back to her bedroom. Pulled on thicker socks and extra woollens and lifted her coat from its hook on the back of the door. Matthias would be rousing soon, and maybe Dathne as well. She wasn't ready to face them yet.

A walk in the woods was what she needed. Solitude, for the strengthening of heart and will. She'd take the pigs.

Pigs were good listeners, and they never talked back.

When Asher stirred again it was to a rising sun whose winter heat barely warmed his chilled and stiffened body. Far beyond caring about such niceties as privacy, modesty, shame, he pissed into the straw. The few remaining yellow stalks turned pink.

In the Square, the diminished crowd stirred and muttered and stamped its feet. A few half-hearted eggs cracked open on the cage roof. These ones were hardly rotten at all. Pale yellow yolk dripped onto his face. He opened his parched mouth and swallowed, because his belly was empty and rumbling. That small act of self-sustenance stirred his audience to anger. Someone shouted. Someone else threw a rock. Two rocks. Four. Five. One hit him, drawing blood. He threw it back, swearing.

The next thing he knew it was raining rocks, until the guards stepped in and stopped the sport. Not out of pity; they just didn't want an accident that might prevent his keenly anticipated beheading. Or to get hit by mistake themselves.

Adrift on a shifting sea of memories, swaddled in a sharp glass blanket of pain, Asher let himself float, praying that the next time he opened his eyes he'd be dead.

Gar woke to the sound of curtains rattling along their thick brass rods and an unwelcome voice. "Your Highness? Your Highness."

He rolled his head on the pillow then frowned. What? That wasn't right. Since when was his pillow made of wood? Someone had crept into his bedchamber and turned his pillow into *wood*. And then they'd rolled it *flat*...

He opened his eyes, blinking in the pale morning sunshine laid over his face like gauze. Oh. This wasn't his bedchamber, it was his library. The pillow was actually his desk, where he'd fallen asleep at some point during the night while continuing his search for Barl's diary.

His fruitless search. If the diary existed he'd failed to find it amongst Durm's books. It must be in Durm's study. If it existed...

He was starting to think it didn't. That the diary was nothing more than a figment of Durm's dying mind. That hope for him, for Asher, for the whole kingdom, was truly dead.

He sat up, groaning as every muscle protested his unorthodox mattress. His eyes were gritty, his mouth tasted like old socks and his head hurt as though it was spiky with nails and the sunlight was a hammer, pounding...

"Your Highness, really," fussed Darran. "You hardly touched your dinner!"

He rubbed his eyes. Glanced at the abandoned tray on the floor with its burden of congealed roast lamb and soggy carrots. "I wasn't hungry. What time is it?"

"A quarter after seven," said Darran, retrieving the tray. "Now, sir, I've drawn you a bath. Please take it, and by the time you're finished breakfast will be ready."

He felt his stomach roil. "I'm still not hungry."

"Hungry or not, Your Highness, you can't miss dinner and breakfast!"

He groaned again. "You're turning into an old woman, Darran, right before my eyes."

Darran sniffed. "Well if I am, sir, you're hastening the transformation. Come along now! Up, up, up! Your bath water's getting cold."

Clearly there was no escape short of dismissing the old man. A tempting thought, but no. Glowering, he shoved his chair back from his library desk and staggered upstairs to his bathroom, where there was indeed a hot bath waiting. Darran had even laid him out fresh clothes.

He didn't know whether to laugh or cry.

Still. The hot bath, scented with oils, did feel good to his cramped and tired muscles. He let himself sink beneath the fragrant water and waited for the heat to suffuse him. For his headache to subside and his aching tension to ease.

But no. With wakefulness and silence came more uncomfortable thoughts. If Barl's diary did exist and was hidden somewhere in Durm's study instead of his book collection, could he hope to find it there? Without falling foul of Conroyd? Without alerting the bastard to his unpermitted wanderings and causing his limited freedom to be reduced altogether? He tried to imagine guards in Conroyd's pay cluttering up his Tower, counting every step he took, every breath, and was forced to stop. Just the idea of it made him sick.

But he had to take the chance. If he didn't it meant he truly was Gar the Magickless again, forever, and faced a life of virtual imprisonment in a kingdom ruled by the wrong man. A life of unbearable guilt and sorrow. No matter what it took, no matter what it cost, he had to believe the diary was real, and contained a means of rescue for them all.

His bath was getting cold. He stood, dripping. Wrapped himself in a towel and staggered into his bedchamber where Darran was fussing over a small dining table. Odd. He couldn't recall having a dining table in here half an hour ago.

"I hope you don't mind, sir," said Darran, buffing silver cutlery with a linen cloth. "But I thought if you ate in here it might reduce the number of rooms to clean." He looked up, stricken. "Not that I begrudge the task, sir! I don't! But—"

"I know," he said. "It's a sensible plan, Darran. Whatever I can do to make your life easier, consider it done. And don't forget to set yourself a place too. We're in this together, old friend."

Darran's sallow cheeks turned pink. "I...I thought an omelette for breakfast, sir. With ham and asparagus. A little creamed cheese. I'll serve it momentarily, if that's agreeable."

Gar sighed. Darran was trying so hard, and his own life was just as disarranged. Lay in equally smoking ruins. Through no fault of his own he'd been reduced to housewifery in the service of a disgraced and impotent prince of nothing. After a lifetime's exemplary royal service he'd earned much better than this ignominious exile.

Eyes suddenly stinging, he smiled. "It's perfect. Thank you." The smile swiftly faded, though, as another unwelcome thought stabbed. "I can only pray Asher is treated so well."

Something in the quality of Darran's silence made him stare.

"What?"

"Oh, sir," Darran's expression was anguished, his voice a strangled whisper. "I don't know how to tell you..."

"Tell me what?"

"About Asher."

His heart thudded. "For Barl's sake, just say it, man."

Darran was wringing the linen polishing cloth as though it were a chicken's neck. "I went and saw him last night."

"Asher?"

"Yes."

He felt his emptied lungs constrict. "Why?"

Very carefully, Darran smoothed out the throttled cloth and laid it on the table. "I was...concerned. I thought you'd want to know if he was all right."

He didn't.

He had to. "And was he?"

Darran shook his head, mute misery in his face. "No. He's in a cage, in the Square. On public display like an animal. Lord Jarralt—the king—has hurt him."

"The king is a cruel and wicked man."

"Yes, sir," Darran whispered. "I'm most afraid you're right."

Towel still clutched about his drying body Gar moved to the window, pulled aside the curtain and stared down into the grounds below where cheerful gardeners no longer worked. With an effort he kept his voice steady.

"And Asher. Did you have the chance to speak to him?"

"Briefly, sir. He asked me to give you a message."

A message. The sunlight hammer resumed its pounding, and the nails drove into his brain. "There's no need, Darran. I can imagine what it was."

"No, sir," said Darran. His voice sounded closer. "In fact, he asked me to say he forgives you. He understands the kingdom must come before all personal considerations, and that in denying him you did what had to be done so Lur might remain safe and at peace. He begs you not to blame yourself for his death."

"Oh," he said eventually. "I see." Slowly he turned from the window and stared into Darran's pale, composed features. "That doesn't sound like Asher. Was he lying?"

Darran shook his head, vehement. "No, sir. Every word he said to me was the truth."

Well. If Darran believed it—and clearly he did—then he'd believe it too. "How was he?"

"His spirits are low," Darran admitted, reluctant. "Which is only to be expected. I think he's afraid, though he'd never admit it. But he loves you, sir. I was wrong to think he never did."

A big admission from Darran. Gar nodded and turned back to the window, unwilling to trust his face, his self-control, to another's scrutiny.

He forgives you.

And did that make things better or worse? He wasn't sure. Might never be sure.

"You should get dressed, sir," Darran said gently. "I'll be back in a trice with your omelette."

But when he returned some ten minutes later, he brought with him not breakfast but Willer. Smirking, resplendent in sky-blue satin embroidered everywhere with House Jarralt's falcon emblem, the horrible little man strutted into the room as though he owned the world.

"I'm sorry, sir," said Darran stiffly. "He insisted."

Gar looked at his former employee. "What do you want? You must know you're not welcome here, Willer."

The smirk widened to a fatuous smile. "On the contrary, *Gar*. As an emissary for the king I am welcome everywhere. His Majesty sends me to say: surrender the Weather Orb and such books and papers removed unwisely from dead Durm's apartments." With a flourish he produced a sealed note and held it out.

Gar, forced to step towards him as though in supplication, raised a hand at Darran's hiss of outrage and took the missive without comment. Opened it and frowned. "This is from Conroyd?"

"From the king, yes. And mind you address him as such, with all his due respect."

Ignoring the little slug's snide tone, the temerity of his scolding, he continued to frown at the note. It was signed *Conroyd the First* and its contents betrayed both character and knowledge. *To quote yourself to yourself: "I disobey, and others suffer." Heed my emissary's demand without delay.*

It was Conroyd's handwriting, no question of that. And yet...and yet...

"Well?" said Willer, grown even fatter with arrogance and pride. "Must I tell His Majesty you kept me waiting? Fetch the Orb at once!"

"Ignore him, Darran," said Gar as his secretary choked on a breathless imprecation. "He's a cur dog yapping from the shelter of his master's shadow."

"Sir," said Darran, and subsided, still bristling.

The Weather Orb was here, hidden safely in his bedchamber. He'd intended to take it back to Durm's apartments then changed his mind in case the Weather Magics transfer to Asher had failed, or faded, and they needed to perform it again. In case he found his cure and was able to resume his role as WeatherWorker.

One thought unnecessary, the other forlorn. He retrieved Barl's gift from its hiding place at the bottom of his blanket box and held it out. "Durm's books and papers are unboxed and scattered. I'll need time to ready them for—the King."

Willer took the Orb's box gingerly, as though it were alive and may bite him. "One hour. House Jarralt servants will come to collect them. Be advised—don't make them wait."

Gar smiled thinly. "And when you give King Conroyd the Orb, Willer, give him this message with it: he would do well to reconsider keeping Asher in a cage. Such unkindness sets a tone for his reign that some might find disconcerting."

"You are the only one who thinks so," retorted Willer. "Didn't Darran tell you? They're lining up ten-deep in the Square to get their look at the traitor from Restharven and pelt him with the refuse from their dinner tables and byres."

A lifetime of controlling his feelings in public kept his face from revealing any pain. Contempt, though; contempt he'd reveal, and gladly. "And I suppose you couldn't wait to join in, could you? You must feel very proud."

Willer flushed, lifted his twice-doubled chin. "Durm's books and papers in one hour...or deal with His Majesty's wrath."

"I'm so sorry, sir," said Darran once Willer had departed. "I'd have kept him out if I—"

Gar held out Conroyd's note. "What do you make of this?"

Baffled, Darran took it. Read it. "I...I'm not sure I know what—"

"It's Conroyd's penmanship. After two years on the Privy Council I'd know it anywhere. So should you by now. But..." He shook his head. "Don't you think there's something *odd* about it?"

Darran examined the note again. "I'm sorry, sir. No." He frowned. "Perhaps it's a trifle unsteady—"

"You do see it, don't you?" Gar said. "It's Conroyd's hand...and yet it's not. As though..." And then he stopped. The idea was too fantastical for words.

"Yes, sir?" Darran prompted. "As though what?"

He took back the note. "As though someone else's hand was laid over Conroyd's as he held the pen to write."

"Oh," said Darran. "I see. Yes. Well. That would be very odd, sir."

"Never mind," he said, and crumpled the paper. "I'm imagining things. Darran, I need your help."

"Certainly, sir," said Darran. He sounded relieved. "Doing what?"

"Durm's books and journals. I want to go through them one last time before I have to give them over to Conroyd. I don't know. It's a slim chance but I keep thinking I might have *missed* it."

"Missed what, sir?"

He took a deep breath. This secret was a luxury he could no longer afford. "As he was dying, Durm told me he'd found a diary. Barl's diary. He seemed to think it was important. I want to find it. I want to keep it out of Conroyd's hands."

Darran's eyes were opened wide. "Sir! If it's true—why, it might change everything!"

"That's what I'm hoping for," he said, and pulled a face. "Praying for. Durm called the diary our only hope and it's *my* hope he was right. He warned me against Conroyd. Somehow I think he knew disaster was brewing. But we've only got an hour. Breakfast will have to wait, I'm afraid. All your hard cooking..."

"Breakfast can burn, sir, for all I care," said Darran firmly. "Let's get at those books."

CHAPTER TWENTY-SIX

When Dathne woke in the trundle bed Veira had made up for her, she saw through the partly closed sitting room curtains that the sun had crawled high in the sky. Around her, the cottage felt uninhabited. As she blinked muzzily, trying to arrange her frothy thoughts, she heard the ringing crack of an axe blade against wood coming from somewhere outside.

After using the chamber pot and dragging on fresh clothes, she poked about the rest of the cottage, just in case her feelings had fooled her and Veira was there to talk to after all.

But no. The cottage was empty of both Veira and Matt, so she let herself outside through the kitchen door and into the cottage's tree-fringed back yard.

Where Matt was chopping firewood.

He glanced at her. Not angrily, but not in a friendly way either. "Veira's taken the pigs for a walk," he said, lining up a fresh round of timber on the block. "There's no saying how long she'll be gone. I left oatmush on the hob for you."

"I smelled it," she said, and perched herself on a handy tree stump. The thought of food was revolting. Her belly was greasy, rolling with nausea. "Maybe later." She kicked her heels against the stump; the three black and white chickens scratching the grass nearby took frightened offence and scattered, squawking.

He nodded.

Drenched with regrets she watched him continue his chopping, distant and entirely self-contained. The man she'd known in Dorana was vanished. In his place stood this stranger with hooded eyes and a grim mouth and no exasperated pleasure in her company. In the mid-morning light the chasm between them looked no easier to cross than it had last night in Veira's kitchen.

Before drifting off to sleep she'd replayed over and over in her mind the sequence of events that had brought them to this time and place. The decisions she'd made, the choices she'd discarded in favour of silence and subterfuge.

Try as she might she'd not been able to imagine herself doing anything differently. And whether that meant that as Jervale's Heir she'd been right and was guided by Prophecy, or as her plain self she'd been nothing but a stubborn slumskumbledy wench, she had no idea at all.

In heavy silence the haphazard pile of wood dwindled as Matt reduced the rough lumps of seasoned timber to tidy logs and kindling, his horseman's hands gripped tight around the axe handle, his weathered face severe with concentration. The useful stack of firewood grew taller and wider and still he did not speak, and neither did she. Her heart and head were aching; she wasn't sure she'd ever been so sorrowed or felt so helpless in all her life.

Because it hurt so much to look at this shuttered and newly unknowable man she looked at her surroundings instead. A goodly garden had been created around the back of the cottage. There was a vegetable patch sprouting carrots and tomatoes and suchlike. Three scraggly apple trees. A riotous herb bed and a hodgepodge of flowers. A clovery lawn patched the spaces between cottage and cultivation. Veira's pony cropped grass in a small paddock attached to a tumbledown stable off to the left, and on the right was a mildly odorous pigpen. Next to that the henhouse, its jaunty red paint faded and peeling. It was all very...rural.

Aside from the sound of Matt's wood-chopping, the sharp calls of hidden birds and the answering cackles of Veira's hens, the forest hush was absolute. Unsettling, after the steady humming bustle of the City. But there was a kind of peace in it too. A balm to her lacerated soul. On any other morning she'd have revelled in the solitude and thought of this interlude as a holiday, embracing it with passion.

But all her passion had died. She'd killed it, with arrogance and pride and a refusal to consider she might be wrong. That Matt could be right. That being Jervale's Heir did not make her infallible.

She wanted to tell him that. To say she was sorry and beg his forgiveness. But his shuttered face defeated her. Made her more tongue-tied, and unfairly angry. So she sat unspeaking and watched him cut wood.

Eventually there was none left. Matt buried the axe blade in the chopping block with one mighty swing and said, sweating, "Could be you were right after all."

For a moment she could only look at him, slumguzzled into silence. Then she found her meagre voice and said, uncertainly, "What do you mean?"

He inspected his palms for blisters. Found one and popped it, frowning. "I mean about not telling Asher the truth."

Asher. Images from the scrying basin swam across her inner eye. She felt her heart constrict and her mouth suck dry. "How so?"

"What you saw was done to him... the way that Jarralt hurt him..."

She thrust away the bloodshed and the haunting echo of screams. "What about it? How can that mean I was right?"

Matt looked elsewhere, into the distance of tangled trees. "Who's to say what a man can know and not talk of when that kind of thing's being done to him? With all the will in the world, if he'd known who he is and what we're about, it's more likely than not he'd have told it to that poxy Doranen bastard and then where would we be?"

She shook her head. "No. Asher's strong. He'd never have broken."

"You can't know that for sure. So the way things fell out it's best you held your tongue and made me hold mine." He glanced at her. "That's the only thing you were right about, mind. As for the rest of it..." Faint colour tinged his face. "The futtering..."

"What about it?" she said tiredly, feeling her own face heat. "You deny Asher's charge that you're jealous 'cause he's known me and you haven't, and never will. But how can I believe you? You act like a man feeling robbed."

For some time he didn't answer. Then he shrugged. Glanced at her again then let his gaze slide sideways into the woods. "Believe me, Dathne, if ever once I loved you I got over it soon enough."

And that hurt, not because she wanted him to love her, at least not like that, but because there was a hardness in him now that before this moment she'd only ever noticed in herself. She'd done that to him, and wasn't proud to learn it.

"I do love him, Matt," she said, worrying at a pulled thread in the fabric stretched over her knee. Needing him to believe her. "It's not an excuse for what I did, but I suppose it is a reason."

He nodded. "I suppose."

"I'm not sure *why* I love him, mind. The purpose behind it, I mean, not the bits and pieces of him that make me soft round the edges. And there must be a purpose, Matt. Mustn't there? Prophecy wouldn't have thrown us together for so long and in such a way that we fell in love if there wasn't a purpose?"

"You're asking the wrong man. I've never much understood Prophecy or its workings."

"And yet you've followed it all your life. Followed *me*. Why?"

He gave her a painful smile. "Why does a dog chase rabbits, Dathne? Because it's in his nature."

In all the years she'd known him she'd never heard him sound so defeated. "We can't afford to doubt now, Matt. We've come too far. Risked too much, and sacrificed more. We must see this through to the end no matter how bitter it might be."

"I know that," he said tersely. "I'm here, aren't I?"

She longed to touch him, but was afraid he'd rebuff her. "What I did with Asher...it was never a trivial thing. I meant what I said about us being sworn in marriage, Barlsman or no Barlsman. His heart is mine, Matt, and mine is his, no matter what."

"I know," he said. "If I thought it'd make a difference, I'd say I wished you happy."

She felt tears well, burning her tired eyes. Never before last night had she cried in front of Matt. It had been a matter of pride and, she thought, necessity. But such things seemed pointless now so she let them fall. "It makes a difference," she whispered, fisting her fingers in the folds of her skirt. "Never think it doesn't make a difference."

"Good," he said. "I'm glad for that."

"I can't believe he has their magic," she said. "He made it snow, right under my roof. How can an Olken do that?"

Matt shook his head. "I don't know. Unless..."

"Unless what?"

"Could he have Doranen blood in him?"

The idea was outrageous. "How? Our peoples don't mix, it's forbidden!"

That made Matt snort. "Olken magic's forbidden, Dathne, yet here we are. Aren't you the one who says all things are possible with Prophecy?"

"Yes, but…" She shook her head. "It doesn't matter. He has their magic and I didn't feel it. How could I not feel it? It's my business to know the Innocent Mage better than he knows himself! And now because I've failed him he might die!"

Matt moved to her then, and folded her in his strong, sheltering arms. He smelled of sweat and leather, his jerkin warm beneath her cheek as he held her against his chest. "You mustn't lose faith, Dath. We have to trust in Prophecy."

"I do," she sobbed. "I do. Oh, Matt, I'm sorry I sent you away. I'm sorry I've always been harsh with you, keeping you distant. I thought it was best. I thought I was protecting you."

"I know that," he said, and rested his cheek on her unruly, unbound hair. "I always knew. And even though it irked me sometimes I never begrudged you your snappishness. It's a sore burden you've been carrying all these years, Dath, and my only true sorrow was in knowing I couldn't carry more of it for you."

"You carried a lot, Matt. You'll never know how much. There were times I thought I could never keep going. I'd have despaired if you hadn't been with me, encouraging. I owe you so much. I owe you my sanity and I never once told you. I'm sorry."

"Hush now, hush," he chided, rocking her gently. "You're Jervale's Heir, you've a task laid on you like nobody else. Especially now, in the Final Days."

She pulled away a little and looked up into his face. "I may be the Heir but you're the Heir's conscience, her wisdom and her strength. Is there anything you can tell me, Matt? Is there anything you've felt that can show me a way out of this mess we're in?" She let out a long and shuddering breath. "That I've put us in?"

He smoothed a tangle of hair from her face. "I wish there was. What do your visions tell you?"

"Nothing," she whispered. "Ever since I lay with Asher they've stopped coming and I don't know why. I've never been so blind in all my life and it scares me."

"Well," Matt said slowly, "could be they've stopped because they'd led you where you needed to be. With him. Could be you're right and Prophecy planned it all along."

"For what purpose? How does me lying with Asher get us through the Final Days? They must be close now, for Asher's revealed as our Innocent Mage. Oh, Matt, are you *sure* you don't know anything?"

"Veira's asked me the same question," he said, "and all I can do is give you the same answer I gave her. There's something amiss with the magic fluxes, but I don't know how or why. It's in the City, because as soon as I left there the uneasiness faded, but beyond that...If I went back I might be able to tell more."

She tightened her arms around him. "No. You can't go back. With Asher arrested they'll want his friends next, and we're his two closest. You're safe here."

"For how long?" Gently, he pulled away and began pacing. "There's not a man, woman or child in all of Lur who'll be safe when Prophecy's finally fulfilled, Dathne, and your dreams become our reality. Our job's not over yet. We still have to save this kingdom from destruction."

"How?" she cried. "For that we need Asher and I can't help him! Can you? Can anyone?"

"I can," said Veira's voice from behind them.

They turned. Stared. Dathne folded her arms about her ribs and held on tight. "How?"

Veira walked out of the forest fringe and across the cottage yard to join them, her brown wool trousers soaked to the knees and her stout leather boots mired in mud. In one gnarled hand she gripped an old tramping stick and at her heels snuffled two enormous mud-covered pigs, tame as dogs. Her wrinkled-apple face was grim.

"With heartbreak, and sacrifice, and a mortal lot of danger," she said. "But we must act swiftly. I had word from the Circle last night: Asher's appointment with the axeman is set for midnight Barl's Day next."

Dathne turned to Matt. "I can't believe the king is doing this. Asher's his dearest friend!"

"If by the king you mean Gar then that's more bad news," said Veira. "Lur has a new king now."

"Not Conroyd Jarralt?"

Veira nodded. "Yes."

"Barl protect us," said Matt, and rested his hand on Dathne's shoulder. "There won't be an Olken safe anywhere."

"Only if we fail," said Veira, grimly. "But if we are to save the Innocent Mage from dying and taking us all with him to the grave, you must do as I say without fratching. What's to come will come. Must come. Prophecy demands it."

Matt frowned. "I don't like the sound of that."

"You're not asked to," Veira snapped. "Dathne, put these pigs back in their pen, child, and see they have a good breakfast. You, Matthias, fetch knife and bowl from the kitchen. Cut me two sprigs from every herb and planting in the last row of the garden there. Tie a strip of cheesecloth over your nose and mouth, be sure to put on gloves, and whatever your opinion of what you see and cut, keep it to yourself. Don't bring the cuttings inside either; leave them on the ground beside the back door. When you're both done, amuse yourselves in the kitchen by making soup for lunch. All the fixings are in the pantry."

Bewildered, Dathne looked over at the herb bed. "Cheesecloth and gloves?"

Veira's severe expression eased, just a little. "For precaution only. I'd not put Matthias in danger." She pulled a face. "Not from herbs at least."

As she stumped past them on her way back into the cottage Matt said, "And I like the sound of that even less."

Troubled, Dathne nodded, watching as the cottage's back door closed behind the old woman. "Nor do I. But we'd best do as we're told, I think. Whatever it is she's planning, it's near torn her heart from her chest."

Despite her village isolation and solitary cottage lifestyle, Veira kept her Circle Stones out of sight, in a hidey-hole she'd dug beneath her bedroom floor and lined with discarded tiles from the village pottery. The neatly rejoined floorboards with their betraying finger holes for lifting stayed hidden beneath an old, fraying carpet.

Alone in her bedroom with the door safely closed and curtains drawn she rolled back the carpet, hoisted up the hidey-hole's lid and leaned it against the bed. Forty Circle Stones winked up at her in the flickering lamplight, looking no more important than a random collection of pretty quartz crystals, a magpie's playthings.

Forty stones, forty friends—no, *family*—forty oaths solemnly sworn. So few, to stand against the coming darkness.

She hunkered down beside the hidey-hole, grimacing as her knees protested. Rafel's stone, a blue as pale as fresh-skimmed milk, drew her gaze like a magnet. She picked it up, cradled it in her palm and called to him. When he answered, tears sprang to her eyes.

"It's time."

For long heartbeats he said nothing. Then she felt him sigh. *When we heard of Asher's arrest I thought it might be. He is the one, isn't he? He's the Innocent Mage?*

She'd told no one save Gilda. Trust Rafel to guess the truth.

"Yes," she said. "It's him. Darling—"

Don't say it. She thought his smile might kill her. *You're crying... and besides, I've had strange dreams.*

"If there was any other way..."

Perhaps I wouldn't have been born.

"We have little time," she said through her tears. "You'll need to meet me tomorrow where the West Road runs into the Black Woods Road on its way to the City. How soon can you get there?"

By mid-morning or not long after.

"You must invent some reason for leaving. Tell as few as possible and depart without an audience; say you go anywhere but to the City. Travel light and as fast as you can without drawing undue attention. Let no one see your sorrow."

I understand.

"I'll see you tomorrow, then."

Tomorrow, he said, still smiling, and out of love was the one who broke the link.

Some time later, after she'd won back composure, she again reached out to Gilda through the rich green stone that kept them in contact. Nearly ten long minutes ticked by before their connection was made.

Sorry, sorry, said Gilda, flustered. *I was with a customer I couldn't get away.*

"No matter, Gilda. My friend, I have a task for you. And not to plunge you into deep dismay I must say this: upon your success lies the future of our kingdom."

The link between them trembled with Gilda's uncertainty, then firmed again. *Of course, Veira. What do you need?*

"I'm coming into the City for the execution and I need you to save me bench space for three beside you, right down the front. Directly before the block."

Beside me? said Gilda, faltering. *So close?*

"Yes. Can you do it?"

Of course.

"Bless you, dear. I'll see you before midnight this Barl's Day."

She replaced Gilda's stone and selected another, this one dark blue-black.

"Rogan. I have a task for you."

Rogan agreed without question, as she'd known he would. Next she contacted Laney Treadwell, whose family business was most useful, and finally she reached out to the ten best-placed and strongest magicians in the group, on whose shoulders she must place a heavy burden. Resolute, they promised to join her in Dorana and carry out their task.

Jervale bless them all. Without such staunch supporters she'd not have the heart to go on.

With all the arrangements in place, and tired almost beyond speaking, she replaced the last Circle Stone, the hidey-hole lid and the carpet that covered them. Eased herself groaning to her feet, and went out to the kitchen.

The soup was on the stove top, bubbling aromatically. Dathne and Matthias sat in silence at the table, each lost in private meditation.

"Please, Veira, what's going on?" said Dathne, looking up. "The herbs you had Matt cut for you—"

"Are deadly," she said shortly. "I know it."

Matthias stirred in his chair. "Then why do you need them?"

She moved to the kitchen window and stared out into the garden beyond, with its undisciplined winter roses and riot of ravenberries. "To serve Prophecy."

"Serve it how?" said Dathne.

"I'll keep my own counsel on that. The less you know, the better. At least until you must."

"And who decides when that is? I'm not a child, Veira, whatever you like to call me! I'm Jervale's Heir and—"

"And you'll learn to follow another's instructions!" she snapped, turning away from the window. Then, seeing Dathne's strained and peaky face, seeing the fear imperfectly smothered, she softened. "Child, child—for that's what you are to me, married lady or not—stop fretting on things you don't control. We've enough worms in the apple without you making room for more."

Dathne looked to Matthias, who shook his head and ventured a brief smile. "No fratching, remember?"

Defeated, Dathne slumped. "All right."

"Good," Veira said briskly, and moved to the stove. "Now let's eat."

Afterwards, once the soup had been consumed in silence and Matthias was sent outside to check Bessie, her shoes, her harness and the rackety old cart, Dathne turned her hand to washing dishes.

"I'm not fratching, truly," she said, her hands in soapy water. "I just wish you'd tell me who those herbs are for."

Veira sighed. Letting the dish towel dangle from her fingers she said, "No one you know, child. I promise."

"But someone you know?"

Grimly, she held her tears below the surface. "Yes. Someone I know."

"Then let me brew the potion."

Oh, it was a tempting thought. Kind and loving too. "No," she said, and touched her hand to Dathne's shoulder. "Though you have my thanks for offering."

Mettlesome as always, Dathne took the refusal as criticism. "I am capable! I have more herb lore than—"

"Herb lore has nothing to do with it. No woman with child should touch those cuttings."

Shocked silent, Dathne stared at her. Pulled her hands from the soapy dishwater to flatten them against her belly and press, softly. "With child? What do you mean?"

Veira snorted. "I'm old, child, not blind or deaf or stupid. I might not've birthed my own but I've done my share of midwifery over the years. There's a look a woman gets. And I felt something different in you too." Then she sighed. "You didn't realise?"

Dathne shook her head. "No. At least...I wondered...for a moment...but I *can't* be. We only lay together twice and I took precautions both times."

"Then could be Prophecy had other ideas."

"Why? What good can come of *this?*"

Veira reached for another plate to dry. "There's always good in the birth of a baby."

"When our world's about to end in flood and fire? *How?*"

"Perhaps to remind us not to give up so easily."

"I'm not giving up!" said Dathne, stepping back. Soap suds dripped heedless to the floor. "I'm lost! I'm frightened! I used to trust myself, trust Prophecy, to believe I was given what I needed to prevail! Instead I'm a fugitive and the man I was born to guide and protect awaits his death. And now there's a *baby?*"

The child was losing hope. Time for a little sharp prodding. "In other words you *are* giving up."

Dathne turned away. "Perhaps I am," she whispered roughly. "Perhaps it's the best thing I can do for all of us. Give up. Walk away. Leave his fate to those who've not made such terrible mistakes."

"I doubt that's best for Asher or his babe," said Veira, and put a snap in her voice. "You're Jervale's Heir, Dathne. You cannot walk away. And besides, who amongst us has never made a mistake? Not me. Not Matthias either. Making mistakes isn't the problem, child. It's not doing our best to fix them after that leads to ruin. And we don't know there's been any mistakes. Could be all of this is what Prophecy planned from the beginning."

"Then Prophecy should've thought of a different plan!" Dathne retorted, flushing with temper. Then she turned back to the sink, seeking refuge in housewifery. "You haven't told Matt about this, have you?"

Raising an eyebrow, Veira held out her hand for the next dripping bowl. "Could be he already knows. Handled enough pregnant mares in his time, hasn't he?"

"Well, he hasn't handled me!"

"Peace. I've not told him, child," she said gently. "And I won't. Time and your belly will tell him soon enough. And he's got himself a full plate already, I'm thinking. I don't need to force-feed him any- thing more to chew on."

Dathne nodded, frowning, and reached for the soup pot to scrub. "We're going back to the City, aren't we?" she said after a moment. "To try and rescue Asher."

Well, not "we." But she was too tired for more arguments, at least right now. So instead of telling Dathne the truth, she said, "Yes. Later tonight, after dark. But there'll be no trying about it. The Innocent Mage will be rescued...and Prophecy will continue."

Asher was dragged from a wonderful dream of Dathne by the sound of banging hammers. Cursing, he rolled painfully onto his other side, closed his eyes and tried to recapture sleep.

She'd been in a green and sweetly smelling place, her fragrant hair unbound, her thin face lit with a smile. There were trees all around her, and pigs, and hens.

He opened his eyes.

Pigs and *hens*?

Barl bloody save him. He was finally going mad.

With some of the novelty worn off, enough of the crowd had returned home or to their temporary lodgings in the City's hotels and hostelries for him to see what all the hammering was about. Brawny palace staff were building a dais on the left-hand side of the Square.

Ox Bunder, condemned to guard duty, noticed him noticing and leered in typically unfriendly fashion. Probably he was grudging because now he'd never get paid that three trins owed to him from their last game of darts down at the Goose.

Ha. Praise Barl for small favours.

Ox wandered over, planted his pikestaff like a walking-stick and leaned. "Going to be a big crowd to see you get your comeuppance, midnight tomorrow," he remarked. "I hear the general councillors are near to drawing straws to see who gets the best view from up on that dais they're building. I hear Guild Meister Roddle's been offering money to make sure he's seated right down the very front."

If he said nothing, Ox would stop leaning and hit him with the pikestaff. If he said something, anything, Ox would stop leaning and—

He sighed.

"Midnight tomorrow, eh?" he answered, as though he didn't know. "You reckon it's goin' to rain?"

Ox stopped leaning and hit him with the pikestaff.

Spitting blood and a broken tooth, Asher rolled his face into his folded arms and took refuge once more in sleep. He didn't dream this time, of pigs or hens or Dathne, or anyone else at all.

Blessedly alone in Conroyd's townhouse, with Ethienne at long last noisily departed, the household staff dismissed and Willer sent to oversee arrangements for the impending Olken curfew, Morg sat in a chair in Conroyd's library and gave himself over to thought.

The Weather Orb, dutifully delivered, sat in its box on a table before him. Teasing. Taunting. Tantalising. All that magic but a thin skin's thickness away.

There *had* to be a way to get at it.

Imprisoned within, Conroyd raged. Unlike Durm, whose guilt-stained soul had wept and wailed and begged Barl for mercy, for aid, Conroyd seemed more affronted than anything to find himself a captive inside his own body. The first shock passed, he now jabbered ceaselessly in the background, demanding explanations, insisting upon answers, offering help.

Help . . .

The fool, to think Morg required the help of a sheep. That he was in any position to bargain, wheedle. Make deals. *Arrangements.*

Morg reached out and stroked the Orb. Its quiescent colours swirled, sensing him. Rejecting him. His flesh belonged to Conroyd, but the spirit within was his own. The Orb would never give him access. *Never.*

Unless . . .

An idea, glimmering. A flickered spark of inspiration. He held his breath lest even a gentle exhalation extinguish hope. Could it be managed? Was it *possible*? Could Morg and Conroyd merge into a single entity just long enough for the Orb not to recognise Barl's bitter enemy? To grant him her Weather Magics that he might use them to bring down her Wall?

It would never have worked using Durm. Even with all his maudlin despair the fat fool had been far too strong. And their minds, at the core, were ultimately incompatible. The only way to control him had been to keep him safely, rigorously caged. Letting him out, even a little, would have been fatal.

But Conroyd? Ah, Conroyd. Here was a soul of a different stripe. One with faint echoes of his own darkness. Even better, he and Conroyd were blood related, ties of family whispering down the centuries. They belonged in each other, as he and Durm had never belonged.

And Conroyd was accepted by Barl.

Sitting back, closing his eyes, he reached inside and touched small Conroyd's mind, gentle as sunshine.

You desire to help me, cousin? You wish to sip from the cup of power only I can hold to your lips?

Little Conroyd whimpered, suddenly uncertain.

Have no fear, blood of my blood. You were born for greatness. Born to raise the Doranen to the heights of all known mastery. Help me and together we shall birth an Age of Glory never before known in this land!

Little Conroyd's greed and ambition flared like a torch at midnight.

Come to me, Conroyd, he whispered. *Let us mingle for a moment.*

Conroyd came to him, unthinking and unaware. Morg lowered the bars of the cage around him. Let him out. Let him *breathe* ...

...and at the same instant breathed him in. Melted Conroyd like butter and soaked him through all his nooks and crannies, flavouring his spirit with the essence of Jarralt. Hiding himself like a fox evading hounds in running water.

Conroyd shrieked once, and was silent.

Time passed. At length something not quite Conroyd, not quite Morg, sat upright in its cradling chair. Removed the Weather Orb from its wooden box and held it in its hands. Sighing, it smiled at the glorious swirl of colour. The promise it held of death and destruction. The spell required to transfer the magic from Orb to waiting mind remained, a legacy from Durm. All it needed to do now was recite the words. Trigger the act of Transference. Steal the bitch whore's precious power.

The part of this new thing that was Morg took a moment to

prepare. To ensure that he continued safely entwined with Conroyd. Satisfied, he sank beneath the surface again and the thing held up the Orb before its shining eyes. Spoke the words of the Transference incantation...

...and waited for victory.

Within the Orb the colours swirled. Deepened. Took on lustre and life. The creature watched, exultant, as they poured out of the Orb and over its hands. Into its hands. As they sank inside it, filling it with knowledge, with power. With the key to this kingdom's destruction.

And then...hesitation. The pulsing Orb trembled, the colours shifted. Darkened. Crimson and gold changed to purple and black and began writhing as though alive, furious, and in pain.

Barl's long-dead voice cried: *No! No! This is not for you, Morg! Never for you!*

But still the Orb tried to empty itself of magic, sensing yet the presence of an untainted vessel. The thing surged to its feet, howling, as the flesh of its fingers seared. Sizzled. As the darkness inside the Orb flooded outside, up its arms and over its body like a wave of foul black ink.

Morg wrenched himself free from Conroyd's cloying presence. Threw back his head and screamed in furious desperation. "Bitch! Whore! You won't keep them from me again, Barl! *I will have them!*"

No, Morgan, her whispering voice replied. *No, you will not.*

The Orb burst into flame. Within heartbeats the air in the library was thickened with the stench of charred flesh and charred magic.

Morg screamed and dropped the ruined Orb. It fell to the floor and smashed into pieces. He collapsed a moment later, crushing its blackened shards to powder beneath his convulsing body as oblivion came to claim him.

It was Darran who found the diary. Fussing, fusspot Darran with his passion for order and symmetry, his determination that things must be just *so*. His busy fingers felt the irregular thickness in the aged leather binding of a text on primer exercises for junior magicians. His critical eyes saw the difference between the front and back covers and made him wonder...

Sitting beside him on the study floor, Gar slit the book's apparently untouched stitching with his dagger and eased the diary out of hiding. Held it in hands that trembled and wondered if he was dreaming.

"Barl save us," breathed Darran, astonished. "There really is a diary!"

Barl save them indeed. And in her own words, no less, if the diary was truly once hers. Was it the miracle he'd been waiting for? Hoping for? Believing in against all expectation of fulfilment?

If it wasn't, it was the closest thing he'd found.

He let the diary fall open. Stared at the swift, untidy writing, the faded ink strokes, the imprints of history. Struggling, he made sense of the first few lines.

It saddens me to think of the magics we
must leave behind, but in this new land
magic must be a thing of order and discipline,
not an everyday indulgence or—

"Gracious," said Darran, peering. "It looks like a lot of old chicken scratchings! Do you think you can read it, sir?"

Gar let his fingertips caress the page. Inhaled the scent of musty dust and time, feeling hope's candle flare. He smiled.

"Yes. I can read it."

Darran released a gusty sigh. "Praise Barl for small mercies," he said. "But might I suggest you read it later? The king's men will be here soon, wanting these books. And for once I'm inclined to believe what Willer says: we don't want to keep them waiting."

So he hid the diary at the back of a bookshelf and hurried to help Darran pack away the rest of Durm's collected life and learnings. When they were done, and the books, papers and journals were neatly boxed and stacked by the Tower's front doors he made himself stand still in the middle of the tiled foyer floor for a moment and breathe, just breathe.

"What now, sir?" said Darran.

"Now?" He shook his head to clear it. Wiped away sweat with his forearm. "Now I have work, Darran. And if Barl is merciful and truly hears our prayers there'll be something in these pages that can not only save this kingdom but Asher as well."

"Then you'd better get started, sir," said Darran. "And have no fear. I'll see you're not distracted or disturbed."

Gar spared him a quick smile. "Good man."

As Darran's tired, drawn face lit up with an answering smile, Gar turned and headed for the spiral staircase. Took it three treads at a time, thinking:

Please, Barl. Please. Be merciful, just this once.

CHAPTER TWENTY-SEVEN

Pellen Orrick sat at his desk and frowned at the reports spread before him. *No sign...no sign...*no sign...

Dathne the bookseller and Gar's former Stable Meister, Matt, were nowhere to be found.

He drummed his fingers on the desktop and frowned more deeply. What did their disappearance mean? Was it a coincidence? Unlikely. Were they merely dismayed that their friend had been revealed as a traitor? Possible. Or were they mired hip-deep in blasphemy beside him, and desperate now to save their own wicked lives? Also possible. Maybe even probable.

Which meant King Conroyd was right and this was a conspiracy. It was a horrifying thought, with implications and consequences too dreadful to imagine. Except that he was the Captain of the City and it was his job, his duty, to imagine them.

Chilled, Orrick sat back in his chair and stared out of the window towards the Square. He could just see the top of Asher's cage over the press of bodies still gathered to marvel and gloat. With the word gone out to all and sundry on his crime and imminent death, the City was as full of visitors now as it had been during the month of mourning for the late royal family. The inns were full again. The hotels too, and all the rustic hostelries.

Death was a booming business these days.

Conspiracy. How far did its tentacles spread, then? How deeply was its rotten abscess buried within the flesh of Olken society and how much blood would be shed in the attempt to cut it out? Would Asher's be sufficient? Or must the guards of the kingdom unite to spill blood enough to make a river?

Starting with Dathne's and Stable Meister Matt's.

Abruptly sickened Orrick left his office, left the guardhouse, and made his way across the Square to Asher in his cage. The four guards on duty dipped their heads in polite greeting and withdrew as far as they could, to give him privacy.

He addressed the prisoner without preamble. "Your friends Dathne and Matt are missing. If you love them, tell me where they would go so I might bring them in sensibly and ask them myself how they assisted in your crimes."

Asher's eyes were dark-rimmed and sunken, and all his wounds had festered. Without bothering to lift his head, or look up at all, he croaked, "Piss off, Pellen."

Despite the vile stench from the cage, the straw, Asher's unwashed body, Orrick stepped closer. "If I tell the king I can't find them he'll order a reckless search. Innocent people might be hurt or arrested for all the wrong reasons. In the end you know they'll be found, Asher. There's nowhere they can run to or hide where I or someone like me won't find them. And then it won't be me and mine asking the questions, it'll be His Majesty...and you know best how that will go. So tell me where they are. Not for me, or for him. For them."

Now Asher did stir and look up. "I don't know where they are and any road, they were never involved and Jarralt knows it. If he wants them it's to hurt me, nowt else. Not that you'd care."

"That's untrue!"

Asher laughed, a harsh and rasping rattle. "Is it?"

"You think you have cause for complaint?"

Lifting one raw and weeping wrist, jangling the chains that bound him, for the first time Asher looked him full in the face. "Wouldn't you?"

"You don't think you deserve this? You don't think it's fair? Why not? You were eager enough for justice when it was Timon Spake facing the axe!"

Asher flinched. "Timon Spake was never hurt with magic. You didn't chain him up like an animal, or put him on show like an animal. For all he was a criminal you treated Timon Spake with decency!"

Orrick clenched his jaw, offended by more than just the stink. "I take my duty seriously, Asher. Your arrest is lawful, your guilt beyond doubt. You *admitted* your crime. However..." He tightened his hands behind his back and lowered his voice. "If the choice were mine, you'd have awaited execution in the guardhouse."

"Really?" said Asher. "Well, I guess that means we're friends again, eh?"

He looked away. "We were never friends!"

"I know," said Asher, softly. "But we might've been."

This was a mistake. Tugging his tunic straight Orrick said briskly, "Reconsider your silence on Dathne and Matt. The longer they stay fugitive the harder I must search for them, and the worse things will be once they're found. If they're innocent—"

"Innocent?" said Asher. "There ain't no *innocent* here, Pellen. Our new King Conroyd's got the bit between his teeth now. He's bolting towards turning all us Olken into cattle, and if you can't see that you're blinder than I thought. You let him get his hands on Dathne or Matt, it'll just be the start. Next thing you know, anyone who ever smiled at 'em will be under suspicion. You wait. It's all rollin' downhill from here."

"And if it is?" said Orrick. "Who's to blame for that? Who was the one caught dabbling with magic?"

Asher slumped into his filthy straw. Frowned at his manacled wrists. "I know."

"For the love of Barl, Asher, tell me where they are. You might be saving their lives!"

"You are blind," said Asher, and closed his bloodshot eyes. "Blind and bloody stupid. The best hope they've got is if I never mention their names again. So I won't. Now piss off, why don't you? I'm a very busy man."

Rebuffed, nonplussed, grudgingly moved and resentful of that, Orrick stood there for a moment, just staring at him. Then he turned on his heel and went back to the guardhouse.

The new king awaited his report...and he had yet to decide what it would say.

Conroyd's townhouse was filling with shadows when Morg returned to himself. He felt pain. Confusion. A bizarre disorientation, as though he were trying to be two people at once. For some time he remained on the floor, struggling to piece together what had happened. The memory of Barl's voice sighed through his pounding head.

He lifted his hands before his eyes and stared. Charred flesh. Blistered meat. Revolted, he healed himself with a word and sat up. Barl's voice faded, chased away by buzzing Conroyd. He sank inside, retrieved all the melted thinness of himself and banished Conroyd deep within.

And felt...different.

Startled, as he had not been startled in centuries, he examined the difference. What was it? What did it mean? Was he still himself? Or had Barl's attack damaged him somehow?

Damn Barl. Had he loved her? Worshipped her? Wanted to spend eternity with her? He must have been mad.

Subduing the flesh emotion he waited for his startlement to pass. Conjured glimfire and considered himself. His surroundings. His beautiful clothes were smeared and stained—*the Weather Orb!*

Crumbled to ash and memory, ground into the carpet beneath him. Almost, almost, he wept.

More time passed. Self-control returned and intellect reasserted itself. Yes, the Orb was destroyed and with it his hope for a swift victory. But at least no other Doranen would have the Weather Magics now, and use them to keep Barl's golden Wall strong. And when Asher died, the last living Weather Magic would die along with him.

But failure to gain it for himself and his own ends meant he was still trapped here. Must wait weeks, months, for the magics to fade and the Wall to collapse beneath the weight of its gradual decay. And waiting meant he must somehow keep the other Doranen at bay, his borrowed body safe, until victory came limping to him.

Assaulted, intellect trembled. It was intolerable. *Intolerable.* He staggered to his feet, healed hands clenched into fists. Opened his mouth to shout aloud his fury, frustration and lingering pain—and gasped.

There was new magic in his mind.

Tentatively, he reached towards it. Brushed his senses against it, feeling it slowly unfurl, and laughed.

Weather Magic.

Not complete. Not all that had been contained in the Orb had passed to him. And what had escaped Barl's clutches was damaged now by the black flames. But it was Weather Magic all the same. This must be the difference he had felt. This, his longed-for victory.

"See, bitch?" he shouted to the empty room. To her lingering, vanquished memory. "You did not beat me! You have not won!"

He now possessed just enough Weather Magic to let him see into the heart of her precious Wall. To show him its weft and warp and how he might tease its threads undone. Tease at the fabric of her genius, unravel it, and so unravel the world she'd made in defiance of him and the sacred vows they'd sworn to one another.

But not here. For such deep seeing he required the Weather Chamber.

He rode there on the back of peasant Asher's silver stallion. Like its former master the animal resisted him at first, but not for long.

Nothing and no one could resist him for long.

He travelled the City streets unnoticed, cloaked in a spell of distraction. Entered the palace grounds unremarked by the guards and turned the stallion's head towards the old palace grounds where Barl's final monstrosity squatted amongst the trees. The closer he got to the Chamber the more strongly could he smell it. Six centuries dead and her magic continued to hold sway. He hated her, *hated* her, and marvelled at her mastery.

Breaking through the trees at last he found himself in a clearing, face to face with the ancient Weather Chamber. Bastion of Barl's magic and seat of his undoing. Teeth gritted, he dismounted and looped the stallion's reins over a handy branch. Lathered, pocked with spur marks, the animal drooped its head to the ground, panting and dripping bloody sweat.

After conjuring glimfire he opened the reluctant door and climbed the stairs two at a time, revelling in his athletic ease. The door at the top of the stairs was open. He shoved it wider, stepped into the chamber and was once more soaked with the drenching stench of Barl's Weather Magic. Faint echoes of her presence stirred like fading, rancid perfume.

He tipped back his head. Stared through the crystal ceiling and into the gold-washed sky. "Do you see me, bitch?" he whispered. "It's Morgan, dearest. Your husband's home."

Unanswered, he turned his attention to the centre of the chamber, and the sympathetic model of Lur so skilfully tuned to the fabric of the kingdom. An unfamiliar emotion speared him: regret. The map was a miracle only Barl could manage. Oh, what they might have accomplished if only she'd stayed faithful.

Sinking to the parquetry floor he stretched out his hands above the model. Closed his eyes and opened his mind to the stolen incantations that writhed in his head like golden snakes, letting Barl's stinking magic suffuse him.

And then, at last, he understood. Everything that until this moment had been opaque was perfectly, beautifully clear. He understood it all...

In this fecund land power flows through all living things, a part of them and indivisible. Not hard and sharp and brilliant like Doranen magic, to be forged into weapons and servitude. Olken magic is soft and slithery, nourishing like blood. Destined to slip through the fingers of any who might think to crudely grasp it. Barl sees this. Accepts this. Comes to realise that her purpose requires a marriage of magics. Night and day she labours to give the union life and so protect her new home forever. In the weather lies the key. She weaves magic like a tapestry, combining Olken and Doranen power into whole cloth. This thread for rainfall, that thread for snow. Here the colour of sunshine, there the shadows of wind. The power builds, feeding into the Wall she is creating, flowing from it to the fertile earth and back to the Wall again. It is an endless cycle of give and take, replenish and diminish and replenish once more. An act never-ending, demanding an endless sacrifice. And at its heart lies the WeatherWorker, living conduit of power and pain. The WeatherWorker is the weaver, with the Wall's separate and delicate skeins threading through fragile fingers of flesh and bone. The WeatherWorker controls the magic, is the magic, weaves the tapestry. Maintains the Wall. Constantly creates and keeps the balance between Olken and Doranen powers. And woe to Barl's beloved kingdom should the WeatherWorker snap a thread...

Morg opened his eyes, struggling to remember how to breathe. Blinked and blinked and blinked again until the chamber resolved itself into the familiarity of hard lines and solid surfaces. Before him pulsed the map of the kingdom, its beating, vulnerable heart.

Which now he had the means to crush.

With the stolen Weather Magics incomplete he would be forced to move slowly. Torture! After interminable waiting he longed to rip Barl's Wall to pieces with teeth and taloned fingers. Sink his power into its entrails and gut it like a rabbit. Fall upon the magic-soaked model-map and pound it to splinters with his fists. Grind it to powder beneath his heels.

But no. Confined in flesh, denied access to his untrammelled powers and her complete incantations, he must still bide his time. Pick apart his dear Barl's tapestry thread by slow and sticky thread. Wait a little longer before being reunited with the best and most of himself, held in limbo on the other side of the Wall.

Morg smiled and soothed himself. Patience...patience...after these six centuries, what were a few weeks more?

By the time the hour came for them to leave the cottage, bent on Dorana and Asher's rescue, Dathne was almost numb with fatigue and dread. Filled with a churning horror, reminded sickeningly of Timon Spake and the orris root, she'd sat in the kitchen and watched Veira concoct her poisonous potion. Seven different plants were used: drogle, witcheye, lantin, dogsbane and bloodweed she recognised; the others she'd never seen before and didn't dare query. One word out of place and she knew Veira would banish her from the room. And this wasn't something the old woman should do on her own, even if all the help she'd accept was a silent, sympathetic witnessing.

Once the poison was mixed, poured carefully into a small jar, stoppered and wrapped twice against spillage, Veira disposed of the leftover muck and went to walk in the forest again. With Matt still pottering outside and not needing help, he said, Dathne went back indoors.

But couldn't. Her hand kept drifting to her belly and her thoughts wouldn't turn from the miracle—the mistake, whatever Veira said—now growing deep inside her.

A baby...a baby...a baby...

What was Prophecy *thinking*?

What did *she* think?

As Jervale's Heir she'd never imagined becoming a mother. Not even a wife, given the danger of the life she lived. The last married Heir had died unhappily two hundred years ago, nearly; Dathne had taken that lesson to heart and sworn never to risk herself or her duty in the name of frivolous love.

But then had come Asher...and suddenly love didn't seem so frivolous. Love, without warning, became as needful as air.

Would he be pleased to discover he'd soon enough be a father? Would she even have the chance to tell him? If this rescue failed, if evil triumphed...

No. She wouldn't let doubt touch her. They'd rescue Asher unharmed—Prophecy wouldn't let it be otherwise. She'd see him again and he would forgive her the lies and the silences and when his task for Prophecy was done they'd settle down and be a family in the brand-new Lur they'd helped create.

Tears prickled, blurring her eyes. She was going to have a *baby*.

Outside the cottage, shadows lengthened. Dusk descended. Matt came inside, looking for dinner. She put the book back on its shelf and gave him some carrots to peel. Veira returned with two fresh rabbits already gutted, skinned and jointed. She set them to frying in butter and sage and so night fell upon them.

With dinner eaten and the dishes done, Veira announced they'd depart at midnight, then retired to her bedroom. Matt retired to his. Dathne returned to the sitting room, tried again to read, gave up, and blew out the lantern to sleep a little before they had to leave.

Sleep eluded her. Eyes open or closed, all she could see was that bottle of poison and the look on Veira's face as she'd stoppered it. Terrible sorrow. Dreadful resolve.

For Asher to be rescued, someone had to die.

The thought was appalling. Haunted her unmercifully so that she gave up the idea of slumber and ventured back to the kitchen instead.

Veira was packing bread and cheese and biscuits into a rough-weave hamper. "There you are, child. I was about to come and rouse you. Matt's outside, harnessing Bessie."

"Good," she said, and looked for a mug. "Is there time for tea?"

There was the slightest hesitation as Veira searched the drawer for a bread knife. "Not for me and Matthias. We must leave in the next quarter-hour."

She looked up. "And me."

Straightening, knife in hand, Veira shook her head. "No, Dathne. You're staying behind."

"Behind? I don't think so! Stay here alone while you and Matt run all the risks of rescue?"

"You won't be alone," said Veira. "You'll have the pigs for company. And the hens too. Don't forget to feed them or they'll raise a mighty ruckus. Few things as tetchy as pigs and hens if they're made to go to bed without their supper."

"*Veira!*"

"It's too dangerous, child. You know they'll be looking for you."

"And for Matt!" she protested. "But he's going back, so why can't I?"

Breathing deeply, Veira tucked the bread knife into the basket. "It's best if you don't. I've a little trick practised to keep the guards from spotting Matthias, but I'm not strong enough to play it on both of you."

"Then show it to me and I'll play it on myself!"

"No," said Veira flatly, and kept on packing the basket.

"No?" she echoed, and felt a flooding rage. "I am Jervale's Heir! You don't say 'no' to *me*, old woman!"

The kitchen's back door opened, revealing Matt. "Don't fratch at her, Dathne. If she says you can't come, accept it."

She turned on him, venomous. "Not without a damned good reason!"

That earned her a scorching look from Veira. "Because I say so is reason enough! You may be Jervale's Heir but Prophecy's brought you here and here is where *I'm* in charge! So hold your tongue if you've nothing of use to say with it, and finish off stocking that basket. It's a long trip back to the City and we'll have no time for stopping on the way."

That said, Veira stalked out of the kitchen. Quietly cursing, Dathne did as she was told, flinging biscuits and fruit scones from their tin onto a clean cloth and then into the basket. Lifting hard-boiled eggs from their saucepan on the stove and tossing them in after. Hotly aware of scrutiny she looked up, and met Matt's understanding gaze.

"Veira's right," he said, still standing in the doorway and letting the cold air in. "She's the Circle Guardian. We must be guided by her, no matter how hard that is."

"Veira's a bossy old besom and don't you try telling me otherwise!"

His lips quirked in a tiny smile. "Actually, she reminds me of you."

"Did I ask your opinion?"

He sighed. "No. So I won't give it. And since the wagon's ready, I'm off to harness Bessie."

"Fine," she muttered through gritted teeth as the door banged shut behind him. "I hope she stands on all your toes and breaks them."

"Not a very charitable wish, child," chided Veira from the other doorway. A padded dark blue coat was folded over her arm. "You ride too roughshod over that young man."

Dathne felt her face warm. "He's got broad shoulders," she said defensively. "He can carry a few harsh words from me."

"It's not if he can," said Veira. "It's if he should, and we both know the answer to that."

Abandoning the basket, Dathne dropped into the nearest kitchen chair, watching as Veira put down the coat she carried and picked up the swaddled bottle of poison from the benchtop. The old woman's expression was unbearably sad.

Abruptly, anger died. "Veira...don't take that with you. Rescue Asher without it."

"We can't," said Veira, not looking around. "This is the way it has to be. One life...for another."

"Why? It's *murder*!"

Three of Veira's hairpins were coming loose. She put down the poison and poked and prodded them back into place. "It's sacrifice. There's a difference."

"Asher wouldn't like what you're planning, Veira. He wouldn't want to be rescued like this. I know him, and he wouldn't want it!"

Veira turned, her kindly, wrinkled face now hard with purpose. "I don't much care for what he wants, child. Or what you want either. This is about Prophecy, not personal desires. You may have forgotten that but others haven't."

The barb was unexpected; for a moment she could hardly breathe, let alone speak. "That's unfair."

A scornful snort. "Life's unfair, child."

Which was, unfortunately, true. She picked up the thread of her original argument, loath to let it go. "As Jervale's Heir I should be coming with you. Please, Veira, don't make me stay behind!"

Veira shook her head. "Behind is where you belong."

It was like telling a tree not to grow, or the sun to rise upside down: pointless. But that didn't stop her from trying. "But, Veira, I need to be there. Asher might not trust you or Matt. He will trust me."

With a sharp sigh Veira took a step closer. "Child, child, emotion is addling your wits. What wise housewife puts all her eggs in one basket? Should this rescue fail, should we be discovered or Prophecy thwarted somehow by the darkness struggling to defeat us, you must pick up the Circle's pieces. You must become Heir and Guardian both. In my bedroom, on my dresser, I've left you instructions. Should the worst befall us, follow them exactly. Do what you can to save as many as possible. Save yourself. Bear your child. For it too is a part of Prophecy's plans and doubtless has some grand destiny whose purpose we still don't know."

All without warning, Dathne felt herself flooded with tears. *"Damn…"*

Veira's eyes were brimming too. "Have faith, child. Trust in Prophecy. Between us, Matthias and Rafel and I will bring your Asher home."

"Rafel?" she whispered.

Veira nodded. "The man we go to meet on the way."

The man who soon would die. Had she really wanted a name? Yes, but now she regretted knowing it. Names were real. Names belonged to the living and called to mind the dead. Feeling unsteady, she forced herself to her feet. "When you reach this Rafel, tell him thank you. Tell him I'm sorry. Tell him I wish there was another way."

Solemn, sorrowful, Veira reached out a hand and touched cold fingertips to her cheek. "I will, child. For all of us."

Dathne looked so forlorn, so abandoned, as she stood waving them goodbye from the cottage's front gate that Matt almost asked Veira to reconsider and let her come with them after all.

But only almost. Because he was in truth quite glad she wasn't coming. Was instead left safe behind in the middle of the Black Woods where no harm would come to her if this mad plan to rescue Asher fell all to pieces, as it seemed most likely it would.

Sunk equally deep in blankets and silence, Veira sat beside him on the little wagon's bench seat and let him get on with the driving. Bessie, a good-natured animal, seemed quite happy to venture out in the dark. Didn't take much driving at all, just the occasional "hup-hup" and rattle of reins to keep her up to the bridle as she jog-walk-jogged along the empty road. For that he felt a little sorry. More energetic driving would give him less empty time to think about things he'd rather not consider.

Veira still hadn't revealed the details of this trip. All she'd said was they'd be travelling without stop until they reached Dorana, except for picking up someone else from the Circle. Someone, he suspected, he'd not long have the chance to know.

It was just one of the many things he didn't want to think about.

Slowly, steadily, the miles unrolled behind them. The night grew colder, marching towards sunrise, and he wrapped an extra blanket round his shoulders. Held the reins in one hand so he could warm the other in his armpit, and swapped them over time and again.

Eventually the morning came. Veira stirred and fed them from the basket. They were well along the Black Woods Road now. Sheep grazed on either side and rabbits scuttled white-tailed as they creaked on by but otherwise they were quite alone. Veira ordered him into the back of the wagon to stretch out and sleep properly. Happy to obey her he lay down, tucked the blankets around him and fell into a dreamless oblivion.

She woke him some little time later and he sat up, stiff and yawning. They stopped long enough to take turns ducking behind some convenient bushes, eat a little more and give the pony a short rest, and then resumed their travelling.

The sun had climbed almost to ten o'clock when they reached the West Road intersect where a man stood patiently with his eyes shaded, staring in their direction. At first, ridiculously, Matt thought it was Asher and his hands tightened on the reins.

Beside him, having a rest from driving and dozing with her eyes half closed, Veira tapped him on the knee and said, "No. It's not him. But looks-wise it could be."

He nodded, feeling suddenly ill. He was beginning to make out the bones of this rescue. "And that's why you chose him?"

"Prophecy chose him, Matthias. Not me." Veira sighed. "Does it ever make your blood run cold with wonder? That we're in dire trouble, needing some kind of a miracle, and here's a young man who looks like another young man near enough to be his mirror self, or a brother, and he's one of us and willing to say, 'Take me to do what's needed'?"

He swallowed bile. "Everything about this business makes my blood run cold. I doubt if it's with wonder. How well do you know him, this young man?"

It took Veira a little time to answer. She smoothed the sleeves of her padded coat. Tucked her hair behind her ears, then tugged it free again. Chewed on a ragged fingernail, making it worse. He waited, not patient, but knowing he hadn't a choice.

"His name is Rafel, and I know him well enough. His mother was my youngest sister," Veira said at last, sighing again. "When Timon

Spake died, and then his father Edvord, the Circle required a new member. Prophecy pointed its finger at Rafel."

Shocked, he stared at her. "And you heeded it? This man's your own flesh and blood, Veira. And in your pocket you carry—"

Her sideways look at him was bleak. Reproving. "I know what he is, Matthias, and what I carry. So does he. He comes to this quite willing."

"And you?" he whispered. "How willing are you, Veira, to kill—"

"Be silent!" she commanded. "Don't you understand yet? Prophecy must be served without fear or favour or it can't be served at all! Did you think this would be *easy*? Did you think we'd save our Innocent Mage without we pay a *price*?"

He wrapped his fingers round her wrist and gently drew her from him. "Not one this costly."

"Then you're a fool, Matthias, and I wonder if I can use you at all!" she retorted.

There were tears in her eyes. Seeing them, he felt ashamed. He was a fool to think she didn't know what she was doing, to think her blind to the consequences of their actions. She'd lived with them longer than he'd been alive. He picked up her hand and kissed it.

"I'm sorry. I'll not question you again."

That made her smile. "Of course you will. I think that's why Prophecy chose you. It's your job, and you do it well. Now hush. Rafe's close enough to hear us and we don't want him to see us brangling. What's waiting in Dorana will be hard enough. Let's not have him thinking we've anything on our minds but the gift he's agreed to give us."

CHAPTER TWENTY-EIGHT

Rafel, who so eerily looked like Asher and shared family blood with Veira, appeared remarkably cheerful for a man going to his death. Up close Matt could see he was younger than Asher by maybe a year or two, and not quite so heavily muscled. He wondered if that would make a difference. Rafel swung himself and his knapsack easily into the cart as it stopped beside him and settled himself behind the driver's seat, with his arms folded neatly along its back.

Veira kissed his cheek, unsmiling. "Rafe."

He nodded, eyes warm with affection. "Veira."

"You ready then?"

"I'm ready." He had a clear, light voice. Not like Asher's gravelly growling at all. Neither of his eyebrows was scarred. Hopefully Veira had brought some scissors, to make a quick adjustment. "So. Do you know yet how—"

She pressed a finger to his lips. "Let's not think on that just now. Best you don't have the details to dwell on till they're needed."

His smile was swift and wry. "Maybe so."

Matt knew he was staring. Couldn't help it. "I'm Matt."

"Good to meet a fellow Circleman, Matt."

Hesitant, he shook Rafel's proffered hand. "Likewise."

"You hungry, Rafe?" asked Veira. "Give me the reins, Matthias, and dig out some food from the basket. I'll have an egg. Peeled, if you please."

So he handed over Bessie's reins and peeled them both an egg. Offered one to Rafel, but he refused.

"Strange days," the young man said, and shook his head. "I never thought I'd live to see them."

"None of us did, Rafe," said Veira sadly, and dabbed salt from her fingers with her tongue. "But it's why we're here. Why the Circle was formed. Sooner or later these days were bound to arrive."

"That's true," agreed Rafel. A small silence fell, bloated with words unspoken. He broke it, eventually, saying, "And it's really him? The Innocent Mage?"

"Yes, Rafe," said Veira. "It's really him."

Matt felt his throat close. He couldn't imagine what this young man was feeling, or know the depth of his courage. His honour. Turning a little so he could see that disconcerting face he said, "I'd like to thank you, Rafel."

The young man looked at the sun-splashed passing countryside. "No need. We're all born with different things to do. This is mine."

"There is need. Asher—the Innocent Mage—he's my friend," Matt said. "You're saving my friend. I wanted you to know that, is all."

"Ah," said Rafel, and smiled. "That's good. That's nice. Saving a kingdom's a grand thing to do but it does feel a tiddle bit impersonal. Saving your friend, though. That makes a difference."

"You won't be forgotten," he insisted. "He won't forget you, although you'll never meet."

"None will forget our Rafel," said Veira, a warning note in her voice. "I'll take the pony now, Matthias. you forage in that basket again and find me some sweet plum cake. And from here on in, I think we'll get used to calling you by a different name. No sense advertising who you are."

"Changing my name is easy," Matt said. "But what about my face? I'm well known in the City. Even with a hooded cloak and darkness to hide in, there's a chance I'll be recognised. I heard you tell Dathne you had some trick?"

Veira nodded. "That I do. But I'll wait a while before I play it. I'm not sure how long it'll hold."

That didn't sound encouraging, but she was looking so sad he didn't have the heart to press further. Instead he smiled and nodded, saying, "Whatever you think best, Veira."

She dug his ribs with her elbow. "I think plum cake's best. Didn't I say so? You're a bit young to be deaf, aren't you?"

As Rafel chuckled and Veira pretended flouncy offence Matt handed over the reins and dragged the basket into his lap. "Here you are, mistress," he said with mock servility, and dropped a lump of moist cake in her lap.

"Why thank you, Meister…Meister…" Her lips pursed as she thought about it. "Maklin, I think," she finished at last. "I knew a Maklin once. A right silly fool if ever I met one, and definitely hard of hearing."

Matt swallowed a snort. Exchanged amused glances with Rafel, and took the reins back from Veira so she could enjoy her cake.

Darran was industriously polishing the staircase banister when Willer returned to the Tower. The foyer doors flung open without so much as a knock and the horrid little man sauntered in reeking of arrogance and pomposity.

He flung down his polishing cloth, not bothering to hide his contempt. "In Barl's sweet name, Willer, what do you want *now?* We gave you all Durm's books, I promise!"

"I've a message for Gar," said Willer, smirking. "From His Majesty King Conroyd."

He nearly slapped the smug and shiny face in front of him. Had to pinch his fingers together behind his back to stop himself. "Not Gar," he said icily. "His Royal Highness, the Prince. Call his name like a commoner one more time and you'll live to regret it."

Willer's eyes narrowed to ugly slits. "Threaten me one more time and you'll not live at all," he hissed. "Bolliton has no relevance now. You're an old man serving a destitute and deluded outcast cripple, while *I* am personal assistant to the king. His strong right arm. His trusted companion."

"His lackey, you mean," scoffed Darran. "His scuttling errand boy. What's this message then? Give it me and I'll take it to His Highness."

Willer went to push past him. "I'll tender it myself. Stand aside, old crow. Don't interfere with the king's own business unless you fancy sharing cold straw with Asher."

Blocking him, Darran leaned his face close. "His Highness is sleeping and I'll not see him woken. Not by the likes of you. And as for threats, Willer? I make you no threats. Only this promise. Harass my prince unduly—cause him a heartbeat's more pain—and you'll never know another day's peace. I will destroy you and no one shall touch me for doing it."

Whatever Willer saw in his face then, it must have been convincing. The little worm turned sickly pale and stepped back a pace. "Very well. Take him the message yourself, it's of no account to me. His Majesty commands Prince Gar's attendance at the execution of the traitor Asher. A carriage will be sent here half an hour before midnight tonight. The prince is advised to be ready and waiting."

"I shall so inform His Highness," Darran said. "Now get out."

For a long time after Willer's huffy departure he stood in the foyer, feeling ill. Feeling old, and helpless. Then, because delay was fruitless, he climbed the staircase to Gar's apartments and prayed he would not weep.

"What is it?" said Gar, not looking up from Barl's diary. He was covered in ink: his fingers, his face. Long blue streaks in his hair. He's wiped his hands on his lovely rose silk weskit, ruining it forever. The desktop was scattered with scribblings, the floor littered with discarded notes. He looked stretched thin as a wire.

Standing in the library doorway, afraid to step in closer, Darran cleared his throat. "A message, sir. From His Majesty."

Gar kept on writing, one inky finger tracing a line in the diary, his brow deep-furrowed with strain. "I'm busy. Tell me later."

"I think, sir," he said carefully, "I should tell you now."

"Then tell me and go away!" Gar shouted. "Can't you see what I'm doing?"

Darran told him. Quickly, to get it over with, then watched, unwilling but unable not to, as the meaning and the meanness of Jarralt's command sunk into Gar's understanding. The prince's fingers trembled and dropped the pen.

"So," he murmured, unseeing. "It's not enough that I condemn

him. I must also watch him die. Oh, Conroyd, Conroyd...is *this* how
much you hated us?"

Darran withdrew and closed the door before it was impossible to
pretend he hadn't seen Gar's grief.

By early afternoon Bessie's unflagging walk-jog-walk had carried
them without incident to the turn-off onto the main City road. Now
there was traffic. Carriages and dogcarts and saddle horses, all bearing Olken, all flowing in a steady stream towards Dorana.

Still driving, his back aching now, Matt stared at them, stabbed
through with a furious dismay. "What's the matter with them?" he
muttered to Veira. "Don't they know it's bloodshed and murder
they're going to see?"

"Judicious murder," said Veira. "There's a difference."

"What difference?" he retorted. "The blood spilled's not as red?"

She shook her head. "It's not red at all, Meister Maklin. It's black.
Black as the heart of the bad man who's dying."

"You don't believe that!"

"Of course not. But they do." She patted his knee. "They have to. If
they let themselves think for one moment this might not be just...well.
Folks like to put an untroubled head on their pillow at night, don't
they? And it's harder still for us Olken. If we don't condemn a dabbling
in magic, it's the same as shouting we'd like to try it ourselves."

It made him so angry he could easily have shouted himself. Behind
them, in the back of the cart, Rafel snored softly, curled up beneath a
canvas coverall. It was no use; he had to ask.

"When the time comes, Veira, how will you do it?"

"Kindly," she said, after a moment. "There's herbs in the brew I
concocted as will ease him gently on his way. When all's said and
done, Matthias, it's not so different from a dog or a cat that's aged
past saving."

Except that it was, and she knew it, and so did he. Nor was it the
answer he'd looked for...but it wasn't in him to press her further.
This time he patted her knee, then took her hand in his to hold, and
squeeze. She didn't pull away.

He guided Bessie onto City Road and let silence fall again for three
more miles. Then, still holding her hand, he said, "It could be me,
Veira, but I think Dath's not looking like herself."

She grunted without comment and started poking in the basket for
a cake crumb she'd missed the last six times she'd looked.

"She had more colour to her, the last time I saw her," he added. "Of course it might just be the worry..."

"Might be," agreed Veira. "There's a lot to be worried about, I know that much."

"And she wasn't eating."

"Worry can do that to an appetite, I'm told."

Wretched old woman. She wasn't going to say. If he wanted to have his suspicions about Dathne's condition confirmed he'd have to ask the question outright, and even then he thought she'd probably feign sudden deafness. He chose another topic instead, one equally as vexing. "If we manage this, Veira, if your mad plan works and we get Asher out of Dorana with his head still attached and ours, too, for that matter..."

She gave him a hard look. "He'll be grateful."

"For how long? Will he still be grateful when he finds out the truth and how it's been kept from him all this time? When he learns how I've lied, and Dathne's lied, all to make some Prophecy he's never heard of come true?"

"He's the Innocent Mage," said Veira, quietly fierce. "He's got Prophecy in his blood and bones whether he knows it or not. He'll do what he's born for, never you fear."

She was the Circle Guardian, wise in things he'd never even thought of, but still he was driven to disagree. "We've all been so set on what we want. How he fits into our plans. But, Veira, what about his plans, and what he wants? Magic's meant nothing but hardship and heart-break for Asher. Look what it's doing to him now! I don't know if there's enough gratitude in all the kingdom, let alone one man's heart, to dull the pain of these past days. Or douse his anger when he finds out how he's been duped...and who's done the duping."

He was making her angry. Her lips tightened and her fingers fisted in her lap. "He loves her, Matthias."

"And she loves him, I know," he sighed. "But she lied before she loved him, while she loved him, after she loved him. Is it 'cause you're both women that you can't see the blow you'll deal his pride?"

She fixed her gaze to the carriage up ahead. "Pride's of no consequence where Prophecy's concerned."

He shut his mouth. Could be she was right and he was wrong. Could be Asher would take it all in his stride, forgive the lies, the manipulation, the nudgings here and there to put him where he was wanted and when. Could be he'd embrace Prophecy and all its mysterious workings as willingly as he'd embraced Dathne when he thought she was only a woman who once worked in a bookshop.

If he did, well and good. And if he didn't...what could they do about it anyway? They lived their lives at the mercy of Prophecy and Prophecy, as always, would do as it willed.

"We'll not discuss it any more," said Veira. "What's done is done and there's no turning back. Why don't you climb in with young Rafel and get a little shut-eye? You need to be rested for what lies ahead."

"What about you? You need rest too, and—"

The smallest flash of teeth, as she smiled. "And I'm old? True enough, Meister Maklin. But I'm old like Bessie's harness leather is old. Tough, well looked after and hard to break. Rest. I'll wake you when we're closer to the City and it's time to play our trick."

She'd have her way, he could see that, so he clambered over the driver's seat and into the cart's cramped belly, trying not to tread on snoring Rafel. How the man could sleep, knowing what lay ahead for him, was a mystery.

Even though she was right, and he was very tired, Matt doubted he would sleep...but a moment after he'd closed his eyes to think on Veira's words the old woman was shaking his shoulder and urging in his ear, "Meister Maklin! Meister Maklin, come along now! Dorana's in sight. Wake up, it's time to fix your face."

She was in the back of the wagon with him. Opening his eyes he sat up and saw the sun had set and the night was flickered with torches. Four burned brightly at each corner of their wagon. Rafel, taking his turn with the reins, had guided them to the side of the road; traffic had dwindled to a trickle and they were, for the moment, alone. Lit up with glimfire the City walls gleamed in the distance, no more than half an hour away. He hadn't thought to sleep so long.

"Lie on your back and keep your head down," Veira told him softly. "And no matter what happens, don't cry out. This shouldn't be downright painful but you might well feel a tingle or two."

"Why?" he whispered, lowering himself to the wagon floor. "What are you planning? What's this trick you've come up with?"

"To be truthful, dear, I'm not quite sure. Something to take the edge off your fine good looks, I'm hoping." She settled on her haunches beside him. "Now close your eyes and let down your defences. I need you quite open for this."

Nervous, but trusting her, he settled into himself, loosening the fetters he kept round his mind, sinking into the fabric of the world around him...and nearly choked on a scream of pain and surprise. It was like breathing in fire, or poison, or something of both.

"What is it? What's happened?" demanded Rafel, peering over his shoulder.

"Matthias? Matthias!"

Veira's voice was an anchor, a saving grace. He clutched at her, desperate for the touch of wholesome flesh beneath his fingers. His mind felt fouled, smeared, contaminated with evil. Gasping, he fought the urge to empty his belly all over her. "It's back! Veira, can't you sense it? Dark—sticky—*wicked*! Worse than ever I felt it before. Stronger—almost *alive*." He pressed his fists against his mouth, to hold the horror inside. Struggled to regain his balance, his serenity, when the thing he could feel pulsing at the heart of the kingdom's magic wanted nothing more than chaos and destruction.

Veira's hands were cradling his head against her belly, she was holding him, rocking him. "All right, all right, just you breathe easy, child. Make sure you're all closed up again. Maybe it's alive and maybe it isn't, but we don't want to go flapping our hands in front of its face if it is, now, do we?"

Heartbeat by heartbeat the awful feeling passed and he was able to sit up. "That was horrible."

"It looked it," said Rafel, shaken. "Are you sure you're all right?"

"I will be." He stared at Veira. "I think it's what Prophecy warned of. The thing we must fight in the Final Days."

She pulled a face. "I don't doubt that at all."

"I don't think we can fight it, Veira," he whispered, starting to shiver. "Not that. It's too big. Too black, and hungry. If this is what Dathne's been dreaming..." A wave of revulsion engulfed him. "I don't know how she can live with it. I don't know how she's not *mad*!"

"She's Jervale's Heir," said Veira. "It's what she was born for. And saving Asher's what *we* were born for so we'd best be on about it. Lie down again, Matthias, and this time don't open your mind. I'm going to try my trick another way."

Reluctantly he did as she bade. Eyes closed, he felt her fingers spread across his face. Beneath their touch his skin grew warm. Hot. Burning. It twitched and crawled and seemed to seethe. He could hear her whimpering. Whimpered a little himself.

"There," she said at last, sounding exhausted, and pulled her hands away. "I call it blurring. Rafel, what do you think?"

"Jervale save us," Rafel said, hushed and fearful. "How did you *do* that? That's not his face!"

"Which would be the idea," said Veira, acerbic. "Matthias—can you hear me?"

He grunted. "Yes, and see you too. Your nose is bleeding. What have you done to my face?"

"Nothing much," she said, fishing in her pocket for her kerchief. "Rearranged the furniture a bit. Made sure no one in that City will look at you twice."

"How? I could feel you channelling energy, shaping me, but..."

Veira dabbed the kerchief at her lip and frowned at the bloodstains smeared on the cotton. "To be truthful I'm not quite sure how it's managed. The idea came in a dream. I practised on my own face a time or several. Gave myself a nasty fright, looking in the mirror. It's not the way our magic's normally used and I wouldn't recommend it as a parlour game. But it'll do the trick tonight and that's all I care about. Rafel? Get this cart back on the road, young man. We've work to be getting on with."

As Rafel obeyed her, Matt sat up and explored his face with his fingertips. It was definitely...different. Pockmarked. Fatter. His lips felt rubbery and his nose was an awkward shape.

He sighed. "You couldn't have made me handsome?"

Veira just laughed and patted his knee.

The rest of the journey was completed in silence. They reached the City's outer stone wall. Passed beneath the shadow of its gates. Trundling by Pellen Orrick's guards unrecognised, unchallenged, Matt felt his crushing sense of dread ease so he could breathe again.

"We've a horse stall saved for us in a private yard down the back of the Livestock Quarter," said Veira. "Matt, you'd best drive us from here. You know where you're going."

So he took the reins from Rafel and guided Bessie and the cart through the crowded glimlit streets to the livestock district, past smelly pens of goats and sheep and yards crammed full of cattle and horses, where Veira directed him to an empty double stable decorated with a flapping green ribbon. Stiff and hungry, they shunted the cart into hiding, unharnessed the pony and saw her safely settled with hay and water.

"Now," said Veira, hefting her bag on her shoulder, "I'm for a chamber pot, 'cause my bladder's a-bursting and I'll bet yours are too. Then we'd best find our places in the Square and settle ourselves for a long and fractious wait."

Matt watched her march away, suddenly numb. Then he turned to Rafel, who hadn't bothered to pull his own knapsack from the cart.

Well, why would he? He wasn't going to need it again.

"Are you sure you want to go through with this?" he asked Veira's calm-faced nephew. "It's not too late to change your mind."

Rafel smiled, softly and sadly, not the kind of smile he'd ever seen on Asher's face. "Thanks, Matthias...but it was always too late to change my mind."

After that there was nothing left to say. Without thinking, Matt embraced him. Felt Rafel's fear and trembling courage. Then, side by side and silent, they followed in Veira's footsteps.

PART FOUR

CHAPTER TWENTY-NINE

*D*amn, thought Gar, and threw down his pen. Ancient Doranen grammar was a quagmire, and he was rapidly sinking. Remembering his blithe assurances that he could *easily* read the books they'd found in Barl's hidden library, he winced. What a shame there was no way of getting back in there. Perhaps his ancestors had thought to bring some school texts with them—an introduction to basic Old Tongue, for instance...

But the long-lost vault's door was warded against him, and there was no way now of breaking in. And besides, he *could* read all the other books he'd taken from those dusty shelves. It was only Barl's diary that was proving a challenge. A deliberate attempt to foil prying eyes? Or was tortured self-expression just one more thing that made her unique?

A tentative knuckle-rap on the chamber's closed door interrupted his profitless inner complaints. He looked up. "What is it?"

The door swung open on soundless hinges, revealing Darran. Gar bit his lip, pinched with conscience. The old man looked tired. It was asking too much for him to caretake this whole Tower by himself and Conroyd knew it. Bastard. Instead of sitting warm and cosy in this library he should be helping Darran, prince or no prince, but nothing was more important than translating Barl's diary.

Not even an old man's precarious health.

"I'm so sorry to disturb you, sir, but I thought you should know: the carriage will be here in an hour."

An *hour*? Was it that late? Had he really been sitting here without stirring for nearly seven hours? Startled, he looked at the clock on the fireplace mantel and saw that yes, he had.

Seven hours, and only five more pages deciphered to show for it.

Abruptly he was aware of muscles aching. Of a belly growling for food and a bladder in need of emptying. Stifling a groan he pushed his chair back and stood, hands pressed into the small of his back.

"I thought you were going to bring me dinner?"

Darran sighed. "I did."

Oh yes. So he did. And there it was, still untouched on its tray, which he'd ordered be put down somewhere, anywhere, just get out and leave him to work! Darran had left it on the side table next to the armchair.

Shuffling out from behind his desk, Gar spared him a swift, apologetic smile. "Sorry."

As he reached out a hand to filch a slice of pinkly tender beef, Darran swooped. Snatched the tray beyond his reach and retreated. "It'll be stone cold by now, sir. I'll just go and heat it up for you."

He nodded. "Fine. And while you do that I'll attend to my appearance. When you come back make sure to bring a jug of icewine with you. Unless of course Conroyd saw fit to confiscate my cellar along with everything else?"

"No," said Darran after a moment's hesitation. "No, you've still a supply of good vintage yet."

"Obviously an oversight on Conroyd's part."

"Obviously," said Darran, sniffing, and returned to the kitchen.

His head full of obscure phrasing and past-participle constructions, Gar drifted upstairs to his bedchamber and set about putting himself to rights. Made sure to keep pondering those recalcitrant participles, because provided he remained focused on the subtle differences between "having" and "keeping," then he was sure not to start thinking about why it was he had to bathe and shave and change his clothes.

If he let himself think about "why," there was a good chance he'd drop in his tracks like an arrow-struck stag and never get up again.

By the time he returned downstairs, clean and refreshed and impeccably attired in black, efficient Darran had contrived to reheat his neglected dinner and unearth a particularly splendid jug of icewine.

Swigging it straight from the jug would be ungenteel, so he poured the icewine neatly into a paper-thin crystal glass—something *else* Conroyd had neglected to steal? Really, the man was slipping—and drank without pause until it was empty.

Assaulted with alcohol, his head spun a little. He smiled and poured a second glass.

This time Darran had pointedly left the dinner tray on his desk, after tidily putting all his scribbled notes to one side.

Gar sat down, speared meat with his fork and ate without tasting as he considered again Barl's diary and the entries he'd transcribed so far.

*I am afraid, she had written. In the madness of war we slipped
away, but I know we can't hide forever. Morgan brooks no
interference, nor leaves unpunished the slightest
transgression—and my crime against him is not slight. We
swore an oath together and he'll hold me to it or see me dead.
By his reckoning he loves me and Talor forgive me, I love him.
Loved him. Loved the man he used to be—not the monster he's
become. I must find a way to defeat that monster, else surely
we are doomed. And all the world with us.*

There was no indication when or where she'd recorded that entry.
Most likely it was during the terrible flight from Dorana. Before she
and her fellow refugees stumbled into the sleepy land of Lur.

Another entry, some time later:

*Two more of our children died today. We buried them in an
Olken graveyard. These simple people are good, and kind. I
can't repay them with bloodshed and destruction. There must
be a way to keep this fertile land safe.*

And another, still later:

*He is coming, he is coming, I can feel it. Tabithe and Jerrot say
I'm just dreaming, they say Morgan is dead, must be dead, the
mage wars were unsurvivable...but I know otherwise. I've not
told a soul of the power we discovered, the key to immortality.
If I told them they'd see me as Morgan in their midst and I'd be
killed out of hand, I'm certain. And if I die, there'll be no
stopping him.*

Immortality? Gar pushed his dinner aside and poured himself
more wine. It seemed no more likely on this second reading than it
had the first. Immortality was a myth. A dream. Not even the ancient
Doranen, magicians powerful beyond the imaginings of their tamer
descendants, could aspire to such a feat.

Could they?

She'd said more about it, further on...

*There is some risk, in the making of this Wall. Not great,
however, and I am a master magician. Morgan's equal, though
he was always loath to admit it. When it is done and Lur is*

forever sealed safe behind it I think I shall honour my oath to Morgan and transmute myself immortal. Not for any base desire for power, or to feed some gross appetite for worship. I am not Morgan. I'll do it because I know he lives, and will change himself soon if he hasn't already. Then he will find us, no matter how long it takes to search each corner of the world. When he does I must be waiting for him. Ten years. One hundred. One thousand. He will come and I must face him. Defeat him. No other magician lives who might stand in his way.

Gar sat back in his chair, shaking his head. Poured himself a third glass of wine and drank it faster than such a superb vintage deserved. Insanity. What he'd translated was insanity, the exhausted ramblings of a woman in shock, in mourning and soaked to the marrow in grief. No one could live a thousand years—which was a shame, really. To speak with Barl? A historian's dream.

"Sir?"

Rudely jerked from gentle fantasy, he looked up. Darran again. Hovering like a—what was it Asher used to call him? A constipated scarecrow?—in the library's open doorway.

Asher. *Damn.* And he'd been doing so well, not thinking of him.

"Sir..." Tentatively, Darran entered the room. "I'm sorry. Lord Jarr— His Majesty's carriage awaits you."

"Does it?" He flicked a glance at the mantel clock: it was a half-hour till midnight, exactly. Slowly, deliberately, he poured himself more wine. Lifted the glass and admired the way the firelight shafted through the pale green liquid within. "How prompt he is. A man of his word."

"Yes, sir," said Darran. "Sir...please...you have to leave now."

He let his gaze shift to Barl's secret diary. His last hope of salvation. Asher's last hope of life. Hours of work and he was only halfway through it, with no answers found. No miracles revealed.

And now time had run out.

He emptied the fresh glass of icewine down his throat in one long, burning rush. Darran's expression was disapproving, but that was just too bad. If he thought his prince could get through this night sober he was very sadly mistaken. With delicate precision he placed the wineglass on the desk and stood for Darran's inspection.

"Well? How do I look? Don't say drunk."

Darran's face was rigid. "You look very proper, sir."

He smiled, as bright and brittle as the icewine churning in his belly. "Are you sure you won't come with me? I expect there'll be room for one more."

Darran flinched. "Thank you, sir, but no. I'm content to forgo the pleasure."

"And it will be a pleasure. For many."

"Alas, sir, yes," said Darran, and stepped backwards, hinting, "Sir..."

"I know, I know!" he snapped. "The carriage is waiting."

Darran followed him downstairs and opened the Tower doors for him. Ordinary torchlight spilled inside; he could've asked Conroyd to arrange for glimfire, but knowing how much pleasure refusal would give he'd refrained. Even though it meant more work for Darran. At the bottom of the Tower steps there was indeed a carriage, blazoned with House Jarralt's crest. The falcon now wore a thunderbolt crown. For a moment he thought he was going to lose his bulwark of icewine down the front of his black silk tunic.

Seeing him, one of Conroyd's lackeys jumped off the carriage's rear travelling step and opened the nearest door.

"I'll wait up for you, sir," said Darran, standing back from the door. His eyes were anxious.

Gar started down the steps. "Don't bother. I might be some time."

"It's no bother," Darran called after him.

At the point of entering Conroyd's ostentatious carriage, he paused and looked back. "Fine. Suit yourself."

He climbed inside. The lackey slammed the door and clambered back onto the travelling step. A whip-crack. A creaking of harness and wood. Then they were moving.

Gar let his head fall against the cushions and wished he were dead. Or really drunk.

The Square was a solid sea of Olken spectators wrapped warm against the midnight chill, packed on three sides around the space in the middle that still contained the cart, and the cage, and Asher. Conspicuous in blue and crimson, stationed at every opportunity amongst the crowd, beside the cage, wherever there was space to stand, and armed with both pikestaffs and truncheons, were Pellen Orrick's City Guard. Looking keyed-up. Looking grim.

The Square's fourth side was taken up with an unusually elevated dais reserved for the king and such dignitaries as still remained in the City. Most of them were Olken too. Gar, staring through the carriage window as it rolled slowly to a halt, saw how few Doranen sat with them and frowned. Odd. He'd imagined they'd be the most eager of all to see the upstart Olken die.

The carriage door opened and he got out, a few paces from the foot of the stairs attached to the dais. Heart uncomfortably thudding, he let his gaze touch the Square and the people, but not the cage or its inhabitant and only briefly, sickly, the block and the straw and the hooded man in black beside them, holding a sharpened silver axe. Was it the same man who'd dealt with Timon Spake? He couldn't tell.

Everything was lit as bright as day by the enormous balls of glimfire hovering overhead. There was a hissing snap as one of them shivered, showering sparks. A moment later a second followed suit. Then a third. A few cries went up from those folks stung by the spitting magic.

Payne Sorvold stood nearby in conversation with Nole Daltrie. Two of Conroyd's closest friends; of course they'd make sure to be here. Doubtless they expected high office in the new Doranen court. Seeing the uncertain glimfire, hearing the loud protests from the crowd, Sorvold broke off his amused rejoinder to some quip of Daltrie's and reinforced the stuttering magic.

Turning back, Sorvold noticed Conroyd's carriage and then the newest arrival. Excused himself to Daltrie and approached, his expression smoothed to a scrupulous politeness. "Your Highness," he said, offering a token bow. "His Majesty asked that I greet you and escort you to your seat. He will be here himself momentarily."

"Hoping for a grand entrance?" said Gar. His head was pounding; he'd not drunk nearly enough wine. "Typical. What's wrong with the glimfire?"

Sorvold's eyes had widened at his comment, and his tone. He said, sounding wary, "Nothing, sir. There's a lot of it up there, and larger than would normally be called, but you've no need for concern."

"Did I sound concerned?" he said.

Sorvold took refuge behind formality. "If you'd like to come with me, sir?"

"Oh, Payne," he sighed. "There is nothing I would like to do less."

"Sir?"

"Never mind," he said curtly. "Let's go."

As he fell into step beside Sorvold he caught sight of Pellen Orrick, resplendent in crimson, standing some ten feet away with his attention focused keenly on the crowd. Feeling eyes upon him, the captain turned. Acknowledged the royal presence with a nod. Gar nodded back, wondering what went on behind that cold, composed face. He'd had the impression Orrick and Asher were friendly, but if Orrick was disturbed by any of this he didn't show it.

But then, nobody with any sense would show sorrow here tonight.

He climbed the dais stairs behind Sorvold and followed him to the seat so thoughtfully reserved for him. Right down the front, of course. Beside the elegant, elaborate chair clearly intended for Conroyd. The good and ignorant people of his dead father's kingdom saw him, and a roar went up that threatened to rattle the stars.

"Gar! Gar! Barl bless our Prince Gar!"

He responded because he had no choice, nodding and waving and pretending he cared, that their wild acclaim meant something and he was glad to be here. Then, as the cheering died down, he took his seat. Breathing deeply, he let his face become a mask. He could feel the speculative glances of those few Doranen lords and ladies who'd decided to attend the entertainment. People who once had begged his attendance at their parties and dances, who'd dreamed of him as a match for their daughters, who now doubtless wished he'd died along with his family. Who found him inconvenient. An embarrassment.

Not one of them spoke to him, or even approached. Which suited him perfectly.

Some minutes later Barlsman Holze arrived, decorated in his most costly clerical robes. The still-jittery glimfire sparked and flashed on the rubies and sapphires sewn into his white brocade tunic. At his heels trailed Willer, swathed in dull green silk. The little man's air of self-importance bordered on the obscene as he shuffled himself into one of the seats to the rear of the dais, where apparently the Olken belonged. Holze sank into the chair on the other side of Conroyd's empty imitation throne. Gar glanced down at the Square, and frowned. Holze up here...and no sign at all of a Barlspeaker's presence amongst the guards. Did this mean Asher was to be denied the consolation of a clerical attendance? No prayers, as there'd been prayers for Timon Spake?

It seemed there was no end to Conroyd's casual cruelties.

"Your Highness," Holze said with an almost imperceptible nod.

Gar unclenched his jaw. "Barlsman."

Behind them a low buzz of voices, as the other attendees distracted themselves with conversation. Holze leaned a little closer. "I hope you're reconciled to tonight's event. There can be no suggestion of... ambivalence."

"You think me ambivalent?" He smiled. "You're mistaken."

A new roar from the crowd below killed Holze's cold-eyed reply.

"The king! The king! Barl brings us the king!"

So Conroyd arrived in a sound-storm of rapture that threatened not only to rattle the stars but rain them down on all their heads. He was the king. He was their saviour, the glorious golden Doranen who'd rescued them from a royal house well loved but bled utterly dry of magic. He arrived draped in crimson, dappled with rubies, studded with diamonds. Riding Cygnet, the beautiful silver stallion Asher loved.

For the first time since climbing out of Conroyd's carriage Gar looked in the cage. Saw Asher, on his knees and staring with eyes gone hollow in a wounded face gone hollower still.

He had to look away.

Overhead the glimfire furiously sparked and sputtered. Four balls extinguished themselves entirely and were hastily rekindled by Sorvold and Daltrie, still in attendance on the ground. All the while Conroyd sat on the fretting silver stallion and waved, laughing, drinking the applause avidly, gluttonously, as though too much could never be enough.

Just as Gar thought he must be sick, Conroyd dismounted and tossed his reins to a waiting Olken servant. Lightly leapt up the stairs to the top of the dais and stood before his empty chair. Not once did he acknowledge his former king's existence.

"Good people!" he cried, and the crowd fell silent. "Your love moves me to tears!" Mellifluous, musical, his glorious voice bathed them all in beauty. "Midnight approaches. Justice awaits. Let it be done, and let all gathered here bear witness to Barl's mercy and might! Captain Orrick!"

Pellen Orrick appeared before him and bowed. "Your Majesty."

"It is time, Captain. Do your duty!"

The crowd shouted, drumming its heels to show approval. On the dais behind Gar no such vulgar display; but the mood of self-satisfaction swelled. He watched, sickened, as Orrick walked with slow deliberation across the Square to the cage holding Asher. In one hand he held a large key.

To distract himself Gar turned to Conroyd, seated now, and said softly, "It was supposed to rain here today. Did you forget?"

Conroyd smiled, his attention on Orrick. "Be silent."

"Or haven't you even taken the Weather Magic yet? Conroyd, you mustn't delay. The people depend—"

"Be silent," said Conroyd, "or lose your tongue."

He flinched. Was it his imagination playing tricks or was there something wrong with Conroyd? Something different about him. His eyes? The way his skin stretched over his face? There was something......and it made his skin crawl.

Three more balls of glimfire expired and one exploded. Before Sor-vold or Daltrie could act, Conroyd replaced them with a wave of his hand. Nodded to Orrick, who unlocked the cage and handled Asher ungently into the Square. Asher moved slowly, painfully, his chains clanking in the sudden hush. He looked up and as their eyes met Gar felt his heart seize. Freeze.

Darran had *lied*. There was no forgiveness in Asher's thinned and bloodless face. No understanding or acceptance. Only hate and hate and hate.

Damn Darran. Damn Asher, too. And Conroyd. The crowd. Above all damn himself. He'd wanted so much to believe in Asher's absolu-tion, he'd deafened himself to the small voice within whispering *what you do is unforgiveable*. Had allowed himself to be deceived... because deception was so alluring, and so desperately desired.

And now was dead. As Asher would soon be dead.

Orrick escorted his shuffling prisoner to the block. Steadied Asher before it and impersonally helped him to kneel. His kneeling broke the taut silence; the crowd shouted. Cheered. Drummed their heels again, ecstatic. Some of them sat so close to the block they were in danger, surely, of being soaked in spraying blood. Of having their clothing ruined. Did they realise? Did they care? Or was it deliberate? An attempt to gain some kind of revolting keepsake?

Remembering the horror of Timon Spake's beheading, Gar couldn't comprehend this lust for blood and death. These Olken who howled for Asher's murder were the same men and women who, scant weeks ago, had fought to call him friend. To buy him ale. To boast to their cronies: *"As I said to Asher himself, just the other day..."*

A touch to one shoulder, and Asher put his head on the block. Gar wanted to close his eyes but couldn't. He owed his friend this much, not to close his eyes.

With his hands and ankles chained Asher couldn't keep his bal-ance. He kept slipping sideways off the block; a final obscenity. Orrick looked up and Conroyd nodded. The chains were removed. Asher once more lowered his head and Orrick stepped back, well out of the way. The executioner came forward. Raised his axe. A gasp of indrawn breath ran round and through the waiting crowd—

—and all the glimfire went out.

Plunging darkness. Screams. Confusion. Conroyd, swearing. One minute passed, and then one more. A ball of glimfire bloomed. Another. Then another. Light returned, revealing Asher still kneeling at the block, passively awaiting death.

"*Kill him!*" screamed Conroyd, leaping to his feet. "*Kill him now!*"

The axe fell. Blood sprayed. The crowd shrieked. A ball of glimfire directly overhead erupted into shooting flame and sank, igniting the bloody straw and Asher's sundered body. Panic, as those closest to the carnage tried to get away. Some of them were on fire. Panic spread and the crowd stampeded.

Forgotten, held fast in some kind of frozen stillness, Gar watched as chaos held sway. Orrick and his guards tried and failed to maintain order. Barlsman Holze shouted prayers and pleas for sanity. Conroyd's guests tumbled pell-mell off the dais, in fear for their lives. Willer was squealing.

Gar couldn't help it; he laughed out loud.

Conroyd turned on him, his altered face livid. The glimfire's dying flames reflected in his eyes. "Is this *your* doing, eunuch? *Is it?*"

Despite his danger, he smiled. "Mine? How could it be? I'm a cripple, remember? Perhaps it's Barl, expressing her displeasure."

Conroyd struck him so hard that a ruby ring opened the flesh along his cheekbone. "If I find this is you, runt, your pain will last *forever*!"

Blood was pouring down his face. He groped for the kerchief Darran insisted he carry and pressed it to the wound. "Are you mad, Conroyd? To assault me in *public*?"

There was madness, or something worse, seething beneath the surface of Conroyd's chalk-white face. "With me!" he grunted. "Now!"

His arm bruised in an inescapable grip, Gar found himself dragged from his seat, from the dais, down the stairs and into the Square where the stench of charred straw, blood and human flesh was hideous. He gagged. Retched. Brought up all his swallowed icewine in a frothy puddle at Conroyd's feet.

Conroyd threw him to his knees in the middle of it. "Look there!" he commanded. "You know him better than any man alive. Is that him? Tell me if it's him! And if you lie I'll see it and no mercy known shall save you!"

The body and its head had caught almost the full brunt of the flaming glimfire. The face was blistered, bubbled, oozing thick boiled blood, but it was Asher's. The rest of the torso and its limbs were roasted, its clothes burned almost away. Only one small section of flesh was left seared but unblackened: the right arm, from shoulder to inches above the wrist. In falling, the body had sheltered it from the worst of the flames.

Gar stared at the smooth, unscarred length of limb. Looked again at that terrible face, still recognisable, and then again at the unscarred arm.

Like immortality, this was impossible.

"*Is it Asher?*" said Conroyd.

Churned with confusion, with the beginnings of a hope too great to admit, Gar pressed his hands to his face and let a sob burst from his throat. "Damn you, Conroyd. Of course it is. He's dead. You've killed him."

Cruel fingers tangled in his hair, dragging his head backwards to break-neck position. "You swear it?" said Conroyd, his terrible eyes on fire. "On pain of every punishment I've ever promised, and many more besides?"

His slashed cheek was burning. "Yes, yes, I swear it!" he said. "Look at his face! See for yourself! It's Asher!"

Conroyd looked. "Yes," he said at last, in almost a whisper. "It is him. I've won. My exile at last is ending!" His grasping fingers loosened and he backed a pace away.

Gar climbed unsteadily to his feet, certain of one thing only: that *none* of this made sense. He stared at Conroyd, who for all his familiar cruelty yet seemed subtly unlike himself. And even as he watched, something rippled across that hated face, some alchemical change that suggested, for a single impossible moment, that he was looking not at one man but two.

As Gar opened his mouth to shout, Pellen Orrick came running to join them, his uniform torn and filthy. "Your Majesty! Your Majesty, forgive the interruption. Asher's friend—Stable Meister Matt! He's taken."

Stunned shock congealed into pain. "Let him go, Conroyd!" he said. "Asher's dead now. It's over. Please, let him go."

Conroyd turned on him, wholly himself again. "Get back to your Tower and stay there, runt! I'll know if you're straying and you won't like my wrath!"

Matt. *Matt.* Anguished, despairing, Gar turned away without looking again at the burned body at his feet. The Square was almost emptied now, the dais entirely deserted. The carriage that had brought him here was waiting a little distance away, the golden crown on the falcon's head flashing in the guttering glimfire. He climbed inside and let it take him home through the thronged and noisy streets. His wounded cheek throbbed, unmerciful.

True to his word, of course, Darran was waiting up for him. Took one look at his cut and bloodstained face and cried out in alarm. "Sir! Sir, what's happened? You're *injured*!"

Either he needed to get properly drunk, right now, or he should never touch icewine again. Ignoring Darran's outstretched hand, his peppering of incoherently anxious questions, Gar paced around the foyer floor. Struggled to make sense of events that were incredibly senseless. Totally impossible. He was brought up short by Darran, who abandoned a lifetime of protocol, grabbed him by the arm and dragged him to a halt.

"Sir! Sir, you're *frightening* me!"

Shocked, Gar looked at the old man. Saw that yes indeed, his secretary—his friend—was frightened. "I'm sorry. I didn't mean to."

Appalled at himself, Darran unclutched his fingers and stepped back. "Please, sir. I understand how you feel. What's happened is a tragedy. But it's not your fault and you mustn't go on blaming yourself. Asher's death—"

Gar held up a silencing finger. Leaned close. Whispered, "Asher's not dead."

From the look on the old man's face it was clear Darran thought he'd lost his mind. "Oh, sir. Please. Let me take you upstairs. Help you lie down and find medicine for your wound. You've had a terrible shock and—"

He seized Darran's black-clad shoulders and shook him. "*Listen* to me. Asher's not dead. Someone is. Someone died tonight, cruelly and bloodily. But that someone *wasn't Asher.*"

Dumbly, Darran stared at him. "Wasn't Asher?" he said at last. "How can you be—"

Shuddering, he saw again that burned and blackened body. Smelled the wrenching stink of fresh-cooked flesh. "A missing scar. You've seen it—on his right arm. An injury he got as a boy. The man killed tonight didn't have it. He wasn't Asher."

"Then who—"

"I have no idea," he said, and let Darran go. Began pacing again, his head pounding with thoughts and ideas and pain. "But it can only mean one thing. Asher was rescued."

"*Rescued?* Oh, sir, I mean no disrespect but—"

He spun about. "Matt's arrested. He was there, Darran. He was involved somehow. I *know* it."

Looking uncomfortable, Darran cleared his throat. "Don't you know? Asher and Matt parted uncivilly, sir. At the risk of sounding ghoulish, isn't it possible that Matt returned merely to witness—"

"*No!*" Frustration was a fire, burning, Perhaps if he banged Darran's thick head on the nearest wall he'd see what had to be seen. "At least—yes. It's possible. But I don't think it's the answer. I can't explain it. Call it intuition. Desperation. Whatever you like. But I know Matt was here to rescue Asher and he didn't come alone. Asher got away, helped by people who wanted to keep him alive. And I doubt they were Doranen."

"Olken?" Darran whispered. "You mean...more of our kind like Asher?"

"I don't know about that. I don't know who they are, or what they want. All I know is we have to find them, somehow. Because they can lead us to Asher!"

"*No*, sir!" Darran was so upset he didn't seem to notice he'd raised his voice to his prince. "It's too dangerous! If Asher's alive then I'm glad of it, for his sake. But you *cannot* meddle further! To do so could mean your life! You could *die!*"

"And if I *don't* meddle, Darran, it could mean the death of this kingdom!"

Darran's face crumpled with despair. "Oh, sir. Sir. Why won't you accept it? The kingdom's dead already. At least, it's dead to you. Conroyd is our king now. Lur's livelihood rests with him."

Again, he took the old man by the shoulders and this time held him gently, as though his bones could break. "You don't understand Darran," he whispered. "There's something wrong with Conroyd."

Darran snorted. "Forgive me, sir, but I've known that for quite some time!"

"No, no," he said, still whispering. Too afraid to give his thoughts full voice. "I saw something. Tonight. In him. Saw...some*one*." He took a deep and shaking breath. Let it out. "Someone who wasn't Conroyd. For a moment, he...he wore *two faces*."

"Your Highness..." Now Darran was whispering. Looking afraid. "I don't know what you mean."

He stepped back. "Neither do I."

"What you're saying...it sounds fantastical."

"I know that. Insane too." He forced a smile. "But I'm not crazy, Darran. Witnessing that execution hasn't robbed me of my wits or filled my head with wild imaginings. I know what I saw. And I know this too. Since the moment we opened Barl's library—since Durm found her hidden diary—something's been wrong in this kingdom. I don't know what but I intend to find out."

Still fearful, Darran stiffened his spine. "Yes, sir. But how?"

Gar glanced up, as though he could see right through the ceiling and into his library. "The answer's in that diary, Darran. I can feel it in my bones. I must finish translating it and there isn't a moment to lose. Very soon now, I fear it will be too late and Conroyd—or whoever, whatever, he is—will bring us all to ruin."

He headed for the staircase, almost running. Darran called after him. "And me? Your Highness? Can't I do something?"

"Of course you can," he said, turning on the staircase. "You can think of a way to rescue Matt!"

CHAPTER THIRTY

Conroyd?"

Morg kept his entranced gaze on the blood-soaked straw around the executioner's block. The glimlit Square was almost emptied of Olken now; a handful of industrious individuals were plucking wet, scarlet wheat stalks from the ground, darting in quickly before a guard could interfere with their relic-taking. The body was already removed, bundled into sacking and taken away to the guardhouse to await its promised ignominious destruction. Willer had gone with it, eager and gloating.

All in all, a good night's work.

Behind him, the cleric shifted restlessly. "*Conroyd.*"

Sighing, he turned. Considered the old fool coldly. "Your Majesty."

Holze's pale cheeks coloured. "Forgive me. Your Majesty. Sir, we need to speak."

He turned away again, this time resting his gaze on the guardhouse wherein languished on Olken of great interest. One who'd been held in firm affection by dead Asher, and might, with judicious winnowing, reveal some knowledge of Asher's unexpected abilities. Just in case there was some other inconvenient Olken somewhere who could yet interfere with his plans.

"Tomorrow, Holze."

Standing at a discreet distance, ever-hopeful Sorvold and Daltrie waited to see if their friend and king required anything more of them. Holze spared them a wary glance and stepped closer. "I'm sorry, but it can't wait," he said, his voice insistently lowered. "Tonight sees the

end of an era for our kingdom. An era that has died with bloodshed...
and a certain amount of unexpected excitement. As Lur's oath-sworn
caretakers it is urgent that you and I confer. In private. Between us, as
Barl's chosen instruments, we maintain the spiritual and temporal
balance in this land. What we do next will set the tone for generations
of Doranen and Olken to come."

Well, no. Because Lur's current crop of milk-and-water magicians
was its last and the Olken were irrelevant. But since he was, for the
moment, forced to continue his charade as the dutiful, dedicated king
he couldn't let Holze suspect that.

And, in truth, there was no desperate need to question the captured
stable meister immediately. Obedient Orrick had him safely locked
away. This Matt would keep a few hours longer—and a night spent
stewing in fear would doubtless render him more pliable. More likely
to speak without encouragement. Searching Asher's mind had nearly
killed the Olken untimely, and Asher had been an Olken stronger
than most. It might well be unwise to kill this one too quickly, and
with magic. Orrick's inconvenient ethics might prompt him to whisper in the wrong ears.

He favoured Barl-sot Holze with a smile. "Efrim, your wisdom as
ever prevails. Indeed, let us talk." With a raised eyebrow he summoned Payne Sorvold to his side.

"Your Majesty?"

He acknowledged Sorvold's bow with the slightest of nods. "Ah,
Payne. Barlsman Holze and I have weighty matters of state to discuss.
See that my horse is taken to the Barl's Chapel stables."

Sorvold bowed again. "Certainly, sir." His public face was impec-
cable; Morg almost laughed to see the churning disquiet behind it.
The barely leashed desire to partake in those weighty state discus-
sions. Sorvold's ambition stank like rotting flesh.

For desultory amusement he touched his fingertips to Sorvold's
forearm. "Patience, friend," he murmured. "Walking, one still reaches
the desired destination...and with far less risk of a fall."

Sorvold's greedy eyes glittered. "Indeed, Your Majesty."

As Sorvold and Daltrie withdrew, conferring, Holze made a little
noise of disapproval. "I confess I had thought better of Payne Sorvold.
Such naked self-interest is displeasing to Barl. Those of us privileged
to be in the upper ranks of Doranen society should care more for her
desires than our own."

Drivel, drivel, drivel. Was there no end to the man's pious platitudes? Suppressing contempt, Morg smiled. "As you say, Efrim. But a

king is confined to the counsel at hand. And if Payne Sorvold's voice is a part of the choir we must assume he sings with Barl's blessing, yes? Her choice may seem dubious to us but is it meet that we question it?"

The rebuke stung fresh colour into Holze's cheeks. He bowed. "Your Majesty."

Morg smiled. "And now let us retire to your rooms, Efrim, that we might best decide how together we can steer our beloved kingdom to its rightful destiny."

"Indeed, Conroyd," agreed Holze. "Let us."

Fuelled by desperation, Gar returned to his study of Barl's diary. There was no more time for a measured, methodical deconstruction of her memories. He had to risk haste, risk racing through each entry in his search for the key words and phrases that would help him explain their current predicament. Had to subdue the historian, whose love of language and detail cried out for a leisurely perusal, and let the king's needs hold sway.

The king's.

Yes. In his heart, though his magic was now a bitter memory, he believed he was still Lur's rightful king, its guardian, its protector, in a way that transcended magic and Weather-Working and trappings of power. The transience of an externally bestowed authority.

His father's words, spoken so long ago, echoed in his mind like thunder. *"Barl has a destiny for you, my son."*

This was it. Finding her diary. Learning its secrets and using them to save Lur from a danger he could not define but knew was upon them. That was connected intimately, inexplicably, to the fate of Conroyd Jarralt.

Ignoring the spiking pain between his eyes, indifferent to the dull ache in his shoulders, his spine, uncaring of the throbbing in his face where Conroyd's ring had cut him open, Gar bent all his energy to those secrets' uncovering. Every time he lifted his gaze from the diary's ancient, faded paper and ink the image of Conroyd's dual face rose before him, spurring him on.

Wisely, Darran left him alone.

The answer came hours later, as the first intimations of light appeared in the sky beyond his library window. Not dawn, but dawn's harbinger.

Exhausted, he'd had no choice but to slow the speed of his reading. The diary's later entries were scrawled hastily, haphazardly, as though Barl had been as pressed for time then as he was now. They were almost illegible. The incantations she'd recorded were of no use to him, of course. Not any more. But if he could find Asher...prevail upon him for assistance one last time...

The Doranen arcane heritage was appalling. No wonder there'd been a war. No wonder Barl had hidden the diary, and Durm after her. No wonder such magics had been erased from his ancestors' memories. The thought of such magic unleashed during Trevoyle's Schism... unleashed now by Conroyd against any who dared oppose him...

Sickened, his fatigued eyes burning, acutely aware of the fast-approaching day, Gar flogged his tired mind onwards.

Barl had written:

But while a locked room is safe, without a key it is also a trap. So I have fashioned one and in time I will use it to open a window in the Wall, that I may see what has become of the world beyond. And if it be safe then we will go home. I swear it, I swear it on my life. One day we will all go home.

A window in the Wall?

Thrumming with tiredness he slumped in his chair and let the implications of Barl's words unfold in his mind. Fragments of her earlier comments resurfaced and clicked into place, part of the puzzle he was trying so desperately to piece together.

I've not told a soul of the power we discovered, the key to immortality...He is coming, he is coming, I can feel it...He will find us, no matter how long it takes to search each corner of the world...

A window in the Wall.

Was *that* the answer? Had *Durm* read Barl's diary from cover to cover? And had he, in all his pride and arrogance, opened Barl's window? Breached their safe, sealed kingdom and placed them all at risk?

He heard again Durm's harsh and dying words: "*Borne...forgive me. I couldn't stop him...*"

Gar dragged his fingers over his face, struggling to understand. Stop *who?* Stop...*Morg?*

No. *No.* It couldn't be that. Morg was dead, *had* to be dead. Immortality was a dream, not reality. There was another explanation, one he hadn't thought of yet.

Behind his closed eyes he saw once more that rippling alchemical change cross Conroyd's face. Remembered the oddness in his writing, as though another hand had guided the pen. Remembered the gaping hole in the fence at Salbert's Eyrie, where horses and carriage had plunged over the edge without any attempt to swerve or stop. Taking with them three powerful magicians without a fight.

A window in the Wall...and an immortal warrior mage, steeped in evil, bent on revenge.

"*Darran!*"

The old man appeared in the doorway a few moments later, shaken and breathless. "Sir? Sir, what is it?"

Gar pushed to his feet, clutching at the desk to keep from falling sideways. "Get down to the guardhouse. Now, before the City starts stirring. Find Pellen Orrick and bring him back here." He pounded a fist against his head, trying to rattle coherent thought free of crippling exhaustion. "No! No, not here. It's too dangerous. Take him—take him to House Torvig's crypt. I'll meet you there."

Darran looked as sleepless as Gar felt. In rumpled clothing, his hair awry, he wrung his hands in agitation. "Sir? Has something happened?"

Slowly, acutely aware of all his aches and pains and his swollen cut cheek burning. Gar nodded. "I think I've figured it out, Darran. I think I know what we're up against. *Who* we're up against."

Darran swallowed. "And do I want to know, sir?"

He shook his head, feeling sick. "No. No, Darran, you really don't."

Pellen Orrick jerked upright in his chair with a snort, furious with himself for dozing, and looked to his prisoner to make sure he was still there and breathing.

He was. Curled on his side against the cell's far wall, draped in a blanket, the stable meister watched his captor with silent wariness.

Perhaps not surprisingly, given the execution and the malfunctioning glimfire and the general air of unrest, the guards who'd apprehended Matt last night had been heavy-handed in their methods. Enthusiastic in their eagerness to restrain him. They'd brought him in unconscious. Now, in the murky just-dawn light, Orrick saw that the man was a patchwork quilt of cuts and bruises. None life-threatening but all uncomfortable...and with more discomfort still to come.

Creaking a little, Orrick got to his feet. Stretched, hearing all the bones in his neck go *pop*, then stared down at the silent, unmoving prisoner on the floor before him.

"His Majesty sent word late last night. He'll be here later today to interrogate you himself. If you're wise you'll tell him whatever you know, and quickly. Asher resisted and paid a heavy price."

Matt blinked his swollen, blood-crusted eyes. "I don't know anything."

"For your sake I hope not. I warn you, Matt, since you're a man who to the best of my knowledge has done no harm: our new king is ruthless in the pursuit of justice. He'll use magic to tear the truth from you, just as he used it on Asher."

"Magic?" said Matt, and sat up, wincing. "But that's forbidden. You're the Captain of the City, how could you sanction—"

"Captains don't sanction," he replied. "Or object." Not when a king commands. Even when their conscience pricked them. Even though they had grave doubts. And was that duty or cowardice speaking? An uncomfortable question he wasn't sure how to answer. "Tell him what you know, Matt. Put an end to all this misery."

"I told you," said Matt, and closed his eyes. "I don't know anything."

Well, if the stable meister was telling the truth surely he had nothing to fear, magic or no magic. And if the man was lying the king would soon dig the truth free. Either way, it was out of his hands. He was weary, and hungry, and needed an hour or three at home.

The guardhouse was empty, save for Bunder on front-desk duty and young Jesip filling out reports. All the other lads, on active duty or recalled for special circumstances, were out patrolling the City, maintaining order after last night's tumult and hastening all the sightseers back to their homes, either in Dorana or beyond it. He sent Jesip out back to keep a close eye on their prisoner and paused for a word with stolid Ox.

"I'm off home for a bit. Stay alert and send for me if there's fresh trouble."

Letting himself out through the guardsmen's entrance he saw that the day promised fair, with flushes of pink on the rim of the horizon. Smothering a yawn, he turned for the small gate leading into the alley... and was accosted from the shadows alongside the guardhouse building.

"Captain Orrick! Captain Orrick, a word!"

He knew that whispering voice. It was the prince's secretary. Darran. A good man, if a witterer. "Sir?" Orrick said, approaching. "Is something wrong? Come out into the light where I can see you."

The old man didn't move. "Captain Orrick, do you love this kingdom?"

And what kind of a question was that? He scowled, feeling fratched and fractious. "Meister Secretary, it's been a long night and I'm in no mood for games. State your business or be on your way. It's a grave offence to loiter on guardhouse property."

The old man inched forward until just his face was visible. His gaze darted left and right, seeking eavesdroppers. "Captain, we must speak in private. Will you come?"

"Come where? And why? What do you want to speak of?"

Darran eased a little further forward. He looked exhausted. Terrified. "I can't say, Captain. Not here. Please, I beg you. Come. In the name of our beloved King Borne."

That name stilled his tongue. He looked more closely at Darran. Recognised honesty, and desperation. "I was on my way home," he grumbled. "I've been on duty now a good long time, sir."

"I know that," said Darran. "I'd not ask if it weren't important."

He sighed. "How important?"

"A matter of life or death," the old man said. "For all of us." He held out a bundled cloak. "Wear this. Pull the hood low over your face. We don't want you recognised."

Orrick took the cloak and shrugged it on as the old man settled the hood of his own cloak over his greying head. "If this is not urgent but a trick or, worse still, some lawless skulduggery..."

"Come with me, Captain," said Darran, "and see for yourself."

Groaning, sighing, Orrick went with him.

He wasn't surprised to find he'd been taken to meet with Prince Gar. The choice of meeting place was more unexpected: House Torvig's family crypt. Chilly, and filled full of candles. And bodies.

The prince looked sleepless. High-strung and backed against an invisible wall. The cut on his cheekbone was scabbed over, the flesh around it bruised and puffy. "Thank you for coming, Captain. Pellen. May I call you Pellen?"

Orrick nodded. "Of course."

"Pellen, I need your help. Lur needs your help. Can we count on you?"

His spine snapped straight. "I am an officer of the crown. My loyalty has never been questioned." Well. Not reasonably anyway. Or more than once.

The prince smiled. There was something ghastly in his eyes. He stood beside his dead sister's coffin, his fingers caressing her—*the effigy's*—cold stone foot. "I know that," he said. "But you're also an officer who's never been asked to face what we are facing. To accept what will sound to you like the ravings of a madman."

Careful...careful...Orrick moistened dry lips. Glanced once at the old man who'd brought him here, standing now in the corner, then settled his attention on the prince. "And what is it we're facing, Your Highness?"

"I believe—the destruction of our kingdom."

Well, yes, that did sound like the ravings of a madman. And he was so damned *tired*. "Sir, you'll need to speak more plainly. You *believe* that we're in danger? From whom? From what? And where is your proof?"

"So speaks the City guardsman." The prince shook his head. "I'm not sure you'd call it proof, Pellen."

Orrick glanced again at Darran. The old man's eyes didn't leave the prince's face. From his expression he at least believed what Gar was saying. Or did he just want to believe it? Hard to say.

Looking back at the prince, he thought for a moment, choosing his words carefully. "Your Highness, have you told the king of your concern?"

The question provoked a harsh, choked-off bark of laughter. "Pellen, dear Pellen. Conroyd is my concern!"

"You're talking treason. I can't hear this," he snapped, and burned Darran with a look. "You shouldn't have brought me here, old man. If you love your prince, take him away. Now. And I'll do my best to forget the three of us ever spoke."

Spinning on his heel, chaotic with regret and sorrow and fury, he headed for the door.

The prince said harshly, "I lied about Asher."

He stopped. Listened to his thudding, hammering heart. "*Lied*, sir?"

Footsteps behind him. A gentle hand touching, tugging him round. The prince's face was stark. No royal mask, no polished public presentation. Raw emotion only, with everything laid bare. He flinched.

"What he told you was true. All of it," the prince said, as softly as though they were in chapel. "I asked him to do magic."

His reply was automatic. "Olken have no magic."

The prince smiled sadly. "Asher does. Did. I can't explain it, but it's true. And he used it to protect this kingdom. When my own powers failed I gave him the Weather Magics myself, willingly. He never conspired to steal my crown. He was the truest subject a king could ever have. The truest friend. In every way that matters, Asher was innocent."

All his life a guardsman. He'd learned—thought he'd learned—to tell when truth was spoken. "But you renounced him!" he said, incredulous. "You signed the execution order yourself!"

The prince nodded. "I had to. Even though I'd sworn to protect him, I had to sign his death warrant. If I refused, Conroyd said he'd slaughter your people. I believed him."

Could a living man be turned to stone? It felt like it. He swallowed, struggling against the pain in his throat, his chest. "He was *innocent*? But I *killed* him!"

"No, Pellen," the prince said. "The law killed him."

"It's the same thing!"

The prince looked to Darran, then. As though he were seeking advice...or absolution. The old man shrugged. "I think you must, sir. We've come too far not to."

The prince sighed. "You're no murderer, Pellen. Asher isn't dead. The man who lost his life last night was unknown to me. Asher lives, somewhere, and if we're to save our kingdom from destruction you have to help me find him."

Orrick felt his legs give way. He stumbled sideways, fending off the hands stretched out to help him. Fetching up against a cold brick wall he pressed a hand across his face and fought to catch his ragged breath.

"This is madness," he muttered. "The rotten fruit of overwork. I must be dreaming." He lowered his sheltering hand and looked at the prince. "Tell me I'm dreaming!"

"If you are, Pellen, it's a nightmare. And the rest of us are snared in it with you." The prince reached inside his buttoned coat and pulled out a battered, leather-bound journal. It looked ancient. "This is Blessed Barl's diary. Durm discovered it and hid its existence. It contains our long-lost magics...and an incantation that opens a window in the Wall."

"A *window*? Your Highness—"

"I know," the prince said quickly. "I know how this sounds, but please, bear with me. I believe Durm used this spell." His face twisted with bitterness and regret. "He was always a curious man. And an arrogant one. Convinced he was never in danger, no matter the risks he took."

Orrick stepped away from the wall and clasped his hands behind his back. Buried beneath confusion and bewilderment there was shame, that he'd let himself be so undisciplined as to show such open dismay. "Very well. A window. But what has that to do with Asher? With anything?"

The prince slipped the journal back inside his coat. "Everything.

When Durm opened that window in the Wall, I think something climbed through it after him and is here with us now, bent on malevolent destruction. I think it killed my family and wants to kill us all. That's why I have to find Asher. He's the only one with magic I can trust to fight against it."

"Against *what*, sir? Nobody knows what lies beyond the Wall! Nobody knows who lives there!"

"We know who used to live there."

It took Orrick a moment to work out the prince's meaning. When he did, he almost fell down. "*Morg?* Sir, you are raving!"

Gar shook his head. "I wish I was. Pellen, Morg knew how to make himself immortal. Understand: he was a magician with powers we can't begin to comprehend. The Doranen of Lur are mere *shadows* compared to our ancestors, and what they could do. Did do. It's all in the diary and I tell you, it's terrifying."

Was madness contagious? He was starting to believe the prince... "If you're right—if Morg really is among us—how is it nobody's noticed?"

"Because he's clever. He's hiding."

"Hiding where?"

The prince's gaze dropped for a moment. He took a deep breath. Let it out. Looked up and answered. "Inside Conroyd Jarralt."

Orrick turned away, one fist pressed to his aching chest. Barl save him... Barl save him... but he believed it. Last night. In all the mayhem. He'd seen King Conroyd's face as he demanded Asher's beheading. Seen him afterwards, gloating over the body. Something inhuman and unnatural lurked there, deep inside his bones.

The prince said softly, "I'm the last living member of House Torvig, Pellen. For hundreds of years my family has shed its blood for the keeping of this kingdom. By all that's holy, in this sacred house of rest, before countless generations of my witnessing family, I swear, I *swear* I've told you nothing but the truth. *Please*. Will you help me?"

Orrick stared at the ground. Time stopped, hanging on his answer. He looked up.

"Yes, Gar. I'll help you. And if it proves we're wrong may Barl have mercy on our souls."

Ox Bunder looked up in surprise as Orrick walked back into the guardhouse. "Captain? Something wrong?"

Only everything. Still reeling from the prince's revelations, from his own mad decision to follow him blindly, break the law, *free a prisoner*, he called upon his twenty-eight years of guarding experience and showed the man nothing but a sheepish smile.

"I tried to sleep but all my leftover paperwork kept tapping me on the shoulder," he said. "You know how I am."

Ox grinned. "Yes, sir, I do."

"No trouble from the prisoner?"

"No, Captain."

"Jesip's still with him?"

"Er..." Bunder looked discomfited. "No. You know his mother's poorly? He just wanted to see if she'd spent the night all right. I didn't see the harm, sir, he's been on duty for nearly two days. I checked the prisoner myself not ten minutes ago and he was out to the world, snoring."

"I see. Well, I suppose that's all right." He headed for the rear door leading to the cells. His heart was pounding so hard he was amazed Bunder couldn't hear it. "But I'll have a quick look at him myself before I go upstairs. Carry on, Ox."

Praise Barl, the guardhouse's other prison cells were empty, all impulse to petty criminalities swallowed by the enormous events of the past few weeks. He hurried along the cell-lined corridor to the room at the end where Asher had been briefly held. Where Matt now waited in equal danger. He opened the outer double-locked door—

—and found the prisoner trying to hang himself with the torn-off sleeve of his shirt.

"No, damn you! *No!*"

With shaking hands he fumbled the keys from his belt, jammed the right one in the lock and wrenched the cell door wide open. The stable meister was on his knees, swaying at the end of his improvised noose, wheezing, choking, his battered face suffused with blood and turning purple.

Orrick lunged at him. Tore frantically at the knot around his neck but had no hope of loosening it. Instead he got his shoulder under the man's heaving chest and bellowed for Bunder.

"Get me a knife!" he ordered as Ox skidded into the outer cell. Gaping, Ox bolted out again and returned moments later with a dagger. Together they freed the strangling prisoner.

"Captain, captain..." Bunder stammered, horrified.

"Never mind that now, Bunder—we'll talk about discipline later!" he growled, watching Matt's face fade from purple to red. His mind raced, seeking a way to turn this near-disaster into success. It wasn't easy. He was the Captain of the City; he spent his time putting people *into* prison, not thinking of ways to help them *escape*.

"This man should have a pother," he said at last.

"There's a pothery two streets over," said Bunder, eager to make amends. "I'll—"

He shook his head. "No. This is an important prisoner. He'd best be seen by the king's own man. Go to the palace and fetch Nix here. But *slowly*!" he added as Bunder made a dash for the door. "After the hullabaloo last night the townsfolk don't need to see you careering through the streets like a scalded cat. Walk there and walk back again. Like you're out for a stroll. With a friend."

"Walk back?" said Bunder, confused. "But doesn't the pother have a carriage?"

"A very nice one, I believe, with royal bits and pieces painted all over it," Orrick said. "Humour me, Ox. Walk. This City's been in a ferment for far too long. It's our job now to set a calm example."

"Yes, sir," said Bunder, still confused but trained to the teeth. "I'll be back with the pother directly."

But not too directly, Orrick hoped, as the sound of Bunder's retreating footsteps diminished. Well. He'd bought himself some time. Now to spend it wisely...

Matt was breathing more easily now, slumped on his side, his face almost human again. "You shouldn't have stopped me, Captain," he croaked, looking up through slitted eyes. "I'm going to die anyway."

Orrick glared. Dragged the fool upright and leaned him against the wall. As a precaution he picked up the dagger and stuck it through his belt. "Well done. You've almost ruined everything. Sit there and do *nothing*. I won't be long."

Turning his back on Matt's bewilderment he hurried to the rear of the guardhouse and opened the door. Beckoned to Darran, once more hiding in the shadows.

"Hurry! One of my lads could return any moment!"

Darran stared in alarm. "Where's Matt?"

"Inside. The damned fool tried to hang himself and besides, there's his escape to be covered! Come *in*!"

Wittering, Darran came. Matt's swollen jaw dropped when he saw the prince's secretary.

"*Darran?* Are you another Circle member? Is Orrick?"

"I haven't the faintest idea," said Darran, kneeling beside him and speaking quickly. "Now hush up and listen. I'm getting you out of here. Prince Gar's orders. The kingdom's in danger and we need your help to save it."

"I don't understand," said Matt, rubbing at his bruised, chafed throat. "If you aren't part of the Circle why—"

Orrick kicked him, just hard enough to get his attention. "Can you take them to Asher?"

Matt's face stilled. "Asher's dead."

"He's not and we all know it. Do you know where to find him?"

"Please, Matt," Darran urged him as the stable meister continued silent. "This isn't a trick, I promise. We're trying to save you. Trust us, we're your only hope. The kingdom's only hope. His Highness is *counting* on you."

A riot of uncertainty in the injured man's face. An agony of indecision. They were running out of time...

Orrick snatched the dagger from his belt. Hauled Matt up and onto his feet then shoved the weapon into his hand.

"Stab me."

"*What?*"

"No one will believe this unless I'm wounded! Stab me, you fool, and be quick about it! Do you want the king to find us? Could be he's on his way!"

Matt lifted the dagger in front of his face, looking at it as though he'd never seen one before. "Say I do it. Say I stab you. Then what?"

"Then we run, Matt! To Asher!" said Darran, on his feet again. "His Highness is outside hidden in a donkey cart. We have to go now, man, before it's discovered we're missing from the Tower!"

But Matt just shook his head, still dazed. "I can't—I don't know—"

Orrick looked at Darran. "This won't work, he's addled with shock. You've got to get out of here, back to the Tower. Think of another way to—"

"There is no other way!" said Darran. His face was flushed, his eyes alight with desperation. "Oh sweet Barl, forgive me!" he gasped. Snatched the dagger from Matt's unresisting fingers and struck.

Orrick choked as the blade sank deep into his shoulder. Magically tempered steel sliced muscle. Scraped bone. The pain was immediate. Shocking. Hot bright lights danced before his eyes and the small cell spun, sparkling like glimfire. Without his permission his knees buckled and he sagged to the floor.

Darran's hands were pressed to his face. "Oh dear...oh dear..."

Oh dear was right. There was sweat on his face, icy as melted snow. His shoulder was on fire. Damn. Who'd have thought such a stringy old man would have such strength in him? "Go," he croaked. His right hand hovered over the jutting dagger hilt. If he pulled the damn thing out would he bleed to death right here on the floor? "Now. Flog that damned donkey till it drops in the road and don't look back. Nix is on his way, I'll be all right. Tell His Highness, good luck. Tell Asher, I'm sorry."

"Yes—yes—" said Darran, shaking, and took hold of Matt's arm to drag him from the cell.

Matt pulled free. "Wait." His dazed confusion had cleared. Beneath the bruises and bloodstains he looked himself again, the calm and competent man who'd run a prince's stables. "We'll never get out of the City unrecognised."

"We might do!" cried Darran. "We must risk it!"

"No," said Matt, and turned to Darran. Spread his hands wide and pressed them to the old man's face. "Stand still. This won't take a moment...I hope."

Pounded with pain, Orrick watched as Matt's battered face contorted and he lost his last colour. Beneath his pressing hands Darran cried out, protesting.

"What are you doing? Stop it! Stop it!"

Matt lowered his hands. Staggered a little, and would have fallen if not for his shoulder pressed hard to the cell wall. "Did it work?" he muttered. "I've never done it before. Just had it done to me, once."

Shocked speechless, Orrick looked into Darran's changed features. A moment earlier they had been thin. Straight-nosed and sharp-chinned. Familiar. Now Darran wore the face of a stranger ten years younger, placid and pouchy, with a bulbous nose and a spider-working of veins across his cheeks. He found his voice and whispered, disbelieving, "It worked. You're disguised, Darran. With magic."

Darran gasped. "Barl have mercy! Not you too, Matt!"

Still leaning on the cell wall Matt pressed his hands to his own face. Groaned aloud, a sound of extreme distress, and nearly slid to the floor, retching. When his hands fell away they revealed a second stranger.

"It's called a blurring," he said hoarsely. His new face was grey and sweating. "But we'll have to hurry. It won't last long."

"Then go," said Orrick fiercely. "Now!"

They bolted. Alone and bleeding he sprawled face-up on the prison-cell floor. Before he could wonder if he'd done the right thing, the world around him turned scarlet, then black. His last clear thought, as consciousness left him, was something like a prayer.

Sweet Blessed Barl...don't let me be wrong.

CHAPTER THIRTY-ONE

Morg woke late in his unattended house, and for some little while indulged himself in the luxury of silence. Silence was an antidote to the memory of Holze's insistent yammering...

"*Conroyd, you must show yourself the Weather Worker in public. Conroyd, you must move into the palace. Conroyd, you must recall the lords and ladies now dallying in the country. Appoint a Privy Council...soothe the worried populace...decide upon an heir... name a Master Magician. Conroyd...Conroyd...Conroyd...*"

He intended to feed the cleric to his demons *personally* when at last the Wall came down.

His regrettably unavoidable meeting with the man had lasted hours. Through it all he'd nodded and smiled and indicated approval, agreement, whatever was required to bring the audience to an end. But it seemed Holze had been storing up an inexhaustible supply of opinions...and he couldn't risk taking action. A swift and surreptitious examination of the prosing cleric's mind showed him a man peculiarly proofed against easy tampering. More of Barl's interference? He couldn't tell. Didn't care; in the end it would make no difference. With gritted teeth he'd survived the lecturing and so had Holze, barely, what he needed now was to bend his will towards the only thing that mattered: the next step in his undermining of Barl's infernal Wall. That exquisite task completed, he would examine the stable meister taken by Orrick's men after the execution and—

The execution.

Beneath his cosseting blankets Morg stretched with delight like a cat.

Interfering, unexpected Asher was dead.

Gar had wept; recollection of the mewling cripple's grief bathed him in more pleasure, leaving him languorous and replete. He was aware, too, of Conroyd's pleasure in that brutal death. Conroyd had hated the Olken with a passion nearly matching his own. Not that his docile prisoner said as much. Subdued at last, run out of words and curses, Conroyd sat silent in his cage now; but his feelings were as loud as any shout.

The glow of sunlight behind the bedchamber's drawn curtains reminded him the day was ageing rapidly. He rose, bathed, dressed, summoned food from his cookless kitchen and then rode Asher's cowed stallion back to the Weather Chamber.

Holze had been right about one thing, damn him: to allay suspicion he must show the people of Lur their expected weather. So he made it rain, but with the magic corrupted, the spell altered, so that every drop of water falling from the sky pulled free a thread of the tapestry binding together the bitch whore's ancient barrier.

Ancient... but not immortal.

Overhead, the golden Wall trembled. Shuddered. Staring through the Weather Chamber's clear glass ceiling Morg laughed and laughed to see it. Rode away light-hearted towards the City Guardhouse where waited the prisoner Matt, ripe for plucking.

But instead of the cripple's former stable meister he found chaos.

"It's a nasty wound, Your Majesty," Pother Nix informed him on the threshold of Orrick's office. "The captain has lost considerable blood. He'll mend, but—Your Majesty, he's not ready for—Your Majesty, I must protest! My patient—"

Thrusting the fool aside, ignoring his irrelevant gabble, Morg confronted Orrick on his makeshift sickbed. "Well? What happened? And why was I not informed immediately?"

Stripped to the waist and swathed in scarlet-stained bandages, Orrick regarded him weakly. His skin had turned sickly and his eyes were rimmed with red. "Your Majesty...forgive me..." His voice was a whispering trickle. "I failed you."

One of the guardsmen, a hulking brute, stepped forward from the background huddle of uniforms and bowed. "Your Majesty, the prisoner tried to hang himself. Captain Orrick sent me to fetch him a pother and while I was gone the prisoner stabbed him near to death. He's escaped."

For one blinding moment his rage was absolute, so that he nearly wiped them from existence with a word: Orrick, Nix, the brutish guardsman.

"Your Majesty..." Orrick again, barely audible. "I'd hoped to find him quickly. Avoid the need to trouble you. I've many men out searching. He'll be recaptured, I swear it."

Rage subsided. So the stable meister was missing. But did it really matter? Attempted suicide suggested secrets worth hiding, true...but equally it could have been fear. Asher was dead and Weather Working had died with him. The Wall even now was crumbling. What matter the fate of one Olken, destined soon for fire wherever he'd run to?

Not that he'd say so. Keeping all eyes focused on recent events would mean less attention paid to him. He smiled, magnanimously forgiving. "Very well, Captain. I accept your apology. Continue your hunt for the miscreant. I trust implicitly your diligence shall find him in the end. Meanwhile, your men can enforce the Olken curfew and the other restrictions arising from this new and criminal action. My man Willer shall advise you of the details."

He left behind him uneasy silence and a horrified exchanging of glances. Inwardly he smiled.

Downstairs in the guardhouse reception area he was accosted by ubiquitous Willer, damp from the still-falling rain and puffing from his minimal exertions. "Your Majesty! Oh, at last I've found you!"

"For what purpose?" he asked coldly. The little toad had pretensions, and required regular squashing.

Willer stepped improperly close. "I have an urgent message, sir."

He had no interest in messages. Frowning at the repellent creature he said, "Did you do as I bid, Willer, and see to Asher's remains?"

Willer stepped back. "I supervised their disposal first thing this morning, Your Majesty, exactly as requested. The dead dogs are burned now, and their ashes scattered. The traitor is no more."

"Excellent. And your message?"

"Your Majesty," Willer's voice was lowered to a sibilant hiss. "Lords Sorvold and Daltrie request an urgent audience."

Of course they did. Puling lickspittles, desperate for advancement. "Inform them I am unavailable for audience."

Willer swallowed, convulsively. "Yes, Your Majesty. Your Majesty, they seemed quite...determined. They'll ask me to ask you again. What shall I tell them?"

"Tell them a king does not account himself to his subordinates. Subordinates account themselves to their king."

Willer looked less than convinced. "Yes, Your Majesty. Er, Your Majesty?"

In the midst of leaving he stopped and turned. Let his displeasure fully reveal itself and waited for Willer to cease his cringing. "Yes?"

Faltering, stooped as though avoiding a blow, Willer crept close again. "There is just one more thing, sir. The palace provisioner was wondering when you thought to—"

"For all I care, Willer, the palace provisioner can drop dead of an ague!" he snapped. "Delay me no further! I am fatigued with Weather Working and must recover my strength. The damage wrought by the traitor Asher is greater than even I imagined. Would you have me weak and incapable of fulfilling my sacred duties? Of saving this king-dom from his black and ugly business?"

Willer blanched. "No, sir! Oh no!"

"Then desist your childish blatherings! And tell those who would tax me with trifles to quickly follow suit! I return now to my town-house. If you're wise you'll see I'm not disturbed."

"Your Majesty," said Willer, his obeisance folding him in half.

Sweeping out of the guardhouse Morg ignored the murmured rev-erent acknowledgements by guards and visitors alike. Paused on the steps he savoured the slurry of rain splashing from the greeny-grey clouds he'd called with a thought. Olken and Doranen in the street beyond the guardhouse gates stopped to bow or curtsey. He ignored them too. Stared instead at Barl's great Wall, clinging tight to the mountains.

Was it his imagination or did the glowing gold seem...tarnished? And along its very top—was that a hint, the merest suggestion, of a tatter? A hem, unravelling?

He rather thought it was.

A lackey brought him the silver stallion. He mounted, smiling, and rode away.

Just as dusk was falling Dathne heard the cottage's side gate creak. She dropped the book she'd not really been reading, convinced at first it was a dream. Three false alarms she'd raised already. Was near worn out with hope and waiting. But this time it wasn't her frantic mind playing tricks. This time there was the sound of a tired horse—no, two tired horses—plodding along the track outside the cottage and the glimpse through the window of a cart rolling past, driven past a bent old woman wrapped tight in a blanket.

Veira. Veira was home. Which meant Asher—

She bolted into the kitchen so fast she banged into the rickety table and nearly fell flat on her face. Rubbing her hip and cursing she shoved the back door open and tumbled into the midst of Veira's vigorously scratching hens. They fled, cackling. The sun was sliding towards the brooding treetops and a chill wind was up, rattling their branches.

Veira slumped alone on the wagon's driving seat, her face half hid-den in the hood of her cloak. Little brown Bessie had been replaced by two tall raw-boned greys, and the wagon they pulled was differ-ent too.

"Veira!" she cried. "I thought you'd never get here! Did it go right?

Do you have him? What happened? And where's Matt? Quick, quick, tell me, quick!"

Veira pushed the hood back on her shoulders. In the fading light she looked exhausted. So, for that matter, did the two strange horses. They were splashed with mud to their bellies and their heads hung almost to the ground.

"Matt and me got separated. I swapped Bessie and my old cart for faster new horses and a wagon with a hidey-hole in it. Now stop your questions, child, and give me a hand with our Innocent Mage."

All she could do was stand and stare. "What do you mean, you got separated? Did you leave Matt behind? *Veira!*"

"Dathne!" the old woman snapped. "I can't lift Asher out on my own! *Help* me. I'll tell you what I can once he's safe inside!"

The bony grey horses stood patiently as Veira clambered down from the wagon and began fiddling with the side of the box seat. Muttering under her breath, she poked and prodded while Dathne watched, feeling sick.

"Asher's in there?" she demanded. "He'll be suffocated!"

Veira ignored her. Poked and prodded some more, then said "Ha!" with a tired satisfaction. The side of the box seat dropped open and Dathne saw the soles of two bare and dirty feet.

Asher.

She leapt forward and helped Veira drag him slowly from his prison until his toe-tips touched the grassy ground and she could wrap her arms around his unconscious body. The weight of him had her staggering.

"He's drugged," said Veira, leaning against the wagon and catching her breath. "It was safer, and easier."

Drugged. That was unlikely to please him. She could feel his slow and heavy breathing, warm between her shoulderblades. The rank smell of him caught in the back of her throat. "Let's get him inside, then," she said. Her voice was rough with pent-up tears and barely realised relief. "Before he wakes and causes a ruckus."

Veira put her arm around him from the other side and together they half carried, half dragged him into the cottage.

"My room," Veira grunted.

They lowered him onto the sagging mattress in Veira's tiny bedchamber and took a moment to recover their breathing. Then, as Veira lit her bedside lamps, Dathne looked into her husband's face.

"Oh, *Veira*," she whispered.

"I know, child, I know," said Veira. Shockingly, she sounded on the verge of tears. "I'd best go see to those horses and the wagon. And the chickens." She sniffed, looking disappointed. "You might have done right by my chickens, child."

Dathne flushed. "I'm sorry, I—"

"And what about my pigs? Did you forget about my pigs as well?"

"No! No, I didn't forget, I just...I've been waiting, worrying. I..."

Veira sighed. "I'll see to the pigs then, too. You stay in here. Make Asher comfortable and sit with him till I'm done outside. Then we'll clean and physick him. In the meantime, if he wakes..." She frowned. "But I doubt he will. I gave him enough grobleroot to—"

"*Grobleroot?*" said Dathne. "Veira, how could you risk—"

"Because I had to!" the old woman retorted. "And it didn't kill him, so let it be. We've bigger things to worry about than whether or not I slipped him a sleeping draught!"

Dathne realised then how close Veira was to collapsing, and felt ashamed. "I'm sorry," she murmured. "Of course you know what you're doing."

Veira nodded. "And mind you remember that. Now I'll be back directly."

The bedroom door banged shut behind her. Dathne frowned at it, then turned her attention to the heavily stuporous Asher. First things first: get him out of his stinking horrible clothes. She'd only undressed him twice before, and both times were occasions for joy.

Now, though...

When she saw the extent of his injuries she wept a little, for what had been done to him. What he'd endured. And what he had yet to face, once consciousness returned. She threw the stained and filthy shirt and trews on the floor, settled his head more comfortably on the pillows, drew a light blanket over him and waited for Veira.

The sun had set completely by the time the old woman returned to the bedroom carrying her medicine tin, a bowl of warm water and a bagful of rags. Working silently, swiftly, they washed the dirt, dried blood and caked pus from Asher's bruised and crusted skin. Spread his wounds with salves and ointments, acridly healing. Now Dathne was glad of the grobleroot because they must have been hurting him. Through it all, Asher failed to stir.

At last the nasty task was done. Clean and physicked, dressed in an old nightshirt and coddled with blankets, Asher slept on. Veira touched her arm. "Into the kitchen, child," she whispered. "I could do with some tea."

She smoothed Asher's hair a final time and followed Veira from the chamber, unspeaking. Watched in continued silence as the old woman waved her to a chair, refusing her assistance, and put the kettle on the hob. She looked pale. Moved slowly, painfully, as she dribbled honey into their steaming tea cups and tipped butter biscuits onto a plate.

"The important thing is," she said as she finally settled down at the table, "we got him here safely."

Yes. Yes, that was important. It was everything. Dathne sipped her scalding tea cautiously, but didn't risk a biscuit. Her occupied belly was unforgiving now. "Please, Veira. Tell me what happened. Rafel. Is he—"

Veira nodded. "Yes. He's dead. Just as I planned it."

"I'm so sorry."

Staring into the depths of her mug, Veira seemed not to hear her. "Rafel's dead and Asher's alive and good Matthias is missing. I wonder if this is what Prophecy wanted."

Matt was *missing*? "I don't know," Dathne whispered. Reached out and covered Veira's hand with her own. "Why don't you tell me all of it and I'll see if I can't answer."

Not lifting her eyes Veira nodded again, then haltingly began to speak.

"He smiled at me, you know," she whispered. "When I gave him the potion and bade him to drink. He smiled, and kissed my cheek, and...and *thanked* me, for the chance to do such service." Tears wet her cheeks, unheeded. "I held him as best I could while the poison worked its will on him. I thought I'd made it painless but...at the end, he felt it. Not badly, and not for long, but I was looking into his eyes at the last and I saw—" She shuddered, and released a ragged breath.

"Don't think about it," Dathne urged. "It's over now, and he's at peace. What happened next?"

It sounded incredible, like something from one of Vev Gertsik's improbable novels. Circle members hidden in the crowd, tampering with Doranen glimfire. The hooded axeman one of their own, striking the head from a man already heart-stopped so living Asher might be whisked away in the shouting confusion. Fire. Alarm. Hysteria.

"I thought for a moment we'd not survive it," Veira admitted after another swallow of tea. "There was screaming. Trampling. I couldn't see a foot in front of me and if I'd fallen no one would've stopped to lend a hand. Our people there saved us. Bundled us into blankets and spirited us to the Livestock Quarter right under the noses of the guards. It was all such pandemonium I didn't even realise Matthias wasn't with us until we'd reached the horses and wagon and it was time to go."

Her hand still on Veira's, Dathne tightened her fingers. "It wasn't your fault. You said it yourself: saving Asher was the most important thing. Matt's a strong man, and resourceful. He'll find his way back to us. I know it."

But she sounded more confident than she felt.

Veira pulled her hand free and pushed slowly to her feet. "I'm sure you're right, child. But what say we see for certain, eh? I'll sleep easier knowing he's on his way here."

"Let me. You're too tired to scry tonight, Veira."

Veira frowned. "And you're with child."

"You mean there's danger?" Dathne said, alarmed, and leapt from her chair, palms pressed to her still-flat belly. "I scried when I got here! Have I harmed the baby?"

"No, no, I shouldn't think so," said Veira, and pressed her back in the chair. "Tanal's not a poison, Dathne. Chewed and not swallowed it does no harm. But better safe than sorry. Besides, I'm old and I'm tired but I'm not so decrepit I can't find our Matthias this once."

"Then at least let me fetch what's necessary. Sit down and finish your tea. Eat another biscuit. You'll need your strength."

Pretending to grumble, Veira obeyed. Dathne gathered the basin, the water, the herbs. Laid them neatly before the old woman then withdrew to lean herself against the sink, one ear cocked in case Asher should wake and make a sound. She was too nervous to sit again until she knew Matt was all right.

Jervale, are you listening? He'd better be all right...

Unhurried and methodical, Veira readied herself for the scrying. Chewed the tanal, spat it out. Closed her eyes, and waited.

It seemed to take forever.

"I have him," Veira whispered at last. A slow smile spread over her tired, wrinkled face. "He's safe. He's coming. And with company..."

"Company?" Dathne leapt to the table and stared into the scrying water even though she knew she'd see nothing. "Who?"

"An old man—Olken—and a handsome young Doranen fellow. They're travelling in a donkey cart."

A handsome young *Doranen*? Could it be—"Gar?" she said, incredulous. "He's bringing *Gar* here? *Why*?"

Veira shrugged. "No doubt he has his reasons, child."

"Not good ones!"

"Who's the old Olken man, do you think?"

"I don't know for certain. But if the Doranen is Gar then that has to be Darran. The royal secretary." Dazed, she paced the kitchen floor. "I don't believe this. What is he *thinking*?" Her pleasure at Matt's survival was doused now with ire. "Once it's realised Gar's missing Jarralt won't rest till he's found him! He'll peer under every blade of grass in the kingdom! We'll all be discovered. When Matt gets here I'll *kill* him!"

Slowly Veira opened her eyes and eased herself out of the tanal's cloying grasp. "No, you won't, child. You'll listen to his story with your tongue behind your teeth. There's been enough killing for now."

That silenced her. When she could trust her temper again she asked, with restraint, "How long till they reach us?"

Veira shrugged. "The countryside is the same for miles and miles between us and the City. I can't quite tell where they are. They'll be here by and by, child. That's all I can say for certain."

Suddenly queasy, Dathne dropped into a chair. "Good. That's... good."

But what Asher would say when he found himself in such a houseful, she hadn't the faintest idea.

"Our Mage'll be waking soon, I'm thinking," said Veira, clearing the scrying things away. "And it's nigh on dinnertime. Cook us a meal, child, and I'll sit with Asher till he stirs."

Dathne nodded. She wanted to feel angry at Veira's high-handedness. To feel outraged and proprietary and indignant for her rights where Asher was concerned—but instead, she felt relieved. And then guilty. She was desperate to see him. She was frightened to see him. All the hidden truths would soon be laid bare...

"It'll be fine," said Veira. Her eyes were warm and knowing. "If we trust to Prophecy, it'll be just fine."

In his dreams, Asher was sailing.

The sky was a blue bowl overhead, with little scudding clouds and the sun playing peekaboo behind them. A salt-stiffened breeze snapped the sail against the masthead, the shirt on his back, the hair on his head. The fishing smack, not brand new but seaworthy all the same, gaily green and blue in her fresh coat of paint, plunged and curvetted like an eager young filly, dipping low into Restharven Harbour with the heaving weight of her nets and the bounty they promised. Her name was Amaranda. Laughing, he reached out his hands to haul the first net back on board. Laughing, Da joined him and together they cracked their muscles, smiling with the effort, as the catch came over the side in all its wet-scaled flapping glory...

"Da!" said Asher and sat up in his bed.

"Easy now," said a comfortable voice to his right. "You might find your head's gone all a bit whirligig."

It had. Dizzy, he flopped back on the pillows and waited for the spinning to stop. The voice was female. Old. Unfamiliar, as was the room. "Where am I?"

"Safe."

There were no lamps lit; he couldn't see the speaker's face. "Where?"

"In my house."

"And who are you?"

"A friend. The friend of friends. Be easy now. Your enemies are behind you and they'll not find you here."

He touched clumsy fingers to his neck. "I ain't dead." It came as a kind of discovery, and a welcome surprise.

A breathy chuckle. "No, child, you ain't."

His mind was a jumble of memories. The cage. The Square seething with sound and faces. The executioner with his axe. The glimfire, which kept on sparking. How the wooden block felt pressed against his throat. The pain in his wrists and ankles as he walked towards his death. The stink of his own piss and sweat. Pellen's grim, unfeeling face.

Gar.

He tried to sit up again. For the first time in forever his body was free of pain. "How did I get here? What's goin' on? Sink me, woman, who *are* you?"

A rough-palmed hand reached out of the darkness and held him down. "People call me Veira."

His muscles felt like soggy bread. "What people?"

"Just people."

"The folk who rescued me?"

"That's right."

He wished there were a few more candles burning, so he could see this Veira's face. "I want to meet 'em."

"You can't, child. Not yet. But one day soon, I hope. Prophecy willing."

Prophecy? What was prophecy? "Who are you to say no to me? I want to meet 'em, I said!"

"And I said not yet!" she snapped, her voice hardening.

Another snatch of memory: loud screaming, and a harsh, urgent voice in his ear demanding: *Do you want to live?*

Then he did sit up, never mind his weakened body or the hand still pressed against his shoulder. "I remember you now! You were there! You saved my life!"

"A lot of people saved your life, child," the old woman said. She sounded suddenly sad. "And one man in particular. I'll tell you about him, by and by."

He sank to the pillows again, his body a traitor. "Call me Asher. I ain't a child."

A breath of amusement. "You are to me. To me, at my age, you're a spratling."

Spratling. "That's a fishing word."

"And you're a fishing man. Or you were, and hope to be again. But if you want that dream coming true there's a thing or two you'll need to do first."

"Show me your face," he said, suspicious. "Why are we sittin' in the dark? Can't you light a lamp or somethin'?"

"Light one yourself," said the aggravating old besom. "The glimfire's in you, along with everything else."

He stopped breathing. Didn't start again till his lungs began clamouring for mercy. "That ain't funny."

"And I'm not laughing. The time for hiding is past us, young Asher of Restharven. Though that's not the name I know you by."

He wasn't going to ask how she knew him. Knew any of it. Wouldn't say another word until she lit a lamp and showed him her face and explained what he was *doing* here.

She answered the unasked question anyway. "For six hundred years, Asher, me and mine have known you as the Innocent Mage. Prophecy named you in the days of Barl and the making of her Wall. When she sowed the seeds we're reaping as weeds today. You've a birthright, child. And the womb of the world is ready at last to spit you out in blood and pain."

He shook his head. "You're crazy."

"Am I?" she asked him. He heard a whispered word and felt a tremble of power. A tiny bloom of glimfire appeared hovering above her palm like a firefly. It illuminated the softly folded planes of her face and turned her dark eyes to gemstones. "You see?" she said, smiling. "You aren't the only one after all. But you are the very best..."

He was too astonished to speak.

She frowned at the glimfire. "Believe it or not this used to be ours. The Doranen took it, of course, just like they took everything else. And our fool elders let 'em. Made their shortsighted bargain and dropped us all in a stinky, stinky soup."

He found his voice at last. "I ain't got the first idea what you're witterin' about. You called *glimfire.* I thought I was—"

"Alone?" The old woman chuckled. "No, child. Not alone. Every Olken's got magic in him. What did you think happens at your Sea Harvest Festival? You think the fish rise for a Doranen, singing? No. They answer the call of the Olken. Lur's fisherfolk using the power they were born with, all unknowing."

"*What?* What d'you mean, what—"

She raised her other hand. "Hush now. There's not much time for story-spinning, so pin back your ears and I'll tell you what's most needful."

The last time he'd let someone tell him a story he'd ended up with his head on a chopping block. He kicked back the blankets. "Don't bother. I ain't interested. And I ain't stayin' neither."

She made no move to stop him. Just watched as betrayed by weakness he crashed to the rug-covered floor. Banged and bashed about finding his feet. Staggered to the bedroom door. Grabbed its handle. Wrenched it open—

"Hello, Asher," said Dathne. Smiling. Shaking. "Please don't go yet. We've a lot to talk about."

After hours on the road the elderly donkey was exhausted, so they climbed from the cart and walked for a while. Matt kept to the poor beast's head, guiding its tottering footsteps along the rutted roadway. Gar and Darran followed behind. It was the dark of the moon and the starlight was faint. Close ahead of them were the Black Woods and the mountains. This near to the Wall there should be a glorious wash of gold to help them find their way, but...

Cold, hungry, plagued with blisters and longing for this journey to end, Gar looked around. Apart from themselves the road was empty; it should be safe to speak. "Are my eyes playing tricks, Matt, or does it seem to you the Wall has...faded?"

Matt's voice floated back to him out of the dark. "No tricks. If what you say is true—if Morg is really among us—then it's my belief he's working to bring down the Wall from inside the kingdom."

Envy prickled. Matt had already explained his peculiar sensitivities. His...magic. It was all he'd explained; up till now the journey had been conducted almost in silence. "You can feel that?"

"I can. Now, Gar, it's best we hold our tongues. Sound travels easier than we do, this time of night."

Beside him Darran bristled, deeply disapproving of his prince's instruction that Matt abandon formality and get used to calling him "Gar." He chewed at his lip for a moment, debating. But it had to be said...before they reached their destination, which promised little relaxation. Now seemed as good a time as any.

He lowered his voice. "You lied to me, Darran."

Limping just a little, likely nursing blisters of his own, Darran kept his gaze pinned to the road. "I'm sure I never did, sir."

"Don't make it worse, Darran. You lied. Asher doesn't forgive me. He hates me. I think he'd kill me if he could."

A fraught pause, then Darran rallied. "His Highness is mistaken. I distinctly recall—"

He raised a finger. "*Don't.* Not if you truly love me."

Silence, save for the creaking of the cart's wheels, the thudding of their feet onto the road's packed clay and the donkey's laboured breathing.

"I only sought to ease your pain, sir," said Darran eventually, harshly whispering. "Asher was about to die, I saw no harm in—"

"I know why you did it," he said, biting back impatience. "And I'm grateful that you care. But it doesn't change the truth. Asher trusted me and I betrayed him to his death. He hates me for that...and I can't say I blame him."

"Well, I can!" said Darran, indignant. "You did what you had to, what any king would—"

"Exactly. I acted like a king...but what Asher needed was a friend."

"You've been a friend without peer, sir! He was a nothing, a nobody, when he came to Dorana!"

Gar shook his head. "And now he's a fugitive, destined for death if he's discovered, and all because of me. I swore on my life I'd protect him, Darran, and instead of keeping my word I abandoned him. I just pray that when we see him again he'll not let his hatred of me stand in the way of helping us against Conr— Morg."

"He won't," said Matt from the gloom ahead. "He might hate you but when he hears what you've got to say, he'll do what's needful. What's right."

"How can you be so sure?" he said, shivering.

"Because he's the Innocent Mage."

He frowned. "And what *is* that, exactly, Matt? I think it's time you told me what's going on. You do know, don't you?"

Darkly silhouetted, Matt nodded. "I do."

"In the guardhouse you mentioned a circle. What did you mean?"

"I meant I'm not alone," said Matt. "Me, Dathne, the folk who helped save Asher—we're magicians. Not like the Doranen. Our magic's different. But we have a power, like your people do. We're joined in secrecy and silence, bound to serve Prophecy and Asher. The Innocent Mage."

"And does Asher know this?"

"He didn't, but I'd say there's a good chance he does by now. By now he likely knows everything."

When last Gar saw him, Asher was kneeling with his head on a block, waiting for a sharpened axe to fall. Remembering that stark, cruel moment he felt his bowels constrict. What would happen when Asher came face to face with the architect of his torment and near destruction?

Matt seemed certain he'd forgive and forget. For himself, he wasn't anywhere close to confident. He had his own suspicions and they threatened to drop him where he walked.

He increased his pace till he fell into step beside his former stable meister. "I think, Matt," he said, letting his concern show, making it an order and not a request, "that if we want to make sure Asher's with us, not against us, it's time I knew everything too."

CHAPTER THIRTY-TWO

Bundled back into the saggy single bed by that bossy Veira, Asher stared at Dathne as though she were a ghost. Nasty suspicions were stirring in his mind. Roiling in his belly.

It didn't help she was having trouble meeting his eyes.

"Dath?" he said softly, willing her to look at him. "Dath, what are you doin' here? What's goin' on?"

Still she kept her gaze pinned to the floor. Now a lamp was lit and he could see her clearly. She looked frightened. He'd never seen her frightened before. Angry. Impatient. Uncertain. But never rigid with fear like this. She stood with her back pressed hard to the closed bedchamber door, her fingers fisted by her sides.

Retreated to the bedroom's shadows, Veira sat like a pile of laundry in a ratty overstuffed armchair shoved in a corner and watched them.

He ignored her. "Dath—*talk* to me. How did I get here? Who's this Veira and what's she to you? To me? *Tell* me!"

In her dark corner, the old woman stirred. "Well, child, you started this. Seems to me you should finish it."

Dathne looked up. Her eyes were enormous. "Asher, do you love me?"

He scowled. "I married you, didn't I? Though it's startin' to look like I made a mistake."

She flinched as though he'd struck her. In a way he had. He didn't care. If she was frightened, he was terrified.

"I've a story to tell you, Asher." Her voice was a whisper. "Will you promise to listen, not judging, till you know all the facts?"

It was the first of *Tevit's Principles of Jurisprudence*. Anger burned him. Did she think it was *funny*, throwing Justice Hall in his face now? After everything he'd been through?

She saw her error. Reached out to him, alarmed. "Please, Asher! Listen! You'll understand everything by the time I'm done."

"Understand what I'm doin' here? What *you're* doin' here? How I escaped, and how *she* can do *magic*?"

Dathne crept to the chair beside the bed and slid into it. Looked where he was pointing, at the silently watchful old woman, and nodded. "Everything. I promise."

"Dathne..." He felt sick, his heart was beating so hard. "Can *you* do magic?"

Tears flooded her eyes. Overflowed down her cheeks. "I couldn't tell you, any more than you could tell me. Secrecy was the only thing that saved us. Remember that, before you judge me."

She could do magic. Everything about her was a lie. He turned his face away. "Reckon I'd rather forget."

"You can't. You mustn't. Or the kingdom will fall into chaos and nothing you love will survive."

Without another word spoken he knew what went on here was dangerous. Madness. Worse than anything Gar had tricked him into. He didn't want to know more. Wished almost he was dead, his head and his body in two separate pieces. Fed to the dogs, as Jarralt had promised.

Jarralt.

As always, Dathne read him. "You're safe, Asher. I promise. No one's hunting you. Conroyd Jarralt believes you're dead."

Still he couldn't look at her. "He'd need a body for that."

"He's got one."

Now he looked. "You *murdered* someone?"

"Jarralt's the murderer, not Dathne," said Veira from the shadows. "Rafel was one of us. He gave his life willingly, because it was needful. And his birthright."

He kept his gaze pinned to Dathne. "So all this is part of a plan?"

She nodded. "Yes. One set in motion centuries before either of us were born."

"And me? What am I?"

She sat a little straighter in her chair. Unclenched her fingers and laid them softly on her knees. "You are the Innocent Mage, Asher. Born to save the kingdom from blood and fire."

He couldn't answer. Could only lie there and stare at this woman, this stranger. Had he kissed her? Had he *married* her? He'd never seen her before in his life.

"I know this is difficult," she said. "It's not easy for me either. Things happened I should've...prevented."

"Like spreading your legs for me?"

She blanched. "Like falling in love."

"Is *that* what you call it?" he said, and laughed. His stomach was full of acid, churning.

She turned her face from him. "Matt warned me this would happen. I was a fool not to listen."

"*Matt* warned—" He struggled to sit up. "*Matt's* a part of this?"

"We're all of us a part of it, child," said Veira from the darkness. "Whether we know it or don't. What's coming comes to everyone trapped behind the mountains. And unless we work together, no matter our pride and hurt feelings, the thing that's coming will kill every last one of us. Is that what you want on your conscience?"

"I don't know what you're talkin' about! I don't know what you *mean*!"

"Then let me tell you," said Dathne. "Forget what hurts I've done you and just listen to the words. I swear they're true."

All the wounded places in his body were awake again, and burning. His head pounded. He wanted to flee but his legs were too weak. He was pinned beneath the blankets, captive. As he'd been captive one way or another all his damned life.

"Have I got a choice?" he said bitterly.

Veira answered him. "Always, child. We can't compel you to do what's right."

No, they bloody couldn't. They couldn't compel him to do *anything*, magic or no magic, and woe to them if they bloody well tried.

He had a little magic of his own. As for right and wrong—Dathne had a hide to think she could give him a lecture on *that*. All these secrets...the people in his life he'd trusted, leaned on...and *none* of them what he'd thought they were.

Veira said, quite kindly, "Your pricked pride is the least of our worries, child. Hear Dathne out then tell me we were wrong."

Pricked pride? Pricked *pride*? He nearly flung the words back in her face, came close to kicking aside the blankets and getting out of there, no matter if it meant crawling on hands and knees...but curiosity won over outrage, just.

"Fine," he grunted, and folded his arms. "I'm listenin'."

The Doranen who came over the mountains six centuries ago were nothing like the Doranen he knew today, Dathne told him. Those Doranen were a bright and brittle people, weary and battle-scarred and desperate for peace. Their magic was a thing of violence. With it they called nightmares out of hiding and gave them life, gave them teeth to bite and talons to tear. Flattened buildings. Razed whole towns. Slaughtered thousands. They were warriors. And in their eyes were memories of the homeland they'd left behind them. Memories of carnage, and what it had cost them to escape.

Led by a young woman named Barl, they'd fled their wartorn Dorana in terror, crossing countless miles of country burying loved ones as they came. Confronted by the mountains they'd not turned back but instead clawed their way over them and down into Lur. And there found the safe harbour for which they'd long been searching.

They had no intention of giving it up. Of struggling back over the mountains, losing even more of their friends and family on the way, so they might die in the monstrous mage war they'd so narrowly, so dearly, escaped. No matter that this new land wasn't theirs to take. No matter it already had inhabitants who loved it. They were a race for whom wanting became having without a second thought. And they wanted Lur.

The people they found here called themselves Olken. They were a gentle race with magic of their own, an earthbound power tying them to the land, to green and growing things. To the ebb and flow of natural energies. They lived in loosely allied independent communities scattered from coast to coast, with no central government, no king or queen. They had no hope of defeating the warrior Doranen. No chance of resisting the lure of Doranen magic. It was splendid. Miraculous. There was nothing it couldn't do. It even let the Olken understand the beautiful invaders, and be understood in return.

Not long after her people's arrival Barl gathered all the Olken community leaders together and explained about the conflict in her homeland, about Morg, and how defenceless they were against him...how he would not rest till he found her and her people and punished them for fleeing, and then take every Olken as a slave, or worse...

It so happened that in that time the Olken people were suffering. Drought and famine gripped their land and not even their strongest earth-singers could save them. Barl saw their dilemma and made them a glittering offer. Share their homeland with the Doranen—abandon their meagre magics and any memory of them—and she would create a paradise safe not only from Morg but from all the natural sufferings their earthbound lives were prey to. The Olken and Doranen would live together in perfect harmony, perfect peace, safe, secure and prosperous, hidden from the rest of the world beyond the mountains, until the end of time.

Dathne stopped talking. The room was so quiet Asher thought he could hear the spiders breathing. "This ain't the story my ma told me when I were a spratling."

She nodded. "It wasn't. That story was...a lie."

"But you know the truth?" he sneered. "How, if the Olken agreed to forget it? Or is this just another lie, made up to get you what you want? From me."

He could see his words hurt her, and was glad. He'd meant them to.

"One Olken voice spoke out against the bargain," she continued, her hands folded tightly in her lap. Her eyes were bright in the dim lighting. "His name was Jervale and I am his last living heir. Inheritor of his visions and the prophecy they foretold."

Jervale was known in his own small community as something of a seer. A man whose dreams had the knack of coming true. As a small boy he'd had visions of a golden-haired people who'd bring the Olken to ruin. He didn't know who they were or when they'd come or what form that ruin would take. Years passed, he grew up, and the visions faded from memory.

Then the Doranen came, and with them returned his foreboding dreams. They told him the heart of the sweet fruit they offered was rotten...and that one day it would lead to his people's death.

"Jervale tried to warn the Olken elders but they were too Doranendazzled to listen," Dathne said. She sounded sad, regretful. "They didn't know him, or have reason to trust in his prophecies. In this prophecy, the most important of all. With children dying of hunger and thirst the Doranen were the answer to our prayers, or so it seemed."

"Seemed?" he said. "Sounds like they were, if folks were starvin' to death! Sounds to me like your precious Jervale didn't give a fart about that?"

"Of course he did! But he could see further than a season's shortage of food. He knew Barl was right: something dark and dreadful *did* lurk beyond the barrier of mountains. And he knew this, too. That for all their fearsome magic the Doranen would not be able to stand against it. Somehow *Olken* magic would have a part to play in protecting Lur. One day an Olken would be born whose destiny was to save us all in the Final Days. He named him the Innocent Mage."

He stared at her, unconvinced. "And you reckon that's me?"

She nodded. "Yes. You are Prophecy's child, Asher. Born to save the world as Jervale foretold."

Born to save the world? *Him*? It sounded so ridiculous he was hardput not to laugh out loud. But he didn't, because her expression was so serious. Clearly she believed every word she'd said and right now he was at her mercy. One word in the wrong ear from her or the old woman in the corner and he'd be back on his knees before the chopping block. Besides, there were still things he wanted—needed—to know.

"And what about you?" he said. "How do you come into this, eh?"

She glanced at Veira then rested her gaze on the foot of his bed. "I am Jervale's Heir, his descendant, inheritor of his visions and knowledge. I've dreamed you most of my life, Asher. Knew you for who and what you are long before we met."

Dreamed him? *Knew* him? Oh, he didn't like the sound of that. Didn't like it at *all*. "And Matt?" He pointed at the old woman, brooding in her corner. "Her? How do *they* fit in with your precious prophecies?"

Now her fingers laced themselves together to still their trembling. And well she should tremble, too. What she'd *done* . . .

"When he realised his warnings would not be heeded, Jervale went home and gathered to him his closest friends," she said. "Those who knew his visions could be trusted and believed his prophecy would come true. Together they swore an oath to hold the Olken's magical heritage in sacred trust, generation after generation, until the Innocent Mage was born and needed Olken magicians to stand with him in the Final Days. Together they devised a way to protect themselves from the Doranen's purge. They called themselves the Circle. Veira, Matt and I are all of the Circle. There are others, scattered throughout the kingdom, but only Veira knows who they are. Like me they are descended from the Olken of Barl's time. Like me, they've lived their lives with only one purpose: to defeat the evil that will come in the Final Days. That *has* come, Asher. The Final Days are upon us now."

He shook his head, rejecting her and everything she'd said. Prophecies. Visions. Secret societies of Olken magicians. It was crazy. *Crazy.* "You're mad," he said, scathing. "Stark staring moonstruck. You expect me to *believe*—"

"You have to believe it!" she cried. "Every word is the truth!"

"The *truth*?" Scalded with sudden fury he kicked back his blankets and lunged off the bed at her, seizing the arms of her chair and prisoning her in it. "You wouldn't know the truth if it bit you on the arse! You been lyin' to me since the day I turned up in Dorana!"

Despite his rage, she didn't shrink back. "No, I haven't! Withholding information isn't telling lies. I was *protecting* you, Asher!"

"Protecting me?" he said, incredulous. "From what?"

"From accident! From yourself!"

He leaned even closer, till he could feel her panting breath on his cheeks. "The only danger I been in is from *you*. You should've found someone to protect me from *you*, Dathne."

"That's not fair!" she cried. "You were *never* in danger from me!"

He flung himself sideways and half rolled, half staggered to his feet. "Of course I bloody was!" He could see it all, now; how she'd duped him, dudded him, played him like a puppet. "You arranged everything, didn't you? I don't know how, but you did. Me savin' Gar's horse that mornin' in the market. Him thinkin' I was right to be his assistant. You practically *dared* me to take the job, when I knew in my guts I shouldn't! Was it you made him think of me in the first place, one day when you were sellin' him a book? It was, wasn't it? For why, Dathne?" He pulled down the neck of his borrowed nightshirt, baring burned flesh to the light. "For *this*?"

She stretched out an imploring hand. "No, no, of course not! I never *dreamed* you'd come so close to dying!"

He stepped back. The touch of her now would make him vomit. "I don't believe you." A cold thought struck him, then. "How much does Gar know? Are you in bed with him too? Did you dream this up together, you and him, with the sweat of your futtering still wet on your skin?"

Tears streaming, she leapt to her feet. "*No!* How can you say so? How can you *think* it?"

Another thought, colder still. He made himself look in her face. "*Timon Spake.*"

Bewildered, smearing those pouring tears, she shook her head. "What?"

"They caught him trying to do magic!" he shouted. "Was he one of yours? Was he part of your precious Circle?"

As Dathne struggled for words—for lies—Veira answered. "He was, child. A good boy, Timon, but foolish."

He turned on her. "And you didn't save him? You let him *die*?"

The old woman stood and came forward into the light. "We couldn't save him. Timon knew that. He died with courage, and will be remembered."

Courage. That poor sickly boy, and all the blood in him, spilling. He stared at Dathne. "He was never your cousin. That was another lie."

Her stricken gaze flicked to Veira, and back. "Forget Timon. Timon's dead. We must—"

"Why'd you bully me to let you see him, Dathne? What was so important?"

Veira took a small step closer. "What's he talking of, child? When did you see Timon?"

"Beforehand. Briefly," said Dathne. "But that's in the past. Asher, *listen*—"

And now he understood. "You were scared he'd talk out of turn. You thought he'd betray you." His breath caught hard in his aching throat. "What was in them cakes you took him?"

"Cakes?" said Veira, frowning. "You made no mention of cakes, child."

"They were nothing," said Dathne. "Nothing that matters anymore."

No, they were something. The memory was there in her dark brown eyes. Eyes he thought had looked on him with love. His belly cramped, rejecting. "They were poisoned. Weren't they?"

"Poisoned?" Veira echoed. "Child, is that true?"

"Damn you, Asher!" cried Dathne, and turned to the old woman. "I'm *sorry*, I *had* to! I couldn't trust he'd keep the faith and stay silent!"

He was so sickened now he could hardly see straight. "But Spake did. You were wrong about him, Dathne, and you're wrong about me. I ain't your Innocent Mage. I'm a fool as was diddled by sweet talk and lies. Yours. Matt's. Gar's. Everyone's."

"No, no," said Dathne, breathless. "Please believe me. I love you. We need you. You're Prophecy's fulfilment, this kingdom's only hope!"

She reached out her hand to touch him and he knocked it away.

Knocked her sideways as the power inside him drew breath like a dragon and threatened to set him on fire.

"Get away from me, bitch! Get her out of here, old woman, or I won't be responsible. Get out, get *out*!"

The magic ignited. Burst from eyes, mouth and fingers in a roar of burning snow and flaming rain. He let it consume him...didn't care if it killed him. Or Dathne, or Veira.

Didn't care about anything.

Sobbing, Dathne let herself be pushed through the cottage and into the kitchen. She heard the door slam shut and felt Veira's hand press her into a chair.

"We...we...have to go back to him. We have to *stop* him!"

"He'll stop himself soon enough," said Veira, filling the kettle. "Best he gets it out of his system before we try another sensible conversation. I've dampened the bedroom, child. He'll do it no damage."

She hiccuped, struggling for self-control. "Dampened it? When?"

"While you were talking."

"You expected this?"

"A tantrum?" Nodding, Veira put the kettle on the stove top then opened the stove's front to rouse the coals with a poker. "Of course. Didn't you?"

"It's more than a tantrum! That's not a fair word. He's angry, Veira, and he's every right to be. I did deceive him. In a way, I did lie."

Veira sniffed. "You did your duty as Jervale's Heir."

"He doesn't think so," she whispered.

"He will, in time."

She felt her eyes fill again. "He called me a bitch."

"And so you are," said Veira tartly. "And so am I. You think this a business for gentle folk?"

She held Veira's challenging gaze for a moment, then looked away. "I'm sorry about Timon Spake. If there hadn't been an accident—the cakes ruined—I'd have told you what I did."

Veira shrugged. "As you say, child. It's in the past. And after Rafel, who am I to judge you?"

On the stove top the kettle bubbled, burping steam. Veira set out mugs and milk and frowned at the almost empty jug. "First thing in the morning you could make yourself useful, if you like, and wander along to the village. Get me more milk, since I'm almost out and we've got company coming."

Oh, yes. Incredibly, she'd forgotten. Matt, and Gar, and Darran.

Would they be here soon? She hoped so. "Why don't you keep a cow? Or a goat?"

"'Cause there's only me, that's why," said Veira, adding tea leaves to the pot. "And my few cuicks help the milkman. Will you go? I'll give you directions. It's easy enough to find."

She nodded. "Trying to keep me out of Asher's way?"

"I think it's advisable," said Veira, making the tea. "For the next little while at least. You can bring back more bacon too. Maybe some ham. There's carrots and greens in the garden and a big jar of pickled cabbage. Lots of eggs. I think provisions will stretch."

She took the mug that Veira offered. "Won't the villagers be curious about me?"

"Curious, yes. Rude, no," said Veira, smiling briefly. "Tell them you're my niece come to visit, that'll answer."

The tea was hot and sweet, a welcome relief to the cold lump in her middle. *Asher.* She swallowed greedily, not caring that it burned. "Will it be much longer, do you think? Before the absolute end?"

Veira blew on her own tea, brow furrowed with thought. "No," she said at last. "Not too much longer."

It was what she thought herself. Didn't know whether hearing the suspicion confirmed made matters better or worse.

"So what now?"

"Now, child, we'll have us some supper. Then you can go to bed and I'll sit up for Asher. And tomorrow will bring us what it brings."

She wasn't hungry or tired but there was nothing else to do. She even managed to doze a little. She heard no alarm from Veira's bedroom. Its door opened and closed three times, and she caught the merest murmur of voices, but no one called for her to come. Asher stayed safely within.

At first light she rose, bathed, dressed and saw to the livestock. The chickens cackled, the pigs snorted, the raw-boned horses snatched for their hay.

Well. At least someone was glad to see her.

She heard the cottage's back door bang and put her head round the corner of the stable. Asher. He was dressed in drab brown jacket and trews Veira must have had stored or brought with her from the City. Grim-faced, he strode across the back yard, kicked open the gate to the forest and kept on walking. She almost ran after him, shouting. The Black Woods were dangerous. There were bears. Wolves. People. He shouldn't go in there alone...

The kitchen door opened again. Veira stood in the doorway and watched the forest's shadows swallow him. Said nothing as he disappeared among the mossy tree trunks. She was calm and quiet. Peaceful, almost. As though she'd reached a place of balance and was happy to stay there for a while. Dathne held her breath, half hoping Veira saw her, half hoping that she didn't.

She did. Nodded, acknowledging, then went back inside. Dathne sighed and followed her.

"Is he all right?"

Close to, Veira looked exhausted. Slumped in a chair, head propped in her hands with her silver hair all which-way, she nodded. "Right enough. And will be better, by and by. He needs more time alone."

"He won't run?"

Veira snorted. "Run where? We're his only haven and he knows it. Make us breakfast, will you, child? I'm almost too weary for breathing."

She cooked them eggs with cream and dill. Settled Veira in the sitting room with tea and a blanket, then went on her little trip to the village. It was surprisingly pleasant, marching through the forest with only a basket for company. A little balm for her lacerated soul. The air was fresh and clean, scented with pine. Unseen birds whistled and called, sounding cheerful. She kept one eye out for Asher but didn't see him. Finding the little forest community without mishap, she told all who asked that she was Veira's niece. As Veira predicted, they seemed happy with that. Gladly they sold her milk and meat and gave her a jar of honey in welcome.

She felt like a fraud, accepting.

Walking back was a slower affair; the provision-filled basket was heavy. There was still no sign of Asher. As she reached the cottage gate she paused and stared down the road, hopeful but not expecting—

Someone was coming towards her. Several someones. And a donkey. And a cart.

She dropped the basket and ran.

"Matt! *Matt!*"

Startled, he jogged to meet her halfway. "Dathne, Dathne, what's amiss?"

She held him like a long-lost sweetheart, hugging his ribs to breaking. Cradled his hurt face gently in her hands and scolded him without mercy.

"I'm all right, I'm all right!" he soothed her, alarm and pleasure mingled. "Is Asher here? Is he all right?"

"Yes." It was all she dared to say.

Matt looked into her face and sighed. "You told him."

"Yes."

"And now he's angry."

She saw again that terrifying torrent of magic. "Very. I know...I know...you warned me."

A tentatively cleared throat turned her head. It was Gar, looking fragile. She hadn't even seen him. She stepped back from Matt and managed a half-hearted curtsey. "I'm sorry, sir. Your Highness."

He shook his head, faintly smiling. "Gar."

"And Darran," she added, nodding at the old gentleman as he leaned against the rickety donkey cart. "Forgive me. You both must be exhausted. Come inside. Veira will want to—"

The cottage's front door opened. "Greet her visitors," said Veira, and joined them. She kissed Matt's cheek and touched a finger to his bruised, rubbed throat. "Welcome back, Matthias. You're a little the worse for wear." Looking Gar up and down she added, "And you'll be our late king's son, then?"

Gar nodded. "At your service, Veira. Matt's told me all about you."

"Well," the old woman said, lips pursed, "not *all* about me, I'm guessing." She turned to Darran. "And who might you be?"

Darran managed a tottery bow. "His Highness's secretary, madam. Good morning."

"This is Darran," said Gar. "A dear, dear friend, and all that's left of my family."

As Darran choked back unseemly emotion, Veira again considered Gar with a narrow gaze. "And why have you come here? To hide? If so, you're doomed to disappointment. There'll be no hiding for anyone in the long dark days ahead."

Gar met her appraisal unflinching.

"I've come to help," he said. "And also...to make amends."

Veira reached out and laid her palm against his pale thin cheek. Stared deep into his eyes. "Good. For you've a lot you can do and much to be sorry for."

Matt cleared his throat. "Not that much. Gar helped me escape the guardhouse. Darran, too, and Captain Orrick."

"Orrick?" said Dathne, startled.

Matt's smile was tired. "It's a long story. I'll tell it properly later. After I've spoken with Asher."

"I don't think that's wise. He's angry with you too, Matt. He knows you've a part in the Circle, and all that's happened."

Veira closed a warning hand about her wrist. "You'll find him in the woods yonder, Matthias," she said, pointing behind the cottage.

"Working out a thing or two on his lonesome. Might be he could use some company round about now. He's had a tricky night."

Matt nodded. "I heard. I also heard he's—"

"Aggravated?" said Veira, eyebrows raised. "It's not surprising. A man has a right to be aggravated when he learns last of all he's born to save a kingdom. We'll see you inside directly, child. Dathne, tend to the donkey."

As Veira ushered the prince and his secretary into the cottage, Dathne rolled her eyes at Matt. "I think she and Asher spent half the night talking."

"Well, he has been hard done by, Dath," said Matt, determined to be reasonable. "He had his head on the axeman's block before we saved him. That'd give any man pause."

She winced. "I know."

He dropped an unexpected kiss on the crown of her head.

"Go coddle the donkey, Dath. I'll see you inside, by and by."

Unwilling to let him go, she twisted her fingers in his shirt front. "Be careful, Matt, please. He really is angry—and there's a power in him you can't imagine."

He kissed her again, this time on the cheek. "I'll be fine. Stop fratching."

And he walked away, without looking back.

Slumped at the foot of a twisted honey-pine, aching and hollow, thrumming still, hours later, with the echoing remnants of power, Asher heard footsteps approaching and scowled. If he had to hear one more story about dear young Rafel he was going to puke. Or worse, do someone a mischief.

"Piss off, ole woman," he said unkindly. "After listenin' to you jaw at me all last night my bloody ears have gone numb. I ain't interested in anythin' else you got to say."

"That's a fine greeting for a friend," said a hurtfully familiar voice. One that once would've been welcome. "If I am a friend. If you're willing to forgive me."

He scrambled to his feet. Felt his hands clench into fists, and didn't unclench them. "Matt."

The stable meister looked terrible. Hollow eyes, sunken and bruised-looking. Charred patches on his face and a livid purple bruise around his throat. He stood at a distance, a little worried. A little wary.

As he should be.

"I hear you're feeling...aggravated."

He smiled unpleasantly. "You might say that. You might say aggravated don't even come close."

"I don't blame you," said Matt. His battered face was sympathetic.

He sneered. "That's right generous of you."

Sighing, Matt slipped his hands in his pockets. "I wanted to tell you months ago, Asher. I wasn't permitted. If I say now I'm sorry, will it make a difference?"

"What's the point? Sorry won't undo what's done."

"You're right. It won't," Matt agreed. Hesitated, then took two steps closer. "But neither will sulking out here in the woods. You are what you are, Asher. I didn't make you a mage. Neither did Dathne, or Veira, or anyone else. It's what you were born. What Prophecy meant you to be. Needs you to be."

"I reckon," he said conversationally, "if one more person says the word 'prophecy' where I can hear it they're goin' to be bloody sorry."

Matt's lips quirked into something near to a smile. "I can understand that."

Bastard. Matt was talking the way he used to talk to fractious yearlings. Calm. Gentle. Soothing. Any minute now he'd reach out a hand to pat him on the bloody forehead...

Asher folded his arms across his chest. "So. Everything those bitches told me. Magic and history and dreams. What I was born for. You reckon it's true, do you?"

Matt frowned. "Don't call them bitches."

"*Is it true?*"

"Yes."

But then, he knew that already. He'd felt the rightness of Dathne's fantastic tale humming in his blood and bones, even as he'd rejected it. Veira had told the truth too, talking gently and softly throughout the long night. But it had taken him till now to admit it.

Sink the truth.

"I could walk away," he said, belligerent. Daring Matt to contradict him.

Matt nodded. "You could."

"I could walk away right now and no one could stop me. Not you, not Dathne. No one." He bared his teeth in a Conroyd smile. "I'm a man of power, Matt. I could burn you with a *look*."

"I know it," said Matt, unmoving. "I felt the change when that power woke within you. Like a thousand roaring furnaces devouring a million trees, it was. You could burn this whole kingdom with a look, if that's what you want. Is it?"

"*I want to be left alone!*"

Matt sighed. "To do what? Go where? There's nowhere to go, Asher. For better or worse, this kingdom's all we have. And unless you do what you were born to do we won't even have that."

Asher raised a hand above his head, despairing. "I'll tell you what I *don't* want, Matt! *I don't want this!*"

A thin stream of fire poured out of his fingers and flamed into the sky, singeing the honey-pine's fragrant foliage. Birds rattled upwards in a panic, screeching. Raggedly panting, not knowing how he knew it, knowing only that he could, he pulled the power back into himself. Slowly lowered his arm and stepped sideways to sag against the honey-pine's crooked trunk. His heart pounded and his blood burned. He spread out his fingers and looked at his hand. His shaking *magician's* hand.

I used to be a fisherman.

Matt was staring at him, wide-eyed but unflinching. Asher scowled. "So what happened to your throat?"

For the first time Matt looked uncomfortable. "In the chaos after your rescue, I was taken. I...tried to hang myself."

"*Hang* yourself?"

Matt shrugged. "Jarralt was coming to question me. I was afraid I'd talk. Tell him everything. Endanger you."

"*Jarralt.*" He felt his fingers clench to fists. "I want to kill that bastard, Matt, with my two bare hands. I want his bones for *toothpicks*!"

Matt's lips twisted in a wry smile. "Stand in line."

"How'd you escape him?"

"Pellen Orrick helped me."

Orrick. Another name with spikes in. "That bastard."

"He knows now he was hoodwinked," said Matt. "I owe him my life, Asher. Don't judge him too harshly. He didn't have all the facts."

Facts. "So he's on your side now?"

"Our side. Yes."

He pulled a face. "Who says there's an 'our side,' Matt? Who says I'm goin' to join you? You savin' my life don't mean I aim to join you!"

Matt dragged a dirty hand across his unshaven face, wincing as calluses scraped burned and blistered skin. "Look, Asher, I wish there was time for you to think on this," he said impatiently. "I wish there was time for a lot of things. But there isn't. You can't see it here, we're too deep into the Black Woods, but you can see it from the road leading in and elsewhere in the kingdom."

"See what?" he said roughly. "What are you on about now?"

Matt looked up, as though his gaze could pierce the forest's ceiling. "The Wall," he said. The faintest tremor was in his voice and his expression was bleak. "Asher, the Wall is falling. The Final Days are here. And without your help—without the Innocent Mage—not a man, woman or child in this kingdom stands a chance of surviving."

CHAPTER THIRTY-THREE

Asher stared at him, dumbfounded. "What am I s'posed to say to that? What d'you want me to *say*?"

Gently distressed, Matt spread his hands wide. "Honestly? That you'll do it."

"Do *what*?"

"Accept your destiny. Fulfil Prophecy. Save us."

"How? How am I s'posed to save you? Does your precious bloody prophecy tell me *how*?"

Now Matt looked uncomfortable. "No. Not in so many words."

No, of course it bloody didn't. That'd be too easy, wouldn't it? "Then what does it say?" he asked, struggling with temper. Old Veira had tried to tell him last night but he'd refused to listen. Now, though, he thought he'd better. "Or is the bloody thing so vague you can't even remember it?"

Matt let out a hard breath and his gaze lost focus. "'In the Final Days shall come the Innocent Mage, born to save the world from blood and death. He shall enter the House of the Usurper. He shall learn their ways. He shall earn their love. He shall lay down his life. And Jervale's Heir shall know him, and guide him, and enlighten him not.'"

"'Lay down his life'? You mean *die*?" He backed away, shaking his head. "Matt—"

"I know, I know, but think about it," Matt said quickly. "In a way you've done that already."

Sharp pain. A furious, bewildered resentment. "Wrong. Somebody else did that." Not that he'd ever asked for it. Not that he ever would.

"But you were about to die," Matt insisted. "It was intended. And you helped Gar knowing it could mean your life. If you look at it that way, Prophecy holds."

He turned away. "Prophecy's a crock of shit, Matt. It can mean whatever you want!"

"Then forget Prophecy and trust in your senses!" Matt urged him. "Barl's Wall is unravelling. I can feel it. You'd feel it too, if you'd let yourself. Don't be afraid of what's inside you, Asher. Embrace it. Extend your senses and feel the world around you. You'll see I'm right. You'll feel what I feel. Do it! Now, before it's too late! Before we're all beyond saving!"

In a different lifetime, he'd called this man "sir." Spurred by Matt's pleading he fell back on old habits. Did as he was told. Closed his eyes and opened his mind.

Darkness, seething. Malevolent power. Stuttering light. Thrashing feebly, Barl's Wall dying...black rotting patches like mould, like slime, smeared across its shimmering surface...

Gasping, he wrenched himself free of the vision—the dreaming— whatever had snared him. That part of himself he'd never dreamed existed, and didn't want to possess.

"You see?" said Matt. "Dathne was right. The Final Days are on us. And you're the Innocent Mage."

Dathne. More anger, more pain. "That's what she says," he muttered. "Take my advice, Matt. Don't go believin' everythin' you hear."

Matt's hard horseman's hand closed about his arm and roughly pulled him around. "Dathne was born with a destiny too," he said fiercely. "To carry Prophecy in her heart and mind. To deny all womanly desires, her dreams of hearth and home. To risk her life, every day, safeguarding Prophecy first and then you. And she did it willingly because she knew it was needful. Even though it hurt her. Even though she knew she was falling in love with you, and what would happen when she finally told you the truth."

Asher broke Matt's grip and retreated. He didn't want to hear this. Didn't want Matt to stand there *defending* the bitch. She'd lied to him, made a fool of him, coaxed out his heart then cut it to ribbons.

"Something evil has entered the kingdom, Asher." Matt's voice was quiet now, ferocity subdued, or spent. "Something you were born to fight. That only you can fight."

No, no, no, he didn't want to *hear* this. Not from Matt. He'd heard enough of it last night from Veira and it was all a load of ole cobblers. "I'm a fisherman, Matt! I ain't a warrior! This evil of yours, you want me to fight it with trout guts?"

"Of course not," said Matt, impatient. "You'll fight it with magic."

"You fight it with magic!" he retorted. "You and your damned Circle! You're the ones been practisin' for the last six hundred years. Me, I ain't got the first idea what I'm doin'!"

"If we could we would, believe me," said Matt. "But Olken magic isn't strong enough, and none of us can wield Doranen magic. Without your help we're doomed."

"Why does it have to be *me*?" he shouted. "Why can't you find someone else?"

"There *is* no one else! There's only *you*! That's why you're the Innocent Mage!"

"Well, I don't want to be the Innocent Mage! I never asked for it! I've a bloody good mind to just walk away right now! Walk away and never look back!"

Matt met his gaze unflinching. "Yes. You can walk away, Asher. I'm not strong enough to stop you. No one is. You can walk away and all of us can die. It's not fair, it's not just, but it is that simple. If you walk away, the rest of us will die."

Badgered, cornered, backed against the wall of his inconvenient conscience, Asher stared at his blunt, square hands. Beneath the surface of his skin the power simmered. If he closed his eyes he could almost see it: a river of fire, flowing through his veins. Ever since his outburst last night his awareness of it refused to fade. He took a deep, resentful breath, and eased it out slowly. He could still feel the sticky touch of darkness, fouling his mind.

"It's askin' a lot, Matt," he whispered. "One man against that kind of evil. One man all on his lonesome."

"You're not on your lonesome!" Matt said sharply. "You've got me. Dathne. Veira. The rest of the Circle."

He snorted. "Thought you said Olken magic was nigh to useless?"

"I said it couldn't defeat the evil we're facing. But there's still work for us to do. All of us have sworn to aid you, Asher. We'll give our lives if that's what's needed." Matt stepped close again, his face a riot of unhappy emotions. "I wish there was another way. I wish we could've told you sooner. I wish you hadn't suffered what you've suffered. When this is over, if you want to punish us for lying, or deceiving, walk away then. Never speak to us again and we'll understand. But I'm begging you, Asher: don't walk away now. Not when we need you. Not when you're all that stands between us and destruction."

Silence, as though the Black Woods was holding its breath. Deeper in, a fox barked. Once. Twice. A predator, prowling. Searching for its next kill, and all the little rabbits unsuspecting...

Matt was right, the bastard. It weren't fair and it weren't just. But it was simple. Maybe he was this Innocent Mage, and maybe he wasn't. That weren't really the point. At the end of the day he was his da's son, and Da had never once in his life turned away from someone in need. Wherever he was now—if he was anywhere—he'd expect his youngest to follow that example.

So he would. But that didn't mean he had to like it, or play nice.

"Wait!" Matt called after him, as he stomped away in the direction of Veira's cottage.

"Thought you said we were runnin' out of time?" he snarled over his shoulder. "You want to get this done or don't you? Make your mind up, Matt!"

"But there's something I haven't told you, Asher! Something you need to—"

"You told me enough! Now are you bloody comin', 'cause I ain't got all day!"

After ten minutes tramping he reached Veira's cloverpatched yard. Scattering chickens he marched across it to the cottage, shoved open the back door and went inside. The kitchen was empty, but he could hear voices murmuring from along the narrow corridor. He followed the sound to its source: Veira's tiny excuse for a sitting room. It was crowded with bodies. Veira. Dathne. Darran? And—

"Hello, Asher," said Gar.

He felt smothered. Disjointed. The room was suddenly hazy with red. A voice—his voice—said thickly, "Get him out of here."

Behind him Matt said, "No. Wait. You don't understand—"

"Get him out or it's *over*!"

As Veira, thunderous, opened her mouth to say something he didn't care to hear and she might well regret Gar stood, dropped the leather-bound book he was holding onto the faded carpet and tugged at his travel-stained weskit. Then he glanced at all their horrified faces.

"I'd like a moment in private with Asher."

"I got nowt to say to you."

Gar held his hot gaze unflinching. "All right. Then I'll talk and you can listen."

"Hear him out," Matt said, his voice low. "Please."

The river of fire burned hotter still. It was almost sweating out of him. "Why should I?"

"Because we need him—and he saved my life."

He wasn't expecting that. Startled, he looked at Matt, who nodded. Something must have changed in his face then, because without a word Dathne and Veira and Darran got out of their chairs and headed for the sitting-room door. He stood aside to let them pass. Refused to meet Dathne's anxious eyes or give Darran the satisfaction of acknowledgement.

Matt nodded. "Thank you."

Then he was gone too, the door was closing and it was just him and Gar. He felt sick, his vision still clouded with scarlet.

"You got two minutes," he said. "Then I walk out of here and you don't exist any more."

Gar's pale lips pressed tight, then he sighed. "You hate me. I understand that. But don't let hatred blind you to the truth. Matt's right. You need me, Asher. You won't defeat Conroyd without my help."

"Conroyd?"

"Well..." Gar bent to retrieve the dropped leather-bound book and frowned at its mottled cover. "The thing that used to be Conroyd."

He didn't want to ask...he didn't want to ask... "What are you bloody on about?" he asked roughly. "What's Jarralt got to do with this?"

Gar held up the book. "This is Barl's diary. Durm found it but didn't tell anyone. He used an incantation in it to breach the Wall. Morg was waiting on the other side. He—"

"Morg? The magician your ancestors ran away from six hundred years ago?" He laughed. "You're crazy."

"I know it sounds fantastic," said Gar. "Impossible. But it's true. He came through the breach in the Wall Durm foolishly opened and masquerades now as Conroyd Jarralt, Lur's king and Weather Worker. I think he's the evil your prophecy spoke of."

"It ain't *my* bloody prophecy!"

"Well, whoever it belongs to it's about to be fulfilled. The Wall is falling, Asher. Matt feels it, and I'll bet you feel it too."

The last thing he intended to discuss with Gar was feelings. "You're mad. How can Morg be Conroyd Jarralt? Don't you reckon someone would've *noticed*?"

"He's lived six hundred years, Asher! He's skilled beyond imagining! And it is him. Conroyd's no longer himself, I've seen...changes. And Durm tried to warn me before he died. I didn't understand him then but I do now. I think Morg used him to begin with. I think he's why my family died. How I got my magic, and why it failed. Morg is behind it all."

Asher rubbed a hand across his tired face, his stinging eyes. "And you want me to confront him, eh? The most talented, vicious magician your people ever bred. One strong enough to survive for six centuries. Strong enough to bring down Barl's Wall, all by himself. Me. An Olken fisherman who can make it rain, at a pinch, and then has to sit around snivellin' for two hours after." He turned for the door. "You're out of your sinkin' mind."

"No! Wait! I haven't finished!" said Gar, and leapt forward to clutch at his arm.

Without thought, without planning, he let the barely leashed power boil out of him. Let it rip Gar's fingers from his sleeve and smash him across the room, knocking an armchair sideways and hurling him into the wall.

Coughing, choking and running with blood, Gar staggered to his feet. "Asher...please..."

"Don't you touch me!" he ordered, shaking with rage. "Don't *ever* touch me!"

The sitting-room door flew open and Veira tumbled in.

"What are you doing? What's going on here?" she demanded.

"It's nothing!" Gar answered, wheezing. "I'm all right. A misunderstanding. Please, Veira. Leave us to talk."

"There's nowt left to say, Gar. You've had your two minutes," he spat. "And now you don't exist."

Veira stood in the doorway, blocking his exit. "What nonsense is this? Two minutes? Pah! You'll stay here and listen for as long as need be! Until you've heard all Gar has to say!"

"I ain't interested in what he's got to say! Listenin' to him landed me in this mess to start with!"

She slapped his face. "Prophecy landed you in this mess, child, six centuries before you were born! Were you listening last night or did I talk myself hoarse for nothing? Did my Rafel die for nothing? Prince Gar is a part of this business! He's of the Usurper's House! And you will hear him, do I make myself clear?"

Ears ringing, cheek burning, he stared at the angry old woman. "You might want to think twice, hittin' me, since I'm the only one as can save your wrinkly hide."

"Child, child, I'll hit you as many times as it takes to drive sense into your fool stubborn head! Don't you know we're out of time?"

Sticky with blood, his legs unsteady, Gar stepped forward. "What do you mean, Veira? What's happened now?"

She didn't answer. Just turned on her heel and stamped along the corridor towards the kitchen end of the cottage.

"Asher," said Gar, his hands upturned. "We should see what she's talking about. It sounded important."

Itching to hit Gar again, he turned on his heel and stalked after Veira. Gar's footsteps followed him, sounding uneven, as though he were hurt.

Good. Let him be hurt. He deserved a few bruises and a whole lot more.

The kitchen's back door stood open. The others were outside already, scattered about the yard. Seeking solitude, he moved over to the henhouse. Gar joined Darran by the pigpen and rested a hand on the ole crow's shoulder. Seeing the blood on him, Darran made to protest. Gar smiled and shook his head. Not dismissive but reassuring. Watching them, Asher scowled. Something had changed there. Some balance had shifted. He looked away. Good luck to 'em, the miserable bastards. They bloody deserved each other. Veira, her tatty cardigan pulled close to her body, had joined Matt and Dathne a stone's throw from the stable.

All of them, silent, stared at the sky.

The morning's blue brightness had almost disappeared. Now the air above the Black Woods was bellicose with clouds. They seemed too close to the ground, low enough nearly for a tall man to touch. Grubby white and dirty grey, they whirled and streamed and jostled like live things. With a kind of mean-spirited deliberation.

"It looks like Westwailing," Gar said, hushed. "Weather run amok. Power without form or purpose."

An ominous rumble trembled the air. Birds exploded from the tree-tops, flapping away. The horses crammed in the stable whinnied in sudden loud fear. There was a crash as hooves kicked timber. The donkey in its little enclosure off to the side echoed their distress with a nerve-shattering bray.

Asher rubbed the prickling skin inside his shirt sleeves. "The Weather Magic's unravelling. The threads binding it to the earth, the mountains, are comin' undone."

Dathne turned. "You can feel that?"

He kept his gaze pinned to the curdling clouds. The unwanted knowledge inside him, transferred from the Weather Orb to that secret place in his mind, was chiming loud alarms. Setting his teeth on edge. It was like standing on the headlands watching a bad storm roll in over Dragon-teeth Reef: the air alive with lightning, with wildness. Contemptuous of kings and their magics. Determined to lash without mercy.

It was just like that...only a thousand times worse.

He looked at Matt. "This is just the beginning, I reckon."

Another rumble of thunder, louder this time. This time the ground beneath their feet grumbled a reply. Matt clapped his hands to his head, groaning. Asher closed his eyes. Letting his woken instincts guide him he stretched his mysterious senses into the air. What he found there made him gag. It was worse now than it had been in the woods. The world around him smelled rotten. Rank and putrid, like a carcass blown with maggots.

He opened his eyes. Spat sour saliva onto the grass. "I can stop this, maybe. I got the Weather Magic in me. I could fight it, stitch up the worst holes, buy us some time—"

"No!" said Gar, alarmed. "Don't you understand? Morg will sense it. He'll know you're alive. The only way to stop this is to stop him. Kill him. And quickly, before it's too late. Before the land tears itself to pieces. The Westwailing storm will be nothing, *nothing*, compared with what's coming."

"Aye, well, you'd know," Asher drawled. "Bein' a cripple and all."

"How dare you!" shouted Darran, pushing forward. "Ungrateful peasant! After everything he risked coming here to you! Endangering his life! Walking for miles! Just to bring that wretched diary where it might do the most good!"

"Good? What's it good for, Darran? Arse-wipin'? Or maybe I should throw it at Jarralt. Could be it'll knock him arse over eyeballs and dash out his brains. Maybe that's what it's good for!"

Lifting a placating hand at Darran, Gar answered. "It's good for more than that, Asher. You didn't let me finish, inside. Barl's diary is full of spells. Incantations. Weapons of war that can bring Morg down. And I can teach them to you."

Asher laughed. "*You* can?"

"All right then," said Gar, flushing. "Perhaps 'teach' is the wrong word. I can translate them. Explain them. Show you in theory how they're performed. I was a magician, Asher, if only briefly. I've not forgotten everything yet. If your friends here are right about you, that might work. You're strong enough to use the Weather Magics, after all. You might be strong enough for this."

"He is," said Veira bleakly. "He has to be. Else Prophecy's misled us and all that's left is death."

"Prophecy hasn't misled us!" said Dathne, angry. "Don't you dare lose faith, Veira. You're the Circle Guardian. You don't have the right to lose faith." She turned to Gar. "These war spells. How long will it take you to translate them? How fast can they be learned?"

Gar shrugged. "Learning them's up to Asher. As for the translations, I'll need at least a day. The language they're written in is archaic and complicated. I think Barl used some kind of verbal trickery, in case the wrong person chanced to read them."

"What does that mean?" said Veira. "Is there danger?"

"Not to me," said Gar, pulling a face. "I no longer have the means to activate the incantations. But if I mistranslate them and Asher tries to use them . . . well. It might get very . . . messy."

He snorted. "Wouldn't be the first time you tried to kill me."

Veira turned on him. "Stop that! Is there time for your petty bickering when we stand beneath a sky like *that*?" She jabbed a pointed finger upwards, and they tilted their heads to look.

The thickening clouds had darkened like a bruise, sickly green and purple. Some were turned scarlet, like blood blisters. As they stared, silenced, scattered drops of rain plummeted groundwards, stinking of sulphur. Stinging where they struck exposed flesh.

"Time to get organised," said Veira, and made shooing motions towards the cottage. "Matt, get that donkey undercover then see to making those horses and the wagon as roadworthy and weatherproof as possible. I should have enough canvas and timber tucked away in the shed there for the makings of a wagon cover. Dathne, set to work in the kitchen preparing provisions. We'll be heading back to the City soon."

"The City?" he said. "Why go back to the City?"

"Because that's where Morg is," Veira answered. "That's where you must confront him." She turned away. "Darran, you help Dathne. Gar, get to work on those translations. Asher—"

He scowled at the old woman, disliking her intensely. "What?"

"You come with me, child. We've Circle business to see to."

Another roll of thunder. A vivid crack of lightning. The last ragged peepholes of blue sky disappeared entirely.

"Hurry!" shouted Veira as the rain fell down in earnest, and they scattered to do her bidding.

Aware of Asher's furious resentment, Veira ushered him into her bedroom and calmly closed the door. Smiled at him gravely and patted his arm. "Have a seat, child."

As he threw himself into the furthest armchair she rolled back the carpet, revealing her Circle Stone hidey-hole. Glancing up she caught a glimmer of interest in his eyes, quickly stifled. With a grunt she lifted the hidey-hole's lid and set it aside. In the dim light the Circle Stones glistened. Beyond the bedroom window the rain lashed down hard.

"Here is the Circle," she said, and drifted her fingers across the stones. They felt warm. Comforting. "Each crystal a person, sworn to wait and serve. Dedicated to you, Asher. Dedicated to your fight. Your destiny. Each one would die for you, as Rafel died, if it meant the defeat of evil. No—don't reject them," she added as he shifted sharply in his chair. "They chose this, Asher. No one forced the burden upon them. They are special, as you are special. Don't hurt them by denying their gift. There is no greater service than service performed on behalf of the Innocent Mage."

"Even though I never asked 'em for it?"

"You didn't have to. Prophecy asked and they answered. That should be enough to satisfy you."

He scowled at her. "And if it ain't?"

"But it is," she said softly. "Why else do you think you're so angry?" She patted the floorboards beside her. "Come sit with me. I think it's time you met them, child. They've a part to play in the battle upcoming and it's best not to fight beside strangers."

Grudgingly, he joined her. "They're all goin' to the City too?"

She shook her head. "That's not possible. We're too far-flung."

"Then how are they s'posed to help me?"

"By lending you their strength when you need it." She touched his knee. "Don't worry. It'll all be clear soon enough."

She reached into the hidey-hole and withdrew the one crystal she'd never yet used. Unwrapped its soft silk covering and held it carefully in one hand. It was the most beautiful crystal in the kingdom, one of a kind, forged from shards of all the other Circle Stones by Jervale himself. She closed her eyes and sank into a light trance, acutely aware of Asher beside her and the multifaceted crystal nestled warm and waiting in her palm. With her other hand she touched each Circle Stone, calling to its owner, summoning them to the link. Not one by one, but all together. Showing each to the other for the very first time in the Circle's history. Three stones she left untouched: Rafel's Dathne's and Matt's. Rafel had already done his part—while Dathne and Matt would lend strength in different ways.

At last the remaining Circle members were united. Through the shimmering, shadowed link she saw their beloved faces. Felt their curiosity and fear. Their excitement and their trepidation. Let it flow through her like a river, like a soft breeze, like a sigh.

Veira... Veira... Veira...

"My dear friends," she greeted them. "Welcome. I've called you now, in this time and to this place, to share with you completely what many already suspect or know. The Final Days are upon us. The Innocent Mage is revealed. The evil foretold has risen...and we are all that stands between it and the end. Now comes the time for the Circle to join hand in hand and deny evil its dominion. Are you with me?"

Thundering through the link, all their separate voices singing as one. *We're with you, Veira. We're with you. Tell us what to do.*

Blindly she reached out and took Asher's hand. Felt his brief resistance, then felt him surrender and submit. Heard him gasp as he was admitted to the shadow world of Circle communication.

"Behold, friends, our Innocent Mage. Young, and fiery, and full of ire. The evil we battle has touched him already. Bravely he carries the scars. Bid him welcome, and share with him your hearts."

Welcome, Asher. Welcome, our Innocent Mage. Know we stand with you. Beside you. Behind you. No matter what may be.

She felt Asher's hand tremble in hers as the Circle's love poured through him. Heard his ragged breathing. "Speak, Asher," she whispered. "The Circle will hear you."

"I don't—I can't—what do I say?" he muttered.

"Whatever comes to mind."

"I don't know why I'm chosen," he said at last, hesitant. "Can't believe there ain't nobody better than me. But since I am, since it don't seem there's anyone else, I'll fight this evil best as I can. Can't promise to win. Just that I'll fight."

Bless you, Asher. And we'll fight with you, never fear.

Veira squeezed his fingers. "And so we will. Dear friends, this Circle forged will stay unbroken. Go about your daily lives until I call you. And when that call comes stop what you're doing wherever you are and pour all your powers, all your strength, into this binding link. Pour it into Asher, that he might in the end prevail."

Call us, Veira, and we will come.

Withdrawing from them was a wrenching pain that sprang tears to her eyes. Reverently she laid the crystal on the floor then looked at Asher, stunned and silent by her side.

"You see?" she said softly.

He nodded, his anger softened, his face pliable with understanding. "Aye. At least...I reckon I'm startin' to."

"Then will you not find a way to make peace with Gar? To put aside the hardships he's caused you, knowing it was all in the service of Prophecy?"

He pulled his hand from hers. "That's got nowt to do with this. What's between me and Gar is between me and Gar. You keep yourself clear of it, Veira. Clear of me and Dathne too. Since I got no choice I'll be your Innocent Mage. I'll fight your battles for you. But that don't mean you got leave to dance in and out of my life on a whim. Understood?"

She sighed. "Understood, child."

Tucked away in the corner of her hidey-hole was a felt-wrapped bundle. She pulled it clear and laid it on the floorboards.

"What happens now?" said Asher. Polite enough, but with hidden flint sharp in his voice.

She looked up, and deep into his eyes. "Do you trust me, Asher?"

He shrugged. "I'm still here, ain't I?"

She unwrapped the bundle, revealing a hammer and a knife. The hammer she lifted and, before she could hesitate or waste time with regrets, struck it sharply to the forged-crystal Jervale had made.

Asher cried out in protest as it shattered into myriad pieces, glittering with all its colours.

"Don't fret," she told him. "The Circle's unbroken. This is just the next step."

Swiftly she sifted through the shards, searching for the perfect piece. Finding it, she put it to one side then again turned to Asher.

"Bare your breast to me, child," she commanded. "On the left. Above your heart."

He stared at her. "What?"

"You said you trusted me, Asher. I swear I'll do you no harm." Then she pulled a small face. "Well. No great harm, and not lasting either."

He wanted to refuse her, she could see it in his eyes. But some lingering memory of the Circle persuaded him. Scowling, he pulled open his shirt. Scowled harder when she lifted the knife. Its sharp blade glinted wicked in the lamplight.

He sucked in a deep breath. "Veira—Veira—"

She struck without mercy, slicing open the thick muscle of his chest directly above his heart. Sliced lengthways then dropped the knife and thrust in her finger, tearing apart the muscle's long fibres, creating a hole. Blood made her fingers slippery. His harsh breath was hot in her face. She picked up the crystal shard and pressed it into the wound, forcing it deep inside the tissue. He was gasping now, grunting with the pain. With indignation, and shock.

She leaned towards him. Put her forehead hard to his, clasped the nape of his neck with her left hand and pressed her bloodied fingers to his chest.

"Breathe with me...breathe with me..." she whispered. "Come, child, it's nearly over. And what is pain but a mere sensation?"

Hidden words rose tumultuous to her tongue. Words she'd been given long years ago but thought never to be called on to speak. His wounded flesh heated. Moulded. Grew cool. She let her hands fall free of him. Sat up straight and smiled into his face.

"Done, then. And well done too. Good boy."

"You bloody mad crazy ole woman!" he shouted, scrambling to his feet. "What d'you think you're doin'? Carvin' me like a Barl's Day roast? What kind of craziness is this?"

Bone weary now, and emptied, she looked at the flesh of his chest. No wound there any more. Not even a scar. Just a faint irregularity, where the crystal shard was hidden. "You're one with the Circle now, child," she told him. "They're a part of you, unremovable. When the time comes and the power is called for you'll have it at your fingertips. In your blood and bones."

Those fingertips were scrabbling at his chest. "What? What? What are you talkin' about?"

"Quiet your mind," she advised him. "Sink deep inside yourself. Can you feel them, Asher? All our good friends of the Circle? Can you hear their heartbeats, waiting?"

Startled, he stared at her. Closed his eyes, then jumped as though stuck with a pin. "Sink me bloody sideways!"

She chuckled. "What I told you last night of our magic, Asher, is only the beginning. There's more to learn yet and much you could teach me, if we had time. There's magic in you I doubt I'll ever understand. But that's how Prophecy wanted it, and who am I to question Prophecy? Have a look in my top dresser drawer, will you? There should be a blue felt drawstring bag in there."

Bemused, bewildered, he found the bag she wanted and tossed it to her. She gathered up the other broken pieces of the hammered crystal and slipped them safe inside.

"Now what?" he said, still rubbing at that place on his chest, though she knew he had no more pain there.

"Now you go clean yourself up. And don't mention this to the others. I'll tell them myself when the time's right."

He snorted. "There's only Matt I'm talkin' to."

"Then don't tell him," she snapped, impatient. "Go and see if he needs help with the horses. Or the wagon. Make yourself useful, at any rate. When those war spells are ready for you to practise, everything else must be done." She looked to the bedroom window, out at the pouring rain. "There's precious little time left."

He nodded. Went to the door, then stopped. Turned. All of a sudden he looked young, and uncertain. "Veira. Can I do this?"

She poured all her hope and believing into a smile. "Yes, child. You can."

He smiled in return, swift and wry. "Crazy ole woman," he muttered, then left her alone.

Heart aching, she creaked to her feet, tidied up her chamber then went to the kitchen to help.

CHAPTER THIRTY-FOUR

In the City unsummoned water poured from the sky, alarming its insect inhabitants. Morg lounged on his townhouse balcony and watched the stinking rain fall, listened to the jabbering insect voices in the street below and savoured the swelling sense of alarm.

In the distance, Barl's dying Wall shuddered.

Blubbery Willer came panting to see him. "Your Majesty—Your Majesty—Barlsman Holze craves an urgent audience! Shall I send him away too?"

Morg smiled. He'd been wondering how much longer he'd have to wait before the Barl-sot came bleating. "No. Show him into the drawing room, Willer."

He lingered a few moments longer, just to appreciate his handiwork, then sauntered downstairs to join Barl's little champion. On his entrance the cleric leapt to his feet. He was looking harried, distressed, no flowers in his Barlsbraid. There was a stain on the front of his workday robes.

"Conroyd!" he said, his reedy voice unsteady. "I confess all my hopes were pinned upon not finding you here. Upon the frail hope that these inclement conditions were the result of your Weather Working inexperience and the lack of a Master Magician. But as you are here, and not at work in the Weather Chamber..." His voice trailed off and his hands clutched each other convulsively. "Conroyd...you must have seen the Wall. Do you have an explanation?"

It was too soon yet to reveal his true face, so he arranged his expression into a mask of sorrow and disciplined alarm. "Efrim, dear Efrim, indeed you've read my mind. I was about to send for you, as it happens. I need your help."

"Anything! Anything!" said fool Holze fervently. "Just tell me what I can do! Tell me what's gone wrong!"

He took a turn about the room, pretending to an agitation he was very far from feeling. "I've not said this to another soul, Efrim, and I must ask you to keep it secret. If word gets out I fear for the people's safety. Barl's Wall is damaged. Not beyond my power to heal, of course," he added as the cleric stifled a shocked moan and sank into the nearest chair. "But certainly it will take some time. Blessed Barl's Weather Magics have shown me how to effect a remedy and I'm doing all I can. In time, I will succeed. But there will be more rain, and other unpleasantness, before I have completely undone the damage."

"Asher," said Holze, uncommonly vicious. "This is the doing of that renegade Olken."

Morg bowed his head in feigned sorrow. "Yes. I fear so."

"Have you spoken to that idiot Gar?"

"No," he said after a moment. "Why would I? Gar Torvig is a private citizen now. Irrelevant and unnecessary."

"Yes, but he was there when Asher tinkered with the weather," Holze said eagerly. Filled with a sudden, false hope. "Perhaps he can tell us exactly what the criminal did, in detail. Perhaps that will help you put things right!"

An ingenious thought, if pointless. But interrogating the cripple would give Holze something to do. Keep him out of the way. He nodded. "Bless you, Efrim. I should've thought of this myself."

"No, no, Conroyd. You are pushed to your limit!"

Morg nearly laughed aloud at that. "I'm afraid, Efrim, all the wonderful plans we hatched the other night will have to wait a little longer. Unless I rescue us from Asher's perfidious treachery we'll have no glorious future."

"Of course, of course!" agreed Holze, standing. "Nothing is more important than the repairing of Barl's Wall. That is your sacred duty, Conroyd!"

He nodded. "Precisely. Now, as it happens, you can serve me in two other matters. Firstly, keep the City's population occupied with prayer. You need not be specific, a supportive exhortation on my behalf should be sufficient. I thought it might help allay the people's worries and let them feel they can contribute to the wellbeing of our beloved kingdom. It will also stop your subordinate clerics from speculating unwisely."

Holze nodded. "Of course. What else?"

"Until this crisis passes I think it would be wise to suspend all council activity, Privy and General."

"Are you certain?" said Holze, frowning. "There is still the business of the kingdom to conduct."

"But will it be profitably conducted while the weather remains... unbalanced?" Morg shook his head, as though it mattered. "I think we both know the answer to that. The guilds will agitate and our Doranen brethren will press for some arcane involvement. As it is, Efrim, I turn away unsubtle requests for an audience every hour."

Unhappily, the dodderer nodded. "Yes. Yes. I fear this latest transition of power has upset a great many people."

Upset? Morg turned away, hiding a gleeful smile. The insects had yet to learn the meaning of the word... "I'd take it as a great personal favour, Efrim, if you could announce my decision in an emergency council session. I'll have Willer notify the councillors. Make sure you exhort them to pray hard for our kingdom's delivery."

Holze bowed. "Of course, Your Majesty. Be assured I will see to it."

Concealing his distaste, Morg embraced the gullible cleric. "I trust you implicitly, Efrim. Go now and minister to our kingdom. Use Willer as you would a servant of your own."

"You won't need him?"

Need *Willer*? "It's a sacrifice I'm ready to make in the service of beloved Lur," he said gravely. "Barl's blessings go with you, dear friend."

Alone again, gloriously alone, Morg stretched out on the study sofa, closed his eyes and listened to the music of thunder as it rattled the vulnerable windowpanes.

Beyond Veira's curtained sitting room the wind howled mercilessly, without surcease. Unrelenting rain hammered the ground outside and hail the size of hens' eggs thudded against the cottage's thatched roofing. Gar glanced up, frowning. He'd heard it smash a window earlier but hadn't gone to look. Someone else would deal with that. He had to stay focused on his own task: the accurate translation of Barl's hoarded, horrible spells. Some half-dozen he'd completed already, and handed over to Veira so Asher might learn their dangerous intricacies. Perhaps a dozen more remained for him to decipher.

They made his head hurt.

The door opened and Dathne came in. "Soup," she said, balancing a tray. "And bread. You've been cooped up here for hours. You should eat something."

Behind her kind concern, deep sorrow. Her eyes were hollow, her lips deeply bracketed with lines of pain. He pushed aside his papers and took the tray from her. Steam wafted from the soup bowl, fragrant—but still unappetising. She went to the window, tugged apart the faded curtains and stared at the pitiless downpour.

He put down the tray, picked up the spoon and made himself swallow a little broth. Chicken. As a child it had been his favourite. He said, watching her, "I take it that where Asher's concerned, you've ceased to exist too?"

She flinched, just a little. "I'd rather not talk about it."

"Fine," he said, and swallowed more soup. Chewed on the bread, which was stale. "What's everyone else doing?"

"Matt's cluttered the kitchen with harness, and he and Darran are oiling it."

He choked. "Darran's oiling harness?"

"He's determined to be useful."

Dear old man. "And Veira?"

Dathne hesitated a moment. "She's outside in the shed with Asher. Helping him learn your war spells."

His spoon dropped into the bowl. "Veira can do war spells?"

"No," said Dathne, turning away from the window. "But since Asher refused to let you help him practise she's just...keeping an eye on him. You know. In case..."

In case he accidentally killed himself. "I see."

"But he's doing fine. Veira says you'd think he'd been summoning war-beasts since before he could walk."

"Did you know that about him?"

"I knew nothing about him, beyond he is the Innocent Mage." She rubbed her hands up and down her arms. "It's cold."

"It is," he agreed. "The trip back to Dorana will be miserable, I think." In more ways than the merely physical.

She nodded at Barl's diary, shoved to one side on the little work table he'd been using. "Can an arrogant dead woman's scribblings really save us?"

"I don't know," he said, stifling a prickle of anger that Barl should be described so. Then he shrugged, his fingers caressing the diary's mottled cover. "I hope so. Or at least, help Asher to save us. If he can. If he really is what you think."

"Of course he is," she said sharply. "Or do you doubt me now? And Veira? And everything else you've seen and heard?"

He smiled at her, feeling sour. "Dathne, with everything that's happened these past weeks, if you told me my name was Gar I'd feel a moment's doubt."

Her face softened. "Yes. I suppose you would. So many things turned topsy-turvy."

So many things. "I'm sorry. I didn't mean to sound critical. If we do survive the coming days—if Lur survives them—we'll have you and your Circle to thank for it."

"And Asher." She bit her lip, turning back to the window and the bleak view beyond it. "Will it never stop raining now, I wonder?"

"What did your visions show you?"

She shivered. "Horrors I'd rather forget."

"Yet they showed you Asher, too. Can we have one without the other?"

"Who knows?" She pulled the curtains closed again, hard, then hugged herself tight. "Not me."

"It appears between the two of us we don't know much at all," he said, and tried to make a joke of it.

Unamused she stared at him, her eyes large and dark. "How could *you* not know, you Doranen?" she said, face and voice accusing. "You're the grand magicians, the ones with all the power. Your father was the *king*, Gar, the *Weather Worker*. You and your family had Morg in your midst, breaking bread with you, breathing the same air! How many hours did you spend closeted with him, studying your precious magics? How is it none of you suspected who and what he was? How could you not *know*?"

"Do you think I've not asked myself that question?" he retorted. "Do you think an hour goes by that I don't look back on every hour, every minute we spent in Morg's presence and wonder how it was we were so blind? You can't blame us for our failures more than I do, Dathne, believe me! All I can say in our defence is that Morg may once have been Morgan, a flesh and blood man, but whatever he is now it's something beyond Doranen comprehension. Not even your Prophecy could name him, could it? Nor all your vaunted visions."

"At least we *had* our visions!" she retorted. "Six hundred years ago Jervale knew you and yours were a mistake, but your precious Barl shouted him down! How better might we be prepared for this day if—"

His fist thumped the tabletop. "You can't know that! Dathne, finger-pointing is pointless. What's done is done. My people came, yours accepted us, and so your fates were bound to ours. It's history and unchangeable. We have to focus on the future...and hope against hope for a miracle."

"We have a miracle," she said fiercely. "His name is Asher."

"I hope you're right," he said, suddenly tired. "I hope he's everything your Prophecy claims him to be. For if he's not, this kingdom's doomed and every soul within it damned."

"I'm right," she said, then nodded at the tray with its burden of half-drunk soup and partly chewed bread. "Are you finished with that?"

He nodded. "Yes. Thank you. I'm sorry I couldn't do it more justice." As she moved to take it away, he held up a hand, pausing her, and sifted swiftly through his haphazard pile of papers. "Here," he said, and slid three sheets under the bread plate for safekeeping. "More spells for our miracle to practise."

She looked at them as though they might bite. "When will you have finished all of them?"

"By tonight sometime, I think. I hope."

"I hope so too," she said, and glanced at the curtained window as a fresh wave of hail rattled the glass. "Matt says the Weather Magic's unravelling faster by the hour. The Wall won't stand much longer now."

He pulled a face. "Then I'd best get back to work. Thank you for the soup."

"You're welcome," she said, and left him to his papers, and Barl's diary.

Cowering behind a pile of old boxes in her weatherbeaten shed, Veira raised her voice above the wereslag's howling screech and shouted, "Kill it! *Kill it!*"

Panting, Asher slashed a sigil through the air and uttered the words of banishment. The wereslag's writhing orange tentacles burst into heatless flame; its eight clawed arms withered; it shrivelled and died, leaving only a ring of smoking dirt on the shed floor where its acid slime had dripped and boiled.

"Sink me bloody sideways," he muttered, and sagged against a handy post. "How many more, eh?"

Sidling out from safety, Veira shuffled through the sheaf of papers in her hand. "That's the last of the spells Matt brought out before."

"Then how many are left to come?"

"You'll have to ask Gar," she said tartly, eyebrows lowered in a challenge.

He curled his lip and looked out of the shed at the drowned garden. At the fringe of the Black Woods, and the trees flogging themselves to death against the leaden sky. He was exhausted. Had lost count of the monstrosities he'd called forth with just a few words and the power of his mind.

It was a mighty uncomfortable feeling, knowing that things like wereslags and trolls and horslirs and gruesomes lurked just beneath his skin. If Da could see him now...

Unsettled, still glooming at the lashing forest, his fingers crept up to his chest and rubbed at the hard little lump of crystal nestled in his flesh. Every time he summoned his power—a feat that came more and more easily, something else he didn't much care for—the crystal tickled. Buzzed, as though woken from shallow sleep.

He'd asked and he'd asked, but Veira wouldn't tell him any more about its purpose. Just: "You'll know when the time comes. Stop fratching me, child."

She said now, close enough to swat his shoulder, "Leave it be! We've more spells yet to conquer and it'll be too dark soon to go on."

He groaned. "Let a body rest a moment, Veira. I been at this for bloody hours."

"And hours are all we have left before we must head back to the City. I—"

"Sorry," said Matt, slopping into the shed from outside. He was festooned with oil-dark horse harness, head and shoulders soaked with the ceaseless rain. "Didn't mean to interrupt."

"You ain't," he said, frowning. All Matt's colour was bled from his face, leaving it drawn and pallid. "You all right?"

Matt let the harness slide free onto a cluttered bench. "The unbalance of magic is getting worse. I'm feeling it more with every hour that passes."

Asher nodded. "Aye." He could feel it too, like sharp fingernails digging into his brain. Scraping over his skin. "You got to block it out, Matt, else it'll tear you apart."

Matt pulled a face. "I'm trying. But I'm not you." He looked at Veira. "Can you spare a moment to help me strengthen this harness?

I've grown more used to needles and waxed thread than bindings—and I never was much good at them to begin with."

"Course she will," Asher said cheerfully. "She ain't got nowt better to do just now, since I'm for a breather." And he made his escape before Veira could shout, or slap him again.

He ran over the squelching grass to the cottage, shoved open the kitchen door and escaped inside, dripping.

The kitchen was full of more cleaned harness, cooking smells and Darran. Who took one look at his face, rummaged in a cupboard, pulled from it an anonymous bottle of something that looked promising, at least, and poured him half a glassful.

He swallowed it in one gulp then staggered around for a while coughing and wheezing and banging his chest.

"You're welcome," said Darran. Flour daubed his weskit, his face, his hair. He was in the middle of rolling pastry. It looked suspiciously lumpy.

Asher held out his emptied glass and waited. Pinch-faced, Darran poured him a stingy second splash, ostentatiously recorked the bottle and returned it to the cupboard.

He wasn't a slow learner. Sipping this time, not gulping, he emptied the glass again and put it in the sink. Glanced at Darran, sighed, rinsed it and set it upside down to dry.

Darran returned to his pastry. "Gar never meant to hurt you."

Another sigh. He had no strength for this. "It's been said before and nowt's changed. Let it be, ole man."

Bang went the rolling pin onto the table. "He saved your life!"

"You mean Matt's."

"And yours. Don't you even care how? Or is hating him more important than knowing the truth?"

Asher looked at him. The ole crow's eyes were blazing with unfair hope and accusation. He didn't want to see that, so he slouched over to the window. Looked at the rain instead of this pleading old man who'd been nothing but a trial and tribulation to him from the first day they'd met.

"Aye," he said, surly. "Hate's a lot more important."

Darran seized him. Pushed up his jacket and shirt sleeve to reveal the ragged scar from his madcap Restharven childhood with Jed. "The other man's arm was scarless. But Gar said it was your body burned in the glimfire. He knew it wasn't and he lied, though he could've died for it then and there. He said it so they'd believe you were dead. That *must* be worth a little forgiveness, surely?"

"No," said Asher baldly. "It ain't."

"Why not?" demanded Darran, pleading. "Have you never done anything you've not been sorry for after? That you did because you had to, even though it led to someone else's suffering?"

Jed. He skewered the ole crow with a scathing glare. "I never went back on a promise. And if Gar'd done the same there'd have been no body to identify at all, now would there? Someone still died, Darran!"

Darran flinched as though he'd been struck. "I know. The prince is most—"

"Good. Then maybe you can ask Rafel to forgive Gar," he said bitterly. "Just don't ask me again, Darran. You'll only be wastin' your time and mine."

Darran picked up his rolling pin and attacked the pastry. "Yes," he said, clipped and cold. "Yes, I quite see that I would."

Furious he'd been goaded into saying more than he'd intended, Asher headed for the inside kitchen door, thinking to change his wet clothes. He hauled it open—

—and Gar was on the other side.

"What?" he said roughly. "What d'you want?"

From the stricken look on his face Gar had been eavesdropping. Mute, he held out his hand. In it was another sheaf of papers covered in his quick writing. "More spells," he said, subdued.

"Fine," Asher said, and snatched them. He'd worry about dry clothes later. Turning on his heel he stalked out of the kitchen. Into the rain. Back to the business of killing with magic.

Shaken, Gar ignored the pleading look on Darran's pale face and returned to the sitting room and Barl's diary. He had only a few more pages left to examine. Relief warred with a sharp, unexpected sorrow at the thought. With the diary wholly translated he'd be leaving Barl behind. Saying goodbye. It hurt, to think of that.

Barl...Barl...how glorious she was. A woman unmatched in the history of their people. Brave...dedicated...consumed with integrity. He could read her handwriting now as easily as his own. She spoke to him intimately, mind to mind, a whispering of desperate confidences. Betraying to him, and only him, the secret torments of her heart. Her doubts. Her fears. Her passionate longings. He understood her as no one ever had; certainly not her faithless lover Morgan.

Pulling the diary towards him he turned to the next page. Blinked a couple of times to clear his fuzzy vision, then focused on the hastily scrawled entry.

Being an incantation I shall call the Words of UnMaking. This
is a terrible thing, and only my overwhelming fears have led me
to it. The seeds of this monstrous spell grew out of my work
with Morgan, though it shames me now to admit it. I do
believe that the Wall I labour to bring forth will protect us
from him. I believe we will be safe behind it forever ... but if my
belief proves false, yet will I prevail against him. For the dread
words recorded hereafter will undo him utterly. Yes, and they
will undo the speaker also ... undo me, for no one else shall
have them.

If I must use them ... if I must die ... I shall be justly
punished.

Silence, as the carved wooden clock on the wall ticked away the
seconds and minutes of what might be Lur's last days.

Mouth dry, hands sweaty, he read the diary entry again then
looked at the recorded incantations. Noted the syllables and the sigils
and the rhythms of the words and saw, his heart hard-beating, that
victory was held here in his hands.

Victory ... and death.

There were no more spells in the diary after Barl's Words of
UnMaking. The spell that would ensure Morg's death, and Asher's
with it.

He read it again. Again. Again. Marvelled at the simplicity of its
structure, its exquisite elegance, so quintessentially Barl. Recognised
its triggers and why without question it would work. With magic a
fading memory in his blood he could barely feel the incantation's
power. Faced with the potential of such dreadful destruction he felt
briefly, guiltily relieved the burden of its utterance would never fall
upon him.

And then—as he read the incantation for the eighth time—his disciplined, scholarly, educated mind went *click*. And suddenly he saw
Barl's spell in a whole new light. Saw it for what it was ... but also
what it could be. Still victory. Still death.

And yet entirely different.

He slammed the diary shut. Shoved away from his makeshift desk
and roamed Veira's small sitting room, banging from mantelpiece to
sofa to window and back again. He was sweating. Could he do it? Did
he even dare try? If the memory of magic wasn't enough, if his vaunted
scholarship were faulty. If he misplaced just one single syllable ...

He could kill everyone. Even perhaps leave Morg alive.

No. He couldn't do it. Shouldn't. The risk was too great. It was arrogance inconceivable to think of altering Barl's final, perhaps greatest work. How long had he been a magician? Mere weeks. It wasn't enough. If what he believed was true, if the powers he'd manifested had never been his but were part of Morg's plan, then he'd never been a real magician. Had never been anything but a magickless cripple. A pawn, used and discarded on a whim.

And yet—and yet—he could *see* it. *Feel* it. *Taste* the changes to her incantation, if only in his mind. He knew Barl as well as he knew himself, now. Knew how her mind worked, how it saw and shaped the world, as completely as he knew his own.

He could do this.

He flung himself back to the makeshift desk. Opened the diary. Pulled a fresh sheet of paper towards him and re-inked his pen.

"I can do this, Barl," he said aloud, as though she was nearby, listening. "I must do this. I know you want me to. And it's the only way to repay my debts. Sweet lady, help me…"

Outside the cottage the last of the daylight was washed away and a rain-soaked night fell. As the cottage clocks struck seven, Veira shepherded everyone into the kitchen for dinner. Just as they sat down to Darran's lumpy rabbit pie one of the villagers, braving the dreadful weather, came calling at the back door to see if she was all right. She shooed the others into the corridor where they hid and held their breaths until Gavin was persuaded she was coping just fine, thank you, and went away.

"Is there news from the Circle, Veira?" said Dathne, as they resumed their seats at the crowded kitchen table. "What's happening elsewhere in the kingdom?"

Veira sighed. "Nothing good, child. I've heard from everyone and every story is the same. Storms rage from coast to coast. There's flooding. Fires. Tremors that tear the earth apart, just as when King Borne was ill. Fear riots unchecked in village and township streets alike."

"And what of my people?" said Gar. "Are there no Doranen attempting to help?"

"A few," she said, shrugging. "But what can they do? They have no Weather Magic. I'm told most of them have gone into hiding on their country estates, panic-stricken like the Olken."

As Gar looked at his plate, clearly distressed, Darran cleared his throat. "What about the Doranen in the City? The kingdom's strongest magicians sit on council, surely—"

She shook her head. "Morg's suspended council business. Barlsman Holze has sent out orders for everyone to pray."

"So not even he suspects Jarralt isn't Jarralt?" said Matt, stabbing his fork into a potato.

Unwillingly, Veira shared her last titbit of gossip. "All the trouble's being blamed on Asher."

Asher snorted. "That's convenient."

"It's very clever—and *in*convenient. We'll have to work hard to make sure you're not noticed once we get into the City." She sat back in her chair, appetite defeated. "We leave at first light. "I'd be happier going soon after supper but the roads'll be too treacherous in the dark and we can't risk glimfire." She looked at Gar. "You all done with your translating, then?"

Gar put down his knife and fork. His expression was wary. Watchful. She didn't like the look of it. "Done?" he said. "Yes, I'm done. But the last spell isn't like the others. It's not a summoning for war-beasts."

"Then what is it?" said Dathne.

"A spell that Asher can say only once. A spell I'll have to teach him myself, on the road to Dorana."

For the first time, Asher looked at him. "You ain't comin' with us. You can teach me it tonight."

"I'm too tired tonight," said Gar, flushing. "I've been working all day and this is a desperately complicated incantation. Much harder than the others."

Seated beside him, Veira put her hand on his arm. "Why?"

He took a breath. Let it out. "Because it's a killing spell. Powerful enough to destroy Morg himself."

"And you're only just tellin' us *now*?" said Asher, glaring.

Gar held his hot gaze steadily. "It was the last spell in the diary. Barl's final defence against Morg. I had to be sure I translated it properly."

"And did you?"

"Yes. It will kill him."

Still Asher stared. "And what else? I know you, Gar, there's somethin' you ain't sayin'. Spit it out."

"Unfortunately, it will also kill you."

His words sparked a tempest.

"Then he can't use it!" cried Dathne. "How can you even *think* he would—"

"There's got to be another way," said Matt, pushing his plate away. "Prophecy says nothing about—"

"I told you he was tryin' to kill me!" said Asher, indignant.

Veira slammed her hand hard on the table, making them all jump and fall silent.

"*Enough!* Nobody's said he has to use it. Might be we'll kill this Morg with an army of those monsters Asher conjured up this afternoon. But we can't afford to ignore any weapon handed us in this war. It's a kingdom and thousands upon thousands of lives at stake." She looked at Asher, willing all kind understanding from her face. "But in the end we're not the ones who'll be called on to use it, and die. That might be your fate, child. Can you bear it? If all else fails could you use *this* weapon...though it cost you your life?"

Asher shoved back from the table. Rubbed his hands across his face, then let them fall to his side. "Why are you even askin', ole woman?" His cold gaze raked across all their faces. "You got me to promise to help you, and you know bloody well I keep my promises—no matter what it costs me. Besides. There's some as might think I'm already dead. That all I am is a man livin' on stolen time."

"Do you think that?" said Matt, into the red-hot silence.

Asher shrugged. "Don't matter what I think. Nowt matters any more, save for stoppin' that monster in the City."

"Yes," Veira said, when no one else could answer him. "No matter what it costs any of us, Morg must be stopped. Now let's all finish eating, shall we, then get ourselves some sleep. It'll be a mortal bad trip back to Dorana."

Returned to the Weather Chamber under cover of darkness, Morg raged and raged round the Weather map till all the polish was worn from the parquetry and the mellow timber shone dim.

The bitch whore's golden barrier was pockmarked with weaknesses now, its intricate incantations fraying apace. Outside the chamber a shrill wind was howling. Trees lashed the cloud-clotted sky and lightning stabbed both air and sodden ground. The world bled rain.

The map itself was suffering too. Leprous patches of decay and destruction marred it from end to end. His listening mind heard a far-distant keening. He lifted his eyes and stared through the clear crystal ceiling at the writhing gold light above him.

"Yes, slut! Scream. *Scream.*"

An unheralded voice said somewhere behind him: "Conroyd? Your Majesty? Might we have a word?"

Startled, he spun around. Stepped back, incredulous. Furious. "*Sorvold?* You vomitous excrescence, get out! All of you get out! You are not wanted here!"

They'd come in a gaggle, like geese. Sorvold. Daltrie. And uninvited back from the country, Boqur and Hafar also. Conroyd's dear friends and confidants.

As they stared at him, slack-faced with shock, he laughed his delight. "You lackwits! Don't you know he *despises* you?"

Foolishly they'd braved the inclement weather. Wet, wind-tossed, plastered with tattered leaves, despite their silks and velvets and their pitiful little magics they looked like destitute vagabonds.

Payne Sorvold said, very slowly, "Your Majesty, are you unwell?"

Victory was vintage icewine, burning in his blood. He spread his hands. "Unwell? On the contrary, gentlemen. I am superb. I said *get out*."

They exchanged uneasy glances. Sorvold spoke again. "Your Majesty, we are here on behalf of your Council. Your people. The weather is...disturbing. The Wall itself seems—its appearance suggests— Your Majesty, clearly something is wrong."

Boqur took a step forward. Neglected to bow. "Conroyd, in plain language: you have refused to meet with us that we might form a proper advisory for you in these early, unquiet days of your reign. Against all precedent and sound precepts of governance you've suspended the kingdom's lawful Council. Anxious messengers pour into the City from districts throughout the kingdom, desperate to know how to proceed in the face of the weather's wildness. And an hour ago your assistant Willer informed us that our former monarch Prince Gar has vanished without trace."

He laughed out loud. He hadn't heard. Didn't care. "Vanished? *Vanished?* Oh, poor little runtling! Running and running with no place to hide!"

It was Hafar's turn to remonstrate. "Conroyd, it's clear you're unwell. Perhaps the transfer of Weather Magic went awry. You should not have attempted it without a Master Magician to aid you. We did try to warn you, sir."

"We must be honest, Con!" said bluff Nole Daltrie. "Your kingship's off to a very bad start! Public executions, missing princes and now this dreadful weather! What are you doing to it? The City's in an uproar! Captain Orrick can barely maintain order. There's panic in the streets! Mobs at the palace demanding explanations! And hardly any Doranen are left to help control the population after your stupid wife summoned them to the country. It's an utter disaster and you're to blame! Now how are you going to fix it?"

He heaved a thundering sigh. "Oh, Nole, Nole...do rest that treadmill tongue of yours. I have no intention of fixing it. Everything unfolds as I desire."

"As you *desire*?" said Boqur. "Conroyd! Are you mad then, if not ill? Have you looked outside this chamber? The Wall itself's in danger!"

He smiled, rejoicing. "The Wall itself is *falling*, fool. And soon you'll all fall with it."

"Barl save us," Daltrie whispered. "I think you have gone mad, Con. Gentlemen, you heard him?"

"Indeed we did," said Hafar grimly. "We come just in time. His Majesty is unfit."

Sorvold stepped forward, his expression rigid. "You must accompany us, sir. Immediately. Whatever ails you, Pother Nix shall discover it and with Barl's blessings put you right again."

"Pother Nix is a pus-pot. I am as well as I have ever been. Gentlemen, you're dismissed."

"No, sir," said Sorvold, still approaching. "You are desperately ill. You must be, for the Conroyd Jarralt I know and admire would never—"

He stopped the idiot with a tender smile. Reached out and laid his palm, so gently, above the bleating fool's heart. Leaned close...and showed him his true self.

"But, Payne," he whispered as Sorvold's face turned grey and his mouth sagged in horror. "Can't you tell? I am *not* the Conroyd Jarralt you know and admire..."

A thought, and the labouring heart beneath his hand stopped beating.

"*Conroyd!*" the rest of the geese cried out. Daring to criticise, and question. So he slaughtered them like geese. Dropped their bodies where they stood, burned them to ash with an incandescent thought, then forgot they had ever existed.

CHAPTER THIRTY-FIVE

The storm was worse come cock crow. Wilder wind. Heavier rain, gusting with hailstones and flurries of sudden snow. The fringe of Black Woods around Veira's cottage was battered and full of gaps where trees had been torn down through the night. The world looked desolate, beyond all hope. The sound of running water filled the sodden air.

As Veira battled through the deepening mud, freeing her pigs and chickens and the donkey, Asher helped Matt harness the unhappy horses to the wagon. Matt looked even paler this morning; instead of sleeping last night, as Veira had ordered, he'd spent hours cobbling together blanket-lined canvas covers for the animals to protect them from the rain and hail.

Checking buckles, tugging knots, Asher said, "What d'you reckon we'll find once we get to Dorana?"

Matt shrugged. "I'm trying not to think. Asher—"

He sighed, knowing what Matt was about to say. "Don't. There ain't any point. If I got to say Gar's killing spell, then so be it. You want to get rid of Morg, don't you?"

"Of course I do! But not like—"

"Like what? Me dyin'?" he demanded. "You mean to say you never thought it'd come to this? Even though your bloody Prophecy says as much?"

"No!" Matt protested. "I never—at least I hoped—"

"Hope? Since when did hope save lives, Matt? I could stand in the middle of the City Square and hope till my head falls off that Morg'll drop dead at my feet, but it ain't goin' to happen unless I *make* it happen."

"That doesn't mean—"

"It prob'ly does," he said. "And you've always known it. Don't go insultin' my intelligence now, Matt. Not after all we've been through."

Matt stared at him, stricken. "Dathne told me not to be your friend. She always knew how bad things might get."

Dathne. He turned away. "You should've listened."

Frowning, Matt eased himself round to check the nearside horse's tail, tied up to keep it out of the mud. "You should make your peace with her. This silence is killing her, Asher."

He felt his heart hitch. "That's my business, Matt."

"You're being unfair!"

"You want I should stop talkin' to you too?" he said, dangerously close to snarling. "Leave it, Matt. I got enough to give me headaches without personal claptrap on top of it!"

The horses tossed their heads and stamped, unsettled by their edgy voices as well as the howling rain. Matt reached out a hand to them and murmured, soothing. Then he nodded, and sighed. "All right, Asher. Whatever you want. It's just a shame, is all. I'll say this for the last time then I'll not say it ever again: she loves you."

Over his shoulder, walking away, Asher answered, "Don't you know, Matt? Love's the bloody least of it."

*   *   *

They left the cottage soon after that. Matt driving, with Dathne on one side and Veira the other. In the back of the wagon, under the makeshift canvas covering drummed with rain, Asher, Gar and Darran and their baskets of supplies. The old man tucked himself up in a blanket and quickly fell asleep, a bundle of snoring bones.

"I fear it's been too much for him," Gar said, fretting. "I should've left him behind in the Tower."

Asher snorted. "You should've done a lot of things, I reckon. Bit late now though, eh?"

Gar looked down at the paper in his hands. His face was closed-off. Unreadable. The way it used to be in the early days, when Gar was still "Your Highness" and friendship never thought of. "I hope not." His fingers smoothed over the paper's creased surface. "I hope with this I can put everything right."

"That's what you call killin' me, is it? Puttin' everything right?" He laughed. "It don't bother you at all, eh?"

Gar's eyes glinted. "What? That this spell I've translated will destroy you? If I said yes, would you believe me?" He let his head fall back against the wagon's temporary canvas wall. "Of course you wouldn't. You've made your feelings plain, Asher. Let's not belabour them now. You've agreed to do this, and I've agreed to help. Let's leave it at that, shall we?"

Asher pulled his knees up to his chest and wrapped his arms around them. Glanced up as, overhead, the sky, invisible, was rumbled through with thunder. "Aye. Let's."

"Good," said Gar tightly. "Now shall we get to work on the incantation? I know we've hours to go till we reach Dorana but this isn't a task for skimping."

"And how am I meant to practise the bloody thing if sayin' it's goin' to kill me?"

"Credit me at least with some intelligence," Gar snapped. "I've broken it into sections. We'll work through them one at a time, out of order, and leave the sigils till last. Once you've committed each section to memory I'll show you the proper order they come in. All right?"

Grudgingly, he nodded. "Aye. Fine. All right."

"Good," said Gar. "Now pay attention..."

Dathne huddled inside her enveloping blanket and kept her gaze pinned to the horses' wet, canvas-covered backs. Poor things. They looked so miserable: ears pinned to their heads, snapping peevishly at each other every other stride, bound-up tails lashing. The waterlogged road unrolled before them, bordered each side with battered trees. The wagon's wheels slipped and slithered and the horses grunted with the effort of hauling it.

Beside her, Matt held the reins in hands reddened with cold. He was swaddled in one of Dathne's blankets too, but she could still feel him shivering. Suffering with the collapse of the kingdom's fabric of magic. Even she, never as adept as Matt, was starting to feel it now... a thin cold scream on the edge of hearing.

She felt like screaming herself. How much fear and sorrow could a body hold before it must spill out in a raging torrent?

Asher would not speak to her. Asher might well soon be dead.

She turned her head to stare at the slowly passing countryside, stuffing her knuckles in her mouth to dam the frightened grief. If he died... if he died without forgiving her... died believing their love was a lie, nothing but pragmatics and a cold, hard using... how could she go on after? What would she say to the child?

Their child...

Unbidden, her fingers danced featherlight across her belly. Was it a boy or a girl? Would it have his eyes? Would she see him in the way it walked? Hear him in the sound of its laughter? Would it even be born? Or was it, like him, destined to die? Did death await them all in distant Dorana?

No. She had to stop thinking like this or she'd be a drooling madwoman before ever they reached the City gates. There was hope, yet. There was always hope. She couldn't—*wouldn't*—believe that Prophecy had guided them so far only to abandon them at the end.

Please, please, don't let him die.

The clickety-clack of busy needles distracted her and she glanced past Matt to Veira. The old woman was knitting. *Knitting.* As though she was at home in her kitchen or in front of the fireplace and these were ordinary times.

Veira looked up. "You fratched about our Mage and his friend tucked up behind us? Don't be. They'll not come to blows."

"I know," Dathne said. Tried to say nothing else, but the words were out before she could stop them. "Veira—he won't have to use that killing spell, will he?"

In between them, Matt shook the waterlogged reins and kept his gaze pinned to the horses' backs. If he was filled with fears too, he wasn't letting them show. He'd gotten good at hiding his feelings lately. Once, she would've welcomed that, but now...

Now it just made her feel more alone.

Veira hissed over a dropped scarlet stitch. "I hope not," she said, making good her mistake. "I've taken steps to join him with the Circle so they can lend him strength when he needs it most."

That got Matt's attention; they exchanged startled glances. "When?" Dathne demanded. "And why aren't Matt and I included?"

"It's too dangerous for you and Matthias. The rest of the Circle is safe out of the way but we're like to be in the thick of things, child. You'd just be a distraction to him."

"Then how can we help him?" said Matt, frowning. "We can't do nothing."

Veira patted his knee. "I don't know yet. We'll just have to wait and see once we get there."

Wait and see...wait and see...yes, but what? Victory, or a bloody defeat? The thought of Asher saying the terrible spell of UnMaking made her want to vomit. Damn Gar, anyway! Why did he have to find it? Why did he have to tell them?

Send me a vision, I beg you, Jervale. Show me he's not going to die.

She closed her eyes then, and waited, but Jervale refused to oblige. *Bastard.* Eyes smarting, throat clogged with tears, she folded her arms across her middle. Let herself slump on the wagon's uncomfortable seat and tipped her head sideways till it rested on Matt's shoulder. He didn't object.

She escaped into sleep, and restless unhelpful dreaming.

Dorana City was dying.

Morg stood on the roof of the emptied palace's residential wing and watched its distant death throes, smiling. Behind him, against a sky of tarnished silver, Barl's Wall was a coruscation of filthy, failing power, flogged in the wind like a tattered flag.

At last...at last...the bitch whore was beaten.

Beneath his feet, an ominous rumble. The rooftop trembled as the palace swayed drunkenly on its foundations. Below him, the sounds of windows, breaking, of bricks and tiles falling to shatter in the buckling courtyards. In the gardens mighty trees groaned and shuddered, their roots tearing asunder the rain-softened ground. After six hundred years the earth was waking. Shrugging its shoulders as the bonds of magic were finally freed.

He heard screaming from the rooftops around him. Saw a few frantic Doranen, many more Olken: former councillors and advisors, palace servants, housemaids, butlers, running to and fro as their gentle world fell to pieces around them. They saw him.

"Your Majesty! Your Majesty!" they screamed, like children. "Help us! *Save us!*"

He raised a fist and stopped their heartbeats, each and every one. The noise was distracting. He wanted to savour victory uninterrupted.

A shadow touched his face and he looked up to see fresh clouds roiling, forming out of nothingness, out of the air, born of the wild and undirected Weather Magic he'd unbound from Barl's Wall. They clotted the face of the faded sun, turning day to murky dusk.

With a grinding rumble the earth heaved again, vomiting gouts of steam and boiling mud. In the distance, in the City, he saw more buildings tumble. Imagined the horror, the terror, and was suffused with a blinding joy.

"Your Majesty? Your Majesty," a small voice croaked behind him.

Without turning he said, "Go away, Willer."

"But, Your *Majesty*..."

So he did turn, impatiently, and looked at the pathetic thing bowing and scraping its way across the rooftop towards him.

"What?"

Willer stared at him, blotchy with fear and reeking of ale. "Captain Orrick sends an urgent message! Many streets are running like rivers and the water's scouring everything from its path. There's drowned dogs—wrecked carriages—furniture—" He choked on the horror. "People. *Children.*"

He nodded. "Good."

"*Good?*" Stunned silent, the little worm groped to understand. "But, but, you're the king! You're the Weather Worker!"

"Fool," he said, contemptuous. "I am neither. I never was."

Tears rose in the fat man's eyes. "Please, Your Majesty. Captain Orrick begs you to come. Barlsman Holze, too. Survivors are gathered in the Square—they're praying—but they need you."

He sighed. "Go away, Willer."

Sweating, weeping, the worm wrung its feeble hands. "Are you unwell, sir? Shall I fetch you a pother?"

Morg considered him. Witter, witter, witter. The bleatings of a sheep. "I wonder, was there a reason for you to be breathing?" he mused.

Willer goggled. Began to back away, very slowly. "Your Majesty?"

"No," he decided. "No, you've served your tiny purpose." He pointed a finger and froze the maggot where it stood. "But before I despatch you, would you like to know what you've done? What miracle your little mind and petty jealousies have wrought in this misbegotten kingdom?"

Lifting his finger, he set the worm adrift in the damp and stagnant air. It shrieked. "No! No! Somebody! Help!"

"Look at it, Willer!" he invited. "The might and the majesty of your blessed Barl's Wall! Do you see that it's failing? Do you see that it's *falling*? Do you know that you're to blame?"

"*Me*, sir? *No*, sir!" the bobbing creature protested.

He laughed at the horror in its face. "Oh, yes, sir! For the only man with the power to stop me was Asher of Restharven, and thanks to you, he's dead!"

The worm began flapping its arms, trying to force itself back to the roof. It looked ridiculous. "King Conroyd—*King Conroyd*!"

"Not Conroyd," he advised the worm gently. "Morg."

Willer shrieked. "*Who*? No! You *can't* be! That's *impossible*!"

Breathing deep of the sulphurous air he flared power round his body in a crimson nimbus. Laughed aloud at the terror, the dawning belief, in the little man's eyes.

"Stop this, *stop* it!" the fool worm babbled. "Before it's too late! Don't you see? You're killing the kingdom!"

"Of course I am. To be reborn all things must die."

"No! No! I don't *want* to die!" the wretched thing wailed. "Please don't hurt me! Please put me down!"

"Put you down?" he echoed, smiling. "Certainly, Willer. Whatever you desire."

And with a flick of his finger he spun sobbing Willer over the roof's stone balustrade then released him to fall to the flagstones below… where he burst in a welter of blood and fat.

Overhead, the first bright spears of scarlet lightning lanced the billowing clouds, striking flesh and buildings with lethal force. The lurid sky writhed—and Barl's dying Wall flailed in useless defiance.

Dreary in the daylight gloom, the wagon trundled onwards. The cloud-filled sky stretched on forever, spitting rain and snow in gusts and eddies, sometimes furious, sometimes sullen. The hours unspooled equally sullen. The wagon's shivering passengers dwindled to silence. They saw not another soul as they travelled through the blighted, sodden countryside towards Dorana City.

Matt unhappily kept the horses moving, stopping only to let them drink and snatch a mouthful of grain. Morning surrendered to midday, surrendered to afternoon, surrendered to night.

"We won't stop again till we reach the City," decreed Veira, lighting torches to leaven the dark as Matt ran his hands over the tired horses and the others staggered about in the puddles and slop, stretching their tired legs and trying to get warm. "If you're hungry, raid the baskets. If you must piss or otherwise, do your business quickly and run to catch up. There's no time left for niceties or coddling." She frowned at Darran. "Sorry, old man, but there's no help for it."

Darran nodded. "I understand," he croaked, and climbed back in the wagon, out of the blighting wind.

"And when will we reach the City?" asked Dathne weakly, rattled almost to pieces and leaning against a wheel.

"An hour or two past sunrise, I'm thinking," said Veira, and pulled a face. "Though I doubt we'll be able to see it."

For Asher, filled to bursting with the prickly magic of Gar's killing spell and trapped in the prince's unwelcome company, that end couldn't come fast enough.

No matter it might bring with it his death.

For the first and likely last time in his life, Pellen Orrick felt desperate. Staring through his office's broken windows he rubbed his pain-burned shoulder and struggled to hold back tears.

The dawn of a new day: the worst of his life. His beautiful City, elegant gracious Dorana, spread smashed and trampled before him. Every second building, it seemed, was collapsed or burning or burned out completely, belching greasy smoke, spilling ruined wares through splintered doorways and shattered shopfronts, even as dirty water swirled around the floors and up the doorjambs. Bulls and cows and horses and sheep and goats, once safely penned in the Livestock Quarter, milled and lowed and bleated through the streets with no one willing or able to pen them up again. Some of them slipped, plunged head first into running water or gaping cracks in the ground, and didn't get up again.

There were more dead people than he'd thought to see in all his life. Crushed and smashed by falling masonry, bludgeoned and drowned by the rivers of debris-choked rainwater raging through the narrower streets. Some of the bodies were abandoned, others clutched hard in the arms of weeping loved ones. Olken and Doranen, this madness had spared neither. Nor had magic saved them.

Most of his guards had deserted their posts. Some had fled the City with family and friends, certain that just beyond the next bend, in the next town or village, lay safety, and sanity. The few who'd remained were dead or had gathered in the Square to pray, ignoring his pleas to uphold their duty and their oaths.

He couldn't really blame them. If he'd had a family he might have discarded duty too. Run away or joined with the crowd crammed into the Square where Barlsman Holze all yesterday led beseeching prayers for deliverance.

But deliverance didn't seem to be coming. Dorana was doomed, and the kingdom with it.

Weary almost beyond walking, he made his way downstairs to the guardhouse's deserted main hall where Ox Bunder held steadfastly to his post.

"Captain!" Bunder frowned. "Where's your sling, sir? That shoulder's nowhere near to healed yet."

"My shoulder's the least of my troubles," he replied tiredly. "Ox, you've a young family waiting. Why don't you go? I'll stay here, for all the good I can do."

"No, sir," Bunder said. Stubborn to the last. "I've got my duty."

Before this he'd never much cared for Bunder; now his heart broke for love of him. "No, my friend, you've got your family. Go to them. That's an order." He held out his hand. "And good luck."

Torn between guilt and relief, Bunder clasped his wrist. "Yes, sir. All right."

Orrick walked out with him. His lovely City stank of burnt bones and death. Stopping at the guardhouse gates, he patted Bunder on the back and watched the man force his way through the milling throng, the frightened animals, the puddles and debris.

Scarlet lightning split the sky, spearing the ground with random vengeance. The Golden Cockerel burst apart. A score of people died then and there, pulped and broken by flying brick even as they ran screaming for shelter. But in the centre of the Square, citizens with more faith than sense stood their ground, eyes fixed firmly on Holze on Barl's Chapel steps, as they stubbornly followed the cleric's desperate prayers.

Some folk even climbed into Supplicant's Fountain. Clustered round Barl's greenstone statue, they stroked and stroked her hands, her feet, the folds of her robe. Begged her in high, shrill voices to protect them, save them, forgive them.

Forgive them for what? What sin could merit such harsh retribution? He was a guardsman, he knew crime when he met it. The people of Lur had done nothing, *nothing*, to warrant the horrors he'd witnessed. The carnage yet to come.

All his life he'd thought himself a man of faith. But what was it he believed in? A cold stone statue? A woman who'd died over six hundred years ago, at an age almost young enough to be his daughter? Magic?

For six long centuries the Olken had been told the Doranen were different. Stronger. Better. But the streets were littered with Doranen dead, as well as Olken. Their magic hadn't saved them.

It wasn't saving anyone.

And neither were the prayers.

Even as he watched, another scarlet javelin lanced from the sky and blasted Barl's statue to rubble. Shards of shattered greenstone whipped through the crowd. There was screaming. Blood. More dead, more injured.

Fleetingly, he thought of Asher—but help from that quarter was clearly a forlorn hope. Asher wasn't coming. Asher was probably dead. Struck by lightning, drowned in a ditch, swallowed by the hungry earth. Asher's survival would be some kind of miracle.

Only fools believed in miracles, and Pellen Orrick had never been a fool.

Numb with despair he stumbled to the ruined fountain. The remains of the poor fools who had believed in miracles, who needed his help, for all the good he could do them now. But he was a guardsman, help was his duty, and duty was all he had left.

"It's no use!" shouted Veira as the panicked horses reared and plunged, threatening to smash the wagon and everyone in it. "We'll have to walk the rest of the way!"

Squashed beside the old woman on the wagon's seat so Dathne could get some rest in the back, Asher could scarcely hear her words above the howling wind. They were halted where the Black Woods Road met the main thoroughfare into Dorana. In the distance they could see the foaming River Gant, its banks burst, spreading like a lake on either side. A flood of carts and carriages poured past them fleeing the City, drivers and occupants blind to the mad folk standing still on the side of the road.

Dorana was a scant two miles away now. Behind it, the terrible Wall thrashed to ribbons against the stricken sky. Asher groaned as his guts thrashed in sympathy. There was a vice clamped around his head, its screws turning tighter and tighter with every heartbeat. Nothing could save Barl's Wall now, it was shredded beyond repair.

He felt like he was shredding with it, all the power in him curdling and boiling, bubbling like engraver's acid sat on a naked flame.

"Hold on, child," said Veira, her cold lips pressed against his ear. "Not much longer, now."

He pulled her to him, shoving her face against his chest, as fresh hail pelted from the sky. He heard the wagon's makeshift canvas covering tear, and someone's stifled shout as the jagged ice found naked flesh; it sounded like Gar. Then the air was full of sound and soaking splinters as a barbed spear of lightning struck the heart of a towering djelba tree, too close to their right. The horses bellowed again, ploughing the mud beneath their maddened hooves.

"Please, Veira, you got to let me *do* somethin'!" he begged. "We'll never make it to the City at this rate!"

He felt her shake her head. "No, child," she answered; even muffled, her voice brooked no argument. "He'll hear you and all surprise will be lost. Don't fratch yourself. Prophecy's protected us this far, it won't abandon us now."

More red lightning whiplashed the air, struck the ground, the river, somewhere out of sight in the midst of the fleeing City folk.

"Don't listen," said Veira fiercely, as he jerked his head towards the terrible screaming. "Your job's ahead, not here. We have to go!"

"She's right!" Matt shouted, holding the horses with all his strength. "Now help me get these damned animals unhitched before they flip themselves over and squash us all to mincemeat!"

Asher let go of Veira and leapt to the ground. As his boots touched mud the earth trembled and shuddered, heaving as though something monstrous and living surged just beneath the surface, battling to be free. The wagon lurched forward as the horses tried to run.

"Get to their heads, Asher!" yelled Matt. "Hold them till I reach you! Veira, down! In the back there, get out!"

Skidding in the slimy mud, Asher reached the nearest horse's head and wrapped his fingers in the bridle. Willed the bloody animal to stand, stand, *stand*, you *bastard*. Digging in his heels he hung on till he thought his arm would tear right off at the shoulder. Then Matt was with him and there was a knife in his hand, sharp blade flashing, severing harness and traces. The horses, sensing freedom, struggled even harder. The knife slipped. A horse squealed. Blood churned into the mud underfoot.

Then the last length of leather surrendered to the steel. Mindless with fear the horses bolted, bridles still intact, canvas blankets slipping and sliding and flapping like sails. Gasping, grunting, Matt and

Asher propped each other upright and watched the animals disappear into the gathering murk.

The lowering clouds pressed lower still, and belched a blizzard of snow.

"Come now!" said Veira, chivvying like a shepherd with her flock. "We'll freeze to death and turn into snowmen standing here, and besides, we've work to do!"

Asher straightened. Managed a wry grimace in Matt's direction, then turned his face towards their destination. Felt his guts spasm all over again, protesting the death of Barl's magic.

"You all right?" said Matt.

He nodded. "I'll manage. You?"

"I'll manage."

There was pain in Matt's face, echoing his own. "Let's go then, eh?"

Staggering and stumbling as the uneasy ground beneath them shuddered and the freshly rising wind flung hail and snow in their faces, with newly bleeding Gar supporting Darran, Matt lending a strong arm to Veira, and Dathne stubbornly alone, they started doggedly towards the City. Towards the failing Wall, which drew them like a magnet.

When he'd done all he could for the dead and maimed of Supplicant's Fountain, and finally convinced that fool Holze to get the people praying *inside* the chapel, even if it meant they had to stand on each other's shoulders and dangle from the ceiling, Orrick stayed in the streets doing whatever else was needed.

Indifferent to the danger, to spears of lightning, squalls of hail, and snow, the wind and stinking rain, abruptly collapsing buildings and lethally panicked livestock, he clambered over chunks of masonry and spars of timber, splashed through red-tinged puddles and stepped over rents in the cobbles, because what else could he do? Go back to his office, his desk, his *paperwork*?

He was trying to force his way into a half-tumbled dress shop in Lace Lane, one street back from the Square, to see if anyone was inside injured when a clutching hand closed round his good elbow. "Pellen!"

He turned. "*Asher!*"

It was him. Whole, alive and not alone. Behind him, shrouded in cloaks and hoods, huddled Matt, Dathne, Darran, the prince, with blood on his face—and a wrinkled old woman he'd never laid eyes on before.

"Asher!" he said again, and was flooded with a complication of emotions. The ending world blurred briefly. "How did you—"

Asher shook him. Pain flared, but he didn't care. "Where's Jarralt? I mean, Morg?"

He pressed a hand to his wounded shoulder. Felt fresh blood, seeping, and a fresh chill of horror at the sound of that name. "No one's seen him. No one knows."

Another crimson whiplash of lightning, shrill and shrieking. The hideous screaming of horses, the bellowing of bulls. A thudding rumble as the Musicians' Guildhouse collapsed. Out of nowhere an icy wind, howling and whirling and tearing the bruised clouds to pieces.

A frightened, ragged cry sounded beyond the line of the lane's wrecked shops. Orrick looked at Asher and unspeaking they ran, splashing and reckless, back to the square. The others followed.

When they reached the open rubbled space at the City's centre, what they saw stopped them in their tracks.

"Barl have mercy," moaned Darran.

The few remaining threads of Barl's miraculous Wall flapped uselessly against the green and purple sky. Once proud and gold and mighty, it was now a ripped and raddled mockery of itself. Even as they and the fools still out in the open watched, pieces of magic tore free of the anchoring mountains, setting fire to the trees at their top.

Then Asher and Matt cried out together, staggering, as the last stubborn links of Barl's great Wall snapped. A booming thunder of enormous energy, released, shivered shaken buildings to ruins. Pressed flesh to brittle bones. Beneath the City's cobblestones the earth turned over in one last, massive protest. Every person standing was thrown to the ground, shouting, and all the sensible folk who'd taken refuge in the chapel came running out again, down the steps and into the Square, to see for themselves what had happened. Holze came out behind them, braid flying, to stand on the top of his precious chapel steps and weakly call them back.

The wind fell silent. No rain. No snow. No pounding hail. Gasping, Orrick and the others clambered to their feet. Orrick looked around him, tried to see what fresh damage was done to his poor dying City. If anyone else was killed. His heart stuttered. Heedless of the pain, he flung up his injured arm and pointed. Shouted.

"Look! *Look!*"

The sorcerer Morg was coming.

CHAPTER THIRTY-SIX

He floated on air, on power invincible, high above the wrecked, rubbled City and over the crowd-crammed Square.

"Barl, my beloved! Your Wall has fallen and I am here!"

A voice assailed him. "Conroyd! If you are indeed Conroyd! In the name of Barl and all things holy, I command you now to leave!"

Ah, Holze. Barl-sodden, mumbling, bumbling Holze. He floated to the chapel, the last refuge of dead men, where the shaking old fool stood on the steps and defied him to the last.

"There is no Conroyd," he said, smiling down at him. "Conroyd is dead."

"I don't believe you!" Holze quavered. "Return him to us, whoever you are, and get you gone from here!"

Still smiling, he reached down and touched Efrim's cheek. Withered flesh scorched and melted. "Efrim, Efrim. Recall your scripture. You *know* who I am."

As the cleric fell backwards, screeching, he turned in the air and faced the vanquished mountains. Shivering with pleasure, with a ravenous hunger, he opened his mind and summoned his power, *all* his power, all of himself that he'd left behind, that for too long had been denied him beyond Barl's Wall. Summoned his glorious victory and received—

Nothing.

The shock was so great he fell like a stone. Plunged into the midst of four-legged cattle. Before they could trample him he turned them to ashes with fire and hate, then took again to the fretful air. Horror was a living thing, beating him almost to blindness.

Nothing? Nothing? How could there be *nothing?* He was Morg, the most powerful magician undying! He was a *mountain* of power, an *ocean* of power, a *sky everlasting* of power!

He opened his mind a second time, strained beyond the confines of flesh, of blood, this outgrown borrowed body—

—and touched his sundered self. Felt it tremble, as he now trembled. Yearn, as he was yearning, to be complete again.

And then it recoiled. Repulsed him. He felt revulsion, rejection, an utter repudiation of his mind and his mastery—as though he were a stranger and this not a coming home.

Deep inside him, Conroyd was laughing.

Morg, Morg, what did you think? That I, Conroyd Jarralt, would lie down and die? How could you swallow me yet not know my flavour? You're far too late, cousin, and too long changed. Our minds are one. Our flesh is one. I am you, and you are me, and there is now no going back. The Wall is fallen and still you are trapped.

Deaf and blind, Morg hung in the air. Trapped? *Trapped?*

He opened his mouth and screamed.

Forgetting he hated her, Asher grabbed Dathne's hand and ran, trusting the others to follow. As Morg dangled helpless above them, keening like a creature in torment, he headed for the nearest safe shelter: the Butchers' Guild common house, half of its roof missing and part of one wall, but with most of its front awning still intact. They scuttled inside and collapsed to the ground, panting.

"The guardhouse would be safer," said Orrick. The shoulder of his tunic was wet with blood. "And I've lots of weapons there."

Asher shook his head. "Truncheons and pikestaffs won't hurt that thing. Veira? What's happenin'?"

Seated on a big chunk of brickwork, the old woman dabbed a kerchief to her bleeding arm. "Don't know. But it's useful. Everyone all right?"

Everyone was. Even Darran beside her, though he looked the worse for wear, pasty-faced, and breathing like a bellows. Gar, his hail-damaged cheek puffed and scabbed with blood, had an arm tight round the old man's shoulders, holding him shakily upright. Matt crouched beside them, and Dathne next, with Orrick closest to the street and trouble. Of course.

He shouldn't have let them come. They couldn't help him, and all their lives were in danger.

Gar let go of Darran's slumped shoulders and wriggled closer. "Asher. I have to talk to you. Privately."

Bits of broken masonry dug sharply into his knees. Ignoring the small discomfort, he didn't take his eyes from the Square. From Morg. "What for? There's nowt left to say."

Gar had never known when to shut up. "Yes, there is. The killing spell—"

He spared the little shit an impatient glance. "I've learned it. I know it. You did your job. Now hold your tongue, why don't you, so's I can do mine. I'm tryin' to think here, if it's all right with you."

"But you don't understand! I—"

Lunging sideways past all the rest of them he shoved Gar hard and sent him toppling. The bastard's head hit the wall with a thud. *"There's nowt left to say!"*

As Darran protested and the others fussed over Gar, Veira leaned over and touched his hand.

Her hood was down, her silver snake of hair rain-soaked and tumbling round her shoulders. "I'll call the Circle to you now, child. Let them in. Let them help you. Don't be afraid."

He wasn't afraid, he was bloody terrified. With the Wall's demise the grinding pain in him was almost faded, but in its place something darker flowed bitter and sluggish through his veins, sticky like tar. The foulness of Morg. From the sick look on Matt's face, his friend was feeling it too. But not as keenly as he did. Or as intimately. Matt weren't the Innocent Mage.

He ain't... but I am.

For the very first time, he truly accepted it. Did that mean he accepted death too?

Veira's finger poked him. "Asher! What is it? What's amiss?"

He waited until his heart stopped galloping and he could trust his voice not to crack, his feet not to run him away from there without asking permission first. "Nowt. I'm fine."

"Then be still and silent, and I'll summon the Circle."

Asher watched as she fumbled in her pocket. Pulled out that blue felt bag and withdrew a shard of crystal. It shimmered in the lowering light, then was hidden between her palms. Her eyes closed... her lips moved without sound... and the crystal shard she'd buried in his flesh burst burning into life. In his mind a chorus of voices, echoing.

We're here, Asher. We're with you. Use our strength when you need it. It's yours for the taking.

Fear faded, and with it some of the blackness in his blood. He felt his power stir, untainted. Felt the remnants of pain ease. A comforting heat was in him now, centred above his heart. Within the crystal.

In the Square outside their shelter, Morg's horrible screaming stopped.

Asher stood. Ready or not, want this or not, his time had come. "Best finish this, I reckon."

The quality of silence behind him changed. Lost outrage. Acquired sorrow. Became heavy, full of unspoken last words. He didn't want to hear them. He was doing this because they'd asked him. Begged him. Because no one but him could do it. Because he'd promised to help them no matter the cost and unlike some people, he kept his word.

Didn't mean he wanted a scene.

"What are you doing? Don't go out there!" said Dathne. "Fight him from here, in safety!"

Pellen Orrick answered her. "How can he, Dathne? There are people in the way."

The Square was full of Olken and a handful of Doranen. Folk who'd had nowhere to run to, or thought they'd be all right. Some of them wore faces he'd known once, surely, when he'd been a different man. Dazed and stumbling they crawled amongst the rubble and debris, the aimlessly milling livestock, the fallen bodies. Some struggled to reach Barlsman Holze, the last authority left in the City. The cleric sprawled on his Barl's Chapel steps, unmoving.

"*Asher!*" Dathne cried as he took another step.

He stopped, fingers tight on the ragged brickwork. *Don't look, don't look, there ain't no bloody point!*

He looked. He had to.

All her love was in her face. Seeing it, something brittle inside him broke, or was broken. He summoned a smile for her. "It's all right, Dathne. The bastard won't touch you."

There were tears in her eyes and on her cheeks. "There's something I have to tell you, I—"

He went to her and dropped to one knee. Let his fingers trace the gentle upswing of her eyebrow, her severely curving cheekbone, and lips.

"Tell me later."

"But—"

He stood, and she fell silent. With a final smile he turned his back on her. On all of them: Veira, Darran, Pellen, Matt, and Gar. Stepping out of their meagre shelter he looked at the creature spinning and spinning and spinning above him, oblivious to everything save its private pain.

But for how long...

In his mind, the Circle waited.

He ran haphazard to the steps of the chapel, dodging livestock, ignoring the fallen who needed his help, even the children. Holze was stirring now, sitting up. Seeing him, the cleric gasped. "*Asher?*"

He held out his hand. Above their heads Morg dangled, moaning. "Holze."

Five charred fingerprints marred the side of the cleric's pain-twisted face. "You're *alive?*"

"No, I'm a ghost," he said, and helped Holze to his unsteady feet. Despite the dirty past they shared he felt a grudging respect: Holze could've bolted, and didn't.

The Barlsman's pale lips tightened. "Do you know what *that* is?" he asked, pointing to Morg.

"Aye. Do you?"

"I think I might," Holze said, frowning. "Though my mind can scarce believe it."

He snorted. "Believe it, Holze. That's Morg."

The last hint of colour drained from the cleric's face, leaving the fingerprints livid, and he kissed his holyring with fervour. "Barl save us."

"If you say so." Asher turned and looked at the dazed people in the square. "These folk can't stay out here. Can you get 'em back in the chapel?"

"Yes, yes, of course, but why? What are you going to do?"

He jerked his head upwards. "Kill that."

Holze choked. "How?"

"How d'you reckon?" he snapped, and conjured flame. Not tame and gentle glimlight but the cruel, greedy heat of warfire. One of the many tricks to be found in Barl's diary, which he could so easily have lived without.

"What is this *blasphemy*?" Holze demanded, staring at the fire leaping from Olken fingers. "That's no magic known to me! How do you come by it? Who taught it to you? *Morg*?"

He grinned, feeling vicious. "No, Holze. Barl."

Holze came close to falling head first down the steps. "No—no—that's not *possible*!"

With a flick of his wrist he extinguished the flame. "We can argue what is and ain't possible when this is over, provided we're both still standin'."

Shaken, Holze looked again at Morg. "You can't kill him, Asher. There's Conroyd to consider."

He could've hit the ole fool. "Of course I can! I have to! And if Jarralt's still in there I'll be doin' him a favour. Now get these idiot folk out of here, would you? I've seen enough dead bodies to last me a lifetime!"

He turned his back on the protesting cleric, trounced down the chapel steps and picked his way across the Square until he was directly under Morg's undulating body. Ignoring the danger, he closed his eyes, and for the first time called willingly to the power within.

The flames leapt, burning away the last of Morg's taint. Crimson, gold, silver, azure: the colours of his peculiar magic poured through his veins like a waterfall. And joining them, power of a different hue: earthy brown mixed with grassy green. Pure Olken magic, from the

Circle. Suddenly he was connected to the natural world with a strength he'd never felt before. As though he were a mountain himself, forged of living rock.

Dimly, through the rainbow haze, he heard shouts. Cries of surprise and wonder. He stopped his ears to them. Looked inwards only, gathering the strands of his multicoloured talent, preparing it for battle. Barl's fierce war spells seethed beneath his surface, straining to be set free.

A woman's scream, abruptly silenced. Wrenched from his trance he opened his eyes—and stared at the face of death itself.

"*Asher!*" cried Morg, hovering before him. Jarralt's beauty contorted, distorted and spittled with hate. "Not dead *yet?*"

He lashed out his mind, fingers blurring the air with sigils even as the words he needed tumbled from his tongue. Somewhere, softly, he felt the Circle's shock and surprise.

Spitefully laughing, Morg deflected the power. Sent the red flame splashing left and right, igniting helpless Olken who stood too close, like statues of stone.

Except statues didn't burn.

Sickened, he turned on the rest of them. "Run, you idiots! *Run!*"

Gleeful, malevolent, Morg whirled above them. "No, no, *don't* run! *Change!*" He pointed his fingers and shouted a string of terrible words, syllables to clot the blood and crawl the skin. Power poured out of him, black and stinking. The fleeing Olken it sullied fell screaming to the ground...and altered.

Became demons.

"*Jervale's mercy!*" cried Veira, watching. "Prophecy protect us!"

Dathne watched, shaking and sickened, as vulnerable flesh boiled and bubbled, stretched and strained, grew fangs and talons and snouts and horns. Became scaled. Sprouted bristles. Thickened, hardened, and lost all humanity. She gasped as the milling livestock mutated with the people: grew steely wings and claws like billhooks and teeth as long and sharp as daggers.

Nothing living touched by Morg's foul magic was spared.

Forced now to focus on Morg's creations instead of Morg himself, Asher tried to stop the terrible transformations. He hurled his own magic after Morg's, light at the dark. The sorcerer extinguished it and flicked him aside with contemptuous ease. Catapulted him through the rancid air and crashed him to the puddled ground where he lay winded and feebly struggling.

"Asher!" said Matt.

Dathne clutched his sleeve. "Don't. You can't help him. We can't fight—*that*."

"Then what good are we, Dath?" he demanded. "What are we *here* for?"

Veira turned on him. "We've done our part, Matthias. We've kept the secret of the Innocent Mage, and brought him to the place he was always meant to be. Dathne's right, we're not made to fight this evil. That's why *he* was born!"

"It's not enough!" Matt shouted. "I can't just sit here and let him face that alone!"

"He's not alone! The Circle's with him!"

"Aren't *we* the Circle?"

"Not any more!" said Veira, sharply. "Our part is played. To interfere now is to put all at risk!"

Pellen Orrick stared at the monstrous things lurching and clattering and flapping and growling into life all over the Square. "But I'm Captain of the City! I should be out there fighting!"

"If you go out there he'll try to protect you!" Veira told him. "Which will likely get him killed. So hold your tongue and stay out of sight! All of you! That's the best we can do for our Asher now!"

She was hurtful, but right. Dathne exchanged stricken glances with Orrick, Gar and Darran, then turned to Matt, anguished beside her, and touched his hand. "He'll be all right, Matt. We have to believe it. We mustn't lose faith, for his sake."

"I'm trying, Dath," he whispered. "Jervale knows I'm trying."

He looked so unlike himself, lost and frightened, it was easier to stare outside than at him.

Dazed and unsteady, Asher was back on his feet. Consumed with vengeance Morg sizzled the air above his dreadful creations. "Kill him, children!" he shouted, pointing. "Kill them all!"

The bestial, grunting, roaring things that moments before had been people, livestock, turned on Asher, slavering. Beat their wings. Lashed their tails. Crashed their tusks against their hides—and charged.

Asher flung out both hands and called forth Barl's warbeasts. The air around him shimmered and seethed as monsters worse than the demons attacking him burst into life from thin air. Creatures torn from the heart of nightmare, towering, stinking, yowling for blood.

Morg howled his fury as Asher's monsters attacked his creations. He called forth his own war-beasts, equally dire. The world filled with the sound and stink of violent death: the living demons' black blood gouted, poured sulphurous to the upheaved ground. The magical war-beasts burst into clouds of stinking acid.

Dathne watched, barely breathing, as Asher fought to destroy the cruelties Morg sent against him. From a vast distance she heard Gar name them: *brilbeests...dog-trolls...wereslags...ruunsliks...*an endless litany of foulness and decay.

Asher held his ground...but only just.

And then shrill screaming wrenched her head around. Not all the demons were trying to kill Asher. Some were in pursuit of other prey. She saw something that once had been a horse, now with eyes of fire and bony spikes all over its scarlet-scaled body, leap through a ruined shopfront then back out again with a Doranen youth in tow, his arm clamped in its teeth. The beautiful blond boy was crying, flailing at the creature with his inadequate, watered-down magic. The demon released him, reared up high, red hooves waving, then pounded his body to pulp on the cobbles.

More screaming, this time from the chapel as its doors burst open and four bull-demons chased a horde of Olken out of their refuge. Most were children. Holze staggered behind them, drenched in blood, but his wounds overcame him and he collapsed to the ground, dead or unconscious she had no way to tell. Asher saw the children—couldn't help them—

And Matt burst shouting from their pitiful shelter. Ran straight at the demons, waving his arms. At his heels, Pellen Orrick, just as demented.

"Come back, Matthias!" Veira shouted after him. "Don't do it! *Come back!*"

Dathne leapt after them. Felt the brush of Veira's fingers as the old woman tried to catch her arm, and shook her off. Heard a curse as Veira followed. She didn't look back, saw nothing but Asher— Asher—

He'd seen Matt and Orrick. They'd reached the first of the running children and were pushing them desperately left and right behind anything that might hide them from the monsters pursuing.

The leading bull-demon reached the slowest of the little ones and gored her. Asher killed it with a spear of fire. Matt and Orrick kept on snatching children, throwing them to safety.

And then Morg attacked. Swooped from the sky like a falcon to the kill, his face a rictus of fury and hate.

Asher flung a massive ball of warfire at him. The writhing flames engulfed the sorcerer, cartwheeling him backwards and sideways into the majestic carved front of Justice Hall. Shattered masonry plunged to the ground, stained glass splintered and smashed and fell. Stunned and burning, Morg plummeted to the unforgiving marble far below and lay there, unmoving.

Slipping in mud, in bloodied water, hurdling rubble and bodies, Asher tried to reach Matt and Orrick and the fleeing children, throwing warfire at the demons as he ran. One of Morg's monsters reared up behind him.

"*Asher!*" cried Dathne, and he turned and killed it. He saw her—faltered—brandished his arms—*get back! get back!*

Then his face changed. Someone shouted: "*Veira! Look out!*"

Dathne staggered round. Saw Veira, hobbling, her frail strength spent. Saw Pellen Orrick running back to her, a long spar of timber in his hands like a javelin. Saw a giant bull with bloodstained horns thundering behind the old woman. Gaining...gaining...

Veira tripped, went sprawling. Orrick lunged and thrust his makeshift weapon into the creature's gaping maw. It bellowed, gouting blood, and crashed to the ground—

—crushing Veira beneath it, and Pellen Orrick too.

Asher cried out and dropped to his knees, hands clawing at his heart, his head, oblivious to the battle raging round him.

"*Veira!*" Dathne shouted, and started running. Children forgotten, Matt ran too.

They reached Veira and Orrick together. Flung themselves to the blood-slicked street and reached for her hand—a way to free her.

No use. She was dead. Her eyes, half-open, stared at the red-hazed sky. Spilled from her fingers a shard of crystal, cracked now, its beauty charred.

"Veira!" Matt whispered. "I'm sorry—I'm sorry—"

A groan, then, filled with pain and confusion. Grief-struck, Dathne looked over the lumpen carcass of the demon-bull and there was Orrick, leg-pinned and living.

Matt pushed to his feet. "Help me, Dathne. I'll lift this monster—you drag him free—"

But they couldn't do it unaided. She looked back to the shelter for Gar, who should be helping—

"Dathne! Watch out!" Matt yelled, and knocked her brutally sideways. She fell across a pile of rubble, feeling her skin tear and blood spill, crying out as her head struck something cruelly hard.

Matt had leapt forward, waving his arms. He danced himself sideways, away from her, shouting like a madman. What—*what*—

An enormous armoured-winged demon, snouted and bestial and no longer human, was lumbering towards them.

"Here! Here!" her crazy friend shouted—her compass—her anchor—her candle in the dark. "*Here*, you evil bastard!"

"No, Matt! Run! *Run!*"

But her voice was reduced to a whisper and around her the world was fading fast...

...but not quite fast enough.

Morg's giant, dagger-clawed monster seized Matt in its massive arms and tore him limb from limb. Hot blood sprayed in a mighty fountain, splashing the cobblestones scarlet.

On his knees and devastated by the sundering of the Circle, Asher heard Matt's desperate cry. He looked up. Through blinding pain saw the demon. Saw Dathne, in danger. Saw Matt shove her to safety—confront the monster—and die in blood and futility.

Time stopped, and the whole world with it.

When it started again he was back on his feet. Raging, weeping and lusting for death. War-beast after war-beast boiled into existence around him. He set them loose to rampage—and then leapt forth to join them.

Kill—kill—kill—

His first victim was the thing that slaughtered Matt.

When it was over, and all Morg's monsters were slain or destroyed, there fell a silence, shot through with the sound of someone sobbing and someone else groaning. The Square was drifted with sulphurous smoke. Slicked underfoot with pools and puddles of blood, thick black and red, looking like a slaughterhouse with the sundered carcasses of demons and the broken bodies of children and their elders. Tired beyond imagining, Asher raised a hand as heavy as lead and banished his surviving war-beasts to nothingness.

Then he staggered to Dathne. Gar was with her, seemingly unhurt, helping her sit up. He didn't give a rat's arse about Gar.

"I'm all right, Asher," she insisted, though there was blood on her face and her eyes were unfocused. "Leave me. *Finish* this. Destroy Morg and end the nightmare."

It nearly killed him, but he left her. Ignoring Gar, who shouted his name.

Morg the sorcerer lay still as death on the steps of Justice Hall.

Brimmed with pain Asher walked to join his fallen enemy. Reaching down, he rolled Morg over. Conroyd Jarralt's unmarked face was as handsome as ever. He was breathing yet.

On his belt, neatly secured in its lavishly jewelled sheath and barely flame-touched, Conroyd's knife. Asher slid it free and hefted it in his palm, admiring its weight and balance. Admiring the Olken craftsmanship. Odd that Conroyd chose an Olken-made dagger, given how he despised all things not Doranen.

Odd...and immensely gratifying.

He felt the merest flicker of sorrow, then. Conroyd Jarralt was a bastard but it was unlikely he'd asked to be consumed by Morg. And now he was going to die. Had to die, so Lur might live.

He shook himself. *Don't think on that, don't think on it. It's him or you and everyone else. You're savin' lives, remember?*

And not by spending his own, after all. When he wasn't so tired and full of pain, and this day's doings were a good ways behind him, he might crack a smile about that.

But not now.

He ripped apart Conroyd's blackened clothing. Bared Conroyd's unburned chest to the air. Blanked his mind, his imagination, and plunged the knife through muscle, between bones, deep into Morg's black rancid heart and twisted with all the might left in him to summon. Flesh quivered. Blood flowed. The sorcerer exhaled once, and died.

Incapable of walking anywhere else, even back to Dathne, Asher let himself slump to Justice Hall's steps. Dropping his forehead to his knees he let the trembling take him.

It was done, then. Done and done. Prophecy appeased. Outwitted, even, since he still lived. The mad world righted. Now he could go home to Restharven. Start a new life with Dathne. His wife. His beloved.

Eyes closed, shaking like a man with ague, he saw the sun rise over the harbour, smelled the salt air, felt the sea spray wet on his cheeks. A sob rose hot in his aching throat. *Home...*

Beside him, Conroyd Jarralt's body coughed.

No. No. That weren't bloody *possible*...

On his feet again and staring, sucking air like a man half-drowned, he watched the knife push slowly but surely out of Conroyd's blood-slicked chest to fall with a metallic thud on the marble steps. Watched the wound seal closed as though it had never been and the rib cage rise and fall, rise and fall. Saw the eyelids flicker a dreadful warning.

Shit. *Shit*. Morg was proof to killing steel, and now he had no choice: he'd have to use Gar's bloody spell. Seemed Prophecy weren't outwitted after all.

It wasn't fair, it wasn't *fair*. He wanted to go home!

The words of the UnMaking spell were in him, and waiting. He called them to the tip of his tongue. Turned his head, just a little, just far enough to see Dathne, on her feet at the edge of the Square with Gar nowhere in sight.

Dathne. *Dathne.*

He nearly howled out loud.

This wasn't bloody fair!

At his feet Morg sighed, and shifted.

Now or never. Time was up.

With a right hand that trembled only a little, with a voice that cracked only just at the edges, he signed the sigils, spoke the spell, and closed his eyes.

Here I come, Da... here I come...

Nothing happened. No surge of power. No flash of light. No death, for him or Morg.

Disbelieving, he opened his eyes. "Sink me bloody sideways!" he shouted, spinning about. "*Gar!*"

"This way, Asher!" the little shit called out, beckoning from deep shadows off to the left. "Quickly! Here! Before he wakes!"

Head spinning, rage like a red mist clouding his vision, Asher slipped and slithered down the steps to join Gar in the narrow walkway between Justice Hall and the City chapel. Grabbed him by the shirt front and shook for all he was worth.

"You said it were translated! You said it'd bloody work!"

Gar fended him off with difficulty. "It is! It will! Let me go, Asher! *Listen!*"

"To *you?*" he demanded. "I'm done listenin' to you! I listened to you and look what it got me! Sink me, *sink* me, what do I do now? The bastard won't die! I stuck a knife in his heart and he still ain't dead! And your spell—your damned bloody spell—"

"Won't work unless it's channelled through me."

He took a step backwards, staring. "*What?*"

Gar's face was bloodless, his eyes hollowed and bruised. "I changed Barl's incantation, Asher. Not a lot. Just a little. Now I'm an integral part of the magic. The power must flow through me before it can kill Morg."

Was Gar raving? Deluded? Had the past weeks' strain unhinged him completely?

Reading the questions in his face, Gar sighed and shook his head.

"I'm in my right mind, I promise you, Asher. And what I've said is the simple truth. It's what I tried to tell you before you tried to dash out my brains."

"You altered the incantation? *Why?*"

"I had my reasons."

Stunned almost speechless, Asher turned away. Turned back again, still struggling. "But...but that means you'll die too, don't it?"

Gar shrugged. "What do you care, so long as Morg is dead?"

"You are mad," he whispered, retreating until his shoulderblades met cold damp bricks. "Stark, staring suntouched."

"You know I'm not. Morg must die and this is the only way."

"It can't be!" he shouted. "You're the smart one, the scholar, the historian! Think of somethin' else! I've already had one man die in my place, Gar, I ain't about to make it two!"

Gar shook his head. "That choice isn't yours. It's mine, and it's made."

"But *why?*"

"Why does it matter? You don't care about me."

No, he didn't, but that weren't the point. "Pretend I do and tell me *why!*"

Gar let out a sigh, and stared at the ground. "I promised Fane I'd not seek her crown, and broke my word. I promised you I'd keep you safe, and broke my word again. I promised Barl I'd protect her people with my life—and that's one promise I intend to keep. I may be a magickless cripple but I'm still Lur's king. I'll not have my legacy a string of broken promises. My father taught me better than that. I told you once, I have a destiny. Do you remember? Well, this is it." He looked up, then, his face as stony as any effigy. "Don't try to stop me, Asher. I'll hate you if you do."

"And if you make me go through with this, *I'll* hate *you!*"

A twisted smile touched Gar's lips. "You hate me now."

"Then I'll hate you *more!*"

Another shrug, uncaring. "Hate me as much as you want. It changes nothing. Asher, there's no other way and we're running out of time..."

Trapped. He was trapped, with no escape. The bastard. The *bastard*. "I'll never forgive you for this, Gar," he whispered. "Never not *ever.*"

"I know that already," said Gar. "Now shut up and listen. We only have moments. Everything I taught you in the wagon holds true. All that's different is the spell's delivery. You hold my shoulder and *you don't let go.* Understand me? If you let go the spell fails and Morg lives *forever.*"

He was numb. Dizzy. "Over my dead body."

"No," said Gar, unsmiling. "Over mine."

He had no answer to that.

Still unsmiling, Gar reached inside his jacket and pulled out the age-mottled journal that had started this mess. Bits and pieces of ragged paper were slid here and there between its pages. Looking at it, his expression softened to tenderness. "I brought Barl's diary with me. It comforts me, somehow, though I know that makes no sense to you." He held it but, his hand unsteady. "Take it. Care for it. It's the last the world has of a grand and glorious woman who gave her life for something bigger and better than she was. Don't let her be forgotten. Please."

Grudgingly, he took the proffered diary and shoved the bloody thing inside his weskit. Gar's unguarded face was too terrible to look at. "Now what?" he muttered.

"Now you put your hand on my shoulder...and we finish what Morg started."

"And you're sure this'll work? You said it yourself, you're a magickless cripple, what if—"

Gar's chin lifted, his face full of pride now and nothing uncomfortable. "You said it better. I'm the scholar. Trust me, Asher. This will work."

Side by side they walked to the mouth of the passageway.

"Begin the incantation," Gar whispered. "But keep us concealed till the very last word. Then we'll confront him. Don't forget: you must see his eyes. And for Barl's sake, Asher—"

"I know, I know, I bloody know! Whatever I do, don't let go!"

The words of the spell were still there, still waiting. He took a deep breath. Let it out softly. Tightened his fingers on Gar's steady shoulder.

"*Senusartarum!*"

Sketch the first sigil.

"*Belkavtavartis!*"

Sketch the second, and the third.

"*Kavartis thosartis domonartis ed—*"

This time it was different. The magic ignited, dark and dreadful, setting his bones on fire. Left arm raised to shoulder level, fingers spread and pointing, Gar stepped smoothly out of the shadows. Shaking, burning, Asher stepped with him.

Morg stood posed at the top of Justice Hall's steps, clothing mended, immaculate and glittering. He saw them and laughed, burnished with power.

"So *there* you are! And look at you! *Look!* The little cripple and his tame brute Olken holding hands on the brink of death! How poetic! How *romantic*!" He lifted his arms and threw back his head. Baleful green fire crackled around him, igniting the sullen air. "Oh, what a *wonderful* way to die! You two first, then whoever is left. Or should I leave you till last?"

Gar was shivering. "*Finish it*, Asher! Quickly, *now*! Before he kills anyone else!"

Yes, yes, more than time to finish it. He could barely contain the maelstrom within. On a choking breath he lifted his head to look deep into Morg's mad shining eyes. Opened his mouth and whispered: "*Nux.*"

Killing magic seared through his veins. Out of his fingers clutched to Gar's shoulder, into Gar's body and down Gar's arm to burst from his fingertips in a stream of pure gold fire.

It struck Morg hard in his knife-proof heart, transmuting him to a pillar of flame. Gar sagged to the ground, gasping, shuddering. Not loosening his grip, Asher followed him downwards as the spell of UnMaking flowed like blood from a mortal wound.

For five slow heartbeats, Morg burned incandescent. Then came a crack of ear-splitting sound. The golden fire bloomed. Blossomed. Swallowed the sun.

Morg disappeared, and his dead demons with him.

Without a word Gar slumped to the cobbles. Fell face upwards, green eyes staring at the cloudy sky. The sky with no Wall. Asher fell with him. He mustn't let go, no matter what happened.

Gradually, he became aware of feet, hurrying by him. Sound, as rubble was kicked away. Voices shouted orders, called for "*Help here, help!*" He wanted to answer but his head was hurting and he was oh, so very tired.

Footsteps stopped beside him. He opened his eyes. *Dathne.* At her shoulder, Darran. Not dead then, the ole crow, even with a groggy heart, and in his face such a ravagement of grief...

He managed to smile as Dathne knelt beside him, her hand pressing hard to his cold, wet cheek. "You were goin' to tell me somethin'," he whispered, his voice a sickly croak.

Her eyes were brighter than any star. "I was, love, wasn't I?" Her forehead came to rest against his. "We've made a baby," she told him softly.

A baby. A *baby*? How had *that* happened?

He turned his head and said to his friend, "Did y'hear that, Gar? I'm havin' a *baby*!"

But Gar was dead, and couldn't hear him.

Darran sobbed then, a thin, broken sound. Asher sat up with Dathne's help, and stared at the rotten ole crow in fury.

"Don't you blame *me*, you bloody ole man! This ain't *my* doin'! It ain't *my* fault!"

His blunt and brutal handprint was burned into the shoulder of Gar's blue coat.

"It *ain't* my fault," he said again. "*I* never thought of it. *I* ain't the scholar. It were *his* idea. All his. Not mine."

He lowered his forehead to Gar's still chest.

"*I forgive you*, Gar," he whispered. "*I forgive you. Please...now you forgive me, too...*"

Silence. And then a long, slow weeping of rain.

EPILOGUE

After the moist heat of the high summer afternoon, the shadowy coolness of House Torvig's royal crypt came as a welcome relief. Asher took a deep breath, tossed a ball of glimfire into the air and let it light his way along the corridor to the place he'd not stepped foot in since the funeral. His palms were damp and his heart was racing.

Sink it, he'd sworn he wouldn't let nerves get to him.

The chamber was cramped. Crowded with memories as well as coffins. As he pressed past Borne, then Dana, and finally Fane he touched a fingertip to his forehead in greeting. Looked into the marble serenity of their faces and with affection recalled them, living.

"Majesty. Majesty. Highness."

They were the last royal family of Lur. The end of a long and proud tradition. One day they'd be nowt but old-fashioned portraits staring down from a wall. Engravings in a history book with no one left alive who'd known them.

One day.

But not today.

He reached the fourth and final coffin. Shoved his hands in his pockets and took another deep breath, then let it out slowly, hoping the ache in his chest would ease. It didn't.

"So," he said, into the somnolent silence. "Here I am. Bet you thought I'd never make it, eh?"

By some kind of miracle he'd managed to get Gar's effigy pretty lifelike. Even though Darran kept insisting the nose was wrong.

Bloody ole crow.

Staring at Gar's proud stone profile he felt a wave of melancholy. A grinding echo of grief. Dathne said he shouldn't come here. *Let the dead lie and the living dance.* That was her motto. But he'd put it off for long enough, so here he was.

With a snap of his fingers he conjured a stool to sit on. No reason he couldn't be comfortable, was there? Heart still heavily thudding, he tilted it onto two of its legs till he reached a precarious balance.

"We had some rain this mornin'. Rain that fell all on its lonesome, without any meddlin' from me." He shook his head. "Rain without magic, like everyone's agreed to. Did you ever think we'd see the like? No more WeatherWorking. Now there's a thing..."

The City folk had danced in the street like children as the dove-grey clouds summoned by no one unburdened themselves without spite or fury. He and Dathne had smiled to see it. He smiled again now, remembering, then swiftly sobered; harsher memories lurked close to the surface. Sometimes he thought they'd never sink.

"Everything's different now, Gar. Everything's changed. For the better, I'm hopin', though I don't deny it's still a mite unchancy. Bloody politics. There's lots of you Doranen of the mind things should go right back the way they were. Seems they're havin' a deal of trouble gettin' used to Olken magic. Good thing I got Holze on my side. Good thing Nix and some healers from the Circle patched him up and kept him breathin'. He's the royal Barlsman. Folk listen when he speaks. He's kept the kingdom together, I reckon, him and his clerics. Kept folk from goin' mad."

He thudded the stool back to the flagstoned floor. Got off it, arms folded over his chest, and started pacing.

"We lost a lot of people, Gar. Yours and mine. The storms savaged every inch of the kingdom, just like the Circle said." Pulling a face he added, "All of Conroyd's family perished. Sad, but I don't deny it's made life easier. Ain't no squabblin' over crowns any more. And it seems I got no brothers left but one. There were waves, you see, from the falling of Dragonteeth Reef. Ferocious, they were, folks say. Taller than treetops and faster than a galloping horse. They washed in from the harbours, up and down the coast. Restharven's most gone now, and Westwailing. Rillingcoombe. Struan's Cove."

The playgrounds of his childhood, smashed to rubble and firewood. He'd not gone down to see them yet. Wasn't sure when—or if—he would. Getting the kingdom back on its feet was a full-time job, and besides, all those survivors, searching for answers. What could he tell them? How could he explain?

Not even the Innocent Mage could save everyone.

He shook his head. "Jervale alone knows how Zeth survived, but if anyone was goin' to it'd be him. I sent a message sayin' he and the rest of the family could come here. That they was all welcome. Folks as spoke for me said he just spat and walked away. Aye, well. That's bloody Zeth for you."

With a shrug and a jerk of his chin he put that memory to bed.

"And Jed survived too, bless 'im. He's livin' here now, with us. Potters round the stables and pastures most days. Cygnet and Ballodair follow him like overgrown dogs. He won't stop feedin' 'em apples no matter how often I ask 'im not to."

Was that glimshadow, or Gar secretly smiling? He smiled himself, a little. Right or wrong he found it hard to grieve for his brothers. But if he'd lost Jed...

"We're rebuildin', slowly. Got a new Council. Dathne's on it, and Pellen Orrick. Me. Holze, of course, and Nix. Lady Marnagh, too; she's a woman with sense. There's talk of makin' Orrick mayor of Dorana, but I don't know if he'll do it. He was born a guardsman, Pellen. Dathne's overseein' all to do with Olken magic." He grinned. "You should hear her speechifyin'. Scares the trousers off me. Veira'd be right proud of her, if she was here. Matt, too."

His breath caught a little at the sound of their names, and his fingers pressed the lump of crystal still buried in his flesh. It was a talisman, now. A part of him, memory, as they were part of him and always would be.

"Bloody Darran's in his element. Fussin' and organisin' and bossin' folk about. Truth is I'd be lost without him, but don't you bloody tell 'im. The ole crow's puffed up enough as it is."

He scratched his chin and watched, for a small while, glimshadows dance on the chamber wall.

"It ain't smooth sailin', not by a long shot, but we ain't quite capsized yet." He snorted. "Some fools want to make me king but I won't let 'em. I *ain't* a king, I'm a bloody fisherman. Just 'cause I got some powerful magic..."

Suddenly tired, he dropped back on the stool. "I don't much care for magic, Gar. Don't like what the wrong person can do with it. Ain't too proud of what *I* did with it, even though I had to. I've kept Barl's diary, like you asked me. Read it, at least what you managed to translate. Your bloody handwriting—I nearly went cross-eyed. I'll keep it safe, no need to worry. But I reckon I'll keep it secret, too. Barl hid the thing for a reason, and I reckon she was right. No one should have that kind of power. Not for any reason."

He'd told not even Dathne he had the diary. He had a duty to safeguard the future, just in case another Morgan—or Barl—was born.

Gar's effigy glowed warmly in the light of the yellow glimfire. In the stone face a silent agreement. Seeing it, he breathed a little easier.

"There's talk started up of crossin' Barl's Mountains, and I reckon we will go, one day. But there's work to do here first. That's what we need to think on now, not rushin' about from here to there, sightseein'."

He stood again, then, and unkinked his back. "Speakin' of work, I'd better go. Just wanted to tell you what's happening, is all. Figured you'd like to know." His fingers touched Gar's shoulder, briefly. "I miss you, my friend. Ain't a day goes by I don't think..." He stopped, his throat closing. It was done, it was done, and nowt could undo it. "Anyways. I just wanted you to know this: I promise I won't waste what you gave me. What you gave all of us. I should've said thank you, Gar. I should've said a lot of things. Sorry. Guess I am bloody rude after all." He heaved a sharp sigh. "Don't know when I'll have a chance to visit again, but I will. I promise. Wait for me, eh?"

With a flick of his fingers he sent the glimfire bobbing towards the crypt's doorway. As he reached Fane's tomb he stopped. Shook his head. Turned back.

"Nearly forgot," he said. "About the baby. If it's a boy we thought we'd call it Rafel. That's a bit more personal than a mouldy ole statue. If it's a girl, Darran says we got to call it *Gardenia*." He grinned. "Darran can suck on a blowfish and die."

And he left the crypt, still grinning.

The recently opened Garden of Remembrance was full of fountains and flowers and flitting, jewel-coloured birds. Asher came out of the crypt into warm sunshine, where families strolled and boys and girls, black-haired and yellow, threw balls of glimfire, squealing with laughter.

Dathne was waiting for him, round as a full moon.

"All right?" she asked, her hand on his arm.

He kissed her cheek. "Aye. All right."

"Good," she said, and tugged him along the path. "Now walk with me."

As he turned, obedience personified, he caught a glimpse of Darran hurrying towards them from the direction of the palace. The light of battle was in the ole crow's eye and a dozen scrolls were clutched to his chest. He groaned. He never should have mentioned he was going to the crypt...

"What?" said Dathne, alarmed.

"Nowt, nowt," he assured her blithely. Slid his arm around her shoulders and matched his stride to hers as they strolled between the budding pink cantimonies. With luck she wouldn't notice...

But Dathne glanced to her right and cursed. "Oh, for Jervale's sake! Can't he leave us alone for five minutes?"

"Doubt it," he said. "Darran lives for his paperwork, you know that."

She gave him a look. "Since when are you so tolerant?"

"I ain't. But you're the one said bygones were bygones and these are brand-new days. *And* you said I had standards to set. Can't hardly show my aggravation in public, can I?"

"Maybe not," said Dathne, and raised her hand. "But I can."

The scrolls of paper leapt out of Darran's sheltering arms. They heard his wail of dismay quite clearly.

"That weren't very nice," he said. Glancing over his shoulder he saw Darran stooping and scooping the scrolls from the ground, and grinned. "Then again, neither's this. Rat's arse to good examples!"

With a whispered word he set the scattered scrolls to dancing. The children, seeing a better game afoot, abandoned their balls of glimfire and joined in the chase. They thought it enormously funny.

Darran didn't.

"*Asher!*" he shouted, his voice carrying on the lively breeze. "You *reprobate*. You *ruffian*. You *sorry* excuse for a king!"

Asher shook his head in sorrow. "What a mouth the ole man's got. And all in front of the baby, too."

"Disgraceful," Dathne agreed, smiling. Took his hand and placed it tenderly on her burgeoning belly.

With Darran disposed of they wandered amongst the flowerbeds and past the statues in the Bower of Heroes: Gar and Matt and Veira and Rafel. The sun shone softly in an eggshell-blue sky. Birdsong drifted from the trees around him. And a lone skirling eagle rode the thermal currents above the top of the Black Woods, up the face of Barl's Mountains...and beyond.

ACKNOWLEDGEMENTS

First, last, and all the stops in between—my incomparable editor, Stephanie Smith.

Julia Stiles, copy editor extraordinaire.

The entire HarperCollins Voyager team, most especially Robyn Fritchley and Samantha Rich.

Fiona McLennan for friendship, feedback and excellent website advice.

The Orbit team and David Wyatt for the cover.

Elaine and Peter, again, for more beta reading above and beyond the call of baby Kate.

The Purple Zone crew, whose enthusiasm for Book One made me smile and smile and smile.

All the folk who gambled on me with their dollars, then made a point of letting me know they didn't consider the money wasted. Thank you.

And last, but never least, the wonderful booksellers who convinced them to take that gamble. Thank *you*.

extras

orbit

meet the author

Mary GT Webber

KAREN MILLER was born in Vancouver, Canada, and moved to Australia with her family when she was two. She started writing stories while still in primary school, where she fell in love with speculative fiction after reading *The Lion, the Witch, and the Wardrobe.* Over the years she has held down a wide variety of jobs, including horse stud groom in Buckingham, England. She is working on several new novels. Find out more about the author at www.KarenMiller.net.

introducing

If you enjoyed
KINGMAKER, KINGBREAKER,
look out for

THE GODSPEAKER TRILOGY

by Karen Miller

Sold into slavery, Hekat dreams of power. Fate leads her to the warlord Raklion, and she begins turning dreams into reality. For the nameless god of Mijak is with her, and it promises her the world.

Far away, the King of Ethrea is dying. His daughter Princess Rhian is ready to rule, but if her enemies have their way the crown of Ethrea will never be worn by a woman.

Dexterity Jones is a toymaker. To protect Rhian and his country, he must place his trust in an exile from Mijak. Yet, as Ethrea comes ever closer to civil war, a greater danger awaits.

Hekat still desires the world . . . and power is no longer a dream.

Despite its two burning lard-lamps the kitchen was dark, its air choked with the stink of rancid goat butter and spoiling goat-meat. Spiders festooned the corners with sickly webs, boarding the husks of flies and suck-you-dries. A mud-brick oven swallowed half the space between the door and the solitary window. There were three wooden shelves, one rickety wooden stool and a scarred wooden table, almost unheard of in this land whose trees had ages since turned to stone.

Crouched in the shadows beneath the table, the child with no name listened to the man and the woman fight.

"But you promised," the woman wailed. "You said I could keep this one."

The man's hard fist pounded the timber above the child's head. "That was before another poor harvest, slut, before two more village wells dried up! All the coin it costs to feed it, am I made of money? Don't you complain, when it was born I could've thrown it on the rocks, I could've left it on The Anvil!"

"But she can work, she—"

"Not like a son!" His voice cracked like lightning, rolled like thunder round the small smoky room. "If you'd whelped me more sons—"

"I tried!"

"Not hard enough!" Another boom of fist on wood. "The she-brat goes. Only the god knows when Traders will come this way again."

The woman was sobbing, harsh little sounds like a dying goat. "But she's so young."

"Young? Its blood-time is come. It can pay back what it's cost me, like the other she-brats you spawned. This is my word, woman. Speak again and I'll smash your teeth and black your eyes."

When the woman dared disobey him the child was so surprised she bit her fingers. She scarcely felt the small pain; her whole life was pain, vast like the barren wastes beyond the village's godpost, and had been so since her first caterwauling cry. She was almost numb to it now.

"Please," the woman whispered. "Let me keep her. I've spawned you six sons."

"It should've been eleven!" Now the man sounded like one of his skin-and-bone dogs, slavering beasts who fought for scraps of offal in the stony yard behind their hovel.

The child flinched. She hated those dogs almost as much as she hated the man. It was a bright flame, her hatred, hidden deep and safe from the man's sight. He would kill her if he saw it, would take her by one skinny scabbed ankle and smash her headfirst into the nearest red and ochre rock. He'd done it to a dog once, that had dared to growl at him. The other dogs had lapped up its brains then fought over the bloody carcass all through the long unheated night. On her threadbare blanket beneath the kitchen table she'd fallen asleep to the sound of their teeth, and dreamed the bones they gnawed were her own.

But dangerous or not she refused to abandon her hate, the only thing she owned. It comforted and nourished her, filling her ache-empty belly on the nights she didn't eat because the woman's legs were spread, or her labors were unfinished, or the man was drunk on cactus blood and beating her.

He was beating her now, open-handed blows across the face, swearing and sweating, working himself to a frenzy. The woman knew better than to cry out. Listening to the man's palm smack against the woman's sunken cheeks, to his lusty breathing and her swallowed grunts, the child imagined plunging a knife into his throat. If she closed her eyes she could see the blood spurt scarlet, hear it splash on the floor as he gasped and bubbled and died. She was sure she could do it. Hadn't she seen the men with their proud knives cut the throats of goats and even a horse, once, that had broken its leg and was no longer good for anything but meat and hide and bleached boiled bones?

There were knives in a box on the kitchen's lowest shelf. She felt her fingers curl and cramp as though grasping a carved bone hilt, felt her heart rattle her ribs. The secret flame flickered, flared...then died.

No good. He'd catch her before she killed him. She would not defeat the man today, or tomorrow, or even next fat godmoon. She was too small, and he was too strong. But one day, many fat godmoons from now, she'd be big and he'd be old and shrunken. Then she'd do it and throw his body to the dogs after and laugh and laugh as they gobbled his buttocks and poked their questing tongues through the empty eye sockets of his skull.

One day.

The man hit the woman again, so hard she fell to the pounded dirt floor. "You poisoned my seed five times and whelped bitches, slut. Three sons you whelped lived less than a godmoon. I should curse you! Turn you out for the godspeaker to deal with!"

The woman was sobbing again, scarred arms crossed in front of her face. "I'm sorry—I'm sorry—"

Listening, the child felt contempt. Where was the woman's flame? Did she even have one? Weeping. Begging. Didn't she know this was what the man wanted, to see her broken and bleating in the dirt? The woman should die first.

But she wouldn't. She was weak. All women were weak. Everywhere in the village the child saw it. Even the women who'd spawned only sons, who looked down on the ones who'd spawned she-brats as well, who helped the godspeaker stone the cursed witches whose bodies spewed forth nothing but female flesh...even those women were weak.

I not weak the child told herself fiercely as the man soaked the woman in venom and spite and the woman wept, believing him. *I never beg.*

Now the man pressed his heel between the woman's dugs and shoved her flat on her back. "You should pray thanks to the god. Another man would've broke your legs and turned you out seasons ago. Another man would've plowed two hands of living sons on a better bitch than you!"

"Yes! Yes! I am fortunate! I am blessed!" the woman gabbled, rubbing at the bruised place on her chest.

The man shucked his trousers. "Maybe. Maybe not. Spread, bitch. You give me a living son nine fat godmoons from now or I swear by the village godpost I'll be rid of you onto The Anvil!"

Choking, obedient, the woman hiked up her torn shift and let her thin thighs fall open. The child watched, unmoved, as the man plowed the woman's furrow, grunting and sweating with his effort. He had a puny blade, and the woman's soil was old and dusty. She wore her dog-tooth amulet round her neck but its power was long dead. The child did not think a son would come of this planting or any other. Nine fat godmoons from this day, or sooner, the woman would die.

His seed at last dribbled out, the man stood and pulled up his trousers. "Traders'll be here by highsun tomorrow. Might be seasons till more come. I paid the godspeaker to list us as selling and put a goat's skull on the gate. Money won't come back, so the she-brat goes. Use your water ration to clean it. Use one drop of mine. I'll flay you. I'll hang you with rope twisted from your own skin. Understand?"

"Yes," the woman whispered. She sounded tired and beaten. There was blood on the dirt between her legs.

"Where's the she-brat now?"

"Outside."

The man spat. He was always spitting. Wasting water. "Find it. When it's clean, chain it to the wall so it don't run like the last one."

The woman nodded. He'd broken her nose with his goat-stick that time. The child, three seasons younger then, had heard the woman's splintering bone, watched the pouring blood. Remembering that, she remembered too what the man did to the other she-brat to make it sorry for running. Things that made the she-brat squeal but left no mark because Traders paid less for damaged goods.

That she-brat had been a fool. No matter where the Traders took her it had to be better than the village and the man. Traders were the only escape for she-brats. Traders...or death. And she did not want to die. When they came for her before highsun tomorrow she would go with them willingly.

"I'll chain her," the woman promised. "She won't run."

"Better not," growled the man, and then the slap of goathide on wood as he shoved the kitchen door aside and left.

The woman rolled her head until her red-rimmed eyes found what they sought beneath the kitchen table. "I tried. I'm sorry."

The child crawled out of the shadows and shrugged. The woman was always sorry. But sorrow changed nothing, so what did it matter? "Traders coming," she said. "Wash now."

Wincing, breath catching raw in her throat, the woman clutched at the table leg and clawed herself to her knees, then grabbed hold of the table edge, panting, whimpering, and staggered upright. There was water in her eyes. She reached out a work-knotted hand and touched rough fingertips to the child's cheek. The water trembled, but did not fall.

Then the woman turned on her heel and went out into the searing day. Not understanding, not caring, the child with no name followed.

The Traders came a finger before highsun the next day. Not the four from last time, with tatty robes, skinny donkeys, half-starved purses and hardly any slaves. No. These two Traders were grand. Seated on haughty white camels, jangling with beads and bangles, dangling with earrings and sacred amulets, their dark skin shiny with fragrant oils and jeweled knife-sheaths on their belts. Behind them stretched the longest snake-spine of merchandise: men's inferior sons, discarded, and she-brats, and women. All naked, all chained. Some born to slavery, others newly sold. The difference was in their godbraids, slaves of long standing bore one braid of deep blood red, a sign from the god that they were property. The new slaves would get their red braids, in time.

Guarding the chained slaves, five tall men with swords and spears. Their godbraids bore amulets, even their slave-braids were charmed. They must be special slaves, those guards. In the caravan there were pack camels too, common brown, roped together, laden with baskets, crisscrossed with travel-charms. A sixth unchained slave led them, little more than a boy, and his red godbraid bore amulets as well. At his signal, groaning, the camels folded their calloused knees to squat on the hard ground. The slaves squatted too, silent and sweating.

Waiting in her own chains, the crude iron links heavy and chafing round her wrists and ankles, the child watched the Traders from beneath lowered lashes as they dismounted and stood in the dust and dirt of the man's small holding. Their slender fingers smoothed shining silk robes, tucked their glossy beaded godbraids behind their ears. Their fingernails were all the same neat oval shape and painted bright colors to match their clothing: green and purple and crimson and gold. They were taller than the tallest man in the village. Taller than the godspeaker, who must stand above all. One of them was even *fat*. They were the most splendid creatures the child had ever seen, and knowing she would leave with them, leave forever the squalor and misery of the man and the village, her heart beat faster and her own unpainted fingernails, ragged and shapeless, bit deep into her dirty scarred palms.

The Traders stared at the cracked bare ground with its withered straggle of weeds, at the mud brick hovel with its roof of dried grasses badly woven, at the pen of profitless goats, at the man whose bloodshot eyes shone with hope and avarice. A look flowed between them and their plump lips pursed. They were sneering. The child wondered where they came from, to be so clean and disapproving. Somewhere not like this. She couldn't wait to see such a place herself, to sleep for just one night inside walls that did not stink of fear and goat. She'd wear a hundred chains and crawl on her hands and knees across The Anvil's burning sand if she had to, so long as she reached it.

The man was staring at the Traders too, his eyes popping with amazement. He bobbed his head at them, like a chicken pecking corn. "Excellencies. Welcome, welcome. Thank you for your custom."

The thin Trader wore thick gold earrings; tattooed on his right cheek, in brightest scarlet, a stinging scorpion. The child bit her tongue. He had money enough to buy a protection like that? And power enough that a godspeaker would let him? *Aieee...*

He stepped forward and looked down at the man, fingertips flicking at her. "Just this?"

She was enchanted. His voice was deep and dark like the dead of night, and shaped the words differently from the man. When the man spoke it sounded like rocks grinding in the dry ravine, ugly like him. The Trader was not ugly.

The man nodded. "Just this."

"No sons, un-needed?"

"Apologies, Excellency," said the man. "The god has granted me few sons. I need them all."

Frowning, the Trader circled the child in slow, measured

steps. She held her breath. If he found her unpleasing and if the man did not kill her because of it, she'd be slaved to some village man for beating and spawning sons and hard labor without rest. She would cut her flesh with stone and let the dogs taste her, tear her, devour her, first.

The Trader reached out his hand, his flat palm soft and pink, and smoothed it down her thigh, across her buttock. His touch was warm, and heavy. He glanced at the man. "How old?"

"Sixteen."

The Trader stopped pacing. His companion unhooked a camel whip from his belt of linked precious stones and snapped the thong. The man's dogs, caged for safety, howled and threw themselves against the woven goathide straps of their prison. In the pen beside them the man's goats bleated and milled, dropping anxious balls of shit, yellow slot-eyes gleaming.

"How old?" the Trader asked again. His green eyes were narrow, and cold.

The man cringed, head lowered, fingers knuckled together. "Twelve. Forgive me. Honest error."

The Trader made a small, disbelieving sound. He'd done something to his eyebrows. Instead of being a thick tangled bar like the man's they arched above his eyes in two solid gold half-circles. The child stared at them, fascinated, as the Trader leaned down and brought his dark face close to hers. She wanted to stroke the scarlet scorpion inked into his cheek. Steal some of his protection, in case he did not buy her.

His long, slender fingers tugged on her earlobes, traced the shape of her skull, her nose, her cheeks, pushed back her lips and felt all her teeth. He tasted of salt and things she did not know. He smelled like freedom.

"Is she blooded?" he asked, glancing over his shoulder at the man.

"Since four godmoons."

"Intact?"

The man nodded. "Of course."

The Trader's lip curled. "There is no 'of course' where men and she-flesh abide."

Without warning he plunged his hand between her legs, fingers pushing, probing, higher up, deeper in. Teeth bared, her own fingers like little claws, the child flew at him, screeching. Her chains might have weighed no more than the bangles on his slender, elegant wrists. The man sprang forward shouting, fists raised, face contorted, but the Trader did not need him. He brushed her aside as though she were a corn-moth. Seizing a handful of black and tangled hair he wrenched her to the tips of her toes till she was screaming in pain, not fury, and her hands fell limply by her sides. She felt her heart batter her brittle ribs and despair storm in her throat. Her eyes squeezed shut and for the first time she could remember felt the salty sting of tears.

She had ruined everything. There would be no escape from the village now, no new life beyond the knife-edged horizon. The Trader would toss her aside like spoiled meat, and when he and his fat friend were gone the man would kill her or she would be forced to kill herself. Panting like a goat in the slaughter-house she waited for the blow to fall.

But the Trader was laughing. Still holding her, he turned to his friend. "What a little hell-cat! Untamed and savage, like all these dwellers in the savage north. But do you see the eyes, Yagji? The face? The length of bone and the sleekness of flank? Her sweet breasts, budding?"

Trembling, she dared to look at him. Dared to hope...

The fat one wasn't laughing. He shook his head, setting the ivory dangles in his ears to swinging. "She is scrawny."

"Today, yes," agreed the Trader. "But with food and bathing and three times three godmoons...then we shall see!"

"Your eyes see the invisible, Aba. Scrawny brats are oft diseased."

"No, Excellency!" the man protested. "No disease. No pus, no bloating, no worms. Good flesh. Healthy flesh."

"What there is of it," said the Trader. He turned. "She is not diseased, Yagji."

"But she is ill-tempered," his fat friend argued. "Undisciplined, and wild. She'll be troublesome, Aba."

The Trader nodded. "True." He held out his hand and easily caught the camel whip tossed to him. Fingers tight in her hair he snapped the woven hide quirt around her naked legs so the little metal weights on its end printed bloody patterns in her flesh.

The blows stung like fire. The child sank her teeth into her lip and stared unblinking into the Trader's careful, watching eyes, daring him to strip the unfed flesh from her bones if he liked. He would see she was no weakling, that she was worthy of his coin. Hot blood dripped down her calf to tickle her ankle. Within seconds the small black desert flies came buzzing to drink her. Hearing them, the Trader withheld the next blow and instead tossed the camel whip back to its owner.

"Lesson one, little hell-cat," he said, his fingers untangling from her hair to stroke the sharp line of her cheek. "Raise your hand or voice to me again and you will die never knowing the pleasures that await you. Do you understand me?"

The black desert flies were greedy, their eager sucking made her skin crawl. She'd seen what they could do to living creatures if not discouraged. She tried not to dance on the spot as the feverish flies quarreled over her bloody welts. All she understood was the Trader did not mean to reject her. "Yes."

"Good." He waved the flies away, then pulled from his gold and purple pocket a tiny pottery jar. When he took off its lid she smelled the ointment inside, thick and rich and strange.

Startling her, he dropped to one knee and smeared her burning legs with the jar's fragrant paste. His fingers were cool and sure against her sun-seared skin. The pain vanished, and she was shocked. She hadn't known a man could touch a she-brat and not hurt it.

It made her wonder what else she did not know.

When he was finished he pocketed the jar and stood, staring down at her. "Do you have a name?"

A stupid question. She-brats were owed no names, no more than the stones on the ground or the dead goats in the slaughter-house waiting to be skinned. She opened her mouth to say so, then closed it again. The Trader was almost smiling, and there was a look in his eyes she'd never seen before. A question. Or a challenge. It meant something. She was sure it meant something. If only she could work out what...

She let her gaze slide sideways to the mud brick hovel and its mean kitchen window, where the woman thought she could not be seen as she dangerously watched the trading. The woman who had no name, just descriptions. *Bitch. Slut. Goat-slit.* Then she looked at the man, shaking with greed, waiting for his money. If she gave *herself* a name, how angry it would make him.

But she couldn't think of one. Her mind was blank sand, like The Anvil. Who was she? She had no idea. But the Trader had named her, hadn't he? He had called her something, he had called her—

She tilted her chin so she could look into his green and gleaming eyes. "He—kat," she said, her tongue stumbling over the strange word, the sing-song way he spoke. "Me. Name. Hekat."

894

The Trader laughed again. "As good a name as any, and better than most." He held up his hand, two fingers raised; his fat friend tossed him a red leather pouch, clinking with coin.

The man stepped forward, black eyes ravenous. "If you like the brat so much I will breed you more! Better than this one, worth twice as much coin."

The Trader snorted. "It is a miracle you bred even this one. Do not tempt the god with your blustering lest your seed dry up completely." Nostrils pinched, he dropped the pouch into the man's cupped hands.

The man's fingers tore at the pouch's tied lacing, so clumsily that its contents spilled on the ground. With a cry of anguish he plunged to his knees, heedless of bruises, and began scrabbling for the silver coins. His knuckles skinned against the sharp stones but the man did not notice the blood, or the buzzing black flies that swarmed to drink him.

For a moment the Trader watched him, unspeaking. Then he trod the man's fingers into the dirt. "Your silver has no wings. Remove the child's chains."

The man gaped, face screwed up in pain. "Remove . . . ?"

The Trader smiled; it made his scarlet scorpion flex its claws. "You are deaf? Or would like to be?"

"Excellency?"

The Trader's left hand settled on the long knife at his side. "Headless men cannot hear."

The man wrenched his fingers free and lurched to his feet. Panting, he unlocked the binding chains, not looking at the child. The skin around his eyes twitched as though he were scorpion-stung.

"Come, little Hekat," said the Trader. "You belong to me now."

She followed him to the waiting slave train, thinking he would put his own chains about her wrists and ankles and join her to the other naked slaves squatting on the ground. Instead he led her to his camel and turned to his friend. "A robe, Yagji."

The fat Trader Yagji sighed and fetched a pale yellow garment from one of the pack camel's baskets. Barely breathing, the child stared as the thin Trader took his knife and slashed through the cloth, reducing it to fit her small body. Smiling, he dropped the cut-down robe over her head and guided her arms into its shortened sleeves, smoothed its cool folds over her naked skin. She was astonished. She wished the man's sons were here to see this but they were away at work. Snake-dancing, and tending goats.

"There," said the Trader. "Now we will ride."

Before she could speak he was lifting her up and onto the camel.

Air hissed between the fat Trader's teeth. "Ten silver pieces! Did you have to give so much?"

"To give less would be insulting to the god."

"Tcha! This is madness, Abajai! You will regret this, and so will I!"

"I do not think so, Yagji," the thin Trader replied. "We were guided here by the god. The god will see us safe."

He climbed onto the camel and prodded it to standing. With a muffled curse, the fat Trader climbed onto his own camel and the slave train moved on, leaving the man and the woman and the goats and the dogs behind them.

Hekat sat on the Trader's haughty white camel, her head held high, and never once looked back.